Who's Who in the
Western Fiction of Zane Grey

Who's Who in the Western Fiction of Zane Grey

JOHN DONAHUE

McFarland & Company, Inc., Publishers

Jefferson, North Carolina, and London

The present work is a reprint of the illustrated case bound edition of Who's Who in the Western Fiction of Zane Grey, *first published in 2008 by McFarland.*

LIBRARY OF CONGRESS CATALOGUING-IN-PUBLICATION DATA

Donahue, John, 1950–
Who's who in the western fiction of Zane Grey / John Donahue.
p.   cm.
Includes index.

ISBN 978-0-7864-6421-0
softcover : acid free paper ∞

1. Grey, Zane, 1872–1939 — Characters.
2. Grey, Zane, 1872–1939 — Bibliography.
3. Western stories — Handbooks, manuals, etc.
4. Western stories — Bibliography.
I. Title.
PS3513.R6545 Z56   2012   813'.52 — dc22   2007047690

British Library cataloguing data are available

Cover art: N.C. Wyeth, *The Chase*, 1916 (PicturesNow.com)

Manufactured in the United States of America

McFarland & Company, Inc., Publishers
Box 611, Jefferson, North Carolina 28640
www.mcfarlandpub.com

TABLE OF CONTENTS

INTRODUCTION

Zane Grey has been called the "Homer of the West." He popularized the western novel in the early decades of the twentieth century to such an extent that his name became synonymous with the genre. In the early days of Hollywood, his novels provided the raw material for western movies, both silent and talking. While Zane Grey himself was indebted to the tradition already established by James Fenimore Cooper, Owen Wister and the dime novels, he established the conventions of a form which he termed "Romance," a form which has influenced many subsequent writers in a genre that remains popular to this day.

The purpose of this work is to provide a dictionary of the major and most of the minor characters in the western novels and short fiction of Zane Grey. Characters include the named horses and other animals that figure prominently in Grey's writing. The novels used for this work are the original publications. New editions with expurgated passages restored have been released in recent years, but as there are no new characters introduced as a result of the restorations, I have used the original published versions. In the case of short stories, there is no complete listing or edition of all of Grey's short

fiction. In some cases, works published as short stories are actually parts of novels. The definitive collection of Grey's short stories remains to be published.

Zane Grey was a prolific writer and in addition to novels and short stories concerning the West, he wrote about sports, baseball in particular, as well as about fishing and hunting. He also collaborated on movie scripts for film adaptations of his novels. This book will concentrate only on those writings which are western in theme. In each entry, the novel or story in which the character appears will be indicated. As well, a summary of the character's role in the novel will be provided together with some commentary on the thematic significance of the character in Zane Grey's fiction as a whole. Grey sometimes employed the same name for unrelated characters in different works, and in these instances the entry contains a numbered list of characters with that name, arranged alphabetically by the name of the story or novel.

For lovers of Zane Grey, this will be a handy reference work compiling memorable characters as well as lesser-known figures in the pantheon of Grey westerns.

CHARACTERS IN THE
WESTERN FICTION OF ZANE GREY

A

Aard, Beryl: In *Rogue River Feud*, Jim Aard's daughter. Like Betty Zane, she is a Heidi-type figure. She knows the woods and streams better than anyone else in the mountains. She is a fisherman beyond compare, tying her own flies. She knows the river and the best fishing spots. She impresses Keven with her knowledge and skill, neither of which he could ever hope to match. She offers to teach him how to improve his fishing. Beryl and Keven had been sweethearts before he met Rosamond and left for the army training camp. The months he spends at the Aard cabin rekindles the old romance. He comes to see in Beryl a woman with compassion, sensitivity and loyalty such as he has never met before. Keven wonders what he ever saw in Rosamond Brandeth. When they decide to marry, they go to Portland. There, she gives him the money to pay for dental work and reconstructive surgery on his jaw. He takes her to a motion picture theater, a new experience for her. They visit his father in Grant's Pass, and visit Minton, the tackle dealer. Keven enjoys watching her in Minton's shop discussing rods and bait and tying flies. Her store of knowledge is a match for Mint's. Beryl reveals that she has spoken with Rosamond, who mentions her engagement to Keven. It seems that since Rosamond broke with Atwell, she thought of Keven again. He assures Beryl that any interest he had in Rosamond has been lost long ago. Beryl also tells Keven that she knows the whole story about the Carstone girls. Her best friend at school, Emily Carstone, was a cousin of the girls and she knows that Gus Atwell is the man responsible for their disgrace. While Keven had scrupulously avoided mentioning the gossip for fear of losing her, Beryl saw her possession of the truth as the strongest weapon in their arsenal to fight Atwell.

Aard, Jim: In *Rogue River Feud*, lives along the Rogue River. Garry and Keven meet him when fishing upriver. He recalls Keven had stayed with them some years ago before going to training camp. He heard that Keven was killed in the accident at the camp and then that he was in the hospital. Aard tells them that the steelhead salmon never make it upriver until early October. He speculates about the fishermen downriver who prevent the salmon runs. Garry comments about Jim Aard that he is a queer duck. Mysterious. He always has money. His cabins are the best on the river and he sends his family out often. He never packs out enough fur to Gold Beach to make that much money. When Keven is looking for some place to hold out when he thinks he will be charged with murder for killing Mulligan, he reaches Aard's cabin at Solitude. He is sure he can stay with him for a while. Aard returns from Gold Beach where he had identified Keven and Garry's skiff. Rumor has it that Keven and Garry were drowned. Aard and his daughter take Keven in and care for him. He is impressed with the cabins at Solitude. The main cabin is eight miles from the nearest road, but has all the comforts of any home. His own cabin is likewise well furnished. Aard explains that he makes this selling furs. His daughter, Beryl, does not approve of his trapping. When Beryl and Keven decide to go to Portland to get married, he tells his son-in-law-to-be that Beryl is a one-man woman, like her mother was. When the two of them return to Solitude, Jim shares a secret. In the cabin, in a secret compartment behind a book shelf, he has several bags of gold. His claims have proven bountiful. Keven has in fact married an heiress.

Abe: (1) The storekeeper in White Sage in *The Heritage of the Desert*. He is a good friend of August Naab's and provides him with supplies and information from time to time. When Naab arrives in White Sage with the outcast Jack Hare, Abe informs him of the trouble between his son, Snap, and Jeff Larsen. Snap had been on a bender and had been cheated in a horse-trading deal. Now sober, he's looking for Larsen to settle the score. Abe hopes that August Naab will be able to prevent trouble. Abe sells August Naab an excellent saddle and a hunting rifle which Naab gives to Jack Hare when he works on the high range. Abe is a devout Mormon and works to maintain peace and harmony between the Mormons and the ever-increasing numbers of gentiles in White Sage. When Jack Hare comes to town to confront Holderness and Dene, he meets them in Abe's store, the gathering place for locals. Likewise, when the "revolt of the meek" begins, it begins in Abe's store, where several of the rustlers are seized.

(2) In *The Man of the Forest*, the village storekeeper and the only man who comes out to speak to Las Vegas (Tom Carmichael) as he patrols the street of the village like a sentry watching for an Indian attack. Carmichael has come to town to confront Beasley and thereby settle the issue over his seizure of Auchincloss's ranch. Abe tells Carmichael that Beasley and his men are up at the Beasley ranch, avoiding riding down to the village. He figures that Beasley cannot put off facing Las Vegas much longer. Even Beasley's own men are growing impatient. Abe gives Tom a cigarette and returns to his store.

Ace: In *Western Union*, Kit Sunderland's horse. Someone throws a pebble at him and, being fractious, he bolts. The reins break and Kit cannot stop the animal. Wayne Cameron comes to the rescue, stopping the runaway horse.

Acker: In *West of the Pecos,* one of the men with Sawtell when he comes to the Lambeth ranch looking for Hod Pecos Smith.

Ackerman, Deuce: In *The Trail Driver*, one of the first cowboys to sign on for the trail. He and the cook, Alabama Moze, are with the herd five miles out of San Antonio. He is the first of the Uvalde Quintet. Under twenty years of age, he is tall, slim, bow-legged — the most forceful personality of the group. He clearly has a lot of experience under his belt. Deuce saves the life of Ann Hardy in the Comanche attack on the wagon train. He remains sweet on her, and when they reach Doan's place, where she and her father are to wait for transport, he proposes marriage to her and she accepts. When the drive reaches Dodge, he leaves by stage to pick up Ann.

Ackers, Bill: In *Arizona Ames*, the real name of Noggin, Steele Brandeth's partner in the horse rustling gang. He is a long-armed, high-hatted gambler, as well as a horse thief. He is ferret-faced and mistrustful. He suspects Arizona Ames is not the outlaw he pretends to be and is reluctant to let him join the gang. He plans to rob Morgan's horses and abduct the daughter, Lespeth, to rape and use as he pleases. When the group heads south towards Morgan's, Noggin makes a surprise attack on his partner, Brandeth, and kills him. He, in turn, is shot by Arizona Ames.

Ackers, Polly: In *Sunset Pass*, an old sweetheart of Trueman Rock. When he returns to Wagon Tongue after six years, he learns that she went to the bad, running off with some gambler who came to town.

Ackers, Muddy: In *Shadow on the Trail*, a member of Simm Bell's outlaw gang. He meets Bell

and Holden when they return to Smoky Hollow from the Texas Pacific train heist. No mention is made whether he survives the ambush in Mercer.

Adams: (1) In *The Desert of Wheat*, Anderson's foreman. Lenore meets him in the field and he shows her the new harvester-thresher, a McCormick. He is also involved in organizing the men for guard duty and later for vigilante action against the union organizers.

(2) In *The Wolf Tracker*, the rancher in charge of the outfit doing the fall roundup. He has a ranch at Spring Valley in the Tonto. Adams is a sturdy, well-preserved man of sixty, sharp of eye, bronze of face, with the stamp of a self-made, prosperous rancher upon him. He has a partner, Barrett, who is back at the ranch. Old Gray, the loafer wolf, has killed several cattle and the men are loud in their outcry against the villain. When Brinks comes into the camp asking for information about Old Gray, Adams says it would take over a week to tell all the stories he has heard about this animal. He is curious about Brinks, a professional tracker, and shares with him all he knows about the whereabouts of the wolf and word of the five thousand dollar reward his partner, Barrett, and the other cattlemen have offered for the "scalp" of Old Gray. They have easily lost over twenty-five hundred dollars in livestock to the predator. Perhaps many of the stories told about the wolf are exaggerated or legends, but he points Brinks in the direction where the Old Gray was last reported. Rumor has it that government agents have been around tracking the old wolf but never caught him. They came upon four animals that he killed that very day. Sometimes it seems the wolf just kills for the pleasure of killing. Adams offers the tracker the hospitality of the camp, food and a bed for the night.

Adams, Beaver: In *The Lost Wagon Train*, a frontiersman, and friend of Kit Carson, Dick Curtis, and Jack Smith. He is a trapper by calling, as his name implies. His voice is deep and quiet, and his stature impresses the major. He is called in to Major Greer's office to help solve the mystery of the lost Bowden wagon train. He has heard many strange stories in his years in the West. The Bowden outfit hit the Dry Trail at the beginning of a bad summer for all travelers across the prairies. The Kiowas, Comanches, Apaches and Pawnees were all on the warpath. Bowden had a small force of men unaccustomed to the frontier. Although Pike Anderson could be trusted, the fifty-one tenderfeet would be of little use in a fight with a large force of Indians. He figures they just got massacred. Beaver Adams comments that direct inquiries will probably lead nowhere. Any valuable information will be revealed accidentally when someone is telling a story or in a drunken state spills what he knows. Beaver Adams goes about making inquiries and arouses the suspicions of Lester Cornwall and Stephen Latch.

Adams, Bert: In *The Maverick Queen*, comes out of the Leave It Saloon just as Bud Harkness is entering on his way to kill Hargrove. He is reported to have said that Harkness was not drunk, but that he had never seen such eyes in a human being. Harkness kills Bannister and Hargrove and fills Nesbit full of lead.

Adams, Wess: In *West of the Pecos*, a rider for Don Felipe González down on the Big Bend. Sawtell had Adams fired for branding mavericks on his range. When Pecos Smith leaves the Healds' ranch, he meets up with Curt Williams and Wess Adams and they begin a business of sorts, rounding up mavericks and branding them, selling them either to ranchers or to government stock buyers. Curt Williams and Wess Adams undertake a further operation unbeknownst to Pecos Smith, rebranding cattle. Some ranchers catch them and lynch them, just as the Comanche attack. Pecos Smith, concerned about their tardiness in returning, goes out to look for them and comes upon the lynch party and the Comanches. Williams has already been hanged, and the ranchers are about to deal justice to Adams when the Comanche attack. Adams' horse moves off, the rope the ranchers have dropped snags on the tree and Adams is shot by the attacking Indians.

Aiken, Jeff: In *The Lone Star Ranger*, a giant of a man, eager to punish the man who murdered his wife. He is a fair man, however, and listens to Buck Duane's story that he was over two hundred miles away the day it happened. Buck decides from Aiken's demeanor that he is the type of man he would want as a judge. Jeff Aiken sends for his daughter, Lucy, who witnessed the murder. When Lucy tells them Buck is not the murderer, Jeff tells Buck that Ranger MacNelly assured him that Buck Duane would not commit such a crime. He further advises Buck that MacNelly is a man to be trusted; he recommends that Buck meet with MacNelly to find out what deal he has to offer.

Aiken, Lucy: In *The Lone Star Ranger*, the daughter of Jeff Aiken. She was the only witness to her mother's murder. She tells the lynch mob that Buck Duane was not the man who committed the crime.

Aiken, Mrs. Jeff: In *The Lone Star Ranger*, the woman Buck Duane learns he has been accused of murdering. Her husband has put up a "Dead or Alive" reward for his capture.

Alabama Moze: In *The Trail Driver*, a prepossessing Negro, baffling as to age. His chuck wagon is a huge affair, with hoops for canvas and a boarded contraption at the rear. He's from Alabama, and a remarkably good and economical cook. He tells Brite what he knows about the Uvalde Quintet. He worked for two or three years for the Uvalde outfit. A Colonel Miller ran the outfit, then sold out to Jones because he wanted to get rid of the five who would tear up the town when drunk, and who, with encouragement, were sparkin' his daughter. Since she could not choose among them, there was more trouble than with the cattle. When the cowboys ride off to ambush the Comanche warriors who are attacking the Handy wagon, Moze hears riders approach the camp. He climbs a tree from where he observes Hite and his men rustle the remaining herd.

Aldham: In *The Maverick Queen*, runs the hotel in South Pass where the Maverick Queen, Kit Bandon, keeps a room. McKeever is taken to her room there for Doc Williamson to patch him up. Thatcher hears Kit and Emery arguing through the window at Aldham's hotel.

Alec: In *The Horse Thief*, one of the three horse thieves Dale Brittenham comes upon in camp, waiting to rendezvous with others of the outfit. He shoots his confrere, Ben. He hears Dale moving about in the trees nearby and is shot and killed in the ensuing gunfire.

Alice: In *The Deer Stalker*, the New York recipient of a letter from Patricia Clay Edgerton, describing how pleased she is to be in Arizona. She explains that she has found herself, that the natural environment of the West has done much to soothe her troubled spirits. At some point, Patricia had "sacrificed her reputation" to save Alice. The details of the case are never specified. Apparently, they are contained in a letter from Alice to Patricia which Patricia offers to show to Thad Eburne. This would explain why she was reluctant to accept his proposal of marriage.

Allemewi: An aged, blind Delaware chief in *The Spirit of the Border*. He is the first of the Delaware chiefs to convert to Christianity.

Allen, Beulah: In *Majesty's Rancho*, one of Madge Stewart's crowd at the university in Los Angeles. She has been engaged several times to Snake Elwell, but Madge questions whether he is interested in her or in her car. They form part of the gang that shows up at the Stewart ranch to spend the summer. Ren Starr describes her as a composite of honey, dynamite and autumn leaves of red and gold. She's so pretty, Ren cannot take his eyes off her. Red-headed, roguish-eyed, with a great shape — a devil clear down to her toes. She flirts with Lance Sidway, who is not amused by her attentions. He tells her that he likes Snake, a decent, regular guy, who does not deserve to be toyed with as she is doing. If she has liked him enough to get engaged to him several times, she owes him the decency of not flirting with others in front of him. She is chastened by Lance's frank assessment of her behavior. When they leave, she tells Madge that if things do not work out with Lance, she will be back to try her luck.

Allen, Lester: In *Raiders of Spanish Peaks*, sells the Spanish Peaks ranch to Lindsay. Laramie Nelson has heard of him, but knows little about the man. When he learns that Luke Arlidge is Allen's foreman, he is sure there is something sinister in the association. In Garden City, Allen is not well known, and no one will say anything either good or bad about him, but Luke Arlidge has quite a reputation. Allen and Arlidge arrive together to finish the deal. Lester Allen is a tall man of striking appearance. He is no longer young and has a face like a hawk. He wears a dark suit, the trousers of which are tucked into high-top boots. He carries a huge, tan sombrero and a whip. He is shy and awkward in the presence of women. He describes the ranch, an old fort built by trappers used in trade with the Utes and the Kiowas. The house has a spring that brings water right into the patio. There are only three ranches within fifty miles of the place, and the closest town, La Junta, is two days' ride away. Denver is six days by buckboard. He gives a bit of advice about what supplies will be needed and assures Lindsay that Arlidge will make the necessary arrangements. As well, he has left Arlidge to work as foreman together with nine men. Harriet Lindsay, the business manager of the operation, is not impressed with Allen. She cannot pin him down to exact figures about the number of cattle. After the Lindsays are established at the new ranch, it does not take Laramie Nelson long to conclude that Allen is a shady cattleman. He got the Spanish Peaks ranch from the Seward Company and he did no work to improve the place. He himself is now ranching on Sandstone Creek. He has fine range, lots of corrals, and a log cabin, but no signs of ranch work being done. When Laramie captures members of Gaines and Arlidge's gang, Nig Jackson agrees to give evidence against Allen in exchange for his life. When they arrive at Allen's cabin, Strickland is there trying to convince Allen to join the Cattlemen's Protection Association. Jackson reveals that the cattle they rustled from Lindsay were delivered to Allen, who arranged their sale. Allen is given the choice of being hanged or leaving Colorado permanently. He forks the dead Arlidge's horse and rides away.

Allen, Nick: In *Shadow on the Trail*, a member of Simm Bell's outlaw gang. He meets Bell and Holden when they return to Smoky Hollow from the Texas Pacific train heist. When Bell reports what happened to Smith and Hazlitt, and Holden's attempt to shoot Blue because he suspects he has turned informant, Allen comments that he had always been suspicious of Blue. It is not known whether he survives the ambush in Mercer.

Allerton, Captain: In "The Ranger," the head of the Texas Rangers, Medill's boss. He was injured in the Cutter rustling fight. He sends Medill on the mission to track the abductors of Roseta Uvaldo and the herd of horses; both incidents may be connected.

Alloway, Chess In *The Lone Star Ranger*, one of Bland's lieutenants. He is fast with a colt and jealous of Duane's speed, resenting it when Bland tells him not to attempt to draw on Duane. Alloway has been trying to persuade Bland to give Jennie to him. He shoots Euchre when they are trying to escape and he in turn is shot by Buck Duane, proving definitely that he is the faster on the draw.

Allson, Annie: In *Raiders of Spanish Peaks,* the niece of Bruce Allson, a rancher. Her mother is Allson's sister, who works as his housekeeper. Annie can't read or write, but is one great looker. All the cowboys on the ranch are in love with her. Lonesome is taken with her, but so is the foreman, Price, who resents the competition. He uses this rivalry as a pretext to accuse Lonesome of cattle rustling. Lonesome complains that his big problem is that all the girls fall in love with him so easily.

Allson, Bruce: In *Raiders of Spanish Peaks,* a rancher for whom Lonesome rode. He was a fine man to work for when he was flush. He has a daughter, Annie, with whom both Lonesome and Price are in love. A fight breaks out over Annie. This leads to the attempt to hang Lonesome.

Alonzo: In *Wild Horse Mesa*, a young, bow-legged, half-breed Mexican vaquero working with the Melberne outfit. He is reputed to be the best horse wrangler in Utah. He is slim, lithe, lightly-built-but-muscular. He has a sharp, smooth, dark face and piercing eyes. He is knowledgeable about the geography of the area, the canyons, the mesas, and the wild horse herds. Like Chane, he disapproves of the barbed wired method of catching mustangs. He doesn't want horses injured or killed. Alonzo is not impressed with Manerube's heartless, brutal methods of handling horses. He is run over in the stampede of animals caught by Manerube in the first roundup, and he reluctantly helps with the hobbling, only to be accused by Manerube of being slow and incompetent. Alonzo stays on with Melberne when the outfit is divided. He helps Chane pursue Panquitch. Chane declares he has never met a better vaquero than Alonzo.

Amador, General Cipriano: In *The Light of Western Stars,* one of the rebel leaders in the Mexican revolution of 1910–1920 executed on orders from General Rojas.

Ames, Arizona (Richard/Rich Ames): In *Arizona Ames,* the new name by which Rich Ames is known after he leaves the Tonto Basin. His life is a series of adventures in which he rescues women from danger or foils the plans of an outlaw gang.

Rich Ames is the eighteen-year-old twin brother of Nesta. He is the head of the family now that his father is dead. Caleb Ames was killed in the Pleasant Valley War and Rich still bears resentment against the Tates who are suspected of killing him. Rich first appears returning from hunting with his friend, Sam Playford, Nesta's fiancé. He receives a new rifle as a present from Cappy Tanner, and he demonstrates his ability with the firearm by shooting holes in a hat, a trick that becomes his trademark. He confides in Cappy that he is worried about his sister's reputation, as she has been spending time with Lil Snell and Lee Tate. Nesta's secretiveness particularly bothers him, as they had always been so close before. Both Nesta and Mrs. Ames, his mother, find Rich a bit overbearing, trying to control other people's lives. He feels he knows best. He does his best to split up Nesta and Tate but it is too late to save his sister's reputation. Nesta tries to commit suicide because she is pregnant with Lee Tate's child and does not want to embarrass Sam Playford by marrying him. Sam marries Nesta in spite of the disgrace. Her indiscretion does not upset him; he loves her enough that it does not matter. Rich then goes to Shelby to confront Lee Tate. The slick young gambler and ladies' man is caught cheating at cards, and although his brother, Slink, tries to keep him calm, Lee draws on Rich Ames, who is much his superior on the draw. Following the episode, Rich leaves the Tonto Basin as friends of the Tates will undoubtedly be on his trail. He sends money back to Nesta and Sam to help them get a start.

And so begins his odyssey through the West, an odyssey in which he becomes an unparalleled cowhand and gunman with an uncanny ability to read men's hearts and souls. He helps people find their way out of crises through compassion such as he felt for Nesta and Sam.

Arizona Ames next appears in the Wind River country of Wyoming. He looks for work at Crow Grieve's ranch, where the first cowboy he meets is Lany Price, a nineteen-year-old who is in love with the boss's nineteen-year-old wife. Arizona learns that Grieve is quite an unpleasant man to work for, a man who beats the wife he acquired in payment for a debt some two years earlier. As well, Grieve abuses the patience of the cowboys, withholding their pay. He has also driven off the smaller "nesters" in the area. Arizona Ames undertakes to help young Amy, who is madly in love with Lany and unhappy with her brutal husband. He also takes up the cause of the Nielsens, a family of Norwegian homesteaders, the first ones into the Wind River Valley, who own the last remaining homestead not seized by Grieve. He has Brick Jones, who helped Grieve build the fence around the Nielsen homestead, tear the fence down. He confronts Grieve in public, before his rancher guests and the cowhands, calling him a wife beater and a coward, a man who mistreats his riders. Arizona declares he will remain until he gets the pay due him, pay Grieve has no intention of giving him. Arizona's action encourages other cowboys to quit Grieve. Warned by Blab McKinney that Grieve is quite the hunter, shooting with his rifle from cover, Arizona Ames spots Grieve one morning as he goes to saddle his horse. Crow is killed in the shootout, and Arizona Ames moves on, having righted several wrongs and set the course of several lives on a new track.

Arizona next meets an outfit of horse thieves who are planning to rob a Mormon horse rancher. Arizona poses as an outlaw and is accepted into the gang by Steele Brandeth. Noggin (Bill Ackers) distrusts him, remaining skeptical of his intentions. Friction breaks out between Noggin and Brandeth, and in the fighting which ensues, both Noggin and Brandeth are killed, Brandeth at Noggin's hand, and Nog-

gin shot by Arizona Ames. Arizona proceeds to the Morgan ranch, where he is warmly received as a hero. Morgan offers him a job on the ranch, and Lespeth, the twenty-one-year-old daughter, falls in love with him, but Arizona, inexperienced with women, is reluctant to get involved.

The next adventure finds Arizona Ames at the Halstead ranch in Colorado. He meets an old cowboy buddy, Joe Caleb, who receives him with open arms. The Halsteads are going through a particularly bad time. Rustlers have almost ruined their operation. Joe Cabel tells John Halstead that Arizona is the man he needs to solve his problem. He cannot praise the man too highly. Arizona is given a job on the ranch. He soon learns that the eldest son, Fred, is involved with Hensler and Bannard, two well-known outlaws. Stevens and Mecklin, two of his riders, are outlaws as well. Arizona Ames meets Bannard in town and gives him a warning, but Mecklin refuses to lie low and proceeds with an attempt to rustle the last of Halstead's herd. The attempt fails, Hensler is killed and Bannard is injured and arrested. The son, Fred, learns his lesson and returns to the straight and narrow. He marries Biny Wood, the daughter of a neighboring rancher. Arizona Ames falls in love with Esther Halstead, the twenty-one-year-old daughter of the rancher. The two are married and Arizona Ames will remain on the ranch as foreman. For their honeymoon, they return to the Tonto Basin to visit Nesta and Sam Playford. Sam has become a prosperous rancher.

Arizona Ames resembles Wetzel in *The Spirit of the Border*, a guardian angel who helps settlers on the frontier, or Chane Weymer in *Wild Horse Mesa*, the man who defends the honor of the Piute woman, Sosie. He is an idealistic man, using his experience and expertise with the gun to right wrongs and defend the weak.

Ames, Caleb: In *Arizona Ames*, the father of Rich and Nesta Ames, husband of Mrs. Ames. He was a Texas Ranger, and took part in the Texas invasion of the Southwest in the '40's. Little wonder that the son, Richard (Arizona), is partial to fighting.

Ames, Dr.: In *Rogue River Feud*, Dr. Ames is a dental surgeon in Portland who does dental work and reconstructive surgery on Keven Bell's jaw. When the work is finished, the war veteran, whose face had been blown apart in an accident shooting a cannon, can barely recognize himself in the mirror. This work does much to repair Keven Bell's shattered ego as well.

Ames, Jess: In *Arizona Ames*, the twin brother of Caleb Ames. He was a Texan, and a fighting man.

Ames, Manzanita: In *Arizona Ames*, one of the young twin girls in the Ames family. Cappy Tanner cannot tell her from her sister, Mescal.

Ames, Mescal: In *Arizona Ames*, one of the young twin girls in the Ames family. Cappy Tanner cannot tell her from her sister, Manzanita.

Ames, Mrs.: In *Arizona Ames,* the forty-year-old mother of Nesta and Rich, and wife of Caleb Ames. She is a handsome, tall, fair-haired pioneer woman, widowed in the Tonto war. Her son, Rich, she says, takes after her husband. He will not let things go but must fight things to their conclusion. She welcomes Cappy Tanner to their home and gratefully accepts the gifts he brings the family, particularly the wonderful white party dress for Nesta. Mrs. Ames tells Cappy she is not worried about Nesta. The young girl has common sense but she's just sowing her wild oats. If Sam Playford plays his cards right, Nesta will marry him. Her infatuation with Lee Tate will not last, and she will rediscover her love for Sam. Mrs. Ames thinks that Rich is making an issue of Lee Tate because his brother, Slink, was suspected to have ambushed and killed Caleb in the Tonto war. Rich and Cappy and Sam Playford keep Nesta's attempted suicide from the mother.

Ames, Nesta: In *Arizona Ames,* the twin sister of Rich "Arizona" Ames. Nesta had been sent back to Texas for education before the Pleasant Valley war. She is eighteen years old and engaged to marry Sam Playford, a young rancher new to the Tonto Basin. Nesta is unusual: at eighteen she is still unmarried, sixteen being the normal age. Of late, she has been very friendly with one Lil Snell, daughter of a wealthy rancher in Shelby. As well, she has been seen with Lee Tate, the devilishly handsome, womanizing son of the Tates, rivals to the Ameses in the Pleasant Valley war. She explains to Cappy that Sam, Rich's best friend, is the first of her beaus to meet with the family's approval. Nesta is troubled and she has no one in whom she can confide. Rich is upset at this because he and Nesta had always been close and now she keeps secrets from him. She explains to Cappy that Rich is too bossy, that he won't give her space to be herself. Nesta suspects that Cappy sides with Rich, although all he has said is that she should take things easy. She does love Sam, and appreciates his loyalty and steadfast confidence in her, but Sam is not good-looking and not exciting like Lee Tate. Nesta is thrilled with the beautiful white dress that Cappy has brought for her. She plans to wear it to Lil Snell's wedding where her beauty stands out, outshining the bride herself. At the party, Nesta dances with Sam and shuns Lee Tate. The next day, she agrees to marry Sam in a week's time at Mescal Ridge. When the time approaches for the wedding, she becomes increasingly distraught and attempts to drown herself in the river. Rich and Sam and Cappy save her, after which she explains that Lil Snell and Madge Low had arranged it that she and Lee Tate would be alone. Lee Tate had tried to force himself on her and she fought him off, but he caught her in the woods and raped her. She is now pregnant with his child. Feeling her disgrace deeply, and the scorn of Lee Tate and her friends, she cannot bring herself to tell Sam or her family what happened. Sam, however, tells her that he loves her, baby and all, and wants to marry her. Nesta and Sam are wed and move to his

ranch farther up in the Tonto. Rich settles the score with Lee Tate in town. Throughout the years, Rich sends money to help Nesta and Sam and their twins. In time, Sam Playford becomes a prosperous rancher. When Rich marries Esther Halstead, they come to visit Nesta and Sam on their ranch, some twenty years after the dramatic events which caused so much pain.

Nesta is unusual in the pantheon of Grey heroines. She is clearly sexually active, curious, pregnant out of wedlock, and a potential suicide. She has disgraced the family honor and is fortunate that she finds a noble young man who forgives her betrayal and marries and cares for her happily.

Ames, Pan Handle: In *Code of the West,* one of the riders working for Enoch Thurman. Like most of Enoch's riders, he is of Texas stock, a rider of the desert Panhandle of Texas before coming to Arizona. He has a homely face, and a serious air. When Mary is looking for someone to drive to town to pick up her sister, Pan Handle reminds her that driving cars is not his forte, as revealed by the disastrous attempt he made to drive her home from school one day. Nevertheless, he does know enough about cars to help Tim Matthews tinker with Cal's automobile when he is driving Georgie back from town.

Ames, Rich(ard): In *Arizona Ames,* the real name of Arizona Ames. In the first section of the novel, he is known as Rich, but when he leaves the Tonto Basin after the gunplay in which Sheriff Stringer and Lee Tate are killed, he acquires this nickname in his wanderings. It sticks and few know his real name.

Ames, Tommy: In *Arizona Ames,* a young son of Mrs. Ames who died recently. The details of the death are not mentioned, except that had they lived in a less remote area, he need not have died. When Cappy Tanner arrives at the Ames ranch, the family are still in mourning for their son and brother.

Amos: In *Arizona Ames,* the jovial, blond giant cook for Brandeth's outlaw gang. When Arizona Ames kills the two leaders, Amos goes off, taking the horses and pack animals.

Amy: In *Black Mesa,* the young woman from Wagontongue with whom Paul Manning had been involved. Wess Kintell describes her as not too tall, very slim and with an incredible shape. She had eyes that could bore through a fellow. Big brown eyes, bold and bright. She dumped Paul for another man.

Ancliffe: In *The U. P. Trail,* an English gentleman, friend of Place Hough, and fellow gambler. He helps Place Hough rescue Allie from Durade. In the fighting which follows, he kills Mex, one of Durade's thugs, and is himself badly injured.

Andersen, Jim: In *The Desert of Wheat,* also known as Montana, a young soldier whom Jim Anderson meets in boot camp. He is a cowboy — tall, generous, open-hearted. He and Jim Anderson become fast friends. Jim writes about his friend in his letters to Lenore. Montana gets into a fight and is hit on the head with a board. A splinter penetrates his scalp and enters the brain, causing paralysis. He is not expected to survive but he surprises everyone and lives. He remains partially paralyzed on one side.

Anderson: (1) In *The Desert of Wheat*, a wheat farmer and rancher in Golden Valley, Washington State. He owns a string of farms that he has acquired with hard work over the years. His farming and ranching operations include fruit orchards, vegetable farms, and cattle-raising. The land is leased out to tenant farmers, the lease paid with a share of the harvest, or is worked by farmhands under the direction of a foreman. He himself oversees the wheat farm. Mr. Anderson is about fifty-five years old and well-preserved. He is owed some thirty thousand dollars by Chris Dorn and has been very lenient about charging interest and demanding repayment. Nevertheless, Chris Dorn considers him a capitalist out to benefit from another's misfortune. His son, Kurt, however, appreciates the fairness and generosity with which Anderson has treated them. He shares what information he has about the I.W.W. agents who have been sowing discontent among the farmhands. He suspects that his car driver, Nash, is an I.W.W. agent and asks his daughter Lenore to get close to him to gather information. His suspicions are confirmed. Nash is working with Glidden and Neuman. He is grateful to young Kurt Dorn for stopping Nash's attempt to abduct his daughter. When Kurt has rescued the eighty thousand dollars his father got for the wheat, Anderson gives him sound advice about where to deposit the money. Anderson organizes the vigilante group that takes action to stop the destructive work of the I.W.W. among the wheat farmers. They have burned wheatfields and grain elevators and intimidated workers. The vigilantes hang Glidden and the ring leaders and prevent the town from being burned. They also drive out Neuman, the rival wheat farmer from Ruxton, who had been supporting and financing the I.W.W. in the area. Anderson buys him out at market value. Anderson is a patriotic American. He sees raising wheat as his contribution to the war effort. He consents to his son's joining the army without waiting for the draft. His son has always been a bit of a hell-raiser and perhaps the army will give some focus to his life. Anderson obtains an exemption from the draft for Kurt Dorn, but young Kurt, anxious to prove his American loyalties to himself, is annoyed at Anderson's interference and enlists anyway. Anderson buys out his farm at market value, giving him enough to repay his debt and to pay off the farmers who had helped him harvest his crop. He promises to let Dorn work the farm for him after the war is over. Anderson goes to see Jim when he learns that Jim is sick. Jim dies of pneumonia resulting from the bad living conditions in boot camp. Anderson regrets having let him go and returns with his son's body. He is enraged at the appalling conditions in which the re-

cruits are housed. All the young men have colds. He concludes the war is being run by profiteers and incompetents. When he hears that Kurt Dorn has returned to the New York, severely wounded and not expected to live, he goes to meet him and brings him back to Washington, to his own home. To the surprise of all, Kurt survives, and marries Anderson's daughter, Lenore. Eventually, when the war is over, Anderson and the I.W.W. find a modus vivendi, with higher wages for the hands and respect for a boss's property.

(2) In *The Dude Ranger*, a former rider and current foreman for the big cattle company across the range, and he strikes Ernest as being a hard-faced, shifty-eyed, taciturn boss. He never speaks to the Red Rock boys, Nebraskie and Ernest, except to give an order which was sure to be the worst possible task. Ernest eavesdrops on a conversation between Anderson and Wilkins. Anderson is now sure that Hepford is not on the up-and-up with the Red Rock Ranch owner, and he hesitates to have further dealings with him. He will not participate in the proposed October cattle drive. Wilkins tells him he has nothing to worry about, since technically, he has no way of knowing what shenanigans Hepford is up to and is not responsible for them anyway.

(3) In *The U.P. Trail*, a scout sent with Lieutenant Brady's detachment to Medicine Bow.

(4) In *Wilderness Trek*, one of Ormiston's drovers. He was friendly with Drake, one of Stanley Dann's men, who was surprised to learn they participated in the rustling of cattle and horses. Anderson is shot when the herd is recovered and the rustlers (bushrangers) captured.

Anderson, Arthur: In *Wyoming*, a good-natured, sandy-haired young man driving a truck along the highway in the Black Hills. He picks up Martha Ann Dixon, suspecting she is a runaway. When she mentions that the knapsack she is carrying had been given to her brother by Colonel Brinkerhoff, a man Anderson knows, he offers to take her to the armory where Brinkerhoff is stationed. She counters that the Colonel is off in Canada on a fishing trip. He then suggests going to the armory until Captain Stevens can be notified, and word sent to her folks, but Martha Ann explains she is going to visit her uncle. He doesn't believe her story, and tells her she cannot lie worth a damn. Martha resorts to tears, and this works. He lets her go, cautioning her to be careful. It is not safe for a young girl to go hitchhiking alone through the Black Hills.

Anderson, Jim: In *The Desert of Wheat*, Lenore's older brother and the only son of Anderson. At the start of the novel, he has signed up for military service, not waiting for the draft. Mr. Anderson has consented to his going because Jim has never been interested in farming and the army discipline might give his life some structure. He wants to be a pilot or mechanic working on planes, as he loves machinery. He writes letters to Lenore about training camp, about one young cowboy from Montana who shares his last name. He catches pneumonia in the poorly heated and poorly ventilated camp. Kurt Dorn comes to visit him in the camp before he ships out for France. Jim envies him. Young Anderson dies of pneumonia and Mr. Anderson brings the body back to Washington state for burial on the farm. The commanding officer at the camp tells Mr. Anderson that Jim was very popular with the men, generous (they all owed him money) and a good influence on camp morale.

Anderson, Joe: In *Fighting Caravans,* arrives on a caravan with Jim Couch and reports to Clint Belmet on the events of their passage.

Anderson, Kathleen: In *The Desert of Wheat,* the youngest sister of Lenore and Jim. She loves to tease her older sister about her new beau, Kurt Dorn. Kathleen takes a liking to Kurt just as Mrs. Anderson does.

Anderson, Lenore: In *The Desert of Wheat,* Mr. Anderson's oldest daughter. She is more interested in wheat farming than her brother Jim, and more involved in the farming activities than his wife. He confides in her more than in any other member of the family. Lenore is drawn to the shy, soft-spoken Kurt Dorn, whom she remembers from high school. His blond hair and gentle features have stuck in her memory. She admires his knowledge of wheat farming and his passion for nature. She, too, has a poetic streak in her. At her father's request, Lenore flirts with the car driver, Nash, and learns that he is an I.W.W. agent, working with Glidden and Neuman. Nash tries to abduct her, but Kurt Dorn prevents his escape. Lenore tries to use her feminine wiles to convince Kurt Dorn to accept the exemption from the draft her father has obtained for him. She does not appreciate the struggle in him between his German and his American halves. Lenore tells him that his self-hatred will prove destructive if he does not come to terms with his dual allegiance. Before he leaves, however, he proposes marriage to her and she accepts. She senses a change in Kurt in the letters he writes home from boot camp and from the front in France. When Kurt is brought home, she is shocked at the nightmares and the fits in which he relives his experiences on the battlefield in France. He imagines that without his arm, he will not be much of a farmer. She promises to marry him as soon as he can sit up in bed. With this promise, a noticeable improvement is seen in Kurt. The two of them marry and return to his old farm to continue farming wheat. Like Madeline Hammond in *The Light of Western Stars,* or Helen Sheppard in *The Last Trail,* Lenore helps the young hero find himself and become a complete individual.

Anderson, Mrs.: In *The Desert of Wheat,* makes a few appearances. Mr. Anderson the rancher and wheat farmer seems to confide more in his daughter Lenore than he does in his wife. Mrs. Anderson tells Lenore that she likes Kurt Dorn because he is so

good-looking and gentle-mannered. He is like an old-fashioned boyfriend. Jim, the first child and only son, was her favorite of the children. She is broken up when he dies of pneumonia at the army training camp. She herself dies shortly afterwards, seemingly of a broken heart, and is buried beside her son.

Anderson, Pike: In *The Lost Wagon Train,* the wagon master who leads the caravan which Bowden and his niece, Cynthia, join on the way to California. Anderson comments on the unusual wagon, a prairie schooner, a cross between a boat and a wagon. Anderson is not keen on taking the Dry Trail although it will shorten the trip to California for Bowden by over three weeks. He does not recommend it for a man with a woman in tow. When Blaisdal's caravan from Texas does not show up on the appointed day, he wants to turn back. In the argument which follows, he shoots and kills Jeff Stover, who tries to take over command of the caravan. When Smith reports back that he has seen a group of white men doling out liquor to Kiowas in a canyon near Tanner's Swale, Pike Anderson knows that the Indians will attack, but that the plan behind the strategy is that of a white man. He expects the worst. Anderson prepares the group for an attack, circling the wagons, herding the cattle into the enclosed circle, and appointing guards for the night. He has faced hazards often and come out unscathed in most instances, but in this case, a cold ache in the marrow of his bones gives him a premonition of death. Anderson and all, except Cynthia Bowden, are killed in the attack. When questions begin to be asked about the lost wagon train, all comments praise Anderson's skill as scout and wagon master, thereby enhancing the mystery of the disappearance.

Anderson, Rose: In *The Desert of Wheat,* Lenore and Jim's fourteen-year-old sister.

Anderson, Tracks: In *The Hash Knife Outfit,* a member of the Hash Knife Outfit. His nickname comes from his reputation as a tracker. He has lived longer than any of the others of the gang in this wild section. He is a serious man, long-matured as shown in the white in his black beard. He has deep eyes. When Jed Stone proposes that the Hash Knife move out of Arizona to find new ranges, he approves. The area won't long be safe for rustlers like them. He predicts that young Jim Traft will settle the score with Bambridge before too long.

Andersons: In *The Hash Knife Outfit,* friends of Glory Traft in Saint Louis, but when she takes up with the disreputable Ed Darnell, gambler, blackmailer, swindler, they desert her.

Andrew: In *The Desert of Wheat,* one of Chris Dorn's farmhands. He is fired after he takes off work thanks to I.W.W. agitation.

Andrews: In *The Lone Star Ranger,* a rancher who helps Jennie and Buck Duane when they are fleeing Bland's camp after the shootings. Even though he knows it could be dangerous to him, he gives Buck and Jennie shelter and they nurse him back to health. Andrews brings back word from Huntsville about the results of Buck's shootout with Bland. Fisher and Hardin are pleased to have Bland removed from the picture, and Hardin has already moved in on Bland's territory, taking over the outlaw town. Andrews says he has heard of Buck before, and of Rodney Brown, the sheriff-rancher who killed Luke Stevens. Andrews was once a prosperous rancher but was ruined by Brown. When Buck asks Andrews what he can do to repay him, Andrews hints that he would like Buck to settle the score with Rod Brown. This request makes Buck Duane think that the victims are as bloody as their assailants.

Andrews, Helen: In *The Shepherd of Guadaloupe*, a former schoolmate and close friend of Virginia Lundeen, and a stunningly beautiful young woman. She is one of the party which visits Virginia as she returns to Cottonwoods from France. Helen gets a crush on Clifton Forrest when the party drops by the Forrests' store, which Cliff is tending. Virginia has been anxious for her brother Jack, a war veteran, to meet Cliff. He went to France, like Cliff, and suffered from influenza and spent a long time recuperating in a hospital before returning to the U.S. Since Cliff has little recollection of the people he met in France, it is possible he and Jack met at some point. She buys many souvenirs, to help Cliff out. When she hears that the store has been burned out, she decides she wants to buy the Payne ranch in Watrous and hire Cliff to run it for her. She is fabulously wealthy and anxious to help out if she can. When things are reaching a resolution at the end of the novel, she goes with Ethel Wayne to visit Cliff at his tent and reports back to Virginia about how he has been transformed by his months in the desert. She expresses her joy that Virginia married him.

Andrews, Jack: In *The Shepherd of Guadaloupe*, the brother of Virginia Lundeen's old schoolmate and intimate friend, Helen. He introduces himself to Jack while the party is touring the store looking for souvenirs of the Southwest. He had been in France, suffered from influenza and spent a lot of time in a hospital recuperating. As Cliff spent a lot of time unconscious and in a very weakened state, it is possible he and Jack met, but he can't recall. He invites Jack to come back some day to have coffee and chat about their experiences. Virginia hopes this camaraderie will convince Jack that his sacrifice in the war was not in vain and that there is hope for the future.

Andrews, Martha: the wife of the rancher in *The Lone Star Ranger* who takes in Jennie and the wounded Buck Duane after the shootout and escape from Bland's camp. She nurses Buck back to health and he and Jennie stay at the ranch for a month.

Andrews, Mrs. Tom: In *The Mysterious Rider*, the wife of Bellounds' former cowboy. She is friendly with Columbine, who comes to her to find out what has become of Wilson Moore since he left the Bellounds' ranch. She reports that Wilson was too in-jured to make the trip to Denver to see a doctor so Mrs. Plummer took care of his leg. Wilson is recuperating in their cabin. When Columbine is sick, after the disastrous fiasco of a wedding day, Mrs. Andrew comes by sled to visit her.

Andrews, Tom: In *The Mysterious Rider*, a former Belllounds cowboy who has set himself up in the stock business with the help of Old Bill Bellounds. His land borders the ranch of his former employer. He has a young wife and several children and a brother who rides for him. Tom Andrews befriends Bent Wade, who fixes his gun and cures some sick cattle that have eaten loco weed (larkspur). The Andrews brothers help Wilson Moore drive his cattle to market when he is laid up, unable to ride.

Andy: (1) In *The Desert of Wheat*, one of the men involved in the vigilante action against the I.W.W. men. He voices patriotic slogans and wonders why all the hanged I.W.W. leaders were cut down except for Glidden.

(2) In *Wild Horse Mesa*, Chane Weymer's white horse. The animal has a few black marks and a nervous disposition.

Anne: In *Black Mesa*, Paul Manning's sister. He picks up two fat letters from her at Belmont's post when he moves in. At the end, when he and Wess Kintell are planning to sell their interest in Belmont's cattle industry at Bitter Seeps, he plans to take Wess Kintell back with him to his farm, where Anne can meet a real fire-eating cowboy and come back West with him to find a ranch.

Annie: In *Betty Zane*, the daughter of the black slave, Sam. She has taken care of Betty since childhood.

Anson, Snake: In *The Man of the Forest*, the worst and most dangerous outlaw in the region around Pine, New Mexico. He is so-named for his serpent-like face and a hissing sound he makes when he speaks. Milt Dale overhears a meeting between Anson and Beasley, one of the two biggest ranchers and sheep-raisers of the White Mountain range. Anson is being commissioned to kidnap the niece of Al Auchincloss, the ranching competitor, whose herds and lands Beasley covets. Anson is to make off with the girl, and he doesn't really care what becomes of her as he wishes. When Milt Dale and the Beeman brothers foil his plan, he recruits Harve Riggs to bring Helen to him. Riggs brings in Bo, the younger sister, by mistake, and Anson is not amused. Riggs suggests that she can be used to get ransom. Beasley is likewise unimpressed with the bungling. Anson expects Beasley to turn on them eventually. Jim Wilson and Snake have a heart-to-heart while they ponder what to do. Snake tells him he was the best partner he ever had. In the years they rustled together they never had a contrary word until he let Beasley fill his ears with promises. He calculates that his years on the range will not be many. Wilson predicts that the disintegration of the group through in-fighting is in the cards for their outfit, as for all outlaw gangs. And as Jim predicts, the gang falls apart. With Milt Dale and his wildcat, Tom, scaring the wits out of the men, they take to shooting. In the confusion, Snake is shot by Shady Jones, whom he kills in turn.

Antelope Clan: In *Blue Feather*, the group with whose princess Taneen fell in love. From their love was born Nashta, Daughter of the Moon. The priests decry their chief's involvement with a woman of this cursed clan. The Antelope Clan has been wiped out by the anger of the gods. Consequently, involvement with a queen of that clan is sacrilegious and sure to be punished by the angry gods.

Aola: known as Whispering Winds in English, the daughter of the Delaware sachem, Wingenund. She is a Pocahontas figure in *The Spirit of the Border*.

Whispering Winds feels sorry for white prisoners and on more than one occasion has secretly freed them. She cuts the rawhide bonds that tie the captive Wetzel in *The Spirit of the Border* and she leaves him a knife to help him escape.

In the trial of Joe and Jim, Aola is called in to make a positive identification of the preacher. Since the two brothers look so much alike, the chiefs cannot tell them apart. And although their dress cannot distinguish them, Aola knows which is Jim. In Pocahontas fashion, she saves Joe from death, and then claims him for her husband.

She is a frequent visitor to the Village of Peace and after her marriage to Joe, she confesses that she is a Christian. With the increasing hostility to Christians among the Indians in the Huron village, she plans to leave with him for the Gnaddenhutten.

Whispering Winds helps Joe find out where Girty has been keeping Kate. She finds the injured Joe after his attempt to rescue Kate. She attempts to patch up his wounds and the two of them set off for the village. Jim Girty catches up with them and murders the two of them. Wetzel, on the trail of Girty, comes upon the bodies and buries them in the Beautiful Spring. Later, Wingenund retrieves the bodies from the water and buries them in a proper grave.

Aola, Whispering Winds, is one of Grey's Pocahontas figures, like Myeerah in *Betty Zane*. As with Pocahontas in Captain John Smith's account, the Indian woman is often the go-between, making possible civil, if not always harmonious, relationships between whites and Indians.

Arab: In *Majesty's Rancho*, one of Madge Stewart's string of thoroughbred horses.

Arallanes, Juan: In *Wanderer of the Wasteland*, the Mexican foreman of the mill in Picacho. He lives with a wife and stepdaughter. They rent a room to Adam Larey when he comes to Picacho. He is well-built, with regular features, a decent, moral man, fair, just, upright. He warns Adam about Margarita, that she is like a wildcat in heat, that she loves to make men jealous and fight over her. His words come true. When Adam returns fourteen years later

to Picacho, he learns that Arallanes moved away when the mills failed. Merryvale has not heard from him since.

Arallanes, Margarita: In *Wanderer of the Wasteland*, the stepdaughter of Juan Arallanes, the foreman of the workers at the mill in Picacho. Margarita is seventeen years old when her mother rents a room to Adam Larey. Margarita wants Adam to go to a dance with her, and he meekly follows. Her stepfather describes her as passionate, always on fire, with as many lovers as a spotted cat has spots. She is alluring and provocative, furious as a barbarian queen when she does not get her way. She has a fit of jealousy when Adam returns from lunch on board the boat with MacKay's friends. Adam describes loving her pretty face and her beautiful body. She glories in her power over men. She seduces Adam, who spends a night with her, then she turns to his brother, who is more handsome and stronger and will fight for her. Margarita does not realize the trouble she can get herself into, playing on the jealousy of men. She ends up being stabbed to death by a jealous Mexican lover, Felix. When Merryvale tells Adam what happened to her, he knows it could only have ended that way. Margarita is also mentioned in the sequel, *Stairs of Sand*. In the Del Toro Saloon in Yuma, some twenty years later, Adam and Merryvale see a young Mexican girl who is the very image of young Margarita. It reminds Adam and his companion of her tragic fate.

Arbell, Joe: In *30,000 on the Hoof*, one of the very young cowboys Logan Huett hires to drive his cattle, since most of the older boys have been recruited for the army.

Archer, Long Tim: In *The Lost Wagon Train*, a cowboy with whom Slim Blue (Corny) used to ride. When he heads to San Antonio to marry Estelle, he hires Slim and several other former trail buddies to drive a herd of five thousand head to their ranch in Latchfield.

Arizona: In *Code of the West*, one of the cowboys working for Enoch Thurman. He is known only by this name. He is small of stature, ruddy-faced, blinking-eyed. He has a reputation for humor that his appearance belies. When asked by Mary the schoolteacher to drive over to pick up her sister at the station, he declines on the grounds that since it hasn't rained in over a month, a storm will surely come up and he must get the sorghum cut before the storm. Nevertheless, he does show up in town with the other cowboys to give Cal a hard time.

Arizona Charlie: In *Stairs of Sand*, appears in the Del Toro Saloon in Yuma. He is a local character whom Merryvale knows by sight. He appears with a group of friends, bent on having a good time. He stands head and shoulders above the crowd, a picturesque frontiersman in cowboy regalia, red of face, blinking of eye with a mouth that is a thin hard line except when he laughs.

Arkansas: In *Shadow on the Trail,* a tall, lanky, red-whiskered outlaw in Bell's gang. He meets Holden when he returns to Smoky Hollow. When discussing what has happened, Arkansas says what Wade Holden is thinking. If Blue has really turned informer, he knows about their hideout in Smoky Hollow. The Texas Pacific job came off because Blue learned about it too late to send the information to the rangers. If they go for the bank in Mercer, the rangers will surely be waiting. Only he and Holden vote against the Mercer job. Arkansas is the first to see the ambush when they ride into town. He helps support the injured Bell in the saddle as they ride out of town, but Arkansas himself is shot and killed.

Arlidge, Luke: In *Raiders of Spanish Peaks,* the foreman and partner-in-crime of Lester Allen. Laramie Nelson had dealings with him before and knows that whatever kind of deal he is involved with cannot be good. When he shows up with Allen to finalize the deal to sell Spanish Peaks, the contrast between the two men is to his benefit. He makes a superb figure of a man, still young, scarcely thirty, with a bronzed, hard, lean face and eagle eyes. He is clearly a man of great experience. His garb is that of a romantic range-rider. He is spurred, booted, and belted over rough, dusty apparel, and most conspicuously, he wears ivory-handled guns that swing from his hip. He clearly knows more about the ranch than Allen, and while his boss does not impress Harriet, Arlidge does. She gauges him as a strong, subtle personality, bold, crafty with a most pleasing exterior. He is shocked when Price announces that Laramie Nelson is to be foreman of the ranch. Laramie had cheated him out of hanging young Mulhall. When Arlidge and Nelson meet, the cowboys move out of the way, expecting gunplay, but Nelson restrains himself, telling Arlidge that he will have to go as the two of them cannot work on the same range. Arlidge leaves, and the crew are divided to whom to transfer their loyalty. Arlidge leaves and supposedly shakes up ranching at Castle Haid with a man named Snook as a foreman, but there is no evidence of any ranching being done on the place. Arlidge, like Allen, maintains a pretense of respectability, operating through cowboys like Gaines and Price. He is interested in Harriet Lindsay, and she is interested in maintaining good relations with the neighbors, although she has no romantic interest in him. Arlidge arrives at the Allen cabin when Strickland and Laramie Nelson are inside. From the porch, he announces that he has had to shoot young Neale Lindsay. Laramie steps outside, Arlidge draws, and Nelson replies, killing him. The arrival of Arlidge confirmed suspicions Strickland had of Allen's dishonesty.

Arrowswift: In *Betty Zane,* the Huron warrior who shoots Isaac Zane in the shoulder as he is escaping. He is reputed to be the best archer in the Huron village.

Ashbow: In *The Last Trail,* a member of the Bing Legget outlaw gang. His claim to fame is his ability as an archer. He shoots an arrow from the island in the Ohio river into Brandt's room, an outstanding feat of strength and accuracy. It is a warning to the rustlers inside the fort that they are under suspicion. He meets Metzar and Brandt down by the river to tell them that Wetzel is on to their game. Wetzel attributes a large part of Bing Legget's success to Ashbow, Wetzel's equal in tracking and in hiding his trail.

Ashbridge, Mark: In *The Shepherd of Guadaloupe,* one of the company of friends that accompany Virginia back to Cottonwoods. He comments that it looks strange not to see any bow-legged cowboys on the ranch, and offers to sign on as a cowboy.

Asher: In *Fighting Caravans,* a teamster on the way to Baruth. He gets up during the night to go hunting jack rabbits. While he is out of the camp, the Indians attack, burning the wagons and killing everyone. He is the lone survivor.

Atelang: In *The Spirit of the Border,* the Delaware name for Wetzel, the "Deathwind," "Black Wind."

Atwell, Gus: In *Rogue River Feud,* the foreman at the cannery, running the operations for John Brandeth. According to Minton, he is a slacker, tardy in paying bills, and showy, driving around in a Rolls-Royce convertible. He has been seen sporting around with Rosamond Brandeth, the cannery owner's daughter. Atwell had been at the army training camp in Washington with Keven. Billy Horn and Emmeline Trapier tell Keven that Gus Atwell has spread the story that Keven got the five Carstone girls pregnant, thereby ruining his reputation back home in Grant's Pass. Gus Atwell himself managed to be discharged for medical reasons to avoid going to Europe to fight. When Keven returns, his hostility continues unabated. Keven confronts him in the hotel, calling him a coward and a liar, striking him. Atwell charges him with assault and attempted murder. The charges are eventually dropped, but Atwell does not let slip by the opportunity to slur Keven again in the papers. Atwell tries to ruin Garry Lord's and Keven's fishing business, making it impossible for them to sell their fish. Keven is nervous about being seen with Beryl Aard around Grant's Pass, but she assures him that when Atwell sees her, he will see things differently. She knows the true story of what happened at the training camp with the Carstone girls. Atwell caused the girls' disgrace, not Keven Bell. He won't dare challenge her.

Auchincloss, Al: In *The Man of the Forest,* owns a large ranch with herds of cattle and flocks of sheep in Pine, New Mexico. Beasley claims he and Al Auchincloss had been partners in sheep-raising for years. Al swore Beasley cheated him at cards and threw him out. He is now on his last legs and is "going to croak." He has sent for his niece, Helen Rayner, in Missouri. He intends to leave her his ranches and his herds. It seems he has no other relatives. When Milt Dale goes to visit him after he has heard of the plot to kidnap the niece from the train station in Magdalena, he finds Old Al sitting on his porch. He is a short man of extremely powerful build and great width of shoulders. He has no gray hairs and he does not look old, but in his face Milt sees a certain weariness, something that resembled sloping lines of distress that tell of age and the ebbing of vitality. Old Al, a hard worker all his life, has never had much use for Milt Dale, whom he considers a wastrel, a good-for-nothing, lacking responsibility and ambition. As well, he has had a bone to pick with Milt over some sheep that he claims Milt's pet wildcat, Tom, had killed. He tells Milt he knew the cat was guilty when the cat looked in his eyes. Milt offers to pay for the damage, but refuses to accept that Tom killed the animals. He also tells Al that Beasley has been plotting to take his land. Old Al gets angry, looking more and more like a pitiful old man. He tells Dale that Beasley has been plotting against him for years; that is not news, but if he really wants to help, he will have to kill Beasley, "that greaser sheep-thief." Milt decides not to tell him about the plot to kidnap Helen. When Milt and the Beeman brothers have rescued Nell, Joe Beeman brings him word that Nell and Bo are with Milt Dale at his senaca. When enough time has passed that Beasley's men are not likely to follow, the Beeman brothers bring Al Auchincloss to Milt's forest retreat to meet his niece. She is the reincarnation of her mother, he says. Nell sees in him a powerfully built man, but one in whose face all the years of toil and battle and privation show something that is not just age or resignation, but something tragic. Al apologizes to Milt for misjudging him. Bo puts in a good world for Tom Carmichael, and Al agrees to give him a job at the ranch. He also offers Milt the job of foreman. He points out that Milt cannot continue forever living in his senaca. Helen will not be able to run the ranch alone. The upcoming fight with Beasley requires a man's touch and Milt has shown he has the initiative and wisdom to handle any problems. Milt refuses the offer saying he would be out of place down in Pine. Back at the ranch, Al introduces Helen to the management of the ranch, preparing her for her new life as manager of the ranch. Within a few months, Al dies, and Helen assumes the reins, running the ranch. Going through her uncle's records, however, she learns that Beasley and her uncle had never been partners. Old Al had taken Beasley in when he was a poor, homeless boy, and raised him like a son. Hence, the particularly bitter conflict between a father and the betraying son.

Auchincloss, Nell: In *The Man of the Forest*, Al Auchincloss's sister and mother of Helen Rayner. She married and lived in Saint Joe, Missouri. Al tells Milt Dale that his niece, Helen, is like her mother, Nell, a strong, determined, courageous and stunningly beautiful woman. He has never seen his niece but from what he has been told, she is another Nell. When he first sees her at Milt Dale's forest retreat, he says she indeed is her mother reborn.

Augustine: (1) In *The Lost Wagon Train*, a Mexican Vaquero in Latch's outlaw outfit. He is a member of the Leighton faction. In the attack on the Anderson caravan, he gets an arrow in his thigh.

(2) In *Stairs of Sand*, a Mexican friend of Wansfell in Yuma. The man is on top of all the goings-on in town and Adam is sure he will be able to help locate Ruth if she is being held there. He is a robust, black-browed Mexican with sloe eyes. He runs a prosperous marketplace. He offers Adam the hospitality of his spacious home. He tells Adam he has seen Collishaw in town, but not Stone. He does know how he can find out, though, since one of Collishaw's drivers is a distant cousin of his. When Merryvale and Adam finally free Ruth from Collishaw, he and his wife take Ruth in to recuperate from her ordeal.

Aull: In *Fighting Caravans*, runs a freighting company employing Clink Belmet and Captain Couch, transporting hides and supplies in the Southwest. Aull's headquarters are in Westport, Kansas City.

Aulsbrook: In *Shadow on the Trail*, trails a herd which the Catlin outfit are planning to rustle. Wade Holden rides into his camp to warn him of the impending attack on his outfit. Aulsbrook has already noticed that he is being followed and as he sees that Holden is a gunman, offers to take him on. His foreman, Bert, suspects Holden is just a plant, pretending to help but really an inside man for Catlin. Aulsbrook gives the reticent Holden the name Blanco, which he uses for the next few years. Aulsbrook's faith in Blanco is proven when the Catlin outfit arrives and provokes a fight in which Catlin and Nippert are killed. When Aulsbrook sells his outfit to Chisum, he invites Blanco to come along with him to New Mexico on his next venture. Wade Holden runs into Aulsbrook about two years later when he is looking for work. Aulsbrook's foreman, Lawsford, tells him about the Pencarrows. He learns from the Pencarrows that Aulsbrook has not been friendly or helpful to them, although his foreman has always been amicable. Eventually, the rustlers' situation becomes so severe that Aulsbrook looks to sell his operation and Wade Holden buys him out.

Aunt Grace: In *The Light of Western Stars*, dies, leaving a huge fortune to Madeline Hammond. This fortune makes it possible for Madeline to move west, to lend her brother ten thousand dollars to pay off debts and to buy and renovate Bill Stillwell's ranch.

Aunt Jane: In *Wildfire*, John Bostril's sister, and Lucy's aunt. She has illusions about the social position they enjoyed back in Missouri, complaining that Bostril's Ford is uncivilized. She wants Lucy to marry one Jim Witherby from Durango. He is a man with prospects, a good match for Lucy. She complains that Lucy is too much of a tomboy and fears that she is interested in young Joel Creech, whom everyone considers an idiot. To please her, Lucy starts wearing dresses around the house. When Lucy starts taking mysterious rides out on the sage and remains away all day, Aunt Jane suspects something, and Lucy tells her about Lin Slone. Aunt Jane complains that it's not respectable for a young woman to meet with a man out on the sage. What will people at Bostril's Ford say when she enters the race with a horse caught and broken by Lin Slone? Aunt Jane is in charge of preparing the feast to celebrate the end of the races when the prizes are given out. Like Hawk Holley, she is upset when Lucy disappears one night, fearing the worst. She does acquiesce in Lucy's marrying Lin Slone.

Aunt Mary: In *The Call of the Canyon*, Carley Burch's aunt. She raised her and when Carley shows her a troubling letter she has received from her fiancé, Glenn Killbourne, who had gone to Arizona, Aunt Mary has some harsh words for her niece. Carley has led a sheltered, selfish life. She does not appreciate the hell that Glenn went through in the war. Aunt Mary tells her that Glenn went west to escape from the shallow life of New York. She advises her niece to go west. In the letter, Glenn is extending a subtle invitation to her. She should seize the opportunity. When Carley confesses that she feels offended by the letter, Aunt Mary tells her it is a good sign that her feelings have been hurt. It's a sign that she does have a heart beneath all the superficial culture of New York.

When Carley returns to New York some months later, Aunt Mary sees a change in her. She examines her with a shrewd, penetrating gaze, and sees that her niece has come to her senses, that she has found herself and her true values. She suggests that the two of them go west together. She wants to visit some friends in California and when she has finished her visit, she will join Carley at the ranch house near the Painted Desert. They travel west by train and visit the Grand Canyon en route.

Although she is a New Yorker, she has true, old-fashioned American family values. For Grey, moving west is a symbolic rejection of the shallow, superficial values of eastern society and a vote for traditional American values.

B

Ba-Lee: In *Blue Feather*, a young maiden of the Rock Clan, betrothed to the young warrior, Tith-Lei, the mole. She is one of the servants who tend to Nashta, Daughter of the Moon and Taneen's daughter. Ba-Lee is impressed with the Nopah stranger, and her interest in him stirs jealousy in Tith-lei. She acts as a go-between, allowing Blue Feather in to visit with Nashta, although this is strictly forbidden. Most of what Nashta knows about men and about love comes from the stories she hears from Ba-Lee. When the Nopah has fallen in love with Nashta, Ba-Lee's love turns to hate, and she betrays both Nashta and Blue Feather. She calls for his death by torture and urges the warriors to kill him. She is killed when the Nopahs take the citadel, having entered through the secret passage revealed by Nashta to Blue Feather's father.

Babbitt: (1) In "Amber's Mirage," the manager of the bank in Pine. Al Shade speaks to him when he comes to deposit the fortune he made in the desert. He comments that Al looks as though he made his fortune the hard way.

(2) In *The Drift Fence* and in *The Hash Knife Outfit*, owns the general store in Flag where Molly gets a job as a salesgirl after she breaks off her engagement to Jim Traft. In *30,000 on the Hoof*, the same Babbitt buys Logan Huett's potato crop and other vegetables. He has gone into cattle and runs a sizeable herd. He is described as one of the cattle barons in the region. In *The Dude Ranger*, Hawk Siebert sends Ernest Selby into Holbrook to pick up an order at Babbitt's store. In *Black Mesa*, Babbitt is said to be running eighty thousand head of cattle on the range. Belmont tells Manning this to impress on him the money that there is to be made in ranching.

Babbitt, Hep: In *The Drift Fence*, named by Ring Locke as one of the larger ranchers in the Diamond who has been affected by cattle rustling. Jim Traft reports this to his nephew, Young Jim, when he appoints him foreman of the ranch.

Badger Clan: In *Blue Feather*, mysteriously disappeared from the escarpment to the south of the Rock Clan.

Bailey, Bill: In *The Border Legion*, one of the two men with Jack Kells when he rides into Harvey Roberts's and Joan Randle's camp. Bill Bailey hobbles the horses and helps with the preparation of supper. Joan describes him as not given to thought, driven primarily by animal instincts. Later, when Kells has abducted Joan, ostensibly for purposes of ransom, Bill grabs Joan's breast when Kells is not around. Joan concludes that his action was motivated purely by animal lust, not by thought or desire to hurt her. Kells returns and catches Bill in the act, and shortly thereafter kills him for his interference with a woman Kells wants for himself. Bill Bailey, it turns out, is a close associate of Gulden. He doesn't die right away, but makes it back to the cabin, where he is found by Beady Jones, who gets word to Gulden about Kells shooting Bailey at point-blank range.

Bailey, Colonel: In *Fighting Caravans*, the newly arrived commandant with little experience on the Western frontier. When Clint Belmet goes to ask for an army escort past Point of Rocks, he comments that it would be more suitable for the frontiersmen to serve as escorts for his inexperienced recruits.

Bailey, Parson: In *The Arizona Clan*, fetched by Buck Hathaway and kept locked up in a cabin to force the parson to marry him and Nan. Dodge Mercer, however, sneaks into the cabin where he is being held with Nan, and the two of them ask the parson to marry them. When Hathaway tries to get Nan to marry him, she runs off before anyone can stop her.

Later, Parson Bailey tells Hathaway he married Nan and Dodge.

Bain: In *Raiders of Spanish Peaks,* one of the honest ranchers who, together with Stockwell, Halscomb and Strickland, have gotten together to form the Spanish Peaks Cattlemen's Protective Association, to rout out dishonest ranchers working in conjunction with rustlers.

Bain, Cal: In *The Lone Star Ranger,* a foolish young man afflicted with a fever that is rampant among young men in Texas, a desire for gunplay. He has already killed one man and has it in for Buck Duane as he suspects Duane has been seeing his girlfriend. He is a "four-flush gunfighter" and wants to build a reputation as a "bad man," aping Bland, King Fisher and Hardin. He announces that he is going to join an outlaw gang and "fix rangers." He has two friends, Burt and Sam Outcott, who try to talk some sense into him, but Bain insists on meeting with Buck Duane. When Buck comes into town, Bain comes out of Everall's with "malignant intent" and forces Duane to draw. When he is shot, his face returns to normal, having been distorted by the hatred he had drummed up to enter the gunfight.

Bain, Jerry: In *The Lost Wagon Train,* a merry little outlaw of whom no stranger would ever think evil. He is a member of Latch's outlaw gang and, like Cole and Johnson, accepts Latch's offer of money and cattle to start ranching. Like Cole and Johnson, he remains active in Leighton's circle, as Leighton holds the threat of revealing their former work to keep them loyal. He doesn't lose any cattle to rustlers, while Latch's herd is decimated. Slim Blue reports seeing him come and go to Leighton's quarters at all hours of the night.

Baird: In *Boulder Dam,* in charge of the scalers and drillers. He has an iron handshake and scrutinizes Lynn Weston with a keen eye. He shows Lynn how to get into the seat and the procedures through which he will be lowered over the rim. He also shows him how to hold the heavy drill, taking him over the rim for a demonstration. He is impressed by the speed at which Lynn learns to do the new job.

Baker: In *The Mysterious Rider,* lives on a ranch near Bellounds. When Buster Jack Belllounds does not return home the day he is expected, one of Baker's cowboys reports that Buster Jack has been seen at Kremmlin' drinking.

Baker, Jim: In *Fighting Caravans,* a famous frontiersman. He was among the first to cross the plains. Baker is married to a Cheyenne woman, Indian fashion. Dick Curtis introduces Clint Belmet to him at Fort Larned. Clint is surprised at the greasy, rough, dirty, disreputable appearance of the man. But for the beard and the talk, mostly profane, he could have been an Indian. Clint Belmet meets him again at Kit Carson's home in Taos, New Mexico.

In *The Lost Wagon Train,* Jim Baker is mentioned at Fort Union, when Major Greer is conducting inquiries into the disappearance of the Anderson wagon train about a year and a half before. He is not at the meeting, but Kit Carson promises to relay the information to him so he can make inquiries among the Indians and other scouts.

Baker, Lucinda (Luce): In *30,000 on the Hoof,* the wife of Logan Huett. The character of Lucinda is one of Grey's fullest treatments of the pioneer woman and wife.

When Logan Huett quits his job as cavalry scout and tracker, he wants to become a rancher and homestead in Arizona, in Sycamore Canyon. Lucinda (Luce) Baker is his first choice for a wife. She was sixteen years old when he left Independence, a robust, blooming girl, sensible, clever, not too pretty. She has become a schoolteacher, and helps her sick mother with the other children. When he cables her with a proposal of marriage, she accepts. Lucinda Baker had secretly dreamed of romance and adventure. She always felt life was preparing her for something big. She had worked vacations, applied herself to household duties. She always knew Logan would never return to Independence, that the West would claim him, and, she had secretly been preparing herself to become a pioneer wife. She had loved Logan since she was a little girl, when he rescued her from some bullies who had dragged her into a mud puddle. Her experience in the West is a question of reconciling her dreams of romantic adventure with her knight in shining armor, Logan, with the reality of pioneer life.

On the platform of the train station in Flagg, she recognizes him immediately. The boy she knew has grown into a man — hard, stern, more than handsome. There is something proven about him. She is amused that he does not recognize her. Logan's haste to arrange the ceremony, to get back to Sycamore Canyon, surprise her, but she accepts the challenge. After the ceremony in the parson's living room, they set about preparations to leave. Mrs. Hardy, the blacksmith's wife, helps her select appropriate clothes at the store. They set off in the prairie schooner. She learns to drive the oxen, as Logan must ride the horse to herd the cattle they have bought. She experiences camping, cooking in the open. It is exhausting and new, but Logan is solicitous, thoughtful, helpful. He does the cooking, and she is surprised to see he is a very good cook. The Holberts give her a dog, Coyote. When they reach the canyon, the reality of their isolation from civilization hits her. They must build a cabin before winter sets in. She marvels at Logan's capacity for work, at his determination. She finds herself lonely. While the landscape is beautiful, she finds the wind a constant reminder of her loneliness and isolation. At times she is angry at Logan for bringing her there, and she occasionally questions her sanity.

During spring she plants a garden and plants flowers around the cabin, but finds herself alone most of the time. She knows Logan must go about putting up fences and hunting cougars and coyotes that prey on their herd, but she sometimes thinks she is going mad. When George is born, her loneliness and resentment are forgotten. The child is great companionship for her. The second child, Abe, is born in the barn, and with the third son, her family is complete. One day Abe, her favorite, is being naughty and has wandered away from the house. When she finds him and George, they have a baby girl with them. She looks around to see who might have left her there, but there are no signs of anyone. That night, Logan goes out and investigates. He returns with a disturbing story. The tracks indicate that two wagons had gone by, and that the child was lifted out of a wagon and placed on the ground. The child had been deliberately abandoned. They decide to adopt Barbara as their own.

The years with the children are fulfilling. She teaches them to read and write and about geography, history and such things, while Logan trains the boys to ride, to hunt, to track animals. With the boys, work on the ranch proceeds apace. When they appear to be at the mercy of Holbert and his called-in mortgage, Luce uses the five hundred dollars that her uncle had given her as a wedding gift to pay the mortgage and to invest in needed stock and equipment. She also shows Logan how they can use the produce from their garden to finance the building up of the herd. Logan appreciates her business sense and determination.

When she thinks the time is right, she reveals to the children that Barbara is adopted. She hopes that Barbara will marry one of the boys, Abe being her first choice. Handsome George has become involved with Milly Campbell, a flirt who loves to have boys fight over her. At the dance, a fight breaks out, George is stabbed and Abe comes to his defense. She knows her children are growing up and will have to make their own way in the world. When the war breaks out, they move to Flagg. The boys sign up for the army. Abe and Barbara are married before he leaves. Luce and Barbara work with support groups for the soldiers, knitting, sewing, and raising funds. She works tirelessly.

Logan is in Washington when she gets word that George and Grant have been killed in combat, and that Abe is missing in action. On his arrival home, she asks him to take them back to the cabin in Sycamore Canyon. That is where they were happy. But there is nothing left there. The place has been robbed. All the furniture has been taken. They have to start over. She hopes that this will restore Logan to normal. He has been depressed with the fortune lost in the swindle and the death of his sons. He has no reason to live. She worries about Barbara, who also seems to be out of her mind with grief over the death of Abe.

When Abe unexpectedly returns, alive and kicking, a miracle happens. Logan is restored to his normal sanguine self, Barbara snaps out of her depression, and they set about restarting their lives.

Lucinda is a tribute to the pioneer woman who faces all challenges with courage and determination.

She learns to adapt, to see what is truly valuable in life. While she entered her marriage with a romantic sense of adventure, she goes through phases where she thinks she hates Logan, but eventually comes to see in Logan a much better man than any knight of her dreams.

Baker, Sheriff: In *Shadow on the Trail,* killed by Billy the Kid in the cattle war in Lincoln County. Shortly after that, Billy the Kid pays a visit to his old friend Jesse Evans.

Baldy: (1) In *The Arizona Clan,* Dodge Mercer's horse. Dodge had acquired the horse as a colt and had made a pet of him. He never strays when Dodge makes camp. When Dodge is looking for Buck Hathaway's still down in the rim, he steps in a hole and injures his leg. Dodge and Baldy spend the night in a cave, to give the leg a rest. The following morning, Dodge is shot by Twitchell.

(2) In "Canyon Walls," Monty Bellew's horse.

(3) In *Code of the West,* Tim Matthew's bronco. He is put up in a bet with Cal Thurman against Pitch. Cal bets Tim he will beat him in a fight before the year is out. Tim beat up on Cal for years, and Cal hopes one day to get even.

(4) In *The Dude Ranger,* one of Anderson's cowboys. He comes upon Ernest Selby in the bushes listening to the conversation between Anderson and Wilkins over the unusual nature of Hepford's cattle sales. Lee tells Nebraskie and Ernest that Baldy puts the cattle count at fifteen hundred and eighty-two.

(5) In *Nevada,* the horse Nevada (a.k.a. Jim Lacy, Texas Jack) is riding as he leaves the Blaine ranch in California. He rides the horse to Lineville, on the California-Nevada border. No mention is made of the horse he rides later in the story.

(6) In *Shadow on the Trail,* Wade Holden's (Tex Brandon's) horse, when Holden is pursuing Drake (Rand Blue) and Joe Steele.

(7) In *Under the Tonto Rim,* the horse Edd Denmeade gives Lucy Watson. She declares he is the finest horse she has ever ridden.

(8) In *Wilderness Trek,* one of the tough cayuses that Red Krehl, now in Australia, recalls from back in Texas. See also **McKue, Baldy.**

Bambridge, George: In *The Hash Knife Outfit,* a crooked rancher working in tandem with the Hash Knife Outfit, selling the cattle they rustle. He is first mentioned by Madden when the Hash Knife are discussing the way things have been progressing for them in that part of Arizona. Bambridge had taken court action against Old Jim Traft over ownership of the Yellow Jacket ranch. Bambridge lost his case in court. Traft accused Bambridge of being involved with rustlers, and Bambridge drew a gun on him, but someone knocked it out of his hand. Traft promised to have Bambridge run out of Arizona. Ring Locke gets word that Bambridge is shipping cattle and he suspects that the shipment consists mainly of rustled cattle. Young Jim Traft, as yet not known by sight to Bambridge and his crew, goes to Winslow to observe the cattle being loaded on to the trains. He finds many cattle bearing his brand. He confronts Bambridge about this and Bambridge readily admits it may be true as they were not that careful when they rounded up the herd. Traft cables East to have a count taken when the cattle arrive. Bambridge tells him to send him the bill. Bambridge is shot by Jed Stone when they argue over the money owed to the Hash Knife for the rustled cattle, some ten thousand dollars. Bambridge, in turn, had been double crossed by Ed Darnell, his partner. Bambridge is buried in front of the porch at the Hash Knife cabin, which is later burned to the ground by Slinger Dunn and the Yellow Jacket crew.

Bandon, Kit: In *The Maverick Queen*, the Maverick Queen, so called because she buys up mavericks from the cowboys. Emery suggests that she provided sexual favors for the cowboys, a maverick calf being the price of such a visit. She is a heroine unique in Zane Grey's novels, a woman of beauty, passion, and arrogant pride whose downfall is brought about by her own excess and hubris. She is modeled on the historical figure, Cattle Kate, the woman who was hanged for her shady cattle deals and her original method of payment for sexual services.

Kit Bandon is Lucy Bandon's aunt, a woman considerably older than her appearance. She could pass for twenty-five and she is vain. Lucy cautions Lincoln about bringing up the subject of her age around Kit. When Lucy's mother died, her sister, Kit, took Lucy in. At first they lived in Louisville, where Lucy received an education. Then, they headed west to Cheyenne, where they lived on a ranch. Kit's involvement with a man whom she ends up killing causes them to leave for South Pass, where they ranch on the Sweetwater River. She is involved in cattle deals and owns the Leave It Saloon in town, although Emery has a part share in the business. Kit knows the power she has over men and she enjoys playing with them. As Lincoln tells the gambler McKeever, she likes men, likes to gamble with them and their gold — and their lives. And she is a little on the fickle side. McKeever adds that men don't betray Kit Bandon and live.

Bradway first sees Kit Bandon in a poker game in the Leave It. She is a handsome, dark young woman, not above twenty-five, wearing a diamond as big as a gooseberry, dressed in some black material becomingly relieved at the yoke and the waist by touches of red. She enjoys the competition. She usually wins at cards, but this time, Lincoln Bradway cleans them all out. Emery is upset, as is McKeever, but Kit is a sport, a good loser. She thrives on excitement and danger and thoroughly enjoys the game, although she loses substantial amounts of money. She taunts Emery that he and McKeever had thought Lincoln a tenderfoot and he cleaned them out. From this point on, Kit tries to force herself on Lincoln. His interest in her is genuine, but it's not love. He knows she is somehow involved in the death of his friend, Jimmy

Weston. No doubt she is the dark woman the letters mentioned, who came between him and Lucy.

Lincoln Bradway cannot decide where he stands with Kit. She appears to be on his side, anxious to use him to kill her enemies. She warns him about Gun Haskel, but then, he's not sure that she would not welcome his own death, as he is probing into areas of her life she wants to remain in the dark. When he has killed Haskel, she scolds him for not having turned his gun on Emery. He will have to do so sooner or later. Kit knows that if Lincoln should learn the truth about Jimmy Weston's death, he will learn the truth about many other things as well. In Rock Springs, Kit sets Lincoln up for a gunfight with Hank Miller. She appears upset that he did not finish him off quickly enough. Kit signs out a warrant with Sheriff Haught to keep him in jail for a few days. Apparently, she does not want him to see the man she is meeting in Rock Springs. Kit tells Lincoln she arranged for him to be in jail so she could have him all to herself. Without question, she shows devotion, staying up at night while he recuperates from his gunshot wound. On the way back by stage, she continues her pursuit of Lincoln, and he reveals that he cannot marry her as he is already married. That doesn't appear to phase her. She asks if he can get rid of the wife, but even if he doesn't, the legalities of marriage don't seem to be a necessity for her.

When Kit learns from Emery that Lincoln and Lucy have gone off together up the valley, she follows them, only to catch them kissing. She goes into a rage, calling her niece a little hypocrite, an alley cat. She strikes Lincoln across the face with a whip. She cannot believe that she has lost the man she loves, that she has made a fool of herself over, to that little slip of a niece. She pulls out a gun to shoot them but Lincoln grabs her arm. She falls backward, striking her head against a tree and falling to the ground. When she regains consciousness, she sobs inconsolably, appearing to have aged ten years in a few moments. She appears resigned to her fate. She has toyed with so many men, it never occurred to her she could not get the man she wanted.

Kit decides that she will change her ways. Despite the warnings that Lincoln has given her that the ranchers who have courted her and whom she has scorned, if not made fools of, are not of a forgiving nature. They know she receives stolen cattle, but they need proof. Kit asks Lincoln, "What can they do to me?" Her voice expresses her pride, arrogance and conviction that she is unassailable.

Thatcher overhears her arguing with Emery about selling the Leave It. Emery threatens to turn the tables on her. Vince cautions Lincoln not to be so quick to accept her conversion. Leopards' spots are deep, he says. Lincoln tests her sincerity. He spends the night hiding in the barn and watches two young cowboys arrive with calves. Both of them go to Kit to request the usual fee for bringing in a maverick. She refuses to take the calves, telling them she is out of that business. Posing as Orville Stone, a cowboy with a maverick to sell, he approaches her window, only to be told that he's out of luck. This convinces Lincoln of the genuine nature of her conversion. Kit hopes to move away to start her life anew elsewhere.

The anger of the ranchers, however, quickly grows hotter. The vigilance committee captures her and Emery. They entice Emery to turn on her, promising him freedom if he betrays her. He says they had crooked cattle deals together, and that she used to provide the cowboys with sexual services in exchange for a calf. Before she dies, Kit reveals that Emery shot Jimmy Weston when he was drunk and asleep. Jimmy wanted to marry Kit and to force her to marry him, he threatened to reveal her crooked deals with mavericks. She did nothing to stop Emery. In all of this, Lincoln cannot discern any terror nor cringing in her appearance. She meets her end with dignity.

Mel Thatcher sums up the cowboys' feelings for Kit: "She used some of us a little rough, and Vince isn't the only one who stopped lead because of her, but nobody in this part of Wyoming, long after we boys are gone, will forget the Maverick Queen. I guess the Lord busted His mold when he made Kit Bandon. There will never be another like her in Wyoming."

Bandon, Lucy: In *The Maverick Queen*, the niece Kit Bandon raised, and Jimmy Weston's sweetheart. The family is from Kentucky. Lucy never knew her mother and Kit took her in when Kit's sister died. She went to school in Louisville for five years. When she was twelve, they traveled west in a prairie schooner. First, they lived on a ranch near Cheyenne, then they went to South Pass. Her aunt is a magnet for men, and over the years she has had to kill three. Lucy liked Jimmy, but Kit didn't think he was good enough for her and forbade her to see him. Jimmy became infatuated with Kit and this brought about their separation. Lucy agrees to meet Lincoln at the same place they met the first time. She doesn't show up, and Lincoln learns that she has gone to Rock Springs with Kit. He follows them there, and meets her and Kit in the Elk Hotel where they are about to dine with Hank Miller. While Kit and Miller are settling a cattle deal with an unnamed Texan, Lincoln and Lucy have a heart-to-heart. She suspects that he, like Jimmy, is infatuated with Kit. Her aunt talks constantly about him and how he has changed her life. Lincoln assures her that he is interested in her, not in her aunt. To prove his sincerity, he suggests they get married at once. He arranges the wedding with a Reverend Smith who is on his way to Oregon and who is temporarily holding meetings at the church next door to the depot. Lucy is discreet about her marriage to Lincoln, as Kit would probably throw her out of the house if she knew. She only meets Lincoln once while Sheriff Haught holds him in jail. Kit eventually finds out about the marriage. Emery has told her that Kit and Lincoln went up the valley in a wagon. She comes upon them kissing, and she flies into a rage. She spews invective on Lucy, calling her an ungrateful little alleycat, a hypocriti-

cal prude. In the screaming that ensues, Lucy reveals that Jimmy was killed while he was drunk and asleep. Kit blames Lucy for having tricked her, allowing her to make a fool of herself over Lincoln. She takes a gun out to shoot them, but Lincoln twists her arm and she falls against a tree, knocking herself out. When she comes to, she accepts things as they are. Lucy and Lincoln plan to make their home in the valley where her trapper friend, Ben Thorpe has his cabin. Lincoln and his boys, Vince and Mel, with Thorpe as supervisor, set about building the road. Before they can move in, however, vigilante action comes to a head and Kit is hanged. Lincoln goes to the ranch to tell Lucy about Kit's death and to take her away till things blow over.

Bank, Captain: In *Wild Horse Mesa,* a former sailor, now turned wrangler. He has a large face, like a ham, and a nose badly burned by the sun. He regales the outfit with sea tales at night. Like the rest of the outfit, he likes Chane Weymer and dislikes Manerube, refusing to work with him.

Banks, Lya: In *Fighting Caravans,* figures in a story told by Jim Baker to Clint Belmet. He was a squaw man, married Injun style to a Kiowa, but he was a good friend to all whites in the valley. When Jim Baker and his partner Denver set out after the Kiowas on Major Greer's orders, they come upon Lya Banks's cabin burned to the ground. Several bodies are inside, Lya Banks most probably among them. Baker and Denver bury the bodies before continuing their pursuit of the Kiowas.

Bannard, Clive: In *Arizona Ames,* an outlaw and thief and leader of the gang preying on the Halstead ranch. He is shot by Arizona Ames when the gang is caught with rustled cattle, but he survives to be arrested by the local sheriff.

Bannister: In *The Maverick Queen,* a big, black-bearded man of Emery's working in the Leave It Saloon. His job is to keep curious onlookers away from the big-money poker games. He is killed when Bud Harkness breaks in, looking to shoot Hargrove.

Barclay, Gwen: In *The Shepherd of Guadaloupe,* a friend of Virginia Lundeen's. She is a member of the party which accompanies Virginia back to Cottonwoods when she returns from France. Virginia also runs into her in Las Vegas when she returns there from Colorado Springs to find a place to stay. She is reputed to be filthy rich.

Bard: In *Twin Sombreros,* the name which Brazos Keene hears used the night he arrives at the cabin where the murdered Allen Neece's body has been hidden in the loft. The same name is heard in the hotel room when Deputy Bodkins meets with Syvertsen and Orcutt. Bard is later revealed to have killed Surface in a gunfight in Dodge. Knight is his real name. He arrives in town posing as a cattleman and allies himself with Bodkins and Miller. He shoots Hank Belyen on the assumption that he was going to draw a gun. Knight was the power pulling the strings, and Surface and Bodkins are his puppets. Knight is killed in a gunfight with Brazos Keene, who exposes him as the power behind the rustling and the murder of Neece.

Barg: In *Majesty's Rancho*, one of the Madge Stewart crowd at the university in Los Angeles. He drives with the gang that comes to spend the summer at the Stewart ranch. He and Nate Salisbury like to go to the village to get an ice cream cone and to flirt with the Mexican señoritas there.

Barlow, Jim: In *Fighting Caravans,* a wagon boss who throws in with Belmet at Kansas City. He has a caravan with sixty-eight wagons and seventy-two men.

Barncastle: In *The Fugitive Trail*, the name the outlaw Quade Belton uses when he poses as a respectable cattleman in Dodge. See **Belton, Quade.**

Barner, Hall: In *Arizona Ames,* the young man who marries Lil Snell. He is a close associate of Lee Tate's.

Barnes: (1) In *Boulder Dam*, a deputy working at police headquarters in Las Vegas. Sheriff Logan leaves a message with him for Lynn Weston that he has taken Anne home to mother.

(2) In *Horse Heaven Hill*, one of the cowboys Lark Burrell meets at the dance in Wadestown. She comments that he was "jolly."

(3) In *Robbers' Roost,* a young cowboy working on the Herrick ranch when Jim Wall arrives with Hays. He cares for the horses. Barnes drives the wagon into Grand Junction with Jim Wall to pick up Helen Herrick at the station. Barnes is from the town and appreciates the chance to visit with his girlfriend. On the way, he asks Jim questions about himself, questions which Jim answers as vaguely as possible. Barnes, in turn, reveals little information about Hays, speculating about the connection between Hays and Heeseman. He does invite Jim to spend the night at his family's home, but Jim opts for the hotel to keep an eye on things in town. Barnes is mentioned several times in conjunction with the Herrick's' stables, but there is no evidence he is in on Hays' plan to rustle their cattle and kidnap Helen.

(4) In *Thunder Mountain,* Dick Sloan's partner who arranges his burial. He delivers Ruth Nuggett's bags to Lee Emerson's cabin.

(5) In *Western Union*, a pony express rider. When Barnes comes to deliver mail and dispatches to Creighton's hand, he brings word as well that he has seen Ruby in South Pass and, moreover, that she clearly recognized him and smiled. Cameron and his crew, who had rescued her from Red Pierce's saloon earlier in the tale, set out to rescue her a second time.

Barnes, Tommy: In *The Arizona Clan*, a young boy who speaks to Mercer when he first arrives in Ryeson. He tells him about the stores in town, and about ranches where he could find a job. He suggests Mercer try the Lilleys, who are poor, but Mrs. Lilley is a great cook. He tells Dodge about Nan's troubles

with Buck Hathaway, who laid claim to her after she returned from Texas. Old Rock Lilley sets a heap of store on Buck and he probably intends Nan for Buck. When the Lilleys come into town pursuing Buck Hathaway, Tommy tells them where Twitchell and Hathaway are holed up. After the shooting, he gets a room for Dodge in the tavern, where he talks to Steve. Barnes also keeps the curious gapers from entering the tavern.

Baroma: In *The Great Slave*, the chief of the Crees. He captures Siena and enslaves his people. Baroma treats the enslaved Crows with contempt. He refuses Siena when he requests Emihiyah in marriage. When the Cree are facing starvation, he tries to starve Siena to death. His daughter, however, brings the slave food at night to keep up his strength. Baroma finally consents to let the slave Siena use the thunder stick to go hunting. Siena saves the Cree from starvation. He asks for freedom for his people, and reluctantly, Baroma permits them to leave.

Barrett: In *The Wolf Tracker*, Adams's partner. He had once been a cowboy as lithe and wild as any of his outfit, but now he is heavy, jovial and weatherbeaten. He is organizing the spring roundup in April. He comes to tell his men that they have to get moving to catch up with Adams's crew. It seems no one has heard of Old Gray for a couple of months. Just as he says this, Brinks arrives on foot. The men wonder who he is, but from his gaunt physique, they read the endurance of body and indomitableness of spirit. They are even more amazed when he unpacks a grey hide which they recognize as Old Gray's. Barrett inquires how Brinks caught the wolf, and he says he walked him to death in the snow. He was on the trail from early October to April 10. Barrett offers to write Brinks a check for the five thousand dollar bounty, but the tracker leaves, taking the hide with him. The challenge and the hide are what he treasures, and the bounty would cheapen the elemental conflict between man and beast, reason and instinct.

Barrett, Sally: In *The Wolf Tracker*, the daughter of the rancher, Barrett. The cowboys tease Thad Hickenthorp because he is sweet on her.

Barsh, Joel: In *Twin Sombreros*, deputy sheriff Bodkin's helper. He is with Bodkin when he arrests and attempts to lynch Brazos Keene. He is instructed to throw the rope with the noose over the tree branch and over Brazos's head. Later, Brazos warns Bodkin to warn Barsh not to try to pull a gun on him. Bodkin says he is only a boy and has never shot at anyone in his life.

Bartlett: (1) In *The Lost Wagon Train*, Latch's closest friend at Latchfield, together with Webb. Bartlett is a squaw-man and stands high in the goodwill of the Indians. When Latch asks them directly why they have been cold to him and avoiding him, Webb admits it is because of Leighton's rumors. Bartlett, however, decides that he will stand by his friend and to show his support he will attend the party for Estelle's sixteenth birthday. Webb refuses to attend.

(2) In *West of the Pecos,* a Texan who maintains a post at Menardsville, freighting supplies at infrequent intervals. Lambeth acquires supplies at the post. Bartlett comments that loaded wagons are a good target for the Comanche.

(3) In *Western Union,* one of the men Wayne Cameron engages in conversation about the doings of Red Pierce, who has left Gothenburg. Bartlett reports that Red Pierce's plan is to travel along with the telegraph line, living off the construction workers until he gets into western Wyoming. He plans to buy up cattle to bring along. As the construction of the telegraph line is advancing by slow stages, it would be easy to take a herd of cattle along with him and sell it for big money out on the Sweetwater.

Bartlett, Wilda: In *The Lost Wagon Train,* Bartlett's daughter and a friend of Estelle's. Latch tells him Estelle will be disappointed if Wilda does not show up at her party.

Barton, Kid: In *Boulder Dam,* one of Bellew's gangsters killed in the fight to rescue Anne Vandergrift.

Bates: In *The U. P. Trail,* the first man in line to get his pay, who promptly loses it all at cards.

Bates, Ranger: In *The Fugitive Trail,* one of the Texas Rangers with Captain Maggard in the attack on the cabin where the rustlers are holding out. He is injured but survives.

Baxter: (1) In *Fighting Caravans,* an old scout who was train boss of an emigrant caravan going south to Texas. He knows the train is being followed. He takes Mrs. Clements and May Bell to the home of a settler, Bennet, who takes them in and keeps them for a year. At this point, they join another large caravan which takes them to Kansas City.

(2) In *The U. P. Trail,* assistant to General Lodge, the man entrusted with the job of ensuring the safety of those constructing the transcontinental Union Pacific railroad. He is the chief engineer, who appears at different points throughout the novel but never plays a major role.

Bay (1) In *The Maverick Queen,* Lincoln Bradway's horse. He buys the horse from Headly, who has bought it from Vince. Lincoln decides to keep the bay, and return Brick to Vince, since Brick is his favorite. Lincoln comes to love the horse as the Virginian loves his Monte. At one point, Lincoln is cheered up when he feels the loyalty of his horse, perhaps the only true friend he has in the valley.

(2) In *Robbers' Roost,* Jim Wall's horse, superior to any of the horses in Hays's string or corral, the envy of the other outlaws.

(3) In *Twin Sombreros,* Brazos Keene's bay horse.

(4) In *Wildfire,* one of the two horses that Bruthwait enters in the annual horse race at Bostril's Ford.

Bayne, Reddie: In *The Trail Driver,* joins Adam Brite's trail drivers. She rides into camp on a beautiful black horse, Sam, asking to be taken on. She can handle the remuda. Brite accepts. Texas and the other cowboys wonder where she comes from and why she says so little about her past. They seem not to suspect that she is a girl. Adam Brite feels sorry for the orphan lad when he watches him sleeping. When Wallen appears, asking questions about Reddie, Brite pretends to know nothing. He has no complaints about the work Reddie does. Eventually she tells him she is a girl, and that "Reddie" is her given name, not a nickname for her hair color. She explains that she is alone in the world, her parents having been killed by Indians. She has to make a living, and has worked in stores and restaurants, but pretending to be a boy has meant she can work with horses and have fewer hassles from men hitting on her. She tells Brite that he reminds her of her father. Brite is fond of her and offers to adopt her as his legal daughter. This might give her some protection. He lets her continue with the pretense, knowing that eventually the secret will come out. When Wallen returns later, demanding they hand her over, a gunfight breaks out and Texas Joe kills Wallen. The behavior of the cowboys to her changes somewhat. San Saba and others are particularly gentlemanly with her. Whittaker claims he knew she was a girl from the start, and Texas Joe confesses that he learned her secret when he accidentally came upon her bathing. Reddie is in love with Texas, but she fears that he dislikes her. He pays her little attention, remaining aloof from the workings of the outfit. Reddie shows herself to be a skilled manager of horses and capable of handling the work of a cowboy in a cattle drive as well as any of the men. Still, she cannot hide her feminine side. She worries that when they get to Dodge, Texas will get drunk and get into a gunfight and possibly be killed. Although he proposes marriage to her early in their acquaintanceship, she puts him off. But in Dodge, she decides that she wants him and puts aside her boy's clothes for women's garb. Texas Joe consents to marry her in San Antonio and he forgoes the pleasure of getting drunk with the boys and visiting the "painted women" of Dodge. Reddie Bayne is one of several female characters in Zane Grey's novels who, like Terrill Lambert in *West of the Pecos,* disguise themselves as men to survive more securely in a rough, masculine world.

Bayne, Sheriff: In *The Horse Thief,* a pompous little man who arrives at the Watrous ranch with John Stafford to arrest Dale Brittenham as a horse thief. He refuses to listen to reason, as there is no proof that Dale has been involved with the rustlers. When Dale confesses to take suspicion off his friend, Leale Hildrith, Bayne believes him. Later, Bayne catches up with Dale at Rogers's cabin, just as the hideout of the rustlers has been found, Big Bill and Ed Reed killed, and Edith rescued. Bayne arrests Dale, and proceeds to hang him. Edith comes out and calls Bayne a fool. She makes them release Dale at gunpoint. Some horse rustlers fleeing the valley shoot at the men in front of Rogers's cabin, killing Pickens, Bayne's most enthusiastic supporter among his posse, and fatally wounding Bayne, who dies a few minutes later.

Beady: In *Raiders of Spanish Peaks,* a member of Gaines's kidnapping outfit. He is a short man, no longer young, with a round, dull, blotched face and leaden eyes. He follows Price around like a dog. Price comments that he is not too intelligent, unable to figure out Gaines's tactics. When the sore Gaines arrives at the cabin, Beady stops Gaines from shooting Price for saying what they all already know. Beady, it turns out, is a gunslinger, a bad hombre, able to make Gaines think twice. When Lonesome arrives at the cabin, Beady is shot by Laramie, who was hiding in the cabin loft. See also **Jones, Beady.**

Beal: (1) In *The Rainbow Trail,* comes into camp with Henniger and Smith. He is guarding the door of the schoolhouse when Lake, Shefford and Ruth Jones come to rescue Mary (Fay Larkin), who is confined there pending an investigation of the death of Waggoner, whom she claims to have killed.

(2) In *Western Union,* a wagon train boss. He and his men go to cut down fir trees to make poles for the telegraph line. He and his men are never seen again.

Beam, Jake: In *Tappan's Burro,* the head of the Beam gang working on the Tonto Rim. He and his wife have a scam whereby they trick a lonely prospector into running off with Madge, under the illusion that he is rescuing her from her abusive brother. Madge deserts him in California, and Jake is shot, the circumstances surrounding the shooting being left undisclosed.

Beam, Madge: In *Tappan's Burro,* with her husband meets prospector Tappan in the desert. Madge introduces herself and calls Jake her brother. She is a tall, lithe-figured woman, dressed in overalls and boots. She makes eyes at Tappan, and the desert man, little experienced with women, is soon under her spell. She offers to make biscuits, to do the cooking, and soon she is confiding in Tappan, who is flattered by her attention. She gradually dresses in a more feminine way and Tappan is seduced by her charms. Madge tells him that she and her brother have a ranch up on the Tonto that they want to sell. Tappan considers buying it. Later, Madge informs Tappan that her brother is lying about the ranch, that they have homesteaded only a hundred and sixty acres but haven't proved up on it yet. She admits to being party to the swindle initially, but tells the prospector she has fallen in love with him and cannot go through with it. She proposes marriage to Tappan, telling him she must get away from her brother. Tappan is willing to marry her but hesitates to leave the burro, Jenet, behind. Madge tells him it's either her or the burro, so Tappan leaves Jenet behind. Madge soon gives him the slip, taking all his

gold with her. Later, Jess Blade reveals that Madge and Jake were husband and wife, part of an outlaw gang that had tricked many old prospectors just as they had done Tappan. Madge leaves her husband in California, according to the story Jake Beam told Blade when he was drunk. There are hints that she met a worse fate. In "The Secret of Quaking Asp Cabin," the same story is narrated by Babe Haught, but Madge is called "Bess." In most other details, the stories are similar.

Bean, Joe: In *The Lone Star Ranger,* one of the two cowboys from Longstreth's outfit to be arrested.

Bean, Judge Roy: In *West of the Pecos,* the famous man reputed to be the law West of the Pecos.

Hal Watson describes to Pecos Smith how Bean moved into the Eagle's Nest and set up his court. He has a house about a block away from Brasee's adobe post. Pecos Smith and Terrill Lambeth go to the Eagle Nest to meet the judge. He marries them, after extorting all sorts of legal fees from them, together with fines for "contempt of court." He is every bit the colorful figure he is reputed to have been.

Beany: In *Captives of the Desert,* one of the young Navajo cowboys with whom John Curry works. Beany reports to him on the fight between High-Lo and Newton. He also brings back word about Wilbur Newton setting up a new trading post at Sage Springs. He avoids telling this to Mary, as he knows she thinks he has returned to Texas.

Bear Claws: In *The Thundering Herd,* an Osage Indian scout who accompanies Pilchuck and Starwell in the campaign against the Comanche. He spots the Comanche camp in the canyon.

Beard: In *The Border Legion,* owns a drinking and gambling establishment in Alder Creek. Gulden's and Kells's men frequent the establishment to drink and gamble. Beard shows up on one occasion at the cabin where the Border Legion meets.

Beard, Ham: In *The Hash Knife Outfit,* a rustler working with Croak Malloy and the Hash Knife Outfit. He is killed by Slinger Dunn and his crew, pursuing rustlers. Beard was a bartender in Winslow till he murdered someone, then he took to rustling cattle. He was a lone wolf, a dead shot. But for the smoke from the campfire which alerted Dunn and the Yellow Jacket to their whereabouts, his gunfire on them could have proven fatal.

Beardsley: In *The Desert of Wheat,* a prominent rancher in the area. He is an intelligent man and a successful wheat farmer. He speaks about the work of the I.W.W. agents among the wheat farmers.

Beasley: In *The Man of the Forest,* one of the two biggest ranchers and sheep-raisers of the White Mountain range. He was taken in as a boy by Old Al Auchincloss and raised as a son. Helen Rayner discovers this when she goes through her uncle's papers after his death. Beasley is a forceful personality as well as a handsome man of thirty-five. He is heavily-built, with swarthy skin and sloe-black eyes. He is reported to be part Mexican. He looks crafty, confident and self-centered. Al Auchincloss and Beasley fell out over a sheep deal, Old Al arguing that Beasley had cheated him. Beasley is anxious to settle the score. The widow Cass tells Milt Dale that recently, Beasley's ranch has been growing apace, matching the decline of Al Auchincloss, his only rival. The old man is dying and plans to leave his herds and ranches to his niece in Saint Joseph, Missouri. She is coming to take over the place. Beasley hires Snake Anson to kidnap the girl from the Magdalena train station. He does not care what happens to the girl, so long as she never makes it to her uncle's place in Pine. Milt Dale has overheard the conversation and decides to do what he can to foil the plot. In town, Beasley meets Milt Dale and tries to win him over to his side with an offer of a job as foreman of his sheep herders. He begins to speak ill of old Al, but Milt contradicts him, declaring that Old Al is the squarest man in the area. The Beeman brothers agree to help Dale because Beasley ruined their father. He has cheated other Mormons. The Beemans have proven to themselves that he gets the sheep Snake Anson's gang steals and he drives the herds to Phoenix. They are glad to join Milt to foil the plot. When Beasley's plan to have Helen abducted and killed is foiled, he approaches Helen directly after Al has passed on. He tells her that he has papers proving that Old Al owes him some eighty thousand dollars. Unless she pays the money, he will seize her ranch and cattle. Helen denies any indebtedness, and says the truth is that Beasley owes the Auchinclosses money. Beasley offers to marry her as a way to solve the problem. She refuses. She reveals that Milt Dale overheard him planning with Snake Anson to have her kidnapped. When Harve Riggs kidnaps Bo, hoping to extort money from Helen, Snake Anson figures that Beasley will eventually turn on them, accusing them of stealing sheep, and hunting them down to make a reputation for himself in Pine. Beasley convinces Jeff Mulvey and others who had worked for Al Auchincloss to abandon the ranch when he dies. Eventually, he moves in on Al's place, forcing Helen's men either to join him or to leave. The three Beeman brothers remain to do what they can for Helen. Both Milt Dale and Roy Beeman impress on Helen that the only way she can get her ranch back is by killing Beasley. Waiting for the courts will mean that by the time anything is done, Beasley will have ruined the place and stripped it of cattle. Tom Carmichael, Bo's friend "Las Vegas," calls Beasley out. He hopes his men will kill Carmichael on the sly, but they respect the old cowboy code. Beasley will have to do his own fighting and face Carmichael in a shootout. His men have lost all respect for him. He tries to buy Las Vegas off. He even offers to return Auchincloss's ranch, but to no avail. He is killed in the shootout and meets his end as a craven coward.

Beatty and Kelly: In *The Trail Driver,* run a store in Dodge.

Beck, Mrs. Elsie Canalton: In *The Light of*

Western Stars, goes west to chaperone the party going to visit their friend, Madeline Hammond, who has just bought a ranch. She is a natural pessimist and hopes something dreadful will happen to punish them for bringing her west. Robbie Weede is reputed to be sweet on her.

Beckett: In *Fighting Caravans,* the Aull company agent in Santa Fe. He fills Clint Belmet in on the latest news about May Bell and Mrs. Clement and Blackstone.

Beckman: In *West of the Pecos,* the rancher for whom Sawtell works as ranch foreman. Beckman was one of the ranchers who was involved in the lynching of Pecos's two associates, Wess Adams and Curt Williams. Adams and Williams had been caught altering brands on cattle. While the lynching was in progress, the Comanche attacked. Beckman's body was recognized from his clothes. He was shot full of Comanche arrows, but Sheriff Brice suspects that Pecos Smith, the third in the party, survived, killed Beckman, then shot arrows into the body to make it look like a Comanche attack.

Bedford, Tom: In *Wilderness Trek,* one of Ormiston's drovers on the trek. He calls Ormiston by his real name, Ash Pell. He too is a bushranger (rustler) planning to rustle Hathaway's herd and part of the Dann herd as well. He wants to finish the job before they reach the Diamantina River, in case the rains don't come and more of the herd perishes. Tom Bedford kills Harry Spence in a drunken fight over an aborigine woman. Bedford beats up Eric Dann when he attempts to return to Ormiston's side of the river . Bedford is shot and killed during the fight to recover the rustled cattle, having beaten Ormiston "to hell."

Beecham: In *Nevada,* runs a corral in Sunshine where overnight visitors can leave their horses and buggies.

Beeman, Hal: In *The Man of the Forest,* one of the four Beeman brothers, close friends of Milt Dale. He helps plan and execute the trick to get Helen and Bo away from the train station before Anson and his men can abduct them as they agreed to do for Beasley. Hal and Joe stay at Auchincloss's to help him resist Beasley.

Beeman, Joe: In *The Man of the Forest,* one of the four Beeman brothers, friends of Milt Dale. They are sons of a pioneer Mormon who settled in the little community of Snowdrop. The four brothers are young in years but hard labor and hard life in the open has made them look mature. Horsemen, cattlemen, hunters, they all possess the long, wiry, powerful frames, lean, bronzed, still faces, and the quiet keen eyes of men used to the open. Joe and his brothers help get Helen and Bo Rayner away from the train station before Snake Anson and his men can abduct them. Joe rides along beside Bill, the driver. He observes a horseman following them who goes past after they slow down. He could be one of

Anson's riders. He and his brothers John and Hal return to get on board the real stage to be there where Anson holds it up. Roy instructs Joe to ride over to Al Auchincloss's to give him the news about Helen and Bo and to offer his services should Anson make trouble.

Beeman, John: In *The Man of the Forest*, the oldest of the Beeman brothers, close friends of Milt Dale. He is one year older than Roy. He helps plan and execute the ruse to get the Rayner girls away from the train station before Anson can abduct them. John Beeman comes to Milt Dale's senaca in mid-March to tell him of the developments down in Pine. He finds him thin and distracted, and guesses that what Roy had told him about Milt's falling in love with Helen Rayner is true. When Milt protests, John tells him that if anyone knows women, it's Roy. He is only twenty-eight but already he has three wives! He also tells him that Al Auchincloss is dead and that Roy was shot, but not mortally injured, in a shootout with Beasley's men in the saloon. They set off for Pine with Tom in tow. They come across horse tracks, and John concludes that someone has been riding a mustang that is being led. When they get back to Pine, they learn of Bo's abduction. When Milt sets off to pursue the kidnappers, he leaves John in charge at Mrs. Cass's.

Beeman, Roy: In *The Man of the Forest*, the second of the Beeman boys, and Milt Dale's closest friend and confident. Milt Dale approaches the Beeman brothers for help. They know what Beasley is and they have lost cattle at Snake Anson's hands. They have fast horses, eyes for tracking and they are all good shots. Roy is the keenest of the four brothers and the one to whom adventure and peril called most. He has been the most often with Dale on many a trail. He is the hardest rider and the most relentless tracker in all the country. Roy and Dale plan the rescue with slow and deliberate attention to details. Roy is respectful and gentle with the sisters, doing what he can to provide comfort on the trip back to the senaca. Roy and Milt Dale are friendly rivals over many things—who has the best horse, who is the better shot. Helen is surprised to learn that Roy is lame. A horse threw him once and rolled over him, breaking his collar bone, five ribs, an arm and his legs in two places. Nevertheless, he is tall and lithe, looking singularly powerful and capable. He never lets down his guard, watching for pursuers until they reach the shelter of the pine forest. Helen is also surprised when Roy confesses that they have been lost for a good half-day. No one, he says, can know the mountains completely, but he is not lost for long, getting properly oriented when the fog lifts and he spots Old Baldy mountain.

Roy Beeman provides Milt Dale with food for thought. While he confesses that he sometimes envies Milt's freedom, his way of life is not life. It is only natural for a man to have a wife and a son to continue his family line and his work. Milt confesses that he has envied Roy's situation. However, they do share a love of the natural world, a respect for the workings of nature, and the struggle to survive that gives variety to the forest and strength and health to deer and other game. Above all, Helen Rayner senses in Roy a proven humility, simplicity and loyalty. When the girls return with their uncle, Roy, who has been observing the growing romance between Milt and Helen, predicts that in the coming months, he will learn the real meaning of loneliness.

When Old Al passes away, Roy remains at the ranch as head horse wrangler. He tells Helen that Dale is in love with her, a fact she chooses to downplay. He also tells her that the ultimate solution to her problem on the ranch is the killing of Beasley. He explains to her that it's in the nature of things that Beasley "pass away before his time." Those of his breed invariably end up that way. Roy is particularly pleased when Tom Carmichael exposes Riggs for the make-believe gunman who pretends to sail under the true, wild and reckoning colors of the West. He narrates the episode with gusto to Helen and Bo. The evening after Helen's rejection of Beasley's offer of marriage, Roy is shot in the saloon. Riggs shoots him, hiding behind Beasley, and leaves him on the saloon floor. Carmichael takes him to the Widow Cass's place to have his wounds tended. He sends his brother, John, to tell his family he is not badly hurt, and to fetch Milt Dale from his senaca. He explains that the law of the West is an eye for an eye. That the only way to deal with a man like Beasley is to oppose him with force. Helen abhors violence and killing, like Jane Withersteen. Roy, like Lassiter, points out that such an attitude is taken as a sign of weakness. Sooner or later, someone will have to shoot it out with Beasley.

All turns out as Roy predicted. Carmichael confronts Beasley and shoots him, ensuring Helen's rights are respected. Her ranch and herds are restored to her. Roy, a Mormon preacher, performs the marriage ceremony for Milt and Helen at the camp in Paradise Park.

Roy Beeman exemplifies the admirable qualities Grey found in the Mormon men who served as guides on his trips west. He embodies the qualities of men schooled by nature with a profound sense of natural goodness, generosity, companionship and justice.

Beeson: In *The Lone Star Ranger*, one of the two rangers on guard outside Captain MacNelly's camp.

Beeteia: In *The Vanishing American*, a young Navajo Nopah chief, a war veteran, who marries Gekin Yashi and takes her in with her illegitimate child. He had loved her all his life, but Gekin had rejected his proposals. When she is in trouble, he shows his love by taking her in and protecting her, and keeping her whereabouts a secret from the missionaries.

Beezy: In *The Arizona Clan*, one of the men in the Hathaway-Twitchell-Quayle outfit. In one of the skirmishes, he shoots at Dodge Mercer and the bullet passes between his neck and the collar of his shirt.

Belding, Mrs. Nellie: In *Desert Gold* is Nell Warren from Peoria, Illinois. She is the disgraced daughter of Jonas Warren and the wife that Robert Burton (Cameron) has been seeking throughout the West for many years. She married Belding after Burton was reported seen prospecting in the desert but no word had been heard from him for years. Nellie is suspicious of Dick Gale's intentions towards her daughter, Nell, fearing she might suffer the same fate as herself. Eventually, she decides that Dick Gale is a gentleman and sincere in his interest. She gives her blessing to his proposal of marriage. When Ben Chase comes to the ranch, she recognizes him as someone from her school days in Peoria, and a former suitor. Around the same time, a letter arrives from an old friend with news that some fifteen years earlier, an old prospector had shown up in town with news that he had been seen Robert Burton at the Sonoyta oasis. This causes her to become withdrawn, quiet. She decides she needs to return to Peoria, and Tom Belding lets her go. He knows she is worrying that people will assume she remarried before her first husband was dead. As well, strange behavior in the daughter makes him suspect Chase has some hold on her. He has threatened to reveal her disgrace just when her future in-laws are at the Belding ranch.

Belding, Tom: In *Desert Gold*, a border ranger, rancher and horse wrangler in southern Arizona. His job is to keep Japanese, Chinese and Mexicans from crossing the border illegally. With a revolution in full swing south of the border, the biggest part of his job is to prevent arms smuggling to the rebels and cattle and horse rustling to supply the various revolutionary armies. Belding is a generous man. He hires Dick Gale on the recommendation of Jim Lash and Charley Ladd. If Gale is a friend of George Thorne, the cavalryman, then he meets with Belding's approval. Likewise, he takes in Mercedes Castañeda because Thorne is trying to rescue her from Rojas.

Belding's passion in life is horse breeding. He has five Mexican bred horses—Blanco Sol, Blanco Diablo (his favorite, but hated by Lash, Ladd, Gale and the women), Blanca Reina, Blanca Mujer and Blanco Torres. They are "desert" horses, prized for their stamina and their speed. Belding knows that these animals are particularly attractive to the revolutionaries. Diablo is taken by raiders but thanks to Ladd, Lash and Gale, is retrieved unharmed. Later, when Ladd proposes a trek to Yuma along the "camino del diablo" to get Mercedes to a place where Rojas will probably not follow, Belding sends his string of prized white horses along to keep them from the revolutionaries.

Belding speaks Yaqui and has great admiration for these desert Indians. He tells Dick Gale about how the Spaniards and the Mexicans made war on these noble people to eliminate them. The Yaqui are men of the desert; they have learned how to thrive in a hostile environment. Belding has seen the savage treatment the Yaqui meet at the hands of Mexican rebels and

there is no doubt about where his sympathies lie. He gives advice to Gale on how to relate to the Yaqui whose life he has saved and who seems to have attached himself to Dick as a servant and companion.

Belding agrees to shelter Mercedes, the young Spanish woman George Thorne has rescued from General Rojas, although it brings Rojas and his raiders to his ranch. He shows her the same kindness he has shown to Nell, his wife's daughter by another man. Belding has a soft spot for hard cases.

Tom Belding is an example of the kind of man the Old West used to breed, a man who believes one's word is as good as a contract, a man who has learned by experience, a man who is close to the natural world and respects the environment. While he is not opposed to development, he is more interested in the benefit it may bring to the local people. He grudgingly acknowledges Chase can develop Forlorn River more efficiently and quickly than he and his rangers could ever hope to, but it's the method Chase has chosen to do it that rankles. When he discovers that Ben Chase has moved in to begin mining operations on land that Dick Gale and Charley Ladd had staked for homesteading, he protests that the land already belongs to others. Chase and his legal team have seized the land on a technicality, since the Homestead Act requires that a house be built on the land to hold the claim. Belding travels to Tucson to protest the seizure, only to learn that it is a lost cause. Chase has powerful friends in the courts and the government. He hears rumors that his competency to continue as border ranger have been circulating. He does lose his job and the injustice of it hurts him more than all Chase's other machinations, hardening his resolve never to leave his ranch or make a deal with the mining company.

Belding resigns himself to the loss of his ranch, since Chase has set off dynamite charges that change the current of the underground water, causing his "spring that never goes dry" to fail. He feels there is no choice left but to sell off his cattle, but he still refuses to grant Chase a right of passage through his land. In desperation, Chase tries to bribe him by getting him reinstated as border ranger and making him a partner in the mining operation. He takes pleasure in Gale's confrontation with young Chase over his attempt to ruin Nell Burton's reputation. Dick Gale's coming into possession of a valuable gold mine proves a just compensation for the struggle.

Beleanth do de jodie: In *The Vanishing American*, a rich Nopah and a good man. His wife, Nolgoshie, is put under a spell by Shoie. Beleanth do de jodie goes to Nophaie for help. Nophaie tries to correct the situation by getting Shoie to tell her he has removed the spell, but Shoie later spreads word that removal of spells does no good. His wife broods and dies of her fear of the spell.

Bell: In *Horse Heaven Hill*, one of Stanley Weston's cowboys who quit the ranch when Howard is fired. He joins up with Hurd Blanding for a wild horse hunting expedition.

Bell, Jim: In *The Light of Western Stars,* one of the cowboys who pretend to need lessons in making bread in order to be with Madeline Hammond in the kitchen.

Bell, Keven: In *Rogue River Feud,* a war veteran, like Glenn Killbourne in *The Call of the Canyon.* He has been injured in an accident, shooting a cannon at training camp. He has lost part of the vision in one eye. Part of his jaw is missing. He spent two years in the military hospital. Most people thought he was dead. When he returns home to Grant's Pass, his father does not recognize him. His mother is dead. He has no friends, no prospects. At twenty-six, his life is ruined. His father brings him up to date on developments in town. Brandeth has become very rich because of the war. His daughter now runs around with Atwell, the foreman at the cannery. Keven's reputation has been ruined thanks to the gossip about the Carstone girls who lived near the training camp in Washington. Keven discovers as he walks about town that he still has a few well-wishers. Emmeline Trapier tells him that she and his chum, Billy Horn, are to be married and that they never believed any of the rumors Atwell spread about him. He meets his old friend Garry Lord and proposes that the two of them become partners in a fishing venture. Garry warns him that he has a bad reputation in town. He is considered a lazy, no-good drunk. Keven has always liked Garry and is willing to take the gamble. When he meets with Minton to buy equipment for the venture, the tackle dealer suggests that there are other things he could do as well. There is still a lot of gold to be found along the Rogue River. He should stake a claim and work at that, if he prefers solitude as he seems to do. He could investigate the problem of salmon runs not making it upriver. Keven does think of these suggestions as things become more complicated and difficult.

Keven confronts Atwell in the hotel, calling him a liar and a coward. He strikes him and later Atwell brings charges of assault and attempted murder against him. Sheriff Blackwood, a good friend of Keven's, keeps him in jail for a month or so, but does not turn him over to Rollins to bring him back to Grant's Pass. Eventually, the charges are dropped. Legal authorities farther up the ladder are on to Atwell and his schemes. Atwell's animosity, however, spreads to the fishermen.

Keven and Garry buy a boat from Mr. Bell, Keven's father, who has taken up carpentry and boat-building since he lost his store. They make quite a haul during the first salmon run. But Mulligan and Priddy are jealous of their success and soon a cartel has developed, blocking their sale of salmon. Atwell at the cannery is behind it. After their nets have been destroyed with sulphuric acid, Keven and Garry start spying on other fishermen and discover that Mulligan and his crowd are using illegal nets. They have a visible strip of eight-inch netting at the top sewn to a bottom net of four-inch netting, which is illegal during the salmon runs. He has solved the mystery of the diminishing steelheads on the Rogue River. But Keven never gets to take action. During a storm which sees a sudden rise in the water level on the river, he gets into a fight with Mulligan and stabs him in the neck. Thinking his partner is dead, he runs off to hide in the mountains. He spends about a year with Jim Aard and his daughter, Beryl. Here, he is nursed back to health, both physical and spiritual. Nature and the river have healed him. His mother always had great faith in the curative powers of nature. His father had reminded him of this.

Keven falls in love with Beryl Aard. He has sweet on her before he went off to the army training camp, and now he discovers that she has become a woman capable of deep love and compassion. She is also an incomparable fisherman and woodsman. She offers to teach him to fish better. When they decide to marry, she offers him the money to go to Portland. They are married at city hall. They go to the movies, a new experience for Beryl, and then visit an eye doctor and a dentist. The eye doctor prepares him a pair of glasses that correct his vision. He had thought he would never see properly again. The dentist prepares a cast of the missing section of his jaw and rebuilds his face and mouth. When he looks at himself in the mirror after the artificial jaw and gold and porcelain teeth are in place and comfortable, he does not recognize himself. They visit his father, to learn that Garry is not dead. He was rescued by Mary Coombs who is now his wife. They run a fish store, and she keeps a sharp eye on his drinking, not permitting him more than one spree a month. As well, Garry and Sheriff Blackwood set about laying a trap to catch the crooked fishermen using illegal nets.

Beryl reveals that Rosamond Brandeth had spoken to her in Grant's Pass, reminding her that Keven had been engaged to her. She seems to be trying to make trouble. Keven assures Beryl that any interest he had in Rosamond disappeared years ago. Beryl also reveals that she knows the full story about the Carstone girls. Keven had avoided mentioning the story, thinking she knew nothing about it. Beryl's best friend at school was Emily Carstone, a first cousin and close friend of the disgraced family. She knows Atwell was the culprit in the case.

When Beryl and Keven return to Aard's cabin at Solitude, Jim Aard reveals a secret to his son-in-law. His new gold claim has proven profitable. He shows Keven a secret hiding place in the logs behind the bookshelves. There are several large, heavy buckskin bags, filled with gold. He has married an heiress!

In the character of Keven Bell, Grey took up again the theme of government indifference to veterans. Keven is another Grey Killbourne, who is restored to physical and mental health by healing power of nature.

Bell, May: In *Fighting Caravans,* the daughter of Sam Bell. At the tender age of ten, she is impressed with Clint Belmet. He lets her come fishing with him. She is impressed with Clint's definition of a pioneer woman's work, adding that they would have to fall in love first. Clint is allowed to drive his father's wagon, and May Bell sits with him. May Bell, however, leaves the caravan when her father decides to stay at Council Bluff and later, she disappears after the stage they are on is attacked and she is abducted. May Bell appears at Maxwell's ranch. She recognizes Buff Belmet and identifies herself to him. Clint is thrilled to see her again, but also intimidated by her new refinement. The Clements family that has taken her in has given her a good education and taught her good "Southern" manners. She flirts with Sergeant Clayborn, and Murdock shows interest in her. She doesn't understand that her social graces make Buff feel beneath her socially. When she disappears for a second time, Clint Belmet tries to find her, following one lead, then another. Their paths cross but never converge. Clint Belmet is finally reunited with May Bell in Las Cruces, where they are married and settle down to ranching on the estate of the wealthy Clements family.

Bell, Mr.: In *Rogue River Feud*, Keven Bell's father. He has not heard from his son in several years. When Keven returns home, he does not recognize him. Mr. Bell has fallen on hard times, and can offer little to his son. He has little good to say about the government that wanted young men to go to war, and let them down when the war was over. He tells Keven that in Grant's Pass, he will find no friends. His reputation has been ruined by stories of the Carstone affair in Washington. He advises him to rise above it. He brings his son up to date on the people of the town. Brandeth is now a powerhouse in the cannery, and Atwell, the gossip monger, is the foreman of his plant. Rosamond, Keven's fiancée, has taken up with Atwell. Mr. Bell himself has survived as a carpenter. What had once been a hobby has been his salvation. He makes boats to sell to the upriver fishermen and to people looking for recreational boats. He suggests that Keven take up fishing. As his mother used to say, the river will cure him, physically and psychologically. He tells him about Garry Lord, his old fishing buddy, who has placed an order for a boat. About two years later, after the dramatic events on the river, Keven's disappearance, and marriage to Beryl Aard, Mr. Bell once again serves as reporter, bringing him up to date on developments. Garry was not drowned, but rescued by Mary Coombs, who is now his wife. He runs a fish store in Grant's Pass and Crescent City. Garry has cleared his name in the death of Mulligan. Garry has also exposed the crooked fishermen using illegal nets. With Sheriff Blackwood, he set up a trap to catch the crooked fishermen.

Bell, Sam: In *Fighting Caravans*, the father of May Bell. He hails from Ohio but like the Belmets, is caught by the lure of the West. Originally he intended to go no farther than Independence, Missouri, but has decided to head west. Belmet advises him to sign on as a freighter, to provide an income to put toward the purchase of land. The Belmets continue on, leaving Bell and his family behind in Council Grove. About a week or so later, Sam Bell gets sick of the frontier and wants to go back home. Rumor has it that he was fleeced out of his cash by a gambler. He takes the first stage for Independence. The stage breaks down and the travelers make camp while the driver goes for help. During the night, Indians attack the camp and Sam Bell is killed. Mrs. Bell and May Bell disappear.

Bell, Simm: In *Shadow on the Trail*, the leader of an outlaw gang specializing in robbing stagecoaches, trains and banks. Surprisingly, Simm Bell himself shows little interest in money. He is generous in dividing the spoils with his men, and his generosity to the locals near their hideout guarantees their silence and cooperation. He is also loyal to his men. He has a particular fondness for Randall Blue, a man who he says befriended him. Wade Holden, Smith and Hazlitt believe Blue has betrayed them to the rangers. They have seen him talking to Ranger Pell and in the telegraph office sending a message. Simm refuses to let Holden shoot Blue, choosing instead to expel him from the group on pain of death should he return. Simm has become reckless as he grows older. Holden advises caution. Since Blue has surely advised the rangers about the coming Mercer job, it would only be prudent not to go through with it. As well, it would be wise to abandon the hideout, well-known to the suspected traitor. Bell, however, decides to go through with the bank heist. The rangers are waiting for them. Simm is shot, and, as he has often told young Wade, he dies with his boots on. But before he dies, he reveals that he is Wade Holden's natural father. Simm Bell was a Missouri guerrilla during the war, a lieutenant of Holden's father's. Since Holden's father was crippled, he practically took care of the family. Jim Holden never knew of his wife's infidelity. Wade Holden now understands Simm's particular fondness for him, his concern that he should quit the outlaw outfit and make a life for himself in proper society. The boy has an education, potential. When Holden offers to shoot the rangers approaching them on the road, he gives him one piece of advice. He has managed to survive this long as an outlaw because he never shot a ranger. This advice Holden follows throughout his outlaw career. Simm's concern that he go straight, that he redeem himself, also shape the young man's life.

Bellefontaine: In *Majesty's Rancho*, one of Majesty Stewart's string of thoroughbred horses.

Bellew, Ben: In *Boulder Dam*, a gangster, bootlegger, and white-slaver in Las Vegas. He competes with Ben Sneed for the whiskey trade. He abducts women to work in his establishments in Vegas and elsewhere under the guise of offering them work. They are drugged and kept locked up until they give in. Anne Vandergrift escapes wearing only a blanket. He offers to sell her to Ben Sneed for ten thousand dollars. Bellew continues his search for Anne and when he finally does find her, she goes along willingly, believing his threat to kill Lynn Weston. Bellew is holding Anne prisoner at Vitte's place. Weston, Decker and Sneed manage to rescue Anne. Bellew is shot and killed by his own Chicago gunman, Gip Ring, in the fighting. Bellew's attempt to hijack Sneed's bootleg trucks is foiled when Weston diverts his interest to the kidnapped girl. Sneed gives Lynn the fifty thousand dollars he took from Bellew's wallet as a reward for saving his bootlegging operation.

Bellew, Monty "Smoke" (a.k.a. Sam Hill):
In "Canyon Walls," rides into Green Valley in Utah looking for work at the Boller ranch. Smoke is running away from his old, wild life. He is tired of gunfights, of two-bit rustling, of gambling and the other dubious means of making a living he used in Arizona. He never considered himself outright dishonest. He had the cowboy's elasticity of judgment in such matters. Bad company and the bottle brought Monty to this point. He is looking for a place where he can hide out and start a new life. He accepts the Widow Keetch's offer of hospitality and in turn offers to work for her for room and board. He tells her he has been a no-good, gun-throwing cowpuncher who got run out of Arizona. She understands his situation, tells him it's time to make a new start, and gives him a new name as a beginning. The ranch is not in as bad shape as the widow thought. That summer, the peaches, the pumpkins, the grapes are abundant. Thanks to his work, the ranch becomes profitable. He has plowed new land. The alfalfa crop will be several hundred tons. Boller's offer to purchase the place convinces the widow that the operation can be made profitable. She offers Monty a partnership in the venture. At this point, Monty is well known to the Mormons in the area and he comes to like their company. When he accompanies Rebecca to Kanab on a shopping spree, he discovers that he is in love with her. On the trip back, they are caught in a snowstorm. Spending a night with him on the trail, she fears, could ruin her reputation. Mrs. Keetch tells Sam that Rebecca is in love with him, even though she may not be aware of it. The widow encourages him to pursue her. The match is made. They are married by the bishop in Kanab, who asks Monty if he will become a Mormon. Never having been religious, he declines the offer, but promises not to put any obstacles in the way of Rebecca's practicing her faith. They have a child a year later, when Sheriff Jim Sneed and three men ride up to the ranch. Sneed tells him he has come to buy cattle for Strickland, but that he also has orders to bring him in. Strickland had heard that he was seen in Kanab, and a little investigation convinced him that Sam Hill and Smoke Bellew were the same man. Sneed sees that Smoke has changed. He accepts his invitation to eat with the family. The wife and child are proof that he has turned a new leaf. Sneed assures Bellew that Strickland will agree to his offer to repay the debt a bit every month. Sneed also tells him about what happened to his old partners. Slim was killed covering Cuppy's getaway. Monty is grateful for the twist of fate that

separated him from the partners of his wild and reckless youth.

Belllounds, Old Bill:
In *The Mysterious Rider*, Old Bill Belllounds is a pioneer, rancher who came to Middle Park in the 1860's when the territory was Ute country. He sought the friendship of Piah, the Ute chief of the region, who was well-disposed towards white men. In the last years of the decade, when prospectors and miners and cattlemen start coming to the area, he persuades the Utes to relinquish the land. Bill Belllounds developed several cattle ranches in Middle Park, residing at White Slides. Over the years, he has been open-handed and open-hearted. He boasts that he has never been taken advantage of, and of the men he has helped, none have failed to make good their debts. The innkeeper in Kremmlin' speaks of tension in the Belllounds house, owing to the wife's fear that her husband loves the foundling daughter more than her son. She fears Buster Jack's inheritance will be shared with Columbine. Buster Jack, however, is Old Bill's one blind spot. Despite all the evidence, he never loses faith in his only son. As a boy, Jack was mean, jealous, selfish, and lazy, picking fights with the cowboys. He used to pick on Columbine mercilessly. Still, Bill believes he will make something of himself. Only a few know where he was for the missing three years, but when Jack returns to White Slides from prison, Bill makes him foreman of White Slides, hoping that this job will whip him into shape and give him a sense of responsibility. He has planned a welcome back dinner for the event but Jack spends his first night of freedom drinking and playing cards in Kremmlin', making his appearance at the ranch the following day. Old Bill gives him some friendly advice, to be gentle with horses and with the cowboys. He reminds him that as a kid he was mean. Old Bill acts with fairness and open-mindedness when he comes upon the men after a fight with Buster Jack. He listens to what they have to say, knowing who is telling the truth and who is hiding something. He gives Wilson Moore the yellow mustang he had broken and ridden for years, resolving a dispute between Moore and Buster Jack over ownership of the animal. When Bent Wade shows up offering his services as hunter to clear out the coyotes and wildcats credited with depleting his herds, he decides to take a chance on him. Some of his best friends, after all, were men he had taken chances on. When Buster Jack shows up drunk for his wedding, Bill Belllounds calls him disgusting and cancels the marriage to Columbine. He frees her of any sense of responsibility to him or to Buster Jack. When Buster begins to behave himself, Old Bill is stirred by hope that the son may reform. Hope springs eternal in his breast. Even when Bent Wade comes to Belllounds and tells him that he is Columbine's father, that he has been observing Jack and has concluded that he will never change, Bill remains unconvinced. He accuses Wade of collaborating with Wilson Moore, his "rustler" partner, to steal Columbine from Jack. Eventually, Bent Wade finds

himself forced to tell Belllounds that Buster Jack is the rustler who has been stealing the cattle to finance his own gambling. Furthermore, he has plotted to frame Wilson Moore for the crime. Still, his faith in the possibility of redemption for his son does not falter. When Buster Jack is killed, he finally consents to Columbine's marriage to Wilson Moore, offering Moore the job of foreman on the ranch. Moore, Jack had said, was the son that Belllounds always wanted.

Bill Belllounds is a common biblical archetype found in Grey's novels. He is the prodigal father, blessed with a generous forgiving heart, betrayed by a feckless, worthless son.

Belllounds, Buster Jack: In *The Mysterious Rider*, the only son of Bill Belllounds. He is a big, rangy boy, wild, handsome, and wicked. He made his younger foster sister's youth unendurable. When the novel begins, Buster Jack is expected back at the ranch after an absence of some three years. The story goes that he had been sent away to work, but Wilson Moore and Bent Wade know he was in prison. Buster Jack begins his new life in freedom spending the night in Kremmlin', drinking and playing cards. When he returns, Columbine, who hasn't seen him in about seven years, describes him as tall, like his father, with a handsome boldness sullied by a sullen, shamed look. He is dressed in high-heeled boots, tight-fitting trousers with a dark, heavy belt with a silver buckle, and a white shirt. He looks like his father, duded up, but his eyes show the old worry and discontent. He has not forgotten the old resentments. He plans to fire Wilson Moore the first chance he gets. Wilson Moore had beaten him soundly in a fight over Columbine. He plans to settle the score now. He's not sure how to approach Columbine. The two of them had not gotten along as children and now, with his father's plan that the two of them should marry, he is not sure how to proceed.

Buster Jack is petty, vindictive and incompetent. He is quick to take offense. When his father does not put him in charge of the roundup and branding, he feels slighted. Bill Belllounds feels he should see the wisdom in keeping the crew together under usual conditions during the heaviest and most dangerous work of the year. Jack sees only that he has been belittled before the hired hands. When Moore is named foreman of the branding operation by Hudson, who has been injured, Jack picks a fight with him over the mustang, Spottie, and tries to fire him. Later, at the roundup, Jack tries to rope a steer and succeeds only in frightening the animal, which then jumps a fence and tries to gore one of Columbine's favorite horses, Pronto. Wilson Moore breaks his leg and foot saving Pronto from goring by the steer. Some of the cowboys suspect that Buster Jack deliberately frightened the steer. Later, when he comes upon Wilson Moore with a wagon taking his belongings away from the ranch, he inspects the wagon on the pretext that Moore is stealing from them. When he finds Columbine talking with Moore, he goes to Moore's ranch house, picks a fight, and deliberately kicks his

broken leg and foot. Playing cards with the ranch hands in the bunkhouse, Jack is a bully, a poor loser and a cheat. He uses poor judgment playing and usually ends up fleeced. He treats Columbine roughly, sometimes causing her to fear he will seriously injure her. She suspects madness may be the cause of his violence. Jack is jealous, suspicious, convinced she is seeing Moore on the sly.

Jack's plot to pin the blame for the rustling of Belllounds stock on Moore reveals his criminal ingenuity, probably learned during his sojourn in prison. Bent Wade had not believed him possible of such organization and shrewdness. He joins a gang of rustlers led by one Smith from Kremmlin'. Smith's real name is Captain Folsom, an unscrupulous criminal who figured prominently in Bent Wade's troubled past. Jack buys a horse that looks like Moore's mustang, Spottie, making a horseshoe to match the triangular shaped one Spottie uses because of a twisted hoof. He leaves a trail from Moore's ranch to the cabin hideout of the rustlers. He calls in the sheriff to "find" the evidence against the cowboy. Then, he makes the accusation in front of his father and the ranch hands, hoping to discredit the much-respected Moore in the eyes of everyone. Bent Wade is not fooled. He later tracks Buster to the outlaws' hideout, where he confronts the rustlers. All get killed in the shootout that ensues except Buster Jack. Wade spares his life on the condition that he renounce any marriage to Columbine. Back at the ranch, however, Buster Jack reneges on his promise. Wade then meets Jack. In the shootout which follows, both Jack and Wade die.

Buster Jack is a character type that appears frequently in Grey's novels. Buster is the wayward son, ungrateful, immature, proud, arrogant, incapable of redemption. He is a man who succumbs to the worst elements in his nature and in his surroundings.

Bells: In *Riders of the Purple Sage,* a powerful bay, one of Jane Withersteen's four favorite horses. She lends him to Lassiter when his own steed has been killed in the stampede of the red herd. Bells is stolen by Jerry Card and Horne, who is riding the bay when Venters catches up with them. Later, as Jane plans to abandon Utah, she gives Bells to Judkins in payment and reward for his loyal service during the crisis.

Belmar: In *The Arizona Clan*, a member of the Hathaway-Quayle-Twitchell crowd. Hathaway and his men hold up at Belmar's ranch, where they have corralled the horses stolen from the Lilleys. Belmar stands out because of his great stature.

Belmet, Clint (a.k.a. Buff, Turk): In *Fighting Caravans*, the son of Jim and Mary Belmet. He is thirteen years old when they set out from Independence, Missouri, for the Southwest. He has a freckled face, clear, steady gray eyes and an intent, quiet manner beyond his years. He prefers going fishing to going to town with his father. His mother comments that he takes after her father in this love of hunting and fishing. He takes an interest in May Bell, the ten-year-old daughter of Sam Bell. The ten-year-old looks up to him with admiration and respect, awed at his knowledge of the frontier, the pioneer life, and their role in shaping the future. She falls in love with him and he with her.

The novel traces Clint Belmet's adventures and adaptation to frontier life. Like Joe Downs in *The Spirit of the Border,* he is in love with frontier life. From Dick Curtis, he learns to shoot, to hunt, to skin and butcher a buffalo, how to move about without making noise, and how to hunt wild turkeys. Belmet's enthusiasm for the frontier endears him to Kit Carson, Jim Couch and Lew Maxwell, experienced frontiersmen. Like Joe Downs, he allows the environment to work its magic on him, transforming him into a Wetzel-like figure. As Grey puts it: "Something strong and strange was at work deep within him." He is strong, broad of shoulder, and fleet of foot, with eagle eyesight and unerring aim. These physical traits are coupled with wisdom and prudence. He is fascinated by the picturesqueness of the frontier, the mountain men, the wagon bosses, the mountains, the herds of buffalo. He always felt that whites were in the wrong, usurping Indian hunting grounds, invading their territory, destroying their livelihood. Despite his admiration for frontier life, he appreciates the need for the skills of the civilized world. He offers to teach Tom Sidel how to shoot and drive a team if Sidel will teach him reading and writing.

Clint Belmet retains his boyish shyness where women are concerned. He hesitates to sit at the place beside May Bell at Maxwell's banquet, and he feels he is too unrefined and uncouth for one with her refinement and style. He is jealous when he sees her flirt with Sergeant Clayborn, but rather than pick a fight with the man, he lets May Bell choose.

Clint becomes a wise, prudent wagon boss. He does not take unnecessary risks. He accepts as accurate the information about Murdock and Blackstone provided by Jim Whitefish and plans a trap to catch them at Point of Rocks, where these renegades had planned to ambush the caravan. He refuses to execute the Pawnee prisoners as ordered by Sergeant McMillan. Despite his many years on the frontier, he is still disgusted by the behavior of the frontiersmen who club to death the Indians still alive after the battle.

Clint Belmet finally is reunited with May Bell in fairy-tale fashion. The two marry and settle down to ranching on the Clements estate in Las Cruces, Texas.

The Belmet character lacks the development of similar figures in novels such as *The Spirit of the Border* or *Wild Horse Mesa.* In Clint Belmet, Grey combines the frontiersman with the medieval knight, the man of decency and integrity, using his abilities to help others, not only to advance his own cause.

In *The Lost Wagon Train,* Buff Belmet is mentioned as a young man who got his formation on the trails West, a man who experienced the hardships and struggle of the frontier and triumphed.

In *Knights of the Range,* Buff Belmet shows up at the Ripple ranch and in Las Animas. He reports what he knows about Renn Frayne. He had been a friend of Holly's father. He recounts seeing Frayne meet the gunman, Wes Hardin, in Abilene several years ago. He summarizes his history, footloose and wild, with a hand for guns. He was classed as one of the best gunmen. While the man may be considered an outlaw in some states, he has no record in Arizona. Buff Belmet praises the man's honesty and integrity.

Belmet, Jim: In *Fighting Caravans,* a sturdy, middle-aged teamster from Illinois. He hails from pioneer stock and the call of the West is irresistible to him. He heads for the Southwest with a wagon train out of Independence, Missouri. He has signed on to haul freight for the Tullt Company over the Santa Fe trail. He advises Sam Bell to do the same as it provides income to put towards the purchase of land at the final destination. After his wife is killed, he takes to drinking and gambling to drown his grief and to escape the boredom of camp life. He recruits John Sidel to freight with him. In a Comanche attack on a caravan, Jim Belmet is killed. In his will, he leaves Buff (Clint) under the guardianship of Captain Jim Couch until he is twenty-one.

Belmet, Mary: In *Fighting Caravans,* the mother of Clint (Buff) Belmet and husband of Jim Belmet. She is a robust, comely woman busy with cooking on the wagon train west. She comments that Clint takes after her father, who loved to hunt and fish. She is killed in the Comanche attack on the wagon train and buried along the trail.

Belmont: In *Black Mesa,* a rugged white man in the prime of life. He has a big voice, a big frame, and a big hand. His boldly cut features are not unhandsome but give an unpleasant impression. For a desert man, he has a pale complexion. His eyes are a shade between green and hazel. And it shows that he is a heavy drinker. He owns the trading post at Bitter Seeps which he bought from the Reed brothers He also deals in cattle and sells illegal liquor to the Navajos. He treats the Indians with contempt. Paul and Wess witness him give the young Natasha an overly familiar pat on the backside. He clearly lusts after her. When Paul and Wess set Natasha and Taddy up with sheep and horses, he laughs at their concern for some dirty Indians.

Paul Manning and Wess Kintell enter into a cattle deal with him and they live at the post. Something in Belmont's appearance inspires immediate mistrust. He weighs the Indians' wool with obvious care and strict precision, which Paul Manning learns to doubt. Wess Kintell hears wagons during the night, possibly deliveries of illegal liquor which he sells to the Indians, but when he asks Belmont about this, Belmont denies any nocturnal activity, adding that Wess is probably hearing things. Some weeks later, Paul witnesses John and Bill unloading kegs of liquor. When Belmont proposes a new cattle deal, buying some two hundred head more, Kintell sees his dishonesty in full swing. Wess recognizes their own cattle being sold to them again. When Paul refuses to pay the full price Calkins advises Belmont to take the deal, as Wintell is wise to their scheme. Louise writes Paul advising him not to pay for the new cattle as she, too, suspects Belmont's cronies have rustled some of their own cattle to resell to them. In order to keep the Indians buying pop, ginger ale and liquor in secret, Belmont adds something to the water of the spring making it virtually undrinkable. When Paul comments that the water is not tasting too bad, Belmont goes out that night to throw something into the pool. The secret of the bad water is now revealed. The bad water caused Tommy, his son by Louise, to get sick.

The greatest mystery surrounding Belmont is his relationship to Sister and Louise. While Sister runs the trading post operation, Belmont makes no mention of her as a wife. Louise, supposedly, is the wife. Wess observes Belmont entering Sister's room and spending the night with her. The truth eventually emerges, that Sister is his wife, that she put up the money for him to buy the trading post and his cattle. This is the hold she has over him. She has been the source of his livelihood. Louise claims to love and hate him at different times. She does not know for sure what the relationship between Sister and Belmont is, but she feels trapped and turns to Paul Manning for help. Kintell pieces together the story with information from Shade and Bloom. Belmont was run out of Utah for a fraudulent deal. He was mixed up in a gold mine, selling stock his partners thought was worthless. They were going to put him in jail and he left the state. Later, silver was discovered and the charges were dropped. Shade brings word of this to Belmont, telling him he is free to return to Utah if he so desires. Belmont is killed when he is thrown from his horse on a narrow mountain trail. He falls to his death over a precipice. Sister is the only one who is upset. She did love him in her own way. She keeps his operation at Bitter Seeps, and Louise marries Paul.

Belton, Quade (a.k.a. Barncastle): In *The Fugitive Trail*, a rustler and a bank robber. He organizes the attack on the bank in Denison, having recruited Barse Lockheart for his outlaw gang. Later, Bruce Lockheart meets up with him again, acting as a cattleman and rancher involved in shady deals. Bruce meets him at the Elks Hotel in Mendle, where he recognizes Barncastle as Quade Belton. In the gunfight, Belton is shot, but not killed. When Bruce Lockheart is working at Melrose's ranch, he hears about Melrose having made a cattle deal with Barncastle. Barncastle owes Melrose thousands of dollars which he is unable to repay. Barncastle has also failed to come through on a cattle deal. Stewart, supposedly his right-hand man, shows up to negotiate a deal. He tells Melrose that he should join with him and Barncastle if he knows what is good for him. Later, Barncastle himself shows up to pay Melrose the money he owes, and to break with Stewart. He accuses Stewart of betraying him to Melrose and of making a deal with Vic Henderson behind his back. The two of them get into a fight and Belton is shot. Stewart pretended he was Bruce Lockheart and others are willing to swear that Stewart and Lockheart are the same man.

Ben: (1) In *The Call of the Canyon*, one of Tom Hutter's hands at the sheep ranch. He is with Charley at the sheep dip and reports to Glenn Killbourne what Ruff Haze has been saying about Carley and what happened at Flo's birthday party.

(2) In *The Horse Thief*, one of the three horse thieves that Dale Brittenham comes upon in camp. He overhears them talking about Big Bill Mason and Leale Hildrith, the head men in the group. Ben is shot by his Alec.

(3) In *Shadow on the Trail*, a young cowboy who works under Aulsbrook's foreman, Lawsford. He tells Wade Holden about Pencarrow's daughters, Jacqueline and Rosemary, and how beautiful they are.

(4) In *To the Last Man*, with Greaves outside the Isbel house. He comments to Greaves that it is strange that they have heard no shots from Somers in the last while. Greaves suggests he go see what has happened to Somers.

(5) In *Twin Sombreros*, one of the men in Bodkin's posse who arrest Brazos Keene for the murder of Allen Neece. He and Frank refuses to stay and help with the lynching that Bodkins is planning.

Bender, Hal: In *The Trail Driver*, a tenderfoot from Pennsylvania. He appears to be a hulking youth, good-natured and friendly, though rather shy before the still-faced, intent-eyed Texans. He has heavy, stolid features that fit his bulky shoulders. His hair is the color of tow and resembles a mop. On the trail, he is hard to wake up in the morning. On the trail, he lives down his reputation as a tenderfoot. He is killed in the massive stampede of buffalo and longhorns near the end of the trail.

Bender, Tim: In *The Wolf Tracker*, one of the cowboys in the Adams roundup outfit. Like Banty Smith, he likes to tease Benson about his attachment to his cattle. Like the other men, he doubts that Brinks will be able to catch Old Gray.

Bennet: In *Fighting Caravans*, a settler in a valley near where the emigrant caravans pass. He is friendly with all Indians. He keeps Mrs. Clements and May Bell for a year until another, larger caravan passes by.

Bennet, Alex: In *The Last Trail*, a boatman on the stretch between Fort Pitt and Fort Henry. He reports information heard around Ft. Pitt to Col. Zane, for example, gossip about a certain man who was seeking the whereabouts of the Sheppards. He reports what Jake Wentz and Jeff Lynn have said about Brandt and Jenks. Alex Bennet is a "lukewarm" suitor of Mabel Lane, who had been abducted by Bing Legget. When she is returned, he decides he wants to marry her. Colonel Zane gives him a plot of land as a wedding gift.

Bennet, Billy: In *Betty Zane*, mentioned by Lydia and Alice as a potential beau for Betty. She dismisses him as "just a boy."

Bennet, Harry: In *Betty Zane*, mentioned as one of the young men competing in the shooting contest celebrating Isaac Zane's marriage to Myeerah. In the attack on the fort, Harry Bennet discovers the opening in the stockade and reports his find to the men. Young Harry dies from bullet wounds.

Bennet, Hugh: Among the original settlers in the area around Ft Henry. They are mentioned in *Betty Zane* and *The Spirit of the Border* and *The Last Trail*. In the first novel, Hugh Bennet is one of the first of the settlers at Ft. Henry to welcome Isaac Zane and Myeerah. He is also one of the principal defenders of the fort during the Indian attack, shouting "To heck with King George" at Captain Pratt, in command of the British forces. Later, Hugh Bennet is one of several men who build a patch out of logs for the hole in the fort stockade while Wetzel fights off the Indians trying to come in through the opening. Hugh Bennet gets shot in the process, but is not seriously wounded. In *The Spirit of the Border*, Hugh Bennet is mentioned in a story told to illustrate Wetzel's phenomenal strength. Bennet's loaded wagon was stuck in the mud and a number of men had gathered around to help him get the wagon out of the hole, all to no avail. Wetzel comes along and lifts out the loaded wagon on his own. Apart from a mention of the name, Hugh Bennet does not appear in *The Last Trail*.

Bennet, John: (1) appears in *Betty Zane* as one of settlers at Ft. Henry, and a neighbor of Col. Zane's. He is a huge man, and when he enters the colonel's cabin to congratulate Isaac on his escape and return home, the floor shakes. It is assumed he is the father of Harry and Billy Bennet.

(2) In *Lost Pueblo*, runs the trading post on the Navajo reservation. Mr. Endicott has come here with the archaeologist Phillip Randolph and his daughter, Janey, on an archaeological expedition. Mr. Elijah Endicott wants to get his daughter as far away from civilization as possible. He and Bennet and Randolph plan a "kidnapping" to shock Janey into more sensible behavior. After the fun with the supposed visit from Black Dick and Snitz, Bennet and Mr. Endicott arrive to bring the "victims" back to the post.

Bennet, Mrs.: In *Lost Pueblo*, the wife of the trader, John Bennet. She prepares accommodations for the Endicotts when they arrive with Phillip Randolph.

Bennet, Tom: In *The Last Trail*, one of the young men Jonathan Zane observes entering the Sheppard cabin when he is trailing the man who gave the signal to the Shawnee warriors to steal horses.

Benny: In *The Spirit of the Border*, a young Indian boy, some four or five years of age. He greets the Wellses and Jim Downs when they arrive at the Village of Peace. Later, he is rescued from the slaughter by Nell Wells, who hides him under her skirts. John Christy then hides him in Heckewelder's house. Benny is the only Christian Indian to survive the massacre. Christy reports that Heckewelder has taken the boy to safety and will ensure that he receives an education.

Benow di cleash: In *The Vanishing American*, the Navajo name that Nophaie gives Marian Warner. The name means "white girl with blue eyes." Lo Blandy calls her this name in private.

Benson: (1) In *Wilderness Trek*, a young rider in his late teens. He works for Slyter, together with Drake and Heald. Benson remains loyal to Slyter and Dann throughout the two-and-a-half-year trek. When they reach the Kimberleys, he is sent to Wyndham to fetch supplies before they settle down in their new home at "Dann's Station."

(2) In *The Wolf Tracker*, the foreman of Adams's roundup crew. He voices a desire to have seen the last of Old Gray, the loafer that had killed four of their heifers that day. One of the animals killed was part of Benson's small herd of twenty cattle. Benson comments that the return of the wolf was unexpected, as he had not shown up in that area for some years. He had been hoping the wolf was dead. Benson, both amused and surprised that Brinks wants to track down Old Gray, tells him exactly where he saw the wolf that day and wishes the tracker luck.

Benson, Alec: In *The Lost Wagon Train*, arrives with his wife at Latch's Field after surviving a Comanche attack down on Red River. They have staked out a ranch at Latch's Field, but in Latch's absence, they have made a home for Keetch and for Estelle, Cynthia's daughter. They took care of Cynthia during the birth and buried her when she died. Alec Benson is about forty years old, a sturdy farmer from Pennsylvania. They came west to grow up with the country. Latch tells Benson that if he has come to make his fortune, he need look no farther. He offers him work as manager of his ranch at Latch's Field. The night of the fateful birthday party, Benson reports on what Mizzouri has told him about Slim Blue picking a fight and killing Tumbler Johnson in the street, and later being seen riding down the alley behind Leighton's saloon just before the building bursts into flame. Benson later reports to Slim Blue that he had ridden to the mouth of Spider Creek Canyon with Latch and Pedro. Latch has gone there to get proof of Estelle's relationship to Cynthia Bowden, niece of the Bowden who had bought the prairie schooner from Tullt. He explains about the lawyer, Bowden, and about Simmons being sent to fetch back Estelle. Slim Blue tells him that Simmons was killed before he had reached her but that he has taken her to a safe place, at Bradley's ranch. Benson helps Slim bring Latch back from the canyon to recover from his wounds.

Benson, Jackrabbit: In *The Lone Star Ranger*, runs the saloon in Bland's hideout. He has a cadaverous face, with an extremely pale complexion and a black mustache. He has deep-set, hollow, staring eyes, that restlessly rove around the room in a nervous manner as if he were hiding from someone. Euchre holds it against him that he pimps for Bland. On one occasion, he went to Mexico to get booze and returned with Jennie, having traded with Mexican bandits for her. He sells her to Bland. There is something about him that makes Duane sense evil. Euchre kills him before he attempts to flee with Jennie and Buck.

Benson, Mrs.: In *The Lost Wagon Train,* the wife of Alec Benson. She and her husband escaped a Comanche raid down on the Red River and arrived at Latch's Field seven years before Latch returned. They settled at Latch's Field, took care of Cynthia when she gave birth to Estelle, and the couple raised the child for the past seven years. Mrs. Benson has made a home out of the ranch. She tells Latch the story of Estelle's birth and Cynthia's death. She and her husband have no children of their own and rejoice when Estelle returns from school in New Orleans. She declares that the daughter will make the place hum.

Bent, Charlie: In *Fighting Caravans,* the real name of Lee Murdock.

Bent, Henry: In *Fighting Caravans,* Charlie Bent is (Lee Murdock's) father. He lives in Kansas City. Murdock asks Clint Belmet not to send word to him when he is dying. He had heard from his father several years ago and the old man believes him dead. He asks Clint to keep the fact that he is Charlie Bent a secret from his father.

Bent, William: In *Twin Sombreros,* with his brothers built a fort in 1874 not far from Las Animas. It is now abandoned, but was a key center in the collecting and shipping of buffalo hides.

Beppo: In *The Lone Star Ranger,* the boy who tends to Bland's horse.

Berkley: In *Wilderness Trek,* one of Ormiston's drovers and rustlers. He is shot by Larry when the Dann outfit pursues and catches up with the rustlers.

Bert: In *Shadow on the Trail,* the foreman of Aulsbrook's crew. He is suspicious of Wade Holden (Blanco) from the start, believing that he is a member of Catlin's gang and planning to rustle the cattle despite what he has told them. When Aulsbrook tells him that sometimes you have to believe what a man says, he remains dubious. He calls Blanco a liar. When Nippert is dead and Catlin has ridden off, Holden confronts him, cautioning him that if he plans to call a man a liar, he needs to back his accusation up with his gun. Aulsbrook tells Blanco that Bert's apology will have to do, as the man has never drawn a gun in his life.

Bescos: In *The Fugitive Trail,* a rancher from the Red River driving a herd west to settle across the Brazos, where Melrose has set up ranching. He has sent out a call for Texas cowboys and ranchers to move into the region.

Bess: (1) In *Boulder Dam,* falls in with an outfit from Montana working the strip in Las Vegas. Their game is to get workers drunk and rob them of their wages. Bess is working with Bink Moore, a man working on the same shift as Whitney. He introduces him to Bess at Rankin's drinking establishment. She gets Whitney Curtis drunk and they rob him of his roll of money. Whitney, however, falls for her, as she does for him. She hides him in her tent until he sobers up. While there, he overhears men plotting to sabotage the construction at Boulder Dam. When Whitney has enough money together to pay off his debts in Vegas, he marries Bess with Bink Moore's blessings. Moore is fond of her but agrees to let her go on condition she marry Curtis and leave Nevada. Bess and Whitney leave to take up ranching on the ranch he has inherited from his recently deceased father.

(2) In "The Secret of Quaking Asp Cabin," Bess is the name given to Madge Beam in Babe Haught's version of the story of Tappan and his burro.

Bess (Elizabeth Erne, the Masked Rider): In *Riders of the Purple Sage,* and *The Rainbow Trail,* the name by which Milly Erne's daughter is best known. She is born during her mother Milly Erne's abduction and captivity. The Mormons who had abducted Milly took the daughter away from her to keep her under control. The daughter was handed over by Elder Tull to Oldring, the outlaw. They hoped that life with outlaws would be her ruination. Oldring, however, gave her an education and a decent upbringing. She learned to ride; her only equal is perhaps Jerry Card. She was taught to read and write, and Oldring protected her from his drunken rustlers. She spent a lot of time alone in the cabin valley hideout and when she is shot by Venters and brought to Surprise Valley, she is pleased to enjoy unprecedented freedom. She declares she does not want to return to Oldring's hideout. Bit by bit, she tells about life among the rustlers, the visits from Mormon elders, the gold in the canyon which is the true secret of Deception Pass. Bess is presented as a Heidi figure, at one with the natural world, a child of nature. The animals in Surprise Valley are not afraid of humans. Bess makes friends with a collection of them. Bess slowly comes to love Venters. Although she has met few men, she knows he is unique. When he returns from Cottonwoods, she undergoes a fit of jealousy when she detects that a woman has packed his gear. When she and Venters are fleeing Utah, they meet Jane and Lassiter on the way. Bess is jealous of Jane, the "other" woman Bern would not talk about and Jane reveals that Bern killed her "father," Oldring. Lassiter clears matters up. The suspicion that he had when he visited Bess and Bern in Surprise Valley was confirmed by his chat with Oldring in Snell's saloon. Bess is the daughter of his sister Milly, whom she closely resembles. When Lassiter shows her a picture of her mother, she dimly remembers her, and Jane Witherly comments that she is the very image of her beloved friend. Bess and

Venters leave Utah taking with them two of Jane's prize thoroughbreds, Night and Black Star. The two steeds make possible their escape from Tull and his henchmen. With the two stallions they start their horse farm in Beaumont, Illinois.

In *The Rainbow Trail*, Bess is Venters's wife. They live on a farm where they raise horses. Shefford describes her as beautiful, quiet but strange. She and Venters seem to live in a world of their own. She is particularly pleased to welcome Jim Lassiter and Jane Withersteen to their home in Beaumont, Illinois. She proudly re-introduces Jane to the prize stallions from her stable in Cottonwoods.

Beulah: In *The Light of Western Stars,* the young wife of Ed Linton, whose bachelor party is being celebrated at the beginning of the novel. She is terribly jealous of her husband, who had the reputation of being quite the ladies' man. She keeps a sharp eye on both Ed and Dorothy Coombs during the golf match.

Bevins: In *Riders of the Purple Sage*, the store keeper in Cottonwoods. He is instructed by Jane Withersteen to provide supplies for the poor gentiles living in the village, this in defiance of Elder Tull and Bishop Dyer.

Big Eyes: In *The Hash Knife Outfit*, the affectionate term Jed Stone gives Glory Traft when he has "kidnapped" her to teach her a lesson about life in the West.

Big Tree: In *Betty Zane*, one of the right hand chiefs of Cornplanter (Yantwaia) in planning the attack on Ft. Henry.

Bill: (1) In *Arizona Ames,* a cowboy who works on Grieve's ranch in the Wind River country of Wyoming.

(2) In *Black Mesa*, one of the men making a delivery of liquor to Belmont's post while Paul Manning is observing from the rooftop.

(3) In *The Border Legion*, the driver of the stage from Alder Creek to Bannack. He is driving the night Cleve and Joan leave Alder Creek. The stage, loaded with Overland gold, is held up by Gulden and the gang and Bill is shot.

(4) In *Boulder Dam,* rows a skiff that approaches Lynn Weston as he tows Ben Brown to shore and safety. Bill helps pull the two of them out of the wild Colorado River.

(5) In *The Dude Ranger,* one of the two robbers who board the stage in Springer, hoping to relieve Miss Hepford of her purse, which contains a substantial amount of money. Bill tries to get rid of Ernest Selby, throwing him a dollar coin and telling him to run and fetch some sandwiches for them at the station restaurant. Bill tries to grab Anne Hepford's purse, but Ernest prevents him, fending him off with his boxing strategies. When the shorter companion cannot get the purse either, they run off, with Ernest shooting at their heels.

(6) In *The Lone Star Ranger*, a member of the vigilantes whose work Buck Duane interrupts as he rides away from Jones's ranch. Bill is told to shoot Duane and ask questions later. When the pursuit has led to Buck being trapped in a cottonwood thicket/bog with only one route of escape, Bill finds the trail of blood indicating that Buck has been shot and he sends the bloodhounds into the brakes to follow Buck's trail. There is a second Bill who appears in Laramie's inn in Fairdale to rob the place. Buck learns that before the robbery, he was seen talking with the mayor, Longstreth. During the robbery, he is grazed on the head by a bullet from Buck Duane's gun and he falls unconscious on the ground. He is taken out but regains consciousness and disappears before Duane can question him.

(7) In *Majesty's Rancho*, drives one of the trucks on to which the stolen cattle from Stewart's ranch are being loaded. He pulls a gun on Gene and is shot by Lance Sidway. "Bored him plumb center," in the words of Stewart.

(8) In *The Man of the Forest*, drives the hoax stagecoach which the Beeman brothers and Milt Dale have used to pick up Helen and Bo Rayner from the train station.

(9) In *Nevada*, a member of the Pine Tree Outfit and friend of Babe Morgan and Burt Stillwell.

(10) In *Raiders of Spanish Peaks,* one of the men helping Price hang Mulhall at the start of the novel. Lonesome Mulhall tells Price this hanging on a pretext of cattle rustling is just to extract revenge because Annie Lakin had dumped Price for him. Sooner or later, Hank or Bill will reveal to Annie what Price has done.

Also, in *Raiders of Spanish Peaks*, Lenta Lindsay mentions that she must write to Bill and Jack, friends back in Upper Sandusky, Ohio.

(11) In *Shadow on the Trail,* one of the men with Urba when he comes to Pencarrow's ranch demanding payment for a herd of cattle that Pencarrow claims he has already paid for twice. Tex Brandon has just arrived at the Pencarrow ranch. He challenges Urba and the men, and Bill draws a gun on him. Bill is killed in the shootout.

(12) In *The Shepherd of Guadaloupe*, one of the men in the car with the unnamed speaker who meets Cliff Forrest as he is herding sheep. The unnamed speaker brings Cliff up to date on what happened to Jim Mason, Malpass, and Virginia. Mason survived his gunshot wounds, Malpass is trying to buy Lopez's herd and Virginia was seen taking the train east. When the unnamed speaker asks if there is anything they can do for Cliff, he asks for cigarettes for Julio. Bill and Pedlar, the other passenger, each contribute a pack.

(13) The oarsman in *The Spirit of the Border* who is steering the raft on which Joe and Jim Downs are traveling down the Ohio. He is shot by Silvertip.

(14) In *30,000 on the Hoof*, John Holbert's son-in-law, husband of his daughter, Mary. He accompanies Mrs. Holbert and Mary when they come to the Huett ranch to help Lucinda deliver her second son, Abe. When Huett and his sons make their first

cattle drive, they meet Holbert, who tells them that the year before, his son-in-law, Bill, had taken up with a band of rustlers and had driven ten thousand head of stock out of the territory before Holbert even knew a hoof was moving.

(15) In *Thunder Mountain,* a big, bearded, red-shirted man. He comes out on the run when Lee Emerson asks if anyone had met his brother Sam. Bill was one of the early miners to arrive at Thunder Mountain, but when he arrived, there was no Sam Emerson around. The quartz vein that Sam found had been taken over by Leavitt by then. No one else has ever heard of his brother.

(16) In *Twin Sombreros,* one of the men in the posse that arrests Brazos Keene for the murder of Allen Neece.

(17) In *The U. P. Trail,* an Irish worker who is typical of the little people who have made the construction of the railroad possible. Men like him do the hard work, drink and gamble their pay, and dream of returning home some day.

Also, in *The U. P. Trail,* a trapper friend of Slingerland. Neale meets Bill and an unnamed companion when he is trying to follow the trail of the men who burned Slingerland's cabin and abducted Allie. The trapper says he saw Slingerland go by about a week ago. He further adds that he thinks the railroad is ruining the country for hunters and trappers.

(18) In *The Vanishing American,* one of the white men who capture Nophaie when they steal some of the sheep he is tending. He is the leader of the group, tall, gaunt, gray-haired, lean, with eyes like a hawk. He decides that they will not kill the boy, but take him with them to release him far enough from the herd to prevent him warning the village. They hand the boy over to people in a wagon train. A nameless woman in the group takes in the child, imagining she is doing a noble thing.

(19) In *Wanderer of the Wasteland,* a tall miner, one of the group that attacks Dismukes and treat him as a slave. He is sent for water by Robbins. Wansfell sees him and follows him into camp. In the ensuing fighting, he is shot and killed by Adam.

(20) In *Wyoming,* one of the hoboes Martha Ann Dixon meets sleeping under a bridge on the highway in the Black Hills. Andrew Bonning drives by as the men are trying to catch her. He rescues her from their clutches.

Billings, Lemuel Archibald *see* Lem

Billy the Kid: In *The Light of Western Stars,* cited as an example of a legendary Western figure and gunman well known to Easterners coming west. In *The Lost Wagon Train,* Billy the Kid shows up at Latchfield, a known haven for outlaws, with one Charlie Bondre. He attends the party in honor of Estelle Latch's sixteenth birthday. Given his reputation as an outlaw, he is very popular, especially with the young ladies at the dance, Marce and Elizabeth, Estelle's two friends from school in New Orleans.

In *Shadow on the Trail,* Billy the Kid is a friend of Jesse Evans, foreman of Jesse Chisum's number ten outfit. At one point Billy the Kid rode for Chisum. Billy is the chain lightning and the poison of the frontier, according to Aulsbrook, who has just sold out to Chisum and found a job for Blanco with him. He concludes that Billy is all the bad of the frontier rolled into one eighteen-year-old boy. Evans, however, has better things to say about Billy. They had been partners. Jesse quit hanging around with him when he went in for banditry, but he still trusts Billy's loyalty to him. Billy would not steal from him in a thousand years. When Wade Holden sees Billy for the first time, there is something about him that impresses the viewer, not his stature or his battered slouch hat or his worn garments and boots, but the way he stood with his gun on the left side. He describes him as having the clearest, coldest eyes he has ever seen. He is not unprepossessing. But for a prominent tooth which he exposes when he laughs, he would be handsome His is a smooth, reckless, youthful face, cold, as if carved out of stone. In it, Wade recognizes the spirit of the wildness of the West at its height, and Billy is what the West has made him. He looks like a boy, with the freshness of a boy, but is a man in whom fear was never born. Billy has come to report that he heard that a Texas Ranger, possibly Mahaffey, has been at Chisum's ranch house asking about Blanco. Billy the Kid invites Holden to join up with him. Holden prefers to go off alone. From Mahaffey he learns about the death of Billy the Kid at the hands of Pat Garrett, when Mahaffey has finally caught up with him, and he is married to Jacqueline Pencarrow.

In *Knights of the Range,* Billy the Kid is mentioned as a rival of Jesse Evans, the faster of the two on the draw. In the Lincoln County War, the two ended up in opposite factions and swore to kill each other. But Billy and Jesse never met face to face. The saloons of Lincoln and Roswell waited and gambled on the meeting of the two former cowboy comrades, but Billy and Jesse avoided the encounter that would mean a draw on sight.

In *Twin Sombreros,* Billy the Kid is mentioned in the context of the cattle rustling. He reportedly sells rustled cattle to the army agents buying cattle for reservations. He is also mentioned as a guest at one of Holly Ripple's fiestas.

In *The Fugitive Trail,* Vic Henderson is compared to Billy the Kid. Bruce Lockheart thinks that Henderson lacks Billy's ability to judge a situation. Henderson makes mistakes, getting himself into situations for which he is not prepared.

Bilyen, Hank: In *Twin Sombreros,* an old friend of Brazos Keene from Las Animas. He comes to the jail to tell Sheriff Kiskadden that he has made a mistake arresting Brazos Keene. He speaks in glowing terms about the work Brazos did for the Ripple Outfit, clearing out the Sewall McCoy outlaw gang. Brazos is the swiftest man with a gun, the fiercest in spirit and the most relentless tracker he has ever known. His eulogy embarrasses Brazos, but Bilyen's assertion that if anyone can solve the mystery of

Allen Neece's murder, it's his friend Brazos. Hank accompanies Brazos out to the cabin where the murder took place and the two of them search for prints, discovering the small boot print of a boy or a young woman, and evidence of how the body was placed in the loft. Bilyen keeps his ears open for gossip and reports to Brazos. The two of them try to make sense of the evidence. When Brazos has withdrawn to Coglan's place in the mountains, Hank remains his contact person in Las Animas, getting word to him of new developments, such as the death of Surface in Dodge, and the arrival of Knight in Las Animas. Bilyen is shot by Knight, who knows he is spying on him for Brazos. Bilyen, however, is not seriously wounded.

Bishop, the: In "Canyon Walls," the Mormon bishop in Kanab marries Sam Hill (Smoke Bellew) and Rebecca Keetch. Before he performs the ceremony, he asks if Sam wants to join the Mormon Church. Sam replies that while he has great admiration for Mormon people, he has never practiced any religion but he will not make any objections to Rebecca practicing hers. And so they are married.

Black: (1) In *Fighting Caravans,* a freighter.
(2) In *Riders of the Purple Sage,* one of the gentile riders who used to work for Jane Withersteen but who quits when threatened by Elder Tull's henchmen. Jane nevertheless offers to move him and his family up to her place, which would be safer, but this offer is rejected. The storekeeper Bevins provides help for his family on Jane Withersteen's instructions.
(3) In *The U. P. Trail,* one of Durade's henchmen assigned to guarding Allie Lee and Durade's gambling establishment. He is killed by Neale in the scuffle surrounding Allie's escape from Stanton's.
(4) In *Valley of Wild Horses,* runs a supply store in Littleton where Pan Handle buys a saddle.

Black, Ace: In *Nevada,* a gambler in the Gold Mine Saloon and tavern in Lineville. He reports to Nevada that Link Cawthorne has beaten up Lize Teller, the cause of the shootout between the two. Later, Ace Black appears as a gambler at Brennan's Ace High Saloon in Winthrop, Arizona, where he presides over card games in a room on the second floor.

Black, Archie: In *Sunset Pass,* a young cowboy who is struck on Thiry Preston. He gets a job at the Preston ranch only to be shot by Ash Preston to scare him away.

Black Bess: In "Lightning," the black mustang mare that the Stewart brothers captured and broke in many years ago. They use her as bait to lure in Lightnin,' the black mustang stallion.

Black Bolly: In *The Heritage of the Desert,* Mescal's black mustang. The mare was given to Mescal by August Naab, and Mescal and the mare are particularly close. She does not fear that the mustang will run away to join the wild herd on the plateau while she is there herding sheep, but she does hobble Black Bolly at night, following Naab's instructions. Black Bolly is used as bait when Naab and his boys and Jack set out to capture the stallion, Silvermane. At this point, Black Bolly does run away with the wild stallion. Later, when Jack has captured Silvermane, Mescal continues to insist that Black Bolly is actually faster than the prized stallion. Mescal takes this horse with her when she escapes into the Painted Desert. A year later, in the race to escape from Snap and Holderness's men when she and Jack are returning to "civilization," Silvermane does prove to be the faster animal, a fact which Mescal reluctantly acknowledges.

Black Dick: In *Lost Pueblo,* a desperado. When the Durlands show up at the site where Randolph and Janey are camped, Janey tells Bert and his mother that Phillip Randolph is Black Dick and that he has abducted her. Later, the "real" Black Dick appears. He scolds Mrs. Durland for the way she dresses and, assuming that Janey is her daughter, scolds her for allowing her daughter to go out half-dressed as she does. He looks through Mrs. Durland's magazine and expresses his disgust at the decadent pictures in it. He makes Mrs. Durland prepare supper, a mixture of everything from the tinned supplies they brought. The mixture would sicken a dog, normally, but Black Dick and his sidekick, Snitz, manage to devour it all. The two of them ride off with Mrs. Durland's purse. It turns out that Black Dick and Snitz were hired by Mr. Endicott to give Janey a scare. Janey runs into him in the bank in Flagerstown and he tells her the full story. She is disappointed that he had not actually met the real desperado. She then hires him and Snitz to kidnap Phillip, who is not planning to return east with them, but stay at the archaeological site. They will kidnap him and put him on the train back east.

Black Hand: In *The Lost Wagon Train,* an outlaw who finds acceptance in Latch's outlaw gang. He is shot in the attack on Anderson's wagon train. He joins the Leighton faction when the fight for leadership comes to a head.

Black Hawk: In *Western Union,* an Indian chief who visits the construction site. He does speak some English. To demonstrate the power of the telegraph, Creighton telegraphs ahead to War Cloud, chief of the Ogallala Sioux. The message which returns does not wholly convince him, and a second message is sent concerning information the whites could not know. This does seem to convince him of the power of the telegraph line. Nevertheless, he still thinks there is something more to the mysterious wire and he promises Creighton that he will spread the word that Creighton means no harm with the telegraph line and promises his people will protect it.

Black Jack: In *The Lost Wagon Train,* the leader of an outlaw outfit second only to that of Jim Blackstone that shows up at Latchfield the day of Estelle's sixteenth birthday party.

Black Kettle, Chief: In *Fighting Caravans,* an Indian chief who agrees to bring his pelts and furs for trade with Couch and Belmet at Maxwell's ranch.

Black, Sam: In *Arizona Ames,* the oldest of the cowboys in Grieve's outfit. He wants to quit his job but hangs around hoping to get his pay.

Black Star: In *Riders of the Purple Sage,* one of Jane Withersteen's favorite thoroughbred horses. He is kept in the barns near the ranch house and trained and exercised by Jerd. Night is stolen by Jerry Card, but rescued by Venters, riding Wrangle. Jane and Lassiter take Black Star with them when they abandon the burning ranch to leave Utah. When they meet up with Venters and Bess, Jane insists that the two of them take Black Star and Night as these horses will outrun anything that Tull and the other Mormons have. Venters and Bess return to Illinois with the two thoroughbreds, the start of their horse-raising business in Beaumont, Illinois. In *The Rainbow Trail,* Black Star appears again. Shefford mentions the spectacular horses that Venters and Bess have on their farm. Black Star was Jane Withersteen's pride and joy and remarkably, he remembers her when she returns to Beaumont after being rescued by Shefford.

"Black Wind": The term used by the Indians to describe Wetzel. It is used in *Betty Zane.* See **Deathwind, Wind of Death, Le Vent de la Mort, Wetzel.**

Blackboy: In *Majesty's Rancho,* one of Majesty Stewart's string of thoroughbred horses.

Blackie: (1) In *Horse Heaven Hill,* Stanley Weston's horse. Blackie is beat in a three mile race by Chaps, Lark Burrell's horse.

(2) In *Shadow on the Trail,* Wade Holden's trusted steed. He knows that Blackie can easily outrun any of the mustangs that the Texas Rangers ride, which are not known for speed, but for endurance over a distance. Blackie is shot by the pursuing rangers, but is not fatally wounded. Wade Holden abandons the horse when he enters the woods to get away from his pursuers. The rangers later mention finding the horse.

Blackstone: In *Wyoming,* Blackstone is one of the young men in whom Andy Bonning's sister, Gloria, is interested. Andrew comments that marrying him might not be interesting, but she would be well taken care of.

Blackstone, Jim: In *Fighting Caravans,* a gambler and associate of Murdock. He is reputed to be a thief. He accepts a thousand dollars to take Mrs. Clements and May Bell to Texas, but they never arrive. Blackstone says their caravan was jumped by Kiowas, but Clint Belmet doesn't buy it. In the fighting which follows, Blackstone hides under a table and sustains only minor injuries. Blackstone is seen in a Kiowa village by Billy Weed, and later leads a band of Indians and outlaws in an attack on Belmet's caravan at Point of Rocks. Before he is hanged by his captors, Blackstone tells Belmet that he and Mur-

dock had taken May Bell to their camp one winter, and raped her in turns.

In *The Lost Wagon Train,* Jim Blackstone is mentioned as the leader of an outlaw gang, the largest in the region, famed for robbing stagecoaches. His gang is holed up somewhere on the Purgatory River. Blackstone is a huge, black-bearded man, formerly one of Quantrell's guerrillas who had turned robber. From operating with a few allies, he had graduated to leadership of a dozen or more of the most hardened criminals on the plains. He and his men had wintered at various forts during the early days of the Civil War, but by its end, he would not have dared to show his face in any of them. No doubt, says Kit Carson, he has been blamed for crimes he did not commit. He and his band show up at Latchfield the day that Latch has planned a party for Estelle's sixteenth birthday.

Blackwell: In *The Trail Driver,* a horse trader in Dodge. He buys Brite's entire remuda for twenty dollars a head, a prince that Brite considers good.

Blackwood, Sheriff (Blacky): In *Rogue River Feud,* a sympathetic friend to Keven Bell. He lost a son in the war and has read about Keven's accident with the cannon in the training camp. He has also heard the gossip about the Carstone affair, which, he adds, he never believed. Blackwood is a good friend of Garry Lord's and approves wholeheartedly of their partnership. The kindly, sad-eyed sheriff added another to the slowly growing number of people who reached to the frozen depths of Keven Bell. Sheriff Blackwood does arrest Keven on instructions from Rollins. Keven Bell had confronted Atwell in the hotel in Grant's Pass, calling him a liar and a coward in spreading the gossip about the Carstone girls. The meeting ended with Keven punching Atwell, who charged him with assault and attempted murder. Blackwood detains Keven, but refuses to hand him over to Rollins. The charges are dropped for lack of evidence when the case makes it to court. In the aftermath of the storm and the fight with Mulligan, Blackwood and Garry set a trap for the crooked fishermen, catching them using illegal nets and thereby solving the problem of the diminishing salmon runs on the Rogue River. Sheriff Blackwood is developed along the lines of Sheriff Haught in *The Maverick Queen.* He is an older man, well-acquainted with human nature, and prepared to administer justice with compassion where common sense and legality conflict.

Blacky: In *The Hash Knife Outfit,* a member of the Hash Knife Outfit who escapes unharmed when Slinger Dunn and the Yellow Jacket attack them, capturing and lynching several of the gang. He is with Malloy at the cabin with Jed Stone and helps Madden dig a grave for Bambridge.

Blade, Jess: In *Tappan's Burro,* a prospector who joins up with Tappan in the mountains after he has returned to the desert after being hoodwinked and robbed by a woman. Blade is a rugged, bearded giant, wide-eyed, with a pleasant face. He arrives with no gear, not even a gun. He meets up with Tappan after he has been robbed by a outlaws, but, being wanted by the law himself, he is in no hurry to get back to the civilized world. Tappan offers to share his grub with him. He has not much left, but the hunting is good in the area. Blade fills Tappan in on Madge and Jake Beam, the woman and her husband who had robbed him. It seems they had played a similar trick on many others before. When the two get snowed in, Blade wants to kill Tappan's burro, Jenet, for food. He thinks Tappan has gone mad in his feelings of love for the burro. When Blade tries to shoot Jenet, Tappan shoots him. The same story is told in "The Secret of Quaking Asp Cabin," but this time, Tappan is reputed to have killed Blade by cracking open his skull.

Blaine: In *Nevada*, Ben Ide and Ina Blaine's first son. He is four years old when the story begins.

Blaine, Archie: In *Forlorn River*, the eldest son of Hart Blaine. He is impressed with his destiny as the eldest son of a cattle king.

Blaine, Bob: In *Forlorn River*, one of Hart Blaine's sons. Like Fred, he has become more interested in white-collar city jobs and pursuing city girls. When Ina first arrives back from school in Denver, she rarely sees Bob and Fred because they rise early and eat with the cowhands.

Blaine, Dall: In *Forlorn River*, Ina Blaine's twelve-year-old sister, the youngest of the three daughters and the second-youngest of the seven children. She is a gawky girl, genuinely pleased to have her older sister back home again.

Blaine, Fred: In *Forlorn River*, one of Hart Blaine's sons. He used to be sweet on Hettie Ide, but with their new-found prosperity, he has moved away from farm work to work in the city and is now only interested in city girls. The Tule Lake Ranch loses him to the city. When Ina first arrives back from school in Denver, she rarely sees Bob and Fred because they rise early and eat with the cowhands.

Blaine, Hart: In *Forlorn River*, the father of Ina Blaine. He owns most of the lowland near Tule Lake. He puts up a bounty of $3000 for California Red, a beautiful wild mustang, a gift for his daughter, Ina. Despite his rise in fortune in the ranching world, he will not give up his humble abode, which pleases his daughter, Ina, and his wife. He tells Ina that cattle have been disappearing in the area where Ben Ides lives with Nevada and Modoc, both of these reputed to have been horse thieves. He finds that his daughter has returned from school in Denver with some strange ideas. She is rather blunt with Less Setter, Blaine's principal business partner. He tries to match his daughter up with Sewell McAdam, the son of another of his business partners. It turns out he owes McAdam some thirty thousand dollars on a land deal, and had hoped that Ina's marriage to the son would sweeten the deal. With a rise in fortune comes a rise in influence. Hart Blaine is an important man on the town council. Hence, the value McAdam and Setter place in him. He moves the family up to Wild Goose Lake for the summer, hoping to fix up the old cabin on the ranch. Blaine provides the money for Setter's deals. He doubts the stories Setter spreads about Ben Ide and rustling, and especially he doubts the story Setter tells about his encounter with Ben. Blaine admires the gumption of his hired hand, Bill Sneed, who confronts Less Setter openly, calling him a liar. Sneed tells what really happened, how Setter had provoked a fight and Ben had beaten him squarely, single-handedly. Blaine asks Sneed to stay on, but he refuses. He wants to maintain his independence. Blaine says he is surprised that Sneed did not draw on Setter. Eventually, Blaine's unspoken suspicions of his business partner come out when Ben Ide is arrested and Nevada returns with Bill Hall and Sheriff Strobel. Hall identifies Setter as the head of the rustler outfit. He now believes Ina's claim that Setter was out to ruin not only Ben Ide, but the Blaines and the other ranchers in the area as well. Hart Blaine is willing to accept that he was wrong about Ben Ide and gladly welcomes him as a son-in-law.

Blaine, Ina: Appears in two novels, *Forlorn River* and its sequel, *Nevada*. In *Forlorn River*, Ina Blaine is the second daughter of Hart Blaine, and the principal female character in the novel. She is the third child in a family of four boys and three girls. Her older sister is Kate, and the younger one is Dall. At the age of nineteen she returns to her parents' farm in California near Tule Lake with Mount Shasta in sight. After spending four years away at college, the sound of the geese flying overhead and the sight of the mountains are welcome. She spent the years with the family of her father's brother, who lives in Lawrence, Kansas. Due to the ill health of some members of this family, Ina remained with them without visits home. She has seen Saint Louis, Kansas City, Denver and San Francisco. City life for her has been confining, and she is glad to be back at the ranch. She thinks she might become a schoolteacher in Hammell, a plan which pleases neither her father nor her mother. Her family's situation has changed in her absence. Tule Lake has been drained and her father has made a fortune for himself with the new land. He is a millionaire, a prominent man in the area, a member of the municipal council, a man to be reckoned with. Being his daughter and of marrying age, she is a prize catch, the "Tule Lake Peach" as Nevada says they call her in town. Ina enjoys milking cows, helping out with the work on the ranch, but her mother does not want her doing that kind of work, now that they are prosperous. She had to do that when she was young but does not want that life for her daughter. Ina, however, sees nothing wrong with that kind of work. It is down to earth, close to the essentials of living. Gossip in Hammell has it that she is hitched to young McAdam, as the waitress in Hammell informs Ben on one of his rare visits to town. Ina still likes Ben Ide, now a man of twenty-four with a ranch of his own on Forlorn River, and Hettie, Ben's sister, worries about the effect local gossip will have on her. His pursuit of wild mustangs is said to be a front for cattle rustling. But when Ina meets Ben on the streets of Hammell, none of this has any effect on her. He is still the same boy who played with her as a child and who tried to kiss her once under the cottonwoods.

Hart Blaine, her father, thinks she has acquired some strange ideas at school. He thinks this because she is not interested in young Sewell McAdam, the son of a business partner. Hart Blaine had hoped that a match between the two would help his business dealings along. Ina, however, finds Sewell a shallow social climber, an insincere young man interested only in her financial prospects and his own career advancement. She rejects his attentions, but Sewell is pretty thick and interprets her rejections and refusals as playing hard to get. Her sister, Kate, suggests that this is just because she's still in love with Ben Ide, a comment she knows will raise their father's hackles. Unlike the other members of her own family, as well as Ben's, Ina understands Ben's pride and his bitterness at having been rejected by his father. He is aware of the gossip that has been spread about him, but he is not willing to give up the life he has chosen as a wild mustang hunter.

Ina is suspicious of Less Setter from the start, and wonders about the hold he seems to have on her father. Through Marvie, her youngest brother, Ina is kept informed about Ben Ide's activities. Marvie also reports to her about things he has overheard. Less Setter is encouraging their father to move against Ben Ide, to buy out his ranch and the neighboring ranches in Forlorn Valley. Ina shares her suspicions with Sheriff Charlie Strobel. She confesses that she dreams of Ben Ide coming to rescue her like a knight in shining armor. Ina accompanies Marvie to Ben's ranch where she meets Nevada, Ben's close friend and partner. She tells Nevada that Ben's sister, Hellie, is sweet on him and he should make his move. She also tells Nevada to make sure Ben collects the reward her father has posted for the man who catches California Red for her. When Judd and Walker arrive with Less Setter, claiming they have come to arrest Ben Ide for rustling, Ina's faith in him is shaken. Ben's confession that he is "guilty as hell" leads her to lose faith in him completely. She does not understand, however, that Ben is referring to his decision to set free the rustlers who had helped him capture California Red, not to a career in stealing cattle.

When the truth finally comes out, she feels she no longer deserves Ben's love because of her loss of faith. Ben, however, forgives her easily and holds her to her promise to marry him. They wed and move to his ranch at Forlorn River. Ben is fully accepted by both his own father, Amos Ide, and her father, Hart Blaine.

In *Nevada*, she is happy with her husband, her son, Blaine, and their ranch. She goes to San Francisco with Ben to bring his mother to consult with a specialist. The doctor recommends a change of climate for her — Arizona, for example. When Ben suggests they sell the Tule Lake ranch he inherited from his father and move to Arizona, Ina's pioneering spirit is awakened and she looks forward to the covered wagon trip to their new home. Her family, however, thinks she is mad. Her sister, Kate, comments that she'll never find decent clothes in Arizona, and her father even offers to let her move back home. Only Marvie is enthusiastic about the move and asks to go with them. Above all, Ina knows that Ben misses his friend, Nevada, and that he wants to go to Arizona hoping to find him and resume their partnership.

Blaine, Kate: In *Forlorn River,* Ina Blaine's older sister. She is twenty-two years old, and engaged to a Klamath lawyer. She is spare, resembling her mother. Ina senses that she is not delighted to have Ina back home. There is something about the way Kate watches her constantly that upsets her. She imagines that Kate is jealous of her city education and clothes. Her beau is one of Sewell McAdam's friends from Klamath. To make trouble for Ina, Kate tells their father that Ina is still in love with Ben Ide and not interested in Sewell. She has become a snob, indifferent to the fact that her beau is only interested in her prospects, rather than her. Ina, unlike Kate, knows that a man like Sewell is only interested in a woman for her prospects and advancement of his own career.

Blaine, Marvie: In *Forlorn River,* a handsome lad of fourteen, tow-headed, wild about horses and fishing. He and Ben Ide and Bill Sneed have always been close. When developments at the Blaine ranch are becoming tense, he asks Ben Ide to let him live with him. He is also the sibling closest to Ina Blaine. He goes fishing with Ina and with Ben Ide. Blaine tells Ina about Less Setter, the horse dealer. He overhears Setter and Hart Blaine, his father, plotting to take Ben Ide's ranch and water source. He reports to Ina what he saw of the fight between Ben and Less Setter. He also tells Ina that Less Setter is after her. Marvie is pleased that Ina has sent young Sewell McAdam packing, as he hopes that Ina and Ben will get together. Marvie Blaine testifies that the so-called evidence of rustling that has been found in the barn on Ben Ide's ranch must have been planted because when he stayed in the loft, there was nothing there, and Ben has not been back to the ranch since then. Marvie is delighted that Ben and Ina marry.

In *Nevada*, Marvie is the only one of Ina's siblings who is happy about her decision to move to Arizona. He is the only Blaine, according to Ina, who has not become a snob as a result of their wealth. For the trip to Arizona, Marvie gets himself an outfit similar to what Nevada used to wear. Ben feels he will have quite a job to keep Marvie from "going wild" at the new ranch. Marvie meets Rose Hatt at the dance in Winthrop and falls in love with her. He had already met her in the woods but was not sure she would show up at the dance. He meets her again secretly in the woods. Ben and Marvie get into a fight over his pursuit of Rose. Like Rose herself, Ben fears for Marvie's safety. Together with Hettie, he visits with Rose and they learn much about the Hatt home and the Pine Tree group. At the last meeting, when he proposes to Rose, they are caught together by Cedar Hatt, Rose's oldest brother. In the fight which ensues, Marvie kills Cedar. Jim Lacy, who has been following them, intervenes to help. Marvie recognizes him as the Nevada he knew in California. Marvie tells Ben Ide that Dillon has been at the Hatt place pursuing Rose, but Ben refuses to take his word. Ben has to eat crow, admitting that Marvie had been right about Rose and Dillon. He apologizes and makes amends and the two are friends again.

In both novels, Marvie Blaine is an example of the inexperienced boy who becomes a man under the guidance of an older brother or friend, a common character type in Grey's novels.

Blaine, Mrs. Hart: In *Forlorn River,* Ina's mother, wife of Hart. She had been a milkmaid on a farm in Kansas where Hart Blaine was a cowhand. They married and took up ranching in California. Now that prosperity has come their way, she doesn't want her daughter working in a barn as she did as a young woman. Ina sees that she is confused by her role as a wealthy rancher's wife, unsure of what is expected of her. She tells Ina about the rift between the Ides and the Blaines. The Ides, who have also become wealthy with land deals and cattle, now consider them stuck up. Mrs. Ide resents the preacher's pointed references to Ben Ide in his sermon on the "prodigal son." She laments that her husband has been changed by money, how he seems to let himself be led by the nose by Setter and McAdam, his business partners. She does not like young Sewell McAdam, disapproves of the proposed match, and tells Ina she is glad that she rejected his advances. Like many wives in Grey novels, Mrs. Blaine has more humanity and common sense than her husband.

Blaine, Pete: In *Valley of Wild Horses,* one of the ropers working on the first roundup in which young Pan Handle Smith takes part.

Blair: (1) In *Arizona Ames,* an old cattleman who is at the Grieve ranch when Arizona Ames gives Crow Grieve his comeuppance. He predicts Crow Grieve's days are numbered as a rancher.

(2) In *The Mysterious Rider,* a rancher in Gunnison. Bent Wade and Sheriff Burley were involved in a fight which took place on his ranch some ten years previous.

(3) Also in *The Mysterious Rider,* lives in a cabin at Trapper's Lake. Bent Wade stops by his cabin on his way to Bellounds' ranch. Blair says that his wife is ailing and asks Wade for tobacco, which he gives him. Blair gives Wade information about Bellounds, describing him as a very generous man, kind, helpful. He heard that his wife had died some years before but that maybe he has remarried. He also says that Belllounds is getting on in years. Wade may be

just the man the rancher needs to control the coyotes and wildcats. He appears only this one time in the novel.

(4) In *Thunder Mountain,* the father of Sydney and a walking target for gamblers and shady dealers because of his lack of common sense and his weakness for drink and cards. Lee Emerson meets him in Salmon, where he is being targeted by Pritchard and Borden. He accepts Lee Emerson's offer to go to Thunder Mountain and dig for gold. He gets a claim, and does make some money. He soon loses it gambling. Blair hopes that Sydney and Lee will marry. He does not approve of her infatuation with Leavitt, but he has little influence over her. He encourages Lee to pursue her and win her. At first, he remains sober. He reports to Lee on developments in the camp. He encourages him to keep a low profile and slowly work on proving his claim. He is convinced that Lee is honest and truthful. Blair, however, is a weak man. His cabin is the most pretentious in the town. He loses what gold he does dig at gambling, and is robbed of his money one night. Eventually, the truth of Leavitt's deception is made clear. After the landslide, Blair and Sydney leave Thunder Mountain with a train of freighters, poorer and not much wiser than when they arrived. They are examples of individuals who fail to meet the challenge of the West to become better people.

Blair, Betty: In *Wanderer of the Wasteland,* the four-year-old daughter of Mrs. Blair. She looks like her older brother, Eugene.

Blair, Eugene: In *Wanderer of the Wasteland,* the son of Mrs. Blair. He first meets Adam and Genie where they are camped not far from their house. He brings them eggs and milk. Gene is twenty years old. When he was sixteen, his father got the gold fever. They left their home in Indiana and headed west. The father pursued his desire to search for gold, but Eugene and his mother are convinced cattle ranching and raising horses offer a more secure future than prospecting. Gene is saving money to buy more land to go into real ranching. Gene is taken with Genie and is quite pleased that his mother has invited her to stay with them. In *Stairs of Sand,* Ruth recalls Gene Blair who married her friend, Genie Linwood, the young rancher who thought her a penniless waif when she was rich.

Blair, Hal: In *Wanderer of the Wasteland,* the five-year-old brother of Eugene and Tommy and Betty. He was a baby when the family came west and was weakened by the hard trip. He is starting to improve. Adam describes him as a "large, red-haired, freckled imp."

Blair, Mrs.: In *Wanderer of the Wasteland,* lives at Santa Ysabel in California. Adam Larey and Genie Linwood camp near their home. Mrs. Blair welcomes Adam and Genie to their home. She tells Adam about Ruth Hunt, the granddaughter of a couple who live on a nearby farm. She offers to take Genie there to see if Ruth's old dresses fit her. She gets a bundle of them for Ruth. She tells Adam that she is willing to take Genie in if she wants to stay with them. Mrs. Blair sees a daughter in her.

Blair, Sydney: In *Thunder Mountain*, the daughter of Mr. Blair. She tells Lee Emerson that she is nineteen years old. The family is from Ohio. They came west when her father decided to sell his business. She is an only child and her mother is dead. Something happened back in Ohio to make her never want to return. She never does reveal what this unpleasant episode was. She worries about her father. He has responded strangely to Western influences. He drinks, gambles, makes friends with everyone he meets and leaves her alone at night worrying about him. Lee rescues her when Cliff Borden tries to force his way into her room and she beats him off. She gladly accepts his help. With her father, she accompanies Lee Emerson back to Thunder Mountain. There, she falls under the influence of Cliff Leavitt. He is a smooth talker, cultured, debonair, and women fall for him. She cannot believe anything evil about him, despite the abundant evidence to the contrary. She does not even see that he has been cheating her father and robbing him. She accepts his proposal of marriage. Lee and Nugget finally convince her of Leavitt's duplicity and when Leavitt's vigilance committee has brought Lee to court, accusing him of attacking and robbing them, Sydney gives evidence on Lee's behalf, asserting that Lee was with her at the time these men claim to have been attacked. When the landslide wipes out much of the town, she and her father leave with freighters. Sydney Blair has elements which lead one to believe Grey has destined her to be the heroine of the novel. She has the spunk, the independence and courage of a heroine. However, unlike Betty Zane or Madeline Hammond or Carley Burch, she fails to learn from experience and take charge of her own destiny. She leaves Thunder Mountain somewhat wiser but no more mature than when she arrived.

Blair, Tommy: In *Wanderer of the Wasteland*, a three-year-old son of Mrs. Blair and brother to Eugene. He's a "ragged, chubby, tousle-headed little rascal."

Blaisdal: In *The Lost Wagon Train*, leads a wagon train from Texas, stopping at Cimarron Crossing. Jeff Stover tells Anderson that this train contains sixty wagons and that they plan to take the Dry Trail west. Anderson questions the accuracy of Jeff Stover's facts, and when Blaisdal does not show up on the scheduled day, Anderson wants to turn back.

Blaisdell, Jim: In *To the Last Man*, one of the neighbors and relatives of Lee Jorth. Blaisdell strikes Jean Isbel as being a lion-like type of Texan, in his broad, bold face, his huge head with its upstanding tawny hair like a mane and his speech and force that betoken the nature of his heart. He has a rolling voice with the drawling intonation of a Texan, and blue eyes still holding the fire of youth. Blaisdell casts an appraising glance over Jean and concludes that

he, like his sister Ann, resembles their mother. He also concludes that any man up against him would have met his match. Blaisdell brings Jean up to date on the quarrel in the valley. He accuses the sheepmen of provoking a fight because rather than keep their flocks on the higher ranges, they insist on bringing them down into the valley where the cattlemen run their herds. As well, he suspects some of the sheepmen are using their flocks to hide their true work, cattle rustling. He tells Jean what he knows about Greaves, and Jorth, the apparent leader of the sheepmen. He suspects that Gaston Isbel and Lee Jorth knew each other in Texas. He witnessed a meeting of the two in Greaves's store. Gaston Isbel looks as if he were about to draw on Jorth, but Jorth did not go for a gun. The hatred between the two could not be missed. There is more there than he knows about. Blaisdell is slightly injured when the Jorths attack the Isbel ranch, and he joins the attack on the Jorths in Greaves store. Somers kills him in the pursuit of the remnants of the Jorth faction.

Blaise, Sam: In *The Lost Wagon Train*, lout that cannot be trusted. He comes under the influence of Leighton, and Latch concludes that he cannot be left behind at Ft. Union. He speaks to him, finding that like many other frontier outcasts, he is dull, negative, indifferent, living from hand to mouth. He tells Latch he was raised around horses and cows, that he is a good farmer and a grafter of fruit trees. As well, he is a fair carpenter, blacksmith and a good cook and not bad as a doctor, either. Leighton points to his gun with the six notches, but Blaise confesses that he stole the gun. He did not earn the notches. Latch offers Blaise a job with his crew.

Blaize, Mamie: In *Under the Tonto Rim*, an old schoolmate of Clara Watson's. She writes her sister Lucy, telling her she stayed with Mamie when their father refused to take her back after her elopement with Jim Middleton.

Blake: (1) In *Forlorn River,* owns the last ranch on the north side of Goose Lake. He is poor and holding on to his ranch by the skin of his teeth. He is afraid of Hart Blaine.

(2) In *The Hash Knife Outfit*, a hotel man from Winslow. He takes part in the big poker game at Snell's on Christmas Day where Curly Prentiss exposes Ed Darnell as a cheat at cards.

(3) In *Riders of the Purple Sage*, one of Jane Withersteen's Mormon riders. Blake is a close friend of Judkins and informs him that the church elders have called in Jane's riders. He hints to Judkins that he and Dorn have been urged to quit working for Jane out of a higher duty. He tells about the vigilance group called "The Riders" that is being organized to pursue the rustlers. Blake later returns to work for Jane. He tells her that he heeded the order from Tull out of fear for his family. His mother, whom Jane had nursed through sickness, had been threatened by masked men. When the mother dies, he returns to work for Jane. In fact, his mother had insisted that

he do so. Blake reports that the white herd is gone and her many horses as well. He also speaks to Lassiter openly to assure him that he is not a spy sent to assassinate him on the sly. Blake is killed when Jerry Card and Horne break into the stables and take Jane's valuable thoroughbreds.

(4) In *Under the Tonto Rim*, the storekeeper in Winbrook to whom Edd Denmeade sells his honey.

(5) In *The U. P. Trail*, sent with Coffee and Somers from Omaha by Baxter to help Neale solve the problem with the construction of a bridge. Coffee, it turns out, is in cahoots with Allison Lee. He and Coffee had not followed the plans, causing the supports for the bridge to fall. When his role in delaying construction of the bridge becomes clear, he is fired by Neale without pay for past work.

Blake, Bill: In *Valley of Wild Horses*, brother to Jim Blake, uncle to Lucy. When Jard Hardman and Dick Hardman try to force Lucy to marry young Dick, she leaves her father's place and goes to live with her Uncle Bill, a fine, honest man. He was shot in the Yellow Mine saloon and gambling establishment, supposedly by accident. Bill Smith and others doubt that was the case and see Hardman's hand behind it.

Blake, Jerry: In *The Dude Ranger*, reports to the cowboys at Red Rock Ranch that Ernest Selby had beaten up Dude Hyslip at the party when he was drunk.

Blake, Jim: (1) In *Twin Sombreros*, a cattleman Brazos Keene meets one morning in Mexican Joe's restaurant having breakfast. Brazos and he talk about the rustling and speculate about who might be behind it. Blake is reticent to say what he suspects, but Brazos speaks his mind. Blake says he has a note to pay at the bank and the rustling is making that difficult. Brazos comments that it seems that the rustlers are rustling from each other, given what he knows about the connections between rustlers and ranchers. He suggests that Blake go to Henderson, the banker and rancher, and use his name as collateral for renewal of the note.

(2) In *Valley of Wild Horses*, Lucy Blake's father. Jim Blake was one of the latest incoming settlers in Littleton. He chose a place down in a deep swale that Pan always crossed when going to visit his uncle. Jim was a young man, pleasant and jolly, a farmer and would-be rancher with no signs of the cowboy about him. Jim Blake and Bill Smith are called in by the teacher, Amanda Hill, to separate Dick Hardman and Pan Handle in the fight, which leaves Dick unconscious and Pan stabbed in the shoulder. When Pan Handle returns after five years riding the range, he learns that Jim Blake and his family have moved to New Mexico. They had not made a success of farming. He also learns that Blake had been Hardman's foreman and had gone west to scout out ranching prospects. In Marco, Jim Blake is in jail. He has been arrested for cattle rustling, a charge that Mr. Smith says is undoubtedly true. Blake had gone

from bad to worse. Hardman, father and son, have had him arrested to pressure him into getting Lucy to marry Dick. Lucy refuses to marry unless they give her papers clearing her father of any crime. When Pan Handle speaks to Lucy, he convinces her to break her engagement to Dick. Pan Handle then arranges to break Jim out of jail. He tells him to sober up and to look them up in Siccane, Arizona, where he has got his life in order. Jim Blake, however, does not leave town. When Pan Handle returns from wrangling the mustangs to earn money to finance the move to Arizona, Jim Blake has been arrested and put in jail again, and this time, has taken money from Dick Hardman to convince Lucy to marry him. Pan Handle finds him drinking in the saloon and once again tells him to sober up and get out of Marco. He leaves, perhaps to join his daughter and the Smiths in Arizona at some future time.

Blake, Lucy: In *Valley of Wild Horses*, the daughter of Jim Blake, and childhood sweetheart of Pan Handle Smith. He was with her mother when she was born. The two of them were best friends throughout childhood. Lucy always resented that cowboy life seemed to draw Pan Handle as much as she did. Still, she calls on him to defend her when Dick Hardman forces her to kiss him. This leads to the monumental fight at the school where Dick is left unconscious and Pan Handle is stabbed with the teacher's paper knife.

Pan Handle meets Lucy again in Marco. She has grown into a strikingly beautiful young woman. She is living with Pan's family. Her father is in jail, arrested on a warrant from Texas for stealing cattle. Dick Hardman is pressing her to marry him to secure her father's release from jail. She is holding out for papers that clear her father of any crime. Pan Handle's reappearance on the scene reminds her of her love for him. She breaks her engagement to Dick Hardman and Pan Handle arranges to break her father out of jail. But Jim Blake is as feckless as ever. He is caught again by Marshall Matthews, Hardman's puppet, and put in jail again. This time, Dick Hardman pays Jim Blake to ensure his cooperation in forcing Lucy to comply. When Pan Handle returns from the horse wrangling expedition, he finds Hardman and Lucy at the stage depot, married and about to leave on their honeymoon. In fear for his life, Hardman flees to the Yellow Mine saloon where he hides in Louise Merrill's closet. Pan and Blinky Moran come to come to get her away from the place. In a drunken stupor, she takes a knife and stabs Dick to death. This frees Lucy to marry Pan Handle. On the trip to Arizona, they are married by a preacher in Green River.

Blake, Mrs. Jim: In *Valley of Wild Horses*, mentioned once only, when Pan Handle helps her when Lucy is born. A bad storm had arisen and Jim Blake and Bill Smith were not able to get back to the farm in time. Pan Handle has just returned from his uncle George's place and he helps her with the delivery in the barn.

Blake, Sam: In *The Maverick Queen*, a rancher in the south of the Sweetwater Valley when the cowboy walkout does not affect. The young cowboy, Tom, is working for him to pay off a debt. He still has three months to go. Lincoln Bradway offers to give him the money to clear the debt so that he can come work for him with his partner Slim Morris.

Blakely: In *Captives of the Desert*, an unspecified number of Blakely sisters from Phoenix provide the rot-gut liquor to Wilbur Newton, Hanley and the Mormon horse wrangler, Tim Wake. They then sell the rot-gut to the Indians on the sly. The Blakely girls appear at the snake dance ceremony at the start of the novel.

Blakener: In *The Deer Stalker*, a ranger working with Thad Eburne. He entered the ranger service when his wife died, and he hopes to continue until he has earned a pension. Unlike Thad, he regards the work with less zeal, taking it as a job rather than a vocation. He, too, loves the forest and the deer, but is resigned to the way things work. He reports to Thad what he has heard about proposals to deal with the deer overpopulation — traps, hunting. He urges Thad to push McKay's proposal to try to drive the surplus deer down the canyon, across the Colorado, to new range where grass and water abound. He gives what support he can to the proposal and rides with Eburne and McKay when the drive is on.

Blakesley: In *Wildfire*, the rider who first notices that the boat to cross the Colorado has gone missing. He assumes it has been washed away with the sudden rise in the river level.

Blanchard, Colonel Eb: In *The Trail Driver*, a cattleman and lifelong friend to Adam Brite. He recommends Texas Joe Shipman as foreman of his next trail drive. He fetches him around, introduces him to the young man and leaves the two of them to iron out the details.

Blanco (a.k.a. Wade Holden, Tex Brandon): In *Shadow on the Trail,* the name that Aulsbrook gives to Wade Holden when he wanders into his camp to inform him that Catlin's rustler outfit is planning to run off his herd. He does not give them his name, but when Aulsbrook starts calling him Blanco, the name sticks for a while.

Blanco Sol: In *Desert Gold*, Dick Gale's horse, given to him by Tom Belding. The horse is one of Belding's prized string bred from Mexican stock. Dick Gale comes to love the horse like a true friend. Only Dick can catch the animal. Some debate exists as to which is the faster steed, Blanco Sol or Diablo. In a desperate race which is to be found in many Grey novels, Blanco Sol proves to be the faster.

Bland: In *The Lone Star Ranger*, the leader of his own gang of rustlers. They steal cattle from the wealthy ranchers in the area, keep them sequestered in hidden canyons, and take them by boat down the Rio Grande River to boats in the gulf from where they are taken for sale in Cuba. Stevens has told Buck about Bland, about his weakness for women, about the fights that break out in his camp over females. He warns Buck Duane that since he is such a good-looking man, he will be a cause of trouble. When Bland meets Duane, he knows he is telling the truth. Buck sees that he is a man who can judge character, and who wields the power here. Bland seems troubled by the stories he has heard about how swift Buck is with the gun. He advises him to avoid four-flushers like Bosomer (nicknamed "Bo"), and he also advises him to be moving on if he does not want to join his outfit. Euchre fills in the picture somewhat. No one knows for sure where he is from, and many stories abound, but few facts. When he started out, he was soft-spoken and gentle in his mannerisms. Many thought he had once been a Southern gentleman. He also was fair at doctoring people and excellent with tools. He has over a hundred men in his gang. Over the years, he has become as hard as flint and violent of temper, through his association with such rough men. He has also become insanely jealous. Both Kate and Euchre tell how he killed Spence for looking at Jennie and Kate. Still, he is well-heeled, spends money freely and gambles. One day, he comes home early with Chess Alloway and almost catches Buck with Kate, whom he has been with while he plans how to take Jennie away. Bland becomes suspicious and tries to strangle Kate out of jealousy, only to stop when Jennie confirms her story that Buck has been coming to see her. Bland then asks Buck to leave as he is causing trouble with his men, having just had a set-to with Bill Black, who had tried to shoot a Mexican peon for the fun of it. Although Bland approved of how Buck handled the matter and prevented a senseless killing, he doesn't like what trouble might be stirred up if he stays. That night, Bland turns on Kate again, and later on Jennie. Buck Duane comes to the rescue, and shoots Bland. The killing of Bland establishes Buck Duane's reputation in the outlaw community and in all of West Texas.

Bland, Kate: In *The Lone Star Ranger*, the outlaw Bland's wife of more than ten years. She is described as a strong, full-bodied, full-blown, bold, attractive woman from Brownsville. She tells Buck she was from a good family. She married Bland at eighteen and only later did she learn that he was an outlaw. He took her with him to live among outlaws. Bland shot the cousin who informed her of his profession. Buck sees two sides to the woman, one kind, one ruthless. She is smiling, seductive, coquettish, youthful, discontent, and capable of kindness. She enjoys Euchre's visits, calling him a harmless old fool. She goes over to Deger's to help nurse Kid Fuller, who was shot in a card game. She has taken in the young girl Jennie, and kept her from the randy outlaws in the camp. Kate herself suspects that Bland is sweet on Jennie and out of jealousy has beaten her on occasion. Kate tries to seduce Buck, and Euchre advises him that this is the best way to keep from arousing her suspicious about their plans to escape, taking Jennie with them. The whole town knows about Kate and Buck Duane. When the moment of crisis comes, and Kate learns that Buck is not in love with her but with Jennie, she tries to shoot him. Buck discovers that she is as strong as a tiger. He throws her against the wall and she passes out. Later, Buck learns that Kate was killed in the struggle, and that he has been blamed for her death. The cause of her death is never established.

Blanding, Hurd: In *Horse Heaven Hill*, the manager of the Wade ranch. He recently arrived from Wyoming and struck up a friendship with young Ellery Wade. The two of them originate a plan to capture and sell wild horses for chicken feed. In his late twenties, Blanding is older than the average cowboy. He has strikingly handsome features and a masterful way about him with women. When he rides into the Wade camp, Lark comments on the stunning figure he cuts on a horse, a description reminiscent of Molly Wood's first glimpse of the Virginian from the overturned stage. All the girls in town are crazy about him, and Marigold Wade, herself engaged to Stanley Weston, who is no slouch in the looks department, is infatuated with him, unafraid to flirt openly with him in the saloon. Blanding spreads gossip that his involvement with her has gone beyond mere flirting, an insinuation that earns him a beating from Stanley Weston for impugning the reputation of a woman. Coil Bruce tells Lark that Blanding lords it over the other cowboys in the women department. His vanity and confidence know no limits. When Lark goes to the Wade barn to get a horse to go riding, Blanding tries out his charm on her. She is both attracted and repelled by his slickness which carries over into his business dealings. He and Ellery Wade, with the help of Chespelem Indians and other hard-riding cowboys, round up and sell three thousand head of mustangs. Blanding gets three dollars a head for them, netting nine thousand dollars. The Indians get a dollar a head to divide among themselves, Ellery Wade gets a thousand, and the cowboys another thousand to divide among themselves, leaving Blanding with four thousand. When Ellery learns that he has been double-crossed in the deal by Blanding, he breaks with him, only to return at a later point when he needs the money. Blanding gathers a crew including Stanley Weston's foreman, Howard, to round up a further bunch of horses. He captures them in a trap in a blind canyon. Many of the horses are injured trying to climb out of the trap. Blanding refuses to shoot the injured horses, leaving them to suffer painful deaths. His cruelty and indifference shock Stanley Weston and Lark Burrell. Lark Burrell and Stanley Weston free the horses. Blanding arrives at the Wade camp to accuse Weston of releasing the horses and to demand compensation of thousands of dollars for the freed animals. When he attempts to draw on Stanley on the sly, Lark Burrell shoots him in the arm with a rifle.

Blandy: In *The Lone Star Ranger,* the man who runs the Hope So gambling house for Longstreth (Cheseldine). The Hope So used to belong to Laramie.

Blandy, Lo: In *The Vanishing American,* the name by which the Navajo, Nophaie, is known while living in the eastern United States. He abandons the name when he returns to live on the Navajo reservation. Marian Warner continues to refer to him on occasion with the name by which she first knew him. Nophaie rejects this name as a reminder of the white world he wishes to put behind him.

Blaze: In *The Light of Western Stars*, one of the cowboys who come with Al to fetch his sister at Florence Kingsley's place. He, too, criticizes Gene's ungentlemanly treatment of Madeline at the train station.

Blazes: In *Code of the West,* Cal's pinto. He has taken a liking to the wild little bronco because Georgie Stockwell always preferred Blazes to any other of the Thurman stock. Since word of Georgie's preference for this pinto has spread, Cal gets many offers to buy the horse, something which would never have happened before. Cal gives Blazes to Georgie as a gift.

Blicky: In *The Border Legion,* a member of the outlaw gang, the Border Legion. He is a lean, bronzed young man, probably still in his teens. Joan marvels at the grace and strength with which he swings his leg over the saddle and dismounts. He reports on the big strike at Bear Mountain (Alder Creek). He speculates about the many pack trains of gold there will be for robbing. Blicky is one of the outlaws who robs the stagecoach and shares in the gold divided up at the cabin in Cabin Gulch.

Bligh: (1) In *Arizona Ames,* owns the ranch which Halstead buys. During Bligh's tenure, a devastating fire destroyed his ranching operations.

(2) In *Wilderness Trek,* one of Stanley Dann's drovers. He stays with the trek until Eric confesses that he lied about knowing the way to the Kimberleys'. He and three fellow drovers, Hood, Heald and Derrick, decide to quit the group and continue on their own. Stanley Dann gives them two of Ormiston's wagons, supplies for the trip and a string of horses. Bligh and Benson are the first to enter Eric Dann's tent after he shoots himself in the head. They help with the burial and the watches that night. The day after they leave, the aborigines attack again.

Bligh, Tom: In *Western Union,* a Texas cattleman associated with Jeff Sunderland in the big wagon train with a herd of four thousand cattle they are driving to Wyoming. The cattle could pose problems for the telegraph line as the cattle rub against the poles and can knock them down if the herd is sufficiently large.

Bligh, Uncle Nick: In *Wyoming,* Martha Dixon's uncle. For thirty years he has remained out of touch with his family. He failed to make his fortune and never troubled himself to write. But with age, poor health, and a realization of false pride that motivated his silence, he writes for news of the family. His niece, Martha, decides she will go west to visit the mysterious uncle.

Nick Bligh has a ranch in Randall, Wyoming, but moves his herd to Split Rock, farther south, looking for better range. This move is a big gamble. Bligh is respected in Randall and in Split Rock. He has a pleasing personality and a sense of fairness and decency in his dealings with people. Bligh, however, is not much of a businessman. Jim Fenner comments that this latest gamble will make or break him. He is too old to start over somewhere else if this venture fails. Bligh takes over the homestead of one Boseman, and he runs his herd with McCall, thereby sparing himself the need to hire a crew of cowboys. Bligh expects an equal share of McCall's stock, but McCall reneges on the deal, claiming Bligh is only to get a share of his own herd that McCall will raise and market. McCall also claims to hold a lien on the Boseman place. In these troubling times, Uncle Nick takes Andy Bonning on as a hired man for room and board. He is willing to take a risk on him as he had done for Jim Fenner, his foreman from Arizona. The arrival of the niece proves to be a surprise as great as the arrival of Andrew Bonning.

Bonning, however, proves to be a welcome addition. He takes Bligh's interests to heart. At the right time, he reveals the plot against Bligh that he overheard between McCall and Texas Haynes. McCall agrees to release Bligh from the deal. Bonning decides to invest the money he inherited from his mother in stock for the ranch. He and Bligh become partners. Bligh has finally found some good luck.

Blight, Sergeant: In *The Fugitive Trail*, a Texas Ranger sent by Captain Maggard to the Melrose Brazos ranch in pursuit of Bruce Lockheart. Trinity met him at Waco several months before and he made up to her. Blight and his men split with Maggard at Mendle. Blight trailed a horse along the foothills just on a chance while Maggard went on to Dodge with three men. Blight has never met Lockheart and could not recognize him. Trinity had first thought of asking Bruce to leave or to stay away, but now is convinced Blight will not know Bruce. She introduces Bruce as her fiancé, Lee Jones from Texas. Blight at first is interested only in pursuing the gunman, while Melrose and his cowboys under Tex Serd tell him he should be after the rustlers that are plaguing the area. When Captain Maggard shows up, he does join up with Melrose's cowboys pursuing Stewart's rustler gang. Blight is killed in the fighting at the cabin where Stewart's men are holding out.

Blinn, Cal: In *Wildfire*, a rider from Durango who periodically comes to Bostril's Ford. He enters the horse "Hosshoes" in the annual race. He is a rival of Bostril's and looking forward to the day when Bostril is taken down a peg with a loss at the race.

Block, Bill: In *The Lone Star Ranger,* described as a typical Texas desperado, stoop-shouldered, bowlegged, wiry, all muscle. He has a square head with a black scrubby beard and roving cruel eyes. He will gamble on anything, on where a bird will alight, whether or not it will move or fly off. He bets he can shoot a bucket out of the peon's hands at fifty yards, but he is really aiming to shoot the Mexican. Buck Duane sees what he is up to and stops him. He walks off alone, and says nothing. Bland warns Buck that Block will not likely let things lie.

Blodgett: In *The Drift Fence,* mentioned by Caleb See in his explanation of the drift fence to Molly Dunn. Blodgett is one of the larger ranchers out near the Diamond who will benefit from the building of such a fence. In *The Hash Knife Outfit,* Blodgett is the rancher who sold the Yellow Jacket ranch to old Jim Traft. Darnell and Malloy make a raid on his range, running off a sizeable number of steers which they sell to Bambridge. The double-crossing among the rustlers leads to Jed Stone shooting Bambridge and Slinger Dunn, and the Yellow Jacket lynching Darnell and other members of the Hash Knife Outfit.

Blodgett, Allen: In *The Hash Knife Outfit,* Blodgett's son. He takes over his father's operation when Jim and Molly move into the Yellow Jacket. He is one of their neighbors.

Blodgett, Miss: In *The Drift Fence,* young Jim Traft runs into Miss Blodgett, daughter of the rancher, in one of the stores in Flag. She teases him about what Curly Prentiss has been telling her about him and the drift fence. She tells him that Curly used to ride for them, that he was the finest cowboy in the world but that when he drinks, his tongue wags. She asks him in jest if he has anyone special to write home to his family about, but he tells her he has fallen in love with his job. From her, Jim learns that Western girls are as deep as Western cowboys, friendly, but hard to read.

Bloom: (1) In *Code of the West,* the new Bar XX foreman. He is first mentioned in connection with stray cattle that Enoch is returning to their range. Bloom is reputed always to be looking for a fight. Bloom turns up in Ryson when Cal goes to pick up Georgiana Stockwell at the station. He comments that Tuck Merry looks like he escaped from a circus. When Bloom makes a comment about Georgie's dress, Tuck challenges him. This leads to a fight in which Bloom is rendered unconscious before he knows what happened to him.

(2) In *Black Mesa,* works with Calkins, rustling cattle for Belmont. They rustle some two hundred head of Manning's cattle and sell them back to him. When Manning does not pay full price on the deal, Calkins and Bloom decide to rustle some cattle to sell. They know Belmont won't dare make a fuss. When Manning and Kintell come upon the trio planning to rustle cattle, Calkins and Kintell are shot, while Bloom and Sparull get away.

Blowy: In *Valley of Wild Horses*, one of the cowboys working on the first roundup Pan Handle Smith joins. He recognizes Ol' Calico, a cutting horse trained by a friend of his.

Blucher, Mr.: In *The Vanishing American*, a German immigrant in charge of the reservation. He is not at the reservation when Marian Warner arrives. Blucher has come to the U.S. after spending a few years in England. He hates England and America with a passion. Blucher, together with Morgan and Friel, constitute the government of the reservation. While the three men do not like each other, they do share a common interest in maintaining their power over the Navajo and in controlling the funding and the personnel of the reservation. The three siphon off funds intended for projects; they trick Indians into signing away water and property rights, acquiring the best land on the reservation for themselves. They control the personnel on the reservation through cajolery, threats, blackmail and intimidation. Blucher has little respect for the missionaries. He tells Morgan that his "converts" exist only in his fertile imagination. He laughs at Morgan's attempts to impose attendance at chapel on the students at the school, saying that if he were Do Etin, he would not let his daughter attend chapel. He does, however, acquiesce to Morgan's demand that Ruhr, Glendon and Naylor be sent to arrest Do Etin. Likewise, he joins in the campaign to discredit Wolterson and have him removed from his position as agricultural consultant. Wolterson's popularity among the Navajo is a threat to his regime. He does his best to make trouble for him. Blucher sends Jay Lord to spread anti–American propaganda among the Navajo. He knows their resentment of the U.S. government, their sense of betrayal over past wrongs, a poison that is deep. Lord tells the Navajo that the registration for the draft is a fraud, that the government will try to force the Navajo to go to war even if they do not want to. Throughout the war, Blucher does what he can to advance the cause of Germany and to vilify the American government. His abuse of power is the cause of the rebellion on the reservation at the end of the novel. For Zane Grey, Blucher is a stereotype of the incompetent and tyrannical system at work on the Indian reservations.

Bludsoe: In *The Mysterious Rider*, a cowboy at Bill Bellounds' ranch. He is with Wilson, Lem and Jim when Buster Jack provokes a fight with Wilson. He leaves the ranch when Buster Jack assumes the foreman's job and new men are brought in who do not know about the boss's son.

Blue: (1) In "The Secret of Quaking Asp Cabin," Richard Starke's young wife. When they come to Arizona to escape life in the East, she is pretty and spoiled, wild with love and freedom from restraint. At nineteen, after several years in the canyon, Blue outgrows her girlish frailty. Outdoors three-fourths of the year, she had grown strong and brown and beautiful. She helps Letith birth her child and the

following summer, she herself gives birth to Hillie. Blue falls in love with Richard's brother Len, a handsome man closer to her in age and passion for life. She does not know that Richard has seen them making love under the trees. It is not clear that she was aware of Len's plans to kill his brother, but when Richard recovers, she remains with him, while Len goes off into the woods to live like an Apache. For over ten years, Richard does not say a word to her. One day, though, after Hillie has died and Matt Taylor has returned with supplies, Richard decides to talk to her. He tells her he forgives her for her infidelity. He tells her he has money hoarded up which he now wants her to take. He has sent Matt to get Len. He wants them to go off together to start a new life. She leaves the cabin, cries out, and the sound of hoof beats tells Richard that Len has come to get Blue.

(2) In *To the Last Man*, the name used by King Fisher. Blue is a Texas gunman. He has come to Pleasant Valley (Grass Valley) to give Gaston Isbel a hand. He underlines that he is there to return a favor. At one point, Gaston Isbel had saved his life, and he has come to the Tonto Basin out of personal loyalty, not because he believes in the righteousness of the Isbel cause. Blue is quiet, unprepossessing. He says quite openly that he believes one of the Isbel faction is involved in the cattle rustling, an accusation which Gaston Isbel conspicuously ignores, and which makes Bill Isbel feel distinctly uncomfortable. When Gaston Isbel is killed by Jorth, Blue devises a plan to rout the Jorths. Jean distracts the men inside by breaking in the back door with an axe while Blue enters from the front. In the shootout, Lee Jorth and Jackson Jorth are killed, and several others are wounded. Blue himself is mortally wounded, dying in Meeker's cabin later. He says his real name was King Fisher, an assertion that the Jorths' gunman, Queen, doubts, but cannot disprove. Blue's spectacular raid on Greaves's fortress is described as genial and spectacularly courageous, in the best tradition of the Texas gunmen.

(3) In *Wild Horse Mesa*, a roan that Chane Weymer captures but decides to keep when he sells his herd. Like Ben Ide, Chane cannot bear to part with some of the wild horses he has captured.

Blue Bo: In *The Man of the Forest*, a horse Tom Carmichael roped and broke to give to Bo Rayner. The horse is named for her. Tom tells her she can have him when she is Mrs. Tom Carmichael.

Blue Feather (a.k.a. Docleas, "The Nopah"): In *Blue Feather*, the young Nopah, Docleas, in the language of the Sheboyahs. Docleas is the son of Nothis Toh, chief of the Nopahs. He has sent his son among the Sheboyahs as a spy to learn their secrets and to make possible the capture of their citadel and treasures. Blue Feather is in his late twenties when he arrives at the citadel of the Rock Clan. They observe him approaching their fortress, and wonder who he is. They are impressed with his height and strength. He speaks a language they do not understand. Within a few months, he masters their language. He discovers the Rock Clan's weaknesses and sets about corrupting the young men. He masters all their games easily and triumphs over the best of their young men in competition after competition. He feeds their appetite for betting and gambling, constantly increasing the stakes. He introduces them to a blue gum the people of his tribe make, an addictive gum that renders them zombie-like.

Blue Feather's popularity with the young women in particular earns him the resentment of the young men. Ba-Lee, servant to Nastha and fiancée to Tith-Lei, in particular is in love with him. Following her one day, Blue Feather discovers the grotto where the Daughter of the Moon comes to bathe in the moonlight. He falls in love with the chief's daughter, and Ba-Lee and La-Clos become accomplices in letting him in to spend the night with her. When Tith-Lei issues a final challenge to Blue Feather, that he leave the citadel and in three days return carrying an antelope carcass up the wall of the citadel unaided, the Nopah returns to his people. There, he tells his expectant father that the citadel is impregnable and the treasures not worth the effort. As well, there is no game in the area and the Sheboyahs are weak with hunger, their women are shiftless, the young maidens married to men of distant tribes. He declares he will look at the homes of tribes farther off, and suggests his father and his warriors move south.

Blue Feather returns to the Rock Clan Citadel with an antelope carcass and climbs the rocky walls unaided. He is unquestionably the most remarkable man the Sheboyahs have ever seen. Ba-Lee, however, betrays him. She tells Tith-Lei that he goes to see Natsha in the kiva. They capture him, and plan to disembowel him ritualistically and tear his body apart, piece by piece, as a sacrifice to their gods. But before they can accomplish this, the Nopah attack, with scaling ladders. The Sheboyahs repel the first attacks and are quite impressed with their own prowess. La-Clos reveals to Nashta what has happened to Blue Feather, and the plans of the priests and warriors to torture him to death the next day.

Nashta decides she cannot live without him. She leaves her cave by the secret tunnel under the citadel and goes to the camp of the Nopahs. There she meets Nothis Toh, chief of the tribe and father of Blue Feather. She offers to show them the secret entrance to the citadel. At first, some of the Nopahs suspect she is luring them into a trap, but Nothis Toh recalls the power of love in his youth and trusts her. The Nopahs appear the following morning and in the fighting that ensues, the Sheboyahs are destroyed and Blue Feather saved. Nothis Toh forgives him, recalling how in his youth he too felt the power of love. He spares Nashta, allowing her to marry his son.

Blue, Jud: In *The Drift Fence*, foreman of Jim Traft's ranch whom the nephew, young Jim Traft, replaces. The cowboys tell Young Jim about how he was killed. Deliberate murder, it appears. The cowboys did not like Jud very much, saying he deserves to be in hell.

Blue, Randall (a.k.a. Band Drake):   In *Shadow on the Trail*, a member of Simm Bell's outlaw outfit. He is under thirty, tall, fair-haired, not bad looking. Others distrust his shifty gaze, his ready tongue and smile, his big, black eyes. Wade Holden, Smith and Hazlitt accuse him of betraying the group to the rangers. They have seen him talking with Ranger Pell, and sending telegrams at the office. When Wade puts a gun in his belly, he confesses to having spoken with Pell, to having agreed to cooperate with the rangers, but he claims he was planning to double-cross the rangers all along. Wade wants to shoot Blue point blank for his treachery, but Simm saves his life. Blue had befriended him, and he cannot allow him to be shot on suspicion. However, he does expel him from the group and threatens to kill him should he come across him again. Blue is there in Mercer when the Simm outfit comes to rob the bank. A year later, he is still with the rangers. He shows up at Chisum's ranch looking for Wade Holden, now going by the name Blanco. Some two years later, Rand Blue appears around Holbrook, Arizona. He goes by the name Band Drake. He has returned to his outlaw ways. Pencarrow bought his ranch and stock. He has sold cattle to Pencarrow and has exacted payment for the herd twice. His henchman, Urba, is sent to collect his horses in payment. Holden kills Urba, who draws on him. Band Drake works with the rancher Mason from Mariposa. Drake's outfit rustles cattle and Mason sells the animals, giving the transaction the patina of legality. Drake is still up to his old tricks of double-dealing his men. He gets into trouble with his men over money for cattle that Mason sold which has not been distributed among them. When Wade Holden, now known as Tex Brandon, leads a campaign against the rustlers, Band Drake is captured and hanged. Before swinging, he does recognize the Wade Holden he had double-crossed in Mercer.

Blue Roan: In *Wildfire*, Creech's horse. Blue Roan is the only horse which has serious possibilities of challenging the Sage King in a race. Creech has entered Blue Roan in the race, together with Peg. Consequently, Bostril maliciously schemes to prevent Creech's horses from getting across the Colorado River before the floods come. The animals are trapped in a box canyon without grass or water. With the help of some Piute Indians, whose admiration for the stallion is as great as that of Creech, he manages to escape from the canyon, but before they can find grass and water, Creech has to shoot the roan. Creech then attempts to get revenge on Bostril by kidnapping his daughter and demanding the Sage King and Sarchedon as ransom.

Bluegrass (Blue):   In *Knights of the Range*, a superb horseman and marksman with a rifle. He works for the Ripple outfit. When things get rough on the range, Britt decides all the cowboys should spend some time every day practicing their marksmanship. Jackson is assigned to work with the Kentuckian, who had hunted squirrels as a boy. He is the best shot with a rifle of the lot. He is with Jackson and Stinger when the Slaughter outfit tries to convince them to join their rustling operation.

Bluegrass: In *The Horse Thief*, one of Edith Watrous's prized horses that Dale Brittenham retrieves from Mason's horse-rustling outfit.

Bo: (1) In *Boulder Dam,* one of the two young men attempting to get Anne Vandergrift's attention as she comes out of a store. His friend tells him the young man who met Anne was Biff Weston. He comments that they are lucky not to have been "biffed."

(2) In *The Deer Stalker*, one of the orphan fawns that Thad Eburne catches in his deer trap. Bo has a companion, Bopeep.

Bob: In *The Mysterious Rider*, a friend of Old Bill Belllounds who had started him up in the cattle business in Kremmlin'. When Bob died, his wife moved to Elgeria and opened up an inn. Lately, the inn has met with stiff competition from one Smith (Captain Folsom) who has opened up a gambling establishment. Mrs. Bob, the innkeeper's wife, tells Bent Wade about the situation in Belllounds's house, where the wife is jealous of the young girl he took in. She is afraid Bill will give some of his money to the daughter and she is concerned that her son's inheritance is in jeopardy. She also tells Wade that Bill mentioned he was intending to marry Buster Jack to this orphan girl.

Bobby: In *West of the Pecos,* the young boy at Eagle's Nest who brings Pecos Smith up to date on the changes around the place and the plight of young Terrill Lambeth.

Bodkin: In *Twin Sombreros*, the deputy sheriff of Las Animas. He is arrests Brazos Keene for the murder of Allen Neece when he finds him at the cabin where the body has been hidden. His story is that three men came to him around two in the morning to tell him they saw a man shoot another in the back and carry the body into the cabin. He forms a posse and arrives at the cabin around daybreak, when Brazos Keene is preparing to leave. He is arrested and charged with murder. On the way to Las Animas, they meet Surface, a big rancher, cattleman, and head of the Cattleman's Association, who calls Bodkin aside. After he returns, he is determined to hang Brazos without further ado. Inskip opposes this action and soon other members of the posse voice similar objections. Inskip arranges for Brazos to get his guns and put an end to these plans. At the hearing the following day, Bodkin tells his story, but it is quickly disproved. Kiskadden fires him for incompetence. When Kiskadden resigns, he has high hopes of being named sheriff by Surface and the Cattleman's Association whose loyal servant he has been. Henderson and others do voice opposition to his appointment but he still gets the position. Brazos, however, knows he is involved with the murderers of Allen Neece. He overhears a conversation among the deputy, Syvertsen and Orcutt in which their complicity with Surface in rustling and murder is clearly revealed. They are also planning to murder Brazos using the same scheme used to lure Neece to his death. When he becomes sheriff, Bodkin boasts that he will arrest Brazos. However, he is not able to made good on his boast. He is killed in a shootout with Keene when he is at supper with some important, influential ranchers.

Boggs, Captain: In *Betty Zane*, Capt. Boggs has been stationed at Ft. Henry by General Clarke. He is a frequent visitor at Colonel Zane's cabin together with his daughter Lydia, Betty's friend and confident. Capt. Boggs is at Ft. Pitt seeking reinforcements when the Indians and British attack Ft. Henry.

Boggs, Lydia: Lydia Boggs is the eighteen-year-old daughter of Capt. Boggs. She has been with him at Ft. Henry for two years. She and Betty Zane are the best of friends. Lydia serves as a foil to Betty. Lydia has come to appreciate the honesty, forthrightness and simplicity of the people on the frontier while Betty is still living according to the norms of Philadelphia, where she had lived with her aunt. Lydia "was rather pleased that some one had appeared on the scene who did not at once bow down before Betty." She likes to tease Betty about her indifference to the young men around the fort. She knows that Betty is interested in Alfred despite her claims to feeling nothing for him. She also wonders why Betty treats him so poorly for no apparent reason. She tells Betty she could take a few lessons in good manners from the less refined folk around the fort.

Lydia, together with Betty, is a bridesmaid at the wedding of Alice Reynolds and Bill Martin. During the attack on the fort, Lydia helps with the wounded, reloads rifles, or makes lead bullets in a mold.

Bold, Ben: In *Valley of Wild Horses*, one of the cowboys working on the first roundup that Pan Handle Smith joins. He recognizes Ol' Calico, Pan Handle's horse, which a friend of his had trained as a cutting horse.

Boldt: In *The Lone Star Ranger*, one of the gunmen in Cheseldine's gang. Buck Duane first sets eyes on him at the cabin in the valley hideout. He is with the group when Knell and Duane fight it out. He is also one of the outlaws to attack the Ranchers' Bank in Val Verde.

Boller, Andrew: In "Canyon Walls," owns a ranch farther down the canyon from the Keetch place. Monty Bellew has been told by a Mormon shepherd that Boller might take him on as a hand. Boller offers to buy the Keetch place after Monty has made the place a profitable ranch. Mrs. Keetch refuses to sell the ranch to him, but does make a deal to sell her alfalfa crop. She figures that the ranch is worth at least double what he has offered; furthermore, if he is interested in buying it now, it must be worth keeping.

Bondre, Charlie: In *The Lost Wagon Train*, rides into Latchfield with Billy the Kid. Latchfield is a known haven for outlaws. Latch welcomes him and Billy the Kid to town. Everyone gets a welcome.

Bonesteel, Avil (Luce Cheney): In *Stranger from the Tonto*, the leader of the Hole-in-the-Wall outfit. Bonesteel had twenty men in his outfit, and three women, one his wife. She knew nothing of his outlaw activities but after she found out, she did not live long. The fair-haired daughter was raised by Bill Elway and Bonesteel himself. She was educated by the two of them but never allowed to leave the canyon. When he and his men leave on a raid, she is carefully guarded. Jeff is her current guardian. Lucy is innocent of the ways of the world, and has no idea of her father's real work. Slotte pulls the wool over Bonesteel's eyes, spreading lies about Elway. He hopes to kill Bonesteel, get the daughter and take over the outfit. He brings in Roberts, boss of a rival outfit of outlaws, hoping to play them off against each other. When Bonesteel learns of his treachery, he eggs him on until Wingfield and Slotte go for their guns. He pretends to make a deal with Roberts, but in reality, he has decided to leave the canyon hideout and return to his other life as Luce Cheney, respectable rancher and cattle dealer. Bonesteel has come to like Kent Wingfield and asks him to take his daughter out of the canyon by a secret road. He knows Lucy loves Kent and trusts he will take care of her. He orders Jeff, her guardian, to prepare the necessary supplies and saddle the horses and put them near the waterfalls for their flight. He hoped that Kent and Lucy would leave before he precipitates the shootout with the Roberts outfit, but Kent insists on joining in out of loyalty. When the fight is over, he asks Kent to tell Lucy that he was killed in the fight with Roberts. When they are well on their way to Wagontongue, Kent tells her about her father's other family in Utah, and assures her that he did survive the shootout.

Bonesteel, Lucy: In *Stranger from the Tonto*, is Avil Bonesteel's seventeen-year-old daughter. Like Bess in *Riders of the Purple Sage*, raised in the outlaws' hideout by Oldring, Lucy has lived her life isolated from the world. Her mother died when she was young. She was raised by her father in the Hole-in-the-Wall hideout, and educated by him and by Bill Elway, her guardian. When he talks with her, Kent Wingfield gets the measure of her education. She can read some, but her supply of books is meager. She has no sense of geography or history. For her, Utah is somewhere beyond the river, Arizona is a Navajo reservation and California is a gold field. As far as she knows, all men buy and sell cattle, drink, gamble and fight. Some plant and harvest in the fields. Morally, she has received virtually no instruction. The worst man is a horse thief, who should be

hanged pronto. She has no knowledge of the outside world, and until she overhears her father talking with Slotte, no idea of his work as a rustler. Bill Elway asks Kent Wingfield to go the canyon and rescue her. Elway knows that eventually, the outlaw outfit will fall apart, and the men will fight over the innocent, young woman who has no experience of the real world. Kent Wingfield overhears Slotte and Neberyull, and their talk confirms Elway's fears for Lucy. Jeff, her current guardian, helps her to understand Slotte's interest in her. She sees that she is seen as a prize by most of the men in the canyon. She is quite ready for Kent's revelations when she finally meets him. He tells her the truth about her father and the danger she may be in before long. He tells her about Bill Elway and his request that he find her and get her out of the canyon.

Lucy agrees to meet Kent, who is hiding out in the hills, and to bring him food. She keeps their friendship secret when he appears leading the horse. Kent ingratiates himself with Bonesteel, and Bunge's story about his membership in the Hash Knife Outfit establishes his qualifications as an outlaw on the dodge. Kent manages to convince Lucy that Ben's story is a lie. When she overhears her father talking and learns of his secret life, she feels no man can be trusted. When she and her father have a fight over his confining her to the valley and keeping the truth about his double life from her, Bonesteel tells her he married her mother because he loved her and he has done his best to raise Lucy to be innocent and good. He decides to enlist Kent's help to get her out of the valley. He asks Kent to tell her that he is dead. When they set out, Lucy tells Kent she knew where the secret outlet was located, but that she had never taken it. The two horses, Clubfoot and Spades, know the road and need no guidance. When they are approaching Logan's trading post, Kent tells her about her father's other family in Utah. He does not tell her the name he uses, but he does reveal that he was not killed in the shootout with Roberts. Kent has long since decided that she is worth ten of Nita Gail.

Bonita: (1) In *The Light of Western Stars,* the young Mexican woman with whom Danny Mains is in love. She is strikingly beautiful, and many men fight over her. Don Carlos, a fifty-something rancher-bandit pursues her much as Rojas pursues Mercedes Castañeda in *Desert Gold*. She first appears in the train station seeking help from Gene Stewart. He gives her his horse, Majesty, to escape. Madeline comments on her gaudy attire, supposing she must be a saloon girl. Towards the end of the novel, she is arrested by Howe, brutally treated, and tied up. She marries Danny Mains during her period in hiding. Madeline, at one point, is angry at Gene because of his attentions to Bonita. She suspects he is in love with her and is jealous. Later she learns that Gene brought supplies to her and Danny, who are hiding out in the mountains. Danny cannot speak too highly of Bonita, the love of his life. Madeline realizes she has misjudged the girl. Bonita appears again in *Majesty's Rancho* where she and Danny are the parents of a young Bonita who is just as beautiful and mischievous as the mother had been.

(2) In *Majesty's Rancho*, Bonita is the bombshell daughter of Bonita and Danny Mains. She is strikingly attractive, aware of her beauty and her ability to influence men. She knows Ren Starr is crazy about her, but she still likes to flirt with the Mexican vaqueros who work for her father. Gene Stewart predicts she will wreak havoc among the young college men that come to the ranch for the summer. Bonita makes eyes at Lance Sidway, but when his partner Ren Starr tells him how he feels about Bonita, Lance backs out. He later speaks to Bonita to put in a word for Ren. Bonita knows she is a flirt, but she does not do it to make Ren jealous, just to have fun. Some of the Mexican vaqueros who come to see her turn out to be involved with the rustlers who have been attacking the herds of her father, Danny, and of Gene Stewart and Spencer. She tells Lance Sidway that there is a raid planned for the night of Madge's big fiesta. Eventually, Ren Starr and Bonita are married.

Bonning, Andrew: In *Wyoming,* a young man who, like young Jim Traft in *Code of the West,* or Glenn Killbourne in *Call of the Canyon,* leaves behind the effete, decadent East, and finds a worthwhile purpose and genuine values in the West. He is the son of Mr. Bonning and brother to Raymond and Gloria. He has not made a success of his life to date. At college, he failed at athletics, not from lack of talent or application, but because he failed to get the favor of the athletic directors and school officials. When the stock market crashes and his father is almost ruined financially, he finds himself turned out of the family home. He refuses the money his father offers him as his inheritance, and sets out on his own. He is determined to make a success of his life. This is probably the push he needs to shake him out of his doldrums. The future is now a chance and a challenge. When he tells his fiancée, Constance, about his situation, she informs him that she had never considered him as a serious suitor. Andrew now knows she was interested in him only for his family's money. Andy drives west looking for opportunities, not certain what he wants to do, but the idea is there in the back of his mind to go to Wyoming to become a cowboy. He turns his back on speed, luxury, idleness, and the women of the East. In the Black Hills, he rescues in true chivalric style a young woman from the clutches of a bunch of hobos. Pulled off the road to nap near Split Rock, he overhears a conversation between two men called McCall and Texas about their plans to fleece a certain rancher called Bligh. When they leave, Andrew knows what he has to do. He decides to find this Bligh and do what he can to foil their plans. He presents himself at Bligh's ranch, offering to work for room and board. Bligh decides to take him on. He trusts Bonning to learn the cowboy trade, but above all, he wants a man who will be loyal to him, as his foreman, Jim Fenner, has been all these years. When

Martha Dixon, the niece he rescued from the hobos, asks her uncle to fire him, Nick stands by Andrew.

Jim Fenner and his wife, Sue, take to Andrew from the start. Fenner fills him in on Bligh's background, the dubious deal with McCall, the great gamble that Bligh has taken moving to Split Rock. He teaches him to ride, to rope, to herd cattle from horseback, to track animals and to shoot a rifle. Andrew spends time out on the range, applying his skills, and trying to spot rustlers or branders of mavericks. He does come upon a man branding a calf after having shot the cow. He gets shot for his pains, but recognizes the man as Smoky Reed, the man he overheard McCall and Texas Haynes talking about. At the rodeo in town, Andrew makes a reputation for himself. Everyone considers him a dude, and his new hat and clothes make him stand out all the more, but when he wins the bull riding contest, outperforming the local favorites, he commands a new respect. Even Martha Dixon admits to herself that there is more to Andy than she had suspected. At the same rodeo he and Smoky Reed get into a fistfight, ostensibly over Reed's attention to Martha. Sheriff Slade puts him in jail for disturbing the peace, and refuses to release him until a fine of a hundred dollars has been paid.

In the summer months, in the saddle for days on end like John Hare in *The Heritage of the Desert,* he grows hard, strong, enduring. He comes to take joy in action and labor. He finds that he is happy. The old habits of bitter self-mockery have almost disappeared. As he sits watching the embers of his campfire, he knows he was never meant for city crowds, work in an office, or business. He feels at peace. His transformation has prepared him to face the final challenge posed by Texas Haynes and the rancher McCall. Texas has grown dissatisfied with McCall over money he is owed. That, together with his promise to Martha to quit the rustling business, bring about the showdown in which the crooked rancher is killed. Sheriff Slade, aware that his own crooked dealings might be exposed, does not press matters farther.

Andrew decides he has found what he wants to do in life. He invests the money he inherited from his mother in equipment and stock. He plans to develop the Bligh ranch in fine fashion. He marries Martha Dixon, and settles down to a partnership in the ranch.

Bonning, Gloria: In *Wyoming,* Andrew's sister. She has been a loyal friend to Andrew. When they get word of their father's hard luck on Wall Street, and his decision to move into a flat, she sympathizes with her Andrew. As Andy has refused the money their father offered him, Gloria offers to stake him to five thousand dollars till he gets on his feet. Andy jokingly tells Gloria she can always marry well to solve her financial problems. Gloria, however, shows more independence and wants to make it on her own. It's not right for a modern woman to think of marriage only to find financial security.

Bonning, Raymond: In *Wyoming,* brother to Andrew Bonning. He is handsome, blond, charming, but worthless. Mr. Bonning has fallen on hard times. He informs Andrew and Raymond on a Sunday morning after breakfast that they are now on their own. He and Gloria will move into an apartment, but there is no room for the boys. They have both been a disappointment to him, but he can no longer support them. Raymond has squandered the inheritance he received from his mother, and now strides out of the room with a check in his hand announcing that they are in for a ride.

Bonning, Mr.:   In *Wyoming,* Andrew's father. Raymond and Andrew, his two sons, have been a disappointment to him. He has been nearly ruined by the crash on Wall Street, and must now live modestly. He gives each of his sons a check, their share of the inheritance, and informs them they are now on their own. He and his daughter, Gloria, will move into an apartment and there is no room for the boys. Andrew refuses the money his father offers, declaring that this is a chance for him to stand up on his own.

Bonny: In *Wild Horse Mesa,* a sandy-haired, thirty-year-old Irishman. He has been ten years in the United States. He hates towns, and has traveled over large parts of the West. He sings in a deep, bass voice. Bonny has no experience wrangling, but is willing to learn. When the work of hobbling begins, he refuses to work with the brutal Manerube.

Booly: In *The Light of Western Stars,* a cowboy on Bill Stillwell's ranch, later Madeline's ranch. He takes part in the golf game organized to entertain the visitors from Newport. He is also one of the cowboys who participate in the raid on Don Carlos' ranch. He is one of the cowboys from the roundup who come up to the road to catch a glimpse of Madeline going by in her car.

Boone: In *The U. P. Trail,* an engineer and crew boss for the U. P.

Boone, Daniel: An historical figure mentioned in both *The Spirit of the Border* and *Betty Zane.* In the former, Wetzel is said to be his equal in tracking and woodlore, but his superior in understanding of Indian ways. In the latter, he is mentioned as one of many prominent guests who have stayed at Colonel Zane's cabin in Ft. Henry. Jonathan Zane tells a story of how he once met Daniel Boone and spent a week hunting with him on the Muskingong river before he set off for his home in Kentucky.

Boots: In *Horse Heaven Hill,* the affectionate nickname Marigold Wade gives Stanley Weston. It harks back to his football days at university. Stanley, in turn, has given this name to his horse.

Bopeep: In *The Deer Stalker,* the second fawn caught in Thad Eburne's trap. Bopeep keeps Bo company.

Borden, Cliff: In *Thunder Mountain,* appears in Salmon, where Kalispel confronts him as he tries to force his way into Sydney Blair's room. He is de-

scribes as a "forceful presence," with protruding, gleaming eyes and a clean-shaven, protruding jowl. Kalispel and Borden fight, and the following day, Borden has the sheriff out after Lee Emerson (Kalispel) on the pretext that he is wanted for cattle rustling in Montana. Lee confronts Sheriff Lowrie and Borden in the street and, fearing gunfire, they back off. Borden shows up at Thunder City where he opens a saloon and gambling establishment, the Spread Eagle, similar to the one he owns in Salmon. He brings with him Nuggett, the saloon girl Kalispel met in Salmon. Borden joins with Leavitt in exploiting the miners of the city. Borden and Kalispel quarrel again over Nuggett, who wants to leave his employ to marry Dick Sloan. Borden supports Leavitt in his endeavors as mayor and judge, but a split comes when his informants tell him Leavitt is planning to sell out and leave Thunder City in the spring. When Sheriff Masters and Kalispel pursue the men who attacked and killed Dick Sloan, Borden is shot and killed. Borden is a villain cut from the same bolt of cloth as Durade in *The U.P. Trail* or Darnell in *The Hash Knife Outfit.* He is an unscrupulous gambler, a tyrannical boss, and an unrepentant exploiter of the weaknesses of hard-working men.

Boseman: In *Wyoming,* a homesteader who had settled in Split Rock but never proved up on his claim. Nick Bligh buys the place, and later McCall, with whom he has a cattle deal, claims he has a lien on the old Boseman place and will seize it if Bligh pulls out of their cattle deal.

Bosomer: (1) In *Arizona Ames,* owns a saloon in Yampa where Bannard's rustlers congregate to drink and play cards. Fred Halstead gets mixed up with the gang gambling at the saloon.

(2) In *The Lone Star Ranger,* a member of Bland's rustler band and former friend of Luke Stevens. He accuses Buck of killing Stevens and stealing his horse. Bosomer is always looking for a fight to kill someone. He provokes Buck Duane into a shootout, but Buck just shoots him in the arm, breaking a bone. Duane preferred not to kill the man and get off to a bad start in the outlaw hideout.

Bossert: In *The Border Legion,* one of the outlaws who rob the stagecoach from Alder Creek to Bannack. He shares in the loot and loses it all in the gambling session which follows.

Bostril, John: In *Wildfire,* the father of Lucy Bostril, and founder of the town of Bostril's Ford, located at the Crossing of the Fathers on the Colorado River. The Bostrils are from Missouri and hard times there push them to go west. His sister believes that back in Missouri, they had some social standing, a claim Bostril firmly denies. Lucy Bostril says that her father has two faults which explain the problems he has had with riders and other ranchers. He never pays his riders in money and he resents any man who owns a horse faster than his. The first practice means he has trouble hanging on to riders; the second is the principal source of friction between him and other horsemen. John Bostril had come to Utah at a time when owning a horse, a fast horse, was a question of life and death. He developed such a passion for horses that he wants the best for himself. Should another man own a fast horse, Bostril will go to any length to acquire the animal. Bostril has good relations with the Piutes and the Navajos in the region, two tribes as passionate about horses as he is. He considers civilization a corrupting force on the Indians, but ironically looks forward to the coming of the railroad and the possibilities of enrichment it offers.

Bostril has organized a horsemen's club which meets to plan the annual horse race at Bostril's Ford. Some of the men in this group are his personal rivals. Creech, in particular, owns two horses, Blue Roan and Peg, which are considered strong rivals of his own stallions, Sage King and Sarchedon. The horse race is a big event in the region. Ranchers and horse traders come hoping someone will have a horse that will put Bostril in his place and end his boastful arrogance. The local Indian tribes come to participate and to watch. The time is one of great festivities. Bostril fears that Cordts, renowned horseman and horse thief, will steal his horses. Consequently, the day of the races is always a day of worry.

The very real possibility that Creech's Blue Roan could defeat Sage King brings bout the worst in Bostril. On the pretext that it needs fixing, he orders removed from the river the boat that ferries animals, men, sheep, and supplies across the Colorado, thereby preventing Creech from bringing his stallions across. But when the river is about to reach full flood, he has the boat put back only to cut the ropes mooring it one night on the sly. The boat is carried downriver in the swift current. Creech and his horses are trapped in a box canyon without grass and water. Bostril feigns great sorrow over the tragic fate of the animals but secretly rejoices in the destruction of his rival. Bostril is truly proud of his masterful hypocrisy. He has fooled no one, however.

Bostril fears that Cordts will someday make good on the threat to kidnap his daughter Lucy. His immediate concern is for the attention young Joel Creech is showing his daughter. Joel has been strange since he got kicked in the head by a horse. He follows Lucy about, races Peg with her horse Buckles, and makes rather suggestive comments to her. Lucy assure him she pities Joel and does nothing to encourage his attention. Like his sister Jane, Bostril feels young Jim Wetherby from Durango would be a better choice of husband, but he will not force the issue at present. When Lucy defeats Sage King, riding the unknown Wildfire, Bostril is stunned. He then sets about intimidating and threatening Lin Slone, hoping to acquire his beautiful stallion. He offers to buy the animal; he offers Slone a job as a rider; he drives Slone off the ranch he had purchased from Vorhees.

Someone takes a shot at Bostril but it's not clear who has done it. There are so many possible suspects. Principal among them are Joel Creech, who suspects Bostril of sabotaging his father, and Cordts, the horse thief who has always threatened to steal his prize stallions. When Creech kidnaps Lucy, demanding Sage King and Sarchedon as ransom to replace the animals he lost as a result of Bostril's scheming, Bostril actually turns the animals over. Lucy herself had told Creech that she seriously doubted her father would choose her over the horses. When Joel delivers the ransom note, and has departed with the horses, Bostril tells Joel to tell Creech that his sins have finally caught up with him. He sees the just retribution in the way events have unfolded. When Lucy is rescued by Lin Slone, they console Bostril, telling him that in the life and death race which saved Lucy's life, Sage King beat Wildfire. He is allowed to retain his illusion.

In John Bostril, Zane Grey has presented a man who has acquired a passion for horses from the environment in which he has lived. He has, however, allowed this passion to become destructive. Bostril resembles August Naab in *The Heritage of the Desert*, a man who likewise was formed by the Utah desert environment and who shared a similar passion for horses, without the obsession with possessing them and destroying other ranchers. In Bostril, Grey studies the potential for self-destruction resulting from excess.

In *Arizona Ames,* Morgan mentions Bostril, who had a trading post down on the Colorado River, as an unparalleled horseman. He also mentions that the post is now deserted.

Bostril, Lucy: In *Wildfire*, the tomboy, eighteen-year-old daughter of John Bostril. She has known no life other than life at Bostril's Ford. Her mother died before they came west and she has been raised by her father and his sister, Jane. Lucy has no desire for the civilized East, unlike her aunt. She feels at one with the desert and the mountains. The wilderness talks to her and she feels her spirit is at one with the natural world. She has lived her life among cowboys and horsemen and feels more at home dressed like them, but as a concession to her more "civilized" aunt, she consents to wearing dresses about the house.

Both Aunt Jane and her father are worried about Lucy's future. Van Sickle, Bostril's best rider and horseman, is in love with Lucy, as are many of the young cowboys. The chief worry, however, is Joel Creech, a young man who had been kicked in the head by a horse and who has been developing ever-stranger tendencies. Joel chases after Lucy, and, out of pity for the young man, Lucy is kind to him. Many at Bostril's Ford think that she encourages him, and Aunt Jane is not sure that Lucy's claims of indifference to the young man are sincere. Both Aunt Jane and Bostril would like her to marry one Jim Wetherby from Durango, a young horse trader with better prospects. Lucy, however, is not interested in anyone for the time being.

Lucy shares her father's passion for horses. She

can ride better than most men, and Bostril explains this ability by saying she was born on a horse. At times, she is said to cling to a horse like a burr. Like Bostril, she has a keen eye for a good horse, and while she may share her father's love of horses, she does not share his obsessions. In fact, like other ranchers around, she would like to see someone stand up to her father.

She does find such a man one day when she is riding out on the sage. Lin Slone is lying half-starved on the ground and nearby he has Nagger, his regular mustang, and Wildfire, the stallion he has captured and broken. Lucy first spots the horse, and immediately appreciates the worth of the spectacular stallion. She agrees to bring Lin Slone some supplies, food and clothing, and agrees to keep her discovery secret. Lucy develops a keen interest in both the horse and the man, falling in love with both. She agrees to enter the horse in the race, to prove once and for all to her father that the Sage King can be beaten in a race. To the surprise of all, Wildfire and Lucy win the race by several lengths.

When the truth of her relationship comes out, as it must, Lin Slone is concerned that her reputation be cleared. He tells Bostril that he has proposed marriage to Lucy, and that she has rejected his proposal. Lucy, however, tells Lin that her father will not leave him in peace until he gets the prized and coveted stallion. She does her best to help Slone set up his ranch and when Bostril has taken that from him, she continues to sneak out of the house to meet him.

Creech kidnaps Lucy to demand Bostril give him Sage King and Sarchedon, his prized horses, as ransom. These horses will replace his own excellent animals, Blue Roan and Peg, whose deaths were due to Bostril's scheming. Lucy understands that Creech, whom she has known since childhood, is not a bad man, that he is grieving the loss of his most valuable possessions. She is well treated and confesses that she herself is not sure whether her father would be willing to part with his stallions to ransom her. The situation becomes complicated when Cordts, the horse thief, attempts to get the two horses and to capture her. Lin Slone comes to the rescue, saving both her and the horses, but killing Wildfire in the process.

Lucy Bostril is a Grey heroine who combines the love of the natural world of Betty Zane with the charm of Madeline Hammond. As Madeline helps Gene Stewart find himself, Lucy helps Lin Slone abandon his lonely life in the desert and accept his place in a community. She embodies the civilizing force which Grey associates with the feminine element.

In *Arizona Ames*, Morgan mentions that Bostril used to boast that his daughter was born on a horse. Morgan claims a similar honor for his daughter, Lespeth.

Bowden: (1) In *The Lost Wagon Train*, a lawyer from Boston who first appears at Fort Union looking for information about Cynthia Bowden. She has inherited a fortune from a deceased relative in Boston and the lawyer has come west looking for her or her children. He makes a deal with Stephen Latch to accept the sign from Tullt's wagon as proof that Cynthia Bowden had been there, that she had married him and that Estelle (Estie) is her daughter.

(2) In *The Lost Wagon Train*, also the uncle of Cynthia Bowden. They are heading to California to start a new life. Bowden has purchased a wagon, a prairie schooner from Tullt and Company, a wagon that draws attention wherever they go. A style of wagon that became popular in later years, it is a blend of boat and wagon, making travel possible both by land and by river. Bowden is particularly anxious to get to California. He urges Anderson to take the Dry Trail, which will shorten the trip by three weeks. He is little-experienced with the frontier. When attack seems imminent, he attempts to bribe Anderson with his gold to get himself and his niece to safety. When the fighting starts, he is described as flopping and thumping around under his wagon like a beheaded turkey. He is killed in the fighting, along with the rest of the members of the caravan.

Bowden, Cynthia: In *The Lost Wagon Train*, the auburn haired niece of Bowden. She is heading west to California with him to start a new life. She has reservations about the trip and questions the wisdom of taking the Dry Trail, especially when there is no military escort. She does not understand why her uncle insists on such haste to get to California. He confides in her that he has hidden his gold in a false bottom of the wagon. In the attack on the wagon train, she hides in the prairie schooner, wondering what the future will be, regretting her foolish rejection of Latch because of the calumny spread by her brother and Thorpe. She alone survives the massacre. Leighton hides her in a wagon, planning to keep her for himself. He shares the secret with Sprall, who soon enough reveals it to Lester Cornwall, as he does to Latch. Latch rescues her from Leighton, killing Sprall and shooting Leighton in the process. The men in the group are divided over what to do with her, share her or kill her like the rest of the caravan. Latch buys her freedom and marries her, the ceremony being performed by Mandrove, a preacher turned outlaw. Cynthia tells the whole outlaw crew the story of her romance with Stephen Latch, the lies spread by her brother who wanted her for his friend, Thorpe, the duel between Thorpe and Stephen and the death which turned him into an outlaw. She is reunited with her lover, oblivious to the horrendous crimes for which he has been responsible. During their stay in Spider Web Canyon, she never ceases in her efforts to wean him away from the outlaw group, and almost succeeds. During the seven years he is away, she continues on alone. She loves solitude and nature, never growing tired of Spider Web Canyon. During his absence, she bears him a child and dies in childbirth. A wealthy relative in Boston leaves her a legacy and lawyer Bowden's inquiries revive interest in the lost Anderson train and stir up questions about the past Latch has done so much to try to bury.

Bowden, Howard: In *The Lost Wagon Train*, Cynthia Bowden's brother. He disapproved of her relationship with Stephen Latch, wanting her to marry his friend, Thorpe. With Thorpe, he spreads rumors about Stephen's involvement with a woman of ill repute. He ruins Latch's career, ensuring that he does not get a commission in the Southern army. Thanks to Howard, Stephen and Thorpe fight a duel in which Latch kills Thorpe.

Bowden, Uncle John: In *The Lost Wagon Train*, Cynthia's uncle, great-uncle to Estelle Latch. He receives Estelle with open arms. He also takes a great shine to Corny, who behaves, according to Estelle, like a perfect gentleman.

Bowers, Aggie: In *Code of the West*, one of the twin sisters in whom Lock and Wess Thurman are interested. Lock says that Wess is interested in Aggie.

Bowers, Angie: In *Code of the West*, one of the twin sisters in whom Lock Thurman is interested but is too shy to approach. His brothers Wess and Serge tease him mercilessly about her.

Bowes, Mrs.: In *Robbers' Roost*, runs a lodging-house where Helen Herrick has a meal before setting out with Jim Wall and Barnes for the Star Ranch.

Boy Blue: In *Wild Horse Mesa*, the affectionate nickname given to Chess Weymer by his older brother Chane.

Boyce, Luke: In "Amber's Mirage," Luke Boyce is an old friend of Al Shade's. He has married Ruby Low and they have a child. Luke married Ruby after Joe Raston unceremoniously dumped her. He is crazy about her and he knows she does not love him in the same way. He knows she loves pretty things and partying, but all goes well until he breaks a leg and gets fired. He was working as a cowboy on Raston's ranch at the time. Al Shade offers to help him out. He tells him he should put Raston in his place, but Luke fears he will be put in jail for assault. After all, Raston is a wealthy, influential man, and he is an unemployed cowboy. Al Shade puts Raston's lights out and leaves Ruby a bucket of gold so that she and Luke can start a new life.

Bozeman, Joe and Seth: In *Shadow on the Trail*, Mormon brothers who run a general merchandise store in Holbrook. The gunfight between Tex Brandon (Wade Holden, Blanco) and Kent takes place in the street in front of their store.

Bradford, Dennis: In *The Desert of Wheat*, a tramp Kurt Dorn meets in a boxcar. Kurt has been captured by the I.W.W. men, who have tied him up and thrown him into a boxcar. He talks to Kurt, explaining his lot in life. He had an oil well in Pennsylvania but a rival set off a bomb nearby which caused his well to dry up. He came west to try farm-ing, but a bigger outfit wiped him out by tapping into his water source for irrigation, making his own farm a desert. He feels an honest man cannot get ahead. This is why he has joined the I.W.W. He tells Kurt that after burning the grain elevator, Glidden is planning an attack on Anderson's home with the intention of killing him. Dennis Bradford asks Glidden what he plans to do with Kurt and he says he will slit his throat.

Bradford, Susan (Sue): In *The Horse Thief*, a friend of Edith Watrous's. She arrives with Edith for the horse auction in Halsey. Her brother, Wesley, is coming to the auction as well. Wesley is a close friend of Dale Brittenham's.

Bradley: (1) In *The Border Legion*, a young man in Hoadley's camp who said something uncomplimentary about Joan Randle in the saloon. Jim Clive beats him up. Harvey Roberts tells Joan what Jim had done to defend her honor in the saloon and she regrets that she was so hard on him.

(2) In *The Lost Wagon Train*, a rancher, a squaw-man with an Indian wife and daughter. He is a friend of Slim Blue's. Slim leaves Estelle there when he brings her from the wagon train taking her friends back to New Orleans. Leighton has sent men out to kidnap her and so Slim has asked Bradley to keep her with his family until the business between her father and Leighton is settled.

Bradley, Colonel: In *The Lost Wagon Train*, he tells Anderson at Council Grove that with conditions as they are in the war, he cannot provide a military escort for his caravan.

Bradshaw: In *Wyoming*, a friend of Nellie Glemm's mentioned as part of a group at the rodeo.

Bradway, Lincoln (Linc): In *The Maverick Queen*, comes to South Pass, Wyoming, on a mission. Zane Grey develops the character in the same vein as similar detective-gunmen, such as Buck Duane in *The Lone Star Ranger*, James Lassiter in *Riders of the Purple Sage* and Arizona Ames.

Lincoln Bradway comes to South Pass by stage to investigate the death of his partner, Jimmy Weston. He had received letters from Jimmy telling about falling in love with a Lucy. They broke up when he became involved with an unnamed dark-haired woman. The landlady, Mrs. Dill, tells him Jimmy was caught cheating at cards in Emery's saloon and killed in a shootout. Lincoln's faith in Jimmy tells him this cannot be true. The Jimmy he knew never cheated at cards in his life. Slowly, like Lassiter, he gathers clues, and pieces together what happened to his friend. His investigation leads him into a troubling situation where ranchers turn on cowboys and set up vigilance committees to catch and lynch rustlers.

In his first meeting with Lucy Bandon, Lincoln gives a summary of his life story. He is twenty-three years old but much older in experience than in years. He was born in Missouri and his father, whom he

had never seen, was a brother or cousin to the notorious Cole Younger the elder, a guerrilla after the
war and later a famous desperado. In fact, Lincoln
had never known either of his parents. A kindly
neighbor named Bradway raised him and sent him
to school. He took Bradway for his name. At fourteen he was on his own, on the cattle range. By the
age of sixteen, he was in Nebraska. There he became
Jimmy Weston's partner and there he rode the ranges
until he heard of Weston's death, and he pulled up
stakes and headed for Wyoming. His life has been
hard. He has been shot several times and most of the
bones in his body have been broken by horses. He
does not drink much, except on occasion. At eighteen, he met a bad hombre, a gun-slinging half-breed,
and killed him on the main street of Abilene in an
even break. That established his status as a killer.
Lucy tells Lincoln that Jimmy had told her many stories about his beloved hero, how he had killed a
dozen men and had had many love affairs. Lincoln
explains that his buddy was given to exaggeration
and he sometimes told him stories about romantic
involvements to satisfy his curiosity. One thing is
clear, though, the depth of loyalty and friendship
was mutual.

Bradway plunges into the fray in the Leave It Saloon. In a high-stakes poker game, he cleans out
Emery and McKeever, two malicious cardsharps, as
well as Lee, a rancher, and Kit Bandon, the Maverick Queen. The last two enjoyed being fleeced by a
skillful poker player, while the first two react with
suspicion, McKeever drawing a gun. Lincoln shoots
him in the shoulder. The episode establishes that he
is a man who can take care of himself and who cannot be easily intimidated or put off. As well, it establishes that he is a fair man. He could have killed Mc-
Keever, but hits him in the shoulder instead. Kit
Bandon decides Lincoln is the man for her. She has
toyed with most of the big ranchers, spurning their
proposals of marriage, and she thinks she can control Lincoln as easily as she does them. Lincoln, however, is a tough nut to crack. He is never sure
whether Kit is trying to save his life or get him killed.
If he does shoot it out with those men who can hurt
her or give her trouble, and kills them in an even
draw, that is good. If one of them should kill Lincoln,
then his investigation into matters that will expose
her crooked deals will be terminated. She figures she
will win either way. Lincoln is always wary of her intentions. As his friend Vince tells him, leopards'
spots are deep.

Lincoln faces down two gunmen, Gun Haskel in
South Pass, and Hank Miller in Rock Springs. Both
of these have been egged on to confront him. In both
cases, Lincoln shows himself to be cool, controlled,
fearless and competent. The same characterizes his
gathering of evidence in the death of his friend. He
recruits Vince, a down-on-his luck cowboy whose
horse he buys. Vince reminds him of Jimmy. He has
branded mavericks, like Jimmy; he loves a practical
joke, and he can read Lincoln's moods, talking when
appropriate and remaining quiet when it is called

for. Vince serves as his eyes and ears, gathering information from sources close to him, given Lincoln's
high profile in town since he shot McKeever and
Gun Haskel. Both of his partners, Mel Thatcher and
Vince, know more about Jimmy's death than they
are willing to reveal.

Lincoln falls in love with the scenery of Wyoming.
Like most Grey heroes, nature is a source of strength
and consolation. He decides he wants to ranch in a
particularly beautiful valley that Lucy loves as well.
He builds a road into the valley and plans to start
building a cabin. Vince and Mel Thatcher will join
him as partners in the ranch. Mel has a sweetheart
in Cheyenne that he plans to marry and settle down
with for good. His plans must be postponed, however, following the lynching of Kit. He takes Lucy
away for a while to forget.

Like Lassiter, Buck Duane, and Arizona Ames,
Lincoln Bradway is a man of compassion and fairness. He does not shoot to kill unless his life is at
stake. He shoots McKeever in the shoulder, when he
could have done much greater damage. He later
apologizes to McKeever for suspecting him of murdering Jim Weston after Doc Williamson's autopsy
proves the fatal bullet was not fired from his gun. He
also proposes that the two of them call it square between them. Lincoln takes Vince under his wing because he reminds him of Jimmy Weston — the same
recklessness, the same passion for life, the same loyalty and devotion. Like Jimmy, Vince needs someone
to keep him on the straight path. Sheriff Haught in
Rock Springs describes both Mel Thatcher and Vince
as cowboys who could go either way, developing into
either first-class citizens or first-class desperados as
circumstances decide. Above all, Lincoln feels sorry
for Kit Bandon, a woman of great beauty and charm,
but ruthless, determined, proud, blind to her weak
side. Lincoln is the only one to speak out for Kit
when the ranchers are preparing to lynch her. He has
some convinced that it is indecent to hang a woman,
that she should be handed over to the law for prosecution. He feels a profound sadness when the
ranchers decide she must be hanged because they
fear her revenge should she get free.

Brady: In *Majesty's Rancho*, the police officer
who stops the speeding Madge in Los Angeles. He is
immune to her charms and is determined to give her
a ticket. His argument with her leads to the "riot" of
the students in her support, which gets her expelled
from school.

Brady, Lieutenant: In *The U. P. Trail,* leads the
detachment near Medicine Bow. The detachment is
attacked by Sioux Indians, but Larry Red King finds
a way out of the trap in which they find themselves.

Brand: In *Majesty's Rancho*, one of the Madge
Stewart crowd at the university in Los Angeles.

Brander: (1) In *The Border Legion*, a miner and
general store owner at Bear Lake. Luce and later Gulder plan to kill Brander, steal his gold, and abduct
and rape his daughter. When Luce proposes this, Jim

Cleve beats him up for proposing to degrade a woman.

(2) In *Rogue River Feud*, the manager of the cigar store in Grant's Pass. He takes a liking to Keven Bell and warns him that Mulligan and his gang are looking for his partner, Garry, who has sold his fish to the rival cannery.

Brandeth, John: In *Rogue River Feud*, Rosamond Brandeth's father. He has gotten control of the canning factory at Gold Beach. He pays big wages. The cannery is an established business now. Brandeth had always been well off but he got rich during the war. He has built a magnificent new house. He owns a big fruit ranch down on the river and he has a finger in everything in Gold Beach. He took over Bell's store. Whether this was done by straight or crooked means, Keven's father does not say. He only adds that John Brandeth could have saved him from failing.

Brandeth, Rosamond: In *Rogue River Feud*, the daughter of John Brandeth and fiancée of Keven Bell. When Keven returns from the hospital, he is anxious to see her as he considers himself honorbound to release her from their engagement. Rosamond, however, shows little interest in talking to him. She is not at home when he drops by one day and she never returns his message to call him. He does see her one day driving by in a car and although her eyes make contact and she knows who he is, Rosamond drives by, pretending she has not seen him. Rosamond is now involved with Gus Atwell, the manager of her father's cannery. Keven understands now that she is a shallow, selfish individual. In the year that Keven is with Aard at Solitude, Rosamond, to her credit, breaks off with Atwell. She shows a renewed interest in Keven and tries to stir up trouble between him and Beryl Aard. She tells Beryl about her engagement to him before he left for army training camp. She gives Keven a call, but whatever spark had been there is now gone.

Brandeth, Steele: In *Arizona Ames,* partner with Noggin. Arizona Ames meets up with the horse thieves in a lonely canyon in Utah. From Steele's talk, he deduces he is from Kentucky. Brandeth wants to steal Arizona's horse, Cappy. When he decides to take Arizona into the outfit, he reveals they are planning to steal horses from a Morman horse rancher called Morgan. In the inevitable confrontation between Brandeth and Noggin, he is killed by his partner.

Brandon: In "The Camp Robber," one of the ranchers that Wingfield has worked for after spring roundup. He lasted only one payday there.

Brandon, Tex: (see also **Blanco, Wade Holden**) In *Shadow on the Trail,* the name that Wade Holden gives himself in Tombstone. It is a combination of a nickname, "Tex" and his mother's family name, Brandon. This is the name he goes by at Pencarrow's Cedar Range ranch.

Brandt, Collier: In *Riders of the Purple Sage*, a prosperous Mormon with four wives and many children. Jane Withersteen drops by his home when she is walking through Cottonwoods on her way to Mrs. Larkin's place. Each of the wives has her own part of the house with a separate entrance.

Brandt, Mary: In *Riders of the Purple Sage*, one of Collier Brandt's four wives. She is a close friend of Jane Withersteen's. Mary Brandt is aware of the predicament in which Jane Withersteen finds herself. Mary, however, does not approve of Jane's resisting the authority of Tull and Dyer. She advises her to consent to the marriage to Tull. Her justification is that a Mormon woman's duty is to submit. She should not look for personal happiness in this life; that will come in the next world. A woman's lot is to submit, to serve, to suffer. Jane cannot accept that a woman is merely born to suffer, to serve and to procreate.

Brandt, Roger: In *The Last Trail*, he is similar to Miller in *Betty Zane*, an insider turned traitor. Brandt is a French Canadian who arrives at Ft. Henry from Detroit. He claims to have been a pioneer, hunter, scout, soldier, trader — a jack-of-all-trades. He helped with rebuilding the fort after Girty's attack. Brandt seemed honest, and had money. He started the river barges between Ft. Pitt and Ft. Henry. The boat service has done the community a good service. He is popular with the young folk at the fort. Jonathan Zane has his suspicions of the man and Brandt is subsequently proven to be the inside man at the fort, selecting the horses to be stolen by his Shawnee associates.

Brandt and Legget arrange the kidnapping of Helen Sheppard. In the in-fighting that subsequently develops among the outlaws, Brandt kills Mordaunt. He and Legget escape to their cabin pursued by Wetzel. When Wetzel sets the cabin on fire with flaming arrows, Brandt manages to sneak out the back of the cabin and hide in a nearby shack. He later sneaks back to the fort where he gives himself up and throws himself on the mercy of the Colonel. When Helen begs for mercy, Brandt is released on condition that he never return to the fort. As his boat moves downriver, Brandt grabs his rifle to shoot Jonathan. Wetzel shoots him from the cliff overlooking the river.

Roger Brandt follows the pattern of Grey outlaws, men corrupted by the worst elements of civilization which are given free rein in the anarchy of the frontier.

Brandy: In *The U. P. Trail*, an Irish worker who is typical of the little people who have made the construction of the railroad possible. Men like him do the hard work, drink and gamble their pay, and dream of returning home some day.

Brann: In *Nevada*, a member of the Pine Tree Outfit. He loves to gamble and play cards and gamble. He wonders why Jim Lacy never plays cards or gambles or drinks. Sober men are not to be trusted.

Brasee, Conrad (Frenchy): In *West of the Pecos,* has taken over Dale Shevlin's adobe post at Eagle's Nest. He has two Mexicans working for him and a white bartender. Brasee works with Don Felipe Gonzalez, the most powerful rancher in the area. He sells Colonel Lambert supplies on credit, and on Don Felipe's orders calls in the debt and puts young Terril in jail.

Brault, Madam: In *Knights of the Range,* runs a finishing school for young ladies in New Orleans. Holly Ripple spends some eight years in her school, where Colonel Lee Ripple hopes she will be made into a Southern lady.

Braverman: In *The Border Legion,* one of the outlaws who helped rob the Alder Creek stage. He shares in the booty divided up back at the Cabin Gulch hideout and then promptly loses it all in the gambling which ensues.

Bray, Sheriff: In *The Drift Fence,* a lawman of whom Jim Traft quickly forms a bad opinion. When in town for the Fourth of July rodeo with his cowboys, he learns that Bray has arrested Curly Prentiss for drunkenness. Bray is a burly man, thick-featured, with a bluish cast of countenance. He wears his sheriff's badge and his gun rather prominently. The cowboys in the pool hall tell Jim that Bray has it in for the Diamond cowboys and that is why he has picked on Curly. When Jim Traft speaks to him about Curly, Bray accuses of the tenderfoot Jim Traft of playing a high hand. When Jim points out that Curly isn't even half-drunk, Bray threatens to arrest him for interfering with an officer of the law as his hand moves to the gun on his hip. Bray finally decides to release Curly into Jim's custody, fearing things might lead to shooting. Jim Traft thanks him graciously. In *The Hash Knife Outfit,* Sheriff Bray is still the ineffective sheriff of Flagg, Arizona. His prejudice against the Trafts is still evident. He prefers not to know about the rustling going on in his jurisdiction.

Brazos: In *The Lost Wagon Train,* Corny's (Slim Blue's) trusty horse.

Breese, Sam: In *The Lost Wagon Train,* a confederate of Leighton. He is a little, wiry man with a wizened face and a formidable look. He accompanies Leighton and Bruce Kennedy to Spider Web Canyon to track down Stephen Latch. He and Kennedy are prepared to betray Leighton and accept Latch's offer to give them the gold in Bowden's wagon in exchange for his life. He is shot and killed by Slim Blue, who arrives with Hawk Eye to rescue Latch.

Brennan, John: In *Nevada,* owns the Ace High Saloon in Winthrop. On the second floor there is a parlor where men can gamble. Brennan himself has the reputation of being square and of dealing severely with crooked gamblers. There are no women about the place.

Brewer: In *The Desert of Wheat,* one of Kurt Dorn's companions at the military training base. He is lean and lanky with dark hair.

Brice, Cal: In *Wyoming,* a friend of Smoky Reed. With Smoky, he makes fun of Andy Bonning, calling him a dude. Cal Brice is a rustler, like Smoky. Andy Bonning beats Cal Brice and his outfit at the rodeo.

Brice, Jerry: In *West of the Pecos,* an old friend of Pecos Smith's. He is about the same age as Pecos, sunburnt, tow-headed, blue-eyed, a fine, strapping fellow. Brice tells Pecos of his new ranching venture with his brother in New Mexico which was progressing slowly but surely. He predicts growth for the area with the herds being driven north to Dodge City and Abilene. He knows about Don Felipe's being run out of Rockport. He is down on his luck, or as Brice puts it, running out of rope.

Brick: In *The Maverick Queen,* Vince's favorite horse and, according to Lucy, the fastest horse in the Sweetwater valley. Vince must sell his horses to get money to pay back a loan to Kit Bandon, but when Lincoln buys the horses from Bill Headly, he gives Brick back to Vince, and the two become partners.

Bridgeman: In *The Lost Wagon Train,* the scout leading the wagon train carrying Estelle Latch is en route to Latchfield. He is a tall, rugged Texan, with gray eyes like gimlets. Corny (Slim Blue) recognizes him but does not know his name. The two greet each other warmly. Bridgeman tells Corny that he has quit his trail-driving days and is heading west to grow up with the country. He recommends that Corny try it himself.

Bridger, Jim: In *The Maverick Queen,* scouted the Wind River country and found the South Pass through the mountains. The famed Oregon Trail went through the South Pass.

Bridges: (1) In *The Mysterious Rider,* a stockman from Grand Lake who comes to Bellounds' White Slides Ranch with Sheriff Burley to confront Wilson Moore.

(2) In *Robbers' Roost,* a member of Hays's robbers' outfit. He is a sturdy, tow-headed, heavy man of forty or thereabouts, who had probably once been a farmer or villager. He has a bluff, hearty manner and seems not to pry under the surface. At Robbers' Roost, he serves as cook. He shares guard duty with Jim Wall on a promontory from which the entrances to Robbers' Roost can be observed. He is killed early in the assault on the roost by Heeseman's gang.

Brinkerhoff, Colonel: In *Wyoming,* the man who gave Ann Dixon's brother the leather knapsack that she is carrying. The young man who has picked Ann up hitchhiking tells her he knows Colonel Brinkerhoff, and, as it is too dangerous to be hitchhiking in the Black Bills, he will take her to the armory. Ann, however, is quick to reply that the colonel is not there, as he is on a fishing trip to Canada.

Brinks: In *The Wolf Tracker,* a professional tracker.

He approaches the camp of Adams's roundup crew on foot, an unusual circumstance out on the range. At a distance he appears to be old and bowed, but a second glance shows his shoulders to be broad and his stride that of a mountain man. He carries a pack on his back and a shiny rifle. His clothes are ragged and patched until they resemble a checkerboard. He has the weather-beaten face of a matured man of the open, mapped by deep lines, strong, hard — a rugged mask lighted by quiet grey eyes. Adams notes the quiet face, the deep chest, the muscular hands, the wiry body, the powerful legs. No cowboy, for all his riding, ever had wonderful legs like those. The man clearly walked a lot. He tells the men he has been a prospector, trapper, hunter — almost everything. He tracks men, horses, cattle, and wild animals, especially silvertips and wolves. The men assume he is after the five-thousand-dollar reward for Old Gray. They share with him what information they have about the wolf, and the following morning, he sets off on the trail of the loafer.

Grey presents Brinks as a natural man, a man formed by nature, living in the wilderness at an elemental level. He develops the pursuit of the great gray wolf as a contest in Darwinian terms, in which the fitter and stronger will triumph. As a boy of three, Brinks captured his first wild creature, a squirrel that he tamed, loved and eventually freed. All his early boyhood he was a hunter in the woods. At sixteen, he ran away from home. At fifty, he knew the West from the Yukon to the desert home of the Yaqui in Mexico. Brinks has only a dim recollection of home and family, vague things far in the past. He never loved a woman. He lived apart from men except when an accident of travel brought him into camps or settlements. Seldom did he dwell on the past unless the present task required it. He loves the solitude and loneliness of the wilderness. He seems to be part of them. When a young boy, a stepmother taught him to hate a house. As a child he had been punished at the table and never in his life afterward could he outgrow his hatred of a dining room. He views the pursuit of the great gray wolf as a challenge, not to better the cowboys and the government agents who had failed to corner the beast, but as a contest between himself and the wolf. He finds the tracks and follows them. The animal behaves in a predictable fashion, from one kill to another. At times, the wolf works with a pack; at other times alone. On occasion, the carcass suggests he kills for the joy of killing, rather than out of hunger. When Brinks spies the animal, he is genuinely impressed by the animal's size, at least four times that of a normal gray wolf. He gains respect for the wily wolf that seems at times to be playing games with him. He tracks the beast to a den, where the pack is sleeping off gorging on fresh blood and meat, but the old loafer has already left, probably sensing his presence. Brinks takes pleasure in the fact that the wolf had been too cunning to be holed up in a den by a hunter. Old Gray has all the earmarks of a worthy antagonist. When Brinks gets the animal in his

sights, he cannot pull the trigger. He lets out a stentorian yell, one that the wolf will be sure to remember. But the contest will be purely hand-to-hand between man and beast. The man gradually overtakes his quarry, guided by reason as well as instinct. The wolf is endowed only with instinct and physical prowess. In the mountain solitude, the five-hundred-thousand-year-old struggle between man and beast is re-enacted. But over the millennia, man evolved intelligence and reason to augment his instincts, while in his four-footed foes, instinct remained static. The deep snow gives the man on snowshoes an advantage over the large wolf that sinks the length of his legs with every step. The animal becomes weary and Brinks finally comes upon the craven wolf. Stories of trapped wolves fighting fiercely are fiction; all there is is fear, resignation. Brink strangles Old Gray with his bare hands.

When Brinks brings the hide in to Barrett's ranch, the cowboys see in him the manifestations of toil, endurance, and privation, but above all the indomitableness of spirit and endurance of body. The cowboys cannot understand him but he looms incomprehensibly great in their eyes. He rejects the reward. Having proven man superior to beast, and having the hide of his admirable foe are reward enough.

The tale of Brinks and the Old Gray loafer is interspersed with Grey's reflections on the evolution of man and of his ability to subdue nature, but also his link to the inescapable processes of the natural world.

Brite, Adam: In *The Trail Driver,* a cattleman in San Antonio who is planning to make three drives to Dodge in the same season. He has just returned from one drive, and has purchased some forty-five hundred head for a second drive. He is trying to find riders for this second expedition. His friend, Colonel Eb Blancahrd, has found him a young man, Texas Joe Shipman, to be trail boss. Shipman brings along his buddy, Less Holden, and he finds several other young men to sign on. Brite himself adds the gunman, Pan Handle Smith, to his crew. En route, a young man called Reddie Bayne rides in. He takes the young man on, and is impressed by the horse, Sam, that the young man is riding, and by the young man's skill with horses. Brite agrees to keep Reddie on when Reddie confesses he is really a young woman. She is alone in the world, and finds it easier to get along if she hides her identity. Brite protects Reddie from Wallen, who is attempting to get her back, as part of a deal he had made with Clay. Brite adopts her as his daughter. He has never been married and regrets having no family. He takes a shine to the young woman and offers her his protection. Brite witnesses the meeting of Roy Hallett and Ross Hite in Snell's saloon in Austin. Back at camp the following morning, he comes to Chandler's defense when Hallett accuses him of making a deal with Hite to betray the outfit and let them rustle the herd. He forgives the young man and keeps him on.

Brite is not directly involved in organizing the trail drive. He leaves that up to his foreman, Texas Joe Shipman. He gets a kick out of watching the romance between Texas and Reddie, and more than once encourages a trick at Shipman's expense. He advises Pan Handle not to go after Ross Hite in Dodge, but Pan Handle does things his own way. Brite recompenses his men generously for their work sharing part of the profits from the extra cattle Hite had collected when he had the herds. Reddie confides in Brite, her adopter father, her love for Texas Joe and her concern that he may become a gunman and get killed. Brite tells her that is something that she and Tex will have to work out. He does take her to Denman's merchandise emporium where she purchases some feminine articles of clothing. Brite and Reddie and Texas return to San Antonio after Hite is killed in a gunfight with Pan Handle, who then decides to accompany them back to Texas.

Britt, Cappy (Cappie, Captain, Cap): In *Knights of the Range*, a former Texas Ranger and Colonel Lee Ripple's foreman on his sixty-square-mile ranch. He has known Lee for many years, loving the colonel's daughter as if she were his own. He himself named her Holly after an old sweetheart. Britt is unmarried. He tries to get Lee Ripple to be more optimistic about the state of his health. The heart problem he has kept secret for so long may not be as serious as he suspects. The colonel, however, had kept this secret from Britt as well. He asks Britt to teach his daughter to manage the ranch, if that is what she chooses. He hopes she will marry some young cowboy and settle down to become a true Westerner. Britt and his friend and boss discuss the future of the area. The days of the isolated rancher are gone. The buffalo are gone. Settlers are arriving, with the accompanying rustling, gambling and other evils that towns bring. The future does not look as promising as the past.

Britt teaches Holly to manage the ranch, to ride like an Indian, to judge horses. Holly plans to continue her father's tradition of hospitality, a trend Britt encourages. Britt approves of her invitation to Frayne to join her riders. He explains to her that Frayne's outlaw status is nuanced. He is a hunted man, yes, but most likely by men who want revenge for the killing of a friend or a relative, or by genuine bad men he got the best of, or by bluff bad hombres who would like the fame of killing him. Britt appoints Renn Frayne to oversee his cowboys, to whip them into shape, teaching them to shoot more accurately and to develop loyalty to Holly Ripple. He is a force behind Holly's concept of "Knights of the Range." Britt instinctively suspects McCoy and instinctively trusts Renn Frayne. The gunman, in turn, trusts Britt and confides in him his most intimate secrets. He reveals his love for Holly to the old Texas Ranger, trusting him to keep the secret. Britt passes on advice from Frayne about the handling of the ranch to Holly without telling her where it comes from. At Christmas, when Holly is feeling depressed,

he tells her what Frayne had told him about loving her, about not feeling worthy of her love. He advises her to be patient, to wait, that all will work out in the end.

When McCoy and his clutch of ranchers appear, demanding that he get rid of Frayne, accusing him of rustling, Britt stands by his friend without hesitation. He alone accompanies Frayne to town to face Jeff Rankin. His faith in Frayne's goodness is never shaken. Like a father, he is pleased to see Holly marry the man she truly loves.

In *Twin Sombreros*, Britt is mentioned as a friend of Sheriff Kiskadden who had served in the Texas Rangers with him under McKelvey. As well, Kiskadden had ridden for Ripple outfit years ago when Britt was foreman.

Brittenham, Dale: In *The Horse Thief*, he's in an awkward position where his best friend and hero, Leale Hildrith, is engaged to the woman he, too, is in love with. As well, he learns that this beloved friend is the inside man in the Salmon River Valley for the horse rustlers. He has been too shy to pursue Edith, daughter of a wealthy rancher, while he is a mere rider. He believes, however, that he can save his friend from ruin before he marries Edith. Dale reveals what he heard at the rustlers' camp. Leale swears him to secrecy and promises that this last raid was the end of his involvement with Mason. Leale, however, says nothing when Stafford and Sheriff Bayne arrive to arrest him. Dale confesses to being a rustler, hoping to give Leale a chance to redeem himself. He plans to go after the rustlers and expose the operation. With the help of his Indian friend, Nalook, he tracks the horse to Halsey, where a big auction is taking place. He recognizes many of Watrous's prized thoroughbreds among the herd. He tells Strickland and other ranchers there that stolen horses are among the animals. Edith Watrous arrives with Sue Bradford and Leale Hildrith, and makes the same claim. The confrontation ends with Edith being abducted by Reed. With the help of his Palouse Indian friend, Nalook, he tracks the thieves to their cabin in the canyon hideout. Big Bill Mason is there. He witnesses the confrontation where Reed accuses Hildrith of betrayal. Big Bill Mason shoots Leale, and Reed is to take Edith back to her father. Dale rescues her, while Nalook fights and kills Big Bill Mason. On a previous visit to the valley, Dale had met Rogers, a homesteader in the valley and neighbor to Big Bill Mason. He takes Edith there for safety until the fight is over. Sheriff Bayne shows up with a posse to arrest him for the previous charge of rustling. He plans to hang him on the spot, but Edith puts a stop to than with skillfully placed shots at the sheriff. The lynch party is also decimated by fleeing rustlers who shoot Bayne and Pickens as they ride past. When Dale returns to Salmon, Jim Watrous consents to Edith's marrying him. As well, he offers Dale a partnership in the cattle business he plans to enter with Stafford. Edith receives the five-thousand-dollar reward Stafford had placed on his head, dead or alive.

Brooks: In *Stairs of Sand,* an outlaw and a prospector. He and Bill Stark capture Wansfell on orders from Guerd Larey. Stark does not know their prisoner is Wansfell. Brooks did recognize him but kept that fact from the other men. He would double-cross Guerd just as quickly as he would carry out the order to shoot him. Brooks had known him as a prospector. He probably thinks Wansfell has found gold in the canyon and that is what Guerd is after. He hopes to get Wansfell to reveal its whereabouts. When Stark learns Wansfell's identity, he sets him free, returning a favor he had shown Stark's wife many years ago. Stark kills Brooks in a shootout.

Brooks, Daisy (Dais): In *The Dude Ranger,* the daughter of Sam Brooks, and cousin of Anne Hepford. She is a pretty young girl, engaged to Nebraskie, but weak and easily influenced by a stronger personality. Ernest first meets her at the ranch where her father has invited him to dinner. He is impressed by her at that meeting. The tidy little cottage, the wholesome, savory dinner attest to her ability as her father's housekeeper. He notes her shy beauty, her timidity, like a modest cornflower. Sam Brooks tells Ernest that Nebraskie and Daisy had been sweethearts until Dude Hyslip cut him out. Nebraskie was serious but Dude is only fast and loose. Daisy warns Ernest not to let her cousin Anne make a fool of him. She loves to string the cowboys along and then unceremoniously dump them. Daisy is so concerned about Ernest that Nebraskie thinks she is interested in him. Daisy feels indebted to Ernest for protecting her from Dude at the dance. Daisy's weakness becomes more obvious to Ernest when he comes across her and Dude at the ranch. Sam Brooks is removed from the picture when Hyslip brings him a bottle, and before long, he is passed-out drunk leaving Daisy at his mercy. She seems incapable of resisting him, although she claims to hate him. When Daisy confesses to Nebraskie what has happened, that she is afraid Hyslip has got her into trouble, he suggests they get married as soon as possible. That "soon as possible" does not happen before Hyslip makes another visit, when Nebraskie catches them and kills Hyslip in a fight. They elope to Snowflake where Parson Peabody marries them. As they are leaving the church, Ernest and Anne show up for the same purpose. Daisy lends Anne her ring for the ceremony.

Brooks, Sam (Uncle Brooks): In *The Dude Ranger,* the father of Daisy Brooks, married to a cousin of John Hepford. Anne calls him Uncle Brooks. Sam Brooks was the original manager of the Red Rock Ranch for Silas Selby. Brooks tells Ernest that Hepford is the kind of cattleman riders won't ride for unless they have to. He has run Red Rock into the ground. Ernest has heard things not exactly complimentary about the way he runs a ranch. Sam Brooks had built up Red Rock for Selby. At one time there were sixty thousand head of cattle. When Selby bought the ranch he gave Brooks a hundred acres of land at the head of the valley of which Hepford, when he had ousted Brooks from his job, could not get possession. He resents that Hepford and his daughter seem to feel they own the ranch. Ernest feels he has found a friend in the old gentleman, and asks Sam if he can come to work for him if things go badly at Red Rock. Sam agrees. Brooks's weakness is his love of liquor. Dude Hyslip comes by, gives him a bottle, and Sam passes out in a drunken stupor, leaving Daisy, his daughter, at the mercy of Hyslip. This happens too frequently for Daisy, who feels defenseless. When Hepford fires Siebert, Nebraskie and Ernest, they come to work at his ranch for room and board. They do a lot of necessary repairs around the ranch, building and fixing fences, tending the cattle, and above all, keeping an eye the ranch house in case Hepford and Hyslip should appear. The day Hyslip is shot by Nebraskie, Sam has succumbed to drink again, and Hyslip has forced himself on Daisy. Sam, however, recovers in time to witness the fight, and with Siebert, reports to the sheriff what happened.

Brown: In *Raiders of Spanish Peaks,* the storekeeper in Garden City, Kansas, from whom Lindsay buys the wagons he needs for the trip to his new ranch. He also orders furniture and other supplies from this man. Brown finds drivers for the wagons as well.

Brown, Ben: In *Boulder Dam,* landlord of Lynn Weston, who boards in the village built to house workers at the dam. Ben Brown is an ironworker — a pipe setter at the construction site. He works long hours and Mrs. Brown is often alone and lonely. Lynn rescues him when he falls into the tunnel through which the diverted river flows. Weston tries to befriend him but the man becomes increasingly morose. He takes a night shift, the one most disliked by the workers. He spends the day sleeping. Lynn Weston learns from Whitney Curtis that Ben Brown is involved with Sproul and Moore, the communist agitators bent on sabotaging the construction at the dam. Brown suspiciously takes his tool bag everywhere with him, arousing Weston's curiosity. He has fixed the pipes so that they will break with the pressure of the cement and the force of an explosion. He leaves Nevada before the police can capture him. They do learn, however, that he was not a convinced communist but a dupe of Sproul's.

Brown, Charley: In *Valley of Wild Horses,* a young miner that Pan Handle meets in the Chinese restaurant in Marco. The young miner has a wife and a child born after he left home. He hopes to make his fortune in the diggings. Dick Hardman and Purcell have attempted to drive him off his claim. Pan Handle invites him to join with the horse wranglers to catch a large number of horses. Brown goes along. Pan Handle invites Charley to join his family on the trip to Arizona, but he returns to his diggings.

Brown, Mrs.: In *Boulder Dam,* the wife of Ben Brown, the pipe setter at Boulder Dam. Her husband is away at work much of the time and she feels lonely. She invites Lynn Weston and Anne Vandergrift to board with them. When the gangsters from Vegas find Anne and abduct her again, Mrs. Brown describes the men and the car used to take her away. Mrs. Brown is unaware of her husband's involvement with Sproul and Moore in the plot to sabotage the construction at Boulder Dam.

Brown, Rodney: A rancher in *The Lone Star Ranger* who pretends to be a respectable businessman but who in reality is a thief. He recognizes Luke Stevens in Mercer and shoots him as he is riding out of town. Stevens dies from the wound two days later. Buck Duane later learns from Andrews that Brown had boasted how he killed Stevens. Andrews tells Buck that Brown had also ruined him with his thievery and asks Buck to settle the score with him.

Brown, Tuck: In "Avalanche," has been to town before Jake Dunton drops by for a visit at the Brown farm. He informs Jake that word has it in town that Kitty Mains is going to the dance with Ben Stillwell.

Broydon: In *Nevada*, Ben Ide leaves word with the Franklidges that he would like Hettie to meet him the morning after the dance in town at Broydon's ranch.

Bruce, Coil: In *Horse Heaven Hill*, a clean-cut youth, one of the cowboys who work on the Wade ranch. He, Red and Hurd Blanding are playing cards when Lark Burrell comes to the barn, dressed like a boy, looking for a horse to ride. He does not realize she is a girl, and ignores her request. Coil meets her again at the dance and Lark says she likes him the best of all the cowboys she has met. Coil is impressed with Lark's ability to handle horses, and she tells him about her ranch back in Idaho, where she had many horses, some tamed, some wild. Horses of all kinds are well known to her. Like Lark, Bruce opposes Blanding's plan to trap wild horses for sale to the slaughter houses. Coil tells Lark how Blanding became friends with Ellery Wade and foreman of the Wade outfit. He and the other cowboys dislike Blanding for a number of reasons, but especially because of the way he lords it over them. Since he has been around, they seldom get invited anywhere. Coil and Red and the other cowboys are glad that Stanley Weston knocked the stuffing out of Blanding over comments he made about Marigold. Coil summarizes the gossip that Blanding has been spreading about his involvement with Marigold, Weston's fiancée, underlining the justification for his jealousy. Coil seems fond of Lark, and at moments, she feels Stanley Weston is a bit jealous of her time with Coil. Lark takes Bruce's rope from his saddle to Coil when she goes to free the wild mustangs Blanding is holding in the corral in the canyon. Bruce identifies the burnt rope when Howard and Blanding come into the Wade camp to accuse Stanley of freeing the captured horses. Bruce cannot explain how the rope got to be out on the range, but he reveals that he has seen Hurd Blanding wandering around their camp at night.

Bruce, Simm: In *To the Last Man,* is a member of the Hash Knife gang and the Jorth faction. He boasts that Ellen Jorth is his girl and he jokes about her "loose behavior" in Greaves's store when Jean Isbel is present. Isbel forces him to retract his lies about her, beating him up, together with Jorth's Mexican foreman, Lorenzo. Back at the Jorth ranch, he tells a fantastic story about how Isbel had beat him up with an axe in an argument over the Isbel-Jorth range war. Ellen confronts him with the truth as John Sprague told her what happened. After the Jorths have retreated to Greaves store after the siege of the Isbel ranch house, the dying Greaves tells all that Jean Isbel had spoken to him before stabbing him. Isbel said he was avenging the insult to Ellen Jorth in his store. Lee Jorth then kills Simm Bruce himself. In many of Grey's novels, men like Simm Bruce are punished for impugning the reputation of a good woman.

Brunelle: In *The Desert of Wheat,* a solider Kurt Dorn meets in France. He is the only survivor of his squad, which fought in the Battle of Verdun. He describes the horrors of battle at the front.

Brush: In *The U. P. Trail,* one of the construction workers who join Neale and King and Slingerland on the buffalo hunt, which ends in a fight with the Sioux.

Bruthwait: In *Wildfire,* one of the six members of the horsemen's club which meets to select the date for the annual race at Bostril's Ford. He enters two horses, Bay and Charley, in the race but they don't stand a chance next to Bostril's Sage King, Creech's Blue Roan and Lucy's Wildfire. Bruthwait would not mind seeing Bostril taken down a peg or two with a loss in the race.

Brutus: In *Wild Horse Mesa,* Chane Weymer's horse. Brutus is a mustang that Chane Weymer captured and broke. The animal is spectacular, inspiring admiration in all who see him. McPherson decides to steal the horse from Chane immediately upon spotting the animal. His attempts do not succeed. When Chane Weymer is pursuing Panquitch, he discovers that Brutus is the faster horse. Brutus is not exactly a giant of a horse, though higher and heavier than average. His chest is massive, broad, deep — a wonderful storehouse of energy. Such powerful, perfectly proportioned and sound legs are unusual in a horse. His body is large, round, smooth, with an arched neck and fine head and an oval white spot on his face. Chane broke him with gentle, kind persuasion and the animal becomes a comrade, a friend and sweetheart and a savior as well as an incomparable mount.

Buck: In *30,000 on the Hoof,* Logan Huett's saddle horse from his days as a scout in the cavalry. Buck learns the trade of cow horse until Huett is prosperous enough to buy some farm horses.

Buck Jones: In *Majesty's Rancho,* Ren Starr compares Lance Sidway in his cowboy gear to Buck Jones, a Western TV star very popular at the time.

Buckles: In *Wildfire,* Lucy Bostril's mustang, the horse she prefers riding. He is fast, but no match for the Sage King, her father's pride and joy.

Buckskin: (1) In *The Fugitive Trail,* Trinity Spencer's horse.

(2) In *The Vanishing American,* the mustang Withers gives Marian to ride to Oljato (Moonlight on water).

(3) In *Wyoming,* a mustang that Fenner bought for Martha Dixon. He is being kept at Stanley's corral.

Bud: (1) In *Majesty's Rancho,* one of the gangsters who holds up the truck Lance Sidway is driving. He has been ordered to steal the bootleg liquor the truck is supposed to be transporting. Lance gives him a bum steer, telling him the trucks have gone on to El Paso, and he points them to a shortcut.

(2) In *The Man of the Forest,* a baby brown bear, one of Milt Dale's pets. He is fearful of Helen and Bo Rayner when they first arrive, staying out of the camp until Milt calls him. Tom is jealous of Bud, and Bud in turn is afraid of the cougar as they compete for Dale's attention.

Budd: In *The Border Legion,* the sixth man who is at the cabin in the Alder Creek, but his name is not given until later. When it becomes clear that the vigilantes are aware of who the members of the gang are, Budd declares at the meeting that there is a "nigger in the woodpile." Kells cautions him that he should not make accusations against legion members without more solid proof. However, all evidence points to a traitor in the group. When the stolen gold has been divided up and the outlaws are gambling among themselves, Budd takes part in a card game with Kells and is accused of having cheated three times. Kells shoots and kills him.

Buell: In *Fighting Caravans,* the new agent for Aull and Company. He makes Couch a take-it-or-leave-it offer to freight a ninety-wagon caravan to Kansas City. If he refuses, he will never again be offered a contract by Aull and Company. When they return from this mission, Buell reports on Mrs. Clement and May Bell joining a caravan en route to Fort Larned.

Buff: In *Fighting Caravans,* the nickname given to Clint Belmet after he kills his first buffalo. The nickname sticks. It is the name that Kit Carson and Dick Curtis always use with him.

Buffalo Bill: In *The Thundering Herd,* mentioned as a great killer of buffalo. He had been hired to shoot buffalo to feed the men working on the construction of the railroads and to help clear the prairie of buffalo so that the trains could pass unobstructed. He is contrasted with Colonel Buffalo Jones who earned his "buffalo" nickname for his desire to preserve the buffalo. In *Twin Sombreros,* Buffalo Bill is mentioned as having lived at Fort Lyon when he worked providing buffalo meat for the army post nearby.

Bullet: In *The Lone Star Ranger,* Buck Duane's new horse. The animal is unusually big, strong, and impressive. All remark on the quality of the mount. As well, the horse has an impressively engraved Mexican saddle and bridle. This is the first horse that Buck Duane has had in years which was not used merely for speed or convenience. This horse is a true friend, a partner, one who shares adventures and troubles. This horse reminds Buck of what he has become in his years on the run — a selfish man, wary, nervous, hard.

Bullon: In *Shadow on the Trail,* the outlaw leader of a group called the Diamond B. According to Lawsford, this group got its share of Pencarrow's initial herd of twenty thousand.

Bunge, Ben: In *Stranger from the Tonto,* a member of the Hole-in-the-Wall gang. He had left the hideout with Kitsap, Neberyull, Goins and Silk Slotte, taking Lucy Bonesteel's horse, Spades, with them. Bunge deserts the group, taking the horse with him. He runs into Kent Wingfield, camped out on his way to fulfill his promise to Bill Elway to rescue Lucy Bonesteel from her confinement in the hideout. He tells Kent he raised Spades from a colt and that the horse was used to gentler hands than his. He explains that he pulled out when Slotte double-crossed him. Slotte and his men at Logan's trading post recognize Spades, and Wingfield explains how he came to have the horse. He repeats what Bunge had told him about the group. Back at the hideout, Bunge reappears some time later. He tells about running into some Piute Indians who had tried to get the horse from Wingfield only to get shot. He tries to impress on Bonesteel that these Piutes are now their enemies. Not giving away that Kent Wingfield is there in the hideout, Bonesteel asks where the horse and the money are. Bunge tells them about meeting Wingfield, a man wanted for killing a sheriff in Payson. He was in a shootout with Slinger Dunn in the Drift Fence War. He rode for the Hash Knife Outfit and he killed Old Jim Stevens and three of his men. He is a wonder with a rifle and a gun. He also says that Winfield had left Wagontongue with an old prospector and returned alone with a lot of gold. He is suspected of having killed the old man. Bunge is taken aback when he is told to go knock on Kent Wingfield's door. Kent shoots at him and he runs off scared, his outlaw companions getting a great laugh at his expense. He has to confess he had lied about the money. Bonesteel tells Kent he should shoot Bunge, but Wingfield spares him. In the shootout between Roberts's outlaws and Bonesteel's men, Bunge is shot and killed.

Burch, Carley: In *The Call of the Canyon,* a twenty-six-year-old socialite in New York City in 1918. She does not remember her father at all, and her mother left her in the care of her Aunt Mary. Independently wealthy, she has traveled to Europe, which she knows better than the United States. She has only visited a few places on the East Coast and some vacation spots in the Adirondacks. The farthest west she has ever been is Jersey City. She is engaged to marry Glenn Killbourne, who has returned from service in France in the Great War and moved west.

As the story begins, Carley is troubled by a letter from Glenn Killbourne who has moved to Arizona, ostensibly for health reasons. Aunt Mary tells Carley she is blind to what Glenn has said in the letter about not wanting to return to New York, but adds that because Carley can feel hurt by what he says, there is still hope for her. She urges Carley to make a surprise visit to Glenn in Arizona. Aunt Mary sees Glenn's letter as a hint that he wants Carley to join him. Carley hesitates about undertaking such a journey. Although she has traveled in groups, she has never taken a trip on her own. She is reluctant to leave New York because everything that really interests her is there.

On her way, she realizes that she knows nothing about her own country. The wheatfields of Kansas do not interest her. The change in altitude, the climate, the people she sees and meets interest her not at all. She regards them as uncouth denizens of an under-developed foreign land. In Arizona, though, the West begins to penetrate her New York shell. She is surprised at the way the landscape can affect her. When she arrives at Lolomi Lodge, she underlines that she is Glenn Killbourne's fiancée, a fact already well-known by all there. She is troubled, however, to learn that the Hutters— Mrs. Hutter, Tom and Flo— seem to know Glenn better than she does. They have heard all about his experiences in the war, his illness, his mental and physical torment, his hopes and fears— things he has not shared with her. Nevertheless, she likes the Hutters and feels at home.

The Glenn she meets is a changed man. He has regained his health, and he is in good spirits. She feels beloved again when he kisses and hugs her. But there is something new about him. She wonders at his aloofness, and feels he is unfamiliar, withdrawn. Carley senses that Flo is a rival for Glenn's affections and determines she will prove herself up to any challenge.

Carley discovers she has the stamina to endure a rough ride into the mountains to view the Painted Desert and to visit the sheep ranch Glenn and Tom operate. Forewarned by Charley that Flo likes to play tricks on greenhorns, Carley shows herself equal to the challenge. She is thrown from an unruly bronc (one Flo has approved for her use), laughs off stories about tarantulas, snakes, and hydrophobic skunks and doesn't run scared when Glenn plays a trick on her, pretending to be a bear poking around the camp in the dark. Her good-humored acceptance of the ribbing wins the day. She secretly wishes Flo would come to New York so she could turn the tables on her.

Carley, however, does see that she is not the kind of wife Glenn expects. She cannot cook. She has mastered none of the skills of a housewife. She over-hears Lee Stanton and Flo discuss Flo's interest in Glenn. They question Carley's suitability as a wife

for him and her willingness to adapt to Glenn's desire to live in the West. Lee Stanton seems to understand Carley best. He stands in relation to Flo as Carley stands in relation to Glenn: both want someone who does not fully want them. Lee notes how Carley is moved by the desert, commenting that she will have to keep returning to view the panorama until she decides what it means for her. Carley thinks to herself, that "hereditary influence could not be comparable to such environment in the shaping of character." Perhaps this explains the changes in Glenn.

The West becomes a test not only of her mettle but of her self-knowledge. Her encounter with Ruff Haze brings out the great difference in values between the New York she knows and Arizona and the true America. At Flo's birthday party, Carley dresses in a provocatively stunning white dress which attracts the attention of everyone. Such a dress, and her flirting, would have been perfectly normal at a New York social function. At Lolomi Lodge, they are risqué and out of place. Later, Ruff Haze makes advances to her, and she rebuffs him, only to meet him later at the cabin on the sheep ranch. Ruff Haze has fought with Glenn about his "insult" to Carley, with Ruff ending up being dipped in the sulphurous sheep dip. He tells her that her behavior at the party had been cheap and superficial and that she had got what she was looking for. No woman dresses or behaves the way she does to grab the attention of men, and then complains when a man is aroused. She's depressed with her discovery of her superficiality, but Glenn cheers her up, commenting that he loves her because she has great potential. She realizes she has missed the most important moments in Glenn's life because she was too self-absorbed, and feels hurt by his suggestion that she is not woman enough to help him rebuild his life in the West.

Before leaving for New York, she buys six hundred and forty acres at Deep Lake, hoping to make a present of the land to Glenn. Tom Hutter arranges the purchase for her and keeps her secret. Carley returns to New York a changed woman. The scenery she found so uninteresting on her way to Arizona now speaks to her American soul. Her old companions and activities in New York appear superficial and self-absorbed. She no longer appreciates the lives of her bosom friends who think that enjoying themselves, attending parties, flirting with men who are not their husbands, or flirting with married women is acceptable behavior. Her friends think she has gone off the deep end — that the West has made her lose her bearings.

"When visiting with Virgil Rust, a war veteran friend of Glenn's, Carley grasps how she appears to the people in Arizona." Virgil's girl had dumped him while he was overseas, marrying a young man who managed to evade his army duties. Carley is convinced she is every bit the shallow woman that Ruff Haze described and as bad as Virgil's faithless friend. She visits another girlfriend who has married and is raising a family, a friend who has been ignored by her in-crowd because she has no time for their frivolous activities. To her surprise, she finds she now has more in common with Elise Ferguson than with Eleanor, Beatrice and Morrison.

The year in New York convinces Carley that her true self lies in Arizona. She tells Aunt Mary that she plans to return west to built a house on her land and to marry Glenn if he will still have her. Aunt Mary offers to join her on the trip, and to settle with her in Arizona. They depart from New York for good, leaving a way of life that is decadent and superficial. Carley is full of hope and enthusiasm for the future. She has finally found herself. Carley builds her house, prepared to meet Glenn with the surprise. Charley, however, tells her maliciously that Glenn and Flo are married and have just returned from their honeymoon. Angry with Glenn and even mores so with herself, she goes to the lodge to offer the couple her best wishes. Thanks to her Western experience, she has learned to face facts. She accepts her fate as the result of her own stupidity and selfishness. To her surprise, Glenn meets her before she gets to the lodge, and tells her Flo married Lee Stanton, and that Charley was just playing one of his practical jokes on her.

Carley Burch is one of several female characters in Zane Grey's novels who discover their true nature and true values in the West. They are wealthy women, with more money than sense, who go west to join a brother or a former lover. The Western environment teaches them what it means to be a woman, a lover, a wife, and an American.

Burley, Sheriff: In *The Mysterious Rider,* an old acquaintance of Hell Bent Wade from Kremmlin'. He is an experienced, shrewd lawman, hard on rustlers but thoroughly professional and no fool. Buster Jack brings him to White Slides to investigate the rustling of his father's cattle and to lay charges against Wilson Moore. Bent Wade follows the rustlers to the cabin and kills them in a gunfight, but he spares the life of Buster Jack, on the condition that he free Columbine of her promise to marry him. When Burley comes to conduct the official investigation, he informs Wade that the evidence points to a fourth man in the cabin, but he does not press the point, knowing Bent Wade has a good reason for remaining silent. He drops the charges against Wilson Moore.

Burnham, Mrs.:   In *Captives of the Desert*, lives in Taho. Mrs. Jenkins, wife of the government agent at Leupp, is spending a month with her. She has just arrived in Taho.

Burrell, Lark: In *Horse Heaven Hill*, grew up on a ranch in Idaho. Her mother was part Nez Perce Indian and she has retained some features of her Indian grandmother. Nineteen-year-old Lark loves the ranch on which she grew up and the wild horses that live in the mountains but when her father dies, she leaves the place in the care of Jeff, an old ranch hand. She moves to Wadestown to live with Mr. Wade, who

was once partners with her father. Lark feels a bit out of place with her cousin Marigold and her family. Marigold has a university education and Mr. Wade runs a merchandise store in town. She herself has only the education her mother could provide at home, and she has always worked for a living. She hopes to work at the Wade store to pay for her keep. The Wades, however, tell her she is like a daughter to them, and will not hear of her working. Lark also discovers that her values are not those of Marigold and her university friends who come to visit. Marigold considers the wild mustangs a nuisance and Blanding's rounding up and selling the animals to a slaughterhouse a sensible move, a sign of progress. As well, she finds Marigold's flirting with Blanding and other cowboys at the dance more than a bit strange since Marigold has been engaged for five years to Stanley Weston, an extremely handsome and honorable young rancher. Lark discovers that she and Stanley Weston have a lot in common. They share a love of the lonely landscape, the wild mustangs, and ranch life and ranch work. She does nothing to encourage Stanley's interest in her, but on occasion she senses that he resents her friendship with Coil Bruce. Lark has a way with horses; Coil Bruce comments that he has never seen a girl with such know-how. Coil shares with her what information he has about Marigold and Blanding, encouraging her to do something to get Marigold to come to her senses. She tries to convince Stanley that Marigold is just high-strung, that she really does love him. But matters in that camp develop on their own. When Ellery Wade and Blanding plan a second roundup of wild horses, she does her best to prevent it. Marigold Wade has organized a camping trip for her college friends to watch the roundup. The cruelty and indifference to injured animals on the part of Blanding convince Lark to do something. Stanley catches her releasing the animals. He warns her that this could mean big trouble with Blanding. When Hurd comes to the Wade camp to accuse Stanley of having released the herd and to demand compensation for the freed animals, Blanding tries to draw on Weston on the sly. Lark shoots him in the arm, preventing a full-fledged shootout. Previous to his showdown over the horses, Stanley informed Lark that Marigold had broken her engagement to him. He proposes marriage to Lark and she accepts. Mr. Weston sees in her the perfect mate for his rancher son. They return on their honeymoon to her ranch in Idaho. Their plans include modernizing the ranch and making it a profitable operation.

Burrell, Mr.:   In *Horse Heaven Hill*, Lark Burrell's father. He had been in the cattle business with Mr. Wade years before Lark was born. Stanley Weston's father says he was a "real Westerner of the old school." Mr. Burrell liked the unfenced ranges while Wade leaned toward the settlements. When Mr. Burrell dies, he extends an invitation to Lark to come live with his family and to make it her new home.

Burridge, Cash: In *Nevada*, a gambler, rustler,

and associate of Less Sutter. Nevada had taken part in a stagecoach robbery with Burridge some years ago. Burridge is back in Lineville when Nevada returns there after saving Ben Ide's reputation by killing Setter and capturing Hall and his rustlers. Burridge has just returned from Arizona, where he was involved in a deal which he swears was on the up-and-up. He is young, handsome, dissolute, loud, with a curling mustache, almost gold in color. He has gleaming, restless blue eyes. Burridge is quite a ladies' man, having taken Lize Teller from Holder, a rancher with whom she was involved. Burridge has much more glitz and charm and can be agreeable and persuasive when needed. Nevada and Burridge talk about Nevada's absence. He figures that Nevada has killed Setter, although Nevada remains mum about the subject. Lize Teller tells Nevada that Setter had given Burridge a hundred thousand dollars to invest in a cattle ranch in Arizona. He has bought a place and is waiting for Setter to return. He complains that the cattle on his ranch are being rustled. He offers Nevada a chance to come in with him on the project. Nevada doubts Burridge will make a success of the job because he's too fond of womanizing and cannot go straight. Prosperity, liquor and women will be the ruination of him. In Arizona, he sells the ranch to Ben Ide. The ranch is ideally located, with spectacular scenery. Ide, however, learns that Burridge has a bad reputation among the ranchers. He sold Ben Ide cattle that he really didn't own, as both Tom Day and Elam Hatt have liens of several thousand dollars on the herds. He palms his debts off on the new owner. Burridge runs into Jim Lacy (Nevada) at the Ace High saloon. Here he confesses to Nevada that he lost the money he had made on the sale of the ranch gambling with Hardy Rue. He is now part of the Pine Tree Outfit. Nevada meets him at the Hatt ranch. Burridge praises Jim Lacy's wisdom in returning the stolen stallion to Ben Ide. He knows various members of the gang but does not know who the leader is. He quits the outfit before the last assault on Ben Ide's and Tom Day's herds.

Burt: In *The Man of the Forest*, one of the outlaws with Snake Anson at the cabin for the meeting with Beesley. He is one of the gang that kidnaps Bo Rayner. He shoots a deer to feed the outfit. He is friendly with Shady Jones and Jim Wilson. When the outlaws start fighting among themselves, he is frightened and runs off uninjured.

Burthwait: In *Wildfire*, a rider from Durango who enters two horses, Bay and Charley, in the annual race at Bostril's Ford. He is a friend and rival of Bostril, looking forward to him being taken down a peg when his horses are beaten in the race.

Burton: In *Nevada*, a local rancher.

Burton, Bill: In *The Lost Wagon Train*, an old scout and wagon master who arrives at Fort Union on April 10 with many dead and wounded, to report a scrimmage with the Comanches. He looks askance at the thousands of Indians from mixed tribes present at the fort. He does not believe there is such a thing as a peace-loving Indian.

Burton, Bloom: In *The Maverick Queen*, up in a tree on a hill spying on the goings-on at Kit Bandon's ranch. He is watching the cattle being gathered for a drive. Lincoln Bradway correctly concludes that he is there to count the yearlings in the herd. Burton has part-interest in Hargrove's ranch and is clearly in league with Lee and the other cattlemen aiming to take the law into their own hands to resolve the rustling problem. From Burton, Lincoln learns that Jimmy Weston was killed at the Bandon ranch and taken to town in a wagon by a cowboy named Hank Miller, a teamster for Hirsh. The wagon was left in South Pass and Jimmy Weston's Stetson was found in it. When Lincoln says he will drop by Hargrove's, he asks him not to mention their meeting. Burton was supposed to be working undercover, and Hargrove will not appreciate word of their subterfuge getting around. Bradway promises not to mention their meeting.

Burton, George: In *The Call of the Canyon*, shares a bunk next to Virgil Rust in a veteran's hospital in New York. He is originally from Illinois and after his release from the hospital, he plans to go to southern Kansas to take up farming. He goes to Carley Burch to ask for financial help to start his farm. He had heard about Carley and her generous nature from Virgil Rust, Glenn Killbourne's friend. He asks her to lend him five hundred dollars to get him started and she gladly offers more help if he needs it. Evidently, Virgil Rust had not told him the whole story about Carley.

Burton (Belding), Nell: In *Desert Gold*, the daughter of Nell Warren and Robert Burton. She is the child who was born out of wedlock, bringing disgrace on her mother, Nell Warren, and her grandfather. She appears in the novel when Dick Gale arrives at Belding's ranch with Mercedes Castañeda. Tom Belding describes her as wild as an antelope, with little interest in boys. She tells Dick that she has traveled a lot, from Lawrence, Kansas, to Stillwater, Oklahoma, to Austin, Texas, then to Waco, Texas, to New Mexico and Douglas, Arizona, and finally, Forlorn River. She quickly becomes friends with Mercedes.

When no word has come from George Thorne, she urges Dick Gale to go to Casita to find out what has become of him. Dick refuses to go on Tom Belding's orders, so Nell sets out herself on Blanco Sol. When she reaches the cavalry garrison at Casita, she learns that George Thorne has gone on leave but has been captured by Rojas and taken to Mexico. Rojas is holding him, hoping he will reveal the whereabouts of his prey, Mercedes. Begging and pleading will not convince the cavalry to cross the border to rescue George, so she goes herself, forcing them to follow her, thereby effecting Thorne's release.

Nell falls in love with Dick Gale. They share a love of the natural world and especially of horses. Nell is the first one to meet the Chases in Forlorn River. She has been accosted by the young Radford. He is self-assured, arrogant, determined to get what he wants. He strikes her as another Rojas in his attitudes and methods of pursuing women. She fights him off, hitting him with her quirt. Later, hoping to achieve his goal, he threatens to reveal that she was an illegitimate child, thereby disgracing her with her husband-to-be's family.

Nell is a less-well-developed version of the Grey heroine. She embodies the spunkiness, energy, and feminine uncertainty found in other heroines, such as Betty Zane, but Grey has not fleshed out her personality and character to the same degree.

Burton, Robert: a.k.a. Cameron in *Desert Gold*. Burton has become a wanderer of the desert. He has come seeking solitude to remember a woman and to do penance of a sort. He finds the meaning of life in the solitude of the desert, where he feels brother to the wolf, hungering for a mate. Burton meets a stranger, a fellow wanderer of the desert, who asks to keep him company. Burton prefers not to travel the desert with another human being but grudgingly accepts his company and comes to admire him. The stranger never complains and more than holds up his end in the work around camp. In fact, he seems more concerned that Burton find gold than himself. Burton, though, is not curious to learn the man's secrets, but the conversation of two men alone in the desert eventually reveals their true natures. The stranger is a douser, able to find water using a "peach fork," a skill that proves extremely convenient. The man, he learns, is Jonas Warren from Peoria. He is the father of the woman Burton has come to the desert to remember. Burton debates whether he should reveal the truth to Jonas. He decides to reveal his identity and tells Warren about the woman. He fell in love with Nell Warren, but left town before he learned that she was pregnant. When he returns to Peoria upon hearing of her predicament, she has left in disgrace heading west. He sets out after her, finds her and marries her. Nell, however, leaves him, taking her baby daughter with her, disappearing into the wide West. He never sees her again. Both he and Warren have been seeking the same woman for years. Burton sees in this "coincidence" the voice of nature's motherhood, a spirit guiding the course of events. He has found peace, and hears the whisper of God in the solitude. Warren and Burton eventually discover a remarkable gold mine in a location covered with prehistoric markings, but both perish in a desert sandstorm before registering their claim. Burton leaves a box with the marriage certificate, and a letter staking their claim to the gold mine, leaving half of the find for the person who discovers the claim and the other half for his wife and daughter. He trusts that the spirit which brought him and Warren together will ensure that his wife and child are led to the spot and get their inheritance.

Bushnell, Dr.: In *Lost Pueblo*, the head of the museum which had commissioned Randolph to undertake an archaeological expedition to find the Lost Pueblo. Mr. Elijah Endicott, Janey's father, writes Dr. Bushnell to corroborate Randolph's claim to have found the pueblo, countering Mr. Elliott's claim that he had uncovered the location.

Buster: In *Under the Tonto Rim*, Sam Johnson's mustang. He tells the teacher that Buster is as gentle as a lamb, that he has never pitched with a girl, that she should talk to the horse as if she had no idea a horse could be mean.

Butler, Sam: In *Robbers' Roost*, plays cards with some of Hays's men in the saloon in Green River. His wife comes in and orders him to get back home. Hays comments that he would have gone straight if he had had a wife like her.

C

Cabel, Joe: In *Arizona Ames*, works as cook and handyman on John Halstead's spread. He also helps manage the cowboys on the ranch, a job Esther gladly surrendered to him, as he can handle the young men better than she can. When Arizona Ames appears at the ranch, he is overjoyed. Five years earlier he had worked with Arizona Ames and developed great admiration for the young man's abilities as a cowboy, as a gunman and especially as a human being. He is reticent about giving specific details. Esther considers this fact and concludes that it is typical of Joe. He has been with them over two years and although he is a great storyteller, he has revealed precious little information about himself. No one knows about him more than he wishes to tell. He tells Esther that he was married at eighteen, that he and his sweetheart had no children, and she died young, but he is happy about the time they had together. He advises her to declare her love for Arizona Ames. He could add matchmaking to his talents. Joe Cabel recommends Arizona Ames to John Halstead in the highest terms. He guarantees that Arizona is a straight shooter, true blue, good as gold and honest as the day is long. He is the man to solve his problem with cattle thieves. Just as Joe Cabel had promised, Arizona Ames soon identifies the "Trojan Horse" on the ranch and within a few months, the rustlers have been put out of business.

Cabeza de Vaca, Alvar Núñez: In *Knights of the Range,* a Spanish explorer mentioned by Holly Ripple in her address summarizing the history of the area and the Spanish influence on the cattle industry.

Caddell, Lieutenant: In *30,000 on the Hoof*, in charge of buying cattle for the army. He witnesses the transaction in which Lee Mitchell gives Logan Huett the hundred thousand dollars-plus in cash, and witnesses his signature on the receipt. The bundle contained pieces of paper, and no money at all. When

Huett tries to get his money, Caddell is the main obstacle. Mitchell has a reputation of being a crooked dealer, but Caddell's testimony gives him credence.

Caesar: Betty's pet bear in *Betty Zane*. At one point, Betty let Caesar drink a bucket of cider and the poor bear wandered around drunk for half a day.

Cairns: In *Riders of the Purple Sage,* one of the very young gentile cowboys that Judkins hires to tend Jane Withersteen's herds after the Mormon riders have been called in by the elders. He is killed when the white herd is stampeded and destroyed.

Caldwell, Bishop: The Mormon leader in White Sage in *The Heritage of the Desert.* He is a close friend of Martin Cole and of August Naab, who brings the injured Jack Hare to him for laying-on of hands. The bishop is a scholar and a thinker, rather than a man of action. Like Naab, he does not believe in violence, but he does foresee a time when the meek will revolt against the outlaws who have taken charge of the body politic. The bishop's house and gardens seem like paradise to Jack Hare as he rests in the hammock while August Naab packs his supplies for the trip to the ranch in the desert. Dene attempts to seize Hare from the house but is prevented from doing so by Naab. When Jack Hare comes into town upon discovering what Holderness has done at the Seeping Spring watering hole, he heads for the bishop's house, where he is well-received and where he is brought up to date on the goings-on in White Sage. The bishop's son, John, is the man who is most in touch with things. His father prefers to remain detached and above what is going on. Later, when Mescal has escaped from Holderness's clutches, she heads for the bishop's home where she is hidden in a cellar and the outlaws cannot find her. When Jack arrives, the bishop comments that the time of judgment seems to be approaching. He also comments on the mysterious comings and goings of men in the house all night. He does not know what is going on or what role his own sons are playing. An old man, the bishop is frail and probably not able to face up to his oldest son, Paul, being one of Holderness's outlaws. August Naab exacts a promise from all who witness the hangings that the truth be kept from the old man.

In Bishop Caldwell, Zane Grey is presenting the best of the Mormon clergy. He is truly a man of God, a thinker, a scholar, a mystic of sorts, and above all a man of peace. Like August Naab, he prays that evildoers will be punished, but he refuses to take a hand in meting out that punishment. He stands in contrast to the Mormon leaders presented in *Riders of the Purple Sage*, leaders who abuse their position of authority in the church to advance their own personal ends.

Caldwell, John: One of Bishop Caldwell's sons in *The Heritage of the Desert.* He is more in tune with what is going on in the community than his father. He reports to Jack Hare how Martin Cole was killed by Dene. He also explains that Holderness has got himself elected mayor and sheriff of White Sage. When the revolt of the meek finally does take place, John Caldwell is the leader. He proves to be the man of action and purpose the Mormon villagers had been hoping for. John Caldwell and his men arrest and put on quick trial the nineteen outlaws they have caught in town. An immediate execution is scheduled, but delayed by Jack Hare, looking to spare the two men who had helped Mescal escape from Holderness. One of these, it turns out, is John Caldwell's own brother, Paul. John Caldwell is similar to Dave Naab in his views. While a devout Mormon, he does not believe in pacifism as do August Naab and Bishop Caldwell. Evil will eventually be punished, he believes, but it will not happen unless someone acts to put an end to evil and injustice.

Caldwell, Paul: In *The Heritage of the Desert*, the eldest son of Bishop Caldwell. Like many of the Mormons in White Sage, he has become an accomplice in the cattle rustling operation run by Holderness and Dene. Although corrupted, he has not completely lost his sense of decency. He is the unrecognized man Jack Hare watches from the hill. While Holderness is sleeping, he releases Mescal from the house where she is being held captive and provides her with her horse Black Bolly to escape to White Sage. Mescal later identifies him by the wart on his hand and his life is spared. When the black hood is removed from his head, all recognize him as the bishop's son. August Naab is particularly angry at the young Mormon who has abandoned his faith to pursue a life of crime. Paul Caldwell would have preferred to die by hanging rather than face the father whom he has betrayed. Naab exacts a promise that no one will ever reveal the truth of Paul's treachery and disgrace to the old bishop.

Calhoun: In *Twin Sombreros,* a neighbor of Holly Ripple who runs into Capt. Britt at the train station and tells him about Brazos Keene's exploits in Casper, Wyoming. He also tells him that Brazos is working in Latimer, Colorado. Holly and Renn address a letter to Brazos in care of the post office in Latimer.

Calico: In *The Call of the Canyon*, Flo Hutter's horse.

California Red: In *Forlorn River*, a particularly stunning wild mustang Nevada and Ben Ide would like to catch. The horse is a clean-limbed animal, red as fire with a mane streaming behind like a flame. California is not a killer of horses, as so many stallions are. Harte Blaine has posted a reward of three thousand dollars for the capture of the stallion, which he hopes to give to Ina. When Ben has caught the rustlers and is returning with them to town, he spots California Red trapped out on the ice of the lake. He makes an agreement with the rustlers to give them their freedom if they help him capture the stallion. Ben returns with the stallion and Modoc and Nevada track the rustlers, helping the sheriff capture them. Ina Blaine insists that her father pay

Ben the bounty he had promised for the capture of the stallion. Four years later, Ben Ide moves to Arizona bringing California Red. The horse is admired by all the ranchers around. The Pine Tree Outfit of rustlers plans to ruin Ben and his neighboring ranchers but the loss of cattle doesn't seem to bother Ben. But when California Red is stolen, Ben wants the animal tracked and the rustlers punished. The horse is believed to have jumped the corral fence, but Raidy, the old hand from the Blaine ranch that accompanied Ben to Arizona, knows the animal was stolen. When California Red mysteriously reappears in the corral, Raidy shows Ben the marks that indicate he has been hobbled and driven through rough country. But the joy of having the horse back is enough to make Ben forgive everything.

Calkins: In *Black Mesa*, works for the trader, Belmont. He is hired to rustle two hundred or so of Manning and Kintell's own cattle to sell back to them. Calkins tells them he drove the cattle from across the river, but Kintell sees from the lack of caked mud on the animals that they were not in water for some time. As well, he recognizes one particularly cantankerous animal from their own herd. When Manning offers to pay only half of what he had agreed to, Calkins advises Belmont to accept. Kintell is on to them. When Belmont has left for Wagontongue, Kintell and Manning get their camping gear and set out to follow Calkins and his men. They come upon them with more rustled cattle. This time, they are planning on driving the cattle across the river to sell in Utah. They are not consulting Belmont on this endeavor. A gunfight breaks out between Manning and Kintell and the rustlers. Sproull and Bloom get away. Calkins is shot. Before he dies, he tells them what he knows about Belmont, that he was a Utah rancher and trader who fell out with his neighbors. He is really married to Sister, and she has some hold on him but he does not know the details. They bury Calkins there, and later Belmont comes back to inspect the body.

Cameron: In *Desert Gold*, the name that Burton goes by to conceal his true identity.

Cameron, Wayne: In *Western Union*, one of the few first-person narrators in the canon of Grey fiction, heads west looking for adventure. His father is a Southerner by birth and strong in feelings against the Yankees. Following his father's wishes, Wayne attends Harvard Law School for a year, then tries medicine for a year, abandoning that as well. He leaves New England for the West feeling that life in the open is what he wants. The construction of the Western Union telegraph line draws his attention and he hopes to get work with a construction crew. The stagecoach driver, Jim Hawkins, fills him in on bits of local history, the Pony Express and such things. His meeting with Williamson provides the link to get work with Creighton and the construction crews for the Western Union. Williamson had stressed his medical school background and Creighton hires him as medic, to patch up bruises and scrapes and broken limbs for the crew. Wayne also makes friends with some cowboys, Vance Shaw and Jack Lowden, and Tom Darnell. They cotton to him despite his lack of experience. Wayne bankrolls the group, getting a wagon properly equipped for their work.

Wayne Cameron learns to adapt to the West, much as John Hare learned the ways of the West in an early Grey novel, *The Heritage of the Desert*. Cameron experiences a buffalo stampede, an Indian attack, the fording of a swollen river, a prairie fire. He helps his friend Shaw rescue the dance-hall girl, Ruby, from Red Pierce, owner of a gambling establishment and saloon, a professional fleecer of the men working on the construction crew. The same rescue is repeated in South Pass, where the same girl has to be rescued again from Red Pierce, who had abducted her from the wagon where she was living, disguised as a Mexican laborer. Wayne himself falls in love at first sight with Kit Sunderland, daughter of a Texas colonel heading west with a herd from Texas to take up ranching with his brothers in the Sweetwater Valley of Wyoming. Kit comments sarcastically about his being a knight in shining armor, rescuing her in Gotenburg when her horse runs away. The romance progresses slowly. Shaw reports that Kit likes to flirt with cowboys but is never serious about any of them. Seeing Shaw with Kit one night convinces Wayne that she is already taken. At the end of the novel, Cameron and his partners, Shaw and Lowden, are setting up ranching in the Sweetwater Valley, near the Sunderland spread. All things point to a future marriage of Wayne and Kit.

The experiences along the trail transform Cameron into a true Westerner. He becomes a good shot, and learns to ride like a cowboy, to track cattle and men, to survive the worst that the prairies have to inflict. He shows himself to be a leader of men, capable of inspiring confidence and loyalty. He also shows that he is a man of vision, like Creighton, a true Westerner.

Campbell: (1) In *Nevada*, one of the names by which Ed Richardson, (a.k.a. Clan Dillon) is known.

(2) In *The U. P. Trail*, a lineman for Baxter. He meets Neale and Red in Benton and gives Neale the letter from General Lodge requesting that he return to work for the U. P. to resolve some engineering problems they have encountered.

Campbell, Jack: In *30,000 on the Hoof*, Milly Campbell's brother. He disapproves of George Huett's courting her, as he has picked his friend Rich Harvey for her. He picks a fight with George at the dance and knifes him in the fight. Jack later signs up for the army and makes a name for himself as a hero in the war. He was the first young man in Flagg to enlist. In France, he crawled up on a nest of machine guns and threw a bomb in on the Germans, just as they riddled him with bullets. That was his finish. Most forget what was once his bad reputation in Flagg.

Campbell, Jeff: In *To the Last Man*, reports to Abel Meeker what his brother Ted Meeker saw in Greaves' place the previous night. Greaves tells all there that Jean Isbel killed him to avenge his brother, Guy, and Ellen Jorth. Lee Jorth kills Simm Bruce for having sullied his daughter's reputation. Jeff is a villager, seemingly neutral in the Isbel-Jorth feud.

Campbell, Jim and Sandy: In *30,000 on the Hoof*, Jack and Milly's brothers. Jack calls on them to help in the fight at the dance.

Campbell, John: In *Valley of Wild Horses*, runs a general store in Littleton. When Pan Handle was little, he would give him a stick of candy whenever he came into the store. When Pan Handle returns to Littleton after an absence of some five years, Campbell is still huge of build with a long beard and ruddy face, but he cannot place Pan Handle. Campbell tells him about his father's troubles, losing his cattle in the deal with Hardman, the departure of Jim Blake, Hardman's foreman, and his family's pulling up stakes.

Campbell, Milly (Mil): In *30,000 on the Hoof*, the girl George Huett is sweet on. She is handsome and lots of fun and she loves provoking fights among the cowboys chasing after her. At the dance, George Huett proposes to her. This angers her brother, who wants her to marry his friend, Rich Harvey. When George is recuperating from his knife wound at home, Logan tells him this is a lesson not to let "dark-eyed cats" throw themselves at him.

Campbell, Tobe: In *30,000 on the Hoof*, one of the wayward boys of the Campbell family who pick a fight with George at the dance. He has joined an outlaw outfit with Joe Stillman and plans to rustle the Huett herd in Turkey Valley.

Campbells: In *Wyoming*, Martha's mother's family. Nick Bligh says that his niece, Martha, takes after them. They are a fine old family, but stubborn, and not quick to forgive.

Campo: In *Desert Gold*, a Mexican revolutionary leader (1910–1912) who is reported to be tearing up the railway south of Nogales on his way to Casita.

Cappy: In *Arizona Ames*, the name Arizona Ames gives to his horse. The animal is spectacular to look at, a great companion for Arizona and a target for horse thieves. Arizona named the horse after his old trapper friend from the Tonto, Cappy Tanner.

Captain: Betty's pet red squirrel in *Betty Zane*. Betty has quite a menagerie of pets, including bears.

Captain Jack: The name Isaac Zane gives to the son of Thundercloud, the war chief of the Hurons. He is a young boy who has a special fondness for Isaac Zane in the Delaware village. Isaac hopes he will remember him in later life and consider whites as friends, not enemies.

Card, Jerry: In *Riders of the Purple Sage*, reputed to be the best rider in Utah. He first appears with Elder Tull at Jane Withersteen's home when they come to whip Venters and drive him out of Utah. He does the dirty work for Elder Tull, arranging for Oldring to rustle Jane Withersteen's red herd. He also steals her prize horses from the barn, killing Blake in the process. In the race to escape from Venters on Wrangle, Jerry Card performs remarkable feats of horsemanship, jumping from Night to Black Star and back again while the thoroughbreds are running all-out. Hiding in the grass following Venters's capture of the horses, he mounts Wrangle and, in an attempt to control the animal by hanging from its neck and biting its nose, Jerry is killed when the animal jumps over a cliff into a canyon.

Card, Lucy: In "Canyon Walls," sister to Joe and Hal Stacey. They come to visit with the Keetches on a Sunday afternoon.

Cardigan: In *Twin Sombreros*, a gambler who shot Brazos's old partner, Herb Ellerslie, in Dodge.

Cardwell, Dr.: In *Lost Pueblo*, the minister with whom Janey Endicott makes an appointment in Flagerstown, to marry her to Phillip Randolph. Dr. Cardwell is from Connecticut. He went to Arizona years ago with lung trouble. His life had been despaired of in the East, but he is hale and hearty now. He has only praise for Arizona's climate and environment.

Carewe, Mr.: In *Boulder Dam*, the chief engineer in charge of the seven-year Boulder Dam construction project. At first, Lynn Weston thinks he must have a colossal ego to imagine he can stop the Colorado River. Weston wonders about the mathematical and constructive genius who could figure out how to harness the forces of nature. Carewe first hears of Lynn Weston after his ride through the tunnel to rescue Ben Brown, who had fallen into the water. He recalls that his nephew, Stan Ewell, was the right tackle for Oregon State in a game with Lynn Weston. Stan Ewell clipped Weston in that game and admits it was his fault. Carewe asks Lynn about the rumors he dropped out of university because he had been framed out of the captaincy and All-American honors. He makes it possible for Lynn to learn most of the jobs at the construction site. He shows his gratitude to Lynn for foiling Sproul and Moore's sabotage plot by giving him an important position in the construction crew.

Carmichael, Tom: In *The Man of the Forest*, a young, Texas cowboy that Helen and Bo Rayner meet at the train station in Las Vegas. He is long, lean, and bow-legged with a young, frank face and intent eyes. He is particularly attractive with his superb build, his red-bronze face and bright red scarf, his swinging gun and the huge, long, curved spurs. His gait is awkward, as if he is not accustomed to walking. The long spurs jingle musically. The girls flirt with him. He has heard of their uncle Al, and Bo suggests that he come to Pine. She offers to put in a good word for him with her uncle. Bo bets Helen he will show up.

And indeed he does. When Al Auchincloss comes to Dale's camp, Carmichael is with him. Bo speaks up for him and Uncle Al gives him a job on the ranch. When Al passes on and Helen takes over, Las Vegas, Tom Carmichael, proves to be her mainstay in all the complex work of managing a ranch. He tells her that Jeff Mulvey, the foreman her uncle set such store by, has gone over to Beasley and is taking many of her riders with him. When Harve Riggs pesters the girls, he exposes him for a craven coward, beating him up in the saloon and throwing him out into the street.

Tom is in love with Bo, but she likes to play cat-and-mouse with him. When Tom goes to the dance with Flo Stubbs, she is angry and jealous. Helen points out that she has not been treating Tom very fairly. If she likes him, she should not play mean games with him.

Tom Carmichael finally takes matters in hand. He confronts Jeff Mulvey and others of Beasley's crew in the saloon in town, killing them in a shootout. The following morning he extends the challenge to Beasley himself. The storekeeper, Abe, tells him Beasley has retreated to his ranch. He could not hire any gang to bear the brunt of the challenge. It is impossible for him to avoid facing Carmichael. Las Vegas goes to the ranch and confronts him. Beasley tries to buy him off, then tries to return the Auchincloss ranch to Helen, but all to no avail. In the inevitable shootout, Beasley is killed.

Tom returns to the Auchincloss ranch. He brings a horse he has tamed for Bo. She can have him if she becomes Mrs. Tom Carmichael. Bo accepts. Roy Beeman marries them in the ranch house before supper.

Tom Carmichael is the instrument whereby justice is served on Beasley.

Caroline (Carrie): In *The Hash Knife Outfit,* Curly Prentiss's old girlfriend. When they have a fight and he tells her to go where it's hot, she takes up with Wess Stebbins and marries him. Curly gets "turrible drunk" to drown his sorrow.

Carpenter: In *Arizona Ames,* a cowhand on Crow Grieve's ranch. On the boss's orders, he built a fence around the Nielsen homestead to prevent their cattle from getting to the stream on Grieve's ranch. He is killed in a gunfight in South Fork.

Carr, Stoneface: In *The Hash Knife Outfit,* the gambler of the Hash Knife Outfit. He is a gray-faced, gray-haired man of fifty. He is killed by Croak Malloy, who has caught him cheating in a card game. His wad of money is divided among the other Hash Knife Outfit members.

Carson: In *Riders of the Purple Sage,* one of the gentile riders who works for Jane Witchersteen but who quits when threatened by Elder Tull's henchmen. Jane comes to visit him to ask him to return but he refuses. His mother has been threatened, and he thinks it is too dangerous to do so. Jane nevertheless offers to move him and his family up to her

place, which would be safer, but this offer too is rejected. He does accept her offer to help tide him over until things get better. The storekeeper Bevins has already been providing help on Jane Witchersteen's instructions.

Carson, Kit: In *The Rainbow Trail,* the legendary frontiersman, trail boss, scout, and guide for the American cavalry in the Southwest. He scouted for the army in a campaign against the Navajo. Carson is also mentioned in *Knights of the Range,* as one of the important early explorers in Arizona, and his marriage to a Mexican woman is an example of the intermingling of Spanish and American traditions in the region.

In *Fighting Caravans,* Kit Carson appears as a character. At the beginning, he is about forty-seven years old, rather slight in build compared to scouts like Baker and Curtis. He has a clean-shaven face, and bright eyes with a piercing quality. He looks every bit the greatest frontiersman of the West. Buff Belmet meets him at Council Grove and Carson takes a liking to Belmet, predicting he will become an outstanding man. Like Jeff Lynn in *The Spirit of the Border,* who sees in Joe Downs a future frontiersman, Carson sizes Clint up and offers him a bit of advice — never play cards, don't drink, and remember the only good Indian is a dead Indian. Buff gets an invitation to his home in Taos, New Mexico. He introduces him to Dick Curtis, Jim Baker and John Hobbs, other famous frontiersmen and explorers. Some fifteen years later, Buff visits the dying Kit Carson, who listens to his account of the fight at Pawnee Rock and of the death of Blackstone. Carson's last piece of advice to Buff is to go to Las Cruces and find May Bell and marry her.

In *The Lost Wagon Train,* Kit Carson is called in to help in the investigation of the disappearance of Bowden's (Anderson's) wagon train. The caravan had left Independence, Missouri, bound for California, and was to take the Dry Trail. It disappeared completely. Carson advises Major Greer to keep the lid on his inquiry, leaving him and his fellow scouts to ask among their Indian friends, scouts and freighters. Should the word get out that an inquiry is being made, parties who do know something may simply vanish. Dr. McPherson introduces Carson to Stephen Latch, who is recuperating in his hospital. Latch is described as another Maxwell, a man with a ranch where all are welcome. Carson comes to visit Latch, who is impressed by the man and does not consider him to be a threat. Carson, however, tells him that Leighton has been under suspicion. He is playing a deep game of some kind, most likely against Latch. He advises Latch to be wary of him. He speaks well of Handy, whom he calls a clean-shooting outlaw who does not play dirty tricks as Leighton does. Kit Carson's friendliness convinces Latch that he is still above suspicion at the fort.

In *Twin Sombreros,* Kit Carson is said to have stayed at Fort Lyon a good deal in the 1860's.

In *Stranger from the Tonto,* Kent Winfield mentions that the few Indians he had met in Wagontongue trace their enmity for the whites to Kit Carson's campaign rounding up Navajos to be placed on reservations, a rude injustice that has never been forgotten or forgiven.

Carstone, Emily: In *Rogue River Feud*, a cousin of the five Carstone sisters that Keven Bell allegedly got pregnant while at the army training camp in Washington. She was Beryl Aard's best friend when she was at school in Roseburg. Emily's father went out there, got the family away and sold the ranch. Her father told Major Atwell to stay away from Roseburg or he would shoot him. Beryl tells Keven that Atwell will stop his persecution of him when he sees them together. Atwell knows she has the true story of what occurred at the training camp.

Carter: (1) In *Desert Gold*, one of Belding's neighbors. He is sent to Casita to by Gale and Belding to deliver a letter to Thorne at the cavalry outpost there. This is one of the few mentions made of the man in the novel.

(2) In *Riders of the Purple Sage,* Carter is one of Bishop Dyer's bodyguards and gunmen. He is killed in the gunfight between Dyer and Lassiter when Lassiter confronts the bishop during the trial of Willie Kern.

Carter, Rain: In *Shadow on the Trail,* a silent, thin-lipped, shifty-eyed man, manifesting a pondering thoughtfulness and no eager excitement. His youth lies behind him. He is a member of Hogue Kinsey's group. He hesitates to give up the old ways and go straight. He does come along to work on the Pencarrow ranch when Tex Brandon recruits them. Lightfoot comments that he distrusts him, and Jerry comments on his strange behavior and his meeting with riders in the woods, where they have a long confab. Back at the bunkhouse, he tries to pump Jerry and the others for something, trying to get them to say they are tired of riding for Pencarrow and looking for a bonanza. He is gone in the morning. He betrays the group for pay, attempting to kill Tex Brandon and young Hal Pencarrow for Harrobin. Hogue Kinsey and his men pursue Carter. Kid Marshall shoots and breaks his horse's leg. Carter is caught and hanged.

Cartwright: In *Black Mesa*, to impress on Paul Manning the profits to be made in ranching, Belmont tells him that the Cartwright outfit runs fifty thousand head of cattle on range no better than theirs.

Case: Mordaunt's servant in *The Last Trail*. He is a short little man with a face resembling that of a jackal. He has a grizzled, stubbly beard and a protruding, vicious mouth, a broad flat nose and deepset, small glittering eyes. He is eager to use his knife in a fight. He attacks Mr. Sheppard in a fight in Metzar's inn and Jonathan Zane has to put a stop to it.

Case joins Bing Legget's outlaws with full gusto. When his former master is killed, he gambles with Legget for the man's gold, and later for Helen Sheppard. When he tries to beat Helen into submission, he falls dead after a rifle shot is heard. Old Horse identifies the bullet as Wetzel's, a sure sign that Deathwind is on their trail. Case is a villain through and through, his physical appearance being a mere outward manifestation of his truly weasel nature. In this he resembles Jim Girty of *The Spirit of the Border*, whose animal nature and instincts were reflected in his appearance.

Casey, Con: In *Code of the West*, a newcomer to the Thurman ranch, an Irishman only a few years in America and not long in the West. He is the most earnest and simple-minded of young men and a source of vast amusement to his companions, who liked him dearly but nevertheless made him the butt of their jokes. He declines the request to pick up Georgie in town on the grounds that he has never been alone with a woman in his life. This comment brings on great guffaws from his mates.

Casey, Pat: In *The U. P. Trail*, a raw-boned, red-faced, hard-featured Irishman, inured to exposure and the rough life in the construction gangs working on the railroad. He speaks with a thick Irish accent. He becomes a true, loyal friend to Warren Neale, who, in turn, sees men like Pat as the true builders of the railroad, rather than the politicians and bankers who enrich themselves with graft and corruption. Casey is with Neale in the buffalo hunt and in the fight with the Sioux Indians which ensures. He is given to drinking and gambling in Benton, as are most men on the work gangs. When Benton is being dismantled, he is one of the men burying the dead left behind. He buries Beauty Stanton and Larry Red King, Neale's closest friend and companion. On Beauty Stanton's body, he finds the book with her letter to Neale explaining that she herself had been in love with Neale and that she played a dirty trick on Allie. Nevertheless, Allie is alive. Casey rides the gravel car to warn General Lodge of an impending Sioux attack on the train. Casey is killed when the car comes to a stop before the general's coach.

Cass, Mrs.: In *The Man of the Forest*, the widow who is the first person Milt Dale visits when he returns to Snowdrop. She brings him up to date on the latest gossip: Lem Harden's horse being stolen, Sary Jones's death. She tells him about the trouble brewing between Auchincloss and Beasley and Old Al's sending for his niece, Helen, to come take over his ranch. She then turns to matchmaking, telling Milt it's high time he got married and Helen Rayner will be just the girl for him. Later, when the fight between Beasley and Auchincloss is in full swing, Mrs. Cass takes in the Rayner girls. As well, Roy Beeman is taken to her house when he is shot in the saloon.

Cass, Tom: In *The Man of the Forest*, Mrs. Cass's husband. Years ago, he went into the forest and never returned. The old woman still looks for him, never giving up hope.

Cassell: (1) In *The Deer Stalker*, a government agent involved in managing wildlife in parklands. His interest is more in furthering the desires of cattlemen than in protecting wildlife. Like Judson, he has little practical experience with deer. He and Ranger Thad Eburne rarely see eye-to-eye on matters concerning the deer. He takes particular pleasure in making Eburne capture deer to see how they react in captivity and if they can be trapped and moved. He also favors a large-scale hunt to reduce the deer population rather than impose restrictions on grazing for cattle. He is on hand to observe the attempt to drive several thousand deer to new grazing land.

(2) In *Stranger from the Tonto*, a cattle baron who runs about twenty thousand head of cattle over a wide range. He's also a big skinflint and never hires more than half a dozen riders till they holler for their wages, then he lets them go. He'll hire any rider that comes along and doesn't bother to brand his cattle. That makes him an easy target for Roberts's outfit and the Hole-in-the-Wall Gang.

Castañeda: A Spanish explorer quoted in *The Thundering Herd*, on the buffalo, an animal unknown to Europeans, which he describes as "a foul and fierce beast of countenance and form of body."

Castañeda, Mercedes: In *Desert Gold*, flees from the Mexican revolutionary bandit named Rojas, who had held her family for ransom only to kill her father when the ransom was paid. Mercedes escapes disguised as a nun after bribing her guards. She is descended from an old, wealthy, aristocratic Spanish family. In revolutionary Mexico, aristocrats were hated viscerally by the lower class and bandits. Mercedes fears death at the hands of Rojas and unmentionable abuse at the hands of his men. George Thorne, a young officer in the American cavalry stationed in Casita, falls in love with her and agrees to help her. George Thorne solicits the help of Dick Gale, and together, they get her out of town and hide her at Belding's ranch. Mercedes is quite a horsewoman, an experienced rider with stamina of steel. She quickly befriends Nell, Belding's daughter. Rojas continues his pursuit of her throughout the novel, attacking Belding's ranch and following the party led by Yaqui into the desert wilderness. Mercedes is deeply in love with George Thorne and they marry before Rojas arrives at Belding's ranch.

Castleton, Lord: In *The Light of Western Stars*, one of Madeline's former suitors, an English lord who has traveled throughout the world. Alfred suspects he is after one of his sisters (either Madeline or Helen) for their money. Castleton can ride, rope, climb, shoot, and hike and is willing to learn everything. He wants to learn the tricks of the cowboy trade, and takes humbly the good-humored ribbing of the cowboys. He wins their respect, admiration and approval when he succeeds in riding Devil, a particularly ornery bronc which the cowboys have put him on in jest. Even Gene Stewart joins in congratulating him. He declares that Castleton makes it clear why the British empire has spread around the world. Castleton uncharacteristically tells a story about a trip to Uganda and an encounter with a man-eating lion. While the story is undoubtedly true, the cowboys think it is a story told to outdo Monty Price, their own master of the tall tale.

Catlee: In *The Thundering Herd,* the name by which Jim Davis is known. Catlee works as cook and camp organizer for Jett. He drives the wagon in which Milly Fayre sleeps. He is a swarthy fellow of perhaps forty years, rugged of build, garbed as a teamster, with a lined face that seemed a record of a violent life. Milly senses in him an antagonism to Jett and a sympathy towards her. In the squabbles that occur between Pruitt and Follonsbee and Jett, Catlee takes no part. He is connected with the outfit, but he doesn't fit in. Follonsbee thinks that Catlee is a tenderfoot like these in some of the outfits they have robbed, like Huggins's. When things start to deteriorate, Catlee offers to help Milly. He confirms her suspicions that Jett is a thief, but he had assumed she knew this all along and didn't care any more than she did about his advances to her. Catlee is not counted in the calculations when Follonsbee and Pruitt and Jett are discussing dividing up the money. Catlee works for wages; he is not a partner in the profits. He defends Milly when the fighting breaks out and is killed by Pruitt after revealing his true identity, Sam Davis, late partner of the Youngers. As she drives her wagon away from the buffalo fields, Milly recalls Catlee as a "good outlaw," a man who confessed he had never been anything but bad, but still good at heart.

Catlin: In *Shadow on the Trail,* the nominal head of a rustler outfit that Wade Holden meets up with when he is wandering aimlessly, avoiding pursuit by Texas Rangers. Catlin welcomes him into the group, hoping he will join them as his skill with a gun could be useful. He explains his plan to rustle cattle from the Aulsbrook outfit a few miles ahead of them. He plans to sell the cattle to Jesse Chisum, who is not too particular about brands and such things. Catlin does not have full control over his outfit. Nippert, the gunman of the group, approaches Aulsbrook to find out what Wade Holden has revealed and Catlin comes along. Aulsbrook tells them he has known for some time they were trailing him. Nippert is killed when he draws on Holden. Catlin leaves with the body. Catlin's group disintegrates as a viable rustling outfit.

Cawthorne, Link: In *Nevada,* an outlaw and gunman working out of Lineville. He is part of Cash Burridge's gang. Mrs. Wood tells Nevada that Link is reputedly thick with Lize Teller. He is extremely jealous, and when he catches Nevada and Lize together in the saloon, he challenges Nevada, who refuses to fight him. This refusal leads Link to believe that Nevada is afraid to confront him. Mrs. Wood tells Jim (Nevada) that he has just postponed the inevitable. Shortly thereafter, Link beats Lize to within an inch of her life and Jim Lacy kills Cawthorne in a shootout. Once again, Jim Lacy finds himself on the run because he has helped someone in need.

Cedar: In *Majesty's Rancho*, one of Majesty Stewart's string of thoroughbred horses. When Lance Sidway comes to the ranch riding Umpqua, the first comment made is that Lance's horse has Cedar beat hands down.

Chalfack, Bud: In *The Drift Fence*, introduced to young Jim Traft by his rancher uncle, Jim. Bud is the peacemaker of the outfit, a diplomat, the slickest, coolest hand on the range. Whenever anyone is in the wrong, Bud is elected to set him right. He is a little fellow, sturdy, bow-legged, and otherwise suggestive of long acquaintance with horses. He has an open, guileless countenance which reminds Jim Traft of a rosy-faced cherub. He comes to Jim to make peace with Hack Jocelyn over the alleged insult. The crew do not want to be broken up because of Hack and they give him a sound thrashing. Bud then approaches Jim with Hack Jocelyn's offer of an apology and a return to work if he does not have to dig fence posts. Bud tells Jim that Hack swears things will come to a fight with the Cibeque outfit if the fence goes ahead. Jim appreciates Bud's openness and honesty and he accompanies him to the bunkhouse to speak to Jocelyn. The recalcitrant Jocelyn, however, does not genuinely appear interested in apologies or making amends. At the rodeo in Flagg, Bud Chalfack climbs onto a horse running at breakneck speed and performs other feats of horsemanship for the crowd. Bud Chalfack sees Jim kissing Molly and spreads the word to the other cowboys. This changes their opinion of their dude foreman. Bud and Curly Prentiss are the first of the crew to side with the tenderfoot foreman and eventually convince the others of his worthiness of their respect. Bud and Curly come upon Jim held at gunpoint by Slinger Dunn. They arrive in the nick of time. In short, Bud and Curly become Jim Traft's most loyal cowhands.

In *The Hash Knife Outfit*, Bud Chalfack is one of the cowboys who work for young Jim Traft. He is first mentioned when Jim shows the cowboys a picture of his sister. The cowboy is awestruck and stares at the photo. Bud is one of the cowboys accompanying Jim to the train station in Flag to pick up Gloria. Later, he is accused of having insulted Jim's sister by commenting on her legs to the other cowboys. Bud helps Jim Traft with the construction of his log cabin on the Yellow Jacket, where he displays his skill as a fisherman. In the campaign led by Slinger Dunn against the Hash Knife Outfit, Bud Chalfack is shot but not seriously wounded.

Chamberlain: In *The Horse Thief*, one of the Montana ranchers who has lost a large number of horses to Big Bill Mason's horse-rustling outfit.

Chance: (1) In *The Hash Knife Outfit*, runs a saloon in Flagg, Arizona.

(2) (a.k.a. **Two Spot**), one of Dene's two principal henchmen in *The Heritage of the Desert*. He is first mentioned in the early chapters when Dene rides into Naab's camp searching for Jack Hare. Chance had threatened him and Jack had set out for Bane, only to get lost in the desert. Later, Chance is the man responsible for filling in the Blue Star water hole, depriving Naab of water for his sheep. Chance draws on Hare at Abe's store when Hare comes to confront Holderness over his seizing of the Seeping Spring water hole. Hare proves to be as fast a draw as August Naab. When Holderness sends Dene and the henchmen to seize Mescal at Naab's ranch, Dave Naab shoots Chance and Culver.

Chandler, Ben: In *The Trail Driver*, the fourth of the Uvalde Quintet. He is a typical Texas youth, long, rangy, loose-jointed, of sandy complexion and hair, with eyes of clear, light blue. Adam Brite sees Chandler at Snell's saloon in Austin. He is with Roy Hallett. Ben Chandler is clearly there to do some drinking, but Hallett tries to get him over to the card table with Ross Hite, who keeps giving meaningful glances to Hallett. Chandler and Hallett fight, Hallett is knocked flat, and Chandler leaves. Adam Brite hopes to catch up with Chandler on the trail to warn him that Hallett is up to something, but he never sees him. The following morning, Chandler appears when Hallett is telling Texas Joe that he had lured him in to town to go drinking. He announces that Chandler was out to double-cross the outfit. Ben then appears, with a bloodied forehead. He calls Hallett a liar, and in true Texas fashion is prepared to back his accusation with a gun. Pan Handle Smith takes matters in hand and shoots Hallett. Ben Chandler then confesses that Ross Hite had paid Hallett five hundred dollars to leave a breach in the line so Hite and his outfit could cut out a big bunch of stock. At first, he agreed, but then he got afraid. He had gone along largely because Roy Hallett plied him with liquor. He asks for another chance, and Brite is willing to keep him on. Ben Chandler is drowned when trying to lead the herd across the river. Part of the herd goes farther downstream, and Chandler gets ahead of them to turn them to the bank. His horse, however, gets into a fast-flowing current and they can't get out.

Chaps: In *Horse Heaven Hill*, the Oregon-bred horse that Hurd Blanding saddles for Lark Burrell when she appears at the stables to go riding. Lark renames the horse "Cream Puff" The horse beats all the others in a three-mile race, including Stanley Weston's black stallion, Blackie.

Charger: In *The Heritage of the Desert*, August Naab's huge and powerful saddle horse. He is almost a match for Silvermane in strength, speed and endurance.

Charley: (1) In *The Call of the Canyon*, one of Tom Hutter's hired hands. He is a bit dotty, having been kicked by a horse once, but for the most part he is sensible. Carley describes him as long, lean, loose-jointed, dressed in blue overalls and muddy boots, with an olive-colored face and beard. He first appears when he meets Carley en route to Glenn's cabin in the canyon. He directs her up the right path. Charley tells her about Glenn and warns Carley about the Westerner's love of teasing greenhorns as they did with Miss Spenser two years before. He warns Carley that Flo might try such a trick on her, especially as she is sweet on Glenn herself. In the novel, Charley serves as a reporter bringing information about others. He reports to Charley about the romance between Flo and Lee Stanton. He also tells Charley about the fight between Glenn Killbourne and Ruff Haze over the latter's unwelcome advances to her at Flo's birthday party. When Carley returns to Arizona after her visit to New York, in order to build a ranch house on the property she bought overlooking the Painted Desert, she runs into Charley, who announces that he and Lee Stanton have left Tom Hutter's employ. He is now working as a shepherd at Oak Creek. He also teasingly misinforms Carley that Flo and Glenn Killbourne have been married. When Carley goes to Lolomi Lodge to wish the newlyweds the best of luck, Glenn tells her that Charley was pulling her leg, that Flo and Lee have been married. Charley is the stereotypical grizzled Westerner who appears in many of Grey's novels to provide color and comic relief, like Jeff Lynn in *The Spirit of the Border*.

(2) In *Wildfire*, one of the two horses Cal Blinn enters in the annual horse race at Bostril's Ford.

Charley Jim: In *Wanderer of the Wasteland*, a sixty-year-old chief of the Coahuila tribe and father to Oella. He comes upon Adam Larey in the deserted Indian village in the desert, after his mule has run off. He nurses Adam back to health, and goes to Yuma to purchase some supplies for him. He teaches Adam how to survive in the desert, to hunt antelope. He teaches him tricks to get the curious antelope to come close so missing a shot is less likely. He supposes Adam has come to the desert to seek gold. He offers to show him where Peg Leg's gold mine is located in the Superstition Mountains. He offers Oella to Adam as wife, but when Adam rejects the offer, he tells Adam he must wander the desert on his own. Many years later, Adam meets Charley Jim. Adam is now known as Wansfell. Charley Jim marvels at how Adam has grown strong and desert-wise. He tells him that Oella died of a broken heart, pining after him when he rejected her for a wife.

Charlie: In *Valley of Wild Horses*, a young wrangler on the first roundup on which Pan Handle works for pay. One morning, he is thrown from a wild horse and breaks his shoulder bone.

Charteris: In *30,000 on the Hoof*, one of the cattle barons around Flagg, Arizona. Charteris, like the other cattle barons, follows the price of cattle due to war speculation. He has heard that the U.S. government is buying cattle from Argentina. Charteris had done some of the banking for Lee Mitchell, the government agent buying cattle. He reports that Mitchell paid so much for stock and padded his report to the government. When Huett sells his cattle to Mitchell, Charteris recommends he take a government draft in payment, but, not trusting Mitchell, he insisted on cash.

Chase, Ben: In *Desert Gold*, a surveyor and miner from Illinois. He is a man with connections in the Southern Pacific Railway, as well as in political and financial circles. Thanks to these connections, a spur line is being built to Forlorn River. He arrives and immediately sees the potential for generating hydroelectricity for mining if the river were dammed. He takes land there and, through a process of intimidation, drives out the local ranchers, and gets Tom Belding fired from his job as border immigration inspector. He explodes dynamite to disrupt the underground water stream that supplies water to Belding's herd. Without that steady water supply, Belding cannot continue to operate his modest spread. Chase then appears at the ranch with a deal to buy Belding out. Chase had known Belding's wife, Nell, back in Peoria. In order to influence Belding into signing over his land to the mining company, he threatens to reveal the daughter's disgrace.

Ben Chase is a typical villain in Grey's Western novels. He is the unscrupulous exploiter from the East who has no understanding of the geography, the people or the history of the West. He is there to make a fast buck, with little concern for the people or the region. His son is equally arrogant and haughty.

Chase, Radford: In *Desert Gold*, the son of Ben Chase and a chip off the old block. He pursues Belding's stepdaughter, Nell, with arrogance and determination. At first, he thinks his automobile will win her heart. Later, he tries to forces his attentions on her, but to no avail. When he learns that she is engaged to Dick Gale and that his folks have come west for a visit, he threatens to reveal the fact of her illegitimate birth to shame her before them. Dick Gale returns, confronts Radford, and reveals him for the bully and coward that he is.

Cheesbrough: In *Raiders of Spanish Peaks,* a stockman who was Lonesome's rival for the affections of the same girl. Spencer had a red-haired, twenty-year-old daughter that Lonesome had a crush on but she was about to marry Cheesbrough. Lonesome provoked a fight with him by calling him a big cheese. Cheesbrough didn't like this, and beat up Lonesome. Ted Williams comes upon them and shoots it out with Cheesbrough. The stockman is killed, Ted Williams rides off, and Lonesome has not heard from him since.

Cheney, Luce (see Avil Bonesteel): In *Stranger from the Tonto*, the name by which Avil Bonesteel is known in Utah, where he is a respectable rancher. He has a wife and family living there, unaware that he is the head of the Hole-in-the-Wall outlaw gang. Roberts says of Cheney that he is hell on rustlers and that he drives big herds to St. George and Nevada. The Mormons do not like him, perhaps because he's a gentile. He also undersells them. Bonesteel reveals to Roberts that he is Cheney, and that he must keep the secret. Roberts suggests a plan to rustle some twenty thousand head of cattle from Cassell. After the shootout, Bonesteel plans to return to Utah and continue his life as a respectable citizen.

Cheney Brothers: In *Wyoming,* run the Cross Bar ranch on the big range south of the Sweetwater.

Cherokee, Jack (Cherry): In *Knights of the Range,* as his name suggests, a Cherokee Indian, and a rider for the Ripple ranch. He is one of the first to accept the gunman, Renn Frayne, as a member of the crew. He goes with Renn Frayne on the cattle drive to sell the Ripple herd. On the return, they run into the horse thieves that Joe Doane has been pursuing. Jackson and Cherry recognize Anne Doane's blue roan.

Cheseldine: In *The Lone Star Ranger,* named by Ranger MacNelly as the most vicious and dangerous of the outlaw leaders in West Texas. He is reputed to be ruthless, to kill at a whim, to show no mercy. No one, however, has ever seen him. He is cunning, leaving no direct evidence that might lead to him. He rules over Fairdale and several of the surrounding counties. Buck Duane overhears a conversation between Granger Longstreth and Floyd Lawson in which Longstreth is identified as the real Cheseldine. The name is purely legend, a mask, but Longstreth tells Lawson that the name more aptly applies to him, as the brutal deeds ascribed to Cheseldine are all of Lawson's doing.

Chet: In *The Lost Wagon Train,* one of the cowboys working for Lanthorpe with Slim Blue and Weaver.

Chippewa: An Indian tribe in *The Spirit of the Border.* Captain Williamson and his men are pursuing a band of Chippewa raiders and renegades who attacked and burned outlying pioneer settlements. In *The Last Trail* one of the Indians involved in the horse-stealing racket is named "the Chippewa." Several of the members of Bing-Legget's outlaw gang are Chippewa Indians.

Chisolm, John (Jesse): In *The Lost Wagon Train,* mentioned as a man who changed the fortunes of the Lone Star State and began a new phase in the history of the West. His idea was to drive great herds of cattle north from below the Brazos River and as far south as the Rio Grande to Dodge City and Abilene, Kansas. The Chisolm Trail soon marked its rut north over the rolling prairie once traveled only by the buffalo. A wonderful breed of young fighting riders, learning their trade of horsemanship from the Mexican Vaquero, and developing their own spirit of fire and dexterity with guns, developed to do their part in the empire–building of the West. This same encomium to Chisolm is made in *The Trail Driver.*

Chissum, Jesse (also spelled **Chisum** in some novels): In *The Lost Wagon Train,* Latch's only rival as rancher in the area. He is not plagued by rustlers, partly because of his unique way of marking his cattle, by cutting the ear of the calf so that the flap would dance up and down. His spread was located on the Pecos River.

In *Shadow on the Trail,* Chisum (new spelling of the name) appears again. The cattle king appears to be in the prime of a wonderful physical life, though rumor says he has some incurable disease. He is a short, square, extremely powerful man, with the cold blue eyes of a Texan, a broad strong face, a thin lip and a prominent jaw. Catlin plans to rustle Aulsbrook's herd and sell it to Chisum. Aulsbrook repeats the story about his unusual brand, and confirms Catlin's claim. Chisum runs a dozen outfits and has over a hundred thousand head of cattle on the range. He moves cattle fast. That's the way cattlemen do it if they are big enough to risk it. Chisum does not ask questions but he knows that some cattle have been rustled. He knows someone else will buy the cattle, particularly the beef buyers for the forts and the Indian reservations, and he thinks he might as well underbid them. Nine times out of ten the rustled cattle he buys will be gone before the rightful owner turns up, which seldom happens. When Aulsbrook sells out his herd and operation to Chisum, Wade Holden joins his crew. He asks to be assigned to a crew working on an isolated range. Chisum sizes him up. It's clear that he has not done much bronco breaking, horse-shoeing, or woodchopping. Chisum, however, likes his looks, and has no objection per se to his being a gunman. Billy the Kid is reputed to have ridden for him. He assigns him to work with Jesse Evans and tells his foreman, Hicks, to arrange things. Some months later, when the Texas Rangers arrive looking for him, Chisum does nothing to defend him. Billy the Kid, a friend and partner of Jesse Evans, reports that the rangers have come looking for one Wade Holden. Rand Blue has tipped the rangers off, recognizing Holden from a description given him by some riders. Chisum would turn in an outlaw, it seems. He will stand for rustlers and horse thieves as long as they are not known to ride for him. The air of respectability is what concerns him.

In *Knights of the Range,* Russ Slaughter and Ride'em Jackson both worked for Chisum. Slaughter learned his trade, as rancher and outlaw, from Chisum, and Jackson, who once rode for him, refers to the man and his success as the result of a combination of business shrewdness and unabashed banditry.

In *Twin Sombreros,* Chisum is mentioned as a rancher who is not too concerned about where the cattle he buys come from. Holly writes in her letter that at one time Chisum had proposed marriage to her.

In *The Fugitive Trail,* Bruce Lockheart meets a cowboy whose boss is a cattle buyer for Chisum. He pays five dollars a head for cattle, asks no questions about where they come from, and sells them in Dodge for considerably more.

Christ: In *Boulder Dam*, mentioned by Lynn Weston as an example of a man who had a vision and set about making that vision a reality. His vision transformed the world.

Christine: (1) In *The Light of Western Stars*, Christine is Madeline's small, graceful, plump French maid and friend. She falls in love with the cowboy, Ambrose Mills, who carries her off to marry her. She and Ambrose help with the camping trip to the mountains. Madeline thinks back on what Christine said about her eloping with Ambrose, "He say he love me ... he ask me to marry him ... he kiss me, he hug me ... he lift me on ze horse ... he ride with me all night ... he marry me." She wonders why her feelings for Gene Stewart cannot be summarized so simply.

(2) In *The Shepherd of Guadaloupe*, Christine is a young French girl Forrest met during the war. She was petite, with black hair and black eyes. She had no parents, no home, but she made a strong impression on Cliff, who saw in her a symbol of her country.

Christy, John: In *The Spirit of the Border*, a preacher who abandons his vocation to preach to Indians as a result of his experiences on the frontier. He appears towards the end of the story. Christy arrives at the Village of Peace with Captain Williamson and his company. They have been pursuing renegades and Chippewas and arrive just as the hostiles are about to move against the Village of Peace. Christy had been a man of the cloth until his betrothed, Lucy, was abducted and killed by a renegade. Later, Jim Girty identifies this renegade as Deering. Christy commiserates with George Young on the abduction of Kate. Both agree that the frontier environment and the practice of Christianity are incompatible. Pioneers are lured out to the frontier by the hope of land, prosperity and a better life, unaware that the frontier environment is one of bitter struggle to survive. Grey uses Christy as an example to illustrate one result of succumbing to the influences of the frontier, a Darwinian jungle fostering cruelty and brutality. "What does this border life engender in a pioneer who holds his own in it?" he asks. "Of all things, not Christianity. He becomes a fighter, keen as the redskin who steals through the coverts." John Christy later helps conceal Benny and save him from the massacre. In the epilogue to the novel, Christy reports to the people at Ft. Henry that forty-nine adults and twenty-seven children were murdered and their bodies burned in the chapel. He reports that Jim Girty himself clubbed fourteen to death with a sledge hammer. He later reports that Heckewelder has taken charge of Benny and will ensure that he is taken care of and educated.

Cibeque: In *The Hash Knife Outfit*, an outlaw outfit operating in Arizona. Slinger Dunn was once a member of the gang.

Cinco: In *West of the Pecos*, Pecos Smith's horse and companion. He is the fastest horse on the range. The rancher brothers, John and Bill Heald, express great admiration for the steed, predicting that the stallion will draw the attention of the horse-loving Comanches.

Clair: In *Code of the West*, Edd Thurman's dancing partner. Old Henry Thurman improvises a song at the dance in which he pokes fun at Edd who has tramped on Clair's toes.

Clanger: In *Fighting Caravans*, mentioned as an outlaw in the same league as Murdock.

Clark: (1) In *The Fugitive Trail*, arrives at Melrose's ranch on a wagon train led by Seever. He sees Lee Jones (Bruce) and tells Captain Maggard of the Texas Rangers that Lee Jones is Bruce Lockheart, the man all the rangers have been hunting for weeks. He insists he saw him shoot Barncastle and kill Whistler at the Elk Hotel in Mendle. Melrose tells him he must be mistaken as the man he claims is Bruce Lockheart is Lee Jones, his daughter Trinity's fiancé. Clark reluctantly concedes he might be mistaken.

(2) In *The Wanderer of the Wasteland*, a miner who is killed at Tecopah. Adam meets his wife and takes revenge on the murderer.

Clarke, Alfred: Appears in *Betty Zane*. He is mentioned in *The Spirit of the Border* as being Betty Zane's husband.

In *Betty Zane*, Alfred Clarke is the equivalent of Joe Downs in *The Spirit of the Border* and John Hare in *The Heritage of the Desert*. He is from southern Virginia, educated in Philadelphia, a true gentleman, with impeccable manners, and speech. As men of refinement are in short supply on the frontier, he becomes extremely popular with the young ladies after his arrival at Ft. Henry from Ft. Pitt. Like Joe, he is rudderless, having run away from home after his father died and his mother remarried. His natural love of adventure induced him to seek his fortune "with the hardy pioneer and the cunning savage of the border." After several months of service with General Clark, he still knew nothing of frontier life. He left the army and offered his services to Colonel Zane at Ft. Henry. He admires men like Wetzel and Jonathan Zane who take "the most wonderful adventures and daring escapes as a matter of course, a compulsory part of their daily lives." He hopes he can find something useful to do, to give his life some meaning. "I never worked in my life until I came to Ft Henry. My life was all uselessness, idleness" he confesses to Betty while they spend an afternoon canoeing.

During this afternoon excursion, Alfred bares his soul to Betty, explaining that his father had intended him for the ministry, sending him to the theological seminary at Princeton, where he studied for two years. When his father died, he left home, and has spent four years wandering, looking for a purpose in life.

As in a typical Zane Grey romance, the hero and

the heroine are often at odds. Alfred starts off on the wrong foot with Betty. The day he begins work for Colonel Zane, he is assigned guard duty on the river road. He stops Betty from riding down the river road and sends her back to the fort. She finds him condescending and arrogant, resenting the smug, superior, patronizing smile he gives her. The fact that he helped save Isaac's life softens her attitude towards him.

Betty and Alfred do have a heart-to-heart while spending an afternoon canoeing and fishing. Alfred kisses her that evening, offending her delicate sensibilities again. Before he can see her to apologize, Alfred is called away suddenly. He leaves a letter apologizing and explaining his sudden departure with Sam. Sam, however, considers Alfred Clarke typical "southern white trash" and conceals the letter. Upon his return, Alfred again faces Betty's wrath, but the Colonel straightens matters out when he gets Sam to produce the letter and clear Clarke's reputation.

Alfred shows his mettle during the attack on the fort when he climbs up on the roof to remove the burning arrows the Indians have shot into the timbers before the arrows set the buildings on fire.

All ends well, and Alfred and Betty are married, but he dies of unspecified causes before the beginning of the third novel in the series, *The Last Trail*.

Like Joe Downs, Alfred Clarke is another version of the Easterner who must learn to adapt to the frontier. He has come west seeking adventure, a chance to prove himself and find meaning in life. He learns that survival on the frontier requires individual effort, strength, determination, versatility rather than social graces and "good breeding."

Clark, Bill: In *Sunset Pass*, the owner of the Range House Hotel. He is the first person Trueman Rock meets when he returns to Wagontongue after six years in Texas. Clark greets him cordially, commenting on how prosperous he looks. Clark still has a card game going upstairs but comments that the stakes at the game are much bigger then they used to be. He fills Trueman in on the gossip, the increase in the sheep business in the area, the new lumber mills, the new arrivals in the area. He tells him about his old flames, Polly Ackers, Killy Rand, Amy Wund, and Cass Seward. He is reluctant to say much about Ash Preston at this meeting, but later, when Rock is working for Preston and in town for the Fourth of July Rodeo, he pumps him for information about the Prestons.

Clarke, General: Military commander of Ft. Pitt. In *Betty Zane,* he is mentioned as one of the distinguished guests to have stayed at Colonel Zane's cabin. He sends Captain Boggs to the garrison at Ft. Henry.

Clay, John: In *The Trail Driver,* a rancher who sells cattle to Wallen. He gave Wallen some cowboys with the deal. Reddie Bayne was one of those riders and resents being sold "like a nigger slave." She runs away from Wallen.

Clayborn, Lieutenant: In *Fighting Caravans,* an army officer, a handsome, debonair West Pointer. He has many qualities which Clint envies, especially his grace, his ease and charming affability of manner which no plainsmen ever attain. Clayborn shows interest in May Bell, buys her candy. May Bell responds politely to his friendly banter, but Clint feels inadequate and jealous.

Claypool, Amy: In *Under the Tonto Rim,* one of the young women in the Tonto, sister to Gerd, and friend of Mertie Denmeade and Sadie Purdue. Unlike Sadie and Mertie, she thinks Edd is a grand fellow, not a boob at all. Amy Claypool takes over teaching school when Clara is too distraught after the fight in which Edd Denmeade kills Harv Sprall, who had been trying to blackmail her.

Claypool, Dave: In *Under the Tonto Rim,* drops by the Denmeades' place to tell them he met Edd on the Winbrook trail. Claypool lets his horses range up there and he ran across Edd some fifteen miles back.

Claypool, Gerd: In *Under the Tonto Rim,* a cousin of Sam Johnson's, a blue-eyed young giant with tawny hair. He is with Sam when they meet the schoolteacher and Mr. Jenks. He comments that the new teacher is a looker. Gerd is a brown-faced young man with a huge paw of a hand. His face is warm, healthy, expressing both eagerness and bashfulness. Lucy sees in him the promise in the Tonto youth that Mrs. Lynn had spoken to her about.

Claypool, Hank: In *Under the Tonto Rim,* one of the Claypool clan. Mr. Denmeade tells Lucy Watson that they live farther up the canyon and are in greater need than they are.

Claypool, Mrs.: In *Under the Tonto Rim,* appears once in the novel when she and her daughters drop by the Denmeades' on Sunday afternoon. She is hard-featured and unprepossessing, bearing the unmistakable marks of hard labor in a hard country. She does, however, put Lucy at ease.

Clegg, Mrs.: In *Arizona Ames,* the housekeeper on Jim Morgan's ranch.

Clement, Hall: In *Fighting Caravans,* arrives at Maxwell's ranch on Dagget's caravan from Texas. He and Maxwell had been good friends years ago when both served in the army during the Mexican War. Hall had later been a Texas Ranger. The Clements head west to Taos, heading for the West Coast and California. May Bell and Sarah Clements remain in Taos, while Hall continues to California. When he returns, he learns that Murdock had been making unseemly advances to his daughter. He meets him in Turner's saloon in Taos, where Murdock kills him.

Clement, Sarah: In *Fighting Caravans,* the wife of Hall Clement. She is introduced to Maxwell and Clint Belmet at Maxwell's ranch. Her husband and Maxwell and Kit Carson had been partners years ago. Mrs. Clement takes in May Bell when she wanders into a caravan, after the caravan she was in was attacked by Indians and all were killed. Mrs. Clements sees to her schooling, and raises her as her own daughter. Mrs. Clement approves of Clint Belmet as a husband for May and is distressed with her flirting with Lee Murdock and Lieutenant Clayborn. When Clint Belmet catches up with them in Las Cruces some years later, she is a gray-haired, sad-eyed woman. She is overjoyed to see Clint, pleased that her belief that he was still alive has been rewarded. The Clements own a ranch just outside of town. The family is rich, and generous with the poor and the Mexicans. She welcomes Clint as a son-in-law who will take over the ranch.

Clements: In *Knights of the Range,* one of the local ranchers running a heard of about twenty thousand head. He shows up at the Ripple ranch with Sewall McCoy to accuse Renn Frayne of rustling. Clements is one of the more vehement in his insistence that Frayne either face the gunman, Jeff Rankin, or be arrested on suspicion of rustling. Brazos Keene, one of Ripple's cowboys, a "Knight of the Range" proves that Clements himself has been buying stolen cattle from Slaughter, whom they have just caught red-handed with stolen cattle. As it happens, Slaughter kept good records of the cattle he rustled and the ranchers to whom he sold them. He protests that he only bought unbranded stock.

Cleve, Jim: In *The Border Legion,* young man twenty-three years old. He is in love with Joan Randle, but her father does not approve of him. He chases after her and Joan feels that people in town believe she encourages him. Joan sees a strangeness about him that she cannot understand. One day he tries to kiss her and she scolds him, telling him she could never marry him. Jim refuses to work, and he squanders what gold he does find. He drinks heavily, gambles and loves to fight. He is fond of his gun. In short, he is shiftless and reckless. Jim then tells her he will go join Kells and Gulden's outfit, where he will make a name for himself.

Regretting what she said, Joan sets off after Jim. She meets Harvey Roberts, who tells her that the previous evening, Jim had defended her honor when one young Bradley had spoken ill of her in the saloon. Joan has the opportunity to witness further examples of Jim's sense of honor and loyalty and willingness to defend a woman's reputation during her stay with Kells and the Border Legion.

The next time Joan hears about Jim, she is Kells's prisoner. Pearce reports that a young man, quite the cardsharp, has been asking about Jack Kells. Wood reports that this same young man had beaten up an outlaw called Luce for proposing that they rob and kill Bradley and abduct his daughter. Woods's account of Cleve's behavior underlines his courage and his reasonableness. He drinks a lot, but he doesn't act drunk. He gambles, but gambles fairly. He takes out Chick Williams and Beady Jones for cheating at cards, but he only wounds them in the arm. He is cool, quick, smooth.

Jim Cleve does not recognize Joan, disguised in Dandy Dale's robber's outfit, when he is introduced to Kells's outfit. But the man who shows up is not the over-grown, sleepy-eyed boy she had known at Hoadley's camp, but rather a muscle bound, "beautiful man" with two guns on his hips. Jim Cleve becomes popular with the gang, but remains a mystery. He tells a story about having gone to the bad because his girl had married someone else. Kells willingly believes that Cleve has joined the gang because of a woman. When Joan reveals her true identity to Jim, he offers to get her out, but she refuses to leave, out of concern for Kells. Jim thinks she is in love with him. He finds her story of continued innocence nearly impossible to believe. Finally, when she tells how she had followed him and was abducted by Kells, he believes her. Jim calculates that their chances of escape will be better at Alder Creek, in the gold diggings. Jim finds a thirty-pound nugget, a quantity that guarantees him a secure living for the rest of his life, but he remains in the camp. He selects a sleeping spot under a cliff not far from the cabin where Joan is staying. He meets her at the back window and they talk into the night. Finally, Joan is convinced to marry him. He becomes jealous of Kells and wants to kill him. Joan understands that this ferocity in him comes from the environment of the camps. Jim Cleve then finds the solution. He has become friendly with a young preacher in the camp. One night he brings him to the cabin and the two of them are married. Jim becomes increasingly reckless in his visits. Pearce suspects something, and reports to Kells, in part, because he dislikes Cleve, in part because he wants to foment disagreement between Kells and Gulden.

Throughout his period in the camps, Jim Cleve proves that a man of principle can survive in the gold diggings. He is popular among the miners, making friends everywhere. The outlaws all admire and like him, with a few exceptions. He is loyal to Kells, despite Kells's interest in Joan, and he is unafraid of Gulden, the heartless cannibal and murderer.

When Jim and Joan return to Hoadley's town, Aunt Jane reluctantly accepts her new son-in-law, but she has no cause to fear. The Jim Cleve who returns is a fully mature young man ready to accept the responsibilities of a husband and respectable citizen. As in the case of Buck Duane in *The Border Legion,* his inherent decency triumphs.

Cliff: In *Thunder Mountain,* one of Rand Leavitt's henchmen who works with Macabe and Leslie. He is one of the men who attack and rob other miners.

Clodothie: In *Blue Feather,* the chief medicine man of the clan. He holds that the twelve-year drought has resulted from Taneen's involvement with a princess of the accursed Antelope Clan. He orders Taneen to return his daughter Nashta to her own people. Taneen replies that there are prophesies which say that Nashta, Daughter of the Moon, will remain hidden from daylight with the Rock Clan forever. Taneen refuses to believe their prophesies of doom and gloom.

Clubfoot: In *Stranger from the Tonto*, one of Lucy Bonesteel's favorite horses, second after Spades. Bonesteel asks Jeff to saddle Clubfoot and Spades for Lucy and Kent and to place them near the falls and the secret exit from the valley. Lucy and Kent do not know the way, but the two horses, Spades and Clubfoot do, and need no direction.

Coates, Jim: In *Arizona Ames*, a member of Bannard's outlaw gang seen in Bosomer's saloon in Yampa.

Cochise: Mentioned by Bill Stillwell in *The Light of Western Stars* when he recounts the history of the Southwest to Madeline. Cochise was a chief of the Chiricahua Apache. He befriended the whites only to find himself betrayed. He was involved in wars with the American army.

In *Majesty's Rancho*, Madge wants to take her college friends on a camping trip up to Cochise's stronghold in the mountains near the ranch. She had visited the place years ago with her father and thinks it would be an unforgettable experience for her friends. Given that they are tenderfeet and the ranch does not have the camping equipment, the proposal is discarded. When Uhl and his gangsters have kidnapped Madge, Lance Sidway takes the party to the stronghold on the pretext that they can hold out there until Stewart has paid the ransom.

Cocky: In *Wilderness Trek*, one of Leslie Slyter's pet birds.

Coffee: In *The U. P. Trail*, sent with Blake and Somers from Omaha by Baxter to help Neale solve the problems with the construction of a bridge. Coffee, it turns out, is in cahoots with Allison Lee. He and Blake had not followed the plans, causing the supports for the bridge to fall. When his role in delaying construction of the bridge becomes clear, he is fired by Neale without pay for past work.

Coglan: In *Twin Sombreros*, lives in a mountain valley, still quite isolated. He is a strapping man, young, half-hunter and half-trapper, brown as an Indian. He survives here because he is friendly to the Utes. He lives with his wife and children. Brazos Keene comes to stay with him for a month or two looking for a bit of peace and quiet after the first phase of his war against the rustlers, the phase which ends with the deaths of Syvertsen and Orcutt and the shooting of Bess. Coglan agrees to make trips to Las Animas to get the gossip. Bilyen knows that Brazos will be staying with Coglan, and advises he go to see him. He reports back that Surface was killed in Dodge, that Bodkins is boasting that should Brazos appear again in Las Animas, he will arrest him. He also reports on the appearance of a cattleman called Knight.

Coglan, Rose: In *Twin Sombreros*, Coglan's wife. She welcomes Brazos to their home.

Cole, Martin: In *The Heritage of the Desert*, is a Mormon and close friend of August Naab. He is with August Naab when he finds John Hare lying on the desert almost dead from exposure and abuse. He warns Naab not to take the young man in because he is known as Dene's spy, and taking him in will bring down the wrath of the outlaws on Naab and his family. Martin Cole is not as devoutly religious a man as Naab. Unlike his devoutly pacifist friend, Martin Cole believes that he must fight to defend what is his. He already has blood on his hands. He points out that at present, Naab lives in isolation in the desert and enjoys the protection of the friendly Navajo in the area, but such good luck cannot last forever. Cole believes that the Mormons, who are slow to anger, will be pushed too far and resort to violence to drive the cattle thieves out. Eventually, Martin Cole's land and cattle are stolen from him by Holderness, and Cole himself is killed in a gunfight instigated by Dene, it is believed, under orders from Holderness. In the novel, Cole introduces the themes of justice through violence. The law of nature is that the strong prey on the weak, and unless the weak band together to defend themselves, they stand little chance against the strong. Eventually August Naab becomes more sympathetic to Martin Cole's position. Martin Cole is transformed by circumstances. Unlike Naab, who can be both a man of action and a man of reflection, Martin Cole cannot reconcile the two strains; the need to take action takes precedence over forgiving pacifism. His religion may teach forgiveness but that does not mean submissiveness to oppression and injustice. Evil, he knows, will triumph unless good men act.

Cole, Seth: In *The Lost Wagon Train*, an old member of the Latch outlaw outfit. He is a big, bland, lazy man who drifted into outlawry because it was the easiest way. He accepts Latch's offer of money and cattle to set up ranching and start over, living straight. He does prosper somewhat, but like Tumbleer Johnson, he never seems to lose any cattle to rustlers while Latch's herds are shrinking. Slim Blue comments that he has seen Cole coming and going from Leighton's quarters at all hours of the night.

Coleman: In *To the Last Man*, owns a house behind Greaves's store. Jean uses the bushes around his yard as cover as he sneaks up to the back of the building to break in the door.

Coleman, Lieutenant: In *The Trail Driver*, is in charge of a detachment en route to Fort Richardson. He advises Brite to stay near the fort for a while. The Comanches have recently attacked and massacred a wagon train, and buffalo herds have moved into the area to the north. If they continue on the trail, they will meet both the Indians and the buffalo.

Coles, Sam: In *The Mysterious Rider*, nursed Bent Wade back to health after a gunfight in Boulder, Colorado. Sam Coles tells the tale to Old Kemp. Bent Wade is a man pursued by misfortune and with each stroke of bad luck, he must tell the story of his troubles to someone in order to move on.

Collin (also spelled "Collier"), Dwight:
In *30,000 on the Hoof*, named by Holbert as a fellow rancher in the area, closer to Flagg. His ranch is ten miles away. He sells out his ranch and stock to Holbert after Tim Mooney is killed. Mooney had been serving as a front for rustlers, and Collin (Collier) was suspected of the same.

Collins:
In *The U. P. Trail*, a telegraph operator. He informs Casey that the telegraph wires are down and General Lodge cannot be warned that the Sioux are going to the attack the train.

Collishaw:
In *Wanderer of the Wasteland*, Collishaw is a former gunfighter and sheriff from Texas. He arrives at Ehrenberg with Guerd Larey. He is a gambler and ruthless adventurer. Before coming to Picacho, he hangs some Mexicans for shooting and robbing miners. He wants to collect a gambling debt from Adam, money he supposedly owes to his brother, Guerd. Collishaw cuts a striking figure for his repellent face, his massive head on a bull neck, his swarthy, leathery skin like wrinkled leather, his thin lips, tight-shut mouth, and chin as square as a rock. His eyes incessantly move from side to side, trained to see all. He witnesses the fight between Guerd and Adam, and pronounces that Guerd is dead. He threatens to hang Adam. Collishaw sets out after Adam when Adam escapes into the desert. At one point, Adam sees Collishaw and Felix on his trail. Collishaw has a white bandage over his eye. Later, Dismukes meets him at Walters stage stop. He is looking for the man who put out his eye — to kill him. Merryvale recalls Collishaw when Adam Larey returns fourteen years later, but he does not know what became of him.

In *Stairs of Sand*, Collishaw reappears in Yuma and at Lost Lake accompanied by Guerd Larey. He runs one of the many gambling saloons in Yuma, and is partner in others, such as the Del Toro, with the Mexican, Sanchez. He has learned from an insider that the route of the railroad will not be along the east side of the valley but on the opposite side, passing through the water holes Lost Lake, Salton Spring and Twenty-Nine Palms. He and Larey scheme to take possession of these to control the water rights, which will be extremely lucrative. Having been a sheriff in Texas, he claims to have investigated the legality of the Spanish grant on which Indian Jim and Caleb Hunt's claims are based. Collishaw plans to harass Hunt until he signs over his station to Larey or forces his daughter to return to Larey. In Yuma, Collishaw is reportedly the only man interested in taking on the position of sheriff when Jim Henshall is shot. The honest citizens of Yuma, however, oppose him. Collishaw and Hal Stone organize the seeming robbery of ten thousand dollars from Larey and the abduction of Ruth Virey from her home in Lost Lake. Manuel Gomez, his Mexican driver, exposes the plot to Merryvale and Wansfell. Adam

knows Collishaw well. Despite his Texas breeding, he is a desert blackguard. He is the worst kind of criminal on the border. A man, once backed by the law, who affects honesty when under his mask he is a desperado. He confronts Collishaw in Yuma, exposing his crookedness. Collishaw finally recognizes Adam, the man who had put out his eye years ago. In the gunfight which follows, Wansfell kills Collishaw.

Colmon:
In *The Vanishing American*, works at Withers's trading post at Kaidab.

Colmor, Andrew:
In *To the Last Man*, the young man who is engaged to Ann Isbel. Jean Isbel takes a liking to him immediately. He tries to discourage Colmor from joining in the fighting, but Colmor insists on proving his loyalty to the Isbel clan. Gaston Isbel got him started in the cattle business and he feels a debt of gratitude. Jean is concerned that Andrew will come out of this with blood on his hands and the profound guilt that accompanies having killed another human being. Jean would prefer that Ann's husband never have to know that feeling. Andrew, however, refuses to be left behind. He is shot by Queen in the fighting at Greaves's store.

Colohan:
In *The U. P. Trail*, boss of a construction gang.

Colonel:
In *The Lone Star Ranger*, the man in charge of the vigilante group Buck Duane runs into as he is trying to distance himself as much as possible from Ranger MacNelly. The colonel gives instructions to send the dogs into the cottonwood covet where Duane is hiding and to set fire to the brakes to drive Duane out.

Colter, Jim:
In *To the Last Man*, a member of the Hash Knife gang and a key figure in Lee Jorth's faction. He first meets Jean Isbel on a trail above the rim, where he gives him directions down into Grass Valley. Jean Isbel feels that sharper eyes had never flashed over him and his outfit. Colter is tall among tall men, with a dust-colored, sun–burned face, long, lean, hard, with a sandy mustache that hides his mouth, and eyes of piercing intensity. Not much in Western experience had passed by this Jim Colter, although he is not old in years. Jean Isbel senses a subtle hostility emanating from him. He sizes up young Isbel to report to the crew back at Greaves's store so by the time Jean Isbel makes his way into Grass Valley, his arrival is anticipated. Colter is the first to return to the Jorth ranch house after the routing at Greaves's store. He announces to Ellen that she must pack up and leave. He tells her that Jean Isbel sneaked into Greaves's and killed her father and Uncle Jackson in their sleep. He also informs her that her father had entrusted her to his care. Colter steals Lee Jorth's gold and some papers. Colter takes her with him up to the cabin that supposedly had been on Daggs's sheep ranch. Here, he tries to force himself on her and she fights him off, finally shooting him with a rifle.

Columbine: In *The Mysterious Stranger,* the adopted daughter of Old Bill Belllounds. Columbine is nineteen years old when the story begins, and has just returned from four years at school in Denver. She is getting reacquainted with the ranch and its environs. Seventeen years before, Columbine had been found by some miners, lying in a clump of columbine flowers. They brought her to the Belllounds, the only family in the area, at White Slides ranch, where they named her for the flowers where she was found. Belllounds imagines that she had been on a prairie schooner that was attacked by Indians. She had probably crawled away from the road and got lost. Her parents were never found and were presumed dead. Columbine feels acutely the need for a mother and for more information about where she came from. Although she herself never learns the full story, the reader is slowly given more information. Various people add pieces to the picture. The innkeeper's wife in Kremmlin' tells Bent Wade that Belllounds wife was jealous of the old man's attention to the orphan, fearing that he would cheat her son out of his full inheritance. This resentment against the girl clearly has made Columbine feel insecure about her place at White Slides, although Old Belllounds has left her half the estate in his will. He has planned to have Columbine marry his son, Buster Jack, thereby keeping his estate intact. Columbine is willing to marry Jack but she doesn't love him. She feels it is her duty to do what Old Bill wants out of gratitude for his taking her in when she was a baby. Nevertheless, she does wonder if he would throw her out if she did not consent to his wishes. Lewis and Mrs. Andrews and Blair mention that Old Bill dotes on his wayward son, the son who has taken after his mother rather than his father. They add that Columbine is sweet on a cowboy on the ranch. Bent Wade completes the picture when he tells Old Belllounds the story of how he came to lose his daughter. Wade was married to a beautiful young Southern belle, Lucy. He was ridiculously jealous of any man who spoke to her. Lucy's brother, Spencer, together with a friend of his, one Captain Folsom, attempted to drive the two of them apart, encouraging a young Southerner to flirt with Lucy, antagonizing Wade. They hinted that the baby was not Wade's daughter, but the daughter of one of Lucy's male friends. No longer able to cope with his insane jealousy, Lucy abandoned Wade, taking the daughter with her. In the fighting which follows, Lucy's father and brother are killed. Lucy left on a prairie schooner, the last Wade knows of her. Columbine never does hear the full story herself, only that Bent Wade was her father.

Columbine is still in love with a cowboy from White Slides, Wilson Moore. She meets him when riding around the ranch. She asks him why he has not come to see her since her return. Moore answers that he had been told to stay away from her. Furthermore, it's not appropriate that she be seen with him given that she is scheduled to marry Buster Jack. The return of Buster Jack, however, is not pleasant.

He gets drunk and gambles before he makes it home. He is scarcely a gentleman, although he is good looking and well-dressed. Buster Jack recalls that Columbine had once been kissed by Wils and that Wils had beaten him in a fight over Columbine. Jack feels threatened by the presence of Wilson, and Columbine's continuing affection for the cowboy.

When Bent Wade arrives at the ranch, he recognizes her immediately as his daughter, bearing such close resemblance to Lucy. He quickly sizes up the situation and determines to do his best to do right by her. She easily comes to trust him, finding him easier and safer to confide in than anyone else. When Buster shows up drunk at the wedding, Bill Belllounds puts off the wedding in disgust. Improved behavior on the part of his son leads him to hope that Columbine will consent to marrying him. Old Bill sees the violent streak in his son, his lack of responsibility, but he cannot give up on him. Columbine feels a debt of gratitude to her adopted father and a strange responsibility to redeem Buster Jack, to sacrifice herself so he can mature into a decent person. Wade tells her that such a plan is doomed to failure because Buster Jack has his own nature and she cannot hope to deceive him into believing she loves him for the length of a marriage. It could merely lead to the unhappiness of both of them. When Buster Jack reveals his truly malevolent nature in his attempt to blame his own cattle rustling on Wilson Moore, the die is cast. Buster Jack's scheming catches up with him and he is killed in a fight with Bent Wade. Columbine then marries Wilson Moore.

Columbine is a typical heroine of a Zane romance. A young woman with charm and grace and a mature sense of responsibility, she is willing to sacrifice her own happiness to redeem Jack. She vacillates between duty to herself and duty to her foster father. Her happiness is assured, but only after a hero figure acts to save her from her own indecision.

Columbus: In *Boulder Dam,* mentioned by Lynn Weston as a man who had a vision and transformed the world when he realized his dream.

Colville, Bill: In "The Ranger," a ranger friend of Vaughn Medill. He was wounded in the fight with the Cutter rustling outfit and has his arm in a sling. He tells Vaughn that plans are afoot to send him across the river into Mexico to pursue horse thieves who have driven a herd across the river at Brownsville. Colville tells Medill he should have been made a captain in the rangers long ago but the authorities in Houston are a tough lot to deal with. Medill talks of retiring, getting married and going into ranching, but as Medill has no girlfriend, he doubts the likelihood of that happening.

Comanche: A tribe of Indians in western Texas, New Mexico and Colorado. In *The Light of Western Stars,* Bill Stillwell says that he had to fight the Comanche for his ranch land.

Con: In *The Shepherd of Guadaloupe,* an Irish

cowboy who works for Virginia Lundeed. He is a sandy-haired, freckled, strong, wide-eyed cowboy. While Jake is a Westerner and learned his trade from birth, Con is a relative newcomer to the trade. He and Jake had taken care of Lundeed's horses in the past, and she is surprised to find they have been fired by Malpass, who has also sent her horses to a ranch in Watrous. Virginia hires him and Jake back. They take orders directly from her, not from Malpass. Con takes the letter from Virginia to Cliff asking him to meet her at night. Con also accompanies the crew on horseback on the excursion to Emerald Lake near Mt. Baldy. Con and Jake inspect the Padre mine and conclude that there is something fishy about the place. They suspect that the "gold" has been planted there to trick some unsuspecting investor. When Virginia leaves for Colorado Springs after her father has kicked her out of his home, he and Jake agree to take care of her horses, taking them to Jeff Sneed's ranch, where they had worked before. When Virginia returns after the death of her father and Malpass, Con and Jake return to work on her ranch.

Conn, Dixie: In *Majesty's Rancho*, one of Madge Stewart's friends from the university. She comes to spend the summer at the ranch with a group from Los Angeles. She agrees with Sidway that Madge should choose a more manageable horse to ride rather than the frisky Dervish.

Conners, Geralda: In *The Call of the Canyon*, one of Carley's crowd in New York City. Like Eleanor Harmon and Beatrice Lovell, she is puzzled by Carley's attitude after her return from Arizona visiting Glenn Killbourne. She thinks that Carley has gone sour on New York and blames them. She gets a particular hoot out of Carley's speech condemning the decadent lifestyle, the empty, meaningless lives of New Yorkers who do nothing more than seek to satisfy their own selfish cravings. Like Eleanor and Beatrice, she sees nothing wrong with her life.

Conroy: In *The Deer Stalker*, drives an automobile for those who have no horses during the deer roundup and drive that Thad Eburne and Bill McKay organized.

Constance: In *Wyoming*, Andrew Bonning's girlfriend from the university. When Andrew tells her about his father's financial plight and his disinheritance, Connie tells him she had never been serious about him. She confirms what Andrew had always suspected, that she is nothing but a gold digger.

Cook, Al: In *The Horse Thief*, shares a mutual friend with Dale Brittenham, Jen Pierce. Al Cook is a member of Stafford's posse from Montana, pursuing horse thieves. Al takes care of the large, canvas-covered pack that Dale has taken from Big Bill Mason's cabin. He asks him to take the package to his wagon to stow under the seat.

Coombs, Dorothy: In *The Light of Western Stars*, an attractive blonde who caddies for Ed Linton during the golf game organized for the Eastern guests. Despite her claims to riding experience, the horse she is riding rears up and Gene Stewart has to come to her rescue. She is pleased to have him take her back to the ranch. Like Madeline's sister Helen, Dorothy is a self-centered, unrepentant flirt. She is superficial, through and through. She is repulsed by Monty Price's face, unable to see the kind heart behind the scars resulting from severe burns when he went into a burning house to rescue a woman and child. She also complains about how revolting it was for him to kiss her. Helen says of Dorothy that she only looks for someone to flatter her. However, when she leaves, she seems to have softened, seeing more in the horrid cowboys than she had first seen. She asks Madeline to tell Monty that she is glad he kissed her after all.

Coombs, Mary: In *Rogue River Feud*, the daughter of a fisherman. She spots Garry's skiff out at sea one day on their way to Crescent City. They picked Garry up. Garry married the young woman. He now runs a little fish market three days a week in Grant's Pass and three days in Crescent City. Coombs supplies the fish. She manages Garry well, allowing him only one spree per month.

Copelace, Jim: In *The Arizona Clan*, a friend of Steve Lilley's. Rock Lilley claims that Jim once stole a hound of his, but Jim argues that the dog came into his camp and wouldn't leave him. He and Steve have been hunting partners for years. Jim is half Apache, and a phenomenal tracker. Steve calls him in to help track down Hathaway and his men. Copelace has an axe to grind with Buck Hathaway on two counts. It seems Copelace sold his white mule to the Apache and has wreaked havoc with his family. As well, Hathaway once made advances to Jim's sister. Copeland sneaks up to the cabin where the Hathaway outfit is holed up and overhears the conversation in which they divide up the spoils: the Quayles want a good still, and Twitchell wants the Lilley ranch while Buck wants Nan. He accompanies Dodge as they trail the gang, but while Dodge has to look for tracks, Jim seems to spot them at a glance from the saddle. He is the first to reach the cabin where Nan is being held.

Copsy: In *Fighting Caravans*, a friend of Benny Ireland, a member of the caravan of freighters attacked at Point of Rocks. He is killed in the fighting.

Corbett, Mr. and Mrs.: In *Wyoming*, give Martha Ann Dixon a lift along the way. They treat her to a movie when they stop in a town for repairs to the car.

Cordts: In *Wildfire*, a horse thief and bad man. He comes to Bostril's Ford and the sage country from the gold fields of California and Idaho, an outcast, one of the evil wave of wanderers who spread over the West when the gold fields failed. For a while, he hunted wild mustangs. As a rider, Cordts is the equal of Bostril and Van Sickle. He has a passion for fast horses like Bostril, greater it is said, than his passion for a woman. In particular he envies Bostril his stallion, Sage King. He has sworn he will steal the horse, and if not the horse, Bostril's daughter. Aunt Jane cautions Lucy about riding alone on the sage in case Cordts is around. When she sneaks out of the house to go find Slone, Aunt Jane and Holley both fear she will be caught by Cordts. Cordts sends an Indian to ask Bostril's permission to attend the races. He comes with his two men, Hutchinson and Dick Sears. He promises not to disturb the peace, and after the race, true to his word, he leaves. Cordts camps out on the sage and when he and his men spot Joel returning to the canyons with Sage King and Sarchedon, he sets off to follow them. Creech and Bostril both have said that Cordts is not able to track very well, and they don't worry about him catching them. Cordts does, however, come upon them as they flee the canyon. He and Hutchinson shoot at Slone and Lucy from a cliff. Cordts' perch on the rock face is precarious and he slips. Hutchinson offers a hand to help him up, but Lucy shoots Cordts and, as he slips from his perch, he pulls Hutchinson with him over the precipice.

Cordy: In *The U. P. Trail*, one of eight gunmen hired by Beauty Stanton to keep order in her place. Both Cordy and Larry Red King are interested in Ruby, the most popular saloon girl in Stanton's. When Ruby wants to punish Neale for his lack of interest in her, she threatens to send Cordy after him. Cordy recognizes Red as a Texas gunman, brother of the famous King Fisher. Red suspects Cordy is implicated in Ruby's death and he kills him in a gunfight.

Coretta: In *Majesty's Rancho*, Coretta is one of Lance Sidway's girlfriends in Hollywood. She is cited as an example of the typical Hollywood girl, loose, easy, fickle, ready to do anything to make it in the movies.

Cork, Latzy: In *Majesty's Rancho*, there are two characters called Cork. The first, called Latzy, is mentioned by Lance Sidway who tells Bee Uhl he beat it out of Oregon before Latzy Cork. Uhl then speculates about whether Cork has been spotting him. The second one, possibly the same man, is referred to as running a "snatch racket" in eastern Arizona.

Corning, Tex: In *Shadow on the Trail*, a member of Simm Bell's outlaw gang. He is described as tall and thin, with a drooping, sandy moustache which gives him a look of solemnity. Wade Holden sees him riding out of town from the ambush in Mercer, and presumably he gets away.

Cornplanter: Yantwaia in the Indian language, appears in *Betty Zane* and *The Spirit of the Border*. Cornplanter is a chief of the Seneca nation. Colonel Ebenezer Zane purchased an island in the Ohio River from him for the price of a keg of liquor. Cornplanter is one of the prominent Indian chiefs in *Betty Zane* plotting the attack on Ft. Henry. He feels that Indians have been unjustly treated by whites and seeks revenge. When Isaac Zane escapes from the Huron village a second time, he is taken prisoner by Cornplanter, who sentences him to death at the stake. Thundercloud and Myeerah appear on the horizon just before the faggots around Isaac are set ablaze. Cornplanter decides that the personal satisfaction he would get from killing Isaac is not worth incurring the wrath of Tarhe and the Hurons. He does not miss the opportunity, however, to insult the Hurons, telling Myeerah to take the "Long Knife" back to her lodge to make into a squaw. At a later time, however, Cornplanter takes a more conciliatory attitude towards the whites. Cornplanter is mentioned as one of the important guests to have visited Colonel Zane's cabin in Ft. Henry.

Cornwall, Lester: In *The Lost Wagon Train*, Latch's right-hand man during his days as confederate of Satana in the attacks on wagon trains. He is younger than Latch, and Stephen loves him as a brother. His lack of feeling, his unflappable cool in the face of fighting, robbery, blood and murder, impress Latch. In the first tension in the group between Leighton and Latch, Lester Cornwall pronounces himself loyal to Latch. He reveals to the colonel that Sprall and Leighton are hiding a woman in the Tullt wagon. In the ensuing gunplay, he maintains his loyalty to Latch and is asked to stand by him during the wedding ceremony. Lester Cornwall, however, refuses, as he has no use for women. Over the years, Cornwall and Latch become close friends. Latch once asks him if he had ever loved a girl, to which Cornwall replies that he would have killed any other man for asking him that question. He explains that his home life was unhappy. He had come between his parents, his mother preferring him to her husband. He confesses that he and his younger brother, Cornie, were very close. At Fort Union, he wanders among the soldiers, traders, and frontiersmen, listening and gauging from the conversations how much they know about his boss's past. He concludes that they are above suspicion, but that the presence of Leighton and his faction could change that. When Latch begins to talk of changing his ways to become respectable again, Lester tells him he's a dreamer. Cornwall understands border life and what is needed to survive. But Latch is really just a good man gone bad. Latch keeps wondering what makes Lester tick. He seems a strange combination of eagle and vulture. He suggests to Latch that they return to the lonely life at the canyon. He'd like to raise horses, to hunt and fish, to live away from the rum holes, the smoke, the crazy men and the hussies. That very night, Lester is killed by Lily in a card game. Lily is a dance hall girl, stuck on Lester. When he refuses to pay her attention, she persists until he calls her a slut, upon which she pulls a gun and shoots him in the head. Latch mourns the loss of his closest friend and confident.

Corny (also spelled Cornie, a.k.a. Slim Blue): In *The Lost Wagon Train*, the younger brother of Lester Cornwall. Lester called him Cornie because his hair was the color of ripe corn. He was Lester's closest friend, perhaps the only person he ever really loved. When Corny first appears in the novel, he has just shot Pitch, the distant relative of Lanthorpe, the owner of the herd his outfit is trailing. Corny was provoked into the fight but the death makes an outlaw of him. His friends, Weaver, Jeff, and Chet, wish him luck and collect some money to give him a break. When he pulls off the trail to rest, sleeping in a clump of trees, he wakes to overhear two thugs planning a kidnapping and ransom scheme. He kills the two men in a gunfight, and prevents the abduction of Estelle Latch, daughter of Stephen Latch, owner of Latch's Field, a rendezvous town of trail drivers, wagon trains, Indians, and outlaws. She is returning from New Orleans to stay. She offers to have her father to give him a job as reward for saving her. Cornwall agrees to accompany her to the Bridgeman caravan and to her father's place, but he does not want any special favors. He tells Estelle his life's story. He is twenty-two years old, born in Santone (San Antonio). He had a brother, Lester, much older than he, but they were playmates and went to school together. He and Lester were close friends with a man who proved Lester's undoing. Lester was madly in love with the prettiest girl, part Spanish, in Santone (San Antonio). She, however, betrayed Lester with his best friend. Lester did something awful which caused him to run away. He was never heard from again. At fifteen, Corny took to trail driving on the Chisolm Trail. He has driven cattle as far as Montana and Wyoming, always hoping to hear word of his brother, but without success. He has lived through all that trail life brings: floods, rain, snow, frost. He has fought Indians and rustlers, and of necessity, become most proficient with a gun. Unfortunately, due to his striking good looks, he is a magnet for female attention, which, given what happened to his brother Lester, he can do without. At Latch's Field, the story of how he killed the two would-be abductors of Latch's daughter soon spreads. Keetch, Latch's manager and assistant, is impressed with him: "He wasn't as skinny as most cowboys. Built like a wedge, all muscle, an' straight as an Injun. Handsome too.... Lean face, tanned dark, cut sharp an' fine. Sort of cold 'cept when he smiled. He didn't take off his sombrero but I reckon he was tow-headed. An' he had the damdest pair of eyes I ever looked into. You-all shore would have liked him.... Fact is, he struck me like one of them trail drivin' vaqueros. Salt of the earth!" Keetch recommends that Latch take him on. Latch, who finds he looks like his beloved friend Lester, is hesitant. He decides not to hire him because he reminds him too much of his friend. Corny, however, stays on. Estelle is crazy about him, jealous of the attention he gives to other young women. Corny, however, is not interested in them. They are a pretext to hang around town picking up gossip about Latch and Leighton. He overhears Kennedy and Johnson talking about rustling Latch's last cattle, and the black-

mail scheme that Leighton has planned. Although he has been barred from attending Estelle's big sixteenth birthday bash, he shows up anyway. Estelle accompanies him outside, where he proposes to her and she accepts. He asks her to keep it quiet as he has work to do. He breaks into Leighton's place, recovers the documents that he has been using to blackmail Latch, and kills several of Latch's enemies. He foils Leighton's kidnapping plot, killing Jacobs and Manley. He hides Estelle at Bradley's ranch, rides to Spider Web canyon with Hawk Eye, and saves Latch's life, killing Kennedy, Breese and Leighton. Latch tells him about his brother Lester, who had been like a son to him. He recounts how Lester was his loyal assistant and confident. He gives Lester's money belt to Corny, the only thing of Lester's that he kept. The money inside has never been touched. Corny and Estelle are married in San Antonio on their way to Boston, where Estelle will collect the inheritance she received through her mother. Corny decides he will return to take up ranching, and in San Antonio invites his old trail buddies to join him in his venture at Latch's Field.

Corny is a hero along the model of Chane Weymer and Arizona Ames, a young man who has experienced both the best and the worst of frontier life and becomes a stronger and more decent individual in consequence.

Coronado: In *The Thundering Herd,* the Spanish explorer who commanded an expedition into the Great Plains. Castañeda was a member of the expedition and he recorded their impressions of the geography, the Indians and the buffalo. Coronado's men brought with them Arabian horses from which the mustangs (mesteños) of the Great Plains were descended. Coronado is also mentioned in *Knights of the Range,* when Holly Ripple gives a speech summarizing the history of the region and the Spanish contributions to the cattle industry.

Cortina: In "The Ranger," mentioned as part of a trio of Mexican bandits—Villa, Quinella and Cortina—as famous as the trio of gunmen—Hardin', Kingfisher and Poggin'.

Corvalo: In *Majesty's Rancho,* caters the big fiesta that Madge throws at the ranch when her friends are there. He makes a potent punch which has most of the men dead drunk by the end of the evening.

Cosgrove: In *The Thundering Herd,* a hard-drinking, foul-mouthed fellow who clashes with Tom Doan on the issue of who stays behind when the men set out in pursuit of the Comanche. Tom calls Cosgrove a coward.

Couch, Captain Jim: In *Fighting Caravans,* a caravan boss. He carries freight from army post to army forts, or freights wagons of hides to trading posts. Jim Belmet and his family join one of Couch's caravans heading west. To make some money to buy land in the West, Belmet signs on as a driver for Couch. Jim Couch is an experienced frontiersman and Indian fighter. Kit Carson and Colonel Maxwell all speak highly of Couch's knowledge of the frontier and of his bravery. They do, however, suggest that at times he takes unnecessary risks. Before he dies in an Indian attack on the wagon train, Jim Belmet names Couch guardian of his son, Clint, until he is twenty-one. This is the beginning of a fifteen-year relationship. Couch introduces Buff Belmet to Col. Lew Maxwell, soldier, rancher, trader, and owner of the largest property in the West. Maxwell predicts that Captain Couch has stuck at the freighting business too long and someday will find his scalp as ornament in some Indian's lodge.

Count: In *Wilderness Trek*, one of Leslie Slyter's prize horses that successfully makes the trek across Australia.

Covell: In *Knights of the Range*, one of the horse thieves that Britt catches at the Dobe Cabin Corral. He and Heaver had rounded up some twenty of the unbranded Ripple remuda. He is killed in a shootout with Renn Frayne.

Coyote: In *30,000 on the Hoof*, the half-shepherd, half-wolf dog that the Holberts give Lue Huett. She becomes very fond of the dog. It is her only companion much of the time when Logan is out hunting or working on the ranch. The dog is also a good tracker of coyotes and wildcats that plague the ranch, attacking the cattle.

Craig: In *To the Last Man*, mentioned as one of the members of the Hash Knife gang helping Jorth in the Pleasant Valley war. Blaisdell calls him "another respectable sheepman" of Grass Valley.

Crawford, Colonel: In *Betty Zane*, in charge of an expedition in pursuit of Delaware Indians who have attacked pioneer settlements. Crawford fails to follow the advice of his more experienced frontiersman scouts when they discover a deserted Delaware village. They have advised that he should return to Fort Pitt, but Crawford, anxious to finish off the Delaware at one blow, continues his pursuit and finds himself in a clever ambush. Crawford is captured by Cornplanter and put to death. Simon Girty tells Isaac Zane he was friends with Crawford at Ft Pitt but that he could do nothing to influence the Indians. Crawford was made to walk on hot coals for five hours before finally being burned to death at the stake.

Crawford, Jim: In "Amber's Mirage," Jim Crawford is an old prospector. He lives in a shack on the outskirts of Pine, near the sawmill. He is particularly fond of a young man, Al Shade, whom he treats as a son. He offers to share whatever gold he finds with Al, helping him pay off the mortgage, stock a place and farm. Al is in love with Ruby Low, the daughter of his no-good, drunken neighbor. Jim offers to take Al Shade along with him on his next prospecting trip into the desert of Sonora. Al has second thoughts about accompanying him, but Jim assures him this trip will net him a fortune. Jim has

seen Ruby kissing Joe Raston, the son of the wealthy rancher in Pine. Ruby tells Jim she loves Al better than any of the other boys but she does not want to be poor and Al is poorer than her family. Jim promises not to say anything. When Al confides in him that he cannot leave because he does not want to lose Ruby and she will not marry him unless he has money, Jim guarantees they will find Amber's Mirage this time out and he will have the money to court Ruby in style. They set out for the desert, seeking the "three round hills" where an old prospector had told him a fortune in gold was to be found. The desert has made Jim philosophical. He tells Al that the desert is like the earth at the beginning. It takes a man back to what he was when he first evolved from some lower organism. He gets closer to the origin of life and the end of life. They are lost for some two weeks, but eventually find the three round hills. Jim, however, grows weak. He advises Al to return to Pine immediately if he hopes to keep Ruby. He knows Ruby will be unfaithful to Al, that she will marry Joe Raston or someone else. Al refuses to leave him alone to die. Before he breathes his last, he has a vision of Amber's mirage. Al buries Jim in a crevice in the mountain, and when gathering rocks to fill in the crevice, he strikes gold — big time. Al returns to the gravesite three years later, after he has been back to Pine. He also has a vision of Amber's mirage.

Crawley, Joe: In *Valley of Wild Horses*, an older cowboy who takes part in the first roundup with Pan Handle Smith, and keeps an eye on him, teaching him the ropes.

Creech: In *Wildfire*, not one of Bostril's friends, but a member of the horsemen's club which meets to select the date for the annual horse race at Bostril's Ford. Creech owns two horses, Blue Roan and Peg, that are serious rivals to Sage King. Blue Roan and Sage King are so closely matched that the difference in weight of the riders might make the difference. When the men meet to select the date, Creech hints that his Blue Roan is going to take the prize this year. He worries that there may be problems getting the horses across the river if the Colorado floods about the beginning of June. Bostril assures him there will be no problem, but when the time approaches, Bostril cuts the boat loose, trapping Creech and his horses in a box canyon without water or grass. Unless the horses can be led up the steep walls and out on to the desert, they will likely die. With the help of some Piute Indians who love the horses as much as Creech and cannot bear to see them starve, they manage to find a way out of the canyon over the walls, but the horses injure their legs and are weak from thirst and hunger, they have to be put down. Creech arrives at Brackton's store leading two half-dead horses. The men tell him what Joel has been saying, that someone cut the ropes to set the boat adrift when the flood waters came, but Creech says the real crime was removing the boat from the river at a time when the horses could have been taken across. He vows to get even with Bostril. To that end, he kidnaps Lucy, Bostril's daughter, and as ransom, he demands that Bostril hand over Sage King and Sarchedon, his prize horses, to replace the animals that died thanks to Bostril's scheming. Lucy does not think that her father will part with his beloved stallions, even to ransom her. Creech says that in that case, he will sell her to Cordts, the horse thief. Lucy tells Creed the whole story about Wildfire, the race where Sage King was forced off the track, and he is pleased that Bostril got his comeuppance. She adds that her father had tried to buy the horse from Slone, and that he wants a rematch, as he can't accept defeat. Creed sympathizes with Lucy, whom he has known from childhood, and to whom he bears no ill will. He suggests Slone could let Sage King win, to satisfy the father, but Lucy cannot see that happening. Lucy realizes that Creech is not a bad man, just angry at the injustice committed against him by her fast-horse-mad father. When Joel arrives at the canyon where they are camped, a fight breaks out between Joel and his father. The father is shot in the struggle.

Creech, Joel: In *Wildfire*, a tall, lean, young rider, bow-legged from long hours in the saddle. Lucy describes him as having a sallow, freckled face, with a fuzz of beard, and a weak mouth and chin. At some point, Joel was kicked in the head by a mustang and the effects of the kick are to be seen in the crushed shape of his head. Over the years, he has become increasingly strange, doing and saying strange things, speaking in a confused, incomprehensible way. Lucy Bostril feels sorry for the young man. Early in the novel, Joel, riding Peg, races with Lucy, riding Buckles. After Lucy has beaten him, he strips off his clothes and jumps into the lake for a swim, asking Lucy to do the same and join him. She is taken aback by his forwardness and to punish him, plays a practical joke, taking his clothes and dropping them along the trail a mile or so away. Joel, however, doesn't wait until dark to make his way back without risk of sunburn. He rolls himself in mud and walks all the way home, ten miles, failing to find his clothes by the trail. By this time the mud has hardened like adobe, sticking to his skin. The riders at Bostril's Ford get great fun teasing Joel. His nakedness arouses some questions about what he was doing out on the sage with Lucy. When he vows to get even with her, Van Sickle gives him a threshing, after which Joel asks Lucy to marry him to save his reputation with the riders. When she says no, he promises to play a trick on her to get even. He also threatens to kill Van. Joel meets Bostril at the ferry one day and tells him his father is anxious about getting his horses across. Bostril has the boat out of the water, ostensibly for repairs. Joel muses about it being better to swim the horses across the river. When the river has risen and the boat is lost in the flood, Joel reveals that he knows someone cut the boat loose; he saw the rope that was cut. He promises to kill whoever it was that caused the loss of his father's horses. Joel takes a job working for

Slone when Slone buys Vorhees's ranch. He admires Wildfire, the splendid mustang, winner of the Bostril's Ford horse race. He tells Slone he knows Bostril sabotaged his father. He also tells Slone that he was out on the sage that morning when Slone kissed Lucy. He threatens to spread the story about Lucy in town. Slone drives him off. Back at the ford, he spreads the story that Slone is the one who cut the ropes on the boat to ensure his victory in the race. He plants the letter for Bostril, informing him that Lucy has been kidnapped and that he must bring the Sage King and Sarchedon if he wants her back. Bostril delivers the horses and Joel takes them back to the canyon. Cordts, however, has seen him and attempts to follow. In the canyon, Joel takes a fit, talking loudly and incomprehensibly. He and his father get into a fight and the gun goes off, killing Creech. The fire he had started spreads to the dry grass, causing a wildfire. The frightened Sage King attacks Joel, rearing and kicking, killing the boy.

Creede: In *The Border Legion,* a hard-working miner in Alder Creek. He is a large, husky man, who looks like Gulden. As a test of Jim Cleve's loyalty to the Border Legion and proof he is indeed an outlaw, Gulden proposes he rob and murder Creede. Creede's partner was seen leaving on the stage so the job should be accomplished without much trouble. Jim Cleve, popular throughout the mining camp, convinces Creede to leave town for a few days. He exchanges his thirty-pound gold nugget with Creede for the gold belt he keeps around his waist. Cleve then reports back to the Border Legion with the gold belt, saying he killed Creede and dumped the body in a deep part of the creek. Gulden, however, meets up with Creede on the trail some time after Cleve claims to have killed him. He murders him, takes the gold nugget, and presents this as evidence to Kells that Cleve is a traitor to the Border Legion.

Creighton, Edward: In *Western Union*, the man making a reality of his dream to extend the telegraph from coast to coast. Vance Shaw tells Wayne Cameron that Creighton is as big as all outdoors and the kind of man who can influence men to go to hell for him. Creighton hires Wayne Cameron as a doctor for his crew when Williamson informs him of Cameron's medical studies at Harvard. He is impatient to get the job done, feeling every obstacle is a personal affront. He runs a tight ship and inspires his workers with the same enthusiasm for the project as he has, making them feel like they are a part of history in the making.

Creighton, John and James: In *Western Union*, reported to have purchased two wagon trains of poles in Julesburg and to be proceeding to meet Creighton's main construction force, replacing the downed poles along the way.

Creik: In *The Lost Wagon Train*, a member of the Leighton faction of Latch's outlaw outfit that attacks and massacres the Anderson caravan. He had been in the employ of Latch's father on their Southern plantation as a slave driver, and in ways other than his huge bulk, he looked the man who could fulfill such a position. Cornwall comments that he's looking for slaves to beat. He is shot in the hand in the attack on the caravan, and is in favor of Leighton's plan of sharing Cynthia Bowden with all the men. Creik and Augustine drag the bodies of Sprall, Texas and Lone Wolf out of the cabin. He has to be ordered by Latch to share with the rest of the men the money he takes off the bodies. He is reported killed in one of the subsequent attacks on caravans.

Cresop, Colonel: In *Betty Zane,* mentioned as the man who led an expedition against Logan, a Delaware chief, annihilating the village, killing men, women and children indiscriminately. Colonel Cresop is cited as an example of the worst kind of white man on the frontier.

Cricket: In *Captives of the Desert,* High-Lo's horse. High-Lo is following Wilbur Newton and Hanley when Cricket trips over a length of barbed wire stretched over the trail. The horse injures his leg, and High-Lo is thrown, breaking several ribs.

Crocker: In *Robbers' Roost,* one of the homesteaders that Herrick bought out. He remains to work for Herrick as blacksmith. He and his farming associates are bewildered by the onslaught of the Englishman upon their peaceful valley, but they are frankly far richer for it.

Crocker, Les: In *The Horse Thief,* a cowboy in Salomn. According to what Dale overhears in the rustlers' camp, Les Crocker is crazy about Edith Watrous.

Crook, General: In *30,000 on the Hoof,* led the U.S. Cavalry in the Southwest in the Geronimo campaigns. Logan Huett worked as scout and tracker in the campaigns. Crook is also mentioned in the story "Avalanche" as background the story of the Dunton boys.

Crothers: In *Stranger from the Tonto,* Slotte's stiff-armed partner. When Slotte returns to the hideout, he tries to convince Bonesteel that Kent has stolen Lucy's horse Spades from them. In the gunfight which follows, Crothers is shot and hilled by Winfield, as is Silk Slotte.

Crow: In *Betty Zane,* the Wyandot chief who recaptures Isaac Zane in the forest near Ft. Henry. He and Son of Wingenund and Wepatomeka were on his trail for two months.

Crowther: In *Black Mesa,* the government farmer in the area. He tells Wess Kintell that Black Mesa is the worst place for wind, and Bitter Seeps gets the brunt of any sandstorm that blows.

Culberton, Doc: In *Fighting Caravans,* the army doctor at Kansas City who patches up Clint Belmet after the Comanche attack on the wagon train. He tries to get the young man to rest up for a couple of months.

Culkins: In *The Thundering Herd,* an old, white-haired buffalo-hunter who is part of Pilchuck's crew in the fight against the Comanche.

Culver: (1) The second of the pair of thugs usually accompanying Dene in *The Heritage of the Desert.* He is mentioned several times in the company of Chance (Two Spot) when Dene has charged them with some mission. Together with Chance, Culver fills in the water hole called Blue Star, forcing Naab to move his sheep herd farther along. He is present at Abe's store when Dene provokes a fight with Martin Cole and he is shot by Dave Naab when Dene goes to Naab's ranch to seize Mescal and kill Hare, if possible. Dene shoots Dave Naab from behind Culver and Chance, and Dave Naab shoots them trying to get at Dene himself.

(2) In *Sunset Pass,* Culver is named as one of the smaller ranchers around Wagontongue.

Cuppy: In "Canyon Walls," Cuppy is one of the bad companions from whom Monty Bellew is glad to get away. He and Cuppy and Slim were up to mischief in the old days, times that Monty wants to forget. Cuppy and Slim are involved in a rustling job in which Slim gets killed covering Cuppy's escape.

Curly: In *Valley of Wild Horses,* Pan Handle Smith's first horse. He is a black pony with three white feet and a white spot on his face. Pan Handle loves the horse from the start. His mother will not let him ride the pony except when she leads it. One day he contrives to take Curly out of the barn without his mother's knowing and he rides down the road. He squeals in delight at first but the delight soon mixes with fear as Curly runs fast downhill. He is thrown not far from his shocked mother. His father, however, tells her she should let him ride. He has the makings of a cowboy. From that point on, he lives on the back of Curly. He learns to ride, to stick on like a burr, to keep his seat on the bare back of the pony, to move with him as he moves. One day, Curly steps in a prairie-dog hole and injures his foot, and Pan Handle is thrown, plowing the ground with his nose and face. One day when Pan is over at his uncle's, a cowboy unwittingly leaves the door to the granary ajar and Curly gorges on wheat, then drinks a lot of water. The horse founders and dies. Pan Handle is heartbroken at the loss of his best friend.

Curry, John: In *Captives of the Desert,* works as a guide and packer for Mr. Weston at Black Mesa. He also works at the trading post. Katharine Winfield first describes him when he appears at Leupp when their car has broken down. On seeing him, she experiences a pleasant thrill. She seems to know him as if he were a composite of pleasing personalities. He is tall, broad-shouldered, possessed of an athletic slimness. The fine swing of his gait is the mark of perfect control and muscular coordination. He manages to get their car fixed up. The contrast between John Curry and Wilbur Newton strikes Katharine. She has already detected the chemistry between John and her friend Mary, and the obvious tension and mistrust between Curry and Wilbur. Mary explains how they met. She had gone riding alone to a place called Cliff Rocks. At the smell of blood, her horse reared up. She found John in a wash, bloodied, face down in the sand. He had been on a mad race from Castle Mesa to get the doctor at Taho to save some Indian youngster's life. His horse tried to clear the wash and had missed and fallen, breaking two legs and pitching Curry against the rocks. He had to shoot his horse. Mary offered him her horse, but he refused, saying he could walk. She went to an Indian hogan about a mile away to get help. He gave her a bridle to thank her for her help and Wilbur cut it up with a knife. Curry saves her again when the horse she is riding runs away. He scolds Wilbur for letting Mary ride such a spirited horse, only to be treated to a sarcastic comment about how Mary and John have been meeting by accident so frequently.

John Curry is well liked by the men with whom he works. He maintains his popularity among the cowboys at the Black Mesa trading post by demonstrating his need for "their counsel." He is their leader by virtue of his power to control and because of his position of trust with Mr. Weston. He is called "good old John," the buddy of every fellow in the place, an unconscious recognition of his leadership, because at twenty-eight, he is younger than four or five of his own men. John Curry considers High-Lo as his own special charge. He had met High-Lo, recently cast out of his hometown, as he was returning to Black Mesa from his brother's ranch in Colorado. High-Lo shared his troubles with Curry, drowning his sorrow in liquor. John adopted the eighteen-year-old and nursed him, extracting a promise he would not drink again. When John found him drinking again, he gave him a sound thrashing. Ten days later, when they reach Black Mesa, High-Lo is a thoroughly steadied new hand for Weston's outfit. The close relationship between the two continues.

High-Lo's secret pursuit of Wilbur Newton and Hanley to investigate his suspicions that they deal in bootleg liquor, gets him into trouble. John Curry finds him lying on the ground, with several broken ribs. He takes him part of the way back to Taho, when they meet Magdaline, who goes for the doctor. Magdaline has just returned to the Navajo reservation after three years at school in California. She feels lost, no longer able to fit back into the old world. She proposes marriage to John, the man she admires and loves and who she thinks loves her too. When he tells her he cannot marry her because she is so much younger than he is and he does not love her as a man loves a wife, she takes up with Wilbur Newton at his post at Sage Springs. When she becomes pregnant, John is willing to marry her to save her reputation. At this point, High-Lo returns John's many favors, marrying Magdaline to prevent John's marrying her out of pity.

John Curry confides in Katharine Winfield that he would like to set himself up in ranching. She offers to put up half the money for the venture, but he refuses her offer. He must make a success of this on his own.

John Curry's relationship to Mary is the center of his life. While he knows Newton does not treat her well, he will not get involved with another man's wife. While others tell Mary that she should divorce Wilbur for desertion, John respects her decision to wait for Wilbur to return. He finds it hard to believe that she really loves Wilbur. He even attempts to deliver Mary's letter to Wilbur, the letter in which she tells him about her ten-thousand-dollar inheritance from her father. They seem destined for each other. Wilbur is shot by Magdaline when he attempts to force her to return to him at Sage Springs. Mary is now free to marry John.

John Curry is a character developed along the lines of Arizona Ames and Nevada, a profoundly decent man, honorable, straightforward, self-sacrificing, a knight in shining armor.

Curtis: In *Raiders of Spanish Peaks,* Lenta mentions the "Curtis kids" in her discussion with her older sister Harriet. The Curtis kids used to pick on her back East. Harriet used to chase them off and threaten them to stop them beating up on Lenta. The young sister tells her older sister that out West, turning the other cheek will not work. The old Harriet who would fight to defend her little sister is what is needed at Spanish Peaks.

Curtis, Dick: In *Fighting Caravans,* meets Buff Belmet at Council Grove, where he is in the company of Kit Carson. Like Carson, Curtis takes a liking to young Belmet and offers to take him under his wing. He helps him pick out an outfit at Tillt's store, and a gun, a knife and a buckskin shirt. Curtis advances him the money to pay for these necessities. As Wetzel undertakes to educate the inexperienced Joe Downs to the ways of the frontier in *The Spirit of the Border,* Dick Curtis teaches Clint how to shoot, skin and butcher a buffalo, how to move about without making noise. He gives the boy the nickname, Buff, which pleases the boy and becomes his handle on the frontier. After the shootout between Clint Belmet, Blackstone, and Murdock, Dick Curtis gets a doctor to look after Clint's injuries and keeps him at his cabin in the mountains while he recuperates. He also finds out what he can about Mrs. Clements and May Bell, whom Murdock has been pursuing. Curtis gets hold of a Kansas City paper which reports the end of the Civil War. Curtis predicts a flood of troublemakers into the West as a result.

In *The Lost Wagon Train,* Dick Curtis appears at Ft. Union together with Kit Carson, Beaver Adams and other renowned frontiersmen. He is not present at the interview with Major Greer concerning the lost Anderson wagon train, but Kit Carson says he will let him know so he can make inquiries among the Indians and other scouts.

Curtis, Whitney: In *Boulder Dam,* a friend of Lynn Weston. He is a cowboy from across the river and regards broken bones much as Lynn does football injuries, all part of the game. When Lynn goes to visit him in the hospital, Whitney tells him he has read about his rescuing Ben Brown after being swept down the diversion tunnel and almost drowning. Whitney had been flashing around his roll of money, an imprudent act which drew attention to himself. Bink Moore and his men beat him up and steal his money. Bess hides him in her tent until the heat is over. Hidden in the tent, he overhears a conversation among a group of men outside. They are planning to ruin the dam. They mention having contacts among the workers who have planted explosives. He is not sure who these men are — gangsters, racketeers, foreign agitators, perhaps. He asks Lynn not to mention his name should he choose to bring this matter to the attention of the directors of the construction companies. Lynn asks him why he had not mentioned this to the authorities, but since he can attach no names to the men nor identify them, he feels no one would believe him. Lynn, however, can keep an eye out for suspicious activity. When Whitney has recovered, he pays off his debt to Greta Green in Las Vegas, marries Bess and leaves to take over his family ranch in Arizona, in the desert near Ashfork. His father has just died, and his mother and siblings are still there. The ranch is badly run–down, but it has the makings of a good cattle operation. He and Bess are leaving for the ranch when they come to say good-bye to Lynn and Anne. Whitney Curtis, it turns out, is a cousin of Sheriff Logan's, the law officer who is sympathetic to Lynn and helps him with the capture of the gangsters who abducted Anne.

Custer, General George Armstrong: In *Fighting Caravans,* meets Clint Belmet on the way to Fort Larned. Custer offers Clint a job as scout for the army but he refuses.

Cutter: In "The Ranger," Captain Allerton and two rangers are injured in the Cutter rustling fight, while Vaughn Medill, with his usual luck, emerges without a scratch.

D

Dabb: In *Stairs of Sand,* works for Caleb Hunt at the Lost Lake post, but he is largely ruled by Guerd Larey. Dabb is promised Hunt's job when Guerd takes over the post but neither Collishaw nor Larey really trust him. In Mexican Joe's restaurant, Dabb and Merryvale discuss Larey and Collishaw's plans to acquire all the water holes in anticipation of the coming of the railroad. Dabb knows Guerd has the local Indians on board at Lost Lake, and it seems to be only a matter of time before he takes over Hunt's holding. He also has powerful friends in Yuma. Dabb plans to explore buying the Twenty-Nine Palms water hole before Larey does. Dabbs and Merryvale will go into partnership in the new project. When Larey is scheming to kidnap Ruth and take her

to Yuma, Dabb buys up Salton Spring, putting an end to his scheme to control a monopoly of water rights along the new railroad.

Dabb, John: In *Sunset Pass,* the richest and most powerful rancher around Wagontongue. It is said he practically owns the town — several businesses, a store, a butcher shop and a lumber mill. He is a well-preserved man of fifty, scarcely starting to gray. He is married to Trueman Rock's old flame, Amy Wund, although he is considerably older than she is. Amy confides in Trueman that the marriage was arranged to settle a debt between her father and Dabb. Trueman was Dabb's foreman when he was involved in the shooting with Pickins. He left without notice. When he meets with Dabb on his return, Dabb is meeting with Nesbitt, a Wyoming rancher new to the area. Dabb introduces Rock as true-blue, honest to the core. When Nesbitt leaves, their conversation touches on matters which would strain the best of friendships. Rock apologizes for his sudden departure, explaining that he had little confidence in Sheriff Cass Seward's goodwill toward him in the matter of the Pickins shooting. He also explains that there is nothing going on between him and Dabb's wife. Trueman tells Dabb he is neglecting Amy. She is lonely and hurt, feeling that her husband is not interested in her. The flirting with cowboys such as Clink Peeples is an attempt to get his attention. He recommends that Dabb spend more time with Amy. During this part of their encounter, "fury and shame competed with fairness" in Dabb's countenance. It is to his credit that he takes Rock's advice and at the masquerade ball, Amy informs Trueman that her husband is a changed man, acting as he did when they were first married.

Dabb likewise has advice for Trueman. He tells him to leave Preston. While locals know his reputation, others, like Nesbitt, do not. Preston may be using him to cover up his rustling and butchering operation. When Dabb suspects what Preston is up to, he cancels the contract his butcher shop has with him. When Trueman Rock has discovered proof of Ash Preston's operation, he goes to Dabb to discuss how best to proceed. Dabb approves of how he handled the situation with Jim Dunne, but he warns him that Slagle has found where the hides are hidden, and that it will not be long before more concrete proof is brought forward against Preston. Together with Lincoln, he brings forward a proposal for dealing with Preston whereby those who have lost cattle will be compensated. Preston and the boys implicated in the operation will leave the country. The situation will be resolved without bloodshed and without resorting to the courts. He gives Rock authority to offer the deal to Gage on behalf of the Cattleman's Association. Dabb and Lincoln ensure that the recalcitrant Nesbitt concurs.

When Ash Preston has been killed, Gage and the boys agree to the deal. Dabb buys out Preston's ranch in Sunset Pass. He offers Trueman Rock the job of foreman, fully in charge of the ranch.

Dageel: In *Blue Feather*, the idiot of the tribe, a pink-eyed, red-haired, deformed young brave, hideous to behold. He is hated and feared by all the Sheboyahs. He makes weird sounds and waves his arms in unusual gestures which Clodothie interprets as signs from the gods.

Dagg, Lefty: In "The Secret of Quaking Asp Cabin," Babe Haught tells the narrator his story. He is the son of the Dagg who was the first to be killed in the Pleasant Valley war. He and Jim Davis end up killing each other. Dagg had killed one of Davis's cowboys in a gunfight, and although rumor on the range is that it was a fair fight, Davis seeks to even the score.

Dagget: In *Fighting Caravans*, a caravan leader who is the first to pull into Kansas City in the spring. He brings word of the outbreak of the Civil War. The Clements, old friends of Maxwell and foster parents to May Bell, are in his caravan. The following year he is reported dead, having been killed in a gambling dive in Las Vegas. His freighters have disbanded and scattered to other caravans.

Daggs: In *To the Last Man*, a typical Texan, superbly built, light-haired and light-eyed. His face is lined and hard. His long, sandy mustache hides his mouth and droops with a curl. He is spurred, booted, belted and packing a heavy gun low down on his hip. In all, a striking figure. Daggs is a close associate of Lee Jorth and leader of the Hash Knife gang. He has come to Arizona with the remnants of the Texas outlaw crew to help Lee Jorth in his war of vengeance against Gaston Isbel. Blaisdell and others suspect he is a professional rustler but have no solid proof. Daggs makes advances to Ellen Jorth, but when she brushes him off, he accepts it without anger and asks her to marry him, only to be rebuffed once more. When Simm Bruce tells about his encounter with Jean Isbel, Daggs puts the best spin he can on the encounter, saying that they probably don't have too much to fear from the Nez Perce Isbel since he has never known a professional gunman to risk damaging his gun hand by getting into a fistfight. When Ellen challenges Simm's account of the fight with the story she heard from John Sprague, Daggs grabs Lee Jorth's arm to prevent him from killing Bruce on the spot. The cool and tactful Daggs showed himself master of the situation. Daggs commands the attack on the Isbel ranch and shoots Guy Isbel. Later, he shows himself, challenging the Isbels to come out of the house and fight. Jean Isbel shoots him, blowing off the top of his head. Daggs made a tactical mistake as foolish as that of Guy Isbel and Bill Jacobs.

Dakota: In *Raiders of Spanish Peaks*, one of the cowboys who had worked for Allen on the Spanish Peak ranch. When the ranch is sold to Lindsay, he first remains loyal to the old foreman, Arlidge, but eventually transfers his loyalty to Lindsay's new foreman, Laramie. Dakota comes upon Hallie learning to ride cantankerous horses in secret. He offers her help learning to ride Western-style. He promises to keep her secret.

Dale, Milt: In *The Man of the Forest*, the "Man of the Forest." He is thirty years old. As a boy of fourteen, he ran off from his school and home in Iowa and joined a wagon train of pioneers. He was one of the first to see log cabins built on the slopes of the White Mountains. He did not take kindly to farming or sheep-raising or the monotonous home toil. For twelve years he has lived in the forest with only infrequent visits to Pine, Show Down and Snowdrop. He loves wildlife and solitude and beauty with the primitive instinctive force of a savage. Like Wetzel in *The Spirit of the Border*, he is a natural man, taught by Mother Nature herself, free from the corruption of the civilized world. He is tall, broad of shoulder, cutting a striking figure in his fringed buckskin suit. His knowledge of animal life, of the forest, and his ability to track are matched only by those of his Mormon friend, Roy Beeman. Roy comments on his incomparable ability with a rifle, either standing on the ground or from horseback, observing that he can shoot flies off a deer's horns for practice. Helen Reyner comments on Dale's strength when she sees him splitting and carrying logs; he could give Paul Bunyan a run for his money.

Milt Dale feels that it was no accident that he happened to stop by the cabin and overhear the plot to abduct and kill Al Auchincloss's niece, Helen. He accepts the facts of life with equanimity and fatality acquired by life in the bosom of nature. Bad men worked their evil ways just as savage wolves hunted a deer. He feels obliged to do something to foil the plot.

His visit to Pine reminds him why he prefers life in the woods. The people of the village, with few exceptions, though they genuinely like him and admire his outdoor wisdom, consider him a nonentity. Because he loves the wilds and prefers it to village and range life, they classify him as not one of them. Some consider him shiftless, others think him an Indian in mind and habits, and some even think him slow-witted. Al Auchincloss makes the point clearly when he tells Milt that he has no ambition, he doesn't support anyone nor does he do any good in the world. Milt points out that he is more honest and truthful than anyone living in town. There's nothing to make him dishonest or untruthful.

Milt and the Beeman boys arrange to rescue Helen and Bo at Magdalena. Milt makes short business of Harve Riggs, who tries to pull a gun on him. He knocks the firearm out of his hand with a sweep of his arm, and cautions him about drawing the weapon — it might go off. Milt's simplicity, sureness and unruffled coolness impress Helen.

Dale keeps the two girls at his camp in the forest. He introduces them to his menagerie of pets — Tom, the cougar; Bud, the young bear cub; Pedro, the loyal hound. He teaches the girls about nature, about the animals. He and Helen have lengthy discussions about the relative merits of nature and civilization.

Milt argues that men in towns and cities are cut off from their instincts, leading unnatural lives. Contact with nature restores a balance, establishing contact with essential human values. Helen believes that life in the wild makes one savage and cruel. She sees the natural world as a bloody struggle. Milt points out that the law of nature is the struggle to survive. The trees and grasses compete for sunlight and scarce resources. The plants that survive are all the stronger for the competition. The same is true of animal life. The cougar eliminates the weak and sickly among the deer, ensuring that the healthiest and strongest reproduce to keep the herd healthy. Milt tells Helen that she thinks too much, that she does not allow her instincts to guide her.

When Helen's uncle Al comes to take her back to the ranch at Pine, Milt learns what loneliness is like. He had always prided himself on his ability to live alone, but now that the love bug has bitten him, he feels isolated. John Beeman comes with word that Al Auchincloss has died and that his brother Roy has been shot. On their way back to Pine, they come across the trail of the men who abducted Bo. Milt sets out after them with his cougar, Tom. He catches up to the group, meets with Jim Wilson in the woods and convinces this "good outlaw" to help him. Together, they scare the wits out of the other outlaws, Bo playing the role of a woman gone mad, and Tom, a cougar, howling through the night. He returns Bo to her sister, just as Tom Carmichael leaves to confront Beasley.

The confrontation between Helen and Beasley is proof of Milt's view of struggle as the law of life. Evil will triumph unless good fights to win. Helen believes killing is wrong; that differences must be settled by legal means. Both Roy and Milt argue that law means nothing unless it is backed up with force. Milt, like Roy, also believes that Beasley's fate is determined by his evil deeds. Sooner or later, he will get his comeuppance. Beasley's evil ways seal his fate. That is the law of nature, a clearly romantic view which sees nature as a moral force, ensuring that good triumphs over evil.

Milt's friend Roy is also a Mormon preacher and he performs the wedding ceremony for Milt and Helen at his senaca that Helen calls Paradise Park. Milt has decided that if he is truly to live according to the law of nature, he must find a mate and reproduce. He comes to this conclusion after much thought and soul-searching.

In the person of Milt Dale, Zane Grey gives voice to his Darwinist views. Milt's exposition to Helen Reyner — of the laws of nature, of the struggle to adapt to survive, of the contrast between civilized man and natural man — embody the tension in Grey's work between his Wordsworthian-Emersonian-Thoreauvian bent and his naturalistic, deterministic, Darwinian side.

Daley, Lee: In *The Deer Stalker*, with his boys succeeds in driving ten buffalo yearlings into a truck to move to a new range. Jim Evers never thought anyone could move those wild buffalo in a truck. Lee Daley had found a new tool for wild life management.

Daley, Tom: In *The U. P. Trail*, the engineer on General Lodge's trail who finds Casey's body under the gravel car he had used to stop the train. He finds the book Casey was carrying containing the letter from Beauty Stanton to Neale.

Dan: In *Thunder Mountain,* one of the vigilantes who arrest Lee Emerson. He is given the job of frisking him.

Danbury, Colonel: In *Fighting Caravans,* signs a contract with Captain Couch to freight government supplies to all the forts between Westport (Kansas City) and Taos, New Mexico.

Dandy Dale: In *The Border Legion,* a California would-be road-agent, "knight of the road," who was shot by a passenger when holding up a stage. He dressed in a stylish outfit with a mask. Kells kept the outfit and it has been a humorous point with the Border Legion. Kells gives the outfit to Joan to wear in camp to conceal the fact that she is a girl. The fitted uniform does more to heighten her feminine attributes than to disguise her identity. Jim Cleve jokes with Joan that she should dress in this outfit when they return to her home in Hoadley's Camp.

Dann, Beryl: In *Wilderness Trek*, Stanley Dann's daughter, beautiful, spoiled and proud. Red Krehl is attracted to her, but she seems to prefer Ormiston, the slick bushranger. Red is jealous and plans to spy on them at night. Beryl has accepted his proposal of marriage by the time he decides he wants to split the expedition. She tells him she cannot betray her father, that if he insists on making her choose, she will stay with her father and go on to the Kimberleys. She asks Ormiston to reconsider and to come with them. He appears to have agreed. He hopes to drive a wedge between the two Yankees and the women by saying that they spend the night with the lubas in the native camp. Beryl and Leslie believe the story. When Ormiston does leave, rustling cattle and horses on the way, Beryl goes with him. Ormiston uses her as a shield when he is caught and under the gun. Beryl sees Ormiston hanged. She gets a fever and becomes delirious for some time, but when she recovers, she tells the story. She acknowledges that she was taken in by Ash Ormiston. She pretends she was taken unwillingly, but she agreed to go because Ormiston will kill anyone in his way. He had planned to kill Uncle Eric, with whom he had plotted. She went to save Eric's life and her father from ruin, if not worse. Ormiston betrayed her, stealing her father's cattle and his thoroughbred horses. With Ash out of the picture, Beryl shows more interest in Red, that romance growing more intense. She becomes very sick after the dust storm, and they fear she will die. She recovers, however, and completes the trip to the Kimberleys. There, her father, an ordained minister, marries her to Red Krehl.

Dann, Emily: In *Wilderness Trek*, the spinster sister of Stanley and Eric Dann, and aunt of Beryl. She is a woman along in years, unused to life in the open and despite what appeared at first to be a certain robustness, she begins to fail. The extreme heat of the desert is more than she can bear. At first, the change is more mental than physical. She dries up into a shadow of her former self and meets death with a wan, pathetic gladness.

Dann, Eric: In *Wilderness Trek*, the younger brother of Stanley Dann. He is short and strongly built with rather stern, dark features. He and his brother are going to trek to Northwest Australia with ten drovers and thirty-five hundred head of cattle. Eric claims to have made the trek to the Kimberleys before and to know the way. Stanley has his doubts. He tells Red and Sterl that he slights the hardships either because he is callous and unfeeling or because he doesn't want to tell what he knows. Eric has failed after several starts at ranching in Queensland. Eric is a weak person and easily swayed by Ormiston. The source of Ormiston's power over Eric is never made clear. Ormiston insists that Eric be the leader of the expedition, and that they take the once-traveled, longer route. Eric appears reluctant to head off along an unknown trail. He is touchy about his role as leader, and when his decisions are questioned, he gets huffy. He camps with Ormiston, coming on occasion to his brother's camp. He is beaten by Bedford and Jack when Ormiston decides to abandon him. Red Krehl and others become more hostile to Eric as it becomes increasingly clear that he does not know where he is or where they should go. He does not recognize the mountain ranges or the rivers that he had to have passed through if he came his way before. He finally confesses that he had never trekked to western Australia, that they are hopelessly lost, just as Heald, Bligh, Hood and Derrick decide to quit the group. He retires to his tent and shoots himself in the head.

Dann, Stanley: In *Wilderness Trek*, a blond, giant of a man, father of Beryl Dann and brother to Eric and Cedric. He is also an ordained minister. Stanley is a fair man, willing to accommodate himself to the will of the majority. Against his better judgment, he acquiesces in accepting Ormiston's presence on the drive. Stanley is interested in learning what Sterling Hazelton and Red Krehl have to teach him about driving cattle. This type of venture has never been attempted in Australia and the two Texans, who have been on many cattle drives, know what to expect. Stanley is a fair man, to Friday, the aborigine, to the foreign Yanks, and to Ormiston. When he loses three hundred cattle crossing the river, he orders that three hundred head of his herd be branded with Ormiston's brand. When Ormiston has rustled cattle and horses and in consequence been captured and lynched, he divides Ormiston's money fairly, keeping part for Woolcott's and Hathaway's heirs, keeping some in compensation for lost cattle for himself and for Slyter, the remainder being divided with the drovers. While others in the group "retrograded to the primitive," Stanley retains his civilized mien. Sterl observes his way of working and comes to admire him more and more. He proved to be the great physical and spiritual leader Sterl had imagined he would be. He remained imperturbable, cheerful, confident. But he seldom talked to his brother and never voluntarily addressed Ormiston, though he often came to Slyter's camp to smoke and talk. He is patient with his brother, who has deceived them viciously by lying about his knowledge of the countryside. When they reach the Kimberleys, he and his family start building cabins to set up Dann's Station. He resorts to his second profession, that of minister. He marries his daughter Beryl to Red Krehl, and Leslie Slyter to Sterling Hazelton. The twenty-five hundred-mile trek would never have been possible without his firm, patient leadership.

Danton, Mary: In *The Rainbow Trail*, the second witness called at the polygamy trial in Stonebridge. She had two children by her husband, Danton, and three others by nameless father(s). She prefers the stigma of being thought of as having illegitimate children than revealing the truth that she is a sealed wife for another man in Stonebridge. She faces the judge with stone-faced calmness.

Dare: In *The Arizona Clan*, a member of the Hathaway-Quayle-Twitchell outfit. He is involved in the big shootout when Nan escapes from the cabin where Buck is holding her to force Parson Bailey to marry them.

Darnell, Ed: In *The Hash Knife Outfit*, a river boat gambler and cattle thief. He gets involved with Glory Traft in Saint Louis. She is taken with his good looks and his roguish air. He leads her to believe he loves her, borrows money from her, embezzles money from her father, and then dumps her. He appears later in Flagg, Arizona, where he is still the cardsharp, but now a dealer in stolen cattle as well. He takes up with young Molly Dunn when she breaks off her engagement to Jim Traft. Ed Darnell is exposed as a cheat by Curly Prentiss in a high stakes poker game at Snell's on Christmas day. Darnell double-crosses Bambridge, a rancher and fellow dealer in stolen cattle, stealing some ten thousand dollars from him. Darnell is captured and lynched by Slinger Dunn and the Diamond cowboys who were on their trail.

Darnell, Tom: In *Western Union*, first appears in Gothenburg, where he is looking to sell his horse and saddle to get money to eat. Shaw, Lowden and Cameron invite him to join up with them as a team on the telegraph construction crew. He tells them his name is Darnell, that he is from South Pass, Wyoming, where he was involved in the war between the ranchers and the cowboys, the subject of Grey's novel *The Maverick Queen*. He shows them the welts and scars on his back from the whipping he received at the hands of a vigilance committee of ranchers. Darnell drives the wagon for the group. He helps rescue Ruby from Pierce's establishment in Gothenburg. Like Shaw and Lowden, his experience is invaluable in surviving the prairie fire, the Indian attack, the buffalo stampede and the crossing of the swollen Laramie River. In South Pass, Darnell is killed in the rescue attempt to finally free Ruby from Pierce (Bill Howard), who had abducted her from the wagon during the Indian attack in Julesburg.

Dartt: In *The Border Legion,* one of the Border Legion members betrayed to the vigilantes of Alder Creek (Bear Mountain) by Red Pearce. Pearce has offered himself as an informant to the vigilantes and betrays Dartt, Singleton, Frenchy and Texas as proof that he can identify the members of the Legion. Dartt is tried before a masked court and sentenced to hang. He is one of the four men hanged that night.

Dash: In "Lightning," the bloodhound that Lee and Cuth Stewart use to chase down wild mustangs.

Davis: (1) In *The Dude Ranger,* a cowboy working on the Red Rock Ranch. He is mentioned only once in the story.

(2) In *Fighting Caravans,* mentioned as a freighter.

(3) In *The Fugitive Trail,* one of the men with Hank Silverman's wagon train. When they reach the end of the trail, Davis is going to the Tonto Basin in Arizona with Silverman and Higgins.

(4) In *The Hash Knife Outfit,* runs a general store in Flagg, Arizona.

Davis, Ben: In *Fighting Caravans,* (not the same as number two above) operates a cannon on one of the freight wagons in Couch's caravan.

Davis, Jeff: (1) In *The Drift Fence,* hired as cook by young Jim Traft for his crew building the drift fence. Jeff Davis hails from Alabama. He recommends himself highly to young Traft, in writing, claiming that he cannot speak since he was shot in the throat by a vicious cowboy. The cowboys first think his not being able to speak will bother them, but after eating what he has cooked, they no longer have objections. When the cowboys leave for the rodeo, Jeff Davis speaks for the first time to warn Jim that he should not wander off into the woods without taking his rifle with him. Jim keeps Jeff's secret, suspecting that there is more to Jeff than he had imagined. He also foresees a good laugh at the expense of the cowboys when Jeff's secret is revealed. Jeff Davis speaks to the crew for the first time when he asks one of them to shut Hack Jocelyn up. He threatens to put coyote poison in their meat if they don't do it.

(2) In *Twin Sombreros,* an old friend of Brazos Keene. He meets Wess Tanner in the Dodge Hotel where June Neece happens to be staying. She has asked him if he knows anyone who knows Brazos. Davis introduces her to Wess Tanner, who accompanies her by stage to Doan's Crossing.

Davis, Jim: In "The Secret of Quaking Asp Cabin," mentioned in a story told by Babe Haught. He owned one of the best cow outfits in Arizona,

running some ten thousand head of cattle on a ranch neighboring the Hash Knife Outfit. Davis and Lefty Dagg, son of the Dagg who was the first man killed in the Pleasant Valley war, fell out over a cowboy Dagg killed and whom Davis set much store on. The story on the range is that it was an even break, but Davis never believed that. The full story of the fight never came out.

Davis, Lize: Mentioned by Mrs. Wentz in *The Spirit of the Border.* She reputedly thinks Joe Downs will make an excellent husband for Nell.

Davis, Paul: In *Fighting Caravans,* was a driver for Jim Waters. He delivers a letter to Clint Belmet from May Bell. In the letter she explains her flirting with Clayborn and Murdock.

Davis, Sam: In *The Thundering Herd,* the real name of Catlee, one of Jett's hiding crew. He was a member of the Younger outlaw gang.

Davis, Shep: In *The Dude Ranger,* one of the cowboys working on the Red Rock Ranch under John Hepford as foreman. He is a member of the Dude Hyslip faction, devoted to making life miserable for the tenderfoot, Ernest Selby. Of the cowboys other than Dude, Shep Davis seems to be the most dangerous and treacherous. He is surprised to be kept on at higher wages when the new owner, the tenderfoot Selby, asks for an apology.

Dawson: In *Majesty's Rancho,* one of Madge Stewart's crowd at the university in Los Angeles.

Dawson, Jim: In *Wyoming,* one of the men who give Martha Ann Dixon a lift. He gives her a piece of advice. He and his friend are on a trip through the Black Hills and both of them are men to be reckoned with. They are tall and strong and between them they have two shotguns, a revolver, a hatchet, a billy and two ferocious butcher knives. He points out that she is a wisp of a girl, alone, hitchhiking through dangerous territory and should be more careful.

Day, Hank: In *Stairs of Sand,* an old friend of Merryvale's and the driver of the stagecoach to Yuma. He fills Merryvale in on the latest gossip about Yuma.

Day, Tom: In *Nevada,* Ben Ide's nearest neighbor in Winthrop, living a mere ten miles away. He is a courteous Texan, who comes to the ranch to introduce himself and to welcome the Ides to the area. Little Blaine takes a liking to him immediately. He is a huge man with graying hair and a wrinkled, brown face that tells a tale of work and endurance. He has shrewd, penetrating, kind, blue eyes under heavy, bushy brows. He expresses an interest in Hettie from the start, but she does not encourage him. Tom offers Ben Ide friendship and advice. Cash Burridge sold him a ranch with a lot fewer cattle than he had claimed, with perhaps six to seven thousand head and not the eight thousand head claimed. As well, Burridge was in debt, with Day and Hatt having a lien on the cattle. Tom suspects that Burridge has cheated Ben. He has never heard of the Nevada about whom Ben Ide questions him. Day is a close friend of Judge Franklidge, to whom he speaks about Ben. He reports that the rustlers in the area have hit the Ide ranch with greater frequency than any other ranch in the area. Day admires Ben's horsemanship, and his taste in horses, particularly California Red. He suspects that Ben's heart is not in ranching, and momentarily, he wonders if he is not a rustler or a man wanted for something. Day and the judge approve of Texas Jack's going undercover to penetrate the Pine Tree Outfit. He agrees to vouch for Jack's honesty. Day, like Ben Ide, has been taken in by Dillon's affable appearance, but he acknowledges his error when Nevada (Texas Jack) exposes Clan Dillon as the head of the outlaw operation. He clears Nevada's name with the sheriff.

Dayes: In *The U. P. Trail*, one of Durade's henchmen assigned to guard duty in the gambling establishment and to the task of recapturing Allie Lee. He is killed by Larry King in the shootout at Stanton's.

De Lesseps: In *Boulder Dam*, mentioned as the engineer who failed to make a reality of the dream of building the Panama Canal. That feat was accomplished by Goethals.

De Soto: In *Knights of the Range*, the Spanish explorer is mentioned by Holly Ripple in her address to the five hundred diners at her fiesta. Her address summarizes the history of the region and the Spanish contributions to the cattle industry.

Deathwind: In *The Spirit of the Border*, the name by which Wetzel is known on the frontier. It refers to the sound which is reported to be heard before Wetzel attacks. Joe and Jim hear it before he appears to rescue them, and Joe hears it again when he and Wetzel attempt to rescue the captured Nell, Jim and Kate. The superstitious Indians believe that this strange sound is an omen of death and they flee. Col. Ebenezer Zane thinks it is a sound which Wetzel makes before he attacks, but no one knows for sure. In *Betty Zane*, however, as Wetzel is fighting off the Indians trying to enter the fort through a hole in the stockade, he emits blood-curdling yells that sound like a demon. See **Black Death, Le Vent de la Mort** and **Atelang.**

Decker: In *Boulder Dam*, works for Ben Sneed, who sends for him to help Lynn Weston find the men who abducted Anne Vandergrift. He learns from Mame that Vitte is the man to look for. At Vitte's place, Ben Bellew has locked Anne in an upstairs room. Decker is instrumental in effecting the rescue and getting Sheriff Logan. He drives the injured Lynn Weston to the hospital.

Declis: In *Blue Feather*, the painter who sifts colored sands of white and copper, making pictures wherein he reads the will of the gods.

Deering, Jake: One of the renegades in *The Spirit of the Border*. He is Jim Girty's equal in animal and barbarous depravity. He kidnaps, rapes and murders John Christy's betrothed, Lucy. He is a council member when the Indians vote on the fate of the converted Indians. He participates in the massacre. Jake Deering attacks Wingenund, Jim and Nell as they escape the Village of Peace. Wetzel kills him in the ensuing fight.

Deger: In *The Lone Star Ranger*, mentioned as providing a place where Kid Guller can recuperate from his gunshot wound.

Dekker, John: In *The Man of the Forest*, said to have had a heifer killed by a lion since Milt Dale's last visit to town.

Del: In "Monty Price's Nightingale," Muncie's daughter. Monty Price suffers severe burns when he rescues her from the grass fire that has burned their home and killed her mother.

Delilah: In *Riders of the Purple Sage*, Jane Withersteen is compared to this Biblical figure who betrayed Sampson and took his power away from him by cutting his hair. Jane is said to have been a Delilah for Venters, whom she emasculated by taking his guns, and Lassiter, whom she has turned into a lovesick lapdog.

Delorme, Sergeant: In *The Desert of Wheat*, survived the Battle of the Marne. He describes battle with bayonets. He describes the sacking and burning of homes by the German army. He feels great contempt for those who got exemptions and stayed at home and did nothing for their homeland. He admires the Americans who have come to help them out.

Dempsey, Jack: In *Code of the West*, the famous boxer that Thaddeus "Tuck" Merry worked for as a sparring partner. From him, Merry acquired considerable skill in the manly art of self-defense.

In *Boulder Dam*, Lynn Weston observes that Regan, the foreman of the scalers, has the physique and strength of Jack Dempsey.

Dene: In *The Heritage of the Desert*, the leader of an outlaw band that rustles cattle from the Mormon ranchers and re-brands the cattle with Holderness's mark. He appears early in the novel when he enters Naab's camp seeking Jack Hare, "Dene's spy." He is a strikingly handsome young man, compact, clean-shaven, cool, with long dark hair and a jaunty, careless mien. He is sure of himself and fearless. At this point, Naab characterizes him as a scourge, but the lesser evil compared to Holderness. Dene has come to White Sage and southern Utah after being driven from Montana, where he got his start at rustling. He has managed to lure many young Mormons into his gang and many ranchers take his side out of fear of retaliation. Dene is only a gunfighter and a thief, a man with a certain likeableness, despite his badness. Dene is Holderness's henchman, the effective arm of Holderness's bid for power. Of the two, Holderness is the more to be feared because he is greedy, unscrupulous, and hard to corner in dishonesty.

Dene shows a physical courage of which Holderness is incapable. When he learns that Jack Hare has been brought into White Sage by August Naab, he shows up at Bishop Caldwell's home demanding that Jack Hare be turned over to him. August Naab teaches Dene a lesson, grabbing him by the arm and applying enough pressure to break it, forcing him to drop his weapon. He also shows him that he is much faster on the draw, a warning that should any future meetings between them occur, he will be up against a man whose speed surpasses his own. Naab warns him that he could break open his skull with his bare fist, but the biblical command against killing restrains him. Dave Naab believes Dene attempts to follow Naab and his family back to the oasis in the desert but he gives up the pursuit after a day.

Dene is responsible for the rustling in the area, the seizure of Martin Cole's ranch at Holderness's behest as well as the shooting of Martin Cole in White Sage. Dene takes a liking to Jack Hare's horse, Silvermane. At one point, he tried to catch the magnificent stallion but had failed. When Jack Hare sees what Holderness has done at the Seeping Springs watering hole, he heads to town to confront him. On his way back, he passes Dene in the street, and Silvermane knocks the gunman over. Later, when Dene has come to kidnap Mescal, he tries to take the horse but Silvermane tramples him to death.

Denman: In *The Trail Driver,* runs a large merchandise store in Dodge. Brite takes Reddie there and turns her over to a female clerk with orders to get her the best clothes available and not to worry about the cost.

Denmeade, Allie: In *Under the Tonto Rim,* one of the daughters in the Denmeade family. She has been attending school for three years. She and Mertie help the mother prepare and serve the food. She asks Sam Johnson about his date for the dance, telling him she already knows he has asked Sadie Purdue. Lucy Watson describes her as huge of build, with a merry face.

Denmeade, Dan: In *Under the Tonto Rim,* has been attending school one year with his sister, Mary. He is a dark-headed youngster, with eyes to match, mischievous, bold and responsive.

Denmeade, Dick: In *Under the Tonto Rim,* with his brother Joe has been attending school for three years. Lucy cannot tell Dick from his brother Joe. Dick carries a gun when they walk to school, for protection from wild animals. He is a lean, rangy young man, with a smooth face and clear eyes.

Denmeade, Edd: In *Under the Tonto Rim,* a young man in his early twenties, the oldest of the Denmeade children. He is the Tonto version of the natural man, schooled by nature rather than by civilization, strong, moral, decent. He first opposes Lucy Watson's welfare work on the grounds that she

is teaching the little ones things that will only make them unhappy with their lives in the Tonto, things they would probably be better off not knowing. Eventually, like the Virginian, he decides that he needs an education and he works hard at making himself a worthy mate for the schoolmarm. Edd cuts a striking figure, not unlike that of the Virginian, when Molly Wood first spots him. He stalks with a flapping of chaps keeping time with clinking spurs. He is six feet tall, slender, but not lean like his brothers He is built like a narrow wedge, only his body and limbs are rounded, with a small waist, small hips, and giving an impression of extraordinary suppleness and strength. He resembles a range rider, but unlike the typical cowboy who shows himself to best advantage on horseback, Edd Denmeade not only cuts a striking figure in the saddle but, dismounted, walks with a long, quick, graceful springy stride. As the civilized teacher, Molly, must confess, her Virginian has learned more from experience than she ever has from books. Lucy Watson must acknowledge that the unflattering comments she had heard about Edd Denmeade are wholly without foundation. After talking seriously with him, she has a higher opinion of him than of any other young man she has ever met. Throughout her stay with his family, she is constantly surprised by his common sense, his faith in his values, his maturity, and his sense of responsibility and duty.

Mrs. Lynn says of Edd that he is woman-hungry, as backwoodsmen get. He is a bit strange, a bee hunter, wonderfully good to look at, but wild like the woods he lives in. He loves his sisters and gives his mother every dollar he earns. Word of Sadie Purdue's rejection of his marriage proposal has been the talk of the place. A rivalry between Edd and Sam Johnson is likewise a lively point of discussion. Mr. Jenks says of him that he is a superior sort of person to most of the boys. He is forceful, strong, simple, natural. Other boys do not understand him and the girls even less. As a result, he is often the butt of vicious gossip and catty putdowns. When she first sees him, Lucy is struck by his self-assurance. He clearly loves his family, his sister Mertie in particular, and enjoys making them happy. He shows little surprise or curiosity at the arrival of the new welfare worker. Lucy thinks the gap between them is so great it could never be bridged. When Lucy talks to Edd about her work, about how she will go stay with the Spralls for a while, he opposes such a move. The Sprall boys don't know how to treat a woman decently and her reputation would be ruined.

Edd invites her to the school dance, and at first she refuses to go with him. He points out that if the schoolmarm stays away from dances, folks will believe she thinks herself too good for them. Edd has to take her by force, ignoring her protests. She is both fascinated and repelled by him. At the dance, Edd is happy. Mrs. Denmeade congratulates Lucy on how happy she has made him. Edd leaves her free to dance with anyone she wants. He shows no rancor, no remembrance of insults. He is an enigma to Lucy.

He seemingly has no conception of his rude behavior, bringing her against her will with utter disregard for her feelings, but at the dance, he eliminates himself, content to see her whirl around with his cousins and friends, simply radiating with the pride of being her cavalier. He fends off Bud Sprall and Sam Johnson, who become too eager to dance with her.

Shortly thereafter, Edd proposes marriage to her. He acknowledges he is not her equal in education and culture but if she is planning to remain in the Tonto, she will end up marrying someone, so he wants to get his request in first. She refuses his offer, saying that it would not be right to marry someone she does not love. He accepts the rejection, but does not give up hope. He comes to her rescue when Bud Sprall goes around boasting he had peeped through a chink in the cabin wall to watch Lucy change dresses for the party. Edd proves his boast is a lie, defending her honor as the Virginian defends Molly's honor at the barbecue. He confides in Lucy his concern about Mertie, how she mistreats Bert Hall, the best of the young men around who is sweet on her. He has tried to protect her from herself, and now despairs of her.

Edd takes Lucy on a bee-hunting expedition. His knowledge of bees, his skill at finding a hive and getting the honey amaze her. Although he is a backwoodsman with little education, he is a perfect gentleman. Like the Virginian, he undertakes to educate himself. Over the winter, he works through the books Lucy has given him. He becomes her best student. When she moves on to stay at the Claypools's he is sad, but tells her he won't turn to white mule or go looking for Bud Sprall to pick a fight.

When the situation with Clara comes to a head, Edd Denmeade once more comes to defend the honor of the Watson girls. He kills Middleton (Harv Sprall), and Bud Sprall rides off, fearing arrest and imprisonment for other banditry that has come to light. Lucy tells Edd that the illegitimate child in question is hers. Edd sees no problem in that. He offers to go to Kingston with her to fetch the child, to marry Lucy and move away from the Tonto for a while and to return after a few years when the fuss will have blown over. This time, she accepts his offer. He doubts that she loves him, but she finally confesses her true feelings. Meanwhile, Lucy's sister Clara has finally found the courage to tell Joe Denmeade, her husband, the truth, that the child is hers by Middleton (Harv Sprall). Joe forgives her, and agrees to take the child. No one need ever know Sprall had not married her before the child was born.

Edd Denmeade is one of the fullest developments in Grey's novels of the natural gentleman, the 'natural man,' the individual whose sense of morality and decency comes from the wilderness environment rather than from formal education. He is a latter-day Wetzel, one of the most memorable figures in the panoply of Grey heroes.

Denmeade, Joe: In *Under the Tonto Rim*, has attended school for three years, like Allie and Dick.

When Joe arrives home, he reports that Mr. Jenks told him about the new teacher's arrival. They passed Sam Johnson on the way home, packing her baggage. Of all the boys, Joe is the quiet one and the nicest. He is the least-given to dances, white mule, and chasing girls. Lucy asks Joe to meet her sister, Clara. She fears Clara may be Joe's downfall, but is willing to risk it. He has already arranged to take Mr. Jenks' buckboard to drive to town. Joe expects the other boys will waylay them on the way, and indeed, they do. Among them is Jim Middleton, but Lucy does not recognize him as yet. Joe is a perfect gentleman, confirming Lucy's confidence in him. He soon falls in love with Clara. She decides to marry him, but keeps her secret from him. She fears he will reject her and the child if he knows the truth. When she does confide in him, however, she discovers that to Joe, it makes no difference. He loves her all the more for confiding her shame to him. He tells her to send for the child and they will raise it as their own. No one need ever know she and Middleton were not married. Joe builds a cabin on a homestead on the top of the rim.

Denmeade, Lee: In *Under the Tonto Rim*, father of the Denmeade clan. Mr. Jenks takes Lucy Watson up to meet the family. He and his wife first walked up to the place where they now live twenty-three years ago. They had a burro, a cow, a gun and an ax and some dogs. They homesteaded the area in sections and raised a family of five girls and four boys, all born in the one-room cabin. Their original cabin was half log, half stone. In the past year, they built a new log cabin. Jenks tells Lucy that Lee Denmeade said he would never live in a place that wheels could go. He is the most influential among the backwoodsmen in the Tonto. Mr. Lynn feels Lucy may have trouble teaching progressive ideas to him, but Mr. Jenks thinks he might be receptive. When she meets him, she is a bit surprised to meet a man not old or gray, though showing the ravages of years. His eyes are gray and piercing, like those of an eagle. He is approachable, but there is something raw, fierce, like the wilds in which he lives. He shows himself more willing to adapt than she had expected. He explains how homesteaders start farming, the slow progress they make. He praises Edd's and Edd's choice of location to homestead. His boys, he says, are ingenious and hard workers, like he has been. Indeed, Lucy can only admire the determination and steadfastness of all the Denmeades.

Denmeade, Liz: In *Under the Tonto Rim*, twin sister to Lize.

Denmeade, Lize: In *Under the Tonto Rim*, twin sister to Liz. At five years of age, they have not yet started going to school.

Denmeade, Mary: In *Under the Tonto Rim*, has been attending the local school for a year. Lucy Watson describes her as a dark-haired, thin, overworked girl who, under favorable conditions, would be pretty. She is the most communicative of the children and talks to Lucy Watson about her burro, the puppies and school. She attaches herself to Lucy, showing her where the puppies are kept and where she plays with pine cones and shards of Indian pottery she found under the tree. She tells about the hens roosting in the trees to keep from being eaten by beasts. She also tells about Edd and his bees, and his trip to Winbrook to get a special birthday present for Mertie, his favorite sister. Mary shows great enthusiasm to learn all that Lucy has to teach her.

Denmeade, Mertie: In *Under the Tonto Rim,* is sixteen years old. Lucy Watson comments that she is the only one of the Denmeade family who seems to pay attention to how she dresses. She looks at Lucy, but not at her; rather, she is scrutinizing her clothes, her hair, her style. Mertie is boy-crazy. She has the best young man around for her beau, Bert Hall, but she treats him with disdain. She wants to party and flirt with all the young men. She is her brother Edd's favorite sister. She appears more worried about not getting the new dress he promised to bring her from Winbrook than about her brother getting injured in the ice and snowstorm he meets on his return. Edd knows she is selfish and vain, and perhaps that is why he is fondest of her. She needs his influence and common sense to control her natural tendencies. She is too much under the influence of Sadie Purdue. Hoping to influence her for the better, the teacher invites Mertie and Bert to go to Felix with her and Edd. Surprisingly, Mertie and Bert get married there and, to Edd's surprise, she gets a "storm" on her return home.

Denmeade, Mrs.: In *Under the Tonto Rim,* mother of the Denmeade clan. She does her best to make the new teacher feel at home, and approves of her work in the Tonto. Here, welcome is simple, cordial, without show of curiosity or astonishment. She embodies the simplicity and seriousness and hardiness of the pioneer woman.

Denmeade, Uncle Bill: In *Under the Tonto Rim,* Joe Denmeade's oldest brother. There are four Denmeade brothers in the Tonto. Lucy Watson meets him the morning after her arrival at their place.

Denver: (1) In *Fighting Caravans,* Jim Baker's partner. He, Jim Baker and Lya Banks pursue and kill a band of fifteen Kiowa.

(2) In *The Mysterious Rider,* a white, yellow-spotted hound.

Derrick: In *Wilderness Trek,* one of Stanley Dann's drovers on the trans–Australia trek. With Bligh, Hood and Heald, he quits the outfit just as Eric Dann declares that he lied about knowing the route to the Kimberleys.

Dervish: In *Majesty's Rancho,* one of Majesty Stewart's string of thoroughbred horses. She wants to ride him when she and her friends plan to go riding. Lance, José, and Ren Starr all remind her that she has not done any riding for several years now

and Dervish is quite a perky animal to handle. Gene Stewart has given Lance instructions not to let his daughter ride the frisky thoroughbred. Madge's friends agree with Sidway that she should ride another horse, but she insists. For the first part of the ride, things go well. When they dismount for a rest and she remounts Dervish, the horse gets the bit between his teeth and takes off running wildly. Madge is not able to control the horse. Lance Sidway rescues her from the runaway stallion. She admits her error in riding the frisky horse, and Lance rides him back to the stables.

Devil: In *The Light of Western Stars,* a particularly nasty bronc. As a trick, the cowboys give this horse to Castleton to ride, expecting him to be thrown. Devil throws the undaunted English nobleman a few times, but persistence pays off and Castleton does ride him. This feat inspires great admiration among the cowhands, in particular, Gene Stewart.

Devine, Jake: In *The Thundering Herd,* a frontiersman, used to fighting Indians. He fights beside Tom Doan in the Comanche campaign.

Devoe, Johnny: In *Boulder Dam,* drives a truck delivering bootleg whiskey for Sneed. When Bellew attempts to hijack the shipment, Devoe drives his truck into Bellew's car.

Diablo, Blanco: In *Desert Gold,* Belding's favorite among his string of white horses bred from Mexican stock. Belding believes this horse is the fastest, but Blanco Sol proves his better in a desperate race. Diablo is taken by raiders but retrieved unharmed by Dick Gale, Charley Ladd and Jim Lash. When Rojas is about to return to the Belding ranch, Tom arranges for Ladd and the party guarding Mercedes to take his prized horses with them to keep them out of Rojas' clutches.

Díaz, Porfirio: In *The Light of Western Stars,* the president of Mexico mentioned as one of the figures involved in the civil war/revolution.

Dick: (1) In *The Border Legion,* an outlaw shot by Gulden and injured. No further reference is made to him.

(2) In *The Horse Thief,* Edith Watrous's black stallion with a white face. Both Edith and Dale Brittenham recognize him in the herd of horses being auctioned in Halsey by Reed, the rustler. To prove he is her horse, Edith calls to the stallion and he comes over to her and starts nuzzling her.

Diego: In *Lost Pueblo,* one of the cowboys working at John Bennet's trading post. He's Mexican. He saw a Western movie once and has never got over it. He dresses up like movie cowboys, especially for Janey Endicott. He arrives with the other cowboys, supposedly to free Janey from Phillip Randolph, her abductor, and they proceed to go to the pretense of lynching Phillip Randolph.

Dietrich: In *The Lost Wagon Train,* a wagon

driver in the caravan led by Anderson. He is appointed to stand guard during the night with Walling. He is killed in the attack by the Kiowas and Latch's outlaw gang.

Dill, Mrs.: In *The Maverick Queen*, runs the boarding house in South Pass where Lincoln Bradway rents a room. She is a pleasant-faced and hospitable woman who asks for her fee in advance. She is up on the local gossip and provides some useful information on occasion. When Linc mentions that he has come to town to investigate the death of his friend, Jimmy Weston, Mrs. Dill tells him Jimmy was killed in a card game when he was caught cheating. She also adds that although she herself finds it hard to believe Jimmy was cheating at cards, most people in town believe this explanation. She gives Linc the impression she knows more than she is willing to say. She warns him it may be dangerous to pursue his investigation. Later, when Lincoln has won a several thousand dollars in a card game and shot McKeever, Mrs. Dill reports that the town has a favorable opinion of him. Rumor also has exaggerated considerably the size of the pot he won.

Dillon, Clan: In *Nevada*, also known as Ed Richardson and as Campbell. He works as foreman for Ben Ide. He's in deep with Stewart, one of the foremen on Tom Day's ranch. He is a likeable man, and both Ben Ide and Tom Day think highly of him. At the dance in Winthrop, he makes advances to Hettie Ide and she repulses him. When he persists, she fires him. She considers his friendliness and helpfulness a mask to hide his true nature and his less favorable intentions. Texas Jack (Nevada, Jim Lacy) picks a fight with him at the dance, giving him a black eye for being so ungentlemanly to a lady. Rose Hatt interests him as well, and supposedly, he is engaged to her, or so her brother claims. She knows him as Ed Richardson. Rose Hatt is the first person that Jim Lacy hears speak ill of Clan Dillon. Jim Lacy knows he is mad about Hettie. Dillon ingratiates himself with Ben Ide by "recovering" rustled cattle on two occasions. He pooh poohs the idea that Hardy Rue is a member of the Pine Tree Outfit just as he pooh-poohs the idea that the stallion, California Red, was stolen. He claims the horse just jumped the fence and ran off. He is genuinely shocked when the horse reappears one morning in the corral. He argues that the horse merely returned and jumped back into the corral. Reluctantly he acknowledges Raidy's proof that the horse has been hobbled and driven through rough terrain. When Jim Lacy meets Rose Hatt with Marvie Blaine after the encounter in which her brother, Cedar Hatt, is shot, she identifies Richardson, Clan Dillon, as the head of the outlaw outfit. His true identity is exposed to all when Jim Lacy finally brings the Pine Tree rustlers to justice.

Dillon, Colonel: In *The U. P. Trail*, commands the troops guarding the construction crews of the Union Pacific. He accompanies Neale and Slinger-

land when they go to help Horn's wagon train. He appears several times in the novel. His wife takes charge of Allie at the army camp when she escapes from Durade.

Dillon, Mrs.: In *The U. P. Trail*, the wife of Colonel Dillon. She takes in Allie Lee when she has escaped from Durade and keeps her at the army camp.

Dillon, Muggs: In *Knights of the Range*, a cowboy who works on the Ripple ranch. Britt comes upon him early in the story with a gang of horse thieves. Frayne is part of the same outfit, but when Heaver and Covell threaten to do violence to Holly Ripple, he breaks with the outfit. He also declares that he did not like the way they worked on Dillon to make him betray his outfit. Dillon and Brazos Keene had been friends. Brazos had vouched for him. At one point, Brazos, Stinger and Laigs Mason had caught Dillon and three other rustlers driving a bunch of steers with the Ripple brand but had exacted a promise from him to go straight. Brazos feels double-crossed. When he meets him in similar circumstances again, Dillon is killed in the gunplay.

Dipper: In *Majesty's Rancho*, one of the men with Bee Uhl in his car when he meets Lance Sidway in Douglas, Arizona. He approves of hiring Lance to drive the empty truck to Tucson.

Dismukes: In *Wanderer of the Wasteland*, a wanderer of the wasteland who helps Adam Larey get his legs in the desert. Dismukes has the most scarred and calloused hands that Adam Larey has ever seen. He is very short, buck-tanned, and, according to Magdalene Virey, he looks like a big frog. Dismukes is a prospector for gold. He has set himself a goal of finding half-a-million dollars of the yellow stuff. He has already accumulated about a third of his target when he first meets Adam. He keeps the gold hidden in different places in the desert or salted away in banks. He hopes to leave the desert, to travel and enjoy himself when his target is reached. Dismukes has had broad experience of the different men who roam the desert and he can read his new friend like a book. When Adam gives him a false name, Wansfell, Dismukes knows he is lying. Dismukes tells him that the desert is the place for secrets and he is a discreet man. The desert, he says, is a symbol for human nature. It is a lens which intensifies human passions. Dismukes's advice is to do to others as you would like them to do to you. The desert makes beasts of many, but others find a new spirituality rising above the conflict for survival. Dismukes sings the praises of burros, the animal that makes survival on the desert possible for a man. He gives Adam his burro, Jinny, and shares half his food and clothes with the young man. He also gives him an oven for cooking. When they part, he wishes Adam luck. Some time later, Jinny returns to him and he assumes Adam has perished. Eight years later, they meet again at Tecopah in the Mohave desert. Adam is much changed, a huge man, muscular, taciturn, formed by the desert. Dismukes has reached half his target now, a quarter of a million dollars. He asks himself if seeking gold has not become an end in itself and he asks Adam if he has found God yet in the desert. When Adam's reply is noncommittal, he points out that Adam has found his God but doesn't realize it yet. He tells him about a man and a woman living in Death Valley that he met on his wanderings. The man hates the woman and she hates him. He has heard about what Adam did to McKue, a man with whom he had a dispute some years before and whom Adam killed for mistreating a woman. He suggests that perhaps Adam can do something for this unfortunate couple. Several more years later, Adam comes across Dismukes at his arrastra where he is being held prisoner by four thieves. Adam rescues the man, killing his attackers. Dismukes has now met his goal of half-a-million dollars. He announces that he is going to leave the desert, and see the world. He plans to spend some of his money to help the needy, and the rest to visit the places he had heard about. He even speculates about the possibility of getting married and having a son, something he's always regretted about his desert life. Several year later still, Adam meets Dismukes, who has returned from civilization to his desert home. Dismukes had traveled for three years. He went to his hometown but no one there recalled him, and he could find no one he had known there. There is no trace of where his family went, so he cannot visit his parents' graves. It is as if they had never existed. He goes to New York, London, Paris, Cairo, India, Japan. In each case, he finds a lot of people, but the same is true of all the cities he visits—people are shallow, corrupt, manipulative, selfish. They are interested in him only because of his money. He decides that he had known a truer life back in the desert and so he returns to the life he had lived for nearly two decades. When Adam and Dismukes part this time, Dismukes is on his way to Death Valley, where he expects to meet a true challenge.

In Dismukes, Zane Grey presents another of his mystics, men formed by loneliness and the desert, hoping to find God and the essence of human existence. In this he resembles Nas Ta Bega and John Shefford in *The Rainbow Trail* and John Hare in *The Heritage of the Desert*.

In *Stairs of Sand*, Adam Larey mentions Dismukes as the greatest influence on his desert experience. He tells Ruth that Dismukes taught him not to fear the desert, to accept its challenge and its influence and to become like the desert, patient, hard, silent, essential.

Dixie: In *West of the Pecos,* Miss Terrill Lambeth's horse. The animal proves valuable on the trip west, surviving the buffalo stampede.

Dixon: In *The Desert of Wheat,* one of Kurt Dorn's companions at the army training camp. Dixon is from Massachusetts, educated at Harvard, son of a wealthy, influential family and is a noted athlete at school. He is lithe and red-faced, with curly hair.

Dixon, Bob: In *Wyoming,* Martha Dixon's brother. Martha thinks that she will never see him again when she runs away from home.

Dixon, Martha Ann: In *Wyoming,* the niece of Nick Bligh. When the letter arrives from the uncle that no one has heard from in thirty years, Martha's interest in Wyoming is stirred. She decides to run away from home. Under pretext of visiting her university friend, Alice McGinnis who lives in Omaha, she sets off with a knapsack. Continuing the pretense, she sends a postcard home from Omaha before setting out hitchhiking. Her goal is to reach her Uncle Nick's ranch in Randall, Wyoming. She experiences a series of adventures, which include a ride with a young man almost ruined by the war who has made good on a farm in Nebraska, a chivalrous rescue from hobos by Andrew Bonning, an offer to be adopted by an elderly couple, and rides with carefully chosen chaperones concerned about her safety. In Randall, she discovers her uncle is well-known and well-liked, but she also learns he has moved south. Mr. Toller, owner of the emporium in Randall, finds her a lift with Mr. Lee Todd, who delivers her to her destination. There, she discovers that the "knight in shining armor" she met is working for her uncle. She tries to get her uncle to fire him, but he refuses. He attributes her behavior to her being high-strung, like her mother's family, the Campbells. Martha cannot get away from Andy. When she is thrown from a horse, he is there to help her out. It is very annoying, but she slowly comes to see there is more to Andy than meets the eye. Her first feelings of respect for him come when he wins the bull-riding competition at the rodeo.

One day riding on the range, she comes upon Texas Haynes branding one of her uncle's calves. She has met him before in town, and found him quite flattering. He explains to her that branding mavericks is not illegal, but when she points out that it is clear who the calf's mother belongs to, the branding is scarcely honest. He promises to quit branding mavericks if she keeps his secret. Riding back to the ranch, they meet Andy Bonning, who gets into a fight with Texas because of the attention he is paying to her. Again, she finds Andy's defending her honor too much to bear.

Andy proposes marriage to her, but she refuses because she is convinced he thinks she is no good, that he has nothing but contempt for her reckless hitchhiking adventure. She resents his condescending superiority, his certainty that he knows what is best for her. When Texas has killed McCall, she tells Andy that he did it for her sake. He had said he would pick a fight with McCall and shoot the gizzard out of him. Her heart softens towards Andy and when he presents her with a beautiful buckskin horse with an elaborate Mexican saddle, she cannot resist him. She writes home telling of her adventures and of her upcoming marriage to her knight.

Martha resembles Georgie Stockwell in *Code of the West,* who must learn more appropriate, responsible behavior. She, too, discovers in the West the values and the purpose that make life worthwhile.

Dixon, Mr.: In *Wyoming,* Martha Ann's father.

Dixon, Mrs.: In *Wyoming,* Martha's mother. She has her doubts about her daughter's intentions when Martha announces that a friend from the university has invited her to her to visit in Omaha. Mrs. Dixon remembers her daughter's madness to go out West, and suspects this is a ruse.

Do Etin: In *The Vanishing American,* the name means "the Gentleman." He is not a wealthy Navajo but he is respected in the tribe because of his fairness, thoughtfulness and intelligence. He is the father of the young girl, Gekin Yashi. Do Etin believes that the reservation school has some useful things to offer the Navajo and he sends his daughter to the school willingly to learn those things. He does not, however, approve of Morgan's regulation obliging the children to attend chapel. Learning hygiene, cooking, agriculture, reading, writing, and arithmetic, can be accomplished without religious instruction. Do Etin proposes that Nophaie marry Gekin Yashi to make possible her removal from the school. Nophaie refuses the offer. Do Etin does agree to the plan to get his daughter away from the school but doesn't want Nophaie to run the risk of punishment for helping her. He sees that white influence will continue to expand in the future, The Navajo have lost the will to resist. They are a vanishing race. Do Etin is killed by Blucher's henchmen when "resisting arrest." Blucher has been trying to discover where Gekin Yashi has been taken.

Doan, Bill: In *The Thundering Herd,* Tom Doan's father. He was a hard rider and hard shooter. During the Civil War, he fought with the Confederate forces and after the war joined Quantrill's raiders. Pilchuck knew him when he rode with Quantrill and tells Tom he takes after his father.

Doan, Mrs.: In *The Fugitive Trail,* Tom's wife. She sees to Trinity's comfort when she is at the post as she does for June Neece in *Twin Sombreros.*

Doan, Tom: In *The Trail Driver,* runs a supply depot on the Chisolm Trail where it splits into the Abilene and Dodge branches. Adam Brite's drive reaches there before his supplies have been exhausted. He gets flour, sugar, tobacco and other supplies in greater quantities than he needs, knowing that he can use them for trade with the Indians. Doan provides the supplies as well as information. The Indians are on the rampage and can make trouble. He advises that they do something about the two Comanche bucks hanging around the store. They will report back to the chief on the size of the herd and the number of wagons. Texas arranges to have them tied up and locked away for several days, but they get away before anything can be done. Doan also informs them that Ross Hite passed through there just two days before. Ann Hardy and her father leave the drive here to catch a coach to Abilene. Hash Williams and Smilin' Pete also leave the drive here.

In *Twin Sombreros,* this same Tom Doan is a friend of Brazos Keene's. After he has cleared up the rustling problem with Knight and Surface in Las Animas, he heads south into Texas. He stops off to visit with his friend Tom Doan at Doan's Crossing. He is surprised to see that a whole town has grown up around the trading post. Doan is now married. He brings Doan up to date on their mutual friends. June Neece tracks Brazos to Doan's Crossing and they are married in Doan's home.

In *The Fugitive Trail,* this same Doan gives Trinity Spencer advice on where to go looking for Bruce Lockheart. He has heard rumors from the cowboys and drivers at the post that are sure he went north, south and east, but Doan feels he would head west into the Llano Estacado (Staked Plain) or into the country west of the Brazos. Tom Doan also holds the sizeable stakes in the bet between Captain Maggard and Luke Loveless. Loveless tells Maggard he is on a wild goose chase pursuing Lockheart, as he was the most honest man he ever met. He bets it will be proven that Lockheart had nothing to do with the Denison robbery.

Doan, Tom: In *The Thundering Herd,* a young man of twenty-four who has come to the buffalo-hunting fields to make money to buy a ranch. He is a stereotype found in many Grey novels, the runaway male, out to find adventure and to prove himself on the frontier. All during his boyhood, before and through the stirring years of the Civil War, he had been slowly yielding to the call that made so many young men seek adventure in the Southwest. His home had not been happy but he stayed on the Kansas farm as long as his mother lived there and his sisters remained unmarried. He got what education he could at the local school. When Kansas refused to secede to the South, Tom's father joined Quantrill's raiders, but Tom's and his mother's sympathies were with the North. Bill Doan, his father, was killed on one of Quantrill's raids and his mother died shortly after that. The sisters married and moved away leaving Tom free to pursue his dreams.

Tom drifted from place to place, always heading farther and father into unsettled country. He meant to be a rancher, a tiller of the soil, a stockman and breeder of horses, for these things he loved. But there was in him the urge to see the frontier and to be in the thick of wild life. He had in him a "perfect blending of the dual spirit that burned in the hearts of thousands of men" which eventually opened the West to civilization. The commercial lure of buffalo hides brought many to the frontier, to brave the elements and the threat of Indian attack. He arrives at Sprague's post where he hopes to outfit himself, but instead, he signs up with Clark Hudnall and Jude Pilchuck as a skinner. At Sprague's post he meets Colonel Buffalo Jones, a famous frontiersman, and Wild Bill, another legend. Jude Pilchuck, a frontiersman equal to the men of legend, helps him get a horse and select the gear he needs. The Hudnall family welcomes him heartily and Tom feels at home.

Before they set off for the fields, he meets a young woman named Milly. Work at the killing fields is strenuous, and Tom discovers it is much more difficult than skinning a steer. On his first day, he skins twenty-four buffalo. Eventually he develops the strong hands and arms of a frontiersman and the work becomes less strenuous. He develops a method for skinning buffalo using the horse to pull off the hide and turn the carcass over. He skins four hundred and eighty-two carcasses in twenty-four days.

At the killing fields, he meets up with Milly Fayre again, and the two fall in love. She tells him of her unfortunate situation with Jett, her stepfather, who has made lewd suggestions to her. They decide to marry when Milly turns eighteen in a few months. Tom keeps his relationship with Milly a secret from the Hudnalls but he does mention her to the cavalry officers who come to take the womenfolk back to Sprague's where they will be safer. While Milly and Tom agree on most things, their attitudes to the buffalo hunt are a bone of contention. Milly thinks the buffalo hunt is a crime against nature, a celebration of greed and cruelty and waste. The killing fields are covered with carcasses left to rot, the plains are black with buzzards and the howl of surfeited wolves fills the night.

When Hudnall is killed, Tom Doan joins Pilchuck in the campaign against the Comanche, after which he goes on a final buffalo hunt with him. Together, they experience a buffalo stampede, surviving by climbing to the top of a rocky hill while the thundering herd passes them by on all sides. Tom returns to Sprague's post where he discovers that Milly is still alive, working as the schoolteacher in the small town that is growing around the post. Burn Hudnall and Dave Stronghurl, married to Sally Hudnall, have taken up farms there. Tom and Milly marry and buy a farm beside Dave and Burn.

Like Clint Belmet in *Fighting Caravans* and Joe Downs in *The Spirit of the Border*, Tom Doan adapts to the conditions of the frontier and proves himself in his own eyes and in the eyes of his beloved, Milly Fayre.

Doane: In *Knights of the Range,* a rancher, neighbor and friend of the Ripples. Holly Ripple and Britt confide in him about McCoy's threats. It appears Doane talked too much and he is mysteriously killed. His entire stock is run off, leaving Joe and Anne penniless. When Anne is living at the Ripple's waiting to be married, she tells Holly a story about her father that her mother told her when she was twelve. Doane had wronged some man somehow or other. This man dared him to come out and fight. Her mother would not let her father go. That ruined him with his friends and neighbors and he had to clear out. That happened at some fort in Kansas where Doane worked and lived during the war. They moved farther west and since then, she has come to understand the value of honor and the need to fight for your reputation.

Doane, Anne: In *Knights of the Range,* the seventeen-year-old daughter of rancher Doane. She is a comely, buxom girl, rosy-cheeked and blue-eyed, stalwart, a daughter of the frontier. Although younger than her friend Holly in years, she is much older in experience. She was born in a prairie schooner crossing the plains. She has only the teaching her mother gave her as a child. She can ride like a cowboy and throw a rope. Her well-calloused hands and fingertips show she has done the work of a pioneer girl. She is strong in character as in body. She is frank, droll, simple, big-hearted and wise in the ways of the range. She is, in short, Western. Anne is looking forward to the fiesta and the excitement it will cause. She predicts there will be a fight, since there are so few young women around and there is such tension between the Ripples and the other ranch outfits, something is bound to start a fistfight. She recalls that at her party last year, a gun fight broke out in which Sam Price was shot, but not seriously. Anne is engaged to marry Skylark, one of Holly's cowhands. She says he is her steadiest boy, and she plans to settle his bad habits when they are wed. The only thing she regrets is not having ended things with other cowboys before choosing him. This could cause trouble. When Skylark and Anne are wed at the Ripple ranch after her father's death, Holly provides them with an empty cabin. Anne provides good companionship for Holly as well. Unlike Holly, she is directly involved with all the cowhands and workers on the ranch. She has an ear for gossip which she repeats to her friend. She advises Holly to marry soon, and discusses the disadvantages of being single when there are so many men around. Brazos Keene and Renn Frayne are the best choices. She detects that Holly is in love with Frayne, although she does not admit it.

Doane, Joe: In *Knights of the Range,* Anne Doane's brother. Joe and two riders from the ranch trail horse thieves driving off some twenty horses. Among them is his sister's blue roan, a gift from Holly Ripple. Joe comes to work at the Ripple ranch and lives in the bunk house with the hands, who welcome him heartily.

Doc: In *The Hash Knife Outfit,* advises Slinger Dunn, who is recovering from gunshot wounds to the lungs, to cut out smoking. Dunn is not pleased with the advice.

Dockery Brothers: In *The Maverick Queen,* run a supply store which provides Lincoln Bradway and Ben Thorpe with the tools and equipment needed to build a road into the valley where Lincoln and Lucy plan to set up their ranch.

Docleas: In *Blue Feather,* son of the chief Nothis Toh. It's Blue Feather's real name among his own people, the Nopahs.

Doddridge: In *Boulder Dam,* works with Lynn Weston and Smitty under the foreman, Regan. He is a scaler, working with Lynn and Smitty the day Regan gets knocked out by falling rock. Together with Lynn and Smitty, he rescues Regan from certain death falling to the bottom of the canyon.

Dodge: In *The Lone Star Ranger*, the name given by Jim Fletcher to Buck Duane. Buck has come to Ord as an undercover ranger, posing as an outlaw. He has little to say about himself except that he is on the dodge. Fletcher thinks it a suitable handle, as does Buck himself.

Dodge Sheriff: In *Raiders of Spanish Peaks*, the sheriff in the town where Tracks Williams is being held in jail. He comes upon Lonesome and Laramie talking to the prisoners through the jail window. The quick-thinking Laramie explains convincingly that they were giving a prisoner some tobacco for a smoke. When Laramie and Lonesome break Williams and the others out of jail, the nine prisoners inside comment that Dodge Sheriff has the reputation of going off "half-cocked."

Doetin: In *Black Mesa*, an old Indian. His bronze visage resembles a mask of wrinkled parchment. He is lean, gray, upright. He has the look of a falcon in his piercing gaze. He was the first Indian that Paul Manning had ever seen with light eyes instead of dark. He predicts a wind storm is about to blow.

Doetin, Hostein: In *The Rainbow Trail*, a sinewy, old, grey-haired, wrinkled-faced Navajo. He appears wrapped in a blanket at the Navajo village. He is kindly, and friendly to Shefford. He organizes the packing of the goat skins and wool for shipment to the trading post with Withers and Joe Lake. He sends to the Piutes to get them to send in their skins and wool for shipment at the same time. Hostein Doetin is the father of Nas Ta Bega and Glen Naspa. He is particularly concerned about the interest his young daughter has in the missionary, Willetts. He himself has no interest in learning about Jesus and religion and wants to prevent his daughter from leaving for Blue Cañon with Willetts.

Dolan, Bill: In *Valley of Wild Horses*, a rancher in Marco who witnesses Pan Handle's confrontation with Hardman and Matthews in the street in from of the Yellow Mine. He reports this, as well as Jim Blake's escape from prison, to Pan Handle's father.

Dons, the: In *The Shepherd of Guadaloupe*, a family that built the Spanish-style mansion in which the Forrests and later the Lundeens live.

Dorn: In *Riders of the Purple Sage*, one of Jane Withersteen's Mormon riders. With Blake, he joins the vigilance committee being organized to pursue the rustlers who have taken Jane's red herd. Jane Withersteen had been particularly generous with his children, but he feels he has a 'higher duty' to fulfill when he quits working for her on orders from the church elders. He reports to Blake that the white herd is gone and Jane's horses have likewise been stolen. Blake later repeats this information to Lassiter and Jane.

Dorn, Chris: In *The Desert of Wheat*, a wheat farmer in Washington state. He loves the land passionately, and his son, Kurt, says he considers the wheatfields his children. He is a fair man with his workers and democratic in his habits. He and his son always eat their meals with the hired men. He emigrated to the United States over 50 years ago, having left Germany for England, where he spent several years before coming to the United States. He married an American woman, and his son, Kurt, is torn between his German allegiance and his American allegiance. Chris Dorn always speaks to his son in German, and Kurt usually answers in English. Chris Dorn is over seventy years old. He is in debt over thirty thousand dollars to Anderson, a wealthy wheat farmer and rancher in the area. Anderson has been very fair and patient in waiting for repayment but Chris Dorn feels intense resentment against him. Chris Dorn has nursed a hatred for England and an even greater hatred for the United States. He believes than men like Anderson are greedy capitalists, buying up the land from smaller farmers when they fall on hard times. Given his feelings for his adopted country and his creditors, he falls under the sway of the agents of the International Workers of the World, German-financed agents bent on disrupting American agriculture and sabotaging the war effort. He sells his crop of wheat for eighty thousand dollars, which Neuman, another wheat farmer and rancher and the only rival to Anderson in the area, and Glidden convince him to donate to the cause. His son manages to wrest the money from him before it is handed over. Dorn had been promised that his wheatfields would be free from sabotage and burning but he soon learns the I.W.W. agents have not kept their word. Thanks to help from the neighbors, the crop is harvested before it can be destroyed. In the intense heat and effort, Chris Dorn dies from a heart attack, telling his son that he was wrong about the United States. In *The Desert of Wheat*, Chris Dorn is a prime example of citizens with divided loyalties forming a dangerous fifth column in a country at war.

Dorn, Frank: In *Stairs of Sand*, sent by Guerd Larey to take over operation of the freighting post in Lost Lake when it was closed following Ruth's abduction and the murder of Caleb Hunt. He is the husband of Mrs. Dorn, the self-righteous, judgmental gossip.

Dorn, Kurt: In *The Desert of Wheat*, the twenty-four-year-old son of Chris Dorn, a young man torn between his German and his American halves. He shares his father's passion for the land and for wheat, and he waxes poetic about the beauty of the golden wheatfields blowing in the wind. He has studied at an agricultural school and seems to have swallowed the textbook on wheat farming. He explains to Anderson and Lenore about the different varieties of wheat currently used in Washington State and explains the various viruses and fungi which may affect a wheat plant as well as the known treatments for them. He is grateful that Mr. Anderson has been generous towards him and his father in the matter of the thirty-thousand-dollar loan. Mr. Anderson also shares with him what he knows about the International Workers of the World and their campaign to disrupt the wheat harvest in Washington. Like Anderson, he tries to keep I.W.W. men off his ranch and he suffers the consequences. Given his father's hatred of the United States, Kurt suspects he may be influenced to help the I.W.W. men. Kurt finds his father with Neuman discussing handing over to the I.W.W. the eighty thousand dollars he received for his wheat crop. Kurt prevents this by grabbing the money as his father is about to hand it over. This means that Glidden's and Neuman's promises not to attack the Dorn wheatfields mean nothing. Kurt finds phosphorous cakes scattered throughout his prize wheatfields. He convinces his neighbors to help harvest his crop, the only decent wheatfields left in the area. During the work, his father dies of a heart attack, but not before he recognizes that he was wrong about the I.W.W. Although the wheat is safely harvested, the I.W.W. sets fire to the grain elevators. With no money to pay the outstanding debt, Kurt sells his farm to Anderson, then joins the army.

Kurt Dorn is convinced he must go to war to prove to himself that he is truly American. He recalls how children at school made fun of his German name. He had the same experience at agricultural school. Embarrassed by his father's virulent anti–Americanism, Kurt feels he must atone for his father's lack of patriotism. When Hall offers him an exemption from the draft because of his expertise at wheat farming, Kurt refuses. And later when he learns that Anderson has obtained that exemption, he accuses him of meddling. In boot camp, the same feelings of isolation and rejection assail him. He is called "Kaiser Dorn" by the men in his outfit. His desire to belong doesn't come to fruition until he is at the front, where he proves to be an excellent soldier, an inspiration to the other men. Corporal Owens reports this to Mr. Anderson when he comes to New York to bring the injured, dying Kurt back home to Washington. Kurt received twenty-five wounds and lost an arm in combat. He finally feels he has proven himself, and is at death's door as a consequence.

Kurt's lack of self-confidence reveals itself in his relationship with Lenore Anderson. He has felt drawn to her from high school, recalling her features, her look. He recalls an occasion when he spotted her on the street in town and she looked straight at him. When she comes to the farm with her father, Kurt can only think of the immeasurable distance between him and the daughter of one of the richest ranchers in Washington. Slowly, he comes to see her interest in him is sincere, but her charm is not enough to keep him from going to war. She agrees to marry him when he returns, but Kurt feels it wrong to place such an obligation on her. His letters to her from boot camp and from the front trace his loneliness, his feelings of not belonging and the conflicting emotions in him. Lenore had told him that he could not kill the German in him by fighting Germans in Europe. On his return, he seems to have conquered his demons, and Lenore's promise to marry him as soon as he can sit up in bed seems to be the catalyst speeding up his unexpected recovery. The novel ends with Kurt and Lenore at the Dorn farm looking out over the fields of blowing wheat.

In Kurt Dorn, Zane Grey explores the immigrant mentality, the conflict of loyalties, the desire to integrate and to prove oneself. It is a new theme, not developed in other novels of a more standard "Western romance" nature.

Dorn, Mrs.: In *Stairs of Sand*, the wife of Frank Dorn, who works for Guerd Larey's freighting company. She is a little woman of middle age, dark like an Indian, with finely serrated skin and sharp eyes and is a passionate gossip. She is eager to spread the word about Ruth Larey running off with the horse dealer, Stone. She has run off with him once before, but this time, they robbed Larey's office. According to her account, when Larey found out, he nearly tore the place down. He was like a madman. Indoors and outdoors he raved and cursed. The Indians ran away and the Mexicans were afraid of him. When Ruth has been rescued by Adam Larey and returned to her home, Mrs. Dorn comes over on the pretext of borrowing some household utensil. She gives Ruth a piece of her mind. Guerd Larey told her husband that Ruth had made a thief of Stone and that he was determined to get her back. She calls Ruth a beautiful hussy, an unfaithful wife, a woman who loves making men mad about her and then flouting them. She concludes that Guerd should ship her naked through the post.

Dot: In *The Dude Ranger*, one of Anderson's cowboys. He and Baldy are not particularly friendly to the Red Rock cowboys, Ernie and Nebraskie.

Downs, Jim: Preacher brother of Joe Downs in *The Spirit of the Border*. Jim also appears in *The Last Trail*.

Jim Downs meets up with his brother, Joe, at Ft. Pitt. He has come in place of another preacher who was to meet up with Mr. Wells and his nieces and proceed to the Moravian mission. Jim has come west hoping to convert Indians, and also to be with his brother, who has been protective of him. Jim is too meek and mild-mannered, not sufficiently aggressive in defense of his own interests. His fiancée, Rose, betrayed him with a womanizing gambler named Jewett. Joe, whose broader experience of women allowed him to see Rose's true nature, tried to warn his brother of her disloyalty but Jim could not or would not see it. Upon his arrival at Ft. Pitt, he admits to Joe that he was right about Rose and regrets not taking his advice.

Through the character of Jim Downs, Zane Grey introduces the question of the role of religion on the frontier and the value of the work of missionaries among the Indians. In later novels, such as *The Vanishing American*, Zane Grey was much more highly critical of missionaries, criticizing, even condemning, their motives and their methods. Joe's teaching exemplifies the contradictions and failures of preachers among the Native Americans.

Before he begins his work preaching, Jim decides he wants to take a different approach to that of Zeisberger and Heckewelder and the other two preachers, Dave Edwards and George Young. These men begin with the premise that the Indian has nothing to teach them. Some of the preachers have not even bothered to learn the Indian language. Jim, however, learns Delaware from the village interpreters and Glickhican, an old Indian chief who has accepted Christianity. From Glickhickan, he also learns about Indian myths and religious practices. This chief is one of Rousseau's "noble savages," a moral individual, who has never lied, or killed, save in self-defense in all his more than eighty years. He speaks of a golden age before the coming of the white man when the Indian lived in peace and harmony with God and man. He is the quintessential romantic "noble savage."

Because of Jim's popularity among the Delaware, Heckewelder organizes a three-day religious festival of sorts at which Jim delivers his first sermon to a huge gathering of converts and hostiles. It highlights the contradictions in the missionaries' teaching. He speaks of the God of the white man, of the mission of the white man to teach the ignorant tribes and bring them to the light of truth. While he tries to establish connections between Indian beliefs and Christian teaching, he ends up condemning Indian customs such as wearing paint, ornamentation, and charms; the dream quest; his belief in spirits inhabiting the woods; and his concept of the afterlife. He acknowledges that many white men are evil and fail to live up to their religion. He asks the Indian to forgive the white man for the sake of peace. When the sermon is finished, a respected chief, White Eyes, stands up and declares he is accepting Christianity. Shortly thereafter, Wingenund, sachem of the Delaware, advises caution. The gifts of the white man ever contained a poisoned arrow. When he can walk to the "big water" without getting shot at, he will believe.

Through Jim, Grey criticizes the Eurocentrism of the Christianity being taught to the Indians. Christianity, it would appear, is not possible in a society that survives by hunting with only a little agriculture. Such a society experiences periods of feasting and famine, at the mercy of the weather and the movement of game. The missionaries use the prosperity and comfort of the Village of Peace as a bait to lure in converts. The fields surrounding the village are full of waving corn and grain, the pens are filled with grunting pigs, cows, and horses. Clearly, the God of the white man has blessed their efforts. The Indians who live in the village have abandoned their Indian ways and labor in the fields and barns and workshops. The hostile Indians regard these converts as belonging to an alien species, having renounced all things that defines their Indian nature.

There is a strong element of Calvinism in Jim's preaching. Several references are made to the prosperity of the village, the abundant crops, the well-being of the converts as proof of God's favor and approval. Implicit is the threat of God's anger if the Indian rejects their teaching.

Jim does, however, make the point that if the Indian is to survive, he will have to change. The technological superiority of the white world will eventually overpower the Indian and his ways. The Village of Peace offers a bridge to the new world, the civilization that will triumph. The converted, Europeanized Indian will walk with the white man as an equal. The Indian must make a place for himself in this emerging civilization by learning new ways. Christianity will be the element allowing the white man and the Indian to become brothers. Simon Girty, one of the renegade brothers fomenting discontent among the Indians, knows that the work of the missionaries can lead to peace on the frontier, an outcome he must prevent if he is to maintain his influence among the Delaware. He provides confirmation of the outcome Jim had spoken of in his sermon.

Wetzel has warned the missionaries that their work is going to lead to a massacre of the Indians living in the village. It would make more sense to abandon the project for the time being, allow the converts to return to their tribes. The head missionaries are unwilling to do that, and the converted Indians themselves are unwilling to return to the old way of life. They prefer to make a grand sacrifice for the sake of the future. The massacre at the Village of Peace is described in language one would expect for Christians being fed to the lions in the Roman amphitheater. Perhaps this sacrifice is necessary for future triumph.

Jim is a pacifist. Unlike his brother, he prefers to turn the other cheek. But as Benjamin Franklin observed about the Quakers of Pennsylvania, they opposed military service themselves, but were quite happy to pay someone else to do the work. Jim does make an effort to solicit help to defend the Village of Peace. He approaches Captain Williamson, a militia leader who has come to the village with a company of men, curious to see what is happening there. He exhorts Williamson to defend these helpless people who cannot and will not defend themselves. He earns the admiration of Jeff Lynn, the grizzled frontiersman, who respects his "spunk." No one, however, is willing to lift a finger.

Jim is married to Nell Downs by the dying Mr. Wells as the couple flee the Village of Peace under Wingenund's guidance. Unknown to Jim, Wingenund is a Christian in private, unwilling to abandon his Indian life, although he, like his daughter, Whispering Winds, has accepted the new creed. Only Wetzel becomes aware of this, when he comes upon Wingenund praying at his daughter's grave.

Through Jim, Grey questions the possibility of living a truly Christian life in frontier conditions. Grey, often described as a social Darwinist, repeatedly questions whether frontier conditions can ever be compatible with civilized values.

Jim also appears in *The Last Trail*. He is now the pastor of the church at Ft. Henry, a position offered to him at the end of *The Spirit of the Border*. He lives with his wife, Nell Downs, who teaches the Sunday school class.

Downs, Joe: Appears in *The Spirit of the Border*. Joe is an early version of a key figure in a Zane Grey novel, the inexperienced Easterner who must learn the ways of the West to become a whole person.

Joe Downs arrives at Fort Pitt in a wagon convoy bringing Mr. Wells and his two nieces, Nell and Kate, to the frontier to work at the Moravian mission at the Village of Peace, the Gnaddenhutten, in the Ohio River valley. Joe has come west seeking adventure, to "hunt Indians" as he says and to get away from the tame life back in Williamsburg, Virginia. Later it is revealed that he got into a fight with a man called Jewett, a gambler and womanizer. Jewett was involved with Rose, his brother Jim's fiancée. Since Jim, a parson, would not act to defend himself, Joe undertook the job of setting things right. He flees the scene of the fight believing he has killed Jewett.

The Joe Downs character embodies one of the favorite Zane Grey types, the "runaway male," the young man who comes to the frontier to seek adventure or to escape the law or adult responsibilities. Joe is in his early twenties. He and his preacher brother, alike enough in looks to be twins, are the only two surviving members of their family. Joe is full of self-confidence, energy, popular with the girls, but not given to thought or planning. He endears himself to Nell Wells, who has grown fond of him on the wagon trip to Fort Pitt, but he has no intentions of settling down and raising a family.

Two characteristics of Joe emerge at Fort Pitt, his thoughtless enthusiasm and his impetuosity. At Fort Pitt, he flirts with Nell, kissing her, and thus leading residents of Ft. Pitt to believe they are sweethearts and sure to be wed upon their arrival at Ft. Henry. He later plays a practical joke on Silvertip, a Shawnee chief, who is at Ft. Pitt to trade furs. Silvertip is sleeping off a bout of drinking outside the trader's cabin. Joe takes his shirt and puts it on the drunken frontiersman, Loorey, who is sleeping at his side. When Silvertip wakes up, he tries to kill Loorey for stealing his shirt. Joe confesses he had switched the shirt. Silvertip, not amused, leaves, swearing to get even.

Joe impresses the frontiersmen at Ft. Pitt with his strength and his eagerness to learn about frontier life. Jeff Lynn, a grizzled, experienced, frontiersman takes a liking to him, understanding his thirst for adventure. He cautions him not to go looking for it, as adventure will surely find him. All the while, Joe's thirst for knowledge of frontier life is insatiable. On the trip to Ft. Henry with the missionaries, he and his brother Joe are taken captive by Silvertip and some Delaware braves. Unlike his brother Jim, who is downcast and disheartened by their fate, Joe appreciates the opportunity to study how the Indians travel, eat, signal to each other with bird calls, and find their way noiselessly through the woods. He tries to imitate their movements but finds he cannot achieve the same noise-free result.

At Ft. Henry, following the rescue by Wetzel, Joe endears himself to the incomparable, veteran frontiersman who uncharacteristically agrees to take the young man under his wing and teach him the survival skills he will need for life on the frontier. In this, Joe embodies another recurring character type in Grey novels, the apprentice. Joe is the Easterner who must give up Eastern ways and adapt to the demands of the harsh frontier environment. Wetzel teaches Joe how to build a fire that emits no light and no smoke, how to track, how to find his way in the forest, how to interpret the signs provided by animal behavior. The flight of crows overhead identifies the location of an Indian camp, the silence of the forest points to an enemy's presence, a trout not rising to a bug on the surface tells that a canoe has passed. Joe impresses Wetzel with his ability to learn, but the lad's impetuosity worries the teacher. On one occasion, when a lone Indian brave takes a shot at Joe, and he, in turn, lays a trap for the Indian, playing dead and luring his enemy into close range, Joe's nervousness and eagerness cause him to shoot wildly, missing his target. Wetzel has to come to the rescue. Later, Wetzel comments that the lad had planned the trap cleverly but needed to take his time, not get excited, nervous. Several months earlier when Wetzel rescued him and his brother from Silvertip, Joe felt sick as he watched Wetzel scalp the dead Indians. Here again, he is disturbed by the sight of the dead brave who had just tried to kill him. The same impetuosity, lack of self-control, lack of self-understanding and sensitivity lead to his own death.

Joe introduces yet another characteristic of newcomers to the frontier in Zane Grey. Life on the frontier engenders a growth in understanding of self, an insight into one's place in society and one's purpose in life. Joe had once told his brother to give up his desire to convert Indians to Christianity and become a hunter of Indians, like him. Following a second capture by Indians, he is saved from the stake Pocahontas-style by Aola, Whispering Winds, daughter of the Delaware Sachem, Wingenund. Aola takes him as her husband, and Joe settles into an idyllic life in the Indian village. Joe discovers he does not hate Indians as much as he thought. Aola reveals she is a Christian and would prefer life at the Moravian mission. She is determined to warn the Village of Peace of the impending attack by hostile Delaware and Hurons. Before they leave, however, Joe decides to attempt the rescue of Kate Downs, who is being held at Jim Girty's "lair." Here he meets up with Silvertip and Jim Girty, and although he does kill the chief in combat, Jim Girty has had the time to murder Kate. While recovering from his wounds as he and Aola make their way to the village, Joe comes to understand how he had overestimated his strength and his ability to survive on the frontier. He lacks the iron constitution of a Wetzel, and the indifference to suffering and bloodshed. His understanding of Indian life and the wilds is clearly deficient. He knows now it would have been better had he taken Jeff

Lynn's advice about not seeking adventure, or had he followed Colonel Zane's advice and remained at Ft. Henry, settling down to farming.

Joe Downs is an early version of John Hare in *The Heritage of the Desert* and Milt Dale in *The Man of the Forest*, Easterners who come to embrace their full humanity through intimate life with nature on the frontier.

Doyle, Al: In *30,000 on the Hoof*, an old friend of Logan's who meets them whey they arrive in Flagg. He tells them about a house that is up for rent. As a young man, Al Doyle had helped build Union Pacific Railroad and the Santa Fe. He had been a pioneer, cattleman, lumberman, teamster and guide. If there was one Arizonan who knew the West well it was Doyle. Recently, he has been guiding geologists and archeologists into the canyon country and hunters down over the Tonto Rim. He tells Logan about the possibilities for making a lot of money selling cattle to the army. After he has sold his thirty thousand head to Mitchell, he goes for a drink with Al Doyle, whom Mitchell and Caddell refer to as a drunkard in their explanation of the swindle. Doyle does his best to support the despondent Huett when the swindle is discovered. He is one of the friends to meet him at the train when he returns from Washington, where he pursued his suit to get his money from Mitchell.

Doyle, Lee: In *30,000 on the Hoof*, the son of Al Doyle. He is hired by Logan Huett as foreman of the outfit that drives his thirty thousand head of cattle from Sycamore Canyon to Flagg for sale to the army. He tells his father, who repeats it to Huett, that rumor has it Mitchell is after his daughter, Barbara.

Drake: In *Wilderness Trek*, rides for Slyter on the trek to the Kimberleys from Queensland. He is middle-aged, honest, and forcible of aspect, strong of build. He works with Heald and Benson. Drake comments that the Slyter and Dann herds have been able to cross the first major river thanks to Ormiston's foolishness, attempting to drive a herd where the banks were too high and the river too deep. The first cattle to wade in and drown, and the following cattle manage to get across walking on the carcasses of the dead animals. Drake suspects Ormiston is up to no good. His drovers prefer not to mix with the other outfits, and he appears to have something up his sleeve. Slyter sends Drake with Rollie and Larry to get ahead of Ormiston and his rustlers. In the fight to recover the cattle, Drake is shot and killed by Herdman.

Drake, Band (see Randall Blue): In *Shadow on the Trail*, the name that Randall Blue uses when he buys a ranch near Holbrook, Arizona, and runs his new rustler outfit in conjunction with the rancher, Lem Mason.

Drill: In *Shadow on the Trail*, always looking for riders, according to Lawsford, but he pays low wages. Brandon considers approaching him to send over some cattle to bait a trap for the rustlers.

Driscoll: In *Shadow on the Trail*, a rancher in the Cedar Range area. He is reputed to razz the devil out of new riders. At one point, Driscoll is nearly cleaned out of cattle by rustlers. Tex Brandon approaches him to send over some cattle to lay a trap for rustlers.

Driver Bill: In *Lost Pueblo*, Mr. Endicott's chauffeur. Endicott tells Mr. Elliott that the story that the Lost Pueblo had been uncovered was phoned in to the newspaper office in Flagerstown by Driver Bill. Elliott treats the news as nonsense, given its source. Endicott confirms that indeed, Phillip Randolph did uncover the pueblo.

Drone: In *Shadow on the Trail*, sells Tex Brandon ten thousand head of cattle. He has been marked by rustlers and is glad to get rid of his cattle, selling cheap. His wife is ill and, in short, he was eager to sell out.

Duane, Buckley (Buck): The last of the Duane dynasty of gunmen in *The Lone Star Ranger* (a.k.a. *The Last of the Duanes*). His is the story of a man who finds himself sought out because of his father's reputation as a gunman and who, although he has never committed a crime, must run from the law. Zane Grey prefaces the novel with an explanation that although the novel is based on an historical figure, he has taken license in his portrayal of the character. Like Wetzel in *The Spirit of the Border*, he is a blend of fact and fiction. As hero of an action story and romance, he exhibits many of the characteristics found in Jack Hare, Dick Gale, Gene Stewart and Lassiter.

In the character of Buck Duane, Zane Grey develops a study of the influence of heredity and environment in the formation of an individual. At twenty-three in Wellston, Buck Duane must live down the reputation he inherits from his father, an infamous gunman, so hard and tough that when he was shot through the heart, he could still hold a gun and fire two shots to kill his opponent. Uncle Jim tells Buck he shares some of his father's bad qualities — a hot temper, and a fighting instinct. Buck is fast on the draw, possibly faster than his own father, having learned from him all the tricks of the trade. He has a hand steady as a rock and a deadly calmness. In his first gunfight, Buck claims that something he is not accountable for compels him. He asks himself if he has any choice. If he is doomed to follow in his father's footsteps. His first killing is in his father's style, with two bullet holes close together at the top of the heart, close enough for both to be covered by the ace of spades. Upon returning home, the reality of what he has done hits home. He will be hunted by the rangers, although he fought in self-defense. He will never be able to return to Wellston or to see his mother.

In his years on the run, Buck Duane learns what it means to be alone, to be able to trust no one, to be unable to settle down for any length of time. He meets Luke Stevens, an outlaw, who gives him some advice about Bland and the outlaws he will meet. In Bland's village, he meets the men Stevens had told him about and appreciates the forewarning he had received. Making friends with Euchre, he finds confirmation in both Stevens's and Uncle Jim's comment that there were decent men among outlaws. Buck plans to rescue Jennie, the young woman Bland had been given by Jackrabbit Benson, who had bought her from some Mexican raiders. In the rescue attempt, he kills Bland and his henchman Chet Alloway. This establishes his reputation as a gunman to be reckoned with, a reputation he already had before he reached the town, but in the eyes of many, he is seen as a good gunman who has rid the country of some vicious criminals. There follow several years of living on the run.

Buck Duane uses his time alone to analyze his feelings and to try to understand the forces that have shaped him. He is prone to violence, to fits of anger and passion. He can no longer appreciate the simple things of life, a woman's love, a good horse, a sunset, a mountain scene. The horse is just a tool to ensure his own safety, nature a possible hiding place to elude pursuers. He concludes that the greatest factor in an outlaw's life is not greed or a desire for fame, but a profound fear of death. Although he dislikes the life he must live, his instinct for self-preservation will not let him commit suicide in a gunfight. He knows also that others see him as coarse, ignorant and bestial, none of which he is. When he has escaped from certain capture in the cottonwood brakes, he comes across a poster promising a reward of a thousand dollars for his capture, dead or alive. He rides into the nothing town of Shirley to find out what he is supposed to have done. He is taken prisoner, about to be lynched for the murder of a Mrs. Jeff Aiken, when a young cowboy, Sibert, and the grieving husband of the murdered woman ascertain that he is not the murderer and set him free. Ranger MacNelly, a rather unorthodox but competent captain leaves messages with all his friends and acquaintances asking him to come to his camp after dark. On Aiken's advice, he accepts Ranger MacNelly's offer to talk. Buck is offered a full pardon by the governor if he joins the Texas Rangers and works as an undercover agent among the outlaw gangs in West Texas. Buck looks on this as a chance to redeem himself.

With this new lease on life, having been redeemed and offered a second chance, Buck discovers another side to himself. He appreciates the joy and companionship of his powerful black horse, Bullet. He finds new interest in the people he meets, enjoying conversation and discussion. He falls in love with Ray Longstreth and dares to dream about life with her and raising a family. He enjoys the beauty of the landscape, and imagines himself as he did as a boy, out seeking adventure. He ingratiates himself with Laramie, the innkeeper in Fairdale, and with Jim Fletcher, his "in" with the Cheseldine gang. He learns about the workings of the outfit, that the name Cheseldine is a front for Colonel Granger Longstreth, a Southern gentleman, mayor of Fairdale, rancher, property owner. By listening to conversations in saloons, eavesdropping on Longstreth and Floyd Lawson, his right-hand man, Buck learns about the gang members and the plans to rob a bank in Val Verde. He sends word to the rangers, the gang is captured and the most powerful outlaw group in West Texas is broken.

Buck is forced to come to terms with what he has become when he decides to face Poggin at the bank. Grey writes: "Long ago he had seemed to seal in a tomb that horror of his kind — the need ... to go out and kill another. But it was still there in his mind, and now it stalked out, worse, more powerful, magnified by its rest, augmented by the violent passions peculiar and inevitable to that strange, wild product of the Texas frontier — the gunfighter. And those passions were so violent, so raw, so base, so much lower that what ought to have existed in a thinking man. Actual pride of his record! Actual vanity in his speed with a gun! Actual jealousy of any rival!" He must fight Poggin to prove to himself he is the faster man. In a scene reminiscent of *Riders of the Purple Sage*, where Jane Withersteen entreats Lassiter not to go after Tull and Dyer, Ray Longstreth entreats him not to fight Poggin. But like Lassiter, or the Virginian, he must meet his destiny. In the gunfight, he kills Poggin and Boldt and Kane. He himself is badly wounded.

Back in Wellston, he is a hero. Uncle Jim worships him like a child meeting his idol, begging to hear about all his adventures. Buck, though, is troubled about his future. Ray Longstreth agrees to marry him. They will move back to her family plantation in Louisiana where they can raise horses and cattle and start life anew.

The presentation of Buck Duane is largely through action, without the depth of development found in Lassiter or in Jack Hare. Nevertheless, Grey has combined his themes of the role of heredity and environment and free will in a memorable character who must choose his destiny.

In *Raiders of Spanish Peaks,* Buck Duane is mentioned as one of the famous gunmen the West has produced. Laramie Nelson is compared to him. In *The Trail Driver,* Buck Duane is mentioned as a gunman of whom his home town in Texas was extremely proud. In *Shadow on the Trail,* Blanco (Wade Holden) is compared to Buck Duane, an unmatched shot, utterly cool and fearless. The aptness of the comparison is seen when Mahaffey acknowledges that Wade Holden has redeemed himself by doing good and clearing outlaws out of the outlaw gang.

In *Knights of the Range,* Colonel Lee Ripple and his foreman, Britt, speculate about whether Arizona will produce its own local gunmen equal to Buck Duane in fame and ability.

In *The Fugitive Trail,* Bruce Lockheart compares the gunman, Vic Henderson, with Buck Duane. Unlike this experienced gunman who is aware of all that is going on around him, impossible to surprise, Henderson gets himself into situations which he does not control, a sure sign of a second-rate gunman. Lockheart knows he has little to fear from him.

In *Boulder Dam*, Sheriff Logan tells Lynn Weston that he is another Buck Duane after the gunfight with the men who had abducted Anne Vandergrift. He adds that Western would make a great Texas Ranger.

Duchess: In *Wilderness Trek*, one of Leslie Slyter's thoroughbreds that successfully makes the trek from Queensland to the Kimberleys in western Australia.

Duke: In *Wilderness Trek*, one of Leslie slyter's prized thoroughbreds that successfully makes the trek from Queensland to the Kimberleys in western Australia.

Duncan: In *Boulder Dam*, the doorman who finds the necessary equipment — such as bed and mattress — for Lynn Weston's cabin at the site housing workers at Boulder Dam.

Duncan, Captain: In *Fighting Caravans*, in charge of the execution of several robbers at Fort Larned. Clint Belmet tries to get information from them about Murdock and Blackstone.

Dunmore, Lord: Lord Dunmore was the military commander of Ft. Pitt. Colonel Ebenezer Zane served under him. Jonathan Zane scouted for him. He is mentioned in all three of the Ohio Valley novels. In *Betty Zane*, he is mentioned as one of the famous guests who had stayed at Colonel Zane's cabin.

Dunn, Arch "Slinger": In *The Drift Fence*, the older brother of Molly Dunn and her closest confident. He is only twenty-one, yet he has killed more than one man. Through many fights, few of them bloodless, he earned his "slinger" reputation. Lack of steady work, drinking, and roaming the woods with Seth Haverly had ruined him. Molly expects that the arrival of young Jim Traft to take over the foreman's job on the Diamond will bring out the worst in Arch.

The Dunns had homesteaded on a hundred and sixty acres some twenty years ago, but they never proved up on the claim. Over half of the claim consists of timberland. For a few years, Arch had plowed the fields and planted beans, corn, sorghum and potatoes. He had spells when he stayed home and worked the farm, but by the end, he had left the harvesting of the crops to Molly and her mother. Slinger feels protective of his family and sister. He and the Haverlys ride into the drift fence construction crew to confront young Traft, who explains fearlessly that the fence is being built to defend his uncle's interests. Slinger's brotherly protectiveness is seen in his defense of Molly. He has heard the stories about Jim Traft kissing her at the party in Flagg. He is concerned about the interest of young men in her ... Hack Jocelyn, and Seth Haverly. She shares with him her desire to marry someone who will rescue her from the Cibeque. Arch challenges young Jim to explain himself and he shoots him, thinking he is defending his sister's honor. Jim keeps this attack a secret. In Flagg, Jim confronts Slinger, telling him the truth about his relationship with Molly, repeating for all to hear that he has asked her to marry him. He beats Slinger in a fistfight, then extends him an offer to come work on the Diamond Ranch.

Slinger Dunn decides to quit the Cibeque outfit when he learns what Seth Haverly, his brother Sam, and Hack Jocelyn have planned. Molly repeats to him what Andy Stoneham had overheard, that these three plan to lay the blame for everything at Slinger Dunn's door. Slinger tracks the group, arriving at the camp where Jim Traft is being held captive just in time to kill Hack Jocelyn and save Jim's life. He settles the score with the Haverlys, who had betrayed him. Jim Traft sends for Dr. Shields in Flag and saves Slinger's life.

In *The Hash Knife Outfit*, Slinger Dunn has accepted work as a cowboy on Jim Traft's Diamond Ranch and later on the Yellow Jacket with young Jim Traft. When the novel opens, he is recuperating from injuries sustained when he fought the outlaws who had taken young Jim Traft prisoner for ransom. Slinger Dunn is a stunningly handsome man with a dark face, smooth bronze skin like an Indian's, and long hair black as the wing of a crow. He is quick with the gun, and an unparalleled tracker. He had once belonged to the Cibeque outlaw gang and Jed Stone had tried to recruit him for the Hash Knife Outfit. Slinger leads the Traft cowboys in pursuit of the Hash Knife Outfit, setting fire to the cabin, capturing and lynching some, killing others in the shootout. Slinger himself is injured in the gunfight.

Like Buck Duane in *The Lone Star Ranger*, Slinger Dunn is a good "bad man," an individual good at heart, but led astray by bad companions and the victim of his reputation. With the proper support, he lives down his reputation and begins a new life, redeeming himself.

In *Stranger from the Tonto*, to impress Bonesteel and the other men with the ferociousness of Kent Wingfield, Ben Bunge reports that Kent had been a member of the Hash Knife Outfit and had fought and almost killed Slinger Dunn in the Drift Fence war.

Dunn, Commissioner: In *The U. P. Trail*, a government official and close associate of Commissioner Allison Lee. He has used his influence to get contracts on the railroad for Lee. He is present at the meeting when Warburton and Lodge inform Lee that they have proof of his dishonest practices and have decided to ban him from receiving any further contracts for the railroad.

Dunn, Jack: In *The Thundering Herd*, a hider whose load of 500 hides is stolen by hide thieves. He and his outfit join up with Clark Hudnall's.

Dunn, John: In *The Drift Fence*, Molly Dunn's father. He is not old in years, but he is in all else. His hair is a dark, shading gray, hanging down over his knotted, pale brow. He is living in the past, broken by some secret association with an infamous war between sheepmen and cattlemen and devoured by passions that had outlived his enemies. Molly tells Jim Traft that her father has lived all his life under a cloud of suspicion because of his involvement with the sheepmen and the Pleasant Valley war.

Dunn, Molly (a.k.a. "Little Wood Mouse," "Snowflake"): In *The Drift Fence*, her character is introduced from the first chapter. She is going to Flag to buy new clothes and shoes. She has rarely left the valley where the Dunns homesteaded. Her father is a broken man and her mother talks of leaving and returning to Illinois. Molly suspects that her mother is jealous of her, given Mrs. Dunn's reputation of entertaining young cowboy lovers. Her aunt and uncle take her to the rodeo and to the dance. There she meets a young man who is not like any of the other cowboys she has met. She is shocked to learn that her admirer is the tenderfoot Jim Traft, the much-talked-about new foreman of the Diamond Ranch and builder of the drift fence that her uncle fears will start a war like the Pleasant Valley war of Arizona. Molly is flattered by Jim Traft's attentions, but she cannot imagine anything coming of the relationship. Her brother suspects that Traft is making fun of her, and Hack Jocelyn and Seth Haverly express their interest in marrying her when the story of Jim Traft's kiss spreads. She is flattered by the presents that Jim sends with young Keech. She is particularly moved by the books he has sent. Unlike Seth or Hack or even Slinger, Jim understands her deepest desire to improve herself and he encourages her. When Andy Stoneham reveals what he has overheard Hack Jocelyn and the Haverlys plotting, Molly decides to save Jim Traft. She tracks her brother and comes upon Jim Traft. She reveals what she has heard, and brings the injured tenderfoot, shot by her brother, the supplies he needs. When Jocelyn and the Haverlys have carried through their plot, Molly goes along with Jocelyn to the cabin where they are holding Jim. She prevents his death by biting into Hack's gun hand. Jim Traft attributes his survival to Molly and her brother. In *The Hash Knife Outfit*, Molly Dunn is now young Jim Traft's fiancée. Jim Traft credits her with saving his life when he was a prisoner of kidnappers. Molly feels insecure and self-conscious, aware that as an Easterner, Jim's family will probably look down on her lack of class. She is studying at school to bring herself up to his social level. She recalls how Jim was a bit of a snob when he first arrived in Flagg. Jim's sister Gloriana, although she is charming and sweet, nevertheless does make Molly feel inadequate and inferior. Consequently, Molly decides to break off her engagement to Jim. She takes a job in Flag working in Babbitt's store as a clerk. She starts flirting with Ed Darnell, Glory's old nemesis from Saint Louis. Gossip begins to spread about her, but at the Christmas Eve dance, she and Jim finally make up. Molly and Glory are taken prisoners by Malloy and Madden of the Hash Knife Outfit and held for ransom. When Jed Stone rescues them, she tells him about Glory's snobbery and condescension, and agrees to go along with Stone's plan to teach her some Western manners. At times, she fears Stone is being too severe, but eventually, Glory is reformed, even offering to stay with Stone if he will let Molly return to her brother. Molly and Jim are married and set up ranching at the Yellow Jacket.

Dunn, Mrs.: In *The Drift Fence*, the mother of Molly Dunn. She is young and good looking enough to be jealous of her daughter. She had come from a station considerably above her husband's, and she was a bitter, unhappy woman. Molly speaks of her claim to come from a Southern family, which probably explains why she fits so poorly into a log cabin. At one point when Molly is lamenting her family's lack of respectability, Mrs. Dunn reveals that her mother was one Rose Hilyard of Virginia, a blueblood. Molly has no cause to feel embarrassed about her family background. Curly Prentiss tells Jim Traft that Mrs. Dunn is reputed to "cock her eye at a cowboy" and Molly herself tells Jim that her mother's reputation as a loose woman is not altogether undeserved. This makes Molly feel that she is not a worthwhile person.

In *The Hash Knife Outfit*, Mrs. Dunn appears briefly at the start of the novel. She is staying at the Traft Diamond Ranch while her daughter is there with young Jim, her fiancé.

Dunne, Jim: In *Sunset Pass*, Nesbitt's foreman on the Half Moon ranch. He came from Wyoming with Nesbitt and his habits are clearly those of a Wyoming cowboy, not those of a Texan or Arizonan. Nesbitt has been hardest hit by rustlers and Jim Dunne is suspicious of the Prestons. Trueman Rock has observed him spying on them from the hills and he observed him one day down around the corrals and cabins near the slaughterhouse. Dunne and several other Half Moon riders come upon Trueman Rock and the three younger boys, Al, Harry and Tom when they are rounding up two-year-olds. Rock makes him examine the brand on all the animals, then tells him the next time he makes an accusation of rustling he had better be prepared to back up the accusation with gunplay. Jim Dunne learns to respect Trueman Rock. Dunne is shot in a gunfight with Ash Preston when the game is up and the Prestons are caught with stolen cattle. Dunne is badly wounded, but survives, thanks to Trueman's help.

Dunton, Jacob: In "Avalanche," Jacob Dunton is a Kansas farmer who moves west after the Geronimo campaigns make it safe to settle in Arizona. He has selected a spot on the Verde River. When they are camped one day, he returns to the wagon to find his son playing with a strange boy. They cannot learn from anyone in the wagon train who his parents or family are, and no one has come looking for a lost child. Many wagon trains in the area have moved on. He decides to raise the boy as his own. Over the years, the two boys become as close as any brothers could be. He intends to divide his ranch and cattle equally between the two of them. When the romance between Kitty Mains and the brothers destroys the fraternal affection they had for each other, he can only stand on the sidelines and hope that they come to their senses. After the famous fistfight at the dance, the boys depart for their secret rendezvous to settle matters. The father is not sure what the outcome will be. When they return in the spring, he is overjoyed to see them. He announces that Kitty was never worth a little finger and has dumped both of them to marry Ben Stillwell.

Dunton, Jake: In "Avalanche," Jake Dunton is the son of Jane and Jacob Dunton. The story of Jake and his brother, Verde, is a retelling of the Greek myth of Damon and Pythias. Jake finds a lost boy one day when their wagon train is camped on the banks of the Verde River. The boy says nothing about his parents, or the wagon train he is with, just mumbling the word "Dodge." Attempts to locate the parents are unsuccessful and the Duntons take the boy in as their own. Jake and Verde are extremely close; their own company is their universe. At twenty-two, he is a lithe, narrow-hipped, wide-shouldered giant, six feet tall, with a rugged homely face like the bark on one of the pines under which he grew to manhood. He has a mat of coarse hair, beetling brows, a huge nose and a wide mouth. But his eyes make up for his defects. They are clear gray, intent, piercing, beautiful. Jake likes hunting best of all work or play. Jake is proficient with rifle and six-shooter as well as with trapping wild animals. Both Jake and Verde are popular with the girls but the arrival of Kitty Mains makes them competitors for her attention. Jake discovers that he and his brother don't talk much anymore, that their old exchanges of confidences have ceased. Jake proposes marriage to Kitty and she accepts, but that very evening, he gets into a two-hour-long fistfight with his brother. To settle the matter, Verde leaves word he will meet Jake in their secret place. Jake goes to their cabin in Black Gorge, their rendezvous for hunting. He expects to meet Verde at every turn in the trail. He is surprised that Verde is not in the cabin when he arrives. A terrible thunderstorm comes up, followed by an avalanche. Jake wonders what has become of his brother. When he goes out to search for him, he finds him caught under a tree. Verde is in bad shape and begs him to put him out of his misery. Jake, however, cannot forget the love he has had for his brother and the love he has received in return. He extricates the unconscious Verde and takes him to the cabin, where he gets the bleeding stopped and sets his broken leg. When Verde revives, however, he cannot disguise the fact that the second leg is badly broken and will soon turn gangrenous. The old, brotherly friendship returns. Helping Verde brings out the best in Jake. Verde tells him he must amputate the leg, and explains how the job is to be done. Jake performs the surgery, and miraculously, Verde survives. They are

snowed in for the winter, but the supplies in the cabin and the game in the canyon prove sufficient. In the spring, Jake makes a sleigh on which to pull his brother. They make their way out of the canyon and back home, where they learn that the "femme fatale" who had brought them to the verge of self-destruction has married another.

Dunton, Jane: In "Avalanche," the wife of Jacob Dunton, and mother of Jake and Verde. When her six-year-old son, Jake, brings a lost young boy home, she takes him in while they make inquiries about his origins. When no word is to be heard of his family or relations, they decide to raise him as their own son. When the romance with Kitty Mains begins, Jane Dunton worries about the boys, who turn against each other in their competition for her attention. She does not interfere, however, hoping and praying they will see the light.

Dunton, Verde (Dodge): In "Avalanche," the adopted son of Jacob and Jane Dunton. They take the boy in when he returns to their wagon with their son, Jake. Attempts to find his parents lead nowhere, so they take him in and raise him as their own. He and Jake are taken with each other, and grow into fine young men. Like Jake, Verde is a rangy, long-limbed, Tonto type, a composite rider and hunter. At twenty-three, he is a few inches shorter than Jake, a bit heavier, but of the same supple, lithe build, fair and curly-haired, ruddy cheeked, with eyes of flashing blue, handsome as a woodland god. Verde was a born horseman, proficient with any of the tasks of the cowhand, without peer in the use of the lasso, the champion bulldogger of the Tonto. Verde and Jake are popular with the young women, often dating the same girls, but never getting serious about any of them. When Kitty Mains comes, however, he becomes Jakes's chief competitor, and the two of them end up in a major fight which leaves matters undecided. The brotherly love has mutated into a passionate hatred. Verde sends word to Jake to meet him at their secret place. Verde is caught in an avalanche, and when Jake finds him, faint with loss of blood and with two badly broken legs, he asks to be put out of his misery. Jake, however, cannot sacrifice the brother he has loved. When Verde regains consciousness, he is in the cabin. Jake has set and splinted one leg, but the other leg has a splintered bone that cannot be fixed. Verde sees in him the brother he wanted those many years ago when he refused to reveal the name of his brutal stepfather because he wanted to stay with Jake, the boy who had befriended him. He advises Jake on how to amputate the leg. The operation proves successful. Verde recovers. Jake cares for his brother over the winter and when spring comes, he makes a sleigh and pulls and carries Verde out of the canyon. Over the winter, the old brotherly love and confidence returns. They come to understand the emotions that had torn them apart, and the nature of Kitty Mains, who had almost destroyed them. Verde hears Jake confess that he always knew Kitty loved Verde better, and Verde acknowledges that Kitty is not the kind of woman to be tied down to a one-legged husband. When they make it home, they learn that the shallow, fickle Kitty has married Ben Stillwell.

Durade: In *The U.P. Trail*, a Spaniard of "high degree" with whom Mrs. Allison Lee runs off from New Orleans in 1850. Durade is a man addicted to games of chance. He uses his "wife" to lure men into his gaming establishment where they are fleeced of their gold. Mrs. Durade comments that Durade has a genius for drawing men to him and for managing them. He is heading east in a wagon train to find Mrs. Durade and Allie when Allie finds her way to the caravan after escaping from the Sioux. Durade does not believe her story that her mother is dead. He wants to get his revenge on her for deserting him. He plans to use Allie for the same purposes as he used her mother. In Benton, Durade sets up his gambling establishment, using Allie to lure men in. In a card game with Place Hough, he loses all his gold and Hough suggests that he will put up all the gold if Durade puts Allie up as prize. In the draw, Hough wins, and takes Allie as his prize. Durade, however, does not accept his loss and sends his five henchmen, Andy, Black, Grist, Dayes and Mex, to take her back. Durade is killed in a knife fight with Warren Neale and Slingerland.

Durade, Mrs.: In *The U.P. Trail*, the wife of Allison Lee, capitalist and later railroad commissioner from New Orleans. As a young woman, in 1847, she was forced to marry him by her family. She abandoned him in 1850, taking with her their newborn daughter, Allie. She runs off to California with one Durade, a Spanish gambler and adventurer. Durade used her good looks and charm as bait to lure men into his gambling establishment. To ensure her cooperation, he would abuse her. Durade was not a victim of gold lust but of games of chance. He loved taking risks, games of chance being his true passion. Mrs. Durade, as she calls herself although she never married Durade, returns east to find Allie's father. Life with Durade in the mining camps had been worse than life with Allison Lee in New Orleans. She fears that Durade will use her daughter as he used her. Mrs. Durade feels guilty about the misfortune Durade has brought to so many miners When the Sioux attack is imminent, she tells Allie the true story of her father. Mrs. Durade is murdered and scalped by the Sioux. Allie witnesses the whole event.

Durade/Lee, Allie: In *The U. P. Trail*, the daughter of Allison Lee and Mrs. Durade/Lee. At the start of the novel, she is on her way back east with her mother to find her real father, Allison Lee of New Orleans. Allie witnesses the slaughter and scalping of the members of the wagon train. When Slingerland and Neale and King find her, she is in a catatonic state, unable to speak. Slowly, the vision of the Indian attack fades and she returns to normal. She stays at Slingerland's cabin, where Neale and King visit her. She teaches Neale how to fish, but she remains

fragile. When she is abducted by Fresno and his three men, she shows spunk and shrewdness in her plans for escape. She tries to bribe Fresno with Horn's gold, and then tries to flee while the men are fighting among themselves over the gold. She is taken prisoner by the Sioux and guarded by an old squaw, but released during the night by a young squaw who is obviously jealous of her beauty. The young squaw shows her a trail through the mountains where, after walking several days without food and water, she comes across a wagon train in which she meets Durade, the man from whom her mother was fleeing. Durade takes her prisoner, not believing the story she tells about her mother's death. He is planning to use her as he had used her mother, as bait to lure men into his gaming establishment. Through Allie, he will get his revenge on the mother. There follow several attempts at escape, followed by recapture. In all this, she retains her love for Neale, the man who had saved her and given her a reason to live after the Sioux massacre. Allie finally gets her freedom from Durade when the gambler, Place Hough, wins her in a card game. She thinks that Neale is in love with Beauty Stanton, and is prepared to lose him. Slingerland visits her in Omaha, where she is staying with Colonel Dillon's wife. He tells her the truth about Beauty Stanton and the confusion that arose at the time of her escape from Durade. Allie and Neale are married the day the last spike is driven on the Union Pacific railroad by the same preacher who had spoken the prayers at the ceremony.

The character of Allie Durade/Lee is similar to Betty Zane, or Nell Downs, or Helen Sheppard, the heroine of a romance. She is frequently a damsel in distress needing the help of the hero to make her way. Nevertheless, she shows moments of great courage and spunk, retaining her goodness and innocence in spite of the circumstances in which she finds herself. Beauty Stanton sees in her the childhood and innocent hopefulness she lost long ago. For Neale, she gives purpose to life, a goal, the possibility of a stable, secure future.

Durland, Bert: In *Lost Pueblo*, one of the reasons that Mr. Elijah Endicott has taken his daughter, Janey, with him on a trip to Arizona. He is a "slick little article" like his social ladder-climbing mother. Endicott wants to see to it that Bert Durland doesn't climb into his daughter's inheritance. Janey tries to coax her father into letting her invite Bert for a visit. She would enjoy going riding with him. Mr. Endicott, however, thinks she will be frightfully bored with him. Janey is thinking more along the lines of making Phillip jealous and letting the cowboys have fun at Durland's expense. When Janey is out with Phillip Randolph at the excavation site, Bert Durland and his mother arrive. Bert is duded up in a ten-gallon sombrero that appears to make him top heavy. He is wearing white moleskin riding pants tight at the knees, high shiny boots and enormous spurs that trip him as he walks. Back east he was the darling of many week-end parties, a slick, dark, dapper young man just out of college. He has his mother in tow. He first meets Phillip and he announces who he is and that he is looking for Janey. Phillip pretends he has never head of him. When Janey appears, she pretends that she is Phillip's wife and that she does not recognize him. Later, she tells him that she has been abducted by Phillip and that he is really Black Dick, the dangerous desperado. Bert insists he was engaged to Janey, and Phillip denies he is married to Janey. The hoax becomes more complicated when the real Black Dick appears and proceeds to rob Mrs. Durland, then makes her fix supper. Finally, the cowboys from the post appear and proceed to rescue Janey from her abductor and pretend to lynch Phillip. Janey makes an impassioned speech pleading for his life because she loves him. Bert Durland is convinced by the speech. He and his mother are to return east on the same train as the Endicotts after the wedding in Flagerstown.

Durland, Mrs.:   In *Lost Pueblo*, Bert's social-ladder climbing mother. She arrives at Phillip and Janey's camp, dressed ludicrously in a riding outfit that is two sizes too small for her. She complains about the ride out through the desert, that Janey is not good enough for her son, and so forth. The Navajo, Ham Face, gets a kick out of teasing her over her being dressed in pants. He tells her that he went to Paris and New York during the war, but for modern-dressed women, she beats them all by a mile. Black Dick tells her that she must be a dreadful parent, allowing her daughter to go around dressed in clothes more suited for a ten-year-old than a twenty-year-old woman. He condemns the pictures in the magazine she has with her. He makes her fix supper, something she has not done in some time. She opens up all the tinned food she has, preparing a smorgasbord that would probably sicken a dog, but Black Dick and Snitz manage to devour everything. She is truly perplexed by the events which follow, the "lynching," the arrival of Endicott and Bennet, and the discovery of her purse, money and jewels intact, hanging from the branch of a tree by the trail. Back at the post, she continues to complain about the ride through the desert. Fearing that Mrs. Durland could ruin her reputation permanently with her gossip back in New York, Janey agrees to marry Phillip in Flagerstown.

Dusty: (1) In *The Thundering Herd*, Tom Doan's saddle horse, purchased at Sprague's post. Tom gives the horse this name because at that time nothing but a full bath could have removed the dust from him. Pilchuck approves of his choice. At the buffalo hunt, Dusty is afraid of the buffalo carcasses and shies away, throwing Tom. Bit by bit, Dusty becomes used to the strange beasts. When Tom is delivering hides to Sprague's post, Pilchuck uses Dusty as his mount while hunting and the horse performs to perfection. He developed into a fleet, tireless steed second only to Pilchuck's best buffalo-chaser.

(2) In *Wilderness Trek*, Dusty is one of the wild cayuses in Texas that Red Krehl recalls when he is in Australia.

Dusty Ben: In *Wildfire*, a huge rangy bay, John Bostril's most faithful horse. He will not even consider giving this horse to his daughter, Lucy.

Dusty Dan: In *The Horse Thief*, one of the Watrous horses that Dale Brittenham recognizes among the stolen horses being auctioned by Reed in Halsey.

Dwire: In "Fantoms of Peace," a prospector in the California-Arizona deserts. He has acquired the habit of silence, having forgotten that life deals shocks to other men. He has met other men during his years in the desert, but has evinced little curiosity about them or their motives for coming to the desert. As a rule, they have come to find graves in the blowing sand. When Dwire allows Hartwell to accompany him into the desert, he does not expect to become friends with the man. Hartwell is the kindest man he has ever met. He takes exquisite care of his burros, always offering water to them before drinking himself. He has a gift for finding water with a dousing stick. Dwire reflects on how the desert affects men. Wild men in wild places, fighting cold, heat, starvation, thirst, and barrenness, facing the elements in all their primal ferocity, usually retrogress, descend toward the savage, losing all heart and soul, becoming mere brutes. But there are those few who become noble, wonderful, superhuman in consequence of the same experience. The desert magnifies what a man is, bringing out in extreme form those innate tendencies. Dwire acknowledges to Hartwell that he has come to the desert to forget a woman he had wronged. Hartwell is there to forget his daughter who was ruined. By accident one day, Dwire gets a look at the picture of his daughter that Hartwell carries in his wallet. It is a picture of Nell Warren, the woman he had ruined. Dwire keeps this news to himself, but eventually he tells Hartwell that his real name is Gail Hamlin. He tells the grieving father that his daughter was never debauched, that the slurs on her reputation were spread by jealous gossips, that she had never been anything but good and decent. The two men are reconciled. They find gold in large quantities, a virtual el dorado, and a pick abandoned there by another prospector. Dwire marks the spot with a pile of rocks. A dust storm hits and the two men sacrifice themselves for each other, pouring water on the sly from one canteen to another. Eventually, they expire, both having found the peace they came seeking in the desert.

Dyer, Bishop: In *Riders of the Purple Sage*, one of the leaders of the Mormon church in Cottonwoods. Together with Elder Tull, he controls the lives of most of the people. Bishop Dyer had been a close friend of Jane Withersteen's father. Many years before, he had gone to Texas preaching the new religion. He worked with a blond bearded, blue-eyed Adonis, Jane's father. Millie Erne was fascinated by the preacher and his friend. Prompted by Withersteen, Dyer planned the abduction of Millie Erne as a wife for Withersteen. Back in Utah, when Millie proved stubborn, he arranged with the outlaw, Oldrin', to abduct her child, in part to have some control over Millie, but also as a final insult to Frank Erne, Millie's husband, should he ever find his wife and child. Dyer hopes that Oldrin' will debauch the girl. Dyer has been a family friend and spiritual advisor to Jane. She had been brought up to believe that he was God's mouthpiece, that God spoke in secret to this man. He makes his first appearance in the novel at WitHersteen House when he comes to censure Jane for conduct unbecoming a Mormon woman. She plans to raise Fay Larkin without giving the child Mormon teaching. She has refused his order that she marry Elder Tull. As well, she is said to have taken on Lassiter, the gunman and gentile, as a hired man. When she tells him that she has taken him on to keep him from learning the truth about the abductors of Milly Erne, Bishop Dyer acquiesces. Jim Lassiter had come into the building during this conversation, and when Dyer sees him, he draws his gun, only to be shot in the arm by the much more adept gunman. This episode causes Jane to think about her allegiance to Dyer. The man scarcely seems like a man of God. He comes into her house without removing his hat. He dresses like any rancher, booted, spurred, covered with dust, carrying a gun which he has been known to use. The episode tells Lassiter that Dyer is the man he is looking for. Bishop Dyer appears again when Lassiter seeks him out after Fay is abducted. Dyer is presiding over a court convened to prosecute the gentile boys who had helped Judkins tend to Jane WitHersteen's herds. As the court is dealing with young Willie Kern for diverting water from an irrigation ditch, Lassiter appears and Dyer draws on him. Lassiter gives him numerous opportunities to back down but Dyer's hatred drives him to keep shooting until Lassiter does fire a fatal shot.

Dynamite: In *The Rainbow Trail*, a gray mare, a mustang. When Withers and the group make camp for the night en route to the Navajo village, the mustang kicks, rears, and falls into the fire before finally calming down.

Dyott, Bing: In *The Deer Stalker*, a former member of the Hash Knife Outfit and partially reformed outlaw. He works with Settlemire, a rancher who opposes the removal of cattle from the lands designated as parkland for wildlife such as deer or buffalo. Bing Dyott and his men come to the cabin in the wilderness into which Patricia and Sue have wandered by accident. In the morning, Dyott discovers a woman's glove outside and women's footprints. He fears he had been overheard discussing plans to disrupt the deer drive with another unnamed man. When the drive is underway, Dyott and his men are around, but not interested in driving the deer to new pastures.

E

Eagle: In *Wanderer of the Wasteland,* the name the Indians of the desert have given Wansfell, Adam Larey. Adam had great admiration for the eagle, keen of eye, soaring above the desert and the world. The eagle knows the freedom and independence that Adam longs for.

Earp, Wyatt: In *Shadow on the Trail,* sheriff of Tombstone in its heyday, he witnesses the encounter between Holden and Monte. He comments that he doesn't like Texas gunmen around his town.

Eburne, Thad: In *The Deer Stalker*, works as a forest ranger at the ranger station, V.T. Park. Thad has sacrificed himself to the cause of forest conservation. In her letters, his mother complains that he has not been home in years. His parents are getting old and she would like to see him. She talks of moving to a warmer climate, perhaps California, so she could see her son once in a while. His father is retired from active business, and his sister is to be married at Christmas. She complains that he has not married. Blakener, his fellow ranger, tells him he should get out of the job when he's still young. He has an education and could get work anywhere.

Thad first sought the ranger life to regain rugged health, but that being accomplished, he never returned to his New England home. Life in the open had always been his dream and the West claimed him. He was past thirty. His ambition had been to work himself up in the service to the point where he could travel from one national forest preserve to another, fostering his ideals of conservation. But that had long since become only a dream. His very love of wild animals, his antagonism to the killing even of wolves and wildcats, and especially cougars, had incurred the enmity of his superiors in the service. Besides that, he had fought the building of roads, and the overtures of lumbermen and miners who would have exploited the beautiful preserve for their greedy ends. There were cattlemen too, who hated Eburne for sternly holding them to their prescribed grazing permits. Graft had not worked with him, and men of little brief authority found him a tough nut to crack. For these reasons he had remained merely a ranger, and had been advised that even his present situation was none too secure.

The deer have multiplied in the park and, unless something is done, thousands of the animals will starve in the coming winter. There are several alternatives open to the ranger service: grazing by herds belonging to cattle companies can be strictly eliminated from public land; hunting of greater numbers of deer can cull the herd to sustainable levels; or deer can be moved to other ranges. The greatest problem of all is that the bureaucrats in Washington and the inspectors and agents on whom they rely have no knowledge of deer, their grazing habits, their reproductive cycles, or the role of predators in keeping the herd healthy and within reasonable size. Men like Cassell and Judson are more interested in their careers, their power base in the organization, than in conservation.

Eburne questions the wisdom of many decisions taken by these uninformed government agents. They hired Jim Evers to kill predators, such as wolves and cougars, with the result that the natural predators that culled the sick and weak from he herd, keeping it healthy, no longer play their role in the natural cycle. Cattlemen have been allowed to graze on the land supposedly reserved for deer, a practice that should be ended. Cassell orders him to use "deer traps" to catch animals so they can be moved elsewhere. Thad Eburne gives the traps a fair trial, but the deer captured are so frightened that they injure themselves terribly and have to be put down. His friend, McKay, suggests that they try a roundup and cattle-style drive, to move thousands of deer from their present range across the Colorado to new pasture. Most think the idea is foolhardy, but then, the same was thought about moving wild buffalo until Buffalo Jones showed it could be done. Eburne does his best to sell the proposal, and finally it is approved.

Eburne knows that the solution is to leave the forest and deer to nature, without roads, cars, men, cattle. Let nature take care of the deer. But he knows that is not possible, because governments appear to be made up of the same kind of men as those who live off the range. They want to run things to suit themselves, and each set of men, ranchers, cattlemen, prospectors, and hunters, changes things according to their idiosyncrasies or personal desires.

Sue Warren speaks of Thad Eburne to Patricia Edgerton, an eastern fashion model at the El Tovar resort. She tells her that Thad is an educated man from New England, a man dedicated to the cause of conservation. He is tall, dark as a Navajo, slender, strong, with piercing eyes that would make a liar tell the truth and a woman fall in love with him. He helped her cowboy friend, Nelson Stackhouse, go straight, and found him a job as guide at the El Tovar resort. When she finally meets Thad, when he rescues them from Bing Dyott's gang, she is taken with him and invites him to visit her at the resort. He eventually makes the trip, intending to propose marriage to her. Clara Hilton tries to turn him against Patricia with stories about how she is a model with a scandalous past, probably out to make a fool of him. He retains his faith in Patricia, however, punching the lights out of a New York broker, Erroll Scott, a former suitor and spiteful loser. He promises that he will be like Nelson Stackhouse in his relentless pursuit of Sue Warren. When the attempt to move the deer herd ends in disaster, Thad returns to pursue Patricia, and this time she accepts him.

Thad Eburne is a Zane Grey hero like Wetzel in *The Spirit of the Border*, or Milt Dale in *The Man of the Forest*. He has been formed by nature, has remained rooted in the earth and the cycles of interdependence that maintain the balance of the natural world. He believes that man reaches his greatest spiritual depth when he resigns himself to nature and her influence, thereby acquiring truly human values.

Eckersall: In *The Vanishing American*, the government farmer at Copenwashie. His job is to teach the Navajo how to adapt to white farming techniques. He is an old westerner, down to earth, not given to hyperbole. He treats the Navajo with respect and fairness. In the winter following the end of the war, he predicts that things will be bad on the reservation. The summer has been dry, and there is not much hay. What hay there is is owned by Friel, who demands an exorbitant price for his alfalfa. He and Marian Warner do what they can to provide hay for the Navajo farmers.

Edd, Juniper: In *The Wolf Tracker*, the star rider for Barrett. He is present when Brinks brings in Old Gray's hide to show them that he has killed the predator. He is impressed by Brinks and his account of the pursuit of Old Gray.

Edgerton, Patricia (Clay): In *The Deer Stalker*, a world-famous, glamorous model, who goes west looking for a change. Like Carley Burch in *The Call of the Canyon*, she is adrift. She wants to be alone where she will see no one and where no one will see her. She knows that there will always be people who will be curious about her. She is deeply moved by the landscape around El Tovar. "It was as if some stupendous monster, alive, merciless with age-old knowledge, had lain in ambush for her, suddenly to strip bare the truth of her heart, the love of beauty, of life, of love, of mystery, of the physical in her and the spiritual that glorified it." She writes to her friend Alice from the hotel, telling Alice that she had come to hate her social group, that idle, luxurious, childless, dancing, drinking crowd. She never had the courage to rebel before to seek what she really wants: a man, children, work. She has had insight into herself. She feels that in the presence of the majestic monuments of nature, she will find herself. A short time ago, life seemed a thing of complete indifference to her. Now it seemed something to cherish. She becomes friends with Sue Warren, a young woman from Flagstaff. Sue has visited the canyon on eight occasions, and is good friends with a young cowboy who works as guide. Sue tells her that Thad Eburne helped set Nelson, the young cowboy, straight, but that if she wants to learn more about him, Clara Hilton claims to know him well. Clara thinks highly of him although she makes fun of his love for deer. Nelson and Tine, the guides from El Tovar, take her and Sue on an excursion into the mountains. They spend the night in a cabin, sleeping in the loft, while a group of seeming outlaws are camped down below. Sue gets away and returns with Thad Eburne, who clears up matters with Dyott. Patricia is smitten with Thad and invites him to visit her at El Tovar.

After the adventurous trip to the north rim with

Nels, Tine and Sue, she formulates her plans for the summer. She will establish El Tovar as her base of operations, then will arrange visits to all the major tourist sites in the area: the Petrified Forest, Monument Valley, Montezuma's Well, Natural Bridge, Rainbow Bridge. She requests that Nelson Stackhouse organize the trips, with Tine Higgenbottom. Sue will accompany her as well. Patricia also commissions Nels to scout around Flagstaff for an available ranch. She wants to live permanently in the area. At the back of her mind, she is interested in getting Sue and Nelson together, and to have him manage her ranch. When Thad proposes marriage to her, she refuses, but does not give a reason, although she tells him she is not married or divorced or anything of the sort. Patricia puts up the money to pay for the Indian cowboys who will help out on the deer drive.

When the snowstorm puts an end to the attempt to save the deer, Patricia learns that Nelson has found an appropriate ranch for her purposes near Flagstaff. Nelson will run the ranch for her. She accepts Thad's proposal of marriage.

Patricia Edgerton is a heroine developed along the lines of Carly Burch, Madeline Hammond and Georgie Stockwell. These wealthy women are tired of the decadent, pagan life of the East and are seeking a life with true values. Zane Grey repeats his theme that the West provides that environment where true human values are fostered and appreciated, where a meaningful, truly human life can be enjoyed.

Edmunds, Old Bill: In *The Horse Thief*, the stagecoach driver who drops Edith Watrous and Dale Brittenham off at Dale's cabin on the return to Montana from Idaho.

Edwards, Dave: One of the missionaries at the Village of Peace in *The Spirit of the Border*. Like George Young, he is hitting forty, and is ugly, and awkward around women. He has a robust, square build, a heavy face and a manner that in most men would suggest self-confidence. Edwards is the first to propose marriage to Kate but she rejects him.

Dave Edwards is put in charge of the mission when Heckwelder and Zeisberger are away, traveling among the Indian tribes, soliciting help to defend the village. Edwards shows himself to be courageous and steadfast. The day of the massacre, he begins to preach as usual and is the first to be shot by the hostiles. Heckewelder manages to remove the bullet from his shoulder and his survival is assured.

Elbert: In *The Mysterious Rider*, quarrels with Buster Jack over cards at Smith's (Folsom's) place in Elgeria. He cheated at cards and when challenged, he went for his gun and shot at Jack. He missed. Jack shot him and three days later, Elbert dies.

El Capitán: In *The Light of Western Stars*, the nickname given to Gene Stewart after his success with the federal forces in the Mexican Revolution (1910–1920). He commands great respect on both sides of the border. He led the forces which took Ciudad Juárez from Porfirio Diaz. In a later skirmish at Madera where the rebel forces are defeated, he is taken prisoner and sentenced to death. Because he was such a brave soldier, he is given a special honor. The day of his execution, he is released into the village square, free to walk around. He will be shot by a sniper at some point in his walk. The day scheduled for the execution, he comes out the door of the prison, dressed in his military uniform, and walks around the plaza. To his surprise, he finds Madeline waiting for him with news of his pardon.

Elkins, Steve: (1) In *Nevada,* reports back in Lineville that he saw Nevada (Jim Lacy) in Hammell, California.

(2) In *Raiders of Spanish Peaks,* one of the prisoners in jail with Tracks Williams. He is freed when Laramie and Lonesome break their friend out of jail. He, alone, bothers to thank them for the rescue. He also comments that Sheriff Dodge is reputed to go off half-cocked, and they had better get away fast.

Ellerslie, Herb: In *Twin Sombreros,* an old partner of Brazos Smith. Tom Don reports that he was killed in Dodge, shot by the gambler, Cardigan.

Ellerton: In *Wyoming,* one of the young men in whom Andy Bonning's sister, Gloria, is interested. Andrew comments that marrying him might not be interesting but she would be well taken care of.

Elliott, Bill: In *The Spirit of the Border* and *Betty Zane*, deserted from Ft. Pitt during the Revolutionary War with the Girtys and spent his life among the Indians, inciting them to violence against white settlements. He votes to destroy the Village of Peace and participates in the massacre.

Elliott, Mr.:   In *Lost Pueblo*, works at the New York museum which had commissioned Phillip Randolph's archaeological expedition to Beckyshibeta to uncover the Lost Pueblo. He has arranged to get Phillip fired as he wants to get credit for the discovery himself. When he gets the word at the newspaper office in Flagerstown that Randolph has discovered the site, he pooh-poohs it as nonsense. But when Mr. Endicott tells him that he can vouch for the veracity of the report, and that he is writing Dr. Bushnell, head of the New York museum, and Jackson, corroborating Randolph's discovery, Mr. Elliott decides it would be in his best interest to rehire Randolph and submit to his overseeing the excavations. He asks Endicott not to mention his having fired Randolph to Bushnell and Jackson.

Ellsworth: In *The Thundering Herd*, a frontiersman scout for the cavalry officer who comes to the hiders' camps ordering all women to be taken back to a post for protection. Milly Fayre overhears him talking with Captain Singleton. Ellsworth tells the captain that the hide hunters have started what will inevitably lead to an Indian war. He compares this rush to the killing fields to the gold rush of '49 in California-outlaws, ex-soldiers, adventurers, desperadoes, tenderfeet, plainsmen, pioneers— all looking to make quick money. It is fertile ground for thieves who prey on the ignorant and inexperienced outfits, killing them, stealing their hides, and making it look like the Indians have done the deed.

Elm, Landy: In *Horse Heaven Hill*, a young cowboy who works for Stanley Weston. He is the son of a farmer and went to school with Stanley. Landy is a young blond giant, a fine horseman, an industrious sober fellow who has recently married a Wadestown girl. He is appointed foreman of the ranch after Howard is fired. Like Stanley and Lark, he dislikes the rounding up of wild mustangs to sell for meat. With Stanley, he helps organize the camping expedition for Marigold Wade's friends. Landy spots the trap in the blind canyon into which Hurd Blanding will drive the mustangs. When the captured horses have been freed and Blanding comes into the Wade camp to accuse Stanley and Lark of having "stolen" his horses, Landy spots Blanding going for his gun and calls out a warning to Stan. Landy proves to be the loyal friend and foreman needed on the Weston ranch.

Elsing, Bill: In *The Last Trail,* brings word about the horse thieves' activities at Yellow Creek.

Elway, Bill: In *Stranger from the Tonto*, a prospector following his sixth sense in his search for gold in the desert. He is convinced he has uncovered the trick the Yaqui used to locate gold. He is accompanied by Kent Wingfield. Elway finds his way through the desert by instinct and that same instinct tells him that on this trip he is going to die. He advises his companion to take Jenester, his best mule, and go back to Wagontongue. He cautions the young man that his fiancée will have deserted him. Elway says there is a lot of bad in Nita Gail, that he saw her and Joe Raston kissing the night before they set out on this expedition. She is the kind of woman who needs a strong man around to keep her straight. Maybe he has been wrong about Nita, but in case he is right, Elway has a mission he would like Wingfield to undertake for him. Elway tells him the story of his life, how he had been a member of the Hole-in-the-Wall gang for many years. He asks Kent to find the hideout and rescue Lucy Bonesteel from her confinement in the canyon. Elway had been Bonesteel's right-hand man until the younger man Slotte, a daredevil caught the boss's eye. Slotte turned Bonesteel against him. Slotte spreads stories that Elway frequented Indian trading posts and Arizona towns, gambled and drank, was hell on girls. They fought and he shot Slotte, leaving him for dead. He fled the hideout and came to Wagontongue. He has heard that Slotte is still alive, but has not dared to return to the hideout. There were twenty men in the outfit and three women, one being Bonesteel's wife. She was a good woman from a good family and when she learned her husband was the leader of the notorious outlaw gang, she did not live long. Bonesteel worshiped the child. He never allowed her to be with other women unless he was there. When the outfit went on long raids, he left Lucy carefully guarded, a job he once performed. Elways says he taught the girl all he knew just as Bonesteel, an educated man, had done before him. The child is unaware that her father is an outlaw, but now being seventeen at least, she will become increasingly attractive to the unscrupulous men. He also asks Wingfield to kill Slotte, if in fact he is still alive. Slotte will inevitably split the gang, killing Bonesteel to get Lucy. He must be stopped. Elway adds that one of the secrets of the Hole-in-the-Wall is that there is gold aplenty in the canyon. Old Bill gives Kent directions to find the canyon, and orders him to leave. Kent will not leave the old man to die alone, and within a day, Bill Elway dies. Shortly after that, Kent finds the wash of gold for which Elway was looking. He collects nuggets as large as eggs, and sets off for Wagontongue. Events unfold pretty much as Elway had predicted: Nita was unfaithful, and so he pursues his mission to rescue Elway's former protégée, Lucy.

Elwell, Snake: In *Majesty's Rancho*, a rosy, cherub-faced young man, one of Madge Stewart's crowd at the university in Los Angeles. He is best friends with Rollie Stevens. He has been engaged several times to Beulah Allen but they have broken off the engagement. They do so again at the ranch. Lance Sidway comments that Beulah is not being fair to Snake. He tells her he does not appreciate her flirting with him when she knows Snake is in love with her. He doesn't want her to get a fight started between them because he likes Snake. He's not flashy. He's a diamond in the rough. If Beulah loved him enough to get engaged to him, she should show him some respect by not flirting with other men.

Ema: In *The Great Slave*, the mother of Siena, the chief of the Crows who leads his people to the shore of the Great Slave Lake.

Emerson (Ralph Waldo): In *Boulder Dam*, mentioned by Lynn Weston as an example of a human mind attempting to fathom the mystery of life and existence.

Emerson, Jake: In *Thunder Mountain*, the second of the Emerson brothers. He, too, has spent much of his life prospecting with little to show for his efforts. He is impressed with Sam's discovery but is not enamored of the valley, which he says will he hot as hell in summer and cold as Greenland in winter since the mountains on both sides virtually obliterate the sun. He is outvoted by his younger and older brothers. He is given the task of negotiating a deal with a mining company in Boise or Challis, to sell the claim for a minimum of a hundred thousand dollars. He has a sample of the ore to display to the miners. Lee and Emerson calculate that their trip will take much longer than anticipated, so Lee goes to fetch the supplies alone while Jake proceeds to Boise. Jake is attacked and robbed. He describes the man who attacked him and Lee identifies him as Selback, the man Leavitt had guarding his cabin and whom Lee shot shortly after he arrived back. Jake had been struck on the temple and was out of his head for several weeks. An old man named Wilson took him in until he returned more or less to normal. Jake is still pale and weak when he returns to Thunder Mountain. To establish his knowledge of the area, he describes the cabin he had built, and the location of the beaver dam and of Sam's claim. Leavitt argues that he had found the claim abandoned and no sign of Sam was to be seen. The miners' court finds in favor of Leavitt, the expected verdict, since Leavitt is the head honcho of the camp. Jake takes up a claim of his own, waiting for things to develop or for some sign of Sam to be found. He has little luck with his claim. Later, he joins with his brother, Lee, in the project, hunting deer and elk to provide meat for the camp. Lee offers him a partnership in the ranch he plans to buy in the valley they passed through en route to Challis and Salmon. When the landslide puts an end to the boom town, Jake and Lee leave to buy the ranch at which they stopped on the banks of the Salmon River.

Emerson, Lee (Old Montana, Kalispel):

In *Thunder Mountain*, known principally by the nickname Kalispel given to him in Montana. He is the youngest of the three Emerson brothers, who make a remarkable gold strike at Thunder Mountain, Idaho. The Emersons are from Missouri. Lee grew up on a farm there. His mother died when he was little and his father married again, but Lee did not take to his stepmother. At fourteen, he ran away from home, joining a wagon train. In Laramie, he got into a fight and left the train. He spent ten years cowboying throughout Wyoming and later in Montana. He rode for the hardest outfits on the ranges. His quickness with a gun often got him into trouble. At age twenty-seven, following a shooting scrape, his brothers Jake and Sam, who had been prospecting in Montana, catch up with him in the nick of time. Otherwise, the wild streak in him would have brought about his downfall. His serious blunders, his shooting scrapes, would surely have made an outlaw of him. What he longs for is a little ranch with cattle and horses of his own, a wife to keep him straight, and chance to realize the promise he knows he possesses. But he never can save a dollar. His several attempts to gather a herd of cattle lead to questions he could only answer with a gun. And all the girls he had been attracted to had led him into trouble. Always willing to help out someone in need, he makes their troubles his own. In this he resembles Buck Duane, Arizona Ames and many other cowboy heroes in Grey's novels.

What impresses Lee about the valley is not so much the gold find as the beauty of the natural surroundings, the effects of sunlight on the scenery, the game, and the stream. It strikes him as paradise. With his brother Jake, he sets off for supplies. En route to Salmon, he spots the Olsen ranch near the Salmon River and decides he wants to buy the place to set up ranching. He goes to Salmon while Jake heads to Boise to negotiate a deal with a mining company to buy the claim. In Salmon, his concern

for others gets him into a scrape defending one Sydney Blair, a young woman fighting off Cliff Borden, who is trying to enter her hotel room. He tries to help her father out, warning him about Pritchard, the gambler, and offering to take him and his daughter back to Thunder Mountain. He tells them about the gold strike, thinking that they can make a fortune and get a new start.

Back at Thunder Mountain, he discovers a tent city with miners galore. Gambling dens, saloons, the typical elements of a bonanza mining town have already been set up. He tries to learn what happened to his brother, Sam, but the claim has been taken over by Rand Leavitt, the boss, it seems, of this new town. Hoping to bide his time until Jake returns or until he learns what has become of his brother Sam, he builds himself a cabin. When he is building his fireplace, he finds an incredible vein of gold. He keeps his find a secret, digging at night, and building the cabin during the day. His cabin is located on a hillside dominating the valley, so Lee can keep watch on the goings-on in town.

Lee and Jake establish a business providing meat for the town. They hunt deer and elk and sell the meat to customers, from individual miners to groups of miners and restaurants. The business proves more profitable than some of the mining claims. It also enables Lee to keep his finger on the pulse of gossip around town. The miners come to respect his honest dealings. The most important of these is Sheriff Masters, a Texan elected to the post by a majority of miners over Leavitt's disapproval.

Lee becomes the principal opponent of Rand Leavitt, the town leader and one of the men who had jumped his brother in Challis. Lee's reputation as a gunman has preceded him. He meets with Hank Lowrie, a "sheriff" he had trouble with in Montana. As well, he and Leavitt are rivals for Sydney Blair's affections. Sydney finds Leavitt attractive because of his suave good looks and his manners. She is easily fooled by him. He is such a contrast to Lee, whom she calls a strange mixture of knightly chivalry and baseness. Leavitt also takes advantage of her father's penchant for drink and gambling, selling a useless claim that he has "spiked" with gold to fool him. Eventually, Leavitt attempts to turn the miners against Lee by spreading the rumor that he is a thief. He organizes a vigilance committee which arrests Lee and takes him before a court. Jones and Matthews, two of the Leavitt faction, testify that he is the man who robbed them. Sydney Blair, however, counters their evidence saying that Lee was with her at the time these men claim they were attacked and robbed.

Lee's stay in the valley is a series of scrapes where he tries to help someone. He saves Blair's father from his own stupidity, exposing Pritchard as a cheat at cards. He retrieves the money Leavitt had stolen from him, giving it to Sydney to prevent him from losing it again gambling. He tries to make Sydney Blair see what Leavitt is really like. Nuggett tells her that Leavitt cheats women and abuses them, but she suspects this is just Lee's way to discredit his rival for her affections. Eventually, she does see through his charming pose. Lee helps Dick Sloan, a young miner, by rescuing Nuggett (Ruth), his sweetheart, from virtual enslavement working in Cliff Borden's saloon.

Lee Emerson's dream finally does come true. When Thunder Mountain punishes the excess of the mining camp, wiping out the worst element in a landslide, Lee, Jake and Nugget, whom he has married, leave for the Salmon River, where they buy Olsen's ranch. They redo the cottage and settle in for the winter. Kalispel now has all he dreamed of, money to acquire the spread and a wife to keep him straight, and the beauty of nature to soothe his spirit.

Emerson, Sam: In *Thunder Mountain*, the oldest of the three Emerson brothers who come to the remote valley by Thunder Mountain prospecting for gold. As Tomanmo, the Indian chief had predicted, gold is discovered, a rich strike. Sam has been prospecting all his life. Of the three brothers, he knows the most about prospecting. He made strikes in the past, but failed to reap the benefit of his discovery as others rushed in and laid claim to the most profitable digs. This remote valley makes him think that their rich strike can be kept secret until they register their claims and get the jump on other prospectors, who will inevitably flood the valley. Like Tomanmo, he foresees a time when the slope of the grumbling mountain will slide down, obliterating the valley. He agrees to remain behind at the digs while Jake leaves for Boise to register their claims and Lee goes to Salmon to get supplies. When Lee returns, he finds a tent city and prospectors galore in what had been an uninhabited valley. There is no sign of his brother Sam, or of their claim. Rand Leavitt has taken the claim that Sam had begun to dig. He tells the miners' court, when Jake Emerson returns to challenge his claim, that he had found the claim abandoned. Lee is not absolutely sure that Sam did not wander off, prospecting elsewhere. Eventually the truth emerges. Sheriff Masters learns from Jones or Matthews that they had killed Sam at Leavitt's instigation. And true to his prediction, the valley is almost filled in when the slope of Thunder Mountain slides down, virtually obliterating the city that had grown up at its foot.

Emery, Jess: In *The Maverick Queen*, co-owner of the Leave It Saloon with Kit Bandon. He is a cardsharp, cattleman, speculator, a "snake in the grass." Lucy Bandon tells Lincoln that Emery and his crew will ambush him and kill him. That's the way they operate. True to form, Emery hires Gun Haskel to shoot Lincoln. The dying gunman confesses to Lincoln and other witnesses that Emery had sent Sealover to hire his services. When Kit decides she wants to go straight and move out of South Pass, Emery threatens to reveal things she would prefer to keep hidden. He tells Kit about Lincoln and Lucy, setting her on their trail to the cabin. Emery himself has proposed marriage to her, but Kit has refused

him. Lincoln wonders why Kit seems so anxious for him to kill Emery in a gunfight. When his creditors put the squeeze on him, he loses the Leave It Saloon. He does not take their advice to leave South Pass as quickly as possible. He is suspected of being involved in crooked cattle deals with Kit Bandon. The fateful night the vigilance committee takes Kit and Emery, they strike a deal with him to set him free if he confesses to crooked cattle deals with Kit. The ranchers let him go, but the cowboys catch and hang him from a cottonwood. Before she is executed, Kit tells Lincoln that it was Emery that shot his friend Jimmy Weston. Jimmy was threatening to expose Kit and Emery if she did not consent to marry him. Emery killed Jimmy in his sleep.

Emery, Tom: In *Raiders of Spanish Peaks*, Harriet Lindsay's only sweetheart. Back in Sandusky, Ohio, she had formed an attachment for a handsome clerk in her father's store. It was her only romance, an unhappy one. Her father's estimate of Tom Emery was justified and Harriet was left heartbroken. She withdraws in secret sorrow, feeling that she wants nothing more to do with men.

Emihiyah: In *The Great Slave*, the daughter of the Cree chief, Baroma. Her name means a wind kiss on the flowers in the moonlight. She falls in love with Siena, the young Crow chief whom her father has enslaved. Siena goes to Baroma asking to marry her, but the haughty chief refuses. When starvation threatens the Cree and the Crow slaves, she brings Siena meat during the night, against her father's orders. She begs Siena to save the Cree. Siena agrees to take the gun only he knows how to use, and he kills enough moose to save the tribes from starvation. When Siena and his people leave, she follows them, dressed in the silver fox and marten coat the Crow chief had given her. Siena takes her as his bride and they move north to the shores of the Great Slave Lake.

Endicott, Janey: In *Lost Pueblo*, Elijah Endicott's daughter. She is twenty years old, acts like fifteen and dresses like ten. She has had all the benefits that wealth and education can bring. After college, she traveled in Europe. Then there followed the usual round of golf, motoring, dancing and all that went with them. She was well aware that her father did not approve of her lifestyle, but he never interfered with her ways of being happy. This trip, however, seems more purposeful than others. They are to meet Phillip Randolph, a young archaeologist, in Flagerstown. She likes Phillip, although he seems somewhat old-fashioned and does not approve of her crowd. She recalls that her father seemed quite taken with him. At the post in the desert, the young cowboys are taken with her as men everywhere have been, but she is surprised when Ray, the most outspoken of the five cowboys at the post, tells her that western men consider her way of dressing, her smoking, hardly lady-like behavior.

She overhears her father and Phillip planning an

"abduction" to teach her a lesson. Phillip will arrange for her to go off with him on an archaeological dig. He is looking for a lost pueblo. The close proximity may spark romance, and Janey might marry a real man of principles. Janey decides to go along with the plan and turn it to her advantage and make fools of Phillip and her father. She proves to be of little help camping. She can't cook; she makes a nuisance of herself when he is digging. She goes wandering off into dangerous places. At one point, Phillip takes her over his knee and spanks her. Janey, however, does make a vital discovery one day. She finds steps cut into the side of a cliff, and when she climbs to the top, she discovers the entrance to a pueblo. She finds what she thinks is a kiva. She keeps the secret to herself, hoping to surprise Phillip with proof of her usefulness.

When the Durlands appear, she tries to play a joke on them, unaware that she herself is the target of a prank. At first, she pretends she does not recognize Bert Durland, then tells him she is Mrs. Phillip Randolph. When Phillip denies they are married, she tells them that Phillip is really Black Dick, a notorious desperado in the area, and that he has kidnapped her. The "real" Black Dick appears with his associate, Snitz, and the two of them proceed to lecture Mrs. Durland on her way of dressing and on the poor job she did raising her daughter. Janey enjoys seeing the Durlands' discomfort. When the cowboys arrive to rescue them, and make like they are going to lynch Phillip, Janey makes a passionate plea for his life, declaring that she loves him. When her father arrives, announcing that he had planned the whole thing to give Janey a scare, Janey feels her reputation has been ruined. Mrs. Durland will surely spread lots of gossip about her back home. She reveals to Phillip where she found the entrance to the pueblo, and sure enough, it is the site he has been looking for. Janey agrees to marry Phillip to protect her reputation, secretly vowing she will get a divorce at the first opportunity. In Flagerstown, she meets the real "Black Dick," who tells her he had been hired by her father. She expresses her disappointment as she had thought she had met a real desperado. She in turn hires him to kidnap Phillip and put him on the train east. Phillip had been planning to stay at the dig while she returned east. That, however, might lead Mrs. Durland to suspect that the marriage was a hoax. But by now, Janey has realized that she is truly in love with Phillip and she wants the honeymoon.

Janey Endicott is a study of a female character type developed in several Grey novels. She is the modern woman, the product of a civilization that has lost its bearings—like Georgiana Stockwell in *Code of the West* or Lenta Linsay in *Raiders of Spanish Peaks* or Majesty Stewart in *Majesty's Rancho* or Carly Burch in *The Call of the Canyon*—who must learn the true values of a mature woman and abandon her frivolous, superficial ways.

Endicott, Mr. Elijah: In *Lost Pueblo*, a well-preserved man of sixty, handsome, clean-cut, a typical New Yorker, keen, worldly, kindly. He has come west with his daughter to get her as far away as possible from civilization. His daughter has become too modern. She drinks, she smokes, she dresses in a scandalous fashion and the crowd she hangs out with makes him despair about the nation's youth. With the help of Phillip Randolph, he hopes to teach her a lesson. Things don't quite work out as he planned, as a storm blows up and the cowboys cannot follow them across the swollen rivers. The situation, however, works out even better than he had planned. Janey discovers the entrance to the lost pueblo and she tells Phillip. Mr. Endicott uses his influence to get Phillip reinstated in his job at the museum. Phillip and Janey are married, and Janey discovers that she really does love the "square peg" who didn't match the round hole, as her friends used to say.

Erne, Elizabeth: In *Riders of the Purple Sage* and *The Rainbow Trail*, the full name of Bess. She is the daughter of Frank Erne and Milly Lassiter. See **Bess**.

Erne, Frank: In *Riders of the Purple Sage*, the husband of Milly Erne and father of Bess (Elizabeth Erne). All information about Frank Erne is provided by Lassiter when he tells Jane Withersteen about his past. Frank Erne was a preacher who competed with other young men for Milly's attention. Milly had always been strong on religion and Frank Erne won her heart. Lassiter, not exactly a religious man, struck up a great friendship with his brother-in-law. He loved him like a brother. Although a man of the cloth, Frank Erne could ride, hunt, and fish like a regular man. He worked at ranching as well as at preaching on Sundays. He once saved Lassiter's life when buffalo hunting. He was the only man Lassiter considered good enough to marry his sister. Lassiter goes off for several years and upon his return, Frank Erne is a ghost of his former self. It seems Milly had fallen under the sway of a Mormon preacher and Frank Erne had denounced him and had him driven out of town. Shortly after that, Milly disappears, most believing she had run off with the new preacher. But not Frank. Returning to the ranch after a year on the trail of Milly's abductors, Lassiter finds Frank in a pathetic state. Like a mad man, he sits on the porch, whittling. Lassiter suspects he knows more than he tells. His farm has gone to weeds, and the house has become so weathered it won't keep out the rain. Lassiter finds papers in a little drawer with letters from Milly to Frank, telling him about the birth of their daughter and asking Frank not to come looking for her and to keep Jim (Lassiter) from pursuing her. She says she wants to stay with the man she had come to love and will not be heard from again. Frank Erne dies of a broken heart.

Erne, Milly: In *Riders of the Purple Sage*, the sister of Jim Lassiter. He comes to Cottonwoods to speak with Jane Withersteen who, he has been told, can tell him where Milly Erne is buried. Jane Withersteen is surprised at the request. Indeed, Milly

Erne had been her closest friend. She promises to take him to the site where she is buried, there on her ranch. It is a hidden spot, known only to her. Bern Venters tells Lassiter what he knows about Milly. She had been in Cottonwoods years when he arrived. He got to know her pretty well, but most of what he knew about her he heard from others. She was a tiny woman, crazy on religion. He was never sure whether she was a Mormon or a gentile, but she had the Mormon woman's locked lips. She had a daughter when she first came to Cottonwoods, and she lived for the child. She was not known as a Mormon wife, but Venters is convinced that she was a sealed wife to someone. Eventually, Milly gave up her job teaching the village school and she quit the church. She began to fight Mormon upbringing for her child. Shortly after that, the child disappeared. That wrecked her. Jame Withersteen was her only friend, but Jane could not mend her broken heart. Milly died, pining for her daughter. Jane Withersteen undoubtedly knows the whole story, but a hot poker could not get her to speak of it.

Lassiter tells Jane Withersteen about the Milly he knew as a sister. She was always crazy about religion and when she married Frank Erne, she set about trying to save his soul. While Lassiter has nothing but admiration for his rancher/preacher brother-in-law, the finest man he ever knew, he quickly tires of his sister's attempts to convert him. When he returns after some two years wandering from Texas to Nebraska, years in which he became an unparalleled tracker and gunman, he finds that Milly is gone, and Frank Erne is a ghost of his former self. Milly, he learns, had fallen under the influence of a charismatic preacher of a new religion. Frank Erne was very open-minded about religion and did not object to his wife's attending prayer meetings and sermons, but when he learned that the new preacher was a Mormon, he had him driven out of town. Shortly after that, Milly disappears one night when Frank is away from the ranch. Everyone, including her mother and father, believe Milly has run off with the new preacher. Frank and Jim, however, do not believe that to be the case. Jim Lassiter trails her, finding the house where she was held prisoner, where she gave birth to her daughter. In a letter he finds in a small drawer in Frank's house, he learns the names of the men who abducted his sister. He finds them, and kills them without learning anything more about Milly's whereabouts. Eventually, he is given Jane Withersteen's name. She can probably tell him something about his sister. Lassiter figures out that Bishop Dyer was the young missionary who lured her away from her own religion, but Jane Withersteen eventually tells Lassiter that her father was the man for whom he had had her abducted.

Eschtah: In *The Heritage of the Desert*, the chief of the Navajo who live on the Painted Desert near August Naab's ranch. He is a good friend of the Mormon patriarch, August Naab, and grandfather of Mescal. He has three wives, an old woman about his own age, a middle-aged woman, and a young wife with a child. He is a Navajo version of the noble savage, like Wingenund in *The Spirit of the Border*. He is tall, thin but strong, a man of exceptional wisdom and dignity. He has reached the age where more time is spent in meditation than in action. He speaks little and thinks a lot. He is close to the earth, to the environment which has shaped him. One night, Jack Hare watches him with Mescal and sees a harmony between them and the desert land that is comforting.

Eschtah first appears when Naab and his family are returning to their ranch from White Sage. Jack is introduced to him when he is sick; Eschtah predicts that Jack will become a strong man. Despite his age, he is a man of exceptional strength and endurance. Jack is struck with admiration for him as he watches the Navajo cross the Colorado River. August Naab comes to Eschtah for help in finding Mescal when she has run away rather than marry Snap. Eschtah agrees to provide some of his best trackers to help in the task. Eschtah understands Mescal's thinking better than Naab does. When weeks of tracking yield nothing, Eschtah accepts without emotion that the desert has called her. This is one of those things that was meant to happen. The blood of the Navajo and the blood of the white man cannot successfully mix. She is with her tongueless peon who can smell water in the desert and follow a trail over rock better than anyone else. She is answering the call of destiny. Eschtah also takes this opportunity to comment on white society from the Navajo's point of view. The white man is never content with life as it is. He believes in progress. Jack Hare learns from Eschtah that the Navajo learn from nature, accept its teaching and do not try to change nature to suit man's whims.

Later, when Naab has decided that he must take action against Holderness and the outlaw gang, he goes to Eschtah for help. Eschtah lectures Naab with irony that the white prophet, despite his gift of prophecy, had not been able to foresee this outcome. Naab has brought this difficulty on himself since he refused to take action at the proper time. Naab has allowed evil to grow and prosper, evil which he could have stopped. Eschtah promises that he will give Naab four days to settle the matter before he comes to White Sage to give help.

Eschtah embodies the noble qualities Zane Grey admired in the Indians of the Southwest. They live in harmony with the natural world. They have rejected the corrupting influences of white civilization. They enjoy a harmony and peace the "civilized" East can only dream about. Naab's ranch is found in the "Garden of Eschtah."

Esperanza, Don: In *The Lost Wagon Train*, a successful rancher in west Texas like Maxwell, and Latch, who has made his home a welcoming spot for Indians, wagon trains, settlers, and outlaws.

Ester: In *The Heritage of the Desert*, one of August Naab's daughters. She reports that Mescal's buckskin clothes are gone from her room and that her wedding dress is untouched. No indication is given of her age or rank among the children of August Naab.

Etenia: In *The Vanishing American,* first mentioned as an Indian who salts his wool to increase its weight when sold in bulk to the trading post. Nophaie asks him to stop this dishonest practice and he complies. He is a wealthy Indian and offers Nophaie his daughter as a wife. When Nophaie refuses, he accuses Nophaie of being Indian in body but white in spirit. When the missionaries and reservation management are trying to remove Wolterson, the agricultural consultant, Etenia is proposed as a favorable witness to attest to his good work and approval among the Navajo. When Nophaie helps Gekin Yashi flee the school, Etenia promises that no Nopha will betray Nophaie to the authorities, but cautions that the Noki who work for the reservation management will not be reliable. Etenia predicts that Gekin Yashi and Nophaie will marry. When war breaks out, he is annoyed at the process of registration and is deceived by Blucher's anti–American, pro–German propaganda. He does not understand why the Navajo cannot be left to volunteer to fight if they so desire. He feels they are being unjustly driven to war and he has no feelings one way or another for the Germans or the issues in the conflict. Nophaie convinces him that Blucher has been spreading false stories about the war effort and Etenia comes over to his side and helps convince young Navajo men to enlist.

Euchre: In *The Lone Star Ranger,* an outlaw living in Bland's village. He was a friend of Luke Stevens and recognizes his horse when Buck Duane rides into the village. He knows Buck is telling the truth when he reports how Stevens wanted to die with his boots off. Euchre is old, with grey hair, and is almost bald. His eyes are so wrinkled that they appear half-shut. He prefers running from a fight to shooting. He invites Buck to stay at his place while he is in Bland's camp. Buck detects in him something kind and eager, traits he saw in Stevens. He concludes there is decency among outlaws too. Euchre says he has only done rustling, not killing, and only stole from rich ranchers who never missed the cattle he took. He is a quiet observer and commentator. He knows a lot about everyone in the camp. He proclaims himself a champion and partner of Buck Duane. He explains outlaw psychology to Buck, confirming some of his own conclusions. Euchre is a good friend to Jennie, the young woman that Bland took in to protect from the other men, but who is badly mistreated by Bland's jealous wife, Kate, who refers to him as a tender-hearted old fool. He helps Buck plan his escape with Jennie, preparing the horses and mules. Before he leaves, however, he goes to settle a score with Benson, killing him in a draw. He himself is shot by Chess Alloway, Bland's right-hand man, in the shooting that erupts when Bland arrives on the spot. Bland is shot by Buck Duane.

Evangeline: In *The Vanishing American,* a three-year-old prodigy. Her Indian mother was glad to get rid of her and gives her to the missionaries to raise. She speaks only English and hates to be called Indian. She is round-faced, black-eyed, very Navajo in appearance. She says her prayers and behaves like a white child. Evangeline is given as an example of a child raised by missionaries who has been taught to despise her Indian background.

Evans: In *Valley of Wild Horses,* brings supplies from Marco out to Bill Smith's place when they are preparing to leave for Siccane, Arizona.

Evans, Jesse: In *Shadow on the Trail,* the foreman of Jesse Chisum's outfit number ten. Chisum sends Blanco (Wade Holden) to work with him. Evans agrees that Holden is the best rider Chisum has ever hired. Jesse is twenty years old, a towheaded cowboy with steel-blue eyes, lithe and bowlegged. He was famous for many things but most notorious for his past friendship with Billy the Kid. Wade develops great respect for Jesse Evans. He sums Wade up perfectly one day when the cowboys are teasing him about how he keeps to himself. Evans describes his job as close to cowboy heaven, but admits he wants to get back to drinking and gambling dens and painted women. Evans tells Blanco (Wade Holden) about Billy the Kid, his old partner. They parted when he refused to go along with Billy's outlaw tendencies. However, he maintains his faith in the Kid's integrity. He introduces Billy to Blanco when he arrives with word that Mahaffey has come to Chisum's ranch asking about him. Wade regrets leaving, but there is no alternative. Evans was about as good a friend as he could hope to find.

In *Knights of the Range,* a slightly different picture is given of Evans. He is mentioned as a gunman, a rival of Billy the Kid. He and Billy manage never to have to shoot it out by avoiding places where the two of them might meet. Evans is said to have accepted that Billy was his superior on the draw.

In *The Fugitive Trail,* Jesse Evans is Bruce Lockheart's model of a Texas cowboy. Bruce thinks he could probably fool Maggard, the Texas Ranger captain, by acting and dressing like Jesse Evans, friend of Billy the Kid and right-hand man to Jesse Chisholm. He is dressed in ragged cowboy garb and looks the part. There is a zest and devil-may-care defiance in the pretense.

Evarts, Jake: In *To the Last Man,* a neighbor of Gaston Isbel. He looks after the flock of sheep that Gaston Isbel keeps. His son met Jean Isbel the day he came into Grass Valley and gave him directions to the Isbel ranch. Jean describes him as a burly, grizzled man with eyes reddened and narrowed by much riding in wind and dust. Gaston Isbel meets him on the way to attack the Jorths in Greaves's store. He rejects Evarts's offer to help in the fighting and tells him that if he does not survive the fight, the flock of sheep are his. Evarts later repeats to John Sprague what Ted Meeker tells him of what happened in the store, when Greaves repeats what Jean said before he stabbed him.

Everall: Cal Bain is over at "Everall's" in *The Lone Star Ranger* when Buck Duane comes to town to face him. Perhaps this is a store or a saloon of some sort.

Everett: In *Majesty's Rancho*, president of the university which Madge Stewart attends in Los Angeles. He decides to expel her for her latest escapade, starting a riot, given that she is already on probation. Madge's friends go to "Mad Everett" to put in a good word on her behalf, but he is adamant. In her meeting with him, Madge says nothing to defend herself, but accepts his decision without protest.

Everett, Bill: In *The Wolf Tracker,* the range hand who first spotted the spectacular, huge grey wolf. He called him an old gray Jasper. The name stuck, but eventually, as the story spread, the Jasper part got dropped and the loafer was called "Old Gray."

Evers, Jim: In *The Deer Stalker*, one of Thad Eburne's few friends. He had once been a Texas ranger and later a predatory game hunter for the government. He and Thad had seen each other frequently when Evers was hunting cougars along the canyon rim. Jim now manages a herd of tame buffalo that his old friend, Buffalo Jones, gave him, along with a pack of hounds. He and Thad discuss the problems of overpopulation in the parklands. He sums up the gossip he has heard, that the government wants to open up the park to hunters to control the deer population. He also mentions McKay and his proposal to have a cattle-style drive to move deer across the Colorado River to empty grazing and forest. He has his doubts that deer could ever be herded and driven like steers.

Ewell, Stan: In *Boulder Dam,* the Oregon State right tackle who collided with Lynn Weston in a crucial football game. He is Carewe's nephew. Stan tells his uncle that he caused the collision and that Lynn Weston never clipped anyone.

F

Fairchild, Charlie: In *Horse Heaven Hill,* one of the cowboys that Lark Burrell meets at her first dance in Wadestown. She found Charlie very likeable.

Farlane: In *Wildfire,* one of the riders hired by John Bostril to look after his horses at Bostril's Ford. Farlane is an older man, experienced in training horses. Lucy says that every hair on Sage King talks to him. He knows how his employer loves his horses and he knows how to humor him. He reports that he observed Lucy and Joel Creech racing, and that Lucy won. When Lucy is to replace Van, who has been thrown by the Sage King and laid up for a few days, Farlane gives advice on how to handle the horse. Throughout the story, Farlane hears gossip about Slone, Cordts, and Joel Creech and reports it to Bostril when he feels it is appropriate. He, like Hawk Holley, questions Bostril's motivations in stalling the ferry across the Colorado to prevent Creech from bringing his two horses across for the race. He understands the petty streak in his boss, but does not condone it.

Farnum, Dustin: A Broadway actor who starred in the stage production of *The Virginian*, is mentioned by Madeline Hammond in *The Light of Western Stars*. Madeline's concept of the West and of cowboys is based on the stage adaptation she saw of Wister's novels. Dustin Farnum was a popular actor of the time, and many took his costume to be representative of the true West.

Farrell, Charlie: In *Sunset Pass,* one of the two Farrell boys. The Farrells and the Prestons are friendly and the girls stay with the Farrells or the Winters when they are in Wagontongue. Charlie Farrell is sweet on Alice (Allie) Preston and takes her to the masquerade ball. He and she are engaged when Gage Preston leaves Sunset Pass.

"Fat Party": In *Robbers' Roost,* a Mormon that Jim Wall and Hank Hays meet on their way to Green Valley. He cheats the young boy who runs the ferry across the river out of his fare by taking one horse on the ferry and letting the other horses in his string swim along behind the raft. Jim Wall and Hank Hays play a trick on him to reward him for his meanness.

Fay: In "The Camp Robber," the name Pegleg Smith gives to the young girl born to a woman he found by the trail. He had taken her to his cabin where she gave birth, only to die a few days later. As it turns out, Fay is the daughter of Lex Wingfield, the cowboy who tracks Pegleg from the cabin on Stimpson's ranch where the payroll has been stolen.

Fayre, Milly (Mildred): In *The Thundering Herd,* the seventeen-year-old stepdaughter of Randall Jett. Milly grew up on a farm in Missouri. She has little recollection of her father, who went missing during the war. When Milly was sixteen, her mother married Randall Jett, only to die several months later. Having no relatives, she was left in Jett's care. Jett had been away for long months hunting buffalo but abruptly returned with a new wife. Milly was then taken along to the buffalo hunt. At Sprague's store, she meets young Tom Doan, who shows her courtesy she has not known. She is drawn to him and dreams of meeting him again.

In Jett's camp, things do not go well. Milly must cope with the jealousy of Jett's new wife and with the drunken propositions of Jett himself. To her joy, she meets Tom Doan accidentally one day and the two of them arrange to meet at night. They agree to marry when she turns eighteen and will no longer be under Jett's guardianship.

One day when Milly has climbed into a tree to escape from a buffalo bull, she overhears a conversation between one Ellsworth and a cavalry officer who stop beneath the tree. They are discussing the hide hunters at work in the hunting fields, men who profit off the effort of others and then try to put the blame on Indians. This sets Milly to thinking about the unusual way that Jett and his men work. Tom Doan tells her about the episode with Pilchuck, when he caught Jett skinning a buffalo he had shot. She is convinced then that Jett is a thief, a fact which explains the odd behavior of the men and the Jetts. Milly does not understand why this buffalo hunt is needed. It is a crime against nature, an orgy of greed and waste. She tells Tom about her disgust for the process, and asks him to give it up. She will not marry him until he does.

Milly is taken to Sprague's with the other women by the soldiers. There, she shares a room with Sally Hudnall. She hopes to stay there until Tom returns to marry her, but Jett and company arrive several days earlier and take her off, this time disguised as a boy to get past the military checkpoint. The return to the killing fields brings even greater trouble. She speaks with Catlee, who seems willing to help her. He tells her he was surprised to learn that she does not like Jett. He had always assumed that she did not mind Jett's advances to her, since she never protested. In the fighting that breaks out, Catlee makes sure nothing happens to her. She learns that his true identity is "Sam Davis," a former member of the Younger gang. She manages to drive her wagon back to Sprague's, through a buffalo herd and across rivers. At Sprague's, she is received by the Hudnalls. She settles down to wait for Tom to return. She becomes the schoolteacher in the growing town. She and Tom are married and buy a farm near Sally and Burn.

Milly Fayre is a heroine in the same vein as Betty Zane and Sue Melberne in *Wild Horse Mesa*. She is young and innocent, but spunky. She manages to drive a wagon back to Sprague's from the buffalo hunting fields, crossing rivers and making her way through a buffalo herd on the move. She proves herself a heroine worthy of the hero, Tom Doan.

Felix: (1) In *The Call of the Canyon*, one of the Mexican herders who work for Tom Hutter.

(2) In *The Wanderer of the Wasteland*, a Mexican laborer working at the mill in Picacho. He draws a knife on Juan Arallanes, the foreman of the mill. Adam comes to Arallanes's rescue and throws Felix around. Felix prowls around, waiting for him in ambush, particularly annoyed because Adam is interested in Margarita, Arallanes's stepdaughter. Margarita is afraid of Felix and asks Adam to kill him. Fourteen years later, when Adam returns to Picacho, he learns from Merryvale that Felix had killed Margarita, stabbing her to death.

Fenner, Jim: In *Wyoming*, Nick Bligh's right-hand man. He has been with him for many years. Jim Fenner is from Arizona. He threw in with Bligh not in hope of profit but because he and his wife liked Nick. They have had a hard time since Jim was crippled and could no longer do a regular cowboy's work. Fenner thinks Andrew Bonning has potential as a cowboy. Andy tells him about the conversation he overheard between Texas and McCall. Jim readily accepts the truth of the story. He understands well the gamble that Bligh has undertaken, moving from Randall to Split Rock. He discusses with Andy the ways in which Bligh could increase his herd and make his ranch a profitable operation. He himself had worked for the Hash Knife Outfit and still carries some of their lead. Jim takes Andy under his wing and teaches him to ride, to rope, to herd and track cattle. In short, he turns him into a true westerner. He also teaches him to shoot a rifle. When Andy is arrested for disturbing the peace at the rodeo, he offers to vouch for him with Sheriff Slade. When he and Andy come upon Hall Pickens branding a maverick, Fenner starts to hang the thief, hoping to scare him into revealing the identity of other rustlers. He points out to Andy that in Arizona, lynching thieves on the spot was the only way to curb the plague of rustling once it got started. Jim Fenner also discerns that Martha Dixon is in love with Andrew, although she pretends that she hates him. He gives fatherly advice to the young man. Andrew Bonning first reveals to Jim the fact that he has some money put aside to invest in a herd.

Fenner, Sue (Mrs.):   In *Wyoming*, Jim Fenner's wife. She undertakes to fix up the living room of Bligh's house as a bedroom for Martha when she arrives.

Fenton, Mr.:   In *The Shepherd of Guadaloupe*, the father of Richard Fenton, childhood friend of Virginia Lundeen. He lends her ten thousand dollars and approves of her plan to buy Don Lopez's flock. There is money to be made in sheep. He also tells her that he always liked her, recalling how he used to watch her and Dick playing together. He thinks Cliff is an excellent choice of husband.

Fenton, Richard (Dick):   In *The Shepherd of Guadaloupe*, an old friend of Virginia Forrest's. He meets her in New York when she disembarks from the Berengaria and takes her to the train station. He is on the train all the way to Las Vegas. He disapproves when Cliff Forrest gives Virginia a book with some of his favorite poems to read. Back at Cottonwoods, he proposes marriage to Virginia, as he has heard that her father plans to marry her off to Malpass. Later, after Virginia has been thrown out of her home and is staying at a hotel in Las Vegas, he meets her for lunch and arranges for her to meet his banker father to arrange financing for herself. He also tells her what happened to Cliff, that he is now working as a shepherd for Don Lopez.

Ferguson, Elsie: In *The Call of the Canyon*, a school friend of Carley Burch who has not been part of her crowd since her marriage. Unlike Eleanor Harmon, Beatrice Lovell and Geralda Conners, Elsie has married a middle-class man and has dedicated her time to raising her family. She lives on Long Island and rarely makes it into Manhattan. Elsie has been ostracized by the group who feel she no longer belongs. Carley envies Elsie's life. She has a family — a baby boy and a little girl. She leads a purposeful life, devoted to her husband and children. Carley envies her, and finds she now has more in common with this outcast than with the "in crowd" she is part of. Elsie is the kind of wife that Glenn Killbourne would want.

Field, Broom: In *Fighting Caravans,* an outlaw in the same league as Blackstone and Murdock.

Filler: In *Betty Zane*, invites Betty Zane to go on a sleigh ride. Betty had been in a depressed state of mind for weeks, not having heard from Alfred Clarke. He drives her and Wetzel to a party at the Watkinses'.

Fire: One of the Shawnee chiefs involved in the attack on Ft. Henry in *Betty Zane*. He is reputed to be a close confederate of Simon Girty. He initiates the tactic of firing flaming arrows at the fort, hoping to set the roofs on fire. Fire is killed in the fighting and at the end of the battle, his body lies on the ground in front of the fort.

Fisher: In *The Dude Ranger*, once worked a homestead near the Red Rock Ranch. All that is left is the cabin.

Fisher, King *see* **King Fisher.**   The spelling of the name and the use of first name and last name varies in the novels. The full entry is found under King Fisher, the most common spelling and arrangement.

Five Plumes: In *The Thundering Herd,* the Indian who came into possession of Hudnall's rifle after Nigger Horse's son was killed. Five Plumes, too, was killed. The Indians came to believe that whoever had Hudnall's rifle would be killed. The weapon was bad medicine.

Flannigan: In *Thunder Mountain,* runs a saloon and gambling hall where Blair has a miraculous stroke of luck at cards.

Flemm: In *Majesty's Rancho*, a mobster who arrives at Bolton (El Cajón) with Honey Bee Uhl. Flemm holds a machine gun on the cowboys while Uhl negotiates the purchase price of the hoses with Sloan. He mistrusts Lance Sidway and tells Uhl that there's something unreliable about him. Uhl was convinced Sidway had been part of Cork's outfit, having misunderstood his reason for being in Douglas some months back. Flemm is knocked unconscious by Sidway when he enters the cabin at Cochise's hideout to rescue Madge. Flemm is later shot by Ben Starr when Stewart and his riders come to help Sidway capture the gangsters.

Flesher: In *The Lone Star Ranger*, a rancher outside of Wellston whose cattle have been rustled, obliging Sheriff Oaks to be out of town the day Cal Bain calls Buck Duane out.

Flesher, Luke: In *30,000 on the Hoof,* the young cowboy who brings word to the Huetts in Sycamore Canyon that war has broken out with Germany.

Fletch: In *The Drift Fence*, the cook of the Haverly-Jocelyn outfit that kidnaps Jim Traft. He first spots Hack Jocelyn coming to the camp with Molly Dunn behind him. Like Matty, he is released from the cabin by the angry Slinger Dunn and he makes his departure as quickly as Matty had done.

Fletcher, Hal: In *Horse Heaven Hill*, a friend of Coil Bruce's. Coil describes him as a truthful fellow and vouches for the accuracy of his report. According to Fletcher, Hurd Blanding has been telling all around town that Stanley Weston had slugged him for making comments about Marigold Wade, his fiancée. He insinuates that Stanley Weston has ample cause to be jealous of him, that Marigold has been double-crossing him. He hints at secret meetings with Marigold and amorous "successes" with Stanley's promised bride.

Fletcher, Jim: A fair-haired, mustached member of the Cheseldine outlaw gang in *The Lone Star Ranger*. He meets Buck Duane in the saloon when he first arrives in Ord and gives him the name "Dodge," since he can get so little exact information out of him. As well, any stranger in Ord must be an outlaw on the run. Duane says it's as good a name as any. Fletcher scrutinizes him like a hawk. Sometime later when Buck Duane reveals to him he knows that Longstreth is Cheseldine, Fletcher becomes more friendly, offering to speak to the gang to request he join them. He is prepared to vouch for him with the gang, calling him his partner. Phil Knell, one of the senior members of the gang, feels that Jim Fletcher is too open, too friendly with strangers. Knell himself thinks he has seen the tall stranger before, and eventually puts the name Buck Duane on the face. He shares his reservations with Cheseldine and the gang at the valley hideout. When Fletcher does bring Buck Duane to the group, he apologizes to Duane for the poor reception he is getting, and after the gunfight in which Duane kills Knell, he helps Duane escape. He is an example of the decent outlaw, like Luke Stevens.

Flick, Boyd: In *The Drift Fence,* a member of the Cibeque outlaw gang. He is in on the plot to cut the drift fence, to rustle cattle from the Trafts and to kidnap young Jim. Flick is sent with the ransom note with orders to deliver it to Traft himself or to Blodgett or the banker, Tobin. Before he leaves on his mission, he comments to his Cibeque partners that allowing Hack Jocelyn into their group has been its ruination. Curly speculates that Boyd will figure out that the kidnapping has gone amiss and will skedaddle with the money. Jim thinks not. Boyd Flick rides into camp with the ransom money but is glad to get rid of it. He and the surviving members of the Cibeque depart, apologizing for their part in the game, revealing that Jocelyn had fooled all of them as to his true intentions. The last heard of Boyd Flick is when he brings back word to Jim from Mrs. Dunn that Molly is fine and Slinger is on the mend.

Flinty: In *Knights of the Range,* a cowboy from Nebraska working for the Ripple outfit.

Flo: (1) In *Western Union,* a saloon girl working at Red Pierce's establishment in Gothenburg. She is in on the secret of Ruby's rescue by Shaw and Cameron, but keeps quiet. Pierce later sets up in South Pass, and Flo is brought west to work there. She tells Cameron and Shaw about Red Pierce abducting Ruby the night of the Indian raid in Julesburg. Pierce kept her at the Atlantic but has now moved her to the new saloon and gambling hall, the Gold Nugget. She explains the note Ruby left saying she was married. She feared that Pierce would shoot Vance in the back. She reveals that Pierce is the man responsible for sabotaging the telegraph line. His real name is Bill Howard, and he is currently planning a big bank robbery in South Pass. Flo has received an offer of marriage from a man called Jim, a young miner. She feels she is not worthy of him, but decides to marry him anyway.

(2) In *Wilderness Trek,* Nan Halbert's best friend. Sterling had flirted with her and word got back to Nan. To punish him, Nan took up with his cousin, Ross Haight, with tragic consequences.

Flying Cloud: In *Fighting Caravans,* a chief of the Utes given the seat of honor at Maxwell's right at the dining table. Flying Cloud has a magnificent bearing but he is not handsome. His head is shaped like a hawk's. Rumor along the border has it that he has massacred more than one caravan, but no definite proof has ever been brought forward. It is an accepted fact that he will never attack one of Maxwell's caravans.

Flynn: In *Boulder Dam,* the foreman in charge of hiring workers for work at the Boulder Dam construction site. He is impressed with Lynn Weston's work and arranges for him to work at different tasks, each more important and demanding than the previous one. When Lynn has foiled the plot to sabotage the dam, Flynn digs up a "real" job for him.

Follonsbee, Hank: In *The Thundering Herd,* a member of Randall Jett's hide-stealing operation. He is a tall, spare man with an evil face, red from liquor and exposure. He appears to have Jett's confidence. Follonsbee feels contempt for Catlee, calling him a Missouri farmer, unaware of his true identity. Mrs. Jett is the first to call Follonsbee a "hide thief." Mrs. Jett has a particular dislike for him. He tells Jett that he has a poor way with Pruitt, and with people in general. Follonsbee joins Pruitt in his rebellion against Jett when he learns that Mrs. Jett, the Harden woman, is running the show and planning to cut them out of their share of the profits. He has been told the true story of their relationship by a man he

knows at Sprague's outpost. He and Pruitt kill Jett and the wife, and plan to divvy up the remaining outfit, sharing Milly between them. Catlee kills Follonsbee in the shooting that ensues.

Folsom, Captain *see* **Smith in *The Mysterious Rider*.**

Folsom, Speed: In *Boulder Dam,* the big ham who is elevated into Lynn "Biff" Weston's backfield position and glory on the university football team.

Ford, Bella: In *Boulder Dam,* the telephone operator at Carewe's office, the headquarters of the administration for Boulder Dam. When she realizes that the payroll is being robbed from the office upstairs, she goes out to get help and, as luck would have it, runs into a couple of Boulder Dam police and a truck full of laborers. They wait for the robbers to emerge from the building and capture them.

Forman: In *Stranger from the Tonto,* a rider for the Hole-in-the-Wall gang. Lucy recognizes him among the men with Slotte in the bunkhouse when he returns. He is killed by Westfall in the shootout between Bonesteel's outfit and Roberts's outlaws.

Forrest, Clay: In *The Shepherd of Guadaloupe,* the father of Clifford Forrest. He is a proud man, and has developed a passionate hatred of the Lundeens, whose change of fortune has now given them all that he once had. Malpass explains that Clay Forrest was a rancher, and had invested all his money in cattle, but after the war, the bottom fell out of the cattle market, and Malpass and Lundeen, who held his loans, called them in. Clay Forrest now lives in the house that formerly belonged to Lundeen. When Virginia brings Cliff home, he is angry that she has entered the house and asks her to leave. He is equally hostile to the interest his son seems to have in Virginia, suspecting that he is in love with her. He is as opposed to their marriage as Lundeen is. When Jed Lundeen storms in with the news that Cliff is married to Virginia, Clay Forrest cannot believe it. He does accept that Clay did it, not out of love, but out of a desire to help her avoid pressure to marry Malpass. He expects the son will divorce her in due time. He throws his son out of the house when he protests that he married Virginia out of love, not out of a desire to help. When Virginia returns the property to the Forrests, since it had been taken from them by fraud, he is reconciled to having her for a daughter-in-law. He goes to meet his son, the shepherd, who has been miraculously restored to health by his time in the desert.

Forrest, Clifford (Cliff): In *The Shepherd of Guadaloupe,* a man of twenty-eight years who is returning from France on the Berengaria. He had been wounded in the war, spent a long time in hospitals recuperating, and his family does not know whether he is alive or dead. He cannot remember much of his time in the hospital. Clifford is cynical and depressed. He has been given a month to live and he wants to get back home, to Cottonwoods, near Las Vegas. He questions the value of his sacrifice and suffering, given the small show of concern and appreciation his own government and people have displayed. On the ship, he meets a man who had been to France to look for the grave of his son. He is the only person who speaks sympathetically with Cliff about the war. A young woman who never introduces herself shows him kindness, pinning a small sprig of violets on the blanket on his deck chair. By coincidence, the young woman is on the same train going west and she shows equal concern for him, helping him when he faints and ensuring that he gets the attention he needs. When he reaches his home, he learns that she is Virginia Lundeen, the daughter of his old neighbor who now occupies the old family home, his father having lost his cattle ranch and his house. Virginia Lundeen used to watch him ride by, and he recalls pulling her hair and teasing her when she was a child.

Recovery is slow for Forrest. He cannot walk for any length of time. He takes over the job of caring for the family store, and insists on walking there and back. On one occasion, he falls, and is crawling along the road, and Virginia finds him and helps him home. The job at the store is easy, but he finds he must work to undo the suspicion and mistrust that the Indians and Mexicans have, thanks to Lundeen's treatment of them at the store. Slowly, he gains their confidence. One day, Virginia Lundeen and her friends drop by, looking for souvenirs. Virginia's friend Ethel tells him that they are fabulously wealthy and that he should double the price of everything for them. He meets Jack Andrews, a brother of Virginia's classmate at school, who had been in the war, was wounded, and suffered from influenza. He too had a slow recuperation. Cliff invites him back for a coffee to chat about the war.

When the gang buys out his supplies for their excursion to Emerald Lake, Malpass, the arrogant partner of Virginia's father, who expects to marry her, pays two thousand dollars for the supplies, but then attacks Cliff for being too friendly with Virginia. Some time later, when Cliff has restocked the place, the store mysteriously burns to the ground. Things get hot for Virginia and she comes to Cliff with a proposal, that he marry her to prevent Malpass from getting her. Cliff dismisses this idea but later, when things become urgent, he does consent and the two of them are married in secret.

Cliff gets a job as bookkeeper/accountant for Hartwell at a construction supply store in Watrous. Malpass comes in one day to order supplies to build a house. He boasts about his coming marriage to Virginia Lundeen and when he sees Cliff, he makes his patronage at the store conditional on Cliff's being fired. Cliff quits, but his tongue gets the better of him and in the fight which ensues, he reveals that he and Virginia are married. Malpass's rage knows no bounds, and an innocent bystander gets shot. Back at Lundeen's, Malpass threatens ruination of Virginia's father if she does not divorce Cliff. The same scene is repeated at the Forrest house. Both Virginia and Cliff end up homeless.

For Cliff, this is the best thing that could have happened. He gets a job with a Mexican sheep rancher, Don Lopez. Together with Julio, Don Lopez's son, he tends sheep on the upper pastures, in the desert, away from civilization and his troubles. The desert works its magic on him as it did on Jack Hare in *The Heritage of the Desert*. Slowly, his strength grows. His lungs heal, his legs become strong, his resistance and endurance are such that he enjoys better health than he has ever known.

He learns from a passerby in a car what had happened to Virginia and to Malpass. When the time comes to bring in the sheep to Don Lopez for sale, the problems of the world he left behind have been resolved. Malpass and Lundeen are dead, Virginia is now the owner of her father's estate and fabulously wealthy. She has restored to the Forrests the ranch and home which Malpass had taken from them by fraud. She has bought the Payne Ranch at Watrous where she intends to live. Cliff is reconciled with his father, but he decides he wants to continue his work as a shepherd, even though he is married to a wealthy wife. She agrees to his request.

Through Cliff Forrest, Zane Grey once more deals with the theme of the shameful treatment of war veterans by both the American government and the American people, a theme he addressed in *The Call of the Canyon*, *Desert of Wheat* and *The Vanishing American*. As well, Cliff laments the sad treatment of Indians and Mexicans by easterners who have settled in the West. He does what he can to set things right. As well, Zane Grey returns to his theme of the restorative power of nature. While it does not figure as prominently here as it does in *The Call of the Canyon* and *The Heritage of the Desert*, once again, Mother Nature performs miracles restoring Clifton Forrest both physically and psychologically. Clifton is healed, thanks to the intimate contact with the natural world, where the false values and crises are forgotten and true values and priorities are instilled.

Forrest, Mrs.:   In *The Shepherd of Guadaloupe*, the mother of Cliff. She has not heard from her son in some time, unaware that he is alive and returning home. She is pleasantly surprised to see her son, even though he has been brought home by one of the despised Lundeens. She does not share her husband's great hatred of the family, and is quite eager to establish friendly relations with Virginia, of whom she is very fond. Virginia drops by to visit her when Clay is away.

Fox: (1) In *Majesty's Rancho*, a gangster in the car with Uhl when he kidnaps Madge and Rollie Stevens. He obeys orders without question. He's not very fit, and moans about the ride up the mountains and the camping outdoors. He is hanged by Starr and Stewart when they capture the kidnappers at Cochise's stronghold in the Peloncillo Hills. Stewart admires him because he was game to the end.

(2) In *The Mysterious Rider*, the most remarkable of the hounds given to Bent Wade to use when hunting down coyotes and wildcats attacking Belllounds'

herd. The hound pursues its prey without barking. The hound is instrumental in solving the mystery of the rustling at White Slides. The dog stays in the cabin with Bent Wade and when he finally quits his job at Belllounds' ranch to go help Wilson Moore, he is given Fox as a parting gift.

Francisca: In *Majesty's Rancho*, a friend of Bonita's, Danny Mains's daughter. When Lance speaks to her about her flirting with the college students who are spending the summer at the Stewart ranch, she says that she has not done as much flirting as Francisca and María.

Frank: (1) In *The U. P. Trail*, cited as an Irish worker who is described by Neale as typical of the people who have made the construction of the railroad possible. Men like him do the hard work, drink and gamble their pay, and dream of returning home some day. There is another Frank in *The U. P. Trail* who is a friend as well as partner to Fresno, who attacks, robs and burns Slingerland's cabin. He survives longer than the other two members of the gang, Sandy and Old Miles. He is shot by Allie when she is escaping from him and Fresno during the Sioux attack.

(2) In *Twin Sombreros*, one of the men in the posse Bodkins organizes to arrest Brazos Keene for the murder of Allen Neece. With Ben, he leaves, refusing to participate in the lynching Bodkins is planning on orders from Surface.

Franklidge, Alice: In *Nevada*, the nineteen-year-old daughter of Judge Franklidge by his second wife. She is a frank, breezy girl, a true westerner, according to Hettie Ide. She and Hettie become fast friends. After the dance, Hettie is to spend the night at her place before returning to their ranch, a day's ride away. Alice comments on Dillon, the foreman at the Ide ranch. She says he seems to be agreeable and winning, but there is a boldness about him which she does not like. She finds him untrustworthy.

Franklidge, Judge: In *Nevada*, owns the Chevelon ranch and is the father of Alice. He is the largest cattleman around Winthrop and president of the bank. He has lent money and staked many settlers in the area. His kindness and generosity are legendary. He has never driven hard bargains or force payment of overdue loans. He has prospered and earned the great respect of all in the region. He is a close friend of Tom Day and Texas Jack. He agrees to let Texas Jack (Jim Lacy/Nevada) go undercover with the Pine Tree Outfit, agreeing that when the matter is resolved he will clear Jim's name. He sings the praises of Jim Lacy to Ben Ide, revealing the mission on which he had sent the man. This is before Ben Ide sees Jim Lacy and realizes that he is his old friend, Nevada.

Frayne, Renn: In *Knights of the Range*, epitomizes the raw, wild spirit of the frontier according to Britt. He is another Lassiter: a gunman, an outlaw, a self-reliant, steadfast man, loyal to a fault, committed to a mission.

As the novel begins, he is a member of Heaver's horse-rustling operation, but when Heaver tries to assault Holly, he turns on his boss, killing him to defend her honor. She sees in him the loneliness, desperation and nobility that Jane Withersteen saw in Lassiter. Frayne, however noble and chivalrous he may be, speaks his mind to her, telling her she is foolish to ride alone, taking unnecessary risks. She is a blind dreamer who refuses to see things as they are. Nevertheless, she offers him a job.

Frayne accepts the job on the Ripple ranch. Information about his past comes to light bit by bit. Buff Belmet tells how he met him years ago. Frayne was involved in a gunfight in which the foreman of a big cattleman in Kansas was killed. The cattleman, like Chisum, indulged in dubious cattle deals, and the truth of this was revealed eventually, but the price on Frayne's head was never removed. Belmet classes him with gunmen like Wes Hardin whom Fayne made "take water" in Abilene. Britt explains his case to Holly. He is a hunted man, perhaps, by the law, but most certainly by men who want revenge for the killing of a friend or a relative, or by genuine bad men he has got the best of, or by bad hombres or wild cowboys who would enjoy the fame of killing him. He is a man more sinned against than sinning.

Frayne himself summarizes his life story when he speaks at Holly's fiesta. He left the East when he was twenty and has been fourteen years in the West. As a boy, he hated cities, crowds, work. He wanted adventure and answered the call of the West. He landed at Independence, Missouri, in 1860. From buffalo hunting, he drifted from one thing to another. He shot a cheating gambler on a steamboat and that started him on his career as a gunman. During the Civil War, he was a soldier. He killed an officer in a fight over a woman, and deserted to hide out with trappers in the mountains. After the war, he became a cowboy and rode the ranges for years—the Panhandle, Nebraska, Wyoming, eastern Colorado, Kansas. He shot one Sutherland, a big cattleman, one of those cattlemen who posed as a respectable, honest rancher only to mask his rustler activities. Sutherland had powerful friends and they egged on the gun-fighters and two-faced sheriffs and they made him an outlaw with a price on his head. Eventually, Sutherland's crooked dealings were exposed, but no one thought to remove the price on his head. He has ridden with some hard gangs and rustlers, branding mavericks and outright stealing. He speaks of the problems of the present, of the rustling, of the lure of fast money, of the difficulty of distinguishing between honest and dishonest men. He fully endorses Holly Ripple's concept of the "Knights of the Range," young cowboys pledged to do good, to redeem themselves, to clear the range of rustlers and outlaws. In short, what Wade Holden did with Hogue Kinsey's men in *Shadow on the Trail*. He pledges himself to the task of helping his fellow cowboys avoid drunkenness and the lure of easy money.

Frayne is a man of broad experience with little patience for games. He fully understands Brazos Keene's resentment of him. He admires and loves the young man, and treats him with patience, knowing that eventually Brazos will reveal what is bugging him. When he does, Brazos acknowledges that Frayne is the better man, and that Holly will be better off with him. He does not mince words about Holly either. He calls her a princess, who wants all the cowboys to adore her and bow down to her. She wants to make a hero out of him but he is no hero out of a romance. He may forget what he was, but not what he is. At the dance, he has little use for Holly's games, her shallow conversation. "Must you chatter such party nonsense? Be sincere or be quiet," he tells her. He has no patience with her petty jealousy. Although he does love her, he keeps it to himself. His commitment to his work extirpating the scourge of rustlers in the area precludes his romantic involvement with her. When he returns from driving her herd to market and returns with a hundred and twenty-five thousand dollars, she kisses him. He pushes her away, merely giving a report of the job he had been sent to do. He confesses to Britt what she did, but asks him not to reveal how he really feels about her.

Frayne organizes the men to fight the rustlers. He has the men work in pairs to improve their shooting, and to practice an hour every day. He assigns teams to work together, selecting the men with specific skills for tracking and surveillance. They track down two outfits and lynch the rustlers. They collect evidence proving McCoy's and Slaughter's role in the rustling industry. He becomes the focal point of the quarrel with other ranchers, just as Lassiter is the focal point of the Mormon elders' wrath. McCoy has powerful friends and he convinces the smaller ranchers and cattlemen that Frayne is the man behind the rustling operations. They come to the Ripple ranch, demanding that Britt send him away. When Britt refuses to do so, they threaten legal proceedings against the man. They offer him options: to shoot it out with Jeff Rankin, a Kansas gunman; to leave the range never to return; or to stand trial. He opts for a trial, but when Holly comes to his defense, he decides to face Rankin. He asks Brazos to make sure none of the men leave the barn, and, with Britt, he goes to the village for the showdown.

Like the Virginian about to face Trampas, or Wade Holden facing Kent, he has not allowed his love to affect his composure. McCoy and Rankin had been hoping this was the case. He makes short shrift of Rankin, and returns to the ranch. Here, Brazos men return with the dead Russ Slaughter. McCoy's guilt is clearly established. Brazos administers justice, and issues a warning to the accusing ranchers that they should be prepared to fight the next time they meet any of the Ripple outfit. Brazos leaves, asking Frayne to name his and Holly's first boy after him.

Frayne and Holly are married. He settles down to manage the ranch, fully effecting his redemption, as Wade Holden's marriage and settling down (*Shadow on the Trail*) mark the forgiveness of society for the former gunman.

In *Twin Sombreros*, Frayne adds a postscript to Holly Ripple's letter to Brazos Keene. He tells Brazos how happy he is to be married to Holly and how things are going on the ranch. He shares with him some news he has heard about a rancher named Surface, over his way in Colorado. The reports say he is another Sewall McCoy, a rustler posing as a respectable rancher. He repeats Holly's offer for him to return to the ranch, to work as a partner with a share in the ranch.

Fremont: In *Fighting Caravans,* the "Pathfinder," whom Kit Carson accompanied on several journeys of exploration in the West. Carson accompanied him on a trip in 1842 to the Wind River Range. On a second expedition, they explored the country beyond the Rockies just south of the Columbia River. In 1843, Carson and his friend Maxwell spent fourteen months with Fremont exploring the West and reporting to the government on the possibility of opening up the country to settlement. Fremont's ambition was to acquaint the East and indeed the whole world with the wonders of California.

Frenchy: In *The Border Legion,* one of Gulden's gang at the cabin in Lost Cañon. Joan describes him as dark, small-featured, with piercing, gimlet eyes and a mouth ready to gush forth hate and violence. He is mentioned several times in the story but the key moment comes when the vigilantes in Alder Creek are about to hang him. He squeals and begs and pleads and consents to turn on the members of the Border Legion to save his own skin. In the confusion, someone shoots him, presumably Kells.

Frenshy: In *Fighting Caravans,* Old Bill's partner in a humorous story he tells about a buffalo hunt.

Fresno: In *The U. P. Trail,* first appears at Slingerland's cabin looking for something to rob. He recognizes Allie Lee, who has been living there waiting for Neale to return. She, too, recognizes him as one of Durade's men from the mining camps in California. Fresno allows two of his companions to kill each other fighting over the gold from Slingerland's cabin, then plans to abduct Allie with his partner, Frank. He manages to escape capture by the Sioux, who come upon him and Allie and Frank. Later, he appears with Durade at the gambling establishment in Benton. On Durade's orders, he kills the gambler, Jones, to show the power he exerts over men. Fresno makes several advances to Allie, although he knows her "special" relationship to Durade. He claims not to be afraid of Durade, a claim Allie tries to take advantage of on several occasions. Durade is finally killed in a gunfight with Larry Red King when King is taking Allie from Stanton's to find Neale.

Friday: In *Wilderness Trek,* an aborigine who works with Slyter and Stanley Dann. He reminds Krehl and Hazelton of Comanche Indians. He is a dark brown, handsome fellow of about thirty, garbed as a drover. He easily makes friends with the two Yankees, especially as Red defends him against the abuse of Ormiston. Stanley says Friday is the best native he has ever known. He is honest, loyal and devoted to Leslie, who was good to his gin (wife) as she lay dying. Friday helps with the aboriginal tribes they meet along the way. He can speak some of the languages but above all, he is familiar with the different tribes, whether they are likely to be hostile or not. Friday discovers that Woolcott was shot first, then speared, probably to hide the fact that he had been shot. Friday is also familiar with the weather that can be expected in different parts of Australia. He knows when the rainy season will begin, how to survive in the desert. He's an aboriginal Squanto, another Chingachgook.

Friel: In *The Vanishing American,* the missionary at Mesa on the Navajo reservation. Mrs. Paxton first speaks of him to Marian Warner. She says he has done more to antagonize Indians against Christianity than to instill in them the true spirit of the religion. The cowboy missionary, Ramsdell, whose success was due to his teaching, his working with the Indians and setting an example of Christian love and morality, contrasts with this power-seeking, exploitative man, ill-suited to his job. He meets Marian when she arrives at the first post on the reservation. He asks her if she has permission to be on the reservation as he is anxious to control who visits the place and above all, who gets to stay. He speaks of giving her a job at Mesa, hoping to endear himself to her. As well, he offers to give her a lift to Kaidab, speaking disparagingly of the Navajo mailman driver. This driver later tells Marian that Friel is known among his people as "head big stick with skin stretched over." Marian finds it an apt description. Friel works hand in glove with Morgan, the reservation administrator. Morgan witnesses Friel making sexual advances to Marian and uses this as blackmail against him. There are suggestions that he and Morgan are responsible for getting Indian girls pregnant, Gekin Yashi being a case in point. As well, Morgan threatens to expose the fraudulent means whereby Friel tricked Noki and Nopah Indians into signing away their water rights to him. Friel is not intimidated by Morgan on this score, as Morgan was equally involved in the scheme. Some time later, Marian sees Friel's stone mansion, built amidst the grinding poverty of the Nopahs and Nokis. In the hard winter following the end of the war and the collapse of the wool market, Friel is the only man around to have hay and alfalfa, as he controls access to water. He sells the feed to Indians at crushing prices. He imposes the obligation to attend chapel on the Indians. At the end of the novel, the Navajo and Noki revolt against the reservation leadership. They are about to hang Friel from a tree when Nophaie arrives and talks them out of the lynching. Friel is an example of the kind of missionary that Zane Grey despised, the kind of missionary unsuited to his job,

a failure in white civilization who through fraud and extortion becomes a petty tyrant among the naive, simple Navajo. He embodies the worst of the white world.

Frisbee: In *Forlorn River*, a horse trade in Hammel eager to buy the wild mustangs that Ben Ide brings in. Ben Ide sends the horses to him with Modoc with instructions to deposit the money he will give for the animals in his account at the bank in town.

Frost, Uphill: (1) In *The Drift Fence*, one of the cowboys on the Diamond Ranch when young Jim Traft is assigned as foreman of the crew building the drift fence. He is grateful that the outfit has an experienced cook on the job. He resents the new foreman and provokes a fight with Jim, only to be beaten soundly by the tenderfoot. Eventually, Uphill Frost becomes a loyal supporter of Young Jim. In *The Hash Knife Outfit*, Frost is still a cowboy working for Jim Traft. Madden reports to Jed Stone that Frost was injured when they tore down several miles of Traft's drift fence.

(2) In *The Hash Knife Outfit,* one of the cowboys who work for Jim Traft at the Diamond Ranch. Frost is one of the hands who accompany Jim to the train station in Flag to meet his sister. He is one of the two cowboys killed when the Diamond cowhands under Slinger Dunn attack the Hash Knife hideout.

Fuller, Kid: In *The Lone Star Ranger,* the youngest of the outlaws in Bland's gang. He reportedly killed his sweetheart's father and stole his horses. He is living life fast. He gets into a gunfight over cards in Jackrabbit Benson's saloon. He is recovering from his wounds in Deger's.

G

Gage: In *Twin Sombreros*, runs a merchandise store in Las Animas. When Hank Bilyen is shot by Knight, he is brought to a room in the back of Gage's store, where Doc Williamson comes to patch up the gunshot. Brazos comes to see him there.

Gail, Nita: In *Stranger from the Tonto*, Kent Wingfield's fiancée. He got engaged to her the Saturday before he and Bill Elway left to go prospecting for gold in the desert. He is hoping that she will be waiting for him when he returns to Wagontongue. Bill Elway tells Kent that it is unlikely she will be waiting for him when he returns, because there is a lot of bad in her. She needs someone like Kent to keep her straight. He suspects that Joe Raston will have her by now. As he travels towards Wagontongue following Elway's death, he recalls how the redheaded Nita had coaxed him in off the wild range and from his questionable involvement with the Hash Knife Outfit. He discovers he can think of her and Joe Raston without a flush of anger, and he concludes he owes her thanks for having taught him to be indifferent to heartbreak. He decides to undertake the mission that Bill Elway had requested, to rescue Lucy Bonesteel from the Hole-in-the-Wall hideout.

Gaines, Chess: In *Raiders of Spanish Peaks,* one of the cowboys working on the Spanish Peaks ranch when the Lindsays arrive. He remains part of the Arlidge faction, a gunman and a rustler. Gaines is the first of the cowboys with whom wild young Lenta Lindsay becomes involved. Mr. Lindsay forbids her to go riding with him, and Lonesome Mulhall catches them together one day. Gaines had been bragging about meeting her, but he did not go for a gun when Lonesome confronts them. Later, Lenta tells Hallie she flirted with Gaines to find out what he was up to. He rides over to Arlidge's place at night. She finds him deep and cute, and she's anxious to lead him along. She does not realize how dangerous a man he is. Laramie reports on an episode in which Gaines locks horns with Slim Red over Lenta. While they are quarreling, two strangers come up. Lenta plays ignorant and Gaines moodily takes her home. Laramie concludes that Gaines will end up hanged or shot. Laramie sends Gaines packing when he comes upon him fighting with Neale. Gaines has been meaner than any of the other cowboys to the boss's son. Gaines's vicious nature reveals itself when he tries to kill Slim Red, shooting him three times when he's lying on the ground. It appears he is settling the score with Slim for being interested in Lenta. To exact revenge, Gaines plans to abduct Lenta, ostensibly for ransom. When Lin Stuart frees her from her confinement in a makeshift jail, Gaines waits for them on the promontory where they usually go riding. He kills Stuart, riddling the body with bullets, and carries Lenta off to a cabin on Arlidge's ranch. Lenta proves more than he can handle. Laramie overhears Lenta cussing Gaines, calling him a mere rustler, Arlidge's right-hand man, a waste of her time. He threatens to teach her a lesson in holding her tongue. Price and Beady protest Gaines's doings, but he turns on Price, pulling his tawny hair out by the roots. The recriminations which follow reveal that Arlidge has fired Gaines as Laramie had, and that Lester Allen sells the triangle bar brand cattle, the brand of the Peak Dot outlaws, in Denver and Nebraska. When he turns on her, Lenta fights Gaines like a wildcat, just as Lonesome arrives, breaking in the door and killing Gaines.

Gaines, Handsome: In *Knights of the Range,* a rider for the Ripple outfit. He is with Stinger when they come upon the rustlers who shoot at them. He helps get Stinger back to the ranch to report on what they have learned.

Gale, Elsie: In *Desert Gold,* Dick Gale's younger sister. She is the only member of the family he has kept in touch with by letter. When the Gales come west, she is the most receptive to the West and its ways and is thrilled to see the changes in her brother and to learn that he has become a true westerner, as he had always dreamed. She finds it amusing that Dick has a job which pays forty dollars a month and he manages to save money out of that. When he was in college or at home in Chicago, he used to spend thousands without noticing. She and Nell become good friends and she is happy to welcome her new sister-in-law to the family. Tom Belding finds that she reminds him of Dick when he first arrived.

Gale, Mr.: Richard's father in *Desert Gold.* He comes west looking for his son as the most recent letters have gone unanswered. Tom Belding feels he oozes power, but without the arrogant edge that he has detected in Ben Chase, also from Illinois. But he detects in him as well a grave, kindly, troubled soul. He asks Belding to tell him about his son, and Tom obliges, praising the work that Dick has done as a ranger. Mr. Gale is pleased to learn that his son has not gone to the bad as he had feared, although he seems unsure whether to believe what he hears or not. Before returning east, he hopes Dick will get back from his mission, but is about to leave just as Jack returns. He is truly proud of the success his son has made of himself. At the wedding, he speaks of "desert gold," and Dick is sure he is not referring to the gold mine that he and Nell now own.

Gale, Mrs.: Dick's mother in *Desert Gold.* She is reserved, proud, distant. Belding detects a hauteur in her. Nevertheless, she appears truly pleased to meet Nell, her son's fiancée.

Gale, Richard (Dick): The "runaway male" in *Desert Gold.* At the end of the novel, his sister, Elsie Gale, comments that Dick has become the western man he had dreamed about as a boy. George Thorne had made the same comment about him earlier. Richard Gale's is the story of a dreamer, a boy who wanted a life in the open with a chance to test and prove himself, to earn the admiration of men who made their living in nature. His dreams came true in Forlorn Valley, Arizona.

Dick Gale reveals his background while talking to George Thorne in a saloon in Casita, Arizona, a town whose main street marks the international border with Mexico. George Thorne remembers him from the University of Wisconsin where Dick (nicknamed "Biff Gale") was quite a star on the football team. He comes from a good family but he has wasted his life, idling, traveling. He could not make it in his father's business world because, as his father put it, he lacked character. So he set out to find himself. Going west, his father was sure, would turn him into an outlaw. In Casita, he sees cowboys with guns, and imagines this is the West of adventures he dreamed about. He has even considered crossing to Mexico to join some rebel group. When Thorne tells him about Mercedes Castañeda and his plans to rescue and marry her, Dick signs on to help. He solicits the help of two cowboys, Jim Lash and Charley Ladd, to create a disturbance and distract Rojas so Thorne and Mercedes can flee. In the scuffle, Rojas is shot. Thorne and

Mercedes have escaped. Dick meets up with them out of town. He convinces Thorne to return to the garrison so as not to be AWOL. He agrees to take Mercedes out to the desert and to meet George later, after he has spoken to Colonel Weede.

Out of town and free of pursuit, Gale stops to think about his situation. He is infatuated with the beautiful young woman. It occurs to him the influence a woman can have on a man. But he also realizes that he is incapable of doing much for her as he has no knowledge of the terrain and no skills to survive in the desert. Fortunately, Jim Lash and Charley Ladd, who had helped him get the brawl started in the saloon, ride by. He appreciates their offer of help and he is particularly pleased that they accept him. They are the kind of men who would have normally ignored him because of his background. They propose taking Mercedes to Belding's ranch where they work. Tom will keep Mercedes until Thorne comes to get her. She will be safe from Rojas. Jack is almost embarrassed by the praise they heap on him when he meets Belding, who offers him a job as a ranger. He gladly accepts the position. He wants a man's job where he must work with his hands, outdoors, a job requiring action. He has no clothes save those on his back, as everything got left behind in Casitas in the hasty exit. Dick accepts this as a potent symbol of the break he is making with his past life. He learns through a letter from Thorne that Rojas had been injured enough to be hospitalized. He realizes as well that he is capable of killing.

Two months later, Dick Gale is a man transformed by the desert. "Heat, thirst, hunger, loneliness, toil, fear, ferocity, pain — he knew them all." He has developed an exceedingly powerful physique, and a hardness forged in the desert crucible. He has learned how to survive, to bear the silence, to cope with utter desolation, sleeplessness, and the pursuit of men. The desert is a teacher, calling to the primal instincts of man. He has forged a bond with his horse, Blanco Sol. Like Jack Hare in *The Heritage of the Desert*, he "fitted the horse as he fitted the saddle." He has learned to trust his horse's desert instincts, the animal having saved his life on several occasions. He has come to appreciate the simple needs of existence. "Like dead scales, the superficialities, the falsities, the habits that had once meant all of life, dropped off, useless things in this stern waste of rock and sand." As happened with Wetzel in *The Spirit of the Border* and Jack Hare in *The Heritage of the Desert*, existence close to nature has put the things of life into their proper perspective. It frees him of prejudice — "Color, race, blood, breeding — what were these in the wilderness?"

At the end of this first two-month stint in the desert, he comes across some Mexican raiders who have guns and a Yaqui prisoner. He follows them across the border, destroys the guns, and rescues the Yaqui. From then on, the Yaqui attaches himself to Dick as a devoted friend and servant to repay the debt of having saved his life. He helps track the seven or eight raiders who have taken the prized horse,

Blanco Diablo. They successfully retrieve the animal unharmed. Later, the Yaqui leads the party across the desert to Yuma along the Camino del Diablo to escape Rojas. He proves invaluable in ensuring their survival in the desert after the fight with Rojas, who had followed them into the wilderness.

In Dick, Yaqui evokes Emersonian reflections on the difference between the "natural" man and the "civilized" man. In Yaqui, Dick sees the product of a life of exposure to the desert, an experience which he feels has transformed him, calling out those instincts suppressed by civilized life and making him a true man. In Yaqui, he sees the desert man, a man tenacious of life, who faces pain and difficulties with stoicism, a man of endurance and strength, but also a man with a deep sense of loyalty, honor, gratitude. To repay his debt, Yaqui shows Dick where a mine is located. There, Dick finds the box with the marriage certificate and the will, signed by Jonas Warren and Robert Burton, leaving half of the mine to the finder of the box and the other half to his wife, Nellie Burton, and their daughter.

At university, Gale had acquired some knowledge of engineering. He sees the potential for mining in Forlorn Valley, and he plans to settle down and work on a project with Belding, Ladd and Lash. He loses this claim to the land when Chase moves in to set up a mining operation. He had not built a cabin on the land to hold his claim.

At the end of the novel, Dick is able to meet his family, to face his father, without fear. He is his own man with nothing to be ashamed of or to apologize for. Mr. Gale refers to him as true "desert gold."

Dick Gale is an example of the western hero in the Jack Hare mode. He is an easterner who has come west to find himself. At first, he is overwhelmed by the environment, but with humility and persistence, he undergoes a transformation. Nature calls him, teaches him, molds him into the kind of man he is intended to be.

Galliard, Tom: In *The Fugitive Trail*, in Couchos trading horses when Silverman and his wagon train pass through. Some of Hank's men hear Galliard talking. He recognized Bruce Lockheart and swore he would send word to Captain Maggard. He's hoping to get the reward for his capture. Silverman had suspected this man was Bruce Lockheart, and he recommends he ride out of Texas where the rangers have no jurisdiction. Bruce looks Galliard up and publicly calls him a rustler. Galliard is killed in the gunfight.

Gamble: In *Western Union*, named by Williamson as the engineer who has started the construction of the telegraph line on the Pacific Coast, working east to meet Creighton.

García: In "The Ranger," García is one of the Mexican bandits who abducts Roseta in order to capture Ranger Medill, who crosses into Mexico in pursuit.

García, José: In *Stairs of Sand*, runs the Mexican restaurant at the Lost Lake freighting post. He had lived at Lost Lake when it was still called Indian Wells and knows everyone and hears everything that is going on. Merryvale turns to him for information.

Garrett, Pat: In *Nevada,* mentioned as the sheriff who cleared up the mess in Lincoln County and killed Billy the Kid. Franklidge and Day consider calling him in to clean out the Pine Tree Outfit in Winthrop. In *Shadow on the Trail,* the story of Pat Garritt and Billy the Kid is narrated by Ranger Mahaffey. (The spelling here is "Garritt.") The sheriff is presented as a coward who fears to meet Billy in the open, and so he waits for him at the home of his friend, Pete Maxwell. When Billy arrives, he knocks on the door and when he enters, Garritt shoots him.

Gekin Yashi: In *The Vanishing American,* a fourteen-year-old girl at the mission school. Gekin Yashi, "the little beauty" in Navajo, is one of the most intelligent of the young girls at the school. Marian Warner becomes fond of her. At age fifteen, she decides she does not wish to attend the chapel services where the preacher, Friel, tries to teach Christianity to the Navajo children. Since Friel intends to make this compulsory, she must escape from the school. Nophaie and her father, Do Etin, arrange for her to come home for the weekend and from there, she is taken by Nophaie to live with a Pahute family in a distant canyon. Noki, a tracker under the control of Friel and the reservation administrators, finds her and returns her to the school. Her father, Do Etin, is killed by Blucher's henchmen in the process. Fearing that Nophaie will also be killed as Blucher and Friel threaten, she consents to stay at the school. She becomes reserved, distant, and cuts off all contact with her old friend, Marian Warner. She becomes pregnant by one of the missionaries. The father is never identified, but she escapes from the school. A young Navajo, Beeteia, who had been in love with her for years and who has just returned from the war, takes her in with her child, and marries her. Gekin Yashi dies of the flu in the epidemic that hits the reservation in 1918.

Gekin Yashi is one of a series of young Indian girls who are abused by the missionaries at reservation schools, and who die as a result of the mistreatment. For Grey, Gekin Yashi exemplifies the Indian who chooses to learn useful things at the white school but who rejects the religious indoctrination that the missionaries wish to impose as well. Gekin Yashi's fate represents the tragedy of destructive reservation and missionary policies.

George: In *Fighting Caravans,* a young fellow from La Crosse, Wisconsin who has lost his parents in an accident when they tried to cross the frozen Mississippi. The wagons broke through and the family's wagon and everything in it were lost. His parents were killed. The neighbors who had coaxed the family to join them on the trip to Kansas left him to fend for himself in Kansas City. He would play his accordion to earn money to eat. Then some freighters took him along. George reminds Clint of himself when he first came west. He gets a job for the lad at Aull's supply store.

Gerald, Mrs.: In *Under the Tonto Rim,* the woman in Kingston, where Clara Watson gave birth to her daughter. Mrs. Gerald has no family. She runs a little restaurant for miners and takes care of Clara when the child is born. Clara confides in Mrs. Gerald the fact that she is not married. As no one knows the story, Mrs. Gerald offers to take care of the child if Clara helps contribute to her support. When Clara is unable to pay her for the child's support, she threatens to write a letter to the girl's father, or to send the child back. Jim Middleton (Harv Sprall) threatens to ruin Clara's reputation in the Tonto by showing the letter to all the young men around.

Gerónimo: In *The Light of Western Stars,* mentioned in Bill Stillwell's account of the history of the Southwest. He, like Cochise, is a chief of the Apache nation who led his people in the wars against the American army attempting to pacify the Southwest.

In *30,000 on the Hoof,* Logan Huett served as a scout in the campaign to capture Gerónimo and his son, Matazel. Logan predicts that Gerónimo will be impossible to keep on the reservation.

Gersha: In *Black Mesa,* the Indian woman who works for Sister in the kitchen at Belmont's trading post. Louise tells Paul that Gersha helps her take care of Tommy when he's sick.

Geysha: In *Stranger from the Tonto,* Cy Logan's daughter. Slotte fancies himself a ladykiller and makes uninvited remarks and gropes at her under the table. Kent Wingfield calls Slotte on his disrespect for the girl. Cy Logan says Slotte and his group have always treated the poor girl like a slut, a completely unwarranted assumption.

Gibbons: In *Raiders of Spanish Peaks,* Lenta mentions the Gibbons kids who used to beat her up. Her older sister, Harriet, would chase them off. Lenta tells Harriet that out west, she should behave as she did then. Turning the other cheek will not work in the West, their new home.

Gilchrist: In *Shadow on the Trail,* the redshirted cook of the Bell outlaw gang in Smoky Hollow. It is not clear whether he is killed or escapes from the ambush in Mercer.

Gino: In *The Call of the Canyon,* one of the Mexican workers hired by Hoyle to build the ranch house Carley puts up on her property overlooking the Painted Desert.

Girty, George: Mentioned as one of the infamous Girty renegades in *The Spirit of the Border.* He is reputed to have become more savage than any Indian. He does not play any significant role in the development of the story.

Girty, Jim: Appears in *Betty Zane* and *The Spirit of the Border.* He is described as an animal in appearance, wolf-like, with a long hooked nose. His ugliness in itself instills fear and disgust. Nell faints when she sees his ugly face in the window of her room at the Village of Peace. He is sometimes referred to as "buzzard Jim" because he talks endlessly about feeding his victims to the buzzards.

In *The Spirit of the Border*, Jim Girty is spoken of in Ft. Pitt as a scourge of the frontier. He first appears in the Delaware village when Wetzel is brought in as prisoner. He taunts Wetzel, who kicks him in the stomach, knocking the wind out of him, to the pleasure of some of the Indians. Later, Joe Downs pulls his nose, likewise provoking much merriment among the Indians, who enjoy seeing Jim Girty taken down a notch.

Jim Girty together with Silvertip and six braves kidnaps Jim, Kate and Nell. Nell is rescued by Wetzel. Jim Girty takes Kate off to his den where he abuses her at will. Jim Girty eventually kills her when Joe attempts to rescue her. Jim Girty later kills Joe and Whispering Winds.

In the council where the fate of the Village of Peace is decided, Jim Girty casts the deciding vote for destruction, condemning the Christians to the "buzzards."

Jim Girty has been responsible for much bloodshed on the frontier. During the massacre, he himself clubs fourteen to death with a sledge hammer. Later that day, he and Deering come upon Nell, Jim, Mr. Wells and Wingenund as they are escaping the village. Wetzel appears on the scene, kills Deering, and leaves Jim Girty pinned to a tree with a hunting knife through the groin. Despite his best efforts to free himself, the knife holds fast. In his last moments, he recalls his childhood, his brothers and sisters, his parents. He dies, eaten alive by buzzards, the fate of many of his own victims.

Girty, Simon: Among the Delaware, known as the "White Chief," in *The Spirit of the Border* and *Betty Zane*. Of the three Girty renegades, he alone retains traces of his civilized, white background.

Simon Girty had been a soldier and respectable individual until he deserted his post at Ft. Pitt in a moment of pique. He did not receive the military promotion he had coveted and so he has devoted his life to making war on his own kind. In *Betty Zane*, Simon Girty helps the British organize an attack on Ft. Henry, one of the last battles of the Revolutionary War. He travels among the Indian tribes to establish the alliance of Hurons, Delaware, Shawnee. He does act to save Isaac Zane by sending word to Myeerah, telling her that Isaac is a prisoner of Cornplanter.

At the beginning of the attack on Ft. Henry, Simon Girty rides up to the gate and demands surrender. He remains out of rifle range and after the three-day attack withdraws uninjured from the fort.

In *The Spirit of the Border*, Simon Girty has been further hardened by the defeat of the British. Simon Girty has aroused the Indians against the Village of Peace. He lies to them with stories that Washington has been defeated and the British are coming back. He convinces them of the danger of white influence through the converted Indians at the Village of Peace. He knows that the Christian Indians are much better off than other Indians but he sees in the spread of their influence the end of his power over chiefs like Pipe and Half King. In the council meeting where the fate of the Gnaddenhutten is to be decided, he speaks for moderation. He suggests the missionaries be driven out, the village burned, the fields destroyed, and the converts returned to their former villages. In time, they will forget and adapt. He soon realizes that the poison he has sown among the Indians cannot be stopped. Simon Girty, however, acquiesces in the murder of the converts so that he may retain his influence and power. In *The Last Trail*, Simon Girty is mentioned. He has not done much to provoke trouble on the frontier since his defeat in the attack on Fort Henry. The day of the renegade and Indian attacks is over and problems like horse thieves have replaced them.

Glemm, Nellie: In *Wyoming*, the daughter of Mrs. Glemm, who runs the hotel in Split Rock. According to her cousin Simpson, she is sweet on Tex, while Smoky Reed is sweet on her. She appears again later at the rodeo.

Glemm, Mrs.: In *Wyoming*, runs the hotel in Split Rock. She arranges for her nephew Sim(pson) to give Martha Dixon a ride out to her uncle's ranch.

Glemm, Sim(pson): In *Wyoming*, Mrs. Glemm's nephew. He gives Martha a lift to her uncle's ranch in his beat-up Ford. He tells Martha not to trust Tex, the handsome, smooth-talking cowboy she had met at the hotel, and especially to warn her uncle not to give him a job. He also mentions that Tex is developing a reputation as a gunman, having crippled a number of cowboys. Smoky Reed, he adds, is another one to avoid. Smoky is sweet on Nellie Glemm, his cousin, but she is in love with Tex.

Glemm, Tom: In *Wyoming*, mentioned only once. He is Nellie Glemm's brother. He appears on the porch of the hotel when all are in town for the rodeo.

Glen Naspa: In *The Rainbow Trail*, the young Navajo girl John Shefford first meets at Red Lake. He finds her with the preacher, Willetts, in a compromising situation and he intervenes to defend her. She rides off from the trading post the following morning and John Shefford, who has little experience traveling in the desert on his own, follows her trail. She next appears in his camp, bringing back the horse that had freed itself from the hobbles during the night. The young girl is in love with the preacher, Willetts, and when he comes to her home, he convinces her to go back to the mission school at Blue Cañon. Despite Shefford's efforts to prevent her departure, Nas Ta Bega says that his sister must choose. She will come home when she is ready. At the mission school, Shefford's worst imaginings come true.

She gets pregnant and dies in childbirth. Her body and the body of the child are returned to the family for Navajo burial.

Glendon: In *The Vanishing American,* one of Blucher's henchmen on the Navajo reservation.

Glickhickan: In *The Spirit of the Border,* an old Indian chief, the first to accept the teachings of the Moravian missionaries. He is a member of the Turtle tribe of the Delaware, a peaceful branch in contrast to the Wolf tribe. From Glickhickan, Jim learns the Delaware language as well as Delaware myths and legends and religious beliefs. From Glickhickan, he learns about the Indian's sense of duty and honor, his respect for nature. In Glickhickan, Zane Grey portrays the noble savage, similar to Chingachgook or Uncas in Cooper's *The Last of the Mohicans.* Glickhickan speaks of a golden age of the Indian before the white man arrived. He is the Indian who is able to blend the best of the Indian world with the influence of the white world. He sees the missionaries' work as providing the best solution for relations between the red and the white races. Glickhickan dies in the massacre at the Village of Peace.

Glidden: In *The Desert of Wheat,* the chief agent of the International Workers of the World. He appears at Kurt Dorn's farm in the company of an unnamed Austrian man, a sallow-faced runt. Glidden, unlike his assistant, is American and speaks unaccented English. He is persuasive and forceful, sometimes threatening those who disagree with him. He is about thirty years old, clean-shaven, square-jawed, with steely, secretive grey eyes. He has a look of intelligence and assurance that does not harmonize with his garb. He treats Jerry and Kurt with "cunning assurance" when they throw him off the farm. Later, Kurt sees him with Chris Dorn and Neuman, a prominent farmer in the area and rival to Anderson for influence in the community. Glidden's group needs money and they convince Chris Dorn to hand over the eighty thousand dollars he has received for his wheat crop to the organization. He organizes the burning of wheatfields by throwing phosphorous cakes into the dry wheat. He leads the fight with Kurt and Olsen while the grain elevator is burning. Glidden is lynched and his body is left hanging from a bridge as a lesson to other agitators.

Glover: In "The Ranger," Glover owns the ranch where Uvaldo works as foreman. Vaughn Medill imagines that his son, "young Glover," will marry Uvaldo's daughter, Roseta, the most desirable young woman around.

Goddard, Harry: In "Amber's Mirage," Harry Goddard is one of the young men with whom Ruby Low flirted. Al Shade beats him up out of jealousy.

Goethals: In *Boulder Dam,* mentioned as the visionary who constructed the Panama Canal.

Goins: In *Stranger from the Tonto,* a member of the Hole-in-the-Wall gang. Kent Wingfield first sees him in camp with Kitsay and Slotte. Wingfield concludes he is the least dangerous of the three. Goins appears at Logan's trading post later, with Slotte and Kitsa. He supports his friend Ben Bunge when he returns to the hideout with a fantastic story about Kent Wingfield's time with the Hash Knife Outfit. When Roberts and Bonesteel decide to split, Bonesteel asks Goins to declare his loyalty to him. Bonesteel's shooting and killing Goins is the start of the shootout in which Roberts's men are killed and many of Bonesteel's men are wounded.

Gomez, Manuel: In *Stairs of Sand,* a distant kin of Augustine, Adam Larey's trusted friend in Yuma. He has been working as a driver for Collishaw. He tells Adam how Collishaw and Stone engineered the abduction of Ruth from her home in Lost Lake and her transportation to Yuma where she is being held. The men treat her brutally, he says, and she fought like a panther. He does not know for sure where she is being held in Yuma.

Gonzalez, Don Felipe: In *West of the Pecos,* a half–Mexican, half–Indian rancher who in the early days ran a large ranch south of the Río Grande. Pecos Smith rode for him for some five years. Don Felipe was an old acquaintance of his family, taking him on when his father was killed in the war and his family busted up. When the Lambeths move on to their ranch, they encounter Don Felipe, who now operates in West Texas. He runs the Eagle Nest, but nobody likes him. He is reputed to have killed seven men, three of them white. When Pecos was with Don Felipe, he was reputed to have killed five men, one of them a white foreigner. Don Felipe is selling cattle to the Chisholm trail drivers. Terrill Lambeth reports that Don Felipe's vaqueros had been stealing their cattle and she suspects Don Felipe's hand behind the killing of her father. To keep themselves in supplies, they had gone into debt with Brassee, who later puts Terrill in jail for lack of payment on Don Felipe's orders. In Texas, Don Felipe has teamed up with Sawtell and together they challenge all claims in the region. Don Felipe shows up at Judge Roy Bean's post when Pecos Smith and Terrill Lambeth are getting married. He tries to stop the wedding. When he hears Pecos is the bridegroom, he gets angry. He pulls a gun on Pecos, only to have it shot out of his hand. Pecos gives him a dressing down, telling how he hires young, ignorant vaqueros and then kills them to get out of paying their wages, how he rustled Colonel Lambeth's cattle and tried to abduct his daughter. Pecos sends Don Felipe off, promising to kill him if he ever sees him again.

Goodman, Mrs.: In *Majesty's Rancho,* runs a café in Bolton (El Cajón). According to Ren Starr, who recommends her establishment to Lance Sidway, she's a nice woman who dotes on cowboys and runs a swell little chuck house.

Gordon, Mrs.: In *Captives of the Desert,* a neighbor of the Newtons' in Taho. She has a baby which dies of influenza the following winter.

Gorsech, Sheriff: In *The Lone Star Ranger*, a sheriff who is tall, angular, yellow-faced with a mustache. He is in Longstreth's (Cheseldine's) pocket.

Grady: In *The U. P. Trail*, mentioned as a conscientious construction boss on the U. P. railroad.

Graham, Captain: In *Fighting Caravans*, leads a detachment of cavalry, eighty-five men, from Ft. Wise to Santa Fe. He meets Couch and Waters's caravan after the attack by Satock. Captain Graham has been on the plains for many years, first in Indian campaigns and later in charge of numerous caravans of forty-niners en route to California and the gold fields. He has had the time to think about the Indian situation. His sympathies are with the Indians. He describes the white invasion of the West as a deliberate steal. He predicts that eventually all the Indian tribes will be as hostile to whites as the Apaches are. The Indians see that the whites cannot be trusted. Nevertheless, historical grievances between different tribes prevent them from taking a united stand against the invading whites. Captain Graham criticizes Waters, who complains about a bullet in his hip he received in a fight with Indians. If Waters had stayed at home on his own land instead of riding across Indian country, he would never have been shot. He praises a man like Colonel Maxwell, who doesn't have an Indian enemy on the plains. He treats every Indian the same as he does a white man. Indian chiefs have told Maxwell that they fear for the future. It is only a question of time before whites turn their guns on the buffalo for their hides, and with the loss of the buffalo will come the end of the Indians. Captain Graham also predicts that war will break out between the North and the South before any greater war breaks out between whites and Indians. Clint Belmet is impressed with Captain Graham. He tells his father that the captain talks like a book.

Grange, Evelyn: In *Horse Heaven Hill*, a close friend of Marigold Wade's from university. She comes to visit the Wades with Doris McKeen. Like Doris, she is anxious to go to the local dances to meet "real" cowboys. She also goes on the picnic camping trip to watch Blanding and his men round up the wild horses.

Graves: In *Majesty's Rancho*, the new employee at the garage in Bolton where Ren Starr works. Graves has helped tank up several canvas-covered trucks, and he lets slip that the trucks are going to be in town all night. This leads Ren Starr to suspect that these trucks will be used to rustle cattle during the night. His suspicion is proven correct.

Greaser: In *The Light of Western Stars*, a term used to refer to Mexicans.

Greaves: In *To the Last Man*, runs the general store and saloon in Grass Valley. His place is built like a fort to resist attack and siege. Blaisdell tells Jean that Greaves is a hard man to figure out. He's a snaky customer in deals but seems to be kind to the poor people in the valley. He claims to be from Missouri but he seems more like a Texan. He rode into the Tonto without so much as a pack to his name. He builds a stone house and freights in supplies from Phoenix. He appears to do a business buying and selling stock. For a while, he appears to steer a middle course between the cattlemen and sheepmen. Both sides use his store as a meeting place. Jean's first defense of Ellen Jorth takes place in this store, where he beats up Simm Bruce for making indecent suggestions about her. Greaves participates with Jorth in the attack on the Isbel ranch house. He is stabbed in the dark by Jean Isbel, but does not die immediately. He lives to tell Ted Meeker that Jean Isbel had stabbed him to avenge his brother Guy and Ellen Jorth.

Green, Caleb: In *The Fugitive Trail*, a rancher neighbor to the Spencers. He and Hal Spencer were in Denison the night Bruce Lockheart confronted Henderson and Belton in Lafe Hennesy's saloon. They meet Trinity on the road. Green is anxious to get home to tell the news.

Green, Greta: In *Boulder Dam*, Whitey Curtis owes a substantial sum of money to Greta Green, and this debt prevents him from marrying Bess and leaving Las Vegas. When he finally gets ahead, he pays off the debt and returns to run the ranch he has just inherited from his father.

Major Greer: (1) In *Fighting Caravans*, commander of Fort Union in New Mexico. The fort is the major distribution point for all of New Mexico.

(2) In *The Lost Wagon Train*, has ten troops of dragoons at Fort Union. Before the Civil War he had twice that number, which he would state was far less than needed. Fort Union is a distributing point for all New Mexico and owing to the increased hostility of the Indians and the movement of freight and caravans, it has become difficult to provide escort for wagon trains. Major Greer begins the investigation into the disappearance of the Anderson wagon train in response to inquiries from a lawyer, Bowden, from Boston. He calls in Kit Carson, Dick Curtis, Baker and John Smith to find out what they know about Anderson and the caravan. Beaver Adams comments that not much will be learned by direct inquiry. Most likely, someone will let something slip and that will provide the clue to unravel the mystery. Greer leaves the problem in their hands.

Gremniger: In *The Desert of Wheat*, a neighbor to Olsen. His wheatfields have suffered from drought and are burned by the I.W.W. men. He abandons his own useless crop to help harvest Dorn's.

Grieve, Amy: In *Arizona Ames*, the nineteen-year-old, hungry-eyed wife of Crow Grieve. She is from Texas, a southern beauty. She was seventeen when she married Crow Grieve, and now has a baby. Amy came to marry Crow Grieve to acquit a debt of her father's. Amy is not happy with Crow. He abuses her, beating her when he is drunk. Amy likes the cowboys on the ranch, particularly Lany Price, whom she meets in secret. Arizona Ames tells her to be cautious. Amy Grieve has been friendly with the Nielsens, the Norwegian homesteaders her husband is trying to drive off their holding. This further angers her husband. After Arizona Ames confronts Crow in the presence of the cowboys and his rancher guests, Amy is kept locked up in a room.

Grieve, Crow: In *Arizona Ames,* a big rancher in the Wind River country of Wyoming. He is about forty years old, a man of fine physique, dark-skinned, with eyes black as a crow. He exudes a bold, virile presence. As a rancher, he has the reputation of being a severe master. He runs everything himself, never hiring a foreman. He is disliked by other cattlemen because he drives hard bargains and has forced others off the range. He is currently attempting to drive Nielsen, a Norwegian homesteader and the only homesteader still around, off his holding. He pays lower wages than any other rancher, but cowboys feel some compensation is provided by the good bunk house and good food. He mistrusts cowboys, and should a cowboy decide to quit, Grieve refuses to pay him his wages. Grieve has a young wife, Amy, of whom he is jealous. God help the cowboy that looks her way. He acquired his wife in payment for a debt. He is also given to drink and beats his wife. He has heard of Arizona Ames, and he backs down in a discussion with him soon upon his arrival, the first time any of his cowhands have seen this happen. When Arizona Ames learns about him beating his wife, he confronts him in front of his business associates who have come to the ranch for a meeting and in front of the assembled cowhands. Grieve is humiliated, but does not dare draw on Arizona Ames. Instead, he sneaks around and tries to ambush him one morning as Arizona is going to saddle his horse.

Griffith, Lane: In *Raiders of Spanish Peaks,* mentioned as one of Lenta Lindsay's old beaux from Upper Sandersky, Ohio.

Griggs: In *The Desert of Wheat,* a young boy who runs the German barrage in France, seven times carrying ammunition to the men.

Grimm: In *The Desert of Wheat,* the only guard left at the elevator where Kurt Dorn's wheat has been stored. The other guards have been driven off by the I.W.W. and Grimm himself is badly beaten by the I.W.W. thugs. They then set fire to the grain elevator.

Gulden: In *The Border Legion,* partner with Kells in an outlaw gang infesting the mining camps in the border region between Idaho and Nevada. He arrives at the cabin in the Lost Cañon when Kells is recuperating from the bullet wound. He is surprised to learn that Kells is married and that he killed Bill Bailey and Holloway for being too "friendly" with his wife. Gulden helps in Kells's recovery by cutting out the bullet in his back. Joan describes him as a giant, the acme of physical power, an animal, a gorilla with light hair, pale skin, and teeth like a wolf's fangs. He

does not seem to be sullen or to brood. In fact, he does not seem to think at all, a fact which fills her with deep fear. When he explains to Pearce and Wood about the name, the Border Legion, resembling the Royal Legion in Algeria, he predicts the fate of the outlaw outfit. The Royal Legion, he explains, was composed of outlaw types, ruffians, villains, who eventually brought destruction on themselves with infighting. Gulden resents the loyalty of men to Kells and he starts most of the dissension and fighting within the group himself.

Kells warns Joan that Gulden is a much more dangerous man than he is. Gulden had once been a pirate, and when he was shipwrecked, resorted to cannibalism to survive. The same thing happened when he was trapped in the snow in the mountains in California. He survived by killing and eating his two Indian companions. He was reputed to have kept a woman as a sex slave in a cave in California. She was kept naked and eventually froze to death.

Gulden controls by brute force. He picks a fight with Jim Cleve in Beard's saloon over the plan to rob and murder Brander and abduct his daughter. Jim hits him over the head with a whiskey bottle and shoots off one of his ears. The brutality is also seen in the different philosophies of banditry of Gulden and Kells: Gulden prefers to murder everyone leaving no witnesses to identify them while Kells's position is that such extreme violence will ensure drastic retribution by the miners and the end to their outfit altogether. Gulden tries to create a rift between Kells and Cleve over the thirty-pound nugget. While the other men are happy for Jim's success, Gulden argues the proceeds should be shared equally with all. He tries to turn Kells and the men against Cleve, arguing that he cannot be counted on to commit a real crime. He is quite pleased to report that Jim has not murdered Creede as required, doing the job himself. When the gang has fallen under suspicion and its members are excluded from the Last Nugget saloon, Gulden accuses Jim Cleve of being an informant. Gulden tries to force Kells's hand by revealing that Jim has not murdered Creede, but Kells forgives him, expressing understanding that he froze at the last minute.

Gulden is put in charge of the last operation, robbing the stage from Alder Creek to Bannack. The gold is divided, and then the gambling begins. Gulden slowly wins all the gold from the men and from Kells. He proposes a final gamble, all the gold for Joan. They cut the cards. Kells gets a king but Gulden gets the ace of spades. In the gunfight which ensues, Gulden and Kells are both killed.

H

Hadley: (1) In *The Arizona Clan,* runs the blacksmith shop in Ryeson, Arizona.

(2) In *Robbers' Roost,* the cattle dealer to whom

Hays sells the cattle that he rustles from Herrick. Hadley guarantees that he will buy every hoof they have to sell.

(3) In *Thunder Mountain*, maintains a mess for several miners. He and his partner Jones are described as "progressive" miners. They readily agree to Kalispel's proposal to provide them with meat. They comment that lack of fresh meat has been a problem throughout the town. Hadley is the older of the two men. He offers to drum up more customers for Kalispel among the miners.

(4) In *Twin Sombreros,* one of the big ranchers who is willing to buck the consensus in the Cattleman's Association concerning the appointment of Bodkins as sheriff, following Kiskadden's resignation.

Hagoie: In *The Vanishing American,* an old Navajo who is swayed by Lord's anti-registration propaganda. He threatens to kill any Nopah Indian who registers for military service.

Haight, Ross: In *Wilderness Trek*, is Sterling Hazelton's cousin in Arizona. Both Ross and Sterling were in love with the same girl, Nan Halbert. Ross is a loveable, sweet-tempered man except when drunk. He is the only son of an ailing father with lands and herds to bequeath. Ross had shot a man who certainly deserved it, but since his cousin had so much more to offer Nan, Sterling takes the blame for the shooting. Ross protests Sterling's taking the blame, but his mind is made up. He advises his cousin to go straight and to take care of Nan, who loves him best. When Red and Sterl leave, Ross gives Red an envelope containing ten thousand dollars.

Hailey: In *Twin Sombreros,* runs the hotel in Las Animas.

Haines, Bill (also spelled Haynes): In *The Maverick Queen*, a big man, broad as a wagon end. He hit it rich up at the diggings and then went into ranching. His ranch is about twelve miles downstream from South Pass. Vince did Bill a good turn once and they have been friends. Haines advised Vince that he should rustle out of that neck of the woods. Thatcher learns from Bill Haines that a cowboy had been caught red-handed and was being held down in the river bottom by the riders who caught him. Thatcher and Vince got hold of Haines and finally got him to tell where the cowboy was being held. This cowboy is Harkness, and Lee and Hargrove try to whip him into confessing that Kit is behind all the rustling in the valley.

Haines, Sheriff Bill: In *West of the Pecos,* arrives at the Lambeth ranch with Sawtell. He has a smug, bold face, a bluff laugh, shifty gray eyes. Terrill mistrusts him immediately. When they have found the money, some twenty thousand dollars that Pecos had entrusted to Terrill, Haines wants to leave but Sawtell insists on remaining to string up Smith. Haines warns that he won't be easy to catch and hang. He points out that Breen Sawtell, supposedly out to avenge his brother, had been double-crossing him himself. Haines reminds Sawtell he had taken up his old Kansas job of sheriff to serve Sawtell's ends and he expects to get his share of the money they have found. Breen Sawtell shoots him dead for his shooting his chin off.

Haines, Sheriff: In *The Man of the Forest*, Bo Rayner reminds her sister, Helen, after they encountered her annoying old suitor, Harve Riggs, that old Sheriff Haines (presumably in Saint Joe, Missouri) had called Riggs a four-flush would-be gunfighter who would be run out of any real western town.

Halbert, Nan: In *Wilderness Trek,* Sterling Hazelton's sweetheart in Arizona. She doublecrossed him with Ross Haight, his cousin. Ross had shot someone who "deserved it" but, since Ross, son of a wealthy rancher with a great inheritance to look forward to, could offer Nan much more than he could, Sterl takes the blame for the shooting and leaves Arizona for Australia.

Half King: "Tellane" in Delaware, is mentioned in *Betty Zane* as one of the chiefs involved in the coalition against Ft. Henry. In *The Spirit of the Border*, Half King is one of the hostile Delaware chiefs. He gloats over Wetzel's capture. He is also the Indian chief who is in charge of the hostile forces which invade the Village of Peace. Before he gives the order for the destruction of the mission, he delivers a speech not unlike that of Wingenund, who warned Indians to take the missionaries' vision of peace and harmony with suspicion. Half King orders the missionaries not to preach that day. He raises his hatchet as he is about to pronounce the death sentence on the Christian Indians when he is hit between the eyes by a bullet from Wetzel's rifle. The shot comes from so far away that the bullet hits when the sound reaches the village. Bystanders at first think it is a sign from the Christian God, who has struck down the hostile chief.

Half Town: In *Betty Zane,* one of the right-hand chiefs of Cornplanter in his plans to attack Ft. Henry and drive out the white man.

Hall: (1) In "The Camp Robber," Hall is one of the ranchers for whom Wingfield worked after spring roundup, before going to Stimpson's.

(2) In *The Desert of Wheat*, "Uncle Sam" with the Conservation Committee of the federal government. He has heard that Kurt Dorn is a progressive farmer and he offers to get him an exemption from the draft so that he can work on his father's farm. He has heard about the elder Dorn's German sympathies, but he underlines the need for agriculture to support the war effort. He tells him that his father has sold his wheat crop and is anticipating that he will hand the money over to the I.W.W. He gives Kurt a lift to Glencoe and goes to Wheatley in time to stop the surrender of the money to Glidden. Later, Anderson reveals that Hall had, at his request, obtained an exemption from military service for Kurt Dorn.

(3) In *The Horse Thief,* one of the men in Sheriff Bayne's posse, which arrives at Rogers's homestead to arrest Dale Brittenham for stealing horses.

(4) In *The Lost Wagon Train,* a wagon driver in the caravan led by Anderson. He is killed in the Satana-Latch attack on the wagon train.

(5) In *Twin Sombreros,* runs a saloon in Las Animas. Knight comes out of his saloon when Brazos confronts him and they shoot it out.

(6) In *Valley of Wild Horses,* a rancher outside of Marco from whom Pan Handle Smith's father rents a farm. He has an option on the farm and it's a bargain, a hundred and ten acres, most of it cultivated with good water, pasture, a barn and a cabin.

Hall, Bert (Bertie):   In *Under the Tonto Rim,* one of Mertie Denmeade's beaus who lives in Cedar Ridge. He is sweet on Mertie and Edd tells Lucy she likes Bertie the best of all the fellows who run after her. He owns a ranch and has a share in his father's sawmill. He wants to marry Mertie, but she wants to run wild, dance, ride, and have a good time, and her friend, Sadie Purdue, eggs her on. Lucky for Mertie, Bert is quiet, easy-going and patient. Lucy arranges to have Bert and Mertie accompany them to Felix, where they get married. Later, on the bee hunting expedition, Edd comments that he never expected Bert and Mertie to get a "storm" after their marriage.

Hall, Bill: (1) In *Forlorn River,* a young man, leader of the rustlers who work near Silver Meadow in the Forlorn River Valley. Ben Ide tracks him and his men to the Ice Caves, where he surrounds them, preventing their escape during a twenty-four day siege. When their food runs out, Bill Hall and his men surrender, confessing to rustling cattle for Less Setter, who took charge of selling the cattle. He adds that he had worked with Setter in Colorado and Nevada, and that Judd and Walker, the two men posing as peace officers representing the Hammel Cattle Association, are really members of their outfit.

In *Nevada,* Bill Hall is mentioned on several occasions when Jim Lacy (Nevada) returns to Lineville. Mrs. Wood and Cash Burridge among others mention that he hasn't been seen around lately and that no one has heard from him. He was known to have gone over the "divide" into California. Hall had told people that he was going to help Setter, who had managed to wheedle some rich cattlemen and ranchers into speculating on some big money project. No one seems to have learned that he was caught. He laughs at Setter's weakness for women.

(2) In *Rogue River Feud,* Minton reports that Bill scoffed when Gus Atwell told the story about Keven Bell having got the five Carstone girls pregnant when he was at the army training camp near Roseburg, Washington.

Hall, Lovelace: In *West of the Pecos,* one of the cowboys that Pecos Smith hires through Slinger and Hudson to go with him to the Lambeth ranch west of the Pecos. He is an extremely tall Texan, red-haired and dark-eyed, the type that Pecos Smith

equates with being "hell on horses, cows an' other ornery things."

Hall, Mr.:   In *Western Union,* one of the two men with Ruby (the other is Joe Slade, the gunman) when Cameron and Shaw come to effect her escape from Red Pierce's saloon. Ruby introduces him to her cowboy friends.

Hall, Tom: In *Code of the West,* one of the riders on the Saunders XX ranch. He reports to Wess on the fight between Cal and Bid Hatfield at the XX ranch. According to Tom, they wrecked the bunkhouse. Cal held his own against Bid in the rough n' tumble, but if Saunders had not put an end to the fight, Bid could have beaten Cal to death. Tom Hall is the only rider willing to take Cal home. He tells Wess he's glad he met him, as a meeting with Enoch and Old Henry would have been too risky.

Hallett, Roy: In *The Trail Driver,* the fifth member of the Uvalde Quintet. Unlike the others, there is nothing distinctive about him. He is a quiet, somber, negative youth. Adam Brite sees him in Snell's saloon in Austin. Brite knows he does not have Shipman's permission to be in town. He is there with Chandler. He seems to have something on his mind. Hallett and Chandler get into a fight and Chandler leaves the saloon. Hallett and Hite pretend to play cards, then go to the bar and chat in low tones. They leave the saloon. At dawn the following morning, Hallett rides into camp, where Texas Joe asks him to explain himself. He tries to pass the incident off as a night in town drinking, which Chandler pulled him into. He is shocked when Chandler presents himself, calling Hallett a liar. Brite then steps up and says he saw them in Austin, and that Chandler's version of events conforms with what he saw. Hallett goes for his gun and Pan Handle Smith shoots him in the left eye.

Halloway: In *The Border Legion,* the second man with Jack Kells when he rides into Harvey Robers's and Joan Randle's camp. He whistles Dixie tunes when working about the camp. He says little but does incur Kells's wrath when Bill is caught with Joan. Kells kills him because of his interest in Joan.

Halscomb: In *Raiders of Spanish Peaks,* one of the honest ranchers who, together with Stockwell, Bain and Strickland, have got together to form the Spanish Peaks Cattlemen's Protective Association, to rout out dishonest ranchers working in conjunction with rustlers.

Halsey, Mr.:   In *Boulder Dam,* president of the California Company, the largest of the Six Companies banded together to construct Boulder Dam. Lynn Weston and Anne Vandergrift meet him in Mr. Carewe's office. He praises Lynn's rescue of Ben Brown as an example of the comradeship of workers on such a colossal, inspiring project.

Halstead: In *Knights of the Range,* a rancher in the same area as Holly Ripple. He is one of the ranchers who appears at the Ripple ranch with McCoy to accuse Renn Frayne of rustling cattle.

Halstead, Brown: In *Arizona Ames*, the seven-year-old son of John Halstead. His passion is fishing. He and Arizona Ames become great friends while fishing. His older sister, Esther, has trouble keeping him from using cuss words which he has learned from his older brother, Fred.

Halstead, Esther: In *Arizona Ames*, the nineteen-year-old, eldest daughter of John Halstead. She is also her father's confidante since her mother died. She went to school in Missouri from age six to age twelve, and has been in Troublesome since age fifteen She has taken over running the household and raising her younger brothers and sister. She also manages the ranch, a job that she finds very demanding. Joe Cabel, ranch cook, has relieved her of the need to meet with the riders on a regular basis. She found their romantic overtures and demeanor trying. She worries about her older brother, Fred, who has succumbed to the wildness of the environment. He has gotten involved with a bad crowd, drinking and gambling. He has been brought home drunk on two occasions by unknown men. The last time, he asks Esther for three hundred dollars to pay off a gambling debt. She refuses to help him. When their father returns, she debates whether she should tell him, but Mr. Halstead has already learned of the disgrace and has upbraided Fred in front of the cowboys. Esther worries about her father, as well. He returns from his trip with presents for everyone. He is a generous man, but given their finances at present, the generosity is foolish. Mr. Halstead comments that she has her grandmother's head for business. Esther is taken with Arizona Ames from his first arrival. She is anxious to find a husband, but has been discouraged by the cowboys she has met. This has increased her sense of solitude. Arizona Ames shows little interest in her, and she is not sure where she stands with him. Like many western heroines, Esther has a peculiar love of the western landscape, which soothes her troubled spirit. Her first personal encounter with Arizona Ames is one day returning from her lonely vigil with nature. Eventually, Esther gets Arizona Ames to overcome the fear he has of his own unworthiness to love a woman and the two of them marry and plan to honeymoon with Nesta and Sam in the Tonto in Arizona.

Halstead, Fred: In *Arizona Ames*, the twenty-one-year-old, eldest son of John Halstead. He has succumbed to the wildness of the environment, and his example is a poor model for the two younger brothers. Fred has gotten in with a bad crowd, drinking and gambling. He is brought home drunk by two unknown men who turn out to be members of a rustling outfit. He has run up gambling debts of over three hundred dollars to Barsh Hensler. Fred tries to get his sister, Esther, to give him the money she has saved, but she refuses. Despite his attempts to keep his drunkenness a secret, his father learns of

it and upbraids Fred in the presence of Joe Cabel and the other cowboys. This sours his relationship with his father, who thinks that perhaps the humiliation will be the correction needed to put him on the right path. Fred is forced by Hensler and Bannard to help them rustle his father's cattle to pay off the debt. When one bunch of cattle are rustled, Fred happens to be at the Woods ranch, where he finds a rival beau with his girl, Biny. When the last bout of rustling occurs, Fred is directly implicated. He is riding with Stevens and Mecklin when Arizona Ames comes upon the group with rustled cattle. He finds Fred among them. Arizona spares him, explaining to the sheriff that Fred had been acting under compulsion. The boy's name is cleared and he has learned his lesson. Fred is sweet on Biny Wood, daughter of a rancher, Jim Wood, whose spread is ten miles away over the mountain. He announces his engagement to Biny at the end of the novel.

Halstead, Gertrude (Gertie): In *Arizona Ames*, the nine-year-old sister of Esther and second daughter of John Halstead. She shares a room with Esther. She helps with the housework, which she does not enjoy much. Her special peeve is sewing, and there is a lot of it to do since the Halsteads must make all their own clothes.

Halstead, John: In *Arizona Ames*, owns a ranch in a remote corner of Colorado near Utah. He had gone west to the gold fields of Colorado but turned to ranching, buying out Bligh's spread after a devastating fire. Arizona Ames tells Halstead the burning should have generated new, lush growth, but the ranch has been failing, largely due to rustlers. Halstead has three sons and two daughters. He is generous to a fault with his children but he does not display much judgment in selecting his riders. His daughter, Esther, has been left to do much of the management of the ranch in his absence. He tells her she has inherited her grandmother's business sense. He also upbraids his son, Fred, in front of the cowboys for his drinking and wild behavior. He thinks that the humiliation might knock some sense into him. His hired hands are unreliable, one of them working in cahoots with the rustlers. On Joe Cabel's advice, he takes on Arizona Ames, who soon observes what dealings are going on between Mecklin, the hired man, and Barsh Hensler, gambler and cattle thief.

Halstead, Mr.: In *The Shepherd of Guadaloupe*, a bank manager in Las Vegas whom Virginia Lundeen consults about her finances. He had once been a cattleman, as his rugged hands and weathered countenance confirm. Virginia knows him from the church she used to attend. She inquires about the money left in her trust fund, money which her father has given to Malpass to "invest." She also inquires about her father's finances. He has no loans from any bank in Las Vegas, and Malpass has never done business with any of the local banks. Halstead does report that Malpass has a poor reputation among local businessmen. Perhaps Malpass pays the workers on the ranch and in the mines with cash, because there are no checks drawn on any account in Las Vegas. This information raises Virginia's suspicions about her father's business operations and Malpass's hold over her father.

Halstead, Plug: In *The Lost Wagon Train*, Keetch reports to Latch that some of his old crew are back for the winter, Halstead among them. He is a bad hombre, described as one of the glinting-eyed fraternity of the border, one to whom trouble gravitated and only the gun could end. True to form, he is killed in a gunfight in Leighton's gambling den at Latch's Field.

Halstead, Ronald (Ronnie): In *Arizona Ames*, the six-year-old son of John Halstead. Esther, his older sister and mother surrogate, describes him as the more malleable of the younger boys. He loves dogs. "Sharp-eyed Ronnie" spots the injured Stevens lying by the road. Stevens is taken to the doctor's and tells about plans to rustle the remaining herd from the ranch.

Ham Face: In *Lost Pueblo*, a Navajo Indian who rides into Phillip Randolph's camp when the Durands are there. Janey cannot decide whether he is young or old. He has great black eyes, piercing and bold, but melancholy as well. He sits beside Mrs. Durand and speaks to her in Navajo. Randolph translates. Mrs. Durand is dressed in riding breeches about two sizes too small for her. Ham Face asks her why she dresses like a man, and he follows her around. She becomes nervous, and Ham Face starts speaking perfect English. He tells her he has never seen a woman as strange looking as her. He had been in Paris and New York during the war, and had seen many "modern" women, but she has them all beaten by a mile. He and Randolph speak in Navajo, and he leaves, bidding Mrs. Durand farewell.

Hamblin, Jacob: A Mormon missionary to the Navajo whom Joe Lake describes to John Shefford in *The Rainbow Trail*. John Shefford had been speaking with Joe Lake about the negative influence of missionaries among the Indians and Joe tells him that this is not necessarily the case. Jacob Hamblin worked among the Navajo teaching them useful things, bits of medicine. He opened up trade with the Navajo, and did not preach religion to them unless they requested it. He made possible friendly relations between the Navajo and the Mormons. Shefford then concludes that the evil element in missionaries' work seems to be their attempt to impose institutional religion which is incompatible with Indian culture.

Hamlin, Gail: In "Fantoms of Peace," Gail Hamlin is Dwire's real name. Most wanderers of the desert go by an assumed name.

Hammond, Alfred: In *The Light of Western Stars*, like Jack Hare in *The Heritage of the Desert* and in *Desert Gold*, a "runaway male," a young easterner who has come west seeking adventure, the opportunity to prove himself, and life close to the earth.

Alfred is the disgraced brother of Madeline and Helen Hammond. He left his home in the east to establish himself in the cattle business. Madeline recalls his practical jokes and at first thinks that the incident in the train station with Gene Stewart and Padre Marcos and Bonita is all a practical joke he has organized. Back at the Stillwell ranch, he explains the problems he had, the debt to a gambler and losing his land to Don Carlos and a cattleman called Ward who is influential in Santa Fe, El Paso and Douglas. The lawsuit over the ranch is still pending in the courts in Santa Fe. He has spoken a lot about his sister and has shown them all the picture of her with her horse. Gene Stewart has kept the picture.

When Madeline has paid off his debts and bought out Bill Stillwell to set up a large ranching operation, Alfred leaves for California. He returns with prospects of setting up a large cattle company with his sister and investors in California. He intends to marry Florence immediately. All the cowboys are invited to the wedding. The reception is disturbed by the disturbance with Sheriff Hawe and Sneek, who have come to arrest Gene Stewart. When Madeline observes how he carries himself, she realizes he is fully western. There is nothing of the effete east left in him.

In *Majesty's Rancho*, Madeline recalls how she had come west to meet Al, and how he is now a prosperous rancher in California. Gene Stewart considers asking him for a loan to get him through the slump caused by depressed prices for cattle.

Hammond, Helen: The younger sister of Madeline and Alfred Hammond in *The Light of Western Stars*. Madeline describes her as easily fooled by glitter and fame and crazy for adulation. Unlike Madeline, she does not see her life of wealth and privilege as shallow and boring. She has planned this trip west in part to see her sister, but also to entice her to return east. She dislikes the cowboys because they are crude, unrefined. She finds Monty Price hideous. She says what she thinks, not caring if she hurts someone. She is easily given to infatuations and just as easily forgets the object of her infatuation. She longs for something exciting to happen, not realizing that the encounter with Don Carlos and his bandits could prove fatal. She leaves, inviting Madeline to return and to bring Gene Stewart with her. Helen had done her best to flirt with Gene, but never managed to get his attention. She correctly attributes her failure to Gene's being in love with Madeline. She has also changed her mind about western men, deciding that Monty Price and Nels are natural gentlemen, despite their lack of eastern refinement.

In *Majesty's Rancho*, "Aunt Helen" has passed away and left her estate to Majesty, Madeline's daughter. The inheritance has been awarded in such a way that Majesty cannot touch the principle. She receives a certain amount every month from the interest generated by the endowment. Madeline and

Gene are thankful that Helen had such foresight in setting up her will, as Majesty has proven to be most spendthrift.

Hammond, Madeline:

In *The Light of Western Stars,* the heroine developed on the model of Nell Wells in *The Spirit of the Border* and Jane Withersteen in *Riders of the Purple Sage.* She is beautiful, kindhearted, independent, manipulative, and out of touch with her true feelings.

She comes west ostensibly to visit her brother Alfred, who is working on a ranch near El Cajón, New Mexico, but in reality, she has come seeking relief from a life in the east which is increasingly meaningless and frivolous. Her family is extremely wealthy and the lifestyle which accompanies such wealth has become false and tedious. Madeline, like most of her class, knows more about Europe than she knows about America and when she sees the Broadway adaptation of Wister's *The Virginian* with Dustin Farnum in the leading role, there awakens in her a desire to learn about the West. Her brother, Alfred, had headed west earlier to escape from the stifling environment in the East and to "find himself." Madeline had cabled Alfred with the details of her arrival but he is not there to meet her. She has no idea of conditions in the West, imagining that telegraphs are delivered as easily and as regularly as they are in Newport.

Madeline's first impressions of the West are not favorable. At the train station, she is accosted by a young cowboy dressed like Dustin Farnum. The cowboy says he knows her brother and explains that he probably has not received her telegraph. There follows what appears to be a practical joke that Madeline suspects her brother has orchestrated. Gene Stewart, the cowboy, brings in a padre who marries them. A young woman rushes into the train station after which some shots are heard, babbling a story that Stewart seems to understand. The cowboy helps her to get away on his horse. Madeline only grasps a fraction of what has happened. Stewart, who has recognized her from the picture Alfred has shown him with her horse, White Stocking, takes her to Florence Kingsley's place to spend the night. Florence, he tells her, is a good friend of her brother's.

Madeline Hammond is an independent woman, eager to show she does not require the efforts of a male to defend her. She has just inherited a large fortune from her Aunt Grace, a fortune sufficiently large to allow her to live in comfort for the rest of her life. Back east, she resented the obsequious politeness of men bowing to her every whim because of her social status and money. Most of her beaux were men like Anglesbury and Lord Castleton, Englishmen who bear a title but who appreciate American wives who are financially well-endowed. She hopes to find "real men" in the West. While she resents what she considers a practical joke being played on her by Gene Stewart, she does admire his size and strength, honesty and forthrightness. The following

day, they decide to put the matter behind them and shake hands on the deal. She later defends Gene when Alfred seeks to punish him for the insult. She admits he was a perfect gentlemen, if overexuberant.

Despite her sense of independence, her first reaction to the news that Alfred is engaged to Florence Kingsley is to declare that she is not "respectable." Alfred tells her than she is still thinking like an easterner and such concerns no longer trouble him. On the fifty-mile ride back to Stillwell's ranch, where Alfred is employed as foreman, she witnesses cowboys herding cattle and roping and branding calves. She finds her attitudes changing and affection for this new environment growing. Never before had she so appreciated the "homely, the commonplace, the natural, the wild."

Madeline decides to use her fortune to do some good. She gives her brother ten thousand dollars to pay off his debts to one Don Carlos and she purchases Bill Stillwell's ranch and the surrounding small ranches to turn the outfit into a large operation. She retains Stillwell as her manager and keeps on all the cowboys. She builds new homes for the Mexican laborers. The new ranch house is equipped with the latest conveniences. She even buys a car and gives the job of driving to Link Stevens, a cowboy who drove horses fast and recklessly and does the same with the car.

Like Molly in Wister's *The Virginian,* she does not believe in violence but in civilized, due process. When Don Carlos is going to be evicted, she is concerned that all be done by the letter of the law. She does not want her cowboys to carry guns. When Don Carlos and his bandits have holed up in her house, out of respect for her wishes, Gene Stewart proposes to get the guests out of the way on a camping trip, before any fighting starts with the bandits. Likewise, when Sheriff Pat Hawe comes to arrest Gene on the pretense he has committed a murder the night she arrived in El Cajón, she speaks up and repeats the story of what happened. When the sheriff pays little attention to the alibi she gives him, Monty Price says that, out of respect for her dislike of violence, he and the other cowboys have held themselves back, but out of devotion to Gene, he challenges the Sheriff, and kills in him the gunfight.

Like Molly as well, Madeline is out of touch with her feelings. She cannot decide how she feels about Gene. In her bedroom at Florence Kingsley's she recalls how beautiful he looked in his cowboy clothes, big, strong, self-assured, but she ascribes that to his resemblance to the character in the Broadway production. Later, when he rescues her from the Mexican bandits, she asks herself if she is falling in love with him. She sees in him a balance between civilized forces and the influence of the natural environment. Her beaus back east had social graces making them her equals, but they lack the essentials of manhood that a lonely life in Arizona had given Gene Stewart. It troubles her that a man with little education and sophistication can understand her so well. He tells her that he knows she has come west to escape from something, to change, but he does not pursue the matter. At one point she sees him silhouetted against the sky, looking at the landscape. He seems perfectly at one with the natural scene and she wonders what thoughts are going through his mind. She makes a trip to bring him back to the ranch, when Nels has found him in jail. He has lost all hope in himself, having succumbed again to his weakness for gambling and drinking. She convinces him to come back to the ranch and work for her for her sake. She imagines herself the lady of a romance helping the poor swain redeem himself. On the camping trip, when she sees him talking to Bonita, she is suddenly jealous. She suspects that he has been seeing her on the side. When Edith Wayne and her sister Helen are leaving, both comment that she and Gene are in love. She asks herself if they have seen something in her that she is not aware of. When Gene confronts her at Monty Price's grave, he asks her why she has been so cruel to him when he has been faithful to her. She strikes him in the face with her quirt, and he kisses her and leaves for Mexico. Shortly thereafter, Danny Mains returns and tells her how Gene helped him and Bonita get married, and how Gene kept them in supplies while hiding in the mountains. Then Padre Marcos, having heard of Gene's departure, comes to tell her something he has been pledged to keep secret. He reveals that she has really been married to Gene since the night at the train station. He tells her that she is a woman unsure of her true feelings and that she should think carefully before she does something that her heart does not want. Only then does she understand that she does love Gene Stewart, and that she has loved him all along, but had refused to face the fact. She then goes into full gear, calling on family friends and political associates of the family in Washington to secure Gene's release through diplomatic pressure. Hearing that he has been sentenced to death, she goes to Mexico to speak to the men in charge to do what she can. Madeline does achieve the seemingly impossible. Gene is pardoned and she arrives at Agua Prieta just as he is released in to the plaza, thinking he is to face execution.

Madeline Hammond is a heroine in the same vein as Jane Withersteen in *Riders of the Purple Sage*. She is a beautiful, wealthy woman with character and determination, with power and influence ahead of her time, feminine, but willing to sacrifice that femininity to maintain her independence but also willing to use it to manipulate others to achieve her ends. Ironically, Madeline comments on the clarity with which she can see the stars in the western sky, but it takes a near-tragedy for her to grasp what they are telling her.

Majesty's Rancho introduces Madeline some twenty years later. The rancho, once thriving and bustling, has suffered the effects of the Depression. The price of livestock has dropped. Meat can be imported from Argentina cheaper than it can be produced in the West. As well, the bank in which her inheritance from her Aunt Grace was kept went bankrupt. Madeline worries about her daughter in Los Angeles. She is willful, stubborn, selfish, much like Madeline herself at her age. She has used up what was left of her inheritance to keep Madge at school in style. All of this, of course, has been kept strictly secret from the daughter. Madeline and Gene recall how her friends from back east came to visit her the summer she purchased the ranch. She thinks it will be wonderful having the house full of such young people again. She and Gene, however, find them a bit annoying at times. Both Madeline and Gene like Lance Sidway and hope Madge will come to her senses and see what a good person he is. Lance reminds Madeline of the Gene she fell in love with so many years ago. The novel ends with Madeline pleased that her daughter has come to her senses.

Hammond, Majesty: In *The Light of Western Stars,* the nickname Alfred Hammond gave to his sister, Madeline. He has given a photo of his sister with her horse to Gene Stewart. When Stewart meets her in the train station in El Cajón, New Mexico, he recognizes her instantly. The brother had used the nickname to tease his sister for her regal attitudes, but Gene and other cowboys see it as a compliment. She is truly a gracious, noble, majestic woman.

Hammond, Mr. and Mrs.: Parents of Madeline, Alfred and Helen in *The Light of Western Stars*. They are extremely wealthy and influential people back east, but seem to have little interest in their children. Neither shows any interest in what has become of Alfred. Mrs. Hammond believes, according to Madeline, that civilization ends at the Hudson River. When Madeline heads west to visit Alfred, the Hammonds take off to Europe for the summer.

Hand, Fanny: In *The Lost Wagon Train*, a young woman in Latchfield who has her eye on Slim Blue. She was brought to Latchfield by Leighton, who makes her work in his saloon. She is called a dance-hall hussy. Slim tells the jealous Estelle that he talks to her because she really needs a friend.

Handy: In *The Lost Wagon Train*, a gunman at Ft. Union. He and Blaise have been hanging around Leighton, and Latch considers it too risky to have them stay on at the fort when he and Leighton leave. Cornwall has been around the saloons and gambling dens. He calls Handy a fox who has been knocking around the forts for years, but Lester suspects he has learned something about Latch from Leighton. Latch asks to see him and is impressed by his sterling qualities. He has a fearless, cool, aloof air, a straight, hard glance, and a voice to match both. He describes himself to Latch as a "gentleman of leisure." He confesses that he can't drive a wagon or throw a lasso. He also tells Latch that he had him figured out before Leighton told him anything about him. At once, Latch realizes that compared to Handy, he is a novice on the plains. He wonders if Kit Carson and the other scouts read him as keenly as had Handy. The outlaw is invited to join Latch and Leighton's party to return to Latchfield.

Hanes, Pan Handle: In "From Missouri," one of the cowboys on Springer's ranch involved in the letter-writing to the schoolteacher from Missouri. Pan Handle, Andy and Tex are surprised to find a letter from the school marm, as they had decided to stop the hoax.

Hanford, Henry: In *The Hash Knife Outfit*, the man in Saint Louis, Missouri, that Gloriana Traft's parents want her to marry. He is old enough to be her father, but Glory's mother wants her daughter to be safe. As an act of rebellion, Gloriana takes up with Ed Darnell, a riverboat gambler.

Hank: (1) In *Nevada*, the cook at the Ide ranch in Arizona.

(2) In *Raiders of Spanish Peaks*, one of the men helping Price hang Mulhall at the start of the novel. Lonesome Mulhall tells Price this hanging on pretext of cattle rustling is just to exact revenge, because Annie Lakin had dumped Price for him. Sooner or later, Hank or Bill will reveal to Annie what Price has done.

Hanley: In *Captives of the Desert*, a partner with Wilbur Newton in the selling of rot-gut, bootlegged liquor to the Navajos. He pulls the strings, and Wilbur dances, according to Mary. The man is brutish in build, tall, thick-bodied, with shoulders heavy and broad, and bowed legs, a condition that intensified his likeness to a bulldog. He arranges accommodations for Katerine, Alice and Mary when they must stop in Leupp because the car broke down. He enlists the women to keep the Blakely sisters company at the Snake Dance. Hanley supposedly is in the sheep business but a sudden prosperity leaves him free to hire hands to tend the sheep while he tends to a second business, buying liquor to sell to the Indians. When they suspect High-Lo is following them, they set the trap with the barbed wire, which causes High-Lo's horse, Cricket, to trip, throwing the rider. High-Lo breaks several ribs in the tumble. Hanley and Wilbur run the new trading post in Sage Springs, from where they distribute the contraband liquor. When High-Lo and John Curry are trying to find Wilbur to deliver Mary's letter, he and Hanley think they are being pursued by the law and a gunfight breaks out. High-Lo shoots and kills Hanley.

Hans, Gus: In *Valley of Wild Horses*, a cowboy from Montana. He and Blinky rode the Cimarron and the Arkansas together. Blinky says they were the only two straight cow punchers in the Long Bar C outfit that was driven out of Wyoming. More than once he has saved Blinky's life. He is partners with Blinky Moran in his horse-wrangling business. His particular talent is breaking and gentling horses. After the capture and sale of the fifteen hundred mustangs, he accompanies Pan Handle and his family to Siccane, Arizona.

Happy: In *Raiders of Spanish Peaks*, a cowboy who used to work for Arlidge and Allen. When Allen reports on the crew that will be waiting for Lindsay at Spanish Peaks, he says there are ten men, but Arlidge corrects the figure to nine, as he "had to let Happy go."

Harden, Lem: In *The Man of the Forest*, his horse has been stolen. When Milt Dale visits Mrs. Cass in Snowdrop, she tells him that since his last visit to town, Lem Harden's favorite horse has been stolen by thieves. Later, Lem himself asks Milt Dale to track and retrieve his horse. Lem Harden also told Al Auchincloss that Milt Dale had spoken up for him in town that day.

Hardin', John Wesley: (1) In *The Lone Star Ranger*, named as one of the outlaw leaders young Texans want to imitate. He is specifically a collaborator with Bland in rustling cattle, shipping them down the Rio Grande to load on to boats for shipment to Cuba. He commands a large outlaw gang of his own. He moves in to take over Bland's operation when Buck Duane kills Bland. Euchre points him out to Buck Duane. He is unassuming in looks, but deadly with a gun. Later, Buck Duane calls him out in the town square in Mercer. Hardin' had beaten and robbed a man who had helped him when he was in need. In the gunfight, Hardin' is killed. Many are grateful that he has cleared the area of another outlaw.

In *Thunder Mountain*, when Sheriff Bruce Masters introduces himself to Lee Emerson (Kalispel) he names Wes Hardin' as a gunman from whom he learned the trade.

In *Raiders of Spanish Peaks*, Wes Harkin (apparently the same man as Wes Hardin') is mentioned as a famous gunman the West has produced. Laramie Nelson mentions that he has met Harkin, and he never tangled with him.

In *The Trail Driver*, Hardin' is mentioned as a gunman of whom his hometown was extremely proud.

In *Shadow on the Trail*, Simm Bell and Wade Holden are compared to him.

In *Knights of the Range*, Colonel Lee Ripple and his foreman, Britt, speculate about whether the Arizona cattle ranges will produce a gunman of the caliber and reputation of Hardin'.

In *The Arizona Clan*, Uncle Bill Lilley tells Dodge Mercer that the Lilleys are lucky that Nan's Texas friend is of the same breed of gunmen as Wess Hardin', Wild Bill and King Fisher.

(2) In *Western Union*, Hardin' along with Siddell, is a ranger friend of Vance Shaw's. Colonel Sunderland reports that Siddell and Hardin' finished off Duke Wells's gang. Before he died, Wells cleared Vance Shaw's name in the shooting of Stanley.

Hardman, Dick: In *Valley of Wild Horses*, the son of Jard Hardman and childhood enemy of Pan Handle Smith. Pan Handle Smith's earliest recollections of Dick Hardman are not pleasant. Mrs. Smith made a deal with Dick to get rid of some skunks who had set up house under the porch. Dick goes in with a torch to chase out the skunks and gets sprayed. When he scurries out, he leaves the torch behind and soon, the Smiths' cabin is burned to the ground. At school, Dick would make fun of Pan, calling him the "little skunk tamer," and he encouraged others to ridicule him. Later, he makes fun of Pan's horses, Curly or Pildarlick, because he rode them without a saddle. Dick grows into a big boy, handsome, bold, with a mop of flaming red hair. Dick and Pan continue getting into fights. Miss Jones asks Pan to avoid Dick, but that is not easy. Pan must cope with being called the "teacher's pet." Dick is older and in a higher grade than Pan. The biggest fight between them breaks out when Dick tries to force Lucy to kiss him. The fight ends with Dick unconscious after stabbing Pan with the teacher's paper knife. The Hardmans' departure from Littleton is precipitated in part by a shooting scrape in which Dick injures a rancher's son.

The Hardman family leaves for New Mexico. When Pan heads west to track down his family, he hears again about Dick Hardman. Charley Brown, a young miner in Marco, tells him how Dick has bullied men off their claims. His father makes the money and Dick blows it. He plays cards and gambles, but he's lousy at both. He drinks like a fish and fancies himself a ladykiller. Dick Hardman has not lost his interest in Lucy. He enlists her father's help in forcing her to marry him. Jim Blake is in jail and Hardman will secure his release if Lucy marries him. Pan Handle arrives just in time to prevent that. Dick catches Lucy and Pan Handle together, and Lucy breaks off her engagement to Dick on Pan's promise to free her father from jail. However, before long, Jim Blake is in trouble again and the same pressure is put on Lucy. When Pan returns from hunting mustangs, he finds Lucy has just been married to Dick. Pan Handle confronts Dick with his mistreatment of Louise Melliss and threatens to kill him. When he goes with Blinky to remove Louise from the Yellow Mine saloon, Louise takes a knife and stabs Dick to death. He had been hiding in her closet. His charred body is found in the ashes of the Yellow Mine saloon that burns down in the chaos and shooting that ensues.

Hardman, Jard: In *Valley of Wild Horses*, father of Dick Hardman and neighbor of the Smiths in Littleton in the early days. The family leaves Littleton after Dick is involved in a shooting scrape, injuring a rancher's son. Rumor also has it that the Hardmans had come into some money. As well, Hardman had cattle deals with Pan Handle's father, deals Pan knew nothing about. More people than Pan's father got stung by Hardman in cattle deals. Jim Blake had been his foreman and left with Hardman for New Mexico. In Marco, Charley Brown tells Pan Handle that Jard Hardman is a force to be reckoned with. He's into everything—mining, ranching, and wild horse chasing, and he's "doing everybody" as well. He has big interests in town. It is rumored he owns the Yellow Mine, the biggest sa-

loon and gambling hole in town. Louise Melliss later tells Pan Handle that he owns half the property in town. Marshal Matthews is in his pocket. Jard Hardman's biggest problem is his son, a hopeless gambler and troublemaker who wastes all that his father makes. When Pan Handle meets him, he looks to be about fifty years old, florid of complexion, well-fed and used to strong drink. Pan confronts him about the crooked cattle deal with his father. Hardman has long been a power wherever he went and fails to realize that in Pan Handle, he has met his match. His backing down in public leads people in Marco to lose respect for him. He tries to bribe Handy Mac-New into betraying his fellow horse wranglers. He accuses him of double crossing Pan Handle and Blinky. In the gunfight which follows, Hardman is killed. The money he has on his person is taken to repay Bill Smith for the cattle Hardman had stolen from him back in Littleton.

Hardman, Mrs.: In *Valley of Wild Horses*, mentioned once only. The Hardmans are the only family near the Smith's place in Littleton when Pan Handle is little and Pan's mother thinks the Hardmans' boy, Dick, could be a friend for her son.

Hardwick: In "Amber's Mirage," the teller at the bank in Pine.

Hardy, Alex *see* **High-Lo:** In *Captives of the Desert*, the real name of the cowboy, High-Lo.

Hardy, Ann: In *The Trail Driver*, the daughter of John Hardy. She and her father survive the Comanche attack on their wagon. Deuce Ackerman saves her when a Comanche buck is chasing her. For several days after her rescue, she is in shock from the horror of the massacre. She recovers, even becomes a bit of a tease with the cowboys. She gets sweet on Deuce Ackerman, and they plan to marry. He leaves her at Doan's freighter station and promises to return to get her when the drive to Dodge is over.

Hardy, Joe: In *30,000 on the Hoof*, the son of the blacksmith and his wife, Mr. and Mrs. John Hardy of Flagg. Joe is fascinated by automobiles and airplanes. He signs up for the air force when recruitment begins for the war. His mother comments that he had always been a rotten horseman. He has already left for France when Mrs. Hardy tells this to the Huetts.

Hardy, John: (1) In *30,000 on the Hoof*, the blacksmith in Flagg and friend of Logan Huett's. He tells him where he can find a preacher to conduct a ceremony. He also shows the newly arrived Luce the prairie schooner she will be driving back to Sycamore Canyon. His wife helps her select clothing more appropriate for a pioneer wife than the dresses she has brought with her from Missouri. Hardy is one of the friends who meet Logan Huett on his return from Washington after he has got the news that two of his sons were killed in action in France and the third is missing in action.

(2) In *The Trail Drive*, the father of Ann Hardy.

He and his daughter were on their way to Fort Sill to join a wagon train there when the Indians attacked. They left them, but returned several days later. John Hardy is shot but survives. Brite's outfit takes him and his daughter as far as Doan's post.

Hardy, Mrs.:   In *30,000 on the Hoof*, the wife of John Hardy, blacksmith in Flagg. She warmly welcomes the new bride, Lucinda Baker, and helps her select clothing at the general store which is more suitable to the pioneer wife. She comments that the clothes do not necessarily have to make a woman look like a man, if they are chosen properly.

Hare, John (Jack):   The hero of *The Heritage of the Desert*. He is the first full development of the quintessential Grey hero. As well, in Jack Hare, Zane Grey develops many of his favorite western themes.

Jack Hare is the 'runaway-male,' the young easterner who, like Joe in *The Spirit of the Border* and Alfred Clarke in *Betty Zane*, has come west seeking a new life and adventure. Jack is twenty-four years old, from Connecticut, and in poor health. His parents are dead, and on the advice of his doctor, he heads west. In Utah, he finds himself deceived by unscrupulous men and at the mercy of strangers like August Naab. He has dreamed of a life of adventures in the West. On a number of occasions, Jack reflects on how his childhood dreams have come true. He is enthralled when he witnesses the "Crossing of the Fathers," the Navajo crossing the Colorado River. He learns to live "close to the earth," to trust the instincts nature had given him but which had been dampened if not extinguished by life in civilization He is pleased with his skill at drawing the gun. He learns to do cowboy work with enviable skill. He becomes an expert horseman, capable of living in the saddle, at one with his horse. He owns the most beautiful, the swiftest, the strongest steed on the range. He learns to survive in the wilderness on his own, submitting humbly to the formative power of nature, the "spirit of the desert." He hunts coyotes and kills a bear about to attack Mescal. He travels through the Painted Desert in search of the runaway Mescal and comes out not only alive but a much stronger man. He takes on the powerful rancher who has tried to ruin August Naab and has oppressed all the small ranchers in the area through his subordinate, Dene. He falls in love with the beautiful Mescal, daughter of a Navajo woman and a Spanish father. She embodies the mystery of the western landscape he has come to love. He marries her at the end, after rescuing her from danger and death on three occasions: when the bear attacks, when she flees into the desert, and when she is taken captive by Holderness. Life in the West has been a dream come true.

John Hare is the weakling who becomes a hero through the restorative, formative power of Mother Nature. Jack has come west because of bad lungs. He is suffering from pneumonia when August Naab finds him lying on the desert. While on the plateau helping herd sheep and protect the flock from coyotes and bears, Jack discovers a new desire to live. And after a couple of months, he realizes that his lungs have been cured by the sage- and juniper-scented air. He can breathe deeply without pain. He attributes his "triumphant health" to the spirit of the wilderness. Living "close to the earth" like the Indians, he has been restored to wholeness.

The Heritage of the Desert traces Jack's transformation from victim to hero. He allows himself to be shaped by the new environment in which he is immersed. He learns to heed the teachings of nature, to embrace the "heritage" of the desert (the struggle for survival in which the strong and adaptable triumph). August Naab and Holderness both see in him great potential that requires only the desert crucible to reach fulfillment. Holderness fears what this may lead to. August Naab assigns Jack different tasks to shape him for the destiny for which Naab feels he has been born. Working with the herds, branding, roping, will teach him to love his horse, to let himself be guided by the elemental instincts with which nature has imbued them. The constant, hard work will make him "grow lean and hard like an iron bar." He becomes "leather-lunged and wire-muscled." In all of this, Naab speaks of a "farsighted purpose." Jack comes to see that he indeed has been endowed with special gifts for a purpose.

Jack's experience of nature resembles the almost mystical rapture Jonathan Zane describes when he observes the natural world in *The Last Trail*. Jack feels the spirit of the desert growing in him. During the trip through the Painted Desert in search of Mescal, he hears the call of this spirit in the silence of the wilderness. The Jack who emerges from the desert is a man sure of himself and of his purpose. He has struggled to survive and has triumphed. The desert has taught him that life is a struggle. Naab's pacifism is unnatural. Nature teaches man to fight, to resist, to survive. To kill or escape death — this is the law of the natural world. Jack then realizes that he is the "tool of inscrutable fate." He undertakes the task of confronting the oppressor, Holderness, and restoring the balance nature had intended. John Caldwell says of his victory over Dene, "it must have been written."

Through Jack, Grey develops his romantic theory of natural justice, that is, the belief that nature is a moral force, not only a teacher of basic morality, but the guarantor of justice, the nemesis of evildoers. Holderness and Dene have pursued evil tendencies nature does not intend for mankind. Jack is the force nature creates to reset the balance of things. This is the "call" that Jack feels, the "destiny," the "fate," the heritage that he has been born for.

Hargrove, Jim: In *The Maverick Queen*, a rancher in the Sweetwater Valley. He is a close ally of Lee. Like Lee, he has proposed marriage to the Maverick Queen, Kit Bandon, and been rejected. Hargrove's ranch borders on Kit's place, about twenty miles down the valley from Lee's ranch. Hargrove has sent his partner, Bloom Burton, to spy on the roundup at Kit's ranch with the specific task of counting the yearlings in the herd. Hargrove is determined to settle the score with Kit. Hargrove is the principal supporter of Lee in his vigilance committee to mete out justice to rustlers. He and Lee capture and whip young Bud Harkness, attempting to get him to implicate Kit Bandon in his maverick branding. The cowboy does not say a word. Several days later, Harkness enters Emery's Leave It Saloon, shoots Hargrove dead and cripples Nesbit, another rancher and vigilance committee member.

Harkaway: In *Stranger from the Tonto*, a member of the Hole-in-the-Wall outfit. He returns to the hideout with Slotte. Lucy recognizes him among the group of men in the bunkhouse. He is shot by Bonesteel trying to escape in the boat after the shootout between Bonesteel's outfit and Roberts's outlaws.

Harkaway, Spades: In *The Thundering Herd,* Spades Harkaway is one of Pilchuck's lieutenants in the campaign against the Comanche. He is from Texas, and known on the range as a man to be feared in a fight. He witnessed the fight in which Tom knocked down Cosgrove. In the fight at the Comanche camp, Harkaway and his money come to join Pilchuck's men just in time as the Comanche turn to retreat.

Harker: In *The Rainbow Trail*, a known outlaw and killer among the ruffians who accompany the group taking the Mormon women back to the hidden village after the polygamy trial in Stonebridge.

Harkness, Bud: In *The Maverick Queen*, the young cowboy who was caught red-handed with a stolen calf. Thatcher reports that Hargrove and his hired men were responsible for tripping Harkness up. Vince and Thatcher witness the brutal treatment of the young man by the night riders. Lee and Hargrove whip him, hoping to extract information implicating others, but Harkness remains silent. Vince tells Lincoln that one night when he got back to Headly's livery stable, he found Harkness foaming at the mouth. He had heard from Headly that Hargrove and other ranchers were in town. Vince gives him some clothes and his gun and a second gun of Lincoln's. Bud negotiates a deal with Headly for a new horse and saddle. That evening, Harkness rides into town. Bystanders comment on the bruises and cuts on his back. He forces his way into Emery's Leave It, killing Emery's man, Bannister. He accuses Hargrove of starting a war between the cowboys and the ranchers and he shoots him dead and fills Nesbit full of lead, but surprisingly, he survives. The last anyone sees of Harkness, he is riding out of town toward Casper.

Harmon, Eleanor: In *The Call of the Canyon,* a member of Carley Burch's crowd in New York. She is a purely modern woman, leading an empty life pursuing pleasure, excitement, selfishness. She doesn't work, and scorns women who do. She is an ornament, a toy in a luxurious cage, as Carley puts it. She leads a useless life seeking only to be "a gratification to the senses of [her] husband." Like Beatrice Lovell, she sees nothing wrong with her life and resents Carley's seemingly insane rejection of her way of life. For Glenn Killbourne, Eleanor and her crowd embody all that is wrong with the decadent America to which he returned after the war in Europe.

Harrington, Elbert: In *The Call of the Canyon*, proposes marriage to Carley when she returns to New York from her trip to Arizona. He is an older man, a lawyer, a man of means, and old-fashioned. He speaks of the empty lives and empty marriages of his friends. None of them have children, and none of them seem particularly happy. He wants a true, old-fashioned American home. Carley refuses his proposal, however, because she is still in love with Glenn. Shortly after this, she decides to return west to build her house on the property bordering the Painted Desert and to marry Glenn Killbourne.

Harrobin: In *Shadow on the Trail,* an outlaw masquerading as an honest cattleman at Mariposa and other places. Tex Brandon vows he will hang the man. Harrobin has been rustling Pencarrow's cattle bit by bit and keeping them in an isolated canyon. Tex Brandon and Hogue Kinsey return the herd to Pencarrow. Eventually Tex Brandon corners Mason and Harrobin with the money from the sale of stolen Pencarrow cattle. Harrobin is hanged, and Mason shot in a gunfight with Brandon.

Hart, Jem: In *Wyoming,* owns the pinto Martha Dixon rides down the street the day of the rodeo.

Hartwell: In *Sunset Pass,* the rancher hardest hit by the rustlers in Sunset Pass, according to Slagle, who reports it to Trueman Rock.

Hartwell, Mr.: In *The Shepherd of Guadaloupe,* runs a hardware and building supply store in Watrous. He takes Clifton Forrest on as bookkeeper. Mr. Malpass comes to him to order supplies for building a house. He boasts that soon he and Virginia Lundeen will be married. He also stipulates that if Hartwell wants to get his patronage, he must fire Cliff Forrest. Mr. Hartwell witnesses the fight that breaks out between Cliff and Malpass, and brings the injured Malpass back to Lundeen's home in Cottonwoods. He is told to keep quiet about the fight, but warns that if the police come investigating the shooting of Jim Mason, he will have to speak.

Hartwell, Mrs.: In "From Missouri," manages to wrench the new schoolteacher, Miss Jane Stacey, from the swarm of cowboys seeking their turn dancing with her. She introduces her to the parents of the children she is teaching, a welcome respite to the exhausted young woman.

Harwell: In "Fantoms of Peace," the father of Nell Warren. He joins up with Dwire to prospect in the deserts of eastern California and Arizona. Hartwell has an unusual talent, to be able to find water in the desert with a dousing rod. Dwire admires his gentle way with burros. Hartwell will always let the burros drink first. He extends this same kindness to Dwire. The two become friends, and in time, share confidences. Dwire comes to realize that Hartwell's daughter is the woman Dwire came to the desert to forget, Nell Warren. Eventually, Dwire tells the grieving father about his daughter, assuring him that the vicious gossip that had been spread about her is all untrue. Harwell appears to be relieved with this revelation. The two men eventually perish in a sandstorm.

Harvey, Boyd: In *The Light of Western Stars*, one of several suitors of Helen Hammond. According to Helen Hammond, he always wants what he can't have. He comes west with Helen and several other friends to visit Madeline at her new home in the West. Boyd Harvey is a true easterner, without interest in the activities that make the West enjoyable. He hates the outdoors, hates any physical activity such as riding. He is extremely wealthy, hence the interest Helen takes in him. He is particularly proud of his soft hands, women's hands, as Madeline observes later. He has never done any manual work and will not walk anywhere if he can help it.

Harvey, Rich: In *30,000 on the Hoof*, George Huett's main rival for Milly Campbell's affections. Jack Campbell, her brother, prefers she marry Harvey, and it seems she accepted his proposal before George made his.

Hash Knife Outfit: Mentioned in several novels and plays an active role in several. In *Nevada*, Sheriff Stoebel mentions the group as one of the outlaw outfits still reputed to have members operating in the part of Arizona where Ben Ide expects to start ranching. In *To the Last Man*, the remnants of the gang appear in the Tonto Basin, led by Daggs. They fight the feud against the Isbels, and Colmor, Somers, Springer, Slater and the Jorths were members of the gang of rustlers. According to Lawsford in *Shadow on the Trail*, the Hash Knife Outfit got their share of the twenty thousand head of cattle with which Pencarrow started off.

In *30,000 on the Hoof*, Holbert tells Huett, who is just about to take up ranching, that before long, outlaw gangs will move into the area, and he names the Hash Knife as the most likely outfit, as they are already at work in the Cibeque, not too far off.

In *Stranger from the Tonto*, Kent Winfield had been a member of the Hash Knife Outfit but had been coaxed in off the wild range by Nita Gail. When Wingfield finds the Hole-in-the-Wall outfit's hiding place, he uses his association with the Hash Knife Outfit as proof of his outlaw status.

Haskel, Gun: In *The Maverick Queen*, the gunman from Atlantic, another mining camp, that Emery sends Sealover to Rock Springs to hire to kill Lincoln Bradway. Lincoln hears of this recruitment from Vince. Haskel is a big whiskered gentleman, toting two guns and boasting he had been sent for

to put some slick cowboy out of the way. Lincoln confronts Haskel in the Leave It Saloon. Kit Bandon calls Lincoln aside to warn him about Haskel. He is a trigger-happy lout, she says, who has been involved in many shooting scrapes, but is not likely to meet his opponent in a fair fight. And true to form, before the shootout in the street, Vince shoots Mike, one of Emery's men, who had positioned himself in an upstairs widow, waiting to shoot Lincoln from ambush. Haskel is no match for Lincoln in the showdown. Before he dies, Haskel tells Lincoln that Emery had sent Sealover to hire him for this job.

Haskell: In *Thunder Mountain*, with his partner Selby, rides into the mining camp and soon is working for Rand Leavitt. He speaks poorly of Lee Emerson, possibly concerning his reputation in Montana.

Hatcher: In *Fighting Caravans*, the agent at Fort Taos, New Mexico, in '52.

Hatcher, John: In *Fighting Caravans*, a wagon boss. His caravan contains forty wagons and fifty men. He had been raised in the Shawnee Nation in Kansas. He was perhaps the best Indian fighter on the plains, according to the frontiersmen. He joins up with Clint Belmet en route to Point of Rocks. He is killed in the attack. He leaves his thick money belt containing a lifetime of savings to Clint Belmet.

Hatfield, Bid: In *Code of the West*, a young, handsome stalwart figure. He swaggers as he walks. His garb is picturesque, consisting of a large beaver sombrero, red scarf, blue flannel shirt, and fringed chaps ornamented in silver. He is a real ladykiller, sure of his success with the women. He approaches Georgie Stockwell at the station, but does not identify himself. His manner, bold and assured, shows some awkwardness, for he had not judged her correctly. He plays the gallant, taking her bags to put in his car, offering to drive her home. Cal, however, tells her that if she goes with him she will never be welcome on the Thurman ranch. Hatfield is angry when Cal removes the bags from his car, but it's clear to him that Georgie is alive to his striking appearance and personality. Georgie meets him on other occasions and when Mary warns her that Hatfield is not well-liked, Georgie comments that the Tonto girls have spoiled him, that she has no interest in him other than to string him along, he's so stuck on himself. At the October dance, Mary gets a close look at him and she is struck by his good looks: a tall, powerfully-built fellow, handsome in a bold way, picturesque in dress, carrying a gun in his right hip pocket. Georgie dances with him, after turning down Tim Matthews and others of the Thurmans. Some time after the dance, Cal comes upon Bid Hatfield talking to Georgie. It becomes clear from her pushing him away with protest, that she is not interested. Cal intervenes, threatening Hatfield. When Georgie is married to Cal, Hatfield spreads rumors about his relationship with Georgie, and Cal gets severely beaten when he confronts him. Georgie herself goes to the Saunders Bar XX ranch. She acknowledges she kissed him, as she kissed many other young cowboys, but she acted out of foolish youthful inexperience. Bid Hatfield is forced to confess that he had lied about her involvement with him. Tuck Merry then administers a beating to match the one he gave Cal. Saunders then promises Enoch Thurman that Hatfield will be sent away from the ranch, either riding his own horse or being packed on another.

Hathaway, Allan: In *Wilderness Trek*, one of the cattlemen taking part in the twenty-five-hundred-mile trek from Queensland to Northwest Australia in the Kimberleys. Hathaway is tall, rather florid, and apparently under fifty years of age. He is the first to leave, with six drovers and a mob (herd) of fifteen hundred cattle. Under pressure from Woolcott, Hathaway joins the Ormiston faction on the drive. Nevertheless, when they hold the first meeting to assess their progress, he praises Stanley Dann's leadership. Hathaway dies unexpectedly one night during the extreme heat they experience crossing the center of Australia. He is buried beside Emily Dann, who also perished from the heat.

Hathaway, Buck: In *The Arizona Clan*, runs the white mule operation, making moonshine from sorghum, and selling the liquor to the Indians and others around. He has acquired a lien on the Lilley ranch and Rock's promise of Nan's hand in marriage in payment for the moonshine. Young Tommy in Ryeson tells Dodge Mercer on his arrival in town that Hathaway has had his eye on Nan since she returned from Texas. At the first dance after her return, he fought off three young men and shot Tommy's cousin, Jim Snecker, crippling him. Tommy adds that he suspects Nan is not very fond of Hathaway, but unlikely to go against her father. On Sunday, Dodge gets his first look at Buck. He is tall with bulky shoulders. His big bear head holds a mop of thick yellow hair that appears to stand up like a mane, giving him a leonine appearance. He is undeniably handsome, with a fierce, godlike cast of features. His profile is singularly sharp and he appears prepossessing. His eyes are large, flaring, gray or light blue, and brutal in expression. His nose is long and straight, remarkable for its distended nostrils. He has large, curved lips, opening in a sneer. He carries a gun on his hip. When Dodge challenges him, he arrogantly instructs Rock Lilley to send him as well as his brother Bill away. Buck strikes Dodge, who strikes back with his left hand, bloodying his nose and knocking him off the porch. His men drag him away. A short time later, Hathaway gives the nod to Twitchell to shoot Ben, who has threatened to quit the group and reveal the whereabouts of the still. Hathaway's cohorts, the Quayle brothers, abduct Nan, and Hathaway gets Parson Bailey to marry them. Dodge, however, thwarts his plans, getting into the cabin and asking the parson to marry him and Nan. Hathaway retreats to Ryeson where he knows the people will not stand for shooting up the town. Dodge again confronts him and Twitchell in

Ryan's saloon. Twitchell goes for his gun and is shot dead. Hathaway, however, runs out of the saloon only to meet Steve Lilley. In the gunfight, Hathaway is shot and killed.

Hatt, Cedar: In *Nevada*, the eldest of the Hatt children. He is described by all as the worst of the lot and extremely dangerous with guns. The Mexican sheep herders fear him as he is known to have murdered sheepmen. His sister says of him that he is just plain cactus and sidewinder rattlesnake mixed up with hell. Rose fears going to the dance because of what Cedar might say. When he catches Rose with Marvie, he shoots at him, and back at home, kicks Rose so that she can't sit down for a week. Cedar plans to double-cross the Pine Tree Outfit by rustling the last of the Day and Ide herds and taking them over the mountains to sell. He is killed by Marvie Blaine when he comes upon Rose and Blaine in the woods.

Hatt, Elam: In *Nevada*, the father of three sons, Cedar, Henny and Tobe, and one daughter, Rose. The three boys are from the first marriage, and Rose is from the second marriage, although there is some doubt about whether he ever married the second woman. He owns a ranch in the remote back country, in the brakes. According to Tom Day, the Hatts have a lien on the cattle that Burridge sold Ben Ide. Ben goes to the Hatt ranch to pay off the debt. When Ben Ide first sees him, he describes him as one more at home in a saddle than on a buckboard. The Hatt ranch is the gathering place for the Pine Tree Outfit which the eldest son, Cedar, seems to lead.

Hatt, Henny: In *Nevada*, one of Elam Hatt's sons. An uncouth, unshaven lout with pale eyes and low mental ability. He can commit murder without hesitation.

Hatt, Rose: In *Nevada*, the sixteen-year-old daughter of Elam Hatt. They live in an isolated valley where the Pine Tree Outfit regularly meets. She has two half-wit brothers and a half-brother, Cedar, who runs the family operation and is co-leader with Richardson (Dillon) in the Pine Tree rustlers gang. She is not sure that her father and mother were married. All she knows is that her mother died when she was a baby. She is a pretty young woman, not used to men's courteous behavior. She is surprised when Jim Lacy takes off his hat to her. She is sweet on Marvie Blaine, whom she meets by accident in the woods one day. Their clandestine meetings blossom into love. They dance together at the party in Winthrop. She is cautious, fearing what Cedar might do. During her meeting with Hettie, she reveals how she has been abused by her father and her brothers and other members of the outfit. She is afraid to reveal what she knows about Cash Burridge and until Cedar catches her with Marvie and Cedar is killed, she will not reveal who the leader of the Pine Tree Outfit is. Eventually she does identify Richardson, Clan Dillon, as the head man in the operation.

Haught, Babe: In "The Secret of Quaking Asp

Cabin," a bear hunter and friend of the unnamed narrator. He and his four sons, a Japanese cook and the narrator's brother are camping in the canyon some ten miles from Quaking Asp Cabin. Babe Haught knows many of the stories associated with the cabin, including the story of Tappan and his burro, Bates, who was bitten by a rabid skunk and Daggs from the Hash Knife Outfit.

Haught, Henry: In "The Secret of Quaking Asp Cabin," Babe Haught's brother. He helped tie Bates to a wagon for transport to Winslow and a doctor after he had been bitten by a rabid skunk. In Winslow, Bates had to be tied down to a bed, dying several days later after going completely mad.

Haught, Sheriff: In *The Maverick Queen*, a Texan and the peace officer in Rock Springs. He comes upon Lincoln Bradway in the streets of Rock Springs after his fistfight with Hank Miller. He accompanies Lincoln away from the scene and takes him to a quiet little hotel, where he finds him accommodations. Haught is interested in learning more about Kit Bandon and Lucy. They spell trouble. The following morning, Haught meets Lincoln in the dining room of the hotel. He has seen Miller already that morning, and he saw Kit Bandon talking to him. The sheriff does not get the impression that she is trying to prevent their meeting. He tells Lincoln where Miller is waiting for him and offers to stay close to him in case Miller tries something on the sly. When the inevitable gunfight takes place, he takes the injured Bradway to his jail, where he holds him on a warrant sworn out by Kit Bandon. She appears to have some reason to keep him out of the way. The sheriff wonders what she is up to. Haught is amused by the doings of Kit Bandon and her concern for Linc's progress. He is also impressed by the two cowboys, Vince and Thatcher, who come to visit Linc. He senses they are on the dividing line between going to hell and going straight. Something has rubbed them the wrong way, something dangerous. When Lincoln has recovered and is released, he thanks the sheriff for the interesting company and friendship he has provided. Haught wishes him good luck with Lucy and cautions him to be wary of Kit. She will not be amused when she learns Lincoln is married to Lucy.

Haverly, Seth: In *The Drift Fence*, one of the key members in the Cibeque outlaw gang. He is a lean range-rider, neither young nor old. He fits the country. At a later point he is described as having eyes that oscillate like a compass needle. And when holding Traft captive, he is described as a thin, wiry young man with blond hair and hazel eyes, clear as light. His beard is like fine, amber moss. He is Arch "Slinger" Dunn's boon companion. Molly blames Seth for having led her brother down the path of rustling and gunslinging. Seth resents the construction of the drift fence, and his first meeting with Jim Traft ends unpleasantly. He, like Jim Traft and Hack Jocelyn, is interested in Molly Dunn. He sends word with Slinger Dunn asking Molly if she will marry him. Molly says she has nothing personal against him but that marrying one of the Cibeque will keep her there in the valley and she is looking for someone who will save her from that fate. With the construction of the drift fence, more cattle remain below in the brakes, and the Haverlys and Slinger Dunn have more cattle deals afoot than ever before. Seth agrees to go in with Hack Jocelyn in his plot to kidnap young Jim Traft and to put the blame on Slinger Dunn. When they have Traft captive, Seth confesses that he likes young Jim and has since the first day he met him at Limestone. Jim comments that Seth seemed to have good sense, something Seth confesses he lost since he broke with Slinger Dunn. Seth is willing to consider Jim Traft's offer to give them the ransom money if they give none of it to Jocelyn. The Haverly brothers are considering the offer when Jocelyn rides into camp with Molly Dunn in tow. Molly appears to have come willingly, a turn of events which confounds Seth, who believed she could not stand the man. He disapproves of Jocelyn's killing young Andy Stoneham. Discord breaks out in the group. When Jocelyn is dead, Slinger settles the score with his former Cibeque associates. In the cabin, Slinger kills both Sam and Seth Haverly.

Haverly, Sam: In *The Drift Fence*, Seth's brother. Blond, almost red of hair and complexion, he is more sturdy than his brother, less lean of face and intelligent of eye. He is more easily swayed by Hack Jocelyn than is his brother, Seth. Sam tells about Jocelyn's plan to kidnap Molly Dunn and bring her along, a development which Seth condemns. In the shootout in the cabin when Slinger is settling scores with the betrayal by his Cibeque partners, Sam and his brother Seth are killed.

Haverly, Lil: In *The Drift Fence*, sister of Seth and Sam, to whom Slinger (Arch) Dunn proposes marriage. When he is delirious, recovering from gunshot wounds, he speaks of her. Molly comments that now, Lil will hate the mention of Arch's name.

Haverlys: In *The Hash Knife Outfit*, members of the Cibeque outlaw outfit. They are double-crossed by Hack Jocelyn, who kidnaps young Jim Traft for ransom without letting them in on it. Slinger Dunn tracks the brothers down and kills them.

Hawe, Sheriff Pat: The incompetent, vengeful sheriff of El Cajón in *The Light of Western Stars*. Pat Howe had put Bonita in jail, where he tried to seduce her. Gene Stewart reports to him the incident at the train station, where Bonita had come running from a scuffle at the Linton bachelor party. Howe mistrusts Danny Mains, and wonders what happened to Stewart's beloved horse. Pat Howe is also in love with Florence Kingsley, Alfred Hammond's fiancée, and this explains his animosity to Madeline's brother. When Gene Stewart returns from Mexico having earned a reputation as a leader and a new name, "El Capitán," he tries to arrest him for an unsolved murder years before. He refuses to arrest Don Carlos, the leader of the Mexican raiders in the area. Later, when pursuing bandits who hole up in Madeline's house, Howe wants to rip the house apart to get at them. He eventually does catch up with Bonita, arrests her, and takes her to Madeline's ranch. He has hired Sneed, one of Don Carlos's right-hand men, as his deputy. With Bonita in chains he comes to the ranch to arrest Gene Stewart the day of Alfred Hammond's wedding. Monty Price challenges him and in the shootout, both Howe and Sneed are killed.

Howe is one of many corrupt law enforcement officers in Grey westerns. They abuse their power to settle personal grudges or to advance the cause of criminal associates.

Hawk: In *Wildfire,* a Navajo chief invited to attend the horse race at Bostril's Ford. Hawk is a lover of fast horses.

Hawk Eye: In *The Lost Wagon Train,* a Kiowa Indian scout who works for Stephen Latch. He is a matchless tracker and rider. He helps Latch negotiate his terms with Satana. Hawk Eye fulfills boyhood dreams Latch had of life on the frontier. He is the embodiment of tales of savage warfare. During the many years that Latch is away from Latch's Field and Spider Web Canyon, Hawk Eye serves as his messenger, taking gold and other valuables to hide at Spider Web or at Latch's Field, and returning with mail from Keetch. Latch trusts him implicitly. When Corny needs to get to Spider Web Canyon to rescue Latch, Hawk Eye leads him there, straight as the crow flies, in pitch darkness, and finds a back entrance to the canyon Corny could never have found in broad daylight. He is to Latch what Chingachgook was to Natty Bumpo in Cooper's tale, *The Last of the Mohicans.*

Hawkins, Jeff: In *The Fugitive Trail,* the sheriff of Denison. He was shot by a strange gunslinger who later made the fatal mistake of bucking up against Bruce Lockheart. Hal Spencer witnessed that shootout. The dead man in the saloon is the man that Hawkins had tried to arrest. In town, Lockheart is highly praised for ridding the town of a gunman.

Hawkins, Jim: In *Western Union,* has been driving the stagecoach for ten years. He is a virtual encyclopedia of information about the frontier to the Bostonian, Wayne Cameron, who is heading west to make a new life for himself. He entertains Wayne with stories about the Indians, about Creighton and his plan to extend the telegraph to the West Coast, and about the Pony Express Riders.

Hawkins, Red: In *Fighting Caravans,* an associate of Blackstone and Murdock. He is killed in the shootout with Clint Belmet. McGill used him as a shield when he shot at Clint.

Hay, Sylvester: In *Wyoming,* one of the four cowboys in the new team Bligh hires for his ranch. He is introduced by Bandy Wheelock as a "girl dodger" from Montana. He is the youngest of the four—fair-haired, blue-eyed, slim, superbly built, short, with a smooth, unlined face. His blushing when he looks at Martha confirms Bandy's description of him.

Haynes, Tex(as): In *Wyoming,* from Texas, as his name suggests. Sim Glemm tells Martha that he is a wonderful cowpuncher and wins all the rodeos at Cheyenne. It's hard not to like him and he has a way with the girls. Nellie Glemm tells Martha the day of the rodeo that he's not only handsome but he's a gentleman too, if rather wild. Sim advises Martha to tell her uncle not to hire Tex because he is starting to get a shady reputation. Andrew Bonning overhears a conversation between Texas and McCall. While Tex has branded mavericks for McCall, a practice that is still within the law, he is loathe to do outright rustling for him. McCall reminds him that he had a reputation before he started working for him. That reputation is mixed. His "bad" reputation was as a gunman and a womanizer. Rancher Jeff Little vouches for him as wild but straight as a string, from old Texas stock. When Martha catches him branding her uncle's cattle, he explains that what he is doing is technically not illegal. But when he knows for sure who owns the animal, the legality becomes questionable. He promises Martha he will quit working for McCall, and she promises not to reveal what she has seen. When McCall attempts to put the pressure on Bligh to force him to surrender his herd and ranch, Haynes puts his own pressure on McCall. He demands past wages which McCall has refused to pay. In the quarrel, Texas shoots and kills McCall. He tells Fenner and Bonning that he had branded about a hundred of their calves with McCall's brand. Sheriff Slade makes no attempt to arrest Texas, who takes to his horse and the range.

Hays, Hank: In *Robbers' Roost,* makes his appearance robbing the "fat party" who has just cheated Johnny, the boy running the ferry, out of his six-bits passage. Hays relieves the fat party of his wallet and gives a bill to the boy to pay for his passage. Hays laughs as the fat party sets off to "seek justice." He makes friends quickly with Jim Wall, who witnessed the episode at the ferry. He introduces him around at Green Valley and offers to put him up for the night and to give him a job in his outfit. He tells him about this Englishman who has bought a ranch up in the Henry Mountains and hired him on as foreman to protect the ranch from thieves. He plans to rustle the cattle slowly, fleecing Herrick of all that he owns. He feels competition from Heeseman, a former partner whom he double-crossed. Jim Wall observes the men in the group, a motley crew, and predicts trouble will result. Hays generously stakes Jim Wall to new equipment, a new saddle, clothes. As the crew packs up to leave, Hays thinks it would give him great pleasure someday to return and rob Sneed, the storekeeper. Hank Hays reveals a little about his background on the return trip to Herrick's ranch. His father was a prospector and founded a town, Hankville. Hank lived there for years, trapping fur in the mountains. He got to know the whole country around. His father was shot by rustlers. Hank Hays says he became a robber thanks to a woman. That's why he no longer has any use for women. At the ranch, they discuss his plan to slowly fleece Herrick. Wall admits the plan is good. Jim Wall comes to suspect that while Hays inspires loyalty in his men by his generous treatment, there is more to him than meets the eye. Herrick takes Jim into his confidence, showing him his gun collection, talking openly of his finances and his plans. He selects Jim to fetch his sister from Grand Junction. Jim's suspicions of Hays's intentions are stirred when Hays twice tries to get him to switch places, letting him go to town to pick up the sister. When Helen Herrick appears on the scene, Hays changes. As they drive in, Jim Wall notes that "he had the stiff, alert posture of a watching jack rabbit that imagines itself unseen." Helen Hays comments that "your Mr. Hays looked for all the world like a giant ring cobra." Hays's behavior becomes more enigmatic to his men. His plan to rustle the cattle has become a plan to rob Herrick. After the men have left, he returns to kidnap Helen, supposedly for ransom. In the process, he meets Heeseman's men, who are there for the same purpose. He kills Progar, Heeseman's right-hand man, in cold blood, thereby ensuring that they will be pursued. At the roost in Dirty Devil canyon, Hays faces the wrath of the men. He divides the money he stole from Herrick with the men, but not the whole amount. The men then proceed to gamble. Brad Lincoln wins all of Hays's share of the money. Fighting breaks out and Brad Lincoln is killed for cheating at cards. His money is divided among the rest. This marks the start of the disintegration of his outfit. Hays builds a cabin for Helen Hays, but keeps close watch on all who go near. When Heeseman and Morley track them into the Roost, a fight to the finish ensues. Hays and Heeseman kill each other.

Hayward: In *Knights of the Range*, a rancher who has been convinced by Sewall McCoy and Russ Slaughter that Renn Frayne is the leader of the rustler outfit that has been attacking their herds. Hayward arrives at the ranch with Halstead, Spencer, Clements and others who have been convinced by the "proofs" that McCoy has provided them. These proofs are never explained or presented. He offers Frayne the option of being arrested for rustling or facing Jeff Rankin in a shootout.

Haze, Ruff: In *The Call of the Canyon*, one of Tom Hutter's hands at the sheep dip. He stares at Carley Burch and she sees evil in his eyes. He is a bit older than Glenn, with grizzled hair and a seamed, scarred visage, coarse thick lips, beetling brows, gleaming eyes. He stares at the women at Flo's birthday party lecherously. Glenn challenges Ruff Haze at the sheep dip over his disrespectful behavior towards Carley. In the fight, Haze falls into the sheep dip. Later, he meets Carley at the cabin on the ranch. His comments give Carley reason to think about her own behavior and her part in this unfortunate affair. He

points out that Carley is a tease. She dresses provocatively to stir men's passion and then pretends annoyance when men act on that passion. At Flo's party, Carley had worn a white dress designed to reveal her form and to draw attention to herself. She made herself the queen of a party given for another woman. Obviously, she wanted to compete for attention. He tells her she is a floozy, a dishonest woman. She plays games with men's affections. Ruff Haze says that he had never before heard of a woman who behaves as she does, being "insulted" by a man's attentions. He dismisses her as a superficial, trifling woman, and wonders what a man like Glenn Killbourne sees in her. Ruff Haze is an uneducated man, but one with enough sense to see through the falseness and pretense typical of decadent easterners. His passion is genuine, coming from the nature of a man, not the game of sexual innuendo Carley plays at in New York.

Hazelett Boys: In *Wyoming*, mentioned at the rodeo in Split Rock. They are friends of Smoky Reed and help make fun of the dude, Andy Bonning.

Hazelitt: In *Raiders of Spanish Peaks*, Lester Allen tells John Lindsay that he cannot give him any wagons for the trek to Spanish Peaks. He has made arrangements with a man called Hazelitt to call on him and get him set up.

Hazelitt, Abe: In *Code of the West*, a young fellow who works at the station in town. He comments to Cal that something unusual has happened. Upon further questioning, it seems the arrival of Georgie Stockwell has been the cause of all the hubbub. She's wearing socks and her bare knees show! When Cal complains about the job he has been given, Abe retorts that some people have all the luck. Cal Thurman suspects that the cowboys from the ranch have called ahead and put Abe up to a trick at his expense.

Hazelton, Cherry: In *The Thundering Herd*, a strapping youngster, freckle-faced and red-headed. Like Tom Doan when he first arrived in the West, he worships frontiersmen and Indian fighters. He and his young comrades, brothers named Dan and Joe Newman, hang around Pilchuck in awe. Tom takes Cherry under his wing, teaching him the tricks of buffalo hunting and skinning, as Pilchuck showed him when he arrived.

Hazelton, Sterling (Sterl): In *Wilderness Trek*, a twenty-five-year-old cowboy from Texas via Arizona who ends up in Australia on a cattle drive, taking some seven to eight thousand cattle across twenty-five hundred miles of jungle and desert and mountains to open a station in Northwest Australia in the Kimberleys. Hazelton's departure from Arizona is due to an affair of the heart. He flirted with Flo, the best friend of his sweetheart, Nan Halbert. To get even with him, she takes up with his cousin, Ross Haight. The cousin is the only son of an ailing cattleman with land and herds to bequeath to him, but he has been involved in a shooting, thoroughly justified. Since Nan loves Haight more, Sterling takes the blame for the shooting and leaves Arizona with his loyal partner, Red. Ross gives Red a package with ten thousand dollars in it. The two of them set sail for Australia. They make their way north to Brisbane and from there to Downsville, where they meet Bingham Slyter, a broad-shouldered teamster who is putting together a crew for a drive across the continent to the Kimberleys in Northwest Australia. Sterling and Red are well-experienced at trailing cattle and have much to offer the expedition. Sterling hits it off with Slyter's daughter, Leslie. She enjoys teaching him about the animals and birds of Australia, and delights in showing him her string of thoroughbred horses. She gives him King, her favorite, to ride on the trail. He and Red explain the formation in which the cattle move, and the reason for that shape. Red has ridden as point man, but Sterling never has. It is perhaps the toughest and most dangerous job on the trail. Sterling and Red explain how the wagons can be used as boats to float them across deep rivers. The two of them caulk the seams in the wagons so that they will float. The experiment succeeds, making rivers less of a problem. Red and Sterling pretend to have a disagreement so that Red can cozy up to Ormiston's drovers to learn what their intentions are. Red's suspicions of Ormiston's intentions are confirmed when he overhears him discussing plans with Bedford and Jack. Red and Sterling lead the drovers in pursuit of Ormiston and recover the stolen cattle, wagons and horses. Red is injured, and on their return, Sterl does his best to patch his partner up. On the last part of the trail, Hazelton provides advice on how to drive cattle in intense heat. Short drives, moving slow, does the trick. When they are crossing the crocodile-infested river, Stanley puts Hazelton in charge of the drovers. When they finally reach the Kimberleys, two and a half years after they left Downsville, Queensland, Hazelton is ready to set up ranching in his new country. Stanley Dann, a preacher as well as cattleman, marries Sterling and Leslie.

Hazlitt: In *Shadow on the Trail,* together with Smith, helps Simm Bell and Wade Holden hold up the Texas Pacific train. Hazlitt and Smith feel that Bell's division of the spoils is unfair and try to force him at gunpoint to give them more. When they attempt to draw on the boss, Wade Holden shoots them.

Headly, Bill: In *The Maverick Queen,* runs the livery stable in South Pass. He is a red-bearded man with a limp. He had been a miner and had done fairly well at the diggings, but when he broke his leg, he was no longer able to continue in that line of work, so he bought out Jeff Smith's livery stable, quite a profitable business. He makes friends with Lincoln Bradway, and brings him and Vince together over a horse trade. Throughout the story, Headly is a source of information about the goings-on in town. His office is the meeting place for Vince, Lincoln and Mel Thatcher.

Heady: In *Arizona Ames,* the loquacious Mormon guide with Steele Brandeth's outlaw gang. He has a wife and two children. He once rode for Jim Morgan, the Mormon horse rancher from whom Brandeth is planning to rustle horses. When Brandeth and Noggin are killed by Arizona Ames, he takes the money belt around Brandeth's waist. With the money, he hopes to make a new start. He thanks Arizona for setting him on the straight path again. At Morgan's, he offers Arizona Ames advice on courting Lespeth.

Heald: (1) In *The Desert of Wheat,* Heald is one of the authors of the book used at the State Agricultural Experimental Station which discusses wheat types, wheat viruses and soil conditions most conducive to growing wheat. Kurt Dorn has learned most of what he knows about growing wheat from Heald and Woolman.

(2) In *Wilderness Trek,* Heald is one Slyter's drovers. He is a sturdy young man not out of his teens and he sits his saddle as if used to it. He remains unquestionably loyal to Slyter throughout the friction between Eric Dann and Ash Ormiston on the one hand, and Slyter and Stanley Dann on the other. After the attempt by Ormiston to rustle part of the herd and the horses, and when they are deliberating about the road to take, Heald, with Bligh, Hood and Derrick, decide they can no longer continue with this group. Shortly thereafter, Eric Dann confesses that he hasn't a clue where they are, that he lied about having been the to Kimberleys before and knowing the way. Heald, Bligh, Hood and Derrick work their way westward toward the coast. They reach fine grazing country where they set up a station. Heald writes a letter to Stanley Dann telling of their safe arrival and their success in setting up a ranching station. He also reports that Ormiston's three escaping bushrangers (rustlers) had been murdered by aborigines. A rumor had reached the coast before their arrival that Dann's trekkers had perished on the Never-never. Heald wrote this letter hoping to get a reply. Stanley Dann is pleased to hear of Heald's good fortune.

Heald, Bill: In *West of the Pecos,* one of the brother ranchers with whom Pecos Smith signs on as cowboy. He sees that Mary has her eye on Pecos. He pegs Pecos as a drifter, not likely to get attached to a woman. When Sawtell comes to get the brothers to fire Pecos, Bill stands by Pecos. When Pecos decides to go to take the heat off the brothers, Bill and John assure Pecos they will tell the law that the shooting of Sawtell was done in self-defense.

Heald, John: In *West of the Pecos,* brother to Bill Heald, and co-owner of the ranch. They take on Pecos Smith as a cowboy. He admits to having worked for Don Felipe. John Heald takes a liking to him at once, pegging him as a likeable fellow with "real Texas stuff" in him. He asks no more questions about his background. Like Bill, he promises to vouch for Pecos should there be any questions about the shooting of Sawtell.

Heald, Mary: In *West of the Pecos,* the sister of John Heald. She takes a liking to Pecos Smith immediately. When she gives a party which all the young men of the area attend, Pecos Smith does not show up, having volunteered to take the night watch on the herd so the others can go. Mary is furious at him and snubs him all the next day. The rumor begins that Pecos is a woman-hater. When Sawtell comes to the ranch accusing him of cattle rustling and murder, Mary, like her brothers, refuses to doubt Pecos's honesty. After the shooting of Sawtell, she begs him to stay. Pecos, however, feels it would not be fair to the Healds if he stayed. Like Nevada and Hettie Ide, Pecos Smith tells Mary her confidence in him would keep him straight if anything can. He does think of her later, musing that he might someday return to court her seriously.

Heaver, Bill: In *Knights of the Range,* one of the horse thieves that Britt catches at the Dobe Cabin corral. He is in charge of the outfit, having recruited Mugg Dillon from the Ripple outfit. He puts up a haughty, arrogant front when confronted by Britt. He angers Frayne, a gunman in his outfit, when he tries to drag Holly out of her saddle. He is killed by Frayne in the gunfight which follows.

Heckewelder: In *The Spirit of the Border,* one of the head missionaries at the Village of Peace. He travels among the Indian tribes spreading the gospel and trying to bring peace between the white world and the Indian world. He welcomes the newcomers to the village and gives them a tour of the place, explaining what work they have done and showing the fruits of their labor, the workshops where converts work, the fields of corn, the cattle in pastures on the hillsides. He leaves on a mission several weeks before the descent on the village, hoping to get help from friendly tribes to forestall the attack. Heckewelder philosophically accepts what will happen as a setback resulting from frontier conditions but he knows that with time, his efforts will bear fruit. He prevents Jim from sacrificing himself as Dave Edwards and George Young do.

Heddon: In *Fighting Caravans,* shot in the hip in the fighting at Point of Rocks.

Heeseman: In *Robbers' Roost,* identified by Hank Hays as the rustler of Dragon Canyon. None of the ranchers around know this about him. He has a small outfit, but effective. He had the same reaction to Herrick's arrival as Hank Hays. Both of them started riding for Herrick, but Hays got the upper hand and came to be boss. Heeseman's persistence annoys Hays. Jim Wall meets him when he drops by the Herrick ranch. He is a man under forty, with narrow blue eyes, reddened by wind and dust. He was a more prepossessing man than Hays. Heeseman gives Wall a careful scrutiny. He informs Wall that he and Hays had once been partners, and, with emphasis, that Hays double-crossed him. He leaves the Herrick ranch with an invitation for Wall to come see him if he gets curious. It turns out Heese-

man also was planning to rob Herrick and abduct Helen for ransom. His right-hand man, Progar, is killed in cold blood by Hays. Heeseman follows Hays and his gang, losing them in the brakes and the canyons of Devil's River. Slocum, however, predicts Morley and Heeseman will eventually find the Robbers' Roost and a shootout will be inevitable. Slocum's prediction comes true in a few weeks. Hays and Heeseman kill each other in a shootout.

Hellbrand: In *30,000 on the Hoof,* the head of a rustler outfit. Tobe Campbell and Joe Stillman, his right-hand man, plan to raid the Huett ranch in Sycamore Canyon. They bring the scourge of rustling to Huett's isolated ranch.

Helm: Mentioned by August Naab in *The Heritage of the Desert.* He was an outlaw, a killing machine, like Dene. He was driven out of Utah when the Mormons rose up against their outlaw oppressors. August Naab intimates that the same fate will eventually befall Dene in White Sage. He is also mentioned in *The Lone Star Ranger,* where it is said that he was unrepentant until the last moment of his life, shouting, "Let her rip" from the scaffold.

Helmar: In *The Desert of Wheat,* a representative of the lumber company from Blue Mountains. He reports to the chamber of commerce about the activities of the I.W.W. agents with the men at the lumber mills. They have threatened to paralyze the industry if the company does not yield to their demands for wages. There are vagrant members of the group camped all over the place.

Hempstead, Bill: In *Twin Sombreros,* drives the stagecoach which brings June Neece to Doan's Crossing from Dodge.

Henderson: In *Twin Sombreros,* a cattleman and banker in Las Animas. He is the sole voice opposing Raine Surface at the Cattleman's Association. He refuses to believe Brazos Keene guilty of the murder of Allen Neece. He hires Brazos's friend, Jack Sain, as a rider and renews Blake's note on Brazos's request. He reveals to Brazos that Surface withdrew forty thousand dollars, all the cash he had available, the day Lura left for Denver. However, Brazos observes that while Henderson knows that Surface is crooked, he does not dare betray him. He swallows his loss and waits for someone else to risk calling the cattle baron a rustler. He enters into a partnership with Neece when the Twin Sombreros ranch has been restored to him. At the Cattleman's Association, he does speak out against Surface's plan to name Bodkins sheriff, but eventually he becomes reconciled to the inevitable. He is at supper with Bodkins and Miller when Brazos confronts the new sheriff and shoots it out with him. Brazos tells Henderson that he is hanging around with crooks, that Miller has merely replaced Surface as the corrupt cattleman running the show.

Henderson, John: In *The Call of the Canyon,* a twenty-two-year-old veteran of the war that Tom

Hutter meets in Flagstaff, Arizona. He is a very sick young man. He had known Glenn Killbourne in France, and he tells Tom Hutter about what Glenn and he had suffered on the battlefields of France. John Henderson refuses to accept help from Tom as he is waiting for his war bonus and the promised veteran's pension from the government — but they never come. Like Glenn and Virgil Rust and George Burton, he feels betrayed by the country for which he was willing to give his life. He works for a while at El Tovar before moving to Flagstaff. He dies of the same injuries as Glenn Killbourne, thereby underlining the perilous nature of Glenn's case.

Henderson, Steve: In *The Fugitive Trail*, is Quade Belton's sidekick. He tells Barse Lockheart to tell his brother to go to hell and let them get on with their card game. Bruce Lockheart continues, calling him a crooked card player. Henderson tries to pull his gun on Bruce but he never had a chance to aim as Bruce shot him. His gun goes off in the air as he topples over backwards.

Henderson, Sue: In *The Hash Knife Outfit*, a young woman from Flagg, Arizona. Glory Traft at first thinks that she is her brother Jim's love interest. Sue Henderson has the reputation of being the second biggest gossip in Flag after her mother. She inquires of Curly Prentiss if it is true that Molly and Jim have split up and will not be attending the Christmas Eve dance together. When she spots Jim and Molly talking together in the street, she sets the rumor mill in motion.

Henderson, Vic: In *The Fugitive Trail*, Henderson enters into a deal with Bill Stewart to rustle Melrose's Little Wichita herd. They sell the cattle to one Jerry McMillan. In Camp Cooper, Melrose's cowboys catch up with him. Bruce Lockheart sizes up the gunman and concludes he is no Buck Duane or King Fisher. Henderson and his men are at a table in the middle of the saloon. Bruce enters and calls him out, calling him a rustler. Stewart is not there, he says, but Henderson soon realizes he is face to face with the real Bruce Lockheart. In the shootout, Henderson is killed.

Henley: In *Wilderness Trek*, one of Ormiston's drovers. He had been friendly with Drake, a drover in Dann's outfit. He is shot by Larry when the Dann outfit catches up with Ormiston and his crew with the stolen cattle and horses.

Hennesy (Scout): In *Fighting Caravans*, mentioned as a freighter. In *The Lost Wagon Train*, this same Hennesy arrives at Latchfield with a caravan from Texas. Several of his party declare that Latchfield is the place of their dreams and they decide to settle there.

Hennesy: In *Raiders of Spanish Peaks*, one of Allen's riders. He survives the gunfight at Allen's ranch when Laramie and his men and Strickland, the representative of the Cattlemen's Association, confront him about his dealing in stolen cattle. Hennesy is warned never to come back to that range, if he values his life. He rides off, grateful to escape hanging.

Hennesy, Lafe: In *The Fugitive Trail*, runs the saloon in Dennison where Bruce Lockheart shoots and kills Steve Henderson.

Henney: In *The U. P. Trail*, the oldest of the engineering corps. He supervises the work of the junior engineers. He has great praise for Warren Neale's work and, like General Lodge, sees a great future for him with the U. P. Henney plays no significant role in the novel, although he is mentioned quite frequently.

Henniger: In *The Rainbow Trail*, one of the Mormon men who come into camp at Navajo mountain. He is cordial and pleasant. He is the guard at the schoolhouse in the secret village where Mary is being confined after the murder of Waggoner.

Henny: In *Majesty's Rancho*, one of the gangsters assigned to hold up the truck Lance Sidway is driving. He is surprised to find it empty, as it should have been carrying bootleg liquor. Lance gives him a bum steer, telling him other trucks have gone to El Paso, and he points him on a shortcut.

Henry: (1) In *Arizona Ames*, a blacksmith in Shelby and friend of Cappy Tanner. The two of them had done some trapping together in the past. He and his chatty wife bring Tanner up to date on the latest gossip about Nesta and Lee Tate. He does not have a good opinion of the Tates, but considers Nesta a lost cause because of her infatuation with Lee.

(2) In *The Fugitive Trail*, Henry is Jerry McMillan's foreman. McMillan has bought a herd of cattle from Vic Henderson. Melrose's cowboys catch up with him and inform him that he has bought stolen cattle. McMillan tells Tex Serks that Henry had his doubts about Henderson's honesty but he could not pass up a good deal. They reach an agreement whereby he will sell the cattle and split the money with Melrose.

Henshall, Jim: In *Stairs of Sand*, declared by Hank Day to be the only sheriff in Yuma who was any good. He was killed in a fight and nobody has taken his place. Rumor has it that Collishaw, Adam Larey's enemy, is the only man keen to take up the job, but he's not very well liked by the solid citizens of the growing town, as he runs the saloon and other gambling establishments.

Hensler, Barsh: In *Arizona Ames*, rustler Clive Bannard's right-hand man. He is a gambler and a thief, and a friend of Fred Halstead, who owes him three hundred dollars in gambling debts. He proposes Fred pay off the debt by rustling cattle from his father. Hensler works with Mecklin, one of Halstead's riders. In the confrontation with Arizona Ames, who has caught them red-handed with stolen cattle, Hensler attempts to draw on Arizona Ames, who shoots him in the forehead.

Hepford, Anne: In *The Dude Ranger*, the daughter of John Hepford and cousin of Sam Brooks, whom she addresses as Uncle Brooks. She is a beautiful, shallow, proud, insincere, manipulative young woman. Ernest Selby first meets her in Springer, where she is waiting for the stage home to Red Rock Ranch. She had been sent to town to make a withdrawal of a substantial amount of money for her father. She feels uneasy carrying such a large amount on her. In her conversation with a cowboy called Jeff, she mentions her resentment of the owner of the ranch, who has left his estate to someone back east. She feels she and her father are the rightful heirs to the estate. On the ride back, three robbers attempt to take her purse with the money, but Ernest Selby, the tenderfoot heir, saves her. She jokes that he probably arranged this to make an impression on her. At the ranch, when he is hired as a hand, she joins in with Hyslip and the cowboys in making fun of Ernest. She sends him to town on an errand, to fetch the mail, to buy certain things for her. She is amused that he bought her some candy. She spreads the word among the cowboys that she will invite him to the dance in Springer, since her date from Saint Louis will not be able to come. Nebraskie and others warn Ernest that she is playing him for a sucker, intending to make a fool of him by dumping him at the last minute. And sure enough, she does. At the dance, she is amazed to see Ernest dressed up. She tells him she had asked him to the dance just to annoy Hyslip. Ernest takes her behavior as proof that she is shallow. Hawk Siebert holds out some hope for her. He suggests Ernest try a different approach, being serious. Most of the cowboys take her for the superficial flirt she seems to be. Maybe a proposal of marriage would make the difference. Ernest tries this, but is spurned for his efforts. Ernest cannot decide if his feelings for Anne are completely without foundation. He cannot believe that his instincts are that wrong. When he has been injured in his fight with Dude over at Brooks's ranch, she takes care of his bruises and cuts, then turns on him. When he is kicked off the ranch together with Nebraskie and Siebert, she shows up at the ranch with Hyslip. Her true feelings come out when Ernest returns to the ranch to get the blue ledger which Anne has told him contains her father's accounts. Hepford returns to the house and he enters the only room with an unlocked door. It is Anne's room, and she is there, in tears. She tells him she has written him a letter explaining her behavior over the past weeks. When she hears her father tell that Ernest has killed Hyslip, she offers to leave with him. Her father and the cowboys will not wait for the sheriff but will surely lynch him should they catch him. They leave together in a wagon, heading for the New Mexico border. They stop in Snowflake, where they meet Nebraskie and Daisy, who have just been married. Ernest and Anne tie the knot there too. When they return to Red Rock Ranch, Anne learns that he is the new owner of the ranch. She did not expect Ernest to be so generous in his treatment of her thieving father. She also ex-

pects some kind of punishment for her own cruel treatment of Ernest, but he tells her he loves her, that she married him for himself, before she knew he was the heir to the ranch. She confesses that she deserves worse, that she certainly does not deserve him.

Anne is an example of the shrew who must learn to treat others with respect and dignity. Like Georgie in *Code of the West*, she must learn to think of others and behave in a manner befitting a mature woman.

Hepford, John: In *The Dude Ranger*, the foreman of the Red Rock Ranch. He has held the position for some fifteen years, running the place for the absentee owner, Silas Selby. His management of the ranch has seen the stock drop from a high of some sixty thousand. In the past three years, twenty thousand have shrunk to little more than six thousand. As well, he has done little to maintain the ranch. He is reputed to have trouble keeping riders. Sam Brooks explains his strange way of selling cattle. He sends bunches of two-year-olds to Holbrook. The big drives don't go to the railroad, but to the reservations, where they are sold to a government buyer named Jones. The reports he has sent back to Silas Selby show no evidence of big drives of cattle. That explains how twenty thousand head of cattle had dwindled to the present six thousand. Hepford was clearly a cattle thief, feathering his nest for the past ten years. He has probably salted away over two hundred thousand dollars. The lawyer, Jefford Smith, tells Ernest that Hepford has money on interest in Holbrook where he is a director of the bank. He does considerable banking in Globe and other towns. He has bought a ranch in New Mexico and everything points to an imminent departure from Red Rock when the last of the cattle have been sold. When Ernest comes to the house the day of the dance to look for Anne, Hepford laughs at him for taking her seriously. Surely he should have realized that her invitation was just a joke. Ernest overhears Anderson and Wilkins talking about Hepford's cattle sales. They speculate about what he is doing, but assuage their consciences, saying they are not responsible for Hepford's swindling the owner of Red Rock. They do decide that things are getting too hot to go through with his proposed drive in October. Hepford fires Siebert, who tells him to his face he knows about his shady dealings. From this point on, the pace of things picks up. Hepford sends Hyslip to put Brooks off his homestead. Young Ernest gets his hands on the blue ledger where he kept his private accounts of cattle deals. Ernest had learned of his book when he dropped in to see Anne in the ranch office where she was doing the accounts. She pointed to this book held closed with an elastic band as records she was never to look at. Hepford tries to blame Ernest for Hyslip's death but Sam Brooks and Hawk Siebert tell the sheriff what really happened. Hepford is shocked when he learns that the young tenderfoot he had treated so dismissively is the new owner of the ranch. Ernest makes him an offer. If Hepford renounces his claim to the ranch, to his Arizona interests in the bank and otherwise, Selby will not prosecute. Hepford accepts the deal and does not have to face prosecution and prison.

Herbert, Ruth: The niece of Longstreth in *The Lone Star Ranger*. She arrives on the stage with Ray Longstreth. She is present in the inn when the robbers break in. She is also present in the Longstreth living room when Buck Duane comes to arrest Bo Snecker. She has little influence on the development of the plot.

Herdman: In *Wilderness Trek*, one of Ormiston's drovers involved in the rustling of cattle from the Slyter and Dann herds. He shoots Drake, one of Dann's drovers. He and Smith get away.

Hernández, General: In *The Light of Western Stars,* mentioned as one of the rebel Mexican leaders executed on orders from General Rojas.

Herrick, Bernie: In *Robbers' Roost*, an Englishman who has set up ranching in the Henry Mountains. According to Hays, he is rich and crazy as a bedbug, with more money than brains. He selected the spot because of the beautiful countryside. He bought ten thousand head of cattle and a lot of horses. Herrick chose Hays as his superintendent and sent him off looking for hard-riding, hard-shooting men. Hays laughs at Herrick. He has bought out the smaller farmers in the area, and all their cattle, chickens, turkeys, pigs, sheep, and burros. Hays underlines that eggs are a staple at the ranch, something unheard of in cattle country. To Hank Hays and most westerners, Herrick is a fool asking to be taken advantage of. When Jim Wall reaches the ranch, much of what Hays has said proves true. Herrick has selected as a site for his home what is undoubtedly the most picturesque point in the valley, not one particularly suited to conduct the ranch business. Herrick himself is a florid, blonde young man, hardly over thirty, and handsome in a fleshy sort of way, dressed as no westerner would ever dress. He explains the advice he had been given in Salt Lake City and Grand Junction, that he should hire a foreman of experience to handle the riders, and gunmen to deal with the rustlers reputed to haunt the region. Jim Wall feels sorry for Herrick, knowing what Hays has in store for him. Herrick speaks openly to him about his plans. He hired Heeseman to keep an eye on Hays. Wall suggests Heeseman is head of the Mount Henry rustler gang, and Herrick says that Heeseman had made the same comment about Hank Hays. Wall has to acknowledge that it is an old strategy to send a thief to catch a thief. Herrick declares that he takes men at their word. Since Jim has some education, he makes him his accountant. He tells them that his twenty-two-year-old sister Helen is arriving from Saint Louis through Denver around the fifteenth of the month. She wants to make Star Ranch her home. She rides like a Tartar and is looking forward to the West. Herrick has brought hounds with him, planning to

hunt, English style. Jim Wall explains that that form of entertainment is a joke in Colorado, as is his English saddle. A western saddle is designed for the working cowboy, with heavy cinches, stirrups, and room to tie a rope, canteen, rifle-sheath, saddlebags, slicker and bedroll. Herrick shows himself willing to adapt. Jim also shows him how to shoot. Herrick is a generous man, willing to learn, deeply devoted to his sister. When he is betrayed and beaten, and his sister abducted for ransom, he willingly agrees to pay the sum. At the end of the story when Jim Wall returns with Helen, he accepts him as brother-in-law and manager of his operation.

Herrick, Helen: In *Robbers' Roost,* Bernie Herrick's twenty-two-year-old sister. She is his only remaining close relative. She wants to make Star Ranch her home. According to Bernie, she rides like a Tartar. Jim Wall thinks that on a ranch peopled by cowboys, a single woman could wreak the havoc that her name suggests. Her arrival at Grand Junction creates quite a commotion. At first, she is not sure whether she should go with Jim and Barnes but when Barnes gives her a message from Bernie, that she should fetch what came by Wells Fargo, she decides all is O.K. She has nineteen bags, a problem for Jim and Barnes to fit into the wagon. Barnes is the first to see her without her hat and veil and reports to Jim that Utah has never seen the likes of her ... red lips, pink cheeks, golden hair, violet eyes, free and easy like her brother. Helen Herrick surprises Jim Wall by the vivid freshness of her youth. She is not in the least frightened, absolutely free from revulsion at the conditions of the town and the facilities it affords. She is thrilled to meet a desperado, as her brother had described Jim Wall in his letters. Young Barnes had spoken to her about Bernie having hired Jim to keep desperados and thieves away from Star Ranch. He has elaborated on Jim's supposed exploits as a gunman in his travels around the West. Clearly he worships Jim as his hero. Helen informs Jim that she lived in London most of her life and she has come to hate the crowded streets, the mud, the clamor, the dark cold rooms, and the endless, hurrying throngs of people. She is answering the call of the primitive blood inherited from her Viking ancestors. At the ranch, Jim learns that Helen's fearlessness borders on recklessness. She has little mistrust of the men on the ranch, and is clearly misled by Hank Hays's handsome face and suave demeanor. Although she calls him a cobra, she never fails to arouse his keen interest when she walks by. Jim comments that Hays watches her like a hawk. When Jim takes her riding and hunting, he tries to caution her that she needs to be more prudent. Jim kisses her to show what men could do to her. She slaps his face, but later at the ranch, admits that he has a point. After she is abducted by Hays and secreted in Robbers' Roost, Hays keeps the men away from her. Suspicion arises as to his true intentions. Slocum and Wall and Sparrowhawk Latimer know that Hayes has doublecrossed the group about the money he stole from

Herrick and they fear he has worse in store for Helen. Hays builds a shelter for her where she can move about without being seen by the men. Jim Wall comes to see her by night. She tells him she regrets not taking his advice before and offers him the ransom if he will protect her. Jim offers his help but rejects the money. He tells her he loves her. When the robber gang falls apart and the Heeseman crew attacks, Jim Wall ensures Helen's safety. He finds the way out of the canyon, crossing the flooded Dirty Devil River, surviving rock slides. He returns her to Star Ranch and her brother, Bernie. By this time, Helen is fully in love with him. He has rescued her like a knight of the chivalrous romances. Bernie takes him on as manager of the ranch and Helen proposes marriage. She has found a true western man who fulfills all her dreams.

Herron, Miss: In *The Vanishing American*, the white woman who teaches at the reservation school. She has acquired her position thanks to Morgan and although she disapproves of his proposal to enforce compulsory attendance at chapel, she acquiesces to him. She takes a particular dislike to Marian Warner and to her protégée, Gekin Yashi. Marian has witnessed her techniques in disciplining the children and disapproves wholeheartedly. Miss Herron is frightened out of her mind when Nophaie comes to the school to confront Morgan. Miss Herron is an example of the incompetent people working at the residential schools who owe their position to their connections rather than to their interest or abilities or concern for the Native Americans.

Hester: (1) In *The Heritage of the Desert*, Martin Cole's daughter and Snap Naab's first wife. She is a vindictive woman with a temper who is not willing to allow Snap to take a second wife. She indicates her displeasure in many ways. When Snap is in a better humor, off the drink and sober, he pursues his courtship of Mescal. Hester does her best to keep interrupting the process by sending the children to make requests of their father or otherwise hinder the meetings. On one occasion, she takes Snap's clothes and hides them so he must go about the house naked and would certainly be unable to court Mescal. Father Naab and the brothers as well as Jack get a good laugh out of this. When she continues to refuse to consent to the marriage, Snap beats her into submission. At an unspecified time in the year when Mescal is in the desert and Snap has gone over to work for Holderness, Hester dies, perhaps from a beating at Snap's hands or from pining over her fate.

(2) In *The Rainbow Trail*, Hester is the name of one of the sealed wives in the hidden village. She tells Ruth Jones that Mary has not had any food, and this gives Ruth and Shefford, who are planning her escape, a believable excuse to get into the schoolhouse, where Ruth switches clothes with Mary, thereby making her escape in disguise possible.

(3) In *Riders of the Purple Sage*, one of Jane Withersteen's servant women. She is caught listening at the door while Jane and Lassiter are talking. She is suspected of stealing documents and deeds from Jane's house and handing them over to Elder Tull.

Heston, Pony: In *Shadow on the Trail*, a member of Simm's outlaw gang. He meets Holden and Bell as they return to Smoky Hollow after the Texas Pacific job. He is shot in the ambush in Mercer, and badly wounded, but seems to have got away.

Hetcoff: In *West of the Pecos*, a rancher on the east side of the Pecos River. The Lambeth party camp near his ranch for the night. Hetcoff himself is from Missouri. He advises Lambeth to pick his range somewhere along the San Saba. The area is near the junction of roads and someday will be heavily populated. He knows little about what lies beyond the Pecos, but what he has heard sounds sinister.

Hevron, Bat: In *Boulder Dam*, a faro dealer at the Monte Palace in Las Vegas. Lynn Weston catches him cheating while dealing cards.

Hickenthorp, Thad: In *The Wolf Tracker*, one of the cowboys on Barrett's ranch preparing for the spring roundup. His buddies tease him because he is sweet on the boss's daughter, Sally.

Hickock, Wild Bill: In *Raiders of Spanish Peaks*, one of the legendary gunmen of the West that Laramie Nelson has met. He saw him shoot five men all in a row at Hays City. In *Shadow on the Trail*, Billy the Kid is declared to be even more deadly than Hickock. In *Knights of the Range*, Colonel Ripple and Britt speculate about whether Arizona will produce its own local gunmen of the caliber of Hickock.

In *The Arizona Clan*, Uncle Bill Lilley tells Dodge Mercer that they are lucky that Nan's Texas friend is of the same breed as Wild Bill, King Fisher and Wess Hardin.

Hicks: (1) In *Captives of the Desert*, Hicks is a cross-eyed, red-haired cowboy who gives Alex Hardy the name "High-Lo." He reports to John Curry that he has been looking high and low for Alex but can't find him. He calls Alex the "High-Low" cowboy, and the nickname sticks.

(2) In *Shadow on the Trail*, the name of three different characters.

The first Hicks is foreman of Jesse Chisum's operation. He assigns Holden to Jesse Evans's crew, which is working on a remote range.

Another man called Hicks appears in Holbrook and appears to run a general store which competes with the Bozeman brothers' emporium. He tells Wade Holden (Tex Brandon) that he is welcome to do business at his establishment as the Bozemans tend to concentrate on Mormon clients.

A third Hicks is a member of Hogue Kinsey's gang, who accepts Brandon's invitation to come work for Pencarrow. He is part Apache — the best man with horses, the best tracker and the slickest man in the woods among Kinsey's crew. Brandon comments that he has all the Indian's matchless horsemanship and all the range rider's daredevil boldness. His tracking skills come in handy trailing

Carter, the rustled cattle, Blue, and Harrobin among others.

Higgenbottom, Tine: In *The Deer Stalker*, one of the guides conducting tours for the El Tovar hotel at the Grand Canyon. His fellow guide, Nelson Stackhouse, keeps bumming cigarettes off him. Patricia Edgerton observes the dynamic between the two of them. Nelson is clearly the leader, but Tine is his loving, loyal follower. Tine and Nelson contrive to get Patricia and Sue to take a camping excursion with them up to the North Rim. Tine accompanies Nelson as he goes about looking for a suitable ranch around Flagstaff for Patricia Edgerton. With Nels, he participates in the deer drive. He will be working on Patricia's new ranch when she takes over.

Higgins: (1) In *The Fugitive Trail*, one of the men working for Hank Silverman on the wagon train. When they have completed their part of the trail, he is leaving with Silverman and Davis for the Tonto Basin in Arizona, where Silverman has two brothers.

(2) In *The Maverick Queen*, one of the ranchers north of the forks of the Sweetwater River. Slim Morris used to ride for him.

Higgins, Brick: In *The Lone Star Ranger,* one of two men in Longstreth's gang who get arrested.

Higgins, Captain: In *Wyoming*, Andrew Bonning says that he never made a success of athletics at university because Captain Higgins and the athletic directors played their favorites and never gave him a chance.

Highgate and Stanfield: In *30,000 on the Hoof*, the lawyers that Logan Huett consults in Washington when he tries to sue the government to recover the hundred thousand dollars that were swindled from him by Mitchell and Caddell. These lawyers take a fee of twenty-five hundred dollars and claim to have started the process of suing to retrieve the money. When things keep getting postponed, Huett goes to Senator Spellman from Arizona only to learn that these lawyers are not part of respectable law firm, and furthermore, they have never filed a suit in the courts.

High-Lo: In *Captives of the Desert*, the nickname that the cowboy Hicks gives to Alex Hardy. He tells John Curry that he has looked high and low for Alex but he is nowhere to be seen. The "High-Lo" cowboy cannot be found if he does not want to be found.

High-Lo is a handsome young fellow short of twenty with a tremendous store of energy which, in his early youth, was misdirected. When High-Lo was seven or eight years old, his father introduced him to whisky and taught him the false notion that the true measure of a man was his ability to drink heavily without passing out. High-Lo tried his best to measure up to this standard. Consequently, he was outlawed before he was eighteen by the community in which he lived. He faced the county judge once too often. Before he left the family homestead in

Colorado, he rustled three of the county judge's own maverick calves, marked them with his father's brand, and presented them to the judge as a gift from his father, who wished to show his appreciation of the judge's leniency towards his wayward son. On his exodus from Colorado, he met up with John Curry journeying to Black Mesa from his brother's ranch in Colorado. The incident of their meeting began a new chapter in the boy's life. High-Lo sobbed his troubles to John Curry over a campfire. Curry adopted the boy at once and nursed him through his drinking sickness, but when he found him drunk again, gave him a good thrashing. High-Lo becomes a hand working for Mr. Weston's outfit with John. He became one of the best and the worst cowboys working for the Black Mesa outfit.

High-Lo does not like Wilbur Newton. He knows about his selling liquor to the Indians, but he keeps quiet about it out of respect for Newton's wife, Mary. The young cowboy falls into a trap laid by the bootleggers, Hanley and Newton. They string a length of barbed wire across the trail. High-Lo's horse, Cricket, trips over the wire, throwing the rider, who breaks several ribs in his fall. John Curry comes looking for him when he does not return home overnight. He finds him unconscious, and tries to take him home, holding High-Lo in front of him in the saddle. Magdaline meets them on the way and rides to Taho for help. Back at Taho, the doctor sets his broken ribs.

When John sets out looking for Wilbur Newton to deliver a letter from Mary, High-Lo accompanies him. They come upon the bootleggers and a shootout ensues in which Hanley is killed and John is shot in the shoulder. It is High-Lo's turn to return the favor of saving his life. High-Lo knows that John is concerned about Magdaline's plight. She is pregnant by Newton and in a depressed state. High-Lo marries her, thereby preventing John from making a big mistake.

Hildrith, Leale: In *The Horse Thief*, an easygoing, generous, open-hearted, blond-bearded giant in his late twenties, Watrous's foreman and close friend to Dale Brittenham. Leale Hildrith had found him out on the range, crippled, half-starved, and frozen. At risk of his own life, he carried Dale through the blizzard to the safety of a distant shelter. A friendship had sprung up between the two men, generous and careless on Hildrith's part, at times, even protective. It engendered in Dale a passionate loyalty and gratitude, almost a hero-worship for the golden-bearded Hildrith. Dale is both shocked and dismayed to hear Ben, Alec and Steve, the rustlers in camp, speak of Hildrith as their inside man in Salmon. When Dale returns with the prized horses, he now notes a look of shocked surprise in his friend's eyes. Later, Leale comes upon Edith kissing Dale out of gratitude for his having retrieved her stolen horses. Edith assuages the jealousy in Leale, but Dale has something more serious to discuss with him. He reveals what he heard in the rustlers' camp.

Leale swears his friend to secrecy, promising to get out of the business before he marries Edith, to whom he has just become engaged. When the sheriff comes to arrest Dale, out of loyalty, Dale confesses to take any possible suspicion away from Leale. He plans to track down the rustlers and clear his name, and Leale's as well. Leale shows up in Hasley with Edith for the horse auction. Leale is rather sheepish when Edith asks him to confirm that the black stallion, Dick, is her horse. Reed tries to force a confession out of him that he is one of the gang. Reed abducts Edith, taking her to Big Bill Mason's cabin in the hideout canyon. There, he denounces Leale as a traitor to the group. Although Big Bill likes Hildrith more than he does Reed, the betrayal is more than the head rustler can tolerate. He shoots and kills Leale Hildrith.

Hiles, Sheriff: In *Shadow on the Trail*, witnesses the exchange of gunfire between Wade Holden (Tex Brandon) and Kent. Brandon calls on him to recognize that it was self-defense. He comes from down Winslow way, and, according to Hogue Kinsey, he's not much good. From the talk which follows with Tex, he is clearly a partisan of Mason and his rustlers, if not directly involved in his rustling scam. He threatens to arrest Brandon if he does not leave town.

Hill: In *Valley of Wild Horses*, one of the three guards at the jail where Jim Blake is being held. He is reputed to be a "tough customer."

Hill, Amanda: In *Valley of Wild Horses*, the teacher at the school when Dick Hardman and Pan Handle Smith get into a fight over Dick's unwelcome kissing of Lucy. It becomes a fight to the death, as it were, for Dick stabs Pan Handle in the shoulder with the teacher's letter opener. Miss Hill has to get Jim Blake and Pan Handle's father to tear the boys apart.

Hill, Archie: In *Raiders of Spanish Peaks*, one of the cowboys that Allen has left to work on Lindsay's new ranch. Lenta has gotten to know the cowboys and has divided them into those that are loyal to Arlidge and Allen, and those who have come over to Laramie Nelson. Archie Hill, however, she has not been able to figure out and is not sure where he stands.

Hill, Sam: In "Canyon Walls," the name the widow Keetch gives Smoke Bellew when she decides to take him on as a hired hand at her ranch in Green Canyon.

Hillie: In "The Secret of Quaking Asp Cabin," the daughter of Richard Starke and Blue. She is particularly fond of her father and remains loyal to him even after he has had his arm shot off and is unable to do much for himself. She is about six years old at this time. She never guesses the reason for her father's moroseness. Her brother, Starke, a year her senior, the bastard son of her uncle Len and the Apache girl Letithe, is very close to her. Ten years after the shooting in which Richard lost his arm,

Hillie dies and is buried not far from the cabin. Starke spends hours standing at the grave. He leaves without a word of farewell to the parents who raised him.

Hills, Miss: In *Captives of the Desert*, takes turns with Mary Newton staying up with Joy in the hospital. She sleeps through the day to be ready to sit up at night. Recalling all that Mary had undergone, she arranged with the neighbors to have Mary's house warm for her return.

Hilton, Clara: In *The Deer Stalker*, works at the El Tovar resort organizing tours for guests to visit the Grand Canyon. When Thad's mother reminds him in a letter that it is time he got married, he can think of no woman he might want to marry except Clara Hilton, and he's not terribly enthusiastic about that option. Patricia Edgerton describes her as hawk-like as she sees to the needs of the guests at the resort. She gives Patricia a strange look, as if trying to place her. Miss Edgerton feels Clara Hilton is a jealous person, calculating, inquisitive. She conceives an instant dislike for the woman, although she is handsome and speaks in an ingratiating way with everyone. Clara, it turns out, has seen her picture in a New York paper left behind by a guest. She learns Patricia's name is actually Edgerton, not Clay, as recorded in the registry. She reads about her career as an international model with a questionable reputation. She wastes no time spreading the word about her. When Thad Eburne shows interest in Patricia, she does her best to try to start trouble between them. She tells him Patricia's name is associated with a great disgrace on two continents. She is worth millions and has had lovers galore. She ruined her reputation and had to leave New York. That's why she's parading under a false name. What interest could she possibly have in a mere forest ranger if not to have a bit of fun. Thad, however, does not lose faith in Patricia.

Hilton, John: In *Twin Sombreros*, the postmaster in Latimer. He signed the receipt delivering a letter to Brazos Keene in the post office in Latimer at 8:10 in the morning. This evidence proves Brazos could not have murdered Allen Keene in mid-afternoon in Las Animas, as no one could ride that distance in that time.

Hilyard, Rose: In *The Drift Fence*, the Virginia grandmother of Molly Dunn. Mrs. Dunn tells Molly that this woman was her grandmother when Molly is complaining about the lack of family pride. Given the poor reputation of her immediate family, her brother, her mother, her father, Molly has little self-respect. This ancestor supposedly proves she has bluer blood than the rich and powerful Trafts and has no reason to feel inferior to anyone.

Hindfoot: In *Stairs of Sand*, located by Merryvale in the saloon in Lost Lake. He is called Hindfoot locally and is one of the tragic derelicts of the desert, ruined by contact with the whites. He understands English, though he can speak it only a little. He is capable in many ways but has become so addicted to drink that he cannot get work. When the saloon opens from morning to night, he can be counted upon to be there. Merryvale recruits him to help track the abductors of Ruth Virey. Hindfoot says it was too dark the night they arrived to see who the men were, but he does not think Larey was one of them. He gets Merryvale equipped to follow Adam into the desert.

Hines: In *Arizona Ames,* homesteaders in the Tonto Basin who had conjoined twins that died shortly after birth. Rich Ames mentions them when he thinks about the quirks of nature. Giving birth to twins runs in the Ames family. Fortunately, none were ever conjoined.

Hirsh: In *The Maverick Queen*, a rancher neighbor to Bloom Burton down in the valley. Bloom reveals that Hirsh's wagon was used to move Jimmy Weston's body from Kit Bandon's ranch, where he was murdered, to the saloon in South Pass.

Hite, Ross: In *The Trail Driver*, a name known to all the trail drivers. Hite has run the gamut of all Texas occupations known to the range. He is a man of about fifty years old, with a visage like a bleak stone bluff and eyes like cracks. He rides into Brite's camp with Wallen, demanding that Reddie be given back. When Wallen is killed, he retreats, commenting that Brite is well-heeled, with two gunmen in his crew. Brite observes that one of the men with Wallen and Hite was riding one of his horses. Pan Handle Smith suspects that Hite and Wallen were responsible for the stampede of horses earlier in the day. Pan Handle says Hite is a cattle-buyer from Abilene, but having got into shady deals, Abilene has become too hot for him. He is surprised though, that he would be involved in such a small thing as stampeding a few horses. He suspects that Hite is planning bigger heists along the Chisolm Trail. Adam Brite finds confirmation of this when he visits Snell's saloon in Austin and finds two of his riders there with Hite. Hallett especially is involved in a low voiced conversation with him, while Chandler appears to have come mainly to drink. The following day, Chandler appears just as Hallett is accusing him of plotting with Hite to arrange the rustling of the herd. Indeed, this is what happens. Hite rustles half of the herd when the cattle get split up crossing a river. He rustles the second half when Brite's men are busy with the Comanches who have attacked the Hardy wagons. Texas decides to let Hite have the trouble of driving the herd, and they keep a close eye on him from a distance. Eventually, they get the herd back from him when most of his riders are killed in a lightning storm. Texas Joe discovers that there are about fifteen hundred more cattle than they started off with. It appears Hite has rustled some cattle along the way to add to the herd. Doan informs Pan Handle Smith that Hite hangs out at Hays City and visits Dodge often. In Dodge, Pan Handle is determined to find him and settle the score. He catches up to him

coming out of the barber shop beside Beatty and Kelly's store. Hite is killed in the gunfight.

Hitwell, Sam: In *The Trail Driver*, in the cattle business before the war with Adam Brite. He set up a merchandise store to supply the men organizing trail drives north. Hitwell comments that if Chisolm had had more foresight, he would have gone into the merchandising business.

Hoadley, Bill: In *The Border Legion*, the man who opened the mining town named after him. He is Joan Randle's uncle, married to her Aunt Jane. He also discovered gold at Alder Creek and is known by the name Overland, as the agent in charge of shipping out all the gold from Alder Creek by stage. Joan is glad that all his years of toil have finally paid off.

Hoadley, Jane: In *The Border Legion*, Joan Randle's father's sister, Aunt Jane. When Joan is abducted, she at first thinks that Harvey Roberts will bring back word that she is all right. When she realizes Roberts has been shot and killed, she worries about her aunt. When she finally returns to Hoadley, she worries that her aunt won't understand why she married Jim Cleve, a young man with the reputation of being shiftless.

Hobbs, John: In *Fighting Caravans*, a famous frontier scout that Clint Belmet meets at Kit Carson's home in Taos, New Mexico.

Holbert, Ben: In *30,000 on the Hoof*, the son of John Holbert. He witnessed the fight between George Huett and Jack Campbell. The story he tells suggests that the Campbells had planned the fight at the dance to dissuade George from seeing their sister, Milly, but they had not counted on his brother Abe being there to help out.

Holbert, John: In *30,000 on the Hoof*, Logan Huett's closest neighbor. When the story begins, he is living with his wife and two daughters and his sister. His youngest daughter is married to a young man called Bill. Holbert sells Logan Huett his first few head of cattle when he takes up ranching in the Sycamore Canyon. He advances him cattle on credit for a number of years, then calls in the mortgage, unexpectedly. A certain jealousy characterizes his dealings with Huett. When Logan kills Tim Mooney, the crooked rancher dealing with rustlers, Holbert is quick to emphasize he has had nothing to do with rustling. Holbert is one of the friends waiting to meet Huett when he returns from Washington, having learned of the death of George and Grant in the war, and Abe's being missing in action.

Holbert, Mary: In *30,000 on the Hoof*, John Holbert's daughter. She marries Bill, who deserts ranching and takes up rustling.

Holbert, Mrs.: In *30,000 on the Hoof*, the wife of John Holbert. She gives Lucinda her dog, Coyote, and helps with the delivery of the second son, Abe.

Holden, Jim: In *Shadow on the Trail*, Wade

Holden's father. Jim Holden was a Missouri guerrilla during the Civil War. After the war he came home a crippled and ruined man. Simm Bell had been one of his lieutenants and for some years had practically taken care of the Holdens. It seems that Jim Holden is not Wade's biological father, as his mother had an affair with Simm Bell without Holden ever finding out. Simm Bell has treated Wade like a son and has tried to get him to leave the outlaw outfit and make something respectable of himself. When he is dying, he reveals that he is Wade's real father.

Holden, Less: In *The Trail Driver,* an old partner of Texas Joe Shipman. He is a flaming-faced youth under twenty ... with eyes of blue fire and an air of reckless insouciance. Texas Joe volunteers him to join the trail drive that Adam Brite is planning to Dodge. Shipman describes him as a "wild hombre." He is from Dallas, and for the past three years has been riding for Dave Slaughter. He has never gone on a trail drive before. He partakes of all the adventures along the trail, the encounter with Wallen, the stampedes, the Comanche attack on the Handy wagon, the rustling of the herd, and the partying in Dodge.

Holden, Lil: In *Shadow on the Trail,* Wade Holden's sister. Wade tells Simm Bell that she is his only relative. His parents are dead, and Lil is married, and she knows he has gone to the bad. Simm Bell and his outlaw gang are the only family he knows. He tells Jacqueline Pencarrow that Lil and his mother are the only women he has ever known.

Holden, Wade (a.k.a. Tex Brandon and Blanco): In *Shadow on the Trail,* a member of Simm Bell's robber gang. Zane Grey develops the character of Wade Holden to answer a question he asks in the preface to the novel: what ever happened to those outlaws who made a momentary splash in some town or some region only to vanish, never to be heard from again? In Wade Holden, Grey explores one possible destiny of such a man.

Simm has a special fondness for Holden, treating him like a son. When the novel begins, Bell and Holden are robbing the Texas Pacific express car. Holden warns Simm that Rand Blue, one of Simm's special friends among the gang, has betrayed them. Holden saw him talking to Ranger Pell, and sending a telegram at the express office. When Smith and Hazlitt argue over the division of the money, Holden has to shoot them to defend Bell. He then confronts Blue, who admits to the betrayal claiming, however, that he was going to double-cross the rangers, not them. Furthermore, Blue tells Simm that Holden is jealous of their friendship and that is why he has made this accusation. Bell stops Holden from shooting Blue. He cannot let Holden shoot a friend because of suspicion. He does, however, let Blue go with the warning that if he should discover that Blue has betrayed him, he will hunt Blue down and kill him.

Back at Smoky Hollow, the issue of Blue's betrayal comes up again. Nick Allen says he has always mistrusted Blue. Arkansas pragmatically points out that they should not go through with the Mercer bank job, just in case he has betrayed them to the rangers. Furthermore, they should quickly vacate the hideout in Smoky Hollow and get out of the area because Blue has been there and reveal its location to the rangers. Wade agrees. However, only the two of them vote to curtail the Mercer job.

Before they undertake the job, Simm Bell comes to talk to Wade. He confesses to a strange feeling that has been creeping over him, the kind people say comes over you when someone walks on your grave. He tells Wade that he feels responsible for him. He is not afraid of jail, planning to be killed before that happens. But he wants things different for Wade. His mother was a good woman and his sister Lil is a fine young woman. He's had schooling and he's a handsome young man. He should ride away and go straight. Just after the train heist, Wade himself was feeling trapped by his life. He does not want to desert Simm Bell, who has been like a father to him, and feels there is no other course open to him.

Simm Bell, strange to say for a bank and express office robber, feels little attachment to money. He is generous with his men and with the locals, who are glad to keep silent about his activities. He gives Wade Holden a large packet filled with paper money. When he opens it, Wade sees packets of fifty- and hundred-dollar bills, as well as smaller denominations, twenties, tens and fives. He sews the money into the lining of his vest and his coat.

After the disastrous ambush in Mercer, Wade and Simm are pursued by the rangers led by Mahaffey. Simm is mortally wounded, and Wade Holden planning to ambush the rangers and pick them off one by one as they approach. He is a wonderful marksman and could kill at least half of the rangers before they could they could get close enough to shoot back. Simm, however, forbids it. He has lasted this long in the rustling business because he had the good sense never to shoot a ranger. He recommends that course of action for Wade as well. Holden leaves Simm leaning against the trunk of a tree with his rifle, ready to shoot the approaching rangers. Perhaps he can slow them down enough to let Wade get away. But before he goes, Simm reveals that he is Wade Holden's real father. Now he understands Simm's protectiveness and concern about his well-being, feelings Simm never had for any other members of his gang.

Wade Holden escapes the grip of the rangers, hiding in Jacqueline Pencarrow's tent while the rangers search the wagon train. She binds up his wounds, hides him overnight, and shows him the best trail to avoid detection. The next months and years fade together. He comes into the camp of some buffalo hunters, from whom he buys a horse and saddle. The hiders promise never to mention seeing him. He comes upon a cattle trail and falls in with the Catlin outfit of rustlers, who are planning to clean out the Aulsbrook drive located about ten miles ahead of them. They offer him a place in their group, but he overhears a conversation in which Nippert expresses suspicions about the man, adding that he looks well-heeled. They would be better off killing him in the night and robbing him. Holden leaves before dawn and approaches Aulsbrook, warning him of Catlin's intention. Aulsbrook's foreman, Bert, is suspicious, thinking that it's part of Catlin's strategy. Holden's honesty is proven when Catlin and Nippert arrive for a fatal showdown. Aulsbrook takes him on as a rider, and when he sells his cattle to Jesse Chisum, leaving his cowboys with the new employer, he invites Wade to continue on with him. Wade, however, chooses to stay with Chisum, who sets him to work under Jesse Evans and the number ten outfit on a remote stretch of range. Jesse Evans praises him, the best man Chisum has hired since he has been with him. His encomium goes like this:

"He come here with all kinds of a rep as a gunman ... shoots the haids off all the jack rabbits ... an you cain't find a tin can without a hole in it. He's been the kind of tenderfoot I never seen before. You cain't make him mad. He'll tend you anythin' but his guns. Give you his last smoke. Stand your watch an' do your chores. He'll play two-bit poker but nothin' higher an' did he ever win a dollar? Hell no.... They say you hail from Texas. But you're no Texan. You came from somewhere north.... You always have somethin' on your mind. You're always lookin' for somebody.... You got the eye, the hand and the draw of a gunman. You've killed men, an' you bet more than them two hombres that Aulsbrook told us about last spring ... we don't like you the less for that. But 'cept in my case, the boys air leery of you. Thet'd pass in time, if you stayed with us. But you won't stay, Blanco. Mark my hunch. You'll be gone before the snow flies."

Holden is amazed at how accurately Evans has read him. Evans acknowledges that all cowboys have a deep side, a bad side. He should know, having been friends with Billy the Kid. But out in cowboy heaven on this beautiful range, there is time to think. Shortly after this, Billy the Kid does appear with word that Mahaffey has appeared at Chisum's looking for Blanco. Holden refuses the Kid's offer to accompany him, leaving instead to wander. He spends the winter with an old trapper who teaches him the tricks of survival in the wilderness. Come spring, he sets out again with a new appearance. His beard has provided him with an excellent disguise, a change in appearance that should help him find a new way. He works as a shepherd in Mariposa, works with a trader who sends him about the Indian villages buying up blankets and other artifacts he can sell in his store. He works on a Mormon ranch where the owner's daughter makes staying on a source of trouble with the other cowboys. He works in a lumber camp, in the mining camps, making himself a small fortune. He wanders into Tombstone, where he acquires a new name after killing gambler Monte in a fight to protect a dancer. The new name is Tex Brandon, a combination of his nickname and his mother's family name.

With this, he travels around Arizona, looking for an opportunity to settle down, to redeem himself. By coincidence he runs into Lawsford, Aulsbrook's foreman. This is the Aulsbrook he had saved from Catlin's robbers. Lawsford mentions the Pencarrows, the family whose daughter had hidden him in her tent while Mahaffey and his men searched the caravan. Pencarrow is on hard times, and Wade decides this would be his chance to repay Jacqueline Pencarrow for having saved his life and given him a chance to redeem himself.

Pencarrow offers to let him work there as foreman. He defends him against Drake's men, Bill and Urba, who try to take his horses in payment for a twice-paid debt. He lends Pencarrow seven thousand dollars to pay off debts. On the advice of a neighbor, Elwood Lightfoot, he recruits Hogue Kinsey and his outfit to work for Pencarrow. Slowly, he brings about great change on Cedar Range. He trains Pencarrow's son as a cowboy, teaching him to ride, to shoot, to herd cattle. He whips his cowboys into a powerful unit of herders and gunmen. He tracks down the outlaw gang in the area — Carter, Harrobin, Randall Blue (who had betrayed his father), Mason and Kent. Slowly he clears the range of the criminal element, making ranching once more a viable operation. He buys out Aulsbrook's operation and settles down to ranching as a neighbor to the Pencarrows. In the process, Jacqueline Pencarrow comes to love him. He had worried that she might recognize him, and on occasion, he thinks that she has placed him. However, she never mentions anything. She and Wade Holden marry. When Ranger Mahaffey catches up with Holden, Pencarrow and Jacqueline speak of him in such glowing terms that he shows no inclination to arrest him. He has been redeemed and can live out the rest of his life as Tex Brandon in blissful isolation and anonymity from the law. It turns out that Jacqueline did recognize him, but kept quiet about it, since he seemed to want it that way.

Zane Grey often develops the theme of the outlaw who redeems himself by changing his way of life, doing good to compensate for the bad he has done in the past, making amends. Grey hoped that Holden's was the fate of other momentarily notorious outlaws who vanished from the pages of history.

Holder: In *Nevada*, from Eureka, California. He is mentioned as a decent man, a rancher, interested in Lize Teller. He bought cattle in Lineville, possibly aware that they were stolen. Mrs. Wood thinks he would have been good for Lize, but Burridge returned loaded with money from some deal down south with money to gamble. Burridge and Holder get into a fight over Lize.

Holderness: In *The Heritage of the Desert*, a cattle thief masquerading as a respectable rancher. Holderness first appears early in the novel when he meets August Naab and Jack Hare in Abe's store. Jack Hare detects in him something different from other men, a power, an instinct, an indefinable subtlety, an indefinable mistrust. In turn, Holderness sees in Hare a threat, a latent possibility. Holderness is an excellent judge of character and he looks at Hare with the keen intelligence of a man who knows how the desert can transform and harden a man. He has heard of "Dene's spy" who had been sent to Lund to count unbranded cattle among Holderness's herds. Rustling in this part of the West is a question of taking unbranded cattle and branding them with one's own brand, or taking branded cattle and altering the brand, then driving the cattle north for sale. Holderness's herds increase at a rate well beyond that sanctioned by the reproductive process of Mother Nature. Holderness hopes to be able to lure Jack Hare to his side, much as he has lured other normally upright Mormons and Snap Naab to his cause.

A second tactic used by Holderness is intimidation. With the help of Dene and his outlaws, Holderness has taken over many of the smaller ranches in the area through a process of rustling combined with harassment. Martin Cole lost his ranch to Holderness in this way. Holderness attempts to do the same to August Naab. First he fills in the Blue Star water hole, forcing Naab to drive his flock of sheep to another watering hole. The herd of over five thousand sheep perish on the way to the Seeping Springs. Holderness eventually moves on to this second water hole. He closes off access to the spring with fences and corrals, staking a personal claim to water, which in the desert is available to all. He builds a cabin at the spring to establish his claim. When he first finds the logs to build the cabin, Jack Hare burns them, but the next time any of Naab's crew ride past the Seeping Springs water hole, Holderness has proceeded apace with the construction of the cabin. This is combined with a systematic rustling of Naab's unbranded cattle and sometimes clumsy attempts at rebranding them. Jack Hare and Mescal see his handiwork as they ride back to Naab's oasis when they return from the desert.

Holderness is the first of type of character to appear in Grey's western novels, the ruthless monopolistic profiteer whose only interest is profit, without regard for other people or the environment. The reader learns this about Holderness during his first appearance at Abe's store. He offers to buy Silver Springs and Silver Cup from August Naab for ten thousand dollars. Naab refuses to entertain the thought, saying that no man has right to own what is needed by all. Naab contrasts the law of the desert with the laws of property, pointing out that one man cannot take possession of an oasis to supplant other ranchers. Holderness and his cattle company care little for the environment or other small cattlemen. It's a question of business and profit to be made as quickly and as effortlessly as possible.

Holderness relies on the mask of respectability to fool people. He consolidates power in White Sage by taking control of the instruments of government. He gets himself elected sheriff, and exerts power over both the Mormon ranchers from whom he steals and over the Mormons in town who have not succumbed to his will. Most are too afraid to do anything. Killings are reported on a daily basis in the community. When Jack finds the goings-on at Seeping Springs, he goes to White Sage to confront Holderness openly in Abe's store. He calls him a cattle thief, a liar, a murderer. His secret is out in the open.

The same ruthlessness is seen in his interest in Mescal. He offers to buy her from Naab to be used as a slave. Later, he offers to marry her. When pressure is put on Naab through the loss of his springs and his cattle, Holderness sends Snap Naab and Dene to seize her. Snap thinks that Holderness has been helping him to get the wife who had been promised to him but who had escaped to the desert. He is surprised to learn that Holderness has intended her for himself from the start. Holderness tricks Snap Naab into a gunfight, having first taken the precaution of unloading Snap's pistol. With Snap dead, Holderness thinks he has finally got her. One of his men, however, frees her from the cabin where she is being held and she escapes to White Sage, where the Mormons hide her. Holderness goes to Bishop Caldwell's place to claim Mescal but when this tactic meets without success, he draws on Jack Hare, only to be shot before his gun is half out of the holster.

Holderness is the prototype of the quintessential villain of many B westerns, the handsome, cool, calculating, slick, superior, manipulating profiteer.

Holley, Hawk: In *Wildfire*, works for John Bostril at Bostril's Ford. He and Farlane are close confidants of Bostril. He has better eyesight than either Farlane or Bostril and is called to describe what he sees in the race between Joel Creech and Lucy. He understands Bostril's love of horses but is less sympathetic to his obsession with owning the fastest horses around and his unscrupulous tactics in obtaining the fast horses of others Holley is the sixth member of Bostril's horseman's club when they meet to plan the races. He himself enters a horse called Rocks in the race. Holley is lean, gray. He is suspicious of Bostril's motives in preventing Creech from bringing his horses across the river for the race. Holley tries to ward off trouble between Bostril and Slone when Wildfire wins the race. He describes himself as an older brother to Lucy and acts to preserve her happiness. Holley serves as a go-between, bringing word from Slone about a proposal to buy Wildfire; he also delivers messages from Lucy. When Joel Creech spreads a rumor that he had witnessed Lin Slone trying to force himself on Lucy, Holley is not quite sure whom to believe. He tells Lin Slone about Lucy's being "hard to control." He also tries to keep the gossip spread by Joel from reaching the ears of Bostril or Lucy. Most of the men, Van, Farlane among them, are inclined to believe Joel's story. Holley is one of the men in the group when they come upon Joel with the ransom note for Lucy. Holley is an admirer of horsemanship and he proclaims Lin Slone the best horseman he has ever seen. Lucy's marriage to Lin, he is sure, will be a "stable" marriage.

Holliday, Lonestar: In *The Drift Fence*, a member of Jim Traft's crew on the Diamond Ranch. He reputedly left Texas over a shooting incident. Lonestar works on the drift fence without too much grumbling. At the rodeo, Lonestar wins a purse for bulldogging steers. Lonestar picks a fight with the foreman and gets soundly trounced. Like the rest of the crew, he comes to like and admire his tenderfoot foreman. In *The Hash Knife Outfit*, Lonestar Holliday is still in the employ of Jim Traft and the Diamond Ranch. His reputation as a gunman is given more prominence here. Pecos of the Hash Knife Outfit points out to the other members that a man like Lonestar Holliday is not to be taken lightly. He accompanies young Jim Traft to Lang to pick up his sister.

Hones: In *The Lost Wagon Train*, a wagon driver in Anderson's caravan taking the Bowdens to California. He is killed in Kiowa attack on the wagon train.

Hood: In *Wilderness Trek*, one of Stanley Dann's drovers on the trans–Australia trek. Just before Eric Dann confesses he has lied about knowing the way, Hood, who has a wife and child, decides to quit the trek, together with Bligh, Derrick and Heald.

Hoofs In *The Horse Thief*, Dale Brittenham's faithful horse.

Hooker: In *Sunset Pass*, Amy Wund mentions this young cowboy crazy with drink and jealousy whom Trueman Rock killed in a gunfight. She feels she was the cause of his death.

Hooley: In *Valley of Wild Horses*, one of the calf ropers working on the first roundup in which young Pan Handle Smith participates.

Hopi John: In *Captives of the Desert*, lives in Taho. He provides John Curry with information about Hanley, the whiskey runner. Hopi John is proud of his English and looks for any opportunity to practice it. Hanley, it seems, was seen in Phoenix negotiating a "sheep deal." The Blakely sisters, whiskey traders, also happen to live in Phoenix.

Horn brothers: In *Knights of the Range*, run a trading post and freighting depot. Their establishment is on land that strictly speaking belongs to the Ripple ranch, but Colonel Lee and his daughter Holly do nothing about it because there are clear advantages in having such a post nearby. However, as the years pass, the freighting station grows to include several saloons and gambling establishments. Holly Ripple resents the riffraff that such a place draws.

Horn, Bill: In *The U. P. Trail*, a burly miner, bearded and uncouth, of rough speech and taciturn nature, absolutely fearless. He is the leader of a caravan heading east through the Wyoming mountains. The caravan consists of men who have been at the mining camps, who have failed to make their fortune and are returning home. Bill Horn had gone west at the beginning of the gold strikes but he did not strike it rich until after the gold strikes of '53. By 1865, he had decided to head back east. When the snow had melted in the mountains, he gathered together a party of men and woman and left Sacramento. In the Wyoming mountains, a mountain man, Slingerland, meets the train and tells them that Sioux Indians have been following them. The trapper offers to go to the railroad construction camp to get some soldiers to help protect them. Meanwhile, he advises them to keep moving. Bill Horn hears the war cries of the Sioux and senses that his end is about to come. He orders the wagons to form a circle for defense. He buries the bags of gold he has with him, telling the group that whoever survives the coming attack is welcome to the treasure. He is rather fond of young Allie Durade (Lee), the daughter of Mrs. Durade, a member of the caravan. The entire party is wiped out in the Sioux attack, except for Allie Durade Lee.

Horn, Billy: In *Rogue River Feud*, an old friend of Keven Bell and Emmeline Trapier. When Em mentions him, he does not recall the name at first. Billy is one who did not believe the calumny being spread by Gus Atwell concerning Keven at the training camp. He has told Emmeline that he heard Atwell telling the story. Em and Billy are engaged to be married.

Horn, Jim: In *Wild Horse Mesa,* one of Manerube's gang. He is a man without character, unscrupulous. He attacks Chane Weymer and the Piutes. In the fight, he is run over by Brutus, Chane's horse, the animal they are attempting to steal.

Horne: In *Riders of the Purple Sage*, a supposedly respectable rancher who helps steal Jane's prize thoroughbred horses. When he is riding across the sage with Jerry Card, he is shot by Bern Venters. Judkins reports that Horne's body was found and identified. All are surprised that he was involved in the theft of Jane Withersteen's prize horses.

Horner: (1) In *Fighting Caravans,* runs a saloon in Fort Larned.

(2) In *30,000 on the Hoof*, brothers suspected of having killed Matazel, Geronimo's son who was found dead just beyond Sycamore Canyon. Once before, their sister had to fight off an Apache buck who tried to abduct her from their cabin. Logan Huett lets people believe this, although his wife knows he is the one who killed Matazel.

Horton: (1) In *The Trail Driver*, the trail driver bringing Dave Slaughter's herd to Dodge. His is the second outfit behind Brite's.

(2) In *Wilderness Trek*, the first person that the Dann crew meet in the Kimberleys. He has already heard about them and the twenty-five-hundred-mile cattle drive they had undertaken. The trek has taken two years and five months, an accomplishment of epic proportions. He tells them they have arrived just in time, as gold has been discovered in the Kimberleys. He tells them where they can buy land at incredibly cheap prices, and points out the road to Wyndham, where they can get supplies.

Horton, Billy: In *Captives of the Desert*, a cowboy working at Taho. Wilbur Newton instructs him to keep his truck and send it to Flaggerston with the first car out, and to express it collect to his mother's place in Texas. Billy reports this to Katharine and Mary, Newton's wife. Horton is asked to drive Mary to Flaggerston in a snowstorm. She decides not to go, however.

Hosshoes: In *Wildfire*, the horse Cal Blinn enters in the annual horse race at Bostril's Ford.

Hough, Place: In *The U. P. Trail*, a Mississippi River gambler who shows up at Benton, in Stanton's place. He loves games of chance but is strictly honest. He sees that Beauty Stanton is in love with Neale and tells him so. He also recognizes Red King as brother of the famous Texas gunman, King Fisher. Stanton devises a plan to rescue Allie, Neale's sweetheart, from her stepfather, Durade. He wins her from him in a card game, then, when Durade welches on the deal, he and Ancliffe fight off Durade's thugs so Allie can escape. Hough is killed in the fighting.

Houser: In *Western Union*, one of the men working on Creighton's telegraph line construction crew.

Howard: (1) In *Horse Heaven Hill*, foreman of Stanley Weston's ranch. Stanley fires him when he learns that he and several of the cowboys have helped Hurd Blanding round up the wild horses to drive to market. As well, Howard has been drinking and Weston will not tolerate drinking among his cowboys. Howard becomes Blanding's right-hand man in the second organized roundup of mustangs. Howard later appears at the camp where the Wade crowd is entertaining guests on a camping picnic, to accuse Stanley Weston and Lark Burrell of releasing the wild mustangs they had penned up in a canyon. Howard gets the worst end of the deal in a fight with Stan and has to be packed on his saddle like a sack of grain by his men.

(2) In *Twin Sombreros*, a gambler. In the saloon, his pale, cold face, enhanced by his dark frock coat, draws attention to himself in a room full of range-garbed men. He hails from Denver. Howard is reputed to be a ladykiller in more ways than one. He is involved with Lura Surface. When she leaves her father's home and is staying in Las Animas with her friend, Delia Ross, she is seen around town with Howard. Before she leaves town for good, Lura explains to Brazos that Allen Neece was killed by her father because he knew why he wanted him out of the way. Howard figured it all out. He had that hold on Surface and they played it for all it was worth, while she was still an heiress. She and Howard manage to extort some forty thousand dollars out of Surface, money they use to go to Dodge.

Howard, Bill: In *Western Union*, the real name of Red Pierce, who runs a gambling operation which follows the men working on the construction crews of the Western Union Telegraph. He is a hardened

criminal whose true identity is revealed in South Pass, Wyoming. See **Pierce, Red.**

Howard, Captain: In *Fighting Caravans*, in charge at Fort Zarah. He sends Lt. Stevens and sixty troopers to pursue some fourteen Comanche braves, whom they catch and execute.

Howe, Eddie: In *Raiders of Spanish Peaks*, mentioned by Harriet as one of her sister Lenta's beaux from Upper Sandersky, Ohio.

Howland, Captain: In *Fighting Caravans*, with Lieutenant Wilcox is in charge of an escort of ninety-eight soldiers to accompany Captain Couch's caravan loaded with furs en route to Westport (Kansas City).

Hoyle: In *The Call of the Canyon*, the superintendent of the construction crew building a ranch house with a view overlooking the Painted Desert. Hoyle praises the choice of location and the plans for the building, but makes suggestions for alterations to those drawings due to the location of the house and the land where it is being built. He is a cooperative, helpful man.

Hoyle, Bill: In *Fighting Caravans*, a former soldier who handles the firing of the cannon in battle with the Indians.

Hubrigg: In *Nevada*, a member of the Pine Tree Outfit. He likes Jim Lacy, unlike other members, who are suspicious of him as he doesn't gamble, play cards or drink.

Hudkins: In *West of the Pecos*, the man in charge of the hiding expedition heading toward the Pecos river. Colonel Templeton Lambeth joins the hiders as he makes his way west to take up ranching. Hudkins and his men return to San Antonio when they have collected their load of hides, while Lambeth and his crew continue west.

Hudnall, Burn: In *The Thundering Herd*, Clark Hudnall's son and Sally Hudnall's brother. Tom notes the resemblance to his father. Burn is a strong, cheerful young man. He helps Tom get settled in. Burn shares his father's enthusiasm for the buffalo hunt and looks forward to the profits to be made so he can buy a farm. Burn helps Tom at the buffalo field, showing him how to train his horse to accept the sight of a buffalo carcass or a buffalo herd. After his father is killed, Burn decides to return to Sprague's and take up farming. Tom gives him his money to bank. Tom and Burn meet up again when Tom returns a year later.

Hudnall, Clark: In *The Thundering Herd*, has entered the hiding venture to raise money quickly to buy a farm. Tom feels in his handshake the mighty grip of a calloused hand that has known the plow and the ax. Hudnall hires Tom as a member of his crew with generous pay. Hudnall brings his wife, Mary and his daughter, Sally, along together with his son Burn and his wife. Hudnall's eagerness to make money blinds him to the dangers of the enterprise, and the danger to himself and to the women. He was not a frontiersman, though brave, and was fool-hardy. Jude Pilchuck, his partner and an experienced frontiersman and buffalo hunter, advises him to do his killing and skinning near the camp. He protests that Pilchuck is too cautious, and pooh-poohs the threat of Indians. Even when Pilchuck has spotted Comanches and Kiowas, he refuses to heed warnings to stay close to camp. Clark Hudnall is killed, scalped and mutilated by Comanches when alone, skinning a buffalo, far from the camp and any help. His gun is taken by the Indians. It becomes an object of legend when every man who owns the gun gets killed. The Comanche say it is bad medicine.

Hudnall, Mrs. Mary: In *The Thundering Herd*, Clark's wife. She is a pleasant woman with a serious face that is lighted with a smile. She welcomes Tom Doan to the outfit. At camp, she does the cooking and washing. Mrs. Hudnall is not terribly fond of the idea of hiding but she accompanies her husband. Together with her daughter Sally, she returns to Sprague's post when the cavalry rounds up the women at the buffalo hunt and returns them to posts where they will be safe. She and Sally take care of Milly Fayre. Mrs. Hudnall is friendly with Sprague's wife and from her she learns about the goings-on in the Jett camp. Mrs. Hudnall greets Tom when he returns to the post after the buffalo hunt, announcing that his beloved Milly is still alive, and in fact is the schoolteacher in the growing town.

Hudnall, Sally: In *The Thundering Herd*, Clark Hudnall's daughter and Burn Hudnall's sister. She is eighteen years old, large of frame, pleasant-faced, with roguish eyes that take instant stock of Tom Doan, who has joined her father's hiding outfit. Sally flirts with Tom, but is rather peeved when he remains impervious to her charms. She approves of his choice of a horse. She is amused at Tom's clumsy efforts to peg his first hides and offers to help, but he rebuffs her. She helps with the cooking in the camp at the killing fields. She returns to Sprague's post when the cavalry rounds up all the women and brings them in. She befriends Milly Fayre, Tom's betrothed, while they are at Sprague's. Both Dave Stronghurl and Orvy Tacks are interested in her. Sally chooses Dave Stronghurl and they are married when he returns to Sprague's with a load of hides, as there is a young preacher in camp at the time. Clark Hudnall is not pleased when he hears the news. When the men return to Sprague's after the Comanche campaign, she and Dave buy a farm next to her brother's place at Sprague's post. A year later, when Tom Doan abandons the hunt, he and Milly marry and buy a neighboring farm.

Hudson: (1) In *The Mysterious Rider*, the foreman of the branding during roundup on Belllounds's ranch. He is injured at work and appoints Wilson Moore to take his place, an appointment which displeases Buster Jack.

(2) In *West of the Pecos*, a hawk-eyed old plainsman from the Brazon country that inspires confidence. Jeff Slinger, Texas Ranger and friend of Pecos Smith's, knows Hudson, who is a bachelor getting well along in years and looking to sell out, wanting a little peace and freedom from rustlers. Slinger had met him in Rockport when Pecos Smith and Terrill Lambeth were there. He agrees to sell his two thousand head to Pecos Smith and Smith takes on his two nephews and his crew as hands.

Huell, Andy: In *Rogue River Feud*, a fisherman on the Rogue River. During the storm and subsequent dramatic rise in the river, his boat was swept over a sandbar. He jumped and waded out of danger but lost his boat. He reports that Mulligan was drowned.

Huerta: In *Desert Gold*, a federal general in the Mexican army who comes to Casita to relieve the federalist garrison.

Huett, Abe Lincoln: In *30,000 on the Hoof*, the second son of Logan and Lucinda. His birth is dramatic. Logan has gone to get the Holberts when the baby is born in a horse stall in the barn. She feels a special fondness for Abe. He is not fond of anything intellectual, but is sweet, patient and plodding. He excels at tracking and hunting and learns these skills from his father. He also excels at shooting with a rifle. He prefers life outdoors, dresses in buckskins, and, according to his brother George, he looks like an Indian. Abe is most helpful around the ranch. He suggests that they capture wild mustangs to sell, and he organizes the hunt and the capture of over eighty mustangs. Likewise, he overhears Tobe Campbell and Joe Stillman planning to raid Sycamore. He organizes the defense of the ranch and sets a trap to catch the rustlers as they attempt to take the herd. Abe comes to George's defense at the dance when Jack Campbell knifes him in a fight. Abe marries Barbara, his childhood companion, before he leaves for France. His father tells an amusing story about his stint in boot camp, training to shoot. Abe is marched out to the shooting range with a lot of green recruits and a red-headed cuss of a sergeant who shoves him up to the mark and hands him a government rifle. He tells Abe to shoot at a target. There are targets at fifty yards, a hundred, two hundred, and so on up to a thousand, targets with a black center and rings. When the sergeant asks if he can shoot, he says that he can, but not very well. And so he shoots at the "first target." He took five shots at the target a thousand feet off. He hit three bull's eyes and two shots inside the first circle. The sergeant gets red in the face, asking why he said he couldn't shoot. Abe replies that his old man says he's not much of a shot!

Abe is reported missing in action, and the family presumes he has been killed and that the body has not been recovered. Abe, however, had been in the hospital, with shell-shock, unidentified. When he comes to his senses, he proves who he is and is sent home. His return home has a miraculous effect on Barbara and his father. The war had not impaired Abe physically. Spiritually, he seems finer, stronger. Abe loves the wilderness, and the old potent loneliness and solitude, the trails and the trees, the cliff walls, and his wife and boy, soon blot out whatever it is that haunts him.

He performs a second miracle when he discovers in Turkey Canyon the remnants of a herd they had not rounded up to trail to Flagg for sale. Over the years, the herd has multiplied so that the few hundred originally there are now eighteen hundred. With cattle selling at over fifty dollars a head, they are not as destitute as they had thought.

Huett, Barbara: In *30,000 on the Hoof*, the adopted daughter of Lucinda and Logan. Abe and George find her one afternoon when they are playing along the road. The tracks indicate that she was deliberately abandoned having been lifted to the ground from wagons that then drove off. The Huetts make inquiries but no word comes as to who her parents might be. They raise her as their own daughter. She grows up to become a beautiful young woman, as attractive to the young men as the notorious Milly Campbell. She and Abe are particularly close. When Lucinda reveals to her that she is not their own child, but adopted, Abe decides he wants to marry her. They do marry before he leaves for the war. The womanizing government cattle buyer Mitchell has his eyes on her. Logan asks her to flirt with him to convince him to buy his herd of cattle, and she agrees. Together with Luce, she works hard with the women's auxiliary doing things to support the troops in Europe. When word comes that George and Grant have been killed and that Abe is missing, she falls into a catatonic state, barely in touch with reality. She returns with her parents and her son to Sycamore Canyon. Only the return of Abe jolts her back into reality. Life returns to normal in the Sycamore with the promise of recaptured happiness and prosperity.

Huett, George Washington: In *30,000 on the Hoof*, the first child of Lucinda and Logan. He is intelligent and quick to learn. He is a born cattleman and cowboy, but he also has a love of automobiles. He slowly convinces his father that they need a car, and when he returns with a second-hand automobile one day, Logan, who dislikes machines intensely, is forced to admit that you can get around a lot faster with a car than on horseback. George grows into quite the ladykiller. He is sweet on Milly Campbell and resents Barbara's comments that Milly is frivolous and enjoys nothing more than to get boys to fight over her. He is much more serious about Milly than the family suspects. At the dance, he proposes to Milly on condition that she break off with her disreputable brothers. Jack Campbell does not approve of his courting Milly, as she is already promised to his friend, Rich Harvey. In the fight, Jack knifes George. Abe comes to his defense. His father tells him this is a good lesson not to go fighting over a

woman or to let himself be seduced by some dark-eyed cat. George and Grant sign up for the army, and get killed in France. Abe says his brothers died courageously, highly respected by their buddies and officers.

Huett, General Grant: In *30,000 on the Hoof*, the third son of Lucinda and Logan and unlike his siblings, is born in Flagg. Grant signs up for the army with his brothers, and is killed in action in France. Abe says his brothers died courageously, highly respected by their buddies and officers.

Huett, Little Abe: In *30,000 on the Hoof*, the son of Barbara and Abe. He is born when Abe is abroad fighting in the war.

Huett, Logan: In *30,000 on the Hoof*, a scout in the cavalry. He has just returned from a mission trailing Geronimo's son, Matazel, who vows to get revenge on him some day. The officers and men he has served with all respect him highly. They agree he was cut out to be a pioneer. He has not enjoyed military service. The cowboy life he led before the Geronimo campaign suited him better. He had dreamed of being a rancher for himself.

While Logan is part romantic dreamer, he is part realist too. Like Wetzel, Lassiter, and the other heroes of Grey novels, he passionately loves nature. He selects Sycamore Canyon for his homestead because of its singular beauty. But at the same time, he knows that working a homestead some sixty miles into the wilderness will demand much hard work. He wants a wife. The life of a lonely ranchman in the wilderness is immeasurably improved by a strong, capable wife. He decides his old sweetheart, Lucinda Baker, in Independence, Missouri, would be his first choice. He cables her, asking her to marry him, and is both surprised and pleased when she cables back her assent. He does not recognize her at the station in Flagg. She recognizes him immediately, in his shirt-sleeves and blue jeans tucked into high boots. She is stylish and dignified.

Logan has arranged the marriage for that very day, for they must set out by prairie schooner for their home. There is a cabin to erect, corral fences to build, supplies to get in for the winter. They have a five-day trip ahead of them. She will have to drive the oxen. He knows that this is a lot for her to grasp all at once, but she takes up the challenge with good cheer. He shows her how to make camp, to start a fire, to make sourdough biscuits. He fixes a bed for her under the schooner where she won't get wet should it rain.

When they reach Sycamore Canyon, he sets about building the cabin immediately. He cuts the stand of pine on the nearby hill, hues and fits the logs, and splits shingles for the roof and boards for the floor. He builds a stone chimney and fireplace. Lucinda is impressed by his strength and endurance and perseverance. He knows the isolation is hard on his wife having been used to family and friends and to the social life of town, but he feels Luce will grow to love the solitude as much as he does and become engrossed in their project.

Money is always a problem for Logan. He has invested all he had in stock, the schooner and supplies, and when the cougars kill most of his stock over the winter, he has to start over. The sale of the potato crop to Babbitt provides him with some cash to buy supplies for the next year, but the same problem presents itself the following winter. He is embarrassed to ask his wife for money but finally he does, and she refuses. She wants to keep the five hundred dollars she received as a wedding gift from an uncle for more serious emergencies. Eventually, that emergency arises when Holbert calls in the mortgage on the cattle. Lucinda makes a proposal that they take the money, pay off their debts, and start over, determined never to get into debt again. She also makes a plan, that they use the money earned from selling the produce of their gardens to slowly build up the herd. Logan feels foolish having to use farming to support his ranching endeavors, but her step-by-step approach to building the herd makes sense. He does as she suggests and by the time his family is grown, he has about thirty thousand head of cattle to market.

When his sons are born, he feels he and his boys can conquer the wilderness. George proves to be an excellent cattleman, a born cowboy. Abe is incomparable at tracking and shooting with the rifle. He takes to the wilderness as his father had. He envisions that his sons will marry and continue to live in Sycamore Canyon and expand the ranching enterprise.

Logan must fight every step of the way to achieve his success. He must clear the canyon of wild cats and coyotes that attack his herd, especially in winter. This project takes several years. He must learn where to plant his crops, how to prevent the crows from eating the seed, how to ensure there is enough water for the plants. Much of this is trial and error. A miracle saves the canyon from destruction by grasshoppers, when wild turkeys appear in flocks to eat up the locusts, saving the crops. He vows not to eat turkey again out of gratitude!

Perhaps the greatest trial is the double blow of losing his fortune to the shyster government cattle buyer, Mitchell, and the death of his sons, his hope for the future. He blames himself for his stupidity with the cattle deal. He had been holding out for a better price, as speculation had been steadily pushing the prices up. Then, the price began to fall, as the army found other sources of beef. He negotiates a deal with Charteris, but when this dealer cannot pay cash, he resorts to Mitchell, the man who had been ogling his daughter, Barbara. Mitchell promises to pay in cash, and when he delivers the "money" in bundles wrapped in foil, Logan foolishly does not open the bundles to count the money. He signs the receipt, leaves with the bundles, goes for a drink with his friends and returns home to discover the swindle. Attempts to recover the money fail because his signature on the receipt was witnessed and he

did not check the contents of the package on the spot. A trip to Washington leads to the loss of a further twenty-five hundred dollars to a crooked lawyer who assures him he can get his money back. Senator Spellman from Arizona tells him he is wasting his time there in Washington. The case is closed as far as the army is concerned. He receives word from Lucinda to come home. In Flagg, he learns that George and Grant have been killed in action and that Abe is missing.

Like Wordsworth's patriarchal figure Michael, he returns to the bosom of nature to be restored. Lucinda asks to return to their cabin in Sycamore Canyon. Nature has not changed. The conditions that had worked to bind them together are still there. Work needs to be done on the cabin, meat procured for the winter. Logan's depression improves somewhat, but when his son Abe returns unexpectedly, the miracle is complete. Abe discovers that the remnant of a herd they had left in Turkey Canyon has now multiplied to some eighteen hundred head. With cattle selling at fifty dollars a head, they have the capital to rebuild their ranch.

The story of Logan Huett and Lucinda Baker and their pioneer experience resembles Willa Cather's tribute to pioneers in her novels. Logan and Lucinda overcome loneliness, despair, tremendous physical hardship, failure upon failure, the loss of their sons in the war. Theirs is the story of the triumph of the human spirit.

Huggins: In *The Thundering Herd*, leads an inexperienced crew to the buffalo hunt. He is attacked and killed by Jett, Follonsbee and Pruitt. His hides are stolen, his outfit burned and it is made to look like the result of an Indian attack.

Huggins, Fox: In *The Lost Wagon Train*, is a cowboy with whom Slim Blue, Cornie, used to ride. When he heads to San Antonio to marry Estelle, he hires Slim and several other former trail buddies to drive a herd of five thousand head to their ranch in Latchfield.

Hunt, Caleb: In *Stairs of Sand*, Ruth Virey's grandfather. He is mentioned in *Wanderer of the Desert* as neighbor to the Blairs. The young woman living with them is friendly with Genie Linwood. Adam realizes he has found the parents with whom Magdalene Virey had left her daughter, Ruth. In *Stairs of Sand*, Caleb Hunt owns the water hole at Lost Lake (Indian Wells). He purchased the water hole from Indian Jim and has made a living from the trading post and water rights. He had come to the desert for reasons of health, and indeed he recovered there. He had money to invest and bought up the water rights at Lost Lake and went into the freighting business. The man who lured him into the enterprise was a young, handsome fellow equally as interested in Ruth as in the business. Caleb Hunt went into the freighting business. Supplies from San Francisco were brought by sea and river to Yuma and from there, freighted in wagons into the interior.

Places like Lost Lake became valuable pieces of property. The young man who had entered the venture with Caleb Hunt threatened to ruin him if he did not get Ruth to agree to marry him. The grandfather pressures her and Ruth marries Guerd Larey. Ruth fears that eventually Guerd will succeed in wrenching the property from her grandfather. This is especially urgent since the railroad company is planning to expand northward through the desert, passing by the principal water holes along the way. Larey has been trying to buy Hunt out but he refuses to sell. The grandfather is given an ultimatum: to keep his property, he must persuade Ruth to return to her husband, Guerd Larey. As the pressure increases on him, he wishes that Ruth would only care enough for Larey to go back to him. Then their problems would be solved. When Ruth tells him the story of her abduction by Stone and Collishaw and her rescue in Yuma by Adam, he is not inclined to believe the story. He confesses he is seriously thinking of accepting Larey's latest offer. Caleb Hunt is murdered, by whom is never established. Somebody hit him behind the ear with a heavy stone or club. He was knocked so his head fell under water. It's not clear whether the blow killed him or he drowned. There is little doubt, however, who expects to profit by his death.

Hunt, Cy: In *The Lost Wagon Train*, with Blaisdal is leading a caravan of sixty wagons from Texas heading west, stopping at Cimarron Crossing. The caravan does not arrive on the scheduled date.

Huon: In *The Desert of Wheat*, an old soldier Dorn meets in France. Huon and his men had been in the battle of Verdun. They welcome the young Americans coming to their aid against the Germans.

Hurd: (1) In *Riders of the Purple Sage*, one of the three men who abduct Milly Erne from her home in Texas and bring her to Utah. Lassiter catches up with him in central Utah some years later but he dies without revealing where Milly has been hidden.

(2) In *The Thundering Herd*, a member of the same outfit as Cosgrove. He denounces Pilchuck's campaign against the Comanche. He is a hard-drinking, loud-mouthed type like his colleague. Hurd, like Cosgrove, is there to make money and not willing to risk his life in the campaign against the Indians.

(3) In *Valley of Wild Horses*, the name Handy MacNew uses when he is in Marco working as a guard at the jail. See: **MacNew, Handy.**

Hurd, Dr.:   In *Raiders of Spanish Peaks,* John Lindsay's doctor back in Ohio. He had recommended Lindsay go west for the climate. He feared that Lindsay's weak lungs would succumb to pneumonia. The trek to Spanish Peaks weakens John Lindsay and he does succumb to a severe case of pneumonia.

Hurley: In *The Rainbow Trail*, a young gentile cowboy who makes trouble while the secret wives from the hidden village are being taken back home after the trial in Stonebridge. He fights with John Shefford, suggesting that he is a whoremaster of sorts, keeping the women at the village for himself.

Hutchinson: In *Wildfire*, one of the men usually accompanying Cordts, the horse thief. Hutch is spare, stoop-shouldered, red-faced and squinty-eyed. He looks every bit the thief. He shows up at the races at Bostril's Ford with Cordts, and like Cordts, agrees to keep the peace. He leaves after the races with Cordts, after these two, it seems, have had a disagreement with Dick Sears, their associate. Hutchinson and Cordts, however, have not given up their goal of stealing Sage King and Wildfire. They follow Joel Creech when he brings back the horses as ransom for Lucy Bostril. Hutchinson is killed in the gunplay which brings the venture to an end. He falls over a cliff while attempting to rescue Cordts.

Hutchinson, Mary: In *The Fugitive Trail*, Steve Melrose's first wife and mother of Trinity Spencer. When Ranger Captain Maggard tells Trinity she looks like the wife of a friend of his who had disappeared with a child of three some twenty years ago, he suggests she visit the Melroses in case she is the lost daughter. Trinity has a keepsake from the mother she does not remember, a locket. Melrose recognizes it immediately. He had bought it from a jeweler who dealt in antiques. The locket was a rare piece and was worn by someone in the court of Louis XV. He gave Mary the locket the day they were married in New Orleans. This confirms that Trinity is Mary's child and his daughter. Trinity looks like Mary come back to life.

Hutchinson, Randolph: In *Twin Sombreros,* a stalwart, erect, keen-eyed man in his sixties. He is well-known in Las Animas and comes forward to speak to Brazos Keene's character. He says there is no finer, straighter, squarer cowboy nor a more honest cattleman on the range.

Hutter, Flo: In *The Call of the Canyon*, the daughter of Tom Hutter, owner of the Lolomi Lodge in Glenn's canyon. She helps her mother run the inn. When Carley Burch first arrives, Flo is bubbly, effusive, energetic and helpful. She greets the easterner cheerfully and appears willing to help out. She shows her how to use the stove in her room and offers to tell her all about Glenn, who had recuperated from his war experience in that very room. Carley senses that Flo is in love with Glenn and, as Charley, one of her father's hands, comments, she's not above playing a prank on a greenhorn, as she did with Miss Spenser. This streak in her comes out when she approves Spillbeans as Carley's mount for the ride to the sheep ranch, knowing as she does that the bronc can be quite a handful for the inexperienced rider. Carley sees in Flo a potential rival for Glenn's affections, although there is a seven year difference in their ages. Although Carley is genuinely interested in Lee Stanton, she pretends not to be; Carley sees in this love game the eternal coquetry of women, pretending lack of interest to encourage a lover's pursuit. At the sheep dip, Flo helpfully explains the purpose of the operation. She also confides in Carley the details of Glenn's long recuperation. He had been gassed during the war, and his lungs were severely damaged. He spent days in bed, coughing up blood, and the doctor thought that his weakened lungs would never heal. The fresh mountain air did much to heal his lungs and his body, but Flo does not know how well the mental problems resulting from the war have been cured. Nevertheless, Glenn has become more optimistic and his outlook on life vastly improved. At Flo's twentieth birthday party, Carley overhears a conversation between Flo and Lee Stanton. She tells Lee that she does love him, but that he pales in comparison to Glenn Killbourne. Glenn had sacrificed himself for his country, nearly giving his life for the cause. He is a true hero. Flo arranges for another girl to make advances to Lee but when he actually shows interest in that girl, Flo gets jealous and angry. Eventually, she and Lee are married. When Carley returns from new York to build a ranch house on the land she had bought on a spot especially dear to Glenn, Charley tells her that Flo and Glenn are married, but when Carley comes to Lolomi Lodge to visit and wish the newlyweds the best of luck, she learns from Glenn that Flo and Lee are the newlyweds, and Charley is just up to his practical jokes once more.

Carley sees in Flo a dramatic contrast to her friends back east. While her circle in New York are interested only in selfish pursuits, in parties, in shopping, in entertainment, in affairs, Flo really likes to work and is genuinely interested in other people. Carley reluctantly admits to herself that Flo possesses more of the qualities that Glenn is seeking in a wife than she does. Flo wants to marry and raise a family, and expects to pull her weight in a marriage with work and devotion. She is a true American, with American values which seem to have vanished in New York women.

Hutter, Mrs.: In *The Call of the Canyon,* the wife of Tom Hutter who runs the Lolomi Lodge with the help of her daughter Flo. When Carley Burch arrives, Mrs. Hutter recognizes her immediately from the picture of her that Glenn Killbourne keeps over his fireplace. Glenn has told her many things about Carley, his fiancée from New York. She gives Carley a warm, western welcome, giving her in the room which Glenn had used when he first came west. She tells Carley about the hard time Glenn had recovering from the dreadful effects of the war, the shell shock, the damage to his lungs from poison gas, and the fever and coughing which nearly killed him. They had all feared he would not survive. Her husband, Tom, takes Glenn on as a partner in his sheep ranching operation.

Hutter, Tom: In *The Call of the Canyon,* Mrs. Hutter's husband, Flo's father and Glenn Killbourne's partner in the sheep ranching business. When Carey meets him, he has just returned from a trip east to Chicago and Kansas City. Tom Hutter is originally from Illinois. Thirty years ago, he came west and this trip is the first back in those thirty years. He finds the east greatly, and to him, unpleasantly changed. Carley likes him at first sight, drawn by his deep, slow voice and the ease and force of his presence. She takes at once to his strong personality. Tom Hutter takes to Carley too; he is amused by her reactions to Lee Stanton and to the test of her stamina on the ride to the sheep ranch. He proposed the trip into the mountains so that Carley could get a first-hand taste of the operation and see the sheep dipping process. Tom Hutter had taken on Glenn as a partner after Glenn had worked for him for several months, until Glenn had built his own cabin in the canyon. He and his family have taken Glenn in and cared for him as a son.

Hyslip, Dude: In *The Dude Ranger,* from Texas, a ladykiller cowboy with a big ego. He has a heart-shaped piece of metal nailed to the heel of his boot. His footprint leaving the imprint of a heart is his trademark, a standing joke among the cowboys on the range. He is reputed to have killed a man in Winslow and probably others elsewhere. Few dare to cross him. When Ernest arrives at the Red Rock Ranch, Dude Hyslip names him Ioway, and makes up a mocking song about him. He leads the other cowboys in their petty persecution of the newcomer. Hyslip invents the story that Ernest had hired the three robbers to attack Anne Hepford so he could come to her rescue and act the big hero. Hyslip fancies himself a ladykiller. He broke up Daisy Brooks and Nebraskie. Daisy describes her relationship with him as that of a snake and a bird. She is mesmerized by him, and he gets his way with women by a combination of charm and brute force. Nebraskie wonders what women see in such a brute. Hyslip has a hold over John Hepford and he lords it over the cowboys on the ranch who follow his lead like sheep. Ernest and Hawk and Nebraskie wonder what it is that he has on Hepford. Ernest Howard gets invited to the dance by Anne Hepford, a turn of events which deals a blow to Dude's ego. At the dance in Springer, he makes drunken advances to Daisy Brooks on the dance floor. Ernest puts his lights out, and he doesn't know who hit him. Some time later when Ernest catches him forcing himself on Daisy at her father's ranch, Ernest reveals that he is the one who beat Dude up at the dance. Having studied some boxing back in Iowa, Ernest has little trouble beating Hyslip in a fistfight, leaving him lying by the brook. Dude Hyslip then begins to spread the story that the tenderfoot had beat him up when he was unconscious. When Hepford has fired Siebert and Howard and Nebraskie, Hyslip becomes foreman. He attempts to drive Brooks off his ranch through intimidation. He is killed when he is caught by Siebert and Nebraskie, trying to force himself on Daisy. At first, Hepford tells the sheriff that Ernest had done the shooting, but Sam Brooks and Hawk Siebert set him straight on Dude's attempt to rape

Daisy, and Nebraskie's shooting him to defend the girl.

I

Ide, Amos: In *Forlorn River,* Amos Ide is Ben Ide's father. He is described as iron of muscle and mind, with clear grey eyes like sunlight on ice, a weathered, wrinkled face, a record of labor and strife. Amos Ide comes into money when he sells land recovered from Tule Lake, which has been drained. He has become conceited about his new-found prosperity. He serves on the town council with Hart Blaine. He considers himself an important man in the community. He and Ben Ide fell out over Ben's refusal to settle down on the ranch and over his pursuit of his passion to chase wild mustangs. He is a religious man, and considers Ben an outcast. Amos Ide never mentions his son's name. When Strobel arrests Ben at the insistence of Setter, Judd and Walker, he believes the worst about his son, trying to convince him to confess to rustling. Even when the truth comes out, he is reluctant to admit he has been wrong about Ben. The son gets great satisfaction in showing his father the bank book with the twelve thousand dollars he has made on the sale of wild mustangs.

Ide, Ben: In *Forlorn River,* the eldest son of Amos Ide. Ben was well born, raised by a hard-working, God-fearing family, educated to the age of sixteen. He is now twenty-four years old. He owns a ranch on Forlorn River in the Clear Lake district. The cabin, the corrals and the barns are in better shape than he is. He thinks more of his wild mustangs than he does of himself. Ben is in love with the open country and mustangs. He thrills at the sight of wild horses, glorying in their beauty, freedom and self-sufficiency. He admires the wisdom of the wild horse. Local ranchers shoot the mustangs that they consider a nuisance, but Ben hopes to make a living catching, breaking and selling them. His love for horses is such that he becomes so attached to them he cannot bring himself to sell them. Ben hopes to expand his operation by buying out the neighboring ranches, which have suffered because of the drought. His own ranch is well watered, with streams and springs that never go dry. He plans to build a dam to do some irrigating in the dry season.

Ben Ide is out of favor with his father. Amos Ide wanted his son to settle down and work on the ranch with him, but Ben's boundless passion for chasing wild horses made such a settled life seem like prison. The father kicked him out, and now will not even speak his name. Amos is all too willing to believe the worst about his son. The mother is upset at this rift between father and son, the strain affecting her health. As well, the local pastor had made pointed references to Ben in his sermon on the prodigal son, thereby giving further credence to the rumors spread about him. Only his sister, Hettie, has retained any faith in him. She communicates with him on the sly.

Ben Ide is a decent human being to the core. He takes in the wounded Nevada, who comes up to his campfire exhausted and half-starved. He tends to his wound and gives him a place to live. Ben never inquires about Nevada's past, accepting his friendship and help without demands. He likewise takes in Modoc, the Indian, whose questionable activities have made him an outcast in town. He has made these men partners in his ranch operation. Likewise, he is generous to a fault. He gives Nevada one of his favorite mustangs, Sandy. He takes Marvie Blaine fishing, letting him stay with him at the ranch. He gives Marvie a pony to ride.

On his trip to town, Ben meets Sheriff Strobel, an old friend from his childhood. Strobel used to take him fishing as a boy. The sheriff does not believe any of the rumors being spread about him and the rustlers, even offering to swear him in as a secret deputy to pursue the rustlers in the Forlorn River valley. Ben refuses the offer but promises to keep an eye out for the cattle thieves.

Ben Ide has been sweet on Ina Blaine since boyhood, but now he feels that he is not her equal. She has a college education, she is refined, her family is wealthy. He doubts she would want to have anything to do with one with his poor reputation and even poorer prospects. Nevertheless, Ina has not lost her interest in him. She has faith in him, even proposing marriage. She believes in him over the assertions of a man like Less Setter. She proposes marriage to him when she goes to visit his ranch but he puts things on hold until the cattle rustlers have been caught and his good name has been restored.

With Nevada urging quick action, Ben buys out the three neighboring ranchers, paying for the land with mustangs. One of these ranchers, Sims, confides in him that he had worked with the rustlers to get some money to make it through the hard times. With the help of Nevada and Modoc, the best trackers around, he finds Bill Hall's rustlers' camp and trails them to the ice caves, where the three of them hold the outlaws besieged for twenty-four days before hunger brings them to surrender.

On the way back to the Blaine ranch with these captives, Ben's love of wild horses overcomes his better judgment. He sees California Red, the greatest of the wild stallions, out on the frozen lake. He promises freedom to any of the captured rustlers willing to help him capture the stallion. This act seems to confirm the worst suspicions that Setter has been able to arouse in the ranchers about Ben. Nevada, however, together with Sheriff Strobel, manages to track down and capture Bill Hall and his men.

Ben Ide's reputation is cleared. He has a substantial amount of money in the bank from the sale of his mustangs. Ina agrees to marry him. Even Amos Ide acknowledges that he had been wrong about his son. The one thing which prevents his happiness from being complete is the departure of his partner, Nevada.

In *Nevada,* four years later, Ben Ide is married to Ina Blaine and the father of Little Blaine. He is the owner of large tracts of land he inherited from his father. His mother's health is poor and when a San Francisco doctor recommends that she move to a more agreeable climate, Ben decides to sell the land and move to Arizona. Ina and Hettie, his sister who owns half the ranch, agree to the move. They both realize that Ben is really motivated by a desire to set out in search of his partner, Nevada (Jim Lacy). Ben does not sell the Forlorn River Ranch as that was where he and Ben had chased after wild mustangs, half of which belongs to Nevada. He wonders why Nevada has not written in the past four years. If he was a gunman, it would make no difference to him. He is anxious to see him after all this time. Getting advice from his friend, Sheriff Stoebel, about the best region of Arizona to set up ranching, he leaves with the family and a few hands from the old ranch in covered wagons, anxious to undergo the full pioneer experience.

In Lineville, he hears a lot about one Jim Lacy from Mrs. Wood, at whose house they spend the night when in town. She recounts all the local gossip, concentrating in particular on her quasi-adopted son, Jim Lacy. He had recently returned from California but due to his penchant for sacrificing himself to help others, has killed one Link Cawthorne in a shootout helping Lize Teller, an old friend. Ben Ide does not realize he has been listening to an account of Nevada's activities.

In Winthrop, Arizona, he buys a ranch from Cash Burridge located sixty miles from town. Burridge tells him there are some eight to ten thousand head of cattle on the ranch, but they are never counted. Ben is not overly concerned. He builds a house on the ranch, and Raidy, his old hand from California, remains with him while the other cowboys return home. Ben quickly acquires a reputation for fairness. His neighbor, Tom Day, informs him that Burridge was not well thought of in the district. He sold Ben cattle on which he and Elam Hatt had a lien for several thousand dollars. Ben settles Burridge's debts with the neighbors, desiring to be fair to all. Tom Day takes a liking to him, lending him several hands to help him get started. Day admires Ben Ide's horsemanship and his spectacular stallion, California Red. Nevertheless, when Ben does not appear concerned about the herds of cattle being stolen, Day wonders if he is a serious rancher at all, even entertaining the idea that Ben is on the run from something or looking for someone by making himself a visible target.

Ben worries that Hettie has invested her share of the sale of the Tule Lake Ranch in his Arizona project. He offers to buy her out so that if things go under, she will not be ruined. He allows himself to be hoodwinked by Clan Dillon, his foreman. Dillon is a sweet talker, interested in Hettie, who sees through his blarney. Dillon causes a rift between Ben and Raidy and between Ben and Marvie Blaine. Dillon ingratiates himself with Ben when he "recovers" some of the stolen cattle on two occasions. Conse-

quently, Ben is willing to take his word that California Red has jumped the corral fence and some weeks later, jumps back into the corral at night. Raidy has great difficulty in getting Ben to see the truth. Ben Ide is about to give up his Arizona project, figuring that he will never find Nevada, just as the rustling crisis comes to a head. Jim Lacy appears, confronting Clan Dillon, the Pine Tree Outfit leader. Dillon is killed in a shootout. Jim Lacy is being held for hanging, and Ben Ide is willing to go through with the process until he sees that Jim Lacy is his friend Nevada, whereupon he orders him released. Judge Franklidge and Tom Day reveal that Jim Lacy had been working undercover to smoke out the leaders of the outfit. Ben Ide has to eat crow and apologize to Raidy and Marvie Blaine, asking them to come back to work for him.

Ben Ide now finds his life fulfilled. He has his ranch, a loving wife, a son, and his best friend and partner, now his brother-in-law, as Jim and Hettie marry.

The Ben Ide-Jim Lacy friendship is one of many buddy stories in Zane Grey's novels. To the westerner, a man's partner was often a more intimate friend, a closer ally, than wife or family.

Ide, Hettie: Appears in two novels, *Forlorn River* and *Nevada.* In *Forlorn River,* Hettie Ide is Ben Ide's sister. She is the only family member who has kept her faith in him. As well, she is the only family member to be in touch with him, through letters. Her letter to Ben tells of their father's new prosperity and his dealings with Less Setter. She tells him about Ina Blaine's return from school in Denver and that Ina is still sweet on him. Hettie tells Nevada, who delivers the letters, about the trouble between Ben and their father. Ben wanted to pursue his passion of hunting wild mustangs and his father wanted him to settle down to life on the ranch. Hettie still has faith in Ben, and thanks Nevada for standing by him. Hettie advises Ben to buy out the homesteaders before Amos Ide and Setter or Blaine go there. She also reports that Less Setter is the main source of defamatory gossip about Ben's activities in Forlorn Valley. Hettie Ide falls in love with Nevada, but he leaves the area after the outlaws have been captured.

In *Nevada,* Hettie has spent four years waiting and hoping to hear from Nevada. She feels closer to her brother and her sister-in-law, Ina, than ever before. Nevertheless, she grieves in secret for her lost love. She understands that Ben misses Nevada and she knows that he has not kept in touch out of fear that they might learn he was a terrible gunfighter and love him the less in consequence. During the four years, ranch hands court Hettie, but she encourages none of them. She sees Nevada in all of them, but not one of them can match her memory of Nevada, who incomparably bestrode a horse, and was the most handsome cowboy she ever saw. Her love for him deepens constantly. She knows what she had been to him, that she had given Nevada hope to change his life. She knows he will not use his gun again except to help someone.

While Ben and Ina are in San Francisco, buyers come to the ranch offering two hundred thousand dollars for the property. A railroad is to be built into the area and the value of the property has increased greatly. When Ben and Ina return with the doctor's recommendation that their mother move to a more suitable climate, Hettie announces that she had received an offer of two hundred thousand for the property. Ben enthusiastically agrees to the sale. Hettie gets half the proceeds. In the new venture, Ben gives her a third share, as he does not want her to lose out if things go badly. Ben builds a ranch in a wild spot. Hettie senses that the spot has been chosen as a lodestone for cowboys, ranchers, cattlemen, gunmen and outlaws through whom he might get word of Nevada.

Hettie is not without her admirers in Winthrop. The neighboring rancher, Tom Day, is interested in her, but she discourages him. Clan Dillon likewise has his eye on her, but she despises him, suspecting that his friendly, helpful demeanor is false. She fires him from the ranch, only to have her order countermanded by Ben, who has been hoodwinked by Dillon. One day while shopping in Winthrop, she spots Nevada, who has just killed Hardy Rue in a shootout in the street. She begins to think that he has fallen back on his old ways and she fears she has misplaced her faith in him.

Hettie becomes Marvie Blaine's confidante in matters of the heart. She goes with him to visit Rose Hatt and learns from the girl about the abuse from her father and brothers of which she has been victim.

Despite her best efforts, Hettie does not succeed in convincing Ben that Dillon is not to be trusted. She intervenes with him on behalf of Marvie, with whom he has had a falling out over fencing not done properly. As well, she advocates on behalf of Raidy, who has lost Ben's favor to the slick Dillon. She alone sees through his pretense, watching his changing expression as Raidy reveals the truth about California Red's disappearance and return. From Rose Hatt, she hears about Jim Lacy in the Pine Tree Outfit. She tries to stop the meeting of Nevada and Jim Lacy to prevent a gunfight. When they meet, she accuses him of betrayal. When the truth of his undercover work is revealed, she asks forgiveness for her lack of faith.

Hettie and Nevada are married and Nevada once again is partner in Ben Ide's ranch.

Hettie Ide is one of many female characters in Zane Grey who retain their faith in a "good" outlaw through thick and thin. The love of a good woman, her faith in a man's goodness, has the power to work miracles.

Ide, Mrs.: In *Forlorn River,* the mother of Ben Ide and Hettie. She is in poor health when the novel begins, in part because she is distressed about the rift between her husband, Amos Ide, and their son, Ben. She hasn't been to church since the preacher gave a pointed sermon about the "prodigal son," clearly aimed at Ben. She is thrilled at Ben's secret visit, and after it, her spirits and health are noticeably improved. She is highly pleased that the two are reconciled at the end of the novel.

In *Nevada,* Mrs. Ide's ill health causes Ben and Ina to take her to San Francisco to consult with a doctor. He recommends that she move to a more suitable climate, such as Arizona. The Tule Lake dampness is not good for her.

She enjoys the return to pioneer days on their covered wagon trip from California to Arizona. She gets into a fight with the cook Ben brings from the ranch and finally takes over the job herself. No mention is made of her after the Ides arrive in Winthrop, Arizona.

Indian Jim: In *Stairs of Sand,* a native and friend of Merryvale. Indian Jim is a Coalmila Indian and had once owned the water hole which had long been familiar to prospectors under the name of Indian Wells. Jim and his people had been prosperous before they sold the spring, which was a mecca for all desert travelers. But they had squandered their fortune and now eked out a living, bitter against the owners of the freighting post and especially Caleb Hunt, Ruth Virey's grandfather. Guerd Virey argues that Indian Jim and his family didn't have a clear title to the water hole, that it had first belonged to an old Spanish grant. Indian Jim had nothing in writing. The Spanish grant went to the state, and Larey has staked a claim to the water hole. Caleb Hunt trusts the legitimacy of his purchase of the land from Indian Jim.

Inskip: In *Twin Sombreros,* a rancher in Las Animas, partner of Kiskadden, his silent partner. Inskip joined Bodkin's posse of his own accord, Bodkin not welcoming his participation. He is a Texan, a man who does not like to be pushed around. He is the voice of opposition to the deputy who, on Surface's orders, plans to lynch the cowboy. He allows Brazos to grab his guns, upon which the posse disintegrates. Brazos is brought to Kiskadden, the sheriff, in Las Animas. Kiskadden plans to investigate the case and conduct an inquiry the following morning. Brazos knows that if not for this brave, stubborn Texan, he would have been hanged.

Ireland, Benny: In *Fighting Caravans,* a little red-headed Irishman, a former soldier who had been a gunner in the army. He has no fear of death or devil and loves to fight. His flaw is his impatience, which he shows in his habit of singing out to the Indians when the freighters are expecting a surprise attack. Benny is killed in the fighting at Point of Rocks when the Kiowas and Comanche attack the wagon train.

Irvine: In *Boulder Dam,* mentioned by Lynn Weston as an example of one of the peaks of human achievement, resulting from vision and determination. Irvine, in his conquest of Mount Everest, on whose summit his great heart cracked, proved the supremacy of mind over matter, of determination and faith over seemingly impossible obstacles.

Isbel, Ann: In *To the Last Man*, Gaston Isbel's only daughter. Like all the Isbels, she is a good shot and can hold her own with Bill and Guy in any shooting contest. She is the family member that Jean Isbel says is most like him. When he arrives in Grass Valley in Arizona, he brings her a special present, a bolt of cloth to make a new dress. Aunt Mary comments that he couldn't have given her a better gift as she is engaged to marry young Andrew Colmor. Jean consults Ann about Ellen Jorth. Ann had tried to make friends with her two years ago. They didn't know each other's names then. Ellen was the prettiest girl Ann had ever seen and they liked each other at once. Ellen struck Ann as sad and unhappy. They met later at a roundup. There were other girls with Ann and they snubbed Ellen. Ann leaves the other girls to talk with Ellen. She talks about herself, how she has no friends, how she hates the people in Arizona but how she loves the countryside. She has no fit clothes to wear. The budding friendship, however, is killed when she learns Ann is an Isbel. Ann meets her later, riding down a trail with a male companion who tries to kiss her. Ellen pushes him away, but when she sees Ann, she holds her head high in defiance. Ann's impressions of Ellen are all favorable. She has had to live with a crowd of wild men without the support of her mother. No doubt she has had to put up with a lot of inappropriate behavior from those men, but Ann is sure Ellen is a good, decent, honest girl. Jean is grateful to Ann for renewing his faith in Ellen. Jean gives Ellen a pair of shoes and stockings he had brought for Ann and when Ellen opens the package with Ann's name on it, she realizes how special she must be to Jean and she recalls her own brief friendship with her. Ann stands by the Isbels in the conflict which begins, and does not stop Andrew Colmor from joining the fight, although Jean tries to convince him to stay out of it.

Isbel, Donna: In *Yaqui*, the dueña, or chaperone for Señorita Dolores Mendoza. When the marriage to Lieutenant Perez has been arranged, she no longer feels it necessary to keep such a sharp eye on her charge, permitting her to meet with Montes.

Isbel, Aunt Mary: In *To the Last Man*, Gaston Isbel's sister, who lives with the family. Jean Isbel remembers her. Aunt Mary is pleased to see him back with the rest of the family. She approves of the gifts he brought the children, and especially of the material he brought Ann which she will use for her wedding dress. Aunt Mary predicts that her handsome nephew will be a killer with the ladies in Grass Valley. When the war breaks out, she is stoically silent. There is no evidence that she has ever been married or has a family of her own.

Isbel, Bill: In *To the Last Man*, the oldest son of Gaston Isbel, who he takes after his father both in looks and ways. He is a born cattleman and a chip off the old block. Bill tends to be jocular, rather than serious. Jean recalls that when they were children, Bill was secretive and selfish. He is married to Kate and they have three children, the youngest boy called Lee. Jean Isbel brings Bill a new rifle. When Jean asks where Bill and Guy were when cattle and sheep disappear and someone shoots at their father, Bill takes offense and tells Jean that at least they are with their father, not up in Oregon. When the all-out fighting starts, Bill takes to drinking heavily. Jean witnesses a fond, tearful farewell between Bill and his wife and children. Jean suspects that Bill has something he wants to get off his chest, but the opportunity for the two of them to talk privately never presents itself. Jean detects the same look on Bill when Blue expresses his doubts about the justice of the Isbel cause, that is, he doubts that this is about punishing cattle rustlers because he knows someone on the Isbel side is involved in the disappearance of Isbel and Blaisdell cattle. Bill is shot by Colter and lies bleeding in the undergrowth. Shepp's howling brings Ellen Jorth to the scene. He asks her to convey a message to Jean, that he had been rustling cattle from his father and Jim Blaisdell. He says that he has been as bad as his father, that Jean is the only decent boy in the lot. He also tells Ellen how her father killed their father on the sly when Gaston proposed a one-on-one meeting to bring an end to the feud and prevent needless bloodshed.

Isbel, Esther: In *To the Last Man*, Guy Isbel's wife. Esther is a young, strapping girl, red-headed and freckled, with wonderful lines of pain and strength in her face. When she was a child, the Apaches had murdered all her family. She faces the death of Guy Isbel with stoical courage. Unlike the men in the family, she is not afraid to go out into the corral to bury her husband when the pigs threaten to desecrate the bodies. Later, she gives Gaston Isbel a piece of her mind. She calls him a coward, unwilling to face Lee Jorth himself without dragging the whole family and their friends into the fight. This style of Texas feuding is cowardly, not the style of Arizona men. The women and children have to suffer the consequences of his selfishness. As a result of her dressing-down, Gaston Isbel decides to face Lee Jorth one-on-one to end the quarrel.

Isbel, Gaston: In *To the Last Man*, the head of the cattlemen faction in the Grass Valley war. Like his archenemy Lee Jorth, he grew up in Weston, Texas. He and Jorth were rivals at school, on the playground and in courting the same woman. When the Civil War breaks out, he enlists. He is badly wounded and recuperation takes a long time. He is left partly crippled. Meanwhile, Ellen Sutton, his fiancée, has betrayed him and married Lee Jorth. In revenge, Gaston Isbel sets a trap for Jorth, catching him branding calves that belong to Isbel. Jorth blames Gaston for his losing the Sutton property and his reputation. Some time later, Isbel gets involved in a card game with Lee Jorth and a cardsharp. In the card game, he is fleeced, and gets into a fight with the cardsharp, killing him. This precipitates his departure from Texas and his flight to Oregon. Jean is a child of his second marriage to a Nez Perce woman in Oregon. Jean is unlike other members of the family, his Indian heritage endowing him with skills and preferences not shared by his siblings. When Jorth appears in the Tonto Basin, the old Jorth-Isbel feud begins to heat up. Gaston Isbel leads the cattlemen and Jorth the sheepmen. Gaston sends for his Oregon son to come help with the fighting. When Jean arrives, Gaston fills him in on the situation, the rustling, the attacks on his life, but he underlines that this is not just a Texas-style blood feud but a war of law-abiding cattlemen against rustlers masquerading as sheepmen. The predicted war soon breaks out and Isbel loses his son Guy in the first round. Guy's wife puts him to shame, calling him a coward, a man too afraid to face his enemy alone, preferring instead to drag his whole family and his friends into the fight. In consequence of this dressing-down, Gaston decides to meet Jorth face-to-face. He sends young Evarts with a message for the Jorths holed up in Greaves Store. Lee Jorth comes out towards Gaston, but someone shoots Isbel with a rifle from one of the store windows. Gaston Isbel falls, and Lee Jorth finishes him off in the dust.

Isbel, Guy: In *To the Last Man*, second of Gaston Isbel's sons. He is smaller than Bill, wiry and hard as a rock, with snapping eyes in a brown, still face. He had the bowlegs of a cattleman. His passion is for horses. Like Bill, he resents Jean's criticism that they have not been doing enough to prevent the cattle rustling and the attacks on their father. When the fight begins at the Isbel ranch, Guy leaves the house to prevent Daggs from stealing his beloved horses. He and Jacobs head for the corral but are shot down by the Jorth faction. Later, pigs break into the corral and are about to devour the bodies. His wife, Esther, and Mrs. Jacobs risk getting shot to come out and dig graves and bury their husbands. Guy was Jean's favorite brother, a beloved playmate from childhood. When Jean kills Greaves, he says it is to avenge the death of his brother.

Isbel, Jean: In *To the Last Man*, the youngest son of Gaston Isbel. He is a child of Gaston's second marriage, to a Nez Perce woman in Oregon. Jean is another example of Grey's "natural man," a blend of white and Indian characteristics, a man as at home in the bosom of Mother Nature as in civilization. He, like Wetzel, is at home in the wilderness, in tune with his instincts which he has not allowed his rational self to snuff out.

Ellen Jorth describes him as she watches him when he comes to their appointed meeting at noon at the lip of the Rim: "He was clad in a buckskin suit, rather new, and it certainly showed off to advantage.... He did not look so large. Ellen was used to the long, lean, rangy Arizonans and Texans. This man was built differently. He had the widest shoulders of any man she had ever seen and they made him appear rather short. But his lithe, powerful limbs proved he was not short. Whenever he moved the muscles rippled. His hands were clasped round a knee — brown, sinewy hands, very broad, and fitting the thick muscular wrists.... He wore a cap evidently of some thin fur. His hair was straight and short, and in color a dead raven black. His complexion was dark, clear tan, with no trace of red. He did not have the prominent cheek bones nor the high-bridged nose usual with white men who were part Indian. Still, he had the Indian look. Ellen caught that in the dark, intent, piercing eyes, in the wide, level, thoughtful brows, in the stern impassiveness of his smooth face. He had a straight, sharp cut profile." She concludes that he was "the finest-looking man I ever saw in my life...!"

In response to an urgent letter from his aging father, Jean Isbel makes the trip from Oregon to Arizona's Tonto Basin, taking a boat to San Diego, then buying a horse and pack animals to trek across the Sierras. Jean is used to the lush Oregon forests, and the dry, desert conditions he has found in Southern California and Arizona do not please him. The Tonto Basin, however, with its abundance of trees and grass, is more to his liking. Thanks to his Indian heritage, Jean Isbel is a man of the forest, attuned to its ways, at home outdoors, capable of moving about undetected. Jean has outstanding eyesight, physical strength, swiftness of foot. He can shoot as well as the best gunmen, and, as Colter says, can track a grasshopper. Gaston Isbel knows in Jean he has an asset without equal in the Jorth faction.

Jean, however, is not willing to sign on to his father's cause without question. He has grown up in Oregon, and the old Texas feud is a dim recollection at best. He questions the need for armed conflict in a valley so well endowed with grazing land, enough to accommodate both herds of cattle and flocks of sheep. He also questions the truth of his father's declaration that this is a war between cattlemen and rustlers. His reason tells him that the rustling would only be possible with help from someone on the Isbel side. Also, he cannot hate the Jorths to the last man with the same unquestioning loyalty as his brothers Bill and Guy. He has met Ellen Jorth, a beautiful young woman with whom he falls in love at first sight. He cannot believe that she is a "hussy," as his father describes her.

In the fighting which ensues, Jean Isbel remains torn between loyalty to his father, and to his own sense of fairness and justice. While he will fight to defend his father's property and the lives of his brothers and sisters, he does not feel the hate that motivates the others. Jean tries to keep Andrew Colmor, Ann's fiancé, out of the fighting, for the sake of his sister and for Andrew's own peace of mind. He sees that Andrew is victim to his sense of manly honor that demands he sign on to the Isbel cause to become a member of the clan. He sees the effect this fighting will have on the next generation when Bill's oldest son comes out and asks his father to kill every last Jorth there is. A touch of Indian fatalism from his Nez Perce background leads him to accept that things must take their course if the disease of hate is to be cured.

Throughout the struggle, Jean maintains his faith in the goodness of Ellen Jorth. Although she has rejected him because he is an Isbel, he has told her that names are of no importance. He leaves her a touching gift; he lets her keep the horse her father has stolen from him. He always treats her with honor and respect. He defends her reputation in Greaves's store when Simm Bruce and Lorenzo besmirch her honor. He refuses to believe her when she tells him she is as bad as others say she is. Even Ellen's father, Lee Jorth, puts in a good word for him. When the dying Greaves reports that Jean Isbel said he was killing him to avenge the insult to Ellen Jorth, Lee Jorth declares he is the only decent man around.

The end of the novel reiterates a theme found in Grey novels, that sometimes for an evil to be eradicated, all those tainted by that evil must be wiped out. As a variant of the Grey hero, Jean Isbel blends Indian and frontiersman instincts with the principles of the medieval knight, a man whose faith in the goodness of a maligned woman and in his own goodness triumphs at last.

Isbel, Kate: In *To the Last Man*, Bill Isbel's wife. She is a stout, comely woman, mother of three children. She says nothing when Bill leaves to fight the Jorths in the village. Like Aunt Mary, she takes a stoical approach to the conflict.

Isbel, Lee: In *To the Last Man*, Bill Isbel's youngest boy. When Jean Isbel arrives, he leads the children in their request to see the gifts he has brought them. Jean thinks about how this feud will affect Bill's children.

Isbel, Uncle Jean: In *To the Last Man*, Gaston Isbel's youngest brother and a "fire-eater." Jean took after their Creole mother, inheriting his fighting nature from her. When the war of the rebellion began, Jean and Gaston enlisted in the army. Jean went through three years before he was killed. His company had orders to fight to the last man. Jean fought to the end, being the last to die. Gaston's son is named after Jean, and Gaston predicts that his fate will be that of his namesake uncle.

J

Jack: (1) In *Fighting Caravans*, Clint Belmet's dog. Jack can smell Indians and on several occasions warns the wagon train of an approaching attack. Clint becomes increasingly fond of the dog after his mother's death. The dog is finally killed in an Indian attack. A Comanche is pulling Clint from beneath a wagon to scalp him and Jack attacks the warrior, biting and holding on to his arm. The Indian stabs Jack to death.

(2) In *The Light of Western Stars*, one of the cowboys who works for Alfred on Bill Stillwell's ranch. He appears at Florence Kingsley's when Al comes to fetch his sister. He is Florence's brother-in-law.

(3) In *The Lone Star Ranger*, one of the vigilantes Buck Duane stumbles onto when they are about to hang a man. Buck Duane shoots Jack, but does not injure him seriously.

(4) In *Raiders of Spanish Peaks*, Lenta tells her mother she cannot accompany her to do shopping as she must write to Bill and Jack about her experiences coming out west. They are old friends back in Upper Sandusky, Ohio.

(5) In *Shadow on the Trail*, one of the cowboys working under Jesse Evans in Chisum's number ten outfit. He comments that Blanco is the best rider that Chisum has ever hired.

(6) In *West of the Pecos*, one of the men with Sawtell when he comes to the Lambeth ranch looking for Hod Pecos Smith.

(7) In *Wilderness Trek*, a drover-rustler working with Ormiston. Red overhears Ormiston, Jack and Bedford discussing plans to rustle cattle before they reach the Diamantina River or possibly earlier, as Bedford wants. In the fighting to recover the rustled cattle and horses, Sterl shoots and kills Jack, fearing he might shoot Leslie Slyter's horse, King.

Jack, Happy: In *Robbers' Roost*, a member of Hays's outlaw gang. Jim Walls comments that Happy Jack, as his name suggests, is an agreeable and likable man who had no business being among robbers. He has no force of character, veering like the wind. The person who last had his ear convinced him. Happy Jack is killed in the attack on Hays's outfit in the Devil's River Robbers' Roost.

Jackson: (1) In *Fighting Caravans*, a black man in the caravan with Belmet.

(2) In *Lost Pueblo*, works at the museum back east which had commissioned Phillip Randolph to undertake an archaeological expedition to find a lost pueblo. He is also a personal friend of Mr. Elijah Endicott, who is going to write to him corroborating Randolph's claim to have found the Lost Pueblo.

Jackson, Nig: In *Raiders of Spanish Peaks*, the only black cowboy working on the Spanish Peaks ranch. He is one of the crew that Allen leaves to work the ranch for Lindsay. Nig remains royal to Arlidge, and helps rustle the cattle from Lindsay's place and deliver them to Allen. He is captured by Laramie and Lonesome and Ted when they pursue Lenta's abductors. He is a pathetic figure, but not without courage. He says in his defense that he was never a rustler until Arlidge made him one. Nig is threatened with hanging until he agrees to turn on Allen and tell all he knows about the rustling. When Laramie and Lonesome reach Allen's ranch, Strickland is there, trying to convince Allen to join his Cattlemen's Protection Association. Nig Jackson tells Strickland what he knows about Allen's operation.

Jackson, Ride'em: In *Knights of the Range*, a Negro cowboy working for the Ripple ranch. He has a colorful background. He rode for Jesse Chisum, under Russ Slaughter. He admits once to having robbed a bank. They took the safe out of the bank and nearly busted themselves lugging it out onto the prairie. They spent two days breaking the iron box open only to discover it contained nothing but pieces of paper. He tells the story with great gusto and humor. He rustled cattle for a while. He is an incomparable man on horseback, with a special trick for staying on a bucking horse. He bites the horse's lip, keeping the animal from concentrating fully on the bucking. He is the secret weapon on the Ripple outfit in the rodeo competition against Russ Slaughter's outfit. Slaughter is not a good loser, demanding to know how he managed his trick. Jackson accompanies Frayne on the cattle drive to sell Holly's herd. He recounts their encounter with the horse rustlers on their return. Jackson helps with the capture and lynching of Talman and Lascelles. He is Brazos's messenger to Holly with the lie that Frayne cannot attend the wedding.

Jacobs, Bill: In *To the Last Man*, a neighbor and ally of Gaston Isbel. He is a thick-set, bearded man, rather jovial, unlike the lean-jawed Texans. He uses a .44 rifle of an old style. He offers to go with Guy Isbel to prevent the Jorths from stealing the horses. His wife asks him not to go, as his life is worth more than a couple of horses, but he insists. He is shot by the Isbels in the corral. His wife comes out later to bury his body when the Jorths open the gate to let the hogs in.

Jacobs, Jane: In *To the Last Man*, the wife of Bill Jacobs. She is a little woman with a homely face and very bright eyes. She entreats her husband not to go out to the corral to protect the horses from the Jorths. When the hogs break into the corral and threaten to desecrate the bodies, she goes with Esther Isbel to bury the bodies, despite the fact that the Jorths could shoot them down. With her husband dead, she says she will return to stay with her aging mother, who will be grateful to have her there. Jane Jacobs shows the stamina, courage and stoicism of Grey's pioneer women.

Jacobs, Slab: In "The Camp Robber," Slab Jacobs is a cowhand on the Selwyn Ranch who returns from the spring roundup to find the bunkhouse ransacked, but nothing missing.

Jacobs, Smilin': In *The Lost Wagon Train*, becomes Leighton's bosom partner in his campaign to ruin Latch. He is a gunslinger, bodyguard to Leighton. He is sent with Wess Manley to abduct Estelle Latch as she returns from seeing her friends off to New Orleans. They are to bring her to Spider Web Canyon where they will try to extort money out of Latch for her release. Smilin' Jacobs is killed by Slim Blue in a gunfight.

Jade: (1) In *The Horse Thief*, one of Edith Watrous's prized horses that Dale Brittenham retrieves from Mason's horse-rustling outfit.

(2) In *West of the Pecos*, Brasee's bartender at Eagle's Nest. He knifes Brasee, killing him.

Jake: (1) In "Canyon Walls," Jake is a young man

hired by Mrs. Keetch in Kanab. He and another new hired hand drive one wagon loaded with supplies while Sam and Rebecca go in the other one.

(2) In *Code of the West,* the stagecoach driver. Abe Hazelitt reports that the stagecoach has arrived early and that Jake has been driving like a crazy fool. Jake makes a gallant of himself, helping the female passenger descend from the coach. He unloads her luggage and when she complains that there is no one there to meet her, he laughs, pointing to all the young men gathered around to watch. He is the first man in the story to be bedeviled by Georgie's charms.

(3) In *The Deer Stalker*, one of the men in the Dyott-Settlemire group that spends the night in the cabin where Patricia Clay and Sue Warren are hiding in the loft.

(4) In *The Desert of Wheat*, a cowboy who works for Anderson. The boss sets him to watching Nash, the driver, and Jake reports that he meets with Glidden and other I.W.W. men. He warns Lenore about Nash and cautions her to be careful. He has graver doubts about the man than her father does. He spots men prowling around in the fields and night and shoots at one, winging him. After that, he advises all the hands to carry firearms. He breaks the word to Lenore that her father has organized a group of vigilantes to deal with the I.W.W. At one point, Glidden and Kurt get into a fight and Jake has to pull Kurt off Glidden to keep him from killing him. When the vigilante action is being planned, he urges Lenore to keep Kurt at home, but she does not succeed. After the I.W.W. men have been dealt with in town, he goes with Bill Jones to Neuman's place to tackle the problem of dealing with the real boss behind the I.W.W. in the area. On the way to Anderson's farm, they pass by the bridge from which Glidden's body still hangs.

(5) In *Horse Heaven Hill*, the short, old, grizzled, wrinkled, honest-eyed farmhand who has remained at the Burrell ranch in Idaho when Lark Burrell goes to live with the Wades. Lark is surprised to find him unchanged when she returns to the ranch with her husband, Stanley Weston, to restore the place to a working ranch.

(6) In *Robbers' Roost*, the young man who takes care of the horses at Red's establishment in Green Valley.

(7) In *The Shepherd of Guadaloupe*, a young cowboy who takes care of Virginia Lundeen's horses. He and Con are close friends, being thrown together because they are the only two non–Mexican cowboys working on the ranch. He is lean, dark-haired and dark-eyed, bowlegged, born on the range. Jake had worked in Silver City and had some mining experience. On Virginia's request, he takes a look at the Padre Mine and concludes that there is something fishy going on there. It appears that no real mining was ever done there, and no silver ever extracted. However, evidence suggests that someone has tried to plant gold dust in the soil there, by scattering the dust then setting off charges to drive it into the

ground. This gives Virginia an insight into how Malpass had managed to defraud her father. Jake and Con take care of Virginia's horses when she leaves for Colorado Springs. They return when she has inherited the properties from her father.

(8) In *Wild Horse Mesa*, a heavyset, square-framed, bald man who works with the Melberne outfit as a cook. He once had a wife, kids, prosperity, but lost them all. His daughter would be the age of Sue Melberne now. Jake had been a cowboy, but he is unable to work as a rider anymore. Nevertheless, he is cheerful and unselfish, and advises Sue Melberne that the only way to face life's vicissitudes is with open-hearted optimism. Bitterness gnaws at the spirit and sours life. He knows that Sue is troubled by Ora's annoyance that Chess likes her, but he tells her that she is just a spoiled girl who will eventually come around. He takes to Chane Weymer immediately, calling him the best rider he has ever seen.

James: In *Wyoming,* the butler at the Bonning home. Andrew knows something is amiss when James tells him that his father would like to speak to him.

James, Frank and Jesse: In *Knights of the Range,* are mentioned by Renn Frayne. He met them in Las Animas when they were on their way back east from a stint in California, where Jesse and Frank reputedly killed six men over a card game. The Jameses extended Frayne an invitation to join their gang but he refused. Frayne also mentions that the Jameses attended one of Holly Ripple's fiestas, but they passed unnoticed in the enormous crowd attending.

Jansen: In *The Desert of Wheat,* one of Chris Dorn's farmhands. He is fired after he takes off work thanks to I.W.W. agitation.

Jarvis: In *Rogue River Feud,* the new cannery man, running an operation that competes with Brandeth. He buys fish from Garry and Keven, angering the cartel that deals with Atwell and Brandeth's operation.

Jarvis, Mr.: (1) In *The Desert of Wheat,* the male nurse who accompanies Kurt Dorn home to Washington state when Mr. Anderson arranges his transfer.

(2) In *The Shepherd of Guadaloupe,* the mining engineer that Virginia Lundeen Forrest consults in Denver. She explains that she suspects the Padre Mine on her father's property had been planted. She asks him to come to investigate. He says it would probably take half a day to conduct the inspection. Jarvis comes to Las Vegas, where Virginia meets him. They go by car to the mine. Jarvis looks about and reports that indeed, the mine had been planted, and in quite a clumsy fashion. Gold dust had been planted around and dispersed through the soil through blasting. He comes back to the mining office just in time to save Virginia Lundeen from Malpass's attack. He gets shot five times, but miraculously survives. He provides the evidence Virginia needs to prove Malpass's fraudulent acquisition of her father's property.

Jason: In *The Horse Thief,* a man from Salmon in Sheriff Bayne's posse, which appears at Rogers's homestead to arrest Dale Brittenham.

Jasper: In *The Lone Star Ranger,* an outlaw in Bland's gang. He bets with Bill Black on anything. He reports back to Bland what Buck Duane did when Bill Bland bet he could hit the bucket the Mexican peon was carrying.

Jed: In *Arizona Ames,* the teamster on Halstead's ranch.

Jeff: (1) In *The Desert of Wheat,* a cowboy at Kurt Dorn's old wheat farm in Washington who has promised to write to him when he is away in boot camp and in France.

(2) In *Horse Heaven Hill,* the old cook who has been in the service of the Wade family for many years. He is a wonderful cook but cranky and methodical in his ways. To be late for a meal is an unpardonable sin and to ask for food at any other time is still worse. In the morning, he is up first, making numerous and unnecessary noises with tin buckets and whatever else comes to hand, just when people want to sleep.

(3) In *The Lost Wagon Train,* one of the cowboys who work for Lanthorpe with Slim Blue (Corny). He rides to catch up with Corny, who has ridden off after the gunfight with Pitch. He brings the money that Weaver and the boys have put together to give him, as they know he is broke. Jeff relays a message from Weaver to write to him at San Antone.

(4) In *Stranger from the Tonto,* a spare gray man of uncertain age with a gaunt visage, softening its "hard record through kindly feelings." He wears high boots and a gun sheath swings from under his coat. He is a member of the Hole-in-the-Wall gang, and confidante of Lucy Bonesteel, Avil Bonesteel's daughter. He has cooperated with Bonesteel in keeping Lucy in the dark about his work, although he knows that they cannot fool her forever. She does not know that her father is the head of an outlaw operation or that the men who stay there are thieves. Jeff tells her that Slotte is in love with her and wants to marry her because she is beautiful. He reminds her that her father has protected her since her mother died and that he has shot men who tried to get to her. Jeff wonders that she does not want to leave the outlaw hideout, but she has never known any other home. Lucy eventually tells Kent that Jeff had shown her the secret way out, but she never wanted to leave. He asks Lucy not to tell her father what he has talked about with her, because her father would surely kill him for being so frank. When Bonesteel decides to leave the hideout permanently and to settle the score with Roberts and his outfit, he gives Jeff the job of preparing things so that Kent and Lucy can escape via the secret route under the waterfalls. Jeff prepares knapsacks with food and the other supplies they will need for their trip. He saddles

the horses to have them ready for the flight near the waterfall. Bonesteel leaves a sack of gold for Jeff in appreciation of his years of loyal service and dedication to Lucy. Kent tells Bonesteel that Jeff did not get back to the cabin before the shootout began. He has survived and will probably accompany Bonesteel to his other home, a ranch in Utah.

(5) In *Under the Tonto Rim,* mentioned by the men chatting in Bill Lynn's place in Cedar Ridge. They say he is "rarin' to plow."

Jeffries: In *Thunder Mountain,* a miner who approaches Kalispel (Lee Emerson) to congratulate him on having exposed Pritchard as a cheat at cards and for having disabled the gunman Selby. Jeffries adds that there are many more miners like him who support what Kalispel has done.

Jenester: (1) In "Amber's Mirage," Jim Crawford's burro. She is his priceless companion in the desert, as she can smell water.

(2) In *Stranger from the Tonto,* Old Bill Elway's favorite burro. She has been indispensable to his traveling around the desert prospecting for gold. Jenester wears a bell which tinkles and the other mules follow her. When Elway dies, he gives the burros to Kent Wingfield, who releases them in the desert when he runs into Ben Bunge, who sells him Spades, a magnificent black stallion.

Jenet: In *Tappan's Burro,* born to Jennie, Tappan's principal burro. Tappan raises the burro and comes to think of her as a person. Jenet has been well trained to stay around camp and to wait until Tappan returns. Others marvel at how well trained the little burro is, offering to buy her. Jenet shows her love for her master on two occasions in the story, when she saves him from death in Death Valley, and when, after Tappan has abandoned the burro to run off with a woman, she is still there in his camp, waiting for him, when he returns about a year later. Tappan learns a lesson in love and loyalty from the little burro, and when he is snowed in with another trapper some time later, he refuses to let Jess Blade kill Jenet for food. Jenet's hooves cut through the crust on the snow and the animal sinks, making travel slow and painful. Tappan makes a sleigh for her out of a tarpaulin. The man pulls the burro along behind him, finally reaching the low country below. That night, the wind blows very cold, and Tappan freezes to death. The following morning, the little burro comes into camp as she had done thousands of mornings before, waiting for Tappan to wake up and break camp. But this time, she gets no answer. In "The Secret of Quaking Asp Cabin," the story of Tappan and his Burro is retold by Babe Haught to an unnamed narrator. He adds that Jenet continued to live for many years after, returning to the wild, but never abandoning the area where Tappan had died.

Zane Grey gained great respect for burros during his travels in the West. Tappan, like Dismukes in *The Wanderer of the Wasteland,* admires the burro for its strength, its endurance, its playfulness and its loyalty. Jenet is perhaps Grey's greatest tribute to the virtues of the desert burro.

Jengessen: In *Riders of the Purple Sage,* one of Bishop Dyer's bodyguards and gunmen. He is killed in the gunfight when Lassiter confronts Dyer during the trial of Willie Kern for the trumped-up charge of diverting water from an irrigation ditch.

Jenkins: In "The Flight of Fargo Jones," Jenkins is one of the men in Sheriff Smith's posse pursuing cattle thieves who brand maverick calves.

Jenkins, Mr.: In *Captives of the Desert,* the government agent at Leupp. He finds accommodations for the Winfields, and for the Newtons when their car breaks down on the way to the see the Navajo snake dance. His biggest problem is tracking down who is selling liquor to the Indians.

Jenkins, Mrs.: In *Captives of the Desert,* has just arrived at the reservation. She will be spending a month with Mrs. Burnham in Taho. When Mary Newton has been deserted by her husband and is considering moving to Flaggerston, Mrs. Jenkins tells her of a photographer who is looking for someone to keep his books and receive his patrons. She recommends Mary for the job. Mary Weston says of her that she has mastered the art of always keeping to herself other people's affairs, whether they reach her accidentally or intentionally.

Jenkins, Sam: In *Twin Sombreros,* an old partner of Brazos Keene. Brazos asks him if he can still palm aces like he used to and sing the herd quiet. He says he can still do the same tricks. He and Wess Tanner have heard about Brazos's work cleaning up the Surface rustler ring in Las Animas.

Jenkins, Wess: In *Shadow on the Trail,* the bartender in Mercer. He is responsible for the failure of the ambush because he comes out and starts shooting too soon. He shoots Simm Bell and in turn is shot by Wade Holden.

Jenks: (1) In *Forlorn River,* one of the rustlers caught at the ice caves with Bill Hall.

(2) In *The Last Trail,* the teamster hired to guide the Sheppards from Ft. Pitt overland to Ft. Henry. Jenks turns out to be unreliable. In fact, he is leading the Sheppards into an ambush. Bing-Leggett of the horse-stealing outfit has heard of Helen Sheppard and, like Jim Girty in previous novels, routinely abducts young women for his pleasure. Jenks is also involved in a later abduction of Helen Sheppard. Jenks is killed by Case when he, in turn, has tried to kill Case and steal his gold.

Jenks, Mr.: In *Under the Tonto Rim,* the schoolteacher in the Tonto basin. He is a slight, stoop-shouldered man whose thin, serious face shows both suffering and benevolence. He is the first male teacher there. The authorities think that a man would be a better choice as the women teachers end up marrying one of the young men. Mr. Jenks is in the high, dry country for his health and he's old enough that the girls won't be making sheep eyes at him. He explains to Lucy that he lives in a tent near the Johnson's home, and walks five miles to school every day. On occasion, he meets wild animals on the way. The pupils, some twenty-seven students from nineteen to four years of age, come on horseback or walk, some from a distance of eight miles. On his way from the Lynn's place at the stagecoach station, he tells Lucy the history of the place, explains the geography and the environment, and talks about the families, in particular about Edd Denmeade, about whom the Lynns had spoken, and his rivalry with Sam Johnson. He talks of the dances held at the school which last all night, and of a lack of pastimes for the young. When Mr. Jenks has to return back east, he recommends Clara Watson for the job. She accepts the job on a two-year contract.

Jennie: In *Tappan's Burro*, Tappan's mule. At the beginning of the story, Jennie gives birth to a floppy-eared baby which Tappan names Jenet. Jennie dies a few years later and Jenet becomes Tappan's principal burro.

Jenny: In *Thunder Mountain*, Kalispel's (Lee Emerson's) burro. She carries a load of over a hundred pounds of gold out of the valley when Lee leaves to buy Olsen's ranch.

Jerd: In *Riders of the Purple Sage*, the young man in charge of the stables. He is responsible for exercising Jane's thoroughbreds and training them. He remains loyal to her, one of the few Mormon riders who remain after Elder Tull has called her cowboys in. He provides mounts for Venters and Lassiter on instructions from Jane. He disappears after the thoroughbreds have been stolen. It is not clear whether or not he has been killed by the thieves.

Jerky: In *Raiders of Spanish Peaks*, one of Laramie's riders. He brings word back to the Spanish Peaks ranch that Lenta has been rescued.

Jerry: In *The Desert of Wheat*, a trusted employee of Chris and Kurt Dorn. He reports to the Dorns on the I.W.W. strangers on the farm. He is a big, lumbering fellow, gnarled like an oak tree, with a good-natured face and honest eyes. He keeps tabs on the I.W.W. men in the area, at one point reporting that a hundred and sixteen have been camped nearby. He agrees with Kurt's plan to get the neighboring farmers to help harvest the wheat. He takes guard duty at night, and is the first to spot the phosphorous cakes in the wheatfields. He organizes the men on horseback to pursue the I.W.W. men, who have set fire to the grain elevators. Thanks to his quick planning, the I.W.W. men do not burn down the whole village.

Jerry: (1) In *The Horse Thief*, one of the men in Sheriff Bayne's posse which arrives at Roger' homestead to arrest Dale Brittenham for stealing horses.

(2) In *Shadow on the Trail*, one of the cowboys from Hogue Kinsey's group that Tex Brandon recruits to work for Pencarrow. Jerry reports on Carter's change of attitude and his attempts to sow dissent among the cowboys. He concludes Carter has betrayed the men. He reports on seeing him have a long confab with some men on the range. His suspicions prove well-founded when Carter attempts to shoot Tex Brandon and Hal Pencarrow.

(3) In *Twin Sombreros*, Abe Neece's stable boy and driver. The young boy is seriously injured in the incident in which Neece was robbed of some forty thousand dollars. Some two years later, he has not yet recovered from the beating.

Jess: In *The Man of the Forest*, one of Milt Dale's horses that is killed by a bear.

Jester: In *Wilderness Trek*, one of Leslie Slyter's prize thoroughbreds. She gives him to Red to ride on the trek across Australia. Jester is stolen by Ormiston when he rustles part of the herd and the horses. He is retrieved by Red and Sterl.

Jett, Mrs. Jane (Harden):   In *The Thundering Herd*, the supposed wife of Randall Jett. He took up with her several months after Milly Fayre's mother died. Mrs. Jett does not reveal her true colors until later in the novel. She is a handsome woman, still young, dark, full faced, with regular features and an expression of sullenness. She is a hard worker, preparing the food for the outfit. She senses a competitor for Randall Jett's affections in the stepdaughter, pointing out that Milly is no more related to Jett than she is. She observes the way Rand watches Milly and her resentment grows. At one point, however, she almost appears friendly to Milly, enough so that the girl contemplates revealing to her that she and Tom Doan meet during the night. Perhaps she could be an ally when Jett discovers the truth. After the outfit returns from Sprague's, where they pick up Milly, who had been taken there earlier when the cavalry rounded up the women at the hiding camps, it becomes clear that Mrs. Jett is the brains behind the outfit. Milly overhears a conversation in which Jane issues orders to Jett. She is the mainspring in Jett's calculated mechanism to recruit new hiders for his operation, and when the other men discovered the truth, the cat is released among the pigeons. She refuses to negotiate, to share her part of the profits. She orders Jett to kill Follonsbee and Pruitt, but during the night, the two of them kill her and Randall and dispose of the bodies.

Jett, Randall: In *The Thundering Herd*, Milly Fayre's stepfather. He married Milly's mother when Milly was sixteen, but she died after a few months, upon which he took up with another woman, Jane Harden. Milly Fayre, the stepdaughter, says of him that his eyes are a hard blue, roving everywhere. They are the eyes of a mistrustful, suspicious man, looking for untoward reactions in people. Pilchuck reports to Hudnall's crew what he has heard at Sprague's about Jett. He is not very civil, avoiding the other hiders. Nobody knows much about him. He has returned to Sprague's on two occasions with two thousand hides. The shadow of doubt hangs over him, but no real proof that he is a hide thief.

Pilchuck does have one unpleasant encounter with Jett when he comes upon him skinning a buffalo that Pilchuck has shot. Jett claims he shot the animal and continues skinning it, but Pilchuck knows that the buffalo was felled by his rifle. He does not make an issue of it, but it confirms the man's reputation as a thief.

Milly Fayre comments that Jett's camp is like no other. There is no good humor, no kindliness, no happy words or pleasant laughing. Jett always selects a spot where the camp cannot be seen, usually in brakes or in a grove of trees. There is a lot of secrecy between Jett and the men, Follonsbee and Pruitt forming one group and Catlee left out of the circle. Jett is addicted to drink and in one of his drunken moments proposes to get rid of Jane, his wife, and take off with Milly. From them on, she avoids being alone with him.

After the last trip back to Sprague's with hides, things take a turn for the worse. Jane Harden, it turns out, is not married to Jett, but she is running the show. She has decided to get out of the hide stealing business. She refuses to share the money with Pruitt and Follonsbee. She orders Rand to kill the men. In the quarreling which ensues, Jane and Rand are killed by Pruitt and Follonsbee. Their bodies are no where to be seen.

Jigger: In *The Drift Fence*, Molly Dunn's horse. Jigger is not shod and he makes no noise along the trail when Molly sets out to follow her brother to warn him of Hack Jocelyn's plot.

Jim: (1) In *The Horse Thief*, one of Edith Watrous's prize horses that Dale Brittenham retrieves from the Mason's horse rustlers.

(2) In *Knights of the Range*, the cowboy in charge of the remuda on the Ripple ranch.

(3) In *The Mysterious Rider*, a good-sized hound, but small compared to Sampson. The hound is old but still vigorous.

(4) In *Shadow on the Trail*, a member of Aulsbrook's crew when Wade Holden rides in with word that Catlin's rustler outfit is planning to drive off their herd.

(5) In *The U. P. Trail*, cited as an Irish worker who is typical of the "little people" who have made the construction of the railroad possible. Men like him do the hard work, drink and gamble their pay, and dream of returning home some day.

(6) In *Western Union*, a young miner in South Pass who wants to marry Flo. She tells Cameron that she is not good enough for him, but he doesn't seem to think so.

Jinny: (1) In *Code of the West*, the mule to which the most delicate and valuable possessions are entrusted in the move to Cal's new homestead cabin.

(2) In *To the Last Man*, Ellen Jorth's burro, a gift from John Sprague. She apologizes for her fickleness to the burro when she is overjoyed with her gift horse, Spades (Whiteface).

(3) In *The Wanderer of the Wasteland*, the mule Dismukes gives to Adam Larey when they first meet in the desert. Jinny is quite mischievous, given to raiding her master's pack and ready to eat anything she can get a hold of. She takes advantage of the inexperienced Wansfell (Adam), poking through his pack, scattering everything on the ground, and setting fire to his kit by chewing the matches wrapped there. Jinny then runs off, and Dismukes finds her. He assumes that Adam has perished in the desert and the burro has returned to him.

Jo: In *Western Union*, a saloon girl at the Gold Nugget in South Pass. She told Flo where Ruby was being held at the Nugget.

Joan: In *The Rainbow Trail*, mentioned as one of the sealed wives in the hidden Mormon village.

Jocelyn, Hack: In *The Hash Knife Outfit*, a cowboy who once worked for old Jim Traft's Diamond outfit. He quit the ranch to join the Cibeque outlaw gang. He loses his head over Molly Dunn, sister to the gunman, Slinger Dunn. Jocelyn caused division in the Cibeque, between the Haverlys and Slinger Dunn. Jocelyn kidnaps young Jim Traft for ransom, planning to collect the money, then kill young Jim. Jocelyn has one drink too many and then tries to take Molly off into the woods. She fights him tooth and nail. Jocelyn ties Jim to a post and uses him for target practice, placing a bottle on his head. He tries to shoot and kill young Jim but Molly prevents it. Slinger shows up and kills Jocelyn. Jim Traft credits Molly with saving his life when she bit Hack's gun hand.

In *The Drift Fence*, the full story of Hack Jocelyn is presented. Jocelyn is a handsome young cowboy who works for the Diamond Ranch and more than any other cowboy in the outfit, he resents the tenderfoot nephew of Jim Traft being named foreman. As well, he resents being asked to work building a fence, carrying barbed wire and digging fence posts. He behaves insolently toward young Jim Traft and incites discontent and rebellion among the remaining cowboys. Hack Jocelyn's attitude is his problem. His face wears an expression of condescending disdain for Jim Traft. He does not lack for cowboy skills. He breaks the local record for calf roping at the rodeo in Flagg, but he refuses to comply with new policy at the Diamond Ranch. Hack provokes a fight with Jim Traft over his comments about Molly Dunn, but Jim, who has trained as a boxer back east, is more than a match for any of the cowboys on the Diamond. Jocelyn is jealous of Jim Traft because he, too, is interested in Molly Dunn. After he quits the Diamond, he proposes marriage to her, but she wants nothing to do with him. Before he quits the Diamond Outfit, Hack has done his best to sabotage the drift fence project, cutting the wire in places and driving cattle through the opening. Jocelyn then plans to make his fortune by kidnapping Jim Traft and holding him for ransom. He and Seth and Sam Haverly decide to lay the blame on Slinger Dunn, Molly's brother. The plot is revealed when Andy

Stoneham overhears Jocelyn and the Haverlys making their plans, plans which Andy repeats to Molly. Hack executes his plot, kidnapping Jim Traft, but Molly and Arch (Slinger) foil his plans. Jocelyn is killed and his Cibeque outlaw gang finished. Jocelyn is an example of the bad cowboy, a man with potential, but unwilling to do the work to make his way in the world.

Joe: In *The Horse Thief*, the stable boy at the Watrous ranch. Edith asks him to take care of the stolen horses that Dale has just brought back.

Joel: In *The Lone Star Ranger*, the driver of the stagecoach in which Ruth Herbert and Ray Longstreth come to Fairdale. He tries to console the girls when a fight breaks out and Bill is shot.

John: In *Black Mesa*, one of the men making a delivery of liquor to Belmont's post while Paul Manning is observing from the rooftop.

Johnny: (1) In *The Drift Fence*, the young boy young Jim Traft sends into Mace's saloon to ask Slinger Dunn to come out to meet him in the street. The young boy obliges.

(2) In *Robbers' Roost,* the young boy at the ferry crossing who is cheated by the "fat party," who outsmarts the boy and avoids paying the ferry fee by swimming his horses behind the raft. Johnny gives the "fat party" his change vowing never to be caught by such a trick again.

Johnson: In *30,000 on the Hoof*, a young cowboy hired by Logan Huett to drive his herd from Sycamore Canyon to Flagg. He is a young Irish man with a thick Irish accent.

Johnson Girls: In *Betty Zane*, the story of their abduction by Jim Girty is used as a warning to scare young girls away from lonely roads in or near the woods.

Johnson, Ora: In *Under the Tonto Rim*, one of the Johnsons who live farther up the canyon from the Denmeades. Sam is his son. Ora Johnson has an old cabin with one room. Counting his wife, there are eight in the family and all live in the one room, with one door and no window.

Johnson, Ranger: In *West of the Pecos,* one of the cowboys Pecos Smith recruits in South Texas to come west of the Pecos to work on the Lambeth ranch. Johnson stands out among the crew for his skill with a rifle, killing two buffalo on the short hunt.

Johnson, Sam: (1) In *Under the Tonto Rim*, one of the family near whose house the teacher, Mr. Jenks, has set up his camp. He readies a horse and wagon to take Lucy Watson to the Denmeade's where she will begin her work. Lucy describes him as a young giant, somewhere over twenty years of age, with clear, hazel eyes and a smooth face. He introduces her to her horse, Buster, whose name suggests unmanageable behavior that is not typical. Sam is gleeful thinking about how Edd Denmeade will react when he sees the new teacher riding his horse. Sam has the reputation of being the best dancer around, and both Sadie Purdue and Allie Denmeade are after him. Sadie, who rejected Edd's marriage proposal, is pushing Sam to homestead on the spot that Edd had picked out. She hopes to make trouble between Sam and Edd.

(2) In *Wyoming,* runs a gas station in Split Rock. He is unable to give Simpson directions to Bligh's ranch but sends him on to Jed Price, who will surely be able to help.

Johnson, Tumbler: In *The Lost Wagon Train*, a mulatto member of the Leighton faction at Latch's Field. He got his name from his former profession as circus performer. He is described as a good friend and a dangerous enemy. He accepts the offer to start up ranching with the money and cattle Latch gives him. He becomes the only Negro on the frontier known to be a squaw-man. However, he continues to work for Leighton, since this man could ruin him if he revealed his former and present outlaw activities. His herds are never bothered by rustlers, while those of Latch are nearly cleaned out. Slim Blue overhears him talking to Kennedy about Leighton's plans to ruin Stephen Latch. Johnson explains to Kennedy that Leighton and Latch had been partners with the Kiowa chief, Satana, in his raids on wagon trains. Also, they once fought over a woman, and Leighton was shot in the quarrel. The woman in question was Cynthia Bowden, Estelle's mother. He has never forgiven Latch and has been plotting revenge for over fifteen years. When the full scale score-settling begins the night of Estelle's party, Slim Blue provokes a fight with Tumbler Johnson and kills him. Mizzouri describes the event to Simmons, who reports it to Latch.

Joker: In *The Deer Stalker*, the name of one of the mules used to bring tourists down into the Grand Canyon. Nelson Stackhouse plays a trick on the tenderfoot Patricia Clay, giving her this mule to ride. Joker likes to frighten tourists by approaching the narrow edge of a trail and stopping to look down into the chasm, scaring the life out of the rider in the process.

Jones: (1) In *The Arizona Clan*, the Jones ranch is across the valley from the Lilleys'. Denton goes to their ranch to get someone to stay with their mother when they set out after the Hathaway outfit.

(2) In *Boulder Dam*, phones the cement mill when Lynn Weston is trying to track down the saboteurs about to set off an explosion at the construction site. He claims to have received inside information that the pipe tunnel is to be filled in with cement that morning. Lynn recognizes the call as a bluff and a sign that the racketeers are involved in the plot.

(3) In *The Dude Ranger*, a cattle dealer for the government, buying cattle for the Indian reservations. John Hepford has made cattle drives to sell him cattle. He is not particularly interested in where the cattle he buys come from.

(4) In *Nevada,* runs the general store in Lineville. He is a long, lanky westerner who has seen days on the range. He offers Nevada work, as he is now doing well and sees even better days ahead. The mines are booming in the area and there is demand for timber. The new prosperity of the town has benefited him greatly.

(5) In *Thunder Mountain*, the younger partner of Hadley. He and Hadley run a mess for eight other miners. Kalispel approaches them with a proposal to provide their camp with fresh meat. They gladly welcome the offer and drum up new customers for Lee Emerson (Kalispel).

(6) In *Thunder Mountain*, a second Jones appears as a witness against Kalispel in the miners' court convoked by Rand Leavitt and his vigilantes. Jones accuses Lee Emerson (Kalispel) of having attacked and robbed him. His testimony is proven false when Sydney Blair proves that Kalispel was with her when the attack supposedly took place. This same Jones and Matthews, another false witness, get into a gunfight with Sheriff Masters after Kalispel has left Thunder Mountain to set up his ranch. One of them confesses to having killed Sam Emerson on orders from Rand Leavitt.

(7) In *The Trail Driver*, buys Colonel Miller's herd and his trail drive wagons. Alabama Moze goes with the herd and the equipment.

(8) In *The U. P. Trail*, a member of the wagon train organized by Bill Horn to return to the East. Jones is a loquacious man, leading the speculation about the fortune in gold Horn is bringing back with him as well as the possibilities of a railroad being built to the West Coast. He is killed in the Sioux attack on the caravan.

(9) In *The U. P. Trail*, a professional gambler who is lured into a card game in Durade's gambling establishment in Benton. Durade picks a fight with him, accusing him of cheating, and Durade's henchman, Fresno, shoots and kills Jones.

Jones, Beady: (1) In *The Border Legion*, the man who found Bill Bailey at the cabin. Bill tells him that Jack Kells shot him at point blank range and left him for dead. He also tells Beady that Joan is not Kells's wife, as he is pretending. Beady Jones is a member of the Border Legion, vacillating between the Gulden and Kells factions. He declares he is happy for Jim Cleave when he finds the thirty-pound gold nugget. Beady is one of the outlaws involved in the holdup of the Alder Creek-Bannock stage. He is also present when the gold is divided at the cabin and the gambling results in the self-destruction of the Border Legion.

(2) In "From Missouri," a tall, handsome cowboy, an unusually good dancer who does not hold his partner in such a manner as to cause difficulty in breathing. He is witty and engaging and has a flattering tongue. The schoolteacher admits that he is charming and appealing, if a bit too bold, self-assured and debonair. Beady Jones had been foreman at the Springer ranch until his slickness angered the boss. Beady's cutting in on Tex's dance with Miss Stacey provokes a fight. Jones shows up the following Sunday, expecting to go riding with the teacher. Springer chases him off, but Jane admits she may have said something to give him the impression she would go riding. Beady Jones does not give up. He waits on the range, hoping she will ride out from the ranch, and one day he does meet her. He makes quite a picture as he dismounts, slick, shiny, booted, spurred with a huge sombrero. Springer meets with them and invites Beady to a fight in which the handsome cowboy is solidly defeated.

Jones, Bill: In *The Desert of Wheat,* works for Anderson. He shares guard duty with Jerry when the I.W.W. is prowling about planting phosphorous cakes in the wheatfields. He is driving the new McCormick harvester-thresher that Adams showed Lenore. Bill Jones participates in the vigilante action against Glidden and the I.W.W. and accompanies Jake to Neuman's to bring him to Anderson's, where he is bought out by Anderson at market value for his property and then driven out of the community for his promotion of the I.W.W. and sabotaging the wheat crop.

Jones, Brick: In *Arizona Ames,* a cowboy working on Crow Grieve's ranch. He is one of Grieve's favorite cowboys because he shares a similar disposition. Brick Jones helped Carpenter built the fence around the Nielsen homestead on Grieve's orders. Brick Jones also made advances to Mrs. Nielsen. When Arizona Ames approaches him, asking him to tear down the fence, he agrees to do it, and apologizes for the crude behavior to Mrs. Nielsen. His excuse is that she was friendly to him and he misinterpreted her intentions.

Jones, Burt: In *The Lone Star Ranger,* a Texas rancher who had known Buck Duane's father and helped him out on occasion. He takes Buck in after the shooting with Hardin, welcoming him to his home and family. He reports to Duane that there are rangers in town looking for him. An unarmed ranger comes to his ranch with a message for Buck to go to MacNelly's camp outside of town after dark. Jones suspects it might be a trap and he advises Buck to ride as far away as he can. He himself will go to MacNelly's camp to try to find out what the game is. He doesn't think that MacNelly would double-cross anyone, but suspects that the man's wide reputation for doing things in an unorthodox way may have given him a swelled head.

Jones, Colonel Buffalo: In *The Thundering Herd,* a noted plainsman who gained his sobriquet for his efforts to preserve the buffalo. He argued for preserving calves to form the nucleus of a herd. He argued that the buffalo was a perfect example of Darwin's theory of evolution, an animal singularly fitted to survive and flourish on the vast, varied environment of the Great Plains. He estimated the numbers as ten million. The blizzards of Montana or the torrid sirocco of the Llano Estacado (Staked Plain) was no hindrance to the buffalo, whose great shaggy, matted head had been constructed to face the icy blasts of winter, or the sandstorms and hot gales of summer. Colonel Jones, however, did not extend his admiration to the Indians who lived off the buffalo. These, he felt, needed to be exterminated so that the plains could be opened up to farming. Tom Doan meets Buffalo Jones at Sprague's post when he joins Hudnall's outfit of hiders.

In *Raiders of Spanish Peaks,* Colonel Buffalo Jones meets John Lindsay in Garden City, Kansas. Lindsay has bought the Spanish Peaks ranch in Colorado from a Lester Allen. Jones knows the place, that it is in great need of repair, and suspects Allen has taken advantage of a naive, wealthy easterner. He volunteers to help Lindsay find a man to take his wagon train to Spanish Peaks and work as foreman. He bumps into Laramie Nelson on the street, and immediately thinks of him for the job. The ranch, an old Spanish home and fort, could become as prosperous and influential a place as Maxwell's ranch. Jones praises Nelson as a sharpshooter and true-grain westerner and highly recommends the two men with him, Lonesome Mulhall and Ted "Tracks" Williams. Jones outlines for Lindsay the problems he will face. The house will probably be completely empty; the cattle will probably be far fewer than the ten thousand Allen claims. As well, the crew left behind will undoubtedly be more loyal to Allen than to the new tenderfoot. Rustling is commonplace on the range, and in many cases, it is an inside job. In all of these things, Laramie Nelson will be an invaluable asset to Lindsay.

In *The Deer Stalker,* Thad Eburne, a deer stalker for the parks service, compares himself to Buffalo Jones, only his concern is to preserve the deer population. The problem arises when the government permits cattle grazing on parkland supposedly reserved for wildlife. To prevent the deaths of thousands of deer, he would like to move the deer to new terrain where they would be safe, just as Buffalo Jones made possible the survival of the American Bison, moving a herd into a protected park.

Jones, Dr.:   In *Code of the West,* disagrees with Dr. Smith's diagnosis of Georgiana Stockwell's condition. He sees no problem with her lungs. Rather, he attributes her condition to her over-active social life. She has merely danced and gadded herself into a rundown condition.

Jones, Fargo: In "The Flight of Fargo Jones," a cowboy who is arrested by Sheriff Smith for branding maverick calves. Fargo Jones is riding along a trail and spots a cowboy branding a maverick calf. He shoots his rifle to frighten the man off. The man leaves in a great hurry, and Fargo proceeds to examine what the man was doing. He finds the campfire still burning and a branding iron still hot. He also finds calves in a ravine down by the river. Fargo, however, has been observed from a hilltop by Pete, one of the sheriff's posse. They come to his camp, Pete identifies him, and he is arrested. Back in town,

the sheriff believes Fargo's story but he must keep him in jail for his own protection until he does track down the thieves. Fargo Jones breaks out of jail, hides in a cabin in the mountains, and manages to remove the handcuffs with great difficulty. A year later, Sheriff Smith appears at the cabin. He knew about the cabin, and had deduced from the tracks he followed where Fargo was going. He tells Fargo that he has caught the real cattle thieves. He jokes that he must take him in, however, because he ruined the best pair of handcuffs in that part of the country.

Jones, Miss: In *Valley of Wild Horses,* the schoolteacher who tries to cure Pan Handle Smith of writing with his left hand. She ties his left hand to the desk and makes him practice writing with his right hand.

Jones, Mr.:   In *Twin Sombreros,* a clerk in the store where Brazos confronts Bodkins. Bodkins points to Jones as a "harmless" man, like Raine Surface.

Jones, Mr. and Mrs.:   In *Wyoming,* an elderly couple introduced by Jim Dawson to Martha Ann Dixon at the hotel in Deadwood. He has arranged with them to take her along as they drive through Wyoming. Martha trusts them on sight. Mr. Jones looks like a retired country merchant and Mrs. Jones appears to be a motherly soul. Mrs. Jones tells Martha they do not believe her story, that they know she is running away from home. They understand she is a spirited, wild thing, and that she is lovably innocent. They offer to make arrangements with her relatives to adopt her, if possible. Martha thanks them for their understanding but she refuses their offer. A farmer takes her on the last part of her journey to Randall.

Jones, Mrs.:   (1) In *Code of the West,* Dr. Jones's wife. Mary Stockwell's mother writes that she does not believe Dr. Jones's assessment of Georgie's condition because she does not like his wife, who puts on such airs.

(2) In *The Dude Ranger,* the older woman who shares the stagecoach with Ernest Selby, Anne Hepford and the two would-be robbers. When Anne complains that Silas Selby had left Red Rock ranch to a brother or a nephew, the cowboy, Jeff Martin, tells her she can marry him if she feels the ranch really should belong to her and her father. Mrs. Jones agrees with the proposition. When Anne expresses gratitude that Ernest did not fill the would-be robbers full of lead, Mrs. Jones comments that it would have been better if he had.

(3) In *The U. P. Trail,* a sober-faced, middle-aged woman, wife of the loquacious Jones. She is happy to be returning to the East. She never liked the big tent cities in the mining camps and the wild, uncouth behavior typical of men under the influence of gold fever. Such mining camps are no place for a woman. She is friendly towards Mrs. Durade and her daughter, Allie. Mrs. Jones is murdered and scalped in the Sioux attack on the wagon train.

Jones, Rang: In *Nevada,* one of two cowboys that Tom Daly lends to Ben Ide when he first starts his ranch. Rang Jones does not like Clan Dillon, the man Ben Ide hires as foreman. The two of them fight and Rang Jones quits the Ide ranch.

Jones, Roland Tewksbery: In *Wilderness Trek,* described as a hulking, craggy-visaged chap some years Krehl's and Hazelton's senior. He's not sure what to make of the two Yankee cowboys who have joined Slyter and Dann's trek. He is amused at their ignorance of Australian wildlife, as is Leslie Slyter. When Henry Ward is trampled to death trying to keep separate Ormiston's herd from the rest of the mob, Jones clearly places the blame for the incident on Ormiston himself, who did nothing to warn Ward of the danger he was in or to call him back. Jones also helps retrieve the stolen cattle and horses Ormiston and his crew have rustled. Rollie is loyal to Stanley Dann and Bingham Slyter to the end of the trek in the Kimberleys in Northwest Australia.

Jones, Ruth: In *The Rainbow Trail,* one of Waggoner's many sealed wives in the Mormon village. She is friendly with John Shefford when he comes to the village delivering supplies for Withers. She remains friendly with him and helps him to plan Mary's escape after Waggoner is killed. Ruth is the first woman called to testify at the polygamy trials in Stonebridge. She shows her anger at the process and replies curtly to the questions put to her. Shefford comments about her when the wives have returned to the village, that she is truly a prisoner in the valley. She is not religious, and remains because she does not have the strength and the courage to cast off Mormonism. She also tells Shefford, when he confides in her that he is planning to rescue Mary from the schoolhouse, that she is helping him out of selfishness as much as altruism. Ruth had given Mary the nickname "Sago Lily," in part out of jealousy of her striking beauty and in mockery of her reserve and reticence. She, too, was married to Waggoner, and although he always treated her well, and kept her in everything she wanted, she is not upset that he is dead. She also vows she will never again be a sealed wife. She goes with Shefford to the schoolhouse to bring Mary some food, and when there, she switches clothes with her so she can escape undetected. She has no reason to fear what the Mormons will do to her. At best, they will scold her, and preach at her, but Mormon secrecy, refusal to call attention to themselves by taking any drastic action, will be her salvation.

Jones, Sary: In *The Man of the Forest,* Milt Dale learns from Mrs. Cass that Sary Jones has died since his last visit to the village.

Jones, Shady: In *The Man of the Forest,* one of the outlaws in Snake Anson's gang. He is one of the gang that kidnaps Bo Rayner. When the outfit falls apart, he stands up for Jim Wilson. Shady shoots Anson, and he himself is thrown from his horse and trampled to death when Milt frightens off the outlaws' mounts.

Jones, Tom: In *Knights of the Range,* a train boss and freighter, friend of the late Colonel Lee Ripple. He visits the Ripple ranch with Buff Belmet. He asks Buff if she is still single, and Britt replies that there is simply too much choice for her to make up her mind.

Jorth, Ellen: In *To the Last Man,* the daughter of Lee Jorth. Both Gaston Isbel and Lee Jorth say she is the image of her mother, Ellen Sutton, at the same age. Jean Isbel is struck by her singular beauty and her free mountaineer step. She is impressed by his gentlemanly treatment of her, removing his hat to talk to her. She feels embarrassed by the fact that she has no good shoes or stockings, explaining to him that her mother died in Texas and she has lived with rough men ever since. Their ways have rubbed off on her. She explains to Jean and to John Sprague that she does not understand why the sheepmen and the cattlemen are at odds since there is plenty of grass for both herds to graze on. She thinks the sheepmen are wrong to move their flocks onto cattlemen's range deliberately to provoke a fight. But should such a fight develop, she would be on her father's side, whatever the right and the wrong of the matter. When Jean Isbel tries to kiss her, she brushes it off as typical male behavior, but the revelation that he is an Isbel and therefore an enemy of her father's means they can never be friends. And so begins a Romeo and Juliet story of love and hate and feuds.

Ellen is curious to learn if Jean will keep their appointment at the lip of the Rim, despite his being an Isbel. She hides and watches. Jean Isbel appears and again she is struck by his strength and good looks. His Wetzel-like form and his suppleness and grace dismounting from his horse mark him as an unusual man, a blend of southern courtesy and Indian grace. He looks like an Indian in his buckskin garb. He is carrying a package which he deposits in her tent at the camp. Ellen is unsure what to think. She convinces herself that she hates him and kicks the package around a bit. When she sees Ann Isbel's name on the wrapping, she remembers the girl who had befriended her two years before at a roundup. She puts the package away. When she does open it up, it contains a pair of shoes and several pairs of stockings. No doubt, Jean had noticed she went barefoot and concluded this would be the perfect gift. His sympathy both please and anger her.

Ellen Jorth is presented as a fair-minded individual who must decide between family loyalty and what is right. She has always accepted her father's story about what happened between him and Gaston Isbel back in Texas. She believes that he is a rancher, although evidence is constantly mounting to show that he cares little for his ranch and does no work that could be called farming or ranching. In fact, there is no farming equipment around and the sheep and cattle are left to fend for themselves under the care of lazy, unreliable Mexicans. The same is true of Daggs, her father's closest associate who is supposed to have a sheep ranch in one of the nearby canyons. But despite repeated efforts to locate the place, Ellen has never found sheep, ranch or cabin.

Grey develops the character of Ellen Jorth in the same vein as Betty Zane. She is a Heidi-like figure, a child of nature, at one with the birds, the animals, the trees. Her moods are reflected in the weather and the landscape. She finds consolation in communing with the wilderness. Like Betty, she both loves and hates the man who loves her. Ellen is clearly in love with Jean Isbel. He has treated her with the respect, dignity and consideration a lady deserves, something she has not known since she left the South. But at the same time, he is the son of her father's archenemy, the man who destroyed him and branded him a thief. She is torn between conflicting loyalties, to herself and to her father. She tries to discourage Jean Isbel, to drive him off by telling him she is the hussy everyone says she is. But John Sprague gives her the same advice Colonel Zane gives to Betty, to be true to herself and to value her good name. Ellen must follow her heart, and defend her good name if she is to be happy. Despite all, Jean Isbel has remained her knight in shining armor, defending her reputation in Greaves's store when Simm Bruce tells all he has been with Ellen many times. He kills Greaves to avenge the death of his brother but also to punish the wrong done to Ellen's reputation. When Jean discovers Ellen with his stolen horse, Whiteface (Spades), he lets her keep the animal. In the end, Ellen Jorth must admit to herself that she does love Jean Isbel, that he is the best man she has ever met. She ends up defending the last of her father's hated enemies, shooting Colmer, who is about to kill the last of the Isbels. In the Jean-Ellen relationship, Grey has developed a Romeo and Juliet-style plot with a western touch and a happy ending.

In *Stranger from the Tonto*, Kent Wingfield recalls how he almost cast his lot with the Jorth faction in the Pleasant Valley war because when he was sixteen, he had seen Ellen Jorth once.

Jorth, Jackson: In *To the Last Man*, a brother to Lee Jorth and uncle to Ellen. He is a member of the Hash Knife gang. He came to Arizona with the remnants of the gang to help his brother. Jackson is given to drinking and gambling. He is killed in the Isbel attack on Greaves's store.

Jorth, Lee: In *To the Last Man*, the father of Ellen Jorth . He had once been a singularly handsome man. He is tall but does not have the figure of a horseman. His dark hair is now streaked with gray and has turned white over his ears. His face is sallow, thin, with deep lines. He has a bitter mouth and a weak chin, not wholly concealed by a gray mustache and pointed beard. He wears a long frock coat and a wide-brimmed sombrero, both black in color. Jorth always wears a white linen shirt, a relic of his Southern prosperity.

Lee Jorth is leader of the sheepmen in the cattlemen-sheepmen war in Grass Valley. Lee Jorth and Gaston Isbel grew up in Weston, Texas. They played together as children, went to school together, fought with each other as boys, and fell in love with the same woman, Ellen Sutton. When Isbel went off to war, Lee Jorth pursued Ellen and she married him. Isbel believes Jorth won Ellen over by telling her lies about him. When Isbel returns from the war, he seeks revenge. Jorth had taken over the Sutton range and after a few years was quite comfortable. Like all cattlemen, he had branded calves which weren't his, but Gaston Isbel set a trap for him. He caught Jorth branding one of his own calves, which he had marked, and he proved him a thief and rustler. He ruined him. Jorth was not strong on the draw, a fact attributed to his being born in Louisiana, and, therefore, not being a true Texan. Jorth left Texas in disgrace. Jorth blames Isbel for his misfortunes, his loss of the Sutton property and his being branded a cattle thief. Some years later, Gaston Isbel meets Jorth and a cardsharp friend. Isbel gets fleeced and a gunfight breaks out. The cardsharp is killed, and Isbel flees Texas for Oregon. Colonel Jorth moved into the Tonto Basin to pursue the feud.

Lee Jorth drinks and gambles too much. He claims to be a sheepman, but Ellen knows he cares nothing for the sheep or cattle he has. He leaves on mysterious missions, sometimes not returning for days. He is often in the company of Daggs, known leader of the Hash Knife gang. Still, Jorth loves his daughter and although she is condemned to live among rough, uncouth and lascivious men, he will kill any man who abuses his daughter. He kills Simm Bruce on the spot when he learns from Greaves the truth about Bruce's sullying Ellen's reputation. He even praises Jean Isbel as the only decent man around for having defended Ellen's honor. Jorth leaves the store to face Isbel in a one-on-one encounter, but one of Jorth's faction shoots Isbel with a rifle, and Lee Jorth finishes the injured man off and returns to Greaves's store. Jorth is killed when the gunfighter, King Fisher, known in Grass Valley as Blue, breaks into the store and shoots him and his brother Jackson.

Jorth, Tad: In *To the Last Man*, brother to Lee and Jackson Jorth, and uncle to Ellen. He was wounded in the fight in Greaves's store. Colter and Springer bring him back to the ranch. He is badly wounded. Ellen thinks to herself that he had been the last man to take orders from anyone, let alone a rustler from the Hash Knife gang like Colter. Ellen feels sorry for him, although she has always hated him. He had been a drunkard, a gambler, a waster of her father's property and now he is a rustler and a fugitive. Ellen does her best to help her uncle, and he apologizes for the way Ellen has been disgraced by them. He calls her the only good Jorth of the lot. He warns her she will be "dragged to hell ... unless." The rustlers leave, taking Ellen with them, abandoning Tad to die alone in Lee Jorth's cabin.

Jose: (1) In *Knights of the Range,* the cook with the Britt outfit working on Ripple's ranch. He is reputed to be excellent.

(2) In *Majesty's Rancho*, Jose is a stable hand and rider on Gene Stewart's ranch. He saddles the horses

for Madge's friends. He and Manuel have tracked the cattle rustlers a distance and then lost the trail near the road. This leads Lance Sidway to conclude that the animals have been loaded onto trucks.

Josh: In *The Call of the Canyon,* drives the stage through Oak Creek Canyon where Glenn Killbourne lives. He takes Carley Burch to the Lolomi Lodge in the valley. He also brings supplies to the lodge, and when he arrives with Carley, Mrs. Hutter asks about the supplies he was to bring.

Joy: In *Captives of the Desert,* a young Navajo girl suffering from influenza that Mary Newton helps nurse back to health and then adopts. Joy is Magdaline's younger sister. She wants to go to white school as her sister did. She is obsessed with becoming white one day. She points to a scar on her arm, saying that she is turning white. She also quotes the parson, who talks about being made white when one repents. Mary tells her that such changes just don't happen. Mary understands that the care and love Joy is receiving from her is estranging Joy from her own race and people. She hopes she can educate the child to preserve the best of Navajo traditions and philosophy and give her the arts and skills of white people, so that she can help the women of her own tribe who are lost in an age of change that is crushing their old faiths and customs without an adequate substitute.

Joyce, Maramee: In *Majesty's Rancho,* one of Madge Stewart's crowd at the university in Los Angeles. She is brown-haired, built like Jean Harlow, a knockout. She is one of the group that comes to Arizona to spend the summer on the Stewart ranch.

Juan: In *Nevada,* the shepherd who spreads the word among the Pine Tree Outfit that Ben Ide has offered a reward for the return of the stallion, California Red.

Juanita: In *The Shepherd of Guadaloupe,* Virginia's maid at Cottonwoods. Mrs. Lundeen assigns Juanita to help Virginia because she knows some English.

Juarez: In *The Lost Wagon Train,* one of Leighton's men. He is at the Leighton house when Slim Blue breaks in to steal the documents Leighton is using to blackmail Stephen Latch. Juarez is killed in the fight.

Juárez, Benito: Mexican leader, president, mentioned in *Desert Gold.*

Judd: In *Forlorn River,* a big, heavy, ruddy-faced, loud man who appears at the Blaine ranch with Less Setter and Walker. He claims to be a sheriff, but is, in fact, a member of Setter's rustling operation. When exposed, he confesses to having planted the steer ears which were found in Ben Ide's barn.

Jude: In *Raiders of Spanish Peaks,* one of the cowboys with Price and Gaines, involved in the kidnapping of Lenta Lindsay. He is sent to water the horses while the others settle into the cabin.

Judith: In *The Heritage of the Desert,* one of August Naab's daughters. No indication is given of her age or place in the family hierarchy. She seems to be unmarried. She comes running to Jack Hare for help when Dene, Chance and Culver arrive to kidnap Mescal.

Judkins: In *Riders of the Purple Sage,* one of Jane Withersteen's gentile riders. He is in charge of the cowboys who tend her cattle out on the range. He is a thin young man who lives in the saddle and is fiercely loyal to Jane, although he freely speaks his mind In the novel, he serves both as a participant advancing the plot and an observer and commentator on other characters. He reports that the night riders did not report for duty. In town speaking to Blake and Dorn and other Mormon riders, he learns that they have been called in on purpose by the church elders supposedly to serve on a vigilance committee to pursue rustlers but in reality, he suspects, to leave Jane's herds defenseless against rustlers. He tells Jane that rumor has it she has taken the bit between her teeth and her churchmen want to teach her a lesson. Jane thinks Judkins is exaggerating. Judkins arranges for some young gentiles in their early teens to help him guard the herds. He reports on the destruction of the white herd and the deaths of three of his boys. Judkins informs Venters about the changes he has observed in Lassiter. Formerly a man he admired for his fearlessness and forthrightness, Lassiter has become like a puppy dog following Jane around. He has become what Venters used to be, putty in Jane's hands. As well, Judkins is mystified by a meeting he witnessed in Snell's saloon between Lassiter and Oldring. None of Oldring's men seem surprised in the slightest to see their boss and Lassiter talking quietly and intimately at the bar with a cordial handshake ending the conversation. Like Venters and Lassiter and Jerd, Judkins knows that the sorrel, Wrangle, is the best of Jane's four prize horses. Jane gives Judkins a bag of gold to divide among his boys in payment and reward for their service and loyalty. When she and Lassiter are putting together the things they will take on their escape from Utah, Jane gives her cherished bay, Bells, to Judkins, asking him to take special care of him. In Judkins, Grey presents the best of the American cowboy, loyal to his employer, sincere, truthful, honest, and generous.

Judson: (1) In *The Deer Stalker,* involved with the government regulation of wildlife in parklands. His status is not clear. He's not a ranger or a supervisor. He claims to be an inspector of some sort, but he has always catered to the rich cattlemen's interests or those of tourists rather than those of wildlife and conservationists. He is all in favor of controlling the deer population by opening up the range to hunters. He is not in favor of moving deer to another range where grass is more plentiful, a range which cattlemen would prefer to be opened up to their cattle.

(2) In *The Mysterious Rider,* a rancher from whom Jack borrows money to gamble. He pays off his debt by working for him for a few months.

Julio: In *The Shepherd of Guadaloupe*, Don Lopez's son. He speaks some English and works with Cliff Forrest tending the sheep. He is in charge of getting supplies as needed. He also teaches Cliff the tricks of the trade.

K

Kaiser, the: In *30,000 on the Hoof*, is reported to have warned the American government that if it should ship contraband goods to Europe, he will sink the boats.

Kalispel: In *Thunder Mountain*, the nickname given to Lee Emerson while he was cowboying in Montana. He is usually referred to by this name, rather than by his given name, Lee. The miners at Thunder Mountain give him the nickname, "Old Montana." See **Emerson, Lee.**

Kane: In *The Mysterious Rider*, a wicked dog from Louisiana, half bloodhound. The hound stays with Columbine, but is used by Wade to track the rustlers to their cabin in the mountains.

Kane, Bishop: In *The Rainbow Trail*, an old, dry, thoughtful Mormon leader who loves to pepper his speech with Biblical quotations. He speaks with authority. Withers tells him about Shefford's coming west to find himself, about his doubts about his religious calling. Bishop Kane sees in him a possible convert to Mormonism and therefore approves of his visit to Stonebridge and to the secret village. Joe Lake also vouches for Shefford with the judge. Bishop Kane thinks highly of Willetts and his work, commenting on the good funding he seems to be able to find for his school and other projects. Bishop Kane is also friendly with Shadd, the outlaw. Shefford sees Kane speaking with him in Stonebridge after the polygamy trials.

Kane, Blossom: In *The Lone Star Ranger*, mentioned as a member of Cheseldine's gang by Frank Morton. Buck Duane first sees him in the cabin in the hideout valley. Blossom and Jim Fletcher have a disagreement about introducing a stranger to the outfit. Blossom is killed in the gunfight at the bank in Val Verde.

Keech, Harry: In *The Drift Fence*, the fourteen-year-old son of the widow Keech. Harry is a messenger for his mother, and sweet on Molly Dunn. He delivers letters to her and other presents from Jim Traft. At first, Molly thinks that Harry is sweet on her and courting her, but soon she realizes Jim Traft is her admirer.

Keech, Mrs. In *The Drift Fence*, a widow with two full-grown daughters and a fourteen-year-old son, Harry. She tells Caleb See about the new line of work she is in when he and his wife and Molly Dunn stop there on their way to Flag. The Keeches had been ranchers and had run a sawmill but the rustling in the valley and the trouble they had finding good riders convinced them they would be better trying another line of work. Mrs. Keech has opened up a sort of hotel for travelers in the Cibeque. They sell butter, milk and eggs in the village. The rude clapboard cabins are better inside than outside, according to Molly. There are a fair number of travelers around now and the business is prospering. And the job keeps her up to date on the latest news. She first brings up the topic of the drift fence that the Trafts are building.

Keene, Brazos: In *Knights of the Range*, by far the favorite of the cowboys on the Ripple ranch. In short, he is "the youngest, the wildest, the most untamable, yet the most fascinating and lovable of all Holly Ripple's cowboys. His slim, round-limbed rider's figure lost little from the ragged garb and shiny leather. His smooth, tanned face, fresh and clear as a girl's, clean-cut and regular as a cameo, his half-shut, wild blue eyes and clustering fair hair, all proclaimed his glad youth and irresistible attractiveness, without a hint of his magnificent lawlessness and that he was a combination of fire and ice and steel." Until Frayne joins the group, he is the natural leader of the cowboys. Britt loves and admires him as he sees in him the embodiment of the best of western manhood. Britt sees his acceptance of the gunman, Frayne, as the key to success of his venture. Brazos, however, does not take to Renn as readily as the other men. Frayne knows that Brazos is touchy and has put up with his digs and the occasional slur, going out of his way to avoid confrontation or giving offense. He does confront him openly about his hostility. Brazos admits Frayne has done nothing to offend him, but will not say what he holds against his new colleague. When gambler Lascelles is thrown into the cold stream with the drunk cowboys, the disgruntled gambler pulls a gun on Brazos. Frayne prevents him shooting Keene. This leads to a handshake of thanks and a confession from Brazos that his resentment of Frayne stemmed from his fear that Holly liked Frayne better than she liked him.

Brazos is called upon to speak at the banquet at Holly's fiesta. He is not one to speak about how he feels openly. He says he comes from Texas stock. He never had much schooling and finds it hard to sign his name. He ran away from home because he was no good and all that a cowboy can do without getting himself killed he has done. He speaks about how they are what the range has made them and they are what Holly Ripple needs to accomplish her goal. His partners of Texas Panhandle days are all dead. Since then, he has never had one except Laigs Mason. He has taken on Renn Frayne. And when a Texan, as he says, "makes a partner of a nigger, something big has happened. I'm sinking race prejudice and all that other damn selfish rot. We've got a common cause, men." He goes on to admit that in the past, he has done his share of disorganizing and disrupting, but promises to do better. He becomes the prime mover of the Knights of the Range.

Although he has a touch of the outlaw in him, Brazos is loyal to a fault. He blames himself for disloyalty to Holly when he caught Dillon rustling and gave him a break, only to be betrayed. Likewise, he feels responsible for the desertion of Talman and Trinidad. He feels it behooves him to ensure that punishment is meted out to the rustlers. His loyalty is also seen in his friendship with Laigs Mason. When Mason takes a shot just below the heart to protect him, Brazos cradles the dying cowboy in his arms, singing his death song, "Bury Me Not on the Lone Prairie." He mourns his death for several months, turning to drink and losing interest in life. His commitment to the Knights of the Range restores him to normal.

Brazos is in love with Holly. When he first came to the rancho she liked him a lot and it kept him straight. She rode with him more than with any of the other riders and he was pleased to see how jealous that made them. He got his hopes up that she would marry him. He puts his case to her. She ought to marry a cowman, as her father wanted. He is as good as any of the other cowmen around. If they married, he is sure she would come to love him some day. He wouldn't ask her to be his real wife until she so chose. He could take care of her. She comments that he is younger than her, that she feels more like his sister than his mother. He insists he may be young in years but in the ways of the range, he is as old as her foreman, Britt. He doesn't stop hoping. At the fiesta, he dances with her, and tells her that Renn Frayne is in love with her, that his pose of aloofness and indifference is all show. Clearly, Brazos understands both his friend Renn and Holly.

Brazos is wounded several times in the campaign against the rustlers. He conducts the final assault which nets Slaughter. His men return to the ranch just as Frayne is returning from the shootout with Rankin in the village. He has the proof in Slaughter's ledger that he worked with McCoy and other ranchers rustling and selling stolen cattle. He shoots McCoy and chases off the remaining ranchers, warning them that should they meet any of the Ripple outfit again, they should be ready to fight. Following this last action, he leaves the ranch, never to return. He asks Frayne to name his and Holly's first son "Brazos" after him. He does, however, arrange with the cowboys to play a trick on Frayne and Holly on their wedding day. He has Jackson, the only cowboy who could pull it off, go to Holly to tell her that Frayne can't stay around for the wedding because he has to chase a gang of rustlers. She is asked to stand on the porch and wave her scarf at him as he rides away. Holly falls for the story, and Jackson confesses that Brazos was behind the prank.

In *Twin Sombreros*, Brazos Keene takes on the role of detective, like Lassiter in *Riders of the Purple Sage*. He is on his way to Las Animas and familiar range after spending five years wandering from Wyoming to Texas. His exploits in Casper, Wyoming, have already become part of the folklore as far south as New Mexico. He picks up a letter from Holly Ripple at the

post office in Latimer. He is pleased to hear that she and Renn named their first son after him. He also appreciates their offer to return to Don Carlos's rancho as a partner. Frayne has shared some information which could prove useful, that he has heard that a rancher named Surface is running a rustling operation posing as a cattleman, as McCoy had done.

Brazos Keene is quickly involved in the murder of Allen Neece and the rustling operation of Raine Surface. Keene meets three men leaving a cabin. They tell him the cabin is free if he wants to use it. During the night, the constant dripping sound makes him think the roof is leaking, but by morning, he realizes it is blood dropping from the loft. He discovers the body of a man who has been shot. As he prepares to leave, Bodkin and a posse arrive and arrest him for murder. On the way to Las Animas, they meet Surface. After this encounter, Bodkin is determined to lynch him. Dissent in the posse is inspired by the Texas rancher, Inskip, who lets him grab his guns, and prevents his demise. The sheriff of Las Animas is a fair-minded Texan named Kiskadden. His investigation shows that the man died from a fall, and Brazos's receipt for the letter shows he could not have committed the murder at the time it happened. Former acquaintances from Las Animas step forward to vouch for his good character.

Brazos remains in Las Animas to investigate the death of Allen Neece. His investigation reveals that the murder was ordered by Surface, the rancher who took possession of Abe Neece's Twin Sombreros ranch. Neece had been robbed of the fifty thousand dollars he had withdrawn from the bank to pay for cattle bought from Surface. Unable to pay and with the ranch heavily mortgaged, Surface takes possession of Twin Sombreros. Brazos establishes a connection between the crooked deputy, Bodkin and the three men he met at the cabin. One of these, with the high-pitched voice, is a young woman, Bess Syvertsen. They are planning to do away with him, using the same scheme they used to lure Neece to his death. Brazos, however, foils the plan. As he had done for the Ripple ranch, Brazos exposes the dishonest ranchers and deputy and leaves town after his work is complete.

There are three romantic entanglements in Las Animas. The first is with Lura Surface, daughter of Raine Surface. She had been involved with the murdered boy. Sure of her ability to influence men, she tries to seduce Brazos, only to find he is not interested in her. She leaves town with the gambler, Howard, making only one request, that Brazos not lynch her father. The second is Bess Syvertsen, who turns on the charm, hoping to lure him to an isolated place where her two accomplices can murder him as they did Neece. Things work out quite differently. Bess falls in love with Brazos and refuses to go through with the plot. She leaves for Illinois, where she hopes to start over. And finally the Neece twins, Janis and June. Brazos falls in love with June, but also finds himself the butt of a practical joke. He can never tell which of the twins he is talking to at any given moment and finds himself engaged to both of them. When he leaves Las Animas and returns to Texas, June follows him, catching up to him at Doan's Crossing. They are married, but Brazos is still unsure which of the twins is his wife.

Keetch, John: In "Canyon Walls," the husband of the Widow Keetch and father to Rebecca. The widow says he had never had much of a head for business and did not make a success of his ranch. Even Tyler tells Sam Hill that John Keetch owed money to a Mormon bishop and when he died, their ranch was confiscated to pay the debt. This explains the widow's absence from church on Sundays.

Keetch, Old Man: In *The Lost Wagon Train*, Latch's deputy in the early phase of his career as thief and outlaw. He later comes to be his closest friend and confidante, occupying the place in his life that had formerly been held by Lester Cornwall. Old Man Keetch is a veteran frontiersman. He was a captive of the Kiowa as a young man and knows their language and their ways. He is also the cook of the outfit. Keetch is crippled in the attack on the Bowden-Anderson caravan. Later, his leg is amputated. When the men are discussing what to do with Cynthia Bowden, he reminds them that they were upset watching the Indians kill and scalp women. Why would they do to Cynthia the very thing they criticized in the Kiowas? Latch sends Keetch back with money to build cabins and corrals at the head of Latch's Field. He buys cattle and starts his ranch and maintains good relations with the Kiowas. Latch trusts him implicitly. He is honest and loyal. Over the years, Latch sends money, gold, and jewels back Keetch to stash, and Keetch keeps him informed about goings-on. He does not tell him about moving Cynthia from the cabin in the canyon to the ranch, nor does he mention Cynthia's death in giving birth to his daughter. When Latch returns to his ranch, Keetch gives him a warm welcome, introducing him to the Bensons, who have settled nearby and who have helped with the ranching and raised his daughter, Estie. Keetch has dug a cellar beneath the ranch house where he has stashed all the valuables Latch sent back rather than trek them to the canyon, to which he might be followed unawares. When Latch spots the village that has grown up, he is enraged. But he soon understands that the closest building is two miles from his ranch. Keetch has preserved his field and his privacy and perhaps made possible his reintegration into respectable society. Latch's reputation of similarity to Maxwell has every chance to grow. The ranch house is enormous, fit for a feudal baron, with an enormous front porch, orchards, trees. With Keetch, he makes an offer to his men to go straight. He will set them up with money to start ranching. When Corny appears, he takes a liking to him at once. He first mentions his resemblance to the beloved Lester Cornwall. He recommends that Latch give him a job. When Leighton's valuable papers are stolen, he takes it out on Keetch. He is the only person who could have known about them. He beats him mercilessly in the hope he will reveal where he put the papers or who else might have known about them. When Keetch refuses to speak, he shoots him. Keetch proved loyal to the end.

Keetch, Rebecca: In "Canyon Walls," the daughter of the Widow Keetch. She is eighteen years old and a stunning beauty. The widow complains that the hired hands have spent too much time ogling her and not doing their work. Sam Hill keeps clear of her, sticking to his job and ignoring the young woman. Eventually, however, he does come to take an interest in her and her mother approves of the match. Like all young women, she is often unsure of her true feelings, resenting Sam and wanting him at the same time. Sam and Rebecca are married by the Mormon bishop in Kanab, and a year later, they have a daughter. The sight of Rebecca and the daughter convinces Sheriff Jim Sneed that Sam (Monty Bellew) has reformed and is going straight.

Keetch, Widow: In "Canyon Walls," has a ranch in Green Valley in Utah, just north of the Arizona border. She takes on the stranger, Monty "Smoke" Bellew as a hired hand. She had offered him hospitality for the night and accepts his proposal to work for room and board. She comments that other young men she had hired had proved to be untrustworthy. They were more interested in flirting with her daughter, Rebecca, than in working. Smoke tells her he had trouble with the law in Arizona. She tells him he needs to turn over a new leaf, that she is willing to take a chance on him, and gives him a new name, Sam Hill, as a symbol that he is burying the past. Sam has agreed to work for room and board. The Widow Keetch is impressed with his work. He fixes the fences, plows new land, cuts wood, and in short, in a few months has transformed the place. When the ranch has been turned around, she offers Sam a partnership. The old deal, she says, does not reward him sufficiently for his contribution to the prosperity. She also sees that her daughter is in love with Sam. She encourages him to pursue her. When the going is rocky, she comments that eventually her daughter will see the light. Rebecca and Sam do marry, and give the widow her first granddaughter a year later.

Kellog, Dr.: In *Captives of the Desert*, the school doctor in Taho. He has to cope with an outbreak of influenza, which takes Mrs. Gordon's newborn. He also cares for Magdaline's sister, Joy. At first, he holds out little hope for her recovery, but thanks to Mary Newton's care, she does pull through.

Kells, Jack: In *The Border Legion*, together with Gulden leads an outlaw outfit which harasses the gold miners in the camps along the Idaho-Nevada border. He is a man with a split personality; the traces of his gentlemanly past have not been wiped out completely by the conditions in the mining camps and his life of crime. The presence of Joan Randle brings out his gentler, civilized side. Zane Grey uses this character to study the effects of environment on the forging of human personality.

Jack Kells rides into the camp Harvey Roberts and Joan Randle have made for the night. Roberts recognizes Kells, and the sight of the outlaw frightens him. He tells Joan he had last seen Kells with a rope around his neck. He was being lynched by vigilantes in California. Kells thanks Roberts for having saved his life, but this does not stop him from abducting Joan and killing Roberts and his two associates, Bailey and Holloway, who are "too interested" in Joan.

Kells tells Joan that he is keeping her as a hostage for gold. But back at the camp in Lost Cañon, his true intention becomes obvious. He tells her of how lonely his life has been, how he came west full of ambition, but in the gold fields, he took to robbing stagecoaches and became a feared road agent. He was hunted, almost hanged. When she tells him she is only sixteen years old, he is surprised. He had thought she was twenty-five, and he hesitates to rape her. In a few days, however, that scruple is put aside and as he tries to force himself on her, she shoots him. At first, Joan thinks she has killed him but closer inspection of the body shows he is still alive. She cannot let him die, so she bandages him and remains with him to nurse him. With the arrival of Gulden and two associates, Joan finds herself forced to play along with Kells, who tells them she is his wife. Kells is decidedly the lesser of two evils.

Joan first describes Kells as pale, grey-eyed, intelligent, amiable. There is something intense about him which makes her recall the dark tales told of him, his career as a California road agent and gunfighter. His speech betrays his background, and his instinct to treat a woman with delicacy bespeaks a former way of life. Kells himself tells Joan that he comes from back east, that he received a good education but conditions in the mining camps have made him what he is. Having Joan around brings out the tender side in him. He proposes marriage, offering to leave with her for California to start over. Joan refuses because she does not love him.

Throughout her captivity, Joan has the opportunity to observe Kells. While the grey eyes suggest a capacity for evil, there remains a tender quality bespeaking a redeemable soul. Joan observes that around her, he is always on his best behavior. He does his best to protect her from the savagery in the camp. Pearce and Wood tell her that Kells has the reputation of being a woman hater, but she seems to bring out the best in him. Several times he proposes marriage to her, promising to abandon his outlaw existence to start over with her but, although she is increasingly fond of him, she does not love him.

Despite her softening influence, Joan observes a heartless killer in him as well. He shoots Harvey Roberts, Bill Bailey, and Holloway without hesitation for no real reason. With the help of Red Pearce to provoke a situation in the Last Nugget saloon, he picks a fight with a young miner and shoots him. He gets Joan to walk down Main Street in a dress in front of the miners, knowing some will make rude remarks to her, thereby giving him an excuse to make a scene and pose as a defender of a decent woman's honor. She comes to the conclusion that he is as much concerned about his reputation as he is about gold.

Kells is a man who commands absolute authority in the outlaw gang. The men obey him implicitly, trusting him. He does not require an oath of loyalty and gives his men broad personal freedom. He is generous with gold, allowing each man to keep his own earnings at the gold diggings. In this, he contrasts with Gulden, whose share and share alike policy is accompanied by the imposition of his authority by force and fear.

Kells takes a liking to Jim Cleve, forgiving him for his failure to execute an order to kill Creede. He understands that committing murder in cold blood is not easy. Likewise, when Gulden robs the stagecoach from Alder Creek to Bannack, the stage on which Jim Cleve and Joan Randle are traveling, Kells confirms Jim's story that he had sent them purposely on the stage. When the truth that Joan is married is revealed to him, Kells is stunned. Later, however, when Gulden proposes a final gamble, all the gold for Joan, Kells is moved to protect Joan from Gulden. Kells loses the gamble, and Cleve takes him from the room to Joan's cabin. There, Jim reveals he is Joan's husband, and Joan tells Kells that she had been in love with Cleve for a long time. She had been looking for him when Kells came upon her and Harvey Roberts. She adds that if she had not been in love with Jim, she would have accepted his proposal of marriage. In the gunfight which follows, both Gulden and Kells are killed.

The character of Kells resembles that of Buck Duane in *The Lone Star Ranger*. He is an outlaw who has retained an element of decency. Through him, the mystery of good and evil is played out revealing Grey's romantic faith in the inherent goodness of man despite the worst of conditions.

Kelly: In *The Lost Wagon Train*, driver of a wagon that joins Pike Anderson's caravan. He and Washburn and an unnamed man have three wagons loaded with rifles and ammunition. This will prove most helpful in the coming attack. Satana's Kiowa and Latch's outlaws divide the rifles and ammunition between them when the massacre is over.

Kelly, Bill: In *Fighting Caravans*, the train boss of the caravan which leaves Taos, New Mexico, with May Bell and Mrs. Clement. There were some two hundred and forty-three men in the caravan and they make it through without being attacked by Indians.

Kemp, Nebraskie: In *The Dude Ranger*, a cowboy in his early twenties working on the Red Rock Ranch when the tenderfoot Ernest Howard (Selby) arrives and is hired on by John Hepford out of gratitude for his saving his daughter from robbers. Hawk Siebert, foreman of the cowboys, assigns him a room in the bunkhouse. Since he offers to take on jobs such as cleaning out the barn and digging fence posts and stacking hay in the barn, demeaning tasks unworthy of a cowboy, the "real" cowboys want nothing to do with him. Selby becomes Nebraskie's bunkmate and at first, Nebraskie is not too keen on the idea as he fears Selby's outcast status might lose him caste. He tells Ernest immediately that he got off to a bad start by offering to do work unacceptable to a cowboy. Furthermore, he will have to fight the cowboys to gain their respect, in particular, Dude Hyslip, who is spreading the story that Ernest had hired the robbers to make an attempt to rob Anne Hepford in order to ingratiate himself with her.

Nebraskie comes to like Ernest, to find in him a friend such as he has never had before, but in spite of that, he never fails to be amazed at his naiveté. Ernest seems to be unaware that Anne is just toying with him. When she sends him to fetch the mail in Springer and to do some errands for her, Ernest appears to believe Anne cares for him. Nebraskie warns him that the invitation to the dance is also just a trick to show her scorn for him. Nevertheless, Nebraskie is loyal to Ernest, promising to stand by him should trouble develop at the dance, as it does. He admits that he has never been able to understand women, but has faith that deep down, Anne is "true blue."

Nebraskie himself is in love with Daisy Brooks, Anne Hislop's cousin, and daughter of Sam Brooks, former manager of the ranch. They broke off their engagement when Dude Hyslip entered the picture. Nebraskie is not sure he can trust Daisy, as she shows interest in Ernest as well. When Ernest learns how his bunk mate feels about Daisy, he tells her he cannot be disloyal to his partners. But Daisy seems unable to resist Dude when he comes around, and Nebraskie is not sure how far things have gone between them. When Daisy confesses that she's afraid Dude has got her into trouble, Nebraskie asks her to marry him as soon as possible. It is not likely Dude will come around again when she is married.

Nebraskie shares with Ernest his doubts about Hepford's honesty. He has pieced together the basics of Hepford's scheme to cheat Silas Selby. He makes a drive of cattle without making a count, sells to a dealer who does not make a formal count, and uses cowboys that are not regular workers on the ranch. The sale is transacted in cash. None of the cowboys could possibly recall exactly how many animals were in the drive or at what price they were sold or even when the drive took place. Nebraskie and Ernest are sent with Anderson to drive the cattle to market. Nebraskie has to come to Ernest's rescue when he is caught hiding in the bushes listening to the chat of Anderson, Wilkins and the cattle dealer from Mariposa.

Nebraskie is kicked off the Red Rock Ranch with Hawk Siebert and Ernest Howard. They go to work for Sam Brooks for room and board. They defend Sam against Hepford's threat to drive him off his homestead. One day, when Hepford is gone from Red Rock and Ernest has gone to the ranch house to look for the "blue book," Hepford's ledger of cattle sales, Nebraskie once more catches Dude Hyslip with

Daisy. They get into a fight which leads to shooting. Hyslip is killed. Nebraskie leaves with Daisy for Snowflake, where they get married. He and Daisy meet Ernest and Anne as they come out of the church, and they stand as witnesses for the new couple.

Nebraskie is pleased as punch when he learns that his tenderfoot partners is the new owner of Red Rock Ranch.

Kennedy, Bruce: In *The Lost Wagon Train,* appears at Latch's Field working for Leighton. He is his right-hand man, but he was not a member of the old outlaw gang that had operated with Satana attacking wagon trains. He learns about Leighton's past, the work with Satana, the cause of Latch's hatred from Tumbler Johnson. Keetch comments to Latch that Kennedy's loyalty is not all that convincing and he could be bought if the price were right. Corny overhears Kennedy propose to Johnson that the two of them turn the tables on Leighton and pull a stunt on him similar to the one he's planning to pull on Latch. Kennedy is with Leighton in Spider Web Canyon where they come upon Latch, who has found the Tullt wagon with the painted name of Tullt's company and the gold that Bowden had hidden in the bottom of his prairie schooner. Kennedy offers to free Latch if he will give them the money that Leighton had been demanding. Unlike Leighton, he has no interest in revenge but in money to buy a ranch. In the fighting which follows, Slim Blue kills him in a gunfight.

Kent, Holbrook: In *Shadow on the Trail,* a gunman and friend of the rustler barons around Holbrook. Harrobin sends word to Tex Brandon via Hogue Kinsey that Rand Blue (Drake) has joined Kent as part of his crew. Kent himself is a little man, lame from a bullet still in his hip. He is not young, with a beardless face full of deep lines. He's cockeyed, and reputed to be like lightning on the draw. He is credited with having killed eight men. He is killed in a shootout with Brandon in the street of Holbrook.

Kenton, Simon: In *Betty Zane,* first mentioned as one of the distinguished guests to have stayed at Colonel Ebenezer Zane's cabin. He is mentioned again later as an example of a good deed done by Simon Girty. He saved Kenton from being burned at the stake by Indians. No further information is given about who he is.

Kern, Willie: In *Riders of the Purple Sage,* one of the young gentiles that Judkins hired as a rider when the Mormon riders were called in by Elder Tull. He survives the stampede of the white herd but is being tried by Bishop Dyer on a trumped-up charge of diverting water from an irrigation ditch when Lassiter appears to confront him.

Ketcham: In *Forlorn River,* a merchant in Klamath. He tells Ben Ide that Sewell McAdam is a "high stepper" and after Ina Blaine. He also reports that her father, Hart Blaine, is reputedly keen on the marriage.

Kettle, Ben: In "The Secret of Quaking Asp Cabin," a hunter from the Tonto who told Babe Haught the story of Bates, who had been bitten on the nose by a rabid skunk in Quaking Asp Cabin.

Killbourne, Glenn: In *The Call of the Canyon*, a twenty-seven-year-old veteran of World War I. In 1918, he returns from France to New York, a broken man, a wreck of his former self. He is dismayed by and disgusted with the society he finds in New York, a society given to hedonism, materialism and selfishness. As well, he feels betrayed by a government whose call he answered when he went to war, but which now treats the returning veterans with the indifference and contumely accorded to vagrant dogs. He goes west to try to recover his health. Glenn Killbourne was gassed during the war, and he suffers from TB and severe bleeding in the lungs during his first few weeks at Lolomi Lodge. He also suffers from shell shock and he cannot get a peaceful night's sleep with the constant interruptions of horrible nightmares about the war. The Hutters, owners of the lodge, fear he will die. After several months in Arizona, he writes Carley, his fiancée, that he has changed. He now hates city life, crowds of people, dancing, drinking, and lounging around — in short, Carley's usual crowd. Glenn writes Carley that thinking about her saved him when he was in France, but that when he returned he could no longer tolerate life in the city. While he has no intention of breaking his engagement to her, he cannot return to live in New York.

Upon her Aunt Mary's advice, Carley goes west to visit Glenn, hoping to persuade him to return to New York. She finds him a much-changed man. Glenn looks older than his twenty-seven years, but he has filled out his tall, broad frame. She barely recognizes him. She finds him withdrawn, aloof, impersonal, unfamiliar. He has built himself a cabin and raises his own sheep and pigs. He has become a man close to the earth. The humble, simple things of life are what he admires. He is looking for a wife who can cook, take care of a house, raise a family. He wants a life where one works to live, not to make money. The West has shown him where true values lie and the emptiness of the East and its alienation from nature are now intolerable.

He introduces Carley to his new world, the sheep ranch, the Arizona desert. She shows remarkable stamina and pluckiness, which he admires. He appreciates the good humor with which she takes the practical jokes of Flo and Charley. In short, he tells her there is still hope for her. Carley's behavior at Flo's birthday party, however, shows that she is still a creature of New York. Glenn feels obliged to defend her honor when Ruff Haze makes crude advances to her. Carley suspects that Glenn is more in love with Flo, who is more in line with the kind of woman he is looking for.

Glenn confides in Carley that he plans to go into ranching with Tom Hutter. There is a tract of land near the Painted Desert that he wants to purchase to start up his ranch. Carley returns east, convinced that eventually Glenn will break their engagement and marry Flo. Glenn, however, remains faithful to her, and when Carley discovers that she too has been affected by the West and now finds New York society intolerable, she returns west determined to become the kind of wife Glenn wants.

Glenn Killbourne is one of many young men described in Grey's novels who go west to find themselves. The West, the natural environment, the return to essential pioneer values, forge a new man with his heart and head in the right place, free from the corrupting influence of civilization.

King: In *Wilderness Trek*, Leslie Slyter's favorite thoroughbred. She gives him to Sterling Hazelton to ride on the trek across Australia. King is stolen by Ash Ormiston when he rustles part of the Slyter and Dann herds and some of the best horses in the mob. He is shot at, but not severely wounded. The horse is retrieved when Ormiston and his crew are captured.

King, Captain: In *Fighting Caravans*, Couch's commanding officer in the Mexican war.

King Fisher (also spelled Kingfisher): In *The Lone Star Ranger*, mentioned as one of the great outlaws that young Texans want to imitate. In *To the Last Man*, he assumes the name Blue when he comes to the Tonto Basin to give Gaston Isbel a hand. At some point, Isbel had saved his life, and he is there out of personal loyalty, not out of faith in the righteousness of the cattlemen's cause. He says that he is not convinced of the pure villainy of the Jorths and the sheepmen, as the rustling that is going on shows all the signs of an inside job. He seems to know that one of Gaston Isbel's sons is involved but he says nothing. He is killed in a spectacular attack on the Jorth fortress in Greaves's store.

In *Thunder Mountain*, when Sheriff Bruce Masters introduces himself to Lee Emerson (Kalispel) he names King Fisher as a gunman with whom he trained. In *The Trail Driver*, King Fisher is mentioned as a gunman of whom Texas is extremely proud.

In *Knights of the Range*, Colonel Lee Ripple and his foreman Britt speculate about whether the Arizona range will produce gunmen of the caliber and fame of a King Fisher.

In *The Fugitive Trail*, Bruce Lockheart compares Vic Henderson to King Fisher. A gunman like King Fisher is aware of all that is going on around him and cannot be surprised. Henderson, on the other hand, allows himself to get into situations for which he is not prepared, the sure sign of a second-rate gunman.

In *The Arizona Clan*, Uncle Bill tells Dodge Mercer that they are lucky that Nan's friend from Texas is of the same breed as King Fisher, Wild Bill and Wess Hardin.

King Fisher, Larry Red(die): In *The U. P. Trail*, a Texas cowboy, slow, easy, cool, careless, with latent nerve, wildness, violence. He is a giant of a man, a cowboy without equal, excellent horseman, quick with a gun, with an unswerving sense of devotion and loyalty to his friend, Warren Neale. Place Hough and Cordy recognize him as the brother of the famous Texas gunman, King Fisher. Larry left Texas when things became too hot for him after he shot a sheriff. When Larry and Cordy shoot it out, Larry's true identity is revealed and the story of his quasi-legendary past quickly spreads throughout Benton.

Larry Reddie King attached himself to Neale back in Nebraska when Neale began work for Union Pacific. Neale describes him as "true as steel." When the rope breaks and Neale falls while inspecting the rock formation at the base of a cliff, Larry descends to find him and carries both Neale and his surveying equipment up out of the canyon. Only after Neale has been seen to by the army doctor does Larry reveal that through all of this, he had been working with a broken hand. Similar acts of Larry's stoicism are found throughout the story. Larry King acts as bodyguard for Neale in the camps. Neale is inexperienced in the kind of life to be found in the cities that grow up at construction sites. He advises Neale to carry a gun and teaches him to use it. When Allison Lee calls Neale a liar at the meeting with the board of governors of the U. P., Larry convinces Lee to retract his accusation. King shoots Smith at this meeting.

Larry accompanies Neale on all his major assignments. He is with him at the construction of the bridge, and in the buffalo hunt, when he buries the engineer, Service. In some ways, he is Neale's alter ego.

Larry King has the southern gentleman's respect for women. While he is fond of Allie Lee, he does not interfere with his friend's growing attachment to the young woman. He understands the motives and the ways of women like Beauty Stanton and Ruby. Larry is fond of Ruby, but when Neale offers them his substantial winnings at the card table so that they can go to California and make a fresh start, Larry feels he is a marked man and could not. He must stay to help Neale in Benton. When Stanton tries to get revenge on Neale by turning Allie into a prostitute, Larry King is the first man she sends in to her room. Larry recognizes Neale's long-lost sweetheart and immediately understands what Beauty Stanton has tried to do and why. He promptly proceeds to take her out of the place to meet Neale. In the gunfight which follows, Larry proves his loyalty to Neale and to Allie, shooting most of Durade's crew and Beauty Stanton. Larry King dies in this attempt.

Larry Red King is a "good" bad man, like Buck Duane. Beneath the reputation of violence and death lies a truly loyal friend, an uncorrupted man willing to sacrifice himself for another.

Kingsley, Florence: Alfred Hammond's fiancée in *The Light of Western Stars*. When Madeline Hammond needs a place to stay the first night in El Cajón,

Gene takes her to Florence's home, where she lives with her sister. She scolds Gene for being so stupid, for playing such a practical joke, and cautions him to keep quiet about the goings-on. She speaks with a slow, southern drawl, due to her Kentucky birth and upbringing in Texas. Madeline thinks how her aristocratic parents would scorn her for her background and speech. It appears Sheriff Pat Hawe is also in love with her, explaining his antagonism to Alfred. She accompanies Madeline on the trip to Bill Stillwell's ranch, pointing out Don Carlos's place, and Al's old ranch. Madeline's brother was cheated by crooked ranchers, she says. He could still make a go of it if he had a chance. She explains about the roundup and the different jobs the cowboys do and Madeline is impressed by her knowledge and common sense about people. When Don Carlos's cowboys have laid a trap for Madeline, they switch clothes and she rides off on Madeline's horse, pretending to be an incompetent eastern rider. Madeline escapes. Florence has high praise for Gene Stewart, lauding his good judgment. He sees things and knows things. She is a member of the party taking the camping trip in the mountains, where she begins the storytelling by recounting the story of Padre Juan and the Lost Mine of the Padres. Little does she know that the mine in question is nearby and that Danny Mains has already found it. Florence marries Alfred when he returns from his trip to California, where he has prospects for setting up a large cattle company in conjunction with Madeline.

In *Majesty's Rancho*, Madeline recalls how Flo was such a help to her when she came west and how they have settled in California.

Kinney, Sergeant: In *Western Union*, arrives with a few of his cavalry to help the wagon train defend itself against the Indians.

Kinsey, Hogue: In *Shadow on the Trail*, Wade Holden's (Tex Brandon's) right-hand man on the Pencarrow ranch. Brandon learns about Hogue from Elwood Lightfoot, who describes him as:

> a cowboy rode down heah, bad shot up.... I pulled him through. He was about the likablest cuss I ever met.... His father had a couple of bad years with drouth.... They got pretty pore. Hogue had a sister he must have been plumb fond of. She fell sick an' to get her into a less high an' cold climate, Hogue stole a bunch of cattle an' sold them. Hogue had a meek an' easy-going disposition, but he was quick tempered.... [H]e drifted over Pine Mound way where he hangs out with half a dozen boys slated for hell ... they're stealin' cattle but in a two-bit way thet's not botherin' the ranchers yet. I reckon his outfit have stolen a few haid from Pencarrow. But I'd add this in Hogue's favor. He's the only cowboy I know who never rode up to Pencarrow's door an' asked for a job.... He wouldn't ride for a cayttleman an' steal behind his back.

Tex Brandon recruits him to work for Pencarrow. He comes upon him in a saloon playing cards where Harrobin is trying to convince him and his men to leave the range willingly or be driven out. Their rustling interferes with Harrobin's larger operation. He offers him the chance to go straight, to make up for past wrongs, not unlike Holly Ripple's "Knights of the Range" in the novel by the same name. On their way back to the ranch, they retrieve the cattle that Harrobin has rustled and hidden in the brakes of a canyon. Hogue introduces himself to Pencarrow, confessing that in the past he had rustled some of his cattle, but that he now promises to go straight and regrets his past wrongs. Rona Pencarrow and Hogue Kinsey fall in love at first sight. Jacqueline worries that things will go too far and Kinsey will disgrace her sister and her family. When she and Brandon eavesdrop on a meeting between the two, Brandon's faith in his friend's decency and nobility are confirmed. Kinsey offers to fight Kent to spare Brandon the risk. He considers Brandon more critical to the fight against banditry than he is. When the Drake-Mason-Harrobin outfit has been defeated, Hogue Kinsey courts and marries Rona Pencarrow and remains on the ranch as the foreman.

Kintell, Wess: In *Black Mesa*, a Texan, a superb figure of a rider, tall, wide-shouldered, small-hipped and wiry, scarcely beyond his teens in years yet exhibiting in his lean, lined face the sadness, the reckless hardness of maturity developed by life on the ranges. He has a steel-like grip, lean, brown hands, piercing gray eyes. Paul Manning gets him out of jail, asks no questions about his shady past, and offers him the job running the ranch he plans to set up. Like Lincoln Bradway with Vince in *The Maverick Queen,* he is willing to take a gamble on Wess, sensing that this Texan is a man with whom to form a bond. Wess tells Paul that he has always been a hard nut, and he always figured that people were against him. He wonders why Paul has taken him out of the worst mess he has ever been in and when he is told that Paul thinks helping someone else worse off than himself is the best way he can solve his own problems, Wess understands him completely. He promises his loyalty and friendship and advice. The two become closer than brothers.

Wess knew the woman that had dumped Paul in Wagontongue and assures his new friend that the desert will wither kill or cure him. He is flabbergasted at Paul's innocence where women are concerned. He himself had been involved with a woman and he became a rolling stone after shooting a man involved with his girl. Wess senses immediately that Louise is trouble. Paul falls for her sad story at once, unaware of the trap into which he is falling. He understands instinctively the triangle at the post, Belmont and Sister, Sister and Louise, Louise and Belmont and Paul. He also knows that Paul is a hopeless case, having fallen for Louise. Several times, he recommends that Paul not get involved with her, and later that he run off with her or buy her from Belmont, a practice still found in that area. When Paul is unwilling to take such action, he concentrates on establishing the legality of Belmont's marriage to Louise.

Kintell is an invaluable asset to Paul Manning. He is well experienced in the cattle business, and teaches Paul the tricks of the trade. He also teaches Paul to ride like a cowboy, to herd cattle, to camp, to survive in a dust storm. He is more experienced with cattle dealers and is surprised that Paul is as naive in these matters as he is with women. Kintell also proves to be an excellent detective. His observation establishes that Belmont is dealing in bootleg whiskey. He catches on to Calkins's trick when he observes that the new cattle show no signs of having been driven through mud and water. He recognizes in the herd one of the cantankerous steers from their own stock. Belmont has hired rustlers to cut out two hundred and sixty head from their herd to resell to them. Wess also learns from Shade and Bloom about Belmont's fraudulent deals in Utah and his relationship to Sister.

With Belmont dead, he arranges for the sale of the herd to Shade or Sister. Paul insists he accompany him and Louise back to his farm, where he plans to introduce Wess to his sister Anne. He expects that Anne will be thrilled to meet a genuine Texas cowboy and that they will all return west together to set up his ranch.

Wess Kintell, like Nevada in *Forlorn River* and *Nevada,* or Vince in *The Maverick Queen,* is the redeemed outlaw, the cowboy who had taken the wrong trail and needs only the friendship and confidence of a good man to set him straight. The western environment can bring out either the best or the worst in an individual.

Kishli: In *Black Mesa*, an Indian rider working for Manning. He saw the tracks on the trail where Red Eye was spooked, throwing Belmont over the precipice. He brings back word of Belmont's death to the Bitter Seeps trading post.

Kiskadden: In *Twin Sombreros,* a proud Texan, the sheriff of Las Animas. He is also silent partner in a ranching venture with Inskip. As a young man, he rode for Colonel Lee Ripple, Holly Ripple's father, and served in the Texas Rangers with Captain Britt under Ranger McKelvey. Kiskadden was selected by the Cattleman's Association, but he remains independent. When Brazos Keene is brought in, he resists the pressure of the association and conducts his own investigation. The doctors performs an autopsy which establishes that Neece died from a fractured skull, probably caused by the fall from a horse. The letter in Brazos's pocket establishes that he could not have committed the murder at the time that it occurred. He fires Bodkins, the deputy, and resigns his position as sheriff. He does continue to help Brazos in his investigation of Neece's death and the rustling activities in Las Animas.

Kitsap: In *Stranger from the Tonto*, a member of the Hole-in-the-Wall Outfit. Kent Wingfield sees him for the first time in the camp with Slotte and Goins and estimates that he is more of a danger than Goins would be. He meets him again at Logan's trading post. He appears later at the hideout with Slotte. He and Goins support Ben Bunge when he returns with a fantastic story about what he has been doing and about his encounter with Kent Wingfield. Kitsap survives the shootout between Roberts's outfit and Bonesteel's Hole-in-the-Wall gang.

Knell, Phil: In *The Lone Star Ranger,* one of Cheseldine's right-hand men, a huge man and powerful gunman. Buck Duane first sees him at Cheseldine's hideout in the valley. He is tall, slim, built like a boy, with a pale, smooth expressionless face. His eyes are grey and cold. He and Poggin do not get along. He has been late getting to the valley because Poggin was delayed trying to break a horse. He suspects Fletcher is too friendly with the stranger in town, a stranger who seems familiar. He tells the group he suspects the stranger is none other than the gunman, Buck Duane. Fletcher feels Dodge should be accepted into the gang because he held up the No. 6 train. Knell, however, reveals that this could not be since he himself did the job. When Jim Fletcher has called a meeting of the group to introduce them to his inductee, Buck, Knell enjoys telling Poggin that the new man, "Dodge," that Fletcher has introduced to the outfit is in reality Buck Duane. Poggin is fearful, but Knell turns on Buck. He was a partner of Hardin's and wants to settle the score with the man who killed his best partner. In the gunfight, Buck Duane kills Knell.

Knight (a.k.a. Bard): In *Twin Sombreros,* the true name of Bard, the man involved in the killing of Allen Neece and the real power behind the rustling in the area. **See Bard.**

Knowles, Bert: In *Western Union*, the young man Kit Sunderland was supposed to marry. It seems that Vance Shaw was a bone of contention between them. Knowles had consistently harped on Shaw's being a bad hombre and when the truth came out, Kit told Knowles where to get off.

Kotoxen: Delaware Indian chief in *The Spirit of the Border*. His name means "the Lynx." In the trial of Joe and Jim Downs, he recommends the death penalty.

Krehl, Red: In *Wilderness Trek*, a twenty-four-year-old cowboy from Texas via Arizona who ends up trekking across the Australian continent and marrying an Aussie lass to settle down to ranching in the Kimberleys in Northwest Australia. He lists his qualifications for Roland Tewksbery Jones, one of Stanley Dann's drovers before the trek: "Outside of possessin' all the cowboy traits such as ridin', ropin', shootin', we can hunt, butcher, cook, bake sourdough biscuits an' cake, shoe hosses, mend saddle cinches, plait ropes, chop wood, build fires in wet weather, bandage wounds an' mend broken bones, smoke, drink, play poker, an' fight." Red earns the respect of Stanley Dann and the enmity of Ormiston when he comes to the rescue of Friday, the aborigine drover that Ormiston is beating and kicking.

Ormiston wants the Yanks thrown off the drive, but Stanley and Bingham stand by him. Red explains the strategies for a cattle drive, the triangular formation, the role of the point man and the drovers. He is familiar with the conditions which give rise to stampedes and has experience controlling frightened cattle. He knows the problems of finding water, crossing rivers, confronting rustlers. He devises a means of caulking the cracks in the floor of the wagons to make them waterproof and capable of floating, similar to the prairie schooners of the wagon trains in the American West. Red has suspected Ormiston of plotting against Stanley Dann and his suspicions are proven correct when he overhears Ormiston, a false name for the bushranger (rustler) Ash Pell, and his cohorts, Jack and Bedford, plotting when it would be best to carry out their scheme. Red is injured in the pursuit, capture and lynching of Ormiston. Likewise, Red suspects that Eric is lying about his knowledge of the route. He cannot predict what the terrain will be like on the other side of a mountain range; he doesn't know where the mountain passes are located; he cannot recognize the rivers he claims to have traversed. When Stanley seems willing to let Eric continue to lead, Red bites his tongue. He is proven right again when Eric confesses that he has misled them, that they are hopelessly lost. Red gives useful advice when they face the sandstorm, and when the cattle stampede. Red and Sterling are a source of good humour and camaraderie on the trek. The vicissitudes of the trail never seem to get him down. He is friends with the drovers, even trying to ingratiate himself with Ormiston's drovers, to try to learn something of their plans. At Christmas, he and Sterling manage to produce gifts for all the women on the expedition. Red has been sweet on Beryl Dann, but jealous of her interest in Ormiston. She is engaged to Ormiston, unaware that he is just using her to influence her father or to put pressure on her father. Red is upset that she is so blind to what Ormiston really is. However, when Ormiston is out of the picture, Beryl having seen him lynched, her affection for Red grows. When they reach the Kimberleys, Stanley Dann makes use of his other profession, that of minister, to marry his daughter and Red.

L

La-Clos: In *Blue Feather*, the second young woman who ministers to the chief's daughter, Nashta.

Ladd, Charley: In *Desert Gold*, helps Jim Lash and Dick Gale create a disturbance in the barroom so that Mercedes Castañeda can make her escape. Ladd understands well the political and class hatred that motivates the Mexican rebels and Mercedes' fear of capture. He also understands Rojas' determination and persistence. Ladd retells the story of the brawl to Belding and recommends the young man to him as a ranger. When pursuing raiders and rustlers into Mexico to retrieve horses, Ladd plans the strategy to lure the thieves out of the canyon. Later, when they are on the trail to Yuma over the "camino del diablo," he explains to Dick Gale the wisdom of Yaqui's shooting the Pagago guide first, as he, more than Rojas, would be able to track them. In this last fight with Rojas, Ladd is wounded and almost dies from loss of blood. He urges the others to leave and return to Belding's ranch, but they refuse to leave him behind. When he has recovered his strength, he once again resumes the leadership of the group.

Lady Jane: In *Wilderness Trek*, one of Leslie Slyter's prize thoroughbreds that successfully treks from Queensland to the Kimberley Mountains in western Australia.

Lake, Joe: In *The Rainbow Trail*, the young Mormon cowboy Withers has hired to trek in supplies to the women (sealed wives) in the hidden Mormon village. He is a large man, but for one of his size, he moves with great agility. Shefford is impressed by the graceful fluid motion as he dismounts from his horse. He has a smooth face, red bronze in color, with soft, dark eyes and a winning smile, like a cherub. He is reputed to be the best horse wrangler around and he more than any other can control horses. When his mustang attempts to bite Shefford and Joe scolds him as if he were a mischievous child, the horse seems to feel ashamed. Joe Lake loves practical jokes, and until Shefford learns how to interpret what he says, Joe plays a few on him, almost getting him to shoot at a pack of mules which in the distance look like deer. Lake agrees to work with Nas Ta Bega teaching Shefford the tricks of survival in the desert. Withers has shared with Joe the story of Shefford coming west to find himself after his congregation had dismissed him as preacher. He understands that he is a drifter and a searcher. Lake is not married, the only single man in the hidden village. He takes a liking to Shefford and speaks up for him with the Mormon elders, obtaining permission for him to visit the hidden village and to visit Stonebridge. Lake also serves as a balancing influence on Shefford. John Shefford has become disillusioned with religion and the civilized world. He is ready to condemn missionaries and civilization for all the wrongs inflicted on the red man. Lake, however, teaches him that not all missionaries have been a bad influence and not all aspects of civilization have been destructive. Joe himself, although a devout Mormon, is one of the younger generation, less given to proselytizing and less zealous about converting the world to Mormonism. He advises Shefford to let Nas Ta Bega's sister, Glen Naspa, decide for herself whether she will return to the mission school at Blue Cañon. He is quietly in the know about what is going on, when the night visits of the polygamous husbands will occur, about the presence of federal agents to spy on movements in and out of Stonebridge in an attempt to catch the polygamous Mormons. Joe Lake is in love with Mary, Sago Lily, but he makes no attempt to force himself on her, nor does he behave jealously toward Shefford. He notices that upon her return to the village, she has become thin from worry and not eating. He has noticed the jealousy of the older Mormon wives and their resentment of her fragile beauty. He asks Shefford to assure him that he did not kill Waggoner. Joe Lake is level-headed, calm, willing to let someone else lead when they plan to go to Surprise Valley to rescue Lassiter and Jane Withersteen. He submits to the greater wisdom of Nas Ta Bega in finalizing plans as the Navajo's experience of the desert, the mountains and the canyons is unmatched. Joe Lake is waiting with boats to pick up the fugitives at the San Juan river and he accompanies them to Willow Springs. From there they depart for Flagstaff and Illinois. He makes a quiet, unceremonious departure, in keeping with his humble, unassuming nature.

Lambeth, Mrs. Templeton: In *West of the Pecos,* belongs to one of the old southern families of French extraction. She bore a daughter to Templeton Lambeth, who in disappointment decides to raise the daughter as a son. Mrs. Lambeth does not openly oppose her husband's attempts to treat the daughter as if she were a boy, but when the father is away during the war, she inculcates in the impressionable child values and virtues which the father's subsequent influence cannot wholly eradicate. She dies when Terrill is fifteen years old.

Lambeth, Templeton: In *West of the Pecos,* the brother of Terrill Lambeth and the father of Terrill Lambeth, Rill, the daughter who should have been a son and whom he named after his beloved brother. Templeton inherits a plantation in East Texas from his father. During the civil war, he enlists as a commissioned officer and returns as a colonel. His wife and brother have died, so Templeton yields to the desire to pull up stakes and move to West Texas. He had hunted as far north as the Texas Panhandle and the lure of the unclaimed land west of the Pecos becomes irresistible. He takes with him two of his former slaves, who refused to abandon him when he freed them. Sambo and his wife, Mauree, accompany him and his daughter to West Texas. They pass through San Antonio, where they join a wagon train of buffalo hunters heading to the Llano Estacado. This venture proves no more successful than the plantation had. On his way west, he buys cattle from a rancher named Wakefield and takes on a number of the cowboys who had worked for him. The herd grows, picking up strays, as they make their way to the plains west of the Pecos. Templeton Lambeth is killed by a vaquero shortly after arriving at his new ranch, leaving Terrill and the two former slaves to run the place.

Templeton had been disappointed that the child was not a boy and when the young girl exhibits signs of being a tomboy, showing clear preferences for the rougher, more virile occupations, he takes full advantage of them. She learns to ride as well if not better than any man. He raises her as if she were a boy and when he sets out for West Texas, Miss Rill is dressed as a man. The disguise proves to be her defense on more than one occasion.

Lambeth, Terrill: In *West of the Pecos,* the brother of Templeton. Their father bequeathed a plantation to each of them. Terrill did well with his plantation. During the Civil War, Terrill enlists as a private in the Confederate army. He falls victim to an incurable disease during the war and was sent home long before Lee's surrender. His death is one reason Templeton decides to leave for the plains of West Texas.

Lambeth, Terrill (Rill): The daughter of Templeton Lambeth, named for her father's beloved brother. Templeton had been hoping for a son, and when his wife presented him with a daughter, he did not let that interfere with his plans. As a child, Terrill showed decidedly tomboy tendencies, preferring the rougher and more virile pleasures and occupations. She excelled at riding, taught by the slave, Sambo, and by the age of ten could stick to any four-footed animal on the plantation. During her father's absence in the Civil War, her mother taught her some feminine values and virtues, which did not supplant her father's influence. Terrill loses her mother at the age of fifteen. She shares her father's passionate thirst for adventure and looks forward to their move west of the Pecos to take up ranching.

Terrill dresses as a young man for the move, helped by Sam(bo)'s wife, Mauree, who tailors her clothes to disguise her feminine shape. Sambo teaches her to shoot, to hunt rabbits, and she brings down a buffalo. She learns to get over her squeamishness about firearms and hunting. In San Antonio, the only city she has ever seen except New Orleans, she runs into Pecos Smith coming out of a saloon. He takes her for a boy and asks her to untie his horse while he sheaths his pistols. She never forgets the look in Pecos Smith's eyes.

Terrill experiences a buffalo stampede and the cattle herds on the plains of Texas, all of which engage her sense of adventure. They meet up with Pecos Smith again before they cross the Pecos river. Some five years later, the ranching venture is at risk. The herd of ten thousand cattle has been decimated by rustlers, and the colonel killed, most probably by one of them. Don Felipe, the half–Mexican, half–Indian rancher from the south ascribes the killing to the Comanches, but she has her doubts. She has seen Don Felipe's cowboys stealing their cattle. Terrill is in jail at Brassee's, supposedly for failure to pay a bill. Pecos Smith saves the day and agrees to stay on with them at the ranch.

While Pecos feels like an older brother towards Terrill, the young woman begins to feel for Pecos as a young woman should. Her frustrated emotions reveal themselves in moodiness and petulant ill-temper. Eventually, Pecos discovers her secret one day when young Terrill almost drowns, but pretends not to know. When Breen Sawtell and Sheriff Haines

come to the ranch looking for Pecos, they discover her secret. They assume that Pecos Smith has known this all along and make the obvious assumptions. When Pecos returns and the inevitable gunplay ensues, Terrill's secret is revealed and Pecos and she are free to express their mutual attraction. After a confrontation with Don Felipe and his henchmen, they are free to continue their ranching in peace. They are married by Judge Roy Bean, the "law west of the Pecos."

Terrill Lambeth is an attempt at a new twist on the figure of the heroine, not overly successful. There are echoes of Shakespearean plays where a young girl disguises herself as a boy for reasons of self-defense. As well, she echoes earlier heroines who are torn between the need to be independent and yet dependent on the hero for support and rescue. Terrill Lambeth never achieves the sauciness of a Betty Zane, nor the independence of a Carly Burch or a Madeline Hammond.

Lance: Joe's horse in *The Spirit of the Border.* Joe tells Nell that next to his brother, his horse and his dog are the only things he has ever loved. Lance is taken by Silvertip when he captures the boys at Shawnee Rock. Silvertip is seen riding the horse at the Village of Peace during the religious festival. Joe later gets his horse back, following Isaac Zane's advice that he demand the return of his horse openly. Silvertip returns the horse and Aola rides the animal triumphantly through the village. Lance disappears after Jim Girty murders Aola and Joe at the Glen of the Beautiful Spring.

Lane, Herb: In *Western Union*, works with Creighton's crew. His wagon is responsible for repairing the line that has been sabotaged or knocked down by buffalo or cattle. He is mentioned as directing the wagons crossing the Laramie River and repairing the line as the construction crew approaches South Pass, where signs of deliberate sabotage are unmistakable.

Lane, Jed: In *Arizona Ames,* witnessed the gunfight between Rich and Lee Tate and Springer in the tavern in Shelby. This is reported to Cappy Tanner by the unnamed man who brings the news.

Lane, Jake: In *The Last Trail*, a pioneer whose farm is located several miles from Ft. Henry. He has several horses of excellent quality that are stolen by Bing Legget's outfit. He is killed and the house is burned to make it look like a raid by Indians. Mabel, his daughter, is abducted.

Lane, Mabel: Jake Lane's daughter in *The Last Trail*. She is abducted by Bing Legget and rescued by Jonathan Zane and Wetzel. She is barely alive when returned to Ft. Henry but under the care of Bessie Zane, she is nursed back to health. She marries Alex Bennet, and the colonel gives them a farm as a wedding present.

Lane, Matty: In *The Wolf Tracker*, one of the cowboys gathered at the corral on Barrett's ranch preparing for the spring roundup. He identifies the hide Brinks brings in as Old Gray's.

Lang: In *The Hash Knife Outfit,* an ex-sheriff who is now a member of the Hash Knife Outfit. He is caught and lynched at the outfit's hideout when Slinger Dunn leads the Diamond vigilantes against the cattle thieves.

Lano: In *West of the Pecos,* a Mexican vaquero, a slim, lizard-like rider, darker than an Indian, stamped all over with incomparable horsemanship. He hires on with Pecos Smith to drive a herd to the Pecos country and to work on the Lambeth ranch west of the Pecos.

Lanthorpe: In *The Lost Wagon Train,* the trail boss of the outfit that Corny (Slim Blue) is riding for. Slim kills Pitch in a gunfight that Pitch provoked, but since Pitch had been one of his favorite riders and a relative as well, the other cowboys urge Slim Blue to fork his horse and get away before he returns.

Laoghaire: In *The Spirit of the Border,* the drunken frontiersman who tries to kiss Nell outside Wentz's trading post. Joe comes to Nell's defense.

Larabee, Mrs.:   In *Under the Tonto Rim,* works for the welfare department, which is experimenting with sending a welfare worker to help the families in the Tonto Rim learn some things about the modern world and improve their living conditions. She comments that Lucy will create quite a stir among the young men there, and predicts she will probably end up marrying one of them.

Laramie: In *The Lone Star Ranger,* the owner of the inn. He is married with five children. He had been a rancher and owner of the Hope So gambling establishment until he lost everything in a cattle deal with Longstreth some two years before. At first he is reluctant to talk about Longstreth and the Cheseldine gang, but eventually he believes that Ranger Buck Duane is sincere in his desire to put an end to the rustling and the tyranny of the outlaws. He is attacked and robbed by Bo Snecker. Buck Duane pursues Snecker to Longstreth's ranch house a few minutes out of town. When the judge refuses to prosecute him, Laramie understands that the ranger may have the solution. He gives Buck the names of Frank Morton and Si Zimmer, two ranchers of impeccable honesty. For helping to form the group, he is shot one night by Floyd Lawson. He is an example of the citizen who has to be pushed to oppose outlaws, preferring to hope that things will get better on their own.

Laramie, Mrs.:   The wife of Laramie, the innkeeper, in *The Lone Star Ranger.* The woman is widowed when Floyd Lawson kills her husband for opposing the Cheseldine gang. She has five children, and despairs about their future, as she herself is sick. She gets help from Ranger Buck Duane and from Ray Longstreth, who takes pity on her and gives her a hand.

Larey, Adam: (a.k.a. Eagle, Wansfell): In *Wanderer of the Wasteland,* goes west looking to find himself. When he arrives in Picacho, he is eighteen years old, darkly tanned, with a handsome face. The desert and the Colorado River symbolize mystery, adventure, alluring freedom. Adam is a troubled young man, unsure of himself and seeking answers to questions about the meaning of life. Adam never knew his father. He was the favorite son of his mother, which caused problems with his brother, Guerd. When she died, the mother left her money to him. He shared his inheritance with his brother Guerd, but this did not settle the ill feelings between them. Adam had always looked up to his big brother, but Guerd's condescension and dismissal of him destroy the warm, intimate feelings he used to have for his idol. Adam believes that he is on the threshold of a new and freer life. He is strong. Merryvale tells him if he avoids drink, gambling and women, he can make himself a fortune in the gold fields. He is a handsome young man and the women will give him no peace, Merryvale warns. But Adam feels freed from a cage and he senses the desert will either do something wonderful or something terrible to him. He rents a room from Arallanes, whose stepdaughter, Margarita, takes a fancy to him. At the mill, he begins with a job in the office, but eventually takes a job stoking the furnaces with coal, the hardest, meanest, hottest, dirtiest job in the place. He proves he has stamina and endurance. He survives the toughest physical tests McKay puts to him. Impressed with Adam, McKay asks him to entertain his guests on the riverboat. That experience arouses his animal passion. Margarita has seen him on the boat with other women and has become jealous. That night, she succeeds in getting Adam to sleep with her. He discovers the strength of his lust. The following morning, Adam feels guilty. He knows he should have been able to do better. Just about this time, his brother Guerd appears in Picacho to collect on a "gambling debt." Adam refuses to pay. Collishaw, Guerd's ex-lawman gambling partner, threatens Adam. The resentment against his brother that has been building up over the years explodes. Guerd taunts Adam, that goody-goody, mamma's boy, who thinks himself so much more moral than anyone else, who took Margarita, a Mexican slut, to bed. They fight. Adam sees what a fool he has been. Margarita and Guerd scorn him. In the fight, Guerd is knocked unconscious. Adam thinks that he has killed his brother, and flees. Collishaw threatens to see him hanged.

Adam sets out into the wilderness. The desert is calling him, bidding him take up his burden. He spots Felix, Margarita's Mexican lover, and Collishaw following him. He meets a wanderer, Dismukes, a man with no family or ties. He is grateful that Dismukes asks no questions, but he knows that Dismukes understands his case better than he himself does. He uses a name that Regan back at Picacho had given him, "Wansfell." Dismukes knows it's a false name, but then, a name is a name. Adam learns a lot about the desert from Dismukes, who provides him with a burro, Jinny, with clothes, and a stove. He advises him to head for the Indian village. The following day, the burro destroys his kit and escapes, leaving Adam alone on the desert. He manages to make it to the abandoned village, where he passes out from thirst and exhaustion. On awakening several days later, he finds Charley Jim and his daughter, Oella, there nursing him. Charley Jim teaches him how to hunt in the desert, how to find water, and basic survival skills. From Oella, Adam learns the Coahuila language, and he teaches her some English. Adam recovers his strength and is slowly transformed into Wansfell, the wanderer. Charley Jim imagines that like most white men in the desert, Adam is seeking gold. He offers to show him the location of Peg Leg's mine, but Adam refuses the offer. He's not there for gold. Later, Charley Jim offers him Oella as a wife, on condition that he remain with the Indians. Adam is not ready to make that kind of commitment, since he is still seeking expiation for his sin. Charley Jim asks him to leave, and Adam sets out on his journey of self-discovery.

Eight years later, he meets up with Dismukes again at Tecopah in the Mohave desert. Dismukes does not recognize him. He has filled out. He is taller and stronger than most men. When Adam tells how Dismukes saved his life eight years ago, Dismukes recalls him. He has heard about Wansfell, the legendary wanderer, who killed McKue for abusing a woman. Dismukes reports that at the last stop on the stage line, he met Collishaw, the ex-lawman turned gambler, looking for the man who put his eye out. Discussion turns to the question of God and morality, the meaning of life. Dismukes sees the workings of divinity in nature. Adam sees only the Darwinian struggle to survive, the strong triumphing over the weak. Dismukes advises him to listen to nature; that is where he will hear the voice of God. Dismukes then tells Adam about a couple he met in Death Valley. He suggests that Adam go there.

In Death Valley, Adam rescues Elliott Virey, who is lying almost dead from dehydration. He takes him home, where his wife, Magdalene nurses him back to health. The couple have heard of Wansfell. Magdalene mocks his desire to help people, calling him "Sir Knight" and "Sir Wansfell." Eventually, she tells him her life story, how she betrayed her husband with another man at the age of nineteen, and how her daughter, Ruth, was the fruit of that amorous tryst. It was also the beginning of her husband's hatred of her, his refusal to forgive and forget. The thoughtless act of a moment, the yielding to passion, has ruined two lives. She remains in the desert with Elliott in expiation of her sin, and Elliott lives to torment and punish her. Adam tells how he left home at eighteen, how he fought his brother at Picacho, killing him. Adam offers to take Magdalene out of Death Valley, but she refuses. She is buried in an avalanche that Elliott has started. Adam then pursues Elliott to punish him for his crime. He dies in a landslide that Adam starts.

On his return from Death Valley, Adam finds the bones of Regan, the Irish man at Picacho who had given him the name Wansfell. The man had died from drinking poisoned water at a water hole. Nearby, he comes upon a group of men who have captured Dismukes and are treating him as a slave, whipping him, forcing him to do grueling work, in order to force out of him where he has hidden his gold. Adam takes on the attackers and kills them all. Dismukes tells him he has found all the gold he had hoped to collect — a half-million dollars worth. He sets off to civilization to enjoy the fruits of his labor.

Adam comes upon Eugenia Linwood, a young woman held prisoner by men who have kidnapped her hoping to find where her father's gold lies hidden. Adam rescues her, and returns her to her mother. Mrs. Linwood is dying of consumption. Adam does what he can to help the woman in her last days. Discussion turns to the meaning of life, the purpose of existence. Unlike Adam, Mrs. Linwood sees the hand of God in everything. She feels no resentment against God because of her illness. The struggle for life does not contradict her faith in the goodness of the Creator. She tells Adam that the God he seeks is within him, the voice of conscience. Before she dies, she asks Adam to take care of Genie. The girl inherits the gold her father had left buried under the floor of the house. He sets off with Genie for the civilized world, hoping to find a family that will take her.

On the way back to civilization, he meets Dismukes, who has returned from three years of wandering around the world. Dismukes tells him that the civilized world is an illusion. People pursue wealth and false goals. They are shallow, manipulative, unthinking. They have not the time to reflect on their lives or on what they are doing. He finds the life close to nature that he knew in the desert more authentic and satisfying.

Adam's wanderings bring him to Santa Ysabel. Here, he and Genie set up camp near the Blair's ranch. Mrs. Blair and her twenty-year-old son, Gene, welcome them. Mrs. Blair offers to keep Genie with them. Adam uses some of her money to buy land neighboring the Blair's. Since Gene and Genie seem taken with each other, Adam imagines they will marry and start a full-scale cattle and horse ranching operation.

The Hunts are neighbors to the Blairs. This elderly couple, it turns out, are Magdalene Virey's parents. Ruth is living with them. When Adam meets her, he sees the reincarnation of her beautiful mother. Adam falls in love with her. He decides he does want to marry her, but he has concluded that before he does anything more, he must go back to Picacho and face the music for killing Guerd. The Picacho he left fourteen years earlier is unrecognizable. The mill has closed, most of the people he knew are gone. Merryvale is there and brings him up to date on the people he knew. Arallanes left when the mills closed, and returned to Mexico. Margarita was knifed by Felix in a jealous rage. But to his surprise,

Merryvale informs him that Guerd is still alive. He was not even badly hurt in the fight that had precipitated Adam's flight to the desert.

In Adam, Zane Grey probes most deeply the conflict in a hero figure between the flesh and the spirit. Adam's meditations echo with phrases from the Bible, Emerson, Wordsworth, Tennyson. The young man cannot reconcile his spirituality with his animal desires. He feels guilty because of his sexual desire for Margarita, for Oella, for Genie Linwood. He sees the sexual urge as something demeaning. Mrs. Linwood had spoken of the need for the species to survive, that the individual is merely part of God's plan to ensure that the species survives. Sexuality is nothing to be ashamed of. Adam, on occasion, acquires that oneness with the natural world that John Hare had envied in Mescal and Eschtah, the Navajo chief. He can look at the desert landscape with his mind free from thought. But he remains troubled by the struggle for survival that marks the desert and society. Surely there must be something more, or perhaps life is truly absurd. Adam finally decides that conscience, being true to oneself and one's principles, is what makes life meaningful. Like Wetzel in *The Spirit of the Border*, John Hare in *The Heritage of the Desert*, and Bent Wade in *The Mysterious Stranger*, Adam is a natural man, whose physical being as well as his moral compass have been formed by close communion with nature. These men, and all Grey's heroes to some extent, are men of the earth, formed out of the primal matter of the earth with which the Creator shaped the first life. The natural religious and spiritual impulse in man arises from his very physical being.

In *Stairs of Sand*, Adam Larey (Wansfell), is now thirty-six years old. He is tall, strong, like an eagle, but wears an expression of sadness. He still pursues his mission of doing good and helping and defending people who are in need. He finally fulfills his promise to Magdalene Virey. Wansfell follows Ruth's trail through the Southwest and Mexico, finally hearing from an old prospector he had known years before that she was with her grandfather at Lost Lake. He comes upon her in the desert with Hal Stone, who is trying to force himself on her. He frees her from Stone's clutches, only to learn that she is in the process of running away from her husband and her grandfather. Like Magdalene, she is acting in a selfish, irresponsible manner. He tells her the story of her mother and Elliott Virey in the desert, how he had taken her there to have her to himself and to punish her for her infidelity, an affair which produced Ruth. He tells Ruth he promised Magdalene he would find her daughter and try to help her avoid making the mistakes she had made. Adam has diagnosed her problem. She is still selfish and inconsiderate. She has refused to accept herself, to know herself, and to face her responsibilities. Adam tells her that the desert taught him that one's purpose in life is to help and serve others. The desert experience is not to be feared. It is a testing ground, a forge which creates a stronger person, as her mother learned. It

is an environment in which the truly godlike qualities in man can triumph over the environmental forces that foster cruelty and brutality.

Adam sets about protecting Ruth from her herself and from Guerd Larey. He rescues her from her abductors in Yuma. He kills Collishaw, Larey's right-hand man for the past two decades. He defends her right to her grandfather's property. All the while, he stays out of town, never speaking of his love for her, in order to protect her reputation. Merryvale speaks to Ruth of Adam as a force of nature, an instrument of the desert. He has been sent to save her, to defend her. He tells her that Adam loves her, but that his sense of decency and honor prevent him from speaking of it to her, since she is married and Guerd is his brother. But he is sure fate will bring them together. Adam himself had revealed to her that he is Guerd's brother. He is prepared to fight and kill his brother if needed to defend Ruth. Merryvale shoots Guerd in the confrontation between the two, as he does not want his partner to bear the burden of guilt of having killed his brother. Adam and Ruth are now free to be together.

Larey, Guerd: In *Wanderer of the Wasteland*, Adam Larey's older brother. He is greatly admired and loved by his younger, shy brother, but Guerd is no good. Haughty and dismissive, he mocks and ridicules his brother, does what he can to thwart anything his Adam does. Guerd urges Adam to quit school and to seek adventure with him in the California gold fields. Here, Guerd falls in with bad companions. In Tucson, he launches his career as a gambler. Ehreberg is a mining camp suited to his taste. With a virile, strong, square chin, hazel green eyes, broad forehead, fair hair, and tanned skin, he is a handsome devil and irresistible to women. He shows up at Picacho with the ex-sheriff from Texas, Collishaw. He pursues his brother's girl, Margarita, and taunts Adam with his weakness and morality. He makes Margarita choose between the two of them, and Margarita, a passionate woman living in and for the moment, is completely taken in by Guerd. Guerd makes fun of his brother, who is so smug and self-righteous, a goody-goody little mamma's boy, who was seduced by a "greaser girl." Adam and Guerd fight, and Adam thinks he has killed his brother. He leaves to wander about the desert for some fourteen years. When he returns to Picacho, he learns from Merryvale that Guerd was not even badly hurt in the fight.

In *Stairs of Sand*, Guerd Larey is married to Ruth Virey, Magdalene Virey's daughter, who was being raised by her parents in California. Guerd Larey is interested in extorting the water rights to Lost Lake which her grandfather, Caleb Hunt, possesses. Merryvale explains to Ruth why Guerd hates his brother Adam so intensely, a hatred which stems from sibling rivalry and jealousy of a mother's preference for one son over the other. Larey is still a striking man to look at but also has the look of one it would not be safe to cross. Ruth consented to marry him for her grandfather's sake, and deserted Larey hours after their wedding. She has never been more than a wife in name to him, and he is determined to have her. Her attempts to get away from him with Stone have proved an embarrassment. He has succeeded in portraying his wife as a wanton hussy to others at the post. He arranges her abduction to Yuma, making it appear that she and Hal Stone have run off together again. When Wansfell and Merryvale have rescued her and brought her home, Larey arranges the murder of her grandfather, pretending it was a disgruntled Mexican client who killed him. Larey returns with the men scouting the route for the railroad. Ruth takes over the post her grandfather had operated, and starts collecting past dues for water from Larey's freighting company. This angers him, provoking a confrontation between Adam and Guerd. At first, he does not recognize his brother, but when he does, the old anger and hatred surge out of him. Merryvale shoots Guerd so that Adam will not have the burden of having killed his brother. In the conflict, Guerd is not solely to blame. Adam sees in the relationship between Ruth and Guerd the same problem that had plagued her mother. Ruth likes men, and enjoys toying with them. She is selfish, not concerned about her responsibilities to others. Virey's passionate desire to possess her, to dominate and control her, derives from the same passionate jealousy that drove Virey to hold Magdalene prisoner, hoping eventually to break her spirit.

Larken, Jud: In *The Horse Thief*, foreman of Stafford's posse pursuing horse rustlers from Montana.

Larkin, Mrs.: In *Riders of the Purple Sage,* the mother of Fay Larkin. She is a gentile woman living in the town of Cottonwoods. Her husband is dead and the woman herself is in extremely poor health. Jane Withersteen comes to help her at her house. Mrs. Larkin tells Jane that the women of Cottonwoods have been telling her that the reason Jane is so interested in helping out is that she wants to get Little Fay to raise as a Mormon. She asks Jane if this is true and Jane replies that she has no interest in the child other than to ensure that she is taken care of. She promises not to give her Mormon teaching and to send her back to the Larkin family in the East when she is of age. Mrs. Larkin is glad to hear this, as she always believed that the other Mormon women had told her this out of spite. Jane offers to bring Mrs. Larkin to her own home where she and her women can more easily take care of her. Mrs. Larkin agrees to go. Several weeks later, she passes away.

Larkin, Fay: (See also **Mary, Sago Lily**) In *Riders of the Purple Sage,* a young child that Jane Withersteen has adopted from a dying gentile woman. She promises that she will not raise the child as a Mormon. This becomes a bone of contention with her Mormon church leaders who feel she is betraying her religion by consenting to do this. Fay Larkin is a delightful child, quickly taking to Jane as her new mother. She also instinctively likes Lassiter, allowing Jane to see a tender side to him which she has never suspected. The child innocently asks if Lassiter is going to be her new father, and wonders why he and Jane are not married. Fay senses that the two of them belong together and sees the goodness in Lassiter to which Jane is blind. The final hope that Tull has to get control over Jane and force her to submit to him and the Mormon church is by kidnapping Fay. Jane Withersteen indeed is willing to do anything to get the child back. While they are fleeing Tull and his men, heading for Surprise Valley, Lassiter rescues little Fay from the men who have been holding her pending final instructions from Tull. With the child in hand, Jane is ready to seal herself in the valley with Lassiter.

In *The Rainbow Trail*, Fay is known as Mary, or by the nickname Sago Lily, given to her by Ruth Jones because of her striking beauty and her reserve. Mary was brought to the Mormon village about a year before John Shefford arrives. Her origins are unknown to any of the other women in the village, although gossip is not lacking. The other women are jealous of her beauty, suspecting that their husbands may also have her as a sealed wife. She meets Shefford at the well, where he offers to help her carry her bucket of water back to her cabin. She talks little about herself, but proves to be a good listener. Mary takes him on walking excursions in the mountains, pointing out the wildflowers, the geographic formations. She moves about with the sureness and speed of a mountain goat, all testimony to her upbringing in nature. Shefford shares with her his stories about life back east, the story of his congregation, his failure as a preacher, his doubts about himself, and finally, he broaches the topic of Fay Larkin, and Lassiter and Jane Withersteen in Surprise Valley. At first, she tells him that Fay Larkin is dead, but after she has been called to testify at the polygamy trials in Stonebridge, Nas Ta Bega tells Shefford that Mary is Fay Larkin. She admits that this is true, and tells how the Mormons and an Indian (Shadd, the Piute outlaw) had found them in the valley, and how they had attempted to hang Jim Lassiter, releasing him when they had seized her as hostage, allowing him and Jane to live as long as she consented to become a sealed wife. When Waggoner comes to visit her, she fights with him and passes out. When she comes to, she discovers him dead on the porch with a knife driven deep into his breast. She is accused of murdering him and is held in the schoolhouse until the Mormon elders can meet to determine her fate. John Shefford, helped by Joe Lake and Ruth Jones, effect her escape. On the pretext of bringing her food, Ruth switches clothes with her and she leaves with Shefford and Joe. Fay leads the group to Surprise Valley with the skill and instinct of an Indian. She is reunited with Lassiter and Jane. At the rainbow bridge, she accepts his proposal of marriage. They return to Beaumont, Illinois, with Jane and Lassiter.

Larry: In *Boulder Dam,* the young man driving Helen Pritchard and her mother when Lynn leaves them at Boulder Dam.

Larsen, Jeff: In *The Heritage of the Desert,* a slick, crafty cowboy who trades horses with the drunken son of August Naab, Snap Naab. Snap's pinto was traded for a mustang, but the mustang is lame in one leg. When Snap tries to get his horse back, he gets into a gunfight with Larsen and kills him. As Naab and his family leave White Sage to return home, some of Larsen's friends follow them at a distance, waiting for an opportunity to get at Snap.

Las Vegas: In *The Man of the Forest,* the nickname that Bo Rayner gives Tom Carmichael because she met him in Las Vegas when the train made a stop there. See **Carmichael, Tom.**

Lascelles, Malcolm: In *Knights of the Range,* a fair haired man whose sharp, cold, handsome features proclaim him to be about thirty years old. His black frock coat and gaudy waistcoat and long hair characterize him as a gambler. He is from Louisiana and had known Holly when she was in her last year at Madam Brault's school. She had met him by accident and out of loneliness and rebelliousness and a taste for adventure, she stole out of the school to meet him again and again. When she learned he was a gambler and adventurer, she regretted her folly and ended the acquaintance. He persistently annoyed her with attempts to reestablish himself in her esteem, getting her into disgrace with her teachers. This had a good side in that the principal wrote her father, who hastened her return home. Lascelles comes west, and hangs around the Ripple ranch making life unpleasant for Holly. He cheats the cowboys at cards. He carries a derringer concealed in his vest pocket. The cowboys dunk him in the cold water when sobering up some of their drunken fellow cowboys, a joke he does not appreciate. Lascelles is lured over to Russ Slaughter's rustler outfit with the promise of fast money. He is caught and hanged by the "Knights of the Range."

Lash, Jim: A young cowboy in *Desert Gold* who helps Dick Gale create a disturbance in the barroom in order for George Thorne to get Mercedes Castañeda out of town. Lash takes Dick Gale and Mercedes to Belding's place. Lash is an experienced, brave horseman and cowboy. He knows the geography of the border and avoids the Mexican rebels who are everywhere, looking for cattle and horses to rustle for the revolutionary armies south of the border. He has great praise for Gale's courage when they arrive at Belding's ranch. Lash proposes the stratagem to get Mercedes away from Rojas by going to Yuma across the "camino del diablo." He brings along Belding's prize horses to save them from the revolutionaries. Lash tells Dick Gale about a place he found in the desert where there is a buried water hole and bleached bones. Yaqui later leads Dick to the spot, which turns out to be the mine that Burton, Nell's real father, had found at the beginning of the story some twenty years before.

Laskin: In *Nevada,* one of the cowboys working on Ben Ide's ranch in Winthrop. Clan Dillon lies about the report he gave on the location of the herds.

Lassiter, James (Jim, Uncle Jim): In *Riders of the Purple Sage,* the gunman from Texas who has spent eighteen years pursuing the men who abducted his sister. He undertakes to defend Venters and Jane Withersteen from the Mormon elders who are seeking their destruction. Like Shane, he is a dark man with a past, but a man who defends the weak and oppressed. He is perhaps the most famous gunman in popular western fiction. Zane Grey's son, Lorne, penned a series of novels with Lassiter as hero, novels detailing the adventures of his father's hero before he appears in *Riders of the Purple Sage.*

Jim Lassiter's family moved from Missouri to Texas and he and his sister Milly were raised there. He considers himself a Texan through and through. He and his sister were particularly close. She was the belle of the town, all the young men wanting to court her. Milly was always strong on religion, trying to convert Jim, but she never succeeded. Her husband, Frank Erne, while a man of the cloth, was also a man's man who loved ranching, hunting, and fishing. He and Jim became the best of friends. After Milly's marriage, Lassiter left home and "went to the bad." He knew hard life in the Panhandle, and in Kansas and Nebraska, where he acquired extraordinary skill at tracking man or beast, and consummate skill with the gun. On his return home, he discovered Milly gone, and his brother-in-law a broken man with little interest in living. He sets out in pursuit of Milly and in a year's time finds the cabin where she was held captive and where she gave birth to her daughter. From letters Milly wrote to Frank asking him not to pursue her, Lassiter gets the names of the men who abducted her. He sets off on their trail and catches up with them in northern Utah. They die without revealing Milly's whereabouts. Eventually he learns that his sister is dead, but that one Jane Withersteen could probably tell him where Milly is buried. Lassiter arrives at Withersteen House just as Tull is preparing to have Bern Venters whipped. Lassiter appears to emerge out of the landscape just as Jane is praying that a hero neither creed-bound nor creed-mad will come to her rescue.

Lassiter is both outlaw and avenger. He confesses to having spent lawless years when he wandered away from home, unable to endure his sister's attempts to convert him. At some point, he and Oldring had worked together, whether for good or for evil being left unstated. Venters tells Jane that the man has acquired a reputation as a gunman, and his swiftness on the draw is unmatched. Rumors abound of his shooting up towns in northern Utah, but Venters cannot say how much of this is true and how much is legend. He has the reputation of being a hater of Mormons. These stories Jane Withersteen takes to heart. She sees Lassiter through the prism of legend. She thinks him a bloodthirsty Mormon-hater. He is intent on killing Tull and Dyer to satisfy a blood lust. He has made many children fatherless. Before he goes to Surprise Valley, he must kill a few more Mormons to satisfy his hatred.

Judkins and Venters see another Lassiter. For them, he is an expert horseman, cowboy, tracker, a loyal friend, a fair man and a gentleman. He lets his horse drink before he slakes his own thirst. Riding his blind horse, he wheels the stampeding red herd, stopping their race to destruction, a testimony to his background as a cowboy. He tracks Venters to Surprise Valley, a spot Venters was convinced was impossible to find. He is concerned about Venters's safety in the valley. When Dyer draws on him at Jane's home, Lassiter defends himself, but he did not start the trouble. Rather than kill the bishop, he wounds him in the arm, causing him to drop his firearm. When he confronts Dyer at the end of the conflict, he gives Dyer the opportunity to back down, but the bishop continues to shoot at Lassiter. The bishop's stubbornness makes the use of lethal force a necessity. Above all, Lassiter is extremely respectful of women. He removes his hat when speaking to Jane, he never comes to the house without an invitation, and he resists her attempts at seduction. Before he leaves Surprise Valley, where he has found Venters with Bess, he exacts a promise from Bern that he will do right by her, and not take advantage of her youth and innocence. As Tull and his henchmen are in hot pursuit, he refuses to roll the rock sealing the entrance to Surprise Valley until he gets assurance from Jane that she is willing possibly to spend the rest of her life with him in the valley.

Lassiter is a man who sees things clearly and whose reaction is appropriate for the circumstances. He intervenes to save Venters from a whipping. He understands the strategy of the Mormon elders and can predict their future maneuvers. He explains to Jane that her pacifism cannot work on the frontier. Men who do not stand up for themselves are trampled. Knowing how to defend yourself, to use a gun, to fight, best assure your rights will be respected. Venters' demise was due to his emasculation when he surrendered his guns to Jane. Her belief that she can wait out the campaign of harassment against her on the part of her church elders is a dream. Lassiter shows her that her churchmen are not interested in the salvation of her soul but in ensuring their influence and power are unopposed. Judkins is given cause to worry about Lassiter when he sees him and Oldring talking quietly in Snell's saloon like long-lost buddies. He fears that Lassiter is becoming weak, like Venters had been, due to Jane's influence. But the man of action, the hero, is still there, biding the right time to act. Jane Withersteen sees Lassiter as hard and unchanging. Lassiter, however, is willing to try her pacifism, but to do so, they must leave Utah. She cannot believe that he can change. She persists in misunderstanding him up to the very end. But in spite of her misunderstanding and condemning him, he loves her and does not abandon her.

In *The Rainbow Trail*, Lassiter appears in the closing chapters when Shefford and Fay Larkin, with Joe Lake and Nas Ta Bega, come to get them out of the valley and out of Utah. The story of Lassiter and Jane's captivity in Surprise Valley was told to Shefford by Venters back in Illinois. Fay Larkin tells about their discovery in the canyon by the Mormons. Waggoner and Shadd had attempted to hang Lassiter, fearing he may have retained his ability with the gun despite the decade in isolation. His life is spared by Jane's entreaties and Fay is taken away to use as guarantee that they will toe the line and remain in the valley. When Shefford and the party arrive, Lassiter tells Jane that indeed, Venters has kept his promise of coming to rescue them. Lassiter has changed. He is now gray-haired and his hands, formerly so skilled with the gun, resemble claws. Shefford wonders if in this past decade he has lost his ability with the gun, but when a rifle is put in his hands, the old memory returns. Lassiter has panned several large bags of gold while in the valley. This gold ensures a quiet old age back in Illinois.

In Lassiter, Zane Grey establishes the pattern of his hero, a man of unparalleled insight, competence, skill, a gentleman, a man of principle, a man willing to take what action is necessary in defense of others. He retains his faith in the goodness of people and life, despite his immersion in the worst elements of the frontier.

Latch, Estelle (Estie): In *The Lost Wagon Train,* the daughter of Stephen Latch and Cynthia Bowden. When Latch returns home after a seven-year absence, he is looking forward to being reunited with his beautiful wife, only to learn that she is dead. Estelle is his daughter, now seven years old. In the seven years, Keetch had never once mentioned Cynthia's death nor the birth of the daughter in any of his letters. When he finally takes a look at her, he sees a striking resemblance to her mother. Until the age of ten, she lives at her father's ranch being cared for by Mrs. Benson, whom she considers as a mother. There follow six years of school in New Orleans with summers at Latch's Field and finally, just before her sixteenth birthday, she returns home for good. In New Orleans, she learns the refined manners of a southern young lady. She is on her way back to Latch's Field by wagon and caravan when Corny foils an abduction attempt. She is taken with the young man and tells him her father will give him a job as reward for saving her. Corny agrees to accompany her to her father's ranch. Estelle speaks to her father about Corny, but he does not want to have him stay around. Corny seems to draw the attention of the young ladies at Latch's Field and this makes Estelle jealous. Corny protests that he is just being friendly. Eventually, Corny succumbs to her charms, and she agrees to marry him. The night of her sixteenth birthday party, Corny proves his loyalty both to her and to her father. He foils a second abduction attempt, and saves Latch's life, eliminating the remaining outlaws who knew of his past, thus ensuring that his reputation will not be assailed again. Estelle's relationship to Cynthia Bowden is established beyond doubt and she receives both the money her uncle had hidden in his wagon, and the inheritance from her mother's uncle. Estelle and Corny are married in San Antonio and then continue east to Boston, where she meets her mother's family and receives her inheritance. They plan to return to Latch's Field to take over Latch's ranch.

Latch, Stephen: In *The Lost Wagon Train*, a good man gone bad. His is a story of disgrace and redemption. He experiences the vicissitudes of fortune, having been born into high society, falling into disgrace and a life of crime, being robbed and ruined, and restored to grace by a twist of fate.

He is about thirty years old, the son of a Louisiana planter, ruined at the inception of the war. His descent into banditry resulted from a failed love affair. Deeply in love with Cynthia Bowden, Latch meets with her brother's disapproval. The brother plans for her to marry his friend, Thorpe. Howard turns Cynthia against Stephen, telling her that Stephen is involved with a cheap harlot. Cynthia then turns to Thorpe. This same rumor prevents Stephen from receiving a commission in the Confederate army, that honor also going to Thorpe. He challenges his rival to a duel in which Thorpe is killed. Stephen then is ruined and takes to the frontier and a career of banditry, having lost all hope or respectability in Southern society. With a distant relation, Leighton, and a motley crew of failed cowboys and ranchers, he plans to join forces with the Kiowa chief, Satana, and attack wagon trains. But the beauty of his plan is that there will be no witnesses. Everyone will be massacred, and the wagons dumped into Spider Web Canyon, where they are unlikely ever to be found. He and his men will keep the valuables on the wagons, the cattle and the horses will go to the Kiowas.

Latch's position of authority among the men is challenged immediately by Leighton. He conspires to keep a woman who had escaped the massacre. When Latch learns of it, he is forced to shoot the man to assert his authority. When he learns that the woman is Cynthia Bowden, he is overwhelmed. He convinces the men with rum and bribery to let him marry her. Cynthia loves the canyon and the beauty of nature and appears happy with him in the cabin. She never tires of trying to wean him away from the outlaws. Latch is intensely happy.

His excursions to attack caravans take him away from the canyon for long periods of time. He commissions his associate, Keetch, to buy land from Satana at Latch's Field and to set up a ranch. He continues to send him the spoils to conceal in Spider Web Canyon. Latch believes that Leighton has changed, but Lester Cornwall, a man he considers like a son, and the scout Kit Carson warn him that Leighton is planning something sinister against him. At Fort Union, he is compared to Maxwell, a southerner who has carved out for himself a place on the prairie where all, white, Indian, outlaw, and respectable citizens are welcome.

When he returns to Latch's Field and discovers

that Cynthia is dead and he has a daughter, Latch decides he wants to change. He offers his men money to establish themselves as ranchers. It's not too late to go straight. Latch sends his daughter to school in New Orleans to learn the graces of a southern lady. Still the fear of discovery haunts him. The shadow of his past never leaves him.

When Estelle returns, things take a turn for the worse. Leighton has stepped up his campaign against Latch. His rustlers have virtually ruined the man. He has bought up all his debts and now plans to collect on them, demanding payment he knows Latch cannot make. As well, he has begun to spread rumors about Latch's past, about his involvement with the outlaws who show up at Latch's Field. Above all, he plans to abduct his daughter, expose Latch's past to her, then rape and kill her.

Latch is saved by several twists of fate. A young cowboy, Lester Cornwall's long lost brother, Cornie, rescues Estelle from kidnappers on her way home. This cowboy becomes a guardian angel to Latch, learning of the Leighton's plot against him, and foiling his plans. He eliminates permanently all of Latch's enemies, and burns the remains of the wagons in the Spider Web Canyon, ensuring that no evidence is left of Latch's outlaw past and his connection to Satana and his raids and slaughter. Latch is restored to fortune by the discovery of gold in the Tullt wagon where Cynthia had been hiding during the massacre. Her uncle had hidden his fortune in a false bottom. No one had known about it. As well, Estie comes into an inheritance from a rich relative of Cynthia's in Boston. Latch is free to live out his old age in the respectability he had been denied.

Latimer, Sparrowhawk: In *Robbers' Roost*, is a member of Hank Hays's outfit. Jim Wall thinks he resembles a horse thief he had seen hanged. Latimer has the same beaked nose, the same small sleek head, the same gimlet eyes of steel. Latimer is shot in the abduction of Helen Herrick and the robbery of her brother. Hays tries to remove the bullet but blood poison sets in. His conscience is bothering him and he wants to get something off his conscience, so he tells Jim Wall and Smoky what happened when they abducted Helen. He asks Jim and Smoky not to reveal what he is going to tell them until after he is dead. He had been told by Hays that they were going to rob Herrick, nothing more, but just before they put their plan into action, Hays brings out a saddled horse he had kept hidden behind the barn. When Sparrowhawk learns what Hays has in mind, he protests that he wants nothing to do with the abduction. Hays beats and robs Herrick. Hays's claim that he was abducting Helen for ransom is not the truth. He picked a fight with Herrick and beat him with a gun, then tied him up. They ransacked the house for money and jewels, collecting over sixteen thousand dollars in cash, not counting whatever was in the Wells Fargo package (bundles of hundred dollar bills) that Helen Herrick had brought with her. Sparrowhawk knows Hays has double-crossed the men, hiding from them the extent of the take in the robbery. The Wells Fargo package does not figure in the total loot which is divided among the men. Sparrowhawk gives his share to Jim and Smoky. He warns Jim and Smoky that Hays's intentions for Helen are dubious. Five days later, Sparrowhawk dies.

Laughing Jack: In *Wilderness Trek*, Leslie Slyter's pet kookaburra.

Lawrence, Jud: In *Raiders of Spanish Peaks*, hired by Laramie Nelson as cook for the trip from Garden City to the Spanish Peak ranch. He proves to be as good a cook as he had boasted. He remains as cook when they reach the ranch.

Lawsford: In *Shadow on the Trail*, Aulsbrook's foreman on his ranch in Arizona whom Wade Holden meets when he rides into his camp. Lawsford describes the job opportunities in the area. Driscoll could hire him but his outfit razzes the devil out of any new rider. Mason's foreman, Stewart, is hell to work for, and Drill, while always hiring, pays poor wages. That leaves Pencarrow, who can't pay for anything now. He explains that Pencarrow has had a rough time with his large herd of twenty thousand being rustled by the Hash Knife, the Diamond B and other outfits. He speaks highly of Pencarrow and his family. When Tex Brandon reaches the Pencarrow ranch and explains how he came there, Pencarrow says Lawsford and Aulsbrook are no friends of his, but his daughter corrects him, adding that Lawsford has always been friendly in spite of his boss's enmity.

Lawson: In *Majesty's Rancho*, a neighboring rancher who has gone into bankruptcy. Gene reports this to Madeline when they discuss the dismal prospects for their ranch in the "Hungry Thirties."

Lawson, Floyd: In *The Lone Star Ranger*, the second-in-command, after Colonel Granger Longstreth, in the Cheseldine gang. In fact, Longstreth argues that the name more properly applies to Lawson than to him since the major rustling has been planned and executed by Lawson. Furthermore, it has been Lawson's cruelty and brutality, his murderous tactics, which have given Cheseldine his reputation. Floyd Lawson is former gentleman from Louisiana, of French extraction. Buck Duane observes him talking with Longstreth in the inn just after the colonel and the girls have arrived. He is supposed to be a cousin of the Longstreths and the colonel introduces him to his daughter, Ray, and their cousin Ruth. Floyd Lawson is under thirty yet gray at the temples, dark, smooth-shaven, with lines left by wildness and dissipation. He has a strong mouth, and a bitter, square chin. There is something recklessly handsome in his sinister face. Buck Duane attributes this to traces of a former genteel existence that have not completely been blotted out by his present life of crime. He is Longstreth's lieutenant and when Buck chases Bo Snecker to the Longstreth ranch, Lawson does what he can to prevent him exercising his duties as ranger. He thinks that it's all a bluff. Lawson is present in the court when Buck tries to bring Snecker before the judge. Floyd tries to force himself on Ruth when drunk. He tells both Ruth and Ray that Buck Duane is out to stir the town up against Colonel Longstreth. Curious to find out what the man is up to, Buck Duane follows him. He meets with unknown men at night. His movements have the signs of someone planning an operation. The day of the planned attack on the Ranchers' Bank in Val Verde, Longstreth and Lawson meet to make the final plans. Things are not going well between Longstreth and Lawson. Floyd is in love with Longstreth's daughter, Ray, but Longstreth is not keen on the idea. The father argues that he cannot force his daughter to do something she does not want to, a problem any father would understand. Ray informs him that she is more interested in the ranger, Duane, than in Lawson. This infuriates him even further. When Buck Duane comes in, Lawson is killed in the gunfight when the ranger comes to arrest them.

Le Vent de la Mort: In *The Spirit of the Border*, the French version of Wetzel's name, the "Wind of Death" or "Deathwind." See **Atelang**.

Leatherstocking: In *Majesty's Rancho*, one of Madge Stewart's string of thoroughbred horses.

Leavitt, Rand: In *Thunder Mountain*, in Challis when he gets wind of a strike at Thunder Mountain. He learns of the strike from Selback, who had attacked Jake Emerson and stolen his gold nuggets. He arrives in the valley and finds the claim that Sam Emerson was working. He quickly takes charge of the emerging mining city that grows overnight, having himself elected mayor and judge according to established law in mining camps. From this position of authority, he gets to decide who will be allowed to work a claim. He sells worthless claims that he has had spiked with a few nuggets to lure suckers into paying high prices. Likewise, he sets up a vigilance committee to enforce his regulations when he learns that the sheriff, Bruce Mastes, elected by the miners, will not submit to his rule. The vigilance committee and the robbers he controls are the same group. When Kalispel challenges his claim to Sam's diggings, Leavitt denies knowing of any Sam Emerson. Jake Emerson later challenges his claim in court, only to have the miners' court rule in favor of Leavitt. Kalispel decides to keep an eye on Leavitt and catch him in criminal activity. The two lock horns over Sydney Blair, who is seduced by his charming manners. Kalispel compares him to one Henry Plummer, who as sheriff hid his criminal activity under the mask of respectability. Kalispel overhears him planning robberies, and discovers where he has hidden his gold. From the cache buried under the floor of his cabin, he retrieves the gold stolen from his brother, and Blair's wallet stolen after big winnings at cards. While Leavitt manages to convince Sydney Blair to marry him, she eventually does see that he is a crook and when he falsely accuses Kalispel of robbery, she testifies that she was with the man when the supposed attack took place. Leavitt is killed in the rock slide that destroys much of Thunder City. From the expression on the man's face, Kalispel concludes he had just discovered that his stash of gold and money has gone missing. Later, Sheriff Masters learns from Jones and Matthews that they had killed Sam Emerson on orders from Leavitt. The death of Leavitt and the destruction of his criminal organization conforms to Grey's view of nature being a moral force, ensuring that the evildoers are not allowed to prosper.

Lee: (1) In *The Dude Ranger*, one of Anderson's riders driving the herd from Red Rock Ranch to market. Lee is the only one of the group that is any way friendly to Ernest and Nebraskie. Lee tells them that Baldy and Dot have counted the herd; Baldy puts the number at eighteen hundred and sixty-eight head and Dot at eighteen hundred and sixty-two.

(2) In *The Maverick Queen*, a tall Texan, a rancher and cattle dealer. He is one of the many ranchers who had proposed marriage to Kit Bandon and been rejected by her. This is a bone of contention between him and Emery, her latest pursuer, and the owner of the cigar store predicts Lee will kill Emery some day. Lee is sometimes referred to as "Colonel," although there is no indication he had served in the army. He is one of the players in the card game in the Leave It Saloon when Lincoln Bradway wins a big pot, several thousand dollars. He is impressed with Bradway's self-assurance and competence and fearlessness. He comments that he has not seen such an interesting game of poker since he came to South Pass, nor someone win such a large sum through strict, honest playing. Several days later, he approaches Lincoln to offer him a job as head of a vigilance group he is organizing. It strikes Lincoln as strange he should offer such a position to a newcomer. Lee fires his foreman, Mel Thatcher, because he refuses to participate in the vigilantes. Lee fires his own cowboys and brings in riders from Casper, precipitating a range war. He is the first to whip Bud Harkness, trying to get out of him a confession implicating Kit Bandon. His right-hand man, Jim Hargrove, is killed in the Leave It by Harkness and a full range war gets underway. Lee is shot by Vince when he and his cowboys reach the clearing where the ranchers are preparing to hang Emery and Kit.

Lee, Clay: In *Raiders of Spanish Peaks*, a member of Arlidge's crew at the Spanish Peaks ranch. At first, he remains loyal to Arlidge, who is in cahoots with Lester Allen, a rancher and dealer in stolen cattle. Eventually, Lee comes to change his loyalty to Laramie and the Lindsays.

Lee, Commissioner Allison: In *The U. P. Trail*, the father of Allie Lee Durade. Mrs. Durade was forced by her family to marry him at an early age. She escapes from him with the gambler Durade. On Horn's wagon train back east, Mrs. Durade explains to Allie that her true father, in New Orleans, is a wealthy and powerful man. Commissioner Allison Lee is currently one of the men hiring crews for the construction of the railroad. He is a corrupt man, using his position of wealth and influence to cheat the government. He orders sections of road to be rebuilt, the contract going to his own construction company. Warren Neale denounces him to the board of directors of the U. P. in Omaha, and he counters the accusation by calling Neale a drunkard and a liar. Later, in a similar scene, Allison Lee is told that the evidence of his efforts to defraud Union Pacific and the government are so blatant that he is banned from any future contracts. Commissioner Lee takes in Allie when he learns who she is. He tries to prevent her from seeing Neale, but fate intervenes in the person of Slingerland. Commissioner Allison Lee is a popular figure in Grey novels, the corrupt capitalist who exploits the environment or the government or his workers for personal gain.

Lee, John D.: In *The Deer Stalker*, Lee's Ferry is named for a man who took refuge there. Lee was the instigator of the dread Mountain Meadow massacre. His ranch, strangely beautiful to the eye weary of desert reds and grays, is in an oval valley just beyond the ferry crossing.

Lee, Marcella (Marcie): In *The Lost Wagon Train*, is a friend of Estelle Latch's from school in New Orleans. Marcella and Elizabeth accompany her back to her father's ranch and stay there until her sixteenth birthday party. She is particularly taken with Slim Blue and the cowboys at the ranch. Like Elizabeth, she is fascinated by Billy the Kid and other outlaws that visit the place. She and Elizabeth return to New Orleans the day following the fateful birthday party.

Legget, Bing: Appears in *The Last Trail*. Legget is a "blond-bearded giant, with steel-blue, inhuman eyes and the expression of a free but hunted animal; [with] a set, mastiff-like jaw, brutal and coarse." He is readily identified by the nasty scar on his temple and cheek, courtesy of a shot by Wetzel. He is a French Canadian from Detroit, and his horse-stealing operation takes horses to Detroit for resale. Legget works in the dark and is the equal of the Girtys and other renegades in his knowledge of the woods. Leggett was obliged to flee Fort Pitt after he murdered a man. He is thick with Metzar, who opened the inn at Ft. Henry. Colonel Zane says about him that since Simon Girty and his renegades have been lying low after their defeat in the attack on the fort, the field has been left open to Bing Legget.

Brandt tells Legget he committed a major blunder when he did not kill Jonathan Zane while he was in his power. Leggett convinces Brandt to get Mordaunt involved, under the promise that they will get Helen for him. In fact, Legget is hoping to get her for himself.

Legget eventually has to retreat to his cabin in a well-hidden ravine. He is tracked there by Wetzel. While he and Brandt hide in the cabin, Wetzel sets the roof afire with flaming arrows. Brandt hides out until the following day and makes his way to the fort, but Legget and his Indian associates escape through the woods, pursued by Wetzel. Jonathan Zane later comes upon the bodies of Legget and the Indians.

Legs: In *The Fugitive Trail*, Bruce Lockheart's horse and companion on his flight from Denison and around Texas to the Melrose ranch.

Leighton: In *The Lost Wagon Train*, a fellow southerner, as well as Latch's distant relation, rival and enemy. Lester Cornwall cautions Latch that Leighton is not to be trusted in things as simple as the amount of rum to be given to the men and certainly not in more crucial matters. Leighton finds a woman in the Tullt wagon and decides to keep her for himself. When Sprall learns the secret, it gets out. Cornwall tells Latch and the first major confrontation takes place. Latch kills Sprall and shoots Leighton in the shoulder and the face. When he discovers that the woman is his old flame, Cynthia Bowden, he convinces the men to spare her and let him marry her. Latch wants to believe that Leighton has changed over the years, but Cornwall warns him that Leighton hates him with a passion that grows every day. He is hatching a plot to get revenge. At Ft. Union, Leighton earns the dislike of nearly everyone. He owes money to everyone, he drinks, he gambles, he whores around. Lester Cornwall feels it is only a matter of time before he spills the beans about their involvement with Satana and the disappeared wagon trains. In the five months that Latch has been sick, Leighton has changed markedly. His face bears a crooked, livid, triangular scar, the result of Latch's shot. It gives him a deformed, hideous appearance. He has grown heavy in body and untidy of person. He appears possessed by a hidden thought. When Latch decides he wants to go straight and become respectable again, Leighton refuses the offer of money to go into ranching. But he does not leave the area. In the town of Latch's Field, he sets up a gambling establishment and saloon which is the haven of the local outlaws. He organizes rustlers, cleaning out Latch's herds slowly but surely. Back at Ft. Union, Kit Carson had told Latch that Leighton was playing a deep game of some kind against Latch. The years prove his assessment correct. When Corny, Lester Cornwall's younger brother, appears on the scene, he learns the gossip concerning Leighton and Latch, and learns of Leighton's plan to ruin his kinsman and former associate. He plans to expose Latch's involvement with Satana, and expose Estelle as a bastard. When he discovers that his papers have disappeared, he suspects Keetch has done it to save Latch. He kills the man when he refuses to disclose what he knows. Shortly thereafter, when he learns that Latch has gone to Spider Web Canyon to retrieve evidence of Estelle's parentage from the Tullt wagon, he trails him to the canyon. He captures him. Ties him up. He has sent his men to abduct Estelle and bring her there so he can reveal to her who and what her fa-

ther had been, and then strip and rape her. He has never forgotten that Latch took Cynthia Bowden from him. Leighton is killed by Slim Blue, who arrives in time to put an end to Leighton, Kennedy and Breese. Leighton is the Jim Girty (*The Spirit of the Border*) of the novel, the lowest form of villain the frontier can produce.

Leland, Allie: In *Majesty's Rancho*, one of Madge Stewart's crowd at university in Los Angeles. She is Madge's best friend, a slim, stylish girl with gray eyes, the best of the bunch, but not in looks. She reminds Madge that she has gotten herself into this predicament by her outlandish behavior. She holds little hope that her friend will not be expelled. She accompanies the crowd to the ranch for the summer, where she continues to serve as a sounding board for Madge. Allie hears Madge's confession that she is angry at Lance because he has not buckled to her will. She has finally met her match, a man who will not give her her own way. She sees that Madge is really in love with Lance and predicts more squabbles between the two before things are resolved.

Lem (Lemuel Archibald Billings): In *The Mysterious Rider*, the blacksmith on the Belllounds' ranch. He declares he will leave the ranch if Buster Jack is made foreman, but he does stay on. His handle among the cowboys is "Lemme Two Bits." He reports the incident with Pronto to Columbine, the breaking of Wilson Moore's leg and foot and the brewing trouble with Buster Jack. When Bent Wade appears at the ranch looking for work as a hunter, Lem summarizes the situation at the ranch in a few words. He plays poker with Jack, fleecing him. Later, he tells Columbine that Bent Wade had offered to be friends with Jack, to help him find himself, but Jack got enraged and wanted his father to fire Wade. Lem is present when Buster Jack accuses Wilson Moore of rustling cattle, and is present at the wedding at the end.

Leslie: In *Thunder Mountain*, one of Rand Leavitt's henchmen who helps Macabe attack Dick Sloan.

Leslie, Jim: In *Sunset Pass*, a tall rancher who is selling out and leaving Sunset Pass. He has some very good horses and Winter and Slagle suggest that Trueman Rock see him to buy a horse. He has one spectacular animal for which he is asking three hundred dollars. He has refused to sell the animal to John Dabb, who wants him for Amy, or to the Prestons, who have also expressed interest. In fact, the Preston children known the horse well, having named him "Egypt." Leslie takes a liking to Trueman and agrees to sell him the horse, confident he will be well used. He throws in a pack horse to boot. Trueman later jokes that he had to buy a spectacular horse to match the saddle he had.

Lespeth: In *Arizona Ames*, the twenty-one-year-old daughter of Jim Morgan, the Mormon horse rancher that Noggin and Steele plan to ruin by rustling the last of his herd. Lespeth's mother was a gentile, which perhaps explains her lukewarmness to Mormonism. She is the only child still with the father. She is reputed to be an unparalleled horsewoman. According to rumor, she has refused all offers of marriage to date, even one from a Mormon bishop. She falls in love with Arizona Ames, invites him to stay on as foreman of the ranch, saying that her father would surely approve of a marriage, since he thinks so highly of Arizona Ames, but Arizona is skittish about marriage.

Letith: In "The Secret of Quaking Asp Cabin," the daughter of the Apache hunter and his squaw who spend a summer in the canyon with the Starkes. She is young, beautiful, passionate. Len pursues her all summer and she has a child. She never says who the father of the child is, but from the way she looks at Len, it is no secret what the relationship between them had been. When her father decides to leave the canyon, he refuses to take the boy with them. Richard Starke decides to raise the boy as his own.

Lewis: (1) In *The Mysterious Rider*, a prospector in the mountains near the Belllounds ranch. He tries to disguise his work, but not very successfully. He is tall, with long gray hair over his shoulders. He has a bronzed, weather-beaten face, a mass of wrinkles. He has a fearless, honest spirit. He speaks well of Bill Belllounds when Bent Wade reveals where he is going. Belllounds had taken care of him when he was sick, sending Wilson Moore up to his cabin with medicine he did not have at the ranch when Lewis was there. He mentions that Wilson is sweet on Columbine, the daughter. Lewis first mentions the activity of rustlers in the vicinity. Lewis appears several times in the novel, and at one point is shot at by the rustlers.

(2) In *Rogue River Feud*, owns a ranch on the banks of the Rogue River.

(3) In *The Trail Driver*, a trail driver that Brite meets in Denman's store while Reddie is buying some women's clothing. They have a "merry" time reminiscing about trail experiences.

Lewis, Bud: In *The Man of the Forest*, one of Al Auchincloss's riders. He is a bunkmate of Tom Carmichael's and Tom reports that Bud came out openly and tried to convince him to go over to Beasley when old Al passes away. He reveals that Jeff and others from the outfit are planning to go over to Beasley. Tom leaves Bud with the impression that he will come round and join them.

Liggett: In *To the Last Man*, one of the greatest rebels the South had, according to Gaston Isbel. Gaston's brother Jean had served as scout under Liggett.

Lightfoot, Elwood: In *Shadow on the Trail*, a neighbor to Pencarrow as well as mentor and advisor to Tex Brandon. He is a lean, gray old fellow whose eyes are light blue and keen as a whip. His homestead is located in a big brake of Cedar Canyon on the west side adjoining land claimed by Aulsbrook. He interests Wade Holden (Tex Brandon),

because Pencarrow said Aulsbrook had been unable to drive or buy him off. His plot of a hundred and sixty acres is a productive little ranch watered by a sister spring to that in Cedar Canyon. Lightfoot does not raise any cattle but makes a living farming. He complains that he can't get rid of the peaches and grapes and melons and corn and other vegetables. Tons of them rot on the ground. He furnishes the Pencarrows with all they eat except beef. When Tex tells him of his plan to form a group of cowboys devoted to doing good and redeeming themselves for past banditry, giving them a sense of purpose and pride in themselves, Lightfoot suggests he approach young Hogue Kinsey. This proves to be an inspired recommendation. Brandon turns the Kinsey outlaw gang into a later version of Holly Ripple's "Knights of the Range," young men as dedicated and idealistic as King Arthur's Knights of the Round Table. Brandon continues to visit Lightfoot for advice and help. Lightfoot warns him about Harrobin and Drake, two dangerous, untrustworthy men. Lightfoot is up to date on the gossip of the range. He mentions that Aulsbrook never lost cattle when he was friendly with Drake. Neither did Discroll. When Tex Brandon has bought out Aulsbrook, ranch and stock, Lightfoot suggests that he hire some new cowboys, divide the outfit, leave Hogue Kinsey as foreman of Pencarrow's ranch, and take the remainder with him to his new ranch. Elwood Lightfoot resembles John Sprague in *To the Last Man* or Bent Wade in *The Mysterious Stranger*, men with wide experience, compassion and wisdom, who give advice and guidance to a younger man or woman.

Lightnin': In "Lightning," a black mustang stallion. A five-hundred-dollar reward has been offered for the capture of the animal. When the Stewart brothers do finally take the stallion, they decide the reward is nowhere enough for such a spectacular horse.

Liligh, Ben: In *Western Union*, the man Ed Creighton places in charge of his wagon train of construction crews. He is a wiry man, gray-faced and gray-haired, dressed in a soiled buckskin shirt, fringed and beaded. His old slouch hat is cocked to one side and he smokes a pipe. He takes on Cameron and Shaw and Darnell as part of his crew. Liligh is described by some as a "slave-driver," sharing the same enthusiasm and impatience to complete the project as his boss, Creighton. He guides the crews through an Indian attack, a buffalo stampede, and crossing the swollen Laramie River.

Lilley: In *Raiders of Spanish Peaks*, a rancher in the area who pays a visit to the Lindsays one Sunday afternoon. The Lindsay girls notice his hands, which reveal evidence of hard work. They, themselves, have soft, white hands, not stained and hardened by hard work.

Lilley, Ben: In *The Arizona Clan*, Steve's younger brother, and accomplice in stealing sorghum for Buck Hathaway. Steve confesses to his involvement and reveals that Ben has been working for Hathaway as well. Ben, however, is more firmly under Buck's control, and when Rock Lilley chastises him for stealing the sorghum and working for Hathaway, he leaves home and does not return, even for his father's burial. Things don't work out with Hathaway, however. He feels that Hathaway is cheating him out of his pay, and he threatens to reveal the location of the still as well as information about Buck's crooked deals. Snipe Twitchell then kills him in a shootout, witnessed by his brother, Elmer, who brings Ben's body home for burial.

Lilley, Denton: In *The Arizona Clan*, one of Nan Lilley's teenage brothers, younger than Steve. He goes to the Jones ranch across the valley to get someone to come stay with their mother while they pursue the Hathaway outfit.

Lilley, Elmer: In *The Arizona Clan*, goes into town to tell his brother, Ben, about their father's death, in case he had not heard. He witnesses Ben's threat to reveal the location of Buck Hathaway's still and other details of his crooked dealings. Snipe Twitchell then kills Ben in a patently uneven shootout. Elmer reports this back to Nan and Steve and Bill at the ranch. He brings Ben's body back to the house for burial.

Lilley, George: In *The Arizona Clan*, one of Nan's brothers, younger than Steve and older than the twins. He is mentioned only once in the novel.

Lilley, Little Rock: In *The Arizona Clan*, one of Nan's younger brothers. He and Rill are twins. He becomes attached to Dodge Mercer from the moment of his arrival. Little Rock is shot in Hathaway's initial attack on the Lilley home when he comes to press his claim to the place after Rock dies.

Lilley, Mrs.: In *The Arizona Clan*, mentioned by Tommy when he is recommending the Lilley place to Dodge Mercer, who inquires about ranches where he might get work as a rider. Tommy says Mrs. Lilley is a very good cook.

Lilley, Nan: In *The Arizona Clan*, Rock Lilley's oldest daughter, and the eldest of the family. She has just returned from Texas and, as Tommy tells Mercer, she's in a peck of trouble. Her father has promised her to Buck Hathaway but she hates Hathaway. She feels duty-bound to honor her father's word as he is head of the clan and his word is law. Dodge describes her as she appears the first time he sees her. She has great dark blue eyes, blankly tragic. Her face is youthful and clear-cut, with a strange and compelling beauty. Her hair is thick and clustering, of a chestnut hue where the sunlight catches gleams of gold. She is annoyed when Dodge Mercer tells her all that he has learned about her from Tommy Barnes. At first she is inclined to be sarcastic when he tells her he has come to save her, even to marry her to keep her from making the mistake of marrying Hathaway. But she does come around to reveal her troubles. Her father has cancer and can't live long.

Her brothers are drinking and idling while the family gets poorer and poorer. They owe a year's debt to Timms's store for supplies and their mother is failing. Things couldn't be much worse. Nan takes him back to the house to introduce him to the clan. Mercer feels right at home with her father, Rock, and her Uncle Bill. Nan has to admit that Dodge's arrival has changed things around the house. He seems to have a beneficial influence on Steve, getting him to quit drinking. When he confronts Buck Hathaway on Sunday afternoon, Nan finds the strength to defy Buck herself. She tells him she will never marry him — that she would prefer to die. When Rock Lilley dies, Steve refuses to hand over the ranch to Buck, but Buck has his own plans. Nan is still inclined to honor her father's word to Hathaway, but Steve, Uncle Bill and Mercer won't hear of it. Steve's Apache cowboy friend, Copeland, overhears Buck and his cohorts discussing what they want: the Quayle brothers want the best still, Twitchell wants the Lilley ranch, but Buck wants Nan. He abducts her, and plans to force her to marry him. Dodge Mercer, however, gets into the cabin where Nan and Parson Bailey are being held. The parson marries Nan and Dodge. When Buck comes to get her, she says she will marry him if he leaves her alone the first night. He has no intention of leaving her alone, and she slips out the door, jumps on a horse and gets away. When the fight is over, Nan recalls her first meeting with Dodge, when he announced that he had come especially to save her. She now calls him Sir Galahad, a knight who came to her rescue.

Lilley, Rill: In *The Arizona Clan*, Little Rock's twin brother. Like Rock, he is fond of the newcomer, Dodge Mercer.

Lilley, Rock: In *The Arizona Clan*, the head of the Lilley clan. His word is law. He has six sons and as many daughters. Not all are named. Dodge Mercer describes him as a superb, craggy-faced man of about fifty years. His visage is a remarkable one, with piercing hazel eyes, beetling high brows, high cheekbones under which his cheeks sank in, and a rugged, scantily bearded chin. His expression makes Dodge feel safe. He and his brother, Bill, had been very close, and when young men, they had both been in love with the same girl. Nan tells Dodge her father is dying of cancer, but it's the "white mule" moonshine he has been drinking that is the cause of his illness. He has gotten the family into greater debt than the value of his ranch and home. As well, he has promised Buck Hathaway his daughter in marriage. Rock is pleased when Dodge bucks Hathaway at the Sunday afternoon get-together. He even tries to give up drinking, but his health has deteriorated too far. He dies and is buried on the ranch. Hathaway expects to take possession of the place, but Steve refuses to hand over the property.

Lilley, Rose: In *The Arizona Clan*, one of Nan's younger sisters. She is mentioned only once, when Dodge Mercer is presented to the family. She helps her sister Sally serve the table.

Lilley, Sally: In *The Arizona Clan*, one of Nan's younger sisters. She helps serve the dinner and wash the dishes the first time Dodge eats with the family. She also appears at the Sunday afternoon get-together.

Lilley, Sammy: In *The Arizona Clan*, the youngest of the Lilley clan. He, like his brothers, Little Rock and Rill, is taken with Nan's new friend, Dodge. He clings to Dodge's legs when he stands on the porch on the way to dinner.

Lilley, Steve: In *The Arizona Clan*, the nineteen-year-old oldest son of the Lilley clan, a man in stature if not in years. Steve and Nan have been especially close. Steve has a sweetheart in Ryeson, Tess Williams. Dodge learns that Steve is involved with Buck Hathaway in his white mule moonshine operation. Knowing that liquor will ruin him as it has his father, Dodge hopes to make a friend of him and save his future. He offers him his friendship and his help. Steve at first is resentful, but eventually explains that he has no other way to earn money. Their father takes every dollar they earn if he hears about it. His girlfriend is run after by the boys in town and they can buy her pretty things. He is in debt at Timms's store. Unless he can find work elsewhere, he has no chance of breaking away from Hathaway. Dodge gives Steve the money to pay off his debts, and this trust works a magical transformation in the young man. Nan comments on the change in Steve. When Dodge confronts Buck Hathaway on Sunday afternoon, Steve backs him up, confessing publicly to his involvement in Hathaway's operation. He thanks Dodge for setting him straight. When their father dies, Steve is opposed to handing over the property to Hathaway, who claims he was promised the ranch by Rock in payment for his debt. Steve figures he is going to have to face Hathaway himself. Dodge teaches him to draw fast, but Nan is worried that Steve will be killed. After the campaign against the moonshine outfit, and the rescue of Nan from Hathaway's cabin, Hathaway's outfit has withdrawn to Ryeson, where people have little tolerance for shooting. Dodge tries to make Hathaway go for his gun when he confronts him in Ryan's saloon. Hathaway does not take the bait but he does face Steve outside. Steve is angry at Hathaway for having interfered in what he thinks was his responsibility. He impresses on Nan that now, as the eldest son, he is the head of the clan. Mr. Williams, Tess's father, gives them a thousand head of Texas cattle as a wedding present, to set them up in ranching. He himself intends to go into ranching as well.

Lilley, Uncle Bill: In *The Arizona Clan*, Rock's brother and best friend. Dodge says that Texas is written all over the stalwart uncle, and Dodge senses that in him he has found a friend, the salt of the earth. Bill was in Abilene last April and witnessed Dodge Mercer's shootout with Strickland. He is impressed with the man, and reports that many in Abilene spoke approvingly of the service he had pro-

vided, ridding the town of Strickland. Uncle Bill takes Dodge into his confidence early on. He explains that the white mule moonshine is the cause of his brother's illness, and that sooner or later, someone will have to confront Buck Hathaway. Rock has promised Nan to Buck, but she hates him. Killing Buck is the only solution. When Bill backs up Dodge's challenge during Buck's Sunday afternoon visit, Buck tries to get Rock to send his brother away. Rock, however, proves his loyalty to his devoted brother. Bill warns Dodge that now he will have to be careful, as Hathaway or his partner, Twitchell, will likely try to shoot him from an ambush. Bill and Steve find Dodge in the canyon, ambushed by Twitchell just as predicted. They find one still and destroy it. This is the first battle in the campaign against Hathaway. After the big shootout at the hunting cabin, Uncle Bill reports that Parson Bailey informed Buck Hathaway that he had married Nan Lilley and Dodge Mercer, thwarting Buck's plans to force her to marry him.

Lily: In *The Lost Wagon Train*, a habitué of the Palace of Chance in Dodge. She is a young, pretty, brazen, wild-eyed girl. Her sleeveless gown is cut extremely décolleté, giving her an alluring charm. She tries to get Lester Cornwall interested in her, but he brushes her off to continue with his cards. She persists in her efforts to get him to notice her and when he calls her a lousy slut, she takes a gun and shoots him in the head.

Lindbergh, Charles: In *Boulder Dam*, mentioned by Lynn Weston as an example of the unlimited possibilities of the mind, of the heroic spirituality in man, of whatever else nature (evolution) intends for the future of humanity.

Lincoln: In *Sunset Pass*, one of the big ranchers around Wagontongue. He is an old cowboy, true grain, and Trueman Rock trusts him. He meets with Dabb and Rock to arrange a deal to resolve the Preston rustling-slaughterhouse business. He does a bit of arm twisting to ensure that Nesbitt joins in. The night of the dinner at Dabbs, Lincoln joins Rock and Dabb in a card game with "big stakes."

Lincoln, Brad: In *Robbers' Roost*, someone to look at twice—a swarthy, dark, restless-eyed man with nothing of the cowboy stripe in his makeup. Lincoln questions Jim Wall about where he is from, if he is on the run, and if he is a gunfighter, as he recognizes "the brand" in him. Hays says Brad Lincoln is curious and blunt and jealous of Jim Wall, suspecting he is a quicker draw than he himself. He is not a skilled card player, losing more than he wins. Lincoln suspects something amiss in Hays's deal with Herrick. It strikes him as bizarre that someone like Herrick would hire men like himself and Hays to ride for him. When they discuss Heeseman's outfit as an obstacle to their plan, Brad Lincoln proposes killing Heeseman and all his men as the surest way to eliminate the problem. When the outfit are hiding out in the Robbers' Roost, Lincoln's irascible temper and weakness for cards leads to a fight with Hays in which he is shot and killed. His death marks the beginning of the disintegration of the outfit in Robbers' Roost.

Linden: In *The Fugitive Trail*, sold cattle to Barncastle and agreed to drive the herd to Melrose's ranch. Melrose is angry because Barncastle has not paid him he money he owes and has not delivered the herd he bought.

Lindsay: (1) In *The Mysterious Rider*, a stockman from Grand Lake who comes to Belllounds' White Slides Ranch with Sheriff Burley to confront Wilson Moore.

(2) In *West of the Pecos*, a trail driver that Jerry Brice met who reports to him on what has happened to Don Felipe. Lindsay has a ranch on the San Saba, in the country where Templeton Lambeth was advised to set up ranching.

Lindsay, Flo(rence): In *Raiders of Spanish Peaks*, the nineteen-year-old second daughter of the Lindsays. A dazzlingly pretty blond with dark, dreamy, thoughtful eyes, she had been the most sought-after girl back in Sandusky. She wonders about her possibilities of finding a suitable husband out west. She is taken from the start with Ted "Tracks" Williams, with whom she elopes a few months after arriving at the ranch. Mr. Lindsay pretends disapproval at first, but is actually quite pleased. She married Ted before learning that he has reconciled with his parents, who have decided to come to Colorado to stake him in a ranch and stock as a wedding present. Harriet is impressed with how quickly Flo has matured at Spanish Peaks.

Lindsay, Harriet (Hallie): In *Raiders of Spanish Peaks*, the twenty-five-year-old and oldest daughter of the Lindsays. She has been her father's right-hand man, serving as bookkeeper for the store back in Sandusky. Her experience there has prepared her well for her job as ranch manager at Spanish Peaks. She disapproves of the speed with which her father negotiated the deal with Arlidge and Allen. She cannot pin Allen down to a specific count of the cattle on the ranch, and her gut feeling is that neither Allen nor Arlidge is to be trusted. On the ranch, she assigns the task of dealing with the men to Laramie Nelson, a man to whom she feels attracted, but who frightens her a bit. She is cautious about revealing her emotions because of an unhappy romance with Tom Emery, a clerk in her father's store of whom he did not approve. Hallie is like Jane Withersteen in *Riders of the Purple Sage* in her opposition to guns and to violence and in her ability to draw strength from nature. Hallie falls in love with the rugged environment, which inspires her with new energy and hope. And like Jane, who tries to shackle the gunman Lassiter who is trying to protect her, she forbids Laramie to use violence or guns to combat the rustlers that have brought the ranch to near ruin. Eventually, she does come to see that the eastern pacifist norms cannot work here. Harriet resents

the truths about herself that Lenta points out. Lenta tells her she has made little effort to adapt to her new life. She is standoffish, not getting to know the cowboys on the ranch, remaining aloof and distant in her office or the house. She fights off Laramie Nelson, who carries her to the house when she has been thrown by a horse. So independent is she that she refuses to see that he is clearly in love with her. She knows precious little about what is going on around her. Hallie tries to change. She teaches herself to ride horses in secret. She talks to the cowboys, trying to get to know them. And when matters have been resolved, she finally confesses her love for Laramie and asks him to stay on as her husband.

Lindsay, Lenta: In *Raiders of Spanish Peaks*, the youngest of Lindsay's three daughters. She is quite the handful. Her sister Hallie comments that there is a mean streak in Lenta than can be very destructive. Lenta declares that in Colorado, she is going to give her sister Flo a run for her money with the cowboys. Back in Sandusky, her time had been taken up by school and friends, but out west, things would be very different. Of the three girls, Lenta adapts the most quickly, showing the greatest enthusiasm for the new life. She predicts that their father's health will improve and he will be rich and powerful on the range. Spanish Peaks will become famous and their mother will be a celebrated hostess as she had been in Ohio. Flo will marry Ted Williams and his wealthy family will reconcile with him. Ted will accept their money, but remain out west and return east for occasional visits. And she will "play the merry devil with these gawky range-riders until retribution overtakes me and I am scared stiff or stung by remorse for my heartbreaking ways — or I fall really in love with some homely bow-legged vociferous little giant." Her flippant comment proves true. Lenta is another Georgie Traft from *The Hash Knife Outfit* or Georgiana Stockwell from *Code of the West*. She flirts shamelessly, exciting all the cowboys, provoking jealousy and fights. She gets to know the cowboys better than her manager sister, or the foreman Laramie. She claims she flirts with them to find out what they are thinking and where their allegiances lie. Hallie is genuinely impressed with her knowledge of the cowboys and her perspicacity where their allegiances are concerned. Lenta, however, makes hurtful observations about how little Hallie knows about the people she is in charge of, and how repressed she is about her feelings for Laramie Nelson. Lenta's behavior outrages her father, who confines her to a room with iron bars on the windows. She convinces her latest beau, Lin Stuart, to get her out, but this caper leads to her capture by Chess Gaines. The confinement reveals her stamina, her courage, her determination, and above all, her fearlessness. She challenges Gaines, calling him a second-rate rustler. She taunts him by revealing how easily she has read his plans, and how much she has been able to trick his men into revealing to her their rustling operation and Allen's role in selling the stolen cattle under his brand. Lenta is finally reconciled with Lonesome Mulhall, the ugly, bow-legged, passionate cowboy who first proposed marriage to her.

Lindsay, Mr. John: In *Raiders of Spanish Peaks,* from Upper Sandusky, Ohio. He is head of the family, an iron gray-haired man of fifty years and of fine appearance except for an extreme pallor which indicated a tubercular condition. He has always wanted to move west and has always had a secret longing to be a rancher. He is caught up in the romance of the West. He has come to Colorado for his health with his wife and three daughters and a son. Buffalo Jones says he has the true pioneer spirit that new arrivals from the East require. He has purchased a ranch with stock from a man called Allen without seeing the place or confirming the count of stock. Buffalo Jones does not think this a very wise move. On Buffalo Jones's advice, he hires Laramie Nelson as foreman of his wagon train and ranch. Lindsay was too trusting to keep Arlidge on as manager. He does come to realize he has been duped by Lester Allen and Arlidge, but he is prepared to make the best of things. His daughter, who had managed his general merchandise store in Sandusky, will be his financial manager here too. She tries to nail Allen down to specific figures for the cattle, but he does not oblige. Harriet tells her father that she mistrusts Allen. She thinks her father has been seriously cheated. Mr. Lindsay provides the funds to buy wagons and supplies and furniture for the new ranch. He suffers considerably from the trip, and at times, Mrs. Lindsay is not sure he will make it. Within a few months, his health has vastly improved. He is able to split wood and do a day's work outdoors. He remains largely aloof from the operation of Spanish Peaks ranch. His daughter Harriet is still in charge, although he thinks she is wrong to try to apply eastern standards to dealing with the cowboys and the rustlers. Lindsay is equally aloof from the doings of his family. He lets his wife take charge of fixing up the house. He allows his son, Neale, to wander about as he pleases, satisfied that Neale is struck with hero-worship for Laramie, whom both parents consider a good influence on the boy. He is surprised when Flo elopes with Ted Williams. He has not completely abandoned eastern norms in the selection of a husband for his daughter. Although he knows this kind of romance is inevitable, and he is quite taken with Ted "Tracks" Williams, he pretends annoyance with Flo to make her regret not having spoken to him before eloping. When Strickland arrives asking Lindsay to join in the Cattlemen's Protective Association, Lindsay points to his daughter as the one with whom he should be holding discussions. When Allen and the rustlers have been dealt with, Lenta rescued, and Flo and Ted reconciled with them, he encourages Harriet to marry Laramie and keep him on as foreman.

Lindsay, Mrs.:   In *Raiders of Spanish Peaks,* the wife of John Lindsay. They have come west because of Neale's weak lungs. Mrs. Lindsay attempts to do cooking on the trek to the ranch, but surrenders the position to Jud Lawrence, who proves to be every bit as good a cook as she herself is. Mrs. Lindsay is described as wide-eyed, motherly, easily taken in by Lonesome's sad-sob fictional description of his youth. Like her husband, she is disappointed with the state of the ranch they have purchased, but like him, she has the drive to make a success of it. Mrs. Lindsay has great confidence in Laramie Nelson. She tells Harriet that Laramie will cure her father and make a man out of her brother. According to Lenta, the ranch will be a big success and her mother can go back to playing the elegant hostess, as she did in Sandusky.

Lindsay, Neale: In *Raiders of Spanish Peaks,* the eighteen-year-old son of John Lindsay, a rather foppish youth. The sisters think of the embarrassing incidents they have had to suffer because of this spoiled, only son. Mr. Lindsay thinks that the raw West will make a man of him. Neale reports to the family at breakfast one morning that they are the laughingstock of the Garden City. They're a bunch of rich tenderfeet who got properly fleeced by Allen in the land deal. Neale gets into a fight with Lonesome at a pool hall, according to Lonesome, over Lonesome's winking at a girl Neale was talking to. His pale face is marred by a darkly swollen eye when he is introduced to Laramie Nelson by his father. Laramie assigns Neale to drive one of the wagons to Spanish Peaks. Laramie sees potential in young Neale. The West will make or break him. Neale, meanwhile, is impressed with Laramie Nelson. At the ranch, Neale amazes them all by his undeveloped ability to stick to hard work, although he has outraged his mother by his drinking and fighting. Harriet suspects that Neale is not all to blame for this, as the cowboys have an itch to play tricks on tenderfeet. Lonesome is one of the worst about such pranks, and Neale and he fail to hit it off. He is shot by Luke Arlidge in the skirmishes accompanying Lenta's abduction and the pursuit of the rustlers.

Linton, Ed: In *The Light of Western Stars,* the cowboy whose bachelor party is being held the night that Madeline Hammond arrives in El Cajón. Gene Stewart is at the party, gets drunk, and bets he'll marry the first pretty woman he meets. Ed Linton appears on several occasions in the story. He is a short, stocky cowboy, who was once quite a lady's man. His wife is extremely jealous and keeps him under close watch. The other cowboys like to tease him about being henpecked, but Ed and the wife seem to get along well enough. He is one of the cowboys playing in the golf game that is organized to entertain Castleton and Harvey.

Linwood, Genie: In *Wanderer of the Wasteland,* first seen when Wansfell (Adam Larey) rescues her from the men who have kidnapped her. She tells him that her mother is alone and sick with consumption and needs supplies. Genie is fourteen years old.

Her mother had been a schoolteacher and has taught her to read and write. Her father died in the desert, looking for gold. She herself was born in Kansas on a prairie schooner as they were going west looking for a more healthy climate. Both parents had consumption and their health improved in the dry desert air. The father's brother, Ed, also comes west looking for gold. Genie's father joins him in his venture and goes crazy looking for gold, killing himself with work. He did find substantial amounts of gold which they have kept hidden under the floor of the cabin. The robbers did not find it when they took Genie. When Mrs. Linwood dies, she asks Adam to take care of her daughter. The two of them become good friends and their conversations touch on a number of topics that Wansfell has been pondering during his wanderings in the desert. Genie finds little love in Indian marriages. The chief selects wives from the tribe, warriors buy wives. Mating is purely for purposes of reproduction without love. She cannot understand this way of things. She has faith in God all around her; she sees order and purpose in the universe, not a competition of various forces. She grows into quite a young lady and Adam feels attracted to her. He takes her to Santa Ysabel and soon finds a family, the Blairs, who receive them very kindly and eventually agree to take Genie Linwood in. At first, Genie is a bit skittish, but comes to like the family and looks forward to her new home. The Blair's oldest son, Gene, is sweet on her. Adam Larey uses some of Genie's gold to buy land adjacent to the Blairs' ten acres. This gift will make possible Gene Blair's dream of setting up a horse and cattle ranch. It will also give Genie a solid financial basis for the future. In *Stairs of Sand,* Ruth Virey recalls her friend Genie, her marriage to Gene Blair, but especially her stories about the Indian God, Taquitch, the god of the mountain. She also recalls her story about how her mother had prayed to God for help and Adam Larey arrived just in time to take care of Genie when she passed away.

Linwood, Mrs.:   In *Wanderer of the Wasteland,* Genie Linwood's mother. The woman is in poor health when Wansfell (Adam Larey) finds her in the shack. Despite her sorry condition, she is optimistic about life. She understands Adam's struggle to come to terms with the contradictions of life, the struggle to survive in the desert, and the seeming conflict between these blind forces and the concept of a providential being looking out for mankind. She points out that his arrival in time to take care of her daughter is proof of God's guiding hand. She asks Adam to look after Genie when she is gone, and gives him the gold that her father had dug and kept hidden under the floor of the cabin. She entrusts him with her future, never doubting that he is a good man and will keep his word. She tells him that the little voice he hears in himself, his conscience, is God. She is one of a series of people Wansfell meets who point his search for God in the right direction. Mrs. Linwood dies and is buried near her cabin in the desert.

Linwood, Uncle Ed: In *Wanderer of the Wasteland,* Eugenia Linwood's uncle. He went prospecting for gold and never returned. Genie says he was kind to her, but when she told her mother that he sometimes put his hands on her, Mrs. Linwood told her to stay out of his way when he was drunk. Adam later comes across his bones in the desert.

Little, Bill: In *The Deer Stalker,* the cook with Nels Stackhouse and Tine Higgenbottom when they take Patricia Clay and Sue Warren on a camping trip up to the North Rim of the Grand Canyon.

Little Girl Gold: In *Wild Horse Mesa,* the nickname Chess Weymer gives Sue Melberne.

Little, Jeff: In *Wyoming,* a cattleman who spoke highly of Tex when Sheriff Slade suggested he was involved in rustling. Andy Bonning meets him at the rodeo. He tells Andy he runs forty thousand head of cattle and that the ranching business is good.

Little, Judge: In *The Lone Star Ranger,* of El Paso, Texas, mentioned as an example of a well-known judge. No further information is given about him.

Little, Lawyer: In *30,000 on the Hoof,* a lawyer and cattle baron around Flagg. Mr. Little tries to help Logan Huett get the money that Mitchell and Caddell have swindled from him in the sale of the thirty-one thousand head of cattle to the army. He cables ahead to Holbrook to have Mitchell taken from the train until the matter can be investigated. He has had reason to suspect that Mitchell's dealings are dishonest. Charteris, who has done some of his banking, has told him that Mitchell pays a certain amount for cattle, but then pads the report on the transactions that he sends the government. Little calls him a slick operator. He asks Huett why he had insisted on cash. Huett had been willing to sell cattle to Charteris, but he did not have enough cash on hand to pay, while Mitchell claimed that he did. Little is energetic and persistent in his efforts to get some court action. He goes to Prescott, the capital, in Huett's interest, and finally gets the state congressman in Washington to take up the case. When Huett decides to go to Washington, he gives him the name of the state senator and other people he might visit to request help. He does not hold out too much hope, however, as there is so much corruption and confusion due to the war that his hundred thousand dollars is small potatoes.

Little, Rolly: In *The Trail Driver,* small and round with yellow hair, a freckled face and flashing brown eyes as sharp as daggers. He survives the stampedes, the rustling, and the Comanche attack, and remains in Dodge when Adam Brite, Pan Handle Smith, Reddie and Texas Joe take the stage to Abilene and San Antonio.

Little Wood Mouse: In *The Hash Knife Outfit,* the affectionate term by which Jed Stone refers to Molly Dunn, Jim Traft's fiancée, whom he has known since childhood.

Lo Blandy *see* **Blandy, Lo.**

Locke, Ring: In *The Drift Fence*, Uncle Jim Traft's right-hand man on the Diamond Ranch. He has been with him for twenty years. He is a man of few words, not given to gossip, a man who watches and observes more than he talks. He is eminently fair and just. He is a tall, sandy-complexioned man whose narrow eyes are almost hidden beneath an old black sombrero. He scrutinizes the young nephew who is pleased to have passed inspection. He says it's not such a bad thing being a tenderfoot as long as one knows it. Young Jim Traft takes a liking to him from the start. He warns Jim that he will likely take a licking at the hands of some of the cowboys but that it will not be for keeps. Jim follows Locke around like a puppy dog, but he discovers that Locke remains kind and aloof. He answers his questions but never offers any range lore or gossip. Jim figures out, however, that Locke has been keeping a keen eye on him and he has met with his approval. When Uncle Jim disapproves of how Jim handled his first encounter with Hack Jocelyn in Flag, Ring Locke says things may work out just fine. When Hack Jocelyn arrives at the camp where Jim is being held captive, he recalls what Ring Locke had said about Jocelyn, that he was one of the breed of far-riding cowboys, outlawed from many ranges, and a dangerous man. Ring's predictions are completely accurate.

In *The Hash Knife Outfit*, Ring Locke still works for old Jim Traft on the Diamond Ranch. He is Traft's right-hand man and confidante and Old Jim often calls on him for advice. Jed Stone of the Hash Knife Outfit tells his men there is no slicker cowman on the range than Ring Locke. He reports to his boss that Bambridge is shipping cattle, rustled cattle most probably, from Winslow. He advises against old Jim Traft going to check up on this as he would surely get shot. He suggests young Jim go as he is not known to the Hash Knife Outfit as yet and could get a good look at the cattle without arousing suspicion. He is pleased to hear about Curly Prentiss exposing Bambridge as a cheat and rustler in the card game at Snell's.

Lockheart, Barse: In *The Fugitive Trail*, Bruce Lockheart's brother. He first appears in a card game in Hennesy's, with Bolton and Henderson. He is trying hard, sweating freely, but getting trimmed. He is in his twenties, soft of face and hands, obviously not a horseman, and from the way he played, not much of a gambler. His brother Bruce comes to get him away from the game, but this leads to a gunfight in which Henderson and another man are shot. Trinity Spencer was in love with him once. Mr. Spencer recalls how there was a time not long ago when Barse was a good boy. But he changed as Denison changed, with money, cattle, and the railroad. He fell in with Quade Belton's crowd and went to the bad. Bruce and Trinity have been hoping for Mrs. Lockheart's sake that he will come to his senses before it is too late. Mrs. Lockheart had always liked Barse best because he was weaker and needed more attention.

Eager to find out what Barse is up to, Trinity rides out, following Barse and the riders he was with. She comes upon them, masked, wearing black hats. They are discussing the robbery in Denison, dividing the take. Bruce catches up with Barse and tries to talk some sense into him. None of the witnesses is sure which of the Lockheart brothers was in on the robbery. He proposes changing clothes with Barse, and running off with the money. He tells Barse that Trinity loves him, and that he should marry her. Bruce rides off. Barse goes into town, making sure he is seen, thereby convincing people he has nothing to hide. The following morning, he speaks with Trinity. He tells Trinity, who already knows the truth, that Bruce was in on the bank robbery, that he had fooled everyone with his preaching and trying to reform him. Shooting Henderson and the cardsharp, Whistler, was just part of his plan. Unfortunately, Mrs. Perry recognized him. Trinity is disgusted with Barse. She screams at him that he is a liar, that he let his brother take the blame for his crime and that she loves Bruce, not him. When Trinity has gone on the trail to find Bruce, Barse resorts to his old ways, drinking and gambling. By the time Trinity catches up with Bruce, Barse has been killed in a fight over a card game.

Lockheart, Bruce: In *The Fugitive Trail*, a dead ringer for his brother Barse, except that he is tough, hard and serious, with a reputation as a buffalo hunter, trail driver and gunman. He feels protective of his brother, who has gotten involved with Quade Belton and Steve Henderson. Bruce tries to get him away from them, to break the hold they have on him, but to no avail. When Simmons says he recognized one of the Lockheart brothers as the youngest of the holdup men, Bruce takes Barse's share of the money and rides off, hoping that this way he can get his brother to straighten out. He tells him to marry Trinity, and she will help him change. Lockheart then leaves for Texas. He joins up with Hank Silverman, trail driver, and spends several weeks with the crew. Silverman, however, guesses who he really is, and when his men report that in Couchos, Tom Galliard was heard telling people he had recognized Bruce Lockheart, Hank advises him to ride west. Lockheart, however, rides into town and faces Galliard in a shootout. He then rides farther west, into the brakes of the Llano Estacado.

Captain Maggard of the Texas Rangers is hot in pursuit of Lockheart. His policy is to "ride the man down"—never to give up pursuit. At Doan's, he and Luke Loveless make a bet about Lockheart. Maggard bets he will have caught him within the year, while Loveless, an old trail driver for whom Bruce had worked, tells Maggard he doesn't know Lockheart. It is Loveless's opinion that Lockheart is as honest as the day is long. He bets that when the truth comes out, it will be proven that Bruce had nothing to do with the Denison bank holdup.

Using the name Lee Jones, Bruce joins up with Tex Serks—Texas trail boss, cowboy, gunman—and his brother Jim, and a Mexican, Juan Vasquez, and the homely Peg Simpson. They are heading to the Brazos country following a call from ranchers there for Texas cowboys. They appear at the Melrose ranch and get work as cowboys. Luke Slaughter gives Bruce a good look-over, as he is not an ordinary cowboy. He tells Bruce there is more to him than meets the eye, but he likes what he sees. Bruce, though, remains mum about his past. Shortly after his arrival, he meets Trinity who explains that Steve Melrose is her real father. She also brings him up to date on his mother's moving in with the Spencers and the death of Barse in a gunfight over a card game. She shares his concern over the rangers in pursuit, but, as none of them have ever seen Bruce in the flesh, he is probably safe for a while. When Sgt. Blight appears at the ranch, she warns Bruce of his arrival, then introduces him to Blight as her fiancé. This brings Melrose to cross-examine Bruce about his past. He tells his father-in-law-to-be that there are things about him that he is not free to reveal at present, but that he is a man to be trusted. Melrose takes him at his word.

Melrose's ranch has been experiencing a plague of rustling. Bill Stewart and Vic Henderson are the men organizing the raids on his herds and the shooting of his riders. These two men are involved with one Barncastle, who, it turns out, is Quade Belton, whom Lockheart had shot in Mendle, leaving him for dead. Seever's wagon train passes by the ranch and one of the men, Clark, recognizes Lee Jones (Bruce) as the man he saw shoot Belton and Whistler in Mendle. Sergeant Blight of the Texas Rangers is there at the time. Melrose convinces the man that he must be mistaken, as the man he called Lockheart is his daughter's fiancé, Lee Jones. When Tex tells him it was a close call, he realizes that his Texas partner had guessed his secret and had been discreet about his knowledge.

Barncastle (Belton) owes Mendle money from a previous deal in Dodge, and has failed to deliver a herd of cattle bought in a more recent transaction. When Stewart shows up, he threatens Melrose with the loss of his herd, his money and what remains of his ranch. Lockheart sees that Melrose has become involved with some pretty crooked dealers. He warns him of their dishonesty and urges his boss to take action against them. Eventually, Melrose persuades the Texas Rangers to help with the job. Stewart kills Barncastle, and in the gunfight, he identifies himself as Bruce Lockheart. Trinity thinks that Bruce is safe now, as people will think that Stewart is Lockheart. Bruce and Tex and the cowboys pursue Stewart and his rustlers, eventually cornering them in a cabin where they put up a fight. Stewart himself is not there for the start of the fight, but arrives as the cabin is burning. Bruce and Stewart shoot it out and Stewart is killed. Maggard thinks it was a clever trick to pretend to be Bruce Lockheart to draw Stewart out. He still believes that Stewart is Lockheart.

With the Texas Rangers content in their belief that they have resolved the issue of the Denison robbery,

Trinity and Bruce are free to marry, without worry of pursuit by the law. Lockheart, however, refuses to live under a false name and confesses to Maggard. He then leaves, expecting to be pursued. He is pursued, but not by the rangers. When Trinity catches up to him, she tells him he left too soon. Maggard had decided that Lockheart had squared himself with the law, and he would let the matter rest.

Grey develops the character of Bruce Lockheart along the lines of Nevada, Buck Duane and Laramie Nelson, a "good" bad man who puts his life on the line to help others and redeems himself in the process.

Lockheart, Mrs.: In *The Fugitive Trail*, the mother of Bruce and Barse. Barse has always been her favorite. Bruce does what he can to keep the truth about him from her, even taking the blame for involvement in the Denison bank holdup. After Barse is killed, she goes to live with the Spencers. Trinity reports to Bruce when she catches up with him that her health is failing but that the Spencers are taking good care of her.

Logan: A Mingo chief, friend of whites, who has smoked many a pipe of peace with Colonel Zane at his cabin in Ft. Henry. In *Betty Zane*, the story is told how Logan and his people in a Delaware village were killed to the last man, woman and child by Colonel Cresop.

Lodge, General: In *The U. P. Trail*, the chief engineer of the corps. In part, the construction of the transcontinental railroad is due to his vision and persistence in lobbying Congress and businessmen. He is put in charge of the army assigned to protect the workers from Indian attacks and to maintain law and order in the rowdy camp cities like Benton and Roaring City that grow up along the way. General Lodge sees great potential in Warren Neale, the young engineer he assigns to solve tough problems. He expects that some day the young man will hold a position of great importance and influence in Union Pacific Railroad Company. After Neale has seemingly closed all doors when he exposes fraud and accuses certain railroad commissioners of lying and cheating to make more money for themselves, Lodge sends him a letter asking him to return. Neale goes to visit the general and is told that the completion of a bridge is holding up the completion of the railroad. Lodge gives Neale the power to hire and fire whomever he needs to get the job done. He is pleased with the results that Neale achieves. Acting on the information Neale has acquired from the engineers Blake and Coffee, General Lodge takes action to expose the fraud committed by Allison Lee and Senator Dunn. On Lodge's recommendation, the board of the railroad bans him from any further contracts on the railroad. General Lodge is given the book found on Casey, the man sent to warn him of an impending Sioux attack. He starts to read the letter from Beauty Stanton to Neale, and stops when he realizes how personal it is. He ensures that the letter gets to Neale. Throughout the novel, General Lodge tells Neale he must make use of his gifts. Thanks to the general's support, Neale is present when the last spike is driven, completing the dream he, like Neale, had for the country. General Lodge combines vision with power and integrity, a rare man in the world of government depicted in *The U. P. Trail.*

Logan, Cy: In *Stranger from the Tonto*, the squaw man who runs a trading post. An old Navajo gives Kent Wingfield directions to the place. When Kent arrives riding Spades, Logan recognizes the horse and tells him that no man who ever owned that horse could sleep in peace. He suggests Kent leave the horse at his camp because there are men inside who will recognize him. Logan tells Kent he can pay for the grain the horse will eat, but not for his own board. At table, he witnesses Slotte's rude and indecent behavior with Logan's daughter and calls him on it, thereby earning Logan's friendship and loyalty. Later, Neberyull learns from Tobiki that Wingfield rode in on Spades and that Logan spoke to Winfield, after which he rode the horse out to his camp and walked back. Slotte challenges Logan, who replies that the horse looked somewhat like Spades. Wingfield then tells Slotte how he came to buy the horse. A fight breaks out, with lots of shooting. Slotte is stunned, Neberyull killed. Winfield apologizes for the trouble and tells Logan about his prospecting with Elway. Logan knew Bill Elway and calls him the whitest man in the Hole-in-the-Wall outfit. He gives Kent directions to get to Segi, where he will start his trek into canyon country.

Logan, Sheriff: In *Boulder Dam,* meets Lynn Weston after his fight with Bat Hevron and Ben Sneed in the Monte Palace. Logan advises him to go back to Boulder City and stay there. Hevron is a gangster from Chicago and a dangerous man. Ben Sneed, on the other hand, although a bootlegger, is basically an honest man. Logan deplores the arrival of gangsters from around the country in Las Vegas since the beginning of the Boulder Dam project. Sheriff Logan, a former Texas Ranger, is a cousin of Whitney Curtis's, and Curtis suggests that Lynn Weston go to him about the men plotting to sabotage the construction of the dam. Lynn goes to see him about the kidnapping of his fiancée, Anne, but Logan cannot act against Ben Bellew without more concrete proof. Logan takes Anne to a safe place after the fight at Vitte's place. He brings her and a minister to see Lynn in the hospital, where they are wed. Logan comments that he would make a great Texas Ranger, with the courage and gunmanship of a Cole Younger or a Buck Duane.

Lone Wolf: In *The Lost Wagon Train*, a gunman in Latch's outlaw gang. He and Texas from the start are itching to find out who is faster. He is one of the few who is not injured at all in the attack on Anderson's caravan, but in the dispute which follows the discovery of Cynthia Bowden in Tullt's wagon, hidden away by Leighton, he and Texas have a shootout in which he is killed.

Lone Wolf, Chief: In *Fighting Caravans*, a Ute chief who promises to bring down all his tribe's furs and pelts and buffalo robes in April to trade with Couch and Clint Belmet. He is a superb warrior, friendly to the whites and dignified. He is introduced to May Bell at Maxwell's ranch, where he proposes marriage to her. Maxwell explains to May Bell that the chief was only speaking in fun, but the compliment was sincere. Maxwell calls him the "salt of the earth."

Longstreth, Colonel Granger: In *The Lone Star Ranger,* the mayor of Fairdale and father of Ray Longstreth. He is from Louisiana, of French aristocratic extraction. Buck Duane first sees him in conversation with Lawson after he has gotten off the stage. Later, he comes into the inn, where a robbery is in progress. From the reactions of Bill and the unnamed robber to Longstreth, Buck Duane concludes that the men know each other. Longstreth's ranch is a few minutes' walk from town, and the robber, Bo Snecker, takes refuge there when the ranger is pursuing him. In court, Longstreth gives instructions to the judge to release Snecker. He further adds that he recognizes no ranger jurisdiction in his part of Texas. Slowly, Buck Duane comes to learn the scope of his influence — ranching, gambling, robbery, corruption — in a conversation he overhears one evening between Longstreth and Lawson. He has followed Lawson to Longstreth's home, and finds a spot between two adobe walls where he can see into the living room and overhear the conversation. No doubt remains that Longstreth is Cheseldine. He accuses Lawson of having gone too far with his rustling and killings. Longstreth argues that evil sooner or later will meet its nemesis. He feels that their time has come and he plans to organize one last operation, stealing the gold from the Rancher's Bank of Val Verde, and then leaving for Louisiana. He warns against taking on the ranger. Longstreth develops a mistrust for Lawson and resists his demands that Ray marry him. Longstreth is relieved when Buck Duane kills Lawson in a gunfight. He willingly submits to arrest, and the terms the ranger imposes on him. He will be stripped of all his property which will be disposed of and divided up among his victims. Also, he will go with the rangers to Val Verde to help entrap the remaining members of the gang. Longstreth submits, on condition that his daughter not learn who he was, although she has already reached that conclusion on her own. Longstreth will be allowed to return to Louisiana, where his reputation will not likely interfere with his starting a new life. Buck Duane explains to Ray how her father came to be an outlaw:

> The line between a rustler and a rancher is hard to draw in these wild border days. Rustling is stealing cattle, and I once heard a well-known rancher say that all rich cattlemen had done a little stealing. Your father drifted out here, and like a good many others, he succeeded. Some way or other, he drifted in with bad men. Maybe a deal

that was honest somehow tied his hands. This matter of land, water, a few stray head of stock had to be decided out of court. I'm sure in his case he never realized where he was drifting. Then one thing led to another, until he was face to face with dealing that took on crooked form. To protect himself, he bound men to him. And so the gang developed. Many powerful gangs have developed that way out here. He could not control them. He become involved with them, and eventually their dealings became deliberately and boldly dishonest. That meant the inevitable spilling of blood sooner or later and so he grew into the leader because he was the strongest.

Longstreth, Ray: In *The Lone Star Ranger,* the daughter of Colonel Granger Longstreth. She comes west on the stage to meet her father, bringing with her her cousin Ruth. She is quiet, melancholy, and doesn't resemble her father very much. Buck Duane describes her as having jet black hair, a chiseled oval face, olive-tinted skin, long eyes, wide apart and black as coal, with a slender, straight nose. She reminds him of a thoroughbred horse. He guesses that she is descended from one of the old French families of eastern Texas. (Later he learns her family is from Louisiana) She comports herself with pride and passion. She behaves courageously when the robber holds her at gunpoint in the inn. She is a figure of contradictions, haughty and aloof, kind and loving. She holds herself apart from Lawson and the other men, but when she learns that Mrs. Laramie is on hard times, she herself comes to lend her a hand. When Mrs. Laramie tells her that Ranger Duane has been supporting her and her five children since her husband was killed, Ray apologizes to Buck for believing the lies spread about him. She admits to Buck that she suspects her father is corrupt. When the adobe wall from behind which Buck has been eavesdropping collapses, she hides Buck in her room until her father and Lawson have given up the chase. Ray is in love with Buck, and she tries to prevent him from getting into a gunfight at the bank in Val Verde. After the Cheseldine gang is finished off, she accompanies him back to Wellston, and nurses Buck back to health. They plan to marry and move to Louisiana where they can live on the family plantation and begin a new life.

Loorey: In *The Spirit of the Border,* the drunken frontiersman that Silvertip attacks thinking he has stolen his shirt. Joe Downs confesses that he switched the shirts, thereby saving Loorey's scalp.

Lopez: (1) In *The Lost Wagon Train,* one of Latch's Mexican hands. He brings fresh clothes and other personal items to Estelle at the Bradley's ranch.

(2) In "The Ranger," a bandit that Ranger Medill has killed. Lopez was a friend of Quinela who concocts the abduction of Roseta to lure Medill across the border to even the score for the killing.

Lord Chester: In *Wilderness Trek,* one of Leslie Slyter's prize thoroughbred horses who successfully make the trek across Australia from Queensland to the Kimberleys in western Australia.

Lopez, Don: In *The Shepherd of Guadaloupe,* an old Mexican sheep rancher who hires Cliff Forrest as a shepherd. He sells his three thousand sheep to Virginia, who is anxious to prevent Malpass from acquiring the flock.

Lord, Garry (also spelled Gary): In *Rogue River Feud,* an old fishing buddy of Keven Bell's. When Keven returns from the army hospital in Washington, he meets Garry down at their old fishing hole. He has a leathery, weather-beaten face, homely and hard, unshaven and dirty, yet despite these features the unmistakable imprint of the bottle, somehow, far from revolting. Garry has bought a new fishing boat from Mr. Bell and Keven proposes the two of them form a partnership and take up commercial fishing. Garry warns Keven that he has a bad name. He is thought of as lazy, no-good, rum-guzzling. It would ruin Keven to be associated with him. Keven, however, has always liked him and is willing to give it a whirl. Garry is an expert fisherman, and the two of them make a good haul with the first salmon run. Garry, however, cannot resist drink and when he has money, spends it on liquor. At one point he wins a pot in a card game at the Sock-Eye, and surprisingly entrusts it to Keven because he knows he'll just drink it. Their success inspires envy, and Mulligan and his thugs organize a cartel, making it impossible for them to sell their fish. Their nets are destroyed with sulphuric acid. During a storm, Keven kills Mulligan when he is beating Garry Lord. Keven thinks Garry has been killed and is sure he will be charged with the murder of Mulligan. He retreats into the mountains. When he finally returns a year or more later, there is Garry, alive and better than ever. He was rescued by Mary Coombs, whom he marries. He clears Keven's name, and with Sheriff Blackwood, has caught the crooked fishermen using illegal nets. Garry now runs a fish store in Grant's Pass and Crescent City. Mary keeps a close eye on his drinking, allowing him a spree once a month.

Lord, Jay: In *The Vanishing American,* one of Blucher's henchmen. He is heavily built. He dresses western-style, with jeans, boots, sombrero. His speech is usually satiric in tone. He has a careless, cool, devilish insouciance about his manner. He arouses Nophaie's mistrust at their first meeting. Jay Lord carries out Blucher and Morgan's orders. He spreads the story about Shoie putting a spell on a squaw. He tracks Gekin Yashi to her hiding place after the Pahutes report where she is. They fear that Shoie will put a spell on them and so they betray Nophaie and turn the girl in. Lord also controls the activities of Walterson and the traders with threats. He is the man in charge of spreading Blucher's antiwar propaganda. When he threatens any who want to register, Nophaie confronts him.

Lorenzo: (1) In *The Call of the Canyon,* one of the hands working at the sheep dip with Ben and Ruff Haze.

(2) In *Nevada,* reports the return of Jim Lacy to Lineville, to Nevada's old fling, Lize Teller.

Loughbridge, Jim: In *Wild Horse Mesa,* Melberne's partner in the mustang operation. He has more experience with ranching than Melberne. Loughbridge thinks that Manerube is the type of wrangler they need and has great confidence in him. He has few qualms about using the barbarous wire method to catch a large number of horses, or the hobbling method to deliver them to the train. He wants a quick return on his investment. When Manerube tells the tale about Chane Weymer, Loughbridge declares that he has heard of Chane before. He is known as a wonderful horse wrangler but he also has a reputation as a loner who has been involved in a number of shooting scrapes. He readily accepts Manerube's assessment of Chane. Loughbridge does not understand Melberne's dissatisfaction with Manerube's results, and he accepts his partner's offer to dissolve the partnership, cancel the debt he owes him and give him half his profit on the sale of mustangs. Loughbridge, like Manerube, suspects someone has opened the gate to release the remaining horses but refrains from making any direct accusations against Sue, the person both he and Manerube suspect of having done the deed. When Loughbridge finally realizes that Manerube is a horse thief and a scoundrel, he is reconciled with Melberne. The two of them decide to set up ranching as neighbors on Wild Horse Mesa. His daughter, Ora marries Chess Weymer.

Loughbridge, Mrs.: In *Wild Horse Mesa,* mentioned as Jim Loughbridge's wife, but other than a mention that she helps with the cooking in the camp, she does not appear in the novel.

Loughbridge, Ora: In *Wild Horse Mesa,* the dark-eyed, sullen, spoiled daughter of Jim Loughbridge. She is sweet on Chess Weymer but he seems struck on Sue. She is jealous and the jealousy makes her spiteful. To make Chess jealous, she flirts with Manerube. Like Sue, she is impressed by the western landscape. Eventually, Chess takes an interest in her and at the end of the story, she and Chess are to be married at the same time as Chane and Sue Melberne.

Louis Philippe, King: Exiled from France by Napoleon, he came to America during his wanderings. He spent several days at Colonel Zane's cabin in Ft. Henry where he was trapped by a winter blizzard. He spent most of his time near the colonel's fireside.

Louise (Louie): In *Black Mesa,* a young woman, sixteen years old, with a young child called Tommy. She is living in a cabin at Bitter Seeps. Apparently, she is married to Belmont and Tommy is his son, but it is some time before Paul and Wess establish exactly the relationship between the two. From the start, Louise looks on Paul as a kind of savior, and Paul contemplates becoming an Adam Larey (*Wanderer of the Wasteland*), devoting his life to helping those in need. Wess Kintell advises caution. Louise tells them that she cannot remember her parents. She lived with an aunt in Peoria where she went to school. When the aunt died, she went to work. Belmont came to visit the people with whom she boarded. They had a farm near town. They were queer people and Belmont had a hold on them. He took her to Utah with him, promised her a job, a home, everything. They lived on a ranch outside of Lund at a place across the big river lost in canyon country. He kept her confined with the woman he calls Sister to keep an eye on her. He married her just before moving to Bitter Seeps. Sister was mean and cruel to Louise. She beat her until Belmont caught her at it. Sister and Belmont quarrel often, but since their arrival at Bitter Seeps, she leaves Louise alone.

Louise falls in love with Paul and shows her jealousy when Paul speaks to Natasha. She imagines he is sweet on the Indian girl. Wess tells Paul that Louise has never met any men as gallant as Paul. She is a powder magazine waiting for a spark. Paul has had little experience with women, and Wess cautions him that Louise has latched on to him because she is so unhappy with Belmont. Louise's big concern is for Tommy, who is often sick. The Indian woman, Gersha, helps her with the baby. Paul and Wess cannot get Louise to tell them if Sister is Belmont's sister or his first wife. Louise does not know. She is not sure how she feels about Belmont either. She does not want Paul to kill Belmont. She tells him that Belmont's indifference has made her love him all the more. Later, in a fit of rage, she tells Belmont that she has always hated him. Sister tries to stir the waters by telling Belmont that Louise lets Paul into her cabin at night, that she has been betraying him. Wess Kintell catches up with Bloom, one of the rustlers Belmont hired to steal some of Manning and Kintell's cattle to sell back to them, and from him, he learns that Belmont has no legal claim on Louise. She is not his legal wife because he is legally married to Sister. As things work out, Belmont is killed when he falls from a precipice and Louise is free to marry Paul.

Louisiana: In *West of the Pecos,* a medium-sized, well-muscled Negro cowboy with a pleasantly handsome face, hired by Pecos Smith to drive cattle west of the Pecos to the Lambeth ranch.

Loveless, Luke: In *The Fugitive Trail,* a trail driver for whom Bruce Lockheart had been right-hand man for three years. He mentions this to Hank Silverman to establish his reputation. Luke Loveless was the most successful buffalo hunter in Texas and is now a big cattleman. He incenses Captain Maggard and hurts his vanity and makes Bruce Lockheart a marked man. Bruce had ridden for Loveless during the wildest range strife Texas had known. Loveless's riders had been a hard crowd and Bruce had been his best marksman and rider. There is no love lost between Loveless and Maggard. He tells the ranger he is on a wild goose chase, pursuing Lockheart. If Bruce has not become a killer and outlaw,

Maggard will make him one. As far as Loveless is concerned, however, Bruce Lockheart is as honest as he himself is and he would be proud to have him for a son. He cautions the rangers that they will never take him alive and if they corner him, a number of them will cash in their checks. The two of them make a bet that becomes famous among the trail drivers and in all the posts around. Maggard bets he will arrest Lockheart or kill him within a year, and Loveless bets that he never will, and that eventually, Lockheart will be proven to have had nothing to do with the bank holdup in Denison of which he is accused. Tom Doan holds the stakes.

Lovell, Beatrice: In *The Call of the Canyon,* a member of Carley Burch's crowd in New York City. When Carley returns east from her visit to Glenn Killbourne in Arizona, Beatrice meets her at the train station. Beatrice, like Eleanor Harmon, is a "modern woman," addicted to the good life, to entertainment, to the pursuit of pleasure, and to making herself attractive to her husband, an appendage on his arm. She resents Carley's criticism of her way of life, seeing nothing wrong with it.

Low, Madge: In *Arizona Ames,* a "friend" of Nesta Ames who spreads gossip about her and Lee Tate. She is pure poison. She has urged Lee to seduce Nesta and ruin her reputation.

Low, Mrs.: In "Amber's Mirage," Ruby's mother.

Low, Ruby: In "Amber's Mirage," Al Shade's sweetheart and Jim Crawford's neighbor. She is a vivacious young woman who loves pretty things and dancing. Although Al is in love with her, she still flirts with the other young men, although she tells Al she loves him best. She confides in Jim Crawford that she does not want to be poor all her life and Al is poorer than her family. Nevertheless, the night before Al's departure with Crawford, they become engaged and she promises to wait for him. Jim tells Al that she won't wait. She is too shallow, too selfish to be true. Al would have to be around to keep an eye on her for that to happen. Nevertheless, when he returns, he learns from Boyce and Raston that she had been true to him until word came that he had died in the Sonora desert. Al leaves the bucket of gold he promised her at the door of her house, to give her and Luke Boyce the chance for a real life.

Lowden, Jack: In *Western Union,* one of the first to befriend the easterner, Wayne Cameron, when he arrives in the West. Lowden announces that he is from Missouri. He is with his friend, Vance Shaw, both of them hard on their luck. His rough, calloused hands and his powerful grip underline how inexperienced Cameron is in comparison. Lowden's appearance is in vivid contrast to that of his friend, Shaw. He is small of stature, sturdy, powerful, with arms too long for his body and legs markedly bowed from a life on horseback. His face is ugly, hard, lined, and his eyes blue and intent. He and Shaw team up with Cameron to work on the telegraph line. Cameron provides the capital for the venture to outfit a wagon. Lowden's skill with a rifle proves useful during the Indian attack on the wagon train. He helps rescue Ruby from Pierce in Gothenburg and later in South Pass. He and Shaw plan to take up ranching in the Sweetwater Valley when the work on the telegraph line is complete.

Lowell, Dr.: In *The Desert of Wheat,* the local doctor who will care for Kurt Dorn at Anderson's home. When Kurt Dorn is brought back home, it is not expected that he will live.

Lowrie, Hank: In *Thunder Mountain,* a sheriff in Salmon in cahoots with the gambler Borden. He appears when Borden and Kalispel have locked horns over Borden's attempt to force his way into Sydney Blair's hotel room. He says he is there to arrest Kalispel for rustling in Montana. Lee Emerson (Kalispel) challenges his authority, calling him a crook and a blow-hard coward, yellow to the gizzard. The confrontation goes no farther as he fears Kalispel's gunmanship. At Thunder Mountain, Hank Lowrie appears in the employ of Rand Leavitt, judge, mayor of the mining camp and head of the vigilance committee and the band of robbers.

Loyals: In *The Hash Knife Outfit,* friends of Glory Traft in Saint Louis. When she takes up with the disreputable Ed Darnell, gambler, blackmailer, swindler, they desert her.

Luce: In *The Border Legion,* an outlaw who haunts Beard's saloon. He plans to rob the storekeeper/miner Brander of his gold and abduct his daughter. Jim Cleve overhears him talking about his plan and he beats him up for his dishonorable intentions towards a woman. This incident is later repeated to Kells and to Gulver.

Lucy: (1) In *The Mysterious Rider,* Hell Bent Wade's wife. Wade suspected his wife was involved with a "southern gentleman" at her brother's establishment in Denver. Wade kills this man, only to learn that his wife and the man were both innocent. Lucy then leaves Wade, taking his daughter with her. Wade knows Columbine is his daughter from the striking resemblance she bears to her mother.

(2) In *The Spirit of the Border,* John Christy's betrothed. She is taken captive by the renegade Jim Girty, raped and killed. Deering mentions this in a conversation with Jim Girty as they take over the Village of Peace.

Luki: In *The Light of Western Stars,* appears as the gun-bearer in a story told by Castleton about hunting a man-eating lion in Uganda.

Lundeen, Jed: In *The Shepherd of Guadaloupe,* the father of Virginia Lundeen. He is from Georgia, originally, going west to take up ranching. He never made a success of it, ending up operating a store. Entering into a partnership with Malpass, his fortunes improve. He comes to own the land which belongs to his landlord, and the two families exchange residences. Lundeen has developed a passionate hatred of the Forrests, a hatred fueled by Malpass, under whose influence he has fallen. Lundeen has given Virginia's large trust fund to Malpass to invest, but only ten thousand dollars are left. As well, Malpass has fired the two cowboys who cared for her horses, which likewise have been sent away to a ranch in Watrous. Jed Lundeen wants his daughter to marry Malpass. Slowly it is revealed that he is heavily indebted to the partner and unless the marriage goes ahead, he faces financial ruin. Lundeen suggests she go through with the marriage to settle financial matters, then she can divorce him later. He is so angry with his daughter that he throws her out of the house. The next time he sees his daughter is when he comes to the Padre Mine, where the mining engineer, Jarvis, is inspecting the tunnels for evidence of gold being planted. He arrives at the end of a fight among Malpass, Jarvis and Virginia. Lundeen and Malpass kill each other.

Lundeen, Mrs.: In *The Shepherd of Guadaloupe*, the mother of Virginia. She is from the South, and has never really adapted to life in the Southwest. Unlike her husband, she is not ambitious nor driven by hatred or a desire to be wealthy. She feels out of place in the large house at Cottonwoods with the Mexican servants. She does not like the influence that Malpass has on her husband, and she does not approve of her husband's plan to marry Virginia off to his ubiquitous partner. She is pleased to see Cliff Forrest, and she is not opposed to Virginia's marrying him. She is not aware that her husband has kicked Virginia out of the house when she leaves with her for the train station on her way to Atlanta. Virginia goes to visit her there after her father is killed by Malpass. Mrs. Lundeen decides to remain in Georgia, her native home.

Lundeen, Virginia (Ginia): In *The Shepherd of Guadaloupe*, the daughter of Jed Lundeen, coveted as a wife by Malpass. She first appears on the *Berengaria*, returning from France. There she meets a soldier returning to the U.S. who is in a very sad state. She shows him concern but not excessive sympathy, and he appreciates the sprig of violets she pins on his deck chair blanket. She meets him again on the train, where she is concerned that the train staff give him proper attention. When her male companion shows disapproval of her interest in him, her sympathy cools. However, the soldier turns up in a cab at her home, Cottonwoods, and she realizes that he is Clifton Forrest. She goes with the driver to take him to his parents' new home, in fact, her old home. Virginia enters the house and speaks to Mrs. Forrest, preparing her for Clifton's appearance. At first, Mrs. Forrest thinks she has come to introduce her husband. When Mr. Forrest arrives, he asks her to leave, refusing to have a Lundeen in his home.

But Virginia is not really a Lundeen at heart, as Mrs. Forrest tells her. She continues to be concerned about Cliff. She recalls how she had been in love with him as a child, how she considered him her knight in shining armor, how she would wave to him from the top of the wall as he rode by. She is still in love with him, although she is shy about expressing that love. She does continue to be concerned about his well-being. One day, she finds him lying on the road, having fallen from exhaustion on his walk back from the store. She brings her friends to the store, the fabulously rich friends who have money to burn. Her best friend, Ethel, always the practical joker and wit, tells Cliff he should charge them double the price on everything and they would never notice it. Malpass, Lundeen's partner who hopes to marry Virginia, is displeased with his interest in her. He fights Cliff, knocking him to the ground.

Virginia and her friends spend some weeks camping up at Emerald Lake. Here, Virginia communes with the natural world, finding peace of mind and a solution to her problem. She refers to the spot where she enjoys solitude as her shrine. She proposes that Cliff marry her, thereby making it impossible to be forced into a marriage with Malpass. Ethel thinks the idea splendid, and Cliff the perfect mate. Cliff, however, does not see the need for such drastic action yet. But in a few weeks when the situation becomes more urgent, he agrees to her proposal. Virginia gets the license and arranges for the marriage with the minister, swearing both of these to secrecy. She continues with life as usual, tending to her horses, avoiding contact with Cliff at the store. When the store is burned down, she is concerned about Cliff and the Forrests, but they reject offers of help. Cliff gets a job in Watrous as a bookkeeper, driving back and forth in a wreck of a car. A fight with Malpass at the store when he comes to arrange for supplies to build a house ends with the truth of their marriage being revealed. Virginia confesses that it is true, affirming that it was not a marriage of love, but of convenience, to prevent marriage to Malpass. Suspecting that she is in love with Cliff, Jed Lundeen throws her out of the house.

Virginia needs time to think over what has happened. She needs to get her father out of the mess he is in with Malpass. She wonders how Malpass came to have such power over her father, and she suspects the Padre Mine is part of it. Her cowboy, Jake, had some experience with silver mining in Silver City. He looks at the mine and concludes that no serious extraction of ore was ever done there. He suspects that someone has been planting gold dust in the tunnels, possibly as a scam for some unsuspecting buyer. He recommends that she get a mining engineer to give it a closer look. Virginia goes to Colorado Springs to visit with Ethel. Her friend praises her for her action, and puts her in touch with a mining engineer who agrees to look at the mine. When she has returned to Las Vegas, she arranges for financing from Fenton, the father of her friend Dick. She also buys out Lopez's flock to prevent Malpass from buying it to make trouble for Cliff. Then, she and Jarvis, the engineer, go to the mine. While she and Jarvis are there, Malpass shows up and a fight breaks out. Malpass attacks her, Jarvis comes to the rescue and is shot some five times. Her father arrives and takes on Malpass. The two men end up killing each other.

Virginia inherits her father's holdings. She returns the ranch and Cottonwoods to the Forrests, from whom they had been taken fraudulently by Malpass. She moves into her old home. She buys the Payne ranch in Watrous where she plans to live. She hesitates to go to Cliff, who, she has been told, has been marvelously transformed by his months tending sheep in the desert. Cliff had always been so independent, refusing help when he was destitute. She thinks he will find it hard to accept that she is now fabulously wealthy. Ethel and Helen have been to visit him at his camp with the sheep and report that he is very well. Virginia and Cliff come together in his tent, and agree that he will continue his work tending sheep, although they will never lack for anything.

Virginia Lundeen is another in the parade of wealthy women who come to the rescue of men in Grey's novels. She rejects the false values of many in her class, seeing sacrifice and compassion as more rewarding than the pursuit of pleasure.

Lying Juan: In *Valley of Wild Horses*, the cook for Blinky Moran's outfit that sets out to catch wild horses. Lying Juan has an unmatched reputation as teller of tall tales. In one of these, he claims to have played poker with Queen Victoria when he was in London. She is an incredibly sharp card player and took him for several hundred dollars.

Lynn, Bill: In *Under the Tonto Rim*, runs an inn at the stage stop at Cedar Ridge. Lucy Watson spends two days there before making her way to the Tonto.

Lynn, Jeff: Appears as a character in *The Spirit of the Border*. Although he does not appear in *The Last Trail*, Colonel Ebenezer Zane refers to Jeff Lynn's reports about certain characters at Ft. Pitt who have made their way to Ft. Henry. He is a frontiersman, hunter, guide who takes Joe and Jim Downs, Nell, and Kate Wells and their uncle by raft from Ft. Pitt to Ft. Henry. For Joe Downs, he is a source of information about people on the frontier, Wetzel, Silvertip, and Jonathan Zane, and a source of advice about what frontier life has in store for him. He leads the party to the Village of Peace and during the invasion by hostile Indians, he attempts to find men among Captain Williamson's company who would be willing to help defend the Christian Indians. When he cannot find enough men, he advises Jim to leave the place when he has the chance. He voices the attitude of many on the frontier, that the Indian is the enemy and not worth pitying.

Lynn, Mrs.:   In *Under the Tonto Rim*, Bill Lynn's wife. She is a motherly person, kind and full of curiosity. She approves of the work Lucy is about to undertake with the families in the Tonto. She expresses doubts about how receptive the families will be. The backwoods people, she says, keep to themselves. They are ignorant, but proud. She tells Lucy about the Denmeades, the Claypools, and in particular,

about Edd Denmeade. Like Mrs. Larabee at the welfare office, she predicts Lucy will be of great interest to the young men. She and Bill wish Lucy well at her undertaking. They admire her spunk and courage.

Lyons, Jesse: In *The Man of the Forest*, when Milt Dale comes to visit Snowdrop, Jesse Lyons asks him to break a colt for him with patience, not violence as is the method of the hard-riding cowboys at Pine.

M

Maahesenie: In *The Vanishing American*, Nophaie's only remaining relative on the Navajo reservation. He lives in the hogan with Nophaie and watches his flocks of sheep. When Marian arrives, she is impressed by his keen eyes, his sense of humor and his concern for her after the long, hard ride. Maahesenie suffers from rheumatism. He does not take shelter when it rains as he watches the sheep. When he gets sick, like a true Navajo, he believes it is the result of evil thoughts. The medicine man comes to give him a massage and say prayers and perform cleansing rituals. He refuses to believe Nophaie's explanation that rheumatism is a disease whose effects can be lessened by avoiding dampness and staying in a warm hogan. Maahesenie's attitude, however, is that his time has come. As a young man, he had carried the testing stone a hundred steps. He has lived a full life and he is not afraid to meet his death. When he passes away, Nophaie buries him with traditional Navajo rituals.

Mac: (1) In *The Arizona Clan*, a member of the Hathaway-Twitchell-Quayle outfit. He is involved in the shootout at the cabin where Buck is holding Nan Lilley hostage, hoping to force Parson Bailey to marry them.

(2) In *Robbers' Roost*, a member of Hays' outlaw outfit. He is the eldest of the group, a cadaverous-faced man, with a clammy skin and eyes like a ghoul. He is always twisting and squeezing his hands, lean, sinewy, strong members. Mac is killed in the attack on Robbers Roost by Heeseman's gang.

Mac(abe):   In *Thunder Mountain*, one of Rand Leavitt's henchmen. He is responsible for the attack on Dick Sloan at his new mining claim. He implicates Cliff Borden in the attempt to abduct Nugggett from Dick Sloan. Lee Emerson admires the integrity of the man who remains loyal to Leavitt to the end.

MacDonalds: In *Captives of the Desert*, run a boarding house at Taho. Katharine and Alice Winfield stay at their place when they visit their friend, Mary Newton. John Curry and High-Lo share a room there when they move into Taho for the winter.

Mace: In *The Drift Fence*, runs a saloon in Flag where Hack Jocelyn and his cronies drink and play cards.

McKay: (1) In *The Deer Stalker*, McKay is a friend of Thad Eburne's. He used to work for the park service but has since gone into drilling for oil on the Indian reservation. McKay has a proposal for dealing with the overpopulation of deer in one region. He suggests that with a hundred Indians and some fifty cowboys he could drive ten thousand deer through the Saddge Gal, down the canyon, across the Colorado River and up Tanner's trail to the rim, right into the forest ranges where there are plentiful food and water. Government officials doubt a large number of deer could be driven like cattle, but McKay's enthusiasm for the project is contagious. Before the project could be undertaken, however, a lot of money would have to be raised to hire the cowboys and the Indians for the drive and to buy the supplies for the men. Patricia Clay provides the money needed for the supplies and to hire the Indians for the venture. Eburne doubts the project will succeed because McKay is a visionary and not given to resolving practical details. He is a good miner and oil driller, a cattleman and a horse dealer, but hopeless when it comes to planning details. The cattlemen from Utah are opposed to the project and the park service has given it at best a lukewarm approval. Everything seems to go wrong. Needed supplies don't arrive on time, and a blizzard hits once the drive is underway. The Indian and cowboy drivers are not able to continue because of the weather. McKay has to admit he is licked. Eburne regrets that he has incurred many debts with this venture.

(2) In *The Wanderer of the Wasteland,* the manager of the mill in Picacho. He gives Adam a job in the office first. McKay is of medium height, powerfully built, with an unshaven broad face, strong and ruddy. He wears a red flannel shirt with a gun in his belt. He is a rough, practical miner. McKay later puts Adam to work stoking boilers to cure him of his desire for more physical labor. He plays a trick on Adam, giving him the most grueling work of all, but Adam survives, even thrives on the work. A good friendship develops between McKay and Adam.

McKay, Bill: In *The Deer Stalker*, the brother of McKay, who is organizing the deer drive. He gets word from his brother to hire some Piutes for the drive.

Mackenzie: In *The Fugitive Trail*, built an old military post at Camp Cooper in 1871. The road through Camp Cooper crosses the Chisholm Trail in Fort Worth and the camp is busy in the summer with the trail drivers passing through. Bruce Wells suggests they head there to begin their search for Vic Henderson and the rustlers who took Melrose's Little Wichita herd.

Macklin, Sheriff: In *Nevada,* the sheriff of Winthrop, Arizona, where Ben Ide has set up ranching and where Jim Lacy is working for Judge Franklidge and Tom Day under the name Texas Jack. Macklin is reputed to be strict with drunken cowboys, Indians and Mexicans, but rather easy-going on gamblers or dangerous characters. Jim Lacy has little respect for him, suspecting he is afraid to take action against the Pine Tree Outfit.

MacNeill: In *The Maverick Queen*, one of the ranchers who supports Lee's secret vigilance committee to punish maverick-stealing cowboys and in particular, the Maverick Queen, Kit Bandon. He is present the night Hargrove and Lee try to whip a confession and information out of Bud Harkness.

MacNelly, Captain: In *The Lone Star Ranger,* the leader of a troop of rangers in West Texas whose mission is to break the hold of the outlaw gangs on that part of the state. He is of slight build, wiry, tough, with a clear face and black mustache and hair. He has sharp black eyes which have a look of authority. He comes from a good, Southern family. He doesn't have a reputation as a gunman, but he does have nerve and experience. His approach to dealing with outlaws is unconventional. He has decided that Buck Duane is a man who does not deserve the reputation attributed to him. There are simply too many decent people who believe in him for the stories to be true. MacNelly leaves word with all the people Buck is known to associate with to come into his camp after dark. When Buck does come into camp, he is received cordially. MacNelly has a pardon for him from the governor if he agrees to join the rangers and work as an undercover agent to infiltrate and destroy the Cheseldine gang. He gives some advice about getting in touch with him and provides some money, and leaves the job to Buck. When Duane has discovered the Cheseldine hideout and the plans to rob the gold from the Ranchers' Bank in Val Verde, he rides all night to telegraph MacNelly about the plans. MacNelly and his rangers are in town, prepared to capture the outlaws. Captain MacNelly tries to convince Buck Duane not to face the outlaws in the bank, but Buck feels it is his duty to finish a job that no one else can do as well as he can. Captain MacNelly is an example of the law officer found in some of Grey's novels, more concerned with justice than with legality. He knows when to bend, and when to be firm.

MacNew, Handy: In *Valley of Wild Horses,* late of Montana, a cowboy who had drifted beyond the pale, one of the innumerable band Pan Handle Smith has helped in some way or other. Handy had become a horse thief and was a suspect in a murder the year following Pan Handle's acquaintance with him. Pan Handle saved him from being strung up when he was working in the Powder River country for Hurley's XYZ outfit. Since MacNew's guilt was not clear to him, he got him out of the mess on condition he leave the country. Handy owes him a favor and agrees to let Jim Blake out of jail. To make things look good, Pan Handle ties him up. Marshal Matthews, however, suspects him of complicity in the escape and fires him from his job as guard. Pan Handle recruits him for the wild horse operation. One morning, Gus kicks over MacNew's coat and discovers that the pockets are full of gold coins. They suspect him of complicity with Hardman. Pan Handle, however, is convinced that MacNew would never betray him. He reserves judgment on the finding. Eventually MacNew comes to Pan Handle and confesses that Hardman did pay him to report to back on their progress in capturing wild mustangs. He says he never intended to betray them to Hardman. When they do come upon Hardman, who tries to take the herd from them, Hardman says MacNew is one of his men. MacNew then draws on Hardman, killing him. Hardman's right-hand gunman, Purcell, shoots MacNew.

Macomber: In *Wildfire*, a rancher near Bostril's Ford. He is a horse trader, and early in the story has just acquired a sorrel in trade for a mustang and cash. He asks Lucy's opinion of the animal and she teases him, telling him he has bad judgment in horse flesh. Like Bostril, he is proud of his horses and anxious to have his animal win the annual race. He is present when Sears attempts to steal Wildfire from Lin Slone. He comments that he has never seen a man more skilled at throwing a lasso than Slone.

Madcap: Betty's Indian pony in *Betty Zane*. Betty loves to ride the horse down the road along the river. The horse is reputedly as fast as Alfred Clarke's purebred stallion. During the plague of horse-stealing in *The Last Trail*, Madcap is taken out of his stall in the barn late one afternoon, together with a thoroughbred horse. Wetzel and Jonathan later retrieve the horses before they are taken to Detroit for sale. When Jonathan and Wetzel see Madcap among the horses penned up, they know they have found Legget's holding area for stolen animals.

Madden: In *The Wanderer of the Wasteland*, a farmer, a neighbor to the Lareys back east. The Maddens had a well on their farm with particularly cold and good-tasting water, "granite water" as it was called. The thirst in the desert makes Adam think of Madden's water.

Madden (Muddy): In *The Hash Knife Outfit*, the cook for the Hash Knife Outfit. Pecos tells Jed Stone that Madden fears Croak Malloy, but he would double-cross Jed Stone any day. He stays with Malloy when the Hash Knife Outfit breaks up and helps kidnap Molly Wood and Glory Traft. He is killed in a gunfight with Jed Stone when the old leader comes to rescue the girls.

Madero: Mexican revolutionary leader mentioned in *Desert Gold* and *The Light of Western Stars*. Gene Stewart joins his rebel army when he goes to Mexico. When Madero's forces are defeated, Gene is arrested and sentenced to death.

Magdaline: In *Captives of the Desert*, a sixteen-year-old Navajo girl who has spent the past three years at a white school in California. She is Joy's older sister. Mrs. Weston has brought her back to Sage Springs. She has become a strikingly beautiful young woman. She complains that she no longer fits into her old Indian world, and is unwanted in the white world. Whites gave her the name Magdaline because they could not get their tongues around her Indian name. John Curry thinks she is every bit an Indian princess in the way she carries herself when High-Lo is injured, looking after him and going for help. At first she thinks High-Lo was running away from her but High-Lo tells John he had been following Newton and Hanley to uncover their bootlegging operation. Mrs. Weston tells Magdaline she could become an important role model among the Navajo, teaching the women the modern ways she has learned. Magdaline despairs of such a mission since most Navajo women are not interested in the new ways, and in the modern white household, appliances all require electricity, a commodity lacking on the reservation. She proposes marriage to John Curry, but he refuses. She asks if it is because she is Indian and he is white. He replies that he is much older than she is and he does not love her that way. High-Lo, however, is in love with her, but she does not realize his shyness, his fear of revealing how he feels. Vowing never to wear Navajo clothes again, she moves in with Wilbur Newton when he sets up the trading post at Sage Springs. Her scorn for the white world grows when she sees he runs the bootlegging operation on the reservation. She is unaware that he is married to Mary. When she gets pregnant, he gives her fifty dollars and throws her out. Magdaline plans to go to Flaggerston to have her baby and to find work. Before leaving, she goes to Mary's home to visit her younger sister, Joy, and learns to her surprise that Mary is Wilbur Newton's wife. John Curry goes to Flaggerston to look for her, but can find no trace of her. He meets High-Lo, who tells him that he has married Magdaline to prevent John from making a terrible mistake. Magdaline appears, happy and at peace. She has always loved High-Lo. When they return to Taho, she stays at the family's hogan. Newton shows up to take her back to his post at Sage Springs. In the fight, she shoots him.

Magdaline's plight is that of Gekin Yashi in *The Vanishing American*, or Glen Napa, Nas Ta Bega's sister in *The Rainbow Trail*, other young Navajo girls educated in the white world, and caught between two worlds, both of which see them as outsiders. Magdaline is another example of the failure of the government policies in dealing with the Navajo.

Maggard, Captain: In *The Fugitive Trail*, a Texas Ranger who is out to catch the men responsible for the bank robbery in Denison. He is determined to "ride down" Bruce Lockheart. Maggard catches up with Trinity Spencer at Doan's and tells her she looks like the wife of a friend of his. As she is heading west, he suggests that she visit Melrose and tell him her story. She could be the daughter that disappeared twenty years ago. At Doan's, Maggard makes a bet which becomes the talk of the cowboys on the range. He bets he will get Lockheart within the year, while Luke Loveless bets Lockheart will be proven innocent of any involvement in the bank holdup in Denison. Doan holds the substantial wagers. He himself appears at the Melrose ranch, but Steve Melrose is not too happy to see him. Melrose had a younger brother who went to the bad after the Civil War. Then, Steve Melrose was hard and not trusting, and he missed the opportunity to influence his brother for the good. He was killed by rangers. Melrose has had little respect for them since then. Melrose thinks the rangers are wasting their time pursuing Lockheart when there is a plague of rustlers in the area. At the ranch, Maggard, like his previous emissary, Sgt. Blight, is introduced to Lee Jones. Since he has never met Lockheart, Maggard does not realize Lee Jones is Bruce Lockheart, the man he is "riding down." Even when Clark on the wagon train insists Lee is Bruce Lockheart, he is convinced by Melrose's defense of his son-in-law-to-be. Eventually, Maggard decides he should pursue the rustlers in the area, in part because he believes that Stewart is the real Lockheart. Even when Bruce has killed Stewart, he does not catch on to the truth. When Lockheart decides he cannot live under an assumed name, he goes to Maggard and reveals he is Lockheart. Bruce then rides off, thinking Maggard is pursuing him. It turns out to be Trinity who brings him word that Maggard has called off the pursuit. He is free. As Maggard said, "He squared himself with me."

Magill, Bones: In *The Dude Ranger,* one of the cowboys working on the Red Rock Ranch. He is one of the Dude Hyslip faction devoted to making life miserable for the tenderfoot Ernest Selby. He is surprised to learn the tenderfoot is the new owner of the ranch and equally surprised when Ernest offers to keep him on the ranch at high pay if he apologizes for his previous mean behavior.

Mahaffey: In *Shadow on the Trail,* the head of the detachment of Texas Rangers pursuing Simm Bell and his outlaws. Mahaffey has placed a reward of ten thousand dollars on Bell's head, alive or dead. Mahaffey is pleased that they have an inside man in the outfit, Randall Blue, who has tipped them off about the planned bank heist in Mercer. Bell and Holden, however, pull a job on the Texas Pacific train, unexpectedly. When Simm and Wade get away, they hide out with a farmer Simm knows. They get clothes, work horses and an old wagon from the farmer. On the road, they meet Mahaffey, who fails to recognize them. He leaves, promising to ride them down. Mahaffey is known for his persistence. Holden and Arkansas vote not to attempt the Mercer holdup but to abandon the Smoky Hollow hideout to which Blue has been. They should head south, out of the country, maybe to Mexico. At Mercer, sure enough, the rangers are waiting. Mahaffey and Pell pursue the escaping Bell and Holden. Bell is fatally wounded, and Holden, while he could have killed Mahaffey and other rangers, heeds his boss's advice not to shoot a ranger. Holden escapes, hiding in Jacqueline Pencarrow's tent. Over a year later, he comes across Blanco, the name given to Wade

Holden by Aulsbrook, when he is working at Jesse Chisum's ranch. It's possible that Chisum himself has informed on Holden. He escapes again. Mahaffey appears at the end, years later, after Wade Holden, now Ted Brandon, has fully redeemed himself by rescuing Pencarrow from ruin and clearing the area of rustlers. Mahaffey's decision not to arrest him is proof of forgiveness. Mahaffey is not as unbending as Wade Holden had believed.

Mains, Danny: In *The Light of Western Stars,* a young cowboy who is robbed at the start of the novel. He was bringing back the payroll for Bill Stillwell. Gene Stewart asks Bonita in the train station if Danny had been involved in any of the gunplay at Linton's bachelor party. Danny disappears, and the sheriff imagines that he has been involved in the shooting in El Cajón the night of Madeline's arrival. After Alfred Hammond's wedding and Gene's departure for Mexico, Danny Mains appears at Madeline's ranch. He has come to repay Stillwell for the payroll money stolen from him. He explains that he and Bonita were hiding in the cabin in the mountains not far from where Madeline and her party came on a camping expedition. He was prospecting for gold and made a wonderful strike. He found the lost padre's mine, the mine referred to in the story Florence told the group one night around the campfire. Gene Stewart had kept the two of them in supplies. As well, Gene insisted that they get married and he brought Padre Marcos from El Cajón up to marry them. They attribute all their good fortune to Gene. When Danny hears she may be going back east, he offers to buy the ranch to give to Gene.

In *Majesty's Rancho,* Danny Mains, one of Gene's wild outfit in those long-past prosperous days, reappears as a neighbor and friend. His bow legs and his sturdy build have not changed, but his homely visage betrays the havoc of the years. Danny is now a rancher, neighbor of Gene Stewart, and father of a young girl, also named Bonita, approximately the same age as Majesty. He worries about her because she is as beautiful and as flirtatious as his wife had been. Danny, like Gene, has lost cattle to rustlers and he suspects they are Mexican, possibly relations of his wife. He and his vaqueros help Gene track the rustlers and prepare the ambush to surprise the men who arrive with trucks. Together with Gene, he plans to sell off half of his herd. The smaller herd would be easier to manage and keep track of, possibly reducing the risk of rustling. Danny encourages Ren Starr in his courting of Bonita. He thinks that Ren, a hard working, level-headed cowboy, would be a good husband and son-in-law. Danny rides with Stewart, Starr and Nels to Cochise's stronghold, where Madge is being held by the kidnappers. He has been a life-long, loyal friend to Gene Stewart.

Mains, Kitty: In "Avalanche," the "femme fatale," the insincere, flirtatious, shallow easterner who drives the Dunton brothers apart. She is the daughter of a reputedly rich Saint Louis horse dealer who had come to Arizona for his health and who was to buy out the Stillwell cattle interests and take up ranching on a large scale. She is strikingly beautiful, small of stature with a graceful, well-rounded form. She has a face that strikes men and women alike as pretty. Her hair is brown, curly, luxuriant, rebellious. Her skin has a complexion that makes the tanned, ruddy skin of the Tonto girls look positively coarse. She has an advantage over the Tonto girls as well in being daintily and stylishly dressed. Her eyes are of two colors, one blue, the other hazel, an indication of her split personality, one sweet, wistful, appealing, and the other a dancing devil. The Dunton brothers, both inexperienced with women, are smitten by her charm. They do not know she is an instinctive flirt, an insatiably greedy little soul who lives on love and never returns it. She has the animal instinct that either garners for herself or destroys. The two lads go silly over her. She flirts with both, seeming to favor one over the other, giving each the impression he is her favorite. Seemingly unwilling to tear the brothers apart, she goes to the dance with Ben Stillwell, but at that very dance accepts Jake's proposal of marriage. She then returns to dancing with her partner of the evening, young Stillwell. A two-hour long fistfight breaks out between the brothers, ending with Jake in the dust. During their winter in the cabin in Black Gorge, the brothers come to see Kitty more realistically. Jake knows Kitty loved Verde more than she loved him, and Verde knows that Kitty is not the type of woman to be tied down to a one-legged husband. When they reach the Dunton ranch in the spring, they learn that Kitty married Ben Stillwell, son of the cattleman with whom her father is in business. Jacob Dunton tells them they had been fighting over a girl who wasn't worth a little finger.

Majesty: In *The Light of Western Stars,* Gene Stewart's bronco. He loves the horse like a father loves a child. He has never used a quirt or a spur on the animal. He names the horse after his friend Alfred Hammond's sister, Madeline, whose nickname is Majesty. When Gene decides that he has been wasting his time trying to get Madeline to love him, he decides to head for Mexico, leaving his beloved bronco with her. It is a tearful parting.

Malloy, Croak: In *The Hash Knife Outfit,* the worst and meanest member of the Hash Knife Outfit and rival to Jed Stone for the leadership of the gang. Croak Malloy has a misshapen body and an ugly face and a sour disposition to match. He is fast with the gun and without scruples or remorse. Killing men or raping women mean nothing to him. He kills young Frank Reed for leaving the Hash Knife and joining the Diamond, and he kills Stoneface Carr supposedly for cheating at cards. He hopes to rape Molly Dunn and Glory Traft when he abducts them. When Jed Stone recommends a bit of caution in the rustling activities, Malloy wants to wage all out war against the ranchers. Stone sees this as the sure end of the Hash Knife Outfit. When young Jim Traft comes to see Jed Stone, Malloy plays games with him, trying

to scare him by shooting the cigarette out of his mouth. Jed Stone kicks the gun out of Croak's hand. Malloy is involved with Bambridge and Darnell in the rustling operations. After the assault on the Hash Knife by young Traft's cowboys under Slinger Dunn, Croak Malloy escapes. During his overnight stay at the cabin with Jed Stone, he assumes leadership of what is left of the outfit, as Jed Stone is planning to leave Arizona. Malloy comes upon Jim Traft and the two girls, Molly and Glory. He kidnaps the girls for ransom, taking them to the cabin. Jed Stone trails them there, knowing that Malloy has no scruples about raping women. He kills Malloy and Madden, rescuing the girls.

Malone, Bill: In *Rogue River Feud,* a friend of Garry Lord. Garry returns with Keven Bell to a campsite on the Rogue River they had used the previous year.

Malpass, Augustine: In *The Shepherd of Guadaloupe,* Lundeen's business partner. He had been a cowboy around San Luis, and superintendent of Lundeen's ranch. He is rumored to be in on every deal in which Lundeen is involved. He is believed to be responsible for the deals which ruined Clay Forrest. He is in his late thirties or early forties, with magnetic eyes, and slick black hair. Although clearly of Spanish origin (on one occasion he is called Brazilian), there is no trace of an accent in his speech. He dislikes references to his Spanish background, but he generally operates within the Mexican environment. He has no bank accounts in Las Vegas, nor does he have any dealings with the businessmen there, who suspect him of shady transactions. The only men he hires are Mexican. He dresses in riding gear, with high boots, and spurs. He comes and goes from the Lundeen house as if he were a member of the family rather than a business associate. He runs the phosphate mining operations in the south, the real source of Lundeen income, as well as the ranches. He ordered Virginia's two cowboys, Pete and Con, discharged, and her horses taken to the ranch in Watrous. He is not used to people crossing him and he has a violent temper. When Virginia and her friends go to Forrest's store to buy supplies for a camping excursion to Emerald Lake at Mt. Baldy, he buys out the whole store for two thousand dollars, then gets into a fight with Cliff, knocking him to the floor. Later, when Cliff has the place restocked, Malpass has it burned down. Virginia is right to call him a snake in the grass. While there is no proof of his involvement in the arson, Malpass himself reveals the fact to Virginia when they are arguing one day. Malpass explains to Virginia how he has her father under his thumb, how he engineered the failure of the Forrest ranching operation and how he has provided the money for all her father's deals. Lundeen is deeply in debt to him and unless she agrees to marry him, he will ruin her father.

Malpass is planning to build a house near Watrous for his wife-to-be, Virginia. He places an order for the supplies in the store where Cliff Forrest is working as bookkeeper. He makes firing Cliff a condition of his doing business with Hartwell. A fight breaks out between Malpass and Cliff in which Jim Mason, an innocent bystander, is shot. Cliff also reveals the fact that he and Virginia are married. He is brought to the Lundeen place where he denounces Virginia to her father, the result of which is that she is thrown out of the house. When Lundeen learns that Cliff has been expelled from his father's house and gone to work as a shepherd for an old Mexican sheep rancher, he tries to buy Don Lopez's flock in order to fire Cliff from his job.

By accident, Malpass discovers Virginia and Jarvis at the Padre's mine. When Virginia explains that she has an engineer inspecting the mine for evidence of planted gold and fraud, Malpass becomes violent. He attacks her, and when Jarvis comes to her rescue, he shoots him. The fight with Virginia is interrupted by the arrival of her father. The two of them fight until Lundeen is shot to death and Malpass falls off a foot bridge to his death in the canyon below.

Mame: In *Boulder Dam*, a friend of Decker's. She lives in a large, plain house on the corner of a street. It looks like the dwelling place of a town merchant. Decker comes to her with Weston, hoping she can give them a clue as to where Anne (Weston's sweetheart) has been taken. Mame has met Anne. She was in the company of a man called Vitte or Vitto. This clue proves crucial in locating the missing Anne.

Manchester, Hoff (Hoof): In "The Camp Robber," foreman of the Selwyn ranch, one of the ranches in the area to have been hit by the mysterious camp robber who never takes anything of value.

Mandrove: In *The Lost Wagon Train*, a sallow, sandy-mustached young man with a shifty gaze who is a member of the Latch outfit that attacks wagon trains in conjunction with the Kiowas. Mandrove was a deserter from the Confederate army, and a former preacher. Cornwall speculates that Mandrove has joined the outfit for the money, not for gambling, but to escape. Mandrove is badly hurt in the attack on the Anderson caravan, but he survives. He performs the marriage ceremony for Stephen Latch and Cynthia Bowden, since he had been a preacher. He holds his Bible with bloody hands. His talk at the marriage ceremony speaks of the need for personal redemption. This becomes the central goal of Latch's life in a few years' time.

Manerube, Bent: In *Wild Horse Mesa*, a wrangler working with Chane Weymer and later with Melberne and Loughbridge. He is a man under thirty years of age, blond, mustached, educated, domineering in manner, secretive, brutal to horses, and a troublemaker with the Piutes. He is stunningly good looking, easily seducing women with his looks and subtle manners, but at heart, is disrespectful and disdainful of them. There are suspicions that he is Mormon, but the question is never resolved.

Manerube and Chane Weymer never get along.

Manerube attempts to discredit Chane. He spreads the rumor that Chane has been shacked up with a Navajo woman and hints that he is Sosie's lover. Manerube himself convinces the willing Sosie to run off with him. He has promised to marry her, but Chane stops them and makes Manerube admit that he had no intention of keeping that promise.

Manerube is with Chane Weymer under false pretenses. While supposedly a mustanger, there to help him drive his mustangs to Wund, he actually knows little about horses and is not very skillful with them, using violence to break them in or control them. He and McPherson plan to steal Weymer's horse Brutus, and the mustangs he has gathered for sale. Their attempt fails, but they do get a second chance.

Manerube signs on with the Melberne-Loughbridge mustanging outfit. Melberne has his doubts about Manerube but Loughbridge is convinced that Manerube is the man they need for their work. Loughbridge and Manerube both are motivated by schemes to make money quickly. Manerube's method is to round up large numbers of mustangs using barbed wire fences. Many wild horses are injured in the process. The hobbling process to quiet the horses down for driving to the train likewise entails a loss of up to a quarter of the animals due to injury. But the pain and suffering inflicted on the mustangs is a matter of little consequence to him. His work shows that he is not much of a horseman and is an abusive foreman. No one wants to work with him. Melberne is disgusted with the process and decides to break with Loughbridge and Manerube.

Manerube boasts about his abilities and his chivalrous treatment of women. He attempts to defame Chane with the Melbernes. He tells a story in which he makes Chane the abductor of Sosie, and himself the defender of her honor. He flirts with Sue and with Ora, but it doesn't take them long to see through him.

Manerube and McPherson catch Panquitch after Chane has already caught the animal and released him. A fight breaks out between McPherson and Manerube over ownership of the stallion. McPherson claims the right of ownership as he caught the horse. Manerube shoots and kills McPherson, while he himself is shot by the Toddy Nokin's sons.

Manerube is one of many villains appearing in Grey's novels, men in whom the western environment brings out the worst in their natures—greed, cruelty, and indifference to human and animal suffering.

Manley, Wess: In *The Lost Wagon Train*, a gunslinger, bodyguard to Leighton. He is handsome and bold and makes advances to Estelle at Smith's store. Manley is sent with Smilin' Jacobs to kidnap Estelle as she returns from seeing her friends off at the caravan to New Orleans. Manley proposes to Jacobs that they kidnap Estelle, but that they hold on to her to extort a ransom out of Leighton before he uses her to extort money from Latch. Jacobs is too scared to cross Leighton, telling Manley that he's a tenderfoot in such matters compared to Leighton. Manley is killed in a gun fight with Slim Blue, who has come to foil their abduction plans.

Mannin, Sam: In *Twin Sombreros,* runs a general merchandise store in Las Animas. He has changed sufficiently in looks that Brazos does not recognize him. He is a spare, gray westerner of venerable and kindly aspect, with a lined face. He heartily welcomes Brazos back to Las Animas. He invites Brazos to drop by his home for a visit.

Mannin, Louise: In *Twin Sombreros,* Sam Mannin's daughter. Brazos Keene recalls that she used to work in the store and had sold him a red silk scarf. Sam reports that she is married now and has two children. He asks Sam to tell Louise he is disappointed she broke her promise to wait for him.

Manning, Paul: In *Black Mesa,* wants to become a writer. He spent a year in Wagontongue, where he had gone after leaving college in Lawrence, Kansas. Still, his experience of the West has been limited. He has come to Bitter Seeps with Wess Kintell hoping to start anew. He has just gone through an unpleasant experience with Amy in Wagontongue. In the desert, he feels that he has the chance to start over and resume his writing. Like other Grey heroes, he finds that nature provides the moral support to face life's vicissitudes. He has just inherited a little money and would like to invest it in a ranch, cattle, horses—the kind of work he has always wanted to do. He selects Wess Kintell to run his ranch. His instincts tell him that Kintell is a man he can trust and who will teach him the ropes of the cattle industry. Wess Kintell scouts out the possibility of a cattle deal with Belmont at the trading post. When a deal is struck, Paul sets up a small writing studio in his room at the trading post cabin.

Paul offers Wess the job of taking care of his accounts. He owns a thousand-acre farm, huge grain elevators, a store, an apartment house and other property back in Kansas. Wess confesses that he can barely write his name and knows very little math. He can fork a horse, sling a diamond hitch, rope and tie down a steer and throw a gun. Paul agrees that those are the skills most needed for a ranch foreman, his right-hand man. And especially, he wants Wess to teach him to be a cowboy. He means to be outdoors in all kinds of weather, by day and by night, to take what comes, to endure the hard life of mesa country, to learn all it can teach. Wess proves to be a good friend and a good, conscientious and compassionate teacher. He teaches Paul to ride all kinds of horses, to rope cattle, to judge the lay of the land, to use the spy glass to watch his cattle, to trail, to camp in the open, to survive a dust storm. In all cattle dealing, Wess has carte blanche to make arrangements and Paul follows his advice assiduously. Wess catches on to Belmont's trick of selling them back two hundred and sixty of their own cattle. His suspicious are aroused by the lack of mud caked on animals sup-

posedly driven across a river, and the recognition of a particularly cantankerous steer from their own herd.

In other matters, Wess proves to be an invaluable friend. He is a source of wise advice about Louise. Paul is remarkably naive where women are concerned, and in his eagerness to help out a soul in need, fails to see the mess he has stepped into. When Wess sees that Paul cannot be dissuaded from getting involved with Louise, he does his best to help. Louise turns to Paul for help with Tommy, and for comfort. He teachers her to read. Paul at first suspects that Wess is in love with Louise, but that proves not to be the case. Paul does not want to get involved with another man's wife, but the exact relationship between Louise and Belmont is far from clear. Again, Wess Kintell's detective work establishes that Louise has never been married to Belmont, as he is already married to Sister.

Paul's sympathy for the downtrodden is seen as well in his concern for the Indians. He sees Belmont's lecherous looks at Natsha, his too familiar slap on her backside. He sees the poverty of the Indians that Belmont cheats. To keep the Indians dependent on him, Belmont puts something into Bitter Seeps spring to make the water undrinkable, forcing the Indians to rely on him for pop and ginger ale or liquor. Despite the scrupulous care he takes weighing the wool they have to sell, Paul knows Belmont is cheating them. Paul and Wess give Natasha and Taddy a flock of sheep and goats, some ponies, saddles, and a camping outfit when they get married. Belmont sneers contemptuously at Paul's sentimentality.

The time at Bitter Seeps has been an invaluable learning experience for Paul. When Belmont is dead, he and Wess will sell their share of the herd to Shade, if Sister does not want to buy them out. Paul is planning to return to Kansas to visit his family and to introduce his partner to Anne. He expects she will be taken with his genuine Texas cowboy and that the four of them, himself, Wess, Anne, and Louise, will return to set up the ranch he has always wanted.

Manuel: (1) In *The Lone Star Ranger,* a Mexican bandit who helps Bland and Hardin.

(2) In *Majesty's Rancho,* one of the Mexican hands who work on Gene Stewart's ranch. He works around the stables. He and Jose track the cattle rustlers to the highway, and then they lose the track. This leads Lance Sidway to conclude that the cattle are loaded onto trucks.

(3) In "The Ranger," one of the Mexican bandits who abduct Roseta and capture Ranger Medill when he crosses into Mexico in pursuit.

March, Charlie: In *Thunder Mountain,* said by Cliff Borden to be one of Rand Leavitt's right-hand men. He has a weakness for drink and when he drinks, he talks. He told Sadie about Borden's plans and she repeated them to him. Borden has learned through them that Leavitt plans to pull out of Thunder Mountain in the spring.

March, Lefty: In *Under the Tonto Rim*, one of the men talking in the dining room at Bill Lynn's place in Cedar Ridge says that he nearly dropped dead when Lefty March paid him the money he owed him.

María: (1) In *The Dude Ranger*, works at the Red Rock Ranch for Hepford.

(2) In *Majesty's Rancho*, a friend of Bonita's, Danny Mains's daughter. When Lance speaks to Bonita about her flirting with the college students spending the summer at the ranch, which offends Ren Starr who is in love with her, she tells him she has not done as much flirting as María and Francisca.

Marie: In *The Maverick Queen*, the servant at the hotel in Rock Springs who helps Kit Bandon watch over the wounded Lincoln Bradway while he is recuperating in the jail.

Marr, Bill: In *The Lone Star Ranger*, presented through the eyes of Euchre. He has been shot so often he is said to be full of lead. He is not the kind to get into fights needlessly, and more likely to run than to shoot. He is the best rustler in Bland's outfit as he is unsurpassed as a rider and cowhand.

Marsh, Bud: In *The Lone Star Ranger*, challenged by Kid Fuller during a card game. Euchre tells Buck Duane that Bud Marsh is as straight at cards as they come. His friends stop him from killing Kid Fuller.

Marshall: In *The Heritage of the Desert*, a small-time rancher whose property neighbors on August Naab's ranch. Prior to the seizure of the Seeping Springs water hole, Dene runs off several hundred head of cattle from Marshall's range and sells them in Lund, to the north.

Marshall, Kid: In *Shadow on the Trail*, one of Hogue Kinsey's group that Tex Brandon (Wade Holden) recruits to work for Pencarrow. Kid makes possible the capture of Carter, who has attempted to kill Tex Brandon by shooting his horse. Among the cowboys, he has the gift of the gab. At the Christmas dinner, he is the only cowboy able to make a little speech in which he thanks the ranch for taking them on despite their bad reputation and giving them a chance to prove themselves and go straight. Likewise, when Pencarrow is nearly broke with no money to pay, he speaks for the group, promising that they will stay on anyway.

Marta: In *Stairs of Sand*, Caleb Hunt's Mexican cook.

Martha: In *The Desert of Wheat*, the cook at Chris Dorn's ranch. She is annoyed when the men don't show up on time for meals. Kurt Dorn makes an arrangement with Anderson to keep her on when he sells him the ranch to clear his father's debt.

Martin, George: In *Betty Zane*, the brother of Will Martin. During the wedding celebrations, he gives Alfred Clarke a run for his money in the "race for the bottle."

Martin, Harry: Mentioned in *Betty Zane* as an eligible bachelor in whom Betty might be interested. He does not appear again in the novel. Presumably, he is a brother to William (Bill) and George.

Martin, Jeff: In *The Dude Ranger*, the cowboy cook on Red Rock Ranch. He is in Springer when Anne comes to withdraw money for her father. He is talks with her before she takes the stage. Ernest Selby hears their conversation about the ranch, the death of the owner, her speculation about who the new owner is, and her resentment about this as she feels the ranch should belong to her and her father, the foreman. Jeff jokes that whoever the new owner is, she can always marry him, if she really wants to own the ranch. Jeff also serves as a messenger for Anne. He comes to Ernest to tell him Anne wants him to pick up the mail when he is town. He also warns Ernest when the cowboys are planning something amiss.

Martin, Will: In *Betty Zane*, first mentioned to Betty as an eligible bachelor. Will Martin later marries Alice Reynolds, Betty's friend. His wedding celebration is featured in one of the chapters of the novel. Will Martin is one of the men inside the fort during the Indian attack. He is killed in the fighting. His wife, Alice, who has been holding him, is hit by a stray bullet. The scene of his death in her arms is one of the most moving episodes in the novel.

Martinez: In *The Lost Wagon Train*, runs a blacksmith shop behind Leighton's saloon. The morning after the big birthday party for Estelle, Benson is having a horse shod at Martinez's shop when he sees Slim Blue ride down the alley behind Leighton's house, just before it bursts into flames. Martinez is open earlier in the morning than Rankin and sons.

Martínez, Don Carlos: In *The Light of Western Stars*, a Mexican rebel leader posing as a respectable rancher and a neighbor of Bill Stillwell. He is suspected of being involved in the cattle and horse rustling to support Mexican rebels. Don Carlos is first mentioned early in the novel when Gene Stewart helps Bonita in the train station. Don Carlos's men were in town and involved in the scuffle at Linton's bachelor party. Don Carlos is after her, to abuse and enslave her. Alfred Hammond owes him money, which Madeline repays. When Madeline buys out his ranch, her cowboys come to evict him and discover his house is an arsenal of weapons for the Mexican revolutionaries. Don Carlos denies any knowledge of the smuggling operation. Don Carlos also attempts to kidnap Madeline to abduct her to Mexico to sell as a prostitute or slave. He takes advantage of her distaste for violence and invades her home. Pat Hawe and his men have been following the bandits and are prepared to storm the house to catch them. Gene Stewart comes up with an alternate plan whereby her guests will leave quietly on a camping trip. While thinking about these plans, Madeline sees Don Carlos in the door of the back room of the house. She and the guests leave on the camping trip not realizing that Don Carlos and his bandits have snuck away during the night. Don Carlos follows them into the mountains, and enters their camp. The visitors hide while Gene Stewart and the cowboys pretend they are alone there. Sneed discovers a wine basket and concludes that the eastern visitors have been there, but Gene beats him in a fistfight and the men leave. Later in Mexico, when Gene Stewart has been taken prisoner by the rebel forces, Don Carlos Martínez has him arrested and sentenced to death. Madeline secures his release, and Don Carlos is himself arrested, imprisoned and sentenced to death by General Salazar.

In *Majesty's Rancho*, Don Carlos is mentioned when Madeline and Gene are reminiscing about the past and their first meeting. They recall how his ranch became the nucleus of their present estate and how rustling has taken new turns since that time.

Martiniano: In "The Ranger," mentioned by Vaughn Medill as one of the greatest Texas vaqueros.

Mary: In *The Rainbow Trail*, the name by which Fay Larkin is known among the sealed wives in the hidden village. The name disguises her true identity, Fay Larkin. She is also known by the nickname given to her by Ruth Jones, the Sago Lily, a tribute to her rare beauty and her reserve. See also **Larkin, Fay.**

Masked Rider: In *Riders of the Purple Sage*, one of Oldring's men whose name is associated with mayhem and terror. The Masked Rider is credited with over a dozen murders and even more robberies. When the Masked Rider goes by, people stay indoors out of fear. The Masked Rider, however, is really Bess, Milly Erne's daughter, raised by Oldring. She is a gentle, guileless, innocent creature. The legend of the Masked Rider is useful for Oldring, as it allows him to operate his rustling business with less interference, and it keeps people out of Deception Pass, where his hideout and gold diggings are located. See also **Erne, Elizabeth.**

Mason, Big Bill: In *The Horse Thief*, assumed to be a leading rancher and horse breeder. He is one of the loudest in calling for a posse to pursue the horse thieves that have been raiding ranches in Montana. Big Bill's operation consists of a two-fold scheme, whereby horses are rustled in Montana and driven across the mountains, to be auctioned off at markets in Idaho, while a similar operation on the Idaho side provides horses for auction in Montana. This makes it unlikely that the rustled horses will be recognized. Mason's right-hand man is Ed Reed, and his spy among the ranchers is Leale Hildrith, Jim Watrous's foreman. Mason has a perfect mask of acceptability, another Henry Plummer, but he also has a gambling habit, and an addiction to high stakes.

He reputedly loses thousands of dollars in card games. The rustlers that Dale comes upon who have taken Edith Watrous's prized horses mention Big Bill as their boss. Later, Dale sees Big Bill himself at the cabin in the rustlers' hideout. Big Bill is greatly displeased with Reed's abducting Edith Watrous. He is friends with her father and knows Jim will have an implacable posse on their trail. Ed Reed tells Big Bill that Leale Hildrith has betrayed them. Big Bill shoots him. Both Reed and Big Bill are killed in the fighting that ensues. The horse thieves that survive, disperse. The gang has been broken.

Mason, Jim: In *The Shepherd of Guadaloupe*, the bystander who is shot in the fight between Cliff Forrest and Malpass outside Hartwell's store in Watrous. He is not seriously injured.

Mason, Laigs: In *Knights of the Range,* one of the "Knights of the Range," a cowboy working for the Ripple spread. He is so named because his legs are so bowed, he cannot bring his knees close enough together to hold a plate. He is the homely clown of the outfit and partner of Brazos Keene. Laigs helps Frayne dunk the drunk cowboys in the cold stream to sober them up for Holly's fiesta, an event they promised to attend sober. He is a spectacular rider, but manages to get thrown off in the rodeo competition with the Slaughter crowd. He manages to get thrown in such a way that it arouses wild mirth, shouts and jeers from the crowd. Laigs wins a hundred dollars in a card game, a feat which is the most important bit of news in months. When the Knights catch the rustlers in their camp at night, Laigs is shot, placing himself in front of Brazos, in the way of the bullet, when one of the rustlers shoots through his blanket. He does not make a fuss about his wound, just below the heart, allowing the men to take the rustlers captive and lynch them. He dies in the arms of his buddy, Brazos Keene, who mourns his death for months, almost forsaking his promise to Holly and his fellow "Knights of the Range." Brazos sings his funeral dirge, "Bury Me Not on the Lone Prairie."

Mason, Lem: In *Shadow on the Trail*, a rancher over at Mariposa. He works with Band Drake (Rand Blue) and the gunman, Kent. He is that vilest of creatures on the range, a crooked rancher. He buys the cattle that Harrobin and others rustle from the other ranchers and sells them. He hides under a mask of respectability. Tex Brandon reports to Pencarrow how he pursued and caught the lynchpin in the rustling operation on Cedar Range. Mason is a big cattle dealer and merchant. He runs the M Bar ranch below Quirts as a blind. He sells his own brand at Mariposa and drives stolen brands into New Mexico. Brandon rounds up Harrobin and Mason in a saloon where they are drinking to the success of their recent venture. Brandon gets the money from Harrobin, money that Mason has just paid him. Stewart, the foreman, never shows up, possibly having been tipped off. In the crunch, Harrobin betrays

Mason. If he is to swing for rustling, then he wants Mason and Stewart with him. Mason draws on Brandon, and is killed in the shootout. Harrobin is hanged. Later, in Holbrook, Joe Steele tells Bill Wood he is in town waiting for his boss to come in on the train, and McComb tells Hogue that Kent and Drake were in the bank, expecting to meet Mason in the afternoon. With Drake and Steele gone, the rustlers in the region have been cleaned out.

Massey, Captain: In *The Lost Wagon Train*, consulted by Major Greer about Anderson's lost wagon train. He is unable to answer and calls in Sergeant Riley, who has been on the frontier longer and probably has heard of the train.

Masters, Bruce: In *Thunder Mountain*, elected sheriff by the miners of Thunder Mountain without the approval of Rand Leavitt. He is tall, lean, wears no star on his vest, and walks with a limp. He wears a huge black sombrero that at a distance hides the upper part of his sallow face, and he wears a gun prominently, where it ought to be. His placid face reveals an interior serenity that Kalispel finds reassuring. At first, Kalispel is suspicious of him, assuming he must be Leavitt's man or he would never have been elected. Masters tells him that Lowrie and his crew have moved to Haskell to set up shop. Masters reveals he is from Texas where he rode with the Texas Rangers under Captain McNelly. He learned to handle a gun from gunfighters like King Fisher and Wess Hardin'. Masters wants to meet Kalispel to judge for himself whether the rumors spread by the Leavitt faction are true. They are saying he was a cattle thief in Montana and the robber currently operating in Thunder Mountain. Masters concludes the accusations are false and, with Kalispel, lays a trap for the robbers. Leavitt is dissatisfied with him and revokes his authority as sheriff. Masters defends Kalispel in court when he is accused of robbery. Sydney Blair comes forward to provide an alibi, clearing him of all blame. When the rockslide puts an end to much of the operations in Thunder Mountain, Masters stays on as sheriff. In a gunfight with Jones and Matthews, he learns that they killed Sam Emerson, Kalispel's brother, on orders from Rand Leavitt.

Matazel: In *30,000 on the Hoof*, one of Geronimo's sons. Logan Huett is the cavalry scout who tracks him and his bucks across a mesa and corners them. In the skirmish, no one is killed and Matazel is taken prisoner. He vows to get even. About two years later, Matazel appears at Huett's cabin in Sycamore Canyon, where he threatens Luce. He tells her he will burn the house and take Logan's squaw. Several months after that, Logan hears from Holbert that some hunters in the Tonto Basin just below Sycamore Canyon found Matazel's body. He had been caught behind a pine tree too small to cover him and he had been shot to pieces. He seemed to have put up quite a fight. Huett makes no comment, but Luce knows that it was her husband who killed Matazel.

Mathews, Luke: In *The Maverick Queen*, a young Mormon rider hired by Kit Bandon to drive her herd to Rock Springs for sale. Lincoln Bradway speaks to him about the herd and Kit's instructions. Mathews acknowledges that he does find it strange that there are so many yearlings in the herd, but he asks no questions. If some of these are mavericks that now have her brand on them, he knows nothing about it. He has been hired to move the herd and that is all. Lincoln advises him not to drive any more such herds to market.

Mathie: In *The Desert of Wheat*, a French soldier Kurt Dorn meets in France. He describe the retreat of the French army from the attacking Germans.

Matokie: In *Stranger from the Tonto*, the Piute chief that Kent Wingfield meets on his way to the Hole-in-the-Wall hideout. He recognizes Spades and tries to take him from Wingfield. Ben Bunge, who sold Spades to Wingfield, reports to Bonesteel that Matokie and another Indian were shot by this rider and now the Piutes are out for revenge.

Matt: In *Nevada*, works in the general store and is at the door when Jim Lacy and Harley Rue shoot it out in the street. He reports to the people inside, one of whom is Hettie Ide, what is happening outside. No last name is given.

Matthews: In *Thunder Mountain*, a miner who testifies against Lee Emerson (Kalispel) in the miners' court. He accuses Kalispel of attacking and robbing him. He is called to corroborate the testimony of one Jones. The evidence of both men is discredited when Sydney Blair proves that Kalispel was with her at the time the attack supposedly occurred. After the landslide, Matthews and Jones are killed in a gunfight with Sheriff Bruce Masters. One of them confesses to having killed Sam Emerson, Kalispel's oldest brother, on orders from Rand Leavitt.

Matthews, Tim: In *Code of the West*, a cowboy working on the Thurman ranch. Like everyone else, he likes to pick on Cal Thurman. Cal bets his favorite horse, Pitch, an animal envied by all, against Tim's bronco, Baldy, that before the year is out, he will beat him in a fistfight. Matthews nonchalantly dismisses this, saying he does not want to take Cal's horse. Tim Matthews and Pan Handle tinker with the car so Cal will be unable to drive Georgie home from Ryson. The day Wess and Tuck Merry have a fight, Cal gets his revenge on Tim Matthews as well, putting into effect the boxing lessons he has been getting from his buddy. Tim Matthews good-naturedly accepts his defeat, unable to believe what happened. He acknowledges that he merely got his just desserts.

Matty: In *The Drift Fence*, described as an important member of the Haverly-Jocelyn outfit that kidnaps Jim Traft for ransom. He offers to write the ransom note that Boyd will deliver to the elder Traft. He threatens that if the money is not handed over within twenty-four hours, they will kill Jim and hang his body over the drift fence. When Slinger Dunn arrives to settle the score with the old Cibeque outfit that betrayed him, Matty is let go. Jim Traft sees him leave the cabin and rush to get his saddle and bridle and stride off to catch his horse.

Mauree: In *West of the Pecos,* Sam(bo)'s wife. She accompanies the Lambeths on their trip west. She is cook for the outfit, and a companion and mother-surrogate for Terrill. She helps Rill maintain her disguise as a man, adapting her clothes to conceal her feminine form. Mauree foresees the romance between Pecos Smith and her mistress, and never ceases to wonder at how easily the young man, and most other men, have been fooled, failing to pick up on the most obvious clues.

Maurine: In *Majesty's Rancho,* one of Lance Sidway's girlfriends in Hollywood. She tells him that she likes him well enough but she has just gotten a role in a movie and does not want to commit herself to anyone. She suggests that he just string along with her and maybe.... She is a typical Hollywood girl, ready to do anything to get a role in a film.

Maxwell, Captain Lew (Lucien):   In *Fighting Caravans,* a friend and exploration partner of Kit Carson. Buff Belmet describes him as a fifty-year-old man in excellent shape, erect, virile, with a dark face displaying a record of his adventurous life. He is a very handsome man, standing six feet one inch in his moccasins. He has never shaved his face.

Maxwell left Illinois for the West in 1822. He became a frontiersman almost as famous as Kit Carson. He fought in the war with the Navajo Indians and came out with the rank of captain. He fought in the Mexican War in 1842 and the Texas invasion in 1846. He was a captain in the Texas Rangers for four years, after which he retired to his ranch. He is the biggest landowner in America, with a ranch that stretches for sixty-five miles from north to south, and fifteen miles from east to west. The closest town is Fort Union. He employs between four and five hundred Mexicans, and raises corn, oats, wheat, and all kinds of vegetables. He operates a flour and grist mill using horse power, and supplies white flour and meal to the forts and settlements. His flocks are estimated at four hundred thousand sheep, fifty thousand cattle and ten thousand horses, mules and burros. He furnishes beef to Indian reservations on government contract, and to the forts as well. He owns the largest trading and supply store in the West. He befriends whites and Indians alike. Captain Graham tells Buff and Couch that Maxwell has no enemies among the Indians because he treats all men as equals, with respect. The main dining room of his ranch house seats a hundred and it often does. The house and kitchen are run by old, experienced Mexican women. He loves to gamble, not caring whether he wins or loses, but if he does win, he is inexorable in collecting his due, even if it takes the last dollar of his opponent. But if anyone needs money, he lends freely, asking only for a date of repayment. No one has ever cheated him.

Maxwell takes Buff under his wing. He welcomes him into his home, introduces him to important people and encourages him to marry May Bell. He even offers to arrange it with Preacher Smith, then a guest at his ranch. He advises Clint to give up freighting. He predicts that the West of the freighters will soon be gone. Buff would be better off setting himself up in ranching. Couch, Dagget and others have kept at the freighting too long. They will lose their scalps one of these days. Maxwell speaks to Couch about Clint, offering him a job at his ranch. Buff, however, rejects the offer, saying that May Bell is too classy for someone like him. A year later, Clint hears that Maxwell is in financial straits and is looking to sell. In 1866, after the reported discovery of gold on his ranch, an eastern syndicate buys all his holdings at a fabulous price. The colonel moves east, and Clint never hears from him again. When the syndicate fails to find much gold on the place, they let the ranch grow up in weeds and shrubs, as they know nothing about ranching. Some years later, Clint visits the place, recalling the glory days when it was a focal point of traders, Indians, ranching. But only ghosts inhabit the once-thriving house and trading post.

In *Raiders of Spanish Peaks,* Maxwell is mentioned as an example of what Lindsay can do with his centrally located Spanish Peaks ranch. He, too, could become a wealthy man dealing in cattle, trading with the Indians, offering hospitality to all who travel by.

In *The Lost Wagon Train,* Maxwell (Grant) is mentioned as a successful frontiersman whose enormous ranch was an oasis of hospitality to all, red and white. Dr. McPherson tells Major Greer at Ft. Union that Latch reminds him of Maxwell. An educated southerner, handsome, a fine type, ruined by the war, a rancher, and on good terms with all, Indian and white. Latch is flattered by the comparison.

In *Knights of the Range,* Don Carlos Valverde's ranch is reputed to be similar to Maxwell's. His tradition of hospitality with Indians, trappers, traders, cowboys and outlaws is said to match Maxwell's. Colonel Lee Ripple and his daughter, Holly, see themselves as continuing in his tradition of hospitality, but they come to see this as a relic of a past era which must change with altered conditions.

Maxwell, Pete: In *Shadow on the Trail,* owner of the place where Pat Garritt shot Billy the Kid, in the version of the event told by Ranger Mahaffey to Tex Brandon. According to this version, Garritt didn't have the nerve to meet Billy in the open. At Maxwell's in Lincoln, Garritt and Maxwell were talking in the dark and Billy came to the door. Maxwell and Billy were friends. When Billy spoke, Garritt recognized the voice and shot him as he came in the door.

Maybelle: In *Fighting Caravans,* the name Clint Belmet gives the horse he acquires after Pickens and his thieves are caught and hanged.

Mayhew, Fork: In *Raiders of Spanish Peaks,* a cowboy who has been working for Allen on the Spanish Peaks ranch. After the sale to Lindsay, he remains loyal to his old foreman, Arlidge, but eventually changes his allegiance to the new owner, together with Dakota and Clay Lee.

McAdam: In *Forlorn River,* a business partner of Hart Blaine. He owns the Big 3C stores, and is reputed to be awfully rich. He goes into a deal with Ina Blaine's father to buy ranch land and horses and cattle. Dall Blaine refers to him as "Mr. Blondy Pop Eyes." McAdam puts pressure on Hart Blaine to have Ina marry his son to seal a deal. He breaks off the deal when Ina refuses to cooperate.

McAdam, Sewell: In *Forlorn River,* the son of the McAdam who is a business partner of Hart Blaine. He is a forward city-slicker, and friend of Kate Blaine's beau. Nevada meets him at the saloon in Hammel, where he is not overly courteous in asking about Ben Ide. He comes to the Blaine home for Sunday dinner under the impression that Ina Blaine is interested in him. He does not take no for an answer. He comes to their summer camp up at Wild Goose Lake in the mountains, where he accuses Ina of breaking a deal their fathers have made whereby he gets to marry her. Ina sends him packing. Sewell McAdam is a salesman, from Klamath Falls, a city man through and through. He looks for a quick turnover with maximum profit. He is as shallow a person as the business transactions in which he deals. His interest in a woman is determined only by her prospects and the possibility that she might advance his career.

McCall: In *Wyoming,* a rancher and rustler. He hires Texas Haynes and Smoky Reed among others to burn his brand on mavericks, or to change others' brands to his. His latest target is Nick Bligh, a rancher from Randall who has just driven a small herd into the region. Bligh has no riders combing the range, making his stock an easy target. Andrew Bonning overhears a conversation between McCall and Tex, laying out this out clearly. Sheriff Slade is also in on the deal. McCall and Bligh had struck a deal whereby Bligh runs his herd with McCall's. This saves Bligh the need to have a crew of cowboys of his own, an expense he cannot afford. McCall has now changed the terms of the deal. He claims he has a lien on the Boseman homestead which Bligh has bought. McCall hopes to drive Bligh out of business and to seize his herd and homestead. McCall forces the issue, threatening to bring the matter to court. McCall's plans come to naught when Texas Haynes demands payment for past services in public. The truth of his crooked deals comes out. He agrees to settle the deal with Bligh for a thousand dollars, but Bonning and Bligh reject the offer. Bonning repeats what he overheard in the conversation between Tex and McCall. McCall then agrees to break the contract with Bligh, but Texas insists on his back wages. In the gunfight that ensues, he shoots and kills McCall. Eager to keep his own crooked dealings from coming out, Sheriff Slade declares the matter resolved.

McClain, Sandy: In *West of the Pecos,* works on the Healds' ranch. He is one of the few people that Pecos opens up to, but does not reveal much about his past. Sandy does get a look at Pecos's gun, reporting to John and Bill that it has six notches on it.

McClellan, Bill: In *Knights of the Range,* drives the stagecoach from Santa Fe to Las Animas.

McColloch, Elizabeth (Bessie):   Best known as Bessie Zane. She is the sister of Sam McColloch and wife of Colonel Ebenezer Zane. Her mother was a Shawnee Indian. She is Zane Grey's great-grandmother, and through her, Grey claimed kinship with the Native Americans.

Bessie Zane is known for her surgical skill. She can sew up wounds with the skill of a surgeon. Her knowledge herbal remedies and potions make her a genuine doctor in Ft. Henry.

Bessie Zane is a voice of common sense in *Betty Zane.* She sees through Betty's "love games" with Alfred Clarke and tells Ebenezer he needs to speak to his sister about her behavior. In the attack on the fort, Bessie is in charge of the infirmary, treating the wounded during the siege. At the beginning of *The Last Trail,* she speaks eloquently to Helen Sheppard about the trials of the frontier woman.

McColloch, Sam: Mentioned in the last two of the three Ohio Valley novels and appears as a character in the first, *Betty Zane.*

Sam McColloch is Colonel Ebenezer Zane's brother-in-law. He was one of the early settlers at Ft. Henry. He shares Wetzel's dislike of Indians but unlike Wetzel, whose campaign is personal, Sam McColloch conducts expeditions of soldiers and frontiersmen against Indians.

Sam McColloch is known among the Indians as the "Flying Chief" because of his famous leap from the cliff. This occurred during one of the attacks on the fort. Sam McColloch was getting people into the fort for protection and found himself caught between an Indian force coming over the top of the hill and another band at the bottom. Rather than face capture and torture, he rode his horse over the cliff, landing in the pine trees at the bottom. He and his horse rode out of the trees and on to the fort uninjured. The Indians thought it miraculous that he survived the leap.

In *Betty Zane,* the colonel is not inside the fort during the attack, having gone to Ft. Pitt to obtain reinforcements for the defense of Ft. Henry.

At the start of *The Last Trail,* Bessie says that Sam was shot and scalped on the river bank as he was going to the spring for a bucket of water.

McComb, John: In *Shadow on the Trail,* a clerk who works in the bank in Holbrook, where Pencarrow does his business. His father owns the bank. He is madly in love with Jacqueline Pencarrow, but she shows no interest in him. McComb reports to Hogue Kinsey that Drake and Kent are in town, lying low, waiting for Mason. He is a director at the bank now, and they had come in that morning to discuss business. He clearly wants to help if he can.

McCormick: In *Valley of Wild Horses*, brings word from Marco about Pan Handle's fight with Hardman in the Yellow Mine and the burning of the saloon. He reports that people in town think more highly of Pan Handle for his facing Hardman.

McCoy, Sewall: In *Knights of the Range*, a rancher and cattleman. He is first mentioned when Jim reports to Britt about Sewall's outfit appearing on their range, branding every unbranded calf with the Bar M brand, sometimes over the Ripple brand. The practice is not really illegal, but certainly dishonest, since the calf branded Bar M has a mother branded Ripple. Renn Frayne knew McCoy before his arrival at the Ripple ranch. He calls him an outlaw and the crookedest cattleman he ever met. Holly is made to feel his rivalry from the moment he arrives. At the fiesta, he approaches her. He is a large, square-shouldered man, over forty years old, handsome in a bold, rugged way, heavily jowled and possessed of the hard eyes and lips characteristic of so many cattlemen. For a heavy man, he dances well, except that he presumes upon the opportunity to hold her more tightly than she likes. He proposes marriage to her on the dance floor, threatening to form an alliance with Russ Slaughter should she refuse. He also tells her that Renn Frayne is an outlaw, a rustler, and will soon implicate her in his rustling operations. McCoy is stronger on the range than Britt, Holly's foreman, had estimated. He has powerful friends who are not friendly to Texans and he dominates the smaller ranchers, those with small herds or with little means. He goes to town and gambles, times at which he is dangerous He makes veiled threats against Britt and his outfit and adds to his own crew a notorious Kansas gunman and enemy of Frayne, one Jeff Rankin. McCoy pursues his campaign against Frayne, eventually showing up at the Ripple ranch to have him arrested or to force him into a gunfight with Rankin. The ranchers with him, Halstead, Clements, and Spencer, among others, are convinced by McCoy's arguments that Frayne is the head rustler in the area. They await Slaughter's proof while Frayne goes to town with Britt to shoot it out with Rankin. McCoy is shocked to see Frayne return, and even more shocked when Brazos returns with Slaughter's dead body over the saddle of his horse. Slaughter, apparently, had not trusted his partner in crime. He recorded every calf, every steer, every sale he made. His records implicate Clements and other ranchers posing as honest cattlemen. Brazos shoots him, and warns the other ranchers that should they meet with any of the Ripple outfit, they should be prepared to fight.

McDermott: In *The U. P. Trail*, an axeman in a construction gang, a close friend of Sandy Shane and Pat Casey. He joins Neale and Slingerland and Larry King on the buffalo hunt which ends in a fight with the Sioux. He helps Casey bury the dead when the Benton construction city is being relocated to Roaring City. McDermott reports to General Lodge about the meeting of Neale and Slingerland and the fight with Durade in which Durade is killed and Allie Lee finally freed. Neale speaks of McDermott and Casey as the little men who gave their all for the construction of the great railroad but whose names will never be known.

McDonald, Hal: In *30,000 on the Hoof*, one of the very young cowboys that Logan Huett hires to drive his herd to Flagg. The older boys have signed up for the army and the war.

McGill: In *Fighting Caravans*, an associate of Murdock and Blackstone. McGill draws on Clint Belmet from behind Red Hawkins and floors him with a bullet in the shoulder. Belmet shoots dead both Hawkins and McGill.

McGill, Smatty: In *Forlorn River*, the owner of the saloon in Hammell. Ben Ide stops in here when he comes into Hammell to get the latest news.

McGinnis, Alice: In *Wyoming*, Martha Dixon's friend in Omaha. Supposedly, Martha is going to Omaha to visit with Alice and her family. Martha sends a postcard home telling her mother she and Alice have reached Omaha.

McKee: In *The Spirit of the Border*, one of the renegades who abandoned Ft. Pitt after the Revolutionary War and lived among the Indians, making life miserable for pioneers. He works with the Girtys to destroy the influence of the Village of Peace. He is mentioned in *Betty Zane*, *The Spirit of the Border* and *The Last Trail*.

McKeen, Doris: In *Horse Heaven Hill*, a college friend of Marigold Wade's who comes to the ranch on a visit. She is a blond, friendly young woman, easy to get to know and very likeable. She is thrilled to go to dances and to meet local cowboys. She and Evelyn accompany Marigold on the picnic camping trip to watch the men chase and capture a herd of wild mustangs.

McKeever: (1) In *The Maverick Queen*, McKeever is a cardsharp and Jess Emery's right-hand man. He is a gambler who will shoot at the drop of a card, jerking a little gun from inside his vest. During the card game in the saloon the day he arrives in South Pass, Lincoln Bradway concludes that McKeever is a more dangerous man than Emery. When Lincoln wins the big pot in the poker game, McKeever accuses him of cheating and goes for the littlegun in his vest. Lincoln shoots him. McKeever loses a lot of blood, but Doc Williamson manages to patch him up. He is kept in Kit Bandon's room in the Aldham Hotel. Lincoln accompanies Doc Williamson on a visit to McKeever one evening. He finds Sealover in the room with him and McKeever is pleased to watch Sealover squirm under Bradway's scrutiny. When Sealover is gone, Lincoln returns McKeever's derringer to him. He apologizes for suspecting he had killed his partner, Jimmy Weston. Doc Williamson's autopsy has revealed the bullet did not come from McKeever's gun. Lincoln proposes a truce between them and McKeever accepts. He learns that McKeever does not know who killed Jimmy, but that he was not killed at the Leave It. McKeever also warns Linc about Kit. She has made a fool of him as she did with Lee and the other cattlemen and as she is currently doing with Emery. She likes men. She likes to gamble with them and their gold and their lives. And men don't betray Kit and live.

(2) In *West of the Pecos,* a trail driver who had a contract to deliver cattle to Santa Fe. Pecos Smith had been working for him but left the cattle drive when he reached the Healds' ranch. On his return from Santa Fe, he stops by the Healds' place. He describes Pecos Smith as the best-natured boy you'd ever want to meet. He gets picked on or gets into trouble trying to help out others but especially he is known for his skill with a gun. He tells Bill and John that "[his] loss is [their] gain.... They don't come any finer than Smith."

McKelvy: In *Twin Sombreros,* named as the Texas Ranger under whom both Captain Britt and Sheriff Kiskadden had served when in the rangers.

McKinney, Blab: In *Arizona Ames,* a seasoned cowboy working on Crow Grieve's Wind River Ranch. He was shot in a gunfight in Granger. When he gets back to the ranch he recognizes Arizona Ames. McKinney is popular among the other cowboys with his stories and teasing banter. He is pleased to meet his old friend again, filling him in on the gossip about Crow Grieve. When Arizona Ames asks why the cowboys don't do something about Grieve, he answers that they are too afraid to. Blab McKinney is the only cowboy who knows about Lany Price and Amy Grieve, but he keeps his mouth shut. When Arizona Ames confronts Grieve, McKinney decides to quit the ranch as well, but, like Arizona Ames, waits around for his pay. He warns Arizona that Grieve will try to shoot him from ambush.

McKinney, Captain: In *West of the Pecos,* the commander of the Texas Rangers who come looking for Pecos Smith following charges made by Sawtell in a letter. The rangers are in Rockport working on the Big Brewster cattle-steal. Captain McKinney is about medium height, of the usual Texan complexion, with a stern face and piercing eyes. Pecos introduces himself to McKinney in the hotel lobby. The captain invites him to his room in the hotel. He knows Pecos is from a fine old Texas family. He knows his uncle, Bradington Smith, and the ranger, Jeff Slinger, both speak well of Pecos's character. McKinney is inclined to believe the account Pecos gives of himself, and to distrust Sawtell. Additionally, he served in the war with Templeton Lambeth, Pecos's fiancée's father. Captain McKinney leaves Ranger Johnson and Jeff Slinger to return on the cattle drive with Pecos Smith and Terrill.

McKinney, Sergeant: In *30,000 on the Hoof,* works under General Crook. He is in charge of the Apache prisoners to be returned to the reservation. The Apache, Matazel, son of Geronimo, was handed over to him when Logan Huett trailed and recaptured him.

McKue, Baldy: In *Wanderer of the Wasteland,* killed by Adam Larey for abusing a woman. Larey broke his arm, his neck and his ribs with his bare hands. The story is told to underline the phenomenal strength of Wansfell and his mission to avenge the weak and defenseless. In *Stairs of Sand,* Adam Larey tells the story. He found the woman beaten and abandoned by McKue. He never learned who she was or her story. She kept her secret. He nursed her, trying to save her life, but he couldn't. She was not strong enough for childbirth and she and the baby died. She did tell him that the baby was not McKue's. At present, Adam has been captured by Bill Stark who is working under orders from Guerd Larey, who wants Wansfell caught and killed. The woman was Stark's wife and the baby was his. Stark confesses that he had driven the woman to ruin and thanks Adam for his kindness to her. He then proceeds to set Adam free.

McLane, Sandy: In *The Wolf Tracker,* one of the cowboys on Barrett's ranch preparing for the spring roundup when Brinks arrives with Old Gray's hide.

McLaughlin, Major: In *Fighting Caravans,* provides an escort for Couch's caravan to deliver government supplies to Fort Wise, Colorado. When they reach Fort Leavenworth, the cavalry escort departs as ordered by McLaughlin. Couch had hoped the escort would continue with the caravan and considers their departure a "dirty trick."

McLelland, Sandy: In *Fighting Caravans,* a friend of Dick Curtis's. He was witness to the gunfight in the saloon in Santa Fe when Clint Belmet confronted Blackstone and Murdock. In the gunfight, Clint killed McGill and Hawkins before being badly shot up himself. Sandy describes the fight as "nifty." Blackstone and Murdock were injured but not seriously.

McMillan, Jerry: In *The Fugitive Trail,* a big cattleman and trail driver out of Waco. Like most drivers, he will not pass up a good buy. MacMillan is a tall man with a lean red face and narrow eyes. He recognizes Tex Serks, who rides into camp telling him that the two thousand steers he bought from Vic Henderson were cattle rustled from the Circle M, Melrose's ranch. He acknowledges that his foreman, Henry, had doubts about Henderson's honesty. Tex Serks has been given carte blanche by Melrose to handle the situation. He tells McMillan to sell the cattle in Dodge for fifteen dollars a head, to take out what he paid Henderson and three dollars a head for driving them to Dodge. He can send the balance to Melrose. McMillan accepts the deal. He asks Tex about the rangeland in West Texas. Tex Serks replies that there's room for a million cattle. He tells Tex to tell Melrose he will move with his family to the new range near Melrose's ranch.

McMillan, Sergeant: In *Fighting Caravans,* with Belmet and the caravans at Point of Rocks. He orders the Pawnee prisoners shot.

McNeale: In *Boulder Dam,* in charge of the pick and shovel squad at the construction site. Flynn sends Lynn Weston to him to be assigned work duties.

McNelly: In *Thunder Mountain,* mentioned by Sheriff Bruce Masters as a captain in the Texas Rangers for whom Masters rode years ago. He speaks in high terms of this man.

McNulty, Captain: In *Knights of the Range,* mentioned as a famous member of the Texas Rangers, older brother to Rebel McNulty.

McNulty, Rebel: In *Knights of the Range,* a cowboy who works for the Ripple outfit.

McPherson, Bud: In *Wild Horse Mesa,* a member of Manerube's outfit. He is a man with energy and spirit, but he is watchful and secretive. His face is a mask to hide thought. He openly admires Chane Weymer's horse, Brutus, and plans to steal him. He is a genuine lover of horses and disapproves of Manerube's brutal methods with them. At the end of the novel, when he has captured Panquitch, he wonders why the stallion was so easy to capture. Chane Weymer tells him that he had already taken the animal and had just released him. Chane also knows that McPherson truly loves horses and that he is probably a decent man deep down. For the sake of the stallion, he convinces McPherson to claim his right of ownership of the animal. This leads to a gunfight in which Manerube kills McPherson.

McPherson, Dr.:   In *The Lost Wagon Train,* works at Ft. Union. He mentions Stephen Latch to the major and to Kit Carson as a man worth meeting. He reminds him of Maxwell of New Mexico fame, the Maxwell who is friend to all Indians, freighters, scouts, trappers, outlaws, desperadoes. The doctor has been treating him for gunshot wounds.

McSween: In *Shadow on the Trail,* mentioned in conjunction with Billy the Kid and the Lincoln County cattle war. Billy and his outfit were on McSween's side. The other faction surrounded McSween and some of his men were killed. Billy survived, coming out of a burning house shooting, with a gun in each hand.

Meade: In *Majesty's Rancho,* runs a garage in Bolton. Smith sends Lance Sidway to his garage to get instructions on how to get to Mike Scanlon's place at the edge of town. Just as he arrives at the garage, Uhl pulls up in his big black car with the kidnapped Madge and Rollie inside.

Mecklin: In *Arizona Ames,* a rider for John Halstead, but a cohort of Barsh Hensler, right-hand man to Clive Bannard, leader of the rustler outfit. Bannard operates behind the scenes but is caught red-handed with the last cattle to be stolen from Halstead's ranch. Mecklin, however, is referred to as the "Trojan horse" on Halstead's ranch. He gets Fred Halstead drunk and involved in card games where he loses heavily. He shoots Stevens in the back, fearing he may suspect what Mecklin is up to. Bannard and Hensler are afraid to challenge Arizona Ames, preferring to hold off on any further attacks on Halstead's herd for a while. Mecklin prefers to call Ames's bluff, and the outlaws are caught red-handed. Arizona Ames confronts him at the outlaws' agreed meeting place and beats the truth out of him. When Arizona Ames brings him back to the cabin to confront Bannard and Hensler, he manages to sneak off in the confusion that ensues.

Mecklin, Bull: In *Thunder Mountain,* runs a drinking and gambling establishment reputed to be the toughest den in the gold-diggings at Thunder City.

Medill, Ranger Vaughn: In "The Ranger," a veteran member of the Texas Rangers. Like other Texas youths, he had enlisted in the famous and unique state constabulary before he was twenty, and he refused to count the years he had served. He has the stature of the born Texan and the lined, weathered face, the resolute lips, the narrowed eyes of cool gray. The tinge of white over his temples did not begin to tell the truth about his age. Like many Texas, he has contempt for Mexicans, but admiration for some remarkable exceptions—Villa, Martiniano, among others. Medill has been given to existential angst over his future. He wants a wife and family, a ranch of his own, but having no girlfriend makes that change unlikely. He has been infatuated with Roseta for years. At dances, she calls him "un señor grande" and "the handsome gringo." But she is rich, the belle of Las Animas, the despair of cowboy and vaquero alike. He imagines young Glover, son of the rancher her father works for as foreman, will take the prize. When assigned to the case of investigating the abduction, he, too, is inclined to think it could be an elopement. Uvaldo himself hints at this possibility. Medill, however, senses that her father is hiding something. The first tracks suggest an elopement, but soon it is clear that the man she met has been killed and she has been taken to Mexico. Medill is caught by these men who have laid a trap for him. It seems the purpose of this abduction was to lure him across the border. Quinela wants to capture him to get revenge for his killing of Lopez, a relative and fellow bandit. Medill manages to lull Juan Mendoz, leader of the trio, into indiscretions. Juan gets very mellow drinking his canyu. He even unties Medill, who takes advantage of the freedom to get his guns and shoot the three of them. On the return, Roseta tells him that she has always loved him. She proposes they get married, that they "elope" before they return to the Glover ranch, to teach her father a lesson. She asks him to leave the rangers, as she would not want to be worrying about whether he will be shot and killed someday on duty.

He has money set aside to buy a ranch in the North, under the Llano Estacado, where they can live secure from border incursions.

Meeker, Abel: In *To the Last Man,* a villager whose house is across from Greaves's store. He is a friend of Gaston Isbel, who asks Meeker to give him his house to use as headquarters. Meeker agrees, and moves his family out of the house to Jim's. He offers to help Gaston Isbel but Gaston rejects his offer.

Meeker, Parson: In *Code of the West,* a tall gray man who marries Cal Thurman and Georgie Stockwell. Tuck Merry has met him several times and they get along well. He knows how to handle him and concocts a story to gain his sympathy. He brings him around the Diamond to Boyd Thurman's cabin. He is tickled pink to be involved in what he takes to be a real love story, as Cal tells him they have eloped because of problems convincing Georgie's sister to let them wed. Meeker congratulates Georgie on her choice of husband, one of the best men in the Tonto. Parson Meeker later marries Enoch and Georgie's sister, Mary, down at the Thurman ranch.

Meeker, Ted: In *To the Last Man,* the brother of Abel Meeker. He had been friendly with Greaves and is in the store the night after the Jorths return from their attack on the Isbel ranch. He hears Greaves's story about Jean Isbel stabbing him to avenge his brother Guy and Ellen Jorth. He reports that Lee Jorth killed Simm Bruce for sullying Ellen's reputation. He gives Ted Meeker a bad wound and he throws him out of the store. Meeker crawls over to Ewarts, where he tells his story.

Melberne: In *Wild Horse Mesa,* has set up an outfit with Jim Loughbridge to hunt wild horses. He has no experience chasing mustangs, but has hired Manerube, who boasts of his great abilities at hunting them. Melberne is a fair man in his dealings with others, open to suggestions and willing to give a man the benefit of the doubt. He has heard that Bud McPherson is a horse thief, and has his doubts about Manerube's honesty. He takes in Chane Weymer when he rides into camp half-starved and nurses him back to health. He does not hold against Chane the story that Manerube had told about him. Melberne solicits Chane's opinion of Manerube's proposed method of catching horses. Chane describes the method, not sparing the bloody details of injury and suffering this will cause the animals. Melberne is tempted to cancel plans to catch animals that way but Loughbridge, anxious to make a quick buck, will not consent. When the first group of horses has been delivered, Melberne breaks his partnership with Loughbridge, wiping out Loughbridge's debt to him. The men in the outfit choose to remain with Melberne. At this point, Melberne tells his daughter, Sue, that he had misjudged Chane. He now considers him the best man he has ever met. He knows that Sue is sweet on him and urges her to marry him. Melberne decides to start ranching on Wild Horse Mesa. He sends word to his brothers in Texas to come join him in the project. Chane Weymer is taken on as foreman of the operation. The friendship with Loughbridge is reestablished when Loughbridge finally understands what kind of man Manerube is. Loughbridge will set up a ranch on the Mesa, as a neighbor to Melberne.

Melberne, Mrs.: In *Wild Horse Mesa,* the second wife of Melburne. She is described as short, stout, pleasant-faced, clever, lovable, and a good mate for her husband. She and her stepdaughter, Sue, get along well. She teases Sue when she sees her "prettied up" for Chane. She is mentioned as cooking, together with Mrs. Loughbridge and Jake.

Melberne, Sue: In *Wild Horse Mesa,* the twenty-year-old daughter of Melberne. She was born in Texas and schooled in Silver City. Her mother is dead, but she gets along well with her stepmother, a woman who is good for her father. She has turned down a job as a schoolteacher in St. George to go along with her father and brother on a mustanging expedition. She prefers life in the open, in the bosom of mother nature, to life in a town. Her reaction to the western landscape recalls that of Mescal, or Jonathan Zane.

Sue Melberne is called "Little Girl Gold" by Chess Weymer, her admirer. She cannot see him romantically, as he is two years younger than she is, but Sue does fall in love with his brother, Chane, initially from the worshipful stories Chess has told about his idealized older brother, and later from personal contact with a man her father comes to describe as the most decent man he has ever met. Chane is good looking and strong, but above all, compassionate, fair, and loyal. She admires the affection between the two brothers, the consideration Chane shows his horse, Brutus, and his friendship with the Indian, Toddy Nokin. Through Chane and Sosie, Toddy Nokin's daughter, she realizes her preconceptions about Indians are false. At first she is jealous of Sosie, but when the Indian girl tells her of Chane's nobility in rescuing her and treating her decently, Sue senses Chane's integrity.

Sue Melberne instinctively mistrusts Manerube. While she is undeniably moved by his handsome face and his slick manners, she senses dishonesty and cowardice in him. When she sees him work with horses and other men, his brutality reinforces her dislike of him. In particular, she dislikes his method of catching large numbers of mustangs with barbed wire fences. The suffering of the captured animals pulls at her heartstrings, and when the men have driven some of the animals, hobbled, to the train station, she secretly opens the gate, allowing the remaining horses to escape. Likewise, when she and Chane have captured Panquitch, the stallion king, she convinces Chane to release the animal. He is a symbol of the freedom and wildness of the West.

Sue and Chane Weymer are to marry at Thanksgiving when her father's preacher brother, Jim, is to arrive from Texas to join them at their ranch on Wild Horse Mesa. Chane will remain as foreman of the ranch.

Melberne, Tommy: In *Wild Horse Mesa*, mentioned as Melberne's son, Sue's brother. He is instructed to go cut wood on one occasion, but there is no further mention of him in the novel.

Melberne, Uncle Jim: In *Wild Horse Mesa*, the brother of Melberne, Sue's father. He is a preacher, living in Texas. Melberne sends word to him that he has found a place suitable for ranching and asks Uncle Jim to come join him. Uncle Jim is to arrive before winter, and Sue hopes he arrives by Thanksgiving, as she wants him to marry her and Chane Weymer.

Melliss, Louise: In *Valley of Wild Horses*, works in the Yellow Mine Saloon. Pan Handle first sees her sitting on Dick Hardman's lap in the saloon. She shows interest in the newcomer, a development which arouses Hardman's curiosity. Louise had met Hardman in San Francisco and he brought her to Marco. She tells Pan Handle she doesn't like Hardman. He made many promises he never kept, double-crossing her. She did, however, take a liking to the bow-legged cowboy who kept telling her he loved her. When they have made a killing selling the mustangs, Pan Handle and Blinky come to take Louise away. She refuses to think of marrying Blinky, saying he is too good for her. She is drunk, unaware of what is going on. When they talk of Hardman, she draws a knife from under her pillow and goes to the closet where Hardman has been hiding and stabs him to death. They take Louise from the Yellow Mine. The parson who had married Hardman and Lucy marries them. With the shooting that breaks out in the saloon, a fire gets started and the Yellow Mine burns to the ground. Hardman's charred remains are found together with those of an unidentified girl that some assume to be Louise. She and Blinky accompany the Smiths to their new home in Arizona.

Mellon, Mr. and Mrs.: In *Fighting Caravans*, he takes Clint Belmet in when he has been released from the military hospital after he had been badly injured in the Indian attack on the wagon train. He and his wife look after Clint, who is in a coma or hallucinating for several months.

Melrose, Jack: In *The Fugitive Trail*, Steven Melrose's sixteen-year-old son. He is a friendly youngster, dressed in cowboy garb, packing a gun rather prominently. He takes a liking to Bruce Lockheart from the start and shares with him what he learns about his father's deals with Barncastle. He reports that his father is worried sick over the deal and Slaughter is madder than a wet hen. His father worries he has been overcautious and oversuspicious and he wants Luke to go slow. Slaughter, however, wants to send Bruce and Tex and the boys out to get proof of Barncastle's crookedness.

Jack arranges to have Bruce take him hunting for venison. He tells Bruce that Trinity "runs" the ranch. She has given Bruce one of her horses to ride for the day. She convinced her father to get Slaughter to assign him to go hunting along the brakes. Slaughter also tells him to keep an eye out for cattle, tracks, and riders out there in the brakes. Bruce notes that young Melrose has the seat of a range rider and makes a fine picture on his horse. He proves to be quite a good shot, and Bruce is impressed when he brings down a two-point buck. They gut the deer and hang the meat in a tree. Then Jack takes Bruce to the high ground to get a view of the ranch. The view is magnificent. Jack notices smoke in the distance. He wants to fetch Serks and his outfit to have a look. Perhaps the rustlers are on the move. Jack is a dynamic, voluble personality and most likeable. Bruce and Jack become partners. When Trinity rides up to them before they reach the ranch, he has the discretion to ride ahead and give them privacy. He waits for them to catch up, apparently seeing or thinking nothing. In the campaign to catch the rustlers, Jack shows himself to be excessively enthusiastic and reckless. Tex and Bruce tease him that when they find Stewart's hole, they will just trail the rustlers to their camp and then send Jack in alone to clear them out. When the rustlers have been caught, Bruce refuses to continue living under a false name. Jack is the first cowboy he tells that he is the real Bruce Lockheart. Jack is impressed, but disappointed that Bruce feels the need to reveal his identity to Maggard and to leave the ranch. Fortunately, Maggard has lost his interest in pursuing the bank robber and Jack and Bruce will now be brothers-in-law as well as partners.

Melrose, Mrs.: In *The Fugitive Trail*, Steven Melrose's second wife. She is mentioned several times in the novel but never appears in any scene.

Melrose, Steven: In *The Fugitive Trail*, a rancher across the Brazos River in Texas. Captain Maggard tells Trinity Spencer that she resembles Steven's first wife, Mary Hutchinson. Steve and Mary lived for several years at Shreveport, and there they had a little girl. Steve went west to buy cattle and find a ranch. After he had located, he sent for Mary and the child. He was anxious for them to join him so he did not wait until there was a big wagon train. Instead, he instructed her to get men and wagons and come on. She left with one wagon and a driver. She was never heard from again. When he gave her up for lost, he married again. He has a wonderful ranch at the head of the Brazos River. He is rich in cattle now but he still speaks to Maggard of his first wife and lost daughter. When Trinity arrives, she first sees him on the porch of his ranch house. He is a tall, stalwart man, with thick silver hair. To Trinity, he embodied all the attributes that seemed so splendid in a Texan. He had a fine, clean-shaven face, lined and drawn, hard and craggy from contact with the elements, but softened on the moment with a smile. He sees the resemblance between Trinity and Mary Hutchinson. Her recollection of wagons and a long drive, campfires, yelling voices of Indians, sounds plausible. She shows Melrose a silver locket with a lock of her hair. It is the locket he had given Mary on their wedding day. The daughter he lost twenty years before has been restored to him. She appears to be Mary restored to life.

Melrose takes Tex, Jim Serks, and Lee Jones (Bruce Lockheart) on as riders. He recognizes their competence and integrity. He gives Bruce Lockheart a good look over, as does Luke Slaughter. He is not an ordinary cowboy by a long shot. When Trinity informs him that she and Lee are engaged, he subjects Bruce to a more careful scrutiny. Lee tells him he cannot answer all his questions at this point but he asks the man to trust that he has both his interests and those of Trinity at heart. Steven recalls how he felt when he ran away with Mary Hutchinson, and gives Trinity and Lee his blessings. When Clark claims to recognize Bruce Lockheart in Lee Jones, Melrose puts up a remarkable defense of his son-in-law-to-be, convincing Clark before the rangers that he must be mistaken in his identification.

Melrose enters into a cattle deal in Dodge with a man he knows as Barncastle. He is unaware that Barncastle is the rustler named Belton. According to their deal, Barncastle is to pay him the money he owes and deliver a herd of cattle he bought. Barncastle is unknown at the bank in Dodge, and the cattle are supposed to be delivered by a man called Linden. Eventually, Barncastle's lieutenant, Stewart, shows up to negotiate. Stewart threatens Melrose, pointing out that he and Barncastle together have fourteen riders, men who have fought Indians, Missouri men who have no use for Texans. He is alone, with fifty thousand head of longhorns. Rustlers have almost cleaned out his Little Wichita outfit. With a range as big and free as this he can lose all his cattle before it is settled. He had better forget his differences with Barncastle and throw in with them. Lee Jones tells Slaughter, Tex and Melrose that Barncastle is an outlaw, a rustler, but that he cannot prove it yet. Melrose convinces the rangers that they should quit their pursuit of a bank robber and take up the problem of the cattle rustlers. He assigns the task to Luke Slaughter, giving him carte blanche. Juan Vasquez, the best tracker around, and Tex Serks lead the pursuit of the rustlers. They corner them in a cabin and in the prolonged shootout, most of them are killed.

Melrose, Trinity (Trin) Spencer: In *The Fugitive Trail*, the daughter of Steve Melrose and Mary Hutchinson. Her father had moved west and sent for his wife and child to join him. Anxious to have them with him at his new ranch on the Brazos, he arranged for them to come west immediately rather than wait for a large wagon train. They never arrive, and are presumed killed in an Indian raid. The Spencers found Trinity, alone, on the banks of the Trinity River. Nothing was ever learned of her origin, and they raised her as their own daughter. Trinity herself has only vague recollections of long rides in a wagon, endless plains of waving grass, black herds of buffalo, camps and fires along dark rivers, fierce, bearded men, gunshots and the blood-curdling war cries of Indians. Captain Maggard of the Texas Rangers meets Trinity

at Doan's post in Texas. He is struck by her resemblance to the first wife of an old friend of his, Steve Melrose. He thinks her recollections of the past match the story of the disappearance of Mary Hutchinson and her daughter. He suggests she visit the Melrose ranch as she is heading west. Sure enough, Melrose sees the same resemblance to his first wife, and the locket Trinity shows him was his wedding present to Mary. Trinity has found her true home.

With the Spencers, Trinity learned the skills of a rancher's wife, but proved equally good at riding, roping and the other tasks normally performed by a cowboy. Mrs. Spencer hopes that she will marry her son Hal one day, but Trinity inclines toward the Lockheart brothers, Bruce and Barse. Bruce is very different from his brother — tough, hard, serious, with a reputation as a buffalo hunter, trail driver and gunman. She wonders about the stories she has heard of his prowess with the gun. Her attentions, however, have been directed at Barse. She has tried to get him to change his ways, to settle down, and she has even promised to marry him if he straightens out. He goes from bad to worse. With the changes in Denison, more cattle, more money, the railroad, Barse hangs around with Belton's gang and Steve Henderson, drinking and gambling. In the Belton gang's assault on the Denison bank, Barse is recognized. Bruce tries to save Barse by taking his place, as though he committed the robbery. Trinity is disgusted with Barse's pretense of innocence, refuses to marry him and sets out to find Bruce.

Her travels take her to Texas, to Doan's post, where Lige Tanner, whom she met on the stage, and Captain Maggard and others try to put her on Bruce's trail. She meets many cowboys who had known him, and learns of their great respect and admiration for their trail partner. Bruce eventually shows up at the Melrose ranch on the Brazos and is taken on as a rider. He calls himself Lee Jones. Trinity pretends not to know him. She brings him up to date on the happenings back in Denison. His mother is now staying with the Spencers, and Barse was killed in a gunfight over cards. At the Melrose ranch, Trinity has become fully accepted. Her brother, Jack, says she now runs the place. He does not say this with feelings of resentment but of pure admiration. She is a better cowboy than he is in many respects.

When the rangers make their appearance at the ranch seeking Bruce Lockheart, Trinity is concerned for him, but soon learns that Sgt. Blight has never seen Bruce and could not recognize him. She introduces Bruce as her fiancé, and Steve Melrose accepts her choice, but only after giving him a close examination. After the many twists and turns of the plot, the rustlers that have been plaguing the ranch have been captured or killed, and Belton and Stewart, who might recognize him, are all dead. Bruce is free of pursuit. When he insists on identifying himself to Maggard and flees on his horse, Trinity pursues him. When she has caught up to him, she tells him that Maggard has abandoned his pursuit, declaring Bruce has squared himself with the law.

Trinity is a heroine developed along the lines of Holly Ripple (*Knights of the Range*) or Hettie Ide and Ina Blaine in *Forlorn River* or *Nevada*. She is a strong, independent woman, fearless in pursuit of her goal, an equal companion and mate for Bruce Lockheart.

Melville: In *The Lost Wagon Train*, comes up in the conversation between Kit Carson and Stephen Latch in the hospital at Fort Union. Melville's caravan had been jumped by Comanches at Point of Rocks in September. Latch tells Carson about the attack in a clean, straightforward, forceful narrative. Kit Carson is impressed. Carson hazards a guess that Nigger Horse was the chief of the Comanches in the attack.

Mendez, Juan: In *Raiders of Spanish Peaks,* one of the crew left by Allen to work on the Spanish Peaks ranch when he sells it to Lindsay. Lenta reports to Harriet that Juan Mendez, like Neg Jackson, is under Chess Gaines's influence. Juan Mendez arrives at the cabin when Laramie and Lonesome are inside. Rather than enter, he turns and rides off, understanding that the game is up and flight is his only security.

Mendoz, Juan: In "The Ranger," leads the trio of Mexican bandits who kill Elmer Wade and abduct Roseta. He reveals to Medill that the abduction was designed to lure him to Mexico. Their boss, Quinela, wants to settle the score with him over the killing of Lopez, a cohort and relative. Juan Mendoz is bringing the ranger and Roseta to Quinela. A bottle of canyu, however, mellows him. Ranger Medill attempts to corrupt him with promises of gold, and even gives him a letter to take to Texas to get the gold from his banker. The drunk and illiterate Juan believes Medill, whose letter really explains who Mendoz is and orders his immediate incarceration. Ranger Medill eventually convinces Juan to untie him. He gets his hands on Juan's guns and kills the trio and returns to Texas with the grateful Roseta.

Mendoza: In *Knights of the Range,* a Spanish explorer mentioned by Holly Ripple in her address to the 500 diners at her fiesta. The address begins by summarizing the history of the region and the Spanish contributions to the cattle industry.

Mendoza, Señorita Dolores: (1) In *Twin Sombreros,* mentioned by Holly Ripple as an old flame of Brazos. She suggests that he return to Don Carlos's rancho, marry Dolores, and settle down as a partner on the ranch.

(2) In *Yaqui,* the daughter of one of the prominent families in Mendoza. Her family has arranged a marriage to Lieutenant Perez, son of Don Sancho Perez, one of the great hemp plantation owners. She is unusual for a young woman of the Yucatan, being blond and fair-skinned. She enjoys the bullfights, not for the demonstration of courage on the part of the picadores or the matadores, but for the killing and the gore. Montes makes love to her, rather surprised that she tolerates his advances given that she is about to marry Perez. She accepts her fate with equanimity. The marriage has been decided. She will do her duty before and after the marriage, but that does not prevent her from enjoying herself with Montes in the meantime. No mention is made of her reaction when the body of her husband-to-be emerges from the bale supposed to contain the spectacular pearls.

Mercer, John Dodge: In *The Arizona Clan*, a Grey hero developed along the lines of Buck Duane, or Arizona Ames. He is a gunman who puts his skills to use to help the Lilley Clan out of a predicament. He understands that helping others is the best way to resolve one's own problems.

Dodge Mercer was born in Philadelphia. He ran away from school and home before he was fifteen. He became a cowhand in Kansas, then drifted west. Dodge has seen a lot of hard life on the Texas Panhandle and the Kansas plains. Then he set out for Arizona looking for a change. He likes the Arizona landscape. In Ryeson, he meets young Tommy Barnes, who tells him about the town and the possibility of employment, either at Simpson's ranch or at the Lilleys.' Tommy fills him in on Nan and her troubles. It seems her father is taken with Buck Hathaway and has promised her to Buck, but she hates him. Dodge takes the story seriously, and decides he will approach the Lilleys. He finds Nan down by the river, and he identifies himself to her and tells her what he has learned from young Barnes. He took the story seriously and has come to get her out of her trouble. She laughs at his presumption, and at first resents a stranger approaching her in this way. She admits that he is different from most men she has met. He tells her that he is ripe for this adventure and he feels that their meeting is not accidental. He proceeds to propose marriage to her. She then explains the trouble she is in and her father's promise to Buck Hathaway. He explains to her that he earned his name, Dodge, because he never dodged trouble in all the ten years he rode the range. He never dodged a night's watch or a stampede of stock or a rustling outfit, or cards or gamblers or women, or fights or bullets, or dealing death. He rode away because he wanted finally to dodge all those things, to find a new life, new faces where there wasn't any trouble. But he has run into Nan and her trouble which he will make his. Life has taught him that whatever befalls him, helping out this backwoods family could only leave him a better person.

Dodge takes a liking to her father and her Uncle Bill, who happened to be in Abilene when he shot it out with Strickland. Bill tells him that many people in the town were grateful to him for ridding them of the man. Dodge agrees to stay on, working at harvesting the sorghum with the boys. Rock has exacted one promise from him, however: that he respect his pledge to Buck Hathaway. Dodge soon learns that Steve and Ben are involved with Buck Hathaway, stealing sorghum. He confronts Steve about this, and learns that the boy has gotten himself into debt over a girlfriend and the need for some spending money. He gives Steve the money to pay off his debts, and makes a friend and confidante of the young lad. Nan is impressed with the change in her favorite brother. On Sunday, when Hathaway shows up for a visit, Dodge brings matters to a head at once. He calls Buck a thief, a moonshiner. He tempts him to draw, explaining that he has never fought with his right hand, or worn a glove on it. Buck strikes Dodge, who strikes back with his left hand, bloodying his nose and knocking him off the porch. He advises him to be prepared to go for his gun should they meet again. Nan's father and uncle are impressed and pleased with the discomfiture inflicted on Buck. Uncle Bill, however, warns him that Buck and his cohort, Twitchell, will not likely face him in the open but rather shoot from ambush.

Dodge sets out to locate the still, on the pretense that he is looking for stray cattle. He follows a trail down into the rim, and when Baldy gets a sore leg, he spends the night in a cave and continues his search the following morning. Twitchell shoots him from an ambush. The bullet goes straight through his upper shoulder, not doing any serious damage, but causing him to lose a lot of blood. Steve and Bill find him and patch him up. Uncle Bill tells him that for a man of his experience, he has not acted very wisely, going off alone and leaving himself open to attack. Steve and Uncle Bill accompany him on a search for the still. They find a small operation, and destroy it. The telltale smoke arouses curiosity and interest among the ranchers around.

When Rock Lilley dies, Buck Hathaway makes his move to take what is his. But Steve, now head of the clan, refuses to hand over the ranch to Hathaway. Nan is of two minds, feeling that their father's pledge should be respected. Dodge repeats his offer of marriage, but he adds that even if she feels she cannot marry him, he will stay on to help them through their troubles. Steve feels that this job is his. Dodge decides to teach him to draw fast and to shoot more accurately. Steve already is a good shot; it's a question of learning speed and remaining calm. The pace of events picks up. Buck decides to abduct Nan and force her to marry him. The Quayle brothers do the deed, bringing her to his hunting cabin. He has brought in Parson Bailey to marry them, willingly or by force. Dodge, Copelace, Steve and Billy track them to the cabin. He makes his way into the shack where Nan is being held. The parson is with her. They convince him to marry them. This way, Nan cannot go through with the promise her father made, and Buck is not likely to force the issue until he faces Dodge. When Buck comes to the cabin, Nan makes her escape. Buck retreats to Ryeson, assuming that there is safety in a town with little sympathy for gunplay. Dodge follows him there, confronting him and Twitchell in the saloon. Twitchell goes for his gun and meets his better in Dodge. Hathaway, however, is not willing to draw his gun, but runs out only to meet Steve, waiting for him outside. Here he makes an attempt to draw on Steve, but he too has met his match.

With the Hathaway menace finally eliminated, Simpson and other ranchers come to thank Dodge for taking care of their problem. Simpson, the cattleman whose ranch is across the valley from the Lilleys, knows his old boss, Josh Turner. He says the ranchers want more riders like him around. Mr. Williams, Steve's father-in-law-to-be, gives Tess and Steve a thousand head of Texas cattle as a wedding present to set them up in ranching. He himself intends to go into ranching. He offers to sell Dodge a further five hundred head at a rock-bottom price to get into the business as well.

Nan now concedes that Dodge's strategy to confront the Hathaway menace had been the appropriate course of action. Something terrible had to happen so that things could get better. She recalls how Dodge had told her when he first arrived that he would make their troubles his, and that by helping others, he would be a better person. She calls him her knight, a Sir Galahad.

Merriwell, Hart: In *The Drift Fence*, a member of the Cibeque outlaw gang. Jim Traft says that he could not have been picked out of a group of cowboys for any distinct individuality. He witnesses Hack Jocelyn killing young Andy Stoneham and he participates in the kidnapping of young Jim Traft. When Hack Jocelyn is killed, Slinger Dunn gathers the remaining members of the Cibeque together in the cabin. Hart Merriwell runs off, but returns after the shooting stops. He tries to help the injured Slinger, placing a saddle under his head. He remains to help Molly take care of her brother. Hart Merriwell, like Boyd Flick, is a young cowboy who has been led astray, needing only positive guidance to keep him on the right path.

Merry, Thaddeus "Tuck":   In *Code of the West*, a friend and confidante of Cal Thurman. He is described as the most singularly built human being Cal Thurman has ever seen. He is tall, extremely thin and so loose-jointed that he seems about to fall apart. His arms are so long as to be grotesque, like the arms of a great ape, and his hands are prodigious in size. He has a chicken neck, a small head, and the homeliest face Cal has ever looked into. He presents a ridiculous, pathetic figure. Cal picks him up on his way to the Ryson station to pick up Georgie. Tuck was a marine in the war, and something about him reminds Cal of Boyd, who had also been in France. Tuck has been hitchhiking around the West and is looking for the Bar XX ranch where he heard jobs were available. Cal tells him that the Bar XX is not hiring but that it should not be hard to find work on a ranch in the Tonto. Tuck and Cal become fast friends. Tuck Merry explains that he got his unusual nickname because he tucks into bed the men he knocks out in fights. He has with him a set of boxing gloves, revealing that at his last job he was a sparring partner for the famous Jack Dempsey. Cal offers Tuck a job at his father's sawmill. He further explains that being the baby of the family, his two older brothers and his seven cousins like to pick on him.

He would love to learn how to fight to even the score with them some day. Tuck agrees to give him boxing lessons. Tuck shows his skill in a fight with Bloom, Bid Hatfield's buddy and foreman of the Bar XX outfit. Bloom doesn't know what hit him. Back at the ranch, Tuck shares a room with Cal, who explains the etiquette among cowboys, a strange etiquette whereby the newcomer has to earn respect by beating the other cowboys one by one in a fistfight. Tuck beats Wess in a bet about reaping sorghum, and later defeats him in a fistfight, earning his unreserved respect and friendship. He also helps his buddy, Cal build his house, and pursue his romance with Georgie. Tuck makes the suggestion that Cal elope with her. He recruits the parson to marry them up at Boyd Thurman's cabin. He himself gets interested in Ollie Thurman at the October dance and later at Enoch and Mary's wedding. He truly celebrates Cal's marriage to Georgie. She turns to him when the trouble with Bud Hatfield has reached a crisis point. She had never known anyone so ungainly but the smile and the light in his eyes show a chivalrous and faithful friend concerned about her welfare. She confides in him what has happened, and Tuck accompanies her to the Saunders Bar XX ranch to confront Bid Hatfield. When the truth is out, he challenges Bid to a fight in which he gives him worse than he gave Cal.

Merryvale: In *Wanderer of the Wasteland*, a fisherman at Picacho. He was a prospector for some twenty years and tells young Adam Larey, who has just arrived, that he has made and lost more than one fortune with drink, faro, and bad women. He offers Adam a word of advice to avoid all three. Merryvale is now a broken-down night watchman at the Picacho mill. He thinks Adam should leave the place as too many young men are ruined in the gold fields or the mines or the camps. He tells Adam the history of the town and takes the young man under his wing. The desert, he tells him, brings out the best and the worst in men. It's a lens which magnifies human strengths, ambitions and passions. "You can never tell what's in a man till he's tried. Not one in a thousand can live on the desert. That has to do with his mind first, then his endurance." He adds to that, saying "Be a man with your body. Don't shirk work or play or fight. Eat an' drink and be merry but don't just live for that. Lend a helpin' hand, be generous with your gold. Put aside a third of your earnings for gambling an' look to lose it. Don't ever get drunk. You can't steer clear of women, good or bad. An' the only way is to be game an' kind an' square." He predicts that when Adam "fills out" he will be one hell of a man. Merryvale takes Adam to the mill and gets him a job in the store. Later, Adam works in the mill doing some of the heaviest, most exhausting work. When Adam returns to Picacho fourteen years later, he finds Merryvale still there. The old man doesn't recognize him or remember him, but when he tells about who he was and when he arrived, Merryvale does remember the shy young man he predicted would become a powerful man. He brings him up to date on the goings-on in the place and the people Adam asks about. He tells Adam that his brother had not been killed in the fight fourteen years ago. In fact, he had not even been seriously hurt. Merryvale is an example of a figure found in many of Grey's novels, the old man who advises the younger man, educating him in the ways of the West. He resembles Jeff Lynn in *The Spirit of the Border* or August Naab in *The Heritage of the Desert*.

In *Stairs of Sand*, Merryvale has been Wansfell's partner for the past four years. He befriends Ruth Virey and her grandfather, Caleb Hunt. Merryvale tells Ruth the story behind Adam Larey's fourteen years of wandering through the desert in expiation for the sin of killing his brother. He also describes him as an instrument of fate, a man formed by the desert, committed to setting wrongs right and defending the weak. Merryvale serves as Wansfell's eyes and ears. A less striking figure than Wansfell, he can go about the freighting station, watching and listening, without drawing to himself the attention that Adam would bring. He diagnoses Ruth Virey's problem easily. She is a woman who has never come to terms with herself. She has neglected her spiritual side, focusing only on selfish satisfaction of her desires. He tells her she will have to learn to accept herself and her responsibilities in life. Merryvale predicts the strategy Larey will take to gain possession of the water holes along the projected railroad line. He and Dabbs contrive to buy up Salton Springs or Twenty-Nine Palms to foil plans to create a monopoly. Merryvale also leads the search for Ruth in Yuma. He finds the room where she is being held, but by the time he returns with Adam, she has fled. He, Augustine and Adam track Stone and force him to release Ruth. Back at Lost Lake, Larey sets his gunmen on the search for Wansfell. Merryvale sets out to warn Adam, but when he reaches the hideout canyon, he discovers his partner tied up under the vigilant watch of Stark and Brooks. Out of gratitude to Wansfell for a favor to his wife many years ago, Start releases Adam. They return to Lost Lake, where Adam confronts his brother. Merryvale shoots Guerd so that his partner will not have the burden of having killed his brother. Merryvale feels that he has accomplished the task he set himself, to bring Ruth and Adam together, as her mother had wished.

Mescal: In *The Heritage of the Desert*, the daughter of a Navajo woman and a Spanish nobleman. She is the granddaughter of the great Navajo chief, Eschtah. She was entrusted by the Navajo to August Naab to be raised. Mescal's name is derived from a type of cactus growing in the Arizona desert. It underlines the intimate connection between her and the natural surroundings. To Jack Hare, she is a kind of earth mother figure as well as the love of his life.

Mescal is introduced in the early chapters. August Naab and Martin Cole have come upon a stranger lying on the desert almost dead from exposure. A devout Mormon, Naab rejects his friend's advice and takes in the young man named John (Jack) Hare. Dene, the outlaw, has been pursuing the stranger and Naab is determined to protect him from the scourge of southern Utah, gives Mescal the task of pretending to make love with Jack Hare outside the glare of the campfire so he will pass unobserved when Dene comes into camp searching for him. Her exotic beauty captivates Jack Hare from the start.

Mescal is seen largely through the prism of Jack Hare's infatuation with her and with the West. The first detailed picture Zane Grey presents of her is while Jack and she are herding sheep up on the high plateau, which they reach by climbing up a three-foot-wide trail which August Naab has cut out of the side of the mountain. Mescal is quiet, reserved, intimately close to nature. Jack asks her about her abstracted look and she explains that when she looks at the landscape, she is at one with it, her mind entirely free from thought. Jack envies this state of harmony with nature.

In spite of her affiliation with the natural world, her Heidi-like ability to make friends with animals, her knowledge of the natural world, Mescal occasionally plays the traditional damsel in distress. A bear has been attacking the flock and when Jack sets off to track the bear, the bear comes upon Mescal at the edge of a cliff. Only Jack's timely arrival and expert marksmanship save the day. When Jack comes upon Mescal in the Thundering Valley, hidden in the Painted Desert where she has survived with her peon for over a year, Mescal plays the helpless damsel once again, begging Jack to help her survive.

Mescal is Jack Hare's source of information about the inner workings of the Naab household. She tells him of the ill feeling between Mother Mary, Naab's first wife, and Mother Ruth, the second wife. As well, there is ill feeling between the other wives in the family. All of them dislike, mistrust and suspect Mescal. Perhaps this is due to her being Navajo but more likely they see in her a rival for their husbands' affections. Jack learns that August Naab might have taken her as a third wife if not for the objections of the previous wives.

Mescal has been promised in marriage to Snap Naab, August Naab's eldest and most rebellious son. Mescal keeps this secret from Jack, allowing him to find out only after August Naab himself has mentioned the topic. Mescal pleads that although she has not embraced the Mormon faith, she feels obliged to marry Snap to please Father Naab, who has been like a father to her. Mescal gives no open indication of dissent. She lets Snap Naab court her. She smiles and looks pleased at his attentions. Only Jack is aware of her true feelings. She gives him a look on occasion, or squeezes his hand under the dining room table, to let him know that she still loves him. When the date for the wedding has been set, Mescal meets Jack outside the house and tells him she loves him and disappears down the road with her peon. Naab and his sons, Jack, and a band of Navajo braves sent by Eschtah, set out to follow her but no trace can be found. Her grandfather Eschtah says that the desert

has spoken. Mescal has chosen to follow her Indian roots.

The disappearance of Mescal, the revelation of her true feelings about Snap and her love for Jack come as a surprise to August Naab. He does, however, resign himself to the fact that he cannot control how things are developing.

A year to the day after her disappearance, Jack hears a call in his sleep and he sets out to find Mescal. Her dog, Wolf, is at the Colorado River waiting for him when he crosses over. Following the dog's lead, Jack eventually makes it to the oasis in the Thundering Canyon where Mescal has been living for the past year. Her peon has recently died, and she fears for her survival. This is the cry that Jack hears in his sleep.

Departure from the paradisiacal oasis and return to the civilized world makes Mescal again the center of trouble. Snap attempts to retake her, claiming her as his wife. Holderness, who had offered to buy Mescal from Naab at the start of the story, now kills Snap to ensure that his rival is out of the way. His plan is foiled when one of his men unties her and lets her escape. She makes it to White Sage, where Bishop Caldwell hides her.

Mescal again becomes the focal point of action when Jack calls upon her to identify the man who had released her in order to save his life. The meek Mormon population has finally developed the gumption to stand up to the outlaws who have been oppressing them for years. The vigilance committee has tried the outlaws and sentenced them to death. Mescal recalls that the man had a wart on his hand. The man in question turns out to be the bishop's eldest son, Paul.

The novel ends with Jack and Mescal's wedding. August Naab gives her away as a father. He blesses the marriage and quietly accepts that perhaps the Mormon way which both Jack and Mescal have rejected is not the answer for everyone.

In the figure of Mescal, Zane Grey has added new elements to the heroine of his western romance. Mescal is a blend of white and Indian worlds. She has the appearance, the style, the elementary survival instincts of a Navajo attuned to the moods of the desert, but as a white woman, she has the charm and the wiles, the independence and the helplessness found in the heroines of romances. She is an earth mother figure capable of healing the body and soothing the spirit. In Mescal, Zane Grey reveals his fascination with the Navajo (American Indian) world and their oneness with the natural world. Mescal is both Indian and nature.

Mesquite: In "The Flight of Fargo Jones," one of the men in Sheriff Smith's posse pursuing branders of maverick calves.

Metzars: Among the group of settlers that accompanied the Zanes into the area around Ft. Henry. They are mentioned in the three Ohio valley novels, *Betty Zane, The Spirit of the Border* and *The Last Trail.* In *The Spirit of the Border,* two Metzars are mentioned, Will and Dick, who are busy cutting timber. They are young men living at Ft. Henry, curious about Joe and his "border fever." When Joe is rescued by Wetzel and brought to Ft. Henry, Will tells Joe that he had once been taken captive by Shawnee Indians, an experience he hopes never to relive. Unlike Joe, these brothers are content to live in the settlement and raise their families. In *Betty Zane*, Will Metzar is mentioned as an eligible bachelor, one who might interest Betty. A Nell Metzar is mentioned by Bessie Zane, an older woman who has been helping her watch over the injured Alfred Clarke. Presumably she is mother to Will and Dick. In *The Last Trail*, a Bill Metzar is reported to have been killed and scalped by Indians. There is another Metzar in this last novel who runs the inn where the horse thieves and other scoundrels meet. He is an active member of Bing Legget's gang, who, together with Brandt, works from inside the fort. He has great contempt for the Zanes and the "fruit picking farmers." Colonel Zane threatens to close his place down if the drunken brawls continue. Metzar's involvement in the outlaw gang becomes clear when Helen Sheppard observes him meeting with Brandt and Ashbow down by the river. The colonel orders him to clean out his place and when he resists, he is placed under arrest in the guardhouse.

Metzger: In *Riders of the Purple Sage*, one of the men hired by Dyer to abduct Milly Erne from her home in Texas. Lassiter catches up with him in central Utah some years later but he dies without revealing the whereabouts of Milly.

Mex: In *The Dude Ranger*, one of the cowboys in Anderson's outfit, driving the herd from Red Rock Ranch.

Mexican Joe: In *Twin Sombreros*, runs a restaurant in Las Animas. Brazos had been a regular customer when he lived in Las Animas five years before. He speaks on Brazos's behalf at the inquiry conducted by Sheriff Kiskadden. Brazos Keene rents a room upstairs from the restaurant.

Michler, Lieutenant: In *West of the Pecos*, mentioned as a member of the U.S. Fourth Cavalry, which had traced out the road west of the Pecos in 1863.

Middleton, Jim (a.k.a. Harv Sprall):   In *Under the Tonto Rim*, the handsome young man with whom Clara Watson runs off. Her father does not approve of him. Middleton is a wild, rodeo cowboy, a handsome devil, but trash. He is no good. He gets her pregnant, then abandons her. Middleton shows up in the Tonto where Lucy Watson is teaching looking for Clara. He supposedly has a letter from Mrs. Gerald, the woman who has been taking care of their daughter. He threatens to show the letter to Joe Denmeade, the young man Clara is going to marry. He plans to show the letter around to disgrace her and Lucy. He is killed in a fight with Edd Denmeade, after which the sheriff identifies him as Harv Sprall, cousin to the outlaw Bud Sprall from the Tonto.

Mike: (1) In *The Maverick Queen*, one of Emery's men who tries to shoot Lincoln Bradway from a balcony when he faces the drunken Gun Haskel in the street outside the Leave It Saloon. Vince had seen him going up the stairs after Lincoln had left the saloon and Haskel had followed. He sees Mike go into a room and open a window and aim his rifle. When he goes to shoot, Vince plugs him and the body falls out the window, over the balcony and into the street.

(2) In *The U. P. Trail*, cited as an Irish worker who is typical of the "little" people who have made the construction of the railroad possible. Men like him do the hard work, drink and gamble their pay, and dream of returning home some day.

Miles, General: In *30,000 on the Hoof*, pursues Geronimo when he escapes from the reservation. Logan Huett tells his young wife, Luce, that she has nothing to worry about, that Miles and his regiment will track the Apaches and capture Geronimo eventually.

Miller: (1) In *The Fugitive Trail*, runs a trading post on the cattle trails where Trinity stops on her trip to find Bruce Lockheart.

(2) In *The Hash Knife Outfit*, owns a ranch on the way from Traft's Diamond Ranch to the Yellow Jacket. Jim Traft, Molly and Glory spend the night with the Millers on their way to the Yellow Jacket. Later, the Millers are said to be moving part of their ranching operation into the valley near the Yellow Jacket where young Jim Traft and Molly Dunn will be living.

(3) In *The Horse Thief*, one of the Montana ranchers. He is a neighbor to Watrous, who has lost many horses to Big Bill Mason's horse-rustling operation.

(4) In *The Trail Driver*, a Missourian who runs a general store in Austin. Brite drops in here to ask him about the herds on the Chisolm trail, and about Ross Hite. He learns that there are only a few men with him.

(5) In *Twin Sombreros*, one of the big ranchers and cattlemen in Las Animas. Together with Surface, he opposes the sheriff. He pushes for Bodkin to replace Kiskadden. When Surface is exposed as a crooked rancher before the Cattleman's Association, Miller takes his place as the driving force behind the organization. His honesty is equally dubious. He is associated with Knight and Bodkin in their pursuit of Brazos Keene. When Brazos has finished off Bodkin, he tells the cattlemen gathered at supper that Miller is a crooked rancher like Surface.

Miller, Blink: In *Nevada*, a cowboy with a face like a weasel. He runs into Nevada (Jim Lacy) in the Gold Mine saloon in Lineville and is insulted when Nevada refuses to drink with him. Mrs. Wood describes him as an outlaw, a "tough nut to crack."

Miller, Bud: In *The Dude Ranger*, one of the three men who plan to rob Anne Hepford on the stage from Springer to Red Rock Ranch. Bud is not on the stage itself, but his two friends trust that he will get the money if they fail to do so. When Bill and his companion fail, Bud makes an attempt when the stage stops for a rest. Bud is younger than the other two. He has a clean, square-cut chin and a dark face. He could pass for a ranchman or a cowboy from his looks. But he has hard, steady, flinty eyes like his two companions. He approaches the stagecoach driver, Jeff Martin, saying his horse is lame and he would like to board the stage. He puts his foot on the step, bends over Miss Hepford, and grabs her purse. Ernest Howard Selby stops him at gunpoint and prevents the robbery. Hawk Siebert is the first to provide Bud Miller's full name, telling Ernest that indeed, Miller is a genuine highwayman.

Miller, Colonel: In *The Trail Driver*, ran the outfit for which Alabama Moze has worked. He sells his stock to Jones to get rid of the problem of the young cowboys tearing up the town and fighting constantly over his daughter.

Miller, Hal: In *Under the Tonto Rim*, a lean, rangy cowboy type, solemn of face and droll of speech. He is one of a group of young men gathering at the Denmeades'. He is a buddy of Sam Johnson and Gerd Claypool. He and his friends show enough interest in the new schoolteacher, Lucy Watson, to stir feelings of jealousy in the local girls.

Miller, Hank: (1) In *Fighting Caravans*, approaches the caravan under the command of Captain Jim Couch. He is running from the law in Santa Fe, having killed a man in a shootout. When Couch decides to hold him until the sheriff can arrive, Miller tries to escape, only to be stopped by Clint Belmet, who sticks out his foot to trip him. Miller is taken back to Santa Fe, where he is tried and hanged. He was a gambler, a cheat and a "bad egg." He killed one man and wounded another. A group of some twenty men take him from the sheriff and string him up in the plaza.

(2) In *The Maverick Queen*, the cowboy who drives Jimmy Weston's body to South Pass in one of Hirsh's wagons. Jeff Slocum, the stagecoach driver, reports seeing him in Rock Springs. He is there to meet Kit Bandon. Lincoln Bradway meets him at the Elk Hotel in Rock Springs. He is a handsome stripling of a cowboy. His presence bears a vitality and a cool demeanor that Lincoln Bradway had learned to associate with cowboys of the hard and reckless school. He packs a gun and wears it low. He moves with grace and assurance, but to judge by the look Kit Bandon gives him, he is evidently on her black list. Lincoln concludes he is a rank poison kind of cowboy, who would fight on the slightest provocation. Lincoln and Miller get into a fistfight when Miller insults Lucy. The following morning, Kit has worked Miller into a fury. Lincoln and Miller shoot it out in front of the hotel. Before the shooting begins, Lincoln gets an edge on Miller by telling him he and Lucy are married. He also learns that Jimmy Weston was already dead when Miller picked him

up at the Bandon ranch. Miller is killed in the gunfight, much to Kit Bandon's satisfaction.

Miller, Molly: In *The Trail Driver*, the daughter of Colonel Miller, Alabama Moze's former employer. She loved to flirt with the cowboys and since she could not make up her mind which one she was in love with, she kept them fighting over her.

Miller, Ralph (Rolfe):   Appears in *Betty Zane*. He is one of Betty's suitors and a traitor to the fort. He resembles a similar villain, Brandt, in *The Last Trail*.

Alfred Clarke reports that Miller was a friend of Simon Girty's and the other renegades, McKee and Elliott, when he was in the garrison at Ft. Pitt. Clarke did not like nor trust him. Mrs. Watkins at the party tells Wetzel that there is something untrustworthy in his looks.

Despite this, Miller is extremely popular with the young ladies, because of his good looks. He does not accept rejection very well. At the Watkins party, Betty is flirting with him to show what little concern she has for Alfred Clarke. When he senses that she is playing with him, he gets angry and Wetzel has to come to Betty's rescue. Miller does not forget nor forgive easily.

Miller is a skilled shooter, and in the celebrations surrounding the marriage of Isaac and Myeerah, he competes for the prize, Betty's embroidered buckskin bullet pouch, against the young men of the settlement. He is the best shot of the lot but Betty asks Wetzel to enter the competition so that Miller will not win. Miller is not amused. He has planned to have Betty abducted and almost tricks her into riding her Indian pony, Madcap, down to the river on a dare, into the hands of waiting Indians that Alfred Clarke has seen lurking in the bushes. In the confusion that ensues, Miller fights with Alfred Clarke, injuring him. That night, Miller ties up the dog, Tige, that suspects nothing. He then attempts to finish Alfred off, and, throwing pebbles at Betty's window to get her attention, offers her and her family safety in the upcoming attack on the fort. When his offer is rejected he vows revenge. Wetzel trails the miscreant to the Delaware village, where he is seen with the most hostile Indian chiefs, Girty and a British officer. Wetzel shoots Miller in his typically dramatic fashion out of regard for Betty's wishes, resisting the temptation to satisfy his own vendetta against Wingenund.

Miller is mentioned in *The Spirit of the Border* when Jonathan Zane thanks Wetzel for having prevented him from harming his sister, Betty Zane.

Miller, Ranger: In *The Fugitive Trail*, one of the Texas Rangers with Captain Maggard in the attack on the cabin where Stewart and the rustlers are holding out. Bates reports that he is "done for."

Miller, Seth: In *Under the Tonto Rim*, head of a family, one of a group of four that live in the canyon under the rim with whom Lucy Watson is going to work. Mr. Denmeade says the Millers will need her more than the Denmeades.

Miller, Tway: In *Wild Horse Mesa,* a member of the Melberne-Loughbridge mustanging outfit. He has given up cowboying and moved north from Texas because he hates barbed wired fences. Tway is a tough, wiry, rugged young man with a face like tree bark. His friends often kid him over his stuttering. He helps Chane look for canyons where a large number of mustangs could naturally be confined without too much difficulty.

Miller brothers: In *Black Mesa,* hoping to impress Paul Manning with the profits to be made in ranching, Belmont says that the Miller brothers run about eighty thousand head of cattle on the range.

Millers: In *The Hash Knife Outfit,* friends of Glory Traft in Saint Louis. But when she takes up with the disreputable Ed Darnell — gambler, blackmailer, swindler — they desert her.

Mills, Ambrose: In *The Light of Western Stars,* first mentioned as a young cowboy who cuts capers to try to get Madeline's attention during the roundup. He offers to rope Don Carlos to keep him from ogling Madeline. He elopes with Christine, Madeline's French maid. He participates in the golf game, and in the camping trip, where he is responsible for keeping the guests hidden and quiet while Don Carlos's bandits enter the camp.

Milly: (1) In *Code of the West,* the girl Lock Thurman is sweet on, but shy about asking to the dance. The brothers and cousins get a laugh at his expense when he returns to the ranch with the horse he had taken along for her to ride to the party. She got tired of waiting for him to ask her and she went with the lady-killer, Bid Hatfield.

(2) In *The Spirit of the Border,* a character in a story told by Jeff Lynn to the party he is taking down the Ohio by raft. She was a young woman whose parents were dead and who was trying to get back to Ft. Pitt to meet her sweetheart. She is on board a boat Jeff Lynn is taking upriver, when Jim Girty attacks. She is shot in the ambush and dies on the island, where she was buried. "Milly's birch" is a landmark on the island.

Minton: In *Rogue River Feud,* the tackle dealer whom Keven had fished with many a summer day. Kevin sees in him faith and loyalty. He never believed the lies about Keven spread by Gus Atwell. He approves of the partnership between Keven and Garry. Like Garry, he is interested in conservation of fish stock on the river. He suggests that Keven investigate why the salmon stock is decreasing. He also suggests that Keven take up prospecting, filing a claim. There is still gold in the sandbars on the river, and if he likes a quiet, private life, that of a prospector would be ideal. He has little respect for Gus Atwell. Atwell was always a slacker, and now that he is rolling in money, he has become worse. He drives around in a Rolls-Royce, but he never pays his bills. It's like squeezing juice out of a rock to get him to pay up, according to gossip around town. He's try-ing to squeeze out the market fishermen upriver. Minton gives Keven equipment on credit, and with the sale of the first haul, Keven pays him back. Minton tells him that the money made little difference to him. He is only interested in doing him a good turn. When Keven goes into hiding up at Solitude following the storm and the killing of Mulligan, Minton, like everyone else, thinks he is dead. When he shows up back in town, he sends Beryl into the shop first. She is as fine a fisherman as Minton himself, and it tickles Keven to have her challenge his assumptions about rods and flies. He predicts that Keven will be a lion in town, now that his reputation has been cleared.

Misseppa: Delaware Indian chief in *The Spirit of the Border.* His name means "the Source." He is present in the Delaware village when Wetzel is brought in as prisoner.

Mitchell, Lee: In *30,000 on the Hoof,* the government agent purchasing cattle for the army in Flagg. The prices he offers fluctuate quickly, from forty, forty-two dollars a head, to a low of twenty-five. He has the reputation of being a womanizer, as well. He takes Barbara Huett to the movies and sweet-talks her. He offers to buy Logan Huett's herd of thirty-one thousand cattle at five thousand a head. He also promises to pay in cash. Mitchell, however, swindles him out of his hundred and sixty-five thousand dollars. When Huett tries to get it back, the scope of the swindle becomes evident. Mitchell had been buying cattle at one price but claiming a much higher price from the government. Because Mitchell has good connections, Huett never recovers the swindled fortune. Mitchell is one of the men Zane Grey detested for having used the war as an opportunity to enrich themselves.

Mizzouri: In *The Lost Wagon Train,* a member of Latch's gang who accepts his offer of land and cattle at Latch's Field and a chance to change his life and go straight. He becomes a rancher, marries and has two children. He is a happy man.

Mobray: In *The Deer Stalker,* the trader who furnishes the equipment and supplies needed to undertake the deer roundup and drive. He goes to the bank in Flag with Patricia Clay (Edgerton) to collect payment due the Navajo Indians at the end of the drive.

Modoc: An Indian name. In a number of novels set in the northern California-Idaho border region, there are references to the Modoc tribe which lived in the area. In *Forlorn River,* Modoc is the name of an Indian who works for Ben Ide. He is taken in by Ben as a horse wrangler after he has been kicked out of a saloon in Hammell. Given his experience with horses, he helps Ben Ide plan his strategy for catching wild mustangs. He tells Ben about the "ice caves" where the horses used to go in times of drought because the springs there never go dry. When Ben is planning his strategy to buy out the neighboring small ranchers, Modoc is entrusted with the sale of his broke mustangs to the horse dealer, Frisbee, in Hammell. Modoc is late returning because the sheriff, who is in Setter's back pocket, has him arrested on a drunkenness charge dating back over two years. Modoc manages to break out of the jail and get back to Ben Ide. Modoc also has the reputation of being the best tracker in the region. He tracks the rustler gang operating in the area to their camp, which, it turns out, is at the ice caves where they plan to catch mustangs.

Mohave: In *Lost Pueblo*, one of the cowboys who work at John Bennet's post. He tells Janey he is named after the desert, which has no beginning and no end. He introduces Janey to the remaining cowboys at the post. He arrives with the other cowboys from the post to free Janey from her abductor. He participates in the pretense of lynching Phillip Randolph.

Mohave Jo: In *The Wanderer of the Wasteland*, runs a place at Tecopah, in the desert. Prospectors visit her establishment on their visits to the town. Dismukes tells Adam Larey about the place and Adam expresses curiosity about meeting her.

Moki: In *The Heritage of the Desert*, referred to as a tribe of Indians, perhaps of Navajo origin, who live in the desert. Eschtah speaks of them as beneath contempt, only good to be slaves. They are in some way connected with the Painted Desert where Mescal has taken refuge.

Monell, Steve: In *The Dude Ranger*, one of the cowboys working at the Red Rock Ranch. He is clearly a supporter of Dude Hyslip. Like all the cowboys except Nebraskie, he gives Ernest a hard time. He lets slip that Hyslip has arranged to have Ernest and Nebraskie and Siebert fired. Like the other cowboys, he gets rip-roaring drunk the night of the dance in Springer and, like the rest of the crew, expects to get fired when he learns that Ernest is the new owner of the ranch. Ernest, however, is magnanimous, keeping them on at higher wages if they apologize. Siebert insisted that Dude Hyslip's influence had sown dissatisfaction.

Monkton: In *Wilderness Trek*, one of the drovers who ride with Slyter and Stanley Dann on the twenty-five-hundred-mile trek across Australia. Having survived the desert and the intense heat, he is bitten by a death adder and for days, he lies delirious, his life hanging in the balance. Monkton survives to complete the trek to Northwest Australia.

Montana: In *Robbers' Roost*, a russet-bearded giant recruited to join the card game in the saloon in Green Valley. He is a member of Heeseman's outfit and is one of the survivors that Hays sees riding off from the attack on Robbers' Roost.

Montana, Jim: In *The Mysterious Rider*, one of the cowboys working on Old Bill Belllounds's ranch, White Slides. He is not thrilled at the prospect of working under Buster Jack and speaks of going to Wyoming when the new foreman appears. He does stay on. He is particularly good at working with horses, and the mustang Whang will let no one but Jim ride him. When a quarrel breaks out between the cowboys and Buster Jack, with guns being drawn, Old Bill asks Jim to give his account of the event. The boss has great confidence in Jim's understated truthfulness. Despite hints that he will be moving on, he remains with White Slides, enduring Buster Jack, playing poker with him and winning much money from him. He is present when Wilson Moore is accused of rustling, a charge he places no credence in.

Montana Slim: In *Black Mesa*, the name by which Wess Kintell introduces Paul Manning to Calkins.

Monte: (1) In *The Maverick Queen*, a cowboy who appears at Kit Bandon's ranch in the middle of the night with a maverick to sell her. He puts the calf in her corral then goes to the house to collect his pay, only to be told that she is no longer involved in that business. He is quite surprised.

(2) In *Shadow on the Trail*, the name of a gambler in Tombstone. A pretty young dancer takes a shine to Wade Holden because of his politeness and kindness to her. It seems she is the property of a gambler named Monte. When he witnesses Monte beating the girl, he calls him every name in the book, provoking him to draw his gun. Holden kills Monte in the shootout.

Montes: In *Yaqui*, a Brazilian government agent in the Yucatan to study the hemp industry. Montes himself is from Argentina, part gaucho in origin. He is fascinated by the seven-foot Yaqui the soldiers take off the Esperanza and sell for slaves on the plantations. He disapproves of the treatment of these Indians, taken from a mountain homeland and enslaved in conditions worse that those of cattle in the sweltering hemp fields. He becomes a conspirator, sneaking food to the Yaqui, supplementing the diet intended to starve the Yaqui while working him to death. He can never forget the scene where the Yaqui had asked not to be separated from his wife and son. The quiet dignity, patience and unsubdued pride of the Yaqui make an indelible impression on Montes. The Brazilian is fascinated by the woman selected as a bride for Perez. With the deal in the bag, her chaperone (duena) no longer feels it necessary to supervise her. The senorita tells Montes she loves him, but will do her duty to Perez, in conformity with the agreement. He notes that she seems particularly fond of scenes of cruelty and gore at the bull ring. Montes makes no comment on her reaction to the body of Perez that emerges from the bale supposed to contain her wedding gift from her husband.

Montes, Señor: In *The Light of Western Stars*, sent with Madeline to deliver the word that Gene Steward has been granted a pardon and is to be released. He is more senior than Don Carlos Martínez, who is responsible for Gene's being sentenced to death as a enemy rebel.

Monty: In *The Maverick Queen*, one of the two cowboys talking with Mel Thatcher outside the Chinese restaurant when Lincoln Bradway walks by shortly after his arrival in South Pass. Monty is upset with Thatcher's telling him to keep quiet about Jimmy Weston and Lucy.

Mooney, Tim: In *30,000 on the Hoof*, named by Holbert as one of the ranchers in the area when Logan Huett asks about his neighbors. He is just past Collier's place on the way to Flagg. Logan Huett kills Mooney in a gunfight. Mooney had been involved in crooked cattle deals. While at first this came as a surprise to many around Flagg, after comparing notes and information, Mooney's guilt stood out indisputably. No one patted Logan on the back for his service in ridding the range of this crooked cattleman, but it did exonerate him from suspicion of crooked deals.

Moore: (1) In *Fighting Caravans*, a freighter in the caravan at Point of Rocks. He is sent to the hilltop with a glass to watch for approaching Indians.

(2) In *Forlorn River*, a homesteader in the Forlorn River valley near Ben Ide's ranch. He is barely surviving and anxious to sell. His wife is the sister of a neighboring rancher, Sims. They hope to move to Washington state and take up wheat farming. Like Sims, he has, on occasion, been involved with the rustlers under Setter's command.

(3) In *Twin Sombreros*, a rancher who is prepared to buck the authority of the Cattleman's Association in the question of electing Bodkins as sheriff to replace Kiskadden.

Moore, Bess: In *Twin Sombreros*, the real name of Bess Syvertsen. See **Syvertsen, Bess.**

Moore, Bink: In *Boulder Dam*, runs an operation in Vegas fleecing unsuspecting workers of their money. He and Bess fleece Whitney Curtis in this way. Moore is sweet on Bess but lets her go on condition she marry Curtis and leave Nevada. She knows too much about his operations to remain in Vegas. Moore is involved with Sproul, who operates a bootlegging operation. Sproul is involved in the plot to sabotage the construction of Boulder Dam. Moore is a communist agitator. When Lynn Weston spots him at the construction site, Moore threatens to detonate a bomb. He is killed when he falls from the rim to the rocks below. He resembles the foreign agitators in *Desert of Wheat*.

Moore, Pug: In *Valley of Wild Horses*, a trail driver who spends the winter with Pan Handle's family, along with two of his cowboys. From Moore and his men, Pan Handle learns all the cowboy songs, and in the evening sometimes skips his chores to listen to them.

Moore, Wilson (a.k.a. Wils): In *The Mysterious Rider*, a young cowboy who works on Belllounds' White Slides ranch at Middle Park. He has been working there for most of his life. He ran away from home at the age of sixteen after a fight with his father and has been working at White Slides ever since. He has something of an education, "Professor" being his handle among the cowboys. Columbine sees him when she is out riding and recalls him as a reckless cowboy for whom no heights or depths had terror. He was a playmate, friend, and brother to her growing up on the ranch. He loves cattle, horses, and life in the open. Tall, slim, round-limbed, with the small hips of a rider, he has square shoulders, hazel eyes and a smiling, bronzed face. He tells Columbine that he still loves her but that he has been told to keep his distance from her, because she is promised to Buster Jack. At one time he had gotten into a fight with Belllounds' son over her, and he recalls how she once slapped his face for trying to kiss her. When Columbine thinks about Wilson, she knows he would be the perfect husband for a rancher's daughter. He is the best rider and roper on the ranch. He handles stock well. He has a gentle way with horses and men. Wilson never looks for trouble, but he won't back away from it either. He never drinks, and saves his money. Bill Belllounds has used him as a model against which he compares his worthless son, a comparison which Buster Jack has resented from childhood. Belllounds tells Columbine he will be a rich rancher some day.

Columbine is not sure how she feels about Wilson because she feels duty-bound to respect her foster father's wishes. She does, however, wish to retain Wilson for a friend. When Jack arrives, Wilson does his best to stay out of Jack's way. Bill Belllounds has planned to give him the job using the hounds to hunt coyotes and wildcats, a job that will keep him away from the ranch. Wilson never deliberately seeks Columbine out; whatever contact there is between them results from her initiative. When he has been injured, he decides to set up ranching for himself in Sage Creek Valley. He recuperates from his broken leg and foot under the watchful eye of Bent Wade and Columbine. He buys cattle, taking care to get signed receipts for all transactions, particularly those involving unbranded stock. When accused of rustling by Buster Jack, he is stunned, but does not lose his cool. He trusts in Wade to help him get out of the mess. When Buster Jack has died, Wilson and Columbine are married. Although Wilson had been offered the opportunity to return home and take over his father's ranch, he decides to stay at White Slides as foreman once he is married. Bill Belllounds has finally found the son and heir he wanted.

Moore is another example of the dedicated, loyal, underappreciated worker, like Gene Stewart in *The Light of Western Stars*. The western environment fosters the best in his nature, just as it brought out the worst in Buster Jack.

Moran, Blinky (a.k.a. Frank Somers): In *Valley of Wild Horses*, an old friend of Pan Handle Smith from Montana. Purcell and Dick Hardman had driven him off his digging (claim) and now he and his partner, Gus Hans, are making a living catching and selling wild horses. Blinky invites Pan

Handle to join up with him. Pan Handle suggests that with a few more people, they could catch a large number of horses, to make a bundle in one swoop. The final group consists of Blinky and Hans, Pan Handle and his father, Charley Brown, Handy Mac-New, and Lying Juan, the cook. Blinky is in love with Louise Melliss who works at the Yellow Mine. Pan Handle has spoken to her about Blinky and she, too, is in love with him, but she is trapped at the saloon, in debt to Dick Hardman. Blinky is given to drinking, spending all his money on liquor or losing it gambling. Pan Handle suggests that after they catch and sell the mustangs, Blinky and Louise join his family and move to Arizona. After the final confrontation with Hardman and the burning of the Yellow Mine saloon, Blinky and Louise are married and join the Smiths in their move to Siccane, Arizona.

Moravians: In *The Spirit of the Border*, were Dutch missionaries who opened a mission among the Delaware Indians. Zeisberger and Heckewelder, the head missionaries, appear in the story as background characters. Both Zeisberger and Heckewelder wrote extensively about their work among the Delaware and their work has provided valuable information about life among the Delaware.

Mordaunt: In *The Last Trail*, a handsome man with fair skin, and a long, silken, blond mustache. Heavy lines and purple shades under his blue eyes have the stamp of dissipation. He is resolute, dissolute, with a devil-may-care attitude. He is the gambler who had been pursuing Helen back in Williamsburg. He follows her to the frontier. He is first reported at Ft. Pitt by Alex Bennet, who works as a boatman on the barges operating between Ft. Pitt and Ft. Henry. He starts questioning Alex when he mentions that people by the name of Sheppard have come to Ft. Henry.

Helen recalls Mordaunt: "She could see him now with his pale, handsome face and distinguished bearing. She had liked him, as she had other men, until he involved her father with himself in financial ruin and had made his attention to her unpleasantly persistent. Then he had followed the fall of fortune with wild dissipation and became a gambler and a drunkard. But he did not desist in his mad wooing. He became like her shadow and life grew to be unendurable until her father planned to emigrate west, when she hailed the news with joy. And now Mordaunt had tracked her to her new home. She was sick with disgust."

At Fort Henry, he is first seen drinking in Metzar's inn. He is later induced into joining Legget's outfit with the promise that they will get Helen for him. When he realizes that he has been duped, he is killed by Brandt in a fight.

Morgan: (1) In *The Desert of Wheat,* a worker on Chris Dorn's farm. He stays on after Glidden has been spreading I.W.W. discontent among the farmhands. He reports to Kurt that his father has fired Jansen and Andrew.

(2) In *The Vanishing American,* a missionary who has been working on the Navajo reservation for twenty years. He is a "bad" missionary, but highly influential with the Mission Board in the East, which rejects any criticism of him as malicious gossip. He has powerful allies in the government in Washington. Morgan keeps a close eye on all that is happening on the reservation and uses whatever dirt he can dig up about employees to keep them in line. Morgan has a weakness for Indian girls, and possibly is the father of Gekin Yashi's child. Morgan sees Friel making advances to Marian Warner, an incident which he uses for blackmail. Morgan attempts to dig up dirt on Wolterson by contacting powerful friends in Texas. Morgan suspects that Marian knew Nophaie before she came to the reservation and suspects she is there as a spy. Nophaie confronts Morgan in the open, underlining the failure of his reservation and schooling policies. This earns him Morgan's enmity. Morgan urges Blucher to move against Do Etin and the thugs end up killing him. Unlike the cowboy missionary Ramsdell, who taught Christianity by example, Morgan believes in imposing Christianity on the Navajo by compulsory attendance at chapel, where he harangues them with the message that their Navajo beliefs will take them to hell. When Do Etin refuses to let Gekin Yashi attend chapel and Nophaie arranges her concealment, Morgan sends his Noki spy out to watch Do Etin's house. Jay Lord tracks her to the canyon where Nophaie had hidden her. Morgan manages to frighten her into confessing that Nophaie was the one who took her away from the school. After that, Gekin Yashi becomes uncommunicative with Marian Warner and increasingly more withdrawn and sullen. After the war, the Noki and the Nophah rebel against the reservation authorities, in particular Blucher and Morgan, who narrowly escape being killed thanks only to Nophaie's intervention. Morgan is an example of Grey's criticism of the reservation system, a system rife with fraud, abuse of power and cruelty.

Morgan, Andy: In *Fighting Caravans,* a freighter with Clint Belmet's caravan. He takes part in the hanging of captured outlaws.

Morgan, Babe: In *Nevada,* is Burt Stillwell's partner. He helped Burt Stillwell steal the stallion, California Red, from Ben Ide's ranch.

Morgan, Bill: In *Shadow on the Trail,* a member of Simm Bell's outlaw gang. He meets Bell and Wade in Smoky Hollow when they return from the Texas Pacific job.

Morgan, Hank: In *Horse Heaven Hill,* an old ranch hand who has been with the Westons for years. He informs Stan that three of the cowboys have quit and left with Howard, a close cohort of Hurd Blanding.

Morgan, Jim: In *Arizona Ames,* a Mormon rancher in an isolated part of southern Utah who raises horses. He lives with his daughter, Lespeth.

He is reputed to be kind and generous, never turning away a wandering cowboy from his ranch. He has been robbed often, and has only a small herd of horses left. He is a superb horseman, boasting that his daughter, Lespeth, was born on a horse. He compares her to Lucy Bostril at Bostril's Ford in *Wildfire.* Morgan receives Arizona Ames graciously and gratefully, as he prevented the last of his mustang herd from being rustled. He offers Arizona Ames a job on his ranch, but Arizona, fearing he will fall in love with Lespeth, rejects the offer.

Morley: In *Robbers' Roost,* claims to be a rancher but is the boss of the Black Diamond outfit. Morley is playing cards in the game where Stud Smith is caught cheating. Morley is reputed to be a good tracker and Slocum predicts that either he or Heeseman or both will eventually find Hays's roost in the canyon. Morley joins up with Heeseman in the attack on Hays's outfit, but runs off with Stud Smith.

Morris, Slim: In *The Maverick Queen*, rode for Higgins in the valley. He quits his job along with all the cowboys north of the forks on the river. The ranchers were planning to fire all the cowboys and bring in others from Casper. Slim takes a job with Lincoln Bradway, who is preparing to take up ranching at the head of the Sweetwater Valley. He is assigned to work on building a road into the area where Linc and Lucy will set up their ranch.

Morrison, Jim: In *The Last Trail*, one of the young men from Ft. Henry that Jonathan Zane observes entering the Sheppard cabin when he is trailing the man who gave the signal to the Shawnee warriors to steal horses.

Morrison, Larry: In *The Call of the Canyon*, one of Carley Burch's set in New York. He will flirt with any woman, married or single. Glenn Killbourne comments that he is amusing, and a great dancer, a real lady's man, but he wonders if he would defend a woman in peril. Morrison managed to avoid military service in the war because of his father's connections. He retained a high-salaried position at the shipyards throughout the war, one of many young men from New York who made a fortune during the conflict at the expense of the valiant men who dutifully joined the army and were sent overseas to battle. He is willful, indolent, rich, effete, self-satisfied, smug. He is not pleased when Carley criticizes his role in the war and his lifestyle. She calls him a slacker who lets others fight so that he can profit from it. Grey uses Morrison as an example of the kind of man to be found in the contemporary East, devoid of manliness, morality, and courage, given only to pleasure and the pursuit of money. He stands in stark contrast to western men like Glenn Killbourne and Tom Hutter.

Morse: In *Western Union*, the inventor of the Morse Code is a friend of Hiram Sibley, who told Jim Hawkins all about Creighton's plans to stretch the telegraph wires across the country.

Morton, Frank: In *The Lone Star Ranger*, recommended by Laramie as impeccably honest when Buck Duane sets about organizing a party of law-abiding citizens to help him fight the Cheseldine outlaw gang. Morton had been neighbor to Laramie in his ranching days. Morton advises Buck not to go into ranching in the area. While Buck Duane believes that rustling will eventually exhaust itself, evil bringing about its own demise, Frank Morton expresses a contrary opinion. The rustlers will be around as long as there is a single cow to rustle.

Mose: Joe's white dog in *The Spirit of the Border.* The epilogue to the novel mentions that a white dog haunts the Glen of the Beautiful Spring where Joe and Aola are buried.

Moss, Charlie: In *Nevada*, dances with Rose Hatt at the party. He seems quite taken with her.

Mother Mary: In *The Heritage of the Desert*, August Naab's first wife and the older of the two. Mother Mary is a much stricter adherent to Mormon teaching than August Naab. When Jack Hare is brought to their home, she tolerates his presence there as it is a duty to receive the stranger with kindness. However, when the children take a liking to Jack and climb up on his bed to get him to tell them stories, Mother Mary becomes alarmed. The fairy tales and animal stories she can tolerate, but not the stories about cities and people in the civilized East. She argues with August about the influence this outsider might have on the children. She insists that they be told nothing of the outside world, in strict conformity to Mormon theology and geography. Mother Mary has her own troubles as well, with the second wife and Mescal, whom she fears has always been the apple of Naab's eye. From Mescal, Jack Hare learns of Mother Mary's hatred for Mescal.

Mother Ruth: In *The Heritage of the Desert*, August Naab's second and younger wife. Mescal hints at problems between this younger wife and Mother Mary. Mother Ruth likes Mescal and feels sorry for her when she is pledged by August Naab as second wife to his eldest son, Snap. The day of the wedding, Hester, Snap's first wife, is still weak from the beating she received from Snap to force her to consent to the second marriage. Mother Ruth cuddles the fragile Hester, seeing in her a woman about to be exposed to the same troubles as she had been.

Moze: (1) In *The Arizona Clan*, one of Nan Lilley's favorite hounds.

(2) In *The Call of the Canyon*, Glenn Killbourne's hound. When Carley has gone back to New York, Glenn writes that the hound resents Flo's new kitten and Pinky, the pet pig Carley had named.

(3) In *The Man of the Forest*, a broad, black-faced outlaw, one of the men with Snake Anson in the cabin where they await Beesley. Later, he is one of the outlaws who kidnap Bo Rayner. When the group falls apart, Anson shoots Moze.

(4) In *Raiders of Spanish Peaks,* the cantankerous

bronc that Harriet eventually learns to control and ride, proof of her adapting to the West.

(5) In *The Vanishing American,* one of the white men who capture Nophaie when they steal some of the sheep he is tending.

Mulhall, Lonesome: In *Raiders of Spanish Peaks,* a young cowboy unable to resist women, and a magnet for trouble. He first appears in the novel when four men are trying to hang him from a cottonwood tree. He is a boy of about twenty, short, sturdy, showing the hallmarks of a rider. He has a homely face, fine eyes neither dark nor light, and an expression of scorn stronger than a somber horror. Laramie Nelson, watching the scene undetected, feels he was too young to face hanging with a spirit of equanimity. He is supposedly being strung up for stealing cattle, but he tells his executioners that it's because he had taken Price's girl from him. At this point Laramie Nelson intervenes to save his life. Mulhall tells Laramie about his troubles, how his partner, Ted Williams saved his life on a previous occasion, two years ago, when he and a cattleman, Cheesbrough, fought over a girl. He was sixteen at the time. Laramie observes Lonesome. He has qualities to make him liked around a cow camp but scarcely those that might secure his survival. He is easy, careless, amiable, probably a drifter, and not above the evils of outdoor life. He does not show signs of being addicted to liquor. The two of them pair up, Laramie feeling that he should take the boy under his wing. In Dodge, they find his old partner, Ted "Tracks" Williams, in jail, and break him out. The three of them form a partnership, "The Three Range Riders." They work together, pool their money and plan to go into ranching together.

When Laramie signs the group on to work for the Lindsays, driving their wagons to the Spanish Peaks ranch, and working on the ranch, Lonesome Mulhall finds himself in a predicament similar to the previous two which nearly cost him his life. He falls in love with Lenta Lindsay, the youngest, wildest daughter of the family. As well, he starts stealing things, Lenta's pocket book, scarves, trinkets dear to the family members. Laramie finds them and makes Mulhall return them. His interest in Lenta gets him into trouble with Chess Gaines. Lenta seems more interested in any other cowboy than him. In a heart-to-heart with Hallie when he tells her that Laramie is in love with her, Hallie tells him he doesn't stand a chance with Lenta, even though he has proposed marriage to her. Laramie gives Lonesome a special task, to go undercover among the cowboys to ferret out the ring leaders in the rustling. Lonesome must act drunk and rowdy among them, listening for clues to detect the traitors among them. When Lenta is abducted, he alone retains faith in her good nature, and when they come upon Lin Stuart's body riddled with bullets, his dead horse, and the tracks of Chess Gaines's horse, the truth of the matter is revealed. Lonesome's faith in Lenta is justified. Stuart had helped her get out of her "cell," and rode with her to

her favorite spot above the ranch, where Gaines knew she liked to go. Lonesome tracks Gaines to the cabin on Alridge's spread, where he breaks in and kills Gaines as he is beating Lenta. The two of them are reconciled, and marriage is possibly in the offing.

Mulhall, Silas: In *Raiders of Spanish Peaks,* Laramie Nelson asks young Lonesome Mulhall, whom he has just saved from hanging, if he is any relation to the large-scale stockman, Silas Mulhall. He isn't.

Mull: In *The U. P. Trail,* a camp boss. He had been a truck driver of horses in New York City before signing up for a construction crew on the U. P. He is a huge man, built like a bull, heavy-lipped and red-cheeked, hairy, coarse-spoken, with sunken eyes. Allie calls him a caveman. He is a heavy drinker, a bully, a gambler, and a pirate. A man who by temperament fits in well with the dissolute life of the construction towns. He works with Durade and is shot by Larry King in the scuffle surrounding Allie's escape from Stanton's.

Mulligan: In *Rogue River Feud,* a bullet-headed Irishman with a shock of red hair and a face like a bull. He is fleeced by Garry Lord in a poker game in the upstairs gambling rooms at the Sock-Eye. Mulligan is a sore loser and possibly this loss to Garry explains his hostility to him on the river. He and Garry had clashed before, and now, Mulligan is keen to prevent him from making a success of his fishing business. He tells Keven they must sell their fish through Priddy. Mulligan and his crew are also using illegal fishing nets, with a strip of netting the legal size at the top, but with a smaller, illegal size at the bottom. Mulligan suspects that Keven and Garry are spying on them and will report their illegal nets to the fish and game authorities. Mulligan is responsible for pouring sulphuric acid on Keven and Garry's nets, causing them to fall apart. During the big storm, Mulligan and Keven and Garry get into a fight. Mulligan is beating up on the unconscious Garry, and Keven comes to his defense. He stabs Mulligan in the throat, killing him. The body is carried away in the storm. Keven expects to be charged with his murder. Garry, however, survived and clears Keven's name, proving the death had been in self-defense. He also proves Mulligan's use of illegal nets.

Mulvey, Jeff: In *The Man of the Forest,* a short, bow-legged horseman, foreman of Al Auchincloss's ranch. He has a sun-bleached face and a boyish grin with bright eyes, although he is not young. Helen Rayner is surprised when Carmichael reports that Jeff Mulvey is planning to go over to Beasley when her uncle dies. Old Al had always relied heavily on Mulvey, and this breach of confidence is hard to believe. When Al has passed away, Jeff Mulvey and six of the riders desert the ranch without a word of farewell or asking for their pay. Jeff Mulvey is involved in the shooting in Turner's saloon when Roy Beeman is attacked. He is shot by Tom Carmichael. Helen is shocked to see the body of her uncle's trusted foreman lying on the floor with a smoking gun in his inert hand.

Muncie: In *Wildfire*, mentioned as a member of Bostril's horsemen's club. He also has employed young Joel Creech, but lets him go as he suspects the young man is crazy.

Muncie, Bart: In "Monty Price's Nightingale," a cowboy who had risen to be a foreman and who eventually went into ranching on a small scale. He acquired a range up in the forest country where grassy valleys and parks lay between the wooded hills. In a wild spot among the pines he built a cabin for his wife and baby. Monty Price went to work for Muncie and rode for him for six months. Then, during a dry spell, with Muncie short of help and with long drives to make, Monty quit in his inexplicable way and left the rancher in dire need. Muncie lost a good deal of stock that fall and always blamed Monty for it. The next time he sees Monty, he confronts him, challenging him to draw, but Monty walks off. Monty rescues Muncie's child during a forest fire which kills his wife and burns down his cabin.

Muncie, Mrs.:   In "Monty Price's Nightingale," the wife of the rancher, Bart Muncie, and mother of the child, Del. She is nowhere to be found in the cabin when Monty Price comes by to get them out of the way of the approaching fire.

Munson: In *The Vanishing American,* a young soldier from Vermont who knew Lo Blandy, as Nophaie was known at school. He meets up with him again in France at the front. He writes to Ted Withers reporting on the heroism of both Nophaie (Lo Blandy) and his Indian compadre, Shoie. Nophaie, he writes, was wounded four times in battle.

Murdock, Lee: In *Fighting Caravans,* the name by which Charlie Bent is known. He is the son of a pioneer named Henry Bent. His name was legend on the frontier and after the government offered a large reward for him alive or dead, his story became known. His father, Henry Bent was married Indian-fashion to a Cheyenne squaw. He sent his son to Saint Louis to be cared for and put in school and educated as a white man. Charley Bent was twenty-one years old when he returned to his father. His mother had died. Bent kept a trading store and the son was put in charge of this. One spring at the end of a good selling season, Charley ran off with the money from the store, with which his father had hoped to retire. Charley spoke the Indian languages fluently. He traveled all over, returning from a long stay in Texas with the name Lee Murdock. The fight in a saloon with Clint Belmet brought attention to him and he was an outlaw again. Murdock enters the picture at Maxwell's, when he arrives with an emigrant train. May Bell happens to be on that train. At Maxwell's, she recognizes Buff Belmet. From Mrs. Clement, Buff learns that Murdock joined the caravan in the Panhandle. He was not a freighter but he claimed he was going west to buy pelts. He said little about himself. He showed himself attentive to the women and Mrs. Clements and May Bell took a liking to him. Mr. Clements, however, did not, partly because of Murdock's attentions to May Bell. Various reports are heard of Murdock over the years. He is a gambler, handy with a gun. He is reputed to be a Texan. Buff Belmet meets him in a saloon in Santa Fe and a gunfight ensues over Murdock's pursuing May Bell across the Southwest. Murdock appears for the last time in the battle at Point of Rocks, where he leads the Indians in an attack on the caravans. He is killed in the fighting, asking Buff Belmet with his dying breath to keep his father from hearing about how he turned out.

Murphy: In *Knights of the Range,* mentioned as one of the various ranchers or businessmen who have tried to buy Don Carlos's ranch.

Murrell: In *The Lone Star Ranger,* named as one of the most infamous outlaws along the Texas border.

Muss: In *The Man of the Forest,* one of Milt Dale's pets, a half-grown black bear. He is abnormally jealous of the cub, little Bud, and he has a well-developed hatred of Tom, the mountain lion. Otherwise, he is a very good-tempered bear. Tom chases Muss out of camp whenever Dale's back is turned and sometimes Muss stays away, shifting for himself. When Bo comes to the senaca, Muss spends a good deal of time around the camp. Muss is not very big nor very heavy and in a wrestling bout with Bo, a strong wiry girl, he sometimes comes out second best. He never bites nor scratches but sometimes gives her a sound slap with his paws.

Myeerah: The daughter of the Huron chief, Tarhe. She appears as a principal character in *Betty Zane* and is mentioned as Isaac Zane's wife in *The Spirit of the Border.* Myeerah is the daughter of Tarhe and a white captive, the daughter of a French woman called La Durante, a woman of aristocratic lineage. She speaks several Indian languages as well as French, which she learned from her mother, and English, which she learned from Isaac Zane. Her name in Huron means "White Crane" or "Walk-in-the-Water."

Myeerah's love for Isaac and her desire to keep him is the cause of Isaac's ten-year captivity. She wants to marry him but he keeps refusing. When Isaac escapes and reaches Ft. Henry, warning them of the impending combined attack on the settlements and fort being planned by the British General Hamilton (the "hair buyer") and the Delaware, Shawnee and Hurons, Myeerah sends her scouts after him. One day when Isaac is out walking alone in the woods beyond the fort, he is recaptured by the Indians. He escapes the Huron village again, but is captured by the Delaware and condemned to be burned at the stake. The morning of his scheduled execution, Myeerah, who has been informed of his capture by Simon Girty, comes to the rescue, appearing with an army of several hundred warriors. She threatens a Huron attack on the Delaware village should they refuse to release Isaac Zane. Cornplanter concludes it is more prudent to retain Tarhe as an ally and he releases Isaac Zane to Myeerah. Outside the village, she sets Isaac free, telling him he may return to Ft. Henry. While she loves him and wants to marry him, she has learned that she cannot accomplish this by force. When Isaac sees that she loves him enough to give him up, he agrees to marry her. The two of them set off for Ft. Henry.

At Ft. Henry, Myeerah is a great hit with the family and the people at the fort. Betty is impressed by her knowledge of English and her education. She is truly a princess in every sense. Isaac and Myeerah return to the Huron village to do what they can to prevent war between the Hurons and the fort. At the end of the novel, Isaac and Myeerah return for the marriage of Betty and Alfred Clarke.

Myeerah, like Aola in *The Spirit of the Border*, is a Pocahontas figure. Once again, the woman is seen as the mediator between the white and the Indian worlds.

N

Naab, August: The Mormon patriarch in *The Heritage of the Desert*. He embodies all the traits Zane Grey admired in the Mormons he met on his excursions to the West. As well, he is the 'natural' man who blends Indian closeness to nature and morality assimilated from her teachings (c.f. Wetzel in *The Spirit of the Border*). Jack Hare says of him that he is free of all the false fears of civilization. He is called the "White Prophet" by the Navajo chief, Eschtah. He is referred to as Father Naab by Mescal, a title John Hare occasionally uses as well. He has two wives, Mother Mary and Mother Ruth. He has numerous children. There are five sons still alive, Snap, Dave, Zeke, George and Billy, as well as several who lie buried in the graveyard on the ranch. Naab also has several daughters, two of whom are mentioned by name, Judith and Esther. There are many grandchildren on the ranch. He takes in Mescal as a baby when her parents die. She has been entrusted to him to raise as a white woman. He also "adopts" Jack Hare, making him a full member of the family and a sharer in his ranch equal to that of his own sons.

August Naab is close to three score years old. He settled and developed his ranch in the desert, in a spot well sheltered from the outside world and well provided with water. He is a jack of all trades: a farmer, a cattleman, a grafter of fruit trees, a breeder of horses, a herder of sheep, a preacher, a physician and an engineer. In addition, he has the gift of healing with natural remedies which he has learned from the Navajo. Naab speaks some Navajo but is not completely fluent in the language. His relations with the Navajo are excellent. He treats them with admiration and respect. Naab is a man of prodigious strength. He grabs Dene by the arm and with only the pressure from his hand, is capable of breaking the bone. He also shows Dene that he is not to be trifled with when he draws with such speed that the gun appears in his hand before Dene's eyes as if by magic. Holderness, Dene and Chance refer to this as "Naab's trick."

August Naab is a devout Mormon, convinced that his religion is not incompatible with the demands of frontier life. When he comes upon Jack Hare in the desert, he does not hesitate to help, despite warnings from his lifelong friend Martin Cole that to do so is to invite the wrath of Dene. The divine injunction against killing he takes seriously. He refuses to shoot Dene in White Sage because God's law forbids it. Likewise, he advises his son, Snap, to let the matter of the horse deal drop and not to go looking for a fight. Despite repeated provocation by Holderness and Dene, despite the destruction of his large flock of sheep, despite the destruction and seizure of his water holes and his pasture, he turns the other cheek, hoping that goodness will come of evil. When Naab arrives in White Sage only to find that Jack Hare and the bishop's sons have already settled matters, he is angry with them. Naab has turned his back on his pacifist beliefs, he has hardened his heart against his fellow man, and then he does not even get the chance to exert the leadership expected of him to mete out the justice he has been called upon to do.

However, he is an unusual Mormon in other ways. Unlike his wife, Mother Mary, who is in charge of the children's education and who holds to the strict Mormon view that they be taught nothing about the outside world, he insists that his children be told the truth. Eventually, they will learn that there is an outside world and if they have been kept in ignorance about this basic fact, they will consider equally false all other tenets of their religion. Untested faith that cannot withstand the truth about the outside world is no faith at all. He would like Mescal and Jack to convert to Mormonism but he will not force this on them. Naab is willing to admit that he was wrong in his approach to the troubles in the area and that perhaps other ways of doing things are as good or perhaps better than Mormon approaches. He admits that perhaps his interpretations of Mormonism have been faulty.

Devout as he is, August Naab knows the ways of the world. He is well-informed about the goings-on in Utah where outlaws like Dene have lured many young Mormons into outlaw gangs. He understands the psychology of a man like Holderness; his understanding permits him to predict his campaign strategy. He can draw a gun faster than anyone and his sons have all been well trained in using fire arms. He shares his knowledge with Jack Hare. When Jack has allowed himself to get shot because he does not want to injure Snap, the oldest son, August Naab is angry. Naab tells Jack that he taught him these skills because he senses the young man has been destined for a special task and he needs to be able to defend himself. He frees Jack of any obligation or debt of gratitude he may feel.

August Naab has experienced much sorrow in his life. He has buried several sons. He has lost many good and dear friends in his struggle to tame the land. His first-born has proven to be a great disappointment. He is a violent, cruel, hot-tempered, trigger-happy drunkard with no sense of responsibility or duty to father, wife or family. Despite his best efforts to be on good terms with all, he finds himself under attack by Holderness. But August Naab is not given to self-pity. When his herd of thousands of sheep fall to their deaths from a cliff in a desperate attempt to reach the water in the river below, he accepts the loss with quiet resignation. Jack Hare is astonished to discover that on the following morning, August Naab is his old sanguine self, quietly planning to get some more sheep from the Navajo to restock his flock.

August Naab is believed to be endowed with the gift of prophecy. He sees in Jack Hare a man with potential, a man who needs to be trained for the role destiny has chosen for him. Holderness reaches the same conclusion about Jack when he first meets him at Abe's store. Just after he has picked Jack up in the desert, the clouds at sunset present a vision of a large fist, clutching with inexorable strength a bleeding heart. Slowly, the closed hand softens its grip and a golden shaft of sunlight pierces the clouds, to be blotted out when the sun sets. Naab intuits that this vision is linked to Jack, the man he has just taken in and saved from death. In Jack Hare, August Naab does find a son to ease the pain of the loss of Snap and Dave.

August Naab embodies the qualities of the frontier which Zane Grey so admired. He is a self-made man, a man close to nature, strong, intelligent, fearless, a man with deep religious convictions, convictions which only partly derive from organized religion. In Naab, Grey presents one of his fullest depictions of the type which appears in many of his western novels.

Naab, Billy:
The youngest son of August Naab in *The Heritage of the Desert*. Billy does not play a large role in the novel. August Naab seems to take particular care to have Billy with him when there is dangerous work being done. Billy helps capture Silvermane up on the high plateau, and he's one of the sons who accompany August Naab in his pursuit of the fleeing Mescal. He rows a boat across the river and arranges the packs on the horses. Billy is away with his father when Dene and his men come after Hare.

Naab, Dave:
In *The Heritage of the Desert*, one of August Naab's sons, the only one who smokes (a pipe). He is loyal to his father, a hard worker, an easy-going, open-hearted brother to Jack Hare, the stray his father has taken in. Dave feels no resentment that his father intends for Jack to share equally with him and his brothers in the inheritance. Dave has greater brotherly feelings for Jack than for his own brother Snap.

Dave Naab is the foreman of Naab's ranch. He is the best horseman of the boys, and a skilled bronc buster. He is the son most frequently entrusted with missions of importance by the father. He leads the group on the way back from White Sage to the ranch. There, he organizes the workers, and assigns the work. When Jack has returned from the upper plateau and sheep herding, now the proud owner of the most powerful horse on the range, he undertakes to train Jack as a cowboy. He teaches Jack how to ride like a cowboy, to rope, to brand cattle, to herd from horseback. He jokes that Jack apparently has more of a natural talent for drawing the gun than for throwing the lasso. Jack had practiced all summer when tending the sheep and hunting coyotes and developed a draw even quicker than that of August Naab. Under his tutorship, Jack becomes a first-rate cowhand.

Dave Naab, a devout Mormon, is more of a realist than his father. He knows that the rustling and tyranny of Holderness and Dene will not end with pious wishful thinking. Someone needs to act. When August Naab tangles with Dene at the bishop's home early in the novel, Dave escorts the outlaw to the gate, warning him that he is not a pacifist like his father, not so "particular about God" and will not hesitate to act more forcefully. On several occasions, he tells his father that action must be taken. He feels that his brother Snap could be the leader that the Mormons require to shake off the yoke of tyranny embodied in Holderness, but when his brother goes to the bad, he comes to the view that Jack is the man for the job.

Dave is a man who speaks what is on his mind. He openly tells his father that his policy is wrong, although he does not act against his father's wishes. He challenges Snap, whom he brands as a cur, a drunken, easily-led fool, to sign up as Holderness's foreman. He points out that Holderness killed his wife's father, stole their cattle and water rights, and is in the process of trying to drive them off the range completely. He always knew that Snap would come to something bad, but he never thought he'd disgrace the Naabs and break his father's heart. Thereupon, he banishes Snap from their home. When Snap tries to shoot Jack, Dave stops him. When Snap and Holderness show up at the ranch to seize Mescal, upon learning she has returned from the desert, Dave is shot on the sly by Holderness. Before dying, he expresses satisfaction that finally something is going to be done to stop Holderness and he asks Jack to avenge his death.

Grey uses Dave as a foil for Snap. In his character, Grey develops one of his biblical themes. He is the loyal son, the faithful one overlooked by the doting father who never gives him the reward he deserves.

Naab, George:
Another of August Naab's sons in *The Heritage of the Desert*. He is one of the cowboys who teach Jack Hare how to cowboy, to ride, to herd cattle from horseback, to rope and to brand animals. He is mentioned a few times, but the only

passage where he is involved in action is when Dene comes to abduct Mescal and he is killed by Silvermane. George also shares Dave's view of what their father should do to confront Holderness. At one point Dave says he knows that George's hand itches for the gun, but they must obey their father's wishes and avoid conflict. When Holderness comes to get Mescal and threatens to burn the house down if she is not handed over, George declares that the time has come for action. He reports on the attack and the shooting of Dave, Mescal's departure riding Silvermane and the death of Dene, run over by the stallion.

Naab, Mary *see* **Mother Mary**.

Naab, Ruth *see* **Mother Ruth**.

Naab, Snap: The eldest and favorite son of August Naab in *The Heritage of the Desert*. He is also the black sheep of the family and the source of great disappointment and sorrow to Father Naab. Snap is given to violence and to drinking. When drunk, he is mean and cruel. The spurs he wears are intended to give pain to a horse rather than a gentle nudge. Jack Hare thinks that his facial features resemble those of the desert hawk. Jack wonders about the rapid changes in his moods. In camp the first night, Hare finds it hard to believe that the Snap Naab he sees had killed a man that morning. The rest of the family seems to avoid mention of the topic. Being the eldest, he is given great latitude.

Snap Naab's name suggests his volatility. He has a quick temper, and matched with his vindictive and unforgiving nature, it is lethal. At the start of the novel, he has been cheated in a horse trade deal by Jeff Larsen. Snap ignores his father's advice to let the matter drop. After all, Snap's drunkenness is in large part responsible for the bad deal. He looks up Larsen and kills him in a shootout. Snap then accompanies his father back to the ranch. Snap takes an immediate dislike to Jack Hare on the trip back. He does not understand why his father has taken in a stray, one who has brought the wrath of Dene down upon them. This dislike is further enhanced when Jack comes upon Snap drinking in secret. Snap threatens dire consequences should Jack reveal what he saw to August Naab.

At times, Snap Naab is almost a pleasant individual. When they brand the cattle, the lack of drink and the hard work seem to calm him down. When the sheep have been lost and Holderness has moved in on Seeping Springs, Snap has great praise for Hare, who had gone to town to confront Holderness in public. He is all in favor of taking immediate action. Snap has an itchy trigger finger.

Mescal has been promised to Snap Naab as a second wife. Jack Hare comments on the courtship. Snap can behave like a perfect gentleman and Jack is afraid that Mescal is really falling in love with him. Hester, his first wife, daughter of Martin Cole, does not agree to the second marriage, and does what she can to embarrass Snap. At one point she takes his clothes and hides them, making Snap lose face with his father and brothers. To get her to consent to the second wife, he beats her into submission. Hester dies of this abuse some months later.

Following the flight of Mescal into the desert and the impossibility of tracking her, Snap deserts his father's home and joins up with Dene and Holderness. Following the death of Snood, Snap takes over the job of foreman of Holderness's ranch. He comes to his father's ranch to get Jack Hare, and witnesses what he thinks is the death of his nemesis. At a later stage, when Jack returns from the desert with Mescal, Snap at first thinks he has seen a ghost.

Despite his cleverness, Snap Naab is easily manipulated by Holderness. When they get their hands on Mescal, Snap naively thinks that Holderness has been helping him get the woman who was to be his wife. Only at the very last does he learn that Holderness had planned to keep her for himself from the start. Holderness tricks Snap into a gunfight. Snap is confident of his speed with a gun, but he had underestimated his rival's treachery. Holderness had emptied his gun of shells and Snap draws an empty revolver. Holderness kills him with a laugh of scorn.

In the character of Snap Naab, Zane Grey develops one of the biblical themes that recur in his novels. Snap is a version of the prodigal son, the father's favorite who knows he is the favorite and takes advantage of his doting father's indulgence. He is the beloved son who has gone to the bad and despite repeated forgiveness, rejects his rightful inheritance. There are echoes of Esau and Jacob, the son who gives up his inheritance for a trifle. Snap is in contrast with Dave, the faithful and loyal son who, despite his resentment of the preferential treatment given the undeserving older brother, remains true to his father.

Naab, Zeke: One of August Naab's sons in *The Heritage of the Desert*. No information is given about his age, but he is younger than Snap, the eldest, and a close friend of his brother Dave. The two of them think alike on the issue of how best to deal with Dene and Holderness. Zeke is present in White Sage at the start of the novel when Dene attempts to take Jack Hare from the bishop's home. He helps with the capture of Silvermane. When Dene shoots Jack Hare, he has the presence of mind to announce that Jack has been killed, encouraging Dene, Chance and Culver to leave. Zeke then bandages Jack up. Thanks to his quick thinking, Jack's life is saved. Zeke still has friends among the Mormons who have gone to work for Dene and Holderness and from them he gets information about their activities. As for the trouble facing the Naabs and the Mormons in the area, Zeke shares Dave's opinion that praying and turning the other cheek will not make Holderness go away. With Dave, he urges his father to face reality and confront Holderness, to fight back and defend what is his. In the attack on the Naab ranch, Zeke helps carry the body of his brother, Dave, into the house.

Nack Yal: In *The Rainbow Trail*, a mustang whose name means "two bits" in Navajo. He is a beautiful, black mustang with three white feet, a spot on his nose and a mane that sweeps down to his knees. The mustang is quite a character. When Withers gives him to Shefford, the mustang looks at the inexperienced rider with disdain. On the trek to the Navajo village to collect hides and wool, the animal brings Shefford's horsemanship into question. The horse constantly turns to the left. Withers explains that he wants to go south to where he was born. Nack Yal is eventually reunited with his mother, who has another young colt. She kicks Nack Yal to make him keep his distance from the colt. Nack Yal feels rejected, heartbroken according to Nas Ta Bega. From this point forward, the horse behaves himself as never before. Shefford develops a deep affection for the animal. Nack Yal is shot by Shadd in the escape from Surprise Valley, but fortunately, the injury is not severe.

Nadglean nas pah: In *The Vanishing American,* tended Nophaie's mother at his birth. She is a woman who lives in the present, and, unlike Nophaie, does not worry about the future. She accepts present wealth and prosperity as proof of worthiness. For Nophaie, she typifies the Navajo attitude to life.

Nagel: In *Forlorn River,* one of the ranchers in the Forlorn River valley who is looking to sell his property. He has been involved with the Setter rustler outfit to earn money to survive. Ben Ide buys him out.

Nagger: (1) In "The Flight of Fargo Jones," Fargo Jones's horse.
(2) In *Wildfire,* Lin Slone's trusted mustang. Slone's companions in hunting wild mustangs declare that Nagger has greater stamina than any horse they have ever known. The animal is huge, with the size and strength of a farm workhorse, and the speed and surefootedness of a thoroughbred racehorse. The horse will follow Slone anywhere. Without this companion, it is doubtful that Lin Slone would ever have been able to capture Wildfire, the fastest mustang on the range.

Nalook: In *The Horse Thief,* a friend of Dale Brittenham's. At one point, Dale saved him from going to jail, a favor which has earned him Nalook's undying loyalty and gratitude. Nalook is a Palouse Indian, and an unmatched tracker and horseman. He helps Dale trail the horse thieves and abductors of Edith Watrous to the cabin in their well-concealed hideout. He helps Dale in the fight against Reed and Mason. His spotting of the rustler lookouts and trails prove invaluable.

Nance: In *Majesty's Rancho,* Lance Sidway's sister, the only relative he has left. She had been sick, but now has recovered after her operation and is soon to be married.

Nancy: In *The Drift Fence,* Curly Prentiss's girlfriend in Flagg. Curly asks Jim Traft for time off to visit her before he returns to the ranch. He does not want Jim Traft to meet her, as he had lost other girlfriends by introducing them to his cowboy buddies.

Nas Ta Bega: In *The Rainbow Trail,* the brother of Glen Naspa and an example of the "noble savage." Nas Ta Bega resembles Eschtah in *The Heritage of the Desert* in his knowledge of the desert and in his spirituality and insight. He also resembles Wingenund in *The Spirit of the Border* in his concern for the vanishing red man and the preservation of Indian culture. He first appears in Shefford's camp returning the horse that had broken its hobbles and wandered off in the night. Shefford describes him as having a noble head, in poise like that of an eagle, a bold, clean-cut profile and stern, close-shut lips, eyes coal black and piercing with an intent look from a keen, inquisitive mind. He has been told by Withers that Shefford is searching for Fay Larkin and Surprise Valley to rescue Lassiter and Jane. He also knows about Shefford's spiritual wandering, his discontent with religion and with God. Nas Ta Bega gives Shefford the Navajo name, Bi Nai, which means brother. He undertakes to teach Shefford to survive in the desert, to find water, to understand the lay of the land. Through a life close to the desert, he will guide him in his spiritual quest to rediscover the God he had lost in the rules and restrictions of organized religion.

Shefford learns of the Navajo's past in part from Withers, from Molly, Withers's wife, and from the man himself. Nas Ta Bega is descended from the Navajo who escaped from the cavalry in the maze of canyons in northern Arizona, thereby managing to evade confinement on a reservation. He was stolen from his parents' home and taken to San Bernadino, where he was interned in a mission school. He spent fourteen years in California, where they tried to make a missionary out of him. But when he was free, he returned to the Navajo and put aside the white man's clothing, knowledge, language, habits, life and religion to resume his Navajo heritage. Nas Ta Bega was born to be a chief, but because he was raised in a mission school, he did not learn to ride until he returned to the Navajo world, and consequently, is no match in horsemanship for the young men in his tribe. Likewise, he has never developed the physical strength to carry the heavy stone, Isende Aha, which marks the initiation rite into manhood among young Navajo braves. Even the burly giant, Joe Lake, cannot lift the rock. Shefford thinks it is truly a crime that missionaries deprived him of his heritage. They had made him something more and something less than an Indian, an alien in two worlds. Molly Withers, a woman raised by the Navajo, had heard of Nas Ta Bega from others. He is reputed to be a sage, a poet, a man in tune with the spirit of the desert.

Like Eschtah in *The Heritage of the Desert,* Nas Ta Bega is a critical observer of the white world. He has concluded that Mormonism is not about seeking God but about building a power base for leaders. The Mormons, for him, are not a people who can see and feel God in the natural world or in their fellow man. The relationship between the different white men — the Spaniards, the Americans — and the Navajo involved a complex mingling of trade and cultural exchange, but the greatest damage was done when the basis of the Indians' faith was undermined. The Indians saw God(s) in the world, in the desert, in the night, in the wind — a palpable presence, not an abstract being known through study and preaching. Nas Ta Bega acknowledges that the white man did provide useful knowledge and technology to the Indians, but the banishing of native religions dealt the death blow to Indian cultures.

Nas Ta Bega proves to be more of a Christian than the cynical Shefford. Nas Ta Bega sees in him a man full of anger who has lost his faith in God and man. He decides to help him find faith in himself and in God again. Shefford learns that people are free to make their own decisions. John Shefford wants Nas Ta Bega to rescue his sister, Glen Naspa, from the mission school at Blue Cañon, but Nas Ta Bega refuses. His sister went of her own free will; she will return home when she decides that is right for her. When Glen Naspa dies in childbirth, a pregnancy resulting from her infatuation with the missionary, Willetts, Nas Ta Bega teaches Shefford that revenge is not wise. Life will punish Willetts. Who is to say that Willetts was completely at fault? Shefford understands that Nas Ta Bega finds in the wildness of his environment a strength no white teaching could ever have given him. The Navajo is above revenge. Revenge is not wise. Nas Ta Bega resembles an "impassive destiny upon which no shocks fell."

Nas Ta Bega assists in the return of the Mormon wives to the village, he helps Fay Larkin escape, and he guides the party to Surprise Valley where they rescue Lassiter and Jane Withersteen. Nas Ta Bega leads them through the desert along trails that only he knows. He outwits Shadd, who is following them but falls into a trap. He delivers the party to the Rainbow bridge where they meet Joe Lake, who has boats to take them downriver. When they have reached Willow Springs, Nas Ta Bega tells Shefford that he killed Waggoner, thereby removing from his mind any doubts he had about Fay Larkin. Quietly, Nas Ta Bega takes his leave. He has accomplished his mission. He has restored Shefford to his faith in God and in man having completed his mission to rescue the prisoners in the valley.

Nash: In *The Desert of Wheat,* Anderson's driver. His real name is Ruenke and he is an agent of the International Workers of the World, a socialist labor organization, reporting to Glidden. He is dark-browed, heavy-jawed, young, with light eyes and hair. He is stuck on Lenore, Anderson's daughter, and wants her to elope with him. Jake warns her that Nash is not reliable, that he has been seen talking with the I.W.W. agents, but her father suggests that she flirt with Nash to get information from him. He reveals his true name, Ruenke, and his German origin and sympathies to her. He proves his sympathies when he deliberately stalls the car, preventing their pursuit of the men throwing cakes of phosphorous into the wheatfields. Eventually, Nash reveals the plot to destroy Anderson's wheat crop and to kill him, as he is the most influential farmer in the area. He tells Lenore he will save her father and farm if she elopes with him. He then tries to run off with Lenore but is stopped by Kurt Dorn before he gets too far. Nash is driven out of Golden Valley.

Nashta: In *Blue Feather*, the only child of Taneen, his daughter with the Princess of the Antelope Clan. Prophecy has it that the "Daughter of the Moon" will never see the light of day and will live with the She-boyahs forever. Nashta is kept in a special cave underground from which she never emerges during the day. She has lived in isolation all her life. Ba-Lee and La-Clos are the two young women who take care of her. Her only knowledge of the outside world comes from her two servants. She pines for contact with people, for a lover such as Ba-Lee knows. When Nashta meets Blue Feather, she falls in love with him, as he does with her. This love convinces him that he cannot betray these people to the warlike Nopahs, his own people. However, when Ba-Lee and Tith-Lei denounce Blue Feather as a traitor who has brought the enemy to attack their citadel, Nashta decides to act to save her lover. She leaves her cave and goes to the camp of the Nophas. She speaks to Nothis Toh, the chief, and father of Blue Feather. She offers to show the Nopah a secret entrance to the citadel. The Nopahs massacre the Rock Clan, seizing their treasures. Blue Feather is forgiven by his father, and returns to his people with his bride.

Natasha: In *Black Mesa*, a sixteen-year-old Indian girl living with her family in a hogan behind the Bitter Seeps trading post. She has been educated in a white school and like Magdaline in *Captives of the Desert* or Gekin Yashi in *The Vanishing American* or Glen Napa in *The Rainbow Trail*, fits neither into the white world nor the Indian world. Paul Manning arouses her interest when he asks her to teach him some Navajo. She confides in him her discomfort, caught between two worlds. Belmont, the trader, makes advances to her. She marries Taddy, a young man from across the mountains. She is anxious to get away from the trading post. Paul and Wess set them up with a flock of sheep and goats, a camping outfit, horses, some ponies, saddles, blankets, clothes, food, and everything they will need to start.

Navajo: In *Wildfire*, referred to as the "Arabs of the Painted Desert" because of their love of horses and horse racing. In *The Heritage of the Desert*, August Naab sends for a Navajo to break in the marvelous mustang stallion he has captured, Silvermane. In *The Rainbow Trail*, the same horsemanship of the Navajo is mentioned. Given Zane Grey's love of horses, he came to love and admire what he considered to be the greatest horsemen of the Southwest.

Navvy: In *The Rainbow Trail*, Joe Lake's horse. When Joe arrives at Withers's trading post in Kayenta, he tries to bite John Shefford. Joe scolds him, as if he were a mischievous child. The horse rears up and jumps and snorts, as if taking a pouting fit, like a child.

Naylor: In *The Vanishing American,* one of Blucher's "policemen" (thugs) on the reservation at Mesa.

Naza: In the short story "The Great Slave," Naza is the god of gods, god of the north wind. Siena prays to the god when there is a time of crisis.

Neal(e):   In *Shadow on the Trail,* one of Harrobin's riders. He and Carter attempt to ambush and kill Tex Brandon. He is the first to shoot from ambush in the trees. Kinsey and Kid Marshall pursue him. Hogue Kinsey shoots him and he falls from his horse, dead.

Neale, Warren: In *The U. P. Trail,* the main character, a young man of twenty-three years from a poor family in New England. He is self-educated, ambitious, wild for adventure and achievement. He is eager, ardent, bronze-faced, keen-eyed, not quite six feet tall and build like a wedge. He is willing to tackle any problem himself. He is nearly killed early in the novel when he climbs down over a cliff to see the kind of rock formation at the base of the precipice. The rope holding him breaks and he falls. Fortunately, tree branches break the fall, and he survives. General Lodge, visionary military man and key figure behind the Union Pacific, has great faith in the young man, predicting that one day he will rise to a position of prominence in the organization. Like Lodge, Neale is excited by the grand vision of a transcontinental railroad and by tackling the challenging engineering problems such construction implies. His faith in the project and his contributions to the construction earn him a place at the ceremony driving the last spike.

Neale has serious character flaws: he is excitable and quick-tempered and moved by emotion rather than reason. Neale gives up his job as engineer and superintendent of maintenance for the railroad after an encounter with Allison Lee, where he exposed the tearing-up and reconstruction of sections of the road for no reason other than to give work to favored construction companies. He acts on hunches. He senses that someone is still alive after the Sioux attack on Horn's wagon train. This hunch leads to the discovery of Allie Lee. Likewise, he senses that Allie has survived the attack on the Slingerland cabin and captivity among the Sioux. He senses that Ruby is basically a good person at heart and he offers her his great winnings so she can leave Stanton's and go with Larry Red King to California. When Lodge asks him to return to the Union Pacific to take charge of the construction of a bridge, he returns out of affection for Lodge, who has been like a father to him. His friend, Larry Red King, cautions him that his temper and his emotions will get him into deep trouble.

His relationship with Allie Lee likewise swings between hope and despair, loyalty and betrayal. He falls in love with her when she is recuperating at Slingerland's cabin. Before he leaves for a year to work on the railroad, he asks her to marry him and she accepts. When he returns to the cabin, finding it burned and no trace of either Allie or Slingerland, he despairs of finding her. These same extremes of emotion are to be seen in his reaction to Beauty Stanton, a woman who runs a gambling establishment and brothel in Benton. A similar pattern is seen in his attachment to the U. P. He is loyal to Lodge, but feels betrayed by the commissioners who allow men like Allison Lee to tarnish the noble project. To Larry Red King, he feels only loyalty and deep friendship. Here is one person in whom he never loses faith or confidence.

Neberyull (Neb):   In *Stranger from the Tonto,* a member of the Hole-in-the-Wall outfit, closely allied with Slotte. He is one of the cowboys that Kent Wingfield meets when he rides into Logan's trading post on Spades. Neberyull is drunk and makes unpleasant advances to Logan's daughter. Outside, Neberyull learns from Tobiki that Kent rode in on Spades and that he was seen talking to Logan and then taking the horse into the trees away from the house. He challenges Kent, and in the shooting, is killed by Wingfield.

Ned: In *The Light of Western Stars,* one of the cowboys working on the roundup when Madeline arrives. He is mentioned on other occasions among the cowboys but plays no significant role in the novel.

Neece, Abe (Abraham):   In *Twin Sombreros,* the father of the twins, Janis and June, and the dead son, Allen. He is a "grand old man," the original owner of the Twin Sombreros ranch. Raine Surface swindles him out of his ranch by stealing the fifty thousand dollars he has withdrawn from the bank to pay for cattle, then calling in the mortgage at the bank. Neece had sent his daughters to Kansas City to be educated. He falls into a depression when they return, as he now feels he has been a complete failure. His son, Allen, was killed when he got too close to discovering the truth. Brazos Keene's promise to find the murderer of his son brings about a marvelous transformation in the old man. When his ranch has been restored to him, he wants Brazos to remain as foreman.

Neece, Allen: In *Twin Sombreros,* the son of Abe Neece. He was murdered the night that Brazos Keene arrived in Las Animas, and stuffed in the loft of the cabin where Brazos spent the night. Brazos is arrested for the murder and almost lynched. When his innocence is established, Brazos sets out to investigate the death of Allen Neece. Abe Neece says Brazos resembles his son in build, but his son was reckless, and Brazos has a proven quality. The boy had made enemies, investigating the robbery in which his father lost forty thousand dollars and the Twin Sombreros ranch. He was lured out to the cabin by Bess Syvertsen, a stunningly beautiful young woman. Orcutt roped him and pulled him off his horse, killing him in the fall when his head struck the ground, fracturing his skull. Then Bard Syvertsen shot him in the back, and the two of them dragged the body into the cabin and pulled it up and pushed it into the loft. Allen had been involved with Lura Surface, daughter of the man who swindled his father out of his ranch. His sisters, Janis and June, dislike Lura because she made a fool of their brother.

Neece, Janis: In *Twin Sombreros*, one of the twin daughters of Abe Neece. She is eighteen years old, and indistinguishable from her sister. The twins love to play tricks on people since they are impossible to tell apart. Their father sent them to Kansas City to school. They returned to Twin Sombreros just as their father lost it to Raine Surface. They showed their spunk borrowing money to open a restaurant, the Twin Sombreros Restaurant, and the Mexican cook from the ranch stayed with them. The restaurant proved a huge success and within a year they had paid back the loan and were making a profit. Janis is reputedly like January, the cold one. She also has the reputation of being more of a flirt than her twin sister, June. Henry Sisk is madly in love with her. At the big party where they plan to celebrate their return to Twin Sombreros, she and June play a trick on Brazos. Janis gets a proposal of marriage out of him, knowing that he has already proposed to June. Brazos then tells her that it was time someone dealt the two of them a bit of their own medicine. At Doan's Crossing, June reports that Janis eloped with Henry Sisk and has since returned married to Twin Sombreros. But Brazos is not sure whether the twin he has just married is June or Janis.

Neece, June: In *Twin Sombreros*, one of Abe Neece's identical twin daughters. She is supposedly the more outgoing and warm of the two. She and her sister Janice run the Twin Sombreros Restaurant, which they opened when the family lost the ranch thanks to the scheming of Raine Surface. Brazos Keene takes a fancy to her, but is never sure which twin he is speaking to. June supposedly has a birthmark on her thigh, the only way to distinguish between the two. June helps Brazos with his investigation of her brother's death. She accepts his proposal of marriage and when he leaves Las Animas, determined to cut all ties with the place, she follows him. In Dodge, she does a bit of detective work herself and learns from cowboys where he is. She shows up at Doan's Crossing, where she professes her love for him. They are married, but Brazos is still not sure which twin he really has for a wife.

Neece, Aunt Mattie: In *Twin Sombreros*, Abe's sister. She is staying with her two nieces, Janis and June, in Las Animas, since they lost the Twin Sombreros Ranch. The twins introduce her to Brazos Keene and she is greatly taken with him. She later learns from Dave Wesley that Abe is doing much better, a change she attributes to the new hope has given her brother that the murderer of his son will be

found and the truth behind the robbery and the loss of his money will be revealed.

Neff: In "The Camp Robber," foreman at Stimpson's ranch. He accuses Wingfield of taking the two thousand-three hundred and sixty dollars, the payroll, that was in his drawer in the bunkhouse. Wally Peters had counted the money with him and saw him put the money in the payroll. Wingfield is the only man to have come into the cabin since the two of them left, as evidenced by the paper he left on the desk.

Nels: In *The Light of Western Stars*, an old cowboy (under forty). He lost his mother at the age of ten and has never had a girlfriend or any woman who loved him. According to Monty Price, he has been involved in gunfights but is modest about his deeds and accomplishments. He is now is stoved up from years of bronc busting and cowboying. He suffers from arthritis in his legs and hands. He is quite the bread maker, but Madeline insists that he learn to use the new machine she has bought for the job. He claims to need special lessons in bread making, which she gives him in the kitchen of the ranch house. Nels is sent to track Gene and he brings back word that the cowboy is in Arizona. A friend of his reports that Gene is there in jail, the result of picking fights when drunk. Nels goes with Madeline to convince him to return. On this trip, he travels in the car, although at first, he wants to follow on horseback. He helps in the raid on Don Carlos's ranch to clean the bandits out. He helps carry out the contraband weapons and ammunition. With Nick Steele, he holds Stillwell back as Stewart pursues Madeline's abductors. He comments that perhaps Helen Hammond's desire for excitement and something bad to happen may come true. He is a watchman of sorts, reporting that Don Carlos and his bandits are approaching and later that the sheriff has captured Bonita. Nels is the man who accompanies Madeline to Mexico to secure Gene's release and freedom. Edith Wayne sees in him an example of the genuinely good man produced by the western environment, but also a lonely man lacking the opportunity to settle down with a family.

In *Majesty's Rancho*, Nels is still working for Gene Stewart. Gene treats him as a father, and for Nels, the Stewarts are his family. He cannot remember his age, and he loves Gene's daughter, Madge, as if she were his own flesh and blood. He taught her to ride, to shoot, to rope, in short, all the tricks of the range. He had told her the terrible stories about her famous father and the lovely and appalling romance of her mother and all about ranch and cowboy life, even before she was old enough to understand.

Ren Starr tells Lance that Nels was one of the best cattleman ever. Gene Stewart accepts his advice without question on matters concerning his herds. But in spite of his wide experience, he has not been able to figure how the cattle disappear without leaving a trace. Nels, like Gene, has little faith in automobiles, and the modern style of cattle rustling had never occurred to him. He is impressed with Lance Sidway and soon comes to trust his judgment in most things. He keeps telling Stewart that Sidway is the best hand that he has ever hired. His admiration for the young man keeps on growing. When Madge is kidnapped, he has no doubt that Lance will save the day. Nels sees that the sparks that fly between Madge and Lance mask a deep affection. The conflict can only be resolved with a dash of humility. Madge has been used to getting her way in everything; she has finally met a man who will not bend to her petulant will. Nels does predict, however, that the battle which began over the wonderful horse Umpqua, will end with Lance giving the horse to Madge. When Madge has been returned to her home, Nels goes to her for a heart-to-heart chat. He points out that she has been unfair to Lance. He has been very hurt by her willingness to believe he was one of the gangsters out to kidnap and rape her. He reveals that Lance has spoken to him about his feelings for Madge, a confidence he has broken by speaking to her. He is pleased when things work out the way they should, as they did between Gene and Madeline over twenty years ago.

Nelson: In *Fighting Caravans*, arrives in Kansas City with a caravan of some one hundred and sixty-nine heavily laden wagons and a number of emigrant families rescued at Point of Rocks in the year after the end of the Civil War, when freighting was very dangerous on the plains. Clint Belmet thinks he has had incredible luck getting through without being attacked by Indians or other renegade outlaws. He is with Belmet's caravan at Point of Rocks.

Nelson, Cliff: In *Western Union*, the brother of Edney Nelson. He and his brother are from Missouri and their wagon joins Creighton's crew just before the Indians attack.

Nelson, Edney: In *Western Union*, brother to Cliff, hardy Missourians who inspire confidence in Wayne Cameron. They join up with the Creighton crew just before the Indian attack. They remain with the group through the river crossing and the buffalo stampede.

Nelson, Laramie: In *Raiders of Spanish Peaks*, presented as a Lassiter-type figure, as Hallie Lindsay is a Jane WitherFsteen. Laramie Nelson is a man in his thirties, a man of deep feeling and experience. He rescues Lonesome Mulhall from a lynching. Seeing much good in him, he decides to partner up with him, to take him under his wing. Together they rescue Ted Williams from jail and the three of them become the "Three Range Riders." They work together, pool their money and plan to go into ranching. The distinguishing thing about them is that they never drink or gamble. The money they had saved to buy a ranch is stolen and when they catch the thieves, the thieves have already gambled away all the money. At this point, Laramie runs into Buffalo Jones, who proposes that he take a job driving the Lindsays' wagon train to the Spanish Peaks ranch in Colorado.

Laramie is introduced to the family and agrees to undertake the job. Buffalo Jones has already told the family about his skill as a marksman in the Comanche war against the hiders. Laramie feels embarrassed by his effusive praise. Harriet Lindsay assesses Nelson when he first appears, and feels a mixture of admiration and repulsion for the gunman. Harriet describes him thus: "He was tall, slim, sandy-haired, slightly freckled, and his eyes gray and intent, shone with something which reminded her of those of Buffalo Jones and Luke Arlidge. His lean face wore a sad cast. He did not smile, even at the irrepressible Lenta, who was nothing if not fascinated with him. His garb was travel-stained and rent. His shiny leather overalls, full of holes, flounced down over muddy boots. Great long spurs bright as silver dragged their rowels on the floor. His right side stood toward Harriet and low down, hanging from a worn belt and sheath, shone the dark deadly handle of a gun. All about him suggested long use, hard service. So this was the killer Laramie Nelson, this strange soft-spoken, singularly fascinating Westerner? Harriet was as amazed as she was repelled. He did not look it."

On Jones's recommendation, Nelson is taken on as foreman, to replace Arlidge whom Allen had left to run the place. Laramie shows himself to be a good organizer, a thoughtful and knowledgeable boss. He selects the men to drive the wagons, to cook, to set up camp. He does everything he can to make the trip as easy as possible for the sick Mr. Lindsay. By the time they reach the fort, Mrs. Lindsay has decided that Laramie will cure her husband and make a man out of their son.

At Spanish Peaks, he sets about cleaning up the house, fixing corrals, setting up an office for Harriet, and assigning cowboys to round up cattle. He clears up the question of foremanship with Arlidge. He tells Lindsay that undoubtedly there are men among the cowboys who have remained that are loyal to Allen and will rustle cattle for him. Harriet is impressed with Nelson's ability to do almost any job, a real jack-of-all-trades. And he shows genuine optimism and concern for her father's interests. He regards this job as a once-in-a-lifetime opportunity to do something worthwhile. He sees a future for himself.

Laramie Nelson is as cynical about women as Lassiter in *Riders of the Purple Sage*. Women manipulate men. They lead them to believe that they are special, and men quickly surrender to a monstrous egoism, believing the lie. He sees this principle at work with Lonesome, Slim Red, Chess Gaines and Lenta, with Flo and Ted, and in himself in his feelings for Harriet. Men, he concludes, are complete idiots where women are concerned, and that's why they are so easily manipulated. He feels the need to temper his love for Hallie, who no doubt looks down on him, a gunman, without the education or the refinement of an eastern gentleman, or the slick manners of a Luke Arlidge. He tells Harriet at one point that she will likely end up marrying Luke.

Laramie Nelson resigns his job as foreman, telling Mr. Lindsay that he cannot solve the rustling problem or deal with the abductors of Lenta doing things Hallie's way. He and Lonesome and Ted track the abductors down. They hang Price, and kill Gaines and Beady in a gunfight. Arlidge also is killed by Laramie when he arrives at Allen's cabin announcing that he has shot Neale Lindsay. Laramie has the chance to think about western justice. It is brutal, crude, hideous and possibly futile. Perhaps Harriet is right. The presence of women on the frontier will bring about a change.

Laramie Nelson, like James Lassiter, expresses the western way of doing things, simple, clear-cut, honest, loyal, but in need of the sophistication and experience of the cultured East.

Nelson, Pequita:

In *Majesty's Rancho*, one of Madge's crowd at the university. She is part Spanish, with creamy, olive skin and great dreamy, and sloe-black eyes, and she is willowy and graceful. She is part of the gang that drives to the ranch in Arizona for the summer. She had gone to speak to the dean on Madge's behalf only to get a discouraging reply.

Nesbit:

In *The Maverick Queen*, one of the ranchers on Lee's secret vigilance committee. He is present the night Hargrove and Lee try to whip a confession out of Bud Harkness or some information incriminating Kit Bandon. Nesbit is shot by Bud Harkness when he confronts and kills Hargrove at Emery's poker table in the Leave It Saloon.

Nesbitt:

In *Sunset Pass,* a new rancher in the area. He comes from Wyoming, but unlike Dabb and Lincoln, he has never been a cowboy himself and he does not have a cowboy's sense of life on the range. He is described as a tough nut to crack and it takes some arm twisting to get him on board with the deal offered to Gage Preston. Jim Dunne and Clink Peeples are his foremen.

Nespelly:

In *Horse Heaven Hill*, an Indian who speaks good English, a member of Hurd Blanding's wild mustang-hunting outfit. Blanding calls on him to tell the crowd at the Wade campsite that he has seen Stanley Weston and Lark Burrell in a secluded spot in the hills, hugging and kissing. Blanding hopes to stir up trouble between Stanley, Lark Burrell and Marigold Wade.

Neuman:

In *The Desert of Wheat,* from Ruxton, one of the biggest wheat farmers in Washington state. He is first seen talking with Chris Dorn in a restaurant in Wheatley, after Dorn has sold his crop to a wheat buyer. Neuman is reputed to be Anderson's only rival in the valley. It becomes clear that Neuman is the force behind the I.W.W. in the area. He is using the organization to sabotage the other wheat farmers so that he can eventually buy them out. He is also acting out of sympathy for the Germans. He is later seen with Glidden and Chris Dorn when the eighty thousand dollars are to be handed over to the I.W.W.. When the vigilantes take action against the I.W.W. and Glidden, Neuman is waiting for them to come harvest his own wheat. He is taken aback by the news of the lynchings. He eventually admits to the plot hatched with Glidden to kill Anderson. Neuman is given the option of being bought out at fair market value and leaving the area, or facing the vigilante justice meted out to Glidden and the other agents. Neuman sells his land for seventy thousand dollars and is escorted to the train station.

Nevada:

(1) In *Forlorn River,* the name Ben Ide gives to a young man with a wounded arm who rides up, exhausted and half-starved, to his campfire. Ben asks no questions but takes him in, tends to his wound, feeds him, and gives him a place to stay. The two become the best of friends and partners. Ben Ide never seeks to probe into his past. He accepts him as he is for what he is. Nevada appreciates the unquestioning confidence and acceptance this friend offers.

Nevada cuts a striking figure in the saddle. He rides a horse as if he had grown up there. He mounts and dismounts with lithe, graceful movements, bespeaking great physical strength and control. He has long black hair, a lean, brown face, a long nose with piercing dark eyes that convey an expression of reckless good nature. Ina Blaine thinks him the most handsome man she has ever seen. She also sees in him a love, a loyalty and a protectiveness for Ben that bespeak his pride in his benefactor.

When the novel begins, Nevada reports back on what he has seen on his visit to Hammell. He is proud that he did no drinking or fighting while in town. Ina Blaine is back, and rumor links her to young McAdam. Rumors abound that the mustangers like Ben are really cattle rustlers. Less Setter is the source of most of this talk. Nevada says he knew Less Setter before he came to California. Wherever he goes, Setter is always the big man, a big spender, a big talker and a power to be reckoned with. Setter has been saying that Nevada was run out of Nevada for rustling. Nevada predicts that he may have to kill Setter before this business is over. He knows Setter's influence on Hart Blaine and Amos Ide cannot be good.

Nevada serves as a messenger between Ben and his sister Hettie. He delivers letters to her and she gives him letters for Ben. Nevada is sweet on Hettie, but he feels that he is not a suitable mate for her, that he is not fit to wipe her boots. He does think of her often, dreaming about what could be.

Nevada advises Ben to purchase the neighboring ranches because without doubt, Less Setter will be making advances on them soon. He has been speaking with the ranchers and knows they are hard up and looking to sell. He and Ben catch horses to give these men as payment for the land. When Nevada sees Ben speaking privately and earnestly with Sims after they have negotiated the sale, he guesses what it is about and he tells him the things he and Modoc have observed, which betray the activities of the rustlers in the mountains.

Nevada and Modoc track the rustlers to the ice

caves, where they had hoped to catch wild mustangs. Bill Hall and his rustlers are surrounded and besieged there for twenty-four days. When they surrender, Nevada and Ben take them back to Blaine's ranch to hand over to the sheriff. When Ben spots the mustang stallion, California Red, out on the frozen lake, they decide to capture the stallion. Ben offers to set free any of the rustlers who help him catch the stallion. When they get back to the ranch with the stallion but without the rustlers, Ben is arrested. Nevada sets off with Sheriff Strobel to recapture the outlaws. Nevada tells the group at Blaine's ranch that Bill Hall denounced Less Setter as the leader of the rustlers. Setter recognizes Nevada and attempts to draw on him, but Nevada is faster. Nevada departs, bidding Ben Ide farewell, saying that the two of them are even.

In *Nevada,* before Nevada returns to Lineville, he looks at the Blaine ranch in the distance. He stops at the ranch he shared with Ben. He is glad he cleared Ben Ide's name, that he put an end to Less Setter. He recalls how close he and Ben had been, and his love for Hettie. He knows she believes in him, but he wonders what they would think if they knew he was a famous gunman from Lineville. He fears that returning to his old haunts will bring back the old ways.

He goes to the home of Mrs. Woods, who was a surrogate mother to him. She had given him room and board in exchange for doing chores around the place. She brings him up to date about Lize Teller and Cash Burridge. Meeting with Cash brings back the old feelings. He does his best to avoid the old Setter crowd. He meets Jones, the store manager, who offers him a job, telling him of the prosperity that has recently blessed Lineville.

At the Gold Mine saloon, he meets some of the old crowd. Lize Teller tells him he was reported seen in Hammell, where Less Setter was known to be. She tells him he is suspected of being involved with Setter's death, although not too many in Lineville as yet can put the two of them together in California. Lize has been playing the field and in order to rid herself of an unpleasant attachment called Link Cawthorne, hopes to provoke a fight between him and Jim. Eventually, her wish comes true. When Link beats her in a jealous rage, Jim calls him out and kills him.

Leaving Lineville for Arizona, Nevada recalls how, as a boy, he was thrown among brutal, evil men. He had worked himself above their bad influence time and again only to be thrown back by accident, by the chivalry in him to redress a wrong done by someone, by a passion to survive. Fate had shaped him into a gunman, a profession for which he seemed unfortunately well-suited. Despite this, when the Ides stop with Mrs. Wood in Lineville en route to Arizona, she tells them that any place is better with men like Jim Lacy around. The do not know she is talking about the cherished friend they hope to find in Arizona.

Two years after leaving Lineville, Jim Lacy, now known as Texas Jack, is working for Tom Day. He overhears Day and Judge Franklidge talking about Ben Ide, how he appears to be on the run or looking for someone. Their suspicions about Ben make him offer his services as an undercover agent to flush out the leaders of the Pine Tree Outfit. The judge offers to deputize him but he merely asks their word of honor that if he comes out of this alive, they will clear his name. Both the judge and Tom Day swear to it. He then realizes that the same old love for Ben and Hettie is still there. He will help them keep their ranch and, although he has made a name for himself and started a new life, he knows he must risk it again for the sake of his friends.

In Winthrop, he gets duded up and resumes his name, Jim Lacy. He meets Rose Hatt and from her story of abuse and fear, he senses that life has tracked him down. He will probably do for her what he did for Lize Teller in Lineville. He is amused at the gossip about Tom Day in town. Some actually suspect he is the leader of the Pine Tree Outfit. He also hears that Ben Ide is being sheeped and rustled off his land. On Day's ranch, he had been deemed anti-social, a woman hater, because he loved to keep to himself. Now, he must make himself known to fulfill his mission. He confronts Dillon at the dance, overhearing Dillon's discourteous encounter with Hettie. He gives him a black eye for his effort, revealing his identity as Jim Lacy at the same time. He meets Cash Burridge in the Ace High saloon. He learns of Burridge's sale of the ranch and his subsequent loss of the money in card games to Hardy Rue, who "holds court" on the second floor of the saloon. He kills Hardy Rue in a shootout in the street, after which Hettie catches sight of him on the sidewalk. From Cash Burridge, he learns about the Hatt family and earns his praise for having the wisdom to return California Red to Ben Ide, thereby making it less likely the place will be swarmed with men seeking to earn the reward. Some people even begin to suspect that he is head of the Pine Tree Outfit. Tracking Cedar Hatt one day, he prevents the killing of Marvie Blaine and Rose. From Rose, he now learns that Ben Ide's foreman, Clan Dillon, is a former Lincoln County outlaw and head of the Pine Tree. En route to the Ide ranch, he meets Hettie. He tells her who Dillon is and she tries to prevent him from going to meet him. In the gunfight which ensues, Dillon is killed. Jim Lacy is being held, facing lynching. Ben Ide is all ready to proceed with the hanging until he realizes who Jim Lacy is. He sets him free. Judge Franklidge and Tom Day tell all that Jim Lacy, whom they know as Texas Jack, had been sent as an undercover agent to flush out the Pine Tree leaders. Nevada and Hettie are married, and Nevada becomes a partner with Ben Ide in the new ranch.

The Ben Ide-Jim Lacy friendship is one of many buddy stories in Zane Grey's novels. To the westerner, a man's partner was often a more intimate friend, a closer ally than wife or family. As well, Jim Lacy is one of many chivalrous cowboys who must resort to the gun to help a friend in need or defend a helpless woman.

(2) In "From Missouri," one of the cowboys on Springer's ranch who vies for the privilege of taking Miss Stacey riding.

Newman, Dan and Joe: In *The Thundering Herd,* meet Tom Doan when they come to the buffalo fields in the last hunt. Like Tom when he first arrived, the brothers are in awe of frontiersmen and Indian fighters and they are anxious to learn from a man like Tom.

Newman, Emily: In *Valley of Wild Horses,* a passenger on the stage from Littleton to Marco, New Mexico. Pan Handle shares her company on the stage for three days and she is eager to hear the stories of his escapades. She reminds Pan Handle of the feminine company he has never had all his years wandering the range.

Newton, Lenora: In *Captives of the Desert,* Mary Newton's sister-in-law, Wilbur's younger sister. When Wilbur announces he is going away on a trip to buy silver for MacDonald at the trading post, he sends for his sister to keep an eye on Mary. Her family cannot afford to give her the money for the trip so Wilbur uses the money Mary has made selling poultry and eggs and produce from the garden. Mary has to give up her bedroom to Lenora and sleep on the couch in the living room. Lenora is a snob, like her brother. Mary overhears Wilbur and Lenora talking about how Mary probably has money hidden away somewhere in a bank where Wilbur cannot get his hands on it. They had thought she was well-heeled. Lenora loves to draw attention to herself, playing the great lady. She invites women from the town over for tea, and then treats Mary as a servant. She likes to draw the attention of the cowboys, John Curry in particular. She tells Mary that Wilbur had asked her to keep an eye on him because he suspected Mary was in love with Curry.

Newton, Mary: In *Captives of the Desert,* Wilbur Newton's wife. Ten years before, Mary left New York to live with relatives in the South. Her father had remarried and he feared conflict between his then-haughty and aloof eighteen-year-old daughter and her temperamental stepmother, barely five years her senior. Her friend Katharine feared nothing good would come of the situation. Mary barely knew the relatives in the South but had Mary been trained to economic independence, she could have escaped her family. Mary's father had chained her to himself to satisfy his creature comforts when her mother had died. Little wonder she married Wilbur Newton before a year had elapsed. She wrote to Katharine that she was marrying a Texan of a branch of one of the oldest southern families. She praised his qualities, his desire to become a rancher to restore the family fortunes. She probably fell in love with an image. He was not unlike John Curry in appearance at that time. He jingled his spurs when he walked. He wore a great big sombrero and his face bespoke kindliness, reserve, power and confidence. Two years later, his ranching and farming ventures had ended

in failure and he found work as an assistant trader on a Navajo reservation in Arizona.

When Katharine writes that Alice has tuberculosis and the doctor recommends a drier climate, Mary urges her friends to come to Arizona. Her own robust health she attributes to the desert. When Katharine arrives, Mary speaks very little of herself and Wilbur during the first three weeks. Katharine, however, makes a lot of correct deductions from what is not said. She sees how dismissive and insulting Wilbur is to Mary. She also sees that Mary has a special friendship with John Curry. Although High-Lo and other cowboys, and eventually Katharine and Alice and others at Taho, know that Wilbur is a bootlegger, selling liquor to the Navajo, Mary refuses to believe anything bad about Wilbur. When Wilbur leaves for several weeks to negotiate "a sheep deal," or to buy silver for the trading post, he asks his sister Lenora to stay with Mary. He uses the money she has made selling eggs and poultry to pay for his sister's bus ticket. Lenora is a snob, treating Mary like a servant, much as Wilbur does. She is there to spy on her, as Wilbur suspects she and John Curry are more than friends. Mary overhears the two of them discussing her. Lenora speculates that Mary is holding out on Wilbur, that she does have money stashed away somewhere but won't let him have it. It appears Wilbur had married her on the false assumption that she was well-heeled. Wilbur abandons Mary, but she refuses to entertain the possibility of a divorce. Katharine and others suggest it would be the best thing for her, but it seems that she does really love him. When she learns she has inherited ten thousand dollars after her father dies, she tries to get word to Wilbur, hoping to get him back, now that she has a bit of money. She eventually learns what many others already know, that Wilbur did not return to his family in Texas, but set up a trading post at Sage Springs to compete with Weston, and that he has been living with Magdaline, a young Navajo woman. Magdaline comes to visit Mary's adopted daughter, Joy, who happens to be her younger sister. During the visit, the truth about Wilbur comes out. He has been living with her at Sage Springs and is the father of her child. Mary regrets having sent the letter asking Wilbur to return. When Wilbur attacks Magdaline in her family's hogan trying to force her to return with him to Sage Springs, he is shot. Mary is finally free to marry John Curry, her soul mate.

Newton, Wilbur: In *Captives of the Desert,* Mary's husband. As a young man, he was impressive to look at. He dressed well, and jingled his spurs when he walked. Mary thought he had a kindly expression but one that exuded confidence and power as well. Six months after their marriage, he had failed in the ranch enterprise. Being such a proud man, he had to flee from his disgrace, so they migrated to southern Arizona. Two years later, his farming project in some remote valley was abandoned and they transferred their meager possessions to Taho on the

Indian reservation, where he worked on salary as an assistant trader. Mary and Wilbur had no children, and it was just as well, as Katharine Winfield puts it, because neither dogs nor children liked Wilbur.

Wilbur, despite his haughtiness and arrogant self-importance, can do very little for himself. When the car breaks down, he hasn't a clue how to go about fixing it. John Curry does the job. When he is angry with Mary, he treats her to contemptuous silence, during which she babies him, catering to his every whim. Katharine is disgusted by her submissiveness. Mary's grandmother had referred to the young generation of Newtons as a lazy, shiftless lot, the frayed-out stock of a broken-down aristocracy. They were always in debt from such unnecessary luxuries as a general-work girl, or a procession of them, who came and left, usually with a threat to sue for back wages. Mary proposes to Wilbur that she get a job in Flaggerston and together they can raise money to start up again in the ranching business bit by bit. Wilbur, however, jumps to Hanley's tune. They run a racket with a Mormon horse wrangler, Tim Wake, peddling liquor to the Navajos. Wilbur abandons Mary, setting up a trading post in Sage Springs. The young Navajo woman, Magdaline, moves in with him. When she gets pregnant, he kicks her out, giving her fifty dollars. But when she has married High-Lo, he goes to her family hogan to force her to come back. She shoots and kills him.

Nichols: In *The Trail Driver,* the trail driver leading the herd which is following Adam Hite's outfit. According to Reddie, they are right on their heels.

Nick: In *Shadow on the Trail,* a member of Aulsbrook's crew when Wade Holden (Blanco) rides in to warn them of Catlin's planned attempt to rustle their herd.

Nielsen: In *Arizona Ames,* a homesteader, a pioneer, one of the first to arrive in the Wind River valley where Crow Grieve's large ranch is located. Nielsen is a farmer, feeding himself and his family with the produce of his fifty-acre holding. He would like to branch into cattle but Grieve will not let him run cattle on the range. He has fenced in Nielsen's holding to prevent just that. He tells Arizona Ames about Grieve's persecution and the advances Brick Jones made to his wife.

Nielsen, Mrs.: In *Arizona Ames,* Nielsen's wife. She is a large, strong woman, mother of several children. She has a naturally friendly disposition. When Brick Jones comes by he misinterprets her friendliness and openness and tries to get fresh with her.

Nigger Horse, Chief: In *The Thundering Herd,* the Comanche chief leading the warriors in the battle with Pilchuck and Starwell's expedition. Jake Devine predicts it will be a fight to the finish since the Indians want to prevent the extermination of the buffalo. Jake Devine shoots him dead.

In *Raiders of Spanish Peaks,* Colonel Buffalo Jones speaks with great admiration to John Lindsay about "Old Nigger Horse," the Comanche chief who had led the Indians against the buffalo hiders down in Texas. Jones has great respect for Old Nigger Horse as a military tactician and a fighter of unparalleled courage. Laramie Nelson was a sharpshooter in that final battle in the canyon on the Llano Estacado (the Staked Plain). When Nigger Horse saw that he was beaten and in danger of being wiped out completely, he sent his son at the head of the hardest-riding bucks straight for the mouth of the gully. The son pranced his horse around at the head of the band. Brave and daring as the son was, he never got more than halfway. He fell at a long shot from one of Jones's sharpshooters, Laramie Nelson. The charge was broken and the Indian attack fell apart. Some escaped by climbing out of the canyon on foot. As a threat to the hiders, the Comanche had been eliminated.

In *The Lost Wagon Train,* Kit Carson concludes from the narrative of the attack on Melville's caravan at Point of Rocks that Nigger Horse must have been the chief of the Comanches involved in the attack.

In *The Trail Driver,* Nigger Horse appears with a band of Comanche to negotiate the terms of passage through Comanche land. He wants flour, sugar, tobacco, and cattle. When he requests guns and ammunition, Brite refuses to surrender any more supplies. He does, however, point out that there will be more herds coming by every few days, and that he can barter similar deals with them. Nigger Horse then allows the herd to continue.

Nigger Jack: In *The Lost Wagon Train,* an outlaw who found acceptance in Latch's outlaw gang. He is killed in the attack on Anderson's wagon train.

Night: In *Riders of the Purple Sage,* one of Jane Withersteen's favorite thoroughbred horses. The animal is kept in a barn near the ranch house and trained and exercised by Jerd. Jane holds that Night and Black Star are the fastest horses, but Venters, Judkins and Lassiter tell her the sorrel, Wrangle, is the best of the lot. Black Star is stolen from the barn by Jerry Card but rescued by Venters on Wrangle in a race which proves that the sorrel is the fastest. When Lassiter and Jane are abandoning the burning ranch, they bring Night and Black Star with them. They meet Venters and Bess on their way out of Utah. Since Tull and his henchmen are pursuing them, they give the thoroughbreds to Venters and Bess as they can surely outrun any horse the Mormons may have. Night and Black Star are the start of the horse breeding farm Venters and Bess establish in Beaumont, Illinois. In *The Rainbow Trail,* Jane Withersteen is reunited with Night when Shefford rescues her and Lassiter and they return east.

Nippert: In *Shadow on the Trail,* a member of Catlin's rustler gang. When Wade Holden makes his way into their camp, he is suspicious. Holden has all the mannerisms of a gunman and could be dangerous. He also suspects that Holden has money on him and he would like to kill and rob him while he sleeps. Catlin, however, is not so enthusiastic. Holden leaves the camp during the night and proceeds to Aulsbrook's camp and warns them of Nippert and Catlin's plans. Nippert and Catlin show up in Aulsbrook's camp to find out what Holden has revealed. Nippert is killed when he draws on Holden.

Noddle: In *The Heritage of the Desert*, Mescal's favorite burro. Hare admires its ability to climb the yard-wide trail up to the plateau with a full load on its back. Noddle accompanies Mescal into the desert and, although left behind in the complications which follow upon Mescal's return to "civilization," the beloved burro appears at Naab's ranch just after Mescal's wedding. She considers Noddle's return the finest wedding present she could have.

Noddlecoddy: In *Black Mesa*, the old Navajo chief who said of Bitter Seeps that the water was not good but that it could sustain life. The mystery of the bad water is solved by Paul Manning.

Noggin: In *Arizona Ames,* the name by which Ben Ackers is known.

Noki: In *The Vanishing American*, both the name of a branch of the Navajo tribe and the name of a man who works as a spy for Blucher and Morgan on the Navajo reservation. He is a tall, dark-haired man with piercing eyes. He spies on Do Etin hoping to learn where his daughter is being hidden. He is an excellent tracker and eventually trails her to the canyon where a Pahute family is keeping her. Noki is responsible for the attack on the home of Do Etin who is killed for "resisting arrest." Noki also makes an attempt on Nophaie's life.

Nolgoshie: In *The Vanishing American,* an expert basket weaver whose name means "loping woman." She is married to Beleanth do de jodie, a rich Nopah and a good man. Shoie tells her he has put a spell on her and she broods on it, her health deteriorating. When Nophaie convinces Shoie to remove the spell, word is brought to her that the spell has been removed and her health improves immediately. However, Shoie again spreads word that the spell removal does no good. The superstitious Nolgoshie slowly withers away and dies.

Nopah: In *Blue Feather*, the tribe to which Blue Feather belongs and of which Nothis Toh is currently chief. This tribe consists of tall hunters and warriors who are intent on conquering the Rock Clan and taking their citadel and treasures.

Nophaie: In *The Vanishing American*, the original Navajo name of Lo Blandy. The character of Nophaie represents the most complete treatment of the theme of the "noble savage" and the "vanishing" Indian in Grey's western fiction. On the one hand, Nophaie is torn between the advantages and progress white civilization offers the Native American, and, on the other, the native culture and world view which must be abandoned in order to accept these "white gifts" fully. His is the tragedy of many Native Americans who are comfortable in neither world.

For the first seven years of his existence, Nophaie lives the life of the "noble savage": The dominant traits of his tribe and his race seemed to be intensified in him. His was the heritage of a chieftain. His mother had died at his birth, whispering strange and mystic prophecies. The old medicine men, the sages of the tribe, had gathered round him ... predicting for him unknown and great feats.... Before Nophaie could walk he had begun to learn the secrets of the life of the open ... all the little wild creatures of the desert were brought to him to tame, to play with, to study and learn to love.... He was unconsciously and unutterably happy because he was in perfect harmony with the reality and spirit of the nature that encompassed him. He wandered in an enchanted land of mystery upon which the Great Spirit looked with love. He had no cares, no needs, no selfishness. Only vaguely had he heard of the menace of the white race encroaching upon the lands of the Indian.... There was no death of spirit for Nophaie and his kind. There was no evil except what he thought and to think evil of himself, of anyone, was a sin. To think evil made it true.... What he loved most was to be alone, out in the desert, listening to the real sounds of the open and to the silent whisperings of his soul....

The events of the first years of his life indeed suggest he is intended for great things. At the age of five, he was tending sheep with other boys of the village. A sandstorm arose and he alone remained with the sheep for three days while the others fled. He was praised and rewarded, and for the past two years had been in charge of the sheep alone. He had proven himself up to the responsibility. He had defended his flock against an eagle and against coyotes. The other boys in the village are jealous of his reputation and stature in the tribe. But one day, he saw his first white men and felt an instinctive mistrust of them. They stole several sheep and took him off with them, intending to abandon him in the desert far enough away that he could not give the alarm. Rather than kill the boy, these white men give him to people in a wagon train. He is sent east to be raised as a young white boy. Eighteen years later, he returns to his Navajo home.

The Lo Bandy that Marian Warner knew in Philadelphia was a scholar and an athletic young man who excelled at football and baseball, setting records at the university, making his way with both academic and athletic scholarships. She recalls him as a slender, bare-headed athlete, with powerful, broad shoulders, and a dark face. He was strikingly handsome, the embodiment of what the ancient Greek athletes competing on Olympus must have been. She had fallen in love with him. He had more principle and better habits than any white boy she knew. She hated the drinking and smoking of women, the unrestrained dances, the lack of courtesy, the undeniable let-down of morals. She felt in Lo Blandy the call to "some subtle innate wildness in her," to a fuller life than Philadelphia could offer.

When Lo Blandy returns to his Navajo reservation, the first thing he does is to strip himself of his white clothes and burn them, a symbol of his rejection of the white world. He writes Marian about his new life. He wants to do something of value for his people but what he has acquired in the white world seems singularly useless here. He has not developed the physical strength and stamina required for this kind of life. Nophaie writes that he lives in the wildest and loneliest part of the reservation because he wants to be away from white people. He lives with his uncle in a hogan and has acquired a small flock of sheep which he raises, work considered as "woman's work" among his people. He has a small herd of mustangs, but no saddle, no gun. He makes his livelihood selling wool and hides and working for rich Navajos. He has planted some corn using a new variety of seed, built a dam to hold the spring run-off for irrigation. Perhaps introducing new methods of agriculture could make a difference on the reservation.

Nophaie discovers that he is an atheist. By this he means that he no longer shares the unquestioning faith of his Navajo people in their spirituality. He lacks the simple resignation in the face of life which he sees in his uncle, Maahesenie, or in Etenia. As he tells Marian, "my developed intelligence makes it impossible for me to believe in the Indian's religion" and he "will not believe in the white man's one." His white education makes it impossible to believe in the power of the witch doctor, the power of spells, the power of magic, the gods which rule the heavens, the winds who live in the valley of the gods. When the witch doctor comes to treat his ailing uncle, he sees that some of the witch doctor's work does have a basis in sound physiological principles, although the witch doctor does not grasp the scientific principles behind his practices.

On his return to the Navajo lands, Nophaie is almost as much of a stranger as any white man. Mrs. Withers, who has spent over twenty-five years among the Navajo, tells Marian that she had to teach Nophaie his language, the legends and myths of his people, the tribal rituals and customs. She knew more about his heritage than he did. Nophaie finds that he must resort to English to talk about his people. He has mastered the language of anthropology and science, the ability to look objectively at things. He cannot see his people as they see themselves, from inside a Navajo cosmology (world view).

Nophaie's rejection of the white world, however, can never be complete. The white man's science and agriculture offer the Navajo great possibilities for improvement of living conditions. Many Navajo share his optimism about the benefits of these things, but like Nophaie, they reject the imposition of the Christian religion at the schools as the price to be paid for learning these practical skills. Nophaie crit-

icizes Morgan to his face, calling him a liar and a hypocrite, a man concerned with enriching himself through cheating the government agencies and depriving the Navajo of those things which would be most beneficial. At one point, his anger is so great that he almost kills Morgan and Blucher in the schoolhouse.

When the attempt to rescue Gekin Yashi has proven unsuccessful, he retreats to a valley in the painted desert, where he gets in touch with his Indian spirit. He can look at the landscape without thought, at one with the world. Withers brings him supplies, and Christmas presents from Marian. He is touched by the fact that it is white men, his supposed enemies, who are most solicitous in his time of need. He understands that nature did not make man to live alone. The community of human beings is needed to maintain a sane perspective.

Marian Warner proposes marriage several times to Nophaie, but he cannot accept. He feels he must marry an Indian woman, to follow the imperative of nature to ensure the continuation of the species, but he cannot marry a woman he does not love. Like Hamlet, he is unable to act.

John Withers brings him word that the United States has entered the war raging in Europe. The government has not imposed conscription, but does require registration of all able-bodied males, Navajos included. Blucher, the passionately pro–German and anti-American reservation manager, takes advantage of the Navajo sense of betrayal by previous U.S. governments. He is busy spreading lies about the registration, telling people that the American government is forcing them to go to war. The Navajo chiefs are not opposed to their men fighting in the U.S. Army, but prefer to do so by choice. They are easily deceived. Nophaie comes back with Withers to counter Blucher's influence. He enlists, and, together with Shoie, convinces many of the Navajo that Blucher has not been truthful. In Europe, Nophaie and Shoie both stand out for their bravery and courage. They are true heroes, Nophaie being wounded four times, and Shoie having his tongue cut out and crucified by the Germans.

On his return to the reservation, Nophaie is hailed as a hero, but he does not find the answer to his dilemmas. Like Kurt Dorn in *Desert of Wheat,* he does not find his god on the battlefields of France. Conditions on the reservation are bad. The wool market has failed with the end of the war; drought and the Spanish flu find many victims. Once again Nophaie saves the lives of the reservation managers, Morgan, Blucher and Friel. The Nophas and Noki have rebelled and are about to hang the men who have made their lives a misery for decades. Nophaie himself falls victim to the flu, and dies in the arms of Marian Warner, his one true friend.

In Nophaie, Zane Grey embodies the struggle he had witnessed among the Navajo to cling to their culture and religion in the face of overwhelming white influence and the heartless exploitation of unscrupulous government agents and missionaries. His hero takes on a Christ-like role, seeking reconciliation with God and man. In fact, his death in the arms of Marian Warner is not unlike the scene captured in Michelangelo's "Pieta."

Nothis Toh: In *Blue Feather*, the chief of the Nopah tribe, a warrior people. He sends his son, Docleas, as a spy, to determine the most effective means to attack the citadel of the Rock Clan. He is surprised when his son returns some months later to announce that the Rock Clan has no treasures worth taking and its citadel is impregnable. He suspects there is something more that his son has not mentioned. He leads the assault on the citadel. The first assault is repulsed, but when Nashta learns that the Sheboyahs are planning to kill Blue Feather, she betrays the secret passage way to Nothis Toh to save her lover. When the battle is over, Nothis Toh forgives his son, after he has seen the beautiful woman who was willing to sacrifice her people for his son, and for whom this son was willing to betray his tribe.

Nugget: In *Captives of the Desert*, the mule that John Curry rides into the desert when he and High-Lo set out to find Wilbur Newton.

Nuggett, Ruth: In *Thunder Mountain*, a saloon girl Lee Emerson first meets in Cliff Borden's establishment in Salmon. She approaches him in the saloon because he looks different from the other men and she takes a liking to him. She comes to Thunder Mountain with Borden to work at his saloon there. Lee Emerson gets her away from Borden and sets her up with his friend Dick Sloan, who is madly in love with her and planning to marry her. She agrees to his proposal. Nugget tries to help Lee by having a heart-to-heart with Sydney Blair, telling her what Leavitt and his crew are really like. Sydney, however, thinks that Nuggett is acting solely to help Lee discredit a rival suitor. When Dick is attacked at his new claim, Nuggett sticks by him, nursing him. When he dies, she moves to Lee Emerson's cabin. She accepts his proposal of marriage, and they buy the Olsen ranch on the Salmon River. Nuggett does not begin with the qualities of a heroine. Her background is similar to that of Sydney Blair. Born in Wisconsin, she went west to Wyoming with her father. At age sixteen, she left Cheyenne to start working in Borden's dance-hall in Salmon. Unlike Sydney, she learns to think of others, to sacrifice herself, and to adapt to the environment which brings out the best in her. She is the mature, serious wife that can keep Lee Emerson straight.

O

Oaks, Sheriff: In *The Lone Star Ranger*, the law in Wellston, Texas. When Cal Bain decides to call out Buck Duane, Oaks is out of town at Flesher's ranch, which had been hit by rustlers the day before.

Oberney: In *Shadow on the Trail*, a member of Simm Bell's outlaw gang. He meets Holden and Simm at the Smoky Hollow hideout as they return from the Texas Pacific job. It is not clear whether he is killed or escapes from the ambush in Mercer.

Oella: In *Wanderer of the Wasteland*, the daughter of Charley Jim. Along with her father, she nurses Adam back to health when they find him at the deserted Indian village. The two become friends. She teaches Adam to speak Coahuila while he teaches her English. She wants to marry Adam, but Charley Jim will not allow it unless Adam consents to stay with the Indians. Adam feels he cannot do that and so Charley Jim tells him he must leave. When Adam Larey meets up with Charley Jim many years later, he learns that Oella died of a broken heart, pining for him.

Old Benei: In *Blue Feather*, the star-gazer, who reads the will of the gods in the sky. None of the omens are favorable to the Rock Clan.

Old Bill: In *Fighting Caravans*, an old timer, freighter, and storyteller, especially when he has had a few drinks. He tells a humorous tale about hunting a buffalo with his partner, Frenshy. He also tells about the pursuit of some Comanche with a Lieutenant Stevens.

Old Brackton: In *Wildfire*, a little, old, gray man with a scant beard and eyes like a bird. He is a member of Bostril's horsemen's club, which meets to plan the annual race at Bostril's Ford. Brackton (Brack) is the owner of the store and tavern at Bostril's Ford. He also runs a freighter business to Durango. Given the establishments he runs, Brackton hears all the gossip first. He reports that Cordts, the reputed horse thief, is around; he has heard that the railroad is going to come to Bostril's Ford, news that is welcome to Bostril and others as they see an opportunity for themselves in land speculation. At the awards ceremony for the winner of the horse race, Brackton reports the news about Joel Creech. He wants to kill whoever sabotaged his fathers' horses. The stallions were trapped in a box canyon together with Joel's father and death by thirst or starvation would be their fate. Brackton, like Bostril, assumes Joel is crazy. Brackton comes to visit Lin Slone at Vorhees' place. He repeats to him the story that Joel has spread about seeing him kissing Lucy. He also believes that Lin Slone had cut the ropes on the boat so that Blue Roan and Peg could not be ferried across the river for the race. Brackton advises Slone to be careful.

Old Butch: In *Stairs of Sand*, a mule. Adam (Wansfell) tells Ruth Virey that eight years ago he became acquainted with the mule in the Mohave desert at a mine where he was working. The packers at the mine couldn't drive him and shot him more than once. Adam catches up with Ruth in the canyon because thirty miles after they left Lost Lake, Old Butch balked and could not be budged any more than you could budge a mountain.

Ol' Calico: In *Valley of Wild Horses*, a horse that

Pan Handle's father got him for his roundup. He bought her from a woman who tried to hitch him up to a wagon but he balked. Pan Handle calls the horse "Old Paint." The cowboys at the roundup recognize the animal and are shocked to see him picket the horse for the night. They tell him Ol' Calico is unmatched as a cutting horse.

Old Dutch John: In *Valley of Wild Horses*, one of the colorful characters Pan Handle meets in his youth. In the spring when the twelve-year-old Pan Handle joins the roundup, he meets Old Dutch John, a famous range character, driving the chuck wagon. At one point he had been a crony of Pan Handle's father and that attracted him to the grizzled old cook. He could not talk without swearing and if he replied to a question that needed only yes or no, he would supplement it with a string of oaths.

Old Freighter, the: In *Fighting Caravans,* not known by any other name. He tells Clint Belmet the story of the fight long ago in Apache Pass between the Spanish and the Apache. The Indians besieged a group of Spanish explorers and soldiers on the top of a mountain. The Spanish eventually starved to death rather than surrender. The mountain is named after the incident, "Starvation Peak."

Old Gray: (1) In *To the Last Man*, a loafer, a gray wolf, that has been attacking the herds in the Tonto Basin. The wolf attacks one of Ellen's ewes and some of the Isbel cattle. Jean Isbel attempts to track the wolf with his dog, Shepp.

(2) In *The Wolf Tracker,* similar to Old Lobo from *The Mysterious Rider,* a huge, gray wolf that slaughtered thousands of dollars worth of stock. The size of this old gray is astonishing, raising questions about its origins. Perhaps ten years ago, a trapper lost a husky, an Alaskan snow-sled dog, and Old Gray is believed to be the offspring of the husky and a range loafer. Another story holds that a wolf escaped from a circus in a railroad wreck and this escaped animal might be Old Gray. The animal is called an old gray, but it's almost white, with a black streak on its neck. Adams tells Brinks that Old Gray is smarter than any dog, too savage and too keen to be caught by ordinary means. As he pursues the wolf, all the things he has been told about the animal's intelligence and cunning prove true. Old Gray seems to take a certain pride in being able to attack and escape from his hereditary foe, man. Brinks develops an admiration for the animal and when he finally does get the loafer in his sights, he cannot pull the trigger. He decides the contest will be between man, unassisted by weaponry, and beast. Brinks tries to put himself into the wolf's head, wondering how the beast sees the contest, whether for him it is a matching of intelligence or merely the clever use of instinct. When the animal realizes it is being pursued by a foe that cannot be deterred, panic and fear take over. The winter snow gives the man on snowshoes an advantage, and when Brinks finally does catch up to the loafer, the animal does not fight. Fear, resignation, cowardice are primary. Brinks strangles the wolf with his bare hands. The contest ends as he had intended, with man unassisted by weaponry and beast in an elemental struggle. Literally, Brinks walked the wolf to death.

In Old Gray, Grey develops his theme of the Darwinian struggle that is embodied in nature, a struggle which is by nature uneven, as nature decreed that man, with his intelligence and reason, forever altered the balance of power in the natural world. The struggle is seen at an elemental level here in the contest between Brinks and Old Gray, but it is equally at work in the human world.

Old Horse: (1) In *The Last Trail*, a Chippewa Indian involved in the horse stealing outfit led by Bing Legget. When Case is shot and killed from afar, Old Horse identifies it as the work of Deathwind.

(2) In *Wildfire*, one of two Navajo chiefs who enter horses in the annual horse race at Bostril's Ford.

Old Joe: In *The Man of the Forest*, Beasley's witness to confirm his claim that Al Auchincloss owes him eighty thousand dollars.

Old Kemp: In *The Mysterious Rider*, the patriarch of a village Bent Wade passes through on his way to Belllounds' ranch. When he hears Wade's name, he recalls what one Sam Coles told him about the man, that trouble seems to follow him mercilessly and after every stroke of bad luck, he must find someone to share his story with.

Old Lobo: In *The Mysterious Rider*, mentioned in a story Bent Wade tells Columbine about a time he was working as a cook on a ranch north of Denver. Old Lobo was a wolf attacking the herd, and had killed eleven yearlings. Bent Wade set out trailing the old wolf, and claims he walked Old Lobo to death.

Old Miles: In *The U. P. Trail*, one of the three men with Fresno when he attacks, robs and burns Slingerland's cabin. He dies in a fight with Sandy over the gold stolen from Slingerland.

Old Montana: In *Thunder Mountain*, the nickname given to Lee Emerson (Kalispel) by the miners at the Thunder Mountain digs.

Old Nigger Horse, see **Nigger Horse, Chief**

Old Paint: In *Valley of Wild Horses*, the name Pan Handle gives Ol' Calico. See **Ol' Calico.**

Old Scotty: In *Arizona Ames*, witnessed the shootout in the tavern in Shelby when Rich Ames kills Lee Tate and Sheriff Stringer. He asserts that it was a fair fight.

Old Tom: In *30,000 on the Hoof*, the name that Logan Huett gives the old cougar that has plagued his herd for years. He finally kills the old cat in a one-on-one fight in the corral where Tom has attacked a calf. Logan keeps the cougar's skin on the wall of the house.

Old White Foot: In *The Heritage of the Desert*, the companion wild mustang stallion to Silvermane. This mustang stallion occasionally raids neighboring ranches, luring away the mares. After Silvermane has been captured and trained and is contented with life as John Hare's steed, Old White Foot makes an occasional appearance, but manages to avoid capture.

Old Wise: In *Code of the West*, Enoch Thurman's white mule. He is famous in Arizona, past his prime but still vigorous, and far from beautiful. He has a well-formed head and keen, intelligent eyes. Old Wise is renowned for many things but especially for his kick. He will not kick anyone he likes, and Mary Stockwell is one of these favored people. She pats the old mule as she thinks about the problems she may face with her younger sister, Georgie, on the way from Erie, Pennsylvania.

Oldfield, Barney: In *Boulder Dam*, Lynn Weston compares a truck driver to Barney Oldfield. There is no further mention of Barney Oldfield in the novel.

Oldrin':   In *Riders of the Purple Sage*, the leader of an outlaw gang that operates in southern Utah near Cottonwoods. Oldrin' is originally from Texas, and it seems at some point Jim Lassiter and he worked together, but the nature of that work is never specified. Lassiter sees a basic honesty in Oldrin', despite his work as a rustler. Oldrin' rustles cattle and sells them in the northern part of the state, up by Sterling. No one knows for sure how he moves the cattle from one place to another, but all assume there is a trail to be found somewhere in Deception Pass. Venters eventually learns the secret of the maze of canyons, identifies the road through the labyrinth and even discovers the entrance to Oldrin's hideout behind the waterfalls. The mystery, though, is that there are cattle there that were rustled up to a year and a half before which are still grazing in the meadows in secret canyons. When Venters has nursed Bess back to health, she tells him that Oldrin' has been doing rustling for the Mormons, Elder Tull in particular. Jerry Card has done the negotiating. But especially, Bess reveals that the rustling operation and the story of the Masked Rider are mere distractions to keep people out of the canyons because he and his men have found gold, and that is the real source of their wealth. Oldrin', Bess says, is educated. One of his men was also educated and taught her to read and provided her with books. He takes special care to keep her away from his men when they are drunk to protect her virtue. Oldrin' reveals to Jim Lassiter when they meet in Snell's saloon that Bess, whom he has raised as his daughter, was brought to him by Tull. She is Milly Erne's daughter. Tull had hoped that living among the rustlers would ensure her corruption but Oldrin' proves to be a true gentleman. He intends to return her to her father's people. Bess refers to herself as Oldrin's girl, but she never elaborates on her relationship with him. Venters imagines the worst and thinks she is his kept woman. He con-

fronts Oldrin' outside Snell's saloon in Cottonwoods and kills him. Oldrin's enigmatic dying words cause him worry and shame when back in Surprise Valley, Bess finally tells Venters that she was Oldrin's daughter. Out of spite, Jane Withersteen reveals to Bess that Venters killed Oldrin', but Jim Lassiter intervenes to explain the role Oldrin' had played in the abduction of Milly Erne's child. Oldrin' is one of several "honorable thieves" to be found in Grey's novels.

Oliver, Handy: In *The Border Legion*, the outlaw companion of the young Blicky. The two are members of the Border Legion. They report to Kells at Cabin Gulch that a big gold strike has been made at Alder Creek. His sympathies are more with Gulder than with Kells. He reports to the gang that Gulder saw Creede, the miner Jim Cleve claims to have robbed and murdered, after the event was supposed to have taken place. He also confirms to Jack Kells the truth of what Red Pearce reported about Joan, that she was meeting someone at night. After Gulden's appearance at the cabin in Alder Creek, the shooting of Red Pearce and the incident of the preacher, and the accusations against Cleve, Handy announces that the vigilantes who had been massing in the town are coming towards the cabin. Red Pearce, he reveals, was either a vigilante or an informer.

Olsen: (1) In *The Desert of Wheat*, one of Dorn's neighbors. Of Swedish origin but unlike the German Chris Dorn, Olsen is passionately pro–American. Kurt Dorn offers to pay him five hundred dollars to help Dorn harvest his wheat but Olsen doe not want to take any pay. Olsen is quite well informed about the doings of the I.W.W. The agents have set his dry wheatfields ablaze with phosphorous cakes. When his crop has been destroyed, he and his men and other neighbors come to help Kurt. Olsen is with Chris Dorn when he dies of a heart attack and he helps Kurt by organizing the funeral. When the I.W.W. sets fire to the grain elevators, he organizes men with guns to pursue the men who have organized the attack. Like Anderson, he feels that they must drive these men and the vagrants out of the area before more mischief is done. Like Kurt Dorn, Olsen sells his land to Anderson but continues to work the land for half-shares. This same deal is offered to Kurt and the other wheat farmers who could not pay their debts thanks to the activities of the I.W.W. agents.

(2) In *Thunder Mountain*, a settler on a ranch where the Salmon River made a wide, slow bend. The land is fertile, bordered by groves of cottonwoods and a log cabin sheltered in the lea of the hill. Lee Emerson falls in love with the spot. The rancher and his family put Jake and Lee up for the night. In their talk, Olsen admits he is anxious to sell. Lee offers to buy him out if he strikes it rich. Lee does return to Olsen and buy the ranch when he leaves Thunder Mountain with over a hundred pounds of gold.

Onate: In *Knights of the Range*, a Spanish explorer mentioned by Holly Ripple in her address to the five hundred diners at her fiesta. The address summarizes the history of the region and the Spanish contributions to the cattle industry.

O'Neill: In *The U. P. Trail*, a telegraph operator.

Orcutt, Hen: In *Twin Sombreros*, one of the three men Brazos Keene meets at the cabin when he arrives in Las Animas. He had helped Syvertseen rob Abe Neece. They handed the money over to Surface. He roped young Allen and pulled him off his horse, the fall killing him. People suspect Orcutt is sweet on Bess, but she denies this to Brazos. He is killed in the shootout with Brazos Keene.

Ormiston, Ash: In *Wilderness Trek*, the name that the bushranger (rustler) Ash Pell uses when he poses as a respectable cattleman and joins the Stanley Dann-Bingham Slyter trek to the Kimberleys. Ormiston has three drovers and about eight hundred head. He is new to Downsville and Slyter does not know him. Nevertheless, Slyter is not keen on his joining the trek. Stanley Dann, however, has allowed him to join the venture. Leslie Slyter also voices her dislike for the man who she says insulted her in their first meeting. Ormiston takes a dislike to the two Yankees and wants them fired. Red Krehl had stopped him from beating and kicking Friday, the aborigine. Dann and Slyter, however, side with Krehl in this matter. Ormiston is interested in the young ladies, Leslie Slyter and Beryl Dann. Beryl, in particular, succumbs to his charms. In the question of which route to take, Ormiston insists that the group let Eric Dann lead. He claims to have made the trek before and to know the route. His brother Stanley prefers to try a new route farther north. Ormiston influences Hathaway Woolcott to vote with him against Stanley. Red Krehl's suspicions of Ormiston continue to grow. Indeed, he overhears Ormiston, Bedford and Jack planning to rustle the herd at the Diamantina River. Red reaches the conclusion that Ormiston wants to partner up with Stanley Dann after the trek or to get control of a big herd of cattle and marry Beryl. He is working things out so that when he threatens to split from the drive, Dann will do anything to keep him. His drovers, however, want a showdown for their efforts or a speed-up of the break. Ormiston is merely after all the cattle he can get. He killed Woolcott when he bucked and wanted to return to Dann. He got Woolcott's herd on the pretext that Woolcott owed him a gambling debt. Having started off with eight hundred cattle, he now controls a herd of over three thousand. Red predicts he will acquire more cattle and at the Diamantina, split with the group and take Beryl with him, willing or not. Ormiston always makes camp apart from the Slyters and Stanley Dann. Red and Sterl comment that he doesn't seem to know much about driving cattle. He refuses to drive the herd as one unit, with the surviving cattle being divided among the cattlemen on a proportional basis when they reach their destination. His herd is branded, and he insists on trying to keep his animals from merging with the general herd. Henry Ward is trampled to death attempting to prevent the herds from merging. Ormiston tries to discredit Red and Sterl by spreading the rumor that they consort with the lubas (aboriginal women) in their camp after they leave Leslie and Beryl. The women, surprisingly, believe him. Ormiston eventually leaves, taking the thoroughbred horses, his cattle and part of the Dann herd. Beryl Dann has gone with him, as is later revealed, under the threat that Ormiston would kill her brother Eric. Red and Sterl organize the pursuit of the rustlers. Ormiston is capture and hanged in western-style justice.

Orozco: Mexican revolutionary mentioned in *Desert Gold* and *The Light of Western Skies*. In the latter novel, he is called the chief of the rebels.

Outcolt, Burt: In *The Lone Star Ranger*, one of Cal Bain's friends who tries to sober him up and talk him out of facing Buck Duane in a gunfight.

Outcolt, Sam: In *The Lone Star Ranger*, one of Cal Bain's friends who tries to sober him up and talk him out of facing Buck Duane in a gunfight, as his brother Burt also attempts to do.

Overland: In *The Border Legion*, the name Bill Hoadley uses in Alder Creek. He ships out all the gold from Alder Creek by stagecoach. He is Joan Randle's uncle and a friend of Harvey Roberts.

Owens, Corporal Bob: In *The Desert of Wheat*, Kurt Dorn's commanding officer in training and later on the battlefields of France. Kurt comments that after a day of fighting at the front, Corporal Owens has aged terribly. Corporal Owens reports on Kurt Dorn to Anderson, who has come to New York to look for him. He tells him that Kurt had been pretty much a loner during training in the States and that in France, he had not been close to his mates at first, until he had engaged in battle. Then, his leadership abilities revealed themselves. He was a natural leader, fearless, an inspiration to his mates.

Owens, Frank: In "From Missouri," the name used by the cowboys in their letters to Miss Jane Stacey, a schoolteacher from Missouri looking for work in the West. These happen to be the two first names of their employer, Frank Owens Springer. When she arrives looking for Mr. Owens, the surprised cowboys admit the hoax but assure her they do need a schoolteacher and their boss will be glad to have her. After the fight with Beady Jones, Springer confesses that he had guessed what his cowboys were up to and had written some of the letters, the love letters, himself.

Owens, Hanford: In *The Lone Star Ranger*, the county judge in Fairdale who presides in court the day Buck Duane arrests Bo Snecker. Hanford Owens is in Longstreth's pocket and refuses to prosecute the case.

Owens, Mrs.:   In *The Hash Knife Outfit*, reputed to be a gossip. Molly Dunn worries what stories she will spread after she spots Molly and Jim Traft talking in Babbitt's store. Rumor has already spread the story of their breakup.

P

Padre Augustine: In *Knights of the Range,* marries Skylark and Anne Doane, and returns to the Ripple ranch for the marriage of Renn Frayne and Holly Ripple.

Padre Juan: In *The Light of Western Stars,* figures in the tale told by Florence when the party is on a camping trip. Padre Juan has a vision of the Virgin Mary when tending his goats. The vision drops golden ashes on the ground and soon plants grow with golden flowers where the ash had fallen. The Virgin appears to him again the next morning telling him to follow the path which will lead him to the gold mine. With the gold, he is to build a church and help his people. He follows the path and finds himself among the Apache Indians. Here he settles down to preach the Christian faith and, given his persuasive and charming personality, he becomes a favorite in the tribe, causing the Apache chief to fear his influence. The chief decides to kill Padre Juan by burning him at the stake. The chief's daughter intercedes to save his life. One day she comes to Padre Juan wearing in her hair the gold flowers that had grown from the gold dust scattered by the Virgin in his vision. When he asks where she found them, she takes him to a mountain overlooking the valley, where gold in large chunks lies about the ground. Padre Juan, however, has fallen in love with the chief's daughter, and he lingers on, meeting her to make love in secret. He feels guilty having betrayed his mission and the Virgin but he cannot leave the young woman behind. When the chief learns of the secret love, he has his daughter burned alive. He spares the life of Padre Juan, knowing that he will suffer the rest of his life, so deep was his love for the daughter. Padre Juan asks the old Indian who had burned the chief's daughter to burn his body when he dies, and to scatter his ashes. They leave a golden trail to the site of the gold. Later, another young missionary follows in his tracks and finds his way to the gold mine. But when he tries to lead others to the mine, he loses his way. This is the legend of the lost mine of the padres.

Eventually, Danny Mains and Bonita find this lost mine about a half-mile from the spot where Florence had entertained the group with this story.

Padre Marcos: In *The Light of Western Stars,* the parish priest of El Cajón. Gene Stewart brings him into the train station to marry him to Madeline Stewart. He also marries Christine, Madeline's French maid, and Ambrose Mills when they elope. When Don Carlos attempts to seize Madeline and has holed up in her large ranch house with his bandits, Gene solicits the help of Padre Marcos to question the servants to find out where Don Carlos and his bandits have hidden themselves in the house. Padre Marcos is brought by Gene Stewart to the mountain retreat to marry Danny Mains and Bonita. Just after Danny has told Madeline about his hiding in the mountains, and observing the camping party below and the discovery of the mine, Padre Marcos comes to Madeline to tell her he must break a promise to Gene. He must do it out of gratitude for what Stewart, El Capitán, has done to help his people in Mexico. Madeline and Stewart are truly married, and have been since that night in the train station. He tells her she does not know what a treasure she has found in Gene Stewart. He suggests that perhaps she does not know her own heart and cautions her not to do anything rash before she reflects on what a good man Stewart is and what her true feelings for him are. When Padre Marcos leaves, Madeline realizes how cruel she has been to Gene and that she does love him.

Pahute: In *The Vanishing American,* works at Kaidab. When Marian Warner arrives, he informs her that Nophaie is with the ewes helping with the lambing. Pahute has a bad reputation, having killed both whites and reds. He is villainous looking, black-haired, round-faced, big-nosed, with a bold, hard look. He feels a sense of joy when Nophaie renounces the white man's ways. Out of admiration for Nophaie, he has not done a single bad thing since Nophaie's return.

Paint Brush: In *Knights of the Range,* the name Holly Ripple has given a pinto she finds among the horses the horse thieves have gathered in the corral at Dobe Cabin.

Pak-a-Guti: In *Stranger from the Tonto,* the leader of a group of three Piute Indians that Kent meets riding towards the Hole-in-the-Wall hideout. The Indian recognizes Spades and wants the animal. He proposes to swap with Kent, and when he refuses, accuses him of having stolen the horse. He tries to grab the horse's reins, and Kent shoots at him, partially knocking him off his mustang. His two companions shoot arrows at Kent, one sticking in his saddle, the second striking Kent in the shoulder. The three Indians ride off.

Panquitch: In *Wild Horse Mesa,* the great wild stallion that Chane Weymer wants to catch. There are other wild mustang hunters out to capture the animal as well. This mustang is called the "king of the wild stallions." It is the color of a lion, except for the black mane and tail. The mane seems to stand erect and fall almost to the sand. He has the points of a racehorse, with the weight and muscle gained from wild life on the desert. But his symmetry and grace, his remarkable beauty, are dwarfed by his spirit. His nostrils dilate and send forth a piercing blast. The stallion is wild, proud, fierce, a creature to stop the heart of a wild-horse hunter.

Panquitch knows the mesas and avoids capture disappearing into twisting canyons unknown to the hunters pursuing him. When he is finally captured by Chane Weymer, in the deep waters of a mountain river, he is almost drowned. Chane describes the animal as the noblest specimen of horseflesh he has ever seen in all his wanderings throughout the West. He also senses in the stallion a spirit incompatible with the rule of man. Chane senses the animal will never be mastered by men. He feels pity for the fallen monarch and on Sue Melberne's request, he consents to free the captured king. Panquitch, however, in his exhausted state, is captured by Manerube and McPherson. Chane convinces McPherson, a true horseman and admirer of the stately stallion, to free the animal. Panquitch remains free on the mesa, a symbol of the unconquered and unconquerable spirit of the West.

Papago: (1) An Indian tribe mentioned in several of Grey's novels about the Southwest.

(2) In *Desert Gold,* the herdsman that betrays Belding by opening the corral for horse thieves. He leads Rojas and his trackers on Mercedes' trail. He is shot by Yaqui, an Indian loyal to Gale and Belding.

Parson: In *Riders of the Purple Sage,* owns a store in Cottonwoods.

Pat: In *The U. P. Trail,* a worker in Reilly's crew who comes to admire the skill and strength of Neale, the engineer who wanted to learn the laborer's jobs.

Patter: In *Lost Pueblo,* one of the horses at Bennet's post. Janey wants to ride him but Ray tells her the horse is mean. She insists.

Patterson: In *Twin Sombreros,* owns the arrow brand. He has recently joined up with Surface, according to Blake.

Paul: In *Riders of the Purple Sage,* one of the young men who work with Jerd in Jane Withersteen's stables.

Paxton: In *The Vanishing American,* a trader at Mesa. Marian Warner meets him when she goes west to visit Nophaie. Paxton is an honest man and is accepted and respected by the Navajos. When Marian is persona non grata at the reservation, he gives her the job of traveling around the Navajo reservation buying blankets and baskets for his trading post. This gives her a legitimate reason to be on the restricted territory. He is the one who brings the news to the reservation that World War I has ended.

Paxton, Mrs.: In *The Vanishing American,* a comely young woman, wife of Paxton the trader at Mesa. She is not a curious woman, and Marian appreciates her discretion. She tells Marian about life on the reservation and points out that she and her husband are probably the only friends the Navajo have among the whites working on this part of the reservation.

Payne, Captain: In *Fighting Caravans,* leads the cavalry unit which has been assigned to escort Belmet's wagon train out of Kansas City (Westport).

Peabody, Parson: In *The Dude Ranger,* the parson in Snowflake who marries the two couples, Nebraskie and Daisy, and Ernest and Anne. It is his second day in Snowflake, and already he has performed two weddings.

Pearce, Red: In *The Border Legion,* first appears when he rides in with Gulden to the cabin hideout in Lost Cañon. Joan describes him as having a lean, fleshless face, a red mask pulled over a grinning skull. He is given to flattery, ingratiating himself with both Kells and Gulden. He tells of Jim Cleve coming into Beard's saloon looking for Jack Kells. Pearce tells Joan that the truth is known about her, that she is not Kells's wife and that she shot her supposed husband. Pearce comes between Gulden and Kells to stop a fight when Gulden confronts Kells about the murder of Bill Bailey. Gulden has learned that Bailey was shot at point blank range by Kells, and the pretext that Bailey had attacked his "wife" is not believable. Pearce tells Joan he had a sister, and he feels sorry about her predicament. He predicts that Kells will "get his own" in the mining camps eventually. Like Bate Wood, he understands Kells's need for attention. He helps Kells find a gambler to shoot and kill in the Last Nugget to get attention. There is more to Pearce than meets the eye. He tries to heighten the discord between Gulden and Kells when he tells Gulden that Jim Cleve has been commissioned by Kells to murder him, as he was commissioned to murder Creede. Pearce had been with the group when Kells assigned the task of robbing and murdering Creede to Jim. Later, Jesse Smith suggests that as his next job, he should kill Gulden. Having revealed this fact to Gulden leads other gang members to suspect his loyalty. Pearce also has observed someone at the rear cabin window talking to Joan. He suspects it is Jim Cleve. He makes an issue of bringing up the question of his whereabouts in front of the group. He apologizes profusely, saying he is not trying to create a rift between Kells and Cleve, but Joan suspects Pearce is a dangerous man. Pearce tells Kells that Joan has been double-crossing him, that he has seen a man climbing through her window at night. Kells pulls a gun and shoots Pearce, killing him. Later, Handy Oliver reveals that Pearce was a vigilante. It is not clear whether he turned informant there at Alder Creek, when the miners' anger at the spate of robberies forced them to take drastic action, or whether he was a plant with the group, informing on them to the law for some time. Handy Oliver theorizes that Pearce betrayed Texas, Frenchy, Singleton and Dartt in order to prove the accuracy of his information, hoping that one of them would betray the leaders of the Border Legion, thus sparing him the need to reveal himself. The reader learns more about Pearce's role in the unfolding of events after his death.

Peckins, Sam: In *Arizona Ames,* a cowboy who shares the bunkhouse with Blab McKinney. Blab wants him to vacate his bunk so that his partner, Arizona Ames, can move in. Sam tells him to go where it's hot.

Pecos: In *The Hash Knife Outfit,* a long-limbed, sandy-mustached Texan, a senior member of the Hash Knife Outfit, having been one of the original members of the gang. He is a silent, mysterious Texan, and has always fascinated Jed Stone. Pecos is a deadly foe, and to a friend, true as steel. He care little for money or drink, not at all for cards, and he shuns women. He and Jed Stone, the leader and founder, are close. Pecos confesses that he would like to see Croak Malloy dead, but he knows he could never beat him on the draw. When Jed Stone decides to quit the Hash Knife and let Malloy take over, Pecos agrees to wait for him at the headwaters of the Little Colorado River.

Pedlar: In *The Shepherd of Guadaloupe,* one of the men in the car with the unnamed speaker who meets Cliff Forrest as he is herding sheep. The unnamed speaker brings Cliff up to date on what happened to Jim Mason, Malpass, and Virginia. Mason survived his gunshot wounds, Malpass is trying to buy Lopez's herd and Virginia was seen taking the train east. When the unnamed speaker asks if there is anything they can do for Cliff, he asks for cigarettes for Julio. Pedlar and Bill, the other passenger, each contribute a pack.

Pedro: (1) In *The Deer Stalker,* one of the men in the Dyott-Settlemire group that spends the night in the cabin where Patricia Clay and Sue Warren are hiding in the loft. He tells Dyott and Settlemire that Ranger Eburne's cabin is about three miles from Long Park.

(2) In *The Dude Ranger,* the stable boy in charge of the horses and tack at Red Rock Ranch.

(3) In *The Hash Knife Outfit,* old Jim Traft's driver. He is killed by Croak Malloy when he is driving Jim Traft and the two girls, Molly Dunn, his nephew Jim's fiancée, and Glory, Jim's sister, to the Yellow Jacket ranch. Croak Malloy holds them up and Jim Traft orders Pedro to drive on, upon which Malloy shoots him.

(4) In *The Lost Wagon Train,* a Mexican vaquero who works on Latch's ranch. He accompanies Latch to Spider Web Canyon to retrieve part of Tullt's wagon to prove Estie's relationship to Cynthia Bowden and thereby claim her inheritance. Pedro is killed by Leighton and Kennedy.

(5) In *The Man of the Forest,* Milt Dale's only remaining hound. He is a dog of unusually large proportions, black and tan in color, with long drooping ears. His head is noble; his eyes shine dark and sad. He seems neither friendly nor unfriendly. The hound is not used to people. Dale had gotten the hound as a pup from a Mexican sheep-herder who claimed he was part California bloodhound. He grew up and became attached to Dale. In his younger days, he did not get along well with Dale's other pets and Dale gave him back to a rancher in the valley. Pedro was back in Dale's senaca the next day. From that day, Milt begins to care more for the hound but he does not want to keep him for various reasons, specifically because Pedro is too fine a dog to be left alone half

the time to fend for himself. When Milt is to join the Beemans on a wild horse hunt, he leaves the dog with a friend. When he gets home months later, there is Pedro, gaunt and worn, waiting for him. The hound had broken a chain and scaled a ten-foot fence to escape. He had trailed Dale to the Beeman camp where he was recognized and put in a wooden cage to keep until Dale returned. He broke out of the box and continued tracking Dale the hundreds of miles following the wild horses. A group of Mexican herders saw Pedro arrive at their camp the day after Milt had moved on. With this show of loyalty, Milt decides to keep Pedro.

(6) In *Raiders of Spanish Peaks,* a Mexican boy working for the Lindsays caring for the horses in the stables. He is in on Harriet's secret, practicing riding in the corral behind the barn.

(7) In "The Ranger," Pedro is the stable boy at the Glover ranch who had saddled a horse for Roseta the morning of her disappearance. He shows Ranger Medill the tracks of her horse to follow.

(8) In *Stairs of Sand,* a young Mexican who works for Guerd Larey at the trading post in Lost Lake.

(9) In *Twin Sombreros,* runs the corral in Las Animas where Brazos leaves his horse. Pedro gives him a vital piece of information in his investigation into the murder of Allen Neece. Late at night when Neece came to pick up his horse, he was accompanied by a second rider who appeared to be a young boy. He also reports to Brazos when he returns from Colgan's place in the mountains that there has been a lot of shooting in town of late.

(10) In *Western Union,* the name Ruby uses when disguised as a Mexican worker with Cameron, Darnell, Shaw and Lowden's wagon.

Peeples, Clink: In *Sunset Pass,* one of the foremen working on Nesbitt's ranch. He has come with him from Wyoming. His trademark is his red scarf. Trueman had seen him looking around the slaughterhouse and corrals at Preston's ranch. He is rumored to be involved with Amy Wund. Exceptionally tall, sandy-haired, with sharp, hawk eyes, he has the reputation of being quite a dandy and ladies' man. He packs a gun and gets his nickname from his habit of clinking coins together at the bar. Before the masquerade party, he is looking for Trueman Rock to size him up. When they meet, Rock gives him a lesson in etiquette, chastising him for his rude behavior to Amy Wund. Peeples is impressed by Trueman, and as a result of their talk, he apologizes to Amy for his behavior. He has heard good things about Rock from cowboys on the range and suggests that Preston has taken him on to take advantage of his reputation as a clear, square rider to cover up Preston's rustling. When things become complicated, he advises Trueman to take Thiry and run away. Peeples takes Trueman to Winter's place in Wagontongue after the gunfight with Ash Preston.

Peffer, Bill: In *Western Union,* a cattle thief from Texas. Cameron and his crew meet him as they are bringing a wagon of telegraph poles. Peffer tells them the poles were cut from his homestead timber. He demands five hundred dollars for them. Vance Shaw recognizes him from his days in the Texas Rangers. He calls him a low-down hombre he put in jail in Brownsville for stealing cattle. Peffer broke out of jail, and killed a sheriff. When his bluff has been called, Peffer makes as though he and his friend are leaving and then he goes for his gun. Vance Shaw shoots the both of them.

Peg:　In *Wildfire,* one of Creech's prize horses. Joel Creech is riding Peg the day he races with Lucy Bostril who is riding Buckles. Peg and Buckles are pretty equally matched, Peg losing the race because Joel is heavier than Lucy. Peg is entered in the horse race but is trapped with Blue Roan in the box canyon without water or grass. Like Blue Roan, she has to be put down before Creech and the Piutes can find sufficient grass and water.

Pell:　In *Shadow on the Trail,* a Texas Ranger who recruits Randall Blue as an informer against Simm Bell. Holden has seen him talking to Pell, and Smith saw him at the telegraph office. When the Bell outfit tries to rob the bank in Mercer, the rangers are waiting for them. Pell is killed by Simm Bell in the shooting when they pursue Bell and Holden out of town.

Pell, Ash:　In *Wilderness Trek,* the real name of Ash Ormiston. Pell is a famous bushranger (rustler) in Queensland. Eric Dann hears Jack and Bedford use this name when addressing Ormiston. See **Ormiston, Ash.**

Pelter:　In *Valley of Wild Horses,* one of two horses Pan Handle's father buys after his first horse, Curly, dies. He is a pinto, snappy and pretty, with a wicked eye. Pan Handle thought he would like Pelter but discovers that he cannot ride the horse. Pelter bucks Pan off every time.

Pen:　In *Shadow on the Trail,* Jacqueline Pencarrow's horse. He is black, fast, and strong. Jacqueline has issued orders she does not want the cowboys riding her horse. She is angry with Tex Brandon because it has been reported to her that someone used her horse. Tex Brandon acknowledges that he had done so because the other horses were exhausted. Jacqueline's brother, Hal, explains how Brandon on Pen prevented his being kidnapped by rustlers. On hearing this, she gives the horse to Tex.

Pencarrow:　In *Shadow on the Trail,* the father of Hal, Rosa and Jacqueline. He had a brother who was a gunman and killed by a Texas Ranger. His daughter Jacqueline mentions an uncle who was a ranger, either another brother of her father's or her mother's brother. Pencarrow and his family first appear when Mahaffey and his rangers come to search for Wade Holden, whom they are pursuing after the attempted ambush in Mercer. They are camped for the night. Pencarrow is not too pleased to have them search his caravan, but tolerates it. He invites the rangers to stay for supper. He and his family are on their way to New Mexico. Pencarrow next appears

when Tex Brandon is looking for a job. Lawsford says that Pencarrow is a Texan and the salt of the earth. He dropped in on the range four or five years ago. He had plenty of money, bought Band Drake's ranch, a wonderful range with the finest view in Arizona. He built a ranch house not matched anywhere before he learned the ropes on Cedar Range. He bought a large herd and several hundred fine horses. Although he had the grass and the water, he could not combat the rustlers and dishonest ranchers. He has heard from Lawsford that Pencarrow cannot afford to pay any riders, but Brandon thinks this will be an opportunity for him to repay his debt to Jacqueline for saving his life. Pencarrow accepts a loan of seven thousand dollars from Brandon, whom he names his foreman and manager. He follows his advice on buying stock, hiring cowboys. It becomes clear that the destruction of the rustler outfits is the only way that honest ranchers will be able to survive. Pencarrow gives his foreman a free hand to do what is necessary. Eventually, Brandon clears the area of gunmen and rustlers, buys Aulsbrook out and becomes a rancher himself. Pencarrow, like his daughter, knows who Brandon really is. When Ranger Mahaffey comes looking for Wade Holden, they speak of his work in glowing terms, to the point that Mahaffey, who vowed to "ride the man down," decides not to make an arrest and leave gunman Holden to his new anonymity.

Pencarrow, Glenn:　In *Shadow on the Trail,* Jacqueline's uncle who was a gunman. He was killed by Texas Rangers. Since then, Mrs. Pencarrow, his sister-in-law, has been opposed to having guns in the house.

Pencarrow, Hal:　In *Shadow on the Trail,* the son of Pencarrow, Rona's twin. The boy is timid, being overprotected by his mother, who has hated guns since her brother-in-law, Glenn Pencarrow, was killed in a gunfight. Hal takes to Tex Brandon immediately. He is the big brother who can teach him to use a gun, to ride, to be a cowboy. He is assigned tasks like the rest of the men. He watches from a hilltop with binoculars for riders who do not belong on the range. At one point, he is shot at in an abduction attempt, a fact which is kept from his easily frightened mother. Hal puts in a good word for Tex with his sister when she complains that someone has been riding her horse without her permission. Tex Brandon makes a man out of Hal, much as Laramie Nelson makes a man out of Neale Lindsay in *Raiders of Spanish Peaks.*

Pencarrow, Jacqueline:　In *Shadow on the Trail,* Pencarrow's oldest daughter. She first appears when she hides Wade Holden from the pursuing rangers. She looks after his bullet wound, patches him up as best she can, watches during the night and sends him on his way in the morning with advice about getting away unseen. When he hears of Pencarrow again, he wonders if she will remember him. There are times when he suspects that she does recognize him, but she never brings the matter up. Jacqueline, like Harriet Lindsay in *Raiders of Spanish Peaks*, is her father's business manager. She does not share her mother's fear of guns, Pencarrow commenting to Tex Brandon, who has shot Urba and Bill, that if he hadn't done it, Jacqueline would have. The relationship between Jacqueline and Tex is similar to that of Laramie Nelson and Harriet Lindsay. Jacqueline feels she has a responsibility to her father and she suppresses her affection for Tex. He, in turn, has little experience of women, as he tells her when they first meet, and he feels that involvement with her would distract him from the work he must do. She does him little favors to show her affection, inviting him to eat with the family, baking pies to leave in his cabin, giving him her horse, Pen. She accepts his criticism when he complains that the Rona-Hogue romance would distress her parents. He tells her that such preoccupation with "bloodline" should have been left behind in the South. Eventually, she turns to him when she fears things have gone too far between the two. Tex again teaches her to trust people. Their spying on Rona and Hogue's meeting restores her faith in her sister's integrity and her confidence in Tex's common sense. She also learns from what Hogue said that Tex is madly in love with her. When things have been resolved with the rustlers, Jacqueline proposes marriage to him. They wed and take up ranching on the Aulsbrook place that Tex has bought. They have a child, a few months old, when Mahaffey shows up looking for Wade Holden. Unknown to Holden, Jacqueline and her father have spoken glowingly of all the good that he has done for them and for the ranches around Cedar Ridge. When Mahaffey decides not to arrest him, Jacqueline says this is evidence that the law has forgiven him. They are free to live their lives in peace without fear of pursuit.

Pencarrow, Mrs.: In *Shadow on the Trail*, plays a minimal role in the story. Her influence is seen mostly in her husband's reluctance to take action, fearing to be killed, leaving the family destitute. Her overprotectiveness has meant that Hal has not learned the skills that a young man normally learns from his father — how to ride, how to shoot, how to herd cattle. To protect her, the family keeps many things from her.

Pencarrow, Rona (Rosemary): In *Shadow on the Trail*, the second daughter of Pencarrow, and Hal's twin sister. When the story begins, she is fourteen years old. She is strikingly good-looking. She takes to Wade Holden (Tex Brandon) the minute he arrives and falls in love at first sight with Hogue Kinsey. The two of them meet in secret at night. Eventually, Jacqueline becomes aware of their meetings and becomes worried. She goes to Tex Brandon to express her fears that Hogue Kinsey will get Rona pregnant and disgrace the whole family. Tex has greater faith in Hogue's decency than Jacqueline does. They hide in the trees and observe Hogue and Rona's meeting. Rona wants to run off, to elope and

get married. Hogue refuses to do that, as it would not be fair to her family. After the meeting, Jacqueline understands that Tex Brandon had a better sense of Hogue's and Rona's integrity than she did. Rona and Hogue are married a year after Tex and Jacqueline are, with Pencarrow's blessing. Hogue Kinsey has become the new foreman of the ranch.

Peon: In *The Heritage of the Desert,* a mute Indian. He was either born without a tongue or it was cut out, according to August Naab. He has been Mescal's constant companion since he was given to her as her personal slave by Eschtah, her Navajo grandfather. Jack Hare comments on his leanness, his straggling black hair, the bird-of-prey cast of his features and the wildness in his mien. Like Piute, Peon helps with the sheep up on the high pasture and with the skinning of the coyote carcasses. He lives in a cave, while Mescal has a tent to herself near the cave entrance. Peon goes with Mescal into the desert. Of him, Dave Naab comments when they have unsuccessfully tried to find their trail: "The man doesn't live who can trail the peon." Eschtah adds that the "slave without a tongue" is a wolf who can scent the trails and the water holes. Among the Navajo, there is no one who can follow his trail. The grandfather has no fear that Mescal will survive, because the peon has been schooled by the desert and knows its ways like no other. The peon finds the oasis at Thunder River and keeps the two of them alive by hunting for a year. When he dies, Mescal buries him. Her anguished cry for help is what Hare hears in his sleep, causing him to set out in her pursuit.

Perez, Don Sancho: In *Yaqui*, the father of Lieutenant Perez. He is the owner of a henequen (hemp) plantation, some fifty thousand acres in size. He has arranged the wedding between Senorita Dolores Mendoza and his son.

Perez, Lieutenant: In *Yaqui*, the handsome son of Don Sancho Perez. He is engaged to Senorita Dolores Mendoza, the unquestioned belle of Merida. He is a particularly cruel young man, taking great pleasure in mistreating the Yaqui slaves brought in to work on the hemp plantations. His father owns one of the largest in the Yucatan. Perez has planned a particular surprise for his wedding, a gift of pearls wrapped in a bale of hemp. He instructs Yaqui in the preparation of the present, but he arrives at the wedding wrapped in the bale himself.

Perkens, Sim: In *The Arizona Clan*, Tommy tells Dodge Mercer that Sim Perkens has looked his last on white mule. Mercer doesn't understand what white mule is, but Tommy explains that he was killed in a shootout over a card game in Ryan's saloon.

Perkins, Hiram: In *Wyoming*, when Andrew Bonning picks up Martha Dixon along the highway, after rescuing her from three hoboes, he tells her he is from Missouri and she asks him sarcastically if his name is Hiram Perkins.

Perry, Mrs.: In *The Fugitive Trail*, heard horses tearing by her house. When she looked out, she declares she is absolutely sure she recognized Bruce Lockheart. Her eyewitness testimony convinces many that Bruce indeed was one of the robbers who attacked the bank in Denison.

Pete: (1) In *Captives of the Desert*, a young Indian boy who works with John Curry and High-Lo on the reservation. John gives him Mary Newton's letter to deliver to Wilbur. He follows him for several days, Newton believing that he is pursuing him with a score to settle. He witnesses Magdaline's killing Newton when he tries to prevent her from leaving the trading post.

(2) In "The Flight of Fargo Jones," the member of Sheriff Smith's posse who spotted Fargo Jones with a branding iron at the campfire where the maverick calves had been branded. He identifies him to the sheriff and Fargo is arrested.

Peters, Wally: In "The Camp Robber," helps the foreman Neff count the payroll and watches him put the money in his drawer. The two of them had left the cabin together.

Piah: In *The Mysterious Rider*, a Ute chief in the Middle Park area. He was friendly towards whites and became friends with Old Bill Belllounds. He allows Belllounds to settle in the area and begin ranching. In 1868 when prospectors and miners and cattlemen come into the region, he agrees the Utes will relinquish the area to whites.

Pickens: (1) In *Fighting Caravans,* the leader of a group of four thieves who try to rob the train. According to frontier justice, Pickens and his men are summarily hanged. Since Clint and Jack were the first to spot them, Clint gets first choice of the outlaws' outfit. Clint selects Pickens's horse and saddle. Clint names the horse Maybell after May Bell, his girlfriend.

(2) In *The Horse Thief*, from Salmon, arrives at the Rogers's homestead with Sheriff Bayne to arrest Dale Brittenham as a horse thief. He is an enthusiastic supporter of Bayne's proposal to hang Dale on the spot. He is shot and killed by the escaping horse thieves who ride past the Rogers's cabin.

(3) In *The Lone Star Ranger*, one of the two rangers on guard at MacNelly's camp.

Pickens, Hall: In *Wyoming,* a homesteader about twenty miles east of Bligh's ranch in Spring Canyon. He is caught by Fenner and Andy rustling cattle. They start to hang him to coax him into giving information about other rustlers. When it is clear he is acting out of desperation and poverty and not as part of an organized group, they let him go with a severe warning. They feel sorry for him. He has a boot on one foot and a shoe on the other, both full of holes.

Pickins: In *Sunset Pass*, the man Trueman Rock shot in a gunfight. This killing caused his sudden departure for Texas six years earlier. John Dabb says it was an even draw, and that is the general opinion of the affair, but Sheriff Cass Seward seemed ill-dis-

posed toward Rock, so he left Wagontongue. Gage Preston and Thiry both tell him that in killing Pickins, he had done them a favor as Pickins was an enemy of the family.

Pierce, Jen: In *The Horse Thief*, a friend of Dale Brittenham's with whom Dale had hunted wild horses. Jen Pierce's friend, Al Cook, is a member of Stafford's posse and he tells Dale that Brittenham's men have stationed themselves at the head of the pass to watch for fleeing rustlers.

Pierce, Red: In *Western Union*, owns a saloon and gambling establishment in Gothenburg where he fleeces the workers on the telegraph line. His plan is to travel along with the telegraph line, living off the construction workers until he gets to Wyoming. He goes by slow stages, and brings along a herd of cattle with him to sell out for big money when he reaches the Sweetwater. He plans to rustle cattle along the way, from the Sunderlands in particular. He treats the girls who work for him like slaves. He purports to be in love with Ruby. Vance Shaw and Cameron manage to free her and keep her with their wagon, disguised as a young Mexican called Pedro. Pierce abducts her from their wagon during the Indian raid at Julesburg. In South Pass, he keeps her at the Atlantic, then moves her to his new saloon and gambling joint, the Gold Nuggett. She is locked in a room in the attic with a girl named Jo. Pierce's real name is Bill Howard, a known crook. His current plans are to rob the bank and fleece the miners. He has sabotaged the telegraph line to prevent news of the bank heist from getting out. Howard (Pierce) is killed by Shaw in the fight to free Ruby.

Pike: In *The Border Legion*, one of the outlaws in Gulden's gang who rob the Alder Creek stage. He shares in the gold divided up at the Cabin Gulch hideout. He proceeds to lose the money in the gambling session which follows.

Pike, Jason: In *The Horse Thief*, arrives at Rogers's homestead with Sheriff Bayne and several other men. He does not approve of Bayne's decision to hang Dale Brittenham on the spot. When the fleeing horse thieves ride past and shoot at the men, Bayne and Pickens are killed. Pike survives and releases Brittenham.

Pilchuck, Jude: In *The Thundering Herd*, Clark Hudnall's partner in the hiding operation. Tom Doan meets him at Sprague's outpost. It happens that Pilchuck had known Tom's father, Bill Doan, during the Civil War. They had ridden for Quantrill. He tells Tom he resembles his father. Pilchuck sizes the young man up and concludes he can do the work of a hider. He proceeds to help Tom select the gear he will need: knives, gun, ammunition, saddle and horse. At the killing fields, he explains how best to shoot a buffalo, where to position oneself and how to skin the beasts. Pilchuck himself hunts from horseback, and while Tom has gone to Sprague's post with a load of hides, he completes the training of Tom's steed, Dusty. Pilchuck sets a record of two hundred and eighty-six kills in a day. Pilchuck warns Hudnall not to take unnecessary risks, but Hudnall ignores his advice. In the campaign against the Comanche which follows the attacks on the buffalo hunter camps, Pilchuck is a natural leader, trapping a Comanche village in a canyon. Later, Pilchuck and Tom continue the hiding and together survive a buffalo stampede by climbing to the top of a rocky hill. Pilchuck is another Wetzel figure, an experienced man of the frontier who takes the inexperienced Tom Doan under his wing.

Pildarlick: In *Valley of Wild Horses*, one of two horses Bill Smith buys to replace Pan Handle's first horse, Curly. Pildarlick is not showy, but is small, strong, easy-gaited and gentle. He soon fills the gap in Pan Handle's heart.

Pine Tree Outfit: In *Nevada*, the name of an outlaw gang. No one is sure who is a member of the outfit, although most ranchers suspect that the Hatt family is at the core of the operation. Others believe that remnants of the Billy the Kid gang from the Lincoln County war in New Mexico may have made their way into the area, or that remnants of the Hash Knife Outfit may still be operating with them. The gang is responsible for rustling to the point that some ranchers are facing ruin. Texas Jack (Jim Lacy/Nevada) agrees with Judge Franklidge and Tom Day to work undercover in the group to flush out the leaders.

Pinky: In *The Call of the Canyon*, a young pig that Carley makes into a pet.

Pinto: In *Majesty's Rancho*, one of Madge Stewart's string of horses.

Pipe: Appears in *Betty Zane* and *The Spirit of the Border*. His name derives from the shape of his face, as his chin resembles the bowl of a pipe. Pipe is a member of the Wolf tribe of the Delaware and a sworn enemy of all white men. In *Betty Zane*, he is involved in the plot to attack Ft. Henry and presses for the execution of Isaac Zane. In *The Spirit of the Border*, he is present when Wetzel is brought into the Delaware village. He attends the religious festival for Jim's debut sermon at the Village of Peace. When the fate of the brothers Joe and Jim Downs is being debated in council, Pipe recommends they be burned at the stake. He is often reported to be consulting with Simon and Jim Girty and readily believes lies they spread about Washington's defeat and the return of the British. He votes in the tribal council for the destruction of the village. He strenuously objects to the return of any converted Indians to their home villages fearing they will contaminate others with their beliefs. He appears at the village to participate in the massacre. Zane Grey uses Pipe as an example of the Indian chiefs who refuse to accept change, presumably loyal to their Indian heritage but ultimately condemning their tribe to extinction. Pipe can also be classified as an ignoble savage ac-

cording to Cooper's classification of Indians. He allows himself to be influenced by the worst elements of white civilization.

Pitch: (1) In *Code of the West*, Cal Thurman's favorite black horse. Pitch was a gift from his brother, Enoch, and he is the best horse ever broke in the Tonto. Cal loves the horse like a brother. He bets Pitch against Tim Matthew's Baldy that he will beat him in a fight before the year is out. Tim teases Cal and beats up on him mercilessly. He comments that he doesn't want to take Cal's favorite horse, so sure he is of winning again.

(2) In *The Lost Wagon Train*, a young cowboy riding for Lanthorpe, a relative of his. Pitch picks a fight with Slim Blue, who kills him.

Piute: (1) In *The Heritage of the Desert*, works as a cowhand and shepherd on August Naab's ranch. He is an outcast from the Piute tribe. Mescal found him on the Coconina Trail five years earlier and he has been with August Naab ever since. His knowledge of the desert and the region is unmatched. Piute helps Jack and Mescal with the sheep. He skins and cures the hides of the coyotes that Jack shoots attacking the herd. "Damn" is his term of approval for things. When Jack has had a particularly good day hunting coyotes, a cry of "damn" from Piute signals approval. At night, when Jack tells tales about life in the East, of trains that run on elevated tracks, of buildings that touch the sky, Piute cannot believe them — "Heap damn lie," he says. Piute is a excellent tracker. He leads the group that sets out in pursuit of Mescal when she runs off with Peon and Noddle into the desert. If he cannot track her, no one can.

Piute is one of several strays that August Naab has taken under his wing and given a home. Naab's ranch is truly a meeting place of the races in the area. Piute expresses his appreciation with undying loyalty.

(2) In *Stranger from the Tonto*, a Piute shepherd dog, half-dog, half-wolf. Piute attaches himself to Kent Wingfield and follows him. The homeless dog that has never heard a white man's voice wanders into Kent's camp one night at supper time. Kent throws him some scraps of rabbit, and the following morning when he sets off, the dog is still around and follows him. Kent asks a young Navajo brave if the dog belongs to his tribe, but he says scornfully that it is a Piute dog. Kent notes that the dog's eyes are a strange shade of grayish-yellow. Piute does not understand affection. He never leaps or cavorts, he never wags his tail or hangs about Kent with glad eyes. The closest he ever gets to such antics is when he sniffs Kent's hand with his cold nose. At Bonesteel's hideout, Piute makes friends with old Jeff's dog, Rover. Piute leaves the Hole-in-the-Wall hideout with Kent and Lucy.

Piutes: In *Wildfire*, referred to as one of the neighboring tribes near Bostril's Ford. They are great horsemen and usually a group of chiefs and braves attend the annual horse race. Some Piutes (Utes) help Creech get his horses out of the box canyon, but before they can find water and grass, the animals have injured their legs and have to be shot.

Playford, Sam: In *Arizona Ames,* a new arrival in the Tonto Basin, homesteading near Doubtful. He is sweet on Nesta Ames, the twin sister of his best friend, Rich Ames. He and Rich go hunting together. He is the first beau of Nesta's to meet with the family's approval. The two are engaged. Sam is several years Rich's senior, making him a man in his early twenties. He is heavier than Rich, with a winning smile on his homely face. He has an enormous nose. Sam is the laughingstock of Shelby because Nesta, his fiancée, is carrying on with Lee Tate. He is known as a "poor, faithful jackass" whose wife-to-be is fooling around on him. Sam, however, is true as steel and pays little attention to the gossip, believing the best about Nesta. He does ask Rich to break up her involvement with Tate or he promises he will do it himself. He confides his troubles to Cappy Tanner, saying that he loves Nesta no matter what. He would break off the engagement if she wanted to, but she has never suggested that. He also knows that the Tates look down on the Ameses and would never allow Lee to marry Nesta. In Shelby for Lil Snell's wedding, he keeps Rich from drinking and starting a fight. He is privileged to be the man Nesta dances with at the party. Together with Rich and Cappy, he rescues Nesta when she attempts to drown herself. He forgives her for her involvement with Tate, telling her he will marry her even though she is carrying Lee Tate's child. They are married and go to his homestead in Doubtful. Rich sends them money to help them out at first. Sam becomes a prosperous rancher.

Plume: In *Wildfire,* one of John Bostril's prize horses, so named for the way her mane sweeps in the wind.

Plummer, Henry: Mentioned in *The Heritage of the Desert* as an example of the criminal who hides under a reputation of respectability. He was a sheriff in Idaho, a man high in the estimation of his townspeople, but he was really the leader of a desperate band of criminals. The deaths of over a hundred men are attributed to him. August Naab mentions him as an example of the type of man Holderness is. A Henry Plummer from Alden Gulch is also mentioned in *Thunder Mountain,* probably the same man. Rand Leavitt is compared to this Plummer. Lee Emerson says Leavitt, the town mayor, judge, and head of a vigilance group and a band of thieves who attack and rob miners, is nearly as successful as Henry Plummer, an officer of the law who leads a large outlaw outfit. In *Robbers' Roost,* Henry Hays, a slick, smooth-talking, handsome outlaw is said to have achieved a mask of respectability almost as good as that of Plummer. He has great admiration for the man. Plummer, says Hays, was an educated man of good family from the East. The gold fever caught him and he was not the kind of man to exert

himself digging. He operated on the placer mines and was an officer of the law while head of the biggest robber gang on the frontier. From Bannock to Lewiston he kept the miners, the stages, the Wells Fargo in terror for years. Hays boasts that, as a young man, he was a member of the gang and proud of the experience. In *The Horse Thief,* Big Bill Mason, a prominent rancher and loud protester against horse thieves, is himself head of the largest rustling outfit in Idaho and Montana. His successful guise of respectability is compared to that of Henry Plummer.

Plummer, Mrs.:   In *The Mysterious Rider,* fixed up Wilson Moore's foot and leg after he was injured in an accident when his horse rolled over on him. She does as good a job as any doctor, saving both his foot and his leg. She is a neighbor to the Andrewses.

Poggin (Poggy):   In *The Lone Star Ranger,* one of Longstreth's (Cheseldine's) gunmen. He has the reputation of being highly skilled with the gun. He and Knell feel great antagonism toward each other. When Knell reveals that the new man introduced to the group by Jim Fletcher is none other than Buck Duane, he is stunned. When Knell draws on Buck Duane, Poggin stands by and does nothing to help. Poggin is killed in the shootout at the Rancher's Bank in Val Verde where he and Cheseldine's outfit attempt to steal a gold shipment. Poggin is killed by Buck Duane in the shootout.

Pollard, Lanky: In *The Dude Ranger,* one of the cowboys working on Red Rock Ranch. He is one of the Dude Hyslip crowd, devoted to making life miserable for the tenderfoot, Ernest Selby. He is surprised to be kept on when the new owner, the tenderfoot Selby, takes over.

Polly: In *The Dude Ranger,* a friend of Anne Hepford's whom she is with at the start of the story when she goes to the bank in Springer to withdraw money for her father. Polly has invited her to stay a while longer but Anne feels uncomfortable carrying such a large sum of money.

Potter, Hep: In *The Lost Wagon Train,* works at Latch's Field. He is a grafter of trees and a farmer. He has had a lot of fruit trees freighted in and has created a fine orchard for Latch.

Powell: In *Fighting Caravans,* a Texan in charge of an emigrant train going to Texas. There are fifty-six in the caravan, thirty-four men and fourteen women and eight children. The caravan has been followed by Indians for several days and when they spot Couch's caravan, they ask to join them for protection.

Pratt, Captain: In the attack on Ft. Henry in *Betty Zane,* the leader of the Queen's Rangers. He asks for the surrender of the fort and after he is shot in the thigh, he retreats beyond rifle range. He gives the signal to retreat from the fort.

Preacher: In *The Border Legion,* the term used for the clergyman who has set up a mission in Alder Creek. No last name is provided for the man. Jim

Cleve has befriended him and asks the preacher to marry him to Joan Randle in secret. Later, Kells sends for the preacher also to marry Joan, but the clergyman recognizes Joan and refuses to perform the ceremony. At first, he says it is a desecration to perform a marriage ceremony where a man has just been murdered. Later, when Joan has removed the Dandy Dale mask, the preacher recognizes her as the woman he had married several nights before. He tells Kells that he married Joan Radley of Hoadley, Idaho, to a young miner.

Prentiss, Curly: In *The Drift Fence,* has just left the Blodgett ranch to work on the Diamond. Miss Blodgett tells Jim Traft that Curly is the best of the cowboys but he has a weakness for drinking. When drunk, he is given to talking too much. Jim Traft makes a friend of Curly when he speaks to Sheriff Bray in Flag. Bray has a particular dislike for Traft's cowboys and is taking him in for drunkenness, to set an example. Curly feels grateful to the foreman, who gives him time to visit his girlfriend, Nancy, before returning to the drift fence. He doesn't want Jim to meet her because he has lost girlfriends in the past by introducing them to his cowboy buddies. Despite the goodwill Jim has shown Curly, cowboy solidarity prevents him from breaking ranks in opposition to the drift fence project. He provokes a fight with Jim Traft and is soundly beaten. Some time later during a griping session, he is accused of having betrayed the other cowboys by siding with the tenderfoot foreman. He points out that he owes Jim Traft special thanks for keeping him out of jail, but that all the cowboys can be grateful to him for favors he has done. He lays the blame for their discontent squarely on Hack Jocelyn. On two occasions, Curly's skill as a tracker saves the day for Jim Traft. He and Bud are Jim's two closest friends among the crew.

In *The Hash Knife Outfit,* Curly Prentiss works for young Jim Traft on the Diamond Ranch and later on the Yellow Jacket. He belongs to a fine old southern family that was rich before the war. He came west after taking offense at something or another. Ring Locke says of him he would be the best of the cowboys if he didn't drink. He is the first to spot the connection between Bambridge (the rancher) and the Hash Knife Outfit, having spotted Madden coming out of Bambridge's one night. He gets into trouble with young Jim when he is reported to have made comments about Glory's legs, and Jim and the other cowboys feign great annoyance. Curly Prentiss is a master at cards, and in the high stakes card game at Snell's on Christmas Day, he exposes Darnell as a cheat. Curly is the first cowboy to figure out Jed Stone's trick to teach Gloriana some western manners, a situation which suits him, as he proposes marriage to the reformed woman and she accepts. They set up ranching near the Yellow Jacket, Jim Traft's ranch.

Presbrey: In *The Rainbow Trail (a.k.a. The Desert Crucible),* the trader who has an outpost at Red Lake and another at Willow Springs. John Shefford meets him when he arrives at Red Lake. Presbrey shares Shefford's dislike of missionaries, and his sympathy for Indians. Shefford tells him he was a preacher but had given up the job. Presbrey understands that preachers lead easy, safe, crowded, bound lives and offers him a job more in keeping with his present situation, hauling freight from Red Lake to his other trading post at Willow Springs. When Shefford first meets him, he is leaving for Willow Springs to get married. He also gives Shefford a gun for protection when he sets out on the trail to find the Surprise Valley his friend, Venters, had told him about.

In *The Vanishing American,* he appears again. He brings Nophaie home in his car when he returns from the war. Blucher, Morgan and Glendon hide in his trading post when the Indians revolt against the abusive regime on the reservation. The Indians threaten to burn down the building to get at these administrators. Nophaie arrives at the trading post in time to put a stop to the riot and save the post from burning.

Presbry: In *Thunder Mountain,* a neighbor of Dick Sloan's. Sloan hires him to work his claim on shares while he goes to work on a more distant, new claim.

Prescott: In *The Lost Wagon Train,* a family in the Bridgeman caravan with whom Estelle Latch is traveling to Latchfield. The family consists of a father, mother, grown son, a daughter about eighteen years old and a lad of ten. Their accent reveals they are from Georgia. They are heading west to win a livelihood out of the soil. The daughter takes a shine to Corny, and the little boy is impressed with Corny's guns.

Prescott, Dave: In *The Lost Wagon Train,* the scout leading the eastbound caravan out of Fort Union. Stephen Latch travels with him. As they settle into the routine, the group becomes more friendly, and Prescott takes a liking to Latch. He inquires how Latch manages to keep his scalp, living in Indian territory. Latch comments that he treats the Indians well. Jim Waters speaks approvingly of such a policy. Indians remember an act of kindness and are grateful. Prescott comments that Latch is becoming another Maxwell. Latch is pleased but adds that he is so only on a small scale. In the talk around the campfire, Prescott reveals that his was the next caravan to follow Bowden out of Dodge. Kit Carson had asked him where Bowden had made his last camp, and Prescott said it was at Tanner's Swale. With more drink, Prescott describes Bowden in detail. He remembered the red-headed daughter, or niece, and the children. He recalls having found a baby's shoe at the swale, something he forgot to tell the commanding officer at Fort Bent.

Preston, Albert: In *Sunset Pass,* one of the younger Preston boys who is assigned to work with Trueman Rock. He takes a strong liking to Rock because he treats them fairly and never asks them to do the hardest work. He reports to his father about the meeting with Dunne when they are gathering up the two-year-olds to move down to the ranch.

Preston, Alice (Allie): In *Sunset Pass*, the sixteen-year-old sister of Thiry Preston. She is Thiry's confidante and go-between with Trueman Rock. She recognizes Trueman immediately at the masquerade ball, and she warns him that her brothers have reported that Ash is in town and will show up at the party. She gets engaged to Charlie Farrell.

Preston, Ash: In *Sunset Pass*, Gage Preston's foster son. His mother asked Gage Preston on her deathbed to take her illegitimate son and raise him. The boy turns out like his father, an incorrigible no-good. Winter calls him a "bad hombre, as bad as ever forked a horse." He is a "cold, shiny rattlesnake waiting to strike." He is suspected of shooting Sheriff Cass Seward and of having killed Winter's son, Nick. He hates cattle, horses, and cowboys and ironically, he is reputed to be a great rider and a hard worker, with a toughness which would be admirable in one less surly. When Trueman Rock first sees him in the corral in Wagontongue, he comments that he "looked and breathed the very spirit of the range at its wildest." He is tall, lean, lithe, handsome, with eyes hot as blue flame. His hair is yellow and scraggy. He wears a gun low down. He is jealous of the attention any man pays to his sister, a jealousy so intense that most people in town suspect the relationship between them is incestuous. He fights with Rock in the corral and when Rock arrives at Sunset Pass looking for Gage, he treats him with un-western rudeness. He takes Rock's horse, Egypt, and tries to break its leg. The horse will not stand for the abuse and after a week-long struggle of wills with the stallion, Ash grudgingly learns to respect the animal. Ash keeps a close eye on all who come near his sister. He comes secretly to the masquerade party for the Fourth of July Rodeo in order to spy on Thiry. He enters and begins to tear the masks off the dancers, finally coming upon Thirty with "Señor del Toro," who punches his lights out. Ash does not return to the ranch for a week, but when he does return, he is hardly repentant. When the game of butchering rustled cattle is up, Ash refuses to stop. He provokes a gunfight with Jimmy Dunne, one of Nesbitt's foremen. Dunne is severely wounded and Ash himself is killed by Trueman Rock. He dies like Bishop Dyer in *Riders of the Purple Sage*— mad, full of hate.

Preston, Burr: In *Sunset Pass*, one of the younger Preston children who meet Trueman when he arrives at Sunset Pass.

Preston, Frank (Boots): In *Sunset Pass*, one of the older sons who works with Ash in the rustling-slaughterhouse business.

Preston, Gage: In *Sunset Pass*, a new cattleman in the area. Originally from Virginia, the Prestons moved to Missouri after the war and then to Arizona. Their southern sympathies are still evident. He has settled in Sunset Pass and his family includes thirteen children. Thiry and Ash are the two best-known in town. Gage Preston is an enigma, and although suspected of rustling, he has a reputation for fairness. Winter reports that he had trouble with Ash over paying the bill at the store, but when the problem was brought to Gage's attention, the matter was settled quickly. Thiry now does the buying for the Prestons and she pays his bills promptly in cash. Preston's ranch is prospering, inspiring jealousy in others. He reputedly pays his cowboys poorly, forty dollars a month, and exacts more work than other ranchers for that stipend. Few cowboys survive there, thanks to the low wages and the work, but especially the unpleasant personality of Ash, who suspects everyone is after his sister. Gage is a tall man, fifty years old, of massive build, dressed like an everyday cattleman. The resemblance to Thiry is obvious, but not at all to Ash.

Preston moved into Sunset Pass five years before. At first, Jem Slagle protested that the land belonged to him, but it turns out Slagle's ranch did not extend into the pass. Previous ranchers had chosen not to build there because of the winds in winter, but Preston has made a success of it. Trueman Rock is impressed with the idyllic location of the cabins. Slagle, however, does not speak ill of Preston. His ruination has been caused by two years of drought and an unwise investment with Dabb, who foreclosed on him. The one incident with Preston involved grazing. Ash kept driving Slagle's herds down from the open range mountain pasture, but when Gage was informed, the practice stopped.

Gage Preston is hospitable, cheerful, courteous. He is impressed by Rock's horse and saddle, both of unparalleled quality. He recognizes Leslie's horse, one he himself had tried to buy. He has heard of Trueman from Range and from cowboys in the area. Range reported on the meeting with Ash and Thiry in Wagontongue and from the cowboys he knows of Rock's reputation for true-blue honesty and reliability. Trueman's cool handling of Ash's rude behavior on his arrival at the ranch is a point in his favor. Preston asks Trueman frankly if he is interested in Thiry, and Trueman confesses that, although she is an important factor, he is really looking for work. Preston gives him a job as foreman of the younger boys, Albert, Tom and Harry. He will have little contact with Ash.

Gage Preston seems to want Trueman around for a reason. He encourages his interest in Thiry, recommending that he propose marriage to her. Preston does not seem concerned about Ash's reaction to the proposal, and Trueman suspects that he may be hoping that Ash does go too far and provoke a gunfight which he would surely lose to Rock. Preston benefits from having Rock as a rider, a man whose reputation for honesty will serve him well.

Gage has allowed himself to be controlled by Ash. The rustling and butchering have been Ash's operation and despite his best efforts to put an end to things, Ash will not stop. He disobeys his father in the question of where they dispose of the hides of the butchered rustled cattle. Gage scolds Ash about his foolish behavior at the masquerade ball, ripping masks of people and destroying Thiry's dress. But none of this seems to have any effect on Ash.

When Rock tells him that Slagle has found the hides and that Dabb, Lincoln and Nesbitt know of his operation and are actively seeking more proof, he is willing to accept the deal that Rock offers him on behalf of the Cattleman's Association. Ash refuses to concede defeat and it is only after Ash is killed that Rock accepts the deal by which he remunerates those whose cattle have been rustled and by which he, together with the three sons implicated in the affair, leave the country. Before he departs, he tells Thiry the truth about Ash, a story which her mother confirms. Ash is not his son, but the son of an old flame of his who, on her deathbed, asked Gage and his wife to take the boy — hence the lack of similarity between him and the rest of the family both in looks and in personality.

Although Gage Preston is a fair man with a sense of right and wrong, he finds himself helpless when faced with Ash, a no-good boy who cannot go straight and who is determined to bring all down with him. He turns to Trueman Rock to set things right.

Preston, Harry: In *Sunset Pass,* one of the fair-haired twins assigned to work with Trueman Rock.

Preston, Lucy: In *Sunset Pass,* one of the younger Prestons. She recognizes Trueman Rock's horse, and tells him that she has ridden him. She tells Trueman that Thiry has already named the horse Egypt.

Preston, Range: In *Sunset Pass,* one of Gage Preston's older sons. He is young, with gray eyes and an intent, expressionless face burned dark from the sun and the wind. He closely resembles his sister, Thiry. Range is associated with Ash Preston and his rustling and butchering operation. Unlike Ash, Range is reasonable and fair. He describes the encounter between Ash and Trueman Rock in the corral in Wagontongue in an even-handed fashion, placing the blame squarely on Ash's hot-tempered jealousy of any man who looks at Thiry. Range leaves Sunset Pass with his father as part of the deal Trueman negotiates with the Cattlemen's Association.

Preston, Scoot: In *Sunset Pass,* one of the older boys who works at the slaughterhouse with Ash. He leaves Sunset Pass with his father as part of the deal resolving the rustling-slaughter house racket.

Preston, Thiry: In *Sunset Pass,* the oldest daughter of Gage Preston. Thiry is in her early twenties. She went to school to the age of seventeen, and then taught her younger brothers and sisters. Gage Preston appears to confide in her more than in his wife. She appears to be the only family member able to influence Ash. The relationship between the two

of them is strange, causing townspeople to suspect that it is unnatural.

Thiry first meets Trueman in Winter's store. She thinks he is a new clerk and asks him to serve her. He is pretty hopeless as clerk and she has to do most of the job herself. He is amused at the boyish way she carries her bags to the buckboard at the corral. She thinks he is like most cowboys who are moonstruck over her. She is a bit shocked when he shows up at the ranch looking for a job. She advises him to leave, warning him that Ash will drive him off. He has shot two young men who came to work there. Her concern is not only for Trueman's physical well-being; she also fears he may find out the truth about the rustling and slaughterhouse operation.

Thiry is always torn between her affection for Trueman and her loyalty to her family. She agrees to meet Trueman in secret to avoid confrontation with Ash. She is thrilled that Ash is not coming to the masquerade party, but learns that he has decided to come after all. She fears what he will do if he should meet up with Trueman. When the inevitable does happen, and "Señor del Toro" punches Ahs's lights out, she fears that Amy Wund, her catty rival, will tell Ash it was Trueman. Her father sends her to Trueman with a proposal that he join with Ash in the rustling operation, and when he categorically refuses to be involved in such criminal activity, she is pleased, Rock having confirmed her faith in his honesty. She offers to elope with him.

Thiry is greatly hurt when Ash is killed, but when her father tells her the truth, that he is not really her brother, she can forgive Trueman more easily. She asks him to marry her and to take her back to her beloved Sunset Pass, where they can run the ranch for Dabb, the new owner.

Thiry Preston is the damsel in distress, the victim of circumstances that overwhelm her, who spurs Trueman Rock to action, bringing out the noblest qualities in him.

Preston, Tom: In *Sunset Pass,* one of the fair-haired twins assigned to work with Trueman Rock.

Price: In *Raiders of Spanish Peaks,* first appears when he is attempting to hang young Lonesome Mulhall, ostensibly for rustling, but in reality to settle a score with the boy who stole his girl. Price is described as a typical cattleman of the period, no longer young, with a lean, hard face of bluish cast under a short beard, with slits for eyes. He looks more at home in the saddle than on the ground and carries a blue Colt gun in the hip pocket of his jeans. The position of the gun reveals much. Laramie Nelson intervenes to stop the lynching. Price is foreman of the Triangle Bar outfit, where Annie Allson, niece of the boss, Bruce Allson, has wreaked havoc among the young cowboys. Several years later, Price is working for Arlidge, as a partner in a rustling operation. He has changed markedly in the face, but Laramie recognizes the coarse, thin-bearded visage. His once portly appearance has become lank. His clothes do not speak of prosperity. Price considers kidnapping

Lenta for ransom a good proposition as there are no more cattle to rustle and sell. When Laramie and his crew have captured Price, Gaines and the other kidnappers, Lenta fears Price will get away. She tells how Price waylaid the party to kill Gaines to get at her. He had been ogling her from the start. Price is executed in the manner in which he had attempted to execute Lonesome Mulhall years before.

"The Price Boy": In *The Drift Fence*, is Ellen Price's younger brother. He is the first boy to dance with Molly Dunn at the party after the rodeo. He cannot dance very well, but he does not spoil things for Molly.

Price, Ellen: In *The Drift Fence*, the daughter of Mrs. Price, who is organizing the dance after the rodeo in Flagg for the Fourth of July when the Sees and Molly Dunn come to town to do some shopping. She is friendly to Molly and the two of them work at a booth at the fair. Ellen tells Molly that the boys do not recognize her and are all guessing who she is and where she is from. Some of her friends are the first to dance with her at the party.

Price, Jed: In *Wyoming*, gives Simpson Glemm directions to Bligh's ranch.

Price, Lany: In *Arizona Ames,* a tanned, tawny, handsome nineteen-year-old cowboy working on Crow Grieve's ranch. He is the son of a poor rancher, a capable rider with a wholesome character. His ambition is to have a ranch of his own. He is the first cowboy Arizona Ames meets when he arrives in the Wind River country. Lany is in a hurry to get a package he is trying to hide up to the ranch house. On the latest cattle drive, his buddies got him drunk for the first time. He warns Arizona Ames that his spectacular horse, Cappy, is a likely target for a horse thief. Lany is cautious about what he says at first, telling Arizona the boss and his wife have been particularly nice to him, making the other cowboys sore. He carries a picture of Amy Grieve, the boss's wife, in his wallet and this arouses Arizona Ames's curiosity, together with Lany's disappearances during the night and his climbing in the window of the bunkhouse. Arizona follows him one day when the Crow Grieve is away and he comes upon Lany and Amy together. The two are clearly in love. Lany reveals that he is in love with Amy, that he is her only friend. Crow Grieve beats her, and he points out the bruises. Lany tells Arizona that he first spoke to Amy when he was asked to drive her wagon home from a neighboring ranch. Amy is so unhappy and lonely, he feels he must do something. Arizona Ames cautions him to be careful. Crow Grieve may suspect something and he has been known to shoot men from ambush. Only Lany suspects that perhaps Arizona is up to something when he deliberately speaks to Amy in Crow's presence and provokes an argument. Arizona Ames clears the way for Lany and Amy to be together when he kills Crow, who is trying to shoot him from behind.

Price, Monty: In "Monty Price's Nightingale," introduced as a man of mystery. Around the campfires, they curse him in hearty cowboy fashion. Monty has no friends. It is said that no foreman or rancher has ever trusted him, that he never spends a dollar, that he cannot keep a job, that there must be something crooked about a fellow who bunks and works alone, who quits jobs every few months to ride away, no one knows where, and who returns to the ranges, haggard and thin and shaky, hunting for another place. Nevertheless, there is no cowboy or rancher who will not admit Monty Price's preeminence as a cowboy. He is a magnificent rider with an iron and cruel hand with a horse. He possesses an Indian's instinct for direction. He never fails on the trail of lost stock. He can ride an outlaw and brand a wild steer and show a vicious mustang as bragging cowboys swear they can. He can endure without complaint long toilsome hours in the piercing wind and freezing sleet and blistering sun. He does extra duty, the hard tasks. He resolves the problems with stock or tools or harness. His famous trick is to offer to take a comrade's night shift for a price, a high price. Still, he never spends a dollar. He saves his money. He never buys fancy boots or spurs or bridles. He scarfs chaps. His cheap jeans and saddles are the jokes of his companions. He has the habit of riding off when he is needed most. This earns him the enmity of Bart Muncie. Muncie, a cowboy who rose to foreman and then to ranching on a small scale, lost a good deal of stock when Monty unexpectedly quit and rode off when Muncie needed men for a drive. Muncie meets him later and calls him out, but Monty walks off. Monty takes a job with rancher Wentworth. When a forest fire is bearing down on the ranch, Monty picks this time to ride off. On his way, he passes by the Muncie cabin. He knows that Muncie is away with Wentworth fighting the fire. He suspects that Muncie's wife and child are still at home. He goes to the cabin and finds the daughter, Del, but no trace of the mother. He rides like the wind but cannot keep ahead of the fire, spreading so quickly, driven by the strong wind. Monty saves the little girl, but is himself severely burned. He finds a home on a ranch far to the south in the shadow of the Peloncillos Mountains. He never rides a horse again. His legs are warped, his feet hobbled. He does not have free use of his hands and seldom does he remove his hat, for there is not a hair on his head. His face is dark, almost black, with terrible scars. He is a burned-out, hobble-footed wreck, but there are those on the ranch who learn to love him, knowing his tragic story.

In *The Light of Western Stars*, this same Monty Price appears as one of the cowboys on Stillwell's ranch. His face is badly scarred, the result of being burned in a fire. He is from Montana, and his injury occurred when he rescued an woman and child from a burning cabin during a prairie grass fire. He participates in the golf game for the visitors, arranging a fake shootout over a golfing disagreement. Monty is a master storyteller. To entertain the company on the camping trip, he tells a tall tale about rescuing a girl in a buffalo stampede, a feat he accomplishes by riding on the back of the buffalo and jumping from the back of one animal to the next. His tale is outdone by Castelton's story of hunting the man-eating lion in Uganda. Monty is a loyal follower of Madeline Hammond's orders. Since she does not want violence and gunplay, he, like the other cowboys, has tried to do things by the book. However, when Sheriff Pat Hawe arrives with Bonita tied to the horse, and Gene is to be arrested on a trumped up charge, Monty decides it's time to do things the old way. He says Madeline's way has not worked and scoundrels like Pat Hawe have thrived in consequence. In the gunfight with Hawe and Sneed, both Hawe and Sneed are killed and Monty Price is fatally injured. Dorothy Coombs, who originally felt he was too hideous to look at, and who was disgusted when he kissed her, concludes that he is a natural gentleman and that she is proud he kissed her. Gene is at Monty's grave, saying farewell before he leaves for Mexico, when he has his confrontation with Madeline.

In *Majesty's Rancho*, Gene Stewart recalls his old cowboy buddy who fought to prevent his arrest some twenty years before.

Price, Mrs.:   (1) In *The Deer Stalker*, a friend of Mary Warren and her niece, Sue. She accompanies them on their tour into the Grand Canyon. She and Mary Warren want old, gentle horses for their ride.

(2) In *The Drift Fence*, the woman at the hotel in Flagg who is organizing the fair and the dance in Flagg for the Fourth of July. She gives Molly and her daughter, Ellen, a booth to take care of at the fair. Mrs. Price invites the Sees and Molly to attend the dance with them.

Price, Sam: (1) In *Horse Heaven Hill*, a cowboy working for Stanley Weston. He quits the Weston ranch when Stan fires Hurd Blanding. Stan is surprised that Blanding has enough influence to convince Sam to leave his employ. Landy Elm later reports that in the discussion of Blanding's departure at the saloon that night, Price went home early and did not contribute to the talk.

(2) In *Knights of the Range*, shot at Anne Doane's party, but not seriously. Anne Doane mentions this to Holly Ripple to acquaint her with what could happen at her fiesta.

Price, Visa: In *Arizona Ames*, Lany Price's sister. Lany carries her picture in his wallet and shows it to Arizona Ames. He tells Arizona she is full of fun and he would like him to meet her.

Priddy: In *Rogue River Feud*, one of the fish buyers allied with Gus Atwell and the Brandeth canning factory. He and Mulligan try to force Garry Lord and Keven Bell join their group and sell their fish to Brandeth exclusively. The group ostracizes Bell and Lord. The canneries will not take their fish unless they sell to Priddy for ten cents a fish.

Prince: In *The Horse Thief*, Edith Watrous's favorite horse, which Dale Brittenham retrieves from Mason's horse-rustling outfit.

Pringle, Adam: In *Sunset Pass*, an old friend, a man of few words, who advises Trueman Rock not to seek employment with the Prestons, who are suspected of rustling.

Pritchard: In *Thunder Mountain*, first appears trying to lure Blair into a card game. Kalispel warns him that Pritchard is a slick gambler. Kalispel himself once sat in a card game with Pritchard in Butte, Montana, and his reputation as a dishonest cardsharp proved true. Pritchard tries to turn Blair against Kalispel, calling him a "bad hombre" who is wanted by the police. Blair does not pay heed to Lee Emerson's (Kalispel's) warning and gets fleeced in Thunder City. To expose the man publicly, Kalispel catches Pritchard in a card game where he is losing and will surely resort to cheating. When Pritchard's turn comes to deal, Kalispel catches him with cards hidden in his hand. Pritchard's reputation is exposed, his cohort Selby is shot in the arm, and Pritchard himself is driven out of town. Jeffries, one of the miners in the establishment at the time, extends his thanks to Kalispel for ridding the place of the crook.

Pritchard, Helen: In *Boulder Dam*, Lynn Weston's ex-fiancée. She loved his physique and his ability as a football player, but beyond that, they had little in common. They part one day when visiting the site of Boulder Dam. Following their parting, Lynn becomes more philosophical, pondering the ambitions and accomplishments of the human race. Helen comes to visit him at Boulder Dam, and her snobbery asserts itself again. Lynn Weston has become a "common laborer." She brings him word that his father has not gone bankrupt and he need not fear being poor. Lynn introduces Anne as his wife, and this shocks her. He tells Helen she has always wanted what she could not have.

Proctor, Elizabeth: In *The Lost Wagon Train*, one of Estelle Latch's school friends from New Orleans. She accompanies her back to Latch's Field. She is fascinated by Slim Blue and the cowboys at the ranch. She in particular is fascinated by Billy the Kid, who makes a visit to the place and attends Estelle's sixteenth birthday party.

Proctor, George: In *Wyoming*, gives Martha Ann Dixon a lift to Sidonia and drops her off at the hotel his uncle runs in town. He describes himself as the "original Sir Galahad" and behaves toward Martha like a gentleman, carrying her bags into the hotel. The uncle and aunt treat her like family.

Progar: In *Robbers' Roost*, the second-in-command in Heeseman's outlaw gang. He and Heeseman have also planned to abduct Helen Herrick for ransom. He arrives at the ranch the same night as Hays and is shot in cold blood by Hays. This ensures that Heeseman will pursue Hays's outfit to seek revenge.

Pronto: In *The Mysterious Rider*, one of Bell-lounds' prize mustangs and one of Columbine's favorite horses. The animal is injured when a frightened steer attempts to gore him. Pronto is saved by Wilson Moore, who rides to distract the steer, getting badly injured himself when his own horse rolls over on him, breaking his leg and foot.

Pruitt, Andy: In *The Thundering Herd*, a member of Randall Jett's hide-stealing outfit. He is a latecomer to the group. He is small of stature, though hardy, with a sallow face remarkable in that its pointed chin is out of line with his bulging forehead. He was a rebel and lost no opportunity to let that fact be known. He is not pleased with conditions at the buffalo hunting grounds and threatens to leave. Jett won't hear of it as he has already paid him an advance. Pruitt leads the rebellion against Jett. He and Follonsbee kill Jett and the Harden woman. They plan to divide up the remaining outfit but meet with opposition from Catlee, who kills both of them.

Purcell: (1) In *The Desert of Wheat*, one of Kurt Dorn's companions at the army training base and in France. Purcell is from New York, born into a rich, well-connected family. His elegant manners and style make him stand out among his comrades-in-arms. He is wounded in battle in France.
(2) In *Valley of Wild Horses*, a gunman and thug who works for Jard Hardman. On orders from Hardman, Purcell runs Blinky Moran and Gus Hans off their claim. He is reputed to have been a claim jumper in Nevada, in Bannock. Purcell comes with Hardman to steal the wild horses that Pan Handle and his crew have captured. When Hurd (MacNew) shoots Jard Hardman, Purcell shoots MacNew and is in turn shot by Pan Handle.

Purdue, Sadie: In *Under the Tonto Rim*, first heard of in the conversation between the men in the Lynn's restaurant. They mention that Edd Denmeade is making up to Sadie again. Sadie possesses little charm. Her face and figure are commonplace, not to be compared with Mertie Denmeade's, and her complexion is pitted and coarse-fibered, well suited to her bold eyes and smug expression. Her shoulders are plump, her hands large, her feet clumsy. Lucy wonders what the boys see in her. There is a mean streak in her, a condescending attitude toward the boys. From the conversation among the young people at the Denmeades,' Lucy learns that Sadie has refused to marry Edd, and there are intimations that she is attached to Sam Johnson. Sadie shows little interest in school. She knows her destiny is to marry, but she's not in too much of a hurry to be tied down. Like Mertie Denmeade, she hopes to marry someone from town. Life on a homestead is too much work. Sadie is often compared to a cat, both in her smugness and in her savage tongue and willingness to attack. At one point, Edd Denmeade tells Lucy she is like Sadie, fickle and dishonest. Sadie and Sam are on the bee-hunting expedition, both getting badly stung when the bees attack.

Q

Quantrill: In *The Thundering Herd*, the leader of the outlaw band of disbanded Confederate officers and soldiers. Bill Doan, Tom Doan's father, rode with the band as did Jude Pilchuck. Tom is embarrassed to admit that his father had been a member of the raiders.

Quayle Brothers: In *The Arizona Clan*, part of Buck Hathaway's outfit that steals sorghum and makes moonshine to peddle around Ryeson. One of the three Quayle brothers shoots Steve, creasing him slightly on the temple. The unnamed brother is killed in the shooting around the hunting cabin. Jim Copeland overhears the Quayles and Hathaway and Twitchell discussing splitting up assets. All the Quayles want is a working still.

Quayle, Diamond: In *The Arizona Clan*, Ruby's twin brother. He and his two brothers, one of whom is unnamed, work with Hathaway making moonshine. Nan recalls the two brothers, identical twins, had pursued her at a dance before she left for Texas. They were terribly handsome young lads. She comments that their names, Diamond and Ruby, are unusual names for men. Diamond helps abduct Nan Lilley at Hathaway's request. He warns his brother not to do anything with Nan because Buck would be greatly displeased. He tells Twitchell about Buck shooting Ruby when he learns Ruby had been kissing her. If Ruby doesn't die, Diamond will take him to the doctor in Ryeson.

Quayle, Ruby: In *The Arizona Clan*, Diamond's twin brother. He and Diamond abduct Nan at Buck Hathaway's request. Ruby tries to carry Nan off into the woods, kissing her all the way. Diamond warns him that he had not dare betray Hathaway like that. When Buck finds out, he shoots Ruby. Diamond is taking him to Ryeson to get patched up.

Queen: In *To the Last Man*, a Texas gunman. Ellen Jorth describes him as a silent, lazy, watchful-eyed man who never wears a glove on his right hand and who never is seen without a gun within easy reach of that hand. Queen shoots Blue in the fight inside Greaves's store. When he learns that Blue was really Texas King Fisher, he hopes to pull a stunt as spectacular as Blue's when he broke into Greaves's store. Queen kills Gordon and Fredericks from the Isbel group, and wounds Jean. The pursuit then becomes a personal challenge, a match of skill and wits between the gunman and the Oregon Nez Perce Isbel. Jean suspects Queen will lay a trap or plan a trick to catch him. He expects to face him in a man-on-man gunfight. But the tracks indicate that the injured gunman's love of life is greater than his desire for glory. He finally comes upon the gunman sitting under a tree with two guns in his hands. He is dead, and Somers and Springer propped him up against a tree to lure in Jean Isbel. Jean sees the trick in time to avoid being shot.

Quinela: In "The Ranger," a Mexican bandit who raids the ranches on the northern side of the border with distressing frequency. His men drive herds of cattle and horses across the border. Quinela and the bandit Lopez were family, according to reports from Mexicans living in Texas, and he is looking for revenge on Ranger Medill, who killed him. Quinela plans a double attack to make sure Medill crosses into Mexico — the rustling of a herd of horses in Brownsville, and the abduction of Uvaldo's daughter, Roseta. He is sure that Medill will undertake one or the other mission. Quinela and Uvaldo have had a standing feud between them for many years.

R

Radford, Hand: In *Western Union*, a cohort of Red Pierce at the saloon in Gothenburg. Ruby tells Cameron and his friends that Radford is mean and brutal, and thinks he owns her. She is pleased to see him get slugged.

Radwell: In *Shadow on the Trail*, has opened a new store in Holbrook.

Raggy: In *Majesty's Rancho*, one of the gangsters with Uhl when he kidnaps Madge Stewart.

Raider: In *The Hash Knife Outfit*, owns a pool hall in Flagg, Arizona, where the cowboys go for a game of pool while waiting for Gloriana Traft's train to arrive.

Raidy: In *Nevada*, one of the cowboys that Ben Ide brings with him from the Tule Lake ranch to Arizona. Raidy is the leader of the caravan on the way south as he knows the country, having gone that way before in a covered wagon. He describes the towns on the way, Salisbar, Lineville, and describes the road farther on in southern Utah and northern Arizona. Raidy is a man knowledgeable about cattle and horses. When California Red vanishes, he is of the opinion that the animal has been stolen, while Dillon, whom Ben seems to trust, argues that the stallion has merely jumped the fence and run off. Raidy resents Ben Ide's apparent lack of confidence in him. When California Red reappears, Raidy examines the horse and finds proof that the horse had been hobbled and roped. Ben is inclined to believe Dillon, but when he examines the marks on the horse that Raidy points out, he sees that his old cowboy friend is right. Dillon is forced to admit that Raidy is right. Raidy also reports on the last herd being stolen, and when Ben doesn't accept his word, he decides to quit working for him. Eventually, Ben must eat crow and apologize to Raidy and ask him to return to work at the ranch.

Ramsdell: In *The Vanishing American*, known as the cowboy missionary. He is no longer at the reservation when Nophaie returns. He combined his missionary work with teaching the Navajo cattle raising and farming techniques. He was a cowboy from Texas. He taught the Indians to plough, to plant, to build houses, and to fix machines. He did not thrust religion down the Indians' throats. He stayed away from Indian women. He is described as a diamond in the rough, a man who worked as hard as any rancher or laborer on the reservation. And this approach to reservation work and spreading Christianity rankled the authorities. Morgan, Friel and Blucher convoke a hearing where Ramsdell is accused of succumbing to heathenism. He dresses in Indian costume and is much too friendly with the traders. Ramsdell is forced off the reservation, much to the dismay of the Indians and Withers and Paxton, who saw in him an exemplary missionary and ambassador to the Indians from the white world. Ramsdell embodies what Zane Grey felt was the proper approach of the reservation agencies towards Indians and their cultures, an approach which shared with the Indian those useful elements of the white culture, making possible a transformation of living conditions without the destruction of Indian culture and beliefs.

Rand, Kitty: In *Sunset Pass*, an old sweetheart of Trueman Rock's. When he returns to Wagontongue after six years, he learns that she married Chess Watkins, a drunken loafer. She worked for a while in the restaurant before they left town permanently.

Randall: In "The Camp Robber," one of the ranchers Winfield worked for after spring roundup before approaching Stimpson for work.

Randle, Joan: In *The Border Legion*, a young woman some twenty years old. She is tall, strong, dark-haired. In Missouri, her father had been a well-to-do, prominent man who "stopped a bullet." She has been the protégée of her uncle, who headed to Idaho to try his fortune in the gold fields. She is a tomboy, more given to riding and wandering around the woods than in doing housework. She undergoes an adventure which teaches her the power of feminine charms to transform a hardened criminal heart.

Jim Cleve, a young man some twenty-three years old, has been chasing her, although she has not given him any encouragement. She does like him but resents that people in town feel she has been giving him encouragement. She tells Jim that he is shiftless, and since he dislikes work, and gambles away what gold he does dig, she cannot consider him as a future mate. When Jim has set off to join the Border Legion to make a reputation for himself, Joan realizes she has been too harsh on him. When she learns from her uncle's friend, Harvey Roberts, that the previous evening Jim had beaten up a young man, Bradley, who had made disrespectful remarks about her in the saloon, she knows she does love Jim.

During her captivity with Kells, Joan realizes that, as Harvey Roberts had told her, she will have to use her feminine wits and wiles to survive. She discovers in Kells an evil intelligence, a man who can control men, who gains their respect with a leadership based on generosity and freedom rather than force and fear. She sense that behind the stories of murder and robbery she has heard about Kells, there is still something of the gentleman in him. She tells him she is only sixteen years old, and Kells at first cannot bring himself to take advantage of one so young. His scruples last only a short while and when he attempts to rape her, Joan grabs his gun and shoots him. When she discovers he is still alive, she cannot leave him to die so she bandages up his wounds and does what she can. Kells seems touched and amazed that she has stayed to nurse him when she could have escaped. When Gulden arrives, she realizes that being with Kells is better than being with Gulden, so she consents to play the role of his wife. She sees a kinder, gentler side to Kells while he is weak. He calls for his mother, and she thinks about how he was once a helpless child whom a mother loved and worried about. Kells offers to marry her, to take her to California where they can start over. He warns her, though, that if they stay in the outlaw camp, he will undoubtedly revert to his evil self when he has recovered.

Joan discovers that she has the power to mitigate to some extent Kells's evil side. He is vain, proud of his power, his influence, his reputation. Part of this pride is in appearing to be a decent citizen, a defender of women. At one point he has Joan dress up and walk down the main street in Alder Creek, hoping someone will make improper remarks which will provide him with an excuse to come to her rescue and thereby establish his reputation. Despite Kells's repeated proposals of marriage, Joan refuses. She does not love the man, although she is grateful for his protection.

When Jim Cleve shows up at the outlaw hideout, Joan does what she can to dissuade him from joining the Border Legion. It then becomes quite a task to control Jim's reckless behavior. He comes to visit her at night, risking getting caught talking to her at the back window. When she finally convinces Jim that she does not love Kells but has stayed with him out of gratitude and pity, Jim proposes marriage and finally brings along a preacher to finalize the issue.

Thanks to Joan's influence, Kells is favorably disposed towards Jim and forgives him transgressions he would never have pardoned in another. When the final showdown is approaching, Joan tells Kells her complete story, how she came to be with Harvey Roberts, how she was the one who had driven Jim Cleve to seek membership in the Border Legion. She adds that if she had not been in love with Jim, she would have accepted Kells's proposal of marriage. This gives Kells the restored sense of pride in himself as he goes to face Gulden in a final showdown.

In the character of Joan Randle, Grey develops another Jane Withersteen, a heroine of romance endowed with the feminine power to tame and transform the violent male, bringing out the better side in him and elevating him to a level of moral responsibility.

Randolph, Phillip: In *Lost Pueblo*, a young archaeologist who works for the New York Museum. He is in Arizona working on an excavation site, hoping to locate a lost pueblo. He is supposed to meet the Endicotts in Flagerstown. Janey Endicott finds Phillip different from the young men in her crowd, but he is as susceptible to her charms as everyone else. He never betrays his feelings by word or action. He is a manly, quiet sort of chap, college-bred, somewhat old-fashioned in his ways, and absorbed in his research work. Janey had liked him too well to let him see much of her. Janey recalls that her father had been quite taken with Phillip.

Phillip explains to Mrs. Bennet that his father and Mr. Endicott had been friends and when he met Mr. Endicott in New York and Endicott expressed interest in getting Janey as far away from civilization as possible, he consented to the expedition in Arizona. Mr. Endicott proposes that Phillip take Janey on an expedition. He loves her, and this would be the opportunity to make her his. If things don't work out, it would still be a memorable experience.

Phillip goes along with the plan. Janey proves to be a nuisance on the site. She digs indiscriminately, possibly damaging artifacts beneath the surface. She wanders around, getting into dangerous places. She can't cook or do anything useful around camp. At one point, he has to spank her, which humiliates her to no end. She does, however, locate the lost pueblo he is looking for, but reveals this to him later.

When the Durlands show up, Phillip enjoys stringing them along. He goes along with Janey's pretense that he has kidnapped her, that he is really Black Dick. When the real Black Dick appears, the Durlands have other ideas about what has been going on. The cowboys from Bennet's post show up, pretending to lynch him. They are a bit too enthusiastic about it, and Phillip thinks they are serious. At this point, Mr. Endicott assures him that they were only acting on his instructions that they should make it look as real as possible. It did bring out a profession of love from Janey as she pleaded for his life. At this point she reveals the location of the lost pueblo. Phillip is overjoyed. He apologizes to Janey for the trick, and proposes marriage. She accepts, but only to protect her reputation from the inevitable gossip that Mrs. Durland will spread back in New York.

Durland had reported that they met a Mr. Elliott, who declared Phillip had been fired from his job for going on the expedition on his own. Randolph, however, declares that he has many witnesses to his discovery. Mr. Endicott and his daughter, John Bennet, the trader, and his cowboys as well as Bent Durland and his mother can substantiate his claims. Mr. Endicott declares he is writing to Mr. Bushnell, the head of the New York Museum, and to Jackson, vouching for Phillip Randolph.

Phillip Randolph and Janey are married by Dr.

Cardwell in Flagerstown. He is planning to stay at the dig, but Janey arranges for Black Dick to kidnap him and put him on the train for the honeymoon trip east. She has decided that she really wants to be married to Phillip.

Phillip Randolph, like Glenn Killbourne in *The Call of the Canyon*, is a young man who rejects the empty social life of the East. In the West, he can live according to his principles.

Randy: In "Canyon Walls," a boy who helps with chores at the Keetch ranch. He chops and hauls firewood.

Range: (1) In *Majesty's Rancho*, one of Majesty Stewart's thoroughbred horses. Gene Stewart gives him to Lance to ride when working around the ranch.

(2) In *Western Union*, Vance Shaw's horse. He boasts the animal is the best horse on the plains, a challenge to Cameron's Wingfoot.

Ranger: In *The Man of the Forest*, Milt Dale's favorite horse. He boasts that Ranger is the fastest and finest horse on the range, capable of beating Roy Beeman's bay. Eventually, he gives Ranger to Helen. At Milt's senaca in the woods, the horse runs wild most of the time. She can give the horse better care than he can.

Rankin: (1) In *Arizona Ames*, a rustler who gave Grieve a hard time some years back. He tells Arizona Ames that whoever killed him had done him a favor. Arizona Ames, it turns out, is that man. Perhaps it is due to this that Grieve gives him a job on his ranch.

(2) In *Boulder Dam*, owns a gaudy gambling palace in Las Vegas. Lynn Weston, Whitney Curtis and others visit the establishment. The bootleggers and the abductors of Anne Vandergrift, Bink Moore and his thieves, also ply their trade at Rankin's.

(3) In *The Lost Wagon Train*, the blacksmith who has two sons. He is an honest man who chose to settle in Latch's Field. Leighton's gossip causes him to feel a certain coolness toward Latch.

Rankin, Edith: In *The Lost Wagon Train*, either the blacksmith Rankin's wife or daughter. She tells Estelle Latch that none of her family will be attending the birthday party.

Rankin, Jeff: In *Knights of the Range*, a gunman from Kansas brought in by Sewall McCoy and Russ Slaughter to kill Renn Frayne and Brazos Keene. Rankin's reputation as a killer gunman is well-known. McCoy has brought him in to further intimidate Holly Ripple and Britt. Word quickly spreads that he and Frayne had clashed in Kansas and that Rankin had killed Frayne's partner. On the way to the village to meet Rankin, Frayne says that he could have killed Rankin in that original confrontation but Rankin was half-drunk and he let him go. Rankin has been led to believe that Frayne has become soft because of his love for Holly Ripple. When the two meet, Frayne is lightning swift on the draw,

and Rankin crumples up on the boardwalk in front of the saloon.

Rankin, Jim: In *The Lost Wagon Train*, the older son of Rankin, the storekeeper in Latch's Field. He is talking to Slim Blue when Latch comes up to talk to him about riding for him after Estelle has spoken to him about what he did to rescue her from abductors on her way home.

Raston: In "Amber's Mirage," the wealthy rancher in Pine who owns the sawmill and buys out Halford's store. On his death, his useless son inherits the businesses in town, and throws his weight around.

Raston, Joe: (1) In "Amber's Mirage," the son of a wealthy rancher in Pine. He flirts with Ruby Low, Al Shade's girl, but has no real interest in her. He drops her unceremoniously. When she marries Luke Boyce, he continues to pursue her. When Al Shade drops by Ruby's place, he tells him that Ruby is a married woman, leading Al to believe he is the husband. Later, to help out Luke Boyce, her real husband, who does not dare fight Raston for fear of being locked up in prison for assault, Al Shade meets Raston, who tells him that Ruby said he was the only man who could make her be disloyal to Luke Boyce. Al gives Raston a knuckle sandwich for good measure, ordering him to leave Luke and Ruby alone.

(2) In *Stranger from the Tonto*, seen by Bill Elway kissing Kent Winfield's fiancée, Nita Gail, the night before the two of them left to go prospecting for gold in the desert.

Rawlins, Bert: In *The Maverick Queen*, one of the two cowboys that Lincoln Bradway witnesses bringing calves to the corral at Kit Bandon's ranch. Rawlins learns from his buddy, Monte, that Kit is no longer buying mavericks from cowboys. He thinks himself quite the ladies' man and bets she will take his calf. He returns disappointed.

Ray: In *Lost Pueblo*, the talkative cowboy who works at John Bennet's trading post. He introduces Janey to the other cowboys. He expresses his shock at the way she dresses and at her rolling her own cigarettes and smoking. He tells her that she will shock everyone around with her very unladylike behavior. Ray and the other four cowboys are in on the trick her father has planned and come to her "rescue" and pretend to be lynching Phillip Randolph.

Ray, Jack: In *30,000 on the Hoof*, one of the very young cowboys that Logan Huett hires to drive his herd to Flagg.

Rayner: In *Betty Zane*, a surveyor. Colonel Zane, hoping to get Betty out of her slump because she has had no word from Alfred Clarke, encourages her to accompany him on a trip to Short Creek to meet a surveyor. He mentions that Mrs. Rayner would be glad to see her. Perhaps this is the wife of the surveyor, but no further details are provided.

Rayner, Helen (Nell): In *The Man of the Forest*, Old Al Auchincloss's niece, to whom he has decided to leave his ranches and herds. She is twenty years old, looking forward to the thrilling adventure of moving west. All her people had the pioneer spirit, and a love of change, action, and adventure. She had taught school, as well as her younger brothers and sisters. Her trip west means tearing up roots, ties to loved ones, but the call of the West is the answer to her prayers. She is glad to leave the yellow, sordid, humdrum towns for the great, rolling, boundless open, to live on a wonderful ranch that will someday be her own. She will be able to fulfill her undeveloped love of horses, cattle, sheep, deserts, mountains, and trees—in short, this is a fairy tale come true. She takes her precocious sixteen-year-old sister, Bo, with her. Harve Riggs, a unpleasant braggart of a suitor, follows her. They meet him on the train, and again at Magdalena. Throughout the trip, Helen feels herself becoming more self-confident; she feels she is taking in the spirit of the landscape of the West. But she also feels that she is inadequate and helpless.

Her resolve and independence are tested as soon as they reach Magdalena. Milt Dale, a tall, broad-shouldered man clad in gray-fringed buckskin, carrying a rifle, approaches her to tell her he has come to meet her. This man quickly puts Harve Riggs in his place, showing him up for the hollow braggart he is. As the first test of her new independence, she must decide quickly if she can trust this stranger. Milt Dale takes them to his senaca in the mountains and forests as it would be too risky to try to reach Pine when Snake Anson's men are out to kidnap her for Beasley. The trip to Milt's forest camp is a challenge to her stamina and determination. The long days riding horseback, the bad weather, the snow, the rain, the wind, camping outdoors, all test her resolve and her strength. As well, she is forced to reevaluate certain prejudices and certainties of her life. Those "civilized" values she prized are challenged. She had always despised hunters, considering them cruel, heartless savages, but out in the wilderness of New Mexico, hunting is a normal part of survival. Milt Dale has spent over a decade in the wilderness, living alone, learning from nature herself; he sees civilized man as cut off from the instincts that nature has placed in him and consequently, his values have become distorted. Helen resists returning to a primitive stage that man abandoned in his progress towards civilization. She knows little about the checks and balances between predator and prey, the need for the mountain lion to keep deer herds healthy. Milt instructs her in the ways of nature, in the "natural law" that controls life beyond man's "civilized" veneer. Milt Dale insists that struggle and competition are the keys to survival. The rot must be cut out for the organism to survive. Civilized man would be a lot more healthy if he listened to his instincts. Helen marvels at the speed with which her younger sister adapts; she is much more willing to give up her eastern ways.

When Al Auchincloss comes to get her and Bo at the senaca, Helen has been well initiated into a more elemental, natural lifestyle which has given her much to think about. She has also fallen in love with her buckskin knight.

When Al Auchincloss dies, she is faced with the problem of protecting her legacy. The cowboys, including her uncle's trusted foreman, Jeff Mulvey, have gone over to Beasley. He is perceived to be the stronger force and Helen the weaker. While she believes that the matter can be resolved peacefully through the courts, Roy Beeman, Milt Dale's friend and helper, assures her that the only way to resolve her problem is to kill Beasley. He is the source of the trouble, the cancer in the body politic, and only when he is removed will the problem be resolved. Like Jane Withersteen in *Riders of the Purple Sage*, she refuses to contemplate violence to preserve her inheritance. Beasley and his men, among them her former suitor, Harve Riggs, move to seize her property. She must take refuge with Mrs. Cass. Roy Beeman tells her that hoping for justice to prevail will accomplish nothing. Unless she is willing to meet force with force, she can forget about getting back her property. Al Auchincloss, Roy tells her, was a hard man. When he was pushed, he pushed back. He made enemies, and now she must live with the consequences. He assures her that in Pine, legal documents mean nothing if you are not willing to back them up with strength. Tom Carmichael, Bo's cowboy friend, eventually brings matters to a close when he faces Beasley in a gunfight. Beasley has been operating through his subordinates, but now he must put his money where his mouth is and face a challenge in person. The western method of finding justice is swift and final, but Helen, while pleased to have her ranch restored to her, cannot accept the methods by which it was made possible. With Beasley gone, Pine returns to its normally peaceful, tranquil existence, thereby confirming Milt Dale's and Roy Beeman's assessment of the cause of the problem and the remedy to be applied.

Helen and Milt are married at the senaca, Paradise Park, by Roy Beeman, who as well as being a good Samaritan and loyal friend, is a Mormon minister. He performs the ceremony uniting the "natural man" and the "civilized woman." Like Nell Downs in *The Spirit of the Border*, or Carly Burch in *The Call of the Canyon*, or Magdalene Stewart in *The Light of Western Stars*, she must abandon those superficial trappings of the East and return to more elemental, genuine values inspired by life in a natural environment.

Rayner, Nancy (Bo, Bo Peep, Pepper): In *The Man of the Forest*, Helen Rayner's sixteen-year-old sister. She is quite the handful. On the trip out, she flirts with a young cowboy at the station in Las Vegas, and Helen tells him Bo will put in a good word for him with her uncle. Bo is convinced he will actually show up in Pine to take her up on the offer. On the trip to Milt Dale's senaca, Bo proves to be the quicker student. She adapts to the conditions and takes the hardship more easily than her more prissy, "civilized" sister. This is due, no doubt, to her love of action rather than contemplation. When Al Auchincloss shows up to fetch them back to the ranch, young Tom Carmichael, the cowboy from Las Vegas, is there. She puts in a word for him and Tom is hired on as a ranch hand. Although Bo is sweet on him, she plays hard to get, and when he takes Flo Stubbs to the dance, she is highly insulted. Helen tells her that she has not treated Las Vegas fairly. If she really loves him she should tell him so. Bo meets Harve Riggs on the range one day and Snake Anson's men kidnap her. She shows little fear of her captors, threatening them with reminders that Las Vegas will soon be after them. Milt Dale and Tom (the wildcat) track the abductors. Milt speaks with Jim Wilson, the best of the bad lot, and convinces him to help. He and Bo together concoct a story that Bo is dying. She acts the part to perfection, pretending to have gone mad. They unnerve Snake Anson's men and Tom's howling fills them with mortal fear. The men start to fight among themselves, Jim Wilson shooting Harve Riggs and Anson and Shady shooting each other. Bo is returned to her uncle's ranch at Pine. After Tom Carmichael has faced Beasley in a shootout, he goes off for a time but returns to marry Bo Rayner. Grey develops the character of Bo as a foil to her sister Helen. While the older sister clings to the norms of the East, Bo quickly adapts to the western environment, absorbing both the mannerisms and attitudes.

Rebecca: In *The Rainbow Trail*, mentioned as one of the sealed wives at the hidden village.

Red: (1) In *Arizona Ames*, a cowboy who works on Crow Grieve's ranch.

(2) In *Horse Heaven Hill*, a young cowboy who works at the Wade ranch. He and Coil Bruce and Blanding are playing cards one morning when Lark comes out to the stables looking for a horse. He comments that Blanding is as lucky at cards as he is at love.

(3) In *The Rainbow Trail*, the name of a mule in Withers's train of pack animals.

(4) In *Robbers' Roost*, runs a hotel where Hays and his outfit stay in Green River.

Red Eye: In *Black Mesa*, a rather spirited horse. Belmont is riding Red Eye along a narrow, dangerous trail in a storm. The horse spooks and rears up, throwing Belmont, who falls over the precipice to his death.

Red Fox: (1) An Indian warrior in the Huron village in *Betty Zane*. He is hopelessly in love with Myeerah and supremely jealous. He hates Isaac with a passion. Red Fox is a swift runner and had often vied with Isaac for athletic honors, but when defeated in this lacrosse game, he struck Isaac on the head with his bat, severely injuring him. Red Fox flees. Myeerah threatens to kill him herself if he should return. Isaac intercedes on behalf of Red Fox. He is a popular brave and many believed that the blow had not been struck intentionally. Red Fox never returned to the village and nothing could be learned of his whereabouts.

(2) A second Indian also named in *Betty Zane*. He is a Shawnee chief. At the beginning of the attack on the fort, he rides up and down in front of the gate brandishing his weapons, making threatening gestures. Wetzel fires the first shot in the battle, killing him.

Red, Slim: In *Raiders of Spanish Peaks,* a cowboy who worked on the Spanish Peaks ranch while Lester Allen was the owner. He remains on the ranch when the Lindsays purchase it. At first, his loyalty is to Arlidge. With insolence, he confronts Lindsay's foreman, Laramie Nelson, who silences him quickly with a punch to the midriff. Later, Slim Red comes to support Nelson. Lenta reports to Harriet that Slim Red is really a bashful young man, not at all the arrogant loudmouth he appeared to be that first night. He reveals to her that Chess Gaines is Arlidge's right-hand man and the source of most of the trouble on the ranch. One day when Lenta rides out from the ranch with Slim Red, they are stopped by Gaines and his men. Gaines shoots Slim three times, but not fatally. Slim slowly recovers. Gaines cannot pardon Slim's going over to Laramie.

Reed: In *Thunder Mountain,* runs a general store in Thunder City. Kalispel accompanies Nuggett to Reed's store and they meet Sydney Blair and Rand Leavitt walking along the boardwalk.

Reed Brothers: In *Black Mesa*, the brothers from whom Belmont bought the trading post at Bitter Seeps.

Reed, Ed: In *The Horse Thief*, from Twin Falls Idaho, Big Bill Mason's right-hand man in the horse-stealing operation. He is sent by Mason with an offer to buy out Rogers, who is homesteading in the valley near their hideout, but Rogers refuses. The price they offered was ludicrously low. Reed runs the auction of the horses in Halsey, where both Dale Brittenham and Edith Watrous identify Dick, a white-faced stallion, as Watrous stock. Reed coolly refuses to surrender the animal. When Edith openly accuses him of being one of the horse thieves, he calls on Leale Hildrith to acknowledge his role in the outfit. Reed abducts Edith from the auction corral and takes her to the hideout at Big Bill's cabin. Big Bill is not pleased to see Reed there with Jim Watrous's daughter. That can only ensure that the influential rancher will pursue them with a large posse. Reed denounces Leale to Mason, who shoots him. Reed is told to return Edith to her father. Dale Brittenham fights and kills Reed, freeing Edith.

Reed, Smoky: In *Wyoming,* a cowboy involved in branding mavericks and rustling. Tex reports that Smoky had been working for the K-Bar outfit and has left there to ride for the Three Flags. He is not likely to last long there either. Tex suspects he will finish rustling Bligh's cattle if McCall asks him. McCall asks Tex to make the proposal to Smoky. Andy Bonning meets Smoky at the rodeo where Smoky makes fun of Andy's new clothes, calling him a tenderfoot dude. A fight breaks out and Sheriff Slade arrests Andy for disturbing the peace. Andy knows that Smoky Reed shot him when he found him branding Bligh's calves. Smoky reveals that Sheriff Slade is involved with bootleggers and rustlers.

Reed, Young Frank: In *The Hash Knife Outfit,* a member of the Hash Knife Outfit. He reports to Jed Stone on the incident in Winslow. Jim Traft showed up when Bambridge was loading stolen cattle on the train. He tells the story to great effect. Reed leaves the outlaw gang to join up with the Diamond cowboys. He is killed by Malloy of the Hash Knife.

Reeves: In *The Hash Knife Outfit,* a member of the Hash Knife Outfit who helps Croak Malloy abduct Molly Dunn and Glory Traft. He is shot at by Jed Stone as he flees the cabin where the abducted girls are being held.

Regan: (1) In *Boulder Dam,* foreman of the scalers at Boulder Dam. The scalers have to go over the cliff suspended in a seat-cage to drill holes in the wall of the canyon for the insertion of metal bars. Regan teaches Lynn to use the drills. One day, a rock slide knocks him unconscious and he almost falls out of his seat. Lynn Weston and Smitty manage to save his life, keeping him from falling to the bottom of the canyon.

(2) In *The Wanderer of the Wasteland,* an Irishman, one of McKay's laborers. He humorously comments on Adam's allure for the women, the guests McKay is entertaining on his boat. He gives Adam the name, "Wansfell" (once fell), a name which he uses in the desert and which becomes his true identity. Adam and Dismukes come across Reagan's body at an oasis in the desert. He had died of thirst. Dismukes and Adam bury him. Adam comments that this man must have seen into him and given him his name.

Reihart: Mentioned in *Betty Zane* and *The Last Trail.* He runs the blacksmith shop. In the former novel, Colonel Zane sends his young son over to watch the blacksmith at work.

Reilly: In *The U. P. Trail,* the boss of the construction gang who gives Neale work as a laborer. Neale is disgusted with the corruption and pretentiousness and greed of the managing class in charge of building the railroad and wants relief in physical labor. Reilly had known Neale as an engineer and is at first reluctant to let him work, but finally sees that Neale is as powerful a man as Pat Casey had been.

Reisenberg: In *The Desert of Wheat,* the head of the local chamber of commerce. He is of German origin, but an American patriot. He is president of the city bank as well. He has called this meeting to discuss the problem of the I.W.W. agents creating disturbances in the area. He reveals that these agents are being financed by German money in the hope that they can compromise the war effort on the home front.

Reynolds: In *The Lost Wagon Train,* works at Latch's ranch at Latch's Field. He is in charge of the Mexican vaqueros.

Reynolds, Alice: A friend of Betty Zane's in *Betty Zane.* She first appears at the start of the novel with Lydia Boggs. They are teasing Betty about her lack of interest in the young men around the fort. Alice Reynolds's marriage to William (Bill) Martin is the occasion for a great celebration. Grey goes into great detail concerning courting rituals, wedding celebrations, etc. on the frontier. At the end of the novel, during the attack on the fort, Alice is cradling the body of Bill, who has died of bullet wounds, when she herself is hit and killed by a stray bullet. Grey uses this incident to illustrate the dangerous nature of life on the frontier and the reason that early marriages are the norm.

Reynolds, George: In *Betty Zane,* the brother of Alice Reynolds, friend of Betty, who marries Will Martin. He is mentioned as a participant in the games held to celebrate Alice's wedding.

Reynolds, Mr.: In *Captives of the Desert,* drives Katharine and Alice Winfield to Taho and from there to Flaggerston. Reynolds speaks with an Irish accent as broad as his red-mottled face. He agrees with Katharine and Alice that Mary Newton is a saint to put up with a husband like Wilbur.

Richardson, Ed: In *Nevada,* one of the names by which Clan Dillon is known. See **Dillon, Clan.**

Rider, Al: In *30,000 on the Hoof,* the only one of the Rider boys who has not gone off to war. He hires on with Logan Huett to drive his herd to Flagg for sale to the army.

Riggs, Harve: In *The Man of the Forest,* a suitor of Helen Rayner. Riggs follows her when she heads west to take over her uncle Al's ranch in Pine, New Mexico. Riggs had been a "sore trial" back in Saint Joseph, Missouri. He had possessed some claim or influence on her mother, who favored his offer of marriage to Helen. He is neither attractive nor good, nor industrious, nor anything that interests her. He is the boastful, strutting adventurer, not genuinely western, but he affects long hair and guns and notoriety. He claims to have been in many fights where he used his guns, but Helen doubts the veracity of his boasting. Riggs is a man of medium height, dark and flashy in appearance, wearing long black hair and a long mustache. His apparel is striking: a black frock-coat, black trousers stuffed into high, fancy-topped boots, an embroidered vest and flowing tie and a large black sombrero. His belt and gun are prominent. His dress excites comment among the passengers on the train. His eyes are hard, with a restless quiver and his mouth is coarse and arrogant. He makes a nuisance of himself on the train and again at Magdalena, where he attempts to show off as a gentleman, carrying Helen's bags. When Milt announces he has come to fetch the girls home, Riggs tries to interfere, threatening to draw a gun on Milt Dale, who puts him in his place quickly, knocking the gun out of his hand and warning him to be careful that the gun might go off. Harve eventually shows up in Pine, where he draws attention to himself with his gambling, drinking and bragging. He makes clear what his intentions are towards Helen, although she makes clear she has no interest in him. Riggs has joined Snake Anson and Beasley in their campaign against Helen Rayner. Riggs meets Bo one day on the range and sends a message for Helen, that if she marries him, he will call off Beasley and his campaign against Helen. Las Vegas confronts Riggs in the saloon, making a fool of him when he refuses to draw. There is nothing a true westerner despises more than a loud-mouthed, bragging phony. Riggs shoots Roy Beeman on the sly, from behind Beasley. Riggs and Anson's gang abduct Bo when she is out riding. Anson is annoyed because Beasley wants Helen. Nell is not phased by her captors and insults Riggs to his face. When Beasley arrives, he curses Riggs for having upset his plans. Bo reminds all that her boyfriend, Carmichael, had called Riggs out and he refused to draw. Riggs was slapped around the saloon and thrown out into the street. Riggs tries to sneak out of the outlaw camp with Bo, but she refuses to go. Jim Wilson comes to the rescue and kills Riggs in a shootout. They find bank notes in his pockets and a moneybelt full of bills. They leave his body where it fell.

Rigney: In *Stranger from the Tonto*, one of the Hole-in-the-Wall gang. Lucy recognizes him among the men who have returned to the hideout with Slotte. Rigney is badly hurt in the shootout between Roberts's outfit and Bonesteel's Hole-in-the-Wall gang, but Wingfield thinks he will survive.

Riley, Sergeant: In *The Lost Wagon Train*, a hard-eyed, square-jawed Irishman who would certainly have looked like a frontiersman but for his uniform. Captain Massey calls him in to ask about Bowden and Anderson's wagon train. He comments that the train is one of several that have gone missing and he knows no more about it than that.

Ring: In *Riders of the Purple Sage,* one of Venters's sheep dogs, half collie, half deer hound. He is particularly well trained, taking turns with the other dog, Whitie, standing guard while Venters sleeps on the open sage. Ring is a faithful companion to the lonely Venters.

Ring, Gip: In *Boulder Dam*, a gunman for the gangsters running the bootlegging operations in Las Vegas. He looks like a boy, barely over twenty, handsome as a girl, with a light complexion and eyes cold as slate. He is a killer from Chicago working for Ben Bellew. Gip Ring is shot and killed in the rescue of Anne Vandergrift.

Ringspot: In *The Horse Thief*, one of Edith Watrous's prized horses that Dale Brittenham retrieves from Mason's horse-rustling outfit.

Ripple, Colonel Lee: In *Knights of the Range,* owner of Don Carlos Valverde's sixty-square-mile ranch. As the story opens, he is discussing with his foreman, Britt, a long time friend and confidante, whether he should tell his daughter, Holly, about his imminent death. He has had two heart attacks and fears that the next will be fatal. He tells the story of how he fell in love with the powerful Don Carlos Valverde's only daughter, Carlotta, when he was fifteen. Don Carlos did not approve of his daughter and the wild young Texan reputed to chase after every pretty face. The two elope and marry in San Antonio, incurring the wrath of the don. He vows to disown his daughter. Lee Ripple regrets being the cause of the estrangement of daughter and father, but in time, Don Carlos comes to forgive Carlotta, and she returns to the ranch. On his death, Carlotta inherits the ranch. After the Civil War, Lee drove a herd of cattle up from Texas and went into ranching in a big way. He has prospered as a cattleman and now wants to leave the ranch to his daughter. At present, he has over fifty thousand head of cattle and over five hundred of the finest horses on the range. He questions the wisdom of sending her off to New Orleans to be made into a refined woman. He wonders whether she will be able to adapt to the uncouth, uncivilized West. His foreman assures him that Holly loves the ranch, that she loves horses, and that he will teach her what she needs to know to run the ranch. Ripple hopes that she will marry some rowdy cowboy and keep up the ranch. Britt has loved her as if she were his own daughter, but he pooh-poohs Ripple's fears of imminent death. He and Britt speculate about what the future holds for the area. With the coming of prosperity, towns will be built and with the cattle and towns, rustlers and scoundrels are sure to follow. He recalls how Kit Carson had prophesied this turn of events. A few months after the return of Holly, the colonel does pass away, leaving the inexperienced young woman in charge of his enormous estate.

Ripple, Holly: In *Knights of the Range,* another interpretation of the Betty Zane heroine, blending elements of Grey's ancestor with elements of the wealthy Mormon landowner, Jane Withersteen, as well as elements from Jacqueline Pencarrow in *Shadow on the Trail*, and Harriet Lindsay in *Raiders of Spanish Peaks.*

Holly is the seventeen-year-old daughter of Colonel Lee Ripple and Carlotta Valverde. At the age of eight, she was sent to Madam Brault's school in New Orleans. Although she is very Spanish in appearance, she has been educated as a southern lady. She comes to complain eventually that her father had educated the Spanish out of her and deprived her of the typical western woman's formation, making her a rootless, rudderless woman. She loves the Valverde ranch, is crazy about horses, but does not know how to ride or anything else about running a ranch. She is aware of her Spanish looks and wonders why she knows nothing about her Spanish heritage, and why she cannot speak her mother's language. She is unable to speak to the Mexican servants and vaqueros on the ranch. She asks her father if there is any special reason for his keeping her from learning about her Spanish heritage. She accepts his explanation that he simply wanted her to get an education, refinement, and an appreciation of her American heritage. Two years later, she has mastered the art of horsemanship, riding like an Indian, according to Britt, but she has shown little interest in the cattle part of her ranch. When she comes upon Britt and the Heaver rustler outfit, she displays the spunk and courage to be expected of the owner of such a large spread. She tells Heaver that although the horses are not branded, she can describe every one of them, proving beyond doubt that they are hers. Heaver tries to pull her off her horse, and the gunman of the outfit, Renn Frayne, defends her. She convinces him to work on her ranch to thank him for saving her life. She is moved by his situation, as Jane Withersteen is by Lassiter's. He is a loner, without a friend in the world. He rides alone, until loneliness drives him to other men like himself; there is a nobility in him, because he killed his outfit bosses to save a girl from harm. Nevertheless, Frayne does not spare her feelings. He points out that she is a child, innocent of the ways of the West, and foolish. She should never ride alone and she should ensure that her stock is branded.

Her lack of a husband becomes an issue. Single women are rare in the West, and as women are outnumbered by men, suitors are not lacking. Holly, like Jane Withersteen and Betty Zane, treasures her independence, and marriage would be a surrender of that freedom. Several cowboys express their interest in her, particularly Brazos Keene. He tells her he wants her to be his wife and proposes to her twice in the course of the novel. She is fond of him, but unwilling to commit. Like Harriet Lindsay in *Raiders of Spanish Peaks*, she refuses to face the truth that her heart speaks, that she is in love with a gunman. At her fiesta, she grows jealous of Conchita Velasquez, who has no trouble using her feminine charms to lure men. She is especially jealous of her because Renn Frayne has danced with her most of the evening. When she finally does get Frayne to dance, he is not amused at her silly party talk and tells her to talk about something important or not at all. He tells her that while the great attendance at the party is testimony to the respect some have for her, this policy of open hospitality is foolhardy. There are many outlaws and criminal ranchers among her guests, but she chooses not to see them. Her encounter with McCoy has not opened her eyes. Like Jane Withersteen, she chooses not to see the truth. When she and Frayne step out to talk privately, they overhear a conversation between Brazos and Conchita, a conversation which clears all doubt about Frayne's interest in her, as Conchita is clearly interested in Brazos.

On Britt's advice, originating with Frayne, Holly establishes her "Knights of the Range," her equivalent of Arthur's Knights of the Round Table. Her cowboys are all devoted to the cause of right, to extirpating the disease of rustling on the range. The cowboys are inspired by the nobility of the cause, pledging their devotion to her.

Holly, though, remains largely an observer of her cowboys, little involved in their personal lives. She does bet five hundred dollars on Ride'-Em Jackson in the rodeo competition with Russ Slaughter's outfit, but in large part, she knows little about what is going on. When Anne Doane and Skylark marry and move into the vacant cabin near the ranch house, she learns more. Anne is a sponge for gossip, which she repeats to her friend. Holly discovers how little she knows about what is going on. From her talks with Anne about the need to marry, she comes to acknowledge that she does love Frayne, and that she wants to be his wife, but she is afraid to act. Frayne's lack of communication with her, his apparent aloofness and indifference, his avoidance of any contact with her, is all a front, according to Britt. Her fatherly foreman reveals Frayne's secret, that he loves her deeply, but he cannot let love of her interfere with what he sees as his mission. Like Lassiter, who apparently loses his will to fight because of his love for the pacifist Jane Withersteen, he does not want his hands tied. Britt advises her to wait patiently.

When the reality of McCoy and Slaughter's hostility to her translates into local ranchers coming to the ranch to accuse Frayne of rustling, Holly does speak up. She tells the ranchers that McCoy had tried to force her into marriage and upon her refusal, promised that he would join forces with Russ Slaughter. The trumped-up charges against Frayne are prompted not only by jealousy and revenge, but fear of Frayne, who knows Slaughter is the robber baron. She also reveals that Clements, one of the most vociferous of the accusing ranchers, has much to explain about his dealings with Slaughter and McCoy.

When Frayne has met Rankin in the village for the shootout and returned victorious, and Brazos returns with the proof of Slaughter's criminal activities and his log book recording transactions of a criminal nature with Clements and other ranchers, the Knights of the Range have largely accomplished the noble task set them of extirpating the rustlers.

Needless to say, Holly and Frayne are married. But the day of the ceremony, Jackson arrives at the house to tell Holly that Renn will not be able to make the ceremony as he has been called away to take care of a rustling problem on the range. Holly is furious, but it soon becomes clear that this is a trick inspired by Brazos Keene to tease her.

Holly Ripple is a powerful woman, largely eastern in outlook, who must allow the West and its values to penetrate the carapace of eastern decorum so that she can discover her real self.

In *Twin Sombreros*, Holly writes a letter to Brazos Keene in care of the post office in Latimer, Colorado. Britt had heard from Calhoun, a neighbor, about his exploits in Casper, Wyoming, and that he had been working with the Two Bar X ranch. She tells him about naming her first son after him, Brazos Ripple

Frayne. As well, she tells about Billy the Kid attending one of her dinners. She talks about what a good husband Renn Frayne has been, and apologizes again for rejecting his offer of marriage, an offer she could not accept as she did not love him that way. She invites him to return to the ranch.

Robbins: In *Wanderer of the Wasteland,* one of the robbers who attacks Dismukes at his mining claim in the desert. He is whipping Dismukes to get him to reveal where he has hidden his gold. Adam throws water on him to distract him from his whipping, whereupon he attacks Adam with a shovel. He is shot by Adam, then two other robbers continue the attack.

Roberts: In *The Thundering Herd,* belongs to Sol White's outfit from Waco, Texas. He reports finding scalped bodies of two dead men with sticks driven into their abdomens. It turns out the camp was Jett's. Tom Doan meets Roberts sometime later after the Indian campaign, when Roberts tells him the story of the superstition with which the Indians regarded Hudnall's rifle.

Roberts, Hal: In *Sunset Pass,* an old acquaintance of Trueman Rock. He rides for Spangler. When he meets Trueman, he tells him that Gage Preston has the reputation of paying his hands poorly and demanding a lot of work from them.

Roberts, Harvey: In *The Border Legion,* a friend of Joan Randle's uncle, Bill Hoadley. Harvey Roberts meets Joan Randle on a trail outside of Hoadley's camp. She is trying to trail Jim Cleve, a young man who is in love with her and whose interest she has rejected because he is shiftless. He has set off to make a name for himself with the outlaws who plague the mining camps along the Idaho-Montana-Nevada border. She meets her uncle, a scarred, grizzled-faced miner. He has seen Jim's trail and offers to go with her, expecting to come upon Jim Cleve before nightfall. Roberts's horse gets a lame foot and they will either have to walk back to Hoadley or camp overnight. While they are making camp, the outlaw Jack Kells rides in with Bill Bailey and Halloway. Roberts had met Kells in the California camps. He came upon a vigilante party attempting to lynch him. Kells recalls that Roberts saved his life but Roberts has little trust in the man. He warns Joan that the man is treacherous and capable of anything. Although Kells behaves like a gentleman, Joan, like her uncle, feels uneasy. The following morning, Kells tells Roberts that he is going to keep Joan. The uncle refuses to leave her alone with Kells, upon which Kells threatens him. He should remember that he has a wife and family back in Hoadley. Roberts retorts that his wife would never forgive him if he left Joan alone with Kells. Tricking Joan to move on, Kells murders Roberts and steals his horse. Kells then tells Joan that he shot Roberts in the arm so that he could not use his gun. He will return to Hoadley to tell her aunt and uncle that she is all right. Later, Joan figures out what Kells has done when she recognizes Roberts's horse among Kells's pack animals.

Roberts, Mr.:   In *Boulder Dam,* works in Carewe's office where the payroll is kept. He is forced by the robbers to open the safe and to hand over the week's payroll.

Roberts, Ney: In *Stranger from the Tonto,* as slick an operator as Slotte. He cuts a striking figure, a brawny, silk-shirted dandy with a bold, handsome face. He has fox features and a drooping mustache, and is the notorious rival of Bonesteel in their nefarious trade, but these have little to do with his singular physical power. Silk Slotte has asked him to come to the Hole-in-the-Wall hideout to meet Bonesteel. Slotte seems to be playing the two against each other. Roberts gives an explanation of his presence, that Slotte had told him Bonesteel wanted to see him. He claims Slotte owed him money and proceeds to take the substantial amount that he had on his person when Kent shot him. Roberts speaks to Kent, perhaps in the hope that he will convince him to join his outfit. He shares with him what Slotte told him about Bonesteel's double life, his wife and family in Utah, but he does not give Kent the name he uses. Bonesteel raids up and down the state, then lies low in the hideout until the ensuing fuss blows over, then he returns to his life as a respectable rancher. Roberts also repeats what Slotte told him about Lucy, a presumed bastard daughter. He suspects Slotte intended to tell her this, hoping to get her. Kent is impressed with Roberts, an honorable thief. He admits Roberts's singular drawing power. If he had really been on the run and looking for an outfit to hide with, he would have considered Roberts's outfit. Roberts and Bonesteel come to an agreement, that they will fleece a penny-pinching rancher up in Utah who has too few cowboys for the twenty thousand head of cattle he runs on his range. They have planned out the strategy to rustle the cattle. But before they undertake the trip, Bonesteel suspects that Roberts will kill him. He takes action before Roberts can. He and his men come into camp. In the shooting that ensues, Roberts is killed and all of the men he had with him. Bonesteel's secret is safe.

Robertson: In *The Fugitive Trail,* runs a trading post on the Brazos River. Trinity stops there on her trip to find Bruce Lockheart.

Rock, Clan: In *Blue Feather,* the group to which Taneen and his people belong.

Rock, Trueman: In *Sunset Pass,* the protagonist in the style of Nevada (Jim Lacy, Texas Jack) in *Forlorn River* and *Nevada.* He is a hero motivated primarily by a desire to help others, in particular, a woman, Thiry Preston.

Trueman Rock was brought up in the town of Carthage in western Illinois, where he attended school to the age of fourteen. The family moved to Nebraska, where the father went into ranching. He didn't make a success of the venture and lost all he had invested. Two years later, the family returned to Illinois but Trueman remained out west. His parents are still living. During the sixteen years since his family's return east, Trueman has lived the life of a wandering, riding, drinking, fighting cowboy. He has acquired the reputation of being a completely honest, trustworthy man whose word is gold. Nevertheless, he was always getting into trouble because of his weakness for the ladies and for drink. He left Wagontongue, Arizona, after a gunfight in which he killed a man. While in Texas, he went in with a pretty big rancher, whose crooked enemies he fought off. When a railroad came their way, the ranch prospered and Trueman sold his part. When he returns to Wagontongue, he has ten thousand dollars in his pockets.

Trueman is now thirty-two years old, and looking to settle down. When he gets off the train, he is surprised to see that the town has not changed all that much in the past six years. His lithe shape, his good clothes, his handsome features still draw the attention of the young ladies on the street. The Happy Days Saloon and the Range House Hotel are still there. At the hotel, Bill Clark fills him in on the latest gossip, in particular the death of Sheriff Cass Seward, and the marriage of Amy Wund, his old flame, to John Dabb, his old boss and the largest rancher in the area. He also fills him in on the new arrivals in the area, the Prestons, who are ranching in Sunset Pass.

Trueman Rock visits Sol Winter, his old friend, father-surrogate and confidante. Winter's store is not as prosperous as it had been. Competition from larger enterprises, together with poor investments have left him in debt. Trueman pays off the bill he owes Winter with interest and then offers to invest in the business. With the money, Winters pays off his debts and invests in new stock and within a few weeks is on the road to prosperity again. Winter gives Trueman more details on developments, in particular, on the Prestons. They are new to the area, and well-liked by some. All of them, that is, except Ash Preston. Some suspect them of involvement in the cattle rustling in the area, others, in true western fashion, refrain from comment. Filling in for Sol Winter as clerk in the store, Trueman meets Thiry Preston and falls in love with her at first sight. The die is cast. He decides to look for work as a rider with Preston's outfit.

Despite warnings from Slagle, a former employer, and Amy Wund, a former sweetheart, that working for the Prestons could harm his reputation, Rock approaches Gage Preston for a job. Preston is impressed with Rock, with the way he handles Ash's rudeness on his arrival, and with his forthrightness in answering questions about himself and his interest in Thiry. He has already heard from his son, Range, how Trueman helped Thiry carry packages from the store to the buckboard and how he dealt with Ash at the corral. All this raises Rock in his esteem, and he gives him a job as foreman of the younger men, his sons, Albert, Tom and Harry. Trueman has his own cabin, not far from the main house. Gage Preston believes Rock is an asset to his ranch, given his sterling reputation for honesty.

The young men under his charge easily take a liking to Trueman. He does the heaviest work himself and does not lose his temper, even when Ash takes his phenomenal horse, Egypt, without permission. Trueman keeps his eyes open, and investigates the rumors he has heard about the Prestons' butchering operation involving stolen cattle. He discovers the old well on the Slagle place where hides are being dumped. The telltale quicklime and Ash's bootprint confirm the worst. Some weeks later on the way to Wagontongue for the Fourth of July Rodeo, he discovers Half Moon hides hidden in a culvert, covered with quicklime and the telltale bootprints in the soft earth. Eventually, others will make the same discovery.

When Jim Dunne comes to inspect the two-year-olds that Trueman, Al, Tom and Harry are gathering, Trueman gives the Wyoming native Dunne a lesson in Arizona etiquette. After he has inspected the brand on each of the two hundred-odd animals, Trueman tells him that next time he accuses someone of rustling, he had better be prepared to back up the accusation with a gun. Dunne, Nesbitt's foreman, is shamed by the encounter. Gage Preston is impressed by the way Rock handled the situation, but erroneously assumes that he is willing to help conceal his rustling-butchering operation.

In town, Trueman visits John Dabb, his former boss and the most influential man in Wagontongue, a town he virtually owns. He clears up a number of things that might strain relations between them. He explains that he quit his job as foreman six years before because he did not trust the sheriff to deal with him fairly in the matter of the Pickins shooting. He also assures Dabb that the romance between him and Amy has been over for a long time. He does advise Dabb to pay her more attention, that she feels neglected and lonely. While Dabb resents these personal comments, he pays heed to what Trueman says and his relationship with his wife improves enormously. Later, Trueman also informs Dabb about the suspicious things he has uncovered. On the advice of Sol Winter, who feels that amends can be made, he approaches Dabb and Lincoln asking for an offer. While these two have not been the most seriously affected by Preston's rustling operation, they are the largest ranchers with the greatest clout. They propose that Preston pay for the animals he stole and butchered and then leave the country. They offer to buy him out at market value. Preston serves as emissary from the Cattlemen's Association. Preston is willing to take the offer, but Ash will not hear tell of it. In the gunfight that this refusal makes inevitable, young Ash Preston is killed and Trueman shot.

Love for Thiry Preston drives Trueman Rock. He always had a weakness for women, but now, at age thirty-two, he is looking to settle down. He seeks employment at the Preston ranch to be close to Thiry. Despite stories he has heard that she has an "unnatural" love for her brother Ash, he feels she is pure and innocent. There is a mystery to her that intrigues him. He cannot understand what binds her so tightly to Ash. While he meets her in secret at the ranch, and then at the masquerade ball for the Fourth of July Rodeo, he is careful not to provoke Ash. Gage Preston even recommends that he propose marriage to Thiry and hints that the two of them should elope. Thiry knows that Preston's love for her is genuine but she fears trouble with Ash and revealing her family's secret. When Gage sends her to ask Trueman to join him and Ash in refusing the Cattlemen's Association offer, she is pleased when he refuses, and offers to elope with him. In the gunfight which ensues, Trueman kills Ash.

Trueman Rock recuperates from his wounds at Winter's home. Thiry comes to visit there, telling him the truth about Ash, that he really wasn't her brother, but the son of an old flame of her father's who had died, asking him to take the boy. She adds that she knew he was no good. She does not want to leave Sunset Pass and asks Rock to marry her and take her back to Sunset Pass, where he can run the ranch as Dabb's new foreman.

Trueman Rock embodies the western hero found in a number of Grey's novels in the middle of his career. He is driven by a desire to right wrongs and to defend the innocent. While he knows that Preston is guilty of rustling, he does not feel that gunfire and killing are the solution. He seeks a peaceful outcome and works with Dabb and Lincoln to negotiate a deal acceptable to all involved. While not as pure as the driven snow, Rock's faults stem from a generous nature, a love of justice and a sincere desire to help others.

Rocks: In *Wildfire*, the name of the horse that Hawk Holley enters in the annual horse race at Bostril's Ford.

Rodriguez: In *West of the Pecos*, a famous vaquero, reputed to have been indefatigable. Pecos Smith's riding and roping are compared to his. Pecos is a whole outfit in himself, never knowing when work is done. He deserves to be a figure of legend, like Rodriguez.

Roger: Alfred Clarke's thoroughbred horse in *Betty Zane*. Alfred brings the horse with him from his home in southern Virginian. There is no horse like the stallion on the frontier. Roger is the envy of everyone at Ft. Henry. The stallion shows his mettle in the "Race for the Bottle" before Alice Reynolds's and Will Martin's wedding celebrations. The animal beats the local animals in speed and endurance over an obstacle course through woods and swampland.

Rogers: (1) In *The Desert of Wheat*, one of Kurt Dorn's mates at the army training camp and in France. Rogers is from the Bronx, a runt in size, but a knot of muscle. He is killed in battle in France.

(2) In *The U. P. Trail*, one of the chief officers of the Union Pacific Railroad. He is mentioned as present in the two meetings of the executives, in Omaha and in North Platte.

Rojas: Rojas is mentioned as a Mexican revolutionary general in *The Light of Western Stars* but he plays no direct role in the plot. In *Desert Gold*, Rojas is a general in the Mexican Revolution (1910–1920). He is handsome in a cold, vain way. His dress, a military uniform with gold lacings and other ornaments, reflects his pride and arrogance. He shares the prejudice of the lower classes against the ruling class, particularly those of Spanish origin like Mercedes Castañeda. He kidnaps her father for ransom and when the ransom is paid, kills him anyway. He looks forward to raping the daughter then turning her over to his soldiers. Mercedes escapes by bribing the guards and disguising herself as a nun. He follows her to Casita to retake her. Here, his plan is foiled by George Thorne and Dick Gale. In the scuffle, he is shot and injured sufficiently to be hospitalized. Rojas has a network of spies among the Mexicans on the Arizona side of the border, and when Thorne takes leave from the cavalry garrison to visit Mercedes, Rojas captures him, taking across the border. He hopes to torture him into revealing Mercedes's whereabouts. Thorne is rescued in a cavalry raid inspired by Nell Burton's brash action. Rojas trails the party to Belding's ranch at Forlorn River. He vows to burn the village, to hang all the women and children. Belding arranges for a party to leave the ranch unbeknownst to Rojas. But Rojas, with a skilled Papago tracker, sets off after them into the desert. In the last stand, Rojas displays the extent of his hatred for Mercedes and his desire to rape and humiliate her. He faces a hail of bullets without flinching, and weaponless, strikes out towards Mercedes. Dick Gale thinks how he has never witnessed such hatred and raw courage. Rojas is shot, pinned against Choya cactus by Yaqui, and eventually plunges from a cliff to his death.

Rollins: In *Rogue River Feud*, a constable from Grant's Pass. He tries to get Sheriff Blackwood of Gold Beach to arrest Keven Bell on a charge of assault and attempted murder. The charge has been laid by Gus Atwell with whom Keven had had a fight in the hotel lobby in Grant's Pass. Atwell is anxious to get rid of Bell, who is a nuisance to his monopoly in the fishing industry and a threat to his dubious reputation. Blackwood does not believe the story but detains Bell. He refuses to hand him over to Rollins to take back to Grant's Pass.

Roosevelt, Teddy: In *30,000 on the Hoof*, Lawyer Little says that if Teddy Roosevelt had been president, he would have prevented Europe from going to war.

Rosalio, General: In *The Light of Western Stars*, mentioned as one of the rebels executed on orders from General Rojas.

Roseta: (1) In *Knights of the Range*, Holly Ripple's Mexican maid.

(2) In "The Ranger," the daughter of Uvaldo, Mexican foreman of the Glover ranch. She is pretty and slight of stature, roguish, coquettish, with the pride of her Spanish forebears. She is young, rich, the belle of Las Animas, and the despair of cowboy and

vaquero alike. Her father has also made it clear that he does not want her to marry south of the border. Ranger Vaughn Medill still entertains thoughts of winning her, despite the great difference in their ages. At dances, she singles him out and calls him "un señor grande" and "the handsome gringo." When she is abducted, Medill is put on the case. Allerton and Colville, as well as her father, Uvaldo, speculate that it may not be an abduction at all, but an elopement. The girl, after all, is kind of wild. Medill follows the trail of her horse, pointed out by the stable boy, Pedro. He finds the grove where someone had been waiting for her, a gringo, to judge from the boot prints and cigarette butts. Perhaps it is an elopement after all. He comes across the prints of other horses and men in sandals, as well as blood. It is an abduction after all. In Mexico, Medill is captured by the men who have Roseta in tow, bound and tied to her horse. They are being taken to Quinela. Roseta asks Medill to kill her should escape be impossible. Medill manages to outfox the captors, killing them. On the way back, Roseta tells Medill that she loves him. She proposes that they get married before returning to Texas, to teach her father a lesson. She convinces him to resign from the rangers. He will buy a ranch under the Llano Estacado, far enough from the border to be safe. Vaughn's seemingly impossible dream has come true.

Ross: In *Horse Heaven Hill*, one of Stanley Weston's cowhands who quit the ranch with the foreman, Howard, to join Hurd Blanding's wild horse hunting expedition.

Ross, Delia: In *Twin Sombreros*, a friend of Lura Surface. When Lura leaves her father's Twin Sombreros ranch, she stays with her friend Delia Ross in Las Animas.

Rover: (1) In *The Lone Star Ranger*, the bloodhound that Bill sends into the cottonwood brakes to trail Buck Duane. The dog just looks at Buck, who is lying on the ground at the foot of a tree, and walks on out of the thicket without a yelp.

(2) In *Stranger from the Tonto*, Jeff's dog, who makes friends with Wingfield's dog, Piute.

Ruby: (1) In *The U. P. Trail*, the most popular saloon girl/whore at Stanton's. She tries to get Neale's attention in Stanton's but he pays her little attention. "The breath, charm and pestilence of her passed over Neale like fire." She is angry that Neale did not succumb to her charms. Beauty Stanton says she is from a good family back east and could go home if she wanted to. She warns that Beauty can mean trouble. Neale takes pity on her, and when he wins a large amount at cards, he offers to give Ruby and Larry the money to go off to California where they can start over. She laughs at the idea that she could lead a normal life. Shortly thereafter, she is found dead in her room, a presumed suicide.

(2) In *Western Union*, a twenty-year-old dance-hall girl working for Red Pierce at his gambling establishment in Gothenburg. Pierce is in love with her and fiercely jealous. She fears him. Young Vance Shaw is the man she likes, and he arranges to get her away from Pierce. She hides out with Shaw and his partners, Darnell, Cameron and Lowden, disguised as a Mexican boy, Pedro. Pierce, however, finds her and abducts her again during the Indian attack on Julesburg. She leaves a message for Vance, telling him not to follow her, because she is already married. She fears that Pierce will shoot Vance in the back someday. Pierce takes her to his gambling holes in South Pass, first to the Atlantic, then to the new place, the Gold Nugget. Shaw and his partners effect a second rescue, and in this escapade, Pierce, whose real name is Bill Howard, is killed. Ruby and Shaw marry and take up ranching with Cameron in the Sweetwater Valley.

Ruckfall, Pan Handle: In *Twin Sombreros*, a gunman that Bodkins and Syvertsen attempt to hire to kill Brazos Smith. Even when they raise the offer to two thousand dollars, he tells them they must be mad to think he would go up against Brazos Keene.

Rudd: In *The U. P. Trail*, one of the chief officers of the Union Pacific Railroad. He is mentioned as present in the two meetings of the executives, in Omaha and in North Platte.

Rue, Hardy: In *Nevada*, Less Setter's second in command. He hates women, never drinks, seldom talks and watches everything with eyes like a hawk. He mistrusts Cash Burridge and keeps a keen eye on his doings. He shows up at the Hatt ranch, speaking of Jim Lacy. When Burridge sells Ben Ide the Arizona ranch he and Less Setter had bought, he loses the money to Hardy Rue in card games. Burridge confesses that Rue and a Spanish girl working with him had cleaned him out. Jim Lacy kills Hardy Rue in a gunfight in the street outside the general store where Hettie is doing her shopping. This is the first time she has seen Nevada in Arizona, and the incident with Hardy Rue convinces her that Jim Lacy has broken his promise to her that he would refrain from gunfighting. Up to this point, some had suspected that Hardy Rue led the Pine Tree Outfit.

Rugg: In *The Lone Star Ranger*, one of Bland's ruthless lieutenants. He is a small, bowlegged man. Half his face has been shot off, and he has the use of only one eye, but that has not impeded his ability to shoot.

Ruhr: In *The Vanishing American*, one of Blucher's henchmen, a "policeman." He enforces the rule that all animals with TB will be shot. He kills Marian's mustang out of spite on the pretense that the animal has TB, although the blood test showed the animal clear of any illness.

Ruskin: English essayist, moralist, philosopher. In *The Deer Stalker*, John Ruskin is one of the big influences on Patricia Clay's outlook on life. When thinking about her experiences, Patricia agrees with Ruskin's classification of the people one meets: some are like thorns, they sting you, while others are like stones that weigh you down, and still others are weeds.

Russ: In *The Light of Western Stars,* one of Madeline Hammond's stag hounds.

Russ, Harvey: In *Stranger from the Tonto,* one of Roberts's men who come to the Hole-in-the-Wall hideout with their chief. When the boat on which they crossed the river to get to the hideout is set adrift, he suspects Lucy Bonesteel did it. Roberts sends Russ to Lucy's cabin see what she has to say. Avil Bonesteel accompanies him to the door of her room. She denies having anything to do with it and calls Roberts a dirty rustler.

Russell: In *The Lone Star Ranger,* Captain Mac-Nelly's assistant at the ranger's camp.

Rust, Virgil: In *The Call of the Canyon,* a young soldier that Glenn had met in France. He is in the hospital in New York, and not expected to recover from the wounds he received in the war. Glenn Killbourne asks Carley to go visit him. Virgil Rust is from Wisconsin, a "rough diamond" in the words of his friend, Glenn. He was deserted by his girlfriend while he was overseas. She married a man who had managed to dodge the war. Like Glenn, Virgil is disgusted by American society, its decadence, its lack of faithfulness or gratitude to those who went to war. He has concluded that America is not worth fighting for. Virgil knew of Carley from Glenn. He idolizes her for having remained true to Glenn during the war. He believes she is a woman of principle. Carley, however, tells him that she and Glenn have drifted apart, that she has been unable to live up to his expectations, that she is as decadent and unfaithful as his own girl. George Burton, another veteran, informs Carley that Virgil Rust died in the hospital some months later.

Ruth, Babe: In *Boulder Dam,* Lynn Weston describes Regan, foreman of the scalers at Boulder Dam, as having the body of Jack Dempsey and the sharp eye of Babe Ruth.

Ryan: In *The Call of the Canyon,* Hutter's neighbor. The party coming from Lolomi Lodge meet him on their way to the sheep dip. The same dip is used by both ranchers. Ryan and Lee Stanton are in charge of running the sheep-dipping operation.

Ryan: In *The Arizona Clan,* runs a saloon in Ryeson. Buck Hathaway and Twitchell hole up there when they come to town after the shootout at Belmar's with the Lilleys and Mercer.

S

Sacky: In *Boulder Dam,* works for Ben Sneed. He takes Lynn Weston to Decker, who helps him find the men who have abducted Anne Vandergrift.

Sadie: In *Thunder Mountain,* reports to Cliff Borden what she heard from Charlie March about Leavitt's plans to pack up and leave Thunder City in the spring.

Sage King: In *Wildfire,* John Bostril's prize stallion, reputed to be the fastest horse in the region. This spirited animal is the color of upland sage, a racer by nature, splendid, proud. The animal has a wonderful disposition, is never ill-tempered, and is easy to catch. Sage King is normally ridden by Bostril's rider, Van Sickle, who has taught the animal a few bad tricks, in the opinion of some. Bostril is fond of Sage King, and refuses to believe that any other horse is faster. In the annual race he organizes, Sage King has always come in first. The year Lucy enters Wildfire in the race, the Sage King is crowded off the track by the wild mustang and is out of the race early. Bostril does not consider this definitive, since the Sage King lost by default.

When Wildfire proves himself faster than Sage King in a race to save Lucy Bostril's life, Wildfire dies from the exertion. Lucy and Lin Slone decide to keep the Sage King's defeat a secret from her father.

Sago Lily: In *The Rainbow Trail,* the nickname given to Mary, or Fay Larkin, by Ruth Jones, one of the sealed Mormon wives in the hidden village. The nickname is a tribute to her beauty and reserve.

Sain, Jack: In *Twin Sombreros,* becomes a friend to Brazos Keene. Hank Bilyen vouches for him. He used to ride for Surface but his friendship with the Neece twins cost him his job. Abe Neece says he was a good friend of his murdered son's. Jack Sain is in love with June Neece, but it's not clear she is in love with him. Brazos asks banker Henderson to give him a job as a rider. When Brazos has cleaned out part of the rustler outfit, with the death of Syvertsen and Orcutt, and the departure of Surface, Jack becomes temporary foreman of the Twin Sombreros ranch.

St. Vrain, Colonel *see page 329*

Salazar: In *Desert Gold,* a Mexican revolutionary leader (1910–1920) who is best known as a horse thief, raiding on the American side to get horses for the Mexican army. In *The Light of Western Stars,* he is mentioned as one of the leaders who has tried to stop attacks on Americans and their property in Mexico. He has two soldiers punished for looting the homes of some Mormons, but other reports suggest he shows little concern about attacks on other Americans. When Madeline Hamond goes to Mexico to secure the release of Gene Stewart, General Salazar is mentioned as the man who will punish Don Carlos for his machinations.

Salisbury, Nate: In *Majesty's Rancho,* one of the Madge Stewart crowd at the university in Los Angeles. He is part of the crowd that comes to the ranch for the summer. He is particularly taken with the Mexican señoritas in the village. He agrees with

Lance Sidway that Madge should ride a more manageable horse than Dervish when they go riding.

Sam: (1) In *Fighting Caravans*, a freighter with Clint Belmet in the fight at Point of Rocks.

(2) In *The Fugitive Trail*, one of the teamsters who drives Trinity to the Melrose ranch on the last leg of her trip.

(3) In *Rogue River Feud*, Beryl Aard's mule. When they go for a ride, Beryl tells Keven that the mule is not stubborn. It's just that he falls asleep on the trail and stops.

(4) In *Shadow on the Trail*, a member of Aulsbrook's crew when Wade Holden (Blanco) rides in with word that Catlin's gang is planning to rustle off their herd.

(5) Colonel Ebenezer Zane's black slave in *The Spirit of the Border* and *Betty Zane*. Sam arrived on the frontier with Colonel Zane and his family. He serves to give a twist to the story line of *Betty Zane* when he destroys the letter Alfred Clarke leaves with him to give to Betty. In the letter, Alfred explains why he has left so suddenly without speaking to Betty. Sam feels protective of the colonel's sister and conceals the letter because he dislikes Alfred, thinking he is an insincere, arrogant Virginian, "southern white trash," to be exact. When confronted by the colonel, Sam confesses that indeed Alfred did leave a letter and he did not deliver it to Betty as requested, hiding it instead. Sam is in the fort during the attack and is the first to spot the Indians with the flaming arrows, about to shoot them into the dry roofs of the buildings inside the fort. Sam comments that his treatment on the frontier is better than what he could expect back in old Virginia.

(6) In *The Trail Driver*, Reddie Bayne's spectacular black horse. The other cowboys in Brite's outfit are jealous of her mount.

(7) In *West of the Pecos*, one of the men with Sawtell when he comes to the Lambeth ranch looking for Hod Pecos Smith.

(8) In *Wilderness Trek*, Horton's cook who prepares a meal for the Dann crew when they arrive at the end of their trek in the Kimberleys.

Sam(bo): (1) In *West of the Pecos*, one of Colonel Templeton Lambeth's slaves, who refuses to leave his service after his liberation following the Civil War. He accompanies the colonel and his daughter on their way to set up ranching west of the Pecos. Templeton Lambeth had taken Sambo with him on his buffalo hunts, finding him a willing and capable hand. Moreover, he was one of the few really good Negro vaqueros. Sam had taught the colonel's daughter to stick like a burr on a horse and to throw a lasso. He was truly devoted to young Terrill. He skillfully drives the wagons through the stampeding buffalo herd on their way west with the hiders. He teaches her to shoot, and soon the young woman becomes a skilled shot, hitting rabbits and other small game and downing her first buffalo. When the colonel is killed, he makes possible her continuing on the ranch. When Terrill is put in jail for failure to pay

a bill at Brassee's place at the Eagle's Nest, Sambo and Mauree remain close at hand, and when Pecos Smith appears, tell him the story and he secures her release. He remains with his mistress when the ranch is attacked by Sawtell, and later after her marriage to Pecos Smith.

(2) In *Western Union*, the Negro driver for Sunderland's wagon in which the recuperating Kit is living. Sambo is mentioned when the caravan must cross the Laramie River in flood.

Sampson: (1) In *The Mysterious Rider*, a gray and yellow hound with mottled black marks, very long ears and big solemn eyes. Sampson is one of the pack of hounds entrusted to Bent Wade for hunting coyotes and wildcats attacking the White Slides herd. Sampson sleeps in Bent Wade's cabin.

(2) Biblical hero. In *Riders of the Purple Sage*, Lassiter and Venters are compared to Sampson, the Old Testament hero whose hair was shorn by Delilah, an act which stripped him of his great strength. Venters and Lassiter are shorn of their power by Jane Withersteen, the Delilah who takes their guns.

San Sabe: In *The Trail Driver*, a youth under twenty, part Indian and part Mexican. His lean shape bears the stamp of a vaquero. He sings to the herd at night, to calm the cattle down. He is also the lookout for the outfit, riding ahead to spy out possible dangers. He spots the Comanche who are about to attack the Handy wagon train. He likewise spies on Ross Hite and his rustlers, who have rustled part of the herd. San Sabe is killed in a night stampede. He and his horse are trampled to death by the stampeding longhorns.

Sanborn: In *The Desert of Wheat*, one of Kurt Dorn's mates at the army training camp and on the battlefields in France. He is from California and is thick-set, sturdy and well-tanned.

Sanchez: In *Stairs of Sand*, a burly man, short, with a head like a bulldog and very dark skin. His attire shows the richness and color affected by the prosperous Mexican. He is a well-heeled Mexican, owner of the Del Toro Saloon, in partnership with Collishaw. He has been able to smooth over some of the hard deals credited to the Del Toro. At first, Adam suspects that Collishaw has sequestered Ruth at his place. Augustine considers Sanchez a friend, and he reports to Merryvale that Sanchez described the fight between Adam Larey and Collishaw, saying that he had at last met one old enemy too many. It was an even match. "Wansfell, the Wanderer, has made a call on Yuma. May he live to come again!" are his parting words to Augustine.

Sanderson: In *Fighting Caravans*, told to help Clint Belmet guard Hank Miller while Captain Couch sends for the sheriff in Santa Fe.

Sands, Mr.: In *Under the Tonto Rim*, the head of the department of welfare work, which is sending Lucy Watson to work with poor families in the Tonto. He tells her that the job she is to undertake will require tact, cleverness, and kindliness of heart and she is the right person for the job.

Sandy: In *The U. P. Trail*, one of the men with Fresno when he attacks, robs and burns Slingerland's cabin. Sandy is killed in a fight with one of his partners, Old Miles.

Santana: Variant spelling of **Satana**.

Santone: In *Knights of the Range*, a swarthy, beady-eyed vaquero who works as a rider on the Ripple ranch. He is one of the contingent of cowboys under Sloan(e) who capture and lynch the cattle rustlers at night.

Sarchedon: In *Wildfire*, a black stallion, seventeen hands high. He is one of John Bostril's prize horses. His daughter, Lucy, rides Sarchedon, but cannot mount the stallion from the ground.

Satana: In *The Lost Wagon Train*, a fierce and bloody chief of the Kiowa tribe who has entered into a pact with Stephen Latch to massacre wagon trains. He is small in stature. His painted face, wedge-shaped, and his broad forehead express tremendous power. No lines are discernible on his face, but it is the face of a mature Indian with a record of blood and evil. Satana had been difficult to deal with, but rum eventually brought him around to deal with Latch. Satana is implacable towards buffalo-hunters, caravans, and soldiers. According to the deal, Satana and his braves massacre everyone in the caravans. They get the livestock as payment. Latch and his men get whatever property is in the wagons. All traces of attacks are wiped out. Latch buys the land where he sets up his ranch from Satana. Others wonder why the place is never attacked, and suspicion arises about the connection between the two. Latch, however, realized early on that Satana would deal with him as he was dealt by, and the Kiowa chief was true to his word. In *The Trail Drivers*, Sa(n)tana is mentioned as a crafty chief of the Kiowas who could be a problem to the trail drivers heading to Dodge. He is reputed to be in league with a band of white outlaws who attack small caravans and kill every man, woman, and child, steal the supplies, and destroy every vestige of the wagons.

Satlee: In *Valley of Wild Horses*, owns a ranch near the gold diggings. When Hardman and Purcell drive Charley Brown off his claim, they chase him as far as Satlee's ranch.

Satock: In *Fighting Caravans*, a notorious chief of the Kiowas who harassed the western border from 1855 to 1863. There are records of attacks on escorted caravans. Satock approaches the wagons warily, asking the men for sugar, coffee and tobacco. He is given what he asked for. He mounts his horse in a single agile action without letting go of the three bags. Satock returns shortly thereafter with some two hundred braves and Waters uses the cannon on them to great effect.

In *The Lost Wagon Train*, Satock is mentioned several times. He has been the regular war chief since 1855, raiding around Santa Fe and up along the Vermigo River. It's a lucky caravan that gets by without a clash with Satock. Satock, however, is not Satana's equal in sagacity and bloodthirstiness. Jim Waters comments that white men have probably committed the attacks on caravans and the tricks for which Satock gets the credit.

Saunders: (1) In *Arizona Ames*, one of the cowboys who works on Grieve's ranch.

(2) In "Canyon Walls," a big gentile rancher in Green Valley. He is expanding southward, and needs feed for his herds. Boller buys up the Keetch's alfalfa crop to resell to Saunders.

(3) In *Code of the West*, owner of the Bar XX ranch. For years there has been a rivalry and enmity between Saunders and the Thurmans. Saunders breaks up a fight between Cal and Hatfield and later, he witnesses the confrontation between Georgie and Hatfield. Because of Hatfield's behavior, Saunders kicks him off the ranch, either under his own steam, or packed on a mule, as the case may be. He and Enoch Thurman shake hands and put an end to the feud that has kept them at odds so many years. Enoch and Saunders discover they really like each other.

(4) In *Fighting Caravans*, the man who drives Clint Belmet's wagon when the cannon is mounted on it after the attack by Comanches in which Tom Sidel and Jim Belmet are killed. He helps Clint load Tom Sidel's body into the wagon for burial later when they have escaped from the Comanches.

(5) In *Knights of the Range*, a cowboy working for Sewall McCoy. He is caught rustling cattle with Beef Falman, Lascelles and Trinidad. He signs a confession naming McCoy and Slaughter as the leaders of the rustling operation on the range. This confession is produced to prove the innocence of Renn Frayne, whom local ranchers and Sewall McCoy have come to accuse of rustling. After he has signed his confession, he is told to fork his horse and to ride out of the region. He is told he will be shot, should he return.

Saunders, Jim: In *Wild Horse Mesa*, a horse dealer from Salt Lake City who informs Malberne and Loughbridge that Bent Manerube had worked for him.

Sawtell: In *West of the Pecos*, shows up at the Healds' ranch demanding that Pecos Smith be fired. He is Beckman's foreman, pursuing rustlers who brand mavericks. He had come across Wess Adams and Curt Williams, suspected of branding over other cattlemen's marks and branding mavericks on the range. Sawtell is drunk and draws on Pecos Smith. He is killed in the fight. The Heald brothers vouch for Pecos's shooting in self-defense.

Sawtell, Breen: In *West of the Pecos*, Sawtell's brother, who takes up the pursuit of Pecos Smith to avenge his brother's death. He writes a letter to the Texas Rangers accusing Pecos Smith of killing his brother and of killing several ranchers, then making the attack appear to have been a Comanche attack. The rangers do not place much credence in his accusation. He enlists Sheriff Bill Haines, formerly of Kansas, to arrest Pecos Smith. He comes to the Lambeth ranch, and holds Sambo, Terrill and Watson hostage. He finds Pecos's money belt containing some twenty thousand dollars. He kills Sheriff Haines, who demands he get a share of the money. Sawtell waits for Pecos to return, to hang him. Sawtell discovers that Terrill is a girl, and assumes she has been living with Pecos. In the fighting that ensues when Pecos Smith challenges Sawtell on his insinuations about Terrill, Sawtell is killed.

Scanlon, Mike: In *Majesty's Rancho*, spots the black car, which turns out to belong to the gangster Uhl, speed by the spot where he discovered the cut, downed telephone wires to the Stewart ranch. He reports this to Smith, the store owner in Bolton, who repeats the information to Lance Sidway.

Scarbreast: In *The Heritage of the Desert*, the war chief of the Navajo who lives near the August Naab ranch. In the "Crossing of the Fathers," the term Naab uses to describe the crossing of the turbulent Colorado River, Scarbreast leads the column of young braves into the water, guiding the reluctant mustang into the current. They form a triangle, the middle of which is filled with pack ponies loaded with bundles of deer pelts. Eventually, the current prevails and the mustangs and the pack animals must flow with the current, coming to shore farther down the Colorado. Jack Hare admires the wildness of it all, the necessity of danger and the calm acceptance of it all. Scarbreast and his braves embody the spirit of the desert for Hare.

Schwartz, Jed: In *Western Union*, a pony express rider. Jim Hawkins tells Wayne Cameron that the stage usually meets Jed just past Ft. Kearney. According to Jim, Jed Schwartz is the best of the lot of Pony Express riders. He is a fearless, hard rider, who packs two guns and knows how to use them. The day of the Pony Express, however, is about to end with the spread of the telegraph across the plains.

Scott: In *Western Union*, mentioned as the master of a wagon train that was attacked by Indians. Ruby's parents were killed in that massacre.

Scott, Errol: In *The Deer Stalker*, a broker from New York City. He appears at the El Tovar resort when Patricia Clay (Edgerton) is staying there. Scott is past thirty, a well-fed, debonair person whose smooth-shaven, red, puffy face shows heat, but not from healthy exercise. His hair is thin at the temples, his eyes are hard, his lips cynical and sensual. He is surprised to learn that she is staying there, as he would have expected her to go to San Francisco or Santa Barbara. When she sees him, Patricia ignores him. Patricia explains to Thad that he was part of her circle in New York City, one of the reasons she has come west. At one point he had proposed marriage

to her. He refers to her as Pat. Later, when Thad Eburne overhears him making remarks about Patricia using the pet name "Pat," which she despises, Thad chides him. When Scott becomes insulting, Thad gives him a punch and he falls to the ground, unconscious. During the deer drive, Patricia tells Thad that Scott had a fractured skull.

Sealover: In *The Maverick Queen*, sent by Emery to Rock Springs to hire a gunman to kill Lincoln Bradway. Gun Haskel tells Lincoln this just before he dies. Lincoln meets Sealover in McKeever's room when he accompanies the doctor to visit the patient. Lincoln confronts him with what Haskel had told him. Sealover claims he merely told Haskel that there was a wild, gun-toting cowboy in South Pass who had won a pile of money. Lincoln Bradway tells him the dying Haskel did not likely lie about who had hired him. When Sealover says he is unarmed, Lincoln advises him to be armed the next time they meet. McKeever tells Bradway he enjoyed watching Sealover sweat a little.

Sears, Dick: In *Wildfire*, a cohort of Cordts, the horse thief. He was reported to have been killed, but early in the novel Hawk Holley reports that Sears has been seen again in the company of Cordts. John Bostril describes him as a little knot of muscle, short, bowlegged, rough as a cactus and scaly like a desert rattlesnake. He comes to the races at Bostril's Ford with Cordts and Hutchinson, but parts company with them afterward. He attempts to steal Wildfire from Slone, but the owner ropes him and Wildfire takes off in an uncontrolled race, dragging Sears behind. The would-be thief is killed before Slone can get the horse stopped.

Sedgewick: In *Knights of the Range*, one of the local ranchers who shows up at the Ripple ranch with Sewall McCoy to accuse Renn Frayne of cattle rustling.

See, Caleb: In *The Drift Fence*, a neighbor of the Dunns and uncle to Molly Dunn. He takes Molly along when he goes into Flagg. Caleb explains to Molly the significance of the drift fence being built by the Trafts, the wealthy, prosperous ranchers of the Diamond. Traft has no right to build the fence as this is supposed to be free range, but being powerful and bull-headed, he does what he wants. The fence is a slap in the face to all small-scale ranchers in the area. Once again, the mighty rule. Caleb predicts this action will produce another Pleasant Valley war.

See, John: In *The Drift Fence*, the son of Caleb See. Molly Dunn says of him that he has more prospects than most of the young men in the Cibeque, but more than his share of demerits as well. Molly is glad he does not go with them to Flagg.

See, Mrs.: In *The Drift Fence*, Caleb See's wife, and aunt to Molly Dunn. She takes Molly along to Flagg where she hopes to buy some new shoes and other clothes. She is kind and protective of Molly in town, and at the party following the rodeo. She is pleased with her niece's popularity with the young men at the rodeo and the dance.

Seever: In *The Fugitive Trail*, the trail boss of the wagon train consisting of some twenty wagons that pulls in to Melrose's ranch. One of the men in the wagon train claims to have recognized Bruce Lockheart among Melrose's hands. He points to Lee Jones (Bruce) insisting he is the man he saw shoot Barncastle at the Elk Hotel in Denison. Melrose convinces him that he must be mistaken. The man he has identified as Bruce Lockheart is Lee Jones, his daughter's fiancé.

Selback: In *Thunder Mountain,* the guard Lee Emerson (Kalispel) meets at Rand Leavitt's cabin when he arrives back at Thunder Mountain. Selback is furtive, cold, calculating. Selback identifies himself as working for Rand Leavitt. When Lee asks what had become of his brother, Selback goes for his rifle and Lee shoots him. It turns out that Selback is the man who attacked Jake Emerson in Challis and stole the sample of ore he was carrying. Selback and Leavitt set out the next day with pack animals for Thunder Mountain. Leavitt tells the miners' court that Selback had got wind of a strike in the valley but he does not know where or how he acquired the information.

Selby: In *Thunder Mountain* with his partner Haskell rides into the mining camp and quickly becomes involved with Rand Leavitt. They speak ill of Lee Emerson, possibly of his reputation in Montana. Selby is shot by Lee Emerson in a poker game with Pritchard, when Kalispel exposes the man as a cheat.

Selby, Ernest Howard (a.k.a. Iowa, (Ioway):

In *The Dude Ranger*, the nephew of Silas Selby and heir to the Red Rock Ranch. He is on his way to Arizona to take possession of his inheritance. He is also interested in investigating the mysterious loss of income and cattle under Hepford's administration. He is extremely grateful to his uncle for having left him the ranch but still more for the opportunity it gives him to forsake his circumscribed life in a small Iowa farming community for the romance and adventure that the West promises. He knows little or nothing about ranching and is unfitted to step in and take over the management of a large ranch. He knows he has to learn the business from the ground up, to gain actual experience of the activities connected with raising stock. He has no idea how to go about investigating possible fraud or uncovering dishonesty and maladministration on the part of Hepford. He decides to ask for employment as a cowboy on his own ranch under the assumed name, Ernest Howard. He has experience working with farm horses; he is strong and husky and feels he can overcome tenderfoot reactions. In this way he can get the inside track on ranch management.

In Springer's store, he purchases himself a cowboy outfit: jeans, spurs, shirt, hat, boots and a gun. He lacks the swagger and the walk of a true cowboy. He's immediately taken for the tenderfoot he is. He overhears Anne Hepford and Jeff Martin talking about the ranch, the death of the owner, and her feeling that the ranch properly belongs to her and her father. On the ride back to Red Rock, he engages in conversation with Sam Brooks, former manager of the ranch and neighbor to Red Rock. He confirms his suspicion that Hepford has not been honest in his dealings with his Uncle Silas. Ernest also gets the chance to be the hero, saving Anne from three robbers who try to steal her purse with the large sum of money she has withdrawn from the bank for her father. On the ranch, he is offered a job out of gratitude for helping Anne. Hawk Siebert looks him over and takes him on, assigning him to bunk with Nebraskie. He does not hit it off with the cowboys because he consents to do jobs no self-respecting cowboy would do, things like digging holes for fence posts, pulling barbed wire, pitching hay. Slowly, he earns the respect of the cook, Jeff Martin, and his bunk make, Nebraskie. He and Nebraskie become fast friends and he learns much about the cowboy life from him and from Hawk. Pleased with his performance without complaint at the unpleasant tasks, Hawk promotes him to range rider.

The cowboys on the Red Rock, however, do not accept him readily. He is made the butt of jokes and ostracized by all but Nebraskie. Dude Hyslip and Anne are the two that give him the most grief. Nebraskie and Hank Siebert, on the other hand, prove to be the salt of the earth, friends who would stand by him through thick and thin.

Ernest quietly sets about investigating the situation on the ranch. He consults with a lawyer in Springer, one Jefford Smith, who is both a cattleman and a lawyer. Jefford acknowledges that things do look suspicious, but advises Ernest to take his time collecting his evidence and not to act until he has definite proof of fraud. From Sam Brooks, Nebraskie and Hawk Siebert he concludes that Hepford has been selling off the cattle and pocketing the money himself. He himself becomes involved in one of these drives designed in such a way that no one has precise figures about the number of cattle on the drive, or the price obtained for the transaction. The cattle are sold to the government agent, Jones, for the reservation. Jones is not too particular about where the cattle come from or other niceties. Ernest also overhears Anderson and Wilkins discussing their suspicions of Hepford's shady deals. After a further consultation with Smith, he asks the lawyer to write his Uncle Silas's lawyer back east, requesting a copy of all cattle sales. He hopes to find some discrepancies with the numbers reported to him at the ranch. By accident he learns where he can find the conclusive proof he needs. He drops by the ranch office to speak to Anne, who does the bookkeeping for her father. She points to a blue ledger held closed by a rubber band, saying that her father forbids her to look into it. The ledger holds his accounts of cattle deals. When Ernest decides the time has come to act, he removes the book from the office and takes it with him.

He surrenders the book to lawyer Smith, who determines that there is now enough conclusive proof to take action.

Ernest finds himself entangled in romantic adventures from the start. He falls in love with Anne Hepford the first time he sees her in Springer. He rescues her from robbers, like a true knight in shining armor. On the ranch, she sends him on errands for her. He rescues Daisy Brooks from the clutches of Dude Hyslip. He helps Nebraskie and Daisy reconcile after Hyslip's interference in their engagement. Ernest proposes marriage to Anne so that she will realize he is not just a flippant cowboy. When he does get the proof to expose Hepford, he does not seek vengeance or a public trial that would disgrace both father and daughter. With the surrender of the money he has in his bank accounts in Arizona and the renunciation of all claims on the ranch, he will not seek further redress. He does not want to start off his married life to Anne with the shadow of revenge hanging over them.

Ernest learns the value of friendship from Nebraskie and Siebert and Brooks. These are men who have gone out on a limb for him, giving him a chance, helping him learn, standing up for him when he is attacked. Early on he decides that when he takes over the ranch, these two will be partners with him, not mere hired hands.

Ernest Selby is another example of the Grey hero, who, like young Jim Traft, inherits a ranch and comes west to prove himself. He shows himself equal to the task and wins the admiration and respect of true westerners.

Selby, Silas: In *The Dude Ranger*, the rancher uncle of Ernest Howard Selby. He owns the Red Rock Ranch and upon his death bequeaths it to his nephew. Ernest is extremely grateful to his uncle for having left him the ranch, but still more for the opportunity it gives him to go west and experience the romance and adventure that the West promises. Silas Selby had been about to go to Arizona to investigate the sudden drop in the cattle herd and in revenues when he died of a heart attack. Uncle Silas Selby had been an absentee landlord for over twenty years. At first, his foreman was Sam Brooks, to whom he gave a strip of land and the ownership of a spring that never goes dry. When Hepford, his brother-in-law, takes over, he cannot get control of his land and spring, although he tries to drive him off.

Seligman: In *The Arizona Clan*, owner of a ranch that is one of the landmarks on the way to Hathaway's hunting cabin three miles below Dead Hoss, on the way to Bull Tank.

Selkirk, Captain: In *Fighting Caravans*, in command of the cavalry detachment at Fort Zarah. Waters reports the Pawnee attack to him when they arrive at the fort. Selkirk sends out a detachment of fifty dragoons to pursue the Indians.

Sellers: In *The Lone Star Ranger*, the man that Buck Duane suspects of abducting Jennie. Buck

catches up to him but Sellers dies without revealing whether or not he had killed Jennie. Her whereabouts are unknown.

Selton: In *The Trail Driver*, a cattle dealer in Dodge. Since Reddie does not want to sell her horse, Sam, Brite arranges for Selton to send the horse back to San Antonio with the first outfit heading there.

Semiramis: In *The Maverick Queen*, a figure from ancient history who burned down cities and fought battles for the man she loved to whom Kit Bandon compares herself. She tells Lincoln Bradway that like this ancient figure, she is willing to destroy black-hearted men to save him.

Semper, Art: In *The Fugitive Trail*, one of the cowboys riding for Steve Melrose on his Little Wichita outfit. He is shot and killed when the Stewart outlaw gang rustles that herd.

Señor del Toro: In *Sunset Pass*, the disguise Trueman Rock wears at the Fourth of July Rodeo Masquerade party. Alice Preston teasingly refers to him by this name later in the novel.

Seris: In *Yaqui*, referred to as a man-eating tribe of desert Indians. In *Stranger from the Tonto*, the dying Bill Elway tells Kent Wingfield that the Seris mined gold at low tide from the rocks along the Gulf shore. They would dig out big hunks of gold eroded and eaten by salt water. They would give the gold to the Papagoes and they in turn would give it to the Yumas.

Serks, Jim: In *The Fugitive Trail*, Tex Serks's brother. He does not play as big a role in the novel as his brother. He is injured in the fighting at the Stewart cabin where the rustlers are cornered.

Serks, Tex: In *The Fugitive Trail*, as his name suggests, a Texas cowboy. He and his outfit are heading west, answering a call put out by Melrose for more Texas cowboys to ride on his ranch at the headwaters of the Brazos River. He meets Bruce Lockheart on the way and invites him to join their group. He suspects that Lee Jones is not his true name, but keeps the secret to himself. Tex is keen on pursuing the rustlers. Jack tells him about seeing campfires from the high country, but when Juan and Peg go out there to investigate, they find nothing. They see no cattle on that part of the range at all. They follow Stewart's tracks down to the brakes and they wait for days, but no one shows. When Bruce Wells returns from the Little Wichita to report the rustling of the herd and the death of two of the riders, Tex is swift, decisive and efficient in treating Bruce's bullet wounds. He is equally efficient in getting organized to pursue the outlaws. Slaughter puts him at the head of the riders. They find the herd Stewart sold to McMillan. This cattle dealer and trail driver happens to be a friend of his. Like most trail drivers, he is not too particular from whom he buys cattle. Tex explains the situation and they strike a deal whereby he will drive the herd to Dodge and take out of the sale what they paid Stewart for the cattle, then give the rest to Melrose. When Clark in Seever's wagon train recognizes Bruce Lockheart, and, thanks to Melrose's intervention, he is convinced he is mistaken, Tex comes up to Bruce and puts an arm around his shoulder, saying, "Close shave.... That man *knew* you." Bruce acknowledges it was a close shave, and straddles a bench and bows his head, overcome by this significant revelation of Serks's knowledge and his loyalty. When Tex and Bruce and the cowboys pursue Henderson into Camp Cooper and find him in the saloon at a card game with his men, Bruce understands that Tex is of the Texas breed of gunfighters, someone to be feared much more in a gunfight than Henderson. He is a useful friend to have nearby. Tex is also well acquainted with the rangers. He explains Melrose's mistrust of Maggard; at some point, he had strung up one of his relatives. Tex is instrumental in getting the rangers to take up the cause of pursuing the rustlers. He leads the attack on Stewart's cabin, where the gang makes its last stand. Tex had guessed the truth of Lee Jones's identity, but he never revealed it. He understands his unwillingness to continue to live under an assumed name.

Serks, Uncle Jed: In *The Fugitive Trail*, Tex tells Bruce Lockheart his Uncle Jed Serks is planning to set up ranching across the Brazos where the Melrose ranch is located. The grass is good, and there is plenty of water, enough for a million steers.

Service: In *The U. P. Trail*, an engineer working at Sherman Pass. He lives alone in a cabin high in the mountain pass. He and Warren Neale discuss the problem drifting snow may pose for the railroad when it is completed. Service likes the loneliness of his cabin but when he slips and falls and breaks an arm and a leg, he freezes to death in the two-day blizzard that keeps Neale and King and Slingerland from getting to him. He is buried in an unmarked grave beside the railroad he helped design.

Setter, Less: In *Forlorn River*, a "big businessman" in Klamath Falls, involved in cattle and land deals with both Hart Blaine and Amos Ide. Dall Blaine refers to him as "Mr. Klamath Falls." Nevada knew him before he came to California, but he does not say much about him and Setter likewise says little about Nevada. Less Setter, however, does brand Ben Ide and Nevada and Modoc as thieves. He knows that wild horse hunters do not get much respect from the ranchers in the area and are easily suspected of rustling to make a living. No one in the area knows anything about Setter. He is a new arrival from the East, a big talker, a big spender. He arranges deals and Hart Blaine puts up the money. He urges Blaine to move in on the small ranchers in Ben Ide's area, and on Ben Ide himself. The land is fertile and there is a year-round supply of water available. He is surprised that Ben Ide has moved to buy out the ranchers. He then provokes a fight with Ben Ide, and spreads a story about Ben Ide attacking him. When

Sneed, Blaine's hired man who had accompanied him to the Ide ranch, protests that Setter is lying, he accuses Sneed of being in cahoots with Ide and the rustlers. Setter arranges to have Modoc arrested on a drunkenness charge from two years earlier. Marvie reveals that Setter is determined to get Ina Blaine. Ina suspects that he has something on her father. It turns out that he holds the mortgages on Blaine's properties and could force foreclosure. When Nevada and Sheriff Strobel return with Bill Hall and the cattle thieves, Setter is identified as the head man in the rustling operation, a profession he had indulged in in Texas and Nevada, before coming to California. Setter is killed in a gunfight with Nevada. The sheriff assures Blaine that all Setter's deals are null and void.

In *Nevada,* some background information is given about him. He is from the Snake River country and is described as a professional swindler who preys on rich, gullible cattlemen. He gets them involved in deals involving speculation, with him doing the planning and them putting up the money. He also has a weakness for women. He tries to get Lize Teller to leave with him. He clashes with Jim Lacy (Nevada) in Lineville before both of them move to California, where Setter attempts to swindle Blaine and Ide, and Jim Lacy is befriended by Ben Ide.

Settlee: In *The Lost Wagon Train*, a rancher who was lynched at Laramie, Wyoming. He had been involved in selling stolen cattle. He was the victim of frontier justice — swift, implacable.

Settlemire: In *The Deer Stalker*, the head of the Houserock Cattle Company which operates in southern Utah and northern Arizona. He is known to get along well with the Mormons and it is suspected that he had influence with someone high in the forest service. His cattle outfit has broken about all of the forest regulations and there is strong mistrust between the rangers and his cowboys. Despite orders to remove his cattle from the parkland, he still has over three thousand cattle running on the west side of the range. Despite the shortage of grass for the deer, he has made no effort to round them up. He has used his influence with officials in Washington to permit the killing of several thousand deer to solve the overpopulation crisis. At the hearings, he succeeds in getting continued grazing rights for local ranchers, if not for big cattle companies, but that is a distinction without a difference. He ridicules the idea of a drive to move deer from one range to another. Thad Eburne regrets that men like Settlemire seem to run the show with Washington bureaucrats.

Seymour: In *The Maverick Queen*, one of the ranchers who joins Lee's vigilance committee to administer secret justice to cowboys who steal mavericks, and on the Maverick Queen, Kit Bandon. He is present the night Lee tries to whip a confession and information out of Bud Harkness.

Shadd: In *The Rainbow Trail*, a half-breed Piute Indian who rides into Shefford's camp the first night he is on the trail, after leaving Prebrey's trading post at Red Lake. Nas Ta Bega and Withers identify him as an outlaw and murderer, head of a gang of outlaws from San Juan country. He was run out of Durango, Colorado, for murder and is said to be well-disposed towards the Mormons. He robs the pack train loaded with hides and wool which Withers and Shefford and Joe Lake are bringing back from the Navajo village. He tried to steal a wad of money from Shefford but couldn't find it. Shadd appears in Stonebridge during the polygamy trials. Mary (Fay Larkin) recognizes him as one of the men with the Mormons who found her with Lassiter and Jane Withersteen in Surprise Valley. He was part of the group attempting to hang Lassiter. He follows Shefford and the party who have gone to rescue Lassiter and Jane from the valley. He is an excellent tracker and horseman, but no match for Nas Ta Bega. He wanders into an ambush. Shefford shoots the horse from under him. The horse falls, knocking Shadd and several other Piutes off a cliff.

Shade: In *Black Mesa*, a driver who makes deliveries to Belmont's post at Bitter Seeps. When he arrives, he gives Belmont two fat envelopes and tells him he has got him reinstated in Utah. Belmont had been involved in selling fraudulent shares in a silver mine. He can now return to Utah if he wants to. Kintell sees Shade in conversation with Crowther, the government farming agent. When Belmont is dead, Shade offers to buy Kintell and Manning's share of Belmont's herd, if Sister does not want it.

Shade, Al: In "Amber's Mirage," a tall, rangy young man of twenty-one. He has a rough, handsome face, keen blue eyes and a square chin covered by a faint silky down. Al works at the sawmill and lives at home with his mother. He appreciates the affection and advice of Jim Crawford, but hesitates to accept his invitation to accompany him prospecting. He knows his sweetheart, Ruby Low, goes with other men, but he trusts her when she says she likes him best. He knows she is shallow, that she likes pretty things and does not want to be poor all her life. He decides to go with Jim Crawford in search of Amber's Mirage in the Sonora desert. He survives the heat better than Jim and when they reach the Three Round Hills, Jim Crawford knows he will never return to Pine. He advises Al to set out immediately, that he must leave at once if he expects to keep his sweetheart. Al will not let Jim die alone and he stays with the old man who has been like a father to him. After Jim dies, he finds a crevice in the mountain in which to bury him. He fills in the crevice with stones, and in the process of finding the stones, he makes a big strike. He has found the gold mountain of the mirage. Two years later, he returns to Pine, well-dressed, dark as an Indian. He deposits his money in the bank. He learns that he was reported lost and dead in the desert. His mother has moved to Colorado and passed away. Ruby is now married to his old friend, Luke Boyce. It takes a while to adjust to the changes, but after a day in his room at the hotel, gazing into the fire in the fireplace, he is reconciled to his fate. He meets Luke Boyce, Ruby's husband. The man is on the verge of becoming a drunkard. He offers to help him get out of debt. He beats up Joe Raston who is still pursuing Ruby, despite her being a married woman. Before he leaves town, he goes to Ruby's home and leaves a bucket of gold at the door, then walks away. He hears the cries of surprise as she realizes what he has left her. Al returns to the Three Round Hills and Jim Crawford's grave, where he also has a vision of Amber's Mirage.

Shade, Mrs.: In "Amber's Mirage," Al's mother. She does not think much of Ruby Low, her son's sweetheart. When Al leaves to go prospecting with Jim Crawford, the two leave her with enough money to cover expenses for the summer, but when Al does not return, Raston forecloses on the mortgage and takes her farm. She moves to Colorado where she passes away without learning her son is still alive.

Shagonie: In *Black Mesa*, tells Taddy that Paul and Wess are looking for Indian cowboys to drive cattle. He also tells Taddy that he knows the cattle that Paul and Wess are buying were rustled from their own herd by Belmont's men.

Shane, Pat: In *The U. P. Trail*, a runt with sandy hair, one of the trio of Irish workers assigned to Neale's crew. He accompanies Neale, Slingerland and King on the buffalo hunt and is killed in the fight with the Sioux as they attack the train. Neale comments that men like Shane have given their all to bring about the vision of a transcontinental railway.

Shanshota: In *Betty Zane*, the chief who planned the ambush in which Crawford and his expedition were annihilated.

Sharpe, Gunsight: In *The Lost Wagon Train*, a cowboy with whom Slim Blue (Corney) used to ride. When Slim Blue heads to San Antonio to marry Estelle, he hires Sharpe and several other former trail buddies to drive a herd of five thousand head to their ranch in Latchfield.

Shaw, Ranger: In *Western Union*, referred to by Bill Peffer's partner when they try to extort money for the telegraph poles out of Cameron's crew. Vance Shaw had put Bill Peffer in jail for cattle stealing in Brownsville, Texas. Peffer had escaped from jail and killed a sheriff in the process.

Shaw, Vance: In *Western Union*, a cowboy from Texas, a dyed-in-the-wool rebel, who teams up with the Harvard man, Wayne Cameron, to work on the construction of the Western Union telegraph line. He is partners with Jack Lowden, from Missouri. They first meet Cameron in the saloon, where Shaw has become sweet on Ruby, one of Pierce's dance hall girls. Shaw is a stunningly good-looking cowboy. He is tall and slim, broad-shouldered, small-hipped, round-limbed, and when he moves, his arm and leg muscles show through his clothes. He wears high-heeled, high-topped boots, practically worn out. He smells of leather, horses and smoke. He is particularly proud of his horse, Range, the best animal on the prairies, he boasts. He invites the Wyoming cowboy, Darnell, to join with their group working on the telegraph line. His kind heart is also seen when he organizes the rescue of Ruby from Red Pierce's gambling den in Gothenburg. He promises to get the first parson they meet to marry them. This escapade requires Shaw to use his guns, and he kills Joe Slade, a gunman friend of Pierce. Shaw disguises Ruby as a young Mexican boy named Pedro. When the Sunderland wagon catches up with Creighton's outfit, Shaw learns from Colonel Sunderland that the escapade which caused him to leave Texas has proven to be fortuitous. What he thought was a crime has turned out to be a good thing for the community. The Stanley that he killed had been living a double life and Shaw was one of the few who knew that he was the head of one of the toughest gangs of thieves along the border. He has been cleared of all charges, thanks to faith in him by his two ranger buddies, Siddell and Harding. They pursued Duke Wells, Stanley's successor, and wiped out the gang. Before Wells died, he cleared Shaw's name. Sunderland also tells Cameron about Shaw's background. He belongs to an old Texas family. His father was robbed and murdered years ago by rustlers. Vance grew into the hardest-riding and hardest-shooting cowboy in Texas. For a while he was in the Texas Rangers, and he rode for Sunderland for three years, killing Sunderland's worst enemy and clearing the Comanches off his range. The colonel has nothing but praise for Shaw. Shaw's experience proves invaluable to the survival of Cameron and his group. Thanks to Vance, they survive the prairie fire, the buffalo stampede, the Indian attack and the crossing of the swollen Laramie River. Vance had been in love with Kit Sunderland, the colonel's daughter. He warns Wayne that she is not very serious, that she likes to flirt with the cowboys who follow her like calves follow their mother. At one point, Cameron sees Vance and Kit talking, and assumes that the old romance has been rekindled. The air is cleared eventually and Shaw assures Cameron there is nothing between them. Shaw organizes the rescue of Ruby a second time after she is abducted from the wagon by Pierce during the Indian raid on Julesburg. In this rescue from the Gold Nugget in South Pass, Shaw kills Pierce, now known to be the outlaw Bill Howard. When the novel ends, Shaw and Ruby are to marry and take up ranching as partners of Cameron in the Sweetwater Valley.

Sheboyahs: In *Blue Feather*, members of the Rock Clan. Their chief is Taneen.

Shefford, John: In *The Rainbow Trail*, a twenty-four-year-old ex-preacher who goes west on a self-imposed mission to rescue Lassiter, Jane Withersteen and Fay Larkin from Surprise Canyon, where they took refuge to escape Mormon pursuers at the end of *Riders of the Purple Sage*. Shefford has heard the story from a member of his congregation in Beaumont, Illinois, from one Venters, who, with his wife Bess, has one of the most prosperous horse-breeding farms in the state. Shefford formed a friendship with the unusual couple and Venters confided in him the story of Jane Withersteen, Fay Larkin and Lassiter. Shefford undertakes to do the job Venters had set himself — to return to free the captives from the hidden canyon in the Utah mountains.

John Shefford had dreamed of becoming an artist, and his reactions to the scenery in the Arizona and Utah deserts are those of a landscape painter. However, his parents had decided he was to be a clergyman and after taking the cloth, he began his work tending his flock in Beaumont. His ideas, however, proved too controversial for his congregation and he was summarily dismissed. John Shefford feels that he is a failure, and in part, on the trip west, he hopes to find himself, to put himself to the test, to discover the real man hidden deep within him that never had been given a chance.

Like John Hare in *The Heritage of the Desert* or Dick Gale in *Desert Gold*, John Shefford returns to the natural world to learn what is truly important in life. He undergoes a transformation in the desert crucible, where the false pretenses of eastern mores are stripped off and the essential man is allowed to emerge. He learns what it means to feel hunger, thirst, cold, and heat; to suffer, to endure, to survive. He adapts to physical labor, to fifty-mile-a-day rides in the desert and mountains. After several months of work in the desert, he emerges hard as iron, cruel and ferocious like a hawk or a wolf, inured to the bitter struggle of everything to survive. He learns to appreciate the simple things in life. Shefford is given to introspection, to self-criticism, driven by fear of failure and fear of appearing foolish. He would like to be able to ride a wild mustang, but to do so he must fight his natural instinctive reluctance to meet obstacles, peril or suffering. He is embarrassed when Nack Yal makes him appear to be an inexperienced, incompetent horseman. He has trouble catching a horse in the morning, and tying the packs onto the packsaddle.

John Shefford transforms his own sense of failure as a preacher to dislike for missionaries and their work, to self-hatred and disgust with the civilized world from which he has sprung. He condemns the work of men like Willetts, unquestionably a poor example of a missionary, but he paints all missionaries with the same brush. Withers, Joe Lake and Nas Ta Bega have to temper his self-righteous condemnations with reminders of the good work that these men have done, of the work they have accomplished bringing better medicine, education, trade and technology to the Indians.

John Shefford imagines himself the hero of a medieval romance. He has come to rescue the damsel in distress, and to free captives from a prison where they have been isolated for over a decade. Shefford could never have accomplished the task without the help of others. But the story ends with Shefford married to Fay Larkin and with Lassiter and Jane Withersteen reunited with their friends, Venters and Bess, and their beloved stallions. Nas Ta Bega sees in him a man with illusions, lacking self knowledge, a wandering spirit that has lost its way. Shefford, in turn, sees in Nas Ta Bega a man who knows himself, who is free of illusions, who is happy with who he is. In the Navajo way of life and religion, he sees a harmony he has never known. For the Navajo, there is a sacramental relationship between the natural world, man, and the deity. The natural world is the source of hope and renewal for man, and man's immortality lies in himself, and in his communion with nature. The desert speaks to the humble listener. The love Nas Ta Bega shows for his fellow man is the true religion. In Joe Lake, the young Mormon who took him under his wing, who helped him learn to handle horses, who offered him advice on how to pursue his inquiries about Fay Larkin, who helped plan and execute her rescue, and in Nas Ta Bega, the man who refused to force his sister to return home from the missionary school, who refused to seek revenge on Willetts, the lascivious missionary who got her pregnant and abandoned her when she died in childbirth, John Shefford sees the best in the human spirit, practitioners of a true religion born of experience, not of preachers and dogma.

Through John Shefford, Zane Grey voices his admiration for the Navajo, for the men of the desert, and his disdain for organized religion and for the mistreatment of the Native American at the hands of the "civilized" world.

Shelley, Mr. and Mrs.:
In *Captives of the Desert*, neighbors of the Newtons in Taho. Mrs. Shelley is from Kansas City but has no desire to reside in any other place. She tells Katharine and Alice Winfield that the desert has become part of her and is necessary to her happiness. She tells them that when the desert gets hold of a person, it never lets go. Katharine and Alice eventually come to feel about the Arizona desert as Mrs. Shelley does. Katharine refers to them as Mr. and Mrs. Bluebeard.

Shepp:
In *To the Last Man*, Gaston Isbel's watchdog. Shepp's father was a timber wolf, a loafer, and his mother a shepherd dog. Shepp shares Jean Isbel's guard duties the first night, growling at the approach of what Jean concludes were some wolves. Shepp runs off with a wolf pack when hostilities break out between the Isbels and the Jorths, but comes back to Jean Isbel when he is tracking Queen and the remnants of the Hash Knife Outfit. Springer comments that Jean Isbel and Shepp could track a grasshopper. After Jean has found Queen's trail, Shepp runs off to join the wolves he hears howling in the woods.

Sheppard, George:
Appears in *The Last Trail*. He is an old friend of Colonel Ebenezer Zane's from back in Williamsburg, Virginia. He has gone west hoping to start over and make a better life for his family. His daughter had been involved with a gam-

bler and scoundrel named Mordaunt. This man was the cause of Mr. Sheppard's losing all his property, and Ft. Henry is a chance to start over. The colonel offers him land to build a cabin and to start farming. No talk of payment is required until he has produced his first crop.

Sheppard, Helen:
In *The Last Trail*, the daughter of George Sheppard. She is a young woman, perhaps in her early twenties, about the age of Betty Zane. Like Betty, she has been a flirt and knows the power of her beauty over men. She is instantly popular among the young men at the fort and the colonel suspects she will be trouble. Her father confesses that he has come west because of her involvement with a certain Mordaunt.

Helen meets her match in Jonathan Zane. She cannot believe that he can resist her charms. At first she feels insulted, diminished, defeated, but eventually decides that he will be a bigger challenge than most and require a longer campaign. She consents to be his helper in ferreting out the horse thieves in the community.

Like Betty, she is stubborn and takes unnecessary risks. She goes for walks in the woods and gets lost, unable to find her way back to the fort, a mere mile or so away. She is abducted by Legget, and gambled over by Case and Legget. She is rescued by Wetzel and Jonathan Zane. At this point, Helen pleads with Jonathan to kill Brandt, who has brought all this on her. Back at the fort, however, when the community has decided that Brandt should be executed, she pleads for his life. The colonel yields to her request, and Brandt is released on condition he never return. Brandt, however, tries to shoot Jonathan, only to be killed by Wetzel. Once again, Helen has misjudged Brandt.

Helen Sheppard, like Betty Zane and Nell Downs, is a typical Zane Grey heroine, and like Betty and Nell, she must learn to accept conditions on the frontier, while hoping to bring civilization. She eventually does "tame" Jonathan, getting him to accept domestic life.

Like Betty, Helen Sheppard is a female character type found repeatedly in Grey novels, the woman who retains the customs and norms of the East, when they are inappropriate on the frontier. Helen's flirting with different men causes ill feeling and dissent, much as Betty's had done at Grandma Wilkins's party in *Betty Zane*. With effort, they eventually do come to accept the norms of the frontier.

Sheppard, William:
Mr. Sheppard's nephew in *The Last Trail*. He is a young man with a frank expression. He accompanies Mr. Sheppard and Helen by wagon train from Ft. Pitt to Ft. Henry. He is beaten and left for dead when Brandt and Legget abduct Helen. He is found by Wetzel and Jonathan and returned to the fort. William and Betty Zane become good friends, going on long walks in the forest, picking flowers and gathering leaves. As the novel ends, there are hints of an imminent wedding.

Sheridan, General Phil: In *The Thundering Herd*, stationed in San Antonio, and reputed to have said that the buffalo-hunters did more in a year to settle the Indian trouble than the entire army did in thirty years. By killing off the buffalo, they kill off the livelihood of the Indians, making their defeat inevitable and opening up the great plains to settlers.

Shevlin, Dale: In *West of the Pecos,* runs an adobe post at Eagle's Nest. When Pecos Smith comes to the post he learns that Shevlin was knifed in the back about a year before and the place has been taken over by one "Frenchy" Conrad Brasee from New Orleans.

Shields, Doctor: In *The Drift Fence*, brought in from Flag to tend to Slinger Dunn's wounds after his shootout with the Haverly brothers. He is a little man, lost in his heavy slicker when he arrives at the cabin. He knows several of the Diamond cowboys. He patches up the six gunshot wounds, and bluntly tells Slinger that he is lucky to be alive. He predicts that Slinger will survive and advises bed rest for several weeks.

Shingiss: In *The Spirit of the Border*, one of the chiefs in the Delaware village when Wetzel is brought in as prisoner. His forehead bears the scar of Wetzel's bullet. In the council meeting to determine the fate of the prisoners, Jim and Joe Downs, Shingiss proposes adopting the brothers into the tribe. He is a moderate, rarely in favor of drastic measures.

Shipman, Texas Joe (Texas Jack): In *The Trail Driver,* worked for Colonel Eb Blanchard for longer than he can remember. Texas has already made two trips to Dodge along the Chisolm trail. He is tall, wide-shouldered, small-hipped, lithe, erect. His boldly cut features are handsome. He has tawny hair, eyes of clear amber, and a lazy, cool smile. He looks to be about twenty-four years old. He accepts the job and brings along his partner, Less Holden, and several other cowboys. Brite thinks he is the kind of man he would have liked for a son. Shipman is given charge of the drive, and Brite lets him handle things his way without interference. He runs a tight ship. There is no drinking, no cards, no gambling in camp. He's not above giving the young cowboys a spanking when they disobey. He is ready to fire Hallet when he returns to camp in the morning after a night in Austin. The infraction turns out to be much more serious than he had first thought, as Chandler reveals that Hallet and Hite had planned to rustle the herd. Texas Joe is aware of all the hazards of the trail. He organizes the attack on the retreating Comanches, who have just attacked wagons of pioneers. He attempts to get the herd back during an electric storm, hoping to scare off Hite's guards. He falls in love with Reddie Bayne, but does his darnedest to hide it from her. She suspects that he really dislikes her, but the problem is that he does not want to look weak before the men. Texas Joe himself is not a bad marksman. He shoots Wallen dead center in the heart, after a quick draw. This causes Reddie to worry that he will take that line and get killed. On Brite's advice, she tries her feminine charm on him in Dodge, where he consents to marry her in San Antonio.

Shivington, Colonel: In *Valley of Wild Horses*, mentioned when Pan Handle and Joe Crawley are riding home after the roundup. They cross the old Indian battlefield where he gave the famous order to his soldiers: "Kill 'em all. Nits make lice!"

Shoie: In *The Vanishing American,* a "half-crazy" Indian. He is twenty years old, with a big head and bushy hair. He is vain, sullen, neither industrious nor intelligent. He tells women they are possessed by evil spirits and that he can put a spell on them. When the superstitious women believe him, he fells terribly powerful. Nolgoshie, wife of Bileanth do de jodie, believes that he has put a spell on her and she broods over it until she dies. This enhances the fear of his magical power among the Navajo and so Shoie is responsible for Gekin Yashi being turned in to the reservation authorities as he threatens to put a curse on the Pahutes who have been hiding her. Shoie does respond to Nophaie's influence, removing the curse from the women and helping him counter the anti–American propaganda being spread by Jay Lord and Blucher. Shoie enlists with Nophaie and serves with him in the war. Shoie applies Navajo hunting techniques in his scouting in the no-man's-land between the American and German troops. He shows great courage and bravery and heroism. He is taken prisoner by the Germans who cut his tongue out and crucify him, nailing his hands and feet to a wall. Shoie manages to work himself free and to get back to the American lines. When Marian sees Shoie after his return from the war, she does not recognize him. He still suffers from shell shock. He looks like one of the devils he claims to possess. His face is lacerated and contorted like a creature possessed by a demon. His clothes hang from him. He cannot speak, his tongue having been cut out. Only unintelligible noise comes from the hollow cavity. Shoie is a symbol of the Navajo whose world is being destroyed and who is destroyed by the new world replacing it.

Shugrue: In *Wildfire*, one of the men who work for Bostril, operating the boat which ferries men, horses, sheep and supplies across the Colorado River. He finds it strange that Bostril orders the boat to be taken out of the river when there are horses to be ferried across for the upcoming races. He wonders what motive might be behind the decision.

Shurd: In *The U. P. Trail*, a surly stage driver who early in the novel kicks Neale's surveying equipment around. This gets him into a fight with Larry King, who shoots him in the arm, breaking it.

Si: In *Valley of Wild Horses*, a horse wrangler and one of two best friends of the twelve-year-old Pan Handle, taking part in his first roundup for pay.

Sibert: In *The Lone Star Ranger*, the young cowboy who breaks up the lynch mob about to hang Buck

Duane. First, he challenges what Abe Strickland has said. Is it believable that an outlaw like Buck Duane would just ride into town, announce who he is and give himself up to an old man? Then, when Duane tells Sibert the same story, he sends for Jeff Aiken to get to the bottom of things. Aiken is mad with grief, but Sibert does manage to get him to listen to reason. When Buck has told his story, Lucy, the only eyewitness is brought out, and she confirms that Duane is not the murderer. He bids Buck Duane farewell with a warm smile of friendship and goodwill.

Sibley, Hiram: In *Western Union*, told the stagecoach driver about Creighton's proposal to string the telegraph wires across the country. Sibley is a friend of Morse, inventor of the code used to transmit messages.

Sickle, Van: In *Wildfire*, a rider working at Bostril's ranch at Bostril's Ford. He is described as a splendid looking young man, tall, lithe, athletic, powerful and an excellent horseman. He is the man to whom Bostril has entrusted the training of Sage King for the upcoming race. Van is the only rider to whom the Sage King will respond. Last year, Van defeated Creech's horses in the races, a feat he expects to repeat. Van is in love with Lucy and is upset that Joel keeps chasing after her. One day, Lucy plays a trick on Joel, taking his clothes when he is swimming, forcing him to walk the ten miles back to town stark naked. When Joel tells the men at Brackton's that he intends to play the same stunt on Lucy, Van gives him a thrashing. Van is riding Sage King in the race when Wildfire forces him off the track. Van describes it as a vicious attack by a mad horse. He feels embarrassed by the defeat. He threatens to tell Lucy the story that Joel has spread, that Lin Slone cut the ropes on the boat to prevent the Creeds from bringing Blue Roan and Peg across the river for the race. Van believes the story that Joel has been spreading. Holley and Farlane convince him to keep quiet.

Sid: In *The Lone Star Ranger,* a rancher whose horse Buck Duane takes and later abandons when he is escaping from the vigilantes. Sid joins the vigilantes and pursues Buck to the cottonwood thicket, where he is trapped. He finds his horse again, abandoned along the trail.

Siddell: In *Western Union*, a Texas Ranger, and friend of Vance Shaw's. Colonel Sunderland reports to Vance that his ranger friends speak very highly of him, that his killing of Stanley proved to be fully justified and he is now regarded as a hero, not an outlaw.

Sidel, John: In *Fighting Caravans,* uncle to Tom Sidel. He joins Couch's caravan at Fort Larned and together with Jim Belmet, negotiates a deal for cattle feed from Judson. He is killed in an Indian attack on the caravan, the same attack in which Jim Belmet is killed.

Sidel, Tom: In *Fighting Caravans,* a devoted admirer and follower of Clint Belmet. As they are about the same age, Tom sees in Clint what he would

like to be. Tom lived in Chicago until a year before, when he moved to live with an uncle in Iowa. The two boys make a pact to help each other. Clint will teach Tom to shoot and hunt and drive a team while Tom will help Clint with his school subjects— reading, writing and arithmetic. The two become fast friends. In the first Indian attack on the caravan, Tom is thrilled with the excitement of combat, much to Clint's chagrin. He really does not understand the danger involved. In a subsequent Comanche attack, Tom Sidel saves Clint's life, shooting a Comanche about to brain Clint with an axe. Tom himself is shot and killed later in the battle. Tom serves as a foil to Clint, a young man with the same enthusiasm for frontier life, but the victim of the vagaries of fate.

Sidway, Lance: In *Majesty's Rancho*, another Gene Stewart or Laramie Nelson, a young man of principle and integrity who puts the good of others above himself. He is a true gentleman, a knight of romance.

Lance Sidway is from Oregon. He grew up on a ranch there, and raising horses was his family's concern. His spectacular horse is his only possession. He is in Hollywood to make money to pay for his sister's operation and medical expenses. His horse, Umpqua, has been used in films, and Lance himself has worked as a stunt man. Hollywood life, however, is not for him. People are shallow, using others openly for the advantage they can find. He decides he is going to ride across the deserts of southern California to Arizona. The horse needs the workout after the easy living in L.A. As well, he looks forward to life in the open. Lance witnesses the altercation between Madge and Officer Brady, who is about to give her a speeding ticket. When the students are stirred to protest and things start to get confused, Lance punches the policeman in the stomach and again in the chin, giving Madge the chance to get the car started and speed off. He is impressed with the way she can handle an automobile. They sit and talk. He tells her of his horse, his sister, his work in Hollywood, and his plans to ride across southern California. They agree to meet in the same parking lot the following day. He debates whether he really wants to see her again, but decides to show up. He arrives early. The valet tells him he can sit in one of the cars while he waits. When Madge arrives, he does not identify himself but rather waits to see what she will do. Uhl comes up in his slick car, and, apparently, the two of them hit it off.

Lance sets off across southern California. He enjoys the ride through the desert. The landscape, the weather, send a thrill through him. He passes through Yuma. In Douglas, he leaves his horse at a Mexican livery stable. He meets Uhl, whom he recognizes from L.A. Uhl, however, does not know who he is. He thinks Lance is one of Latzy Cork's men. Uhl pays him a hundred dollars to drive an empty, canvas-covered truck to Tucson. He is told the truck will be stopped. Lance figures out that the truck is a blind to fool other bootleggers. When he delivers the empty truck, he laughs at having sent the men who stopped him on a wild goose chase to El Paso along a very rough road. This escapade convinces Uhl that Sidway is really a driver for a bootlegging operation.

When he reaches Bolton, in ranching country, Lance meets Ren Starr at the local garage. They take a liking to each other at once. Ren suggests he apply for work at Gene Stewart's ranch. Since he is willing to work for room and board, Stewart will likely take him on. He also writes a letter introducing him to Stewart, a rancher whom he regards as a second father.

Stewart is impressed by the horse, and by the young man, praised in glowing terms in the letter of introduction. He still suspects, however, that Lance is there because of his daughter. To Lance's surprise, the daughter, Madge, is the girl he helped out in Los Angeles. She is convinced he came there to see her, and will believe no denial. As well, she wants to buy his horse. In L.A. she told him it was just as well she would not see the horse because if she liked him, she would want him. This question of Umpqua becomes a permanent bone of contention between the two. He is a better horse than any of her thoroughbreds, and she cannot bear the humiliation of having an employee better mounted than her. Gene is amused at the sparks that fly.

Lance meets all Starr's expectations. He explains that the rustlers plaguing the ranch are not easily traced because they drive cattle to a spot on the road where they can be loaded onto trucks. Stewart and Nels appreciate the fresh thinking he can bring to their operation. Lance saves Gene's life when they ambush the rustlers, shooting Bill, who was drawing a gun on Gene. Lance also puts Stewart's accounts in order, revealing that the situation is not as dismal as thought. He also sees that Gene and Madeline have been sacrificing their ranch for their daughter. Gene swears him to secrecy on this matter. Lance learns from Bonita that the rustlers are planning another raid for the night of Madge's fiesta. He does not tell Gene immediately so that the festivities will not be spoiled. The following morning, he organizes the search for the rustlers. When he becomes aware that Uhl has kidnapped Madge, he quickly forms a plan to lead the gangsters into the mountains, where their inexperience with life in the open will quickly turn to his advantage. Since they think he is a driver for Latzy Cork, they think he is one of them. Lance continues with the pretense and rescues Madge, returning her to her home. She is convinced until the reach the ranch, that Lance was taking her to Mexico or out of state to demand the ransom himself.

The relationship between Lance and Madge is similar to the dueling between the Virginian and Molly in Wister's *The Virginian* or between Lassiter and Jane in *Riders of the Purple Sage*. Lance fell in love with Madge from the first moment he laid eyes on her in L.A. But Madge, headstrong, arrogant, proud, stubborn, insists on being worshiped, as her name Majesty suggests. She must be the center of attention. She calls him a liar when he says he came to the ranch for a job, not to see her. She is angered when he refuses to sell her his horse. She will not take his advice when he tells her she should not ride Dervish, since she has not ridden in several years and the horse can be quite a handful for an inexperienced rider. Lance finds himself rescuing her constantly. He saves her from the runaway horse. He rescues her from the hayfork at the roof of the barn. He carries her home when she sprains her foot, jumping from the moving car. He rescues her when the drunken Rollie Stevens tries to force himself on her. He always seems to be around when she needs rescuing and this infuriates her. As Madge says to Allie, her best friend, "Isn't it conceivable that I should finally fall foul of a real man who sees through me — who has my number — whom I can't fool or intrigue or fascinate or seduce — who has fine ideals and who consequently despises me?" Lance thinks Madge is a spoiled brat, selfish, arrogant, treating others as her subjects. He tells her that her extravagance has ruined her father. He has had to sell half his herd to pay her debts and during her extravagant party, the last of the cattle have been rustled.

Lance has spoken to Gene, to Ren Starr, and to Nels about his feelings for Madge. He cannot forget, however, that she was willing to believe he was a gangster, and that he originally came to the ranch on false pretenses. Nels goes to Madge and give here a bit of fatherly advice, telling her she has been unfair to Lance and that she has hurt him deeply. Lance has decided to leave after Bonita and Ren are married. He tells Gene he loves Madge so much he cannot hang around with things they way they have been. Gene tells him frankly he wants him for a son, and wonders why he hasn't asked Madge to marry him. When Madge finally does come around, he still thinks she's acting, planning yet again to make a fool of him. Madge does acknowledge how she truly feels and, like her mother Madeline, puts aside her pride before it is too late.

Lance Sidway is a young hero, constructed along the lines of Cal Thurman in *Code of the West* or young Jim Traft in *The Hash Knife Outfit*. He is a young man with a clear sense of who he is, what he believes in, what he wants. He is generous, reliable, responsible, putting the good of others ahead of himself. He is truly a knight of romance.

Siebert, Hawk: In *The Dude Ranger*, the foreman of the cowboys on the Red Rock Ranch. He needs riders but has a hard time keeping his outfit up because of the manager, Hepford, and his minion, Dude Hyslip. When Ernest arrives at the ranch, Hepford is grateful for his helping Anne, and sends him to Hawk Siebert to discuss employment. Ernest is impressed with Siebert at first sight, noting the similarity between his features and his first name. Hawk Siebert agrees to take him on if he will do jobs like digging fence posts, stretching barbed wire, pitching hay, jobs most cowboys don't want to do.

Ernest was not aware of it, but Hawk had been testing him, and by the day of the dance, he has taken his measure. Hawk is impressed with the way Ernest has put up with the meanness of the cowboys and his working without complaint. He promotes him to a range rider. The day following the dance, Ernest tells him about the fight with Hyslip and Siebert tells Ernest that Dude doesn't know who hit him. He advises him not to tell anyone else about it and the fuss should blow over. He also advises Ernest that he should not dismiss Anne completely. She is a spoiled brat, but deep down, she is a good person. He suggests Ernest approach her from a new angle, for example, proposing marriage. All the other cowboys have treated her as a superficial flirt because that's the way she presents herself. Maybe a more serious approach would change her. She was just a tyke when he first came to the ranch, and he watched her grow up into a young lady. She is one reason he stayed on at the ranch, and he has not lost his affection for, nor faith in, her.

Siebert also expresses doubts about the honesty of Hepford's cattle deals. Like Nebraskie, he tells Ernest that the deal seems designed to ensure no one can provide exact details about the transaction. He gets into Hepford's bad graces when he comments that the Wilkins cattle deal was a big mistake. He expects to get fired soon, but promises to take Nebraskie and Ernest with him. When Ernie defends himself with the cowboys who are spreading the story that he beat up Hyslip at the dance when he was drunk on the floor, Siebert fires Steve Monell, who threatens that he'll soon be fired himself. Indeed, Hyslip replaces Hawk as foreman and he is sent packing, but not before he tells Hepford that he has a good idea about his shady deals with Anderson. He tells him he can keep what wages are owed him to spend on a real ledger in which to keep cattle accounts. While they are in the bunkhouse packing to leave, Ernest reveals to Siebert he is Ernest Howard Selby, the new owner of the ranch. He asks him not to reveal this to Nebraskie or anyone else. Siebert accompanies Selby and Nebraskie to Brooks's ranch where they work for room and board. Siebert is wounded in the fight to defend the Brooks from Hyslip. He and Sam Brooks tell the sheriff that Ernest was not involved in the fight as Hepford had claimed. When he takes possession of the ranch, Ernest rehires Hawk as foreman of Red Rock.

Siena: In *The Great Slave*, a young Crow Indian, convinced he has been chosen by the gods to perform a special service for the Crow people. One day, he meets some palefaces going downriver in a canoe. Siena has heard about these white men but he has never met one in the flesh. The men ask for food, and Siena shares his fish with them. The paleface leader offers him a shooting stick in thanks for his help. He shows Siena how to load the gun and how to shoot. He also provides him with a supply of lead balls and powder and flint. With the new weapon, Siena becomes a great hunter, saving his people from star-

vation. When the Cree attack the Crow and take them prisoner, Siena is tied up in the middle of the village, where the passersby spit on him. Baroma takes possession of the thunder stick but as he does not understand its use, the gun remains in his lodge above the head of a moose. Baroma's daughter, Emihiyah, takes pity on him, bringing him water and food. Siena attempts to court her, despite Baroma's disapproval and the attempt on his life by Tillimanqua. When the Cree are threatened with starvation, Siena and his Crows seem to fare better than their captors. Emihiyah brings Siena food at night, keeping his strength up. Finally, Baroma yields, and asks Siena to save his people with his shooting stick. Siena goes hunting, bringing down five moose, providing meat to save the starving village. Baroma offers him his freedom, but he refuses to leave without his people. Seven nights, Siena sits in the dark, watching the northern sky, where he sees the message of his future greatness from the gods. He goes to Baroma's lodge, takes the shooting stick and outside, fires it off, proclaiming that he has killed Baroma. The Cree believe his story, and allow Siena and the Crow slaves to leave. They trek north, followed by Emihiyah. Siena takes his bride with him and establishes a new home for his tribe on the shores of the Great Slave Lake.

Silver: In *Wildfire*, one of two Navajo chiefs who enter horses in the annual race at Bostril's Ford.

Silverman, Hank: In *The Fugitive Trail*, reputed to be a real Texan and an old trail boss and scout. Bruce Lockheart catches his wagon train as he is riding west. He tells Silverman he was Luke Loveless's right hand for three years. Silverman accepts this as a strong recommendation. He heard that Loveless had made a big bet on one of his boys. Bruce travels with them on the way to the Santa Fe Trail where Silverman will be delivering the wagons to another boss. The men come to accept Bruce and he feels at home in their company. Shortly before the end of the trail, Silverman tells Bruce that he heard Tom Galliard, Loveless's worst enemy, tell a ranger he had recognized Bruce Lockheart. Hank has already figured out that his man is Bruce Lockheart. Silverman and two of his men, Higgins and Davis, are heading to the Tonto Basin in Arizona where he has two brothers. He invites Bruce to look him up there. If he gets out of Texas, the rangers can't follow.

Silvermane: In *The Heritage of the Desert*, the mustang stallion that is captured, tamed and given to Jack Hare as his principal steed. Silvermane, together with Old White Foot, leads the herd of wild mustangs that lure away the horses from the ranches. For years, the Naabs have been pursuing Silvermane but have failed to catch him. When Jack is on the plateau helping Mescal herd the sheep, Silvermane appears. Following Naab's instructions, Jack closes off the outlets from the plateau, effectively trapping Silvermane. August Naab and his sons arrive to help

Jack, but first they send for the Navajo horse trainer, and in a matter of days, the wild stallion has been broken to the saddle without any violence or dampening of the animal's spirit. August Naab then gives the horse to Jack.

Jack and Silvermane become as close as brothers. Jack takes great pride in riding this spectacular animal. Snood looks at him with envy, as he once had tried to capture the stallion. When learning the cowboy trade, roping and herding cattle, Silvermane catches on much faster than Jack. When Jack sets off into the desert to find Mescal, he comes to trust his horse as he has never trusted another man. He feels the love this animal has for him and the debt of gratitude he has to Silvermane for leading him through the desert. Like the Navajo, Jack learns to trust the animal's instincts. Silvermane (and Mescal's dog, Wolf) finds water in the desert and the oasis where Mescal has been living for the past year. When Jack and Mescal return to "civilization," Silvermane's great speed saves them from capture by Holderness and Dene.

Zane Grey loved horses. Every novel has its equine hero who serves his master and proves unequaled in a race. Silvermane is the first of these stallion heroes in Grey's novels. These animals are presented as fully and as lovingly as any human character.

Silvertip: In *The Spirit of the Border*, a Shawnee chief, first seen trading furs at Ft. Pitt. He is reputed to be sly, vengeful, humorless and grim, and a bosom buddy of Jim Girty. At Ft. Pitt he is found lying drunk outside the fur trader's post. Joe plays a trick on him, switching his shirt with that of a drunken frontiersman. Silvertip vows he will get revenge for the "squaw play." He devises a scheme to stop the raft Joe and Jim are on going downriver. In the wilds, Silvertip is truly a chief, a remarkable specimen of physical strength and courage. Joe develops a grudging admiration for his physical prowess and skills. Silvertip is with Jim Girty when he abducts Kate and Nell Wells and Jim Downs from the Village of Peace. In the Village of Peace, he is seen riding Joe's horse, Lance, at the opening of the three-day religious festival. In the Delaware village, he is a looked upon with suspicion by the Lenni Lenape (Delaware) chiefs, and when Isaac Zane advises Joe to confront Silvertip over ownership of the black horse Lance, Silvertip backs down. Silvertip, however, attempts to get his revenge on Joe when Joe tries to free Kate. Silvertip surprises him and the two engage in a furious fight in which Silvertip is killed and Jim mortally wounded.

Grey uses Silvertip as an example of a Cooperesque ignoble savage, an Indian who sacrifices the good of his tribe for his own petty and selfish interests, who has allowed himself to be corrupted by white man's liquor and white men like Jim Girty.

Simmons: (1) In *The Fugitive Trail*, shoots the hat off one of the bank robbers, loosening the mask over his face. He recognizes the man as one of the Lockheart brothers, but he is not sure which. See **Sims, Mr.**

(2) In *The Lost Wagon Train*, works at Latch's ranch at Latch's Field. He is in charge of Mexican vaqueros. When all hell breaks loose after Estelle's party, Simmons witnesses Leighton's attempt to force Keetch to name who else knew about the papers he had to blackmail Latch. He comes to Keetch, who has been shot several times by Leighton. Keetch sends him to find Latch with the message that he has something important to tell Latch. He dies before Latch returns. Latch sends Simmons to fetch his daughter Estelle back from the caravan with whom she has been riding to accompany her friends part of the way back to New Orleans. He is killed by Jacobs and Manley, who have been sent by Leighton to abduct the girl. Slim Blue comes upon the body and the horse.

Simms: In *Stranger from the Tonto*, Roberts's right-hand man, whom he consults before making any decisions. Simms is shot by Kent Wingfield in the fight between Bonesteel's Hole-in-the-Wall Gang and Roberts's outlaws.

Simpson: (1) In *The Arizona Clan*, Tommy tells Dodge Mercer that Simpson's ranch is across the valley from the Lilleys but he's not poor like them. Nevertheless, he has never hired a rider in ten years. Copelace introduces Simpson to Dodge Mercer after the shootout with Buck Hathaway and Twitchell. He tells Dodge he has heard about him from Josh Turner, an Abilene cattleman. He congratulates him on behalf of other solid cattlemen from the area. They would like a few more riders like Mercer around.

(2) In *Fighting Caravans*, the train boss of the caravan which brings May Bell and the Clementses to Taos, New Mexico.

(3) In *The Maverick Queen*, works for Kit Bandon on her ranch. After the lynching, Lincoln Bradway breaks the news of her death to him first.

Simpson, Peg: In *The Fugitive Trail*, part of Tex Serks's outfit. He comes to work for Melrose with Tex, Jim, Juan and Lee Jones (Bruce Lockheart). He shares a room in the bunkhouse with Lee Jones. Simpson is the cook of the outfit.

Simpson, Bill: In *The Lost Wagon Train*, a driver for Latch of Latch's Field. He is driving Latch's daughter and two of her friends to join up with Bridgeman's caravan. Bill Simpson, it turns out, is quite a good cook. Estelle jokingly says she will marry any man who can cook as well as he can.

Simpson, Wade: In *Sunset Pass*, tells Gage Preston that the "Señor del Toro" who put out Ash Preston's lights at the masquerade ball was really Trueman Rock.

Sims: In *Forlorn River*, a homesteader at Forlorn River together with Moore and Nagel. With the drought, he is anxious to sell, and both Hart Blaine and Ben Ide are anxious to buy him out. Ben Ide is the first to approach him with an offer. He pays him over his asking price with horses from his catch of wild mustangs. He gives them thirty horses to sell; they can divide the profits among themselves as they see fit. Sims tells Ben he is going into wheat farming in the Big Ben country in Washington state. He also advises Ben to be wary of his dealings with the big land buyers. He confesses to having helped the horse thieving outfit out of desperation to survive and he reveals his suspicions about the link between the thieves and the land speculators.

Sims, Mr.: In *The Fugitive Trail*, the cashier in the bank in Denison that Belton and his outfit hold up. Sims began to shoot and a bullet knocked the hat off one bandit's head and loosened his mask, exposing his face. Sims recognized one of the Lockheart boys but he could not say which.

Simmons (see Sims, Mr.): in the novel, the same action is attributed to Simmons and Mr. Sims.

Sinclair, Young (a.k.a. the Saint Louis Gazabo): In *The Dude Ranger*, a young beau from Saint Louis who comes to escort Anne Hepford to the dance in Springer. Anne asked Ernest Selby to accompany her when she thought Sinclair was not coming, but when he does show up, she unceremoniously dumps Ernest.

Singleton: In *The Border Legion*, one of the outlaws in Beard's saloon. He is one of the men betrayed to the vigilantes by Red Pearce. He is tried before a hooded court and lynched that same evening. He dies without betraying any other members of the group.

Singleton, Captain: In *The Thundering Herd*, the cavalry officer who comes to the buffalo hunting fields to tell the hiders to send their women back to the post where they can be protected. The captain is accompanied by Ellsworth, a frontiersman scout. Tom Doan asks Captain Singleton to help Milly, who is at Jett's camp. The captain already knows about Jett's reputation and promises to keep an eye out for her.

Sisk, Henry: In *Twin Sombreros*, Janis Neece's beau. Jack Sain comments that he is very popular with the women. Brazos is at times tempted to think than Janis is stringing him along, but June informs him that Janis and Henry eloped and returned home married.

Sister: In *Black Mesa*, appears to be cook, housekeeper, and saleswoman for Belmont at his trading post at Bitter Seeps. She is a large woman, under forty, dark-eyed, hard-featured, a silent, watchful, repressed person of strong passion. She speaks Navajo and deals with the Indian customers at the post. The mystery of Sister's relationship to Belmont unravels slowly. Louise tells Paul and Wess she was at Belmont's ranch when Sister was brought there. Sister treated her badly, beat her until Belmont caught her at it and made her stop. One night, Wess observes Belmont going to Sister's room and spending the night there. He concludes that she must be

his wife, too, that Belmont is a polygamist Mormon. The dying Calkins tells Paul and Wess that in Lund, it was rumored Sister was Belmont's wife, that she has some hold on him. Later, this hold is revealed. She put up the money for Belmont to buy Bitter Seeps and take over the Reed Brothers trading post. Paul tries to get into her good graces, telling her that Belmont is planning to get rid of her. He feels sorry for this woman, and thinks that maybe this sympathy will lead to some revelation. Sister's jealousy of the younger wife erupts when she tells Belmont that Louise lets Paul into her cabin at night. Louise reveals that Sister provided Belmont with the money to buy cattle and the trading post, that he denied he was married to Sister, that their relationship was purely a business relationship. Before the ultimate crisis, Belmont told Louise that he would kill Paul and the baby if she did not run off with him. He admitted he was married to Sister, and that he had destroyed the marriage certificate, and, since the courthouse where they were married burned down with all the records, there was no proof left. When Shade brings word that Belmont is dead, Sister is genuinely upset. It seems she will buy out Paul and Wess's share of the cattle business when they plan to set up a ranch elsewhere. Louise asks them to make sure Sister gets to keep the trading post. She has already suffered enough because of Belmont.

In Sister, Grey explores once again the question of polygamy, the jealousy, the deceit, the betrayal, the exploitation of women that the institution entails. The wives of the polygamous husband are strangely silent, thereby allowing the practice to continue.

Skylark: In *Knights of the Range*, a young cowboy working for the Ripple outfit, one of the "Knights of the Range." Skylark reports that he has seen Lascelles cheat at cards, playing with the cowboys. He is engaged to Anne Doane—one of her many suitors. She tells Holly he has some annoying habits that she will cure him of when they marry. When her father is killed and she is destitute, Skylark insists they marry immediately. Holly arranges for the padre from the village to perform the ceremony in the Ripple ranch house, followed by a fiesta. Holly looks at Anne and Skylark with some envy and regret. As Skylark put it, with the situation as it is with rustlers, he could be shot at any time and he and Anne "might as well have each other while we can."

Slack: In *Riders of the Purple Sage*, one of the three men who abduct Milly Erne from her home in Texas and bring her to Utah. Lassiter catches up with him in central Utah some years later, but he dies without revealing the whereabouts of Milly or the name of the man who ordered her abduction.

Slack, Hod: In *Wild Horse Mesa*, an outlaw working with Bent Manerube. He is described as a man with no force of character. He participates in both attempts to steal Weymer's horses. In the second encounter, he is shot and killed by Toddy Nokin's sons.

Slade: (1) In *The Fugitive Trail*, one of the teamsters who drives Trinity Spencer on the last leg of her trip to the Melrose ranch.

(2) Mentioned in *The Heritage of the Desert* as an outlaw, fatal on the draw, who had oppressed Mormons up in Utah. He was driven out of the state. August Naab predicts that Dene will meet the same fate as Slade.

Slade, Frank: In *The Light of Western Stars*, one of the cowboys who claims to need special lessons in bread-making in order to be with Madeline Hammond in the kitchen. He is also a rival of Ambrose Mills for Christine's attention. He participates in the golf game organized to entertain the eastern visitors.

Slade, Joe: In *Western Union*, not much of a gunman by Texas standards, but a killer nonetheless. He has a dozen men to his credit or discredit. He appears pleasant enough on occasion but when he has a grudge against someone, he's bad medicine. Liligh points him out to Vance Shaw in Red Pierce's saloon in Gotenburg, where he is in the company of one Black Thornton. Ruby introduces him to Vance and Cameron, and his manner is pleasant. Joe Slade is in charge of the herd of cattle Pierce is bringing from Texas to Wyoming, following along behind the wagon train with Creighton's construction crew. Shaw and Cameron learn later that Slade got drunk and killed one of his riders for no apparent reason. When the men come to rescue Ruby, Vance Shaw and Joe Slade have a shootout in which Slade is killed.

Slagle, Jem: In *Sunset Pass*, a rancher in Sunset Pass. Trueman Rock had worked for him years before and en route to Sunset Pass to seek work with Preston, he stops off to visit with him. Rock is surprised that Slagle is in such dire straits. Slagle tells Rock that he will be leaving for Missouri before winter. His new wife has inherited some money and they will be moving there. He gives him the rundown on what has happened over the past six years. When Gage Preston moved into Sunset Pass, there was some dispute over the boundaries of their ranches, but it turns out Slagle had overestimated the extent of his claim. Nevertheless, he does not blame Preston for his bad luck. He tells Rock that two years of drought, sheep, a bad deal with Dabb which didn't pan out and just plain bad luck are the cause. He had sold cattle and put the money in a bank which failed. At one point, there was a problem with the Prestons. Ash Preston would not allow his cattle to graze in the pass, but when he addressed the problem to Gage himself, Ash was reined in. When Trueman runs into him in Wagontongue at the Fourth of July Rodeo, he is drunk and talking about the crookedness of the Preston slaughterhouse business. He discovers the suspicious hides with the Half Moon brand hidden in the culvert. He has spoken of this to Dabb, as Trueman Rock learns. When the deal is arranged with Lincoln and Dabb, Trueman buys his silence for twenty-five hundred dollars.

Slater: In *To the Last Man*, a member of the Jorth faction and the Hash Knife gang of cattle rustlers. He is at Greaves store when the Isbels attack and he later appears at Jorth's ranch in the mountains as they prepare to flee from the pursuing Isbels. He is killed in the fighting which follows.

Slats: In *Valley of Wild Horses*, one of the two cowboys with "Pug" Moore who spend a winter boarding with the Smiths. He is quite a singer and teachers Pan Handle all the cowboy songs around the campfire in the evening.

Slatten, Bud: In *Shadow on the Trail*, a good friend of Jesse Evans. He used to ride with Billy the Kid and Jesse. He puts Billy up for the night and tells him the news about Mahaffey being at Chisum's place asking questions about Blanco. Billy then relays the information to Jesse and Blanco (Wade Holden).

Slaughter, Abe: In *West of the Pecos*, one of the Slaughter brothers who hire on with Pecos Smith He is a typical Texan, born on the range, a stalwart six-footer, like enough to his brother to be a twin.

Slaughter, Dave: In *The Trail Driver*, a cattleman for whom Less Holden has ridden for over three years. After Brite's herd has left San Antonio, Slaughter himself sends a big herd north in charge of Horton. This herd is the second in line after Brite.

Slaughter, John: In *West of the Pecos*, one of the Slaughter brothers who hire on with Pecos Smith He is a typical Texan, born on the range, a stalwart six-footer, like enough to his brother to be a twin.

Slaughter, Luke: In *The Fugitive Trail*, Steve Melrose's foreman. He is a Texan, a wiry, rangy man, past middle age, with the eyes of a hawk. Slaughter looks over Tex Serks and his brother Jim, Peg Simpson and the other men who have come looking for work as riders. But Luke Slaughter's scrutiny concentrates mostly on Lee Jones (Bruce Lockheart). He questions him about his Texas connections, whether he is one of the Big Bend Joneses, the good or the bad family. Lockheart confesses he is from the bad side, but that one cannot help how one is born. Slaughter comments on his bay horse, Legs, and Bruce assures him he was not stolen and he can sure run. Luke Slaughter offers him a job and Bruce says he can do anything, cook, wash dishes, chop wood, dig postholes. Slaughter takes him on, adding that Bruce interests him. He is no ordinary cowboy, and speaking as a Texan who has seen the range, he has not missed that he is a gunman. The job may require his gun skills, and Bruce puts them at Melrose's service. When Melrose undertakes the job of pursuing the rustlers who have taken his Little Wichita herd, he places Luke Slaughter in charge of the men and gives him carte blanche to do what is necessary.

Slaughter, Russ: In *Knights of the Range*, the effective leader of the rustlers on the range. He worked as a foreman for Jesse Chisum, where he learned the art of the cattleman. He also left Chisum with a taste for appropriating other men's cattle. Ride'-Em Jackson rode for him on Chisum's spread. When Slaughter meets him and Blue, he invites them to join him and his outfit with the promise of a hundred dollars a month in wages. Slaughter recruits the cardsharp Lascelles into his rustler outfit. And, as Frayne points out, he uses the fiesta at the Ripple ranch to scout out possibilities for rustling. Like his boss, Sewall McCoy, he proposes marriage to Holly, accompanying the proposal with a threat of an alliance with McCoy which would work against the interests of her ranch. Slaughter and his cowboys hope to humiliate the Ripple outfit at the local rodeo. Brazos and the boys know they have an unmatched bronc buster in Ride'-Em Jackson. The first riders give a good show, but deliberately lose to encourage betting before they play their trump card, Jackson. Slaughter does not appreciate losing large amounts of money in the betting when the Ripple crew trounces his boys. Slaughter lures two of the "Knights of the Range" from their noble purpose with the promise of money. Eventually, Brazos and Jackson and his men corner Slaughter and his rustlers. Slaughter is shot and hanged. His body is brought back to the Ripple ranch, just as Frayne returns from his fight with Rankin. Slaughter had been a very meticulous bookkeeper, recording all his transactions, possibly as security against betrayal by fellow rustlers. His books record the transactions with McCoy and Clements, among others. His records provide the strongest evidence against the respectable ranchers who have been running the rustling operation against their fellow cattlemen.

Sleepy: In *Shadow on the Trail*, one of the riders working under Jesse Evans in Chisum's outfit number ten.

Slick: In *Valley of Wild Horses*, a horse wrangler on the first roundup on which the twelve-year-old Pan Handle Smith works for pay. He and Si are Pan's two best friends.

Slim: In "Canyon Walls," with Cuppy, Monty's partners. When he attends a dance in Green Valley, he wanders what these two partners are now doing. They had "torn through the corral" at many dances together. When Sheriff Jim Sneed meets up with Monty in Green Valley some two years after he has settled in with the Keetches, he learns that Slim and Cuppy were involved in a caper in which Slim was killed covering Cuppy's escape.

Slim Blue: (1) In *Arizona Ames*, a lithe, slim young cowboy working on Crow Grieve's ranch. He cuts a striking figure of strength and competence. He got his handle from the fact he always dresses in blue jeans and a blue shirt. He is a close friend of Blab McKinney. He tests out Arizona Ames's vaunted skill with a gun by asking him to repeat his trick shooting holes in a hat thrown into the air. His hat ends up with three holes in it. Slim Blue quits the

ranch with Blab McKinney when Arizona Ames confronts Grieve.

(2) In *The Lost Wagon Train*, the trail name given to Corny (Cornie), Lester Cornwall's brother. See **Corny.**

Slinger, Jeff: In *West of the Pecos*, an old friend of Pecos Smith's who vouches for his good name to Captain McKinney. He tells the cavalry Texas Ranger officer that the accusations of murder against Pecos Smith in Sawtell's letter are false. Slinger has been in the force for some ten years. Jeff Slinger recommends a team of vaqueros to Pecos Smith to drive cattle west of the Pecos to the Lambeth ranch.

Slingerland, Ab: In *The U. P. Trail*, a mountain man and trapper, developed in the model of Lew Wetzel in *The Spirit of the Border*. He is a "natural" man who prefers life in the wilderness, living in harmony with the natural world and the Indians. He comes to warn the wagon train guided by Bill Horn that a party of Sioux Indians has been following them. He offers to go to the railroad construction camp to get soldiers to help, and in the meantime, offers to take young Allie Lee with him. She refuses to leave, preferring to face whatever fate has in store with her mother. By the time Slingerland returns with the soldiers and men from the construction camp, the Sioux have massacred the whole party except Allie Lee, who crawled off into the brush under a cliff where she remained undetected by the warriors. Fearing she might not survive a ride back to camp, Slingerland offers to take her to his cabin. There, Warren Neale and Larry Red(die) King nurse her back to health. During the months of recuperation, she falls in love with young Neale, and when he goes off working on the railroad, she remains with Slingerland. For a whole year, he doesn't let her out of his sight, but the one day when he is out checking his trapline, four thugs rob Slingerland's cabin and abduct Allie. Slingerland follows their trail for two days but a heavy rainstorm wipes out whatever trail was left. Slingerland gives up the chase, assuming that with men like that, she could not have survived more than a few days. He decides to retreat farther into the more inaccessible wilderness. In the fate of Neale and Allie, he sees the result of civilization marching westward. For him, civilization is a destructive force. He has lived for many years in harmony with the Indians. The greed of the men overseeing the construction of the railroad destroys the peace and tranquility he has known, and risks turning the Indians against him. Slingerland next appears in Benton, where he runs into Neale and Larry King. He has signed on as a buffalo hunter, shooting buffalo to feed the workers on the construction line. He and Neale and King and several other men are involved in a dramatic buffalo hunt which ends in a battle with the Sioux Indians. At this point, Slingerland leaves for the mountains, inviting Neale to join him to enjoy true peace and quiet. He disappears for some time, to appear later in Benton when Neale has been given the letter from Beauty Stanton informing him that Allie Lee is still alive. In Benton, Slingerland is with Neale when they meet Durade, who is in pursuit of Allie Lee. Allie has been wrested from his power by the gamblers Hough and Ancliffe, and Durade is on her trail. Slingerland kills Durade with his hunting knife. Like Wetzel in *Betty Zane*, who brings Betty and Alfred Clarke together, Slingerland goes to visit Allie in Omaha, where she is staying with Colonel Dillon's wife. He brings her the gold Bill Horn had buried at the site of the massacre, with regards from Neale. He witnesses their wedding at last, and then retreats from civilization into the more remote parts of the mountains.

Slingerland is an example of the "natural" man which Grey develops as a Cooper-like Natty Bumpo figure. He is a man formed by communion with nature, a man living in harmony with the natural world and the Indians. He is a simple man who accepts things as they but who still understands the motives of more "sophisticated" easterners. He is willing to sacrifice himself to help complete strangers, making their plight his own. Like Wetzel, he is a type only the frontier could produce.

Sloan: In *Shadow on the Trail*, runs a general merchandise store in Holbrook.

Sloan, Dick: In *Thunder Mountain*, a fair-haired, frank-faced young man of twenty-two, recently arrived in Thunder City. He makes friends with Kalispel, whom he asks for help to get his girlfriend Ruth Nuggett away from Cliff Borden and the Spread Eagle. He proposes marriage to her, offering to vacate his cabin so she can live there until marriage arrangements are made. When his claim plays out, he acquires another one, at some distance from his cabin. While working at this claim, he is stabbed by robbers. He dies of his wounds some days later, and he is buried on his first claim by his neighbor and partner, Barnes.

Sloan, Tom: In *Majesty's Rancho*, a young cowboy riding for Spencer, a neighbor of Gene Stewart. Lance Sidway meets him near Bolton when he is following the herd that was rustled during Majesty's party. Tom says he has seen the rustlers and the herd over the ridge in the valley, about half way down. He agrees to help Lance pursue them in the morning. They set up camp for the night and Lance goes into town for some extra food. When Lance returns, the gangsters are with him and offer Sloan a thousand dollars for his horses and outfit. Sloan is amazed to see Uhl peel ten one-hundred-dollar bills off a wad. Under the guns of Fox and Flemm, they saddle the outfit. Sloan later reports this to Stewart, adding that he did not realize that they were kidnappers until after they rode off. Sloan was assigned the task of reporting that they want fifty thousand dollars in ransom. If they do not get it, Madge will be raped or murdered or both. Tom Sloan could not deliver the message earlier as the phone lines to the ranch had been cut. He waited in town, knowing Stewart would be coming in pursuit of the stolen herd.

Sloane, Rebel Ben: In *Knights of the Range*, a member of Britt's outfit at the Ripple ranch, valued for his ability at tracking and following a trail. He has been assigned the task of following Talman and Trinidad to spy on them. These two cowboys are suspected of disloyalty. He reports to the cowboys in the bunkhouse that Talman is responsible for the loss of some three thousand head of cattle from the Ripple ranch. Talman watches from a hill with binoculars warning the teams or four or five cowboys who rustle several hundred head at a time. Sloane heads the contingent of cowboys which captures and hangs the rustlers at night, netting Trinidad, Talman, and surprisingly, the cardsharp Lascelles.

Sloane, Tully: In *Wyoming*, one of the four cowboys in the team that Bligh hires for his ranch when he and Andy set up ranching on a bigger scale. Tully Sloane is the tallest of the four, almost bald. His head shines like a polished nut. His face is thin and weathered, like Cordovan leather. He has clear gray eyes that twinkle.

Slocum, Jeff: In *The Maverick Queen*, drives the stagecoach from South Pass to Rock Springs. He is the kind of westerner that Lincoln regards as the salt of the earth. Raw-boned, rugged of build, with a leathery visage and eyes like slits of gray fire, he showed his years of hard contacts with the frontier. He was born in Westfork before they called it Kansas City. He has never been a cowboy but has been almost everything else associated with the West-scout, soldier, pony-express rider, teamster. He tells Lincoln he reminds him of his old partner from Injun days. Slocum had reported to one of Hargrove's riders that he saw Hank Miller in Rock Springs. He remains thoughtful when Lincoln explains that he suspects Miller of having transported his dead friend to Emery's saloon in South Pass. Slocum tells Lincoln something he never mentioned to anyone else, that Hank Miller had told him to give Kit Bandon a message, that she had better meet him in Rock Springs as they had agreed. It's a message he was not able to deliver, as Kit had already left her ranch. Like Lincoln, Slocum does not feel inclined or obliged to knuckle under to Kit Bandon.

Slocum, Smoky: In *Robbers' Roost*, a member of Hank Hays's outlaw gang that rustles the Herrick cattle and robs them blind. He is a slight, wiry, freckled of face and hands, with cold blue eyes. Slocum is a gunman who mistrusts Jim Wall. He is a realist. Hays speaks of harmony among the men in the outfit, but Slocum points out that harmony among a bunch of grown men, all hard, bitter, defeated outlaws is a pipe dream. Sooner or later the outfit will turn on itself. Slocum is often a spokesman for what the others are thinking. He disapproves of Hays's incremental approach to rustling Herrick's cattle and takes it upon himself to rustle the last of the herd ahead of schedule. This angers Hays, who has other plans that must now be hurried along. Smoky and Jim Wall become friends, brought together by a desire to protect Helen Herrick from Hays. Smoky is with Jim when Sparrowhawk reveals that Hays has double-crossed them all by dividing up only a small part of the take at the Herrick ranch. He promises to shoot Hays when the time comes. Jim comes to feel that Smoky is the salt of the earth, if such a tribute could be paid to a member of an outlaw gang. When Helen Hays pulls a gun on Herrick, Slocum ties his boss up. When Heeseman's gang attacks them, Slocum is killed in a shootout with the gambler, Morley. The one regret Jim has leaving Robbers' Roost is that he did not have the chance to go back and give Smoky a proper burial.

Slone, Lin: In *Wildfire*, a wild horse hunter. Together with Bill and Abe Stewart, he has been hunting wild mustangs for some five years. Lin Slone was ten years old when his parents were killed in an Indian raid on a wagon train in Wyoming. He has wandered about the West, spent time in Texas, and become quite adept at his trade. He becomes obsessed with catching Wildfire and breaking him. He doesn't know what he will do with the horse if he should catch and break him, as he has never made any money by selling a horse. He pursues Wildfire because he loves the excitement of the game, the lure of the desert. He has great respect for his horse Nagger, a "warhorse," as large, strong and broad-backed as a farm horse but with the speed of a racing thoroughbred. Nagger has suffered with him the privations of the desert. Unable to understand his obsession with Wildfire, the Stewart brothers leave him to pursue the stallion on his own. When the grub they leave him has run out, he survives by hunting deer and rabbits. Some days he has no food at all. He can imagine the frightening image he would present to someone from the civilized world — emaciated, bearded, wearing soleless, ripped boots and clothes little better than rags. But he does catch Wildfire. Lucy Bostril comes upon him lying on the ground in the desert, half-starved, but with the broken Wildfire. The mustang takes a liking to Lucy; she is able to ride him without the fit of bucking and kicking that inevitably accompanies Slone's stepping into the saddle. Lucy brings Lin some new clothes and sneaks some food out of the house. She brings him the supplies the next day, and thus begins a daily ritual whereby Lucy sneaks out to the sage to help Lin Slone. He shares with her his history, and she admires his strength and skill with horses. He is the finest rider she has ever met, strong, lithe, powerful yet gentle. He decides to give Lucy the horse, since she works so well with him. Slone falls in love with Lucy and decides that he will ask Bostril for her hand when (if) he wins the race. Wildfire is entered in the race with Lucy as owner. Wildfire, a complete unknown, walks off with the first prize, beating the closest competitor, Whitefoot, by several lengths. Slone explains to Bostril how he came to meet Lucy. He tells how she helped prepare the horse for the race and how he proposed marriage to her. Bostril offers to buy Wildfire from Slone, but he refuses. When Slone has saved him from Dick

Sears, he offers Lin a job as one of his riders, but again, Slone refuses the job. Slone buys the Vorhees ranch and settles in. The ranch has particularly well-built corrals, virtually rustler-proof. Slone has trod on dangerous ground by refusing Bostril's offer to buy Wildfire. He has refused to let Bostril bully him the way he bullies Van, Farlane and Holley. Lin Slone hires Joel Creed to help him set up at the ranch. Joel tells about Bostril's sabotaging his father's crossing of the Colorado. He also tells Lin he saw him kissing Lucy out on the sage before the race. Slone beats Joel for threatening to spread the story about Lucy. Holley arrives on a mission from Bostril, again asking if Wildfire is for sale. He tells Holley that Wildfire actually belongs to Lucy. He had given her the horse before the race. Four days later, Slone has to go to Brackton's store for supplies. Here, he meets Bostril, who announces that Vorhees had deceived him, selling him a ranch that didn't belong to him. Slone makes no fight, but makes a proposition. He will race his horse for a major wager, Wildfire for Lucy. Holley delivers Slone a letter from Lucy. She asks to meet him out on the sage where they first met. There, she tells him that the cowboys laughed at how Bostril had gotten the better of him in the deal over Vorhees's ranch. Lucy manages to sneak out of the house when her father is away in Durango, but on her way to meet Slone, she is caught by Creech, who announces his plan to hold her for ransom to get Sage King and Sarchedon. When Lucy does not show up as scheduled, Slone goes to look for her and finds Creech's trail. He follows the trail, and spots Joel leading the horses, then he sees Cordts and Hutchinson in the distance, moving in the same direction. In the confusing maze of canyons, he corners one of Cordts's men who reveals Cordts's plans to take Lucy and the horses from Creech. He finds Joel, Sage King and Lucy in the canyon, and the wildfire spreading. Sage King sets off running wildly, and Slone sets off in pursuit on Wildfire. He manages to rope Sage King, bringing the terrified horse to a stop. Just then, Cordt and Hutchinson begin shooting at them from the cliffs around the canyon. Slone is hit, but not seriously. Lucy shoots Cordts, Hutchinson reaches down to help him up the cliff, Cordts loses his footing and the two of them fall over the precipice. Back at Bostril's Ford, Lucy and Slone tell Bostril that in the race, Sage King proved the faster, but Wildfire was killed. Lucy and Slone are married, and live at Bostril's Ford.

Lin Slone is another version of Grey's western hero. Like Jack Hare, he has been formed by the desert environment. He is man whose strength and wisdom come from experience and suffering. Like Jack Hare, Gene Stewart, Dick Gale, and Buck Duane, he is a gentleman through and through, a defender of a good woman's honor. He is willing to sacrifice himself to help others. In the presentation of Slone, however, less time is spent philosophizing about the formative power of nature. The character is largely presented through action. He reflects Grey's passion for a good horse.

Slotte, Henry "Silk":   In *Stranger from the Tonto*, Bonesteel's right-hand man in the Hole-in-the-Wall Gang. He has leonine features and wide shoulders, and his appearance tells he is clearly a formidable man. His nickname "Silk" comes from his preference for silk shirts. Lucy says of him he is as slick as the shirts he likes to wear. Slotte was a younger man and caught Bonesteel's eye and soon replaced Bill Elway as the boss's confidante. Slotte leaves the hideout with Lucy's horse, Spades. Ben Bunge, one of his outfit, takes off with the horse and sells him to Kent Wingfield. Shortly afterwards, Kent finds Slotte, Kitsap, Goin and Neberyull in camp. He hides in the bushes and listens to their talk, which confirms much of what Bill Elway told him. Slotte had hated Elway because he was close to Lucy and she liked him. She was also fond of Ben Bunge. Slotte pooh-poohs all this, saying Lucy only loves her horse, Spades. The speaker reminds Slotte that he has been in love with Lucy since she was a child but Lucy never gave a damn for him. Furthermore Slotte must realize that Bonesteel will never let him marry Lucy. He tries to retrieve the horse from Wingfield at Logan's trading post but is shot in the shoulder. When he returns to the hideout, he won't believe the story he is first told, that the horse wandered back on his own. Bonesteel informs him that the horse was brought back by Kent Wingfield, who proceeds to tell Bonesteel about how Slotte stole the horse, how Ben Bunge stole it from him, how he shot him in the shoulder at Logan's, then trailed him part of the way home. He accuses him of plotting with Roberts, his new partner, to kill Bonesteel. In the gunfight that ensues, Wingfield shoots and kills Slotte and his cohort, Crothers.

Slover: In *Betty Zane*, a friend of Jonathan Zane's and one of the frontiersman scouts with Crawford's expedition against the Delaware. Like other experienced frontiersmen, he suspects the Indians have planned an ambush, but Crawford will not listen to the advice of more experienced scouts. Crawford's whole company is wiped out in the ambush. Only a few of the older, experienced scouts manage to survive. Colonel Zane says he is glad to hear that Slover was one of these.

Slyter, Bingham: In *Wilderness Trek*, the father of Leslie Slyter and one of Stanley Dann's drovers in the trek across Australia. Red Krehl and Sterling Hazelton meet in at the merchandise store in Downsville where Watson has introduced them. The Danns are planning a trek across Australia, and the two Yankee cowboys offer to sign up for the job. They have experience driving cattle and are familiar with all the possible hazards of the trail, including fighting off rustlers. Slyter is a loyal supporter of Stanley throughout the trek. He supports him against Ormiston in the question of which route to take. He approves Red's attempt to turn the wagons into boats to cross the rivers, like the old prairie schooners of the West. Slyter participates in the pursuit of the rustlers, the crossing of the desert, the crocodile infested rivers, and the arrival in the Kimberleys.

Slyter, Cedric: In *Wilderness Trek*, Bingham Slyter's older brother. He is trampled to death in a cattle stampede. Red Krehl identifies the body, which has been trampled to a pulp, all except the head. The cause of death, however, was a bullet in the back of the head. He was shot in the back of the head while on guard, before the cattle were stampeded. Stanley Dann wants to believe that his being shot was an accident, that the drovers were firing to control the cattle and he was hit by accident.

Slyter, Leslie: In *Wilderness Trek*, the sixteen-year-old daughter of Bingham Slyter. She is fascinated by the two Yankee cowboys, and amused at their ignorance of the animals and birds of Australia. She enjoys pointing out the new birds and marsupials to the two newcomers. She has a string of thoroughbred horses that she loves. She gives Jester to Red to use during the trek and her favorite, King, to Sterling. She dislikes Ormiston and fears him. He insulted her with his insinuations the first time they met. Hazelton advises her never to be alone with him and never to ride out of sight of one of their drovers. Although she is fond of Hazelton and Red, she believes Ormiston's story that they cavort with the aborigine women in their camp. Later, she apologizes for her lack of faith in them. She is overjoyed when Sterling and Red return her horses when they have captured the rustlers and lynched Ormiston. Like Beryl, she gets sick after the sandstorm, but not as severely as Beryl. When the group reaches the Kimberleys, Stanley Dann marries Leslie and Sterling Hezelton.

Slyter, Mrs.:   In *Wilderness Trek*, a buxom, pleasant woman, mother to Lestlie and wife to Bingham. Her willingness to undertake a two- to three-year trek across Australia to take up ranching in the Northwest bespeak the strengths and endurance of a pioneer woman. She is welcoming to the two Yankee cowboys, Sterling Hazelton and Red Krehl. Unfortunately, she believes the rumors that Ash Ormiston has been spreading that Sterl and Red consort with lubas (aboriginal women) after they leave Leslie and Beryl.

Small, Dan: In *The Border Legion*, a cowboy shot and killed one morning for no apparent reason by Gulden.

Smeade: In *The Maverick Queen*, one of two cowboys talking with Mel Thatcher at the entrance to the Chinese restaurant in South Pass. Lincoln Bradway hears Thatcher caution him about mentioning openly what had happened to Jimmy Weston. For Lincoln, this tells him that Mel Thatcher is a possible source of information about what had happened to his partner.

Smilin' Pete: In *The Trail Driver*, with Hash Williams meets Brite and his trail drivers on the trail and asks to join them up to the Little Wichita River. They are good hunters and know the area well, and Brite lets them join his riders.

Smith: (1) In *Arizona Ames*, works on the Halstead ranch. He is in charge of the farming operations. He also helps out Esther from time to time.

(2) In *Boulder Dam*, works at the Boulder Dam site. When Weston is pursuing the saboteurs, he meets Smith leaping down the steps from the second floor, covered in cement dust. He calls to him to watch the mills and to keep the man in the office from getting away.

(3) In *The Last Trail*, Jonathan and Wetzel come upon the body of Smith, Jenks and Mordaunt. Jonathan identifies him as Metzar's man at the inn.

(4) In *The Lost Wagon Train*, one of the men driving a wagon in the caravan Anderson is leading across the Dry Trail. He is not too keen to continue without the larger caravan from Texas, and he comments that Jeff Stoffer has lost some of his enthusiasm for the trip, lagging behind the other wagons. Smith goes out to scout around and spots the Indians and a band of white men in a canyon near Tanner's Swale. The whites are doling out liquor to the Indians. It strikes him as a strange coincidence. Smith is the first to spot the line of Kiowas against the horizon. He is a good shot, killing an attacking Kiowa with every shot. He is eventually killed in the attack.

(5) In *Majesty's Rancho*, runs a store in Bolton. He tells Lance Sidway about the telephone wires to the Stewart ranch having been cut. Mike Scanlon had told him this just ten minutes before. He had seen a black car speeding away from the downed, cut wires.

(6) In *The Mysterious Rider*, runs a hotel and gambling establishment in Elgeria. Smith is an alias for Captain Folsom. He has provided stiff competition to Bob, the innkeeper, who is a friend of Bill Belllounds. Smith has had words with Belllounds about Columbine in the past. Smith (Folsom) is the leader and organizer of the rustlers who have been robbing cattle from Bill's ranch. Buster Jack Belllounds is a member of the gang. Smith does not understand why Buster is stealing from his father. He assumes it's just to finance his gambling. Folsom was involved with Spencer, the brother of Wade's wife, Lucy. Folsom and Wade did not get along back then, and Folsom and Spencer try to break up the marriage by encouraging a young southerner to make advances to Lucy. Smith is killed by Wade in the gunfight in the rustlers' cabin.

(7) In *The Rainbow Trail*, one of the Mormons who come into the camp at Navajo Mountain. He is cordial, pleasant. He is on guard at the hidden village with the sealed wives when Mary (Sago Lily, Fay Larkin) is being held after the death of Waggoner.

(8) In *Shadow on the Trail*, a member of Simm Bell's outlaw gang. He helps rob the Texas Pacific train. He is a freckled, evil-eyed man. He disagrees with the way Simm Bell divides the money from the robbery. Simm gives Blue a share, because he has ridden with him on other ventures, but Smith and Hazlitt feel he deserves nothing as he did not do much to help with this gig. Smith draws a gun on his boss, but young Wade Holden, whom Smith barely even deigns to notice, shoots him and Hazlitt before they can shoot the boss. They bury them under freshly cut branches.

(9) In *Sunset Pass,* one of the small-scale ranchers around Wagontongue.

(10) In *The U. P. Trail*, an associate of Allison Lee, commissioner of the Union Pacific. He is shot by Larry King in the scuffle surrounding Lee's accusations against Warren Neale.

(11) In *Wilderness Trek*, one of Ormiston's drovers and rustlers. He manages to escape when the Dann outfit catches up with them.

Smith, Alice: In *Valley of Wild Horses*, Pan Handle's younger sister. He has not seen her for some five years and is amazed at how she has grown into a beautiful young woman. She does not recognize him when he arrives at the new home in Marco. She is a great help to her mother around the house and to Lucy, Pan Handle's girl.

Smith, Andy: In "From Missouri," one of the three cowboys involved in the letter-writing to the school marm from Missouri. He, Pan Handle and Tex, are surprised when a letter arrives after they decided to discontinue the hoax.

Smith, Banty: In *The Wolf Tracker*, the little arguing rooster of Adams's roundup outfit. He loves to tease the other cowboys— Benson, for instance, who has lost one of his heifers to the old gray wolf. Banty enjoyed a certain reputation among the cowboys as a hunter, a reputation that he has cherished and which, to his humiliation, he could not live up to after several futile hunts after the gray loafer. He doubts that Brinks will succeed and cracks jokes at Brinks's expense, to the great amusement of his cowboy friends.

Smith, Bill: (1) In *The Drift Fence*, mentioned by Andy Stoneham as one young man whom Molly Dunn has hugged and kissed. Bill Smith has been boasting about this to the other young men.

(2) In *30,000 on the Hoof*, one of the young cowboys Logan Huett hires to drive his herd to Flagg for sale to the army. The older boys have signed up for the army and the war.

(3) In *Valley of Wild Horses*, Pan Handle's father. He sets up ranching near Littleton. He encourages Pan Handle in his love of the cowboy life. Despite his wife's opposition, he gets the boy his own horse, Curly, and introduces him to cowboy life, working on the roundups in the area. At sixteen, Pan leaves to ride the range. When he returns, he learns from the storekeeper, Campbell, that things have not gone well for his family. His father had to sell the farm after being stung in a cattle deal with Hardman. Bill went west following Hardman, seeking compensation for the stolen cattle. In Marco, he comes upon Hardman. He gets work as a carpenter at Carter's Wagon Shop and rents a hundred-acre farm from a rancher called Hall. Smith is overjoyed that his son has returned. Pan promises to set things right with

Hardman and to move the family to Arizona to start afresh. Pan Handle calls his father to join in the wrangling expedition. Whatever mistakes his father may have made in business deals, he was always a skilled cowboy and horseman. He proves a valuable addition to Blink Moran's crew. Smith leaves with his family for Arizona when the score has been settled with the Hardmans, and Lucy and Pan Handle are married.

Smith, Bobby: In *Valley of Wild Horses*, Pan Handle Smith's young brother, born after he had left home to ride the range. Mrs. Smith is determined she will not let him become a cowboy like Pan Handle. Bobby is fascinated by his big brother and especially his guns. Bobby sits on Pan's knee and follows his every move with eager anticipation.

Smith, Brodington: In *West of the Pecos,* Pecos Smith's uncle, and a member of the Texas Rangers. Captain McKinney is a friend of Brodington Smith's and knows Pecos's family. The accusations against his friend's nephew appear unfounded.

Smith, Dr.: In *Code of the West,* reported to believe that Georgiana Stockwell's right lung is affected and he recommends she seek a drier climate, like Arizona. Hence her trip to the Tonto to stay with her older sister, Mary.

Smith, Elsie: In *The Lost Wagon Train,* Smith's daughter. She is crazy about Slim Blue (Corny) and she tells Estelle Latch what a handsome man he is. She thinks Slim Blue spends so much time in the store to catch her attention. She does manage to make Estelle very jealous.

Smith, Hale: In *Wyoming,* runs the Triangle X ranch.

Smith, Henry: In *Boulder Dam,* a friend of Anne Vandergrift's father. He has moved to Los Angeles and before her father's death, he had agreed to give her work. Mr. Smith sends her to business school for six months and then employs her. She lives with his family. When the Depression came, his business was ruined and he committed suicide.

Smith, Hobart: In *The Fugitive Trail,* witnesses the holdup at the bank in Denison. He swears that there was only one heavy, mature man in the outfit. The rest were lean, young riders.

Smith, Hod James: In *West of the Pecos,* other names by which Pecos Smith is known. Sawtell knew him as "Hod" Smith and this is the name he uses when he comes looking for him at the Lambeth ranch. "James" is the name Pecos uses when he goes to Judge Roy Bean to get married. It was his given name at birth.

Smith, Jeff: In *The Maverick Queen,* the original owner of the livery stable in South Pass. When the miner, Bill Headly, breaks his leg and cannot continue mining, he buys out Jeff Smith and takes over what proves to be a lucrative business.

Smith, Jefford: In *The Dude Ranger,* a lawyer, a westerner and a cattleman in Springer. His practice of law was a side business and had been taken up as a matter of necessity for the country. Ernest Selby approaches him about his uncle's estate and the seeming fraud committed by the foreman. Smith looks over his uncle's papers and concludes that Hepford has been cheating him, but proving it is another question. Hepford, he says, has more money gathering interest in Holbrook than has ever been paid Selby all together. Hepford is also a director of the bank in Springer. He does banking in Gloe, too, and other towns. But Ernest will have to prove his case. Smith advises him to go slow and not to act until he has gathered unquestionable proof. After Ernest has been investigating matters for a while and suspects Hepford has kept doctored books, he asks Smith to request that his lawyer back east write Hepford, requesting a report of all cattle sales up to date and other necessary details important to the new owner. When Ernest decides to act, he approaches Smith again, who informs him that Hepford is planning to clean the ranch out, and that he has purchased a new ranch in New Mexico. When Ernest informs the lawyer he has married Hepford's daughter Anne, he questions the wisdom of this. Hepford has robbed him of some two hundred thousand dollars. Ernest has recovered some forty thousand dollars through Anne, and he has in his possession the little blue book, Hepford's private ledger. This confirms the crooked deals that Hepford has made cheating Selby. Jefford Smith drives out to the ranch before Ernest returns to the ranch. Smith announces that the new owner has arrived, the tenderfoot cowboy he already knows. When Ernest has dictated his terms to Hepford, Smith makes the arrangements to settle the deal. Jefford Smith is impressed with the speed at which Ernest learned about the cattle trade and the ranch, and with the magnanimity with which he treats Hepford.

Smith, Jerry: In *Nevada,* works on Franklidge's ranch. When Texas Jack (a.k.a. Jim Lacy, Nevada) decides to go undercover to flush out the leaders of the Pine Tree Outfit of rustlers, he gets duded up in town. When his friend Jerry Smith passes him in the street, he doesn't recognize him. Jim Lacy is sure that his new "disguise" works.

Smith, Jesse: In *The Border Legion,* Blicky's partner. He comes into camp with Blicky and the two report on the great gold strike on Alder Creek at Bear Mountain. Jesse had been at the gold strikes in California in '49 and '51 and he thinks this strike exceeds the previous two in potential. There will be many pack trains loaded with gold to rob, millions of dollars' worth. He expresses pleasure at Jim's good fortune. When Gulden has left after proposing a job to test Jim Cleve's ability and loyalty to the Border Legion, Jesse Smith proposes a second test, killing Gulden. The other members of the gang approve the proposal, on condition they don't have to help Jim. They are all afraid of Gulden. Jesse Smith is one of the outlaws who robs the Alder Creek stage. He is present when the gold is divided and the outlaws gamble among themselves. He is killed in the shootout which rips the Border Legion apart.

Smith, John (Jack): In *Fighting Caravans*, a famous frontiersman. Like his partner, Jim Baker, he has been on the frontier for some twenty-five years. He was among the first to cross the plains. Smith is married to a Comanche woman, Indian fashion. His wife is a pretty young woman who can speak some English. Dick Curtis introduces Clint Belmet to him at Fort Larned. Clint is surprised at the greasy, rough, dirty, disreputable appearance of the man. But for the beard and the talk, mostly profane, he could have been an Indian. Clint Belmet finds that Smith's wife is a more interesting person than her renowned trapper husband. Smith had made a good deal of money buying furs from the Indians and selling them to the whites.

In *The Lost Wagon Train*, Jack Smith is one of the frontier scouts that Major Greer calls in to make inquiries about the Bowden (Anderson) wagon train which went missing on the Dry Trail over a year and a half before. Smith is described as a lean giant of a plainsman who has been on the border for over twenty years. He has indeed heard of the Bowden train, but he doubts that anything more will ever be heard of it.

Smith, Josh: In *The Shepherd of Guadaloupe*, a tour guide in Colorado Springs. He is a relic of a westerner who claims he is over eighty years old. He was orphaned when his parents were killed in an Indian raid. He claims to have been a teamster on the plans, a construction worker on the Santa Fe railway, a scout, a cowboy, a miner, a gambler, a bit of everything. He is a colorful figure for tourists. Josh Smith drives a dilapidated vehicle, conducting tours through the "Garden of the Gods." He points to rock formations that look like animals—an elephant, a tomcat, a mud turtle—and others that resemble mythological figures. Ethel, who has been through the place many times, teases him that he changes his story every time she takes the tour.

Smith, Jud: In *The Lost Wagon Train*, runs a general store at Latchfield's village. Slim Blue spends a lot of time in there, as Smith believes to see his daughter, Elsie, but in reality, he is listening to the gossip around the place to learn what Leighton and his men are up to. Latch notes a certain coolness in Jud Smith's attitude, indicative of the influence of Leighton's gossip. Jud Smith was an honest man who had chosen to settle at Latch's Field, and Latch appreciates his friendship and support.

Smith, Lieutenant: In *West of the Pecos*, mentioned as a member of the Fourth Cavalry which had camped at the old post, Camp Lancaster, as early as 1849. This was the beginning of settlement in West Texas.

Smith, Margaret (Mrs. Bill): In *Valley of Wild Horses*, Pan Handle's mother.

Smith, Mother: In *The Rainbow Trail*, the wife of the Smith who deals with Withers and Shefford. She is an older woman, head of the sealed wives. Like Smith, she shows a fondness for Shefford, believing she sees in him a possible convert to Mormonism. She welcomes him to the village and gives him the freedom to talk to any of the women who are willing to talk to him.

Smith, Mr.: In *The Shepherd of Guadaloupe*, a sheepman who appears at the restaurant in Las Vegas where Virginia is dining with Dick Fenton. He has a message for her about Don Lopez and his sheep. Malpass has been talking to him, offering to buy the flock from him in order to fire Cliff Forrest from his job as shepherd. He tells her that there is good money in sheep at present, and she could make a good profit on the deal. Virginia thanks him for his advice and relishes the opportunity to spoil Malpass's plans. It is possible that this Mr. Smith is the man who was driving the car and stopped to speak to Cliff when he was herding sheep.

Smith, Mr. Matty: In *Valley of Wild Horses*, the agent who runs the express office in Littleton, New Mexico. He has been doing the job since he was a boy and he knows everyone in town. Matty Smith is the first person to tell Pan Handle what became of his father. Smith recounts the story of his losing the ranch to Hardman and working at Carter's Wagon Shop as a carpenter. Smith has heard of Pan Handle's reputation and is thrilled to make his acquaintance.

Smith, Pan Handle: In *The Lone Star Ranger*, mentioned by Frank Morton as one of Cheseldine's gunmen. When Buck Duane spies on the group meeting in the secret hideout, Pan Handle Smith is the red-faced cook, merry, profane, short, bowlegged. He reminds Buck Duane of Luke Stevens.

In *The Trail Driver*, the same Pan Handle Smith signs on for the trail drive to Dodge. He does not want any pay, expecting to get a stake at Dodge. Brite is pleased to have this famous Texas gunman as part of his crew. He is confident they can now handle the worst of emergencies on the trail. Pan Handle Smith comments that whoever shot the horse with a needle gun was trying to get a stampede started. He also observes the accuracy of Texas Joe's aim when he shoots Wallen through the heart, dead center, a remarkable feat considering how fast he had to draw. Pan Handle dispatches Hallet quickly. Hallet and Chandler are about to pull guns on each other, and he fears that it will involve Texas Joe and possibly others. He finishes the matter quickly and simply. Pan Handle and Texas Joe ride out in an electric storm to try to retrieve the herd that Ross Hite has stolen. Brite admires their iron nerve and courage. At Doan's, he learns that Hite and his men have just gone through and that they hang out at Hay's in Dodge. When the trail drive reaches Dodge, Pan Handle looks up Hite at his watering hole, and kills him in a gunfight. He then takes the stage back to San Antonio with Brite, Texas Joe Shipman and Reddie.

Smith, Pan Handle (Pan): In *Valley of Wild Horses*, the oldest son of Bill and Margaret Smith, homesteaders in the Panhandle of Texas. Pan Handle himself mentions three main influences on his early years, Curly, cowboys and Lucy Blake. Curly is the pony his father gave him when he was about six years old. His mother did not want him to ride the horse unless she was leading him, but one day, Pan Handle got the horse out of the barn and went riding on his own. His escapade left him on the ground near the barn, but with his father's overriding his mother's restrictions on his riding. They boy was old enough to learn to handle a horse on his own. From then on, he lives on Curly's back, acquiring a cowboy's seat, dreaming of adventures riding the range. The second influence on his life, perhaps the strongest, is cowboys. His father allows him to watch the round ups and help out with the work. He falls in love with the cowboys on the range and these in turn love to tease him. One winter, Pug Moore and his crew board with the Smiths for the winter and Pan Handle learns from them all the cowboy songs and stories. At the age of twelve, he takes part in his first roundup for pay. All he felt was the wild delight of it all, the thrill of the risk, the excitement, the constant stirring of life and motion. The third formative influence is Lucy Blake. He was the only one present when she was born. He was returning from his uncle's place, delayed by a storm, and passed the Blake place as Mrs. Blake was calling for help. Jim Blake and Pan's father had been delayed as well. Pan Handle helped the woman deliver her child. Lucy became his playmate and best friend. At the birthday party his mother prepares for him when he turns fifteen, he looks at Lucy as a girl, rather than a playmate, for the first time. He feels a tingling sense of proprietorship of her. At school, he defends her against bullies like Dick Hardman, who has forced her to kiss him. This leads to a major fight with the handsome school bully who does not know how to fight fair. He grabs the teacher's paper knife and stabs Pan in the shoulder.

Lucy, however, was no match for the lure of the open range. At sixteen, Pan set out to ride the range. His adventures began on the ranges of the Lone Star state where he rode for two years, inevitably drifting into the wild, free life of the cowboys. Sometimes he sent money home, but not often, because he was always in debt. Thoughts of Lucy returned now and then, but he never heard a word from her. He fell in with an outfit driving cattle to Montana, and he learned that stories of his wildness had preceded him. He feared that the gossip would reach his mother. He spent a year in the northern states before heading south again. At twenty years of age, he looked older, inured to the hard life, the hard fare and the hard companionship that had been his lot as an American cowboy. He had absorbed all the virtues of that remarkable character and most of the vices. He had always kept aloof from women, a source of humor among his cowboy pals. One night while guarding the herd, the solitude, the loneliness finally hit home, and Pan Handle felt homesickness.

He returns to Littleton to find that no one recognizes him. Campbell, the storekeeper, tells him his family had run into a streak of bad luck and sold the farm. His father had lost his cattle in an old deal with Jard Hardman. They had gone west looking for Hardman.

Pan Handle leaves for Marco, New Mexico. Jim Wells, the old-timer stagecoach driver, has heard of some of his exploits in Cheyenne, Wyoming, and insists on relating them to Emily Newman, the young female passenger. In Marco, he learns from Mr. Smith, the express office agent, that indeed his family is there. His father is working for the Carter Wagon Company as carpenter. He also farms a hundred acres that he rents from a rancher called Hall. Pan Handle also learns that Jard and Dick Hardman are forces to be reckoned with here. Jard Hardman is into everything — mining, horse wrangling, cattle. He owns half the town, and controls the marshall.

The family situation has changed. His sister Annie is now a fine young woman, and there is a baby brother, Bobby, that he has never met. Little Bobby is thrilled to have a big brother and he is fascinated by Pam's guns. His mother and sister are overjoyed to see him. His mother fills him in on their misfortunes, and the role that Hardman has played in them. Above all, he learns that Lucy is living with his family, that she is again being pressured by Hardman. Jim Blake is in jail on charges of rustling cattle in Texas, a charge Pan's father says is undoubtedly correct. Hardman, however, has agreed to get the charges dropped if Lucy marries Dick. She is holding out for papers clearing her father of any crime. Pan Handle comes to her rescue on two accounts. When they meet, Lucy realizes that she still loves him very much and that she cannot marry Dick Hardman and Pan promises to get her father out of jail.

Pan Handle wants to free his family from their present situation and break all connections with Hardman and his ilk. He proposes that the family move to Arizona. To get the money for this, he joins up with Blinky Moran and Gus Hans in a project to capture a large number of wild horses to sell. His father, the young miner, Charley Brown who had befriended him, Handy MacNew, a cowboy whose life he had saved years ago in Montana and who had helped him free Jim Blake from jail, sign on as well. They capture some fifteen hundred horses which they sell to Wiggate for ten dollars a head. With the money, they plan to set off for Arizona.

Pan Handle must settle the score with the Hardmans. He confronts Jard Hardman and his puppet, Marshall Matthews, in the street outside the Yellow Mine saloon. He accuses Hardman of stealing cattle from his father and demands compensation. He challenges them to a shootout and they back down. This causes them to lose face in town. When Pan and his friend Blinky have rounded up fifteen hundred mustangs, Hardman tries to steal them, buy them or force Pan into dividing them with him. Hardman had tried to bribe MacNew to betray Pan and his men, but when that backfires, MacNew kills Jard in a shootout. Pan takes the money he has on him to pay his father for the cattle stolen years ago.

As he did when he was fifteen years old at school, he rescues Lucy from the clutches of Dick Hardman. She breaks her engagement when Pan promises to free her father. He rescues her again when she has married Hardman to save her father, who had taken money from Dick to pressure her. Pan Handle extends his chivalrous efforts to help Blinky rescue his sweetheart, Louise Melliss, from the Yellow Mine saloon. They find her drunk in her room. She is reluctant to leave with them as she feels she is a terrible person and not worthy of marrying the faithful cowboy who had fallen in love with her. In a drunken stupor, she stabs Dick Hardman to death. He had been hiding in her closet. Her action has freed Lucy to marry Pan Handle. The family, together with Blinky and Louise, set off for Siccane, Arizona. Lucy and Pan are married by a preacher in Green Valley on the way.

The character of Pan Handle Smith is developed along the lines of Arizona Ames, Buck Duane, Lassiter and John Hare. Formed by the western environment, he uses his intelligence and skills to help others. He is the embodiment of chivalry and decency, cowboy style.

Smith, Pecos: In *West of the Pecos,* the hero of the novel, a "good" bad man, as it were. No one ever gets the full story of his background. Captain McKinney knows him from his uncle, Bradington Smith, and from McKinney's ranger, Jeff Slinger, who vouch for his good character. He is from one of the best old families in Texas. His father was killed during the Civil War and the family fell apart. Following this, Pecos went to work as a rider for Don Felipe Gonzalez in Mexico. He cowboyed with him for five years. He travels north, with McKeever, the trail driver, who had a contract to deliver cattle to Santa Fe. They stop at the Heald ranch and when the herd continues on, Pecos remains with the brothers. To the cowhands at the Healds' ranch, he is the best horseman, the best shot, the best roper that had ever ridden up out of Southwest Texas. But that was about all they ever learned. Pecos remains with the Healds for two years. McKeever tells the Healds that Pecos is a good-natured young man, the best you could ever meet, but he gets into trouble trying to help out others. (In this he resembles Arizona Ames.)

When Pecos Smith arrives at the Healds' ranch, he is about twenty-five years old, just above medium height, not so lean and rangy as most horsemen. He has wide shoulders and muscular, round limbs. He is an amazing cowboy and horseman, superior even to the legendary Rodriguez. His horse is outstanding, and his ivory-handled gun is yellow with age. Because of his knowledge of the area, the Healds give him the job of rounding up all Heald cattle scattered over the outlying ranges and observing the roundups of the other cattlemen. During the two years with the Heald brothers, none ever learn much about him.

The cowboy who gets to know him best is Sandy McClain, but even there, the confidences are few. He does not go to parties, taking night herd duty instead. This annoys Mary Heald in particular, because she had planned a party especially hoping to get to know him better there.

In the autumn of his second year with the Healds, Beckman's foreman, Sawtell, working with Don Felipe, shows up to convince the Healds to fire Smith on suspicion of branding mavericks. The drunken Sawtell draws on Pecos, who kills him in self-defense. Rather than bring trouble to the Healds, he leaves, taking up with Wess Adams and Curt Williams, branding mavericks to sell to ranchers or to cattle dealers. At this time, maverick branding is not illegal, but unknown to him, the two partners also indulge in some rebranding of other cattlemen's animals. They are captured by ranchers and are being lynched when Smith finds the party. At the same time, the Comanche attack. The lone rancher survivor tells Pecos Smith that Sawtell was jealous of him, as he too was interested in Mary Heald and sought to discredit Pecos Smith in her eyes.

Pecos Smith first runs into the Lambeths in San Antonio, where Terrill bumps into him as he is coming out of a saloon, shooting. Later, he leads them to the crossing of the Pecos River. He comes upon them again at Eagle's Nest where he pays off Terrill's debts to get her released from jail, where she had been confined on orders from Don Felipe to his man, Brasee. This is after his departure from the Healds' ranch and his discovery of the lynching party being attacked by the Comanches. Pecos takes over the running of the Lambeth ranch and does much to get the operation going. He likes Terrill, thinking the lad needs an older brother as guide. He is quite surprised to discover that Terrill is a girl, one day when he saves her from drowning. He does not let her know that he has discovered her secret, but he becomes all the more protective of her. Maruee, Sambo's wife, marvels at how little experience he has with women not to have guessed the secret before.

When Breen Sawtell, some henchmen and Sheriff Bill Haines come to the ranch, they hold young Terrill hostage, and tie up the neighbor Watson and Sambo. They have discovered the money belt and Terrill's secret. Breen Sawtell is waiting to hang Pecos on his return. The fighting that ensues when Pecos returns is not to recover the money but to avenge the insult to Terrill's reputation. Sawtell calls her a hussy, implying she and Pecos have been living together without benefit of clergy. Sawtell is killed in the gunfight which follows.

Pecos then undertakes to stock the ranch. He meets the Texas Rangers and clears his name. Captain McKinney assigns Lt. Johnson and Jeff Slinger to accompany the cattle drive back to the ranch. At Eagle's Nest, they go to Judge Roy Bean to get married. Don Felipe Gonzalez attempts to stop the wedding, having set his eye on Terrill for himself. Pecos gives him a dressing-down in public, threatening to kill him should he return.

The development of the character of Pecos Smith is uneven. The character appears to be a mixture of several hero types that Grey develops in greater detail and with greater success in other novels, such as *Arizona Ames* and *The Lone Star Ranger*.

Smith, Pegleg: (1) In "The Camp Robber," a prospector who travels around with a burro. He is known to all the cowboys in the area. He is an old man with a face as gray as his hair and beard. He is now thin and sick. Lex Wingfield tracks the camp robber to his cabin. The tell-tale trail, one footprint and a round impression, identify Smith as the robber in question. He explains that he has stolen for the child, the daughter of a woman he had found by the trail some five years previous and who died shortly after giving birth. He returns the money he stole, every dollar. He explains that he has robbed to support Fay. The mother died calling for her husband, "Lex." Lex Wingfield is Fay's father.

(2) In both *The Wanderer of the Wasteland* and *Tappan's Burro*, mentioned as a prospector who found a mine in the Superstition Mountains. He died before he could reveal its location. It is sought by every prospector in the California desert.

Smith, Preacher: In *Fighting Caravans,* says grace at the banquet at Maxwell's ranch. Maxwell tells Clint Belmet he and May Bell should take advantage of the preacher's presence to get married.

Smith, Reverend: In *The Maverick Queen*, marries Lincoln Bradway and Lucy Bandon in Rock Springs. The reverend is on his way to Oregon and is temporarily holding meetings at the church next to the depot. He tells Lincoln that the ceremony was quick, but nonetheless binding, as he hands him the marriage certificate.

Smith, Sheriff: In "The Flight of Fargo Jones," leads a posse in pursuit of rustlers who are branding mavericks. He catches Fargo Jones, who was seen at a campfire where a rustler had been branding mavericks. When he hears Fargo's story, he believes he is innocent, but nevertheless keeps him in jail. Fargo breaks out, knocking the sheriff unconscious. The sheriff, however, knows the area well and deduces from the tracks that Fargo has gone to a remote cabin in the mountains. A year later, Sheriff Smith shows up at the cabin, and tells Fargo that he has caught the real rustlers, but that he is going to arrest him for having ruined the best pair of handcuffs in that part of the state. The two of them enjoy a good laugh.

Smith, Stud: In *Robbers' Roost,* a member of Hays's robber outfit. He is a loud fellow, with a plaid vest and two guns inside the vest, one in each pocket. He is a little fellow but forceful, not one you would want to meet in a narrow, dangerous place. He cheats at cards in a game with Hays, and Jim Wall exposes his cheating. He attempts to draw on Hays but decides not to, although he has the reputation of being quick on the draw. Wall comments that men who are good with guns do not pack them the way Stud does. Stud Smith joins Heeseman's outfit and is at the roost in Devil's River Canyon when the Hays outfit routs Heeseman's attackers. He cuts and runs with Morley.

Smith, Uncle George: In *Valley of Wild Horses*, Bill Smith's brother, who has a ranch in the Littleton area. Pan Handle is late returning from a visit to Uncle George. His father and Jim Blake have not yet returned to the ranch and Pan Handle finds himself helping in the delivery of baby Lucy.

Smith, Uncle Ike: In *Valley of Wild Horses*, an older brother of Pan's father. He was a queer old bachelor, lived alone, and did not invite friendliness. Pam was told to stay away from him. Old Uncle Ike was crabby and hard; when a boy, his heart had been broken by an unfaithful sweetheart; he had shot her lover and run away to war. After serving through the Civil War, he fought Indians and had lived an otherwise wild life. Pan, however, did not find the old man unfriendly. He was always welcome at Old Uncle Ike's and soon the two became fast friends. He would ride over to his place every Saturday, stealing some of the time he was supposed to spend with Lucy. She complained about this but he would only laugh at her.

Smitty: In *Boulder Dam*, works with Lynn Weston as a scaler. He had been a bridge painter and was in good shape. An unusually careful scaler, he managed to get his work done without waste of energy. He helps Lynn rescue their foreman, Regan, who is knocked out by falling rock.

Smoky: In *Lost Pueblo*, a Navajo Indian who follows Janey when she goes riding at the post. Ray tells her that Smoky is not all there. He's not to be trusted. He might follow her around out of curiosity, but then, if she were nice to him, things might happen. This story may be a trick the cowboys are playing on Janey.

Snap: In *Boulder Dam*, one of the gangsters with Bellew and Gip Ring in Vitte's house when Lynn Weston and Decker come to rescue Anne.

Snecker, Bo: In *The Lone Star Ranger*, tries to rob Laramie's inn. He beats Laramie, and takes off with the money, but Buck Duane pursues him to the Longstreth ranch some minutes outside of town. He identifies himself as a ranger and insists on searching the house. Bo Snecker is taken from there directly to the courthouse. Despite Buck's insistence that he be put in jail, Longstreth, the mayor, and Owens, the judge, set him free. In part, his release results from the disdain for the Texas Rangers on the part of many, the governor of the state among them, and in part from Longstreth's desire to impress on Duane that he runs the show in Fairdale.

Snecker, Jim: In *The Arizona Clan*, a cousin of Tommy in Ryeson. The first dance after Nan Lilley got back home from Texas, Buck Hathaway saw her and set his eye on her. He beat three fellows and shot Tommy's cousin, Jim Snecker, crippling him.

Sneed: (1) In *The Light of Western Stars*, a guerrilla, hired as a deputy by Sheriff Pat Howe. Sneed first appears as one of Don Carlos' bandits. He comes to the mountain camping site where he finds the wine basket, a telltale sign that the women and the remaining members of Madeline Hammond's visiting party have been there. Sneed is with Sheriff Pat Howe when he arrests Bonita. He is responsible for the cruel treatment she receives. In the shootout between How and Monty Price, he is shot and killed.

(2) In *Twin Sombreros*, Sneed is a rancher that Brazos questions when he is investigating the three men involved in the killing of Allen Neece. Sneed has a bad reputation and Brazos is wary of him. When asked if he has seen three men, a horse with three white feet, and a kid on a black horse, he answers that he hasn't see that kind of horse, which leads Brazos to assume he has seen the two men and the boy.

Sneed, Ben: In *Boulder Dam*, a "square" bootlegger. Lynn Weston first meets him at the Monte Palace in Las Vegas after he has slugged the faro dealer, Bat Hevron, for cheating at cards. Anne Vandergrift had been working for Sneed before Lynn Weston offer her sanctuary in his cabin. The handsome Sneed had put up ten thousand dollars for information on her whereabouts. Sneed himself is interested in Anne, and had offered to "buy" her from Ben Bellew, who claims he had sent her to work in California. Sneed offers to help him get his fiancée back from Bellew. He gets his man, Decker, to guide Lynn around Vegas looking for information and useful rumors. Sneed rewards Lynn for foiling Bellew's attempt to hijack his whiskey trucks. He slips an envelope full of money under his pillow in the hospital. It contains some fifty thousand dollars he had taken from Bellew.

Sneed, Bill: (1) In *Forlorn River*, a ranch hand for Hart Blaine. He is a clean-cut, red-faced man, a special friend of Hart Blaine's son, Marvie. He appears in the novel when the Blaines have moved to Wild Goose Lake for the summer. He reports that Ben Ide has returned to his ranch at Forlorn River with a herd of wild horses, and that Ben has caught California Red. He is one of the cowboys who goes with Less Setter to Ben's ranch and witnesses the fight between Setter and Ben Ide. He holds Setter on his horse on the way back to Blaine's ranch. Setter lies about what happened at Ben Ide's place, and Sneed protests to Blaine that Setter's story about three men beating him up is untrue. Setter, in turn, accuses Sneed of being a rustler in cahoots with Ben Ide, upon which Sneed quits Blaine's outfit. He tells the true story of the encounter. Later, he reports that Setter has gone to Klamath to visit a dentist to get the tooth he lost in the fight with Ben put back in. Sneed returns to work for Blaine when the rustlers have been captured and Setter's complicity in the outlaw outfit fully exposed. He had refused to return to work for Blaine because he wanted to maintain his independence and to distance himself from what to him was a rotten situation.

(2) In *Thunder Mountain*, runs the Dead Eye saloon in Thunder City. Kalispel calls on him to kick Mac and his gang out or he will burn the place to the ground. Sneed then throws the men out of his saloon to be caught by Sheriff Masters.

Sneed, Jeff: In *The Shepherd of Guadaloupe*, a rancher for whom Jeff and Con used to work. They plan to take Virginia's horses with them to his ranch. They know he will gladly take them back.

Sneed, Josh: In *Robbers' Roost*, runs the general store in Green Valley. He is reported to be friendly to Mormons. Hays outfits his crew here.

Sneed, Sheriff Jim: In "Canyon Walls," comes into Green Valley from Arizona, looking to buy stock for Strickland, who also gave him orders to bring "Smoke" back. Word had come that he had been seen in Kanab. And when he made inquiries in White Sage, he knew who Sam Hill was. When "Smoke" explains that he is now married and has a young child, that he is working on the Keetch ranch, Sneed accepts his offer to repay his debt to Strickland, sending him a bit every month until the debt is paid. Sneed assures him he will get Strickland to agree to the deal. Sneed also tells him that his old partners, Cuppy and Slim, were involved in a rustling operation. Slim was killed covering Cuppy's escape.

Snell: (1) In *The Hash Knife Outfit*, runs a saloon where high stakes poker games are held on the second floor. The Christmas Day poker game where Curly Prentiss exposes Ed Darnell as a cheat takes place here.

(2) In *Riders of the Purple Sage*, runs a saloon in the town of Cottonwoods where Oldrin' and his men gather to drink, play cards and gamble. Lassiter meets with Oldrin' in Snell's saloon and Venters calls Oldrin' out in this saloon.

(3) In *The Trail Driver*, runs a saloon in Austin, Texas. Hallet meets Ross Hite here to finalize plans for rustling the Brite herd. Brite happens to be in the saloon the same night and sees the men speaking in low tones over a supposed card game.

Snell, James: In *Arizona Ames*, the father of Lil Snell. He owns a prosperous ranch in the Tonto basin. The big wedding celebration is held at his house.

Snell, Lil: In *Arizona Ames*, Nesta Ames's friend. Of late, Nesta has been spending a lot of time with Lil. She will be her matron of honor at the wedding. Lil is marrying Hall Barner, who is in tight with Lee Tate. Lil has also been arranging things so that Nesta and Lee will be alone. Nesta does not realize that the Snells look down on her family nor that Nell is setting her up with Tate to ruin her reputation, if not her life. When Nesta shows up to the wedding dressed in the elegant white dress that Cappy Tanner gave her, Lil becomes jealous of the attention her matron is getting. She offers to buy the dress from her. Eventually Nesta realizes what an untrustworthy friend Lil has been.

Snitz: In *Lost Pueblo*, Black Dick's assistant. He is a little, red-faced, red-headed, bow-legged person with a greasy blue leather shirt. He complains that Bert Durland is finely duded up but has no money. He then takes his mother's purse from her hip pocket. It's full of money and jewels. He leaves the purse hanging from the branch of a tree along the trail. He and Black Dick were hired by Mr. Endicott to give Janey a scare.

Snood: In *The Heritage of the Desert*, Holderness's foreman at what had once been Martin Cole's ranch. Jack Hare first meets him when he follows the trail of those who had been building a cabin, and a corral to fence in the Seeping Spring water hole. Snood admires Hare's horse, impressed with the mustang stallion he had tried to catch himself. He recognizes Hare as "Dene's spy." When Jack recounts what he found at Seeping Spring and the trail leading to Holderness's ranch, Snood disavows any knowledge of such doings. He promptly resigns his position as foreman to underline his disapproval of the goings-on. Later, in White Sage, Snood is shot by Dene when he takes Jack Hare's side in an argument.

Snook: In *Raiders of Spanish Peaks*, owns a ranch neighboring the Lindsay's Spanish Peaks spread. Ted Williams tracks his stolen horse to Snook's corral. Snook is reportedly the foreman at Arlidge's ranch, Castle Haid. Snook is involved in the kidnapping of Lenta. Ted Williams shoots him in the fighting when she is rescued.

Snowball: In *Betty Zane*, Betty's pet albino squirrel.

Snowflake: In *The Drift Fence*, the nickname given to Molly Dunn by the cowboys at the rodeo in Flag.

Snyder: In *Valley of Wild Horses*, owned a now-abandoned ranch where Pan Handle and his horse wrangling crew stop for the night on the way back to Marco.

Somers: (1) In *To the Last Man*, a member of the Jorth faction. During the attack on the Isbel ranch, Greaves mentions to Ben that he hasn't heard Somers shoot lately. After the attack by the Isbels on the Jorth stronghold at Greaves's store, Somers appears at the Jorth ranch in the mountains with Slater and Colter. He plans the trick, propping the dead gunman Queen up against a tree to lure Jean Isbel into the open. Isbel is tricked, but when Somers and Springer fail to kill him, he shoots and kills Somers before he runs out of ammunition. He is eventually killed by the pursuing Isbels.

(2) In *The U. P. Trail*, a lineman and engineer. Somers, Coffee and Blake are sent from Omaha by Baxter to help Neale solve the problem with the construction of a bridge. Somers, it turns out, is in cahoots with Allison Lee. He and Blake and Coffee had not followed the plans, causing the supports for the bridge to fall. When his role in delaying construction of the bridge becomes clear, he is fired by Neale without pay for past work.

(3) In *Wildfire*, the second employee of Bostril's who operates the boat ferrying men, horses, and supplies across the Colorado.

Somers, Abe: In "Monty Price's Nightingale," describes Monty Price as the best cowpuncher from the Little Big Horn to the Pecos, but says he's too unreliable. He will pack up and leave just when he is the boy most needed. Abe speculates that there is some mystery about Monty.

Somers, Frank: In *Valley of Wild Horses*, the real name of Blinky Moran. He reveals this to his friends when the question of marriage is brought up.

Son of Wingenund: In *Betty Zane*, one of the Indian chiefs sent by Tarhe and Myeerah to recapture Isaac. Isaac recognizes him as a Delaware chief who married a Wyandot woman and spent most of his time with the Hurons. He went hunting and on warring expeditions of the Delaware and Wyandot against enemy tribes. Isaac had hunted with him, slept under the same blanket as him and had grown to like him. The death of Son of Wingenund allows Grey to describe the death ritual of a chief.

Sonora: In *The Hash Knife Outfit*, the Mexican sheep herder and scout for the Hash Knife Outfit. He is loyal to Malloy. He keeps an eye on the Traft cowboys working on the Yellow Jacket ranch from on top of the rim. Slinger Dunn comes upon him there, prepared to shoot young Jim Traft. Slinger kills him just in time.

Soronto: In *The Lost Wagon Train*, mentioned as one of the most fearful of Comanche chiefs responsible for attacks on wagon trains.

Sorrel: In *Wilderness Trek*, one of Leslie Slyter's prize thoroughbreds that successfully makes the trek across Australia.

Sosie: In *Wild Horse Mesa*, a young Indian woman, daughter of Toddy Nokin. She has spent the last nine of her sixteen years at the government school. She is pretty compared to the older Indian women, and has retained the clean, tidy habits taught her at school. Her father believes it is a good thing for Indians to learn white ways and teach them to other Indians to improve their lives. Back in the Indian world, however, she finds Indian customs backward. Toddy Nokin wants her to marry a young Piute who already has a wife, and he cannot understand her objection. She says that Indian boys who go to the government school revert to the dirty habits of their people upon returning to Indian villages. When she tries to teach her people white concepts of cleanliness, bathing, washing clothes, and clean food, they tell her she thinks herself too good for her own people. She does not want to live in the white world because there, she could only find work as a servant and be treated with condescension. She is looking for a white man to take her away and she falls for Manerube and goes off with him on his promise to marry her. Manerube has lied, of course, and Chane Weymer stops them before Sosie learns the truth, that Manerube is using her with no intention of marrying her. Sosie describes her fate saying "I am what the white men have made me." Later, Sosie comes into the Melberne camp with her father and brothers, who are bringing in Chane's mustangs. She tells Sue Melberne about her childhood tending goats and sheep on the desert, her time at the government school and later about living in California, where she learned the language and habits of the whites. Indian religion was schooled and missionaried out of her, but when given the chance to choose between the Indian and white worlds, she chose to return to her people, like Nophaie and Nas ta Bega, hoping to do some good. She marries a young chief from her tribe, one who also received an education at the government school, someone with whom she has something in common, in that they understand what each other has been through and the fatality of their situation. She describes Chane's rescue for Sue. He fought Manerube, and she had hoped he would kill the liar. Back at home, her father beat her, threatening to kill her if she ever ran off with a white man again. She praises Chane's honesty and fairness. She says he is the kind of man that the missionaries should be.

Southards, Tex and Mex: In *Knights of the Range,* half-breed vaqueros who work on the Ripple ranch. They speak a mixture of Spanish and English. They are slow and impassive in all they do. They volunteer for Sloan's contingent to capture and lynch the rustlers at night.

Spades: (1) In *Stranger from the Tonto,* Lucy Bonesteel's horse that Slotte takes with him when he leaves the hideout. Ben Bunge takes the horse from him and sells it to Kent Wingfield, who rides horse back to the hideout to return to Lucy. The horse is a spectacular creature, well known to many. The Piute Tobiki recognizes him and tells Neberyull that Wingfield rode him into Logan's. On the way to the hideout, another Piute, Matokie, also recognizes the animal. Spades knows the way home and it is possible that Kent Wingfield would never have found the hideout but for the horse. When Lucy and Kent are leaving the canyon, Spades and Clubfoot know the way out of the canyon by the secret trail known only to a few of the outlaws.

(2) In *To the Last Man,* the name given to Jean Isbel's horse, Whiteface, which Lee Jorth gives to his daughter Ellen, cautioning her never to ride the animal outside their valley. When her father gives her the horse, Ellen asks what the animal's name is and Slater says he's called Spades, an ironic comment on the fact that they have paid back the Isbels "in spades." When Jean Isbel tracks the animal to the Jorth ranch, Whiteface (Spades) comes to him immediately and Ellen recognizes that the animal is answering the call of a beloved master. She understands that her father has indeed stolen the animal. Jean Isbel, however, lets her keep his horse, which be-

comes a confidante and source of comfort to her in trying circumstances.

Spangler: In *Sunset Pass,* a rancher operating near Wagontongue.

Specks: In *The Thundering Herd,* one of the horses pulling the wagon which brings Milly Fayre back to Sprague's station. On the trip back, Milly develops a particular affection for Whitey and Specks.

Spellman, Senator: In *30,000 on the Hoof,* the representative from Arizona that Logan Huett visits in his attempt to retrieve the hundred thousand dollars that Mitchell and Caddell swindled from him. Spellman tells him the case is not winnable, since he signed the receipt for the money without checking that the money was actually in the bundle. Mitchell and Caddell have testified that he had gone drinking with friends and had left the package unguarded. He recommends that Logan return home.

Spence, Harry: In *Wilderness Trek,* one of Dann's drovers, part of the rougher element of the crew, according to Sterling Hazelton. Spence and Tom Bedford get into a fight over some aborigine women that Ormiston has allowed to work around his camp. The two men are both drunk.

Spencer: (1) In *Knights of the Range,* one of the local ranchers who shows up at the Ripple ranch to accuse their foreman, Renn Frayne, of rustling.

(2) In *Majesty's Rancho,* the rancher for whom Tom Sloan rides. He too has lost cattle to the rustlers who drive them across the border into Mexico.

(3) In *The Mysterious Rider,* Bent Wade's brother-in-law, Lucy's brother. He runs a gambling place in Dodge. He never liked Bent Wade. Spencer was good friends with Captain Folsom, a confederate officer and Louisiana planter. He and Folsom do their best to drive a wedge between Wade and Lucy, encouraging a young southern aristocrat to pay her attention. Then, they spread the story that Lucy's child is not Wade's. They eventually provoke a fight between Wade and this young man. Wade kills the man he thinks is his wife's lover only to learn that the man is innocent.

(4) In *Raiders of Spanish Peaks,* a cattleman, owner of the B-Bar outfit that Lonesome Mulhall rode for over in Nebraska. Lonesome fell in love with his daughter but she is to marry another stockman called Cheesbrough. A fight breaks out with Cheesbrough over her. Ted Williams, Lonesome's partner "Tracks," kills him in a gunfight during the quarrel. Lonesome mentions him in his account to Laramie of his misfortunes due to his weakness for women.

Spencer, Hal: In *The Fugitive Trail,* the son of Mr. and Mrs. Spencer, and foster brother to Trinity. He is genuinely fond of her and she knows he is the best of the young men around but he is her brother. Hal returns from Denison with Caleb Green, full of stories about what has just happened. He has the latest gossip about the robbery. Sims, the cashier, shot the hat off one of the robbers and loosened his mask. He recognized one of the Lockheart brothers, probably Barse. He reports also on the gunfight between Bruce and Henderson and Whistler. Bruce was not the first to draw, but he must have been hunting trouble. He is awed by Bruce's speed with a gun, adding that there will never be any doubt in Denison again about all the trail drivers' stories of his fights. He tells Trinity that Barse was the cause of the fight, refusing to leave when Bruce tried to get him away from a poker game. When questioned by his father, he adds that Sheriff Jeff Hawkins had tried to arrest the dead gunman the day before. When the story spreads that Bruce, not Barse, was involved in the holdup, Hal, like Trinity, cannot believe it. Bruce was a grand fellow while Barse was no damned good. He suspects that all about the bank robbery is not as it seems.

Spencer, Mr.:   In *The Fugitive Trail*, Trinity's foster father. He is a typical Texan of lofty stature, lean face, white hair and piercing eyes. The Spencers found Trinity beside the Trinity River. She had been abandoned as a child and nothing had ever been learned about where she had come from or who she was. The Spencers raised her as their own daughter. Trinity feels she can discuss anything with him. He has one son, Hal. Like his wife, he understands Trinity's problem choosing a husband, but he reminds her that Barse, her apparent favorite, has gone to the bad. As a child, he was a decent sort, but he has been corrupted by the drinking and gambling that has taken over Denison with the arrival of the railroad.

Spencer, Mrs.:   In *The Fugitive Trail*, Hal's mother, Mr. Spencer's wife and foster mother to Trinity. She has hopes that Trinity will marry her son, Hal. She complains that Denison was pretty bad before the railroad work came with its gold and the riffraff workers, gambling halls and dance-hall hussies. Now, it's the worst Texas town she has ever lived near. She sympathizes with Trinity, who cannot decide which young man she likes best. No wonder, since she is so pretty. She praises Trinity's devotion to work. She can do any task required of a ranch wife, as well as most of what a cowboy does with horses, ropes and guns. She advises Trinity to take the man she likes best. She is fond of Barse Lockheart, but Mrs. Spencer cautions her about hoping she can reform him. He's bad by nature and marrying someone in the hope that he will reform later is a bad idea. When the story of the bank holdup and Barse's involvement in it reaches her, she tells Trinity that it is beyond her comprehension how she can prefer a man like Barse to Hal. She adds angrily that they will all be glad when she is gone if that is how she goes about selecting a husband.

Spense: In *The Lone Star Ranger*, an outlaw in Bland's camp who is killed by Bland. Spense was friendly with Kate Bland and Jennie. Kate admits she was in love with him. Some suspect Bland killed Spense at Kate's behest, as she suspected Spense was in love with Jennie. Kate herself tells Buck Duane that Bland killed Spense because of some disagreement years before.

Spenser, Miss: In *The Call of the Canyon*, a greenhorn from the East who spent a holiday at Lolomi Lodge. Flo and others played tricks on her when she went on a horseback ride into the mountains. Miss Spenser got a bad cold, a peeled nose and skinned shins, not to mention multiple saddle sores. She had to spend two days in bed recuperating from the experience. She didn't ride another horse for the rest of her stay. The locals got a great kick out of her misery and inexperience. Carley Burch senses that Miss Spenser is mentioned to caution her about what she can expect during her stay.

Spillbeans: In *The Call of the Canyon*, a balky bronc that Carley is given to ride when she sets out on a trip to the Hutter's sheep ranch in the mountains. The mustang is attractive to look at and Carley selects him out of ignorance and pride. The bronc throws her on the way, but eventually Carley masters the animal.

Spot: In *Wilderness Trek*, one of the wild cayuses that Red Krehl, now in Australia, recalls back in Texas.

Spottie: In *The Mysterious Rider*, a mottled white mustang, beautiful, but not too graceful or slick. The horse is a good worker, raised and broken by Wilson Moore, the only man who has ever ridden him. Although strictly speaking the property of the White Slides ranch, Spottie has known no master other than Moore. The animal is high-strung and nervous. When Buster Jack tries to ride him, asserting his ownership of the animal, he gets thrown off. This provokes a fight between Moore and Buster Jack. When he hears about the cause of the quarrel, that Buster Jack wanted to assert his authority over Wilson by taking his horse, Bill Belllounds declares the horse is Wilson's personal property. Spottie has a deformed front foot which requires a special triangular-shaped shoe. In order to make it appear that Wilson is one of the rustlers taking Belllounds's stock, Jack finds another mustang similar in color and size to Spottie and makes a special shoe which will leave a triangular print like Spottie's. Wade spots Jack riding this horse, deliberately leaving a trail from Wilson's place to the rustlers' cabin.

Sprague: (1) In *The Thundering Herd*, a man from Missouri who runs a post which collects hides and sells supplies to hiders en route to the buffalo hunt. Tom Doan meets up with Hudnall at Sprague's and Jude Pilchuck selects Tom's outfit at his post. Pilchuck is friendly with Sprague, from whom he learns about Jett and his crew and the rumors about his unusually large shipments of hides. The women brought in from the buffalo hunt are housed in tents at his station. Catlee likewise is friendly with Sprague and he tells him about Milly and Tom. Eventually, Sally and Dave, Burn Hudnall and his wife, and Tom and Milly settle down in the vicinity of the post, taking up ranching.

(2) In *Twin Sombreros,* a big cattleman around Las Animas. His herds have been hit hard by the rustlers.

(3) In *Valley of Wild Horses,* sells his homestead to Bill Smith because his wife wants to go home to Missouri. Their homestead had water, good soil, some timber, and an undeveloped mining claim that turned out well. Jard Hardman came along with claims, papers, witnesses and the backing of the law claiming he had gotten possession of the homestead from the original owner, and the Smiths are thrown off the land.

Sprague, John: In *To the Last Man,* an old man who raises burros in Chevelon Canyon. He lives in a rude, one-room cabin with a leaning, red stone chimney on the outside. He has lived there a long time. Rumor has it he had once been a prospector, one of the men in the area who searched for the Lost Dutchman gold mine. He knows the Tonto Basin better than anyone else around. He knows every trail, canyon, ridge and spring and reputedly can find his way to any of them in the dark. His claim to fame is that he raises nothing but black burros with white faces. They are the finest bred in the Basin and in great demand. He sells a few every year, hating to part with them. He gave Ellen Jorth one of his favorite burros, Jinny. Uncle John Sprague is perhaps the only friend that Ellen has. When she comes to see him, troubled, he lifts her spirits. Sprague is pleased that Ellen has a sensible approach to the imminent sheepmen-cattlemen war. There is no reason why the two factions cannot share the range, as there is plenty of rangeland for both. Sprague suggests that she go stay with relatives until it is over, but Ellen confesses that she has no one. Sprague tells her about the fight in Greaves's store which he witnessed the previous day. He tells her how Jean Isbel defended her honor when Lorenzo and Bruce Simm were besmirching her reputation. Sprague tells her that "[she] must never let anyone think bad of her, much less, help them to." He underlines the need for personal integrity, and honor. Later, when the war is in full force, he tells her about what Greaves said before he died, that Jean Isbel had killed him to avenge the insult to Ellen Jorth. Even Lee Jorth spoke well of Jean Isbel, calling him the only real man in the valley. Sprague resembles Friar Lawrence in Romeo and Juliet, who tries to bring the young couple together. Sprague is a voice of common sense and sanity in a valley divided by hatred.

Sprall: (1) In *The Lost Wagon Train,* one of Latch's outfit involved in the attack on the Anderson caravan. Sprall is part of the Leighton faction. Cornwall comments that he is always itching for a fight and will probably get killed before long. Leighton tells Sprall that not all the whites were killed in the massacre. He has a woman in his wagon. Cornwall later reveals that Sprall knew of Leighton's breaking Latch's orders. He is killed by Latch in a gunfight in which Latch establishes his authority over the outfit.

(2) In *Under the Tonto Rim,* Mr. Jenks, the teacher, tells Lucy that a family named Sprall used to live in a log cabin they pass on the way. They have moved into some remote canyon under the Tonto Rim.

Sprall, Bud: In *Under the Tonto Rim,* Tom Sprall's son. The first reports of him describe his reckless drunkenness. A woman would not feel safe around him. Lucy makes the mistake of dancing with him at the party. Mr. Jenks explains to her that she has danced twice with him and has appeared to enjoy it. He is handsome, and a good dancer, but he's disreputable, not the kind of man with whom a woman in her position should be associated. His true nature comes out when he starts spreading stories that he peeked through a chink in the logs and watched the teacher undress to change clothes before the dance. Edd has to settle the matter with him in a fistfight. There has been bad blood between Bud Sprall and Edd Denmeade for many years. On the way to meet her sister, Lucy and Joe Denmeade meet Bud and Jim Middleton. Joe tells her that Bud is reputed to be thick with cowboys in the Rim outfit. When Middleton attempts to blackmail Lucy and Clara, things lead to a fight in which Middleton is killed and Bud leaves the country. It is not clear how much Bud knew about his cousin Middleton (Harv Sprall) and Clara, but he said nothing. The sheriff's investigation reveals his unsavory reputation and, with one thing or another, he is liable to be sent to state prison. The judge gives him time to leave the country on condition that he not return.

Sprall, Harv (a.k.a. Jim Middleton): In *Under the Tonto Rim,* Jim Middleton's real name. He was killed in a fight with Edd Denmeade. He is a cousin of Bud Sprall and the other Spralls in the canyon. He was not well known in the Tonto but men from over in Winbrook have told the sheriff and the judge about his outlaw activities with his cousin, Bud. He was a wild, handsome, rodeo cowboy with whom Lucy Watson's sister, Clara, had run off. He got her pregnant then abandoned her. He threatens to show a letter from Mrs. Gerald, who has been keeping their daughter. This letter would ruin her reputation and, he hopes, make trouble with the Denmeades.

Sprall, Tom: In *Under the Tonto Rim,* one of the Sprall family that lives farther up the canyon from the Denmeades. He is mentioned once, by Mr. Denmeade, when he is explaining the situation of the other families in the area to Lucy Watson, the new teacher-welfare worker. Tom Sprall has two cabins, but no room for the teacher.

Spraull: In *Black Mesa,* works with Calkins rustling cattle and selling liquor to the Indians for Belmont. When Calkins has been killed by Kintell, Belmont is sure Spraull and Bloom will keep their mouths shut.

Springer: In *To the Last Man,* a gambler and member of the Jorth faction and the Hash Knife gang. He first appears at the Jorth ranch with Queen and Rock Wells. After the Isbel's attack on Greaves's store, he returns with Colter to the Jorth ranch to pack up for the flight from the Isbel pursuers. He is with Somers when they plan the trap to use Queen's body to catch Jean Isbel, but unlike Somers, he manages to escape. He and Colter are alone with Ellen Jorth at Daggs's cabin hideout. After Colter is killed by Ellen to defend the injured Jean Isbel, Isbel shoots Springer.

Springer Brothers: In *The Dude Ranger*, run the merchandise store and post office in the town that bears their name, Springer. The stagecoach leaves from their store in town. Ernest Selby is sent to town to pick up the mail and to make purchases for Anne Hepford at their store.

Springer, Frank Owens: In "From Missouri," the shy, rich, bachelor owner of a ranch. His cowboys initiate a correspondence with a young woman from Missouri who advertised for a position as a schoolteacher in a Kansas City newspaper. They used his first two names in the correspondence and when the new teacher arrives, they are hard pressed to explain there is no Mr. Owens. Springer comes upon them, reads the letters the young woman shows him, and apologizes for the trick some of his cowboys have played on her. He assures her, however, that her services as schoolteacher are welcome. Springer is businesslike, cool and serious. At the ranch, the presence of the young woman improves the dress and behavior of the cowboys when off duty. Springer is amused at how they compete for her attention. He himself invites her to the dance. There, however, she is in great demand. Springer has little time with her all evening. When Beady Jones comes around, he warns him off, and eventually has to engage him in a fistfight to finally discourage him. On the return to the ranch with Miss Stacey, Springer confesses that he is Frank Owens. He had caught on to the cowboys' prank, wrote several love letters himself and intercepted some of the correspondence at the post office. The shy bachelor proposes marriage and she gladly accepts.

Springer, Joe: In *The Dude Ranger*, asks Daisy Brooks to go to the dance.

Sproul: In *Boulder Dam*, a Communist agitator bent on sabotaging the construction of Boulder Dam. He has recruited workers at the dam and at the cement factory, including Ben Brown and Bink Moore. While sabotage of the dam is part of his plan, extorting money from the directors of the project is his immediate goal. He hopes to steal the payroll from director Carewe's office while his agents set bombs. His plot is revealed when Whitney Curtis overhears him plotting with several of his associates and confides this in Lynn Weston.

St. Vrain, Colonel: In *Fighting Caravans*, owns a ranch near Mora, across the Pecos River. He is one of the oldest frontiersmen still living. He came west in 1819, hunted, and trapped for years, fought through the war with the Navajos in 1823, became a major of a regiment in the Texas invasion of 1842 and retired from the army in 1849 to take up residence on his ranch. Clint Belmet meets the old frontiersman on his ranch. To him, the colonel looks like a Southern planter. In *The Lost Wagon Train*, Latch is compared to Colonel St. Vrain and to Maxwell, men who established impressive ranches providing hospitality to all, proof that white men and Indians could get along. In *Knights of the Range*, Don Carlos Valverde and Colonel Lee Ripple's ranch is compared to those of St. Vrain and Maxwell.

Stacey, Jane: In "From Missouri," the "under forty" schoolteacher who advertised for a position in the Kansas City newspaper. She exchanges correspondence with some cowboys, thinking she is writing to a rancher called Frank Owens. When she arrives and meets the cowboys at the train station, she confesses to some deception herself. She is well shy of the forty years she had mentioned in her letters. Jane Stacey is popular at the ranch. The cowboys' dress and behavior shows marked improvement since her arrival. They compete for the privilege of riding with her. At the party, she agrees to dance with all of them, in alphabetical order, and by the end of the night, she is exhausted. She is plagued by visits from Beady Jones, a handsome, slick, silver-tongued cowboy who cannot take no for an answer. The persistence of this lothario finally prods Frank Owens Springer to declare his love for her and propose marriage.

Stacey, Joe: In "Canyon Walls," brother to Hal and Lucy Card (her married name). They come to visit the Keetches one Sunday afternoon. The Staceys accept Sam Hill's presence at the dinner table as a matter of course, but he feels uncomfortable at first. The Staceys put him at ease. They are quiet, friendly, and far from curious about him. His worry that they might know of his past is groundless.

Stacey, Hal: In "Canyon Walls," brother to Joe and Lucy Card (her married name). They come to visit the Keetches one Sunday afternoon.

Stackhouse, Nel(son): In *The Deer Stalker*, a friend of Sue Warren who is working as a tour guide at the El Tovar resort near the Grand Canyon when Patricia Edgerton visits. Nelson was a cowpuncher at the Bar Z ranch near Flagstaff. He had the reputation of being a wild, bad boy. He drank, gambled and fought. He swore he was in love with Sue Warren. Nelson got into trouble and Thad Eburne helped him out of jail. He persuaded Nelson to take a job at El Tovar. Patricia gets her first glimpse of him when he and Tine Higgenbottom come to get the group ready for the descent into the canyon. He is tall, slim, keen-faced, well-muscled, lean-cheeked and square-jawed, with eyes of deep blue. When he walks, he jingles his spurs. Nels mounts his mule with effortless ease and grace. Nels and Tine plan to lure Patricia and Sue into going with them on a horseback excursion to the north rim. Patricia overhears the two of them planning their strategy to convince the women to join them. Patricia keeps mum about her overhearing this and plays along, appearing to be seduced by their charm. The trip through the forests and mountains is most agreeable to the women. They find a cabin when they are walking around stretching their legs and go inside. Patricia and Sue discuss Nelson's proposal of marriage to Sue. Patricia comments that he has a good record at the resort. He is well-liked, straight, sober, industrious, a perfect gentlemen. She herself would prefer a man who had been bad and turned over a new leaf than one who had been good all the time. Their discussion is interrupted by the arrival of men on horseback. They climb into the loft when they realize they are not Tine and Nelson. These turn out to be Bing Dyott and his outfit. Nelson and Tine appear later, having deduced that the women had found the cabin. Nelson enters, identifies himself, and, when speaking to Dyott, spots Sue and Patricia up in the loft. He tells Dyott that he and Tine had come up to have a look at the deer herds. He and Tine spend the night in the cabin, but when Dyott finds Patricia's glove and women's footprints outside, Nelson's quick wit fails him. Sue jumps on a horse and rides off. She meets up with Thad Eburne who returns to settle matters with Dyott. Patricia senses that Nelson feels humiliated that he had planned a trip that ended in disaster without his being able to set things right himself. Patricia announces that her plans for the summer involve visiting all the sights in the region, the Petrified Forest, Rainbow Bridge, Natural Bridge, Monument Valley, Montezuma's Well and the like. She wants Nels Stackhouse to be her guide, and Tine Higgenbottom his assistant. Then, she plans to have him scout out a ranch for her to buy. She plans to have him run the ranch for her when he marries Sue Warren. Nels accepts the job. By the time the deer drive comes about, he has found a suitable ranch for Patricia near Flagstaff. He and Tine help with the unsuccessful deer drive. At the end of the story, he and Sue are to be married.

Stafford: In *West of the Pecos,* told Hal Watson that the Eagle's Nest had changed beyond recognition. With the cattle drives heading north, the site has known unusual prosperity and growth.

Stafford, John: In *The Horse Thief,* a neighbor and friend of Jim Watrous. When Dale Brittenham has returned five of Edith Watrous's stolen horses, Stafford arrives at the ranch with Sheriff Bayne to arrest Dale as a horse thief. He suspects Dale is the inside man helping the thieves, and that the return of the five favorites is a ruse to take suspicion off himself. Later, Stafford puts a five-thousand-dollar reward on Dale's head, dead or alive. He sends a posse after the horse thieves, pursuing them into Idaho. His men catch up with Strickland's posse of cowboys and miners and for a while they shoot at each other, unaware that the thieves have left the valley following a secret trail behind the hideout cabin.

Sheriff Bayne plans to hang Dale when he catches up to him at Rogers's cabin, thereby earning the reward. Stafford acknowledges he was wrong about Brittenham and pays the reward to Edith for bringing him back. Stafford, Watrous and Brittenham go into the cattle-raising business as partners.

Stagg: (1) In *Desert Gold*, the boxing/football coach at the University of Wisconsin. He saw great potential in Dick Gale.

(2) In *Nevada,* a member of the Pine Tree Outfit. On Jim Lacy's request, he returns the stallion, California Red, which Burt Stillwell and Babe Morgan had stolen, to Ben Ide's corral. He explains how he went about returning the stallion without being noticed. Stagg agrees with Lacy (Nevada) that the stallion should not have been stolen. Ben Ide can tolerate the loss of his cattle but not of his beloved stallion. The theft would surely bring him into the pursuit of the Pine Tree Outfit. He confirms this opinion when he reports that on Burton's ranch, the hands told him that Ben Ide was offering a reward for the return of the stallion.

Stanley: (1) In *Western Union*, an outlaw that Vance Shaw had killed in a shootout in Texas. Vance's ranger friends, Hardin' and Siddell, have told Sunderland that when they wiped out the gang, Duke Wells lived long enough to confess Stanley's treachery and clear Vance Shaw's name. Vance is now thought of as a hero in Texas.

(2) In *Wyoming,* proprietor of a shady poolroom and rooming quarters for cowboys. He also runs a feed store and a livery stable in connection with a large corral. He tells Fenner he can have the pick of horses for him in ten days. Stanley witnesses the showdown between Bligh and Bonning, on the one hand, and Texas and McCall on the other. He takes the dying McCall into his livery stable, but nothing can be done for him. Stanley says he told McCall not to rile Texas; McCall brought this all on himself. He is willing to testify about what happened.

Stanton, Beauty: In *The U. P. Trail,* runs a saloon, brothel, and gambling establishment called Stanton's. She takes a liking to Warren Neale, but advises him to go back home. He's too good for a place like Benton. When Place Hough and Ancliffe rescue Allie from Durade, Ancliffe takes her to Stanton's, and Beauty agrees to hide her there. She sees in Allie traces of her old self, back in New Orleans, when she was young and innocent, happy with her brothers and sisters, when life was much simpler. She goes to find Neale, but when she tries to tell him that Allie is hiding at her place, Neale will not listen to her and insults her before the crowd, calling her a whore. In anger, Stanton decides she will ruin Allie to get revenge on Neale. She gives the key to the room where Allie is hidden to the drunken Red King, thinking he will make her into a whore. Larry, however, recognizes her and sobers up quickly, offering to take Allie to Neale. In the scuffle which ensues when he tries to leave the place, he shoots Beauty and

Durade's henchmen as well before being killed himself. Beauty does not die immediately, but in the tent awaiting treatment for her wound, she writes a letter to Neale, apologizing and explaining all that happened. She is buried in an unmarked grave beside Larry Red King by McDermott and Casey. Casey takes her letter when he goes to warn General Lodge of the impending Sioux attack. From there, the letter eventually makes its way back to Neale. Beauty Stanton is an example of a stereotype found in novels about the frontier, the whore with the heart of gold.

Stanton, Lee: In *The Call of the Canyon*, a young cowboy who works on Tom Hutter's ranch. He is sweet on Flo. When he arrives at the ranch, Flo runs off, feigning disapproval, hoping that he will chase after her, as he does. He makes a favorable impression on Carley Burch. He steps out of the saddle with a lazy, graceful action. He is a tall, lithe figure, singularly handsome in his black sombrero, flannel shirt, blue jeans, high boots and rowelled spurs. He embodies the romantic west Carley has known in pictures. He is the overseer of the sheep hands working at the dip. Lee Stanton accompanies Flo and Carley when they go to view the Painted Desert. Unlike Flo or Tom Hutter, he understands how the scene has affected Carley and tells her that she, like himself, will have to return to the seen again and again before she will feel comfortable with its implications and hauntingness. Lee is deeply in love with Flo, but he knows she is sweet on Glenn. Flo tells him she does love him and admire him, but Glenn the war hero has captured her heart. Lee asks if Carley Burch loves Glenn the way Flo does. Carley admits she does not understand the dynamics between Glenn and herself, but she intends to get Glenn to return to New York. Lee questions any depth in Carley, and doubts Glenn will return east. This conversation causes Carley to do some soul-searching about her relationship with Glenn. At the party, Lee learns to do the fox trot from Carley. When Flo tries to show her indifference to Lee by sending another girl to flirt with him, Lee turns the tables on her and pretends to be interested in the new girl. When Carley returns to Arizona, she learns that Lee Stanton has left Tom Hutter's employ to set up his own operation. As well, Lee and Flo have been married. Like Ruff Haze, Lee Stanton has the westerner's common sense and true values.

Star: In "The Ranger," Ranger Medill's horse, a big-boned chestnut, not handsome except in regard to its size. For speed and endurance, Vaughn had never owned his like. They have been on some hard jaunts together and Star has never let him down.

Stark, Bill: In *Stairs of Sand*, with Brooks captured Wansfell on orders from Guerd Larey. Stark does not know their prisoner is the famous Wansfell. When he does, he recalls how he is reputed to have killed Baldy McKue, breaking his arms, his ribs and his neck with his bare hands. Wansfell had killed

McKue for abusing a pregnant woman. It turns out this woman was Stark's wife. Out of gratitude for this service to her, Stark sets Wansfell and Merryvale free. He kills Brooks in a shootout, and leaves with the other outlaws, telling Wansfell they are now even.

Starke: In "The Secret of Quaking Asp Cabin," the name Richard Starke and Blue give to the bastard son of his brother Len and the Apache girl Letith. Dissatisfied with things in the canyon, Letith's father leaves the canyon taking her with him, but refusing to have anything to do with the boy. Len still does not acknowledge his paternity, so Richard adopts the boy to raise as his own. The boy learns English from his parents, but Blue teaches him Apache as well. The boy is fond of Richard and vice versa, and after the shooting where the father loses his arm and barely survives, Starke remains faithful to his father. He continues to plant the crops and hunt to provide for the family during some ten years. When his sister dies, Starke feels as if his heart is buried in the grave with her. He leaves Quaking Asp Cabin without a word of farewell to his parents, never to return while they are alive. He is the half–Apache hunter and guide with whom the narrator has taken hunting trips on three different occasions. He looks young, perhaps in his late twenties, but he tells Grey he is now almost fifty years old. He has heard that the narrator (Grey) wants to learn the full story of Quaking Asp Cabin and the ghosts that seem to haunt the place. He proceeds to tell him the story that no one else knows completely. The narrator, he says, is the only person to whom he would ever tell the story. He was born in the cabin. He says he learned his English from Hillie's mother, Blue. She was from the East, and educated, and taught both him and Hillie. He was never sure which of the brothers was his father. But when his heart broke at Hillie's death, and he drifted from hunter to hard-nut cowboy, to rustler and gunman, he suspected that Len was his father, the brother who cast the evil spell over the homestead. Old Matt Taylor, the Mormon friend and helper, now over eighty years old with a poor memory, is the only other person who could reveal the secret of Quaking Asp Cabin.

Starke, Richard: In "The Secret of Quaking Asp Cabin," a settler. A half–Apache hunter tells the unnamed narrator (possibly Zane Grey) the story which explains the ghosts around Quaking Asp Cabin. It is the story of Richard Starke and his brother, Len. Richard Starke goes west to find a place to live. He and his brother and his wife settle at Quaking Asp Cabin with Matt Taylor, a Mormon, as helper. The Mormons from whom he bought cattle and seeds for planting help erect the cabin and Matt remains to give a helping hand. At first, they prosper. Richard and Blue have a girl, Hillie, Richard adopts the bastard son of his brother Len and the Apache girl, Letith. The boy and girl are particularly fond of their father. One day Richard sees Blue and Len making love under the trees. He is surprised and hurt, but then comes to find excuses for his no-good brother. Perhaps he has made a mistake settling in so isolated and remote a place. Len is much more handsome than he, and Blue is closer in age to Len than to him. Both of them share a similar unrestrained sensuality. Richard has decided to let Blue leave with Len, on condition she leave the children with him. But before he can announce his magnanimous decision, Len attempts to kill him. Richard cannot forget the burning hatred in his eyes. He is determined not to die and to learn if Blue had any part in this. He has lost his right arm, and the top of his lung. He makes it back to the cabin, where Matt Taylor bandages him up. He lies in the cabin for days, everyone expecting him to die. But he does not. He remains morose, sullen, never speaking to Blue. He hears her and Len talking in whispers when they think he does not hear. Len goes off to live in the woods like an Indian, rarely returning. Blue remains out of guilty duty. Matt Taylor remains a friend, helping when he can. The children and Blue do what farming they can, but the prosperity they once knew is over. At age sixteen, Hillie dies, and following that, the boy, Starke, goes off. Richard decides to speak to Blue, telling her he has forgiven her. He tells her he has money hoarded away, enough for her and Len to go off and start over. He has already sent Matt Taylor to find Len to ask him to come back. He asks Blue to help Len go straight. She leaves the house shortly afterward and Richard hears her call. He hears a horse approach and he listens as the hoof beats fade into the distance.

Starke, Len: In "The Secret of Quaking Asp Cabin," the younger brother of Richard Starke and the natural father of Starke, the narrator's Apache hunter and guide. He was an unwanted child, born when Richard was ten years old. All of Len's nineteen years Richard had loved him, shielded him and at last saved the weakling from jail if not from disgrace. He was a handsome stripling, careless, loveable, too weak to curb his bad instincts. One summer when an Apache family lives in the canyon, he gets the daughter, Letith, pregnant. He never acknowledges his paternity, but Letith's way of looking at him speaks volumes. Eventually, the Apache father takes his daughter away, abandoning the child. Len then pursues Blue. Richard becomes aware of their betrayal, but makes excuses for them. Len shoots his brother. Richard loses his arm and part of a lung. Matt Taylor expects him to die, but Richard survives. Len leaves the cabin to live wild in the woods like an Indian. Blue remains with Richard out of a sense of guilt. Richard eventually overcomes his hatred for the pair, forgives Blue, and gives her the money he has hoarded up. He asks her to go off with Len to start a new life. As Richard lies dying in the cabin, he hears Len's hoofbeats fade in the distance.

Starr, Ren: In *Majesty's Rancho*, works at the garage in Bolton when Lance Sidway rides up on his horse, Umpqua. Starr comments on the splendid mount, and the two of them become fast friends. He talks about the depressed cattle industry, the ranches where one might possibly find a job. He recommends Mrs. Goodman's café for a good meal, and Gene Stewart as an employer. Stewart will "cotton to him" as Starr did. Starr loves him as if he was his own father. Ren tells Lance the story of El Capitán in the Mexican Revolution and how he came to marry the new owner of Don Carlos's ranch. He also mentions Stewart's stunningly beautiful daughter who is away at school. He writes Stewart a letter praising young Sidway's abilities. Gene Stewart tells Lance at a later point that Ren had called him a "whiz."

Lance has concluded that trucks are the favorite tool of rustlers nowadays. He had come to understand this when he drove a truck for Uhl, supposedly to distract men out to hijack a bootleg liquor shipment. Trucks used for shipping liquor could just as easily carry stolen cattle. Ren Starr comes to Lance with the news that some canvas-covered trucks have been tanked up at the garage, and word has it they are staying overnight. He learned this from Graves, the new employee at the garage, who had let this piece of information slip. As well, he saw a rider, a stranger, hanging around all day, go into the lunchroom. He was the go-between with the truck drivers. He predicts that a cattle raid is planned for that night. Ren Starr expects to see some wild action when they meet the rustlers. He promises to tell Lance some stories about Stewart and Nels. They have seen the wildest of western days. Nels was a Texas Ranger before coming to Arizona and Gene was not only a tough cowboy but a genuine gunman. The encounter meets his expectations for excitement and action.

Ren signs up as a rider for Gene Stewart. Danny Mains comments to Stewart that he reminds him of their old friend, Nick Steele. Starr is good with horses, and good with a gun. When Lance Sidway tells Madge she should not be riding Dervish, Ren sides with Madge. He confesses that she has a way of talking him into seeing things her way. When Madge is kidnapped, he pooh-poohs any talk of Lance being in cahoots with the gangsters. When they reach Cochise's stronghold, he shoots Flemm, supervises the hanging of Fox, and kills Uhl in a genuine old-fashioned shootout.

He is terribly stuck on Bonita but her flirting with the vaqueros has soured things. Lance talks to her to let her know that her flirting hurts Ren. She says she has not done it on purpose to hurt Ren but just to have fun. By the end of the story, she and Ren are to be married.

Starwell: In *The Thundering Herd*, with a partner, Black, runs a freighting company that buys hides. They go out into the field and buy the hides from the hunters and freight them back to the train station themselves. He is with Pilchuck when they come across the remains of Jett's outfit and try to understand what happened there. Starwell, together with Pilchuck, leads the campaign against the Comanche.

Stearns: In *Twin Sombreros*, a cattleman in Kansas with whom Raine Surface had a major disagreement. Surface shot Stearns, but not fatally. Lura Surface tells Brazos that her father would never draw on another man unless he had the advantage.

Stebbins, Wess: In *The Hash Knife Outfit*, the young man who marries Caroline, Curly Prentiss's old girlfriend.

Stedman, Widow: In *30,000 on the Hoof*, reaches an agreement to graze her herd on Huett's range on the halves. When she dies, she leaves her herd to Logan.

Steele, Joe: In *Shadow on the Trail*, Bilt Wood's rival for the affections of Susie in Holbrook. Joe is quite a ladies' man, a fancy dresser and boastful of his success with women. He rides for Band Drake (Rand Blue) and Mason over in Mariposa. He tells Bilt he is in town waiting to meet his boss, who is coming in on the train from Winslow. When Bilt tries to pick a fight with him over Susie, he says he does not fight with runts like him, especially not in front of a lady. Steele later forces Susie and her family to put Blue and three other men up for the night, nearly frightening her parents to death. In the morning, they leave, taking several of the family's farm horses. When Tex Brandon and his men catch up with them, Steele goes for his gun and is killed in the shootout.

Steele, Nick: In *The Light of Western Stars*, a slim, broad-shouldered cowboy, some six foot, four inches tall. He is the roundup boss for Stillwell and Alfred, an experienced cowman. Gene Steward puts him in charge of holding back Stillwell while he pursues the abductors of Madeline. He is one of the cowboys involved in the golf tournament Madeline organizes to entertain her eastern guests. He tells a tall tale of being a leading golfer in Saint Louis and Kansas City. He is also one of the cowboys involved in the camping expedition in the mountains designed to get the guests out of danger when Don Carlos has invaded the ranch.

In *Majesty's Rancho*, Danny Mains comments that Ren Starr is another Nick Steele, a cowboy and loyal fighter.

Steen: In *The Horse Thief*, runs a saloon in Halsey where Big Bill Mason has won a huge amount of money in a card game.

Stemm: In *Rogue River Feud*, works on the Rogue River. He takes Keven and Garry's first catch of fish to the cannery for sale. He also identifies Garry and Keven's skiff which has washed out to sea. Both Keven and Garry are presumed dead.

Steve: In *The Horse Thief*, one of the three horse thieves that Dale Brittenham comes upon in camp, awaiting the arrival of other members of the gang. He is killed by Dale.

Stevens: (1) In *Arizona Ames*, a rider on Halstead's ranch. He brings Fred home drunk one night.

He is a close associate of Mecklin's and this association casts doubt on his integrity. He is brought into the ranch all shot up and Jed takes him to town to the doctor. He recovers and is fortunate not to be caught with the rustlers.

(2) In *Fighting Caravans*, a freighter with Clint Belmet. He spots Blackstone and the Indians approaching Point of Rocks and gives the warning signal.

(3) In *Twin Sombreros*, a large-scale cattleman in the Las Animas area. He is willing to buck the Cattleman's Association in the question of the appointment of Bodkins as sheriff following Kiskadden's resignation.

Stevens, Captain: In *Wyoming*, in charge of the armory near the Black Hills. Arthur Anderson tells Martha Ann Dixon that he will take her to the armory and keep her there till the captain can be notified.

Stevens, Hump: Appears in *The Drift Fence* and *The Hash Knife Outfit*. In *The Drift Fence*, Hump Stevens is identified as the first cowboy to sign on for the Diamond Ranch some six years ago. He is referred to as a "dyed in the wool" cowboy. While he is not keen on the idea of building the barbed wire drift fence, he volunteers to carry the rolls of barbed wire and to dig posts. He accepts the new state of things under Jim Traft's foremanship. In *The Hash Knife Outfit*, Hump Stevens is still one of the cowboys who work for Jim Traft at the Diamond Ranch. Stevens among others accompanies Jim to the train station in Flag to meet his sister. He is one of the two cowboys killed when the Diamond cowhands under Slinger Dunn attack the Hash Knife Outfit hideout.

Stevens, Jeff: In *The Fugitive Trail*, one of the cowboys riding for Steve Melrose in his Little Wichita outfit. He is shot and killed when the Stewart outlaw gang rustles that herd.

Stevens, Jim: In *Western Union*, a Texas cattleman driving a herd of four thousand cattle to the Sweetwater Valley in Wyoming. They meet Creighton's construction crew, who are worried that the cattle could pose problems for construction, knocking over the poles as the buffalo do.

Stevens, Link: In *The Light of Western Stars*, the cowboy who becomes Madeline Hammond's chauffeur. He loves cars, fast cars. The cowboys say of him that he never had any sense with a horse and has even less with a car. He got banged up busting broncos and has trouble riding now, so he has taken on these new duties. He drives Madeline's family and friends from back east from El Cajón to the ranch. He also drives Madeline to get Gene Stewart to give up drinking and gambling and return to the ranch. Later, he drives her to Mexico to rescue Gene Stewart, El Capitán, from the firing squad.

In *Majesty's Rancho*, Gene Stewart and Nels are reminded of Link Stevens when they see Madge driving over seventy miles an hour along the dirt road to the ranch. Like Link, she loves fast horses and even faster cars, and is just as reckless as he had been.

Stevens, Lieutenant: In *Fighting Caravans*, sent in pursuit of some Comanche braves with sixty troopers. The Comanche are surrounded, captured and executed.

Stevens, Luke: Appears in *The Last of the Duanes* (a.k.a. *The Lone Star Ranger*). Buck Duane runs into him as he is running away from his home in Wellston. He has just killed his first man and has inherited his father's reputation as a gunman. Luke Stevens is also on the run. He's small and wiry, slouchy of attire, with dancing brown eyes and a bold, frank, deep-tanned face. He is straddling a fine bay horse. Stevens has heard of Buck, of his father, and understands immediately why he is on the run. Stevens, himself an outlaw, takes Buck under his wing and gives him some advice about survival among fellow outlaws. He explains what the outlaw towns are like, about the difference between King Fisher and his outfit and Bland, the worst of the lot. Bland would be especially hard on Duane. Bland keeps women in his camp and with his stunningly good looks, Buck Duane would be a sure target for Bland's suspicions and jealousy. He advises Duane to keep to himself as much as he can. It's hard to do, but it's the safest way in the long run.

Luke Stevens is a likeable outlaw, willing to share his experience with Duane and willing to learn from Duane in return. Duane exacts a promise from him that when he goes into Mercer to get some grub, he won't go looking for trouble. Stevens, however, is recognized and he is shot. Stevens advises Duane to leave him behind and to look out for himself. Buck refuses to abandon the man and does his best to tend to his wounds. Stevens dies two days later, thanking Duane for having the kindness to stand by him. There is honor among outlaws.

Luke Stevens is an example of the decent outlaw, a figure that appears regularly in Zane Grey's novels. Stevens seems particularly concerned that he not die with his boots on. Only outlaws and thoroughly corrupt men die with their boots on. Buck removes his boots every night, and indeed, Luke Stevens does die as a decent man dies. Stevens is a man who has yielded to the worst influences in the environment and in his own nature. As well, he is an example of the man in whom decency has taken deep root, although he has not been able to live up to the best in his nature all the time.

Stevens, Old Jim: In *Stranger from the Tonto*, one of the men Kent Wingfield is supposed to have killed according to the story that Ben Bunge spins about the gunman, Kent Wing Field. According to his story, Wing Field's reputation rests on the job he did in the Verdi. He was out with some riders trailing a bunch of rustlers, the Old Jim Stevens outfit. Young Field got separated from his outfit and ran into Stevens with three of his men. While they were

drawing their guns, Wing popped them out of their saddles like so many turkeys from a roost, and he was shooting from a jumpy horse.

Stevens, Rollie: In *Majesty's Rancho*, one of Madge Stewart's crowd at the university in Los Angeles. He urges on the students gathered around when Madge and Officer Brady are arguing about her speeding ticket. The situation gets out of hand, turning into a riot of sorts. Rollie is a decent young man, but Madge treats him more like a messenger boy. He comes to the ranch in Arizona for the summer. Rollie criticizes Madge's treatment of Lance Sidway. Because she has not been able to get her way with Lance, she is mean to Rollie. Rollie likes Lance, He is a real man, not a sap. If Madge were nicer to him, even if she doesn't like him, he would soon fall into line. Rollie has proposed marriage to Madge three times. He has spoken with Madeline about his intentions and told her about his family's position and wealth and his own prospects. He is a likeable young man, according to Madeline, but she doubts he would want to live at the ranch. Lance witnesses a drunken Rollie trying to force himself on Madge in the bower during the fiesta. He and Rollie have a fight. Rollie Stevens is with Madge when she is kidnapped. He fully believes that Lance is one of the gangsters involved in the plot. Stevens actually participates in the hanging of Fox, pulling on the fatal rope.

Stevenson, Captain: In *Fighting Caravans*, leads a detachment of ninety-five soldiers to escort Captain Couch's caravan of freight wagons from Kansas City to Santa Fe.

Stewart: (1) In *The Deer Stalker*, Jim Evers recalls the Stewart boys who were wild horse wranglers. He wishes he had young men like the Stewart brothers to drive the deer from the overcrowded range to a new, unpopulated range. These boys could drive anything that could walk.

(2) In *Nevada*, foreman at Day's ranch. Day has doubts about his honesty. He drinks, and is in close with Clan Dillon. It turns out both of these were part of the Lincoln County gang in New Mexico.

(3) In *Shadow on the Trail*, Mason's foreman. Lawsford says he is hard to work for, and does not suggest Tex Brandon look for work there. Stewart is involved in Mason's scheme to sell rustled cattle. When Brandon is waiting for him in the saloon, he does not show up, someone having tipped him off. He is never heard from again.

Stewart, Abe and Bill: In *Wildfire*, two wild horse hunters who have been working with Lin Slone for some years. Like Slone, they admire the wild stallion whom they have named Wildfire, but unlike Slone, they grow exhausted from the pursuit and conclude they will never catch the wily mustang. They have developed techniques for catching wild horses but Wildfire has managed to avoid them all. When they pull out, they leave Lin with most of the grub and supplies for his continued pursuit of the mustang. Slone comments that these have been the most generous friends he has known.

Stewart, Bill:

In *The Fugitive Trail*, a cattleman involved in a deal with Barncastle and Melrose. He shows up at the ranch just after Bruce Lockheart has come to work there. He declares he is Barncastle's right-hand man. He looks contemptuously at Luke Slaughter, Melrose's foreman. Lockheart recognizes in him a force more powerful than Belton (Barncastle) and realizes that Melrose has gotten involved with some pretty bad men. Stewart and his cowboys have a matured hardness that reminds Bruce of Billy the Kid's outfit. He is not easily perturbed, and concludes by threatening Slaughter that he had better convince his boss of the wisdom of joining with him and Barncastle. He hints that Melrose will likely lose both his money and his cattle. Later, Barncastle comes to see Melrose to settle the deal. He runs into Stewart, who has made a deal with Henderson to rustle Melrose's herd. In the fight which follows, Belton is killed. He tells Belton (Barncastle) that he'll give him another Bruce Lockheart trade-mark. Slaughter and other cowboys from Melrose's ranch overhear the fight and witness the shootout and are convinced that Stewart is the name Bruce Lockheart is currently using. Stewart and Henderson rustle the Melrose herd and sell it to Jerry McMillan. Melrose's cowboys under Tex Serks strike a deal with McMillan to get payment for the cattle when they are delivered to market in Dodge. Then, they pursue Stewart. With the help of the Texas Rangers, who are finally persuaded by Melrose to undertake the task of eliminating the scourge of rustlers, they surround the cabin where Stewart's men are holed up. Stewart comes face to face with Bruce, and in the shootout, he is killed by the man whose name he had appropriated.

Stewart, Gene:

In *The Light of Western Stars*, the hero of the story, a cowboy with a kind heart and great strength, but with little faith in himself and his own goodness.

Gene appears in the opening chapter where he meets Madeline Hammond at the train station. He has made a bet with his friends at Ed Linton's bachelor party that he will marry the first pretty woman he meets. He checks her finger to be sure she is single, brings in Padre Marcos and the two of them are married. She thinks it's all just a big practical joke her brother has organized for her benefit. The scene is confusing; a young Mexican woman, Bonita, comes in, asking for help to escape Don Carlos. Gene gives her his horse, and she rides off into the night. Gene takes Madeline to Florence Kingsley's place to spend the night. Florence is Alfred Hammond's (the brother's) fiancée. Florence scolds him for being so foolish and cautions him to keep quiet about the episode. He returns the next day to apologize to Madeline and to face the music with her brother. Florence say of him that he can't save his money, that he drinks too much, but that he has the best horse in the area, a horse he loves like a family member.

Madeline admits to herself that she is thrilled by the look of this "splendid, dark-faced barbarian" who looks like Dustin Farnum on Broadway.

Gene Stewart, the reader learns, is from the East. He was from a good family and attended college, but went to the bad in the West. His drinking, it seems, is provoked by bouts of remorse over the disgrace he has brought on his mother and sisters. His has been the fate that Mr. Gale expected for his son, Dick, when he went west.

Gene Stewart alternates between living in Mexico and living in Arizona. He gains a reputation for himself in a battle when Madero's forces seize Ciudad Juárez, defeating the forces of Porfirio Diaz. He earns the nickname "El Capitán," popular among Mexican vaqueros on the American side of the border. On his return to Arizona, to Yuma, he turns to drinking, and pleas from Nels and Bill Stillwell to return to the ranch and stop drinking and raising Cain are to no avail. Madeline, however, makes a trip to Chiricahua to see him and convinces him to return. He has a tearful reunion with his horse, Majesty.

On his return, he becomes foreman of her ranch. He commands the raid on Don Carlos's ranch to evict the bandits still there. According to her wishes, all is done by the letter of the law. The ammunition is removed from the house and burned. When Madeline is abducted to Mexico by some of these bandits on orders from Don Carlos, who plans to sell her to a brothel after he has done with her, Gene follows them. He is recognized as "El Capitán" and his reputation allows him to secure her release for two thousand dollars. Gene points out to Madeline that her way of doing things, by the letter of the law, could never have brought about her release. He apologizes for not having killed the bandit who injured her, but he has done things as she would have wished. Her eastern ways need to be adjusted to conditions in the West.

When the visitors come from the East, Gene is friendly, but distant. He disappears on secret errands which he never explains and which cause Madeline and Stillwell to wonder. He refuses to participate in the golf game, pointing out that work still needs to be done. He is particularly worried that Don Carlos will take advantage of the laxity of security at the ranch to do something untoward. Both Helen Hammond and Dorothy Coombs try their best to get his attention by flirting or by playing the helpless female, but all to no avail. They finally give up, assuming that he is in love with Madeline.

When Don Carlos is holed up in the ranch house, Gene Stewart ensures that the revolutionary does not manage to get a war started between the U.S. and Mexico by getting the guests out of the house and up into the mountains where they are safe. On this camping expedition in the mountains, Madeline observes him giving a package to Bonita, whom no one has seen in quite some time. She assumes that Bonita is his woman. Gene sees her tracks on the trail and tries to speak to her to explain, only to be dismissed in a haughty manner. He is about to ride off in a pique when Nels brings word that Don Carlos and his bandits are approaching. They hide the eastern guests and when the bandits come into camp, pretend to be alone. The bandits do discover evidence of the guests' presence, but a fight encourages them to pull out.

The day of Alfred Hammond's wedding, Sheriff Hawe comes to the ranch to arrest Gene for a murder that took place some time ago. When he sees that Hawe has abused Bonita and has her tied to the horse, he offers to surrender himself if Bonita is released. In the gunfight which follows, provoked by Monty Price who is tired of doing things the "eastern" way, Hawe is killed and Bonita set free. Later, over Monty Price's grave, Gene is saying his farewells to the place, as he plans to leave for Mexico again. Madeline comes up to him and he asks her why she did not let him explain about Bonita. Again, she doesn't give him a chance to explain, striking him in the face with her quirt. He tells her how he has loved her all along and been loyal to her, doing things her way only to be dismissed scornfully. Madeline sees in his eyes the same hopelessness and despair she had seen earlier in Chiricahua. He leaves his horse with her and sets off for Mexico.

In Mexico, he is captured and sentenced to death. He is prepared to meet his death with dignity. Given his reputation as "El Capitán," he will not face a firing squad. Instead, he will be released into the plaza dressed in full military uniform. He is free to walk around, knowing that his executioner will be a marksman, hidden on a rooftop. To his surprise, Madeline is waiting for him at the end of the plaza. Padre Marcos has told her that she is indeed married to Gene, and that she should not reject the love of such a decent man. Madeline then puts to work her network of connections in political circles in Washington and arranges his pardon and release.

In Gene Stewart, Grey has produced a variant on his western hero. While Gene has the physical strength, courage, and knowledge of the environment of the usual heroic figure, he lacks the confidence in himself found in a Jack Hare or a Wetzel. Gene needs the encouragement and guidance of the heroine to become a better person. The relationship between Madeline and Gene appears to have been inspired, in part, by the Wister romance of Molly Wood and the Virginian. Molly sees her role as the guide, the moral half of a platonic relationship through which the hero will rise to a new moral level.

Gene Stewart appears again in *Majesty's Rancho*. Some twenty years have passed since he returned with Madeline Hammond from Mexico. He has become a legend of sorts. Ren Starr tells his story to Lance Sidway. It's a story well known to every cowpuncher in the West. The ranch Gene now owns is close to the border and was once the property of a Mexican named Don Carlos. During the Mexican Revolution, Don Carlos had the old Spanish grant. He was selling contraband across the border. Gene was a tough cowboy in those days, great with the rope, with horses and the gun. Hombres came no cooler than Gene. He joined the revolutionaries who called him El Capitán. When Madero was assassinated, he returned to the states just when a rich girl from New York came and bought Don Carlos's ranch. Stillwell was foreman and had gathered the hardest bunch of cowboys that ever rode the range. Nobody could boss them until he put Gene on the job. They ran Don Carlos and his men off the range and built the ranch into the finest known in the West. Gene married the new owner and that story is quite a romance.

The ranch had been remarkably prosperous but has fallen on hard times. The Depression has seen the price of beef plummet, and the future does not look very bright. Gene feels somewhat guilty that the loss of Madeline's fortune with the failure of the eastern bank has not been compensated for by the ranch. He and Madeline have a daughter, Majesty, who is as bright, determined, and pig-headed as Madeline herself had been when he first met her. Gene dotes on his daughter; he is unable to deny her anything. To keep her at the university, he and Madeline have virtually impoverished themselves.

When Lance Sidway appears at the ranch, offering to work for room and board, Gene is impressed most of all with the spectacular horse, Umpqua, the young man is riding. He questions him about his motives for seeking work at this ranch of all places. He suspects Lance is interested in his daughter, but at this point, Lance does not know she is the young woman he met at the riot in Los Angeles. When Madge comes out of the house to inspect the horse, she recognizes Lance as the young man who rescued her from the riot. She suspects he has come to see her. Gene, however, accepts Lance's account of the coincidence.

Gene likes Lance because he sees in him a reflection of himself at that age. Young Sidway never ceases to impress him with his ingenuity, responsibility and initiative. He reveals the mystery surrounding the rustling of his cattle: the rustlers drive the steers to a road where they can easily be loaded on to trucks and transported across the border to Mexico or out of state. In the ambush to catch the thieves, Gene's life is saved by the quick shooting of Lance Sidway. When Madge's friends come from Los Angeles to spend the summer, he puts Lance in charge. Lance is carrying out the same kind of tasks he did when Madeline's family and friends from back east came to pay a visit. Lance remains detached, cool, with his eyes focused on his task, not on the girls. He refuses to get caught up in their games. Gene asks Lance to straighten out his books. Lance learns that the situation on the ranch is not as dismal as Gene had thought. With the sale of half his herd, he should be able to clear his debts and have a bit of money ahead. Lance also learns from the accounts that they have been accumulating debts to keep Madge at the university. Gene swears him to strict secrecy about this sacrifice. Stewart tells Lance that Ren Starr had pegged him perfectly when he called him a "whiz."

The night of Majesty's grand fiesta, Gene gets drunk on Corvalo's remarkable punch. It's the first drinking he has done in many a day, having sworn off the liquor which had nearly ruined him in his youth. When Madge is kidnapped by Bee Uhl, he remains loyal to Lance. Sloan reports that Lance seemed familiar with the gangsters in the car, and wonders if he was not part of the plot. Even Madge and Rollie Stevens have their doubts about his honesty. Stewart sees the wisdom in taking the gangsters up into the mountains, along the Cochise Trail to the mountain stronghold. Such a trip would surely wear out men not accustomed to hard riding. When they reach the stronghold, Stewart grasps immediately what Lance Sidway's plan had been. Lance has gotten away with Madge while the gangsters were out trying to round up the horses. Stewart administers justice the old-fashioned way. Fox is hanged. Flemm is killed in a shootout as is Bee Uhl. He reports back to Madeline about the fight, commenting that the sheriff in El Cajón (Bolton) will be more understanding that Sheriff Hawe had been twenty years ago.

Gene is tremendously pleased when Madge comes to her senses and sees Lance Sidway for what he is, a sincere, honest young man who is deeply in love with her, but who has no patience for her games. With Sidway as foreman, Gene rests assured of future prosperity.

Stewart, Lee and Cuth: In "Lightning," two tall, lean Mormon cowboys, as bronzed as desert Navajos, cool, silent, gray-eyed, still-faced. Both wear crude homespun garments much the worse for wear, boots that are worn out, laced leather wristbands thin and shiny from contact with lassoes and old gray slouch hats that would disgrace cowboys. Their equipment, however, shows a care not bestowed on their clothing. The boys are selected by their ranch foreman to catch the wild stallion, Lightning. A five-hundred-dollar reward has been posted for the capture of the mustang. They use their mustang mare, Black Bess, as bait. Bess has long been broken and is so loyal she can be left loose at night without fear of her running off. The lure of the desert and the call of the mustang stallion, however, prove too strong, and Bess returns to the wild. The boys keep following. Bess loses a shoe and starts to limp. Eventually, the boys catch up with her, and the black stallion, Lightning, has remained by the mare. When the boys see the prize animal they have caught, they decide not to collect the reward. It is nowhere near enough for such a spectacular specimen.

Stewart, Madge (Majesty): In *Majesty's Rancho,* the daughter of Gene and Madeline Stewart. She is a chip off the old block, resembling her mother when she first came west. Madge is developed along the lines of many Grey heroines, such as Betty Zane, Jane Withersteen, and Hallie Lindsay in *Raiders of Spanish Peaks.* She is a selfish, haughty young woman who needs to learn respect for others and to understand and follow the dictates of her heart.

Madge lords it over her crowd at the university. They attend to her as courtiers to a monarch. When she is dismissed from the university, she invites them all to come to her ranch to spend the summer. She has never bothered to discuss this with her parents. She drives back to the ranch, meeting Uhl in Yuma and giving him the slip. She doesn't realize with whom she has been dealing.

At the ranch, she meets Lance Sidway, the young man who had helped her get away from the policeman in L.A. She refuses to believe his meeting her there is purely coincidental. And she insists on buying his horse. This sparks a resentment and determination that she will not be gotten the better of by someone like him. Deep down, she really likes Lance, but his refusal to give her adulation and to bend to her will are intolerable. Lance seems to see through her and this further fuels her resentment.

On her return to the ranch, she decides she is going to remodel her room. She goes to great expense buying furniture and curtains for the room, spending money she doesn't have. Her parents have never told her that they are experiencing hard times, and that they are not able to continue paying for her debts.

Throughout the summer, Lance happens to be around whenever she gets herself into trouble. He rescues her from the runaway horse, much to her embarrassment in front of her friends. He takes her down from the hay fork at the roof of the barn. He carries her home when she sprains her foot, falling from a moving car. He is there in the bower when the drunken Rollie tries to force himself on her. When Lance rescues her from the gangster kidnapper, Honey Bee Uhl, Madge is convinced that he is taking her to Mexico or out of state somewhere so that he can demand the fifty thousand dollars' ransom for himself.

What Madge resents most about Lance is that he is right. He tells her she is inconsiderate, selfish, extravagant, arrogant. She shows little respect for her parents who have sacrificed so much for her. She likes to play games with people, to make fun of them. She has to acknowledge that he has her number.

The trouble is that Madge does not listen to her heart. She acts in ways that counter what she really feels and knows. Nels points out to her that she has been unkind and unfair to one who truly loves her. This she finally does come to see before it is too late. In this she resembles her mother, who almost lost the best man she had ever met because of stubborn pride.

Sticks: In *Wildfire,* a rider who comes to Bostril's Ford for the annual horse race. He is a friend of Blinn, Carlson, Burthwait and, like them, anxious for someone to beat Bostril's horses in the race.

Stillman: In *Arizona Ames,* a rancher in the Wind River country, neighbor to Crow Grieve. Lany Price gets to talk to Amy Grieve for the first time driving the wagon back from Stillman's ranch.

Stillman, Joe: In *30,000 on the Hoof,* one of the Stillman family who live in the canyons near the

Huetts. Together with Tobe Campbell and six other young men, he plans to rustle the Huetts' herd in Turkey Canyon.

Stillwell: In "The Camp Robber," one of the ranchers for whom Wingfield rode during spring roundup. As there was no further need of him after that, he moved on to ride for Brandon, Hall and Randall.

Stillwell, Ben: In "Avalanche," gets to take Kitty Mains to the dance. He arrives, spick-and-span in his dark suit and pale with suppressed excitement, leading a slender young woman, Kitty, wrapped in a fur coat covering her white dress, dainty and alluring. At this same dance, Jake Dunton proposes marriage to her and she accepts. Later, a fight breaks out between the brothers, Jake and Verde. It lasts two hours and ends with Jacob lying in the dust. The fight is the talk of the town until Kitty marries Ben Stillwell during the winter when the Dunton boys are snowed in in the Black Gorge Canyon. They get the news of her marriage to Stillwell when they make it out in the spring.

Stillwell, Bill: In *The Light of Western Stars*, the owner of the ranch where Al Hammond is working. Madeline is not sure what to make of him, but it is clear he does like her brother Alfred and the cowboy, Gene Stewart. The ranch is in rundown condition but very scenic. Bill is an old man, whose wrinkled face looks like stone. He loves to talk, telling her all he knows about the different cowboys working on his ranch. Monty got badly burned saving a baby in a prairie fire, Nels is stove up and crippled after years of hard cowboying. He knows much about the goings-on across the border in Mexico and the doings of the bandits who plague the ranches north of the border with cattle rustling and arms smuggling. When Madeline buys out his ranch and the smaller neighboring ranches to form one large operation, she retains Bill Stillwell as manager and goes to him for advice about ranching matters, and personnel. According to Florence Kingsley, Al's fiancée, Bill Stillwell is too slow to become suspicious of people because of his deep Christian nature. When Don Carlos and his bandits move in and occupy the house, Stillwell accepts the blame because he had allowed the cowboys who normally would stand guard to participate in the golf game. He blows up at Sheriff Pat Howe when he comes to arrest Gene at Al Hammond's wedding party. Later, he helps Madeline in her quest to get Stewart released from the Mexican prison by sending telegrams and conveying messages to her.

Stillwell, Burt: In *Nevada,* a member of the Pine Tree Outfit and a former associate of Billy the Kid from the Lincoln County war in New Mexico. He wants to shoot Cash Burridge but holds off believing that Cash Burridge is Jim Lacy's partner and Stillwell knows he is not able to face Lacy in a shootout. He steals Ben Ide's stallion, California Red, and keeps the animal hobbled in a corral. Jim Lacy

frees the horse and returns it to Ben's ranch on the sly.

Stimpson: In "The Camp Robber," hires Wingfield to work on his ranch. He is willing to take a chance on him, although the man has a history of moving from ranch to ranch after a few weeks of work. Stimpson is willing to give him a chance when circumstantial evidence suggests he has taken the payroll from the foreman's drawer.

Stimpson, Mrs.: In "The Camp Robber," reports that her daughter's doll has gone missing, probably taken by the mysterious camp robber.

Stine, Charley: In *West of the Pecos,* one of Don Felipe Gonzalez's men who works for Hal Watson. He is branding Don Felipe's mark over his employer's brand. Watson does not see him after the first shots fired when rustlers come to his ranch.

Stinger: In *Knights of the Range,* a young cowboy working on the Ripple ranch. Mugg Dillon reports to Heaver that he left Stinger for dead when they gathered the horses. He is shot, but not mortally wounded. Renn Frayne helps patch up the gunshot wound. Stinger and Brazos had caught Dillon rustling before and gave him a break on condition he promise not to do it again. Stinger, like Brazos, is disappointed at being betrayed a second time. When pursuing the rustlers with whom Talman is involved, he is shot a second time.

Stitt: In *The U. P. Trail,* the mute guard to whom Durade has assigned the task of permanent guard duty on his stepdaughter, Allie. He is killed in the fighting surrounding her escape from Stanton's with Red King.

Stockwell: In *Raiders of Spanish Peaks,* one of the honest ranchers who, together with Bain, Halscomb and Strickland, have gotten together to form the Spanish Peaks Cattlemen's Protective Association to rout out dishonest ranchers working in conjunction with rustlers.

Stockwell, Georgiana (Georgie) May: In *Code of the West,* Mary Stockwell's seventeen-year-old sister. She is coming west to stay with her sister because her parents can no longer control her. Georgie is one of the "new" breed of women to emerge from the social conditions following the war. She arrives on the stage to Ryson wearing a flimsy dress, low at the neck and shockingly short, a garment unsuitable for nights in the Tonto. She is quite pleased with the attention she draws from Jack the stagecoach driver, and Abe Hazelitt, the young man who works at the station. The cowboys vie for her attention and she flirts openly with Bid Hatfield. In this first encounter with him, she reveals that her self-possession is largely put-on, that her sophistication is not very old or very deep. Her sister Mary says of her that she is shallow, selfish, thoughtless, mindless, soulless. Her only apparent object in life seems to be to make herself attractive and irresistible to the opposite sex and to trifle with them — to run, dance, flirt. She seems to care little about what others think of her. She preaches a gospel of feminism, proclaiming liberation to think, talk, act as she wants with no concern about what the "lords of creation" feel. She declares religion and churches "back numbers" she abandoned at the age of fourteen. She assures her older, conservative sister, that she is too worldly-wise to be caught by a man like Bid Hatfield. She considers the cowboys on the Thurman ranch backward boobs and brushes off her sister's concern that they consider her cheap and easy. Their sense of decency, loyalty, honor, and chivalry are quaint and amusing.

When nineteen-year-old Cal picks her up at the station, she flirts with him from the start, but he does not take offense. He shares with her his love of the Tonto landscape, his attachment to the land. He enlists her help playing a trick on the ranch hands who have tried to make fun of him for offering to drive Georgie home. She pretends to have been injured when the car stopped, thanks to their fooling around with the car. She plays her part to perfection, and strikes a good note with all that first day. Georgie likes Cal, but she resents his sense of propriety; she feels he thinks he has something on her because of her willingness to go along with his prank on the other cowboys. She complains that he is too serious, too bossy, too jealous, and she rejects his proposal of marriage. Mary tells her Cal is too good for her, that she cannot see his true value. Georgie tells Cal that she is a modern flapper, a queer type. She won't be bossed, she must have her own way, she defies all conventions, she will be as free as a man. She has no interest in making a home for a man, certainly not a caveman like a Thurman cowboy. At the October dance, Georgie makes a fool of herself with her wild dancing, her provocative dress, her outrageous flirting with all, in particular her dancing with Bid Hatfield, the rival of the Thurmans. Fights break out over her. Uncle Gard Thurman addresses her in front of the assembled dancers, telling her that they have held parties in the old schoolhouse for many years and will not put up with an outsider coming in and making the dance an indecent spectacle. Mary feels both pity and admiration for her little sister, who makes no apology or excuse. She bravely goes to Cal Thurman, whom she has ignored all evening and asks him to take her home. Of all the men present who had seen her humiliated, he was the one least calculated to stand by her in her moment of shame, but Cal does not hesitate to take her to the car and drive her home, without reprimands, without recrimination, without criticism.

Nevertheless, despite the chivalrous treatment by Cal, she continues to see Bid Hatfield on the sly. Cal sees the two of them talking one day down the road from the house. Her behavior has reached the point that the embarrassment to the Thurmans is so great her sister Mary fears they will throw her out. Cal and Tuck concoct a plot to abduct her and, with the help of a preacher, elope. Georgie goes through with the ceremony, aware that she must do something to make amends to her sister for the embarrassment she has caused. Georgie and Cal are married at Boyd Thurman's cabin. Her things are brought to Cal's homestead. Cal makes no demands on her. She is free to do as she wants. She does learn to prepare breakfast and meals for him. She has a lot of time to think about her behavior, especially after Mary has pointed out that the marriage to Cal was the only possible honorable solution to her predicament. Nevertheless, Bid Hatfield and Bloom spread rumors about Georgie's loose, immoral behavior with them. Georgie slowly comes to see herself in a new light. She knows she has been vain, selfish, thoughtless, cruel. The stunning truth comes with the realization that in spite of all the arguments she brought west with her which had so distressed her sister, she would not want a daughter of hers to think and act as she had done at the Thurman ranch. What might be done with impunity in the "sophisticated" East could not be done in the Tonto. She does not regret that Cal Thurman had fought for her; the pity is that she is not worth fighting for. Her conscience troubles her and she knows she will never have peace of mind until she somehow makes amends. Anxious to prevent another confrontation between Cal and Hatfield, Georgie then confronts him herself, calling him a liar in front of his crew. She acknowledges her inappropriate behavior which earned her the reputation of being loose but forces a confession out of Hatfield that he had lied about her.

Georgie had first thought she would stick it out with Cal until the heat had blown over. Cal makes no demands of her, sleeping in the living room leaving the bedroom to her alone. She manages to keep up the pretense of being happily married with her sister and with the Thurman family at Christmas. However, when she inherits money from an aunt back east, she is forced to think about her future. While she no longer has to worry about how she will support herself, she is not sure she wants to leave Cal. After the confrontation with Hatfield, she knows she would never want to leave him. When Cal tells her that she was mistaken when she thought he had hit her, that it was a tree branch that had struck her, Georgie comments that he should have hit her, that she deserved it. All's well that ends well.

In the character of Georgiana Stokwell, Zane Grey has revisited Shakespeare's *The Taming of the Shrew* and given his fullest development of the theme of the western environment as the cure for the social and moral ills of the decadent East of the United States. Georgiana, like Carley Burch in *The Call of the Canyon* and Georgiana Traft in *The Hash Knife Outfit* is a thoroughly modern woman who embodies the decadence of the effete East. She learns true American values in the Tonto Basin of Arizona from people who are less sophisticated, perhaps, but better in touch with their humanity and their environment. Like Shakespeare's shrew, she learns humility, respect for others and a willingness to sacrifice herself for the sake of a loved one.

Stockwell, Mary: In *Code of the West,* the schoolteacher at Green Valley, Arizona, in the Tonto Basin. She lives with the family of Henry Thurman, in a cabin near the main ranch house. She has been in the West for six years and teaching in the Tonto for two years. In that time, life back east has changed immeasurably; the old ideals have been dethroned and a new order of things represented by Georgie and her attitudes promises to change America permanently. Mary receives a letter from her mother telling her that her younger sister, Georgiana May, is on her way west. Mary does not quite know how to react, with resentment at the new responsibility thrust upon her, or with pleasurable anticipation of seeing her golden-haired sister. Despite her angelic appearance, Georgie is quite the devil. Mrs. Thurman's letter speaks of an out-of-control seventeen-year-old who pays no heed to the advice of her parents and who shows little respect for traditional ways. She is one of the new women created by conditions following the war, the modern feminist unwilling to submit to supposedly outworn social codes and styles. Mary thinks how out of place she will be in the Tonto, where men outnumber women and where casual eastern relationships are considered improper if not outright immoral. In Arizona, the roles of men and women are still clearly defined in traditional terms and conservative values still obtain. The Tonto country has claimed Mary forever. She loves the people, the children in need of an education, the countryside, and the simple, honest, sincere, profoundly human cowboys and ranchers with whom she lives. Mary has spoken of her new home in Arizona in such glowing terms that Mrs. Stockwell thinks the new environment may be just what Georgie needs to set her straight. Mary has her doubts.

When Georgie arrives, she does create quite a sensation. She wears short skirts which reveal her knees and she wears socks. Her dress is made of light, flimsy material. She is a hopeless flirt and all the young men are crazy about her, vying for her attention. Georgie plays with the cowboys like a cat with a mouse. She doesn't really understand her destructive influence among these inexperienced, naive young men. Mary speaks to her about her behavior all to no avail. Georgie merely points out that she is uptight and afraid to acknowledge her own emotions. Mary warns Georgie about Bid Hatfield, the ladykiller cowboy who works at a rival ranch. She speaks well of young Cal, who is deeply in love with her and who embodies the best of western manhood. Georgie, however, sees no need to change her ways. What bothers Mary is that some of what Georgie says to her she must admit is true. She is in love with Enoch Thurman, but has never dared to reveal her secret love.

The night of the October dance, Enoch drives her to the dance in the car and proposes marriage to her. He begins by praising the work she has done with the children, expressing his hope she will stay on. As well, he hints that she must be getting lonesome for the East and wanting to return. When Mary confesses that she loves Arizona and does not want to leave, he shyly asks her to marry him and she accepts. The party then becomes a celebration of their engagement, spoiled only by the fight that Georgie's behavior provokes among Hatfield and the Thurman boys.

When Cal abducts and marries Georgie, Mary is happy. She does not realize that Georgie did not go along willingly with this, but she explains to her that the marriage has saved the honor of Cal, the Thurmans and herself. Georgie begins to realize the importance of honor and behavior to these Tonto folk.

Mary Stockwell is a heroine in the vein of Molly Wood in Wister's *The Virginian.* As a teacher, she is the embodiment of culture and refinement, an instrument to polish the uncut diamond of western society. Mary serves as a foil to her sister Georgie, the embodiment of the decadent, effete East, corrupted by selfishness and materialism and refinement, in need of the true American values still found in frontier Arizona.

Stockwell, Mrs.: In *Code of the West,* Mary and Georgie Stockwell's mother. She writes her daughter, Mary, who teaches school in the Tonto, asking her to receive her younger sister, Georgiana. Georgie has developed into a thoroughly modern girl, beyond their ability to control. She does not believe that her daughter is bad, but certainly gone astray. She asks Mary to do what she can to set her straight. Perhaps the West her daughter boasts about will be Georgie's salvation.

Stokes: In *Twin Sombreros,* a cattleman in Abilene who worked with Raine Surface. Surface bought cattle and Stokes sold them. At some point they quarreled, and the story was that Stokes began to suspect where Surface was getting his cattle. After their disagreement, Surface left Abilene for Las Animas. This occurred about a year before.

Stone, Hal: In *Stairs of Sand,* works for Guerd Larey's freighting company at Lost Lake. He has eloped with Ruth Virey, who desperately wants to escape her life with her grandfather and the empty marriage to Guerd, a man she despises. Hal Stone has been seduced by Ruth, knowing that Guerd will probably kill him if he is caught. He complains to Ruth that she has lead him to risk his hide, then flouts him when he wants what he has a right to expect. He tells her no one believes her story that she is Guerd's wife in name only. It's a story she invented to make it easier for men to want her. Stone tries to force himself on her when Adam Larey, Wansfell, comes upon them and beats him up. Ruth eventually confesses that she had been using Stone in order to escape her husband and her life at Lost Lake. Larey does not make too much of the incident, but Stone tells Merryvale that Ruth is as fickle as the desert wind. She'll purr at a man one minute and the next scratch his eyes out. He is convinced she will turn her attentions to him before too long. Hal

Stone cooperates with Larey when he plans to abduct Ruth to force her to submit to him in order to save her grandfather. Collishaw and his driver, Sanchez, provide the wagons. As Stone has already run off with her once, the logical conclusion of people at Lost Lake is that Ruth has run off with him again, all of which inspires sympathy for Larey. In Yuma, Stone tries to force Ruth to accept his attentions by offering to protect her from Collishaw. Adam Larey and his associates catch Stone and force him to reveal where he has kept Ruth hidden. He is also forced to reveal to Ruth that Larey had planned this whole escapade to force her to submit to him.

Stone, Jed: In *The Drift Fence,* mentioned by Jim Traft as the leader of the Hash Knife Outfit, which he fears will move into the area when the Cibeque outfit has been eliminated.

In *The Hash Knife Outfit,* Jed Stone is the leader of the Hash Knife Outfit, an example of the "honest outlaw" and the real hero of the novel. He has a fine, lithe figure, still a cowboy despite his forty years and more of hard Arizona life. His profile in no way hints at the evil repute that has long branded him as an outlaw. Jed Stone had ridden for Jim Traft, been his partner, and still holds his old friend in high regard. Old Jim tells his nephew that there was never a finer or squarer cowboy in Arizona than Jed Stone. He says Stone must have been driven to outlawry, that he had never been nor ever would be a cattle thief at heart. Stone accepts the offer of ten thousand dollars to move off the Yellow Jacket. Stone and Traft have long disagreed over the ranch. Traft bought it from Blodgett but Stone continues to consider the area open range. Impressed with Young Jim, Jed Stone accepts the deal and the Hash Knife moves out.

Stone is faced with the slow disintegration of his once virile Hash Knife Outfit, and the betrayal of men that trust him. Loyalty had always been the dominant trait of his personality. Loyalty to a friend had lost him his place among honest cattlemen. When a young man, he had shouldered the sin of his friend for the sake of a girl they both loved, and the noble deed earned him these years of loneliness, misery and infamy. Stone is considering leaving the Hash Knife and leaving Arizona. He sees Croak Malloy as the rival for his leadership in the Hash Knife. Uncle Jim Traft tells Jim that Jed Stone will keep his word about leaving the Yellow Jacket, but that this decision will likely lead to a spate of rustling and killing on the part of Malloy and his faction in the outfit. Stone himself predicts the end of this group. He is true to the old creed of the Hash Knife and so he lets Malloy go his way, to build up another rustler outfit and meet his inevitable end. He plans to leave Arizona, disappear, and never be heard from again.

On his way out of Arizona to meet up with Pecos, Jed Stone comes upon his old partner, Jim Traft, and his murdered driver. The two young ladies he was driving over to the Yellow Jacket have been abducted by Croak Malloy. Stone offers to help, as he fears that Croak Malloy, rejected by the whores of the towns because of his misshapen body and repulsive face, will rape and abuse the women he has abducted. He trails them to the old cabin, where he fights and kills Malloy and Madden, then sets about returning the girls to the Diamond Ranch. Aware of the snootiness of Glory Traft, he decides to teach her a lesson in western values. He gets Molly Dunn, whom he has known since childhood, to help with the ruse. On the way back to the ranch, Glory is subjected to the "leveling power of the wilderness," whereby Glory learns to work, to care for others, and to sacrifice herself. When the lesson has been learned, he releases the girls near the Diamond Ranch. With that act, Jed Stone feels free. His Hash Knife Outfit is finished. He has no more enemies. He has squared himself, and can lie down and sleep worry-free.

Like young Jim Traft, Jed Stone loves nature. He loves the rock walls, the colored cliffs, the canyons, the byways and the rims of the Mogollans. While undoubtedly this landscape provides refuge from pursuit for men of his profession, there was more to his obsession than a sense of security. He resents the encroachment of civilization, which means the loss of the wilderness he so loves. And like Jim, he knows the leveling power of the wilderness, the power in nature to instill a true sense of what is valuable in life.

Stone, Judge: In *The Rainbow Trail*, the federal judge sent to conduct the polygamy trials when the government attempts to stamp out the practice among the Mormons in the newly created state of Utah. The judge goes through the motions of questioning the sealed wives on the assumption that one of them will reveal a polygamous marriage, but all to no avail. The judge has sensed from the start that the job is futile. He treats the women with dignity and courtesy.

Stone, Orville: In *The Maverick Queen*, the name Lincoln Bradway uses when he presents himself at Kit Bandon's ranch in the middle of the night to test the sincerity of her supposed reform. He comes to her window, telling her he has a maverick to sell. He had heard from cowboys on the range that she would buy the animal. Kit tells him he has been misinformed, that she is no longer in that business. See **Bradway, Lincoln.**

Stoneham, Andy   In *The Drift Fence,* the clerk who works at Enoch Summers's store. He has a crush on Molly Dunn. He also has a keen eye and ear for what is going on in the valley. He reports to Molly about seeing Hack Jocelyn and the Haverlys in Mace's saloon. He reports on the good reputation that Jim Traft earned when he renounced any claim on the part of the Diamond Ranch to the stray cattle that had wandered into the brakes to the west of the drift fence. The Haverlys have made a lot of money selling the stray cattle, up to a thousand head. He also tells Molly that rumor has it Arch has quit the Cibeque outfit. He tells Molly how Seth and Sam and Hack are planning to double-cross Slinger, hoping to lay the blame for their cutting the fence and kidnapping and killing young Jim at his door. Andy asks her not to reveal that he has given her the information. A number of shooting incidents occur, one of which involves a shot aimed at Andy, returning home from the Dunn's place. Hack Jocelyn kills young Andy Stoneham on the pretext that he was spying on the outfit and telling Molly Dunn their plans. He killed in cold blood. Sam and Seth Haverly disapprove of his action. Molly regrets the death of a young man who loved her and put his own life at risk to save her and her brother.

Stonewall: In *Knights of the Range,* Holly Ripple's spirited horse. She is riding Stonewall when she comes upon the horse thieves at Dobe Cabin.

Stover, Jeff: In *The Lost Wagon Train,* introduces himself to Bowden at Council Grove and asks to join the caravan. He and his family and two drivers are from Missouri and scheduled to meet a Texas wagon train at Cimarron Crossing, a caravan of some sixty wagons under Blaisdal and Cy Hunt. When the train does not show up at the appointed time, Anderson wants to turn back, but Stover insists they continue on along the Dry Trail. He is killed in a gunfight with Anderson.

Strickland: (1) In *The Arizona Clan,* shot by Dodge Mercer. Uncle Bill Lilley tells Dodge Mercer that he heard about his gunplay in Abilene. Strickland was a big man in Abilene, but Uncle Bill heard more than one say Mercer had done the city a service by shooting him.
   (2) In "Canyon Walls," a rancher from whom Monty Bellew had rustled cattle in the past. When Sheriff Jim Sneed comes upon Monty Bellew in Green Valley, he is acting on orders from Strickland to pick him up, along with the cattle he has bought. Sneed, however, promises Bellew he will get Strickland to agree to the monthly payments to make good the debt. Bellew has straightened out, and the offer to repay the debt is proof he has mended his ways.
   (3) In *The Horse Thief,* a big-time rancher in Halsey, Idaho. He is present at the horse auction organized by Reed. Strickland is convinced by Dale Brittenham and Edith Watrous's story that the horses being sold are actually livestock rustled from ranchers in Montana. He organizes a posse of miners and cowboys to pursue the gang.
   (4) In *Knights of the Range,* a powerful rancher in Kansas. Anyone who crossed him had sheriffs and jails to deal with. Renn Frayne killed his foreman in a shootout.
   (5) In *Raiders of Spanish Peaks,* a cattleman from La Junta. He is the largest-scale cattleman in eastern Colorado. He is a tall, eagle-eyed westerner, past middle age. He is head of a Cattlemen's Association concerned about wiping out the menace of cattle rustlers, who are threatening the ranching business. He arrives at the Spanish Peaks spread the day Mr. Williams arrives. He discusses the goals of the group with Harriet, the manager of the Lindsay's Spanish

Peaks ranch. The association presents a list of ranchers whom they have checked out. There may be names on the list of dishonest ranchers just as there may be honest ones whose names have been left out. Strickland speaks about Allen, from whom they purchased the ranch. Allen is known to sell stock with mixed brands and most suspect him of working with outlaws to sell the cattle they steal. He has also heard of Laramie Nelson from Buffalo Jones, the man who had found him for the Lindsays to lead their wagon train to the ranch and to act as foreman. Harriet reveals that Laramie has resigned as foreman to pursue the kidnappers of her young sister. Strickland appears at the Allen ranch just as Laramie and his crew appear to settle the score with the rustlers and kidnappers. Strickland has been trying to persuade him to join the Cattlemen's Protective Association. Laramie, however, reveals the truth about Allen. Nig Jackson, whose life was spared in exchange for testimony against Allen, reveals how Allen sent Arlidge to rustle the cattle off Lindsay's ranch and then deliver them to Allen, who in turn sold them. Strickland protests hanging Allen, as there is not sufficient proof to convict him in court of rustling. The crooked rancher is given the choice of facing hanging or leaving Colorado permanently. Allen flees the ranch, forking the dead Arlidge's horse.

Strickland, Abe: In *The Lone Star Ranger,* an old man in the town, Shirley, who tries to arrest Buck Duane when he comes into town to find out for what crime there is a "dead or alive" reward of a thousand dollars on his head. Buck clearly identifies himself, and Strickland holds a gun on him and orders him bound. Stickland feels terribly important having captured such a dangerous outlaw! A lynch party is quickly organized but the cowboy, Sibert, puts a halt to things and talks some sense into the crowd.

Stringer, Sheriff Jeff: In *Arizona Ames,* the sheriff of Shelby. He is not well liked in town, in part because he favors the Tates. He dislikes Rich Ames, and when the young man comes to town for the wedding of Lil Snell, Sheriff Stringer goes out of his way to threaten Rich and Sam Playford. A week after the wedding celebration, Stringer is playing cards with the Tate brothers in the tavern when Rich catches Lee Tate cheating. In the ensuing gunfight, Stringer is killed. No one in Shelby seems upset by this turn of events.

Strobel, Sheriff Charlie: In *Forlorn River,* sheriff of Hammell. Ben describes him as lean-jawed, narrow-eyed, and a man he can trust Ben Ide has been a friend of Charlie's for many years. He had taught Ben to fish when he was a boy. Ben Ide meets him on the streets of Hammell. The sheriff tells him of the rumors that have been spread about Nevada and Modoc. Charlie has no doubts about Ben's honesty and offers to make him a secret deputy to spy on the rustlers in the Forlorn River area. Ben refuses. Charlie Strobel comes to the Blaine ranch investigating reports of rustling in the area. He asks Ina about Less Setter, and she tells him about the power this man has on her father. The sheriff tells her that the Cattlemen's Association is putting pressure on him to catch the rustlers; his job is on the line. When Nevada helps him catch Bill Hall and the rustlers, he informs Hart Blaine that any deals that had been made with Sutter are null and void.

In *Nevada*, Strobel is invited to Ben Ide's to talk about Arizona. He had lived and worked there and Ben wants some advice about where to set up ranching. He explains about the geography of the state, recommending an area in the center of the state which is neither too hot nor too cold for ranching. He recommends the Springerville-Snowflake region, which is about a hundred miles from a railroad and where there is good grazing land. He suggests that they buy a winter place in San Diego where Mrs. Ide could go. San Diego, he believes, has the best climate in the world. It's easy to reach by train from Arizona. He warns Ben, however, that the ranch country he has recommended is plagued by outlaws, some of whom have come from troubled New Mexico, where the recent wars between sheepmen and cattlemen had caused them to seek a new range of operation. He suggests that they take the train to Arizona.

Stronghurl, Dave: In *The Thundering Herd*, a member of Hudnall's hiding outfit. His name reflects well his physiognomy. He and Orvy Tacks compete for Sally Hudnall's affections. Sally leaves the hiding outfit to go to Sprague's, where the cavalry have relocated the women in their interest of their safety. When Stronghurl comes to the post with a load of hides, Sally proposes the two of them get married. There is a preacher in the camp and they might as well take advantage of the opportunity. He reports the marriage to Clark Hudnall, who is not pleased with his new son-in-law, and Orvy Tacks is downhearted, having lost in the game of love. Stronghurl returns to Sprague's to meet Sally just after Hudnall is found killed by Comanches. He buys a ranch at Sprague's and settles down to safer work.

Strothers, Bill: In *Shadow on the Trail*, one of Hogue Kinsey's men that Wade Holden (Tex Brandon) recruits to work on Pencarrow's ranch. He is present when Steele is shot and Blue Rand is hanged for cattle rustling.

Struthers: In *Thunder Mountain*, one of Rand Leavitt's henchmen, involved in the attacking and robbing of miners.

Struthers, Sheriff: In *Nevada*, from Southern Arizona, where he made things so hot for outlaws that they have migrated north. He comes to Winthrop to help out Sheriff Macklin, who has been prone to go soft on gamblers and gunmen while taking a hard line with drunks and cowboys.

Stuart, Lin: In *Raiders of Spanish Peaks*, first described as Lenta's latest acquisition. He is a young rider from La Junta. He is certainly handsome. Beside him, Lonesome Mulhall looks like a little banty rooster. Stuart is absurdly attractive, young, redcheeked, fire-eyed, lithe, graceful. He whistles gaily, as if he had not a care in the world. He does not carry a gun, a fact which pleases Hallie Lindsay who, like Jane Withersteen in *Riders of the Purple Sage*, is opposed to violence and guns. Mr. Lindsay does not approve of young Stuart and wants him off the ranch. Laramie orders him never to show up again at Spanish Peaks. Other than his being penniless and shiftless, Ted Williams learns that he is married to an Alice Webster of La Junta, a young waitress that he married and abandoned. Stuart frees Lenta from the room with bars on the windows to which her father has consigned her because of her reckless behavior. Together they ride off. Ted Williams tracks them, and in a few hours comes across Stuart's dead horse, and later, the body of Lin Stuart, riddled with bullets, his pockets turned inside out. Further investigation reveals Stuart had been persuaded by Lenta to get her out of her prison. They rode up to the bluff to get away, probably to make Mr. Lindsay worry a bit. Stuart and Lenta ran smack into Gaines and his crew, who had been camped out there waiting for just such an opportunity. Stuart was killed by Chess Gaines, who had planned to abduct Lenta for ransom. Laramie and Ted conclude that they had misjudged Stuart and Lenta.

Stub: In *Captives of the Desert*, one of the cowboys who work with John Curry on the Navajo reservation near Taho. High-Lo plays a trick on him, tying him up and shaving him bald.

Stubbs, Flo: In *The Man of the Forest*, taken by Tom Carmichael to the dance when Bo Rayner has refused his invitation. Bo calls her an ugly, crosseyed, bold little frump. Helen tells her that Flo is not beautiful but she is very nice and pleasant. She suggests that Bo should show more appreciation for Tom if she expects to hold on to him.

Stube, Joe: In *The Heritage of the Desert*, a friend of Zeke Naab's. He is currently working for Holderness at what was once Martin Cole's ranch. He tells Zeke that Holderness has rebuilt the corrals that Jack Hare had burned earlier. He reports as well that a cabin has been built there and that Snap, Holderness's new foreman, had gotten into a fight with Snood in White Sage and killed him.

Stuffy: In *Captives of the Desert*, one of the cowboys with whom John Curry works at the reservation.

Stuke: In *Twin Sombreros*, one of the men in Bodkin's posse that arrests Brazos Keene for the murder of Allen Neece.

Sullivan, Captain: From the garrison at Ft. Pitt, arrives in time to take shelter inside Ft. Henry during the attack on the fort in *Betty Zane*.

Sullivan, Con: In *30,000 on the Hoof*, one of the very young cowboys that Logan Huett hires to drive his cattle to Flagg. All the older boys have signed up for the army and the war.

Sultan: In *Majesty's Rancho*, one of Majesty Stewart's string of thoroughbred horses.

Summers, Enoch: In *The Drift Fence*, runs the general store in the village. Andy Stoneham clerks for Mr. Summers. The store is the clearinghouse for local gossip and rumor, a virtual post office. Mr. Summers comments that young Jim Traft is in charge of building the drift fence for his uncle and that this drift fence will be sure to cause a lot of resentment if not fighting. He also expresses admiration for young Traft and this ability to pull off the building of the fence.

Sunderland, Colonel: In *Western Union*, with his daughter Kit and his brother Jeff are part of a wagon train from Texas heading to the Sweetwater Valley in Wyoming. They meet up with Creighton's wagons working on construction of the Western Union telegraph line. Colonel Sunderland plans to set up ranching with his brothers. He and Jeff are driving a herd with them. He recognizes Vance Shaw in Cameron's wagon crew and informs him that his problem in Texas has been resolved. Shaw's Texas Ranger friends shot it out with Duke Wells, who confessed as he was dying that Stanley was responsible for the trouble ascribed to Vance. He further adds that Shaw rode for him for three years, during which he killed Sunderland's most bitter enemy and cleared the Comanche from his range. He has nothing but praise for the cowboy. Shaw is only thirty years old, he says, but in experience he exceeds most men in Texas or in the West itself. The Sunderland wagon train is attacked by Indians, the herd is stampeded, and rustlers take half their herd.

Sunderland, Jeff: In *Western Union*, with a wagon train from Texas meets Creighton's wagon trains on their way to the Sweetwater Valley in Wyoming. Jeff is a Texan, easily distinguished by his accent and dress. He is light-haired and light-complexioned and somewhat tanned. He has penetrating, kindly blue eyes and a lined, strong, serious face to which a long, drooping, tawny mustache gives a dolorous touch. His brother in Wyoming is Jim Sunderland, and his other brother is Colonel Sunderland. Jeff and the colonel are driving a herd of cattle to Wyoming.

Sunderland, Jim: In *Western Union*, a cattleman and brother to Colonel Sunderland. He and the colonel have equal interests in a cattle venture in the Sweetwater Valley of Wyoming near where the Western Union telegraph line will pass. When Cameron and Shaw rescue Ruby from Red Pierce in South Pass, they take her to Sunderland's ranch until the matter is fully resolved.

Sunderland, Kit: In *Western Union*, the daughter of Colonel Sunderland. Wayne Cameron falls in love with her at first sight when the stagecoach passes the Sunderland wagon train. He meets her again in Gothenburg after stopping her runaway horse. She had heard about him, the Harvard man working on the Western Union telegraph crew. Shaw, it seems, was once in love with her. He reports to Cameron that Kit likes to flirt with cowboys. Not that she leads them on, but that her looks naturally make cowboys foolish over her. She burns her foot badly in the prairie fire and Cameron has to tend to her injury. At this time, he learns that Kit has discovered Ruby's presence in their wagon, but she has not mentioned this to anyone. Cameron comes upon Shaw talking with Kit one day, and this causes him to be suspicious of his friend, but eventually, Shaw confides that the love had all been on his side. Kit is at the Sunderland ranch when Wayne and his friends bring in the rescued Ruby. She comments sarcastically on his penchant for rescuing damsels in distress. Wayne and Shaw become partners in the cattle industry and set up a ranch near the Sunderlands. Kit and Wayne's marrying is hinted at when the novel concludes.

Surefoot: In *Lost Pueblo*, the horse Janey is riding when she and Randolph are crossing a flooded river at the archaeological site. The horse is not keen on walking into deep water.

Surface, Lura: In *Twin Sombreros*, the only daughter of rancher, cattleman and rustler, Raine Surface. She speaks out to the men about to lynch Brazos Keene, voicing her opposition to the plan and her belief that the man is innocent. Lura has quite a reputation. She is in her early twenties, beautiful, tall, sure of herself. Allen Neece had been in love with her and her father disapproved. The Neece sisters dislike her because she is a snob, and they feel she made a fool of their brother. She casts her eyes on Brazos Keene and the young man is tempted. Lura becomes involved with the gambler, Howard. The cardsharp has figured out Surface's role in the rustling and the murder, and they use their knowledge to squeeze forty thousand dollars out of him. They leave for Denver on the train. Lura asks only one favor of Brazos, whom she meets just before she leaves: that he not hang her father. She knows Brazos will catch him eventually and she makes no effort to conceal her father's guilt.

Surface, Raine: In *Twin Sombreros*, a big-time cattleman and rancher in Las Animas. He arrived from Abilene, where he quarreled with another rancher and cattleman who questioned his connections with rustlers. Surface swindles Neece out of his ranch, selling him cattle, then arranging for Syvertseen and Orcutt to rob him of the fifty thousand in cash needed to pay for the herd. He seizes the ranch. Surface is responsible for the murder of Allen Neece, the son of the dispossessed rancher. Two factors influence his decision to eliminate the boy, his investigation of the swindle is proving too successful, and Allen's involvement with his daughter, Lura. Surface is the most powerful rancher in the Cattleman's Association. He got Kiskadden elected sheriff and is disappointed when the Texan does not bow to his wishes. He also got Bodkin appointed deputy. On Surface's instructions, Bodkin arranges to have

Brazos lynched for the murder of Allen Neece. Rancher Inskip, in the posse, manages to spoil his plans. Brazos Keene takes up the investigation and uncovers Surface's involvement with rustlers and Syvertsen. Once again, Surface commissions the Syvertsen trio to murder Brazos. The plan backfires. Brazos exposes him before his peers at the Cattleman's Association, and, honoring his promise to Lura, Keen allows Surface to leave town, rather than be lynched. Surface is killed by Knight in a shootout in Dodge.

Susie: In *Shadow on the Trail,* Bilt Wood's sweetheart who drops him for Joe Steele. When Bilt comes to town and sees her with Steele, he gets jealous. She goes off with Steele. Later she returns to find Bilt Wood to complain that Steele had forced her and her family to put Rand Blue (Band Drake) and his men up for the night. They have ridden off towards Pine Mound.

Sutherland: In *Knights of the Range,* a big-time cattleman in Kansas shot and killed by Renn Frayne. He was one of those cattlemen who operate in two ways, one open and honest, the other hidden and crooked. Sutherland had powerful friends and they egged on gunfighters and two-faced sheriffs and tough cowboys to put a price on Frayne's head. When Sutherland's true nature was exposed, they forgot to take the price off Frayne's head.

Sutton, Ellen: In *To the Last Man,* the cause of the feud between the Jorths and the Isbels. Both Lee Jorth and Gaston Isbel were in love with her. She belonged to one of the old families of the South. She was a beauty and much courted. She found it hard to choose. She became engaged to Gaston Isbel. When the war broke out, Gaston and his brother Jean enlisted. Jean advised Gaston to marry Ellen before he left, but he wouldn't. After a while, her letters ceased to arrive. Gaston was injured in the war and when he got back home, she had married Lee Jorth. When he was able to move around, he confronted them. Lee Jorth had told her lies about Gaston, but in short, she had been faithless. What Gaston resents most is that she loves Jorth as she had never loved him. She shows no regret for having betrayed him while he was away at war. She clings to Jorth through thick and thin, when Isbel ruins him and forces him to leave Texas. Ellen Jorth is the spitting image of her mother. When Lee Jorth or Gaston Isbel look at her, they see the woman with whom they both were in love.

Swan, Dick: In *Thunder Mountain,* an old miner, neighbor to the Blairs. He informs Blair, who had bought a useless claim, that the bar in front of his cabin had been planted. It was a common trick, to plant a few gold nuggets on a claim, to lure someone into buying the spot at exaggerated prices.

Swearengen, Captain: Mentioned in *Betty Zane* and *The Last Trail.* In the former, he is mentioned as one of the available bachelors at the fort. He never appears as a character in either of the novels.

Syvertsen, Bard: In *Twin Sombreros,* a splendid specimen of Norwegian manhood, lofty of stature, fair-haired, with eyes like blue ice and a handsome craggy face. He is all of forty years old. Syvertsen organizes the murder of Allen Neece on orders from Raine Surface. He hides the body in the loft of the cabin where Brazos Keene is going to spend the night. He gets the deputy, Bodkins, to go to the cabin in time to arrest him for the murder. He and Orcutt and Bess disappear from sight for a while, until they are recalled to perform a similar job for Surface, to eliminate Brazos Keene who, like Neece, is getting too close to discovering the truth. Bess tells Brazos that Bard is a cattle buyer. They travel all over, from Kansas City to Denver. They are currently negotiating deals with Miller and Surface. She calls him "father," although there is no relationship between them at all. When she reveals her true background, she does say that Bard and Hen always respected her. The story that he is her father is to keep tongues from wagging. Brazos overhears Syvertsen and Orcutt and Bodkins talking in the room next to his. The missing pieces all fall into place. Bard is upset when Bess is reluctant to execute this second plot. In the confrontation among Bess, Hard, Hen and Brazos, Bard and Hen accuse her of betraying them. Brazos reveals that he knew the truth already. The two men try to draw on Brazos but are killed in the shooting.

Syvertsen, Bess: In *Twin Sombreros,* the mysterious young boy with the high-pitched voice that Brazos Keene heard at the cabin the night Allen Neece was killed. Bess Syvertsen's real name is Bess Moore. Bard Syvertsen is not her father, although most think he is. She never had any parents that she knew of. She was brought up in a home for illegitimate children. She and Bard and Hen Orcutt were contracted by Surface to get rid of Allen Neece and later, Brazos Keene. Brazos thinks that she would be a strikingly pretty woman but for the hard, ruthless hawklike cast to her features. While he knows she is about to lure him into a trap similar to the one set for young Neece, she can walk past him unaware of his presence. She is a consummate actress. But there is a good side to Bess that comes out in this second scheme. She had plotted to use her beauty and her person to lure another cowboy somewhere so that her associates could murder him, but having gotten to know her victim, possibly fallen in love with him, she did not want him murdered. She refuses to go through with the plan. She and Surface have a very public argument in the lobby of Hailey's hotel. Her associates accuse her of having betrayed them, of having revealed everything to Brazos. She didn't have to, as Brazos knew already what had happened. When they accuse her of letting herself be used by Brazos, she gets angry. In the shooting which follows, Bard and Hen are killed. She pulls a gun on Brazos, and he shoots her in the shoulder. She thinks she is dying, and makes a confession which Kiskadden writes and she signs before passing out. Doc Williamson examines the wound and discovers it is not serious. When she has recovered some, she decides to leave Las Animas and go to stay with friends in Illinois. Brazos apologizes for having deceived her, and Bess decides that she wants to go east to start over.

T

Tacks, Orville (Orvy): In *The Thundering Herd*, a member of Dunn's outfit which joins up with Hudnall after their hides have been stolen. Orvy Tacks finds himself in competition with Dave Stronghurl for Sally Hudnall's attentions. He is broken-hearted when Dave returns from Sprague's with the news that he and Sally are married. Orville is shot in the campaign against the Comanche. Tom Doan tries to save his life but the shot in the abdomen proves fatal.

Taddy: (1) In *Black Mesa*, a young Indian man, a friend of Natasha's. His people live over the mountains where there are no traders. He wants to marry her and she accepts. She wants to go back in the canyons to get away from men like Belmont. Paul Manning and Wess Kintell buy them a flock of sheep and goats, some ponies, saddles, blankets, a camp outfit, clothes, and food — everything they need to start.

(2) In *The Vanishing American*, one of Nophaie's sheep dogs when he is a boy on the reservation.

Takhhashi: In "The Secret of Quaking Asp Cabin," the Japanese cook for the hunting party.

Talman, Beef: In *Knights of the Range*, a cowboy working on the Ripple ranch. He helps with dunking the drunk cowboys in the cold stream to sober them up for Holly's fiesta banquet. Talman, however, likes money, and this weakness leaves him open to corruption. McCoy lures him into rustling with money, and he brings Trinidad along with him. Talman is seen with glasses surveying the range to warn the rustlers of oncoming riders. He is caught with his rustlers' outfit and hanged.

Taneen: In *Blue Feather*, the chief of the Sheboyahs of the Rock Clan. He has aroused the suspicion and enmity of his priests. They warn that the gods are angry with him because he wed a princess of the cursed Antelope Clan which has been wiped out by the angry gods. Taneen is an old man. He has no son to take his place, only a daughter, Nashta, whom he keeps hidden in a special cave and of whose existence only a select few are aware. The girl comes out to bathe only by night in a hidden pool. There has been a twelve-year drought, and many of the nearby clans have moved or been wiped out. Taneen has ordered the tribe to fill the storehouses to prepare for even worse times. The priests observe the depressing omens, and blame Taneen's sins for their plight. When the Nopah stranger arrives, Taneen is impressed with the young man. He can outperform the Rock Clan at everything, game or competition, thereby earning the envy of the young men and the admiration of the women. When the treachery of Blue Feather is revealed, the tribe turns on Taneen.

Tanner, Cappy: In *Arizona Ames*, a trapper who comes to the Tonto annually to visit the Ames family. He has his own log cabin near the Ames's which has been inhabited by a bear since his last stay. He finds the place little changed. The fences he helped Rich build are the same, the cabins are the same, but he senses something different in Nesta. Cappy is loaded with presents, as usual, for the young twins Mescal and Manzanita (that he cannot tell apart), a rifle for Rich and an elegant party dress for Nesta. Rich tells him that Nesta, his twin sister, is engaged to Sam Playford, a young rancher new to the Tonto. But she has been seen fooling around with one Lee Tate, the local womanizer and gambler whose brother, Slink, is believed to have killed Mr. Ames. Rich fears for Nesta's reputation. The crowd she hangs around with, Lil Snell, Madge Low, and Lee Tate, have little respect for her. For the first time in their lives, Nesta is secretive with him. Cappy finds himself caught between Nesta and Rich. Nesta needs someone to confide in. She tells Cappy that Rich keeps bothering her about her engagement to Sam and her flirting with Lee Tate. She needs some space, some time to herself. Cappy feels for her and advises her to take it easy. A talk with Mrs. Ames puts another perspective on the problem. Nesta is a young woman, sowing her wild oats, as it were. She genuinely loves Sam, but can't help being attracted to Lee Tate. Mrs. Ames sees nothing to be concerned about, attributing the worry to Rich's hatred of the Tates, who are suspected of killing his father. Sam Playford, Rich's best friend, tells Cappy he is concerned about Nesta, his fiancée. He knows she loves him, and he is not jealous of Tate. The local gossip is nothing to him, but he does fear for her well-being. Tanner advises him not to give up hope. Cappy goes to town for Lil Snell's wedding. He stops to visit with his friend, Henry, the blacksmith in Shelby. Henry updates him on the latest gossip about Nesta and Tate and Sam. It is clear that Nesta's reputation has already been ruined. But gossip also reveals that most people in Shelby approve of Rich Ames's stand against Sheriff Jeff Stringer and Lee Tate, neither of whom are well-liked. Cappy is pleased that Nesta is the belle of the ball in her new dress, so much so that the bride, Lil, is jealous of her. The party over, Nesta returns home, apparently returning to normal, agreeing to marry Sam by the weekend, but she attempts suicide, throwing herself into the river. Rich and Sam and Cappy save her from drowning, after which she tells the story about being having been raped by Lee Tate and bearing his child. She was too embarrassed to tell Sam the truth. Cappy soothes the unhappy girl, encouraging her to accept Sam's offer of marriage. Several days later, a rider comes to the Ames ranch looking for Cappy to tell him the story of Rich's meeting with Stinger and Tate at a card game. Tate and the sheriff are dead, Slink badly wounded, and Rich has left Arizona. Cappy Tanner had felt older as he made his way into the Tonto, but in all his years he had never experienced such trouble as confronted his beloved Rich and Nesta Ames. Cappy Tanner resembles Jeff Lynn in *The Spirit of the Border* and Old John Sprague in *To the Last Man*. He is a grandfather figure, a source of advice and comfort to a young girl sadly in need of a friend.

Tanner, Cash: In *Wyoming*, one of the four men in the team that Bligh hires for his ranch. Bandy Wheelock describes him to Martha as the "ladykiller" of the outfit. He is a handsome, florid-faced man of at least forty, large of frame, with a huge bow-shaped mustache and big ox-like brown eyes under busy eyebrows. He speaks with a deep, cavernous voice. Martha likes him at once.

Tanner, Joe: In *The Hash Knife Outfit*, a cowhand from Winslow. He is first mentioned by Bambridge when he comes to Jed Stone's cabin, the rendezvous for the rustlers. Madden mentions a big row with Croak Malloy that took place at Tanner's ranch. He is hanged by the Slinger Dunn vigilantes who pursue the Hash Knife rustlers.

Tanner, Lige: In *The Fugitive Trail*, a Texas cowboy from down Nueces way. He befriends Trinity when she is on her way to Doan's Post looking for Bruce Lockheart. He tells her about the life of a trail driver. He and his buddies are returning south, having just completed a trail drive. They are returning to take another herd north. As it turns out, Tanner is a friend of Bruce Lockheart's. He saved his life down on the Colorado. Lige admires his speed with a gun. The two of them had spent half a year hunting buffalo and fighting Indians. They took a trail drive together which ended only six months ago. Bruce had told him about Trinity so he is glad to meet her at last. At Doan's, he makes inquiries and learns that indeed Bruce had been through there, but no one knows for sure in what direction he went when he left.

Tanner, Sam: In *The Hash Knife Outfit*, brother to Joe Tanner of Winslow, likewise a cohort of Croak Malloy. He escapes wounded from the Slinger Dunn attack on the Hash Knife cabin. He shows up at Jed Stone's place with Malloy and Madden, where his wounds are treated. He rides off during the right, unable to continue with the outfit under Malloy's leadership.

Tanner, Wess: In *Twin Sombreros*, a partner of Brazos Keene. Tom Doan at Doan's Crossing tells Brazos that Tanner drove by there some weeks ago and is expected back. He arrives on the stage from Dodge. He has heard about Brazos's work cleaning up Las Animas. He also has a surprise, June Neece.

In Dodge, he was introduced to a young lady by Jeff Davis. She was looking for someone who might know where Brazos was. Thanks to Tanner, she is at Doan's Crossing, staying with Mrs. Doan.

Tappan: In *Tappan's Burro*, an old prospector in the desert of western California and eastern Arizona. He has no "front handle"—at least, none he can remember. He has made quite a fortune for himself prospecting. He has sought out the Peg Leg Mine in the Panamint and the Superstitious Mountains, and the lost Dutchman's mine. He has a burro named Jennie that gives birth to Jennet, a burro he raises and trains, a burro that is the envy of other prospectors. He credits Jennet with saving his life in Death Valley. He has never had cause to question her loyalty. Tappan has little experience with other people but he has come to love his burro, Jenet, as if she were human. He converses with the burro, and, makes promises to her as if she were a real woman. When Tappan meets Madge Beam, he is easily hoodwinked by her, believing that she loves him and that she needs to be rescued from her abusive brother. She and Jake try to sell him a ranch up on the Tonto, but Madge tells Tappan that they do not really own the ranch, never having proved up on it. She regrets being party to the proposed swindle. She tells him she is in love with him and proposes they get married and run off. Tappan hesitates to leave his burro behind, but Madge gives him an ultimatum, her or the burro, but not both. Tappan opts to leave Jenet to her fate, and he flees with Madge. She deserts him, however. She leaves him a note confessing that she is Jake's wife, and that she has double-crossed him. Jake and his gang, she says, suspected her and are close on their trail. She chased off the horses and sent Tappan after them in order to save his life. The old prospector sets out after the thieves, tracking them to Globe, then to Phoenix, and Tucson. In each town he hears of them cashing in his gold, over twelve thousand dollars worth, and then gambling it away. He tracts them on to California, to Yuma, El Cajon and San Diego. There he loses track of Madge, and Jake kills a Mexican in a brawl and crosses over into Mexico. He spends a year in San Diego posing as a peddler, as a ruse to visit houses, but he finds no trace of the woman. Finally, he thinks of his little burro and returns to his old haunts in the Tonto Rim country. To his surprise, Jenet is there at his old camp waiting for him. She had been waiting for the past year for his return. He promises the burro he will never desert her again. Tappan has lost his wanderlust, and his desire to find gold, but in the mountains he feels close to Madge, holding no grudges against her for the taking of his gold. His love for her had been an ennobling experience. Jess Blade wanders into his camp, looking for grub. He has no horse and no equipment. He is not anxious to return to a town, having had some undisclosed trouble with the law. He has heard of Tappan and his escapade with Madge Beam. Tappan wasn't the first one to be duped by the Beam gang that haunts the

Tonto Rim. Tappan offers to share what little he has left of his grub and to share any meat from hunting. When they get snowed in, Blade thinks Tappan has gone mad when he refuses to kill the burro for meat. He is convinced the man is mad when Tappan wants to make a sleigh on which to carry the burro out of the mountains. Tappan has to shoot Blade to save the burro's life. Tappan then, out of gratitude to the burro, pulls the little burro down from the mountain on a sleigh made from his tarpaulin. When they reach the bottom of the mountain, a vicious storm hits. Tappan freezes to death during the night, and Jenet comes to camp in the morning calling to Tappan but he gives no answer. Tappan has saved her life, as she had saved his before. This same story is narrated again in "The Secret of Quaking Asp Cabin" by Babe Haught. A few of the details are changed, but it is essentially the same.

Tappan resembles Dismukes in *The Wanderer of the Wasteland*, the prospector who owes his survival to his relationship with his burros, who has learned to trust their judgment and instincts, which are more reliable than his own. As well, he is a man formed by the desert, inexperienced in the wiles of the civilized world, and easy prey to unscrupulous operators like Madge Beam.

Taquitch: In *Wanderer of the Wasteland*, is an Indian god. Legend has it he sends the lightning and thunder in the summer, the storms and winds in the winter, and rolls rocks at night. In *Stairs of Sand*, Ruth Virey remembers Genie Linwood's stories about this Indian god, whom she associates with the spirit of the desert.

Tarhe: Appears in *Betty Zane* and *The Spirit of the Border*. He is a great Huron chief, father of Myeerah, father-in-law of Isaac Zane. In *The Spirit of the Border*, Tarhe is approached to join in the campaign against the Village of Peace. He decides not to join the alliance. He has a more prominent place in Grey's first novel, *Betty Zane*. Tarhe is the chief of all the Wyandots, a branch of the Huron tribe that migrated south in the late seventeenth century. He is over seventy years old, but still walks erect. His movements and speech show no signs of his advanced age. He is annoyed that Isaac's escape and recapture has cost him the lives of several warriors. Tarhe points out Isaac's dubious situation; Wingenund and Cornplanter want to kill him to avenge the death of Delaware chiefs and warriors. Tarhe offers to make the White Eagle, as Isaac is known among the Delaware, his son and a chief. He will give him land and honors, and never ask him to fight against his own people. He hopes Isaac and Myeerah can resolve their differences soon. He does permit Myeerah and Thundercloud to rescue Isaac when he is captured by Cornplanter and Wingenund.

Tartar: In *The Light of Western Stars*, one of Madeline Hammond's favorite stag hounds.

Tasker: In *Robbers' Roost*, the Mormon farmer who takes in Jim Wall and Helen Herrick when they escape from Robbers' Roost. Tasker and his wife put them up for the night then he accompanies them as far as Torrey. He agrees to sell back the horses Jim Wall had traded with him and deliver them to the Herrick ranch north of Grand Junction. He mentions that he is particularly taken with Jim's bay.

Tate, Slink: In *Arizona Ames*, brother to Lee Tate. He has the surly look of a hound. He has a bad reputation that has stuck to him. He reputedly was involved in the killing of Caleb Ames in ambush. He bears little resemblance to his brother, Lee, the handsome one. In the confrontation in the tavern in Shelby, Slink tries to calm Lee down to avoid a shootout. Lee is killed, and Slink badly injured. The unnamed man who reports on the fight to Cappy Tanner adds that few people in Shelby are praying for Slink's recovery.

Tate, Lee: In *Arizona Ames*, a twenty-two-year-old young man, olive-skinned in complexion, tall, dark-haired, dark-eyed, with a look of desperation in his eyes. He dresses in dark clothes, spurs, and polished boots. There is the air of a dandy about him. Lee Tate is quite the womanizer thanks to his handsome looks, his clothes, and his slick ways. Nesta Ames is taken with him, and Lil Snell and Madge Low arrange for them to be alone together. Lee Tate forces himself on Nesta one day in the woods and when she rejects him, he rapes her. He spreads the word that Nesta threw herself at him and that he has had his way with her. At the wedding party for Lil Snell, he approaches Nesta to dance but is rejected. When Rich Ames comes to Shelby to settle the score about Nesta, he finds Tate in the tavern with his brother Slink and the sheriff and two men from Globe. He nails Lee cheating at cards. Lee draws on Rich, who neatly outdraws him, putting a bullet into his forehead

Tates: In *Arizona Ames*, neighbors to the Ames family in the Tonto basin. There are a number of families involved in a prosperous ranching operation. The men all have the reputation of being hard riders, fighters and quick with the gun. Lee and Slink are the two Tate boys mentioned in the story.

Tay-Tay: In *Lost Pueblo*, the fifth cowboy Janey meets at Bennet's post. He is so called because he stutters. The cowboys like to tease him, making his stutter all the worse. He is one of the cowboys who come to rescue Janey from her abductor and he participates in the mock lynching of Phillip Randolph to scare Janey.

Taylor, Lee: In *Knights of the Range*, had known Holly in New Orleans, where his sister attended Madam Brault's school as well. Holly is not particularly pleased to meet him. He hangs around, together with Lascelles, another suitor from Louisiana.

Taylor, Matt: In "The Secret of Quaking Asp Cabin," a one-armed Mormon who tells the anonymous narrator (probably Zane Grey himself) the story of the Pleasant Valley war. He was intimately involved in the mysterious events surrounding Quaking Asp Cabin. When the Starkes decided to move into the remote canyon, the Mormon rancher from whom they buy cattle and supplies and who helps them build the cabin, leaves Matt Taylor, a young, experienced farmer and hunter, to help out. Matt Taylor is a good friend of the Apache with whom he hunts. Young Len has little disposition for farming and goes hunting with him in the canyon. Matt is a close friend to both Len and Richard. He patches him up when he is shot by his brother and expected to die of his wounds. He continues to bring in supplies to the valley, observing the gradual deterioration of the place. The cattle are rustled, the farming is less productive. He serves as a link between Richard and his brother Len. After Hallie has died and Starke has gone off on his own, he asks Matt to get Len. When Starke tells the story to the anonymous narrator (Grey), Matt Taylor is now over eighty years, and becoming forgetful. Other than Starke himself, he is the only one to know the secret of Quaking Asp Cabin.

Teller, Lize: In *Nevada,* lives in Lineville. She had been involved with Nevada before he went to California, where he worked with Ben Ide catching wild mustangs. Mrs. Wood knows that Lize was crazy about Jim Lacy and will undoubtedly try to take up with him again. She meets Jim at the Gold Mine saloon. She has heard through Lorenzo that he is back, and a changed man. Nevada had been like a brother to her. He knows how she loves to play with men, making fools of them, and she never managed to seduce him completely. She wants him to kill her enemies, Cash Burridge and Link Cawthorne. At present, she is working as bookkeeper and bartender at the Gold Mine. She tells Jim (Nevada) that she was engaged to Cash Burridge but it fell through when Holder, a rival with whom she had been involved, told Burridge about her. Link Cawthorne is her current love interest, but she finds him troublesome. She tells Jim the gossip she has heard reporting his presence in Hammell and linking him with the death of Sutter in California. Lize Teller knows she can count on Jim Lacy's pity for women in distress and so she tries to arrange things so that Jim and Link Cawthorne will come to a shootout. Ben manages to keep things cool until Link beats Lize up, and then he feels obliged to act. Killing Link Cawthorne in a shootout leads to his leaving Lineville and heading for Arizona. Lize's manipulations have finally caught up with her.

Tellson: In *Raiders of Spanish Peaks,* runs the Diamond Bar saloon, where the reputation of the Three Range Riders, Nelson, Williams and Lonesome, as non-drinkers is firmly established.

Tennessee: In *Knights of the Range,* a sallow-faced, towheaded young southerner who works as a rider for the Ripple ranch.

Terrill, Mrs.: In *Arizona Ames,* the buxom widow of forty who works as the housekeeper at Crow Grieve's ranch house. She is not averse to flirting with the cowboys, and loves to talk. Arizona Ames approaches her when he wants to confirm that Grieve beats his wife, Amy. While she is cautious about what she says, she does confirm Amy and Lany's story of abuse.

Tex (Dillon): In "From Missouri," one of the three cowboys at the post office when a surprise letter arrives from the school marm in Missouri after they had decided to discontinue the hoax. Their boss is a shy man, and the cowboys had thought they would bring in a single teacher who might interest him. At the dance, he gets into a fight with Beady Jones, who has taken his turn dancing with Miss Stacey.

Texas: (1) In *The Border Legion,* mentioned several times as one of the outlaws in Beard's saloon or in Kells's cabin at Alder Creek. He is present in the saloon playing cards when Gulden comes to pick a fight with Cleve by proposing the two of them kill Brander, steal his gold and abduct his daughter to use as they please. He reports this back to the group at the cabin. He is one of the men betrayed to the vigilantes by Red Pearce. He is tried before a hooded court and lynched that same evening. He dies without betraying any other members of the group.

(2) In *The Lost Wagon Train,* a gunman from the Rio Grande country. No one mentions his real name. Lester Cornwall observes that he is itching to have a shootout with Lone Wolf, just to see which is faster. He is a member of the Leighton faction in the outlaw outfit, but is opposed to Leighton's proposal to share Cynthia Bowden with all the men and then kill her. He provokes a fight with Lone Wolf and kills him in a gunfight.

Texas Jack: (1) In *Nevada,* the name that Jim Lacy (a.k.a. Nevada) uses when he moves to Arizona. It is the name by which he is known to Judge Franklidge and Tom Day. The name reflects his Texas background and accent. Franklidge calls him a man you can swear by. He went to Lincoln County, New Mexico, on a mission for Judge Franklidge. He speculates that remnants of the gangs involved in the New Mexico–Johnson County war are probably operating with the Pine Tree Outfit. Tom Day has a special admiration and affection for Texas Jack, a man he considers the salt of the earth. See **Lacy, Jim.**

(2) In *West of the Pecos,* one of the cowboys that Pecos Smith hires through Jeff Slinger and Hudson. He is a bullet-headed, jolly-featured, bow-legged cowhand who appears to be an extremely tall Texan. Pecos Smith figures he could be an equally good enemy and a friend.

Thatcher, Mel: In *The Maverick Queen,* Lee's foreman and close friend of Vince. Lincoln Bradway first meets him outside the saloon, where he cautions a friend to hold his tongue or he will end up like Jimmy Weston. This mention of his friend's name arouses Lincoln's curiosity and he arranges to meet Thatcher the following day in the Chinese restaurant. Thatcher seems to Lincoln to be an exceptional cowboy. He is younger and less experienced than Lincoln, but he is certainly no novice at things pertaining to cowboy life, and he wears his gun low on the hip as do most gun-throwers. Thatcher remains tight-lipped about what he knows concerning Jimmy's death. Thatcher is fired by Lee for refusing to join his vigilante group. Lee tries to drive him out of the valley. Vince keeps him from doing something silly. Since Lincoln is looking for cowboys to work on the ranch he is planning to start, Vince brings Thatcher to talk to him. He highly recommends the man. At their meeting, Thatcher tells about Jimmy being brought to the Leave It Saloon in a wagon, but that he knows Miller did not do the shooting. He does not elaborate on how he knows this. Like Vince, Thatcher becomes eyes and ears for Lincoln. He overhears a fight between Emery and Kit, Bandon and her ultimatum to him and his threat to expose her. He also reports on the secret meeting of the cattlemen about to deal with the rustling problem with a vigilance committee. When Lincoln's plans about the ranch start to take shape, Thatcher mentions that he has a sweetheart in Cheyenne and he wants to settle down for keeps on Lincoln's ranch. Linc welcomes the news. Mel comes to Lincoln's room at Mrs. Dill's boarding house with word that things have reached a crisis. The ranchers have taken Emery and Kit, and Vince has disappeared, probably with the cowboy outfit out to fight the ranchers. When the killing is over, Mel promises to take care of the burial of Vince and of the Maverick Queen, while Lincoln goes to Lucy to take her away from the valley for a while. Mel Thatcher is a young Lincoln Bradway, a cowboy decent at heart, needing only proper conditions to go straight and develop into a responsible citizen.

Thompson, Ben: In *Knights of the Range,* Colonel Lee Ripple and his foreman, Britt, speculate about whether the Arizona cattle ranges will ever produce a gunman like Thompson.

Thorndyke, Al: In *The Thundering Herd,* joins the campaign against the Comanche.

Thorne, George: In *Desert Gold,* a young cavalry officer who organizes the rescue of Mercedes Castañeda from the revolutionary general, Rojas. Thorne had known Dick Gale at the University of Wisconsin and recalls his prowess as a football player. He enlists his help in getting Mercedes out of Casita and in hiding her where Rojas cannot find her. He is willing to desert from the army to do this. He is so bewitched by her beauty that he is not thinking straight. Dick, however, convinces him that he should return to the garrison, offering to take charge of her.

Thorne takes a leave to go to Belding's ranch to see Mercedes, but he is taken prisoner by Rojas and sequestered across the border. His cavalry mates are unwilling to cross the border to rescue him. However, Nell Burton comes to the garrison seeking Thorne only to learn of his imprisonment in Mexico. She brashly rides into Rojas's camp, shaming Thorne's cavalry mates into following her and affecting his release.

Reunited with Mercedes at Belding's ranch, Thorne gets the padre from Casita to marry them, thereby risking revealing their location to Rojas. When Thorne is discharged from the cavalry he meets up with Mercedes at Belding's ranch. Rojas pursues them there, attacking the ranch. A party is quickly formed to flee through the desert and escape from Rojas. Thorne is shot, and his recovery is slow, but both he and Mercedes survive the ordeal and Rojas is killed.

Thorne, Jim: In *Shadow on the Trail,* a Texas Ranger who recognized Wade Holden among the outlaws who come to Mercer to rob the bank.

Thorne, Selma: In *Majesty's Rancho,* one of the Madge Stewart crowd at the university in Los Angeles, a blonde that can give Madge a run for her money. She is one of the gang that comes to the ranch for the summer. She helps Madge pack for the trip home when Madge is expelled from university.

Thornton, Black: In *Western Union,* Red Pierce's right-hand man in the saloon and gambling business, as well as in the cattle venture. Thornton appears later in South Pass, Wyoming, where he and Pierce are planning to rob the bank and the miners.

Thorpe: In *The Lost Wagon Train,* the young man that Cynthia's brother, Howard, wanted her to marry. He spreads rumors about Stephen Latch to turn Cynthia against him. He had received the commission as a colonel in the Confederate army that should have gone to Latch. With her brother's connivance and treachery, Thorpe disgraced Stephen so that a commission was denied him. Stephen challenged Thorpe to a duel in which he kills him. As a result, Latch became an outlaw.

Thorpe, Ben: In *The Maverick Queen,* a trapper and a friend of Lucy Bandon's. Like John Sprague in *To the Last Man,* he befriends the young woman and serves as a mentor and confidante. Lucy would like to build her ranch house near Ben Thorpe's cabin. Thorpe had been a trapper and has lived alone in the Sweetwater Valley for many years. She brings Lincoln to meet him. Ben Thorpe is clad in buckskin. His shaggy head bears a great shock of silver and tawny hair, but unlike most trappers, he wears no beard. His face is lined and weatherbeaten and his gray eyes are clear. He tells the couple he is looking forward to having some company after all the years of loneliness. He agrees to help Lincoln build a road into the valley to start his ranch. Lincoln puts him in charge of his cowboys, to direct the project.

Three Ranger Riders: In *Raiders of Spanish Peaks,* Laramie Nelson, Lonesome Mulhall and Ted 'Tracks' Williams refer to their partnership as "The Three Range Riders." They are an inseparable trio, all for one, one for all. They end up partners in a ranching venture with the Lindsays.

Thuber, Jess: In *Arizona Ames*, a young man courting Biny Wood. He is at the ranch on the Sunday that Fred Halstead, another beau, appears to visit her.

Thundercloud: In *Betty Zane*, the war chief of the Hurons. He is the father of Captain Jack, the six-year-old boy who is particularly fond of Isaac Zane. Thundercloud, riding a black stallion, arrives at the Delaware village with Myeerah and two hundred warriors to rescue Isaac Zane, who is about to be burned at the stake.

Thurman, Boyd: In *Code of the West*, brother to Enoch and Cal. Boyd had been a marine in the war and served in France. He returned uninjured and seemingly unaffected by what he had seen in the war. He is the best rider, roper, axman, and hunter of the lot. He is big-shouldered, of strong rugged face, hard as bronze, and his blue eyes are as frank as a child's. Boyd has found a homestead three miles from Green Valley, toward the Tonto Rim. The homestead is not as fertile as the main ranch in the valley. Of the hundred and sixty acres of his property, eighty are under cultivation in sorghum. Since Boyd still lives at the main ranch house, the sorghum harvest is the responsibility of whole clan. The property is not well-watered, the little stream being merely surface water. A few cabins and a barn, weathered, and in need of repair, are built around a pool of water in the rocks. Since Boyd proved up on his claim, Boyd has lived at the main ranch house. The cabin is free, and serves as the wedding spot for Cal and Georgie. Tuck fetches Parson Meeker to the cabin to perform the service.

Thurman, Cal: In *Code of the West*, the nine-teen-year-old, youngest son of Henry Thurman. Five-foot eleven in height, he is a superb specimen of cowboy manhood. He is the only one of the cowboys who does not crowd around Mary Stockwell to get a look at Georgie's picture, apparently not interested in girls. While all the cowboys seemingly have a good reason not to volunteer to fetch Georgie from the station in Ryson, Cal alone accepts the task. Mary Stockwell considers him the finest of the Thurman boys. He has the hardiness, simplicity and ruggedness of the Tonto natives and somewhat more intelligence and schooling. He seems more modern and fairly well read. He spent his last year of school under Mary Stockwell and had been a good student. His grandfather had been a Texan and a rebel, noted for his wild, fiery temperament, which Cal has inherited. Cal loves horses and, as a rider and cowboy, is second only to his famous brother, Boyd. He hates cars and cannot understand what makes them run or stop or break down. He never grasped mathematics at school and his father never managed to teach him the workings of a threshing machine or the steam engine at the sawmill. Cal suspects that his cousins and cowboy pals will not miss the opportunity to play a trick on him. He figures they will do something to make the car stall, or embarrass him in Ryson by

showing up and swarming Georgie. He's right on both counts. The crew who had begged off on the pretext of work obligations show up in Ryson and jinx the car. Cal, however, gets Georgie's help to pay them back in spades. She pretends to have been injured by their prank with the automobile, and continues with the act until they are at the ranch.

Cal is taken with Georgie from the start. While he hates driving the car, he wishes that the eighteen miles back to the Thurman ranch were a hundred and eighty. Georgie flirts with him, and he likes it. He comments openly that her dress is not suitable for the Tonto. It's made of flimsy material, providing no warmth. The Tonto is at high elevation and nights are cool. Georgie would be better off adapting her clothing to the conditions. "It's too thin, too low and a mile too short" he says of her dress, adding that "I can't see the sense of being uncomfortable for the sake of what you call style." He ends the ride with a bit of advice: "You've got some Western ways to learn ... an' I'm sorry I was fool enough to open my mouth. We don't savvy each other.... And as for what you said about Bid Hatfield — let me tell you out straight — you're bein' driven home now by a gentleman, even if he does live in the backwoods — an' if you had come with Hatfield you'd have learned what he thought of your rolled-down stockings."

The romance of Cal and Georgie knows more downs that ups. Cal takes her riding, sharing with her his love of nature, and showing her the spot at Rock Springs he has selected to homestead. He shares with her his dreams of the future, his homestead, his cabin. He voices Zane Grey's belief that the pioneers embody the best of American values. Cal gives Georgie his pinto, Blazes, her favorite horse from the corral. While Georgie likes Cal, she resents his old-fashioned values and his jealousy. She wants to flirt with men, to toy with them. She quickly gets the reputation of being free and loose. All the cowboys are after her. Cal goes to her sister, Mary for advice. Mary advises him to be patient, that Georgie will eventually appreciate him. When she makes a complete fool of herself at the October dance, she turns to Cal to take her home. Everyone there expects Cal to turn his back on her as she so fully deserves, but he puts his arm around her and takes her to the car. Mary Stockwell hopes that Georgie will appreciate the generosity and love in Cal's gesture.

Cal's decency and good nature come out in his friendship with Tuck Merry. He picks him up hitch-hiking along the road on the way to Ryson. Although Tuck is one of the strangest-looking men he has ever seen, he reminds Cal of his brother Boyd. The fact that Tuck had been a sparring partner for Jack Dempsey inspires great interest. Tuck can teach him to box and defend himself. He will finally be able to settle the score with all his cousins who have been beating up on him over the past many years. He gives Tuck a job at his father's sawmill. He shares his room with his new friend and confidante. They become the closest of friends. And thanks to Tuck's boxing lessons, he beats Tim Matthews in a fistfight, winning his bet that he would beat the tar out of him before the year was out.

When Georgie's behavior has reached embarrassing proportions for the family, Tuck comes up with the suggestion that Cal abduct Georgie and marry her. He knows a parson who can be convinced to perform the ceremony. Boyd's empty cabin would be the ideal spot. When Cal spots Georgie fighting off Bid Hatfield, he warns his rival to stay away. He then takes Georgie to the cabin, where he tells her she will have to marry him. Fearing what Cal's anger might lead him to do, she goes through with the ceremony. They go to Cal's cabin at his homestead at Rock Springs. There, Cal makes no demands of her. She is free to spend her time as she sees fit. He expects only that she prepare meals and clean the house. Georgie gradually comes to see that her life could be much worse. Georgie has the time to think about her situation. She does not understand why Cal is so popular with everyone. Even his rival for her affections, Bid Hatfield, likes him, calling him a "square shooter." She plans to tell everyone what a brute he has been to her, to turn people against him. She will get the marriage annulled. Her conversation with Mary leads to a reassessment of her priorities, and seeing Cal in a new light. He has aged years in a day. He is a more serious, proven man. When Cal risks his life to defend her reputation against the insinuations of Bid Hatfield, she finally understands what kind of man he is, and how much he does love her. Wess Thurman tells her the full story of the fight, and to prevent further conflict, she and Tuck head off to the Saunders ranch to confront Hatfield. Her courage and bravery endear her even more to the Thurmans and to Cal.

Cal is a typical hero of a Zane Grey romance. A knight in shining armor, willing to defend a woman's honor, to protect her from herself. He is a gentleman in every way, a man formed by the western environment, the embodiment of true pioneer values, much-needed to reinvigorate society.

Thurman, Edd: In *Code of the West*, one of the numerous Thurman clan in Green Valley of the Tonto. He is a giant of a man and dances like a lumbering rhinoceros. Those assembled at the party have a good laugh at his expense. He tells young Cal that when he gets married, they will "storm this here cabin."

Thurman, Enoch: In *Code of the West*, over thirty and the eldest of Henry Thurman's three sons. He is the chief of this clan, a lofty-statured rider, the sight of whom has always thrilled Mary Stockwell. He has wonderfully clear, light-gray eyes with a piercing quality that softens into a twinkle. His smile softens the rigidity of his lean, dark face. Enoch cannot volunteer to pick up young Georgie because there is too much work to do on the ranch. Cal volunteers, but when speaking to Mary about the trip to Ryson, he tells her Enoch finds her the best-looking woman he has ever seen, and Cal has great faith in his brother Enoch's judgment in most things. Cal tells Tuck and Georgie after the incident in Ryson that Enoch and Bloom are set against each other, and they all side with Enoch. Georgie is quick to see that Enoch is as much in love with Mary as she is with him, but being "backward," he is afraid to speak to her of how he feels. Georgie thinks he's afraid of Mary because he believes she's too far above him to want him for a husband. She has observed Enoch watching Mary when she's not aware, and has reached her own conclusions. On the drive in the car to the October dance, he gets up the nerve to tell Mary how he feels. He has been in love with her since she first arrived in the valley but he never had any hope that she would notice him. He takes the gamble, proposes to her and reacts to her acceptance with his typical understatement. The dance becomes a celebration of their engagement. Enoch and Cal have always been close, and Enoch is a bit jealous of anyone that Cal likes. He is jealous of the friendship between Cal and Tuck. His unfortunate comment about Tuck's height and big hands leads to insults about the size of Enoch's nose, and a fistfight in which Enoch is knocked out. Tuck figures that a knockout is the only option, or Enoch will never cease his teasing. Enoch takes his defeat with grace, and the tension between the two is put to rest permanently. Enoch and Mary are married at the ranch about a month after Cal and Georgie are married by the same Parson Meeker. Enoch Thurman embodies the masculine virtues that Grey so admires in western men, simplicity, sincerity, honesty, strength, chivalrousness, morality, loyalty, and resourcefulness.

Thurman, Henry (a.k.a. Old Henry and Uncle): In *Code of the West*, Cal's father and owner of the Thurman ranch in Green Valley in the Tonto. He boasts that there has never been a black mark against any of the Thurmans. Mary Stockwell says of them that she had never seen any under the influence of liquor. They did not lie. If they made a promise, it would be kept. Old Henry's sons are clean, fine, virile, manly young giants. They smoked cigarettes of their own making and would fight at the drop of a hat. They were cool, easy, tranquil, contented, strong, resourceful, and full of latent fire and reserve force. Henry Thurman also owns and runs a sawmill. He is an old man, but still in charge of assigning the tasks to the riders and sons, distributing work and ensuring that harvesting of sorghum and other crops is done. He plays the fiddle at the dance. Like his brother, Gard, he disapproves of Georgie's outrageous behavior at the dance, but welcomes her as a daughter-in-law.

Thurman, Lock: In *Code of the West*, a son of Gard Thurman, and nephew of Henry's. His brother is Serge. Mary Stockwell describes him as dark-skinned, dark-eyed, dark-haired, a young man of superb stature, and the quietest of the clan. He is teased by his brothers who say he is afraid of women, particularly the Bower twins. Serge comments that Lock cannot tell the twins apart, so there's not much fear of any marriage happening there. He is sweet on a certain Milly and rides over to her place to bring her a horse to ride with him to the dance, but Milly got tired of waiting for him to ask her and she agreed to go with Bid Hatfield, the local lady-killer.

Thurman, Mary: In *Code of the West*, the eldest daughter of Henry Thurman, and sister to Cal. Her opinion of his outfit is solicited before he heads off for town to pick up Georgie Stockwell at the station.

Thurman, Molly: In *Code of the West*, Cal's seventeen-year-old sister. She helps with the cooking on the ranch. She asks to go to town with Cal when he agrees to go fetch the schoolteacher's sister at the station.

Thurman, Mrs.: In *Code of the West*, Cal's mother. She is a slight, tall, gray-haired woman with a wonderful record of pioneer service and sacrifice. She sends Cal off to town to pick up the schoolteacher's sister, Georgie, with some advice on the need to be courteous to the easterner. She comments that in her youth, the Thurmans of Texas knew how to be courteous but that in the hard, Tonto country, such niceties are almost forgotten. Mrs. Thurman remains optimistic about Georgie, despite her outrageous, eastern behavior, and welcomes her as a daughter-in-law.

Thurman, Mrs. Gard: In *Code of the West*, a woman whose face shows the hard years of pioneer life. She looks after the babies at the dance, putting them to bed in a back room while their mothers dance. She receives Georgie for the Christmas dinner at the Thurmans' with motherly generosity and hospitality, commenting that she is picking up and "them's real roses in your cheeks." Her welcome puts the anxious Georgie at ease.

Thurman, Mytie: In *Code of the West*, at six years old, the youngest pupil in Mary Stockwell's school in Green Valley.

Thurman, Ollie: In *Code of the West*, first mentioned as the girl Tuck Merry wants to take to the October dance. At one point she is said to be sitting on the fence outside, between Tuck and Abe Turner. At Enoch and Mary's wedding, the relationship between them has become much closer, and Georgie comments on the look of pleasure and proprietorship in his approach to Ollie.

Thurman, Richard (Dick): In *Code of the West*, at the age of sixteen, the oldest pupil in Mary Stockwell's class at Green Valley in the Tonto. He is also the youngest of the sons of Henry Thurman. He offers to drive Georgie home but cannot take the time away from his lessons, being behind as he is in his homework. Georgie teaches him some of the new eastern dances and they try them out at the party to the amazement and admiration of many. He is more willing to try the "new" eastern ways than his brothers.

Thurman, Serge: In *Code of the West*, the yellow-haired young giant, brother of Wess Thurman. He is the most gallant as well as the best dancer of the Thurman clan. Serge works at herding the cattle, helping Boyd and Enoch round up strays. Serge suspects that Thurman stock is being rustled. He had marked some calves the previous month and some of them have gone missing. Suspicion falls on some at the Bar XX ranch.

Thurman, Uncle Gard: In *Code of the West*, the brother of Old Henry Thurman. Together they run one of the largest ranches in the Tonto. Gard reports that Hatfield on the Bar XX has his eye on Rock Springs, where Cal has his heart set on homesteading. This spurs the young men into building Cal's cabin there to stake his claim. Gard and Henry do the fiddling at the October dance at the school. He is also the man who criticizes Georgie's outrageous dress and behavior at the party, humiliating her in front of all. Gard helps with the building of the cabin for Cal up on Rock Springs. When he meets Georgie after her marriage to Cal, he merely comments that eastern women don't take the bridle easily, but she's a Thurman nonetheless. He accepts her wholeheartedly, without reserve, like his wife and the rest of the family.

Thurman, Wess: In *Code of the West*, the twenty-two-year-old cousin of Boyd and Enoch Thurman, son of Gard Thurman and brother of Serge. He is tall, with wide-open eyes. Wess is proud of his strength and endurance and loves to tease his cousin, Cal, who, when the sorghum crop must be harvested, has the temerity to bet that his tenderfoot friend, Tuck Merry, can beat Wess at harvesting. Wess has long enjoyed the preeminence at this Tonto game of sorghum harvesting and is tenacious of his record. Old Henry comments that Tuck is the best hand he has ever had working for him at the sawmill. Wess comments that Cal has a poor record of betting recently, having waged his favorite horse in a challenge to whop Tim Matthews within the year, and having given his pinto to Georgie, another sure losing proposition. Nevertheless, Wess is easily beaten by Tuck and in the fistfight which follows, Wess is knocked down a peg but takes the loss good-naturedly. Tom Hall entrusts the injured Cal to Wess when he brings him back from the Saunders Bar XX ranch where he fought with Bid Hatfield. Wess tries to hide the truth from Georgie but she guesses that the fight was with Hatfield. Wess assures her that none of the Thurmans believe any of Bid's mouthing off. "For Gawd's sake don't believe any of us Thurmans take stock in what Hatfield says. Reckon Cal feels as we all do. He shore acted like he does.... Wal, we've all talked this over among ourselves an' we figgered this way. You was new to the Tonto, an' a high-stepper at that, as the boys say. You liked Bid and made no bones aboot it. Same way you liked Tim Matthews, an' Arizona, an' of course Cal. You didn't know which one you wanted an' you wasn't in a hurry. Wal, you married Cal, an' thet settled thet.

It sure squared everythin'. An' if Bid Hatfield hadn't been a low-down skunk, you'd never heerd again of your foolin'." In short, Wess explains the "code of the west" to Georgie in terms she can understand.

Tige: (1) In *The Arizona Clan*, Nan Lilley's favorite hound. He takes to Dodge Mercer readily. Tige is given the duty of keeping guard over Dodge, a needful precaution in the view of the attempt on his life which had almost proven fatal. Tige has a particularly sensitive nose and is reputed to be able to follow any trail. He follows Nan and Steve and Bill in pursuit of the Hathaway outfit, and they put him to work tracking the enemy clan.

(2) Colonel Ebenezer Zane's great wolf dog in *Betty Zane* and *The Last Trail*. The dog was with him on the hunting expedition when he first saw the valley where he later returned to found Ft. Henry. In the first novel, Tige finds Isaac Zane on the shore of the river. He recognizes him as a white man. Tige is supposed to be able to smell out Indians and track them with unparalleled skill. Tige goes with Wetzel as he follows Miller, who has fled the fort and gone to join the party about to attack the fort. Miller had plotted to lure Betty down to the river where waiting Indians would kidnap her. After Wetzel has shot Miller, he sends Tige back to the fort with Betty's bullet pouch and a bullet, a sign that it is from Wetzel and that he has shot Wetzel. The dog is treated royally as a messenger.

Tillimanqua: In *The Great Slave*, the son of Baroma, the Crow chief. He attempts to kill Siena by shooting him in the leg. Siena beats him decisively, humiliating him. Siena later suspects that the person clothed in the fur coat following the Crows on their trek northward is Tillimanqua dressed as his sister.

Tillt: In *Fighting Caravans*, owns a freight company that hauls supplies needed for posts on the Santa Fe trail. They have large warehouses stocking wagons, guns, tobacco, leather goods, food, paper and even bags of candy. Jim Belmet signs on as a freighter on his way west, as does Sam Bell.

Tinny: In *The Vanishing American*, one of Nophaie's sheep dogs when he is a boy on the reservation.

Tith-lei: In *Blue Feather*, the greatest warrior of the Rock Clan of the Sheboyahs. He is betrothed to Ba-Lee. When Blue Feather comes, Tith-Lei finds his position in the tribe challenged. Blue Feather defeats him at all athletic contests; Blue Feather can carry the rock which tests a warrior's accession to manhood and strength without apparent effort. He climbs the wall of the citadel with an antelope carcass unaided. More than any other young man in the tribe, Tith-Lei resents Blue Feather's popularity with the young women. He and Ba-Lee become the chief persecutors of Blue Feather, calling for his death by torture. Tith-Lei is killed when the Nopahs, aided by Nashta, make their final assault on the citadel.

Tobiki: In *Stranger from the Tonto*, a Navajo Indian who tells Neberyull that Kent Wingfield rode into Logan's trading post on Spades, Lucy Bonesteel's horse. The Indian knows the horse as well, as Slotte and the Hole-in-the-Wall men do.

Tobin: In *The Drift Fence*, the bank manager in Flagg. Jim Traft's kidnappers want the ransom note taken directly to old Jim Traft, to Blodgett or to Tobin, who they hope will pay out the ransom money without hesitation.

Todd, Lee: In *Wyoming*, asked by Mr. Toller, the emporium owner in Randall, to drive Martha Ann Dixon from Randall to Split Rock, where her uncle is now located. Lee knows her uncle well, and calls him the "salt of the earth." He promises to have her in Split Rock by ten or eleven that evening. He himself is on his way to Lauder.

Toddy Nokin: In *Wild Horse Mesa*, a Piute Indian, father of Sosie and several sons, friend of Chane Weymer. He is a chief, an expert on horses, scrupulously honest, loyal to a fault, a man of few words. Toddy Nokin sent his daughter to study at a white school, but when she returns, he wants her to marry a Piute and to share with them what she has learned at the white school. He is distressed when she shows constant inclination to run off with white men. Toddy Nokin is like Do Etin in *The Vanishing American*, interested in acquiring the best of what the white world has to offer. He and his sons help Chane get the mustangs across the San Juan River before McPherson and his gang can steal them. The animals scatter when the outlaw gang attacks. Chane on Brutus manages to get across the Colorado river and to safety, but Toddy Nokin and his boys are left behind. Later, Toddy Nokin arrives at the mustangers' camp, where he vouches for Chane to Melberne and Sue. He refutes Manerube's claim that Chane was a squaw man, having shacked up with a Navajo woman years ago, and reveals that Manerube attempted to abduct his daughter, Sosie. Chane had rescued her and driven Manerube off.

Tohoniah bi dony: In *The Vanishing American*, a Navajo chief. Nophaie proposes calling him as a witness to testify on behalf of Wolterson.

Toller, Mr.: In *Wyoming*, runs an emporium in Randall, Wyoming. When Martha Ann Dixon arrives in Randall, she goes to the emporium to ask about her uncle. He tells her that Nick Bligh left his ranch on the Belle Fourche several months ago and drove his cattle south to new range at Split Rock. He arranges a lift for her to the new location.

Tolls: In *Sunset Pass*, mentioned as one of the smaller-scale ranchers operating around Wagontongue.

Tom: (1) In *The Horse Thief*, one of the men in Sheriff Bayne's posse which arrives at Rogers's homestead to arrest Dale Brittenham as a horse thief. He survives the ride by shooting at the escaping horse thieves.

(2) In *The Man of the Forest*, Milt Dale's pet

mountain lion. Old Al Auchincloss claims that Tom killed some of his sheep, and he has held this against Milt for some time. Tom is a full-grown cougar (mountain lion). Milt has raised him as a pet. The cougar is jealous of Milt's affections, chasing off Muss (the bear) and Pedro (the hound) to have Milt to himself. Tom tells Jim Wilson that Tom looks dangerous but he is not, no more than a kitten. He only looks fierce. He has never been hurt by a person and he has never fought anything himself but deer and bear. He can trail any scent. Milt tells Wilson that he could not make the cougar hurt anybody. Still, he can be made to scare the hair off anyone he does not know. He emits a cry that sounds like a woman screaming, a sound that curdles the blood.

(3) In *The Maverick Queen*, a partner of Slim Morris. Slim recommends him to Lincoln Bradway, who is looking for cowboys to work building a road into the valley where he and Lucy will set up their ranch. Tom would appreciate the chance to work with his buddy, but tells Lincoln he cannot quit Sam Blake's ranch, as Blake has advanced him money and he has another three months' work to do for him to repay the debt. Lincoln suggests Tom speak to Blake to find out if he would release him if the money were repaid. Lincoln offers to put up the money to clear the debt. Tom comes to work for Lincoln.

Tomanmo: In *Thunder Mountain*, the leader of a group of Indians, warriors with women and children, outcasts from various tribes, who move into the hidden valley beneath Thunder Mountain. They settle in the remote valley where not even animal trails are to be seen. They are the first to discover gold and predict that in time, the valley will be overwhelmed with white men in pursuit of the cursed yellow rock.

Tomepomehala: In *The Spirit of the Border*, Colonel Ebenezer Zane's trusty Shawnee guide. He is reputed to be able to travel a hundred miles in a day. He advises Joe to be wary of Silvertip. When Joe first sees him in Ft. Henry, he thinks he is carved out of wood, he stands so perfectly still.

Tommy: In *Black Mesa*, Louise's son by Belmont. He is often sick, and Louise has to take him to a doctor on one occasion. The bad water is making him sick.

Topsy: In *Captives of the Desert*, one of the mules at Weston's Black Mesa post. Topsy has the reputation of being stubborn. High-Lo is the only cowboy that can convince the mule to do what he wants. When Topsy goes missing, none of the cowboys are particularly disappointed.

Traft, Gloriana Mary (a.k.a. 'Big Eyes'): In *The Hash Knife Outfit*, young Jim Traft's sister and niece of old Jim Traft. As the novel begins, she is heading west, supposedly for reasons of health. Her arrival at the ranch causes quite a commotion as she is a stunning beauty and an incorrigible flirt and snob. Jim Traft expects she will have the hands

fighting over her. Back in Saint Louis, Missouri, Jim had never gotten along with her. She could not bear to hear any criticism of her actions or have any restrictions on her freedom. Her first meeting with Jim confirms some of his worst expectations. She complains that he has become too western, and when he speaks of his fiancée, Molly appears to be an unsuitable wife for a Traft. Gloriana eventually confesses that she has not come west for health reasons, although she had cajoled Dr. Williamson into telling her parents she needed to go west for her that reason. In reality, she needs to escape from an embarrassing situation her recklessness has produced. Her parents had always worried about her lack of discipline and wanted her to marry Henry Hanford, a man old enough to be her father. Glory reacted by getting involved with one Ed Darnell, a handsome young man her father disliked but who drew eyes to him wherever he went. The other girls envied her, and for Glory, that was a feather in her cap. Believing herself to be in love with Darnell and engaged to him, she made a fool of herself. He borrowed money from her and embezzled money from their father. She had turned her former friends into enemies because of her connection with this riverboat gambler. A trip west would save her from embarrassment. Darnell, however, met her at the train station in Saint Louis and she fears he has followed her west where he could embarrass both her brother Jim and her uncle. She imagines he will try to blackmail them to keep quiet about her past. Gloriana soon has all the cowboys a-twitter over her. When Uncle Jim Traft is taking her and Molly over to Jim's new cabin on the Yellow Jacket, she is kidnapped for ransom by Madden and Malloy of the Hash Knife Outfit. Jed Stone comes upon Jim Traft and the abandoned wagon, learns the story and pursues them to the cabin, where he kills the outlaws and rescues the two young women. Molly tells him about Gloriana's wild streak, her snobbishness and her infatuation with desperadoes. Jed Stone decides she needs to be taught a lesson. He makes her haul water, make bread, clean the cabin, sleep outdoors, load a pack onto a mule, and ride for long hours through brush and down steep trails. By the time they reach the Yellow Jacket, she has been reformed, like the shrew in Shakespeare's play. She even offers to go with Jed Stone as his slave if he will release Molly. Gloriana learns to accept western ways. She marries Curly Prentiss, and they settle down on a ranch near the Yellow Jacket.

Gloriana Traft is a variation on the "runaway male" motif, or rather, the "runaway female." She leaves the East to escape an unpleasant situation and eventually learns to give up her shallow eastern ways and acquire true values. She resembles the more substantial heroines of earlier novels, such as Madeline Hammond in *The Light of Western Stars* or Carley Burch in *The Call of the Canyon*.

Traft, Old Jim: In *The Drift Fence*, the bachelor uncle of young Jim Traft. He is first pointed out by Molly Dunn's uncle, Caleb See, who had explained to her his arrogance in building the drift fence. He is a big man in his shirt sleeves, with dusty boots. He has a shrewd, weather-beaten face, hard around the mouth and chin, but softened by bright blue eyes that do not miss anything. Molly thinks that if he had not been Jim Traft, he would be easy to like. Jim Traft treats young Molly with great charm and civility, speaking about having known her father. He commends her for sticking by her kin.

Jim Traft was fond of his brother's son, who had been named for him. As a boy, Young Jim always enjoyed his uncle's stories about Indian fights and road agents, rustlers and gunmen. Uncle Jim writes that he wants to leave his property to his nephew and suggests that the boy, if he is strong and resourceful, could become a rancher. Ranching is a growing industry and though cattle-stealing is still a problem, there is a good future for the business. When Young Jim arrives, his uncle is quite changed. He is a stalwart figure of a man, nearing seventy, but still erect and rugged with a lined, hard face, expressive of life on the frontier. He introduces his nephew to Ring Locke and the two take to each other at once. The uncle sees potential in his nephew, the closest thing he has to a son. He is impressed with Jim's straightforwardness speaking to Ring Locke. Old Jim makes Young Jim foreman of his crew and assigns him the task of building the drift fence, a task which will either make or break him. While Old Jim doesn't fully approve of some of Jim's decisions at first, he gives him free rein to do things his way. Young Jim soon proves himself capable of doing the job and worthy of inheriting the ranch he had built up.

In *The Hash Knife Outfit*, old Jim Traft is the owner of the Diamond Ranch. He has been in this part of Arizona for many years. He had once been partners with Jed Stone, current leader of the Hash Knife Outfit, and he still retains admiration for the man as a straight shooter and a man of his word. Jim is preparing his young nephew to take over his ranching operations and Young Jim has proven up to the challenge. Old Jim remains in the background in much of the novel. His broad experience of the West has given him a wisdom about men and ways that is invaluable to his nephew. He resembles John Sprague in *To the Last Man* and Bent Wade in *The Mysterious Stranger*. Old Jim is taking Molly Dunn and Gloriana over to the Yellow Jacket when they are held up by Madden and Malloy. They take the girls for ransom, leaving Old Jim with the broken wagon and the dead driver. Jim meets Jed Stone, who tells him he has left the Hash Knife. He offers to find the girls and set them free. Jim Traft is back at the Diamond Ranch when Jed Stone returns the girls.

Traft, Young Jim: In *The Drift Fence*, is old Jim Traft's nephew, "Missourie," to whom he intends to bequeath his ranch. When he first gets the news from his father, Young Jim feels humiliated and furious and is not interested in going to Arizona. But his father prevails. The uncle was caustic and crude, having grown up in the stern school of the

ranges, but he was the very salt of the earth with genuine affection for young James. He would be terribly hurt if Jim refused. As Young Jim travels west, the latent spirit of adventure begins to grow in him and when he reaches his uncle's ranch, he has grown quite enthusiastic about his prospects. Young Jim had done a lot of riding, worked a farm for two years and then started up a tree planting and landscaping business, all by his early twenties. Uncle Jim is impressed with his entrepreneurial spirit and his openness and straightforwardness speaking with Ring Locke.

Young Jim likes everything he sees about the ranch — the landscape, the ranch house, the horses, the cowboys, and his mentor, Ring Locke. He follows Ring around like a little boy, anxious for his instruction and his approval. His uncle appoints him foreman of a crew with the task of building a drift fence a hundred miles long. Young Jim knows his being a tenderfoot will be a sticking point with the cowboys, and the building of a fence an even greater challenge. Nevertheless, he sets about the task of learning his job with humility, honesty and enthusiasm. His uncle warns him that the cowboys will play tricks on him, but that in itself is a good sign, showing hope of ultimate acceptance into the fold.

Young Jim learns to ride any horse in the corral, starting off with the more recalcitrant animals. He treats his men fairly, never asking them to do anything he himself will not do. He endures their practical jokes with good humor, getting in a few tricks of his own in return. After a few weeks, he has worked and ridden out the tenderfoot soreness of muscle and bone that had been so painful at first. He is strong and hard, can stick in a saddle, and can dig fenceposts all day. He feels healthy and strong, transformed by this new, western environment. Even the periods of depression he feels due to the lack of acceptance by the cowboys is relieved by communion with the tranquility and majesty of the natural world. In town for the rodeo, he is full of pride in the accomplishment of Bud Chalfack, Hack Jocelyn, Curly Prentiss, Hump Stevens, Uphill Frost and others, longing for their approval and acceptance.

In his fistfight with Curly Prentiss, Young Jim discovers that the boxing lessons he had taken in his teens prove particularly useful. Curly was born on a horse, and is incredibly skilled in the saddle, but clumsy on his feet. Jim can dance circles around him and deliver blows without getting hit himself. Since respect from his peers is proportionate to his ability to defend himself and to command the respect of others in a fistfight or a gunfight, Jim knows it is only a matter of time before he has beaten all of them. One by one, he defeats the cowboys in a fight, until they grudgingly respect him. But the respect comes not only from victories in fistfights but from his genuine, good-natured decency. He saves Curly Prentiss from a night in jail by confronting Sheriff Bray in Flag at the rodeo. He apologizes to Slinger Dunn for having suspected him of cutting the drift fence. He apologizes in public, in the main street of

Flag. When he has beaten Dunn in a fistfight, he then offers him a job on the Diamond Ranch. When the drift fence is cutting off some of the smaller-scale ranchers from the higher range, he posts notices that the Diamond will not lay further claim to stock in the brakes west of the drift fence. The cowboys and the small-scale ranchers are taken by the generosity of this action, winning young Jim support and approval both from his own men and from the cattlemen who profit greatly from the gesture. When the homesteaders come to call at his camp, their attitude is unmistakably friendly and grateful.

On the romantic front, Young Jim wins Molly Dunn's heart at the rodeo. He stands out from the rest, treating her with respect and courtesy. At the dance, he does not mingle with the others, keeping apart. He kisses her out on the porch, an impulsive action witnessed by Bud Chalfack and promptly reported to the cowboys of his outfit. Molly feels inferior to him, given her family's reputation, but Jim pays little attention to that. He sends her gifts, school books among them, knowing that she is anxious to better herself. Molly is truly impressed by his thoughtfulness and respect and courtesy. He is concerned that her association with him not be misunderstood. He is not jealous of other men, and not too proud to learn from her. When Molly learns of the plot to kidnap him, she sets out to warn him. She herself prevents his being shot and killed when she bites into Hack Jocelyn's gun hand.

The Hash Knife Outfit continues the story of young Jim Traft, old Jim Traft's favorite nephew, whom he plans to make the heir of his ranching interests. Now, Young Jim has been in Flagg, Arizona, a year, and quickly adapted to the western way of life, shedding his snobbish eastern ways. Uncle Jim has given him the Yellow Jacket ranch which he bought from Blodgett. Young Jim intends to set up ranching there when he marries. Young Jim had been kidnapped by Hack Jocelyn for ransom and rescued by Slinger and Molly Dunn. At the start of the novel, Jim is engaged to Molly Dunn and planning the date of their wedding. When Jim's sister, Gloriana, arrives from Saint Louis under the pretext of improving her health, he wonders what effect she will have on the cowboys not accustomed to such a flirt. He worries as well about his insecure fiancée. Young Jim goes to Winslow to inspect the herd Bambridge is shipping east. He discovers many animals with the Diamond brand. He makes himself known as a man to be reckoned with. Young Jim goes directly to the Hash Knife cabin to speak with Jed Stone. He informs him that he will be moving onto the Yellow Jacket ranch and asks the Hash Knife to move out of the valley. He comments that some three thousand head of cattle they had in the valley have gone missing. Croak Malloy tries to frighten Jim as he is leaving the cabin by shooting a cigarette out of his mouth. In short, Young Jim impresses Jed Stone, the Hash Knife leader, as a courageous, straight-shooter, not unlike his uncle, Old Jim, who had once been Stone's partner. He agrees to move out, off the Yel-

low Jacket. Young Jim starts to build his cabin on the ranch, but when they take time off to celebrate Christmas at the Diamond Ranch and in Flagg, they return to find the cabin and the logs burned to the ground by the Hash Knife Outfit. Young Jim sends the Diamond cowboys under the leadership of Slinger Dunn in pursuit of the outlaws. They shoot and kill a number of them, burn out some more and lynch three from a tree outside the outfit's cabin.

Young Jim's relationship with Molly has its ups and downs. Molly comes to feel she is not good enough to marry a Traft, that her low-class origins make her unsuitable as a wife. She breaks off the engagement and gets a job at Babbitt's general store and starts seeing Ed Darnell. Eventually, Jim convinces her that her feelings of inferiority and insecurity are unfounded. They marry and move onto the Yellow Jacket.

Like John Hare in *The Heritage of the Desert*, Jim Traft arrives in the west seeking to prove himself. He learns to adapt, to shed frivolous eastern ways and return to the essentials inculcated by the western environment. He becomes a better person, happy with himself, confirmed in his principles and values, a worthwhile contributor to society. Like most Zane Grey heroes, Jim Traft is moved by the beauty of nature. He is happiest when his mind is free from thought as he contemplates nature. He turns to the wilderness for comfort and restoration when things are trying. He selects the Yellow Jacket ranch to be his home for the beauty of the valley.

Trapier, Emmeline: In *Rogue River Feud*, an old friend of Keven Bell's in Grant's Pass. When she meets him on the street, she does not recognize him at first. She welcomes him back wholeheartedly, never having believed the stories Atwell spread about him at the training camp. She invites him over to her house to meet the family. Her brother was killed in France, so she is sympathetic to the wounded Bell. Em is delicate about bringing up the topic of Rosamond Brandeth, Keven's feckless fiancée who is now going around with Gus Atwell. She says she has little contact with her now. Emmeline announces that she and Billy Horn, another chum of Keven's, are engaged to be married. They part with Em wishing Keven all the best and offering their continued friendship.

Trapier, Hal: In *Rogue River Feud*, Emmeline Trapier's brother. He was killed in France in the war. Em is sensitive to Keven Bell's plight when he returns, injured, from training camp.

Trash: In *The Horse Thief*, one of the Montana ranchers who has lost large numbers of horses to Big Bill Mason's horse-rustling outfit.

Trinidad: In *Knights of the Range*, a cowboy working on the Ripple ranch. He is corrupted into rustling by Talman. The two of them have a disagreement when Talman refuses to divvy up the money from the rustling. Trinidad refuses to return to the bunkhouse on the ranch and so they are in the camp when Ripple's cowboys capture and lynch the group. Trinidad runs off in an attempt to escape and is shot.

Trumbell, Vic: In *Horse Heaven Hill*, has the reputation of being quite the ladies' man. He is tall, good-looking and the best dancer in Wadestown. Lark tells Stanley about Vic holding her so tightly while they were dancing that she could scarcely breathe. Rumor has it that Marigold, Stanley's fiancée, has been seen with Trumbell in the saloons and at the dances.

Tull, Elder: In *Riders of the Purple Sage,* one of the head churchmen in Cottonwoods. He first appears at Jane Withersteen's home to whip Bern Venters and drive him out of Utah. Jane has befriended this gentile against the wishes of her clergymen and they will settle the matter by force. Tull is prevented from carrying through his threat by the arrival of Jim Lassiter. Tull is described as ruthless, cold, arrogant, a consummate, polished actor, able to disguise his true feelings and thoughts and to deceive many.

Through his presentation of Tull, Grey voices his strongest criticism of religion and the Mormonism he witnessed in places in the West. Tull is presented as the worst type of clergyman imaginable. He uses his influence as a religious leader to enrich himself and expand his control over his followers. His interest in religion is purely as a tool to personal aggrandizement. Jane Withersteen wants to believe that Tull is a good man, a truly religious man, with her spiritual interests at heart. She is torn between loyalty to her Mormon faith and revulsion at this man's abuse of power. Jane cannot reconcile the two sides to Tull. He appears to be a devout religious man, anxious to do the will of God, but she also knows he is a plotting tyrant, out to ruin her, to marry her to get control of her property. In Cottonwood, Jane Withersteen owns the most prosperous ranch, the best race horses, and Amber Spring, the source of water for the town. It seems her father had wanted her to marry Tull, but Jane has a mind of her own. She will not marry a man she does not love, nor submit to being one of several wives.

Tull is responsible for abducting Milly Erne's daughter and entrusting her to Oldrin.' He is shocked to learn that Lassiter is looking for Milly Erne's grave. He knows that Jane will keep their secrets. While he and she seem to be co-conspirators on this matter, Tull nonetheless pursues his campaign to force Jane to marry him. He has her riders called in to form a vigilance committee to pursue rustlers he already controls; he orders her servants to spy on her, to steal documents and deeds from her, to report on her every movement; he tries to have her cattle stampeded; he orders Jerry Card to steal her horses. In short, he plots the ruination of her ranch and livelihood to force her to submit to him. Bern Venters confronts Tull in the town hall beside Parson's store. He reveals all these underhanded dealings of Tull in front of the Mormon men of Cottonwoods.

But public humiliation does nothing to dull Tull's pursuit of his goals. The abduction of Fay Larkin follows shortly upon this denunciation.

Tull pursues Jane and Lassiter, who are fleeing Utah, having burned the ranch house and the barns. Nothing is left for Tull to take. He has accomplished one of his goals, the ruination of the Withersteen estate, but not quite as he had intended. At first, he pursues Bess and Venters, who have taken Black Star and Night and are racing across the sage. When he realizes he has been duped, he resumes his pursuit of Lassiter and Jane, only to be killed in the landslide which follows their rolling of Balancing Rock, closing the entrance to Surprise Valley.

In *The Rainbow Trail*, Tull is mentioned as the leader of the Mormons from *Riders of the Purple Sage.* He was the Mormon leader who led the persecution of Jane Withersteen, and who worked in conjunction with Bishop Dyer and other outlaws to steal her property. He pursued Lassiter and Jane to Surprise Valley. He was buried in the rock slide when Jane and Lassiter pushed over Balancing Rock, causing a rockslide which buried their pursuers.

Tull, Sam: In *Nevada*, a young rider that Tom Day assigns to Ben Ide to help him get started with his ranch. Sam is killed by the rustlers who begin to decimate his herds.

Tullt: In *The Lost Wagon Train*, runs a store in Fort Union that outfits caravans heading west. He builds a wagon especially for Bowden and his daughter, Cynthia. Years later, he tells the lawyer who is looking for proof of Cynthia's death and possible heirs that he recalls her very well. He describes in detail the wagon he built for them and the red lettering. The lawyer decides that if Latch brings him this board with the Tullt and Co. label, he will accept this as proof that Cynthia had come to Latchfield. Tullt and Co. are also mentioned in several other novels, including *The Thundering Herd* and *Fighting Caravans.*

Tunstan: In *Shadow on the Trail,* an Englishman, a friend of Billy the Kid. The Lincoln County outfit killed him. Billy left Chisum over a disagreement involving Tunstan, whom Chisum did not like.

Turk: In *Fighting Caravans*, one of the nicknames for Clint Belmet. He is called Turk because he loves turkey meat and hunting wild turkeys.

Turner: (1) In *Arizona Ames,* owns the Reception Hall and Bar in Shelby.

(2) In *Fighting Caravans*, operates a saloon in Taos, New Mexico.

(3) In *The Man of the Forest*, one of Beasley's riders who is hot after Bo. He is a fine-looking, strapping cowboy and lucky with the girls. He is a good dancer and interrupts Bo and Tom Carmichael to ask for a dance. Bo obliges him. There is a second Turner, presumably young Turner's father, who runs a saloon in the village. Riggs reports to Helen Rayner that Turner witnessed the shooting of Roy

Beesley in the saloon. Riggs holds it against Turner that he did nothing to help Roy, who lay bleeding on the floor. In the final confrontation, Tom Carmichael makes Turner hold out a bottle and he shoots it out of his hand.

Turner, Abe: In *Code of the West,* a young man keen on Ollie Thurman at the dance.

Turner, Josh: In *The Arizona Clan,* an Abilene cattleman, related to Simpson. Dodge Mercer rode for him for two years. Turner speaks highly of Mercer to Simpson, a rancher whose spread is across the valley from the Lilleys.

Turner, Red: In *West of the Pecos,* a scout with Hudkins buffalo hiding outfit. He has been across the Pecos and reports to Templeton Lambeth on the great numbers of cattle roaming the plains and on the threat from the Comanche. Red Turner is also the Lambeths' source of information on the roads, the rivers, and the suitable places to ford them.

Turner, Reggy: In *Arizona Ames,* a young man who turned to rustling to make some quick money. Arizona Ames comes upon men trying to lynch him and declares that Reggy is innocent, as he (Ames) is the man who did the rustling. Arizona Ames then challenges the lynchers to take him on. Arizona frees the young man on the promise that he will never take up rustling again. He hopes young Turner has learned his lesson and that when he marries his sweetheart, he will stick to the straight road, this scare teaching him the consequences of rustling.

Twitchell, Snipe: In *The Arizona Clan,* Buck Hathaway's partner. He shoots Dodge Mercer from ambush when he is looking for the still. Twitchell provokes Ben Lilley into going for his gun and kills him in the shootout. Copelace overhears the outfit deciding how to divide up their assets, and Twitchell indicates that he wants the Lilley ranch. When Nan escapes from the cabin and they learn Parson Bailey married her to Mercer, they withdraw to Ryeson, where they hope things will quiet down. Dodge Mercer confronts them in Ryan's saloon. Twitchell is killed in the shootout. Twitchell is related to the Quayles in some way but the link is never established.

Two Face: In *Wildfire,* one of John Bostril's prize horses, known for her varied nature. The mare can be coquettish, slick, and glossy, but equally given to cunning treachery. Bostril warns his daughter that Two Face can't be trusted.

Two Spot: In *The Heritage of the Desert,* the nickname by which Chance is known.

Tyler, Eben: In "Canyon Walls," with his brother, Mormon wild-horse hunters with whom Sam Hill (Monty "Smoke" Bellew) goes hunting.

Tyler, Sue: In "Canyon Walls," a friend of Rebecca Keetch's. She offers to take her to go shopping in Kanab. Sam Hill is called upon to comment on this proposal, and voices the opinion that she is too young and too boy crazy to go on such a trip.

Tyler, Wade: In "Canyon Walls," with his brother, Even, Mormon wild-horse hunters with whom Sam Hill goes hunting. Wade explains to Smoke that the Widow Keetch's husband, John, had owed money to a Mormon bishop and when he could not repay the debt, their ranch was confiscated on his death. This clarifies for Smoke the widow's failure to attend church. The brothers plan another wild-horse hunting venture after Sam gets married and becomes one of them. They assure him he will get the mustang pony for Rebecca on this venture.

U

Uhl, Honey Bee: In *Majesty's Rancho,* a Hollywood-type gangster. In him, real life imitates the silver screen. He first appears in Los Angeles, where he drives around in a flashy car. He meets Madge Stewart when she is waiting in a parking lot for Lance Stewart. Uhl sweet talks her, and, to the unseen Lance, she appears to be soaking it up. She leaves him to return to the university, but Uhl makes more of the encounter than she intends. Uhl won't take no for an answer.

On the drive home to the ranch, Uhl bumps into Madge in Yuma. He tries to impress her with his wad of money. She tells him she's engaged, and doesn't want to see him, but he will not take no for an answer. She offers to meet him for breakfast, but then Madge gets up early, and tells the clerk that if anyone asks for her, she got an emergency call and has to return to Los Angeles. Lance runs into Uhl in Douglas, Arizona, where he has stopped for the night. Uhl offers him a hundred dollars to drive a truck to Tucson. Uhl does not know who Lance is, but Lance recognizes him as the slick customer talking to Madge at the parking lot in L.A. Uhl thinks that Lance is a driver for bootlegging operators. He lets him know that the truck will be stopped at Tucson but not to worry.

Uhl materializes again at the end of the novel when the rest of Stewart's and Mains's herds are being rustled. His appearance, however, has nothing to do with the rustling. He is there to settle a score with Madge. Nobody makes a fool of him and gets away with it. Uhl has discovered who Madge is and where she lives. He cuts the telephone wires to the ranch and kidnaps Madge and Rollie Stevens. He wants to demand fifty thousand dollars in ransom. Madge tells him her father could never pay that, but that she could get the money. Part of the threat is that unless the money is delivered, he will rape or kill Madge. When Uhl sees Lance, he still thinks that he is a gangster. Lance offers to take them up to Cochise's stronghold, where they can hold out until the ransom is paid. Uhl, who doesn't know much about riding or camping, agrees to go along. He pays Tom Sloan a thousand dollars for his horses and equipment. They set out for the mountains. Uhl and his thugs do not endure the ride very well. Uhl never realizes that he has been outsmarted by Lance Sidway. Lance rescues Madge, and shoots Uhl. Honey Bee, however, is not dead. He comes out of the cabin just as Stewart and his men arrive. Uhl imagines he can buy his way out of his predicament. In the world he comes from, everyone can be bought; it's just a question of price. He finds himself forced into a genuine gunfight with Ren Starr, a fight which leaves him dead.

Umpqua: In *Majesty's Rancho*, Lance Sidway's spectacular horse. Umpqua, an Indian word meaning "swift," was given to him when he was a colt. He's cowboy bred, on the Oregon range. He is big and rangy, mottled black, with white feet and nose, and bright soft eyes, spirited but gentle. Lance brought Umpqua to Hollywood to work in the movies to earn money for his sister's operation and special treatments. The horse worked in the movies, and Lance rode as an extra. But the soft living was good for neither Lance nor Umpqua so they set off through the desert of southern California. Umpqua can do up to fifty miles a day. Everywhere they go, cowboys marvel at the beautiful animal. At Stewart's ranch, Gene is first impressed by the horse, commenting that the ranch keeping him would likely be hit by rustlers. These don't prove to be so much of a problem as Madge Stewart, who is determined to buy the horse. She quotes a passage from the Arabian Nights describing a dream horse, in short, Umpqua. She offers ten thousand dollars, and when Lance refuses, she swears she will get him eventually. Throughout the novel, Umpqua remains a bone of contention between Lance and Madge.

Uncle Charlie: In *Forlorn River*, tells Ina that she is a true pioneer in spirit, unlike the other members of her family who have been influenced by their new prosperity.

Uncle Jim: In *The Lone Star Ranger*, Buck Duane's uncle. It is never mentioned whether he is an uncle on the father's or the mother's side. When the novel begins, Uncle Jim tries to give Buck Duane some sound advice, that he should hold his temper and not go looking for trouble. He acknowledges that Buck has a reputation to live down. Most expect him to be like his father, and no doubt he has inherited much from him. What kind of a man, he asks Buck, can be shot in the heart and still hold a gun to shoot twice? Buck's father was an incredibly fast gunman, who could place two shots in a man's heart close enough to be covered by the ace of spades. Uncle Jim warns Buck that Texas is changing. The rangers are becoming a potent force in maintaining law and order. Eventually, the scofflaws so admired by young boys will be brought to justice. Uncle Jim sees that all his talking is having little effect on his nephew. He warns him that if he gets into a gunfight

with Cal Bain, it will ruin his life. Even if he shoots in self-defense, he will be a marked man, on the run from then on. He tells him he will have a horse saddled for him when he gets back from town. A short while later, Buck does return, having killed Bain in a fair fight. Buck is coming to terms with the emotions he felt when he shot Bain. Uncle Jim tells Buck he killed in self-defense, and as such is no outlaw. Nevertheless, the family doesn't have the money to hire good lawyers to fight this out in court, and Buck would be tried for his father's reputation more than for anything he himself did. He advises him not to drink, not to gamble and to live as honestly as he can among outlaws. There are some decent men among them. When Buck leaves, he doesn't expect to see him again. Later, when Buck returns after joining the rangers and destroying the Cheseldine gang, Uncle Jim, now childish, is Buck's biggest fan, anxious to hear about all his doings—the gunfights, the action. He takes great pride in his gunfighting nephew.

Urba: In *Shadow on the Trail*, a cowboy in the employ of Band Drake (Rand Blue)—a gunman, a cheat and a thief. He comes to the ranch with a man called Bill and several others just as Wade Holden arrives. He demands payment for a herd of cattle that Pencarrow claims he has paid for twice already. Urba intends to take Pencarrow's horses in payment. He tries to provoke Pencarrow into a gunfight in which he will surely be killed, leaving his ranch free for the taking. Wade Holden (Tex Brandon) challenges him. When Bill goes for his gun, Brandon shoots him. Urba then confesses that Drake's real objective is to get Pencarrow to agree to marrying his daughter Jacqueline to him. Urba tries to draw on Brandon as he is leaving and he, too, is killed. Brandon tells the men to report to their boss, Drake, that Urba turned on him and that should he encounter these men again, he will shoot them on sight.

Uriquides, Juan: In *Thunder Mountain*, a freighter who had packed in a mill over perilous trails and down into the valley on the backs of mules. He received ten cents a pound for this packing and thereby set a price for all supplies and merchandise to be freighted in.

Utah: In *Wild Horse Mesa*, one of the hands working with the Melberne mustanging outfit.

Utsay: In *The Vanishing American*, the god of the Navajo who resides on the mountain, Nothsis Ahn.

Uvalde Quintet: In *The Trail Driver*, the term that Brite uses to refer to the five riders from the town of Uvalde, Texas, that sign up for his drive. Deuce Ackerman, San Sabe, Rolly Little, Ben Chandler, and Roy Hallet make up the quintet of cowboys. Adam Brite has a great love and respect for Texas riders.

Uvaldo: In "The Ranger," the foreman of the Glover ranch. He is Mexican, claiming descent from the Spanish soldier of the same name. He has an American wife, owns many head of stock and is partner with Glover in cattle deals. His daughter, Roseta, was born on the American side of the river and was educated in an American school, an advantage lost on most young Mexican women. Uvaldo raises doubts in Ranger Medill's mind. He is clearly hiding something. Vaughn believes Uvaldo has some connection with Quinela, and he suspects the story about her eloping is a distraction. In Mexico, Medill learns from Juan Mendoz that Uvaldo had wronged Quinela, who now seeks revenge.

V

Vail, Jimmy: In *Riders of the Purple Sage,* one of the young gentile boys that Judkins hires to ride for Jane Withersteen when the Mormon riders have been called in by Elder Tull and Bishop Dyer. He is killed in the stampede of the white herd.

Valverde, Carlotta: In *Knights of the Range,* the daughter of Don Carlos Valverde. At the age of fifteen, she fell in love with Colonel Lee Ripple. As her father did not approve of her involvement with an American, she eloped with him and they married in San Antonio. Her daughter, Holly, is said to resemble her in beauty and poise.

Valverde, Don Carlos: In *Knights of the Range,* the Spanish owner of a large tract of land in Arizona. His reputation for hospitality and generosity resembles that of Maxwell, St. Vrain and other ranchers of the early frontier. He disapproved of his daughter's involvement with Colonel Lee Ripple, and when they were married, he disowned her. When her daughter, Holly, was born, he slowly relented, eventually leaving his enormous ranch to his daughter when he died. This ranch is the basis of Ripple's current operation. In *Twin Sombreros,* Don Carlos is mentioned several times as the founder of the largest and most famous ranch in New Mexico.

Vandergrift, Anne: In *Boulder Dam,* a young twenty-year-old woman from Salem, Illinois. When her father dies, she moves to Los Angeles to live with a Mr. Henry Smith, a friend of her father's, who sends her to business school then employs her in his company. When the Depression hit, his business is ruined and he commits suicide. Anne then takes a series of jobs which she quits because her employers make advances to her. Unable to pay her rent, she loses what few possessions she has and is thrown out on the street. Anne answers an ad in an employment agency window for a job as a waitress in Las Vegas. When she gets off the bus, a dark-faced, sharp-eyed man meets her and takes her to a house where she is shown to an upstairs room. The following morning, after breakfast, her clothes are taken from her and she is locked in the room. She realizes that she is a captive. Ben Sneed tries to buy her from Ben Bellew but she gets away the next day when they are busy trying to subdue another unwilling woman. She has nothing to wear but a blanket. Anne gets into a car to hide — Lynn Weston's, as it turns out. He feels sorry for her and agrees to hide her in his tent out at Boulder City where he works. He gets her clothes — men's clothes — at the company store, and finds her a boarding place with Mrs. Brown, whose husband is a pipesetter at the dam construction site. Lynn slowly falls in love with her, and takes her to visit St. Thomas, an archaeological dig site. She considers him her knight in shining armor. Ben Bellew eventually catches up with her and takes her captive, threatening to kill Lynn Weston if she does not cooperate. He takes her to Vitte's place in Las Vegas. Lynn, Decker and Sneed effect her rescue, killing Bellew and some of his gangsters. Anne is reunited with Lynn in the hospital, where the minister whom Sheriff Logan brings performs the service.

Van Horn, Mr.: In *Nevada,* a rancher who is Alice Franklidge's escort to the dance. He drives Alice and Hettie home to the judge's ranch after the party. He fills the women in on the Hatt family. Marvie Blaine seems to be struck on the daughter, Rose. He knows the names of the three boys and the girl, but admits that little is known about them, just suspicions.

Vasquez, Juan: In *The Fugitive Trail,* a partner of Tex Serks who has ridden with his outfit for years. He comes to work for Melrose with Serks and Peg Simpson. He has a reputation as an excellent tracker, a skill that proves useful when Slaughter assigns them the task of tracking down the Stewart gang of rustlers.

Velasquez, Conchita (Con, Connie): In *Knights of the Range,* the Mexican bombshell on the Ripple ranch. She is not ashamed of her beauty and her power to attract young men, getting a decided thrill out of playing one against the other and watching them fight over her. Holly Ripple feels jealous of her ability to get any man she wants. Holly suspects she has her claws into Frayne, but he tells Holly that Conchita is just being herself. She is fun to be with, dances well, makes no demands. There is nothing between them. Later, he and Holly overhear Conchita and Brazos talking, and it is clear that she has her eye on Brazos, not Frayne.

Venters, Bern: In *Riders of the Purple Sage,* a young gentile man in his late twenties who works for Jane Withersteen. He is a particularly close friend of hers, her lover, according to Mormon gossip, and as the novel begins, he has been seized by Tull's men and is about to be whipped in the hope that he will abandon Jane's service and leave the state of Utah. Venters is saved by the timely arrival of Lassiter, whom he recognizes from his crouch when drawing his guns.

Venters tells Lassiter about his past, how eight years earlier he had run off from his home in Quincy,

Illinois, where his mother still lives, to seek his fortune in the gold fields. He never got any farther than Salt Lake City, where he wandered here and there as a helper, teamster, shepherd. He drifted south, to the more isolated border settlements where he became a rider of the sage, acquired stock of his own and for a time knew prosperity, until that very prosperity made him unwelcome to Mormon authorities. After a campaign of ostracism, robbery and intimidation, his prospects and prosperity are destroyed. He came to be employed by Jane Withersteen as a ranch foreman. Venters understands the forces that are at work against Jane. He himself has been ruined by the invisible hand of Mormon authorities who are trying to rid Utah of all non–Mormons by making it impossible for them to make a living. He sees these same tactics being used against Jane to force her into submission. He regrets having submitted to her request that he hand over his guns to her. A man without guns for self-defense is considered a legitimate target, a weakling, a man commanding little respect. He warns Jane that her Mormon leaders have no interest in her spiritual needs but only in her vast ranch, her cattle, her spectacular thoroughbred horses and Amber Spring, the only permanent supply of water in the area. She is to be punished for her independence and forced into submission by any means available. Venters reiterates the theme of Jane's blindness to the forces that are against her, and her deliberate refusal to see those forces. Lassiter later takes up the same theme.

Venters is Lassiter's first source of information about Milly Erne. He tells about her being the schoolteacher in Cottonwoods, about her daughter, her decision to reject Mormonism for herself and her daughter, and the subsequent campaign to force her into submission by the kidnapping of the child. Venters suspects that she was a sealed wife, but does not know who the husband might have been. He does know that she and Jane were very close friends and that Jane surely has the answers to Lassiter's questions, but she is unlikely to give any answers willingly.

Venters makes the connection between Tull, Jerry Card and the rustling operation. He discovers the secret of Oldrin's canyon, the location of the hideout and the truth about the Masked Rider. Commissioned by Jane to go to Deception Pass and learn about Oldrin's operation, Venters finds the way through the labyrinth of canyons used by the rustlers. He discovers Jane's red herd hidden in a lush canyon which they share with the cattle that have been rustled from various ranches in the region over the past year and a half. He observes rustlers riding through a waterfall which conceals the entrance to the hideout, and the canyons which exit to the north, making possible the movement of cattle unobserved. He also shoots the Masked Rider who turns out to be young Bess, Elizabeth Erne.

Seeking a secure place to hide the injured Masked Rider, Venters comes upon a valley inhabited long ago by cliff dwellers. Here he nurses Bess back to health. The valley is a virtual Garden of Eden, and

Venters allows himself to learn from nature. He becomes transformed, finding himself and his mission. He falls in love with Bess, and sees himself as her knight in shining armor, saving her from the depravity of the outlaws. He is jealous of her relationship with Oldrin', suspecting that she was a whore for the outlaw. He returns to Jane to get supplies, planning to spend the rest of his life in Surprise Valley. Back in Cottonwoods, he confronts Tull, exposing publicly his machinations against Jane and his fundamental dishonesty and criminality. When Lassiter tracks him to the valley, he realizes that the paradise is not as secure as he thought. Others will surely be able to find him, and he especially fears Oldrin's men in search of Bess. He decides to leave the valley and the state and head back east, taking Bess for his wife. Back in Cottonwoods, he meets Oldrin' and kills him in a gunfight, only to learn on his return to the valley that he was Bess's father. He cannot bring himself to tell her what he has done.

Venters and Bess meet Lassiter and Jane on the sage as they leave Surprise Valley. In the meeting, the truth about Oldrin's death at Venters' hand and the fact that Bess is Lassiter's long-lost niece are revealed. Jane gives Bess and Venters her two best horses for their race across the sage and out of Tull's hands. Jane and Lassiter go to the Surprise Valley to take up residence where Bess and Venters had been planning to spend their lives. The valley is fully equipped for survival. Venters and Bess marry and head for Illinois, where they intend to take up horse breeding with Black Star and Night, Jane's prized thoroughbreds.

In *The Rainbow Trail*, Venters is a member of Shefford's congregation in Illinois, and an intimate friend, even after Shefford has been fired by the congregation. He has told John Shefford the story of Jim Lassiter, Jane Withersteen, Fay Larkin and Surprise Valley. He inspires in him the desire to go to Utah to rescue them, since Venters cannot leave his wife and young child to do so. Venters appears at the end of the novel when Lassiter and Jane have been rescued. They are at his farm in Illinois where he has raised prime racehorses from Black Star and Night. When Shefford reaches Surprise Valley, he recognizes everything from what Venters had already told him. Venters had killed off the coyotes in the valley, and had gathered supplies and cattle, having been prepared to live there himself with Bess. His preparations made it possible for Lassiter, Jane and Fay to survive for ten years.

In Venters, Grey has developed his theme of the "natural man," the easterner who comes west and allows himself to learn from the wholesome, natural environment. Venters is transformed by his time in Surprise Valley, where God speaks directly to him through the natural world. He becomes a force of nature, a man with a purpose, in tune with his true self and his environment.

Villa: In "The Ranger," a Mexican bandit whom Vaughn Medill admires and to whom he owes his life.

Vince: In *The Maverick Queen*, a young cowboy, sturdy, bow-legged, towheaded, so down on his luck he must sell his two beloved horses to raise money to pay back a loan to the Maverick Queen (Kit Bandon). He has negotiated a deal with Bill Headly at the livery stable to sell them for a hundred dollars. Lincoln Bradway happens to be looking for horses and pays Headly two hundred for the two. He keeps Bay for himself and returns Brick, Vince's favorite, to Vince. According to Lucy, Brick is the fastest horse in the valley. This generosity on the part of Lincoln earns him Vince's gratitude, friendship and loyalty. Vince reminds Lincoln of his partner, Jimmy Weston, whose death he has come to investigate. He tells Vince that he takes him for what he is. He asks no questions. Vince is free to tell him about his past or not to talk at all. Like Jimmy, Vince can sense Lincoln's moods and knows when is the right time to talk or to keep silent. Vince becomes Lincoln's eyes and ears, able to learn things that Bradway's more high visibility would prevent him from discovering. Vince is fiercely loyal to Kit Bandon, and a friend of Lucy's. He knows more about Jimmy Weston's murder than he is willing to reveal to Lincoln. He brings word that Emery has sent for a gunman, Gun Haskel, to kill Lincoln. Rumor has it that Haskel rarely meets men in an open fight, preferring to shoot from ambush. When the moment of crisis comes, Vince saves Lincoln's life by following Mike, one of Emery's men, upstairs to a bedroom overlooking the street. Mike is preparing to shoot Lincoln when Vince plugs him. Having had first-hand experience with Kit Bandon, Vince is constantly warning Lincoln that the woman is deadly and not to be trusted. He predicts she will be the death of him. Like the leopard, her spots are deep. He doubts very much that Kit's conversion is sincere, when she supposedly has quit buying up mavericks from cowboys. When Lincoln marries Lucy and they spend a day planning out where they will build their cabin, Vince spots Kit heading up the valley towards Thorpe's cabin. He hears gunshots, and thinks that Kit has killed the two of them. He takes it with a grain of salt when Vince tells him Kit had shot at a gopher to let off steam. Vince also reports on the plans of Lee and other big ranchers to set up a vigilance committee of "night riders" to pursue cowboys involved in rustling. He senses that Kit is the object of their search. Vince partners up with Thatcher and Lincoln to build a road into the valley at the headwaters of the Sweetwater River. However, when Bud Harkness has been caught red-handed with a branded maverick, Vince recalls how he himself had been caught and how Bill Haines, a rancher friend, advised him to get out of South Pass and Wyoming. Things develop quickly. When the ranchers declare war on the cowboys, bringing in riders from Casper, Vince becomes the head of a cowboy resistance group. When Lee has captured Emery and Kit and is preparing to hang them, Vince and his cowboys arrive to put an end to the proceedings. Vince shoots Lee, but is killed himself. He fails to rescue Kit Bandon. Lincoln and Thatcher give him a decent burial in the valley where they had planned to set up ranching.

Virey, Elliott: In *Wanderer of the Wasteland*, the husband of Magdalene Virey and father of Ruth Virey. Adam first finds Elliott lying in the desert, almost dead from dehydration. He takes him back to his house in Death Valley, where he and Magdalene nurse him back to health. Elliott Virey has built their house at the bottom of a cliff that appears about to collapse on top of the house in an avalanche. Virey is the most hateful man Adam has ever met. He is brutal to his wife, always speaking with caustic bitterness. He mocks his wife because she cannot cook. At night, he rolls rocks down the cliff, almost hitting the house, to frighten Magdalene. His face reflects the torture of his soul. Magdalene reveals that Elliott had loved their daughter and had loved her until she revealed that she had betrayed him with a lover who is actually Ruth's father. From that point, Elliott's passionate love mutates into an equally passionate hatred focused on the daughter, Ruth, to the point that Magdalene fears leaving her with him. She gives her daughter to her parents in California and she follows Elliott into Death Valley. Elliott has heard of Wansfell from the Indians and other wanderers. He wants to kill Wansfell for being kind to Magdalene. His is a life possessed by hatred and misery resulting from his inability to forgive. He eventually does start an avalanche which crushes the house and Magdalene as well. Adam pursues him and in turn Elliott is crushed in an avalanche. Elliott Virey is an example of a man in whom the desert has magnified the passions, the loves and the hatreds, transforming them into the brutality and savagery that lurks in the hearts of all men. In *Stairs of Sand*, Adam Larey tells Ruth the story of her parents in Death Valley. She recalls only that her parents did not get along. Virey is an object lesson in the way the desert magnifies the natural tendencies in men. Virey's emotions grew into grotesque brutality and savagery. But while Virey's is the fate of the majority of men on the desert, it need not be that way.

Virey, Magdalene: In *Wanderer of the Wasteland,* the mother of Ruth and wife of Elliott. Adam comes across her and her husband in Death Valley. They are the couple that Dismukes had told him about. Adam is struck by her beauty when he sees her in Death Valley. She appears completely out of place. She refers to him as "Sir Knight" and "Sir Wansfell," mocking his need to do good deeds for other people. She is amused that Dismukes, whom she calls a large frog, was interested in saving her and she finds it even more amusing that Adam thinks he might possibly change Elliott. Adam (Wansfell) finds her a classy woman, a "thoroughbred" in manners and style. Her husband is nothing to her. She accepts that her house will be her grave. She has no wifely talents, cannot cook or keep house. Adam shows her how to make bread, but she manages to make a mess of the job. Eventually, as Dismukes had told Adam about the desert being the place where secrets are revealed, Magdalene reveals why she and Elliott are there. She abandoned her daughter, Ruth. At nineteen, recently married, she experienced an insane spell of love for another man, the result of which was her daughter, Ruth. Moved to seek expiation for her sin, she confesses her disloyalty to Elliott. He in turn, refuses to forgive her. His passionate love is turned to an equally passionate hatred, which also extends to the daughter, Ruth. Magdalene fears that he will harm Ruth, so she entrusts Ruth to her parents in California, and returns to face her punishment with Elliott. She tells Adam how he torments her, insults her, berates her, and attempts to frighten her at night by rolling stones at the cabin risking an avalanche. Magdalene takes a bizarre pleasure in Elliott's jealousy of Adam, and feels a thrill when the two of them fight over her. Nevertheless, she is pleased that Elliott is beaten. She warns Adam that Elliott means to kill him too. Long proud of her ability to arouse men's passions, Magdalene marvels at Adam's ability to control his sexual desires. He is the only man she has met who can embrace her as a brother. Discussion turns to the ways of the desert, to the struggle for survival, and she affirms that nature is right. The weak should perish and the strong survive. When she senses that her end is near, she commissions Wansfell to find Ruth. Eventually she is killed in a landslide which buries the house that becomes her grave. Adam sees in Magdalene a representative of thwarted human nature, passion, desire, and guilt destroying the potential of human fulfillment. His acquaintance with her is an object lesson, a parable in his quest for understanding.

In *Stairs of Sand*, Adam Larey has tracked down the daughter, Ruth. He tells her the story of her mother and Virey in Death Valley, not leaving out her mother's infidelity, which caused the great hatred her father had for her mother. He attributes Virey's unnatural hatred of her mother to a mad, insane jealousy. Conditions on the desert only serve to concentrate that hatred. He underlines what Magdalene learned from the desert, that she had come to see who and what she was, willingly accepting Virey's punishment in expiation for her transgressions. Ruth has inherited her mother's recklessness, her ability to attract men and her pleasure in toying with them. She needs to learn her mother's lesson of service to others and duty. Adam recalls Magdalene as one of the most powerful influences on his spiritual growth in the desert.

Virey, Ruth: In *Wanderer of the Wasteland*, the daughter of Magdalene Virey but not by Elliott, her husband. Magdalene had had a romantic liaison with a man and became pregnant with Ruth. At that time, she was married to Elliott. She confessed her sin to her husband, but rather than forgive her, he hates her with a passion, a hatred that is directed particularly at the daughter. Fearing that Elliott might harm the child, Magdalene leaves Ruth with her parents in California. Wansfell meets Ruth when he returns to civilization at the end, looking for a home for Eugenia Linwood. It happens that she lives with the Hunt family, in Santa Ysabel. Adam gives Ruth information about her mother. He tells Ruth she is buried in Death Valley. Adam sees in Ruth a recreation of her beautiful, haunting mother. He falls in love with her. He dissuades Ruth from pursuing her idea of visiting Death Valley to find her mother's grave. He also avoids answering her queries about why her father hated her. Adam decides to go back to Picacho to face the consequences of killing his brother, and Ruth asks him to stay with her. All indications are that he plans to return to her.

In *Stairs of Sand*, Wansfell, now thirty six, has tracked Ruth over much of the Southwest and Mexico to come upon her with Hal Stone in the desert north of Yuma. She has run away from Guerd Larey, her husband, and from her grandfather who runs the freighting post at Lost Lake. Stone says she is as fickle as the desert sand, a woman who likes to toy with men to get her way. Wansfell brings her back to her grandfather. Merryvale tells her Wansfell's history, and what he sees as his mission, to help people find themselves and to defend the weak. Adam tells Ruth the story of her mother and her death in a rockslide in Death Valley. He tells her as well that she is the child of a love affair Magdalene had with another man, and that this infidelity had been the cause of her father's hatred for her mother and for her. In many ways, Ruth is like her mother. She is a desirable woman who can inspire great passion in men but she lacks a sense of responsibility. Adam mentions that he had hopes of marrying her, but Ruth tells him that will not be possible as she is already married to Guerd Virey. Adam tells Ruth that she must take charge of her life. She must return to her grandfather and to her obligations. She must overcome her loathing of the desert and learn to endure and to serve. This will make her a better woman. If she runs off alone, footloose, reckless, beautiful, she will ruin herself as her mother did. Magdalene had asked him to save Ruth from making the mistakes she did. Adam explains that the desert magnifies the good or the bad qualities in a person. Most succumb to the bad side of their character, becoming brutal and savage. A rare few, however, become more spiritual, learning patience, endurance and service to others. Ruth could be one of those, as Magdalene wished she could have been. Slowly, Ruth does come to see that she has inherited her mother's dark side. Virey tells her that he has never forgiven her for running away from him two hours after they were married. She made him the laughingstock of gamblers, greasers, and freighters, the riff-raff of the desert. For years, he has watched her flirt with other men. She has run off with Hal Stone twice. He has accepted her insults. He swallowed his jealousy but the rottener she was to him, the more he loved her. She made him love her until it has nearly killed him. He is determined to have her, and is now using her grandfather as a pawn in his game. He will ruin him and take his property unless Ruth submits to being his wife for real. Ruth is abducted to Yuma, and rescued by Adam. With her grandfather dead at the hands of one of Larey's henchmen, no doubt, she takes over the running of Lost Lake. She attempts to collect past dues for water from Larey's freighting company. This inspires even greater wrath. Virey puts out the word he will pay a reward to whomever kills Wansfell. When Merryvale shoots Guerd in the confrontation with his brother, the last obstacle to Adam and Ruth being together is removed. Magdalene's wish has been fulfilled. Her daughter will be saved from the mistake she made by marrying a man who can save her from herself.

Virginia: In *Majesty's Rancho*, one of Lance Sidway's girlfriends in Hollywood. She is cited as an example of the typical Hollywood girl, fickle, flirting, ready to do what is necessary to make it in the movies.

Vitte: In *Boulder Dam*, brings Anne to Las Vegas and keeps her locked in a room upstairs in his house. Weston and Decker are put on his trail by Mame.

Vorhees: In *Wildfire*, the man who sells his ranch and corrals to Slone. His ranch is on the sage under a bluff with corral enclosures so high they are reputed to be impregnable to rustlers. He is moving to Durango because he has family there and better prospects of finding work. He sells his place at a bargain price. Slone later learns that the property was mortgaged to John Bostril and that it was not his to sell.

W

Wade, Abe: In *Horse Heaven Hill*, the father of Marigold and Ellery Wade. He is a well-preserved man, not much over fifty, with keen blue eyes and a tawny beard, sprinkled with grey. Marigold got her features from him. According to Marigold, he dotes on his son, Ellery, who has turned out to be no good. Mr. Wade hopes to see him married and settled, and Marigold warns Lark that Ellery will target her for his attentions. Mr. Wade runs a general merchandise store in town and lives on a ranch. Attracted by the strong demand for cattle, he rounded up most of his stock and sold them. The money went to pay off debts and to modernize the store to meet the competition. The unprecedented sale of the livestock left his cowboys with more leisure time and they organized a roundup of wild horses to sell. Mr. Wade had been a partner of Mr. Burrell, Lark's father, and when his friend passed away, he invited Lark to come live with them on their ranch in Oregon.

Wade, Bent (a.k.a. Hell Bent Wade, Ben): In *The Mysterious Rider*, the mysterious rider. He has been wandering through Colorado seeking the daughter he lost some seventeen years ago. He is convinced that disaster follows him and, like Coleridge's Ancient Mariner, he feels compelled to find someone to whom to tell his story. He had been married to a beautiful woman named Lucy, and they had a daughter. Lucy's family, however, did not cotton to him. Her brother, Spencer, owner of a gambling establishment in Denver, and his colleague, Captain Folsom, did their best to drive a wedge between Bent and Lucy. They encouraged a young southern gentleman to pursue Lucy, and, given Wade's jealous nature, he was convinced that his wife was unfaithful to him and that the daughter was possibly not his. He kills the man, upon which his wife leaves him, taking the daughter with her. He pursues her, and in a fight, kills her father and brother. Lucy, though, disappears. He learns of the massacre of a group traveling in a prairie schooner; Lucy was one of the party, but the young girl is never found. He has spent all these years searching for clues. When he hears about the Belllounds and the foundling child they have raised, he suspects this may be the child. He presents himself at the Belllounds ranch, applying for a job hunting coyotes and wildcats. Old Bill gives him the job. Columbine, he is sure, is his lost daughter; she looks exactly like her mother, Lucy. Wade decides to make friends with her, and she finds it easy to confide in him, the only person on the ranch not directly involved in her predicament. Wade also befriends Wilson Moore, the young man who would make the perfect husband for his daughter. But out of respect for Old Bill Belllounds, a man he finds admirable, he tries to befriend his son Jack as well, hoping that perhaps he can effect some change in the boy. Bent Wade has developed a sixth sense about people as a result of his travels. He recalls seeing young Jack in prison in Denver and easily concludes that Buster Jack is beyond redemption. Wade takes care of Wilson Moore's broken leg, succeeding in preventing the onset of gangrene. He helps him set up his ranch. When the young cowboy is accused unjustly, he trails Buster Jack and catches him in the mountain cabin with the rustlers. When Buster Jack fails to live up to his promise to give up Columbine, he tells Belllounds the truth about his son's rustling and framing of Moore. Then, in a one-on-one confrontation with Jack, the two of them die. Wade had felt that he was "hell bent" because trouble followed him. He dies knowing he has ensured a better future for his daughter than he or Lucy had. Bill Belllounds reveals to Columbine that Bent Wade was her father.

Bent Wade resembles Robert Burton in *Desert Gold*. Both have spent their lives looking for a lost daughter, and both succeed in finding redemption in doing good for that lost child. The father searching for a lost daughter is a motif which appears in a number of Grey's novels.

Wade, Ellery (El): In *Horse Heaven Hill*, the ne'er-do-well son of Mr. Wade. Following the death of Lark's father, Marigold persuades her father to invite their orphaned cousin to come live with them. Marigold tells Lark Burrell that her brother Ellery is no good. He's the only son and he's been spoiled rotten. He imagines himself a devil with women and she predicts that he will be chasing after Lark. Their father and mother are blind about Ellery. They think the sun rises and sets on him. They cannot see him as he is. For the mother, no woman is good enough for El, and the father wants him settled. Ellery hangs out at the store where, according to Marigold, he "pretends" to work. Ellery and Hurd Blanding originated a scheme with a selected outfit of hard-riding cowboys and a force of Clespelem Indians to chase and trap three thousand head of wild horses. By a trick called tailing, that is, tying the tail of one horse to the head of another, they plan to drive the band to the railroad for shipment to Montana to be slaughtered for chicken feed. Ellery makes a thousand dollars on the deal. This despicable business earns him the contempt of Lark Burrell When Ellery learns that Wade had sold the horses for three dollars a head, he realizes that Hurd has double-crossed him and he tells his father he has quit the wild-horse hunting operation. Later, he returns to Blanding, as Landy Elm learns when he goes to their camp to inform them they cannot cross the Weston range with the captured mustangs. Ellery Wade is with Hurd Blanding when he rides into the Wade camp to accuse Weston of releasing the captured horses.

Wade, Elmer: In "The Ranger," the young man that Roseta would ride out to meet in the grove of trees. The morning of her abduction, they meet and ride off, only to be captured by Juan Mendoz and his men, who kill Elmer and abduct Roseta to Mexico.

Wade, Marigold (Mari): In *Horse Heaven Hill*, the college-educated sister of Ellery, and oldest daughter of Mr. Wade. She convinces her parents to invite Lark Burrell to come live with them when her father has died. Marigold is a tall, perfect blonde, and dresses with style and flair, displaying her beautiful figure. Marigold has been engaged to Stanley Weston for over five years. Mrs. Wade urges a quick marriage, hoping to get her daughter settled. The Weston ranch has great potential and young Stanley is the man to take over and make the place profitable. Marigold, however, has changed considerably since she went to college. She loves to party, to flirt with the cowboys and especially, to have her own way. Stanley tells Lark that things are not going smoothly between them. They are an unlikely couple. He loves the open range, ranching, and the beauty of lonely landscapes, and when he speaks to her of his love of these things, she laughs and ridicules him. Lark hears from Coil Bruce about Marigold's carrying-on in town, her involvement with Hurd Blanding. He knows that the two of them meet out on the range at least three times a week. Lark does not know what to make of the conflicting signals from Marigold. When Stanley speaks to Marigold about setting a date for their wedding, she shows little interest in making a decision. She claims she still loves him, but wants to retain her freedom as long as she can. She

does not want to have children or to live out on the sage on a ranch. She is town girl. Her tastes are not those of a rancher's wife. Mr. Weston tells Stanley that Marigold does not behave like a woman deeply in love. Stanley finds himself duty-bound to defend her honor and reputation, but the stories about her and Hurd Blanding continue to grow. Lark herself comes upon Marigold and Blanding kissing in the parlor of the Wade house. Coil Bruce tells Lark that it is an open secret that Marigold meets with Blanding when she goes riding, and that they meet regularly in the saloon. This has been going on since her return home from college. Coil advises Lark to catch Marigold in the act and try to shame her into coming to her senses. Lark, however, is uncertain how to proceed. Marigold finds Lark's concern about the wild horses amusing. She and her folks think the horses are a nuisance to the ranchers and their rounding up is a good riddance. When two college friends arrive for a visit, she organizes a camping expedition to watch the roundup of the mustangs. During this roundup, Marigold and Stanley have a final showdown, where she gives him back his engagement ring. She has realized that they are too incompatible to marry. She already knows that he is in love with Lark, as she is with him. Lark would make a much better wife for a rancher, as their interests coincide. She takes measures to clear her reputation. Most of the stories Blanding has been telling are exaggerations. The meetings on the range have not been planned by her. She confronts Blanding, forcing him to admit he lied about his insinuations that they had gone beyond mere flirting and a kiss or two. Marigold Wade is developed along the lines of Gloriana Stockwell in *Code of the West* or Carley Burch in *Call of the Canyon*. She is too modern for the West, where old-fashioned, wholesome American values still prevail.

Wade, Mrs.: In *Horse Heaven Hill*, Abe Wade's wife and mother to Ellery and Marigold. Mrs. Wade is anxious to have her daughter settled. She cautions her that she cannot live the carefree lifestyle she has been accustomed to when away at college. The money they made on the sale of the cattle has gone to pay off debts and to restock and modernize the store to meet the competition. She recommends that Marigold marry Stanley Weston, who will likely be rich soon when he takes over his father's ranch. If she puts him off too long, she will end up losing him, the best catch in the area. Mrs. Wade is not keen on the idea of Lark working at the store. When Marigold breaks off her engagement to Stanley Weston, telling her mother about her decision is the hardest part of it all.

Waggoner: In *The Rainbow Trail*, a sixty-year-old Mormon elder, physically strong with a secretive face, intelligent, aloof and powerful. He is reputed to be the wealthiest landowner in southern Utah. He lives in Stonebridge, and is one of the men who comes secretly to the hidden village to visit his sealed wives, two of which are Mary, the Sago Lily (Fay

Larkin) and Ruth Jones. He has the reputation of being a skinflint and hostile to gentiles. Shefford describes him as having a cropped beard and a wolfish jaw. He had five known wives and fifty-five children before the federal law prohibiting polygamy was enacted. Fay Larkin reveals that Waggoner led the party of Mormons that abducted her from Surprise Valley and threatened to hang Lassiter. Waggoner reveals to Ruth Jones that he suspects that Fay Larkin, another sealed wife, is seeing another man. He tries to force the truth out of her. Nas Ta Bega kills him on the porch of the house with a powerful knife thrust through the breastbone.

Wainwright, Bob: In *Western Union*, works on the crew constructing the Western Union telegraph line. At a crucial point he arrives with two wagonloads of poles to replace those knocked over by buffalo and cattle. Wainright is mentioned at the crossing of the Laramie River in flood, and during the buffalo stampede and the prairie fire.

Wake, Tim: In *Captives of the Desert*, a Mormon horse wrangler in Gallup who is in a liquor-running deal with Hanley and Newton to sell whiskey to the Indians. The Blakely girls are mixed up in the buying end of the deal.

Wakefield: In *West of the Pecos*, a rancher living just west of Menardsville, from whom Lambeth buys the nucleus of his herd. Wakefield also supplies him with a couple of his vaqueros to help with the cattle. He advises against going to the Pecos country because, although it does provide good grazing land, it is hard and lonely and sure to be a hotbed of rustlers some day.

Waldron: In *The Lost Wagon Train*, a member of Latch's outlaw outfit that attacks and massacres the caravan. Waldron is described as a gloomy man with a bad conscience. He is killed in the attack on Anderson's caravan.

Walker: In *Forlorn River*, a deputy sheriff from Redlands. He arrives at the Blaine ranch at Wild Goose Lake with Less Sutter and Judd. He claims to have been called in by the Hammel Stock Association to pursue the cattle rustlers. He supposedly finds proof in the barn at Forlorn River that Ben Ide is one of the rustlers. He arrests Ben when he comes to Hart Blaine's ranch with California Red. Walker is, in fact, not a peace officer but a member of Less Sutter's outlaw gang with which he worked in Colorado and Nevada.

Walker, Sam: In *The Arizona Clan*, runs a general store in Ryeson, Arizona.

Wall, Jim: In *Robbers' Roost*, the hero, a "good" outlaw, a black knight who redeems himself. He is a young man in years, but has the hard face and eagle eye of one matured in experience of the wild country. He bestrides a superb bay horse, his pride and the envy of many. Jim Wall is a large man, tall, broad-shouldered. He prides himself on his ability

to judge men by their looks. It has become a habit with him, if not a form of self-preservation. Others read him the same way. Brad Lincoln, to whom he is introduced in the saloon in Green Valley, pegs him as a former cowboy and a gunman. He has the cut, the eye, the movement and the hand of a gunfighter, in short, "the brand." Wall has been different things at different times. He tells Hays he was a country schoolteacher before he was twenty. He once tried to rob a bank. Two of his gang got away. They held up a train, and blew open the safe in the express car. They got away with sixty thousand dollars in gold. Both of these deals were pulled off in Iowa. He is presently on the run, having broken out of jail in Cheyenne, where he was awaiting hanging for killing a man. He had to kill the jailer to get out. This happened some years ago. He has been shooting his way out of one jam or another. Trouble seems to follow him. He has come far out west where no one has ever heard of him. Wall knows that life out here is raw. There is no law except that of the gun. Back in Wyoming and Montana, there were certain restraints bound to affect any man — sheriffs, courts, jails, the law of the noose. In this land, though, a man must be able to take care of himself. He has developed the habit of caution, never turning a corner till he sees what's on the other side, never walking past bushes or trees in the dark or entering gates until he has searched for signs of movement. He feels glad to have fallen in with Hank Hays and his cronies. Although he has been a lone wolf for a long time, he feels the need for the society of any class of man for relief. Nevertheless, he tells Hank that the deal, as he sizes it up, will come to the awfulest mess ever.

Like Cal Thurston in *Code of the West*, or Buck Duane in *The Lone Star Ranger*, or Chane Waymer in *Wild Horse Mesa*, Jim Wall is never more content than when on horseback with open, unknown country ahead. He has seen Texas, Kansas, Colorado, Wyoming, Montana, and Arizona, but Utah is stunning and breathtaking. The hours in the bosom of nature never drag. He can forget all that he has turned his back upon and can look ahead to the beckoning horizons. On the trek from Green Valley to Star Ranch, he is stunned by the magnificence of the scenery and would have halted Bay to enjoy the view, but Hays is waiting for him. A moment's sight seems to take in "a thousand years of man's comprehension." He trembles at the sensations the scenery stirs in him. It would take many years to make Utah his own.

He tells Helen Herrick that nature develops the men who spend their lonely, hard, bloody lives with her. Mostly she makes them into beasts with self-preservation the only instinct, but it is conceivable that one now and then develops in the opposite direction. In this sense, Hank Hays and Jim Wall are examples of these two extremes. Jim shares this love of nature with Helen Herrick, who is equally passionate about the western environment. When the men are holed up in the Robbers' Roost in Dirty Devil Canyon, he prefers those hours on guard duty when he is alone, free to enjoy the scenery and the tranquility and the sounds of nature. He understands what motivated Bernie Herrick to select the Henry Mountains for his ranch, and that particular spot with the spectacular view for his ranch house. Hays, in contrast, finds all of this sentimental twaddle amusing and foolish.

Jim Wall is a spectacular shot. He teaches Bernie Herrick how to handle a rifle, and is the first to be shown his vast collection of firearms. Herrick marvels at Jim's ability to hit three out of five jackrabbits that run past, shooting from horseback. At the roost, Jim repeats his feat of marksmanship, shooting rabbits for meat, shooting them through the eye at over twenty paces. Brad Lincoln and Jeff Bridges jokingly comment that they better be sure Jim never shoots at them.

Jim Hunt inspires confidence. Hank Hays tells him that he looks like the kind of man he wants to hitch up with and hang onto. He appreciates Jim's loyalty when he exposes Stud Smith's cheating at cards and the two guns hidden in his inside vest pockets. Hays shares with him the story of his upbringing in Hankville. He quickly makes friends with the young cowboys not part of the rustler outfit at Star Ranch. Young Barnes talks freely with him on the ride to pick up Helen Herrick. He fills him in on the gossip about Hays, his partnership with Heeseman, and his interest in the ranch. Young Barnes looks up to him as a hero. Helen Herrick is impressed with his person and his gentlemanly behavior. She shares with him her love of nature and her hopes for the ranch. Jim Wall gives her advice about how she should dress and behave around men like Hank Hays. He grabs her and kisses her to show her the risk she takes going out alone with men she does not know. Helen strikes him across the face with her quirt. Later, at the roost, she apologizes for her rash behavior. She should have followed Jim's advice. Among the outlaws, Jim Wall inspires the friendship of Sparrowhawk Latimer and Smoky Slocum. The former reveals to him what Hays had done to Bernie Herrick and Progar. He also reveals that Hays has betrayed the men, hiding the bulk of the take for himself. Jim Wall comes to see in Smoky Slocum, a fellow gunman, the qualities of a true friend and gentleman. Jim Wall's loyalty to his employer earns him the offer of partnership in the ranch when he returns his sister and Helen Herrick proposes marriage. She has come to appreciate his self-sacrifice and chivalrous rescue of her.

In Jim Wall, Zane Grey has created a character to illustrate the natural gentleman (nobleman) that nature can turn out. Exposed to the worst elements that life on the frontier offers, he nevertheless preserves his inherent decency and goodness, and is a "diamond in the rough," as Wister refers to his Virginian.

Wallen: In *The Trail Driver,* a man of about fifty years of age, with a visage like a bleak stone bluff and eyes like fiery cracks. He has been working in Braseda but he hails from the Big Bend country. He first appears in Brite's camp asking if a young man named Reddie Bayne has come by. Brite refuses to say whether he has seen Bayne or not, and Wallen leaves. Texas Joe, however, says he has heard the name before and doubts he is much good. Reddie reveals that he was the foreman of the Clay outfit and when he found out she was a girl, she left. He has been following her since, not because he is in love with her, but because he feels she is his property, like a slave. Wallen returns later with Ross Hite. At this point, Texas Joe notes that some of the five men with him are carrying needleguns in their saddle sheaths. One of the horses in their remuda had been shot with a needlegun. When Brite will not return Reddie to him, gunplay follows. Texas Joe shoots him in the heart.

Walling: In *The Lost Wagon Train*, a driver in the caravan led by Anderson. He is appointed to stand guard duty with Dietrich. He is killed in the attack on the wagon train by Satana's Kiowas and Latch's outlaw gang.

Walton, Isaac: Mentioned in *Betty Zane* when Alfred Clarke and Betty are canoeing one afternoon. Betty mentions Isaac Walton's book on fishing as a must for any serious fisherman. She expresses surprise that Alfred Clarke has not read it. The book was a standard treatise on the subject in the eighteenth century in both England and America.

Wansfell: In *Wanderer of the Wasteland*, the name Regan at Picacho gives Adam Larey. The name means "once fell," referring to the need Adam feels to do penance for the sin of sleeping with Margarita and later of killing his brother. The name embodies his lifelong search for redemption and forgiveness. See **Larey, Adam.**

Wapatomeka: In *Betty Zane*, one of the Delaware chiefs sent by Tarhe and Myeerah to recapture Isaac Zane. Isaac knows him to be one of the most respected and shrewd chiefs in the tribe.

War Cloud: In *Western Union*, a chief of the Ogallala Sioux. To demonstrate the power of the telegraph line to Chief Black Hawk, Creighton sends a message ahead to War Cloud. When the answer that returns is not fully convincing, a second message is sent concerning matters the whites would know nothing about. This answer from War Cloud does convince Black Hawk of the power of the telegraph, and he gives Creighton his assurance that his people will protect the magical line.

Warburton: In *The U. P. Trail*, one of the head officers of the Union Pacific Railroad. He is impressed by young Warren Neale, who is willing to risk his reputation denouncing fraud and corruption on the part of construction companies and their lobbyists. In particular, he denounces Allison Lee, who has ordered rebuilt a section of track surveyed by Neale. The rebuilt section of road, at a cost of hundreds of thousands of dollars, followed the original specifications to the letter. Warburton's desire to promote Neale to a position of greater importance and influence is not realized because Allison Lee calls Neale a liar, and the young cowboy friend of Neale, Larry Red King, forces Lee to confess at gunpoint that he has lied. Some two years later, Warburton attends a similar meeting at North Platte called by General Lodge, and this time Warburton approves a ban on granting any further contracts to Allison Lee. He again praises Neale. Warburton, a capitalist, industrialist, and man of vision, retains his sense of decency and fairness, an example of a man who is not corrupted by power and money.

Ward: In *The Light of Western Stars*, a rancher and cattleman with whom Alfred has had trouble. It is not clear exactly what the trouble was, but most likely it had to do with buying and selling stock.

Ward, Henry: In *Wilderness Trek*, one of Ormiston's drovers. Ormiston had instructed him to go ahead of his mob (herd) crossing the river, to prevent Ormiston's cattle from mixing with Dann's or Slyter's herd, an impossible task. In the stampede, Henry Ward is trampled to death by the cattle.

Warner, Bill and Jeff: In *30,000 on the Hoof*, named by Holbert as other ranchers in area. They run a lot of cattle out on the desert between Clear Creek and the Little Colorado River.

Warner, Marian (Benow di cleash):   In *The Vanishing American*, a young woman from Philadelphia. She is independently wealthy and without close family. Marian met Lo Blandy (Nophaie) at university in Philadelphia. She was struck by his strength, suppleness, speed and grace. Watching him play football or baseball, she is reminded of the Olympian athletes of ancient Greece. She admires his ability as a scholar, his sense of morality and his principles. He reminds her of an eagle, keen, strong, above the common herd. They become fast friends and fall in love.

Marian heads west in response to a letter she receives from Nophaie. Unlike Carley Burch in *The Call of the Canyon*, Marian does not need to be convinced that the West is young and virile, free of eastern fetters of materialism and hedonism. She rejects the falseness of such a life and hopes to contribute something to Nophaie's people. She arrives at the trading post run by Paxton and his wife. Mrs. Paxton describes accurately the situation on the reservation, the mismanagement by agents and missionaries like Friel, who has offered Marian a job and a lift to Kaidab. Here, she sees the reality of life for the Navajo, the dirt, the poverty, the smell of sheep, the wool packed into sacks, flies everywhere. She also meets Mrs. Withers, the trading post man's wife. They have been on the reservation for over twenty-five years. They repeat Mrs. Paxton's story of corrupt management and incompetent missionaries. Mrs. Withers had known Nophaie's mother, and Nophaie himself. She knew him as a shepherd, she knew the woman who took him east, and when he returned,

she taught him about his own people to make possible his reintegration into the tribe.

John Withers takes her to meet Nophaie at Oljato, perhaps the most remote part of the reservation. Marian shows herself to be no tenderfoot, impressing Withers with her stamina and adaptability. He shows her where Nophaie had been kidnapped, where he herded sheep as a boy, where he lived. They visit Pahute Canyon, the Valley of the Gods, the crag of eagles, scenes few white people have ever seen. Her meeting with Nophaie is joyous. He shares with her his new life, and introduces her to his uncle, his hogan, his flock of sheep and his mustangs. Nophaie shares with her some of the Navajo rituals. Marian is touched by his poverty and wants to give him something he could use to make life a bit easier. A saddle? A gun? More sheep? But Nophaie asks nothing of her. He gives her a beautiful, black mustang, so she can ride to meet him, but the two of them plan to meet in secret.

Marian obtains a job working at the reservation office. She sees first-hand the fraudulent practices of Morgan, Blucher, and Friel. She knows all mail is opened and unfavorable comments are censored or letters go astray. Marian makes friends with Gekin Yashi at the school and, with Nophaie, arranges for her to be taken away from the school She suggests that Nophaie marry Gekin Yashi as her father, Do etin, had suggested. She sees Friel's stone mansion and irrigated fields beside Navajo hogans and dry fields.

Marian reflects of how the environment on the reservations brings out the worst in the incompetent government agents and missionaries. With little supervision, the temptation to cheat and steal proceeds unabated. As sexual inhibition is unknown among the young Indian girls, the agents and missionaries misinterpret signals from young women. She has witnessed Miss Herron's abuse of children, Blucher's beating a young boy.

When Nophaie comes to the school to get Gekin Yashi back, she manages to control his rage and prevent the killing of Morgan and Blucher. She points out that although his actions may be justified, no one would believe him in a court of law and those who do believe him can do nothing to help him.

After this, Marian quits her job at the reservation office and goes to live with the Paxtons. By now, Morgan and Blucher's campaign against the agricultural agent, Wolterson, is in full force.

Marian returns to Philadelphia briefly but finds life there insufferable. She returns to the reservation and takes a job with Paxton as a buyer of blankets and baskets. This gives her an excuse to be on the reservation without Morgan and Blucher's permission. She sees Blucher's work to turn the Navajo against the American government. Marian accompanies Mrs. Withers to California but returns to Kaidab. She witnesses the episode of the revolt, where Nophaie prevents the lynching of Blucher and Morgan. She works with Withers, keeping his accounts. She provides money to buy hay for the

Navajo farmers and she witnesses Withers's generosity to the Navajo, buying handicrafts he can never sell and buying hay to keep the Navajos' sheep alive through the drought. No one appreciates the work he has done.

Marian proposes marriage several times to Nophaie. She understands his desire to return to his Indian roots, but she tells him she is willing to share his humble hogan and asks for nothing more than his love. While Nophaie does love her and appreciates her kindness and her willingness to share his choice of life, he cannot bring himself to marry. Marian is with Nophaie when he dies of influenza. She has proven herself to be the truest friend he could ever want.

Marian Warner is one of several wealthy young women in Grey's novels who go west because of a young man. She finds in the West true American values and life with a purpose. But unlike women like Carley Burch in *The Call of the Canyon*, or Madeline Hammond in *The Light of Western Stars*, her life is one of sacrifice and service, never to know the fulfillment of marriage and a home.

Warner, Silas: In *The Desert of Wheat*, an old, gray-haired farmer who has been working with Anderson since before Lenore was born. Lenore watches him work in the fields.

Warnock, Tom: In *30,000 on the Hoof*, traveling south with his wife and mother when Logan Huett meets them. The women volunteer to help Lucinda give birth to George, her first son. They stay three days with the Huetts. Warnock advises Logan to move out of the canyon. That, although it has good range and is fertile and requires few cowhands to tend herds, it is a delusion and a snare. This bothers Logan, but Lucinda convinces him that he should not pay any attention to Warnock's comments. He is just envious and mistaken about the merits of the canyon.

Warren, Jonas: In *Desert Gold*, the stranger Burton (Cameron) meets in the desert prospecting for gold. He never grumbles about the heat. He is tireless, patient, built of steel fiber. He has the gift of divining, that is, the ability to locate water with a "peach fork," a skill of great value in a desert. He helps look for gold, Burton often having the impression he is more concerned about finding gold for Burton than for himself. Gradually, he and Burton come to talk about themselves and Jonas reveals that he has come west looking for his disgraced daughter. She had fallen in love with a young man who got her pregnant and then deserted her. Rather than face the disgrace, she ran off and he has been looking for her and the child ever since. They make a remarkable gold strike, but perish in a dust storm. Before he dies, though, Burton reveals the truth. He is the man Warren's daughter had fallen in love with. He tells Warren that he had returned to find her gone but pursued her, and married her, only to have her run off again. He too has been searching for her for many years.

Warren, Mary: In *The Deer Stalker*, Texan visiting the Grand Canyon with her friend Mrs. Price and her niece, Sue Warren, who lives in Arizona. This is their first visit to the canyon. They are on the same excursion into the canyon as Patricia Edgerton Clay.

Warren, Nell: In "Fantoms of Peace," Harwell's daughter. She is the young woman that Dwire has come into the desert to forget. He had been in love with her, but he abandoned her. The young woman's reputation is ruined by vicious gossip. Dwire loses track of her, and retreats to the desert to forget her. He meets her father, who is grieving the loss of his daughter and her ruined reputation. Dwire reveals he is the man responsible for her lost reputation but he assures Hartwell that Nell had never been guilty of any of the things gossip had spread about her.

Warren, Sue: In *The Deer Stalker*, at the Grand Canyon with her Aunt Mary and Mrs. Price. They are from Texas and are visiting the canyon for the first time but for Sue, it's her eighth time. She and Patricia Clay (Edgerton) become fast friends. They take a trip with the two guides, Nelson Stackhouse and Tine Higgenbottom, to the North Rim of the canyon. There, they pass the night in a cabin loft, while Bing Dyott and his outfit are below. In the morning, their presence is discovered. She explains they had come up from the El Tovar resort to view the herds with Nelson and Tine, and quick as a flash, she jumps on a horse and rides off. She runs into Thad Eburne, who returns with her to the cabin to straighten matters out with Bing Dyott. Sue Warren accompanies Patricia on her trips around the state visiting all the famous tourist sites. She encourages Patricia in her quest for a place to live. Patricia is eager to bring Sue and Nelson together. The young man is very much in love with Sue. She herself gives support to Patricia, who is looking for a change of life, by telling her that westerners judge you by what you are and what you do, not by rumors of the past. She thinks Thad Eburne and Patricia would make a good couple and she does her best to get the two of them together. Sue and Patricia both take part in the deer drive organized by McKay and Thad Eburne. Sue and Nelson Stackhouse get engaged to be married at the end of the novel.

Washburn: In *The Lost Wagon Train*, a driver of a wagon that joins Pike Anderson's caravan. He and Kelly and an unnamed man have three wagons loaded with rifles and ammunition. This will prove most helpful in the coming attack. Satana's Kiowa and Latch's outlaws divide the rifles and ammunition between them when the massacre is over.

Waters: In *Nevada*, an outlaw associated with Cash Burridge. Mrs. Wood describes him as a "tough nut to crack."

Waters, Jim: In *Fighting Caravans*, heads a caravan of freighters, all of whom are experienced Indian-fighters. Waters had been a sergeant of artillery in the Texas invasion of 1842. Waters has a cannon in his caravan, a piece of artillery that has proven most successful in fights with Indians. The fame of the cannon has spread from the Missouri to the Pecos. Waters joins his caravan with Couch's to be able to fight off Satock more effectively. Clint Belmet sees the cannon work in an attack a short while later. Clint Belmet wonders how long Waters will survive. Although he is one of the best freighters around, he takes reckless chances.

In *The Lost Wagon Train,* Jim Waters is a young man, a giant in stature, western-born and already a trained, experienced scout. Years later, he would lose his life at the great Comanche raid at Pawnee Rock. At this point, he is at the start of his career. He approves of Latch's policy of treating the Indians fairly and kindly. As the discussion of Indian attacks progresses, he comments that he will install a cannon on his wagon, a characteristic of his caravans that becomes famous later.

Watkins, Dan: Appears in *Betty Zane.* He is one of the oldest settlers along the river. He located his farm several years after Colonel Zane founded the settlement. He is noted for "kindness of heart. He had loaned many a head of cattle which had never been returned, and many a sack of flour had left his mill unpaid for in grain. He was good shot, he could lay a tree on the ground as quickly as any man who ever swung an axe and he could drink more whiskey than any man in the valley." Dan Watkins throws a party to which Wetzel and Betty Zane and others are invited one winter night.

Watkins, Grandma: In *Betty Zane,* Dan Watkins's mother, a little dried-up old woman with white hair and bright dark eyes. She is so old no one knows for sure how old she is. She can still do a day's work with energy and pleasure. Grandma Watkins sees immediately that Miller is a bad customer. There is something about his face that suggests dishonesty. She sees that Miller is in love with Betty but deduces that Betty is just flirting with him. She expects trouble from him. Grandma Watkins also sees that Wetzel is in love with Betty and advises him to speak his heart to the girl. She advises him that it's not gifts a woman wants out in the West. She needs a strong arm to build cabins, a quick eye with a rifle, and a fearless heart.

Watkins, Susan: In *Betty Zane,* Dan Watkins's daughter. She is not pretty but is strong and healthy, and with her laughing blue eyes and sunny disposition, she numbered her suitors by the score. She is the mistress of ceremonies at the party in her father's home.

Watrous, Edith: In *The Horse Thief,* the daughter of Jim Watrous. She is engaged to Leale Hildrith, the foreman of the ranch. Dale is a good friend of hers as well, and secretly in love with her. Edith is overwhelmed with gratitude when he retrieves the stolen horses, and she thinks it absurd that anyone could suspect him of being the inside man for the rustlers in the Salmon River Valley. Edith tells Dale that that evening, she finally acquiesced to her father's wishes in agreeing to marry Leale Hildrith. Her father wants Hildrith, his current foreman, as a partner in his horse-breeding and trading business. She is nonplussed when Leale comes upon her kissing Dale. She tells him she is so grateful to him for having retrieved her horses she could not control herself. Edith does not believe it for a minute when Dale confesses to being a horse thief. She is pleased to meet with him in Hasley, where she has shown up for the horse auction. She and Wesley and Sue Bradford had been following him. There, she identifies Dick as her horse, and when Reed refuses to return the stolen animal to her, she calls on Leale to back her up. He does, in a way, much to Reed's dismay. Refusing to release the animal, Reed also abducts Edith, taking her to Mason's cabin in the rustlers' hideout canyon. There, she learns the truth, that Leale was a member of the gang. Mason wants Reed to return her to her father, his old friend Jim Watrous. He hopes this will prevent Watrous from coming after them with a posse. She witnesses Mason's shooting Leale in punishment for his betrayal. Dale rescues Edith as Reed tries to leave with her. He takes her to Rogers's cabin, where he plans to leave her until the business with the rustlers is over. Sheriff Bayne shows up with a posse to arrest Dale on the old charges of rustling. They plan to hang him on the spot. Edith puts an end to the attempted lynching, holding the sheriff and the men at gunpoint. When the adventure is over and they have returned to the Watrous ranch, Jim Watrous offers Dale a partnership in the ranch and Edith agrees to marry him.

Watrous, Jim: In *The Horse Thief,* a big-time rancher in Montana near the Idaho border and father of Edith Watrous. When Dale Brittenham returns with five of his prize horses that have been rustled, he is pleased, of course, but tells Dale that suspicion has been cast on him as the inside man for the thieves. Watrous believes Dale, but he cautions him that Stafford and others are not so willing to believe. Jim Watrous is anxious for his daughter to marry Leale Hildrith, his right-hand man. Watrous and Stafford organize a posse to follow the horse thieves into Idaho. The posse arrives after Big Bill Mason and his right-hand man, Reed, and Leale Hildrith, the real inside man, have been killed. He approves of Edith's marrying Dale, and offers the loyal young man a partnership in his ranch.

Watson: In *Wilderness Trek,* the manager of the merchandise store in Downsville who puts Red Krehl and Sterling Hazelton in touch with Bingham Slyter, teamster and drover for Stanley Dann. The Danns are planning a trek across Australia to the Northwest, a distance of twenty-five hundred miles, and drovers are needed.

Watson, Clara: In *Under the Tonto Rim,* the younger sister of Lucy Watson. She runs away from home with a wild, handsome young rodeo cowboy called Jim Middleton. He promises to marry her but never does. He gets her pregnant, and abandons her. She has the child in Kingston while staying at the home of a Mrs. Gerald, who runs a restaurant for the miners. Only Mrs. Gerald and the kindly local doctor know her secret. Mrs. Gerald has consented to raise the child if Clara pays for the support. Clara writes her sister telling her story, asking to come stay with her, but she neglects to mention the part about the illegitimate child. Lucy feels sorry for her vagrant sister and sends for her to come stay in the Tonto. Joe Denmeade picks Clara up and drives her home. Before long, he is in love with her. When Mr. Jenks, the local teacher, has to return east, she takes over the job of teaching school. But all is not well in the remote Tonto. Jim Middleton, whose real name is Harv Sprall, is cousin to Bud Sprall, local bootlegger and outlaw. He has received a letter from Mrs. Gerald asking for payment for child support. He plans to use this letter to blackmail Clara into paying him for his silence. He threatens to show the letter to the young men, making her a laughingstock and a pariah. Clara marries the gentle Joe Denmeade, and fears Joe will abandon her if he learns the truth. Lucy tells Edd Denmeade that the child is hers. Edd is prepared to leave the Tonto, retrieve the child, live somewhere for several years then return, with no one the wiser. Clara, however, decides to tell Joe the truth about her past. He forgives her, and accepts the child as his own. Since Middleton is killed in a fight with Edd, and Bud Sprall, seemingly unaware of the truth about his cousin and Clara, has ridden off, no one is any the wiser. There is no need to mention that Middleton had neglected to marry Clara before the baby was born. Clara has learned from her experience and appreciates the love of a truly good man.

Watson, Hal: In *West of the Pecos,* from Rockport. He runs cattle on the river about ten miles below the Lambeth place. He has had trouble recently with Don Felipe. He became aware that a hand of his called Charley Stine was rebranding his cattle with Don Felipe's mark. He is wounded and Pecos and Terrill and Sambo take him in. He is tied up by Sawtell who comes to the ranch looking for Pecos Smith. Watson is killed by a stray bullet in the fighting that follows.

Watson, Lucy: In *Under the Tonto Rim*, Grey's version of Wister's Molly Wood, the schoolteacher who brings "civilization" to the wilderness. Lucy has no family ties, and signs up with the welfare office of Arizona to go to the Tonto to educate the backwoods families. She herself had always felt the stigma of being the daughter of a saloon-keeper, and her sister ran off with a rodeo cowboy. She thinks that working with families in the wilderness to help them make better homes will be her missionary work. She sets out on her journey to the Tonto with a mixture of enthusiasm and dread. The people she meets admire her for her courage in undertaking the job, and express misgivings on the success of such a venture.

Mr. Jenks, the local teacher, meets her and drives her to the home of the first family with which she will be working. He speaks of the beauty of the natural world around them, about the wild animals, the primitive conditions, but especially of the basic goodness of the people. He warns her that being a looker will make her a target of all the young Romeos.

Lucy's first encounters with the Denmeades and the Claypools are encouraging. The families welcome her cordially and generously. She is not used to the primitive conditions, but she has no cause to complain about their humanity. She is a bit taken aback by the simplicity of their lives, their lack of expectations from life. The children have never known toys, or pretty things. They are not concerned about appearance. They sleep in their clothes. The teenage girls seem only to be interested in boys. There is a high level of viciousness to the gossip.

With the help of Mr. Jenks, she orders new tools for the Denmeades. A sewing machine meant the making of sheets, pillows, towels, curtains, tablecovers, wearing apparel. Tools meant the construction of chairs, tables, closets, shelves, and many other household articles. She tries to teach hygiene, changing clothes more often, sleeping in nightclothes.

At first, she cannot imagine herself marrying a backwoodsman, but as she gets to know Edd Denmeade, she is forced to alter her prejudices about him. He is a man with rock solid common sense and moral principles as well as a self-assuredness of the rightness of his views. He takes her to the first dance at the school, against her will. If she does not go, he tells her, folks will think she is stuck up. At the party, Edd is a perfect gentleman. He leaves her free to dance with anyone she chooses. Like Mr. Jenks, he tells her to avoid dancing with Sam Johnson and Bud Sprall; although they are the most handsome men and the best dancers around, these two have a bad reputation and a schoolmarm should not be seen to enjoy associating with them.

Shortly after rejecting Edd's first proposal of marriage, Lucy learns that Edd defended her honor when Bud Sprall was spreading lies that he had watched her changing her clothes for the party through a window. She receives word from her sister asking her to let her come stay. Lucy agrees. She selects Joe Denmeade to go fetch her from the stage. Joe is a gentleman, and she feels she can trust him. Joe, however, knows that the other boys will probably waylay her, and indeed, they do. Reunited with her wayward sister, Lucy is not quite sure what to make of her.

Clara notes that her sister is in love with Edd, although Lucy herself denies this. She considers herself his friend and mentor, but not a suitable mate for marriage. But with the topic out in the open, she becomes more aware of how much she does like Edd, how good a person and how talented a man he is. Edd takes her hiking, fixes her boots with studs for walking on the cliffs and for climbing. He shows her how he lines bees and finds hives. She goes to dances with him without coaxing.

When she moves on to stay with the Claypools as her job requires, Edd is upset. He accuses her of being unfaithful. She has influenced him, getting him to give up white mule and fighting. He has changed for her, but he cannot stand the idea of her trying to work the same transformation on Sprall. As he leaves the Claypool house, she listens to his spurs jingle as he walks away.

When the truth about Clara's escapade with Jim Middleton threatens to come out, Lucy is at a loss to know what to do. She cannot understand why Clara married Joe Denmeade without telling him the truth. She is disgusted by her sister's selfishness and lack of responsibility. Lucy tells Edd that the child in question is hers by Middleton. He offers to marry her, to take the child, to move away for a while till the fuss blows over. But meanwhile, Clara does find the gumption to tell Joe about her past. He forgives her, agrees to take the child. Since Bud Sprall has left the Tonto and Middleton is dead, no one need be any the wiser about the irregularities surrounding the birth of Clara's daughter. Lucy decides to marry Edd. She knows she could never find a better man. She attributes the happy conclusion to Clara's troubles to the Tonto environment, where life is real and earnest, beautiful and terrible but above all, meaningful.

Though to a lesser extent, Lucy Watson is a heroine in the vein of Madeline Hammond in *Light of Western Stars* or Harriet Lindsay in *Raiders of Spanish Peaks*, an educated woman who finds her true purpose in life from contact with people more rooted in life in the natural world.

Way, Jack(son):   In *The Drift Fence*, one of the cowboys in the outfit that Jim Traft takes over for his uncle on the Diamond Ranch. Jim admires his horsemanship at the rodeo in Flag when he rides two beautiful horses, standing with one foot on each, beating his opponent by a full length. Like the other cowboys, he resents the tenderfoot Jim Traft taking the foreman's job and building the drift fence. He offers to fight Jim together with Uphill Frost and Cherry Winters. In the fistfight which follows, Jackson and Uphill are beaten. Eventually, Jackson and young Jim Traft come to be on very good terms.

In *The Hash Knife Outfit*, Jackson Way leaves the Diamond and accompanies young Jim Traft as a member of his crew at the Yellow Jacket. He is one of the cowboys who go to meet Glory at the train station. Later, when Jim and Molly Dunn are married and moving to the ranch at the Yellow Jacket, Jack Way sets up ranching near the Yellow Jacket, sponsored by his wife's father.

Wayburns: In *Code of the West,* friends of the Stockwells in Erie, Pennsylvania. They are "motoring" out to California and offer to take Georgie along with them to drop off at Mary's place at the Thurman ranch in Green Valley.

Wayne, Edith: In *The Light of Western Stars,* an old friend of Madeline Hammond's from college days. She comes west with Helen as part of a holiday party to visit Madeline's new home in the West. At first, she shares Helen's supercilious attitude towards the cowboys and the place, but she does come to see the charm that has brought both Madeline and her brother Alfred to the West. She confesses that when she came out west, she was sickly and now is healthy. Like Madeline, she is sick of the idleness, the uselessness of life in the East, and the foul smells of life in the city. She understands that cowboys are "natural" men. Their real nature is not hidden behind masks of propriety or class. They are natural noblemen. Monty Price is a "natural nobleman," and Nels would make a perfect husband. She predicts that Helen Hammond will eventually see the light and reject both Castleton and Boyd Harvey, who have little interest in her but for her money.

In *Majesty's Rancho,* Madeline recalls her best friend from the East who had come west to visit her ranch, much as Madge's college friends are now coming to spend the summer with her and Gene Stewart on that same ranch.

Wayne, Ethel: In *The Shepherd of Guadaloupe,* Virginia Lundeen's best friend and confidante. She is from the south, Louisiana, and now lives in Denver. She is a very energetic woman, full of life and a practical joker. She speaks her mind with exaggerated good humor. She is with the party to welcome Virginia back from Europe. She declares that she could fall in love with Clifton if Virginia doesn't, although she confesses that she has a secret beau back in Denver. Ethel organizes the excursion to Cliff Forrest's store. She tells Cliff they are extremely rich with lots of money to burn and he should double his prices for them. She makes the suggestion to Virginia that she should marry someone, Cliff for instance, to get out of Malpass's clutches. When Virginia comes to her in Denver, having married Cliff, she is thrilled. Even though her friend claims to have done this purely out of practicality, Ethel believes it is for the best. She knows that Cliff is mad about Virginia. When Virginia's father and Malpass have died and Virginia has inherited the estate and returned Cottonwoods to the Forrests, Ethel urges Virginia to go to Cliff, but Virginia prefers to let things occur gradually, fearing Cliff will reject her when she learns how wealthy she is. Meanwhile, Ethel and Helen Andrews go to Cliff's camp for a peek at the new man he has become, according to Clay Forrest, his father. They return singing his praises, urging Virginia not to waste another moment waiting for him to come to her. Ethel Wayne is a foil to Virginia; unlike her friend, who must think about things before acting, Ethel is spontaneous, open and generous.

Wayne, Mrs.:   In *The Shepherd of Guadaloupe,* Ethel's mother. She is at the Lundeen home when Virginia arrives home from France. Virginia also meets her when she goes to Denver to spend three weeks with Ethel after her father has thrown her out. Mrs. Wayne thinks Clifton Forrest is a very handsome man and a good catch for a girl.

Weatherby, Ranger: In *The Fugitive Trail*, sent by Captain Maggard to follow the rustlers. He accompanies Tex Serks and the men from Melrose's Brazos ranch. He detects the smoke of campfires and the dust rising from moving cattle through his spyglass. He is ordered by Maggard to "ride the men down."

Weaver: In *The Lost Wagon Train*, Slim Blue's trail boss and friend. He urges him to ride off after shooting Pitch. He tells him about a wagon train leaving in the morning. He also collects money from the other cowboys to give him, since he won't be collecting his pay. Slim Blue tells Weaver he will try to find his brother, Lester. Weaver suggests he put that notion out of his head as he's not likely ever to find him. He suggests riding to Latch's field, or getting a job as a drover on the Chisolm trail.

Weaver, Bim: In *The Lost Wagon Train*, a cowboy with whom Slim Blue (Corny) used to ride. When he heads to San Antonio to marry Estelle, he hires Bim Weaver and several other former trail buddies to drive a herd of five thousand head to their ranch in Latchfield.

Weaver, Buck: In *The Man of the Forest*, one of Beasley's cowboys. Towards the end of the conflict, he reports to Beasley that Las Vegas had been in town looking for him. He saw Carmichael shoot Jeff and Pedro when they drew on him. Beasley asks Weaver why he didn't shoot Carmichael and he replies that he will not shoot anyone from behind doors. He has nothing against Las Vegas; the fight as he sees it is between Beasley and Carmichael. Weaver had been a rider for Auchincloss before going over to Beasley. He has had doubts about Beasley's campaign against old Al and his niece, Helen. As he leaves, he gives Beasley a scrutinizing look which suggests he has no respect for a man who expects others to do his fighting for him.

Webb, Colonel: In *The Lone Star Ranger*, meets Buck Duane in Laramie's inn. Colonel Webb had come west to settle the estate of his brother, a rancher and sheriff, but he can find no legal claim to a ranch nor to a job as sheriff. There seems to be no estate left to settle. Colonel Webb has great respect for the rangers and their efforts to bring law and order to West Texas, despite the governor's opposition to them. He is well informed about the goings-on in Fairdale, and Buck Duane realizes he is a worthwhile person to get to know. He provides useful information about Cheseldine, underlining that the man appears to be more legendary rather than real, a suspicion which proves true. Cheseldine himself has never been seen, never been witnessed committing a crime, conducting all his work through his lieutenants, Phil Knell and Poggin. Nevertheless, Colonel Webb deduces that there must be a clever mind organizing the group's activities. Zane Grey makes use of similar figures in all his novels which feature a detective element in the plot.

Webb, Mrs.: In *The Lost Wagon Train*, her behavior towards Estelle Latch in Smith's store alerts Estelle to the effects of the gossip that Leighton has been spreading about her father.

Webb, Sam: In *The Lost Wagon Train*, has a runaway team stopped by Slim Blue (Corny) in the streets of Latchfield. Sam Webb is not a southerner. He had come from Illinois with his large family and was a man of means and influence. Webb has been one of Latch's best friends in the valley. When Latch is planning a party for his daughter's sixteenth birthday, he gets word that the Webbs are not planning to attend. Latch confronts Webb and Bartlett to ask why. Webb tell him it's because of the rumors about his past that Leighton has been spreading. Webb repeats the gossip, that Latch has made his ranch and the town a haven for outlaws. Webb claims he would never have settled in Latchfield had he known that Latch was associated with outlaws. Although Bartlett decides to attend to show his support for Latch, Webb tells him he cannot come. When Latch tells him he should be ready to go for his gun when next they meet unless he takes back his comments, Webb asks Latch why he doesn't make Leighton go for his gun, since he is the one spreading the stories.

Webster, Alice: In *Raiders of Spanish Peaks*, Stuart's wife in La Junta. He ran off with her, married her, then abandoned her. She returned to work in La Junta. Stuart is now pursuing Lenta Lindsay.

Weed, Billy: In *Fighting Caravans*, a trapper. He came by a Kiowa village on the Purpatory and saw Blackstone there. He has been a scout and a plainsman and there is no question of the accuracy of his report. Clearly, Blackstone and Murdock are involved with the Indians.

Weede, Colonel: In *Desert Gold*, commander of the cavalry stationed at the garrison in Casita. George Thorne plans to ask him for advice about Mercedes, and perhaps to arrange a leave to get her to a safer place.

Weede, Robert: A member of the party which came west to visit Madeline in *The Light of Western Stars*. He is only interested in being near Elsie Beck. He is described as a large, florid young man.

Weedon: In *Fighting Caravans*, a gambler shot by Murdock in Santa Fe.

Weeks, Bill: In *The Desert of Wheat*, a cowboy with Anderson's cattle ranching operation. He reports that he has seen 500 I.W.W. men camped at Blue Spring.

Weeks, Parson: In *Thunder Mountain*, marries Lee Emerson and Ruth Nuggett. He performs the ceremony on the roadside outside of Challis as they are going to Salmon and the Olsen ranch. Lee explains that he has rescued her from a dance hall. The preacher says that he fully understands that in the West, women make their living as best they can, and men who need wives take women whose jobs would have earned them reputations that would make them unfit for wives to men back east. However, he has great faith in the power of love and of the western environment to redeem men and women.

Ween, Sam: In *The Vanishing American,* a half-breed interpreter working for Morgan and Blucher for a salary of twenty dollars a month, although the reservation authorities are given more money than that to cover the work he does. He is a Noki Indian, more loyal to the authorities than the Nopha Indians. Sam Ween also serves as a driver for Morgan and Blucher.

Wells, Buster: In *The Fugitive Trail,* a rider for Steve Melrose on his Little Wichita operation. He rides in to the main ranch house to report the rustling of the herd and the killing of Art Semper and Jeff Stevens by the rustlers. He accompanies Serks and the men in their pursuit of Henderson and the rustlers, suggesting that they head for Camp Cooper, an old military post built by Mackenzie in 1871 and since abandoned by the cavalry. There is a settlement there with stores and a saloon. The Mackenzie Road runs from Santone through Cooper Camp and is pretty much traveled in the summer. The road crosses the Chisholm Trail at Fort Worth.

Wells, Duke: In *Western Union,* takes over the leadership of Stanley's outlaw gang when Shaw has killed the Stanley. Duke Wells is killed when the rangers under Hardin' and Siddell ambush the outfit. Wells lives long enough to confess Stanley's treachery and to clear Vance Shaw's name.

Wells, Henry: In *Fighting Caravans,* freighter with Clint Belmet when the caravan is attacked at Point of Rocks.

Wells, Jim: In *Valley of Wild Horses,* an old timer who had been a pony express rider, miner, teamster and freighter and now, stagecoach driver. He drives the stage Pan Handle takes from Littleton to Marco, New Mexico. He tells Emily Newman, a passenger frightened of Indian attacks, about Pan Handle's escapades in Wyoming, including one in which he dragged a bolt of red calico behind his horse through the streets of Cheyenne.

Wells, Kate: In *The Spirit of the Border,* Nell Wells's older sister, dark-haired, quiet, not given to the displays of emotion of her younger sister. She is effective in her own, quiet way. The two bachelor missionaries at the village are both in love with her and Heckewelder tells them to settle the matter as they are too distracted from their work. Dave Edwards is the first to propose but Nell rejects him for George Young. Kate is kidnapped by Jim Girty the morning of her wedding day. Wetzel is unable to rescue her and Jim Girty takes her off to his lair where he ties her to his bed with leather tongs. He rapes and beats her at will. Kate goes mad with his treatment of her. When Joe attempts to rescue her and return her to the Village of Peace, Jim Girty arrives and stabs her to death. Her fate is shared by many young women on the frontier who are abducted by renegades like Jim Girty.

Wells, Mr.: In *The Spirit of the Border,* an old man, a missionary, coming to preach at the Moravian Mission, the Village of Peace. He is accompanied by his two nieces, Nell and Kate. The man is advanced in years and poorly suited for the trip and the work he has undertaken. He is rarely mentioned in the course of the story. He goes downriver from Ft. Pitt to Ft. Henry on a raft with Nell and Kate and Jeff Lynn, the raft that does not get stopped by Silvertip and his braves. Through Mr. Wells, Grey introduces the theme of nature as paradise. While they travel downriver, Mr. Wells comments that the forest, untouched by human hand, is nature as created by God. He also announces the "noble savage" theme, that the Indian exists in the state of nature, unspoiled by civilization. Mr. Wells's health degenerates over the months. He flees the Village of Peace with Nell, Jim, Benny and Wingenund. The flight is too much for him and he dies near the Beautiful Spring where Joe and Aola are buried. He marries Jim and Nell before he dies. He is buried in a cave nearby.

Wells, Nell: Heroine of *The Spirit of the Border.* She appears in the opening chapters of the story at Ft. Pitt and Ft. Henry. Nell has come west with her older sister, Kate, and her aged uncle. Nell is the embodiment of the qualities of a typical Zane Grey heroine. She is beautiful, compassionate, responsible, spunky but often unsure of her emotions. Nell is fond of Joe but feels he is too irresponsible, too immature. She is flattered that he tried to kiss her but she does not want the people at Ft. Pitt to misinterpret her interest. She decides to punish Joe, slapping his face, only to learn to her embarrassment that she has slapped his brother Jim in the face. Talking in her sleep as they pass the first night of their trip down to Ft. Henry on an island in the Ohio near Milly's birch, she mutters that she loves Joe but that she wishes he were more like Jim (more level-headed and settled). As a Zane Grey heroine, she is refined, a symbol of civilization, of home, of the future. She is a sensitive soul, unable to bear the sight of the animalistic Jim Girty. When she sees his face looking in her window, she promptly faints. She faints again when Girty, Silvertip and six braves kidnap them the morning of Kate's wedding day. Nell is rescued by Wetzel and returned to the Village of Peace. She remains in a comatose state for a week, at which time Jim tells her that her sister Kate is dead, although this is not yet the case. When the Village of Peace is about to be destroyed, Nell shows she is capable of courageous, resolute action. The crisis has brought out the pioneer qualities in her. She hides young Benny, a boy of some four or five years of age, under her skirts as the houses are searched by the Girtys and their drunken Indian helpers. Nell and Jim flee the village with the help of Wingenund. With them is Mr. Wells. Nell marries Jim and the two of them settle at Ft. Henry. In *The Last Trail,* the next in the series of the Ohio River Trilogy, Jim becomes the parson and Nell the schoolteacher.

Wells, Rock: In *To the Last Man,* a member of the Hash Knife gang from Texas and the Jorth faction in the Jorth-Isbel feud. Rock Wells tells the men at Jorth's ranch that he had once worked for Gaston Isbel in Texas, and that the treatment Simm Bruce received from Jean Isbel is typical of the Isbels. They don't want to be the first to start shooting. Rock Wells participates in the attack on the Isbel ranch house and survives the Isbel attack on Greaves's store. He is killed by the pursuing Isbels on the flight back to the Jorth ranch.

Welsh: In *Forlorn River,* the owner of a ranch where Sheriff Strobel and Hart Blaine have a disagreement.

Wentworth: In "Monty Price's Nightingale," a rancher who hires Monty Price, in spite of the reputation he has on the range. When a forest fire is bearing down on the ranch, Monty rides off, but is almost killed rescuing Bart Muncie's child from the approaching fire.

Wentz, Jack: The fur trader at Ft. Pitt in *The Spirit of the Border.* He is also mentioned as Jake Wentz in *The Last Trail.* His trading post is a meeting place for Indians and pioneers. He cautions Mr. Sheppard against taking Jenks on as guide to Ft. Henry.

Wentz, Mrs.: In *The Spirit of the Border,* the wife of the fur trader and a typical busybody. She observes Nell and Joe kissing and assumes they are sweethearts. She tells Nell there is no need to hide her affection for Joe as people on the frontier are glad to see young people sparkin'. She adds that Joe is a fine catch who will take to the frontier like a duck does to water.

Nell observes that Mrs. Wentz, like most frontier people she has met, accept as true what appears to be true, and do not question the evidence of their eyes. Mrs. Wentz typifies people who have been living a long time on the frontier — they: "took everything as a matter of course' manifesting no surprise, concern or any of the 'quick impulses' common among other people. They were 'simple, honest and brave; they accepted what came as fact not to be questioned and believed what looked true."

Wesley (Bradford): In *The Horse Thief,* a friend of Dale Brittenham's in Salmon. He is the first person Dale speaks to when he returns with Edith Watrous's horses that everyone knew had been rustled. Wesley tells him that many ranchers have lost large numbers of horses, in particular, Big Bill Mason, who is said to have lost a hundred head. Wesley also tells him that there has been talk in town of Dale's involvement with the thieves. The return of the horses only serves to enhance that suspicion. Wesley's sister, Sue, is a good friend of Edith's and she has told Wesley that Edith loves Dale. He does not believe this as he knows Jim Watrous wants her to marry his foreman, and Dale's best friend and mentor, Leale Hildrith. Wesley cautions Dale that he thinks too highly of Leale, that the man is not deserving of his love and respect.

Wesley, Dave: In *Twin Sombreros,* a friend of the Neece family. He reports to Aunt Mattie that he had stopped by Bilyen's ranch to visit Abe and had not seen him so well in a while. Mattie attributes this change in his spirits to the hope Brazos Keene has brought that the murderer of his son will be caught, and his ranch restored to him.

Westfall: In *Stranger from the Tonto,* returns to the Hole-in-the-Wall hideout with Slotte. In the shootout between Roberts's gang and the Hole-in-the-Wall men, "the thin-lipped" Westfall kills Ben Bunge and Froman and in turn is shot by Wingfield.

Westfall, Reddy: In *The Lost Wagon Train,* a cowboy with whom Slim Blue (Corny) used to ride. When he heads to San Antonio to marry Estelle, he hires Westfall and several other former trail buddies to drive a herd of five thousand head to their ranch in Latchfield.

Weston, Hosteen (Mr.): In *Captives of the Desert,* runs the trading post in Taho and the Black Mesa ranch. John Curry works for him as a cowboy, and a foreman for his sheep and cattle operation. He and his adopted son, High-Lo, came to work there several years ago. All agree that Mr. Weston is an exceedingly pleasant man to work for. Wilbur Newton opens up a post in Sage Springs from where he sells liquor and, for a while, takes all the trade from Weston.

Weston, Jimmy: In *The Maverick Queen,* Lincoln Bradway's partner whose death brings Lincoln to South Pass to investigate the circumstances. Mrs. Dill, who runs a boarding house, tells Lincoln she knew Jimmy and liked him. Rumor has it he was killed cheating at cards. When Lincoln protests that Jimmy never cheated at cards in his life, she adds that she and most people in town believe the story. The cigar salesman tells him about Jimmy's standing on the saddle of his horse to paint out the "Take it" part of the "Take It or Leave It" Saloon. People agree that "Leave It" is a more appropriate name for the saloon anyway. He also hears of his involvement with Kit Bandon and Emery. Slowly, Lincoln Bradway pieces things together. From Lucy, Jimmy's sweetheart, he learns of Kit's involvement. Kit's desire to get her hands on Jimmy's letters further reinforces his certainty of her complicity in his death. From Bloom Burton, he learns that Hank Miller drove Hirsh's wagon to town with Jimmy's body. Burton does not know who shot him, but the murder took place on Kit's ranch. Later, when Kit comes upon Lincoln and Lucy kissing, a humdinger of a fight breaks out in which Lucy reveals that Jimmy was shot in his sleep at the ranch. The full truth only emerges when Kit is about to be hanged. She tells Lincoln that Jimmy wanted to marry her. In order to force her to do so, he threatened to expose her crooked cattle deals. Emery shot him, but she did nothing to try to stop him. Jimmy had two weaknesses, according to Lincoln, for mavericks and for women, both of which culminated in the Maverick Queen.

Weston, John D.:   In *Boulder Dam,* Lynn Weston's father. Lynn feels he would have been all right if not for his prissy relatives. Mr. Weston was disappointed with his son's interest in football at college. He ridiculed him, kicking him out of the family home, telling him he could kick his way into a good job. At one point, business was going poorly for him, but Helen Pritchard tells Lynn that he did not go bankrupt. Lynn wonders what his father would think if he should hear about him working at Boulder Dam and foiling the plot to sabotage the place.

Weston, Lynn "Biff":   In *Boulder Dam,* a Californian, former backfield for a university football team, disowned son of a wealthy industrialist, who works as a laborer at Boulder Dam. He is a young man, drifting through life, dissatisfied with himself and unsure of what he wants in life. He finds himself involved in two rescue operations, one involving Anne Vandergrift, who has been abducted by a white slaver, and another involving gangsters seeking to sabotage Boulder Dam and to steal the company payroll. He discovers that he has much greater potential than he had ever given himself credit for.

Lynn was engaged to one Helen Pritchard, the daughter of a wealthy family who was impressed with his football abilities, but had little interest in his more philosophical bent. When visiting Boulder Dam with Helen and her mother, he decides to stay there at the site. After a night in town at a gambling establishment, he returns to Boulder City to discover a young woman clothed only in a blanket is hiding in his car. Believing her story about being held prisoner for purposes of white slavery, he agrees to hide her in his tent. He gets clothes for her, and finds her a place to stay with Mrs. Brown. Their friendship deepens and before long, he is in love with her. Unlike Helen, she can understand his philosophical bent, his fascination with the megaproject and the destiny of humanity.

Lynn Weston is eager to learn all the different jobs at the dam site. He comes to the attention of the chief engineer of the project, Mr. Carewe, after he rescues Ben Brown from drowning when he falls into the diversion tunnel. Carewe recognizes his name; his nephew had been playing for the opposing team in the last football game Lynn played in college. Through his friend, Whitney Curtis, he learns of a plot to sabotage the construction site. Curtis had overheard men talking about placing bombs in pipes at the site. He hesitates to bring this to the attention of the foreman, Flynn, but he keeps a close eye on the goings-on. He learns from Bess, Whitney Curtis's girl, that Bink Moore and Sproul and Brown, his neighbor, are involved in the plot. Seemingly, it involves not only doing damage to the construction site but stealing the company payroll as well.

While Lynn is caught up foiling this plot, Ben Bellew finds and abducts Anne Vandergrift. With the help of Ben Sneed and Decker, Lynn effects her rescue, and is injured in the process. He is taken to the hospital. Sheriff Logan brings Anne and a

preacher to visit and the two of them are married. Sheriff Logan comments that Lynn would make a great Texas Ranger. He has the courage and marksmanship of a Cole Younger or a Buck Duane. Carewe rewards him for his heroic saving of the dam with a "real" job at Boulder Dam.

The character of Lynn Weston resembles that of Kurt Dorn in *Desert of Wheat,* the young man who foils the attempt of enemy agents to sabotage the wheat harvest. He also echoes the concerns of Milt Dale in *The Man of the Forest,* who ponders man's place in nature's plan for the universe.

Weston, Mr.:   In *Horse Heaven Hill,* Stanley Weston's invalid father. He had been one of the pioneer settlers in that section of Washington state, having traveled there from Pennsylvania as a young man. He has a fine shaggy head and a gray, rugged face. His son resembles him in stature. Mr. Weston has given over the running of the ranch to his son. He heartily approves of his firing Howard for drinking and for participating in the wild horse roundup. He comments that Stanley has finally seen the light where Howard is concerned. His son is too willing to believe the best of people. He needs to be more cautious. Mr. Weston gives Stanley sound advice about Marigold. He advises him to marry her as quickly as he can. She has become too modern thanks to her years at college, and she needs to have a halter put on her. She has made quite a reputation for herself going to parties and flirting with other cowboys, while engaged to Stanley. Mr. Weston comments that love doesn't last forever. It is clear to him, at least, that Marigold does not love Stanley very much or she would not behave as she does. Nevertheless, he tells his son that if he is convinced Marigold is the woman for him, he should give her the benefit of the doubt, be good to her, and not nag or fight. When Stanley brings Lark home as his wife, Mr. Weston is pleased that his son has finally found a woman who shares his view of life and his love of the land.

Weston, Mrs.:   In *Captives of the Desert,* Hosteen Weston's wife. She is a rather short, stout person with a round face, and a brisk, bright smile that came freely. She accepts Katharine Winfield as she accepts everyone, like a mother suddenly recognizing a strayed member of her brood. She invites her to visit at Black Mesa. She is a kind soul, devoted to the Navajo. She tries to help Magdaline reconcile her white education with her Navajo traditions. She urges her to be an example for her people, showing how elements from the modern world can be introduced into their lives.

Weston, Stanley (Stan, Boots):   In *Horse Heaven Hill,* the fiancé of Marigold Wade. He is broad of shoulder and well above medium height and pleasing to look at. He had gone out for football in college, where Marigold gave him the nickname "Boots." Upon completing college, he returned to his father's ranch. He lives alone with his father, an invalid. Stanley loves the ranch and hopes to carry on there. The ranch house, built of massive logs cut from the nearby hills, commands a view of the mountains and the range. The Westons own a fine stand of timber, hundreds of horses in a fenced, thousand-acre pasture, and no end of cattle. They also own wheat farms south of Wadestown. Mr. Weston tells Stanley that he has one weakness—an unwillingness to see anything but good in people. Stanley likes to think his college education has made him more open-minded and tolerant than his father. He refuses to believe the gossip about Marigold and Blanding, being willing to ascribe it to her being high-strung and flirtatious by nature. Likewise, he has been excessively tolerant of his foreman Howard. The Westons do not allow drinking among the cowboys in the bunkhouse and Howard has transgressed and been warned several times. When Stanley finally fires him and gives Landy Elm the job, Mr. Weston comments that it is about time. It does not take Stanley long to discover that he has more in common with Marigold's Idaho cousin, Lark Burrell. She knows about horses and ranching. She shares his love of the landscape, ranch life and wild horses. Lark comments to him that he and Marigold seem completely unsuited to each other. Although she herself likes Stanley, she does nothing to encourage his interest in her. On the contrary, she speaks well of Marigold, downplaying the rumors about her and Hurd Blanding, optimistically assuring Stanley all will work out between them with patience and time. Stanley catches Lark Burrell releasing the second herd of wild horses that Blanding and Ellery Wade have corralled in a box canyon trap. He warns her that there could be serious repercussions to her freeing the mustangs, which are Blanding's property. Nevertheless, he helps her finish the job. When Blanding rides into the Wade camp demanding compensation for his "stolen" horses, Stanley counters all the evidence he provides of Lark's handiwork with a logical explanation. When Blanding tries to draw on him on the sly, Lark shoots Blanding in the arm with a rifle. The night before this episode, Stanley and Marigold had met, and Marigold broke their engagement, returning his ring. With the end of the wild-horse episode, Marigold points out to Stanley that Lark is the ideal mate for him. She encourages him to propose to Lark. They are married and honeymoon on her ranch in Idaho. Stanley Weston is a true gentleman hero, developed along the lines of Hal Thurman in *Code of the West* or Laramie Nelson in *Raiders of Spanish Peaks*. He is a man shaped by the western environment who preserves the values instilled by life close to nature, despite the influence of a modern education and modern values.

Wetherby, Jim: In *Wildfire*, a young man from Durango that Aunt Jane and John Bostril think would make a good husband for Lucy. For Aunt Jane, he is a gentleman, a man with class and respectability, like the men she knew back in Missouri. She suspects Lucy has stayed out riding on the sage to avoid having to meet him. For John Bostril, Wetherby's a more welcome alternative to Joel Creech, who follows Lucy around like a puppy dog. Both the aunt and her father suspect that Lucy might like Joel, at least, that is the popular opinion at Bostril's Ford. Wetherby himself says and does little in the novel. He is with Bostril at Brackton's store when Bostril challenges Slone to have a rematch between Wildfire and Sage King.

Wetherill: In *30,000 on the Hoof*, a rancher who sends his sons to fetch some young Navajo boys to help herd cattle. There is a decided scarcity of young cowboys as most have signed up for the army.

Wetzel, Lewis: Known by many different names among the Indian tribes in the area. The Shawnee call him "Long Knife," the Hurons, "Destroyer," and the Delaware have named him "Deathwind," or "Black Wind." The French fur traders call him "Le Vent de la Mort." Wetzel appears in all three Ohio Valley novels. He is Grey's version of Cooper's Natty Bumpo, Hawkeye, of the *Leatherstocking Tales*.

When Lewis Wetzel, then aged twenty, and his two brothers, Martin and John, returned from an extended hunting trip, they found "the smoking ruins of the home, the mangled remains of father and mother, the naked and violated bodies of their sisters, and the scalped and bleeding corpse of a baby brother." From that point, he vowed eternal vengeance on the Indians. He is said to live only to hunt Indians.

The Indians see in Wetzel an implacable, insatiable foe. The pioneers see Wetzel as the guardian angel of the settlements. At times, he warns them of impending Indian attacks. Other times, settlers open the house door in the morning to discover the scalped body of an Indian on the ground. Such events are attributed to Wetzel. Colonel Ebenezer Zane describes him as the right hand of the defense of the fort. He spends his time trailing Indians through the forests. He seems aware of any movement on the part of the Indians and consequently, he is able to forestall their plans for an attack on Ft. Henry. In *The Last Trail*, the days of the wild frontier which required the skills of a Wetzel are passing. The Indians are no longer a menace. The greatest threat to the area is the outlaw gang which steals horses and destroys pioneers' homes. Wetzel and Jonathan Zane become detectives of sort, isolating the insider who is giving the thieves information about the whereabouts of the best horses and the movements of people at Ft. Henry. Wetzel plays the role of detective, undertaking to break up the operation of a gang of murderers and horse thieves who steal horses and then drive them north to sell in Detroit to the British in Canada. Wetzel's tracking skills make possible the pursuit of these outlaws, the last of the border ruffians in that area of the Ohio Valley. He and Jonathan Zane take on the band on their own and emerge victorious.

Wetzel is a man shaped by the environment. He is unexcelled on the frontier as hunter, tracker, marksman. All three novels provide memorable examples of these skills. He is reputed to be able to reload his musket while on the run, a claim which is seen in *Betty Zane* when Wetzel is being chased by several Indians. He loads his musket, turns and shoots the lead Indian closest to him. The others quickly take shelter behind trees to evade his unerring aim. Wetzel then takes off running again, to repeat the procedure until his pursuers are all eliminated.

Most memorable, like the shooting competition in Cooper's *The Last of the Mohicans*, are Wetzel's outstanding feats with a gun. In *Betty Zane*, he participates in a shooting contest at Betty's request, as she does not want the prize, a bullet pouch she has made, to go to Miller. The target is a board with a nail partly driven into it. The contestants shoot from a hundred yards away. To hit the board close to the nail is an accomplishment. Wetzel hits the nail on the head and drives it fully into the piece of wood. In *The Spirit of the Border*, Wetzel's target is a small turtle on the end of a log at a similar distance. He hits the target dead center, shooting with an old-fashioned gun Mr. Wells has just given to him. In the same novel, he puts a bullet into the forehead of Half King from a distance of over three hundred yards. Similar feats of shooting are seen in *The Last Trail*, when Wetzel and Jonathan Zane attack the horse thieves in their well-concealed hideout.

Few people know the real Lewis Wetzel. Most pioneers consider him to be mad, filled with bloodlust and hatred for Indians. One scene in *Betty Zane* reveals the Wetzel who goes mad with love of killing in the heat of battle. Ft. Henry is under siege by Indians and British soldiers. During the night, some Indians succeed in cutting a hole in the back of the stockade and begin to enter the fort. Wetzel stands in the opening with an axe fighting off the Indians as they come through the opening: "Just then, Wetzel in all his horrible glory was a sight to freeze the marrow of any man.... He was covered with blood.... At every swing of the gory axe he let out a yell the like of which had never before been heard by the white men. It was the hunter's mad yell of revenge. In his thirst for revenge, he had forgotten that he was defending the Fort with its women and its children; he was fighting because he loved to kill."

Each of the three novels presents a different aspect to Wetzel. *Betty Zane* looks at the relationship between Wetzel and Betty Zane. Given that he spends his life wandering the forests and rarely stays in a settlement for any extended period, he has had little experience of home life and women. Consequently, he keeps his love for Betty a secret. On several occasions, he has to save Betty from herself. At a dance at the Watkins home, Betty has been flirting with Ralph Miller, in part to make Alfred Clarke jealous. Miller does not take the flirting very well and Wetzel must come to Betty's rescue. Mrs. Watkins advises Wetzel to open his heart and speak his mind to Betty (the wise old lady has guessed his secret), but Wetzel says that he is not the marrying type. No woman would put up with him. "Fightin' is all I'm good for," he tells her. At a later point, he confesses

to Betty his love for her, a love he has felt since she was a child, but he tells her she and Alfred Clarke are made for each other. He promises his enduring friendship and help when she needs it. He has the opportunity to show it when he saves her from Miller's kidnapping plot.

In *Betty Zane*, Wetzel recounts an episode when he spared the life of a young Delaware. He nurses the Indian until he is able to get about safely on his own. The Delaware promises to repay him the favor. At a later occasion when Wetzel has been captured by a band of Delaware, the young brave sets him free, thereby repaying his debt. Wetzel speaks with great admiration of the Indians' respect for their word. In *The Spirit of the Border*, Wetzel expresses similar admiration for Wingenund, the noble foe.

Wetzel is arguably the "spirit" in *The Spirit of the Border*. Zane Grey lists clearing Wetzel's name as one of his goals in writing the book. This novel studies the character of the man of nature, the white man who has let the natural world of the American frontier shape him. He is the white "noble savage." In *The Spirit of the Border*, Wetzel performs several chivalrous rescues, as well as several formidable feats of marksmanship. Wetzel takes under his wing the young Joe Downs, who is afflicted with border fever. He teaches the lad how to track, how to hunt, how to pass through the woods without leaving a trail. Joe marvels at his mentor's strength and speed. Wetzel can crawl through the tall grass to sneak up on a buffalo herd faster than Joe can walk and causing no more of a ripple than a grass snake. Wetzel, a forty-year-old man, can run across a five-mile-wide open stretch of prairie and reach the other side showing no sign of exertion in his breathing. Wetzel even shares with Joe the location of his secret hideout, and confides in him his deep abiding love for nature. The mentor advises the disciple to return to Ft. Henry as life as a hunter frontiersman requires greater stamina and skill than he has. Joe, however, does not listen and pays the price. Wetzel is said to return every year to the grave of Joe and Aola in the Glade of the Beautiful Spring.

The Last Trail is the story of the friendship between Jonathan Zane, Colonel Ebenezer Zane's younger brother, and Wetzel. Jonathan, like Joe in *The Spirit of the Border*, but with greater success, has learned from Wetzel the ways of a frontiersman, but unlike Wetzel, whose first love is hunting Indians, Jonathan loves the outdoors for its own sake. In fact, he loves nature more than he loves women. Helen Sheppard learns she must accept this about him if she is to win his heart. The novel is about accepting the need for change, abandoning the wild, free life of the forest, and settling down. Jonathan feels that to marry would be disloyal to his friend, surrogate father, and mentor Wetzel. The older man, however, tells Jonathan that he too had been bitten by the love bug but that Jonathan, unlike Wetzel himself, is still young enough to change. He also underlines that this current campaign against the horse thieves will probably be the last which will require his and

Jonathan's particular gifts. Assured that he is not being disloyal, Jonathan marries, and names his first son after Lew Wetzel. In the novel, though, Wetzel is the main force in ferreting out the Leggett gang's hideout deep in the forest. His tracking skills make possible the rescue of Helen Sheppard and Mabel Lane. Colonel Zane describes him as the strong arm of the law at the fort.

In Wetzel, Grey has created a memorable frontier hero, as striking and noble as Cooper's Hawkeye.

Wetzel, Martin and John: Mentioned in *The Spirit of the Border*. When Colonel Zane is telling Joe Downs the history of Ft. Henry and of the famous frontiersman, Wetzel, he identifies these two brothers of Lewis's. They arrived home from an extended hunting trip to find their home in ashes and all the family members murdered by a party of raiding Shawnee. On the ashes of their home, the three brothers swear eternal revenge on the Shawnee. They have spent their lives on the trail of Indians to exact their revenge. In *Betty Zane*, Martin Wetzel is mentioned as one of the men helping to get pioneers into the fort before the attack. In *The Last Trail*, Colonel Zane mentions that Martin Wetzel was killed and scalped by Indians.

Weymer, Chane: In *Wild Horse Mesa*, a thirty-four-year-old hunter of wild horses. He loves the freedom of his profession, life in the open, free, healthy, active, without restraint. He loves the wild desert. He is a lone wolf, hard-fisted and fast with the gun. His dream is to have a ranch where he can raise horses.

Chane's character is constructed along the lines of Ben Ide and Nevada (Jim Lacy) in *Forlorn River*. Like Ben, Chane resented his father who, like Amos Ide, disapproved of his son's passion for mustanging. He started hunting the wild horses in Colorado and later moved farther afield into Nevada, Arizona and Utah. When his parents died, he assumed guardianship of his younger brother, Chess, whom he affectionately has nicknamed "Boy Blue." The Weymer family was close and his early years in Colorado were happy. His father had been a rancher, cattleman and horse dealer. His brother Chess worships him, and for the first few years, had been amenable, until he got the urge to break out on his own. When the novel begins, he has just left his brother at home when he set off to chase mustangs with the Piute, Toddy Nokin. Chane Weymer prefers hunting mustangs with the Piutes rather than with white men, because the Piutes are better horsemen and more trustworthy. He finds himself with Bent Manerube, Jim Horn, Hod Slack and Bud McPherson, none of whom he trusts, and he correctly suspects they intend to steal his outfit. Only by taking preemptive action does he escape.

Chane Weymer is free of the prejudice men have towards Indians. He respects and admires Toddy Nokin for his horsemanship and personal integrity. Chane knows that rumors abound that he has been a "squaw man." As the story has it, he shacked up with a Navajo woman, but there is no truth to the rumor. He does confess to having been with Indian girls when lonely, but he has always been honest with them. He feels that young Indian women are too eager to love white men, most of whom abuse their affection. Sosie, Toddy Nokin's daughter, is clearly in love with him, but he refuses to take advantage of her, despite her willingness. He rescues her from Bent Manerube, who has run off with her. Manerube is made to admit he was taking advantage of her with no intention of fulfilling his promise to marry her.

When Chane meets up with the Melberne outfit of mustangers after his escape from the ambush planned by Manerube and McPherson, he has to prove himself to Melberne and Loughbridge. These men have heard about him from Manerube, who has ingratiated himself with Loughbridge, the two of them sharing a similar greedy bent. Manerube has portrayed Chane as a ruffian, a gunman, and an abuser of women. Sue Melberne believes what Chess Weymer has told them, but it takes a while for the men to be convinced. Like Ben Ide and Nevada, Chane is seen as an outlaw, a scoundrel.

In the camp, Chane impresses all with his horsemanship. Jake, the cook, declares he's the finest rider he has ever seen. His knowledge of the mustanging business is also impressive, but does not promise the quick profit that Loughbridge is seeking and which Manerube promises. Chane explains why the "barbed wire fence" strategy is not advisable because of the many horses maimed and killed in the process. As well, the process of hobbling horses, making them run on three legs to the train for shipment, results in a loss of perhaps a quarter of the animals to injury and damaged limbs. Nevertheless, Melberne and Loughbridge opt for the bloody method, so eager are they to turn a quick profit. The mustanging done in Manerube's fashion produces the results Chane had predicted. Sue Melberne is disgusted with the suffering of the poor animals, and the experienced cowboys and the Melberne crew all feel that the process has been degrading and barbaric. When the first group of horses has been hobbled and driven to the station, Sue releases the remaining mustangs to escape back to the mesa. Chane is the first to detect her footprints at the corral gate. He sympathizes with her and promises to keep her secret, but warns her that Manerube probably read her tracks as easily as he did.

Chane's good nature is seen in his admiration for and treatment of horses. Like Lin Slone in *Wildfire*, he believes that kindness and gentleness are the tools to be used to break in a horse. His spectacular mount, Brutus, was trained this way. Chane gets attached to the mustangs he takes, acquiring particular affection for some, like Blue, a roan, which he cannot bear to sell. The same feelings are there when he captures Panquitch. Although finally outsmarting and trapping the stallion marks the culmination of many months of pursuit, he returns the King of the Stallions to his domain. It would be wrong to keep him in captivity.

Chane's decency is finally recognized by all when Toddy Nokin and his family arrive with mustangs. The truth about the incident with Manerube and Sosie is revealed, and Melberne declares Weymer to be the most decent man he has ever met. He tells Sue he is glad she is in love with him. He has seen her look at Chane in the same way that his wife used to look at him. He urges her to marry him. The wedding will be soon, at Thanksgiving, possibly, when Melberne's preacher brother, Jim, arrives to join them at the ranch on Wild Horse Mesa. Chane is to be the foreman of the proposed ranching operation.

Chane and Alonzo and Sue pursue Panquitch, the king of the stallions on the mesa. Chane had been pursuing the animal before he hooked up with Manerube and McPherson, the chase interrupted by McPherson's attempt to seize Brutus and the mustanging interlude with Melberne and Loughbridge. When he has caught Panquitch, he releases the animal, partly because he sees the horse can never be subdued, and partly because he agrees with Sue that the stallion does not deserve to be imprisoned. McPherson and Manerube, however, have no such scruples, and when they find the exhausted animal, they capture and hobble him, Chane convinces McPherson to let the animal go. McPherson is a true lover of horses, and when Chane explains that he had caught the stallion and released him, McPherson realizes that is why they were able to catch the horse so easily. He argues with Manerube, claiming his right to the Panquitch. According to the law of the plains, the man who captures an animal is the owner of the animal. Manerube kills MacPherson, and is in turn shot by Toddy Nokin's sons. Panquitch is set free to return to his kingdom, Wild Horse Mesa.

Weymer, Chess: In *Wild Horse Mesa*, "Boy Blue," the eighteen-year-old brother of Chane Weymer. He has worshiped his older brother all his life and cannot imagine him doing anything disgraceful or degrading. Chane sets off in pursuit of his older brother, joining Melberne and Loughbridge's mustanging outfit heading for the Wild Horse Mesa. He is sweet on the twenty-year-old Sue Melberne. She, however, considers him a child, and while she does see admirable qualities in him, she is not interested in him romantically. Chess then decides that she would be the perfect wife for his older brother, Chane, whom he hopes they will find. Ora Loughbridge is sweet on Chess, and, annoyed at his lack of interest in her, she flirts with Manerube, to make him jealous. When Manerube tells the story painting his beloved brother as a scoundrel and abductor of women, Chess fights to defend his brother's honor. When Chane does arrive, Chess is in his glory. The romance he hoped for between Sue and Chane does materialize. Ora and Chess marry and plan to set up ranching with the Loughbridges and Melbernes on Wild Horse Mesa. Like Marvie Blaine in *Forlorn River* and *Nevada*, Chess is an idealistic young man eager to imitate his hero, who makes it to manhood without losing his childlike innocence.

Whang: In *The Mysterious Rider*, a half-broken mustang Lem and Jim are trying to shoe at the start of the novel.

Wheaton, Jeff: In *The Horse Thief*, buys Big Bill Mason's ranch when he decides to sell out in a hurry. This sudden sale at less than rock-bottom price confirms that Mason is the linchpin in the horse-rustling outfit and that the rustlers are clearing out of the region.

Wheelock, Bandy: In *Wyoming*, the leader of a group of four cowboys who arrive at the Bligh ranch. They have been hired by Nick Bligh and he jokingly presents himself and his group to Martha Dixon. He is older than most cowboys, and so bow-legged he could never have stopped a pig in a lane. But Martha finds him irresistibly charming.

Whisner: In *The Rainbow Trail*, Withers's helper at the trading post. He is a Mormon, cold, uncommunicative and aloof. Shefford feels that his presence there is resented.

Whispering Winds: The English translation of the Delaware Aola. She is Wingenund's daughter in *The Spirit of the Border*.

Whistler: In *The Fugitive Trail*, the second man shot and killed when Bruce Lockheart confronts Barncastle at the Elk Hotel in Mendle.

White Bear, Chief: In *Fighting Caravans*, with his Comanche warriors, attacks Jim Waters's caravan.

White, Sol: (1) In *The Lone Star Ranger*, a tall, rawboned Texan with a long mustache, waxed to sharp points. He tends bar in his saloon. He reports to Buck Duane that Cal Bain is looking for him, and later that he is over at Everall's. He also informs Buck that Sheriff Oaks is out of town at Flesher's ranch, which rustlers had hit the night before.

(2) In *The Thundering Herd*, a hider from Waco, Texas. His man, Roberts, comes upon the remains of the Jett camp.

White Eagle: The name the Wyandots give Isaac Zane in *Betty Zane*.

White Eyes: In *The Spirit of the Border*, an old Indian chief who decides to accept Christianity after hearing Jim's sermon at the start of the religious festival at the Village of Peace. He emphasizes his choice dramatically when he rises, removes and discards his chief's headgear and crosses the open area separating the converts from the pagans to sit among the Christian Indians.

White Stocking: (1) In *The Light of Western Stars*, Madeline Hammond's horse back in Newport, Rhode Island. Alfred has a picture of his sister with her horse, a picture which he gives to Gene Stewart.

(2) In "The Secret of Quaking Asp Cabin," the name of the unnamed narrator's horse.

White Wolf: In *Fighting Caravans*, described as a wise old Apache chief. He is reportedly on the war path when Clint Belmet and his father make a trip to Santa Fe.

Whiteall: In *Rogue River Feud*, a prospector on the Rogue River. Minton tells Keven Bell that he might be better off prospecting for gold. Whiteall has been working a claim at Whiskey Creek for years and has been doing all right for himself.

Whiteface: (1) In *To the Last Man*, the black horse with a white face that Jean Isbel selects from his father's corral of horses. The animal is well proportioned and swift, gentle and a joy to ride. The animal is stolen by the Jorths and given to Ellen, who names him Spades.

(2) In *Wilderness Trek*, one of the tough cayuses from back in Texas that Red Krehl recalls when he is in Australia.

Whitefish, Jim: In *Fighting Caravans*, first appears in a story told by Old Bill about an Indian of an unidentified tribe whom he helped after he had escaped from a Pawnee war party. Jim Whitefish, part white, was going to see his girl and ran into the Pawnee, who made him come along. They kicked and beat him and insulted him, calling him a squaw because he would not fight the Mexicans. Old Bill takes him to the fort, and pays the doctor to take care of Jim. He asks Old Bill his name and promises never to forget him. Four years later, when Old Bill has been shot in a fight with Indians, Jim Whitefish comes upon him and hides him from his pursuers in his home and helps him to get back to Fort Larned. Old Bill has not shot at Indians since then. Later, Jim Whitefish warns Couch and Belmet of an impending Indian attack on their wagon train at Point of Rocks. He is with the Indians and Murdock, but he has betrayed the plot to the whites and prevents a massacre, although many Indians are killed in the battle.

Whitefoot: In *Wildfire*, the horse which Macomber enters in the annual horse race at Bostril's ford. The horse comes in second, several lengths behind Wildfire.

Whitie: In *Riders of the Purple Sage,* one of Venters's sheep dogs, part collie, part deer hound. The animal is well trained, standing guard at night while its master sleeps on the open sage. Often, Whitie and Ring provide the only companionship Venters has.

Whiting, Hal: In *Western Union*, mentioned as one of the men working on Creighton's telegraph line construction crew.

Whittaker: In *The Trail Driver*, from the Carolinas. He is a red-faced, sleepy-eyed young rider of twenty-two, notable for his superb physique. He tells Reddie that he had guessed she was not a boy from the start. Whittaker is killed in the mass stampede of cattle and buffalo at the end of the trail.

Whity: In *The Thundering Herd*, one of the horses pulling the wagon which brings Milly Fayre back to Sprague's station. On the trip back, Milly develops a particular affection for the Whity and Specks.

Widing: In *Western Union*, mentioned as one of the men working on Creighton's telegraph line construction crew.

Wiggate: In *Valley of Wild Horses*, a broad, heavy man with a thin gray chin beard. He is a dealer who buys wild horses. Blinky Moran and Gus Hans tell Pan Handle about their wild horse catching proposal and Wiggate is one possible buyer. He and Hardman pay twelve dollars and four bits a horse on the hoof in Marco. Bill Dolan reports to Pan Handle that Wiggate had started the horse-buying business, then Hardman had to get his finger in the pie. When Wiggate became a big man with plenty of money, he broke with Hardman, possibly as a result of Pan Handle's calling him. Wiggate has always had a good reputation in Marco. When Wiggate gets wind that Pan Handle and his crew have taken a large number of horses, some fifteen hundred, he rides out to make a deal. He offers thirteen a head delivered to Marco. Pan Handle settles for ten dollars a head in cash, delivered where they are. Pan Handle feels obliged to give him the true story about Hardman's death as he undoubtedly has heard the story told by Hardman's men who had returned to Marco. Wiggate accepts the evidence Pan Handle offers.

Wilcox: In *The Deer Stalker*, one of the men participating in the deer drive attempting to move a herd of deer to new range.

Wilcox, Lieutenant: In *Fighting Caravans*, together with Captain Howland in command of a detachment of ninety-eight soldiers assigned to escort Couch's caravan and its incredible, magnificent stock of furs en route to Kansas City.

Wild Bill: In *The Thundering Herd*, mentioned as one of the famous frontiersmen that Tom Doan meets at Sprague's hiding post. He is a superb giant of a man, picturesquely clad, straight as an Indian with a handsome face, wonderful in its expression of the wild spirit that had made him great. Wild Bill is reputed to have fought and killed twelve men in a dugout cabin on the plains. He was shot and cut to pieces himself, but recovered.

Wildfire: (1) In *The Last Trail*, a Shawnee Indian member of Bing Legget's horse-stealing operation.

(2) In *Wildfire*, a red mustang, the color of fire. Lin Slone, a veteran hunter of wild horses, spots Wildfire and makes it his goal to capture the stallion. He chases Wildfire over two hundred miles, finally cornering the animal in the desert highland not far from Bostril's Ford at the Crossing of the Fathers on the Colorado River. Wildfire accepts that Slone has captured and broken him, but refuses to submit peacefully. Whenever Lin Slone gets into the saddle, Wildfire jumps and bucks to protest. As Lin tells Bostril, sometimes he gets to ride, sometimes he

doesn't. Wildfire, however, takes a liking to Lucy Bostril, permitting her to ride him without protest. Lin gives the horse to Lucy, given that the two of them seem to have bonded. In the annual horse race, Lucy enters Wildfire as her mount, and wins the race by several lengths. The race is uneven, since Wildfire pushes the Sage King, ridden by Van Sickle, off the track, and as Blue Roan and Peg have been prevented from getting across the river in time, there is no other animal that could possibly match the stallion. Bostril, who cannot tolerate another man owning a horse faster than his own, tries to buy the stallion from Slone, who says the horse is not for sale. Slone fears that someone will attempt to steal the horse, and indeed one of Cordts's men, Sears, does make an attempt. Slone, mounted on Wildfire, ropes Sears and ties the rope around the saddle horn, and Wildfire takes off on a mad race, dragging Sears behind. Before Slone can get the stallion under control, Sears is dead. Later, Cordts attempts to steal Wildfire, Sage King and Sarchedon. To get the animals to leave the canyon where Creech has sequestered them, he starts a prairie grass fire. In the race to save Lucy Bostril, mounted on Sage King, Slone pushes Wildfire beyond his limits, and the animal, already injured by fire and smoke, expires. Wildfire is similar to Silvermane in *The Heritage of the Desert*, another example of the love Zane Grey bore for horses.

Wiley, Ben: In "Amber's Mirage," runs the blacksmith shop in Pine. Al Shade stops by to visit when he returns from his desert excursion with Jim Crawford. Ben barely recognizes him. This friend fills him in on the events of the last two years. He learns about his mother moving to Colorado and her passing away the previous summer. He also learns from Al that Ruby is married to his old friend, Luke Boyce. Wiley invites him over to dinner with his family.

Wilkins: In *The Dude Ranger*, works with Anderson, foreman for a big cattle company across the range. When Anderson expresses doubts about the honesty of Hepford and his cattle deals, Wilkins advises him not to worry about it. If Hepford is cheating the true owner of Red Rock Ranch, it does not concern them. Wilkins has brought in a buyer from Mariposa to whom he and Anderson sell the cattle they bought from Hepford.

Willet: In *Riders of the Purple Sage*, one of the gentile riders who used to work for Jane Withersteen but who quit when threatened by Elder Tull's henchmen. Jane nevertheless offers to move him and his family up to her place, which would be safer, but this offer is rejected. The storekeeper Bevins provides help for his family on Jane Withersteen's instructions.

Willetts: In *The Rainbow Trail*, the missionary John Shefford meets at Red Lake. He is a missionary to the Navajo at Blue Cañon, where he lives and teaches. When Shefford first meets him, he is with Glen Naspa, a young Navajo girl, in a compromising position. Shefford thinks the preacher is making indecent advances to the girl and intervenes to rescue the girl, Shefford beats him up. Later, at the Navajo village, Willetts appears again, this time convincing Glen Naspa to return with him to Blue Cañon. The young girl thinks that Willetts is in love with her. Again, Shefford tries to interfere, insisting that Willetts wait until Nas Ta Bega, her older brother, returns and consents. Later, Willetts tries to defame Shefford by spreading the rumor that he is only pretending to be interested in Mormon teaching in order to be with the sealed wives in the hidden village. He calls Shefford a heretic, an atheist, a man driven out of his congregation for blasphemy — facts he has learned from Presbrey. Willetts is also friendly with Shadd, a Piute outlaw, who helps him spread the rumors about Shefford among the Mormons. Willetts gets Glen Naspa pregnant and the young girl dies in childbirth. The two bodies are returned to her parents and brother for Navajo burial.

Williams: (1) In *Arizona Ames,* a gambler in a lumber camp who recognizes Arizona Ames when he walks into a saloon.
(2) In *Fighting Caravans,* mentioned as a freighter.
(3) In *The Last Trail*, one of Bing Legget's men, a heavy drinker.
(4) In *Wildfire*, mentioned only as a member of Bostril's horsemen's club which meets to plan the annual horse race at Bostril's Ford.

Williams, Bill: In *Wilderness Trek*, the cook for Stanley Dann and Bingham Slyter's camp. He has a share in the herds being trekked across Australia.

Williams, Chick: In *The Border Legion*, mentioned by Joan Randle as one of the younger, clean-cut young men in the outlaw gang. He is mentioned at a number of points in the novel. He expresses pleasure at Jim Cleve's success in finding the nugget. When it becomes obvious to the Border Legion that the vigilantes have an informer on the inside, he suggests that Red Pearce has been acting strangely of late. Pearce is eventually exposed as the traitor.

Williams, Curt: In *West of the Pecos,* a rider for Don Felipe González down on the Big Bend. Sawtell had Williams fired for branding mavericks on his range. When Pecos Smith leaves the Healds' ranch, he meets up with Curt Williams and Wess Adams and they begin a business of sorts, rounding up mavericks and branding them, selling them either to ranchers or to government stock buyers. Curt Williams and Wess Adams undertake a further operation unbeknownst to Pecos Smith, rebranding cattle. Some ranchers catch them and lynch them, just when the Comanche attack. Pecos Smith, concerned about their tardiness in returning, goes out to look for them and comes upon the lynch party and the Comanches.

Williams, Edna (Kitty): In *Raiders of Spanish Peaks,* Ted's sister. She comes west with her father when they receive word from Ted of his marriage to Flo. Kitty is rather shy, but curious about western cowboys. She has heard about Laramie and expresses an eagerness to meet him, an eagerness which annoys Harriet and sets her to thinking about him in a new way.

Williams, Hash: In *The Trail Driver*, with his partner, Smilin' Pete, asks Brite to join their outfit. They are buffalo hiders who are making their way north to Doan's freighting post. They are good hunters and know the area well.

Williams, John: In *The Horse Thief*, a fictitious horse dealer from whom Reed alleges he bought the horses that he is auctioning off in Halsey. Dale Brittenham tells Reed that he is from the Snake River Valley and knows that there is no such man as John Williams living there who deals in horses.

Williams, Mr.: (1) In *The Arizona Clan*, the father of Tess Williams, Steve Lilley's future father-in-law. He appears at the end of the novel when the troubles between the Lilleys and Buck Hathaway have been resolved. He and Uncle Bill are discussing the great possibilities of raising cattle on the range now that Dodge has taken an iron hand and cleaned up the Twitchell-Quayle-Hathaway outfit that was ruining the place. He plans to set up Steve and Tess in ranching with a gift of a thousand head of Texas cattle. He offers to sell Dodge another five hundred head at rock-bottom price and to wait for payment. He also plans to set up a bigger ranch himself with more cattle from Texas.

(2) In *Raiders of Spanish Peaks*, Ted "Tracks" Williams's father. Mr. Williams had hoped his son would become a lawyer. Ted was preparing to enter Yale when they quarreled. He refused to become a lawyer, upon which his father vowed to disinherit him if he did not pursue his career in law. Ted ran away from home and has not been in touch with his family in Boston since then. When Ted and Flo are married, he cables his father about the marriage and his whereabouts. Mr. Williams goes west to surprise his son. He reaches the Spanish Peaks ranch before Ted and Flo have returned from their honeymoon. He tells the Lindsays he has changed. He is willing to take things as they are. For years he had feared that Ted had made a disgrace of himself, that he had become an idle, drunken cowpuncher. He apologizes for mistrusting his son. He has decided he will set his son up with the money to buy a ranch and go into the cattle business. He has heard from men in Kansas City that the cattle business is due for a boom and millions are to be made in a ranching venture.

Williams, Ted "Tracks": In *Raiders of Spanish Peaks*, partner to Lonesome Mulhall for two years. According to Mulhall, Ted could track a bird, hence the nickname he gave him, "Tracks." The name stuck. He is slick with a gun, leaning toward being a gunman. He saves Lonesome in a fight with Cheesbrough, a stockman to whom Spencer's daughter was to be married. Williams shoots Cheesbrough

and takes off. Lonesome has not seen him since. Lonesome and Laramie find him in a jail in Dodge. He got picked up when the sheriff made a sweep of town, rounding up newcomers. Lonesome and Laramie promise to return at suppertime, when they break him out of jail. The three of them form a partnership, calling themselves the Three Range Riders.

According to Laramie, Ted Williams has a handsome, thin white face, lighted by eyes black as night and sharp as daggers. Black locks hang disheveled over a fine brow and a thin downy beard bespeaks youth. When he offers to go off on his own so as not to break up the new partners, Laramie and Lonesome, Laramie senses his loyalty to others. "He belongs to the best of the fine-spirited breed who ride the West." Williams talks very little about himself. Laramie learns of his background when they are invited over to the Lindsays' for dinner. Tracks is from Boston, a Yankee. He ran away from home eight years ago, when he was sixteen. It seems his father had decided he would go to Yale to study law. Ted had little interest in the law, and ran away from school. Mr. Williams threatened to disinherit him if he did not pursue a career in law. Ted has not heard from them since then.

Ted signs on with Laramie and Lonesome to work for the Lindsays at Spanish Peaks ranch. They accompany them to the ranch, and then set about putting the place in order. Not long after arriving at the ranch, Ted's favorite horse disappears. He tracks the pinto to Snook's corral. Laramie decides it would be better not to confront Snook over the horse until they have more evidence against him on the rustling score. Later, another of his pintos disappears.

Ted falls in love with Flo, Lindsay's second daughter, and elopes with her. Although Lindsay feigns opposition, he is quite happy to have Ted as his son-in-law. However, some six weeks before eloping, he writes his parents telling them of his wild life and how he has fallen in with a fine family and a young girl who has promised to marry him. Two days before the elopement, he receives word by letter that his parents are coming west to set him up in the cattle business. It will mean a big ranch for him, but he wants Laramie and Lonesome to throw in with him. He had not mentioned anything to anyone because he wanted to see if Flo would marry him as he was, a range rider without a future.

Ted and his skills as a tracker are indispensable to the recovery of the abducted Lenta. They follow Gaines, and discover the body of young Stuart, who had ridden off with her. The trail leads them to a cabin, where Lenta proves a very uncooperative prisoner. The rescue of Lindsay's daughter also resolves the problem of rustling on the ranch.

Williams, Tess: In *The Arizona Clan*, Steve Lilley's girlfriend. Dodge Mercer compares her to a wild rose. She appears at the Sunday get-together at the Lilleys' and at the end, when her father proposes setting them up with cattle for a ranch. Nan worries at one point that if Steve should run into Tess before calling Hathaway out, she will make him nervous and this will probably give Buck Hathaway an edge on him. Tess is only a child and she gets scared when Steve goes bear hunting.

Williamson: In *Western Union*, tells Wayne Cameron about the crew constructing the telegraph line which could use a young man with his talents. He introduces him to Creighton, emphasizing his medical background. Creighton hires young Cameron to take care of the medical needs of the men in his crew.

Williamson, Captain: Appears in *Betty Zane* and *The Spirit of the Border*. He arrives with his company numbering some eighty men just as the Indians and the renegades move in to destroy the Village of Peace. This militia consists of assorted frontiersmen, hunters, and ex-soldiers from the garrison at Ft. Pitt. He and his men had been pursuing a band of renegades and Chippewa Indians who had attacked and murdered pioneers in outlying areas and burned their cabins. They caught up with the marauders and slaughtered nearly the whole group. When they were at Goshocking, they heard about the planned attack on the Gnaddenhutten and stopped by to see what was happening rather than to help. Both Heckewelder and Jim attempt to convince him to help prevent the massacre but, largely indifferent to the fate of these Indians, Williamson refuses to do anything. Williamson is an historical figure, and it is suspected that he and his men were participants in the destruction of the village, not merely observers of the event. Grey has Williamson slaughtering Chippewas in retaliation for their attacks on settlements. Grey uses Williamson as an example of the cruelty and indifference engendered by life on the frontier. In *Betty Zane*, Captain Williamson and his militia reach Ft. Henry just after the British soldiers have retreated and the Indian bands have returned to their villages. Perhaps word of their company hastened the departure of the attackers.

Williamson, Doc: (1) In *The Maverick Queen*, performs an autopsy on the body of Jimmy Weston at the request of Lincoln Bradway. He extracts a .38 caliber bullet from the body, proving that McKeever did not shoot him. Doc Williamson is also called to patch up McKeever at the Aldham hotel. Lincoln Bradway accompanies him one evening when he is going to check up on his patient. There he meets Sealover, the man Hasket told him had been sent to hire him to shoot Lincoln. Williamson complains that Sealover is disturbing his patient and asks him to leave.

(2) In *Twin Sombreros,* doctor and coroner of Las Animas. Sheriff Kiskadden asks him to determine the time of death of Allen Neece. He concludes that the cause of death was a fractured skull and bleeding. He was shot post mortem. Doc Williamson also patches up Bess Syvertsen, who was shot by Brazos, and Hank Bilyen, who was shot by Knight.

Williamson, Doctor: In *The Hash Knife Outfit*, the Traft family doctor in Saint Louis, Missouri. When Gloriana wants to escape the embarrassing situation in which she finds herself, he consents to play along and tells her parents that she needs to go west for her weak lungs.

Willis, Captain: In *30,000 on the Hoof*, works with General Crook in the Geronimo campaign. He had predicted that Geronimo would break out of the reservation.

Wills (Willis), Joe: In *Riders of the Purple Sage,* one of the gentile boys that Judkins hires to ride for Jane Withersteen when the Mormon cowboys have been called in by Elder Tull and Bishop Dyer. He is killed in the stampede of the white herd.

Wilson: (1) In *The Hash Knife Outfit*, a rancher in Holbrook who was killed by Madden, the cook of the Hash Knife Outfit.

(2) In *30,000 on the Hoof*, one of the cattle barons in the area around Flagg, Arizona. He, like the other ranchers, is interested in the fluctuating price of cattle due to war speculation.

(3) In *Thunder Mountain,* an old man who took pity on Jake Emerson when he was attacked and robbed in Challis. Wilson took care of him during the worst of his recovery, when he was out of his head. Wilson tells him that he saw Leavitt and Selback pack up and leave for parts unknown. Men who were in thick with Leavitt left the next day with mules loaded down with supplies and mining tools. In this way, Jake Emerson learns that Leavitt is behind the death of his brother.

(4) In *Western Union*, Colonel Sunderland's driver. The colonel sends him with Cameron to South Pass to get Ruby.

Wilson, Hardy: In *Knights of the Range,* one of the local ranchers who shows up at the Ripple ranch with Sewall McCoy to accuse Renn Frayne of rustling.

Wilson, Jim: In *The Man of the Forest*, a member of Snake Anson's outlaw gang. He is the only member of Anson's gang that Milt Dale recognizes in the cabin where he is hiding in the loft. Jim Wilson had been well known in Pine before Snake Anson had ever been heard of. He is the best of a bad lot and still has many friends among honest people. It is rumored that he and Snake do not get along together. Tom Carmichael later reveals that Jim Wilson had been a Texas Ranger. When Riggs has kidnapped Bo, Jim Wilson is impressed with the way she challenges him before the band of outlaws, calling him a coward, telling how Milt Dale handled him at the train station in Magdalena and how Tom Carmichael (Las Vegas) drove him out of Pine. Bo later tells him that her uncle, Al Auchincloss, had spoken well of him, praising his gunmanship and expressing regret that he was an outlaw. He is kind to her, insisting that she not be tied up. Where could she go? He and Anson disagree on this point. When Beasley arrives, Jim Wilson is equally unimpressed with the man and his plans. While all the others stand up on his arrival, Wilson remains seated. Bo threatens to send Tom Carmichael after Beasley; a true Texan and defender of women's honor, he will surely kill him. Jim Wilson advises Beasley to listen, to take the threat seriously. Wilson builds a lean-to for Bo, and keeps an eye out for Riggs. When Riggs decides he is going to sneak off with Bo, Wilson puts an end to the attempt, killing Harve in a shootout. Milt Dale meets Dale Wilson in the woods outside the outlaw camp where he has been hiding with his cougar, Tom. The outlaws' horses have smelled the cougar and are nervous. Wilson tells Dale that Bo is the spunkiest girl he has ever met. He mentions that the group is falling apart, and Milt suggests that he help him free Bo. Dale assures Jim that the cougar is a pet and poses no threat to him. Letting the cougar go into the camp would surely scare the living daylights out of the men. Wilson thanks Dale for being square with him and offers to help. He meets Bo and tells her about the plan he and Milt have prepared. Bo plays the role of Ophelia, pretending she has gone mad. Tom emits frightening noises from the woods, the horses and the men expecting an imminent attack. Jim Wilson assures Anson that they have been pursued and are probably now surrounded. The frightened horses run off. The men start fighting among themselves. Anson is killed by Shady Jones. Wilson delivers Bo safely into the arms of the waiting Milt Dale, who, in gratitude, urges him to shake the gang and go straight. He replies that the gang is finished. Bo praises him for having lived up to the reputation of a true Texan.

Wilson, Red: In *Wildfire*, so called because he has red eyes from the red dust of the trail which covers his clothes. He is the freighter who brings in supplies by wagon from Durango to Bostril's Ford. He arrives with a load of freight at Brackton's store and comments on the dry weather and the possibility of one more trip out and back before the rains begin. He has with him the package containing the birthday present Lucy has been expecting.

Wind of Death: In *The Spirit of the Border,* one of the names given to Wetzel. See **Wetzel.**

Wind River Charlie: In *Raiders of Spanish Peaks,* one of the crew left at the Lindsay ranch by Lester Allen. He is a tall, fair-haired young man. Lenta says of him that he is a big, wonderful-looking fellow, simple as a, b, c, but under the sway of Gaines. Eventually, he comes over to Laramie Nelson's side. Lenta Lindsay tells Gaines that she learned from Wind River Charlie that he was Arlidge's right-hand man. When Nig Jackson starts to tell what he knows about the rustling, Wind River Charlie acknowledges he was part of the outfit, but that he did not know they were rustling. Charlie helps in the hanging of Price.

Winfield, Alice: In *Captives of the Desert*, Katharine Winfield's sister. Alice and her sister have come to the Arizona desert because she is suffering from tuberculosis and the family doctor had recom-

mended she move to a drier climate. Mary Newton had written Katharine about how robust her health had become living in the desert and the two of them make the move. Alice, like Katharine, comes to love the desert. She and Katharine share their concerns about Mary and Wilbur and the steady deterioration of their marriage.

Winfield, Katharine: In *Captives of the Desert*, a close friend of Mary Newton. She comes to Arizona to accompany her frail sister, who is suffering from tuberculosis. The family doctor had recommended a drier climate. The landscape and the silence of the desert stir in her religious feelings. She thinks of the prophets of old who went into the wilderness to commune with God. She understands the hold that the desert has on her friend, Mary. She asks herself if Mary had surrendered to this force, this power, this unnamable magic that gave inner peace. Mary takes Catherine to see the Navajo Snake Dance and explains to her the symbolism of the rituals. Katharine detects the chemistry between Mary and John Curry from the start. Mary explains briefly her husband's resentment of her friend, whose life she had saved on the desert. She is troubled by Mary's willingness to believe in Wilbur when everyone else knows he is a dishonest lout. He tells her he has gone to buy silver for MacDonald or to arrange a sheep deal, but it is rumored and known as a fact by some that he is buying rot-gut liquor to sell to the Indians. When Wilbur has abandoned her, she sends Katharine with a message for John, telling him that she may move to Flaggerston to take a job if she can find one. She asks him to pass her by without recognition should he meet her in the street there. Katharine and Alice think she should divorce the man but Mary will not hear tell of such a course of action. It would leave her in permanent disgrace. Katharine confides in John that Wilbur treats Mary like a servant. When John Curry talks about his plans to set up a ranch of his own, Katharine offers to put up some money to help with the venture. She has inherited some money and it has been sitting in a bank at low interest and it could be put to better use. John is reluctant to accept her help. Katharine and Alice go away for a while and return to Taho just as things come to a head. Wilbur is killed by Magdaline, and Mary is free to marry John Curry.

Wingenund: The sachem of the Delaware in *The Spirit of the Border*. He also appears in the earlier novel, *Betty Zane*, where he participates in planning the attack on Ft. Henry. He is an example of the "noble savage." Zane Grey has modeled him on Cooper's Chingachgook. He is a wise man, a gifted tracker superior even to Wetzel, wise in the ways of animals, Indians and whites. Above all, he is cautious, prudent, deliberate. He puts the best interests of his tribe over his personal interests. He is just, giving every man his due, regardless of race.

Wingenund is first seen in the Delaware village when Wetzel is brought in a prisoner. Several years previous, Wingenund had captured Wetzel, made him run the gauntlet and sentenced him to death at the stake. His daughter Whispering Winds (Aola) had free Wetzel. Each has sworn to get revenge on the other.

Wingenund, together with Aola, travel to the Village of Peace for the religious festival. The description of Wingenund here is a classic depiction of the noble savage: "Among all these chiefs, striking as they were, the figure of Wingenund, the Delaware, stood out alone. His position was at the extreme left of the circle, where he leaned against a maple. A long, black mantle, trimmed with spotless white, enveloped him. One bronzed arm, circled by a heavy bracelet of gold, held the mantle close about his lofty form. His headdress, which trailed to the ground was exceedingly beautiful. The eagle plumes were of uniform length and pure white, except the pointed tips. At his feet sat his daughter, Whispering Winds."

After the old chief, White Eyes, has expressed his decision to convert following Jim's preaching, Wingenund speaks, advising the Indians to be cautious. The golden promise of peace and harmony between Indians and whites must be put to the test. After all, the gifts of the whites "ever contained a poisoned arrow." He advises that the Delaware let time prove the truth of the missionaries' promises. When he can walk to the ocean without getting shot at, he will believe what these missionaries teach.

Wingenund presides over the trial of Joe and Jim. He courageously overrides the decision of the chiefs who have called for the death of the two men. His decision is like that of Solomon or of Tamemund in Cooper's *The Last of the Mohicans*. Jim, the preacher, has done no harm to the Delaware and preaches peace and brotherhood. He will be released to return to the village. Joe, the friend of Deathwind, will be burned at the stake. When doubt arises as to which of the two men is the preacher, Aola, Wingenund's daughter and frequent visitor to the village, is called in to settle the matter. Not only does she identify the real missionary but she uses her privilege as the chief's daughter to save Joe's life, Pocahontas style. She takes him as her husband. Wingenund acquiesces in her decision.

When Whispering Winds announces to her father that she is a Christian, Wingenund banishes her from his home and sends her to the Village of Peace. Wingenund declares he must be true to this race.

Wingenund is unable to influence the decision to destroy the village, and no mention is made of his participation in the council that votes on the matter. He is at the village, though, and helps Nell, Jim and the aged and failing Mr. Wells to flee the village. He helps bury Mr. Wells, who expires on the way. Wetzel meets the group who have been stopped by Deering and Jim Girty. Deering and Girty are dispatched by Wetzel, who is convinced by the pleading of Nell and Jim to spare Wingenund. Wetzel gives him until noon before he sets out on his trail.

Wingenund displays his incomparable ability to make his way through the woods without leaving a trail. Wetzel feels the chief is doing this to make a fool of him. He finds the chief at the Glade of the Beautiful Spring, where Wingenund has returned to give his daughter a proper Christian burial. The sachem, it seems, has been a Christian in secret. He could not deny his Indian heritage by surrendering his Indian ways to those of the converted Indians in the village. No further mention is made of Wetzel's pursuit of Wingenund. Wetzel merely tells his inquirers at Ft. Henry that he had had the chief in his sights.

In Wingenund, Grey presents his version of the "noble savage," the Indian who has been formed by Mother Nature, who is a great orator, a great chief, wise, just, true to his origins. He accepts what may be useful to the Indian from white civilization but he never denies or forsakes his heritage. He is a cynosure of physical and moral beauty.

Wingfield, Kent: In *Stranger from the Tonto*, sent on a mission by his friend, Bill Elway, to rescue Lucy Bonesteel from the Hole-in-the-Wall hideout where, like Bess in Oldrin's hideout in *Riders of the Purple Sage*, she has been living since childhood. Like Venters in that same novel, he is concerned to defend her innocence and dignity.

Kent Wingfield's range riding and hunting had embraced the cattle region of Arizona down to the black-timbered Tonto Basin. But for his mother, he would have cast his lot with the Jorth faction in the Pleasant Valley war because he was struck by Ellen Jorth's beauty. She was the only survivor of that fight. Red-headed Nita Gail in Wagontongue had done Kent one good turn: she had coaxed him in off the wild range and from his questionable involvement with the Hash Knife Outfit. Kent has acquired remarkable dexterity with a gun, being able to shoot a rabbit in the head from a moving horse. He is equally proficient with a pistol. Ben Bunge tells the story that as member of the Hash Knife Outfit, he had faced four outlaws, Old Jim Stevens and three men, killing them all. This story, however, is fiction, but serves to establish his qualifications to join the Hole-in-the-Wall gang as an outlaw on the run.

Kent Wingfield had gone prospecting with Bill Elway, trying to track down the stream where the Indians found the gold they traded. He is an old man, and senses that this trip, he will not make it back. He tells Wingfield about his past membership in the Hole-in-the-Wall outfit and asks him to go back there to kill Slotte and rescue Lucy, who by now would be a prime target of lust for all the men in the outfit. Kent is engaged to Nita Gail in Wagontongue, but Old Bill tells him he saw her kissing Joe Raston the night before they left. Nita is a woman who needs a strong man who stays around to keep her straight. Old Bill wants Kent to leave him to die alone in the desert, but he refuses to leave. When Bill dies, he sets off for Wagontongue and on the way finds the gold deposit that Bill was looking for. He returns to town with much gold to put in the bank there. Nita had been unfaithful, as Bill had said. So Kent sets off to fulfill his promise to Elway.

It is not long before he meets Ben Bunge, who sells him a horse called Spades that he has taken from Slotte. Following Bunge's trail, he gets to the Slotte camp where he hides in the bushes to listen to their talk, which confirms Elway's fears for Lucy. He meets up with the group again at Logan's trading post where he gets into a shootout with Slotte and Neberyull over the horse. Kent follows their trail part of the way back to the hideout, but Spades himself finds his way through the maze of canyons to the entrance to the hideout. He is impressed by the size and beauty of the canyon. At night, he sneaks up to the lighted cabin, where he overhears Lucy and Jeff talking. She is worried about her horse and about Slotte's interest in her.

The following day, Kent meets Lucy by accident. She asks if he is one of her father's riders or if he is there to hide out. He tells her he is there to get her. He tells her about Bill Elway's request and shows her the watch he gave him with a lock of her hair inside. He tells her the truth about her father's outfit and the danger she will face should he be killed or should Slotte take over. Lucy now understands many things that puzzled her about life in the canyon. They agree to meet in the hills. She will bring him supplies and keep his presence there a secret. He returns Spades to her. One day, Lucy tells him of a terrible fight she overheard between her father and Slotte. She fears he is plotting to kill her father. Kent realizes that he must make his presence known. He appears at the cabins telling them he had been following Slotte's trail from Logan's trading post. He accuses Slotte of stealing the horse and double-crossing Bonesteel with Roberts. Crothers and Slotte are killed in the shooting which follows.

Bonesteel is impressed with Kent, as is Roberts, who comes to recruit him for his outfit. He tells Kent about Bonesteel's double life, which he learned about from Slotte. In Utah, Bonesteel is a rancher and cattle dealer with another family. No one suspects he is the leader of the Hole-in-the-Wall outlaw gang. Kent is impressed with Roberts. If he were really on the run, he would consider joining Roberts's outfit, but at present his loyalties are to Bonesteel.

Bonesteel and Lucy get into a great fight. She has learned of his double life, of his other family, and she asks why he has kept her isolated in this valley. She tells her father that she loves Kent, and would leave with him. Bonesteel then asks Kent to take her away. He is planning a showdown with Roberts and his men and wants them to leave before the shooting starts. Out of loyalty to Bonesteel, Kent remains to help out. Bonesteel survives uninjured and sends Kent off, requesting that he tell Lucy he was killed. He gives them several bags of gold to set themselves up in the outside world. Kent and Lucy leave, with Spades and Clubfoot leading the way. When they are close to Logan's trading post, Kent tells Lucy that her father survived the shooting and that he was returning to Utah to continue his other life as Luce Cheney.

Grey develops the character of Kent Wingfield

along the lines of Nevada, Arizona Ames, and Adam Larey, a man with a past as a gunman, who sees his mission to rescue or help someone and to use his skills for the good of others and to set wrongs right.

Wingfield, Lex: In "The Camp Robber," a wandering cowboy who takes jobs at various ranches. He can't stay anywhere long. He is twenty-nine years old, restless, irritable, friendless. He cares about nothing. He promises Stimpson that he will try to overcome his anti-social behavior. He explains that some years ago he lost his wife and that has knocked the wind out of him. He makes no friends at the ranch and when Neff reports that the payroll has been stolen, he is suspected. The evidence is circumstantial and there is no real proof against him, and he promises Stimpson he will clear his name. Wingfield understands now that he should have opened up to the other men about his wife. He and his wife had fought and she had run out on him. The men would have understood and perhaps have even helped him. He regrets his isolation. Wingfield sets out to investigate the robbery. He finds the footprints of the robber, and follows them to a cabin where there is a child and an old man. Pegleg Smith confesses he stole the money and returns every dollar. Smith has been stealing to provide for the child, Fay. Five years ago Pegleg had found a woman along the road. She was crazed, ill, suffering. He brought her home, where she gave birth to a child, and died a few days later. He has raised the child since then. No one has ever found him until Winfield tracked him. The dying woman had called for "Lex" and Wingfield realizes he has learned what happened to his wife. Fay is his daughter.

Wingfoot: (1) In *Raiders of Spanish Peaks*, Laramie Nelson's powerful, tireless horse.

(2) In *Western Union*, Wingfoot is Wayne Cameron's horse, reputedly so fast he appears to fly. When crossing the Laramie River in flood, the stallion is said to be part duck, he can swim so well.

Winstonah: Delaware Indian chief in *The Spirit of the Border*. His name means "War Cloud." Winstonah is present in the Delaware village when Wetzel is brought in as a prisoner.

Winter, Sol: In *Sunset Pass*, a storekeeper and surrogate father and confidante of Trueman Rock. He welcomes Rock back to Wagontongue, and fills him in on the gossip about town. His business is not able to compete with some of the larger stores in town, especially Dabb's. Trueman insists on buying a stake in the business and on depositing the remainder of his ten thousand dollars with Winter, together with instructions for sending the money to his family in Illinois should anything happen to him. With the investment, Winter is able to pay off his debts and restock the store, and in a few weeks is on the road to prosperity.

Sol Winter is a fair man, not given to idle gossip. He tells Trueman about the trouble he had with Ash Preston about unpaid bills, and the confrontation between his son, Nick, and Ash Preston. Some weeks later, Nick was found shot dead on the road to Sunset Pass. Winter suspects Ash Preston ambushed and shot him. Sol assures Trueman that the stories about "unnatural" love between Ash and Thiry Preston are malicious gossip. He speaks well of Gage Preston, of his fairness and honesty, but he cannot deny that suspicion of rustling lies heavy on him, especially since he is the only rancher in the area who is prospering, while the others are barely surviving.

When Trueman confides in him that he has found hides of Half Moon cattle in a culvert, the truth is clear. But Winter recalls an incident with a rancher involved with rustlers who managed to save his hide by negotiating a deal to remunerate those whose cattle had been stolen and thereby avoid court proceedings and imprisonment. On Winter's advice, Trueman approaches Dabb and Lincoln, the two biggest ranchers and men with reputations for honesty and fairness. On the Thiry front, he suggests that Trueman elope with her, if confrontation with Ash is to be avoided.

Winter and his wife take Trueman in after the gunfight in which Ash Preston is killed. They tend to him as if he were their son while he recuperates.

Winter, Mrs. Sol: In *Sunset Pass,* declares that Trueman Rock is just the man for Thiry Preston. She tends to his gunshot wounds after the showdown with Ash Preston.

Winter, Nick: In *Sunset Pass,* Sol's son. He helped his father in the store. Nick had a set-to with Ash Preston over an unpaid bill. Ash attacked him in the store. Later, Nick is found dead by the road. There were four empty shells in his gun. It is not clear whether his death was an accident or the result of a fight, but Sol Winter has always suspected that Ash Preston confronted him and fought it out there on the road. Sol has never breathed a word of his suspicion to anyone.

Winters, Cherry: In *The Drift Fence*, one of the cowboys in the outfit Jim Traft assigns to building the drift fence. He complains that they have to walk, not ride, to camp. Such work is insulting for a cowboy. Cherry comes back from Flagg, drunk, with Curly Prentiss holding him in his saddle. Cherry, however, is a humorous drunk. He picks a fight with the tenderfoot foreman and gets soundly trounced. Eventually, like all the crew except Hack Jocelyn, he comes to like Jim Traft. In *The Hash Knife Outfit,* Cherry Winters is still one of the cowboys who work for young Jim Traft. He accompanies Jim Traft to the train station to meet Gloriana.

Wipple, Mrs. Sam: In *Sunset Pass,* reports that Alice and Thiry have been staying at the Farrell's since their father left Sunset Pass, having sold the ranch to John Dabb.

Wirth, Bob: In *Wyoming,* the young man that Martha Ann Dixon's mother is urging her to marry. He is from a wealthy family and if she marries him, she will never have to worry about money again.

Wise, Sam: In *The Drift Fence,* one of the young men who boasts of having kissed Molly Dunn, establishing her reputation as a "loose" young woman. Andy Stoneham tells Molly that Sam Wise had told him of his exploits with Molly.

Withers: In *The Rainbow Trail*, the trader at Kayenta who brings in supplies from Colorado and New Mexico to his trading post, which is located in the wildest part of Arizona. He is young, muscular, friendly, with weather-beaten features. He offers Shefford work packing in supplies to the Mormon and Navajo villages and bringing back loads of hides and wool. He is on good terms with the Mormons, trying to be fair-minded about their religion. They are much misunderstood, he tells Shefford. Withers says that he has managed to survive thanks to the goodwill among the Indians made possible by his father-in-law. His wife, Molly, was raised by the Navajo and is highly respected by both the Navajo and the Piute. There is no white person around who knows more about these two Indian tribes than she does.

Withers listens to Shefford's story about why he has come west, about his desire to rescue Lassiter and Jane and Fay Larkin from the hidden valley. Withers knows Stonebridge, and many of the Mormon leaders in the area. He has heard of Cottonwoods and Amber Spring where Jane Withersteen lived, but they have been abandoned for over a decade. He has heard the name Fay Larkin at the Mormon village, but knows nothing more than the name.

Withers sees in Shefford a man who has lost his faith in himself and in God and who needs a guiding hand. He tells Nas Ta Bega the story of Shefford's dismissal by his congregation. If anyone can restore his faith, it's the Navajo sage and mystic. Withers, like Shefford, has little respect for troublesome missionaries who mistreat the Indians.

As Withers is in good standing with the Mormon elders, he convinces them to let Shefford visit the secret village. He tells them about his crisis of faith and self, and Bishop Kane takes it that Shefford is a potential convert to Mormonism. Withers advises John to take it slow, to ingratiate himself with the women, and to listen to what they have to say. He can learn much that way. Withers confesses that he has fallen in love with Mary, the Sago Lily, and that his wife understands how this could happen. Withers predicts that the federal judge's polygamy trials will be a waste of time, as none of the women are going to betray their husbands. He also stands up for Shefford when Willetts spreads the rumor that Shefford is merely faking a crisis of faith in order to seduce the sealed wives.

Withers is a stock figure found in many Zane Grey novels. He resembles Abe in *The Heritage of the Desert* and Wentz in *The Spirit of the Border*, although he plays a more central role in *The Rainbow Trail* than the others do in their respective novels.

Withers, John: In *The Vanishing American,* a trader at Kaidab. He is "a good man, a trader who helped the Indians and did not make his post a means to cheat them." When Marian arrives, he recognizes her immediately from the description of her given him by his wife. Marian describes Withers as keen-eyed, with dusty, rough boots, and a kindly glance. She likes him immediately. He agrees to take Marian to find Nophaie, several days' ride across the reservation. He explains to Marian about Indian customs and "medicine" — healing potions, but also prayer, straight talk, and mystical power. He points out the place where Nophaie was kidnapped as a boy of seven, the place where he tended his sheep, the Valley of the Gods so sacred to his people. He speaks of all the good that Nophaie has done since his return. He first informs Marian about the situation on the reservation, the destructive influence of some missionaries who are unsuited for their work. Young men who have been failures at other work back east come west as missionaries and succumb to the worst elements in themselves and in the new environment. Not understanding the Indians, they take advantage of them. Withers tells Marian about Ramsdell, the cowboy missionary, whose approach to the Navajos earned the admiration of both red men and white men.

John Withers is the epitome of fairness and justice in his dealings with the Navajo. When he buys Nophaie's mustangs, he gives him more than his asking price. He delivers the supplies and Christmas presents to Nophaie in the lonely canyon, giving him the companionship and support he needs. When the drought sets in following the war, Withers buys Indian blankets and hides and baskets for which he has no market at prices he can ill afford. As well, he buys alfalfa from Friel to give to the Navajo neighbors. He receives no thanks for his work and sacrifice. No one but Marian is aware of his situation.

Withers exemplifies the best of the white world, the white man who treats the Navajo as an equal, with dignity and respect. Men like Withers are the hope of mankind.

Withers, Molly: In *The Rainbow Trail*, the wife of the trader at Kayenta. She is a slight, comely woman, with small, keen, earnest dark eyes. Shefford describes her as serious and quiet. She makes him feel at home. Withers tells Shefford that she grew up among the Navajo and Piutes and that there is no white person who knows more about Indian habits and religion than she does. She is held in peculiar reverence and affection by both tribes. She had heard of Nas Ta Bega before she met him. He has the reputation of being a sage and a poet who embodies the spirit of the desert.

Withers, Mrs. John: In *The Vanishing American,* the wife of the trader at Kaidab. She first came to the reservation twenty-five years before. She loves the Navajo and they love her. She has learned to speak their language like a native, and she has learned their dreams, their religion, their prayers, their poetry, their medicine dances. She tells Marian Warner the Navajo are "children of nature," with noble hearts and beautiful minds. They live in a mystical world of enchantment peopled by spirits, music, voices, whisperings of God. They are as simple as children. When Nophaie returns to the reservation, she teaches him to speak Navajo again. She had known him before he was kidnapped and met him the day he returned. She helped him to relearn his Navajo heritage. She knows he may never fit into the Navajo world completely, but he will never return to the white world either. Although Nophaie does not tell her, Mrs. Withers knows intuitively that he is in love with Marian Warner. She knows that Marian has come west to be with him. She keeps their secret. Mrs. Withers understand very well the situation of the Navajo on reservations. They are really prisoners. They are too powerless to do anything, and no one in Washington is willing to listen to voices pleading for change. Mrs. Withers does more for the Indians than any other person had before. She wants Nophaie to set Shoie straight on the business of putting spells on superstitious women. She predicts that Noki will find Gekin Yashi for Morgan and that Gekin Yashi will eventually be forced to attend chapel. During the time Nophaie is away fighting in France, Mrs. Withers must go to California for a while for health reasons and Marian accompanies her there. They return just after Nophaie returns from France. For Zane Grey, Mrs. Withers and her husband exhibit the true spirit of Christianity and offer the Native Americans a glimpse of what the white world can offer.

Withers, Ted: In *The Vanishing American,* the son of John and Mrs. Withers. He is overseas in France. He writes his mother about Munson and what Munson reports about Nophaie and Shoie's exploits during the battles at the front.

Withersteen: In *Riders of the Purple Sage,* the father of Jane Withersteen. Although he does not appear in the novel, having died some years before the story begins, he is a presence to be felt. Withersteen House bespeaks a man who built a fortress to withstand the attacks of enemies and the weather. It bespeaks a man of great power, determination and wealth. Withersteen was an able administrator, and Jane, his only daughter and only child, has been taught the managerial skills to maintain the estate. She knows about managing staff, riders, cattle breeding, irrigation, and accounting. He was a man with an iron will. Jane fears that she has inherited his temper. She recalls how her father would fall into an insane rage when he would lose all control of himself. Withersteen, it seems, sent a young "clergyman" to seek out wives for him. Bishop Dyer, it turns out, was the man who selected Milly Erne for abduction. She was to be a sealed wife to Withersteen. This secret Jane has kept, revealing it to Lassiter only in a desperate attempt to prevent his killing the bishop.

Withersteen, Jane: In *Riders of the Purple Sage,* the only daughter of Withersteen, a powerful Mormon leader and rancher in southern Utah. She is twenty-eight years old when the story begins, and at odds with her church leaders. She is an unusual woman for her religion and her time. She has inherited her father's vast land holdings, and three herds of cattle, numbering in the thousands. She is experimenting with different breeds of cattle as she is with breeding horses. She has thoroughbreds of great value which she treats like her children. She owns Amber Spring, the principal source of water for the neighboring farms and town. She has gold galore which she uses to pay her hands. She has been trained as a manager and bookkeeper. She knows how to manage the sale of cattle, and shifts of cowboys tending the herds. In short, she has all the knowledge and power of her father, but she does not have his insight and ruthlessness. She does discover that she has inherited his blind anger, a trait she attributes to their Viking ancestry, an emotion which no doubt favored the warrior about to go into battle. This tendency she keeps under control, although on two occasions in the story she does succumb.

Jane Withersteen is presented as a woman of contradictions. These contradictions affect her views of religion, and her attitudes towards men. Jane Withersteen considers herself a devout Mormon woman, but she finds she cannot accept certain precepts of her church. Jane will not marry Elder Tull, although this is her father's wish and the instruction of her bishop. She does not wish to be a second wife, nor to marry a man she does not love. Her friend Mary Brandt points out that a true Mormon woman does not seek love, self-fulfillment or happiness in marriage. That will come in the next life. Jane sincerely believes that if she is firm and resolved, her church elders will eventually see things her way and leave her alone. She may suffer the loss of property and prestige temporarily, but she is certain it will all be restored to her in time. She represses her inchoate suspicions that Tull and Dyer are after her estate and are willing to tolerate her independence because she may be able to control Lassiter.

Jane's changing view of religion unfolds through the novel. From a devout Mormon, as she sees herself, she becomes more broadly Christian in spirit. She sees no reason why Mormonism should be forced on people who do not believe in its tenets. While her church seeks to create an exclusive society in which all truck with gentiles is cut off, she hires a gentile to lead her cowboys and to act as foreman of her ranch. She instructs the man who runs the town's general store and administers her properties in town not to collect rent from the poor gentiles who live there, and to provide them the supplies they need to live at little or no charge. She takes Mrs. Larkin to her home to care for the woman herself, promising to raise her daughter, Fay, without Mormon teaching. She promises to take Fay back to her family in the East when she is of age. She helps Carson and Willets and other gentile cowboys who are on hard times, even though they refuse to come back to ride for her out of fear for the safety of their families. Hers is a truly catholic Christian view. Mrs.

Larkin comments that although they belong to different churches, their God is the same.

Jane, nevertheless, is not interested in marrying a non-Mormon. When Lassiter proposes that they leave Utah, where he can give up his guns without losing face and where she can love a gentile without censure, she will not consider the idea. Her loyalty to her faith will not permit such a betrayal of her beliefs.

Jane Withersteen is a beautiful woman and fully aware of the power that beauty has over men. When Lassiter arrives and has saved Venters, she invites him to stay for supper. She goes into her room where she preens in front of the mirror, taking pride in her beauty. She fully intends to use those charms to the maximum to keep the gunman in line. She has already used her charms to devastating effect on Bern Venters, who allowed her to take his guns from him, thereby exposing himself to attack from Mormons who oppose his friendship with a Mormon woman. Her stunning beauty is a source of vanity, a sign to her Mormon elders of a major character flaw.

On several occasions, Jane attempts to seduce Lassiter. Perhaps two of the most powerful seduction scenes in popular western fiction occur in *Riders of the Purple Sage* when Jane tries to take Lassiter's guns and when she begs him not to go after Dyer. In the former scene, the seduction is loaded with sexual innuendo, as she reaches for his guns, only to be rejected by Lassiter with a firm declaration that guns are a necessity on the frontier and a man without his guns is like Sampson without his hair. Even the Mormon elders carry guns and have been known to use them. The second scene reminds the reader of a similar incident in Wister's *The Virginian*, when Molly Wood tries to stop the Virginian from shooting it out with Trampas. Jane throws herself at Lassiter's feet, offering herself to him if only he will spare the life of Bishop Dyer. It is one of the most powerful scenes in the novel if not in popular western fiction. Lassiter tells Jane that her flirting with him shows her insincerity. She feigns friendship and love for him merely to manipulate him. He overhears her telling Bishop Dyer that she has kept him on as foreman of her ranch and she has offered friendship to him to bind his hands. If he loves her, he will not want to take action against Mormons. She does not know her own heart.

While Jane is an insightful woman in some ways, she chooses to be blind in others. She refuses to believe that Wrangle is a better horse than Black Star and Night, her favorites. She cannot believe that Elder Tull has ordered her riders to desert her. Judkins, her gentile rider, tells her that Blake and Dorn have told him they were ordered to quit their jobs at the Withersteen ranch and to join a vigilance committee to pursue rustlers. Judkins, not given to pulling punches, tells that in town, she is seen as a woman who has "taken the bit between her teeth" and needs to be taught a lesson. She cannot believe it when Lassiter tells her that her servant women are spying on her and reporting everything that happens to Tull. She cannot believe that the house is surrounded and that her every movement is known, making her a virtual prisoner.

Above all, Jane wants to be loyal to her father's memory. The truth that Lassiter is seeking is that the abduction of his sister, Milly Erne, by a handsome Mormon preacher, now Bishop Dyer, was at the instigation of her father. Milly was abducted to become a sealed wife for Withersteen. The extent to which this marriage was a reality, she does not know, but she is determined to keep the secret. Only when she has already lost all that is dear to her does she tell Lassiter the truth.

Jane's inability to see things as they are is particularly true in her perception of Lassiter. At first, she sees him as a savior, a man who materializes out of the sage to rescue her friend Bern Venters from his enemies. But she also sees him as a heartless gunman, out to get revenge on the men who abducted his sister. She sees him as both dangerous and protective, and while she hopes to stay his hand against Elder Tull and Bishop Dyer, she also finds him a useful tool to protect *her* from *them*. Jane believes all the evil things she has heard about Lassiter. When little Fay Larkin becomes fond of him, she finds it unusual that a man she thinks has made many children fatherless should have such a kind and loving way with a child. Likewise, she misinterprets his motives with respect to her. Since she is using him for her purposes, she imagines that he is equally manipulative. She fails to see that he has genuinely fallen in love with her. When they are escaping from Tull and have parted with Venters and Bess, Lassiter hides Jane, asking her to wait for his return. She assumes he has gone off on a bloodthirsty mission to kill more of their pursuers. She is shocked to learn that he had gone to retrieve little Fay from her abductors. Only when the time comes to roll the rock, and Lassiter is unwilling to force her to be with him in the canyon perhaps for the rest of their lives, does Jane realize she does love Lassiter, and that he is genuinely a good person.

In *The Rainbow Trail*, Jane Withersteen appears in the final chapters when Shefford, led by Fay Larkin and Nas Ta Bega and Joe Lake, arrive to rescue them and take them out of the valley and out of Utah. She is referred to as the Mormon woman who incurred the wrath of Mormon leaders by showing kindness to gentiles. The Mormon leaders had resented her wealth (she owned the village of Cottonwoods, and Amber Spring, its source of water). She is the first person that Shefford meets in the valley. Back in Beaumont, Illinois, she is pleased that her prize horses, Black Star and Night, still remember her after twelve years.

Jane Withersteen embodies the characteristics of the western heroine found in certain films with Barbara Stanwyck, such as *Forty Guns*, *The Maverick Queen* or Joan Crawford in *Johnny Guitar*. This heroine breaks the mold of the role of the traditional woman. She is torn between her independence, her business sense, her freedom and her feminine instincts. She is the model on which the women in the aforementioned movies are based. She is also a break with the heroine found in other Grey novels.

Wixy: In *Horse Heaven Hill*, a large black dog that had come from some unknown place to make his home at the Burrell ranch in Idaho.

Wolf: In *The Heritage of the Desert*, Mescal's faithful dog. Wolf is half-shepherd and half-wolf, the only surviving offspring of one of Naab's dogs and a wild wolf. Mescal has raised the dog from puppyhood and the dog is loyal to the death to her. Wolf's job is to herd Naab's Navajo sheep, a task he can accomplish without barking. His movements show he will tolerate no opposition and the sheep quickly obey. Wolf accompanies Mescal into the Painted Desert when she escapes from Snap, and Wolf, as if sent by fate, is waiting for Jack Hare when he crosses the Colorado River in search of Mescal. The faithful dog leads him through the desert to the oasis where she has been living with Peon for the past year. Jack learns to trust the instincts of the dog. The animal is more in tune with nature and nature's intentions than the civilized man.

Wolf Clan: In *Blue Feather*, has entirely disappeared through a combination of drought, failed crops, the disappearance of game and enemy attacks. The Rock Clan fears it may share the same fate.

Wolterson, Bob: In *The Vanishing American*, the government stock inspector on the Navajo reservation at Mesa. Wolterson is young, tall, lithe, clean cut, tanned, not rugged, and dressed in cowboy boots and sombrero like a true Texan. Nophaie praises his work among the Navajo, who have great respect for him. Wolterson reminds him of the cowboy missionary, Ramsdell. He has come west for health reasons. Wolterson warns Nophaie to be careful when he confronts Morgan and Lord. Wolterson is dipping sheep at Do Etin's when Gekin Yashi is spirited away from the residential school. Although he wants to help, Marian and Nophaie do not want him involved. When orders come to test cattle for TB, Wolterson takes a measured approach to the problem, refusing to destroy cattle unless they test positive for the disease. This angers Blucher and Morgan, who begin a campaign to get him fired from his position as inspector. Although Wolterson's test shows that Marian's mustang is healthy, Blucher orders the animal to be killed. Bob Wolterson and his wife are transferred to King Point during the war while Marian is back east in Philadelphia. Wolterson is an example of whites on the reservation who act with honesty and good will but who are thwarted by corrupt reservation officials.

Wolterson, Mrs. Beatrice ("Mrs. Bob"): In *The Vanishing American*, the wife of Bob Wolterson, the agricultural consultant working with the Navajo. She is a striking woman, dark as an Indian, very pleasant. When Marian has returned to Philadelphia while Nophaie is fighting in France,

Mrs. Bob writes her with the news of Mesa. They have been relocated to another part of the reservation called King Point. She does not like this place as well as Mesa. Mrs. Bob herself has two brothers in the army fighting in France. She reports that Blucher's days on the reservation are numbered as someone has countered his anti–war, anti–American propaganda. She writes as well that Gekin Yashi has vanished from the school. She also explains that Morgan and Blucher have devised a scheme whereby they have taken control of the water rights on many parts of the reservation. This prepares for the crisis soon to develop where the large Navajo farms have no water and must buy it at exorbitant prices from Morgan and Blucher.

Wood, Bate: In *The Border Legion,* a member of the Border Legion outlaw gang. He is an older man, having seen the gold rushes in California in '49 and again in '51. He predicts a big strike in Alder Creek, perhaps bigger than the previous two. He describes the turmoil in the camp with disillusioned miners from California, new hopefuls inexperienced in the ways of mining camps, and Civil War soldiers looking for a new life. Wood reports to Kells on a new man he has seen in the Last Nugget, one Jim Cleve, who beat everyone in the saloon at cards and who shot two men in the arm, just winged them, to settle arguments. He is quite impressed with the man. He also reports on the episode where Cleve beats up Luce for proposing the robbery and murder of a man and the abduction of his daughter. Wood tells Joan that the men know that she is not Kells's wife, that she was abducted. He warns her that in California, Kells had the reputation of being a woman-hater. He suspects that she is the one who shot Kells, just as he and Gulden already know that Kells murdered Bill Bailey and Halloway. Bate Wood brings Jim Cleve to present to the gang. Bate Wood is a bit of a philosopher and observer of human nature. He explains to Joan why Kells has organized the walk down Main Street. He knows the men in the camp will ogle her, make cat calls, and shout at her, thereby giving Kells the opportunity to pose as the defender of an insulted woman and focus attention on him. Kells seems to be more concerned about his reputation than about gold or anything else. Bate professes goodwill toward Joan, offering to help if needed. At the meeting discussing Gulden, he points out that Gulden knew things that had been said at their previous meeting, a meeting he did not attend. This tells Bate that Gulden had an informer reporting to him about what went on.

Wood, Bill: In *Knights of the Range,* one of the local ranchers who show up at the Ripple ranch with Sewall McCoy to accuse Renn Frayne of rustling.

Wood, Bilt: In *Shadow on the Trail,* one Hogue Kinsey's gang that Tex Brandon recruits to work on Pencarrow's ranch. He is the one who first notices Carter's absence from the bunkhouse. Carter later tries to kill Tex Brandon. Bilt is sweet on a young girl in Holbrook called Susie. She dumps him for a good-looking young cowboy called Joe Steele. Bilt is wild with jealousy but she tells him to get lost. Later, she returns to ask his forgiveness, telling him that Joe Steele had forced her and her family to hide Rand Blue for the night. Hogue Kinsey, Tex Brandon and others pursue them. Bilt is looking forward to settling the score with his rival in love.

Wood, Biny: In *Arizona Ames,* the daughter of Jim Wood, neighboring rancher to the Halsteads. When Fred comes to see her one day, she is with Jess Thuber, a rival beau, and Fred is jealous. She gets engaged to Fred at the end of the novel.

Wood, Jack: In *Nevada,* the deceased husband of Mrs. Wood. She refers to him as a man who learned to use a gun for his own protection. She sees in Jim Lacy the same desire to help other people, a desire which often gets him into trouble.

Wood, Jim: In *Arizona Ames,* owns a ranch some ten miles away from Halstead's. His cattle never cross the mountain to Halstead's range. His daughter Biny, is in love with Fred Halstead.

Wood, Mrs. Jack: In *Nevada,* a surrogate mother to Jim Lacy (Nevada). When Nevada flees California and returns to Lineville, he goes to her house, where she welcomes him back. He resumes the old arrangement he had with her, doing chores around the house, splitting wood etc. in exchange for room and board. She detects a change in him. He seems older, but the look in his eyes shows he is possessed of a new confidence. Mrs. Wood knows everyone in town and brings Nevada up to date on the latest happenings and gossip about Lize Teller, Cash Burridge and Holden. There is a new stagecoach line passing through town en route to Salisbar, the latest gold strike. She tells him that Less Setter has not been around for some six months, and that there is much speculation as to what has become of him. When Lize Teller tries to renew her relationship with Jim Lacy in order to make Link Cawthorne jealous, Mrs. Wood tells Jim that eventually, he is going to have to fight him. Link Cawthorne has been bragging that Jim is scared of him, making matters worse. Indeed as predicted, Cawthorne beats up Lize and, to defend the woman, Jim shoots and kills Cawthorne, upon which he leaves town for Arizona. When the Ides pass through Lineville en route to Arizona, they stay with Mrs. Wood. Again, she tells them about the new prosperity in the area and the doings of Jim Lacy. At this point, they do not know that he is Nevada. When they express shock at the violence, Mrs. Wood assures them that Jim Lacy is an honorable man, and that Arizona, the home of many famous outlaws, will be a better place thanks to men like Jim Lacy.

Woodbury: In *Thunder Mountain,* owner of a claim taken over by Rand Leavitt after Woodbury was voted out by the miners' court. The miners gathered at Jones's and Hadley's mess talk about the event, giving Lee Emerson what information they have about the way Leavitt proceeds to dispossess miners of their claim. This Woodbury, it seems, stepped high, wide and handsome when he stepped off his claim. The men on the miners' committee were all thick with Leavitt and voted Woodbury off the claim and out of the camp. In short, his claim was seized by Leavitt with the sanction of the miners' court.

Woolcott: In *Wilderness Trek*, has twelve hundred head of cattle when he joins the trek. Woolcott is under Ormiston's influence, and through Woolcott, Ormiston controls Hathaway as well. He is a man seemingly in his sixties, with a beard and deep-set eyes and a gloomy mien. He votes with Hathaway and Ormiston in favor of Eric Dann's choice of route. In the first attack on the group by an aborigine tribe, Woolcott is killed. Friday points out to Red and Sterl that Woolcott had been shot before he was speared by a native, if in fact it was by a native. Stanley Dann is not willing to believe it was murder, holding that perhaps in the confusion of the attack, he was shot by accident.

Woolman: In *The Desert of Wheat*, one of the authors of the book used at the State Agricultural Experimental Station which discusses wheat types, wheat viruses and soil conditions most conducive to growing wheat. Kurt Dorn has learned most of what he knows about growing wheat from Heald and Woolman.

Worthington, Jack: In *Sunset Pass*, came to the Preston ranch seeking employment but also because he was struck on Thiry. Ash Preston frightened him away by shooting him in the leg,

Wrangle: In *Riders of the Purple Sage*, a half-broken sorrel which Jerd saddles for Venters when he sets off to find Oldrin's hideout in Deception Canyon. The animal is full of energy, and loves to run. Venters is an excellent horseman and comes to love the animal. He shares Jerd and Judkins's opinion that Wrangle is the best horse that Jane Withersteen owns, although she casts her vote for Black Star or Night. When Venters moves into Surprise Valley, Wrangle is left to his own devices in the valley. Venters has trouble catching him again when he needs to return to Cottonwoods. In the race to stop the horse thieves, Wrangle proves himself every bit a match for Jane's preferred thoroughbreds. Jerry Card catches Wrangle and tries to control the animal by hanging around his neck and biting his nose. Wrangle, however, refuses to submit and to get rid of the pesky human hanging around his neck, jumps into the canyon, killing himself and Jerry Card. In *The Rainbow Trail*, Wrangle is mentioned as the under-estimated horse that died in the race with Jerry Card in *Riders of the Purple Sage*. He proved to be a faster horse than the thoroughbred Black Star.

Wright: (1) In *Fighting Caravans*, a trader who was in Taos, New Mexico, in Turner's saloon when Murdock shot Hall Clements. He reports on the fight to Clint Belmet, adding that he helped bury Clements.

(2) In *Riders of the Purple Sage*, one of Bishop Dyer's bodyguards and gunmen. He is killed when Lassiter confronts Dyer during the "trial" of Willie Kern for diverting water from an irrigation ditch.

Wrong Wheel Jones: In *The Thundering Herd*, met by Tom Doan when he returns to buffalo hunting after the campaign against the Comanche. Jones got the nickname when he was stranded with a broken wheel on his wagon and didn't have enough sense to take a wheel off another broken wagon to replace the wheel on his own vehicle.

Wund, Amy: In *Sunset Pass*, an old flame of Trueman Rock and wife of John Dabb, the most powerful rancher in the area. Amy played fast and loose with many cowboys, but she was particularly sweet on Trueman. She tries to flirt with him again, but Trueman now wonders what he ever saw in her. He's not interested in getting involved with a married woman. Amy married John Dabb to settle a debt her father owed him. She is not happy, complaining to Trueman that Dabb pays her no attention. She offers to get Trueman a job as foreman on Dabb's ranch, but he refuses. She is friendly with Thiry Preston, but when she learns Trueman is interested in Thiry, she does her best to destroy the relationship. She tells Trueman that Thiry has an "unnatural" love for her brother, Ash. Amy herself has been flirting with one Clink Peeples, a Wyoming cowboy and foreman of Nesbitt's ranch. Peeples thinks her a bit of a slut until Trueman Rock sets him straight. He apologizes to her, much to Amy's surprise. Amy is afraid that if Trueman stays on at the Preston ranch, eventually he will have to kill someone again. Amy Wund organizes the Fourth of July Rodeo masquerade dance, decorating the hall and arranging for the refreshments. She dances with Trueman at the party and tells him about the changes in Dabb, his increased interest in her, as when they first married. She senses Trueman has had something to do with this, but is not sure just what. Amy Wund is a jealous vixens similar to Stanton in *The U.P. Trail*.

Wyandot: The Hurons' name for their own tribe.

Y

Yan as Pa: In *The Rainbow Trail*, Yan as Pa is a Navajo squaw Shefford meets at Withers's trading post at Kayenta. Withers mentions her as a wealthy Navajo, with more flocks of sheep and mustangs than she knows what to do with. She is a careful and cautious trader, hence her wealth. Her virtues typify the Navajo, according to the trader.

Yaqui: (1) In *Desert Gold*, a tribe of Indians in the Sonora Desert of northern Mexico, sometimes referred to as the "Mountain Aztecs." They have resisted the armies of Spain and of Mexico through hundreds of years, defending their homeland against the invaders. Because of their fierce defense of their lands, they have earned the respect of some and the hatred of others. The Mexicans have a particularly fierce hatred of the Yaqui. The Mexican bandits who capture "Yaqui" enjoy torturing him. For Belding, the Yaqui are symbols of independence and harmony with the environment.

(2) In *Desert Gold*, the name used to refer to the Yaqui Indian whom Dick Gale rescues from the Mexican bandits. This Yaqui had survived an attack on his village by troops of the Mexican government in a war of extermination against his people. He was taken prisoner but escaped and made his way to New Orleans, from where he slowly makes his way back across Texas and New Mexico to Arizona, where he is taken captive by bandits. Dick Gale frees him from his captors. Since Dick has saved his life, Yaqui becomes his devoted friend and companion out of gratitude.

Yaqui is a tracker of unparalleled ability. He helps Gale, Lash and Ladd track the bandits who have taken Belding's prize horses. He leads the party into the desert to escape Rojas. He knows where the water holes are located. He knows which plants can provide water, or ointment to heal wounds. He knows horses well, getting them to stand so still they appear to be made of stone, and invisible against the desert background. He knows how to hunt the wild desert goats. Above all, he displays courage, bravery and loyalty to the man who had freed him. He lays a trap for Rojas and his bandits, who have been following them into the desert. Yaqui himself kills Rojas and leads the party back to Belding's ranch. Yaqui's final act of gratitude is to show Dick Gale the location of a gold mine which, as it turns out, is the mine that Nell Burton's father and grandfather had come upon twenty years before.

For Dick Gale, Yaqui is an example of the "natural" man, a "noble savage," a man shaped by nature, a man who lives in tune with the environment. He inspires Emersonian-like reflections about the contrast between nature and civilization. Knowing Yaqui has made Dick Gale see the foolishness of prejudices in civilization against men such as him. In Yaqui, Grey has developed one of his many examples of the "noble savage," like Wingenund in *The Spirit of the Border*.

(3) In the novella *Yaqui*, Yaqui is a chief who in the face of unrelenting attacks against his people in Sonora, Mexico, retreats into the desert, establishing a home for his people in an isolated canyon. His people thrive, away from the threat of the Mexican army. His wife gives him sons and a daughter. He catches a wild stallion, breaks the horse, and teaches his son to ride. But the happiness is short-lived. Several years later, the Mexican army arrives, trapping the Yaqui in the valley, and capturing and enslaving the entire tribe. Yaqui watches as the soldiers take aim at his escaping son and shoot him. He is tied with a lasso, bound like an animal. He is taken by boat, the Esperanza, to the Yucatan, where the Yaqui are enslaved on the henequen (hemp) plantations. Yaqui at first does not expect to be separated from his wife and son, but the cruel Perez seems to take particular pleasure in separating the members of the family. Yaqui, a giant of a man, seven feet tall, with great strength, is assigned work in the fields, gathering the henequen leaves from which hemp is made. Montes, the Brazilian government agent in the Yucatan to study the hemp business, takes a particular interest in this noble Indian, who reminds him of the gaucho of his native Argentina. The dignity, patience, and unsubdued pride of the man appeal to Montes. He sneaks the Indian extra food to supplement the meager rations of bread, a starvation diet designed to kill the Yaqui through exhaustion and weakness. A mountain people, the Yaqui are not accustomed to the sweltering heat of the Yucatan and the henequen fields. Yaqui constantly looks north, dreaming of escape to his mountain home, but eventually he gives up that dream. He is also assigned work removing the carcasses of bulls killed in the ring, then the job of covering up the bloodstains with fresh sand. He is such a good worker that he is eventually given a job in the mill, selecting the fiber to be pressed into bales. He becomes the most skilled operator of the baling machine. Perez plans a special surprise for his comprometida, Senorita Dolores Mendoza. He plans to have a set of expensive pearls delivered to the bride on her wedding day, wrapped in a bale of hemp. The day of the wedding, the groom is late arriving. Yaqui produces the bale and brings it to the ceremony. Instead of the pearls, the opened bale exposes the body of Lt Perez, the missing groom. Yaqui had got his revenge.

Yaquis: In *Stranger from the Tonto*, as he is dying, Bill Elway warns Kent Wingfield about the dangers in the desert, encounters with Yaqui Indians being among the most to fear.

Yantwaia: Indian name for Cornplanter, a Delaware Indian chief in *Betty Zane*.

Young, Brigham: In *Western Union*, the leader of the Mormons in Salt Lake City, mentioned as leading a construction crew bringing the telegraph through Utah to meet with the crew working from the east through Nebraska and Wyoming.

Young, George: One of the missionaries at the Village of Peace in *The Spirit of the Border*. Like Dave Edwards, he is hitting forty, a bachelor, awkward around women, and not pleasing to the eye. He is one of two suitors of Kate Wells, the dark-haired, quiet Wells sister. He is slight in build, with a nervous, timid manner. When Dave Edwards informs him that Kate has rejected his marriage proposal, Young rushes to find Kate, tripping over chairs, in his eagerness to propose to her. The scene offers some comic relief in the novel.

When Jim Girty, Silvertip and some six braves come upon him, Jim, Nell and Kate picking flowers near the Village of Peace, he is left tied to a tree while the other three are abducted. About a week later, after Wetzel returns to the village with the rescued Nell, George learns that Kate is in the clutches of Jim Girty. George goes to Wetzel and begs him to find Jim Girty and kill him. His hatred of the man makes him momentarily forget his Christian calling.

George Young is an example of an individual who has made no attempt to adapt to life on the frontier. He admits that he would be hopelessly lost if he went out into the woods on his own. He has never shot a gun in his life. Yet at one point he is about to grab a rifle and take off to hunt down Jim Girty and rescue his betrothed. He is resigned to his death in the village, calling it God's will. A fatalistic attitude seizes him after Kate's abduction and intensifies with the deteriorating situation at the mission.

Young is the second person to be shot during the massacre at the Village of Peace. When Dave Edwards gets up to preach and is killed, Young takes his place to continue preaching and in turn is shot by one of the hostile Indians. The bullet passes through his body causing serious bleeding. The last time he is mentioned, Heckewelder says his medical expertise can do no more for him and his survival is in God's hands.

Younger, Cole: In *Knights of the Range,* appears in Las Animas to meet the other members of the James-Younger Gang. The Jameses have been in California and are on their way back east. Renn Frayne meets and talks with Younger and the Jameses. They extend him an offer to join their gang, an offer he rejects.

In *The Maverick Queen,* Lincoln Bradway tells Kit Bandon that he is related to Cole Younger the elder. Lincoln had never known his father, who was either a brother or a cousin of the elder Cole Younger, a guerrilla after the war and later a notorious desperado. Lincoln was raised by a neighbor named Bradway and he took that family name. In some ways, Lincoln has inherited the skills of this relative.

In *Boulder Dam,* Sheriff Logan compares Lynn Weston to Cole Younger when he shoots at the men who had abducted Anne Vandergrift. He adds that Lynn would make one hell of a Texas Ranger.

Z

Zane, Andrew: Mentioned in *Betty Zane,* one of the brothers of Colonel Ebenezer Zane. He was taken captive with Ebenezer, Jonathan and Isaac, but was killed by his pursuers when attempting to escape, swimming the Scioto River.

Zane, Betty: The heroine in the novel by the same name. She is the only sister of Ebenezer Zane and the youngest of the family. She had been living with an aunt in Philadelphia and has only recently come to live at Ft. Henry. Much of the novel concerns Betty's abandoning of the city ways and norms she had acquired and learning the ways of the frontier community. She is especially close to her brother Isaac.

Zane Grey develops Betty as a kind of Heidi figure, innocent, natural, at one with the animals. She has a whole menagerie of pets, a bear, Caesar, and a collection of pigeons and squirrels, including Captain, a red squirrel, and Snowball, an albino squirrel.

Betty is in her late teens, a young woman sure of her beauty and quite a flirt. She is accustomed to having her own way. She plays games with her beaux, flirting, teasing. Her friend Lydia Boggs points out that on the frontier, such behavior is inappropriate. Young men here show their affections shyly, expecting to be taken seriously. Being used is a serious slight. Betty has a feminist streak in her that her friends do not share: "I have not a single doubt that your masculine remedies are sufficient for all your ills. Girls who have lost their interest in the old pleasures, who spend their spare time in making linen and quilts and who have sunk their very personalities in a great big tyrant of a man are not liable to get blue. They are afraid he may see a tear or a frown. But thank goodness I have not yet reached that stage."

Betty is said to be the equal of her brothers in running, riding, and shooting. She rides her half-broken Indian pony like an Indian. She can handle a canoe as well as any man, a skill she demonstrates as she and Alfred Clarke go downriver through rapids and down a small waterfall. Alfred admits she is more of a canoeist than he is, more willing to take risks than he.

This last aspect of her character gets her into trouble on more than one occasion in the novel. At the wedding celebration for her friend Lydia, during the sporting events which are part of the festivities, she tells Miller she swam Madcap across the river. He pretends not to believe her and dares her to do it again. She does not know what Miller is up to nor does she know Wetzel and Alfred have already spotted Indians skulking in the bushes by the river. Only the threat by Wetzel to shoot the horse from under her gets her to stop her wild dash to the river and come back.

This spunkiness, however, saves the day when she agrees to go to the colonel's cabin to bring back gunpowder. The fort will surely fall for lack of powder, but with so many British soldiers and Indians around, going the short distance to the colonel's cabin would be suicidal. When a female comes out, the attackers are stunned at first, but Betty's extraordinary speed, coupled with the element of surprise, makes a success of the escapade. The gunpowder she brings back in her apron is sufficient to sustain the defense of the fort. She becomes a legend for her feat.

In *Betty,* Zane Grey develops the prototype of all the heroines of his romances. She is young, beautiful, spunky, emotionally confused, willing to learn and adapt. She is unusually stubborn, unwilling to surrender her independence to a man. Betty needs to be taught a lesson by her brothers Ebenezer and Isaac. She has treated Alfred Clarke in an unacceptable manner. Not until the end does she confess that she has loved him all along.

In *The Last Trail*, Betty is a widow. No explanation is given of how Alfred Clarke died. She undertakes to help Mabel Lane when she is rescued by Jonathan and Wetzel and to guide Helen Sheppard in her adjusting to the frontier. Betty also finds a new friend (husband?) in Helen Sheppard's cousin, Will.

Zane, Colonel Ebenezer:

Appears in the three novels of the Ohio trilogy, *Betty Zane, The Spirit of the Border* and *The Last Trail*. Colonel Ebenezer Zane was the great-grandfather of the author Zane Grey. The events narrated in the three novels are reputedly based on his journals, which were concealed in the back of a picture frame and luckily rescued from the fire by the author's mother. The circumstances of the recovery of the journals are recounted in the preface to *Betty Zane*.

In *Betty Zane*, the colonel is concerned with the defending Ft. Henry from a combined attack of British soldiers and Indian tribes. Colonel Zane had been a soldier in the army of Lord Dunmore, stationed at Ft. Pitt. He had risen to the rank of colonel. Upon retiring from the army, he assumed leadership at Ft. Henry. He is looked up to by the settlers at the fort and often serves as judge in resolving disputes or maintaining law and order. He is also seen as a peacemaker with the Indians. Given his knowledge of Indian languages and customs, he is consulted on matters concerning relationship between the fort and the Indian tribes. He is a man of patience and reason, not unsympathetic to the Indians' sense of victimization. He treats all with fairness and justice.

In *Betty Zane*, the Colonel's role in establishing the settlement is underscored. His cabin, which has been burned to the ground on three occasions, is unofficial city hall. He is the man who is consulted on all issues concerning the welfare of the settlement. He seems to have a major say in the allocation of lots to newcomers. In *The Last Trail,* he allots land as a wedding present to young Alex Bennet, who had been waiting until he had the resources to purchase land before asking Mabel Lane to marry him. Likewise, he gives land to Mr. Sheppard, telling him not to worry about making payments until he has produced his first crop. Colonel Zane takes drastic action in the case of Metzar's inn. It has been the meeting place of the horse thieves and other ruffians, so the colonel, in order to put an end to the mischief being planned there, has the furniture removed and burned in the yard and the inn destroyed as punishment.

Colonel Zane is also a kind of family patriarch. His home is the focal point of Zane family events. Betty comes to stay with him when she leaves her aunt's home in Philadelphia. The colonel is concerned that Betty's behavior, — she is a flirt, and her treatment of Alfred Clarke defies understanding — will bring disfavor on the Zanes. He is concerned about Isaac, about Jonathan. Together with Betty, he plays matchmaker, facilitating Helen Sheppard's quest of Jonathan as husband.

Ebenezer Zane is largely responsible for maintaining the fort in good order and ensuring that all is in a state of preparedness should there be an attack.

In *The Spirit of the Border,* the colonel is largely a reporter of information to the new arrivals, Joe Downs and the Wellses. He gives advice about preparations for the trip downriver and shares stories about the frontier with the young man overcome with border fever.

In the final novel, *The Last Trail*, Colonel Zane appears as a patriarchal figure who takes care of the fort as a father and protector. "Colonel Zane was commandant of the fort, and, in a land where there was no law, tried to maintain the semblance of it. For years he had kept thieves, renegades and outlaws away from his little settlement by dealing out stern justice. His word was law, and his bordermen executed it as such. Therefore Jonathan and Wetzel made it their duty to have a keen eye on all that was happening. They kept the Colonel posted and never interfered in any case without his orders." When fights start breaking out at Metzar's inn, in part due to the drinking, the colonel threatens to shut the place down unless Metzar cleans his act up. He supervises the campaign against the horse thieves and the punishment of those who are captured. By the end, the settlement he founded is finally safe and secure for future generations.

Zane, Isaac:

Called White Eagle by the Hurons, the youngest and best-looking of the Zane brothers. He is a central character in Grey's first novel, *Betty Zane*. As a boy, he was taken captive by the Hurons together with his brothers, but when Jonathan, Silas and Ebenezer were ransomed, Isaac was not released due to the influence of Myeerah, daughter of Tarhe, chief of the Hurons. Myeerah was in love in Isaac and refused to let her father release him.

The plot of *Betty Zane*, is, in part, the story of Isaac's escape, his recapture by Indian chiefs sent in pursuit by Tarhe, his return to the village where he is again kept in a golden cage, refusing to marry Myeerah. He escapes again to be captured by Cornplanter, who makes him run the gauntlet and condemns him to death. Simon Girty gets word to Myeerah who, together with Thundercloud and two hundred warriors, appears at the Delaware village just as the faggots are about to the lighted around Isaac bound at the stake. Following his dramatic rescue by Myeerah, who now suspects that Isaac does not really love her and that she cannot force him to marry her, Isaac is set free and shown the road to the fort. Isaac decides that he will marry Myeerah and the two of them go to the fort together to meet his family and to be married. Shortly before the attack begins, Isaac and his Huron bride leave for the

Wyandot village to do what they can to ease tensions.

Among the Indians, Isaac Zane (White Eagle) has been a model prisoner, the kind readily adopted into the tribe. He speaks their languages, he lives by their customs. Isaac is a proficient player of lacrosse, he knows Indian legends and traditions. When taken prisoner by Cornplanter, his feat in running the gauntlet impresses the chiefs who have sentenced him to the stake. His courage in the face of torture and death serve him well.

Betty Zane ends with the family expecting Isaac and Myeerah to return for the wedding of Betty and Alfred Clarke.

Isaac Zane is called the Indianized Zane in *The Spirit of the Border*. He meets Joe in the Delaware village and gives him advice about how to get his horse back from Silvertip. He also provides information about the latest movement in the Indian villages against the Village of Peace.

In *The Last Trail*, Isaac Zane is only mentioned as a Zane family member, but he does not appear in the story.

Zane, Jonathan: Appears in all three of the Ohio Valley novels. In *Betty Zane*, he is described by his brother Ebenezer as a frontiersman, guide, tracker, and scout for the army. His name is mentioned in conjunction with Lewis Wetzel, an older man and intimate companion in the woods from whom he has learned much of his woodlore. Like Wetzel, he is a man formed by nature, blending the survival skills and knowledge of the forest with elements from the white world. Jonathan is said not to be a hunter of Indians like Wetzel, but rather a man who loves life outdoors. He is intimately involved in the defense of the fort.

In *The Spirit of the Border*, Jonathan is named as Wetzel's companion and appears in conjunction with Wetzel. They are pursuing the renegades when, from a hill some three hundred yards away, Wetzel shoots Half King as he is about to pronounce the death sentence on the Christian Indians. Jonathan lets Wetzel take the shot, as he knows his friend's aim is much more accurate than his.

Jonathan Zane is the hero of *The Last Trail*. This novel concentrates on his transition from man of the forest to husband and father. Helen Sheppard sets her eye on him and despite her attempts to flirt with him and exert her feminine charm, he remains impervious. She takes this as a personal challenge, as never before has she met a man who was immune to her allure.

Jonathan appears not to be interested in women. His first love is nature. He can remain for hours staring at a beautiful scene. Like Mescal in *The Heritage of the Desert*, or Nophaie in *The Vanishing American*, he is at one with the scenery, free from the intrusion of conscious thought. For him, the sunset, the light on the Ohio, the forest in autumn are companions. More so than for Wetzel even, nature has been his teacher. "The fragile ferns and slender-bladed grasses peeping from the gray and amber mosses, and the flowers that hung from craggy ledges, had wisdom to impart ... harkening thus with single heart to nature's teachings, he learned her secrets." The settled life of the community is not for him. Helen Sheppard's charm, though, does penetrate into his psyche and only after long thought does Jonathan see that this is not unnatural. One night, on the top of Bald Mountain with Helen during a thunderstorm, Jonathan goes through a "dark night of the soul" in which he must come to terms with his feelings for the young woman. As a man so close to nature, Jonathan understands that falling in love and marrying are perfectly natural processes. However, he is unwilling to abandon his free life in the forest and his companion Wetzel. His mentor and friend, Wetzel, however, confesses that even he had once been bitten by the love bug. He points out that their way of life will no longer be possible within a few years, as the settlement expands and the wilderness diminishes. Perhaps it would be well for Jonathan to reconsider his feelings for Miss Sheppard.

Jonathan co-opts Helen Sheppard as a helper in the quest for the horse thieves, especially in the identification of the insider who is passing on information about the best horses in the fort and their location. Helen, he feels, has access to information that he could never have. The two achieve a working relationship, and, when Helen is taken by Bing Leggett and Brandt and Mordaunt, he is genuinely confounded.

The novel ends with Jonathan married to Helen, and Wetzel coming to visit them after the birth of their first boy. Jonathan has successfully made the transition from frontiersman to farmer. The frontier in the Ohio Valley is passing away.

Zane, Noah: Mentioned in *Betty Zane*. He is Colonel Ebenezer Zane's eldest son. The colonel plays with him, tells him stories about Wetzel etc. At one point, the colonel sends him over to Reihart's blacksmith shop to watch the smith at work.

Zane, Rebecca: Colonel Zane's third child. She is born at the beginning of *The Last Trail*, the first girl born to one of the Zane brothers.

Zane, Sammy: Colonel Ebenezer Zane's second son. He is mentioned in *Betty Zane*. When Betty is getting over a slump of ill humor because she hasn't heard from Alfred Clarke, she recalls that she hasn't played with Sammy lately.

Zane, Silas: One of the colonel's brothers. He is mentioned in *Betty Zane*, *The Spirit of the Border*, and *The Last Trail*. He was ransomed together with Ebenezer and Jonathan at Detroit. Silas is married to Mary Bennett, presumably John Bennett's sister. Silas does not play a major role in any of the novels. He is referred to as the manager of the fort in *The Last Trail*, ensuring that the garrison is kept up to the necessary level of preparedness. He fulfills the same function in *Betty Zane*, organizing withdrawal of the pioneers into the fort and the provision of gunpowder and weapons. In *The Last Trail,* he ensures that the colonel's decisions as chief law enforcer and judge are carried out. Silas is the brother who helps get Isaac up from the river when Alfred has found him. He alone is not depressed over Isaac's recapture by the Hurons, knowing that Myeerah has special interest in him.

Zeb: In *The Hash Knife Outfit,* one of old Jim Traft's cowboys. He drives the wagon that Jim takes to town to pick up his sister Gloriana at the train station.

Zebra: In *Wyoming,* Andy Bonning's horse.

Zeisberger: One of the founding missionaries at the Moravian Village of Peace in *The Spirit of the Border.* He is not an active character in the story. On occasion he is referred to as the man in charge of the village, and at other times he is clearly subordinate to Heckewelder, who is the man responsible for the western Moravian missions

Zimmer, Si: In *The Lone Star Ranger,* recommended by Laramie to Ranger Buck Duane when he is attempting to organize a group of law-abiding citizens to combat the Cheseldine outlaw gang. He is reputed to be unquestionably honest.

Zoroaster: In *Lost Pueblo,* carries Janey Endicott's hat boxes into the post. He is the fourth of five cowboys working at the post and by far the handsomest of the lot. He stares straight ahead, ignoring Janey completely. Ray explains that he is a Mormon cowpuncher and scared of women. He has never seen any but Mormon girls, so he won't look at Janey. He arrives with the other four cowboys to rescue Janey from the abductor, Randolph, and participates in the mock lynching of Philip Randolph to give Janey a scare.

INDEX

401

www.ingramcontent.com/pod-product-compliance
Lightning Source LLC
Chambersburg PA
CBHW081401090726
47908CB00012B/2751